WHY WE FIGHT

"You lost children?" Others shushed that voice, someone in a leather cloak, but Gird answered it, counting them on his fingers.

"My first two sons died of fever; the lord refused us herb-right in the wood. My wife lost two babes young, one from hunger and one from fever. My eldest daughter they raped; killed her husband. The babe died unborn. My youngest son they struck down; he lives. Another daughter they struck down, breaking her arm; I know not if she lives or dies. And my brother's children, that I'd taken in: two of them dead, by the lords' greed. And that's children. I lost friends, my parents, my brother.

"You ask yourselves: if they can take one child, will they stop there? Will all your submission, all your obedience, get you peace and enough food? Has it *ever* worked? You can sit here and let them take you one by one, or you can decide to fight back."

THE LEGACY OF GIRD

BAEN BOOKS by ELIZABETH MOON

Sheepfarmer's Daughter
Divided Allegiance
Oath of Gold
The Deed of Paksenarrion
Surrender None
Liar's Oath
The Legacy of Gird

Hunting Party
Sporting Chance
Winning Colors

Remnant Population

Sassinak with Anne McCaffrey
Generation Warriors with Anne McCaffrey

THE LEGACY OF GIRD

THE LEGACY OF GIRD

ELIZABETH MOON

BAEN

THE LEGACY OF GIRD

The Legacy of Gird has been published in two parts as Surrender None, copyright © 1990 by Elizabeth Moon, and Liar's Oath, copyright © 1992 by Elizabeth Moon.

A Baen Books Original.

Baen Publishing Enterprises
P.O. Box 1403
Riverdale, N.Y. 10471

ISBN: 0-671-87747-X

Cover art is a computer-generated composite from the art for Surrender None, by Larry Elmore, and Liar's Oath, by Gary Ruddell

First printing, September 1996

Distributed by
SIMON & SCHUSTER
1230 Avenue of the Americas
New York, N.Y. 10020

Library of Congress Cataloging-in-Publication Data

    Moon, Elizabeth.
        The legacy of gird / Elizabeth Moon.
           p. cm.
        "A Baen books original"—T.p. verso.
        ISBN 0-671-87747-X (trade pbk.)
        I. Fantastic fiction, American. I. Title.
  PS3563.0557L4 1996
  813'.54—dc20   96-2957
                                                CIP

Printed in the United States of America

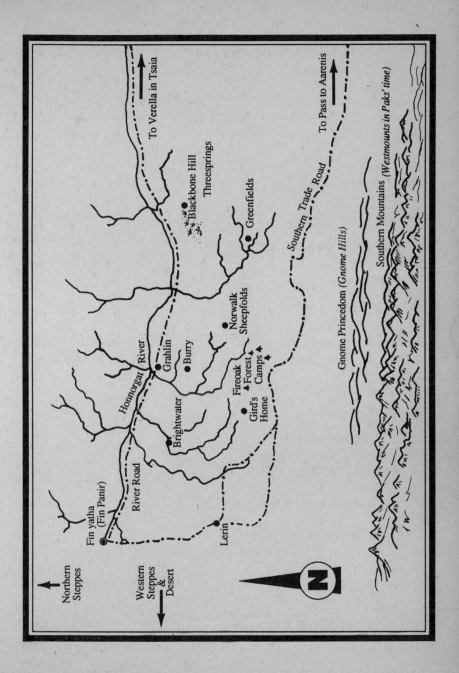

SURRENDER NONE

In memory of Travis Bohannon
a country boy from Florence, Texas
who gave his life to save his family from fire.

Not all heroes are in books.

━━━━━━━━━━━━━━━━◆━━━━━━━━━━━━━━━━

Acknowledgements

Too many people helped with technical advice and special knowledge to mention all, and leaving any of them out is unfair. But special thanks to Ellen McLean, of McLean Beefmasters, whose stock has taught me more than a college class in Dairying ever did, to Joel Graves for showing me how to scythe without cutting my ankles off, and to Mark Unger for instruction and demonstration of mixed-weapon fighting possibilities. Errors are mine; they did their best to straighten me out.

PART I

Prologue

The Rule of Aare is rule one:
Surrender none.

"Esea's light on him," muttered the priest, as the midwife mouthed, "Alyanya's sweet peace," and laid the wet pink newborn on his mother's belly. The priest, sent down hurriedly in the midst of dinner from the lord's hall, dabbed his finger in the blood and touched it to a kerchief, then cut with silver scissors a lock of the newborn's wet dark hair, which he folded in the same kerchief. With that as proof, no fond foolish peasant girl could hide the child away from his true father. The stupid slut might try that; some of them did, being so afraid of the lord's magic, although anyone with wit enough to dip stew from a kettle ought to realize that the lords meant no harm to these outbred children. Quite the contrary. With a final sniff, the priest sketched a gesture that left a streak of light in the room long after he'd left, and departed, to report the successful birth. Not a monster, a manchild whole of limb and healthy. Perhaps this one would inherit the birthright magic . . . perhaps.

Behind, in the birthing room, the midwife glowered at the glowing patch of air, and sketched her own gesture, tossing a handful of herbs at it. It hung there still, hardly fading. The new mother grunted, and the midwife returned to her work, ignoring the light she was determined not to need. She had the healing hands, a legacy of a great-grandmother's indiscretion in the days when such indiscretions meant a quick marriage to some handy serf. She hardly believed the change, and having a priest of Esea in the birthing room convinced her only that the high lords had no decency.

In the lord's hall, the infant's future was quickly determined. His mother could be his nurse, but his rearing would be that of a young lord, until his ability or lack of it appeared.

The boy showed a quick intelligence, a lively curiosity; he learned easily and could form the elegant script of Old Aare by the time he had seen six midwinter festivals. He had no peasant accent; he had no lack of manners or bodily grace. He also had no magic, and

1

when the lord lost hope that he might show a useful trace of it, he found the boy a foster family in one of his villages, and sent him away.

It could have been worse. His lord provided: the family prospered, and the youth, as he grew to be, had no trouble finding a wife. He would inherit a farmstead, he was told, and in due time he had his own farm. With his father's gifts, he started well above the average, and as well he had the position of a market judge in the nearest town. It was not enough to live on, but it supplemented his farm's production. He knew he was well off, and shrugged away the hopes he'd once had of being adopted into the lord's family. Yet he could not forget his parentage, or the promise of magic.

In the year of his birth, and far away, the boy already lived who would make his parentage worthless.

Chapter One

"You're big enough now," said the boy's mother. "You don't need to be hanging on my skirts any more. You're bold enough when it's something you want to do." As she spoke, she raked at the boy's thick unruly hair with her fingers, and wiped a smudge of soot from his cheek. "You take that basket to the lord's steward, now, and be quick about it. Are you a big boy, or only a baby, then?"

"I'm big," he said, frowning. "I'm not scared." His mother flicked her apron over his shirt again, and landed a hand on his backside.

"Then get on with you. You're to be home right away, Gird, mind that. No playing about with the other lads and lasses. There's work to be done, boy."

"I know." With a grunt, he lifted the basket, almost hip-high, and leaned sideways to balance the weight; it was piled high with plums, the best from their tree. He could almost taste one, the sweet juice running down his throat . . .

"And don't you be eating any of those, Gird. Not even one. Your Da would skin you for it."

"I won't." He started up the lane, walking cantways from the weight, but determined not to put the basket down for a rest until he was out of sight of the house. He wanted to go alone. He'd begged for the chance, last year, when he was clearly too small. And this year, when she'd first told him, he'd—he frowned harder, until he could feel the knot of his brows. He'd been afraid, after all. "I'm not afraid," he muttered to himself. "I'm not. I'm big, bigger than the others."

All along the lanes he saw others walking, carrying baskets slung over an arm or on a back. A handbasket for each square of brambleberries; an armbasket for each tree in its first three years of bearing; a ruckbasket for each smallfruit tree over three years, and a backbasket for apples in prime. Last year he'd carried a handbasket in each hand: two handbaskets make an armbasket, last year's fee. This year was the plum's fourth bearing year, and now they owed the lord a ruckbasket.

And that leaves us, he thought bitterly, with only an armbasket

3

for ourselves. It had been a dry year; most of the fruit fell before it ripened. He had heard his parents discussing it. They could have asked the lord's steward to change their fee, but that might bring other trouble.

"It's not the name I want, a man who argues every measure of his fee," said his father, leaning heavily on the table. "No. It's better to pay high one year, and have the lord's opinion. 'Tis not as if we were hungry."

Gird had listened silently. They had been hungry, two years before; he still remembered the pain in his belly, and his brother's gifts of food. Anything was better than that. Now, as he walked the lane, his belly grumbled; the smell of the plums seemed to go straight from his nose to his gut. He squinted against the bright light, trying not to think of it. Underfoot the dust was hot on the surface, but his feet sank into a coolness—was it damp? Why did wet and cold feel the same? He saw a puddle left from the rain a week ago, and headed for it before remembering his mother's detailed warnings. No puddles, she'd said; you don't come into the lord's court with dirty feet.

The lane past his father's house curved around a clump of pick-oak and into the village proper. Gird shifted his basket to the other side, and stumped on. Up ahead, just beyond the great stone barn where the whole village stored hay and grain was the corner of the lord's wall. The lane was choked with people waiting to go in the gate, children younger than Gird with handbaskets, those his own age with armbaskets, older ones with ruckbaskets like his. He joined the line, edging forward as those who had paid their fee came out and left room within.

Once inside the gate, he could just see over taller heads one corner of the awning over the steward's table. As he tried to peek between those ahead of him, and see more, someone tapped his head with a hard knuckle. He looked around.

"Good looking plums," said Rauf, Oreg the pigherd's son. "Better than ours." Rauf was a hand taller than Gird, and mean besides. Gird nodded, but said nothing. That was safer with Rauf. "They'd look better in my basket, I think. Eh, Sig?" Rauf nudged his friend Sikan in the ribs, and they both grinned at Gird. "You've more than you need, little boy; that basket's too heavy anyway." Rauf took a handful of plums off the top of the basket, and Sikan did the same.

"You stop!" Gird forgot that loud voices were not allowed in the lord's court. "Those are my plums!"

"They may have been once, but I found them." Rauf shoved

Gird hard; he stumbled, and more plums rolled out of the basket. "Found them all over the ground, I did; what's down is anyone's, right?"

Gird tried to snatch for the rolling plums. Sikan kicked him lightly in the arm, while Rauf tipped his basket all the way over. Gird heard some of the other boys laughing, a woman nearby crying shame to them all. The back of his neck felt hot, and he heard a wind in his ears. Before he thought, he grabbed the basket and slammed it into Rauf's face. Sikan jumped at him; Gird rolled away, kicking wildly. In moments that corner of the courtyard was a wild tangle of fighting boys and squashed fruit. The steward bellowed, the lord's guards waded into the fight, using their hands, their short staves, the flats of their swords. And Gird found himself held immobile by two guards, with Rauf lying limp on the stones, and the other boys huddled in a frightened mass behind a line of armed men.

"Disgraceful," said someone over his head. Gird looked up. The lord's steward, narrow-faced, blue-eyed. "Who started it?"

No one answered. Gird felt the hands tighten on his arms, and give a shake. "Boy," said a deeper voice, one of the men holding him. "What do you know about this. Who started it?"

"He stole my plums." Before he spoke, he didn't realize he was going to. In the heavy silence, with Rauf lying still before him, and the courtyard a mess of trampled fruit, his voice sounded thin. The steward looked at him, met his eyes.

"Your name, boy? Your father?"

"Gird, sir. Dorthan's son."

"Dorthan, eh? Your father's not a brawling man; I'd have thought better of his sons."

"Sir, he stole my plums!"

"Your tribute . . . yes. What was it, this year?"

"A ruckbasket, sir. And they were fine plums, big dark ones, and he—"

"Who?"

Gird nodded at Rauf. "Rauf, sir. Him and Sikan, his friend."

"Anyone else see that?" The steward's gaze drifted over the crowd of boys. Most stared at their feet, but Teris, a year older than Gird and son of his nearest neighbor, nodded.

"If you please, sir, it was Rauf started it. He said they were good plums, and would look better in his basket. Then he took some, and Gird said no, and he knocked Gird aside—"

"Rauf struck the first blow?"

"Aye, sir."

"Anyone else?" Reluctant nods followed this. Gird saw a space open around Sikan, who had edged to the rear of the group. Sikan flushed and moved forward when the steward stared hard at him.

"It wasn't so bad, sir," he said, trying to smile around a bruised lip. "We was just teasing the lad, like, that was all."

"Teasing, in your lord's court?"

"Well—"

"And did you hit this boy?" The steward pointed at Gird.

"Well, sir, I may have—sort of—sort of pushed at him, like, but nothing hard, not to say brawling. But he's one of them, you know, likes to make quarrels—"

The steward frowned. "It's not the first time, Sikan, that you and Rauf have been found in bad order." He nodded at the men behind Gird, and they released his arms. Gird rubbed his left elbow. "As for you, Gird son of Dorthan, brawling in the lord's court is always wrong—always. Do you understand?"

"Yes, sir." There was nothing else to say.

"And you're at fault in saying that *your* plums were stolen. They were your lord's plums, owed to him. If Rauf had given them in, the lord would still have them. Instead—" The steward waved his hand at the mess. Very few whole fruit had survived the brawl. "But your family has a good name, young Gird, and I think you did not mean to cause trouble. So there will be no fine in fruit for your family . . . only you, along with these others, will stay and clean the court until those stones are clean enough to satisfy Sergeant Mager here."

"Yes, sir." And he would be late home, and get another whipping from his father.

"Now as for you, Sikan, and Rauf—" For Rauf had begun to move about, and his eyes opened, though aimlessly as yet. "Since you started trouble, and moreover chose a smaller boy to bully, you'll spend a night in the stocks, when this work is done." And the steward turned away, back to his canopy over the account table where the scribes made marks on long rolls of parchment.

Gird found the rest of that day instructive. He had scrubbed their stone floor often enough at home, and scraped dung from the cowshed. But his mother was no more particular about the bowls they ate from than Sergeant Mager about the courtyard stones. He and the other boys picked up pieces of the squashed fruit and put them in baskets—without getting even a taste of it. Then they carried buckets of water—buckets so large that Gird couldn't carry one by himself—and brushed the stones with water and long-handled brushes. Then they rinsed, and then they scrubbed again.

Just when Gird was sure that the stones could be no cleaner had they just been quarried, the Sergeant would find a scrap of fruit rind, and they had it all to do over again. But he did his best, working as hard as he could. By the time the Sergeant let them go, it was well past midday, and Gird's fingers were raw with scrubbing. He called Gird back from the gate for an extra word.

"Your dad's got a good name," he said, laying a heavy hand on Gird's shoulder. "And you're a good lad, if quick-tempered. You've got courage, too—you were willing to take on those bigger lads. Ever think of being a soldier?"

Gird felt his heart leap. "You mean ... like you?"

The sergeant laughed. "Not at first, of course. You'd start like the others, as a recruit. But you're big for your age, and strong. You work hard. Think of it ... a sword, a spear maybe ... you could make sergeant someday."

"Do you ever get to ride a horse?" That was his dream, to ride a fast horse as the lords did, running before the wind.

"Sometimes." The sergeant smiled. "The steward might recommend you for training. A lad like you needs the discipline, needs a place to work off his extra energy. Besides, it's a mouth less to feed at home." He gave Gird's shoulder a final shake, and pushed him out the gate. "We'll have a word with your dad, this next day or so. Don't start trouble again, eh?"

"Holy Lady of Flowers!" His mother had been half-way down the lane; she must have been watching from the house. "Gird, what did you mean—"

"I'm sorry." He stared at the dust between his toes, aware of every rip in his clothes. They had been his best, the shirt actually new, and now they looked like his ragged old ones. "I didn't start it, Mother, truly I didn't. Rauf stole some plums, and I thought we might have a fine—"

"Effa says Rauf hit you first."

"Yes'm." He heard her sigh, and looked up. "I really didn't—"

"Gird—" She put a hand on his head. "At least you're back, and no fine. Effa says the steward didn't seem angry, not like she thought he would be."

"I don't think he is." Suddenly his news burst out of him. "Guess what the sergeant said—maybe I can train to be a soldier! I could have a sword—" Excited as he was, he didn't notice her withdrawal, the shock on her face. "Sometimes they even ride horses, he said. He said I was big enough, and strong, and—" Her stiff silence held him at last; he stared at her. "Mother?"

"No!" She caught his arm, and half-dragged him down the lane to the house.

The argument went on all evening. His father's first reaction to the story of the plums was to reach for his belt. "I don't brawl," he said. "And I didn't raise my sons to be brawlers."

Arin, as usual, stood up for him. "Da, that Rauf's a bad lot, you know that. So's the steward: they've got him in stocks this night, and Sikan too."

"And I'll have their fathers down on me, did you think of that? Oreg's no man to blame his own son, even if Rauf tells the tale aright. If Gird hadn't fought back, Oreg would've known he owed me sommat, a bit of bacon even. And Sikan's father—I want no quarrel with him; his wife has the only parrion for dyecraft in this village. As for this way—it's no good. We can't be fighting each other; the world's hard enough without that. They'll have to know I punished Gird, and I'll have to go to them and apologize."

So it was a whipping on top of his bruises, and no supper as well as no lunch. Gird had expected as much; he saw from Arin's wink that he would have a scrap to eat later, whatever Arin could sneak to him without being caught. But his father was as unhappy as his mother to hear of the sergeant's offer of training.

"It's never good to come into notice like that. Besides, we follow the Lady: would you take sword against your own folk, Gird? Break the village peace in blood and iron?" But before he could decide whether it was safe to answer—the answer he'd thought of, while waiting for his father to come from the fields—his father shrugged. "But if the steward comes, what can I say? They have the right to take you, no matter what I think about it. The best I can hope for is that the steward forgets it."

The steward did not forget. Gird spent the next day wrestling with the family's smallest scythe—still too long for him—mowing his father's section of the meadow. He knew he'd been sent there to get him out of sight, away from the other village boys. He knew his mother had baked two sweet cakes for Rauf's family and Sikan's, and his father had taken them over in the early morning. It was hot, the steamy heat of full summer, and the cold porridge of his breakfast had not filled the hollows from yesterday's fast. But above him, in the great field, his father was working, able to see if he shirked.

He kept at it doggedly, hacking uneven chunks where his brother could lay a clean swathe. There had to be a way. He paused to rub the great curved blade with the bit of stone his father had given him, and listened to the change in sound it made on different parts of the blade. When he looked sideways up the slope to the arable, he saw his father talking to another of the village men. Gird leaned on the scythe handle, the blade angled high above him, and picked a bur from between his toes.

When he looked again, his father had started back up the arable. Gird dared not move out of the sun to rest, but he tipped his head back to get the breeze. Something rustled in the tall grass ahead of him. Rat? Bird? He scratched the back of one leg with the other foot, glanced upslope again, and sighed. Someday he would be a man, and if he wasn't a soldier, he'd be a farmer, and able to swing a bigger scythe than this one. Like his father, whose sweeping strokes led the reapers each year. Like his brother Arin, who had just grown out of this scythe. He grunted at himself, and let the long blade down. Surely he could find a way to make this work better.

By nightfall, with all his blisters, he had begun to mow a level swathe. He'd changed the handles slightly, learned to get his hip into the swing, learned to take steps just the right length to compensate for the blade's arc. The next day, he spent on the same patch of meadow. Now that he had the knack of it, he was half-hoping the steward would not come. He would grow up a farmer like his father, leading the reapers in the field, guiding his own oxen, growing even better fruit. . .

It was the next day that the steward came at dusk, when his father had come in from the fields, and Gird had begun to feel himself out of disgrace as far as the family went. The children were sent to the barton out back, while the steward talked, and his father (he was sure) listened. He wanted to creep into the cowbyre and hear for himself, but Arin barred the way. He had to wait until his father called him in.

There in the candlelight, his father's face looked older, tireder. His mother sat stiffly, lips pressed together, behind her loom. The steward smiled at him. "Gird, the sergeant suggested that you were a likely lad to train for soldier: strong and brave, and in need of discipline. Your father will let you choose for yourself. If you agree, you will spend one day of ten with the soldiers this year, and from Midwinter to Midwinter next, two days of ten. It's not soldiering at first, I'll be honest with you: you'll work in the barracks just as you'd work here. But your father'd be paid the worth of your work, a copper crab more than for fieldwork. And the following year, you'd be a recruit, learning warcraft, and your father will get both coppers and a dole off his fee. 'Twould help your family, in hard times, but your father says you must do as you wish."

It was frightening to see his parents so still, so clearly frightened themselves. He had never really understood them before, he felt. Behind him, in the doorway, Arin and the others crowded; he could hear their noisy breathing. Could soldiering be so bad as they thought? All his life he'd seen the guardsmen strolling the village lane, admired the glitter of their buckles, the jingle of their harness. He'd been too young to fear the ordersticks, the clubs . . . he'd had strong hands rumpling his hair, when he crowded near with the other boys, he'd had a smile from the sergeant himself. And the soldiers fought off brigands, and hunted wolves and folokai; he remembered only last winter, cheering in the snow with the others as they carried back the dead folokai tied to poles. One of them had been hurt, his blood staining the orange tunic he wore, but the world was hard, and there were many ways to be hurt.

He wanted to stand on one leg and think about it, but there stood the steward, peering at him in the dimness with eyes that seemed to see clear into his heart. He'd never spoken to a lord before, exactly. Was the steward a lord? Close enough.

"It would not be a binding oath," the steward said, a little impatiently. Gird knew that tone; his father had it when he asked who had left the barton wicket open. It meant a quick answer, or trouble. "If you did not like it, you could quit before you started the real training . . ."

Gird ducked his head, and then looked up at the steward. From one corner of his vision he could see his father's rigid face, but he ignored it.

"Sir . . . steward . . . I would be glad to. If my father allows."

"He has said it." The steward smiled, then. "Dorthan, your son Gird is accepted into service of the Count Kelaive, and here is the *pirik*—" The bargain-sum, Gird remembered: not a price paid, as if he were a sheep, but a sum to mark the conclusion of any bargain. The price was somewhat else.

The very next morning, Gird left at dawn to walk through the village to the count's guards' barracks. None of his friends were out to watch him, but he knew they would be impressed. The guard at the gate admitted him, sent him straight across the forecourt to the barracks. The guards were just getting up, and the sergeant was crosser than Gird remembered.

"Get in the kitchen first, and serve the food; then you can clean for the cooks until after morning drill. I'll see you then. Hop, now."

The porridge was much like their own, if cooked in larger pots and served in bigger bowls. Gird carried the dirty bowls back, and scrubbed them, under the cook's critical eye, then scrubbed the big cookpots. Then it was chop the onions, while his eyes burned and watered, and chop the redroots until his hands were cramped, and then fetch buckets of clean water. All the while the cook scolded, worse than his oldest sister, while mixing and kneading the dough that would be dumplings in the midday stew. The sergeant came in while Gird was still washing down the long tables.

"Right, lad. Now let's see what we've got, here. Come along." He led Gird out the side door of the kitchen, into a back court, a little walled enclosure like a barton with no byres. In one corner was the kitchen well, with the row of buckets Gird had scrubbed neatly ranged along the wall.

The sergeant was just as impressive as ever, to Gird's eye: taller and broader than his own father, hard-muscled, with a brisk authority that expected absolute obedience. Gird looked at him, imagining himself grown into that size and strength, wearing those clean, whole, unmended clothes, having a place in the village and in his lord's service more secure than any farmer.

"You're a hard worker, and strong," the sergeant began, "but you'll have to be stronger yet, and you'll have to learn discipline. Begin with this: you don't talk unless you're told to, and you answer with 'sir' any time I speak to you. Clear?"

Gird nodded. "Yes . . . sir?"

"Right. You're here to learn, not to chatter. Dawn to dusk, one day of ten . . . can you count?"

"Not really, sir."

"Not really is no. Can't count sheep, or cows?"

Gird frowned. "If they're there . . . but not days, sir, they don't stay in front of me."

"You'll learn. Now, Gird: when you come here, you must be clean and ready to work. If you can't wash at home, come early and wash here. I'll have no ragtags in my barracks. Is that your only shirt?"

"No, sir, but th'other's worse."

"Then you'll get one, but only for this work. Do you have shoes? Boots?"

Gird shook his head, then remembered to say "No, sir." Shoes? For a mere lad? He had never had shoes, and wouldn't until he wed, unless his father had a string of good years.

"You'll need them later; you can wear them here, but not at home. Did you have breakfast at home this morning?" Of course he had not, beyond a bit of crust; the porridge had just gone on when he walked up to the barracks. The sergeant hmmphed at that. "Can't grow soldiers on thin rations. I'll tell the cook, and you'll eat here all day on your workdays. Now—about the other boys. I want no brawling, young Gird, none at all. If they tease you about going for soldier, you learn to let it pass. No threats from you, no catcalling at Rauf or Satik or whatever his name was. You'll be where they can't bother you, if you keep your nose clean. Hothead soldiers cause more trouble than they're worth; you have your chance, for you and your family: earn it."

An answer seemed required; Gird said "Yes, sir."

The rest of that day was more chores and little that Gird could see as soldiering, although he did see the inside of the barracks, with the lines of wooden bunks and thin straw mattresses, the weapons hung neatly on the walls, the jacks (*inside!* He wondered, but did not ask, how they were cleaned. Surely they were cleaned; they smelled less than his own family's pit.) He swept a floor that seemed clean enough already, carried more buckets of water to the cook, ate a bowl of stew larger than his father ever saw for his lunch, washed dishes until his hands wrinkled afterwards, fetched yet more water (he felt his feet had worn a groove from the well to the kitchen door) and sliced yet more redroots, had a huge slab of bread and a piece of meat for supper, and was allowed to stand silent in a corner and watch the ordered marching that preceded the changing of watch before dusk.

He ran home along the dark lane his bare feet knew so well, bursting with excitement. Meat! He didn't know if he would tell them, because they would see no meat until harvest . . . but it had tasted so good, and the stew and bread had filled all the hollows in his belly. He burped, tasting meat on his breath, and laughed.

They were waiting, and had saved a bowl of gruel and hunk of bread for him; he felt both shamed and proud when he could give it to the others.

"So—they'll feed you well?" His mother wasn't quite looking at him, spooning his share carefully into other bowls.

"Yes. Breakfast too, but I must get there early."

"And do you like soldiering?" she asked, a sharpness in her voice.

"It's not soldiering yet," he said, watching the others eat. "I helped the cook today, chopping onions and carrying water . . . I carried enough water for two days."

"You can carry my water tomorrow," his mother said. His father had yet said nothing, watching Gird across the firelight as he ate.

The time from summer to Midwinter passed quickly. One day in ten he rose before dawn, at first cockcrow, and ran up the lane to the gate where the guards now knew him by name and greeted him. Into that steamy kitchen, larger than his own cottage, where the cook—never so difficult as that first day—gave him a great bowl of porridge before he served the others. As the days drew in with autumn, that kitchen became a haven, rich with the smells of baking bread and roasting meat, savory stews, fruit pies. It was a feast-day, however plain the soldiers found the food (and he was amazed to hear them grumble), he had his belly full from daylight to dark. With a full belly, the work went easily. Hauling water, sweeping, washing, chopping vegetables, chopping wood for the great hearths. He learned the names of all the guards, and knew where everything was kept. Two of them were recruits, one from his village and one from over the fields sunrising, tall boys he would have thought men if he hadn't seen them next to the soldiers. He began to learn the drill commands as he watched.

The other nine days passed as his days always had, in work with his family. He was growing into the scythe, or managing it better, and he was allowed in the big field for the first time. Arin took him up to the high end of the wood, where the village pigs spent the summer rooting and wallowing, to help gather them into the lower pens. They ate their meager lunch in a rocky cleft up higher than others ever came, a place Arin had shown him the first year he went to help gather pigs. He spent a few days nutting in the woods, with his friends, laughing and playing tricks like the others. They all wanted to know what he was learning. When he explained that so far it was just work, like any work, they wondered why he agreed.

"It *will* be soldiering," Gird said, leaning back against a bank and squinting up at one of their favorite nut trees. "And in the meantime, it's food and coppers for my family—what better?"

"Good food?" asked Amis. He was lean and ribby, as they all were that year.

Gird nodded. "Lots of it, too. And that leaves more—"

"Can you take any home?"

"No." That had been a disappointment, and his first disgrace. Sharing food was part of his life: everyone shared, fast or feast. But when he tried to take home a half-loaf being tossed out anyway, it had brought swift punishment. "The sergeant says that's stealing. They're getting enough for me, he says, more than I'm worth. That may be so, though I try. But not one crust will they let me take out, or a single dried plum." The stripes had not hurt as much as knowing he could not share; he had not told his father why he'd been punished.

Terris made the closed-fist gesture against evil. "Gripe-hearts, is what they are. You watch, Gird, they'll turn you against us."

"Never." Gird said it loudly, though he could already sense a rift between him and his friends. "I can share from my own, when I earn my own: then you'll see. Open heart, open hands: the Lady's blessing."

"Lady's blessing," they all said. Gird made sure to put a handful more than his share into the common sack, that would go up to the count's steward as their fee for nutting in those woods.

At Midwinter Feast, he stood once more before the steward, this time in the Hall, and agreed to his next year's service. His father had stayed home, shrugging away Gird's concern for his cough. Two days in ten, he thought, they will not have to feed me, and there's the coppers besides. He was proud of the thought that his pay might help with the fieldfee.

Two days in ten made one in five. In the short days of winter, the sergeant set him to learning counting and letters. Gird hated it. Sitting with cold feet and numbed hands over a board scrawled with mysterious shapes was far harder than fetching water from the well, even when that meant breaking the ice on it first. At home he could read tallies well enough, the notched sticks all the farmers used to keep count of stock and coin. But here were no helpful hints . . . you could not tell, from the words, who wrote them. Without the clue that this tally was Oder's . . . when everyone knew that Oder had only a double-hand of sheep . . . you had to know *all* the words and numbers to find out what it said.

Some of the men laughed unkindly at his struggles. "Thickhead," said one, a balding redhead whom Gird had rather liked before. "Perhaps the knowledge could get in, if we cracked it open for you?"

"More like his little wit would fall out," said another. "He thinks with his hands and feet, that one, like most peasants."

Gird tried to concentrate on markings that seemed to jump and jiggle about in the flickering candlelight. Was the sign for three supposed to stick out *this* way, or that? He wiggled his fingers, trying to remember. The sergeant's sword was on the same side as that hand . . . he shook his head, confused once more.

"Here," said the redhead, handing him two pebbles. "Put this in your hand—no, *that* hand—and hold it there. Now call that your left hand, eh? Stonehand. Some signs are stonehand, some are empty hand—you can remember that much, can't you?"

He might have, but he was angry. He clenched his teeth against the temptation. The sergeant intervened. "Let him alone, Slagin. The stone's a good idea, but leave the rest of it. Some boys take longer, that's all. All right, Gird, the cook needs more water."

By spring, the two days in ten of plentiful food had begun to show. He had always been heavier built than most of his sibs. "More like my brother," his father had said, of an uncle dead before he was born. Now his broader frame began to carry thicker muscle. He had grown another two fingers up, and was straining the seams of his shirt. And that summer he carried a ruckbasket of plums without difficulty.

All that year, Gird worked his two days in ten, and his family settled into the knowledge that he would almost certainly become a soldier. His father continued to teach him the crafts and skills of farming, but with less urgency. His mother let out his old shirt, and made a new one, without pleading with him to stay home. His brothers admitted, privately, that life was a bit easier when he got part of his food elsewhere, and the coppers came in on quarterdays. Rauf tried once to tease him into a fight, calling him coward when he backed off; a few months later he noticed that Rauf crossed the lane to avoid him. And his friends seemed glad to see him, when any of them had time off for foolery, which wasn't often.

So at Midwinter, he gave his oath to the steward, and entered training as a recruit, to sleep in the barracks with the others and learn the arts of war.

Chapter Two

"Your oath to the steward's one thing," said Sergeant Mager. "It's me you've got to satisfy."

Gird, along with three other recruits, all from other villages, stood uneasily in his new orange uniform while the sergeant stalked back and forth in front of them. The other soldiers were inside, enjoying the Midwinter Feast. They were in the little back courtyard he knew so well, with an icy wind stiffening their skins.

"If you make it through training," the sergeant went on, "you'll give your oath to our lord or his guardian. You'll go where he sends you, and fight his battles, the rest of your time as soldier. Some of you—" He did not look at Gird. "—some of you started your training as boys. But you needn't think you know much yet. You all start level."

Level meant the bottom. The senior recruits, that Gird had seen cuffed and bullied by the older men, now cuffed and bullied the new ones. Gird was no longer the cook's helper, but he still hauled buckets of water, scrubbed floors, and now had his uniform to keep clean and mended, besides. The boots that went with it kept his feet from the snow, but chafed badly until he learned how to pack them with oily wool. He had never had to do anything to a bed but fall into it and fight his brothers for the cover: now he had to produce as neat a mattress, as tightly rolled a blanket, as the others. And, lacking a boy to do the work, all four new recruits washed dishes.

Yet none of them complained. Like Gird, they had all been peasants' sons, only one of them the son of a free tenant. It was worth all the abuse to have a full belly all winter long, somewhere warm to sleep. Gradually they got used to having enough to eat, a bunk each, with a warm blanket, whole clothes that fit, boots.

Gird had been hoping to move quickly into training with weapons, but the sergeant had other priorities. They would all, he said firmly, with a hard look at Gird, learn their letters well enough to follow simple orders. They would learn to keep count, so they could help the steward or his agents during tax-time. Ifor, who had been sent from the nearest trading town, could already read a little, and use the pebble-board for figuring. He didn't mind the daily session with letters that was still torture to Gird.

"You'll never make sergeant, Gird, if you don't learn this," the sergeant warned. Gird was beginning to think he didn't care, if making sergeant meant making sense of reading and writing and numbers. He could see, as clear as his hand on the table, how many legs two sheep had, but trying to think of it and write it down made the sweat run down his face. He was the slowest in this, as he was strongest in body. The sergeant insisted that it didn't have to work that way, that many strong men were quick-minded in learning to read. Gird eyed the others wistfully, wondering what the difference was inside their heads. He struggled on. He knew all the marks, now, that stood for numbers and sounds; he could read the simplest words, and write his own name in awkward, shaky letters. But it got no easier, for all his labors.

Besides that, they had to learn about their lord's domain: the correct address for the lord himself, for the steward, for the various officers who came through on inspections. The names of all the villages, and the headmen of each, and the sergeants in all the places the guard was stationed. Once in the lord's guard, they might be sent anywhere within his domain. Most men served away from their homes, at least until they were well along in service. Gird had never really considered the possibility that he might leave and never come back. Going off to war was one thing, but leaving this village—the only place he'd ever known—to make a life somewhere else—that was new and disturbing. He frowned, but said nothing. At least this was better than reading and writing. The lists went on and on. They had to know the right name for each piece of equipment in the barracks, from the tools used on the hearth to the weapons hung on the walls. Each weapon had not only a name, but a name for each part—for each movement with which it could be used—for the command given to make each movement.

When they did begin what Gird recognized as soldier's training, it was hardly different from the games boys played. Wrestling—he had wrestled with the other lads all his life. He was good at it. When the sergeant asked him if he thought he knew how, he answered briskly that he did, and stepped out. Someone chuckled, but he ignored it. They laughed at everything the new recruits did, good or bad. He eyed the balding redhead he'd been told to work with, and cocked his arm, edging in as the boys always did. Something like a tree trunk suddenly grabbed him and he felt himself flying through the air, to land hard on the cold stone floor.

"It's not a game, any more," said his partner mildly. "Try again." Some five falls later, when Gird was breathless, bruised, and much less cocky—and the other man had hardly broken into a sweat—the sergeant called a halt.

"Now you know what you don't know. Convinced?"

"Yes, sir."

"Remember: if we have to crack your head to let in wisdom, we will." The sergeant was serious, but Gird grinned at that. It made sense. His father said much the same, and he'd known all his life that his own head was considered harder than most.

Besides wrestling, there was drill. Gird found he liked that, although he had trouble with some of the sequences, and more than once turned in the wrong place and got trodden on. And pounded, when the sergeant caught up with him. But when it worked, when all the separate individuals merged into one body, and the boots crashed on the stones together, it sent shivers down his backbone. This was really soldiering, something the village folk could watch and recognize, something to show off. *If* the sergeant ever let them past the gates, which he had not for tens and tens of days.

One late winter day, shepherds came to ask the guard's help in hunting a pack of wolves. The steward agreed, and the sergeant, now mounted on a stout brown horse, led them all out into a miserably cold, bleak day with neither sun nor snow to commend it. Gird marched for the first time in uniform down the lane past his cottage, where his younger sister peeked through the leafless hedge and dared a shy wave. He could not wave back, not with the sergeant's eye on him, as it surely was, for all he rode ahead. But he knew she watched, and admired her older brother, and someday all the others would too. He could imagine himself receiving admiring glances from all the villagers, when he saved their stock from wolves or folokai, or protected them from brigands.

Gird enjoyed the wolf hunt, though it meant that he and the other inexperienced ones spent three whole days trudging through cold damp woods and across even colder wet pastures, looking for wolf signs. It was not until much later that he realized the sergeant never expected them to find any—that's what the gnarled old tracker with his hounds was for—but it kept them out of trouble and far away from the actual hunt. They returned in the glow of a successful hunt, behind the lucky ones who had actually killed two wolves and so got to carry them through the village (Gird and the other recruits had carried them most of the way back, while the hunters themselves told and retold exactly how each spear had gone into its prey.)

With the coming of spring, they spent more of their time outside, and more of it in things Gird recognized as soldierly. Marching drill, and long marches across the fields and pastures. Archery, not with the simple and fairly weak bows his own people used for hunting small fowl in the woods, but with the recurved bows that took all his strength to draw. They learned the use of stick and club, facing off in pairs and later with the older recruits in sections. Gird collected his fair share of bruises and scrapes without comment, and dealt as many.

Days lengthened with the turning year. Soldiers as well as farmers had to put in their due of roadwork, and Gird's weapon on that occasion was a shovel. He hesitated before jamming it into the clogged ditch: was this like a plow? Did he need to perform the spring ritual of propitiation before putting iron in Alyanya's soil? He muttered a quick apology as he saw the sergeant glare his way. It would have to do. He meant no disrespect, and he had brought (on his own time) the sunturning flowers to the barracks well. Although the sergeant had brushed them away without comment, surely the Lady would understand.

He might have known his mutter would not go unnoticed. Even as he tossed the second shovelful of wet clay and matted leaves to one side, the sergeant was beside him.

"What's that you said, Gird?"

"Just asked the Lady's peace, sir, before putting iron to 'er."

The sergeant sighed, gustily, and looked both ways to be sure the others were hard at work before he spoke. "Gird, when you were a farmer's brat, you paid attention to the Lady, and no doubt to every well-sprite, spring spirit, and endstone watcher. I've no doubt who it was tied that bunch of weeds to the wellpost."

Gird opened his mouth to say it wasn't weeds at all, but the proper flowers, picked fresh that morning, but thought better of it.

"But now you're a soldier, or like to be. You need a soldier's patron now, Gird, not a farmer's harvest matron. Gods know I'm as glad of the Lady's bounty as anyone, and I grant her all praise in harvest time. It's right for farmers to follow all the rituals. But not you. Will you stop to ask the Lady's blessing every time you draw steel, in the midst of battle? You'll have a short life that way."

"But sir—"

"You cannot be both, Gird, farmer and soldier. Not in your heart. Did your folk teach you nothing of soldiers' gods?" Gird shook his head, still shoveling, and the sergeant sighed again. "Well, 'tis time you learned. Tir will take your oath in iron, same as mine, and asks nothing but your courage in battle and your care for your comrades. The lords say he's below Esea, their god—" He peered at Gird's face, to see if he understood. Gird nodded, silently; his father had had a lot to say about Esea—a foreign god, he'd said, not like their own Lady, and not like the Windsteed. "But to us it doesn't matter," said the sergeant. "He's god enough for me, my lad, and that should be enough for you. Think about it. And no more flowers around my well, is that clear?"

"Yes, sir." He had not thought soldiers *that* different. Everyone knew the capriciousness of the *merin*, the well-sprites . . . how the water rose and fell, regardless of local rains, how even its flavor changed. Had that well in the barracks yard gone years without proper care? He was sure the water had tasted sweeter after his offering. But he could not argue with his sergeant.

After the roadwork, after the bridge repairs that followed the spring rains, the recruits had their first chance to mingle with the villagers. Gird spent most of that time helping his father and brothers with their work, but found an hour now and then to meet with his old friends. At first they were properly impressed with his growing strength and martial skills, but that didn't last long.

"It's not fair," said Teris, when Gird had thrown him easily for the third time one evening. "You're using soldier's tricks against friends, and that's not fair." He, turned away. So did the others.

"But I—" Gird stared at their backs. He knew what that meant.

If they shut him out, he would have no one in the village but his family. And his family, just lately, had been irritating him with complaints about his attitude. If the sergeant forbade him to remember all the Lady's rituals, his family insisted that he perform them all perfectly. He could not lose his friends: not now. "I—I will teach you," he offered. "Then it would be fair."

"Would you, truly?" Teris turned around again.

"Of course." Gird took a deep breath. The sergeant might think he knew nothing—or that's what he kept saying—but here he knew more than any of them. "We can say we have a guard unit—we can have a sergeant, a captain—"

"I suppose you'll want to be captain," said Kev.

"If he's teaching us," said Teris, shrugging, "he can be captain. For awhile."

"We need a level field," said Gird. He would teach them marching, he thought to himself. Maybe if he taught them, he wouldn't forget the commands himself. Somewhere in the back of his mind he remembered an oath not to teach "peasants and churls" the arts of war. But marching in step wasn't an art of war. They'd all tried it when they were little boys; they just hadn't known how to do it *right*. And wrestling wasn't an art of war; no one fought battles by wrestling. And archery . . . all boys played with archery. Nonetheless, he took care that the level field they decided on was well out of sight of the guard stations.

In a few weeks, Gird's troop of boys was moving around the back horse pasture with assurance. Bit by bit, as he learned from the sergeant, he transferred knowledge to the boys.

"The little groups are called squads," he said one day. "We have enough to have three of them; it's like pretend armies. Every squad has a leader, and marches together, and you can do real things with it." They built a sod fort in the field, and practiced assaults. Teris, in particular, had a gift for it; he remembered everything Gird told him, the first time.

Now, rehearsing his new knowledge with his friends, Gird felt that his life as a soldier was well begun. That first summer as a recruit, he spent all his free time with them; he saw no reason why their old friendship should ever end. He wished he could show them off to the sergeant. If he could train them, he had to be learning himself, didn't he?

But as time passed, Gird's friends were working too hard in the fields to have time for boyish play. First one, then another, failed to turn up for drill, and then the others refused to do it. They wanted to lie in the long grass and talk about things Gird didn't know: whose brother was courting whose sister, which family might have trouble raising the field-fee this year, all that timeless village gossip. When he tried to argue them into drill or wrestling, they simply looked at him, a look the sergeant had taught him to think mulish and stupid. He gave in, since arguing would not serve, and wished he could live in two places at once.

After harvest, he had less time off himself, and rarely came into the village all that winter. The recruits had begun to learn sword-work, and even Gird knew that he could make no excuse for teaching his friends to use edged weapons, even if they had had them to practice with. No one did; the strictest of the laws forbade any but soldiers to have weapons, and even the free smiths feared the punishment for breaking that law. Besides, the sergeant still insisted that he keep trying to learn to read and write. None of his friends could, or cared to. His father admitted that reading was a useful skill, but wasn't at all sure that it was right for a farmer to know. Gird opened his mouth to say "But I'm not a farmer!" and shut it again. That was the whole point, and they all knew it.

There were other barriers growing, too, between them He could not tell them what the sergeant said about Alyanya, or what he felt himself. Even the rituals of harvest had seemed a little silly; the twisted wisps of straw, the knotted yarn around the last sheaf, all that was peasant lore, far removed from his future as a soldier. He felt guilty when he listened to the other soldiers' jests; those were his people, his family and extended kin. Yet he wished that the villagers would somehow impress the soldiers—would somehow be more soldierly, so that he could feel pride in them.

And there was the matter of soldiers' discipline. For himself, Gird could stand a few buffets when he made a mistake, a few lashes for coming back drunk from the harvest festival trying to sing "Nutting in the Woods." Being clouted by the others was no worse than being mauled by Rauf and the older boys when he'd been younger. For that matter, many families were almost as rough; his father had taken a belt to him more than once, and his oldest brother had pummeled him regularly before he married and moved away.

What he did not like was having to do the same to others. When Keri, a lad from one of the distant villages, mishandled a sword, and the sergeant had them all join in the punishment, Gird told himself that someone who couldn't stand a few buffets wouldn't stay strong in battle, but he didn't like to think which bruise on that battered face had come from his fist. He got a reputation for being strong enough but unaggressive, a little too gentle. The sergeant shook his head at him after seeing him flinch from Keri's punishment. "And I thought you'd be the quarrelsome sort, glad enough to clout others. Well, better this way, as long as you don't mind killing an enemy. But mind, lad, soldiering's not for the faint heart or weak stomach." He was sure he would not mind a battle; it was having to hit someone helpless that made him feel sick to his stomach. This was another thing he could not share with boyhood friends; he knew they would not understand.

Past Midwinter Feast, in the slack of late winter, he found another troubling presence in the barracks. Three of the soldiers, all from Finyatha and rotated here from the count's household, favored Liart. Gird had never heard of Liart before that second winter, when he came back from the jacks one night to find the three crouched before the hearth with something that whimpered between them. When they heard him, one of them whirled.

"Get away!" he'd said. "Or by Liart's chain, you'll rue it!" He had gone to the sergeant, unsure, and seen the sergeant's face tighten.

"Liart, is it? Liart's chain? I'll give them Liart's chain!" And he had stormed out, bellowing. But in the end he had gone to the steward, and come back shaken. "A god of war is a god of war," he'd said then, in the bleak light of a winter morning. "Our lord approves, if someone chooses Liart for patron."

Gird tried to ask, and was sworn at for his pains. Then, later, one of the other men, Kadir, explained. "Liart's followers buy his aid with blood; 'tis said he likes it best if it comes hardly . . . d'you see?" Gird didn't, but knew he didn't want to know. "Liart's chain . . . that's the barbed chain, like the barbed whip they use on murderers, up in Finyatha. Some lords use it, more than used to. Mostly it was thieves and outlaws, in the old days, so I heard. But the thing is, Gird, don't you be asking trouble of Liart's followers; they'll torment you as glad as anyone, if you bring notice to them. I'd be careful, was I you."

A few days later he found a short length of barbed chain on his bunk, as they came in for inspection. The sergeant's eyes met his; he took his punishment without complaint; they both knew he had not put it there. He himself had declared for Tir, as his sergeant had suggested the previous summer, although he had not yet given his oath of iron. That would require a Blademaster, and the sergeant said they would have the chance after they'd given their final oath to the lord when training was over. The sergeant had told him what was lawful for him to know, though, and it was very little like anything the villagers taught.

So when the days lengthened again into spring, there were many things he could not share with old friends. They would have questions he could not answer—that was the best face he could put on it. Likely it would be worse. And he himself, as tall now as any of the guards, would be promoted from recruit come Summereve, when the lord was home from Finyatha.

Later he would remember that spring as one of the happiest times of his life, drenched in honey. He was young and strong and handsome; when he walked along the lanes to visit his family, with the brass badge of his lord's service shined and winking in the sun, the little children smiled and waved at him, tagging along behind. "Gird," they called. "Strong Gird . . . carry me, please?" Girls near his age glanced at him sideways; he felt each glance like a caress. Boys too old to tag him like the younger children watched nonetheless, and when he stopped to speak to someone they'd come close. "Is it hard to be a soldier, Gird?" they'd ask. And sometimes he told them tales of the barracks, and watched their eyes widen.

Once, twice, he had leave to go to the gatherings in the sheepfolds around, where the young men and girls met and danced. He was too young yet—he merely watched—but he enjoyed the music, and the respectful, if wary, glances. His old friends still joked with him, cautiously, but none ventured to wrestle or match arms. He didn't mind that; he didn't want to hurt them, and he knew now that he could.

Even at home, it was a good spring. His father's eyes still showed concern, but his older brothers were clearly proud to have a brother in the guards. Other lads his own age were still "lads" only—too young to marry, too young to inherit a farm, and most were younger sons. "Sim's boys" or "Artin's boys," they were called, in lumps like cattle. But he, Gird son of Dorthan, he had a name for himself in the village, and a nickname to match, for even the veterans called him "Strong Gird." And on his rare days off, when he helped his father and brothers on the farm, he knew he deserved that nickname: he could outlift any of them, could haul more wood and dig a longer line of ditch. Now he could handle the longest scythe they had, and mow as level a swathe as his father.

"I can't say they've spoiled you for work," his father said one of those nights, when Gird was enjoying a last few minutes by the fire before walking back to the barracks. "You're a good worker; you always were, from a little lad. You're strong, and you've no foolish ideas about it. But I still wish—" He left the wish unfinished. Gird knew what he would have said, but he had never understood it. He would never forget his family, the people of his heart.

And, strong as he was, he wouldn't die in battle far away—he would come home to them. Couldn't they understand that?

"I'll be all right, Da," he said, patting his father's shoulder. "I'll be good, and someday—" But he could not name his private dream, not then. It trembled on the edge of his mind, half-visible in a cloud of wishes too vague to express. He would do something wonderful, something that made the village and the sergeant both proud of him. Something very brave, that yet hurt no one but bad men, or monsters.

"Go in peace, Gird, as long as you may," his father said. "I pray the Lady forgives your service of iron."

His father always said that, and it always annoyed him now. Alyanya, the Lady of Flowers, the Lady of Peace, the Lady whose permission they must have each spring to touch the land with plow or spade—Gird thought of her in his mind as a more beautiful form of the village maids. Rahel, maybe, with shining hair down her back, or Estil whose perfect breasts swung dizzyingly with every stroke of the scythe during haying. Those girls, those flower-scented soft-skinned girls with their springtime bodies swaying along the lanes, those girls didn't mind his "service of iron." No, he had seen them glance, seen them smile sideways at him, while farm lads his age received no flicker of eyelash at all.

And surely the Lady herself, whatever else she was, understood the need for soldiers—surely she also admired broad shoulders, strength, the courage of a man with bright weapons in his hand. The sergeant had told him an old tale about Alyanya and Tir, in which the Lady had her Warrior guardian, and was glad of his service. He had never heard such a tale at home, but it made sense, the way the sergeant told it. That the iron of plow and spade was but another form of the iron of sword and spear, and the Lady's consent to one was as gracious as her consent to the other. "Bright harvest," the sergeant's tale had sung, "born of this wedding, child of this marriage—" Girl and Lady, he thought to himself, both know and want the strong arm, the bright steel. But he did not argue with his father, as he had once the year before. His father was a farmer, born and bred, and would die as a farmer— may it not be soon! he thought piously—and he could not expect a farmer to understand soldiers' things.

He walked back through the late-spring night, with starlight glittering in the puddles alongside the lane, as happy as he could imagine being. He was Gird, the local farmer's son who had made good, had made a place for himself in the lord's household, by the strength of his arm and the courage of his heart.

*   *   *

Then the lord count arrived from the king's court. All the guards
stood rigid in the courtyard for that: Gird in the back row, with
the other recruits. Tall as he was, he had a good view of the cavalcade. A halfsquad of guards, looking somehow older and rougher
than those he had met, on chunky nomad-bred horses, followed by
two boys that looked younger than Gird on tall, light-built mounts.
Behind them, a prancing warhorse with elaborate harness embroidered and stamped on multicolored leathers. And on the warhorse,
their lord—Gird's liege lord, Count Seriast Vanier Dobrest Kelaive—a sour-faced young man in orange velvet, black gloves, tall
black boots, and a black velvet cap with an orange plume. He
looked, Gird thought, like a gourd going bad in storage—a big
orange gourd spotted with fungus.

Immediately he suppressed the thought. This was his lord, his
sworn liege, and for the rest of his life he would be this man's
loyal vassal. His eyes dropped to the horse, the saddle, the tall
polished boots. There were his spurs, the visible symbol of his
knighthood, long polished shafts and delicate jewelled rowels. The
steward came forward; the squires dismounted, handing their
horses to grooms. One of them held the lord's bridle; the other
steadied the off stirrup while he dismounted. Gird watched every
detail. So far he had not had a chance to ride more than the mule
that turned the millsweep. But in watching the horse, he heard
everything, heard the steward's graceful speech of welcome, the
curt response.

He knew, as did they all, that the young lord had been educated
at the king's court in Finyatha; this year, at Summereve, he would
take over his own domain, and the steward's rule would end. Everyone had liked that idea—or almost everyone—and had told one
another tales of the steward's harshness. A young lord, they'd said,
their own lord, living finally on his own domain, would surely be
more generous. The steward would have to do his bidding, not
make up orders of his own.

But now, seeing the young lord in person, Gird had a moment
of doubt. For all the complaints he'd heard of the steward's harshness, most years no one went hungry. The sergeant had told him
of other lands where brigands or war brought famine. Here, despite
the fees, a hardworking family could prosper, as his had, with one
brother tenanting his own cottage, and Arin soon to marry. Would
things be better under the young count?

Still, Summereve, only a few days away, would bring a great day
for both of them. The lord's investiture, in the moments after

midnight. He could not imagine what solemn rituals gave one of the
lords dominion; the sergeant made it clear that it was none of
their business. Perhaps the sergeant himself had never seen. Village
rumor, he remembered, had it that the lords gained their great
powers when they took office. But he had never seen any lord, or
anyone with powers beyond the steward's ability to ferret out the
truth when someone lied. He could not begin to imagine what kind
of powers their young lord might have, or use. He pulled his mind
back from this speculation to his own prospects. His promotion from
recruit to guard private, the next afternoon, would be part of the lord's
formal court, the first occasion on which the count would show his
wisdom and ability to rule well. Gird had his new uniform ready, had
every bit of leather oiled and shining, every scrap of metal polished.

He let his eyes wander to the rest of the entourage. Behind the
lord's horse came others equally gaudily caparisoned: young nobles in
velvets and furs, sweating in the early summer heat. Young
noblewomen, attended each by maids and chaperons, riding graceful
horses with hooves painted gold and silver. They began to dismount,
in a flurry of ribbons and wide-sweeping sleeves, a gabble of voices
as loud and bright as a flight of birds in the cornfield. As the young
lord passed his steward's deferential bow, and led the party into the
house, Gird felt a surge of excitement. The real world, the great world
of king's court, the outside world he had never seen, had come to
him, to his own village, and he would be part of it.

Chapter Three

Behind the main mass of the lord's hall lay the walled gardens.
To the east, the fruit orchard, with its neatly trimmed plums and
pears, its rare peach trained against a southern wall. To the west,
the long rows of the vegetable garden, mounds of cabbage like a
row of balls, the spiky blue-green stalks of onions and ramps, the
sprawling vine-bushes of redroot. Ten-foot stone walls surrounded
each garden, proof against the casual thief and straying herdbeast.
But not, of course, against the daring of an occasional boy who
would brag the rest of his life about a theft of plum or pear from
the lord's own garden.

Meris, son of Aric, now the tanner's apprentice, had taken a plum the year before, but it was partly green. This year, he determined to take a sackful, and share them out, and they would be ripe ones, too. The lord's best plum tree, as Meris knew well (for his uncle was a skilled pruner of trees, and worked on them), was the old one in the middle of the garden, the only survivor of a row of plums grafted from scions of the king's garden in Finyatha. Its fruit ripened early, just before Summereve, medium-sized reddish egg-shaped plums with a silver bloom and yellow flesh.

It seemed to him that the young lord's arrival would be an excellent time to make his raid. The lord and his retinue would be busy, and nearly everyone else would be watching the excitement in the forecourt. So as soon as the first horns blew across the field, signalling the approaching cavalcade, Meris left off scraping the hair from the wet hide he was working on, and begged his master to let him go.

"Oh, aye, and if I don't you'll be so excited you'll likely scrape a hole in it. Very well . . . put it back to soak, and begone with you. But you'll finish that hide before supper, Meris, if it takes until midnight."

With the prospect of a belly full of his lord's best plums, a delayed supper was the last thing Meris needed to worry about. He grinned his thanks and darted from the tannery. He had hidden what he needed behind a clump of bushes on the east side of the lord's wall . . . a braided rawhide rope with a sliding loop. Other boys used borrowed ladders, and he'd heard of the smith's boy using some sort of hook tied to rope, but he had found that the looped rope could nearly always find a limb to fasten on. With a little support from the rope, and the skill of his bare feet on the rough-cut stone walls, he had always managed to get over. And the rawhide rope, without a hook or other contrivance, never attracted the suspicious attention of the guard. Once they'd found it, and he watched from the bushes as they shrugged and left it in place. A herdsman's noose, they'd said, dropped by some careless apprentice. Let the lad take his master's punishment, and braid another.

He waited, now, in the same clump of bushes, watching people stream by from the eastern fields. Soon no one passed. He heard a commotion around the wall's corner, from the village itself. Let it peak, he thought. Let the lord arrive. He waited a little longer, then glanced around. No one in sight, not even a distant flock. He swung the noose wide, as he'd practiced, and tossed it over the fence. He heard the thrashing of leaves as he pulled, and it tightened. He tugged. Firm enough.

Standing back a bit from the base of the wall, he threw himself upward, finding a toehold, and another. Whenever he found nothing, he used the rope, but most of it was skill and scrambling. At the wall's top, he flattened himself along it and gave a careful look at the hall's rear windows. Once he'd been seen by a servant, and nearly caught. But, as he'd expected, nothing moved in those windows. Everyone must be watching the forecourt, and the young lord's arrival. He pulled up his rope, and coiled it on the top of the wall. He could gain the wall from the inside by climbing one of the pears trained along it; he needed the rope only for getting in. This time, though, he planned to use it to lower the sack of stolen fruit on his way out. He checked his sack, took another cautious look around, and climbed quickly down a pear tree to the soft grass under the trees.

He heard a blast of trumpets from the forecourt, and grinned. Just as he'd planned: complete silence in the gardens, and everyone out front gaping at the lord. Silly. He was going to be there long enough for all to see, so why bother? Meris glanced around, still careful. No sign of anyone. One of the gates between the fruit orchard and the vegetable garden was open; he could see the glistening cabbage heads, the spikes of onion.

He moved forward. None of the pear trees had ripe fruit, but all were heavy with green pears. One of the golden plums was ripe; a single fruit lay on the grass beneath. Meris snatched it up and bit into it. Sun-warm and sweet, the juice slid down his throat. He spat the pit into the grass and plucked several of the golden plums for his sack. He took a few red plums from another tree, and then found himself at the old one, the "king tree" as his uncle called it.

It was loaded with ripe and overripe plums; clearly the steward had decided to leave it for the young lord's pleasure. Ordinarily, Meris knew, the trees were picked over every day to prevent loss to bird and wasp. But here the limbs drooped, heavy with plums, and the grass beneath was littered with fallen fruit. Wasps buzzed around these; the air was heavy with the scent of plum. Meris stepped forward, careful of the wasps beneath, and started picking.

He had nearly filled his sack, when he heard a door slam at the far end of the garden. He looked over his shoulder. Surely the welcoming ceremonies would have taken longer than this! He could see nothing between the trees, but he heard voices coming nearer. To go back, he would have to cross the central walk, in clear view of whatever busybody gardener had come back to work. But on this side, only a few steps away, was the open door to the vegetable gardens. He could outrun any gardener, he was sure, but he might be recognized. If he could hide for a little . . .

Quietly, he eased through the garden door, still without seeing whose were the oncoming voices, and found himself in unknown territory. To his left, rows of cabbage and onion stretched to the rear of the stable walls. Ahead were the beanrows, tall pole frames with bean vines tangling in them, only waist-high at this season. In a few weeks the beanrows would have been tall enough, but right now he'd have to crawl in between the poles. Scant cover, and once he was among them, a long way to any of the walls. On his right, the low matted redroots, with gourds beyond them, and some feathery-leaved plants he'd never seen before. The wall he'd come through was covered with some sort of vine; it had orange flowers and was trimmed off a foot or so below the wall-height. He saw no one, in the whole huge garden, but he saw no place to hide quickly if someone came, in.

He flattened himself against the wall by the open door, and listened. Guards, they sounded like, rough voices. Perhaps the lord had sent them to check on everything—though Meris thought he should have trusted his local sergeant. The voices had passed beyond, and then he heard them coming back, heard the steady stride, the faint chink of metal on metal. Guards, sure enough. He dared a look, saw a broad back in the orange and black striped tunic, no one he recognized. Guards who had come with the young lord, then. They were through; they passed by, and kept going. He listened to their heavy step all the way down the main walk.

He grinned to himself. His luck was holding. In a mad impulse, he darted forward and yanked two onions out of the ground and stuffed them in his sack. And a ramp. Ramps, the onion cousin that none of the peasants was allowed to grow, brought from the old south, so they'd always heard, and sold sometimes on market days for high prices—he would have a ramp of his own, the whole thing. He might even plant it, under the forest edge, and grow more. Then he stood up.

"Hey—you there!" In the time it had taken him to pull a ramp, one of the gardeners had entered by the stable doors. Meris did not wait to see what would happen; he bolted straight for the door into the orchard. Behind him, the gardener's yell had started others yelling. He slammed the door behind him and threw the latch; it might slow them an instant. Then he was off, running between the trees as hard as he could pelt, the sack of stolen fruit banging his thigh.

He hardly saw the group of people strolling along the main walk before he had run into them, knocking one man flat. He heard high-pitched cries, and deeper yells of rage, and kept going,

knocking aside someone's grab at his arm. It seemed the orchard
had grown twice as wide; tree limbs thrashed his face. Behind him
now were the heavy feet of guardsmen as well. When he came to
the wall, he swarmed up the pear tree as fast as a cat fleeing a
wolf, and gained its top, Here he paused a moment. The guards
were too heavy for the pears; they'd never be able to climb so high,
he thought. Of course, they'd bring ladders . . . He caught a flash
of bright orange between the trees below, and someone yelled.
Hardly thinking, he snatched an onion from his bag and fired it at
the shape. Another bellow; he turned to leap into the thicket below.
He'd have to risk mashing his fruit. He had no time to lower it
carefully; in fact, he'd have to run off without it if he didn't want
to be caught.

The sergeant kept them on parade in the forecourt even though
the young lord had gone on into his hall. He might come back out;
besides, the peasants were still milling about in the lane near the
gates. When the noise began, a reverberant yell from somewhere
deep in the hall, the sergeant sent squads in at once, one through
the hall itself. Almost as soon as they disappeared into the hall,
they came boiling back out again, running for the gates. Gird, with
the other recruits, knew that something had happened, but not
what; the sergeant silenced them with curses when they asked, and
finally sent them off to the barracks. There they shifted from foot
to foot, nervous as young colts in a pen. They dared not sit on the
bunks made ready for inspection; they dared not do anything, lest
it be the wrong thing.

Not long after, they were called back. The sergeant looked as
grim as Gird had ever seen him; no one dared speak. He hurried
them into formation, marched them once more to the forecourt.
This time they were told to form a line dividing the forecourt in
half. On one side, the lord and his steward, and the guardsmen.
On the other, the villagers, crowding in behind Gird and the other
recruits. And between them, his shirt torn half off his back, Meris
son of Aric.

Gird stared at the scene before him, bewildered. He had known
Meris all his life; the younger boy had a name for mischief, but
Gird had thought him safely apprenticed to the tanner. What could
Meris have done, to cause such an uproar?

The boy, held tightly by two guardsmen, stood as if lame, leaning
a bit to one side. Gird could see a bruise rising over his eye. On
the far side of the court, the lord started forward, slapping one

black glove against the other. The steward laid a hand on his arm, was shaken off with a glare, and stepped back.

"What's his name?" asked the lord. No one answered for a moment; Gird thought no one was sure who should, or how the young lord should be addressed. Then the steward spoke up.

"Meris, son of Aric," he said. "A tanner's apprentice."

The young lord flung a glance back at the steward, and nodded. "Meris, son of Aric . . . and is Aric here?"

"No, my lord. Aric is a herdsman; your cattle are in the pastures beyond the wood right now; he is with them."

"And the tanner, his master: where is he?"

A movement among the villagers, and the tanner stepped forward. "Here, sir."

"Sir *count,* churl." The lord looked him up and down. "A fine master you are—did you teach your 'prentice to thieve, is that it?"

"Sir?" The tanner's face could not have been more surprised if he'd found himself dyed blue, Gird thought. The young lord barked a contemptuous laugh at him.

"You mean to claim you did not know where he was? You did not know he was stealing fruit from my orchard? From the way he ran straight for that pear tree, I daresay had done it often before. You know the law: a master stands for his apprentice's misdeeds—"

"Stealing fruit?" Gird did not know the tanner well; the man had moved into the village only three years before, when old Simmis had died and left the tannery vacant. But he seemed honest enough now, if perhaps none too bright. "But he begged the time off to see your honor's coming—"

"While you, I presume, were too busy to see your liege lord's arrival, or to supervise your apprentice properly?"

The tanner looked from lord to steward and back again, seeing no help anywhere. "But—but sir—I didn't know. I thought he—"

"You should have known; he was your apprentice. Be glad I don't have you stripped naked and in the stocks for this; the steward will collect your fine later." The lord smiled, and turned to the boy. "And as for this young thief, this miscreant who was not content to steal my fruit, but boldly assaulted my person—you'll climb no more walls, and steal no more fruit, and I daresay you'll remember the respect you owe your lord to the end of your life." The steward moved, as if he would speak, but the young count stared him down. "It is your laxness, Cullen, that's given these cattle the idea they can act so. You should have schooled them better."

The courtyard was utterly silent for a long moment. Then a soft murmur began, like the first movement of leaves in a breeze, rustling just within hearing. Gird felt a wave of nausea, as he realized with the others that the young lord intended far worse than the steward ever had. Even now he could not believe that Meris had assaulted the lord: Meris had never assaulted anyone. His mischiefs were always solitary.

It was then, as his eyes slid from one to another, not quite meeting anyone's as their eyes avoided his, that he noticed the pin clasping the young count's cloak. A circle, like the symbol of Esea's Eye, the Sunlord, but sprouting horns . . . like a circle of barbed chain, the barbed chain the followers of Liart had left on his bunk. And those three, of all the soldiers, were untroubled by the count's malice . . . were eager, he realized, for whatever the count wanted.

What the count wanted, as events proved, was threefold; to terrorize his peasantry, to impress his friends from the king's court, and to leave Meris just enough life to suffer long before dying. Long before the end of it, Gird and many others had heaved their guts out onto the paved court, had fallen shaking and sobbing to their knees, trying not to see and hear what they could not help seeing and hearing. Not even his sergeant's fist on his collar, the urgent "Get *up*, boy, before it's you—" could steady him. He staggered up, shook free of the sergeant's hold, and bolted across the empty space into the crowd, fighting his way to the gate like a terrified ox from a pen.

He had moved so suddenly, with so little forethought, that no one caught him; behind him the villagers reacted to his panic with their own, screaming and thrashing away from the scene of torture. That kept the rest of the soldiers busy, though Gird didn't realize it. He ran as if he could outrun his memories, down the long lane past his father's cottage, out beyond the great field, the haymeadows, fighting his way blindly through the thickets beside the creek, and through the rolling cobbles to the far side. Then he was running in the wood, staggering through briar and vine, falling over the gnarled roots of the old trees to measure his length again and again. He never noticed when his uniform tore, when thorns raked his arms and face, tore at his legs. Higher in the wood, and higher . . . past the pens where they fed the half-wild hogs, past the low hut where the pigherder stayed in season. He startled one sounder of swine, so they snorted and crashed through the undergrowth with him for a space. Then he was falling into another branch of the creek, and turning to clamber upstream, instinct taking over where his mind couldn't, his legs finally losing their stride to let him topple into the rocky cleft his brother Arin had shown him all those years ago.

For some time he knew nothing, felt nothing, and the hours passed over him. He woke, with a countryman's instinct, at dusk, when the evening breeze brought the hayfield scent up over the wood, and tickled his nose with it. He ached in every limb; his scratches burned and itched, and his mouth tasted foul. Until he was up on his knees, he did not remember where he was, or why— but then a spasm of fear and shame doubled him up, and sourness filled his mouth. He gulped and heaved again. Meris, a boy he had known—a lad who had tagged behind him, more than once—would never walk straight again, or hold tools, and he had worn the uniform of the one who had done it.

He could hear his mother's voice ringing in his head. This was what she'd meant, about taking service of iron, and leaving the Lady of Peace. This was what his father had feared, that he would use his strength to hurt his own people. Scalding tears ran down his face. He had been so happy, so proud, only a few days before . . . he had been so sure that his family's fears were the silly fears of old-fashioned peasants, "mere farmers," as the sergeant so often called them.

Arin came to the cleft before dawn, sliding silently between the trees. "Gird?" he called softly. "Girdi—you here?"

Gird coiled himself into an even tighter and more miserable ball as far back as he could burrow, but Arin came all the way in, and squatted down beside him.

"You stink," he said companionably, one brother to another. "The dogs will have no trouble."

"Dogs?" Gird had not thought of dogs, but now remembered the long-tailed hounds that had gone out with the tracker after wolves.

"I brought you a shirt," said Arin. "And a bit of bread. Go wash." The very matter-of-factness of Arin's voice, the big brother he had always listened to, made it possible for him to unclench himself and stagger to his feet. He took the shirt from Arin without looking at it, and moved out of the cleft before stripping off his clothes. In the clean chill of dawn, he could smell himself, the fear-sweat and vomit and blood so different from the honest sweat of toil. Arin smelled of onions and earth. He wished he could be an onion, safe underground. But the cold water, and a bunch of creekside herbs crushed to scrub with, cleansed the stench from his body. His mind was different: he could still hear Meris scream, still feel, as in his own body, the crack of breaking bones.

"Hurry up," said Arin, behind him. "I've got to talk to you." Gird rinsed his mouth in the cold water, and drank a handful, then another. He pulled on the shirt Arin had brought; it was barely big enough across the shoulders, and his wrists stood out of the sleeves, but it covered him. Arin handed him the bread. Gird had not thought he was hungry, but he wolfed the bread down in three bites. He could have eaten a whole loaf.

By this time it was light enough to see his brother's drawn face, and read his expression. Arin shook his head at him. "Girdi, you're like that bullcalf that got loose and stuck in the mire three years ago—do you remember? Thought he was grown, he was so big, but once out of his pen and in trouble, he bawled for help like any new-weaned calf." Gird said nothing; he could feel tears rising in his eyes again, and his throat closed. "Girdi, you have to go back." That opened his eyes, and his throat.

"I can't!" he said, panting. "Arin, I can't—you didn't see—"

"I saw." Arin's voice had hardened. "We all saw; the count made sure of it. But it's that or outlaw, Girdi, and you won't live to be an outlaw—the count will hunt you down, and the fines will fall on our family."

It was another load of black guilt on top of the other. "So—so I must die?"

"No." Arin had picked up a stick, and poked it into the moss-covered ground near the creek. "At least—I hope not. What your sergeant said was that if someone knew where you were, and if you'd turn yourself in, he thought he could save your life. And we'd not lose our holding. The steward . . . the steward's not with the count in this. You saw that. But you have to come in, Gird, on your own. If they chase and capture you—"

"I can't be a soldier," said Gird. "I can't do that—what they did—"

"So I should hope. They don't want you now, anyway." Even in his misery, that hurt. He knew he'd been a promising recruit, barring his slowness in learning to read; he knew the sergeant had had hopes for him. And now he'd lost all that, forever. His stomach rumbled, reminding him that he'd also lost plentiful free food. "We can use you," Arin went on. "We always could."

His mind was a stormy whirlwind of fear and grief and shame. He could imagine what the sergeant would say, the sneers of the other men, the ridicule. And surely he would be punished, for disgracing them so, and breaking his oath of service. Would he be left like Meris, a cripple? Better to die . . . and yet he did not want to die. The thought of it, hanging or the sword in his neck—and those were the easy ways—terrified him. Arin's look was gentle.

"Poor lad. You're still just a boy, after all, aren't you? For all the long arms and legs, for all the bluster you've put on this past spring."

"I'm—sorry." He could not have said all he was sorry for, but a great sore lump of misery filled his head and heart.

"I know." Arin sighed. "But I'm not sorry to think of you working beside me, Gird, when this is over. Come now: wash your face again, and let's be going back."

He felt light-headed on the way, but the stiffness worked out of his legs quickly. His soiled uniform rolled under his arm, he followed Arin down paths he hardly remembered.

"We need to hurry," said Arin over his shoulder. "They were going to start searching again this morning, and I'd like to get you down to the village before they set the dogs loose."

"What—what happened, after—"

"After you bolted? Near a riot, that was, with everyone screaming and thrashing about. It took awhile to settle, and the count had more to think of than you. Then your sergeant came to our place, and talked to father. Said you'd deserted, and they'd have to hunt you unless you came back on your own, and even if you did it might go hard with you. He didn't like the count's sentence on Meris any more than the rest of us, but . . . he had to go along. He took out a few of the men late in the evening, calling for you. I was sure you'd come up here."

"I didn't think," said Gird. "I just couldn't stand it—"

"Mmm. Then the steward came, after dark." Arin stepped carefully over a tangle of roots and went on. "Said we'd lose the holding, the way the count felt. He'd come down to show off his inheritance to his friends from court, all those fine lords and ladies, and then Meris hit him with an onion—"

"He what!"

"That's right. You probably don't know what really happened. Meris was stealing fruit, thinking everyone would be busy out front, but the count wanted to show the ladies the garden, and hurried through. So when Meris was spotted, he ran straight into the count and knocked him flat, in front of his friends, and then fired an onion at him from the top of the wall. Probably thought it was a guard. Poor lad."

Gird was silent, thinking what sort of man would cripple a boy for such a ridiculous mistake.

"He was wrong, of course, and now we're all in trouble, from the steward on down, but—" Arin flashed a grin back over his shoulder. "At least you didn't take part in it—and if they want to call it cowardice, well, I say brave men have better to do than batter rash boys into ruin."

"I don't want to die," said Gird suddenly, into the green silence of the wood.

"No one does," said Arin, "but sick old men and women. Did you think a soldier would never see death?"

"No, but—but I didn't think it would be like this. If it is, I mean." He didn't expect an answer to that, and got none. Early sun probed through the leaves, shafts of golden light between the trees. The wood smelled of damp earth, herbs, ripening bramble-berries, a whiff here and there of pig or fox or rabbit. He was afraid, but he could not shut out the richness of the world around him, the springy feel of the leafmold under his feet. Air went in and out his nose despite his misery.

They came to the straggling end of the lane without being seen. Gird hesitated to follow Arin into the open, but his brother strode on without looking back, trusting him. He could see no one, but a distant shepherd far across the fields. Up the lane toward the village. Now he could see the first cottages, his father's well, the lane beyond, the great fields to his right. A few women at the well, someone (he could not tell who) behind the hedge in front of their cottage.

Arin spoke again. "It's better if you go alone, Gird. Can you do that?"

Cold sweat sprang out all over him. Alone? But he knew Arin was right. The sergeant and steward would know that his brother had gone to bring him in—the whole village knew already—but if he went the rest of the way alone it could go unspoken. Less chance that more punishment would fall on Arin.

The soldiers were just starting out from the gates when he came in sight of them; the sergeant must have delayed as long as he could. They paused, and the sergeant gestured. Gird walked on. His legs felt shaky again, and it was hard to breathe. When he was close enough, he didn't know what to say. He couldn't salute, not with his filthy uniform under his arm, and a peasant shirt on his back. The sergeant's face was closed, impassive.

"Well, Gird," he said.

"Sir," said Gird miserably, looking down at his scuffed and dirty boots. He forced himself to meet the sergeant's eyes. "I—I was wrong, sir." One of the men guffawed; the sergeant cut it short with a chop of hid hand.

"You broke your oath," the sergeant said. He sounded weary and angry together, someone who had come near the end of his strength as well as his patience. "Right in front of the count himself—" He stopped. "You're carrying your uniform? Right. Give it here." Gird handed it over, and the sergeant took it, his nostrils pinched. "Take off your boots, boy." Gird stared a moment, then hurried to obey. Of course the boots were part of the uniform; he should have thought of that. His feet, pale and thin-skinned from more than a year of wearing boots daily, found the dusty lane cool and gritty. The sergeant jerked his head at Keri, one of the other recruits, who came to take the boots, and the uniform both. "We'll burn them," said the sergeant. "We want nothing tainted with cowards' sweat." Gird felt himself flushing; the sergeant nodded at him. "Yes, you. You were wrong, and so was I, to think you'd ever make a soldier. I should have known, when you flinched from it before . . ." His voice trailed away, as the steward came out the gates with the village headman.

The steward gave Gird the same sort of searching look. "So. He came back, did he? Or did you track him down?"

"He came back, sir. Brought his uniform; he'd got a shirt from somewhere."

The steward looked Gird up and down. "It's a bad business, boy, to break an oath. Hard to live down. Reflects on the family. The count would make an example of you, but for the sergeant's report: you're strong, and docile, and will do more good at fieldwork than you will feeding crows from the gibbet. See that you work, boy, and cause no trouble. One more complaint of you, and your family's holding is forfeit." He turned to the headman, ignoring Gird.

The sergeant said, "You heard him. What are you waiting for? Get along to work, boy, and thank your Lady of Peace that you still have the limbs to work with. I wouldn't mind laying a few stripes on your back myself."

Chapter Four

In time Gird thought the stripes would have hurt less. He walked back to his father's cottage, that bright morning, with his feet relearning the balance of walking bare, and his skin prickling with the knowledge that everyone knew he had been disgraced. Had disgraced *himself*, he reminded himself firmly. That first time along the lane, no one said anything, though he was aware of all the sidelong glances. He made it home without incident, to find Arin waiting for him.

"You're to clean out the cowbyre," said Arin, handing him the old wooden shovel. "He thinks it better if you keep out of sight."

Gird glanced at his mother, busy at her loom. Her expression said "I told you no good would come of it," as clearly as if she'd spoken aloud. His youngest sister Hara had obviously been told to keep quiet. He wondered if she'd been the one peeking through the hedge earlier. Probably. He took the shovel and went to work.

Across the barton, Arin was mending harness. Beyond the barton wicket, Gird could see a cluster of men in the greatfield. Midmorning now; they'd stopped work for a chat and a drink. He shoveled steadily, piling the dirty straw and manure in the basket, to drag across the barton and toss on the pile just beyond the gate. He wasn't sure why Arin was staying close—did they think he would run again? And Arin hadn't asked what happened up at the manor gates. Gird felt as touchy as after his first sunburn each spring. Every glance Arin gave him seemed to be made of flame.

At noon, Hara passed through the cowbyre with their father's lunch wrapped in a cloth; she gave Gird a cool nod that cut him to the bone. Arin stopped punching holes and lacing straps together, and stretched. He smiled; by then Gird was not sure what that smile meant.

"Come on, then, long-face. It's not what you're used to, but it is food." Arin hardly needed to wash, but Gird was muck to the knees and elbows. He remembered to flick a spatter of clean water out for grace, and washed carefully enough to please the sergeant before going in to get his bowl of mush. It hardly seemed to touch his hunger, but then the look on his mother's face tightened his throat so that he could not have swallowed another bite.

By late afternoon, he had cleared the cowbyre, and when the cowherd brought the animals back to the village, and Arin led their own three into the barton, he had the stalls spread with fresh straw. He washed up quickly, and started milking. He had always liked the cows, even the crook-horned red cow who slapped his face with her dirty great tail and did her best to tread in the bucket. His father appeared as he was milking the second, but said nothing before going on inside. Gird leaned his head into a warm, hairy flank, and let his hands remember the rhythmic squeeze and pull that brought the milk down quickly and easily. The milk smelled good, no taint of onion or wild garlic. He leaned closer, and gave himself a warm, luscious mouthful.

"I saw that," said Arin, from around the rump of the third cow.

"You know better." It was the old bantering tone of their boyhood, but it didn't seem the same.

"Sorry," said Gird, wishing he weren't so conscious of the taste of that milk, the richness of it. Their milk was traded to the village cheesemaker; grown men did not drink milk. He felt he could drink the whole bucket He finished the last quarter, and carried the bucket into the kitchen. From there he could hear the voices in the front room: his father and the steward. What now? he wondered. But his mother, square athwart the kitchen hearth, sent him back to the barton with a wave of her spoon.

He ranged around it, doing every chore he could think of, until his father called him in. It was much like the night the steward had visited to offer him the chance to train: his mother and father sitting stiffly on one side, and the steward at their single table. Arin followed him in. Hara, banished to the kitchen, was as close to the door as she could be, and not be seen by the elders.

"You should know," said the steward without preamble, "what your rashness will cost your father. He must appear at court, the afternoon of the count's investiture. I have spoken with the count, and pled what I can: your youth, your father's record of work, your brothers. But the fact is, the count is angry, and with reason. And your father, head of your family, will be fined. I came to tell him, that he might have it ready to pay, and save himself a night in the stocks."

Gird met his father's eyes. His father in the stocks? For his running away?

"You will attend as well, boy, and it may be the count will have something to say to you. He is your lord; he may do as he pleases. Remember your rank, and try—" the emphasis was scornful, "to cause no more trouble."

When the steward had gone, Gird's father patted his shoulder. "It's all right, Gird. You're here, and alive, and—it's all right." Gird knew it was not. For the first time in his life, he realized that he could do harm he could not mend. He felt at once helpless and young, and far removed from the boyish confidence of a few days before.

"What—how much is the fine?" he asked.

His father cleared his throat. "Well. They want repaid all they spent on your training. It's all in the steward's accounts, he says. Food, clothing, the coppers he sent me, even barracks room. And then a fine for oath-breaking—" Gird had never really mastered figures, but he knew he'd worn clothes worth far more than his family could have bought him. And eaten more, of better food. His father turned to Arin. "I'll have to ask you—"

Arin nodded. "Of course. Will it be enough?"

His father scrubbed at his face with both hands. "We'll see. Gird, you were too young before: come here, now, and see where our coins lie hid."

He had known it was under some stone in the fireplace; everyone hid valuables that way. But not which—and before his father levered out the stone, he would not have suspected that one. Within was a leather pouch, and in that his father's small store of coppers and silvers. His father counted it out twice.

"I saved most of your wages, for Arin's marriage-price, and Hara's dower. There's a hand of coppers, and another hand of coppers. But a fine of double the fieldfee—that's a silver and a hand of coppers, and doubled—" He laid it out as he spoke, handling the coins as gingerly as if they were nettles to sting him. Gird held his breath, thinking of the hours of labor, baskets of fruit and grain, that each represented. "And the uniforms—" The last of the coppers went into a row, and his father frowned, shaking his head. " 'Tis not enough, even so. They might have let you keep the boots, at least, if we must pay for them."

"How much?" asked his mother.

"Eight copper crabs, and that's if the count holds to the steward's say. I doubt he will. It'll be a sheep, then, or a furl of cloth."

"I have a furl, set by," his mother said. "It was for—"

"No matter what it was for," said his father harshly. "It is for Gird's life, now."

"I know that," said his mother. Gird watched as she opened the press that stored her weaving, and pulled out a rolled furl of cloth. His father touched it lightly, and nodded.

"We'll hope that will do," he said.

The lord held court in the yard, with the count seated beneath an awning striped orange and yellow. None of his noble friends was with him; having sat through his investiture at midnight, they had all slept late.

Despite Gird's father's oath to the steward that they would appear, one of the soldiers came that morning to march them up to the manor gates. He had studiously ignored Gird; others had not, small children who had stared and called and been yanked back within cottages by their mothers. Gird's feet were sore, not yet toughened to going bare, and his shirt had already split. His

mother had patched it the night before. He was acutely aware of
the patch, of his bare feet, of the difference between Gird, Dorthan's son, peasant boy, and Gird the recruit.

That contrast was sharpened when he watched the other recruits
accepted into service as they gave their oaths to the count, and
pinned on the badges of guard private. None of them met his eyes,
not even Keri. One by one they came forward, knelt, swore, and
returned to the formation. Gird's heart contracted. For one
moment he wanted to throw himself before the count and beg to
be reinstated. Then his roving eye saw the stocks, with the stains
of Meris's blood still dark on the wood.

Another case preceded theirs. The steward had intended it, Gird
knew, as the ritual single case the new lord must judge; he had
saved it back from the spring courts. Now he rushed the witnesses
through their stories of missing boundary stone and suspected
encroachment on someone's strip of arable. Clearly not even the
plaintiff and defendant thought it was as important as before,
compared with Gird and his father. The count concurred with
the steward's assessment, and the loser didn't bother to scowl as
he paid his two copper crabs to the winner, and another to
the count.

Then it was their turn. The steward called his father forward;
Gird followed two paces behind, as he'd been bidden. To his surprise, the sergeant came too.

The count's face was drawn down in a scowl of displeasure that
didn't quite conceal an underlying glee. The steward began,
explaining how Gird had been recruited.

"A big, strong lad, already known as a hard worker. He seemed
brave enough then, as boys go—" He turned to the sergeant.

"Willing to work, yes. Obedient, strong . . . not too quick in his
mind, my lord, but there's good soldiers enough that can't do more
than he did. Never gave trouble in the barracks."

"And he gave you no hint of his . . . weakness?" The count's
voice this day was almost silken smooth, no hint of the wild rage
he'd shown before.

The sergeant frowned. "Well, my lord, he did in a way. He didn't
like hurting things, he said once, and he never did give up his
peasant superstitions. Flowers to the well-sprite, and that sort of
thing."

"Complained of hard treatment, did he?"

"No, my lord. Not that. Like I said, a willing enough lad, when
it came to hard work, not one to complain at all. But too soft. I

put it down to his being young, and never from home, but that was wrong."

"Indeed." The count stared at Gird until he felt himself go hot all over. "Big lout. Not well-favored, no *quality* in him. Some are born cattle, you know, and others are born wolves. You can make sheepdogs of wolves, but nothing of cattle save oxen in yokes. He looks stupid enough. I can't imagine why you ever considered him; if you want to stay in my service, you'd best not make such mistakes again."

"No, my lord," said the sergeant and steward, almost in the same breath.

"Well," said the count, "to settle young oxen, put stones on the load. You had a recommendation, steward?" The steward murmured; Gird heard again the terms his father had told him. The count nodded. "Well enough, so far as it goes, but not quite far enough. Let one of my Finyathans give the boy a whipping, and if his father wants him whole, let him pay the death-gift for his life. Else geld the young ox, and breed no more cowards of him." His eyes met Gird's, and he smiled. "Do you like my judgment, boy?"

Beside him, his father was rigid with shock and fear; Gird bowed as well as he could. The death-gift for a son was a cow and its calf that year. A third of their livestock gone, or his future sons and daughters. He knew his father would pay, but the cost!

The steward muttered again; the count shook his head. "Let the father pay now. What is it to be, fellow?" Gird's father stepped forward, and laid the pouch of coins, and the furl of cloth, on the table. The steward took the pouch and counted the coins quickly.

"The cow?" he said without looking up. Gird's father nodded, and the steward noted it down. "Go fetch the cow," he said brusquely.

"Sir, she's with the cowherd—"

"Will you fetch the cow or not?" The steward's face was white. "It's all one to me whether you have grandsons from this boy."

Gird's father bowed. "I'll go now, sir, may I?" he said, his voice trembling, and backed away. The count laughed.

" 'Tis no wonder the boy's a coward, with such a father. At least he's docile." The count waved a hand, and one of the Finyathan guards went off, to return in a few moments with a long rod bound in leather. "And you, sergeant, as you erred in choosing him, I don't doubt you'd like a chance to leave your mark on him?"

Whether he wanted to or not, Gird could not tell, but the sergeant had no choice. That much was clear. Nor did he. He went to the stocks without resistance, hoping he could keep from crying out. He felt the scorn more than the blows, but the Finyathan guard, when the sergeant gave up the rod to him after four or five stripes, had evident delight in his work. The count watched, leaning on one elbow and chatting to the steward without taking his eyes off Gird's face. By the time his father came back with the cow, Gird had bruises and lumps from more than the rod. He had closed his eyes before they swelled shut, not wanting to see his former friends in the guards as they joined in.

He woke face-down in a puddle of water that had been thrown over him, with the count's waspish voice saying "Take the oaf away, and pray I forget all this." His father's arm helped him up; outside the gates Arin too waited, to help him home.

His head rang. He could not have made it without help. His mother and Hara cleaned the blood off, and muttered over the damage done to the shirt. The rest of that day and night he lay wrapped in a blanket, sipping the bitter brew his mother spooned down him at intervals. For himself, he'd have been glad to have wound-fever and die of it, to be at peace, for his old dreams tormented him like haunts, making mock of his pride. He twisted and groaned, until Arin woke and held him.

"It's all right, Girdi. It's over now." But it was not over, and wouldn't be. He was sour with his own sweat, disgusted with himself, and shaking with fears he could not express. If things had gone so wrong so fast, what was safe? Arin's reassurance meant nothing. He remembered the look on the count's face, the delight in cruelty. He might have been killed—really killed—his life had hung on the count's whim.

The next morning he forced his stiff, aching body out of bed. He was not sure he could work, but he knew he must. His mother had yet to remake his shirt from the ragged scraps left after his punishment, so she insisted he stay indoors. His father and Arin agreed. Indoors, then, he worked—back to childhood, he thought, scrubbing the stone hearth, washing dishes and pots, carrying buckets of water from the well. It was hot indoors, breathless as Midsummer usually was. Sweat stung in the welts and scrapes; he ignored it, shrugged away his mother's attempt to put a poultice on the deepest ones. She glared at him.

"You may want a fever, to get out of work, but we've no time for that, lad. Stand you there and no more shifting, while I clean this out again." He felt himself flush, but stood. What else could he do? He had forfeited his chance to adult status. Her fingers were gentler than her voice. The sharp fragrance of herbs worked its way past his misery for a few moments as she stroked the heavy ointment on his back. " 'Tis a bad world, lad, where such things happen. But you see what comes of taking iron to mend them. Remember this: no matter how bad it seems, soldiering makes it worse. It always comes hardest on those with the least. Mind your father, keep out of the lord's eye: that's best. Notice brings trouble, no matter if it seems good at first. Remember what tree the forester chooses."

He'd heard that often and often before. It was not in the Lady's ritual, but it was the village's favorite truth: notice brings trouble. As bad to be always first in reaping as always last; as bad to be richest as poorest. The tall tree catches the forester's eye, and the fattest ox suggests a feast. He had never liked it, since he could not have hidden among others even if he wanted to. What, he had wondered, was the tall tree supposed to *do?* But his trouble would prove the truth as far as the village was concerned, and he expected to hear it many times again.

He was young and strong and healthy; his body healed quickly and he was soon hard at work with his father. But he could not escape the knowledge that he had brought trouble to his family. They had been prosperous, for peasants: three cows, eight ewes, extra cloth laid away, the copper and silver coins that took so long to earn. His father had had a good reputation with the steward, and had no enemies in the village itself.

Now Arin could not marry until they earned the marriage-fee, but before that came the field-fee and house-fee, and the harvest taxes were coming soon. He could help with the work, but he had to eat, and he brought no more land with him, on which more crops could grow, or beasts graze.

His father said nothing of this. He had no need to say it; Gird knew precisely what it meant, what it would cost them all in labor and hunger to regain even a scrap of safety. His feet toughened quicker than his mind. Daylong in the fields he caught the tail end of comments that seemed intended for his ear. The other men said nothing near his father, but left him in no doubt what they thought. Young lout, they said, set himself up for a soldier and then shamed us all with his weakness. He knew some of them had been as sickened as he, but if they remembered it at all, they didn't say so around him. It was convenient to blame it all on him. He knew, on one side of his mind, that this had always happened so, that once he had done the same, but it still hurt. His former friends stayed away from him, whether because of their fathers' orders or their own scorn he didn't know, and soon didn't care. He was in a deep wallow of misery, just like the bullcalf in the bog Arin had mentioned.

In that first month of trouble, between the event and the harvest, only one mercy intervened. The young count and his entourage left to visit another of his holdings, and the steward conveniently forgot to put Gird on the workroll. In the required workdays, he could work his family's garden and fieldstrip, while his father and Arin worked the greatfield for the count. And he could do day-labor for anyone hiring work done, taking his pay in a meal away from home more often than hard coin. Most of this was unskilled labor, fetching and carrying. Gird carried water for the masons brought in to raise the count's orchard walls, and lugged baskets full of clay and broken rock. It was hard work, even for someone of his strength, and he soon felt the difference the change in food made. He came home so tired he could hardly eat, and fell onto the bed as soon as he'd cleaned his bowl.

At harvest, Gird could not avoid the other men and boys. Harvest time gathered in more than crops; the village people worked together and celebrated together, and the year's stories began to form into chants and tales that would be retold over and over during long winter nights. It was no fault of Gird's that his disgrace so neatly fit the measures of an old song, "The Thief's Revenge" and needed but little skill to change a few words. He never knew who sang it first, but its jangling rhymes followed him down the lanes. "He gave a cry and ran away, as fast as he could run—" jibed the little boys. "Eh, Gird, can you outrun a fox? A pig?"

Now his former friends had their own say. A shrug, a wink between them, a shoulder turned to him. Teris even said "If you were going to make such a fuss, you could at least have saved Meris," which was completely unfair. He could not have saved Meris; no one could. They hadn't. But they blamed him for Meris, and for trying and failing. Some—Amis among them—said nothing, just watched him. Were they waiting for him to defend himself, to argue? But he had nothing to say. He was too tired to argue, too hungry and too miserable.

The girls never looked his way at all, and he was sure they laughed about him in their little groups. He was careful not to watch them openly and court more ridicule, although he had come to the age where the mere sight of a girl leaning to pull a bucket from a well could send his blood pounding. It was slightly easier

to ignore the girls if he wasn't with the boys. He quit trying to talk
to anyone, soon, and kept to his own family.

With all they had lost, that winter was hard. They could not
afford to butcher an animal for winter meat; they would need every
calf and lamb next spring to pay the fieldfee. Gird's scanty earnings
had gone for the fall taxes, along with two of their sheep. That
meant less wool next spring, for his mother to spin and weave, and
less cloth to trade or sell. At least they had fodder in plenty, for
that had been gathered before they lost the extra animals. And
Gird roamed the wood bringing back loads of firewood and sacks
of nuts. He avoided the nutting parties of the other boys and young
men, avoided the last autumn gatherings of dancers at the
sheepfold.

Later, he remembered that winter as the coldest, hungriest, and
most miserable of his life, although he knew that wasn't true. There
was no real famine; they had beans and grain enough, some cheese.
Except for the ritual cold hearth at Midwinter, they had a good
fire yearlong. His mother had managed a whole shirt for him,
pieced out of scraps, and he had rags enough to wrap his feet. It
was the sudden difference, from more than enough to barely
enough, that made it seem so bleak.

Meris died in the long cold days after Midwinter. Gird had tried
to visit him once, but his family, suffering under a heavy fine as
well as Meris's injuries, wanted no contact with another unlucky
boy. Meris had had few friends, but those boys loosed their frustrated rage on Gird when they caught him alone, and battered him
into the snow. He might have fought back, to ease his own frustration and grief, but one of them got a bucket over his head. The
guards heard the noise, and broke it up; when Gird wrestled the
bucket off his head, the sergeant was standing there sucking his
teeth speculatively. He said nothing, just watched, as Gird made
it to one knee, then another, and staggered off down the lane.

That was the last direct assault, but by then Gird was convinced
that everyone was against him. The next time he got a bit of work,
and a copper crab, he took it to the smelly leanto behind Kirif's
cottage, where a couple of other men hunched protectively over
mugs of sour ale. He knew it was wrong. He didn't care. For a
crab he got more ale than his head would hold, mug after mug,
and his father found him snoring against the wall.

That loosed his father's tongue, where the other had not. "A sot
as well as a coward! I didn't work so hard to save a drunken oaf,
lad; this had best be the last time you spend our needs on your
own pleasure." It didn't feel like pleasure then; his head was

pounding and his stomach felt as if it never wanted food again. His father was not finished, however. He heard the full tale of his misdeeds, from the time he'd run off to follow Arin on the pighunt as a child, to the stupidity of going for a soldier, right down to his selfishness and sullenness in the past months. He had not told his father about Meris's friends attacking him, or what Teris had said; he realized that it wouldn't do any good now.

He felt almost as guilty as his father seemed to want. It *was* his fault, no getting around it, and if some of the consequences weren't fair, nothing ever had been. Only one of the gods cared about fair, that he knew of, and the High Lord was far away, nothing much to do with the village folk or the soldiers, either one. He went back to work doggedly, determined to pay back enough of the debt he owed so that Arin could marry within a year. He didn't visit the aleshop until after Midsummer, and then with a basket of mushrooms to trade, not good coin his family could use. And he stopped with a single mug, that put a pleasant haze between him and the other villagers.

Arin's wedding briefly lightened his miseries, for his favorite brother would include Gird in the celebration despite anything he'd done. "Besides," Arin said, "you've worked hard to get my fee together. You might have done much less; it wasn't all your fault, after all. I know I can depend on you."

For a wedding, all quarrels ceased. Oreg even donated a pig to the feast. Gird was old enough to wait in the barton with the men, to watch his brother's dance, and join the drinking afterwards, when the newlyweds were safe abed and women were cleaning up the last of the feast. This was not like Kirif's leanto; here was a cask of the strong brown brew from a neighboring vill, and hearty voices singing all the rollicking old songs he'd grown up with, from "Nutting in the Woods" to "Red Sim's Second Wife." He had enough ale to soften the edges of any remarks about him, and joined his loud voice to the others without noticing anyone's complaint.

But this did not last. Arin and his wife took over the bed he had shared with Gird, as was only right; Gird slept on the floor near the hearth that winter. Arin's wife, soon with child, began to have the childsickness, waking early every morning to heave and heave, filling the cottage with the stink of her illness. Gird, now on the work rolls, had his own duties to fulfill when the required days came around; he could no longer replace his brother and free one worker for the family. When Arin's first child was born, another mouth to feed, they had not yet put by enough for the fieldfee. That year was leaner than the one before.

Soon Gird felt that he would never get anywhere at all. Arin's wife lost a child, but was soon pregnant again. As hard as they all could work was barely enough to feed them; they had no chance to save towards replacing the sheep or cow Gird had cost them. Year flowed into year, a constant struggle to survive. Gird could not miss the gray in his father's hair, the cough that every winter came sooner and lasted longer.

Chapter Five

"I don't see why you care." Gird hunched protectively over his mug. The mood Amis was in, if he turned around to argue, Amis would grab it away. He didn't have anything to trade for another, and this one would barely fuzz the edges of his misery.

"You're turning into a drunk," said Amis, far too briskly. "It's been what—three years?—and all you do is work and drink—"

"And eat," said Gird. "Don't forget that—they tell me all the time at home."

"And eat. You never come out with us—"

Gird shrugged, and took a swallow. Worse than usual, it tasted, but the bite in his throat promised ease later. "You may want me; the others don't."

"It's past, Gird. So you're not a soldier, so what? We didn't like it that much when you were—"

"That's true. You don't much like anything I do: fight or not fight, run or not run, drink or not drink. If I gave up ale, Amis, would that make me friends? Not likely."

"You know what I mean. Drink for celebration, yes—with all of us, a lot of singing and dancing and rolling the girls—but not this way. Come with us tonight, anyway."

Gird swallowed the rest of the mug he allowed himself, and tried to think past the rapidly spreading murk in his head. Walk across the fields to some sheepfold, listen to a wandering harper play, dance with—it would have to be girls from the other village, none from here would have him. And then back by daybreak, to work— his feet ached, his back ached, all he wanted was his bed. But at home his father's eyes would question silently: what did you take, to trade for that drink? What will you take next? It was my own, he answered that unspoken question. I found the mushrooms, I picked them when you were resting, it's my right—

"All right," he said gruffly. Amis grinned at him, steadied him as he stood. He did not look to see the reactions of the other men drinking in Kirif's hut; he thought he knew exactly what he'd see if he did.

Somewhere on the walk, two others joined them: Koris and Jens, he'd known them all his life. His skin prickled; he was sure they were none too happy to find him coming along. But nothing they said led that way. It was all the common talk of their village, Jens courting Torin and her father's dislike of it, a wager between Koris and his older brother on the sex of an unborn calf, Teris's problems with his wife's mother, how the last spring storm had damaged the young fruit on the trees. The thought passed through his mind that, but for subjects, it was much like the talk of his mother and aunt and sisters, that nearly drove him mad when he had to be indoors listening to it. For all that Jens and Koris talked of the girls, while Effa and Hara talked of the boys, it was the same talk. Who liked, who spurned, who loved secretly—who would be honest, and who lied in all encounters—whose work could be trusted, and who put rotten plums in the bottom of the basket.

He said nothing, having nothing to say, as the cool night air gradually blew the fumes of ale away. They were walking over the higher pastures sunrising of the village—east, as the lords called it. Under his feet the turf made an uneven carpet; overhead the spring stars blossomed as the night darkened. It had been a long time since he'd been out in the dark looking up, his gaze unmisted by drink. Some night-blooming plant—he knew he should know the name, but he'd forgotten—spread rare perfume on the air, and every lungful he took in seemed important, as if it carried a secret message.

They could see the sheepfold from the ridge, dark against the leaping flames of the fire built in the outer enclosure. As they came down the slope, the harpsong came to greet them, first the more carrying notes, then all of them, a quick rhythm that made them hurry. It ended, and voices rose in noisy swirls of greeting, flirtation, argument. Gird lagged as the others moved forward. He saw Jens edge toward a darker corner. There was Torin, who must have come earlier with her friends. Koris glanced back at him, and Gird stepped into the brighter firelight, not quite sure what he was going to do. He hadn't been to one of these since he was old enough to be serious about it. Boys the age he'd been lounged against the low stone wall, or crouched atop, knocking elbows and joking about the older ones.

At least three times a growing season, from early spring to fall, the young unmarried men and women of five villages met at this communal sheepfold. Gird had no idea how the dates were set, only that the word would spread through the young men—tomorrow night, tonight—and those who wished would go. One cold autumn evening, the first year he'd gone, there'd been only three young men and two women, and the music had come from a ragged lad playing a reed pipe. Usually there were more, and always someone from outside, a stranger, to play the music they danced to. But he had not come since he left the guard's training.

He heard someone say his name, across the fire, and his head jerked up. He couldn't see who, even when he squinted against the flames. So. They'd heard the story too, no doubt, and it would all be told over again. He glared at the coals beneath the burning wood, that half-magical heap of colored lights and mysterious shapes that seemed to be struggling to say something. A long hiss ended in a violent *pop,* and he jumped.

"I wonder what it said that time." The girl's voice held humor, as well as warmth. Gird didn't look at her.

"What all fires say," he said.

"Here's home and safety," she said. And then, surprisingly, "Here's danger; here's death."

Gird turned. She had a broad face, boldly boned for strength, not beauty, and all he could tell of her coloring in that uncertain light was that she was darker than he. Big capable hands held the ends of her shawl; she looked like any other young woman. Except for those eyes, he thought, watching the perfect reflection of the fire in them. Except for the mind that said those words.

"You're Gird," she said. "The one who left the guards."

"Yes." He wished he hadn't looked at her.

"Are they hard on you?"

He looked again, once more surprised. "Now?" She said nothing, and he wondered whether he dared be honest. Silence lengthened. No one else came near them; he could feel no other attention, no other pressure than her quiet interest. "At first," he began, "it was worst on my family—my father, my brothers—" He told her about that, the fines they'd had to pay, the extra labor on the roads. She said nothing, only nodding when he broke off. Tentatively, warily, he told her more. The guards themselves had bothered him least— even now that surprised him, that the sergeant, after that one explosion, had been fair, if distant, and the other soldiers neutral. "I'm just another farmer's son to them. They don't bother me, if they see me; they treat me no differently than the others. They never teased—" His head went down, remembering those who did, whose taunts he could not answer.

"It's like rape," she said. He stared at her, shocked and ready to argue, but she was still talking. "They blame the blameless, the victim: they always do. When the young count's houseparty went hunting our way, and one of them took my cousin, took her there in the street just for the excitement of it, everyone blamed her. My aunt said 'Oh, if you hadn't loitered there,' and the lad who loved her—or said he did—had nothing to say but blame. All her fault, it was, but how could she help it? They blame you, for not preventing what they never moved to prevent."

"But I wasn't—"

"Not your *body*," she said, in a tone that meant he should have understood. Then, "Never mind. If you're not killed, you're still alive; so my cousin said, and married elsewhere a year later, after the babe died. She survived; you will; that's how we all live."

"It's not right," Gird said, in a voice that he remembered in himself from years past.

Her brows went up. "Are we gods, to know right and wrong beyond the law? I hate the way it is, but no one made me a lord."

He would have answered, or tried to, but the music began again. At close range, the harp drowned out soft words, and the others had begun a song. Gird didn't know it, but the girl did.

> *"Fair are the flowers that bloom in the meadows*
> *Fair are the flowers that bloom on the hill*
> *Each spring brings more to brighten the season*
> *Each winter snowstorm the bright flowers kills—"*

She had a husky singing voice, melodic but not strong, that clung to the melody like a peach to a twig, half-enfolding it. Gird could feel her singing along his body, a warm, slightly furry touch. He wanted to sing with her, at least hum the melody, but his throat was too tight. Another song followed that one, this time an even sadder lament that they all knew. He sang, feeling his voice unkink and lengthen into the line of the song; her voice rolled along beside, rich and mellow. At the end of the many verses, he realized that others had fallen silent to listen, and at once his voice broke harshly, ruining the ending. Someone laughed, across the firelight;

Gird flinched as if he'd been slapped, but the girl's hand was on his arm.

"Never mind," she said, under cover of the harper's quick fingering—it would be a jig, this time, and someone had found sticks to patter. Without really looking at the girl, Gird eased back to the angle between wall and fold, not at all surprised to find she had come with him. She stood closer than he found really comfortable; he could have put his arm around her and found her no closer.

"You know my name," he said, gruffly, unwilling to ask what she might refuse to answer.

"I'm Mali, from the village near the crossing—some call it Fireoak." He remembered that name, from his guards' training; with the name he called up the location, the number of families, all the details he'd been taught. It surprised him; he didn't know he could remember all that. He looked down at her.

"You knew of me—"

She shrugged, and the shawl slipped back from dark hair. Something marked the side of her face: a scar, a birthmark. Hard to see in that light, but he could just make out a paler path across her cheek. "Most do; that kind of tale spreads. But Amis told me of you, and your past before the Guards. So I wanted to see you, see what they'd made of you."

"A failure," Gird said, then jumped as she slugged his arm. Hard: he would have a bruise there.

"Only you can make yourself a failure—and you a great strong lad with a head of solid stone—"

He was wide awake, now, as if he'd been dipped in a well. "What *are* you, some foretelling witch—?"

Firelight and shadow moved on her face; he could not read her expression. "I? I'm a farmer's daughter, as you're a farmer's son. I'm headstrong too, so they say of me, and a dangerous lass to cross. If you married me you'd have a strong mother of your children, and a loyal friend—"

"Marry—I can't marry—I'm—"

"A whole man," she said. Gird could feel his ears go hot; he wanted to grab her and shake her, or disappear into thin air. He knew he was whole; his body was as alive to her as his ears, and far more active. Was *this* how girls his age bantered? Surely she was bolder than the others.

"I'm sorry," she said then, in a quiet voice. He could feel her withdrawing without actually moving; she slid the shawl back over her hair. The withdrawal pierced him like a blade. He could not stand if it she left.

"Wait!" he said hoarsely. "I—you—I never heard anyone—"

"It's no matter." She wrapped the shawl tightly around herself, hugged her arms. "I'm overbold and wild; I've been told often enough. But I'd heard of you, and how you had changed, refusing your friends. I thought perhaps I could help, being a stranger—"

"You did." Gird rubbed his own arms, feeling the texture of his clothes and skin for the first time in—when?—years? He felt alive, awake, inside and out, and not only in that way which proved men whole. His skin tingled. "I'm—I'm awake," he said, wondering if she'd understand. Hot tears pricked his eyes; his throat tightened again.

She was looking at him, dark eyes hard to see in that flickering firelight—but he could feel the intensity of her gaze. "Awake?"

"It—oh, I can't talk here! Come on!" Without thinking, he grabbed her arm and led her around the wall to the entrance. She had stiffened for an instant, but then came willingly, hardly needing his guidance. He barely noticed someone by the gate turning to look, and then they were out beyond the walls, on the open fields, with the firelight twinkling behind them and stars brilliant overhead.

He stopped only when he stumbled over a stone and fell, dragging her down too. He had been crying, he realized, the roaring of blood in his ears louder than any night sound, the smell and taste of his own tears covering up the fragrance on the wind. She had pulled free when he fell, and now crouched, a dimly visible shape, an armspan away. When he got his breath at last, he sat up; she did not move, either towards him or away.

"I'm sorry," he said. "I don't—I've never done that before—"

"I should hope not." The tone carried tart amusement, but not hostility.

"I had to get away—I couldn't talk about it there, with those—"

"Only a few of them would still mock you, Gird."

"It's not that. It's—oh, gods, I'm awake again! I didn't know I wasn't. I didn't know I'd gone so numb, and now—"

"Does it hurt, like a leg you've sat on too long?"

He drew a long breath, trying to steady his breathing. "Not—hurt, exactly, though it does prickle. It's more as if I'd been sick, shut indoors a long time, so long I forgot about the colors outside, and then someone carried me out into spring." He turned to her, wishing he could see her expression. "Did you mean that about marrying?"

To his surprise, she burst out laughing, a joyous rollicking laugh that he could not resist. He didn't know why it was funny, but he laughed too. Finally, after a last snort, she quieted down, and apologized.

"I shouldn't laugh at you, I know that, but for someone just waking after long illness, you do move fast. Was this how you courted the girls, back when you were in the guards?"

"I didn't, back then—I was too young." Even in starlight, he could see that she'd let the shawl slip back again, revealing her face. His body insisted that he was not too young *now;* he tried to stay calm. "Mmm—would you sit with me?"

She moved closer, spread her skirts, and sat down almost hip-to-hip. "I thought I was, with you the closest person to me on this whole dark night."

She had a scent he had not noticed before; now it moved straight from his nose to his heart. Did all women smell like this? He cursed himself for a crazy fool, to have wasted the years in which he might have learned how to court such a girl. He clenched his fists to keep from reaching for her.

"But surely—" His voice broke, and he started again. "But surely you have someone—someone in your village—?"

Her low chuckle warmed his heart. "Alas no, Gird. For I'm the forward, quick-tongued lass you heard tonight; I will not guard my tongue for any man's content, though I swear by Alyanya there's no malice in it. And though I'm big and strong enough, and a good cook, I'm not much for threadcraft. My spinning's full of lumps, and my weaving's as bad as a child's. My family's parrion has always been in threadcraft, though my great-aunt taught me her parrion of cooking—she said I'd been born with a gift that way."

"My mother and sisters have threadcraft enough," Gird said. "But a parrion of cooking they'd welcome, even more in herblore than bakecraft." He could hardly believe they had come so fast to discussion of parrions. Wasn't that the last part before formal betrothal? He could not remember; he could not think of anything but the girl herself—Mali, he reminded himself firmly—and the smell and feel of her.

"Mine is that," she said, the weight of her coming now against his arm; he shifted it around her shoulders, and she leaned into him. Where she touched him, her body seemed to burn right through their clothes; he felt afire with longing for her. It was a struggle to speak calmly. He took another long breath of the cold, clean night air.

"Your father?" Gird thought it likely her father wouldn't agree, given his own reputation. But she shook her head, in the angle of his arm, where he could feel it.

"Grandmother's our elder, and village elder too—the magelords don't like it, but they agreed. She'll be glad enough if anyone wants me, and you're a farmer's son, in the same hearthing. But what of your mother?"

"She'll be happy." He leaned closer, to smell her hair. Was he really talking of marriage with someone met just this night, and by firelight? Could she be a witch—or, worst of all, a magelady pretending to be peasant, disguised by her magic?

"I have to tell you about this," said Mali, struggling upright for a moment. He looked at her; she had one hand to the mark on her face. "I'm no beauty, besides my loud tongue. Many call me ugly, for this scar if nothing else."

"What happened?" It was a chance to breathe, to remind himself of the customs of his people.

Mali made a curious noise that Gird could not interpret, somewhere between a sniff and a snort. "I wish I could claim it came from defending my cousin against the magelords—it happened the same day—but in fact it was my own clumsiness. I was carrying a scythe to my brother in the fields, and tripped. When I came running back, looking for sympathy, there was my cousin in the lane. No one had time for me then, and no wonder. I thought to save my grandmother trouble by treating it myself, but failed to put herin in the poultice, so it scarred. My own fault." She laid her warm hand on his. "But I will understand if you change—I mean, it's not fair. I've landed on you this night like a fowler's net on a bird. You must have a free choice, a chance to make up your own mind. See me in daylight and then if you still wish—"

Contending thoughts almost silenced him. Gird eyed her. "Is it that you think you can get nothing better than the coward of the count's own village? Was I just a last chance for you, is that what you're saying?"

She sat bolt upright. For an instant he thought she was going to hit him again; the place she'd slugged him before still ached. "You *fool!* If you don't want me, just say so. Don't make it my fault."

"I didn't—"

"You did." She was breathing fast, angry, and he waited. Finally she went on. "I was curious. I'd heard—what I told you. For myself, barring I like a roll as well as anyone, I'd live alone rather than marry anyone's last chance. Then meeting you—Amis said you were gentle, but he didn't say how you sang." Her voice trailed away. "And you're no coward, whatever *you* think."

"You don't think a man knows himself best?"

Laughter burst out of her again. "Who could? Can water know

it's wet, or stone know it's hard? What could it measure itself against? I know my feelings, but my grandmother knew I was meant for herblore, not needlecraft or weaving. So with you—did your father or mother think you would make a soldier?"

Surprise again. "I—don't know. Not really, I suppose, although they feared I could be—"

"Cruel?" He could see her head shake in the starlight. "No, not like that. You can do what you must, but you take no pleasure in giving pain." He was eased by that, and his suspicions fled. A strange girl, like no girl he'd known (but what girls had he known?) but not a cunning one. If she said she liked him, then she did. Gird cleared his throat.

"I would like to—" Lady's grace; he didn't even know how to ask. But Mali had moved nearer to him again, her shoulder against his, her fragrant hair once more against his face.

"You should wait until sunrise," she said. "You might change your mind."

Gird laughed. "Sunrise," he said, "is too far away. Or do you want to go back and find witnesses to make it formal?"

"I want no witnesses," she said, in a low voice that was almost a growl. "Not for this." She folded her shawl, and lay back upon it, arms wide. "I swear by the Lady, that for this night I am content."

And content were they both by sunrise. Gird had thought he knew how it went between men and women; it was no secret after all, and any child saw it often enough growing up. But Mali's body, sweet-scented and warm on the cool hillside grass, was nothing like his imaginings—or far more. He could not get enough of touching her smooth skin, her many complex curves all ending in another place to enjoy with tongue and nose and fingers. And she, by all evidence, enjoyed it all as much as he did. They had fallen asleep at last, to be wakened by the loud uneven singing of Gird's friends on their way home. Mali chuckled.

"They want to let you know it's time to go, but without interrupting. You know, Gird, they are your friends. You must forgive them someday."

Right then he would have forgiven anyone anything, or so he felt. A pale streak marked distant sunrise. With a groan, he pulled his clothes together. "I don't want to leave."

Mali was already standing, shaking out her shawl. "If you wish, you know where."

"You know I want to marry you."

"I do *not* know. I know you enjoyed my body, and I enjoyed yours, but there's more to marriage than that. But I like you, Gird.

I say that now, after hearing you sing, laugh, and cry—more than many girls do, before they wed. Look on my face in daylight, and decide." She turned away to start home. Gird caught her arm.

"Why not now?"

"What of your work today? What of your family? Go home, lo— Gird. Go home and think whether you want a big, clumsy, loud-voiced wife with a scarred face. If you do, come see me in daylight. Ask me then—"

"I'm asking now!"

"No. I'll not answer now. Daylight for both of us then." And she pulled away and was gone. Gird stared after her, then followed the distant voices of his friends toward home.

He caught up with them within sight of home. By then it was light enough to see their expressions; he could feel himself going red. Amis elbowed Jens.

"You see I was right. He just needed to get a little fresh air—"

"He got more than fresh air, I'll warrant. Look at his face. If I'd gone out like that with Torin—"

"You wouldn't. You'll be learning how in your marriage bed, Jens."

"I know how." Jens shoved Koris, who shoved back. "It's just that with her father—"

"Come on, Gird," said Amis, throwing an arm around his shoulders. "Tell us—you drag the girl out in the middle of the dancing, did you just throw her on the ground, or what?"

He could hear the undertones in their voices—they weren't sure if he was going to be angry, or sulk, or what. He felt like singing, and instead burst out laughing.

"That's new," said Amis. "I like that—Gird laughing again."

"Be still," he said, ducking away from Amis's arm and the finger that was prodding his ribs. "You were right: I admit it. I needed to go dancing—"

"You didn't dance," said Jens.

Gird shrugged. He could feel more laughter bubbling up, like a spring long dry coming in. "I did well enough," he said.

"Watch him go to sleep behind the hedges today." Koris grinned, but it had no bite to it. "You may be tired by nightfall, eh?"

Gird grinned back. He felt that the bad years had never happened; he felt he could work for two days together. He drew a long breath—sweet, fresh air of dawn—and said nothing more. He had never expected to be happy again, and now he was.

He came in through the barton, aware of the stale, sour smell of the cottage after the freshness outside. All very well to fall for a girl, to marry her—but where would they sleep? He'd have to build a bed. He'd have to earn the marriage fee for the count, and the fee to her family for her parrion. He'd have to—

"You're looking blithe this morning," said Arin, from the flank of the red cow. Milk hissed into the bucket. Arin's voice had sharpened, in the difficult years, but he sounded more worried than angry.

"Sheepfold last night," said Gird. He took down the other milking stool, and a bucket.

"You? I thought you'd gone to Kirif's."

Gird washed the cow's udder with water from the stable bucket and folded himself up on the milking stool. The brindle cow flapped her ears back and forth as he reached for her teats, and he leaned into her flank and crooned to her. "Easy, sweetling—I was at Kirif's first, and then Amis came along and we went over to the fold—"

"Good for you," said Arin. "Meet anyone?"

He might as well admit it; it would be all over the village by the time they came to the field. "You always meet someone at the fold," he began, but he couldn't hold the tone. "Someone," he said again. "Arin, there's a girl from Fireoak—"

"Where?"

"Fireoak. Sunrising of here. You know, Teris's wife's sister married into Fireoak. And her parrion is cooking and herblore—"

"Teris's wife's sister?" said Arin, with maddening cooless.

"No. Mali's parrion. The girl I met."

"Arin's eyebrows went up. "You were talking parrions? In one night?"

"We did more than talk," said Gird, stripping the first two teats and going on to the next.

"You can't mean—you're not betrothed? Gird, you know you have to ask—"

Gird grinned into the cow's flank and squirted a stream of milk at Arin, who had come to stand by her hip. "Not betrothed, but more than talk. Lady's grace, Arin, you know what I mean. And I will ask for her, just you wait."

"But are you sure? The first time you've been out with the lasses since before—" he stopped short, and reddened. Gird laughed.

"Since before I left the guards, you mean, and you're right. So you think it's like a blind man's first vision, and I should wait and see? So she said, but I tell you, Arin, this is my wife. You'll like her."

"I hope so," said Arin soberly. "Best tell Da."

"After milking." He finished the brindle cow, and took both buckets into the kitchen.

His mother gave him one look and said "Who?" Gird looked at her. "Is it so obvious?"

"To a woman and a wife? Did you think I was blind, lad? No, you're a lad no more. Man, then. You've found a woman, and bedded her, and now you want to marry."

"True, then. What d'you think?"

She looked at him, a long measuring look. "About time, I think. *If* you're ready. You've spent long enough sulking—"

"I know," he said, to forestall what was coming. She shook her head at him, but didn't continue the familiar lecture.

"Well, then—I don't know where the fee's coming from, but you can earn that. What's her parrion?"

"Herbcraft and cooking." He held his breath; his mother had always talked of finding a wife with a parrion to complement hers: another weaver or spinner, perhaps a dyer.

"Well enough. No lad—man—takes advice of his mother, but you think now, Gird—is she quarrelsome? The house will be no larger for cross words." That was said low; Arin's wife was still in the other room, and she had brought, his mother had said once, a parrion of complaining.

"Not—quarrelsome." She had said she was freespoken, but nothing in her voice had sent the rasp along his skin.

"Best tell your father." She gave him a quick smile. "If she's brought you laughter again, Gird, I'll give her no trouble. It's been a long drought."

His father, still hunched over his breakfast, brightened when Gird told him. Arin's wife said nothing, briskly leading her oldest out the front door. His father leaned close.

"Comely, is she?"

"She's—" Gird could not think of words. She had been starlight and scent, warmth and strength and joy, all wrapped in one. "She's strong," he offered. His father laughed.

"You sound like the lad you were. Strong didn't give that gleam to your eye, I'll warrant. There's more to the lass than muscle. When will you go to her father?"

"Soon. I—I'm not sure."

His father whistled the chorus of "Nutting in the Woods" and laughed again. "Young men. By the gods, boy, I remember your mother—" Gird was shocked. His mother had been his mother—that capable, hard-handed woman in long apron, spooning out porridge or carding wool or weaving—all his life. His father had gone on. "Hair in a cloud of light around her face, and she smelled like—like—I suppose all girls do, in their spring. Never a young lad can resist that, Gird; we all go that way, rams to the ewes and bulls to the cows, and spend the rest of our days yoked in harness— but it's times like this make it worthwhile."

"Eh?" He had not followed all that; his father's words brought back Mali's scent, as if she stood next to him, as if she lay—and he pulled his mind back with an effort.

His father thumped the table. "To see sons ready to wed themselves, strong sons: that's what's worth the work, Gird. To see you with your eyes clear and your mind on something but the past."

Gird shrugged. The self of yesterday, the self that had had nothing to hope for, was gone as if it had never lived.

"'Tis the Lady's power," said his father. "She can bring spring to any field." This no longer embarrassed Gird; he had returned whole-hearted to his family's beliefs.

His visit to Fireoak began auspiciously. Mali's own mother had seen his mother's weaving at the tradefair years before.

"She has the parrion for the firtree pattern," the woman said. She was as tall as Mali, but spare, her dark hair streaked with gray. "If she has not the parrion for the barley pattern, I would be glad to trade." Gird knew that his mother had wanted the barley pattern for years, and had never been able to work it out herself. She had bestowed the firtree pattern on Arin's wife's aunt; surely she would trade with his wife's mother. He nodded: no commitment, but possibility.

Mali herself was kneading bread, her arms flour-smudged to the elbows. The scar she'd told him of was obvious enough, along the right cheek, more broad than deep. He didn't care; he had known he would not care. It was hard to be that close to her, in the same air, and not holding her. Her eyes twinkled at him: agreement. Then she looked back at the bread dough and pummeled it again. He could feel once more her fist on his arm, the strength of her. She was strong inside and out; his knees weakened as he remembered the feel of her body all along his on the starlit grass.

"Mali's not the quietest girl," said Mali's father. He was not so dark as Mali and her mother, a brown square man with a graying beard, almost bald. "She's got a quick tongue."

"Gird knows that," said Mali, flipping the dough and slamming it down again.

"Like that," said her father. Gird smiled at him.

"Better a quick tongue than one full of malice," he said, misquoting the old proverb on purpose.

"Oh, aye, if it's not quick into the pot. Good cook; her parrion's valuable." That began the bargaining phase. A daughter's parrion was a family's most valuable possession, the secrets and inherited talent of generations of women passed to a chosen carrier. A valuable parrion enriched the household gaining it, and impoverished those left behind. The lords' fee for marriage was the same for all of the same rank, but he would owe Mali's family for her parrion.

At least it meant that her family found his acceptable, and she must have agreed as well. Despite all the lords had done, the people had never come over to thinking that girls had to go where their families bestowed them. Marriage was, in the old rituals, the mingling of fires on a hearth—and if either failed to kindle, the marriage could not be.

Arin had come along for the bargaining phase, since Gird was neither holder nor heir. Gird and Mali escaped to the smallgarden, there to stand awkwardly staring at each other, in full view of her village. An amazing number of people seemed to need to go back and forth in the lane. Gird knew none of them, but noticed the same small boys driving the same goats up and down, a girl in a red skirt carrying a basket—full, then empty, then full again—past the gate. Mali finally began to laugh.

"It's true—they're just seeing how long we can stand here, and expecting one of us to turn tail and run."

"The scar doesn't matter." The words were out before he thought; she flushed and it showed whiter. "I'm sorry," he said.

"No—I'm used to it. I *thought* you'd come anyway, and I thought you'd still—but I'm blushing because it's my fault."

"Fault?"

She looked away past his shoulder. "I had heard of you; I went there to meet you, and no one else. And meeting you, I wanted you—and then—"

"And then I wanted you. So?"

"So—I still want you, but—don't bring it back to me, years from now."

"No." He moved closer to her, ignoring the women now carrying buckets past on their way to the well. "No, it was meant. The Lady meant it, maybe, or some other god." He put his arm around her waist, and she leaned on him. He could have carried her off to the barton, then and there, but Arin came out looking pleased.

"So—we have work to do, Gird, to earn your fees."

He knew he had turned red; he could feel the heat on his face. "Ah—yes. Mali—"

"Don't tarry," she said. Then she leaned against him again, and kissed him, and whispered in his ear. "We may have a Lady's blessing already."

Chapter Six

The only awkwardness came when he had to bring Mali before the count's steward, to have her transferred on the Rolls. Luckily the count himself was not in residence, but the steward might have decided to invoke the rule himself.

"So—you're marrying, young Gird?"

"Yes, lord steward." Gird kept his eyes down.

"About time—you've loafed long enough." The voice was chilly; Gird watched the fingers holding the pen tap on the edge of the parchment. "Look up at me, boy."

The steward's face was older, grayer, but otherwise unchanged. Gird met those ice-blue eyes with difficulty.

"You brought the marriage fee?" Gird handed it over, the heavy copper coins slipping out of his hands much faster than they'd come in. "And this is the girl—" The steward looked her up and down, and then glanced at Gird. "You chose strength, eh? A good worker, I'll be bound—none too pretty—" Gird felt his ears burning; Mali's face had gone mottled red. Her scar stood out, stark white, from brow to jawline. "Wide hips—good bearer. Any mageblood in your line, girl?"

"No, lord steward." Her voice was husky, almost a growl.

"No, I daresay not. Nor would breed mages, is my guess. Waste of his lordship's time, your sort, bar the fun of it." The steward looked back down at the parchment. "Mali of Fireoak, daughter of Kekrin, son of Amis, wed to Gird of this village, son of Dorthan, son of Keris. Fee paid, permission granted to farm with Dorthan. That's all then."

They ducked their heads and went out quickly, both of them flushed and angry, but too wise to speak of it. First to Gird's father's house, for Mali to lay her first fire on the greathearth; every old grannie in the village was there to cry the portents of that flame. Gird held his breath. She put the splinters down in the Star pattern, and above them the tripod of fireoak, brought from her own family's hearth, and then struck the flints. Once—would have been too soon. Twice—a fair omen, but not the best. On the third strike, a spark leapt from her tools to the tip of the fireoak splinters, and kindled living flame. Now she moved quickly, laying the rest of the fire in ritual patterns: this twig over that, this herb, a twist of wool from her father's sheep, an apple-seed from their tree. The grannies muttered and flashed handsigns at each other; Gird was worried, but his mother smiled happily. It must be all right, then.

He and the other men left then, trudging through the back kitchen, then the cowbyre, into the narrow, cramped barton where the women had laid out the wedding feast on planks. This would be the refusing, he knew: Mali's parents would come, and try to persuade her to go home. She would first refuse them, with the door open, then—when they argued longer—close and bar the door to them. After a ritual greeting to her mother-in-law, and a prick of the finger to get two drops of blood, one for the fire and one for the hearthstone, her parents would knock again. And now, as a member of this household, she would greet them as honored guests.

All this time, Gird endured the jokes of his friends and his brothers and father. He had heard such jokes all his life, finding them funny once he was old enough, but now, waiting for Mali to become his wife, and not her parents' daughter, he was not amused. What did these grotesque fantasies have to do with Mali? He swiped irritably at his brother, when Arin tried to tie the traditional apron on him.

"You have to, Gird. You're her husband now; don't you want children?"

Gird looked at the apron, its ancient leather darkened by generations of celebrants. It was ridiculous. Bulls didn't need such a thing; why did the gods demand it of humans? He could remember sniggering in the corner when Arin danced in the apron, and wondering how his brother could approach his wife in his own skin afterwards. His friends had come nearer, warily, ready to help Arin force him into it if necessary. He sighed, and let his arms fall.

"All right. But I still think—" He said no more; their hands were busy with thongs and lacings. "I wonder how old this custom is—"

Mali, when she came out, bit her lip to keep from laughing. At least, he hoped that was suppressed laughter on her face. He felt a fool enough, strutting around like a young bull first meeting heifers, and nearly as big. She wore the maiden's vest of soft doeskin embroidered with flowers, laced tightly behind, where she could not reach it, a tradition as old as his apron. The men began to stamp the beat, their deep voices echoing off the barton walls as they chanted. Gird stamped as hard, feeling his face redden, hating it—but the old rhythm began to move him.

The steps were only partly traditional: part was each new-married man's invention. The jiggling thing on the apron was ridiculous, yes—but it was not *merely* ridiculous. Gird strutted the length of the barton, whirled, skipped a step, backed—and closed on Mali. Her eyes were bright, twinkling with laughter; she glanced down, pretended shock, looked skyward and reeled backwards, to catch herself with a clutch at Gird's shoulder. The watchers howled. She snatched her hand back, a maiden caught in indiscretion, and turned away. Gird circled her, faced her again, put his hands behind his back and waggled his hips. For an instant she grinned delightedly, then covered her face with her hands, brushed past him close enough for her skirts to catch on the apron, and then leaped like a startled deer.

Clearly, the dance was not embarrassing Mali—she played into the jokes as heartily as most men. Gird took heart, then. They could make their families laugh—their private joke, if their red faces came from exertion, and not from the shouts and laughter of others. They spun it out, circling and dodging between others and the tables, playing parts they only half understood. When they were both dripping sweat, Gird gave her a little nod, and his next rush carried them both into the cowbyre, where a stall had been laid with fresh straw for this occasion.

Here she had to unlace his apron, and he to unlace the maiden's vest she wore, to replace it with the matron's looser vest, his wedding present to her. Her fingers on his legs, his waist, brushed tantalizingly; the apron would be hardly more obvious than his response if she didn't hurry. He fumbled with the vest lacings.

"Did they have to lace it so tightly?"

"That was my sister," said Mali, breathless. "She wanted to see me faint, I think. Don't break the laces, remember." If he broke the laces, they'd have to give her family a sheep. He grunted and worked carefully. Finally the last knot came loose, and Mali drew a deep breath. "Ahh. Better." She worked her arms out of the vest carefully, and turned to him.

Gird handed her the matron's vest his mother and sisters had made. "You'd best get this on, if you don't want to spend the rest of the feast in here."

Mali chuckled as she looked him up and down. "Eager, are you?" She twitched her shoulders, putting the vest on, and Gird felt his pulse quicken. "But we'd better hang these out, or they'll come in to help."

"I'll do it," said Gird. The apron and vest had to be returned to each family, and the first step was to hang them on the appropriate pegs outside the cowbyre. A roar greeted him as he came out and put them up. Two of his friends were ready to grab him and keep him out, but he was quicker and managed to dart back into the stall with Mali.

Someone outside began another song, in which the women joined as well. Mali hummed the melody, and sat swaying a little back and forth. Gird stared at her. He wanted her—wanted her even more than on a hillside in the dark—but on the other side of the wall the whole village was waiting for this. It was one thing to be roused by someone else's marriage rites, he was discovering, and quite another to fulfill all the rituals with everyone watching him. Or not exactly watching, but not indifferent, either.

Then Mali turned away, and burrowed into the straw. Gird watched, bemused. There was nothing in this stall; he'd cleaned it himself, that morning, and laid the clean straw carefully. Mali grunted, and came up with a stoppered jug and something wrapped in a cloth.

"You are a witch." Gird pulled the stopper out when Mali passed him the jug. He sniffed. "What's this?"

"My aunt's favorite. And I'm not a witch, but you don't know all the rituals. Groom prepares the stall, but the bride bribes her new mother-in-law to supply it."

Gird sipped cautiously; a fiery liquid ran down his throat and made him blink. "Lady's blessing—that would bring—"

"Trouble if the lords knew of it." Mali took a swig, and opened her eyes. "My. No wonder she wouldn't let me taste it before." She unwrapped the cloth, and Gird saw a half-loaf of bread and some cheese. They ate quietly for the rest of that song, and the beginning of the next. Then either Mali's aunt's potion or Mali herself—warm and spicesmelling beside him—drove out his lingering embarrassment. He rolled toward her on the clean straw, and she embraced him. It was as satisfying as the first time, even when he roused to the ring of faces peering down at them.

"You went to sleep," Amis said, grinning. "We could hear you snore all through the singing."

Gird looked past them at the opening; it was nearly dark. Mali, her skirts back down around her knees, started rebraiding her hair. When he looked at her, she winked, and wrinkled her nose. "Well," he said, "did you eat all the food, or can we have some?"

They had to lead more dancing, that night, in the final Weaving that took them in and out of every cottage in the village, and around all three wells. Then at last it was over: all the food eaten, all the songs sung, all the dances danced, and a few hours to sleep (this time only sleep) until dawn brought work and their first day as a married pair.

Despite his mother's approval, Gird had worried about Mali's quick tongue in the house, when she had to share that cramped kitchen with two other women and the children. His mother's health had begun to fail; she was querulous sometimes, and Arin's wife could never weave to suit her. But Mali left the loom alone, and took over all the kitchen work. The other two had no more scouring and scrubbing to do, no more washing of pots or kneading of dough. Gird had never known how much difference a parrion for cooking could make. All women cooked, and many men; food was food. Now he realized that food differed as much as weaving. Mali's bread was lighter, her stews more savory, her porridge smooth, neither lumpy nor thin. She gathered herbs in the wood, and hung them to dry; they gave the cottage a different, sharper smell. She even knew how to make cheese.

With no kitchen work to do, Gird's mother could concentrate on weaving, and let Arin's wife do all the carding and spinning. They traded Mali's cheese for extra wool; his mother sent three furls to the trading fair in the next village, which brought them precious coppers, almost as much as the marriage fee even that first year. Gird's mother had always liked weaving better than anything else. Now she produced furl after furl, trading to the dyer for skeins of colored yarn, rich golds and reds and dark green. With those, she could weave patterned cloth that brought a higher price, combining the barley pattern Mali's mother had taught her with color.

The other cheesemaker in the village was getting old, and people began to bring Mali milk. She traded herbs to the older cheese-maker for one of her tubs, and made more cheese. For every five, a hand, she could keep one. Her cheese was not as good as some, she admitted—she would not try to sell it at a tradefair—but in the village it brought them what they needed to feed the extra mouths.

Gird's first child was born just after Midwinter. Mali had gathered the herbs she said she needed back in the summer, and as usual the village grannies came to help with the birthing. Gird had not realized how much his status would improve, first as a married man, and then as a father. Now all the grown men spoke to him by his own name. In the rest breaks they would wait for him before starting a conversation. Teris, who had been married more than a year, now treated him as an equal, an old friend. For a few days he resisted this, remembering Teris's accusations. One bleak day when they were both in the cowbyre, Mali wormed the old quarrel out of him, and counseled forgiveness.

"You can't change the past, love. If he's a good friend now, why not?"

Gird found that his old grudge looked very different when he got it out and tried to explain it to Mali. "You make everything so simple," he complained.

"It's not simple, but it's over. He erred, back then—did you never err?"

"You know I did, but—"

"Well, then, let be. He blamed you unfairly; if you refuse his friendship now, you'll be blaming unfairly."

"Are you ever angry?" He looked down at her; she had the baby at her breast, and he could smell her milk and the baby's scent overlaying her own.

Mali knotted her brows, thinking. "Angry . . . yes. When things happen, not later. If I'd been here, and seen someone hurting you, then I'd have been angry. Otherwise—'tis like a bit of old milk in the pan that sours the new. All life would sour if we held anger. So I yell, and throw things, and scour it all away, right then, so the next day won't sour."

"But when things aren't *right*—"

Mali shifted the baby to the other breast; he noticed how the baby's sucking had changed the shape of her nipple before she pulled her vest across to cover it. "Is this about Teris, or something else?"

Gird chuckled; he wasn't sure why. "Something you said that first night. And talking with the men in the village council. Things have changed since my father was a young man, and more since his father's day. And not for the better."

"Taxes?" Taxes were up again, the field-fee higher for the third year in a row.

"Not only that." Gird rolled on his back and tried to think. "The law itself has changed. Old Keris was telling us yesterday about the way it was back then. No guards here, for one thing, and fewer everywhere. No lockups. No stocks, no whippings."

"Old men always think their youth was golden," said Mali, stroking the baby's back.

"He saw the lords' magic himself, he said." Gird looked for a reaction to that and got it; Mali stared at him, shocked that he would speak of it openly. "He said they used to show it all the time, use it for aid in drought and storm."

"What was it like?" Her voice was barely above a whisper.

"He saw them call rain, he said. Bring clouds out of a clear sky, gather them up as a shearer gathers the tags of fleece, and then call rain down." Gird cleared his throat and looked around. No one else was in hearing. "He said, too, that the old lords would warm the heart to see, not like our count. That everyone wanted to please them."

"Old men's tales," said Mali, but without conviction.

That year the spring rains came timely, and a rich harvest rewarded their labors. Arin's wife had another baby in the fall; by Midwinter, Mali told him she was pregnant again. The cottage seemed to bulge at the seams already . . .

The dun cow lowed, her hoarse voice as loud as if she'd been in the cottage. No, she seemed to cry. No, no, no . . . o . . . o. Gird palmed his burning eyes and wanted to groan a refrain to it. No. He was not ready to get up and help that cow; he wanted to lie where he was and sleep. But the cow was not giving up; with the stubborn insistence of a deprived bovine, she let out another long plaint. Most cows tried to edge furtively into the woods when about to calve, but this one wanted someone there . . . yet refused to do it where it was convenient. Gird rolled on his back, grunting at the ache in his shoulders from plowing, and slowly sat up. He heard his father's harsh breathing, the catch in every inhalation. One of the children snored: probably Rahel. The cow called again, this time answered by the two in the cowbyre. Gird stifled an oath, and sat up, feeling around on the floor for his boots.

Outside, the predawn light in the sky only made the barton itself darker. Gird carried a splinter of oak from the fire, its tip bright orange, almost flaming in the breeze of his movement. Tucked in his tunic was the scrap of candle he'd light if he needed it when the time came: no use to waste candle if daylight came before the crisis. The dun cow had stayed out of the byre last night, as she did every time she calved. She would be in the thicket near the creek, if he was lucky. Outside the barton, the lower meadow looked silver-gray under a sky sheened with dawn. Heavy spring dew wet his boots through before he came to the thicket, guided more by the cow's voice than his sight, though it grew lighter moment by moment.

In among the gnarled and twisted scrub, though, he could barely see, and staggered more than once over root or stone. Stupid cow, he thought, as he had thought for three years now. Staying out in the cold and dark, hiding yourself in the thicket, when you know you'll want my help. There she was, a large hump of shadow among lighter, flickering shadows. Down already, grunting and panting, her tail thrown back out of her way. He pulled out the candle, found a smooth stone to set it on, and with a wisp of dry grass and breath, blew the splinter into a flame. The cow's big eyes reflected it, making three flames where there had been one. For a moment his mind wandered: did the cow see a reflection of flame in his eyes? Was that why she looked afraid? He lit the candle, picked it up, and walked closer, crooning to the nervous cow. *Have a heifer,* he begged silently. *Have a heifer this time.* A contraction moved across her girth; a bulge extruded below her tail. A pearly blot inside . . . a hoof. That was good, unless the other leg was back. He couldn't quite see. Another contraction, and he could: two hoofs and a nose. A normal delivery, so far, with the shiny black nose already free of the sack. Now it was light enough to see the shapes he needed to see. He tipped the candle, quenching it against the damp grass with a hiss, and tucked it back into his tunic. His feet were cold. The cow groaned again, a softer sound but eloquent of struggle. Gird stroked her flank, and began the calving chant.

"So, cow, gentle cow, quiet cow, so . . . Birth calf, milk calf, little calf grow . . . so cow, kind cow, good cow, so . . . Life come, growth come . . ."

Another contraction, and another, this one longer, pushing the shoulders out. The shoulders came, all in a rush, as always, and the wet calf lay still a moment, hind end still in the cow. Then the rest of the body followed. The cow made a noise Gird never heard save in those moments after calving, almost a murmur. The calf's ear flicked. With a lumbering rush, the cow heaved herself up, and the cord broke. She shook her head at Gird, who went on chanting until the wildness left her eyes, The cow nosed around the calf, licking it clean of the birth sac, licking it dry, murmuring, encouraging. The dun cow was a good mother cow. The calf shook its head, waggling both ears, and tapped its tiny front hooves on the ground as it tried to figure out how to stand. The cow licked on, still murmuring. The calf pushed one front leg out, then another, and heaved itself to a sitting position, then fell over. But it tried again, and again, its ridiculous little ears flicking back and forth with each effort. And it was a heifer, the year's good luck, for he could keep it.

Gird was never sure what made him look away from the calf, to glance between the knotted limbs of creek plum and hazel, but there across the meadow walked a creature of grace and light. Tall, lithe, so inexpressibly lovely that his throat closed. What was it?

The creature turned, as if feeling his glance, and looked toward him. A voice came, bell-like but slightly discordant.

"And what are you thinking, human, alone before dawn on this unlucky day?"

Gird could find nothing to say, only then remembering that it was the spring Evener, the day and night of equal length, when the creatures of night ruled until truedawn, and the creatures of day could not wander the dusks unscathed.

"The cow called," he said finally. The black-cloaked figure came nearer, hardly seeming to touch the ground.

"The cow called. Cattle to cattle: as your masters would say of you. Less than cattle, we think you, worse."

He could see the face now, inhuman but beautiful with a beauty that called human hearts and eyes. Pale against the black cloak, wide eyes starry bright. Was this a treelord? He had heard tales of them but no one he knew had ever seen one.

"No, I am not one of those dreamsoaked lost singers," the figure said. Gird shivered. He had said nothing; it had picked the thought out of his mind. "I am what they were, and should have stayed, had they any pride or wit at all. Your kind, when they know us at all, call us kuaknom."

He had never heard that word. Kuak, that was the old word for tree—and the nomi were the windspirits that hated order and served chaos. Kuaknom: that would be—

"Old lords," said the being, now just outside the thicket. "Very old, human slave. Firstborn of the elder races, lords of power and darkness—"

"The fallen treelords," Gird said, having finally put it all together. The treelords who had quarreled with Adyan the Maker, so the tales went, and turned against their kin, and riven the forests that used to cover the land in a great battle.

"Not fallen, little man," said the kuaknom, with a smile that sent ice to Gird's heart. "Not fallen—but *changed*. And on this night, until truedawn, those witless enough to wander abroad are our lawful prey. You, little man—"

Gird flinched as the kuaknom reached for him. The cow grumbled, in the way of new mother cows, and rattled her horns against the hazels. And a shaft of red sunlight, sharp as an arrow, stung his eyes; he flung up his hand, and the kuaknom backed away, muttering in its own language. Then again, to him:

"You are safe, human, by that one gleam of sun, but I curse you for it. May your loins wither, and your beasts fall sick, and the strength of your arm fail when you need it most." Even as Gird squinted against the sunlight, it was gone, a shadow across the field.

He sat a long time, bemused, until he heard Raheli's shrill voice calling for him. Was such a curse dangerous? Would he die, lose his manhood, his cattle, his strength? The cow continued to groom and nurse the calf, who showed all the sturdy life of a healthy young bovine.

Nothing befell to make him think the curse had force until the following winter. He had consoled himself that it was, after all, delivered in sunlight, which ought to make the words of the dark powerless. He had given more than his usual share to the rituals of Alyanya and even contributed freely to the lords' offering to Esea. Esea was, after all, a god of light, who might be expected to offer protection against the powers of darkness. When the rest of the year went well (the other two cows also calving heifers), he counted himself lucky.

But that was the winter of the wolves, the worst that had been seen since Gird's childhood. It began even before Midwinter. They had heard the wolves howling night after night, but none of the stock had yet been touched. The headman had gone to the steward, asking the guards' help to hunt the pack, but the steward had refused. Some of the men had gone out to the more distant folds, to help the shepherds watch. Arin went, over his mother's objections, twirling his long staff and grinning at Gird as he walked away.

Gird was hauling dung to the pile when he heard the shouts. He hauled himself to the top of the barton wall. There they came, across the snow, a cluster of men moving awkwardly. Carrying something—no, someone—he slid down, and went through the cottage without stopping to speak. His father was already out in the lane. Together they moved toward the group—and then he could see it was Arin they carried, Arin whose blood stained his clothes and dripped scarlet on the snow.

They got him into the house and stretched on the table. Gird felt his own heart pounding, slow but shaking his whole body, as he saw Arin's wounds. Then his mother pushed him aside.

"Go fetch water," she said. And to Arin's wife, "Get those children out of here—into the kitchen—"

Gird went out to the well; the men stood around silently, shoulders hunched against the cold. He lowered the bucket into icy black water and drew it up. As he turned to carry it in, Amis turned to him. "Is he—?"

Gird shook his head. "I don't know."

"Kef's gone for the steward," Amis said. Gird nodded and went back inside with the bucket. Coming in the clean air, he could smell the blood as if it were a slaughterday. He gave the bucket to Mali, who reached for it, and went to stand behind his father.

Arin had long bleeding gashes on his legs and arms; one hand was badly mangled. "He was trying to choke one of them with it," offered Cob, one of the men who had carried him in. Gird's mother said nothing; she and Mali were cleaning the wounds with one of Mali's brews, and wrapping them with the cloths the women kept. Arin looked as white as the snow outside against the dark wood of the table; he did not move or speak. "He bled all the way back," said Cob, into the silence.

Gird's mother gave him a fierce look. "You might have tied these up then," she said.

Cob spread his hands. "We had nothing but our dirty clothes; I would not give him woundfever."

Gird's mother opened her mouth and shut it with a snap. Gird could imagine what she would have said to him. But Cob had done the best he knew, and Cob was not her son.

The door opened, and someone coughed. Gird turned. The steward was there. No one said anything; the steward came nearer. In the dim light his face was stern as usual, but Gird thought his eyes softened when he saw Arin's wounds.

"Wolves, or folokai?" he asked.

"Wolves, sir," said Cob. "At the sheepfold, they were, and Arin come to drive them off—"

"Alone?" asked the steward.

"No, sir. But he went first, and it seemed the wolf drew away— just the one, that we could see. He went to chase it a bit, and that's when the pack ran at him, and then the rest of us ran out with torches, and drove them off him."

The steward moved closer yet. Gird's mother put out a hand, as if to stop him, and drew it back. The steward laid his hands on Arin's shoulders.

"Heal him, sir?" asked Gird's mother in a choked whisper.

The steward looked startled, then shook his head. "No, I can't do that—I have not the power." He looked closely at Arin's wounds. "I doubt he'll live—he looks to have lost too much blood—"

"No!" Gird's mother grabbed at his sleeve. Gird felt his heart contract with pity for her and Arin both. "It's not fair—he alone against the wolves—"

The steward pulled free. "I'm sorry. It's a shame—I'll take his name off the work rolls—if he lives, he'll be unfit to work until well into summer. If he dies, I'll remit half the death fee; he deserves that much."

"And more," someone muttered behind Gird. The steward's head came around, but the mutter had been too low to identify. Even Gird had no idea who it was.

"And I'm sending down a sheep," said the steward. "He will need meat broth to mend, if he can."

"Thank you, sir," said Gird's father. His mother nodded. The steward glanced around the room, as if looking for an excuse to say something else. His gaze lit on Gird.

"At least you have another son, a strong one. And this one—Arin, is it?—has sired already, hasn't he?"

A wave of hot fury rolled over Gird. He knew the lords considered them cattle, but the steward rarely made it so clear. Arin had bred; Arin's children lived; Arin himself—the laughing, steadfast, honest brother who had saved his own life more than once—that Arin did not matter to the steward, and even less to the lord who ruled the steward. He himself was just another bullcalf; if he died, the steward would shrug as easily. By the time he'd mastered his anger, the steward had left, and the other men not of the family. Gird's oldest living brother, a cottager in his own holding, had come; he and Gird stood beside the table.

Arin opened his eyes and stared vacantly at the ceiling for a moment. Then his eyes roved until he met his mother's. "Lady bless you," he said. "This is home?"

"Home," she said. "We'll soon have you well . . ."

"Not so soon." His voice was so weak Gird could hardly hear it. "If I die—"

"You will not die!" Arin's wife had come back in, and clasped his hand.

"If—you will take care of the children?" He looked at Gird, not his older brother or father, and Gird answered, feeling in an instant the weight on his shoulders.

"I will, as my own."

"Good. The wolf—I was—frightened." His eyes sagged shut, and his head rolled sideways.

It was late that night before he spoke again. By then the sheep had come, a carcass already cleaned, and Mali had a broth cooking, rich with herbs as well as meat. By then, too, they knew the old tracker and the guards had already gone after the wolves. Too late, Gird thought bitterly. But he held his tongue. Arin roused briefly, asked for water. He could not lift his head to drink; Gird put an arm under his shoulders and lifted him. He could feel the heat through his shirt. Was it a good sign, that Arin was warm again, or a bad sign of woundfever? He didn't know. He felt the trembling of Arin's muscles as he drank; when his mother had wiped Arin's mouth, Gird let him down as gently as he could, and pulled the blanket straight. Arin's eyes were bright, but not quite focused.

"Issa?" His wife moved up and took his good hand. "I will try, but—I am afraid the wolves have done for me."

"No—" she breathed.

"Yes. You will have a place here. Gird will take care of you."

"Arin—" began his father. Arin interrupted him, talking in broken phrases, without heeding any of them.

"I saw—a place—the Lady's garden. Flowers in the snow. Gird. Little brother—remember what I said."

"Yes, Arin," said Gird. He had no idea which of the things Arin had said over the years had come to him now, but he would forget none of them.

"You are more a soldier than you know. But don't give up the Lady's bounty, Gird."

"I won't." His vision blurred, and he realized he was crying. It felt strange to be looking *down* at Arin. Arin's eyes roved, and found his father's.

"You—told me not to go—" he murmured. His father shrugged. Gird looked at him sharply. Could he say nothing? But the firelight glittered on the tears that ran down his face. Although tears were nothing unusual among the village men, Gird was still surprised. His father cried rarely; now his shoulders shook with silent sobs. "Don't cry," said Arin, quite clearly. "I chose, or the Lady chose my time—" He said nothing more; his eyes closed. Gird watched the blankets for the rise and fall of breath.

In the hours of watching that night, in the flickering firelight, as their words to each other gradually failed and all was silence but for the snoring of Arin's oldest and the thin wail of Gird's youngest when he woke hungry in the turn of night, Gird felt the weight of manhood settle on his shoulders. He looked from face to face, seeing in the exhaustion of his father's the truth that he was now—must be now—the head of their family, in fact if not in law. Here, in this room: all that his father had made was now his to protect, support, defend.

When Mali had fed the baby, she came to sit beside him, her hand on his. He looked into her eyes, and saw her absolute confidence that he could do what he must, that they were safe with him. It was not true. He felt simultaneously the cold menace without, all that winter stood for, of famine, wolves, cold, even the lords' ravaging taxes, and the cozy seeming security within. How could he stand between, one mortal man? Cold sweat came out on his face;

he felt himself shiver as if someone had poured a bucket of icy water over him. Mali squeezed his hand. Her warmth, her strength leaned against him. He was not alone, then—there was another pair of arms, another strong back. Enough? It had to be enough. He could feel through his skin her awareness of his feelings, and her impossible joy that fought all his despair with laughter. His fear did not frighten her, nor his weakness weaken her.

Arin was still alive at dawn, when Gird and his father began the day's work. Gird eyed his father, noticing what he had not before—how weak his father had become in the past few years. That great frame had bent; the broad hands that had frightened him were stiff, knobby with swollen joints. His bush of yellow hair had gone gray. Had this begun while Gird was sulking, before his marriage, Gird wondered? Not that it mattered; somehow his father had become an old man.

All that day, he thought about it while doing his work. Sim would not come back—some old quarrel that had been far over his head when he was a boy had sent Sim out to make his own way. Now that he had cothold, he would be a fool to give it up. And if Arin died—he hoped fiercely that Arin would not die, but knew that hope alone could not save him. If Arin died—when Arin died, since even if he lived through this he might die before Gird another way—Gird would have it all to care for. Arin's wife Issa—the children—Mali—his own children now and to come—his parents. In the bleak light of that late-winter day he admitted to himself that his parents might not live long.

Arin lived another two days. He said nothing more that they could follow, although once the fever rose he muttered constantly, tossing and turning restlessly. He could not drink the broth Mali had made; Gird was almost ashamed to take a bowl of it, but they could not waste food. The sheep was already dead. They all drank quietly, avoiding each others' eyes and trying not hear Arin's moans.

Not long after Arin died, just after the first thaw, Gird's father dropped suddenly one day, and lay twitching. By morning he, too, was dead. The steward came again, to value the cottage and the lord's property therein. Gird had the death-fee to pay, part in coin and part in livestock—his precious heifers, two of them—and then the steward confirmed him in his father's place, as "half-free tenant of this manor," whose clothes and few personal tools might be handed down to his heir. The rest—the land, the cottage, the livestock, the major tools such as ox-yoke, plow, and scythe—were the lord's and he was "allowed" to use them.

Chapter Seven

He loved the feel of the scythe, the oiled wood smooth under his hands, the long elegant curve ending in its shining blade. Facing the uncut grain, with the sun over his left shoulder throwing his shadow ahead of him, he paused for the first of the harvest prayers.

"Alyanya, gracious Lady, harvest-bringer . . ." That was the oldest reaper, away on the other end of the field, to his right.

"Lady of seed and shoot, Lady of flower and corn . . ." That was the oldest granny in the vill, holding a wreath of harvest-daisies high.

"As the seed sprouts, and the green leaf grows, as the flowers come, and the seed swells . . ." And that was the Corn-maiden, who would wear the wreath while they reaped.

"So we with our blood offer, and you with your bounty reply . . ." All the reapers, their response ragged with distance, but sincere— and Gird with the others had nicked the heel of his palm with the scytheblade, and squeezed a drop of blood to flick on the ground. Then he smeared the rest on the blade itself, to return his strength to the cut grain. Garig, the headman, blew a mellow note on the cow's horn, and the harvest began.

Gird swung back his scythe and swept it forward and around. The wheat fell away from his stroke, as if swept by a gust of wind. Step forward, swing, sweep . . . and another swathe turned aside for him. That old rhythm reclaimed him, required—so early in the day—hardly any effort. Step, swing, sweep, return. Step, swing, sweep, return. On one side the standing grain, and before him the diminishing row he worked, and on his left side the bright stalks lying with their heads on the short green grass. The ripe wheat gave up a smell almost as rich as bread baking. Beneath the stalks lay a secret world, tiny runs that showed as he worked his way along.

He looked up, to see his way, and realized he was nearly halfway. Pakel, the oldest reaper, was only a third along his row—but no one expected him to be fast, not at his age. Still, he moved as smoothly as ever, and Gird knew he would be working just that well at day's end. Gird went on. Step, swing, sweep, return.

Something flickered in the stalks ahead of him, and he smiled. So the little ones, the harvest mice, had realized their day was come? He took another stroke, and another. Another mousetail, just escaping his blade to leap deeper into the wheat.

Gird reached the end of his row long before Pakel was through. He stopped to whet his blade from the stone looped to his belt. Behind him, three men worked on the half-field he'd begun, in staggered rows, as three others followed Pakel. It was the custom to harvest in halves, all reapers in each half working the rows one way, to "fold the field" as it was said. Gird walked back up, outside the fallen grain, and took a pull from the water jug one of the women held. He didn't need it yet, but it was wise to drink on every row. Then he began another row behind the last man on his half.

The little cut on his hand itched, as it always did. The sun was higher, and the smell of the ripe grain richer. A little breeze ruffled the wheatears and brought up the green smell of the haymeadows nearer the river. Step, swing, sweep, return. This was the best time of the harvest-day, when he had one swathe down, and his body had warmed and loosened to the work. The scythe swung and sliced almost on its own; his body was merely the pivot for its swing, leaving his mind free to wander. He enjoyed the evenness of his cuts, the smooth stubble he left behind, the proof of his skill. He saw every tiny blossom of the weeds within the grain: the starry blue illin, the delicate red siris, like drops of blood. Overhead arched a cloudless sky, a harvester's boon, and out of it came the song of a kiriel, sweet and piercing. He felt the prickle of stubble on his feet, the sleeves of his shirt on his arms as they swung.

This—not the other—was the right use of his strength. He felt as if he could swing the scythe forever without tiring. Row after row, selion after selion, flowed away behind him. The sun's heat, which a few years ago had worn him down by midday, now seemed to give him its energy. He remembered, as clearly as if it had been that morning, the first time he'd taken a scythe to swing. Arin's scythe, that had been, and his first cuts down in the haymeadow had been ragged as if he'd ripped at the grass with his hands. Now Arin was three years dead, and he was the leading reaper, the strongest man in the village, able to provide for his own and his brothers' children as well. He did not let himself think of the children who had died, his two eldest sons, one of Arin's, in a fever. It might have been that kuaknom's curse, or chance, but it was over.

He stopped to drink at the end of the row, and rubbed his hands together. He could just feel the pressure at the base of his thumbs

from the grips; the right had shifted. He spat on the handle and
worked the grip back and forth slightly. There. He tapped a splinter
under the bindings to tighten it, and swung the scythe lightly to
check . . . yes.

Across the field he could see Arin's oldest lugging water up to
the fieldmasters. Another selion or two, and it would be time for
the noon break. He was not tired, but he was hungry, his belly
reminding him how long it had been since that crust of bread
before dawn. He could smell cooking food even over the rich smell
of ripe grain around him. They were supposed to lunch on the
lord's bounty when harvesting the great field, but that bounty had
been less each year. Back before Arin's death, it had meant meat
as well as bread, and barrels of ale. In his childhood he remembered harvest meals of roast meat, bread, cheese, and sweet cakes,
heavy with honey and spices. Last year, bread and meat broth only;
the men had grumbled, but what good did that do? The steward
would not kill one of the lord's sheep or cows for grumbling alone.
He had not grumbled; he could not afford to, with two families to
support. It did no good to become known as a grumbler. He'd
eaten his bread and broth, taking an extra helping while others
complained.

He looked ahead critically. They might finish the great field in
two days, at this pace, and then begin the harvest of the individual
strips. Would the weather hold? It had been a dry spring, and
they'd all prayed for rain, but rain now would add nothing to the
harvest.

At the noon meal, the steward handed out round dark loaves
and bowls of thin soup. This year no one grumbled. Gird ate
silently, steadily. The more he could take of the lord's bounty, the
better for his family. Arin's boy, as a water carrier, could eat with
the harvesters this year. He came to sit by Gird, a boy as quiet
and shy as Arin had been cheerful and open. Gird wondered if
seeing his father die had changed him—but he'd been a quiet baby,
for all that.

"Mali's coming out to bind," said the boy—Fori, his name was,
though they seldom called him by name. He was "Arin's boy" to
the whole village. Gird frowned.

"She should not: she's too near her time."

"Ma has the sickness," said Fori, ducking his head. Gird sighed.
Issa loathed fieldwork, and although she was not as good a weaver
as his mother had been, she would spend all her time at the loom.
Leaving all the other work for Mali, Gird thought—but she also
had the sickness, no one could deny it. No one with the sickness

could come into the harvest field; throwing up on the first day of harvest was the worst of bad luck. And it was no fault of Fori's, what Issa did or did not do. But he worried about Mali. Big and strong as she was, every child seemed to take more out of her; she had not looked well this time.

"Make sure she has enough water," said Gird. Fori nodded. He had not finished his bowl of soup, but sat dangling his hands.

"Eat! You take all you can get, lad." The boy slurped up the rest of his soup.

"It's not as good as Mali's," he said through a mouthful of bread.

"No, but Mali didn't have to cook it. It's not from our stores. When you're doing the lord's work, you feed from his bounty: that's custom."

Gird followed his own advice, and went back for more. At least the steward wasn't stinting them on amounts—no one frowned when he picked up another half-loaf of bread and refilled his bowl.

When he was full, he lay back in the shadow of the old fireoak at the field's corner until the horn blew. The afternoon's work was always harder: the field seemed to swell with heat, lengthening every selion. Gird was soon back in the rhythm of the work. His mind seemed to hang on every close detail now, unwilling to soar abroad as it had in the morning. His shadow, at first a squat dark figure close beneath him, lengthened with the hours. He was still far ahead of the others, overtaking one after another on their selions, and swinging away beyond them. Yet no one minded: he was, he sensed, their pride as well as his own. Gird Strongarm, they said, grinning as he came past.

On the outer edges of the field, the women and older girls were binding the cut grain into shocks. None of his or Arin's girls were old enough yet: only a woman who had bled could gather in harvest. But he could see Mali's peaked hat busy among the others. Some years she worked first among the women, almost as much faster than others as he was. This year, she lagged, slowed by the coming child that made bending difficult.

By dusk, when he could feel the damp coming out, more than half the great field was down. Now the men joined the women in binding the last grain. Again tonight, they would eat the lords' bread and meat—if there was any meat, Gird thought. Surely there would be. He found Mali, and led her up to the serving line. She moved heavily, and beneath the day's sunburn, her skin was pale.

There was meat, although the steward's men doled it out one slice to a loaf of bread. A pottage of beans, cheese, and a wooden cup of ale completed the meal. "No sweet cake?" Gird heard

someone ask. The steward's men said nothing, handing a serving
to the next in line.

"I heard the steward tell the cooks they need not kill another
sheep—that the great field would be done early enough that there'd
be no evening meal tomorrow." Mali kept her voice low.

"What?" Gird stared at her. "That's—we can't be done by noon,
and if we work the afternoon, he has to feed us."

Mali, her mouth full of meat, merely shrugged. Gird tore off a
hunk of bread and chewed it, thinking hard. The custom had always
been to feed them for any part of a day spent on the lords' work.
When they finished harvest a bit early, they had time for a rest
before the meal, even a bit of singing. He worked his way through
the bean porridge, which lacked the flavor of Mali's, and wondered
what could be done.

As it happened, Mali was not the only one to have heard the
steward's words. The men gathered cautiously after dark, in the
lane near Gird's cottage.

"Not fair," said Teris. "We work faster, and they punish us—"

"So we can work slow, if Gird can hold back," said Amis's uncle.

Gird felt himself flushing. "It's not my fault," he said.

"No one said it was. But if being fast loses us a feast, maybe
being slow will get it back."

"'Course, he's already told the cooks," said Amis. "Might be even
if he has to feed us, it won't be much. No meat, anyway. And he'd
be angry with us. Is it worth that?"

"Where's Garig?" asked Pakul. "What does he think?"

"Garig's in the steward's back pocket," said someone too softly
to make out.

"We can't do aught without him," said Gird. "It's not fair, I'll
stand to that, and do what I can, but we need Garig. It's only he
can speak for us to the steward, anyway."

"I'll say what I can," Garig sighed, though, and Gird was sure
he'd come back with nothing. "The steward— the steward's told
me some of it."

"Of what?"

"What's gone wrong. There's a place—somewhere far off, I don't
know—where the lords come from, back when they come. It's
where they traded, over the mountains. It's gone."

"Gone? How can a place be gone?"

"Raided, I suppose, like a town the nomads have burned. Anyway, the lords got gold and jewels that way, and now they don't."

"So what's that got to do with us?" asked Teris. "We need to eat, same as always, and it's always been if we do the work on the lord's field, he feeds us."

"The count's squeezing *him,*" said Garig. "So he's squeezing us— that's the truth of it. He has to send more—"

"We can't." Mutters of agreement with that, a low voiced growl. "Might's well join the Stone Circle—"

"None o' that!" Garig's voice rang out. "We'll have none o' that talk here. D'you want the guards down on us? They're outlaws, no better than brigands, that bunch."

Gird agreed, but silently. He had heard more than one mention of the Stone Circle in the past two years. All he knew about them came from such brief encounters. The steward had warned Garig that anyone found helping a member of the Stone Circle would be turned out, if not killed outright. According to him, they were lawless, lazy farm lads who tried to get higher wages by threatening the farms—burning grain and hayfields, tacking herds in pasture, and so on. The other stories Gird had heard were of young men who saw no chance of marrying or having a place to farm—whose families could not spare the food, no matter how hard they worked. He tried not to think about it, about the disappearance of four or five younger sons from his own village in the past three years. Somewhere, the stories went, was a great circle of stones bigger than any mortal man could move, and into that circle fell miraculons showers of grain and fruit, more than enough for all who came. And the stones protected anyone who found the way inside, that was in the tales too. From that mysterious place, the movement took its name, promising peace and plenty in the days when "all men are stones of the circle, and none must run and hide."

"I'll speak to the steward," Garig said, sounding more angry than understanding. "I'll try—but no promises. And if there's slacking tomorrow, we could all be in trouble."

The men stood awhile in the lane, grumbling softly, when Garig had gone into his cottage and slammed the door. Gird was glad enough to stand there, in the warm darkness. Inside his own cottage, Issa's sickness fouled the air, and the children bickered over their meager supper. He tried to tell himself that they were doing all right, better than some others, but it was poor comfort.

The next day, Gird worked as slowly as he could. Garig had said that the steward had consented to another evening feast, if the work took them past mid-afternoon. Mali could not come, but Issa was doing her best raking up the fallen heads of grain into baskets. He was worried about Mali. She had not looked really well since losing the one of the twins. This baby should be her last—would be, if he had to force the herbs into her himself. He grinned at that thought. Mall might be weaker, but she was as headstrong as ever.

They finished the greatfield before dark, but not long before. Gird noticed that everyone came to the feast quietly, with none of the usual songs and laughter. There was meat, sure enough—not abundance, but some, and plenty of bread and cheese. He made sure that Fori and Issa ate heartily, and stuffed himself. Tomorrow he could begin cutting their own strip, grain that would feed them and help pay the fieldfee.

It was dark, the thick dark of a cloudy night, with enough wind to keep the leaves rustling uneasily.

"What?" Gird asked softly.

"We want to talk to you." That was Teris, he could tell. Gird sighed.

"Do you have nothing better to do than—"

"Shhh. Not here. Come along with us."

"Who's us?"

"I told you he'd make trouble." Tam's voice, this time.

"I'm not making trouble. I just want to know what—"

"Come *on.*" Teris had his arm, and shook it. "We'll talk, but someplace safe."

Gird let Teris lead him along the lane, between two cottages that he was sure were Garig's and Tam's, and down between a barton wall and the gurgling stream. The night air smelled wet and green; he could pick out scents he never noticed by day.

"There's someone here needs to talk to you," Teris said. Gird felt his heart begin to pound. Someone in the dark, someone he didn't know? He remembered all at once that Teris's mother was reputed to be a dire witch, laying curses on those who crossed her. "Go on," Teris said into the darkness. "Ask him."

Someone he could not see cleared his throat and said "Teris says you know about soldiering."

"No."

"Yes," hissed Teris, "You do."

"We need—we want someone to teach us."

"Who?" asked Gird. He thought he knew already. Instead of a spoken answer, he heard the click of stone on stone, and then felt a stone pressed into his palm.

"You know," said the voice. "The farmer's only hope . . . the only thing what won't burn in the fire that's coming . . ."

"But you're not soldiers," he said. "You don't—"

"We need to know how. We're getting enough, almost, now—if we only knew how to fight, and had weapons—"

"It won't work." Even here, where he was sure no one listened, he kept his voice low. "Running at 'em in a mob, like—they'll just ride over you and ride over you—"

"We have to *try*." His eyes were more used to the dimness; he could just make out Tam's face and the gleam of his eyes. Tam's weaker eye wandered off-focus, then came back. "We can't be soldiers; we don't have the training—"

"You!" Gird snorted. Tam couldn't throw a rock straight, let along make a soldier. "You'll just be killed, and they'll take it out of your families and the rest of us. Use sense, man! You'd have to know how to march, how to use your weapons together—"

"You could teach us," said the stranger, now a hunched black shape against the faint gleam of the water. "You were teaching them to march, Teris said. It was forbidden, but that didn't stop you. And then—"

No one had brought up his cowardice to him for years. They'd accepted him, he thought, once he grew up and married, once he was bent to the same lash as the rest of them. What had they told this stranger, that his voice changed when he said "And then—?"

"I—can't," he said hoarsely. "I—I don't remember enough of it."

"You remember enough to know that an untrained mob is hopeless. You can't have forgotten it all. I didn't." Teris again, hectoring as usual.

"I—"

"You're scared still, aren't you? After all these years—"

"He was my *friend!*" It came out louder than he meant, and he muted the rest of it. "I could not be part of what did that to him. *That's* why I ran, and if you want to call that cowardice, fine." He had never explained it to his friends before. Now the words poured out of him. "If you think I feared blood or pain, why d'you think I stayed in 'til then? If you remember so well, Teris, you must remember the beatings I got. You saw my bruises."

"Well—yes. But they said—"

"*They* called it cowardice, and my father bade me accept that. 'Twas hard enough on us, without causing more trouble. And that's what's really wrong with them—that they'd think cowardice is not wanting to cause pain."

"But you haven't joined—" and the stones clicked again.

"No. I had the family to think of, not just my own but my brother's. Once already I'd caused them all trouble; my mother died of the young lord's enmity, when he refused us the herb-right in the common wood. And the Stone Circle when it started was young lads, unmarried and mostly orphans: they had no family to suffer if they were caught."

"So—?"

Gird sighed. That bleak vision of his nightmares edged nearer, tried to merge with reality. "So—who will feed my wife, my children, if I go off to teach the Stone Circle how to march in step? Who will plow the field, or tend the beasts? If it could happen, and an army of peasants took the field, who would feed *them?* Some must plow and plant, some must spin and weave, or that army would die hungry and ragged, too weak to fight the spears."

"Is that what you plant for? That army, or your family alone?"

Gird spat rudely at the stranger's feet. "I plant for the lord, like all the rest, and we live on the spillage from the tax-cart—dammit, you ask questions like the steward laying blame for a cracked pot! You know my name, but hide yours; why should I listen to you?"

The stranger's head moved, as if listening for something, then gave Gird a long, neutral stare. "You know it's getting worse. You know we have no chance to resist without the knowledge you have. And you sit there, smug as a toad, giving good reasons to a bad argument—why *shouldn't* I put a thorn in your backside? You think I have no family, or these others? Those lads who joined Stone Circle years back are fathers now, just as you are. Those that didn't rot on the spikes. You think your children will thank you, for leaving them helpless before enemies?"

"They would not thank me for throwing them in prison to starve, either."

"Take 'em with you."

"No."

"At least tell us something, something we can use."

"I—" Gird looked around; there were four or five crouched nearby. He was sure of Teris and Tam, but not the others. Was Amis there? He could not tell. "I don't think it will work, even if I taught you—even if real soldiers taught you. The best way for us is to work and keep our peace; what you do only makes the lords angrier, raises the taxes higher—"

The stranger growled, and stood. Gird stood too, and they faced one another a long moment. Then the stranger laughed softly. "It's coming, Gird, whether you like it or not—you will see, and I hope you see before you suffer more deeply than a man can stand. I lost family; I would not wish that on anyone. My name is Diamod, when you want to find me again."

Gird turned away, wondering if they would let him go. No one touched him. He felt his way along the wall of Tam's barton, and then let his feet remember the way along the lane to his own cottage. Teris. Tam. Three or four others, who had not spoken so that he could not know who they were. Did they think he would tell Garig or the steward? His heart ached at that. His hands ached to strike something, anything. He would help them, if he had no family to think of. He could imagine himself teaching them as he had taught Teris and Amis and the others. But he could not risk Mali and Issa and the children.

He got back to bed without waking anyone up, and fell into heavy sleep. Dreams troubled him. In his mind's eye, he could see them, ragged, workworn, scarred, hungry, running in uneven clumps and strings to strike at the horsemen with their poles and scythes, their sickles and clubs. Behind the horsemen, the lords' army waited, trained soldiers in good armor, with their sharp swords and pikes. But they had nothing to do, for the horsemen could deal with the peasants. At the end— He woke with a jerk and a chopped-off cry. Beside him, Mali turned over and groaned softly, then snored.

In the thick darkness of the cottage, he seemed to see the past years as a painted streamer like the ones the lords sometimes carried on horseback. Hard work and hunger now, yes—but he had known hard work and hunger as a child. Yet his children were thinner than he had been, hard as he worked. He had never accumulated the store of coppers and silvers that his father had had beneath the hearthstone when it was needed. If something did happen with his own children, or Arin's, he would not be able to do what his father had done.

The next morning, he was still thinking about it as he shoveled manure. What could he do? He could not imagine sneaking away from the village some nights, to train Stone Circle members, coming back at dawn to work, but he could not imagine taking his whole family into an uncertain future, either. He was mulling this over when he heard shouts from the lane, and the heavy roll of hoofbeats.

He went through the kitchen to find Mali and Issa and the children starting out the front door.

"Get back!" he shouted. They made way for him. He could see, now, people in the lane nearer the center of the village. Amis was headed out his front gate, and Gird moved slowly toward his own. He could hear the loud complaints, the bellowed orders of the guard sergeant, the cries of children. It must be the Stone Circle man, Diamod, he thought, but he didn't see him. Had someone seen him? Reported him? He realized suddenly that his friends might think he had, if that was indeed who the guards were after.

It looked as if the guards were trying to search each cottage and barton. The noisy crowd surrounded them, not actually resisting but somewhat obstructive. The guards, some mounted and some afoot, moved toward Gird's end of the village. Now he could see faces he recognized, guards and villagers alike. An old woman, Teris's mother, was arguing with one of the soldiers, clinging to his arm, shaking it. He wrenched free of her and she staggered away, to be caught by her daughter. A child darted out into the lane ahead of the horses, and Amis went after him. The soldier riding the lead horse yelled something at him; Amis, intent on the child, shook his head and lunged forward.

Although he was behind the others, hardly out of his own dooryard, Gird saw exactly what happened. The soldier's arm moved, and Amis turned, his shoulder already hunching against the expected blow. The soldier's mace caught Amis full in the face, that familiar flesh disappearing instantly in a mush of blood and broken bone. One tooth flew free, a chip of white spinning in the hot sunlight before it fell out of sight behind the other bystanders. Gird felt something prick his hand, and looked down to see the handle of his shovel broken like a dry stick; he opened his hand and let the pieces fall.

As if in a dream, all motion slowed. One by one those at the back of the crowd turned to run, their eyes white-rimmed, their mouths open. Even before Amis fell to the ground, they had opened a path for the soldiers, those in front scrambling back, afraid to turn, afraid . . . and the soldiers' horses, their high necks streaked with sweat, ridged with lather where the reins rubbed, setting their ironshod hooves down one by one, so slowly that it seemed they could hardly catch the terrified fugitives. Amis lay huddled, blood pooling in the lane, soaking into the dust, both hands covering his ruined face. One of the horses, bumped hard by another, placed a front hoof in the center of his back so slowly, with such precision, that Gird had to believe it was a deliberate choice. He could hear a terrible crunch over the other sounds, the thunder of hooves, the screams—

And motion returned to normal, the crowd flowing back along the lane in a panic, the leaders running flat out, arms wide. Behind, the horses surged, the soldiers yelled, their weapons slicing from side to side. Gird stepped back, between the plum trees; it was all he had time for before they were past, horses bumping and trampling over the slow and clumsy, in pursuit of the fleetest. From the corner of his eye, he saw Diamod, cause of the whole incident, slipping quietly from the back of Amis's cowbyre to make his way over the fields.

Gird swallowed the same bolus of rage and fear that he had chewed and swallowed so often before. Now it was Amis on the ground, dead or dying he was sure and then it had been Arin torn by wolves, and before that Meris.

Amis breathed in difficult, jerky snorts. Gird laid his hand against his neck; the pulse was thin, irregular. Was Amis conscious at all? He should say something. What could he say?

"Amis? Can you hear me?" Stupid enough, but something. Amis's hand twitched; Gird laid his own over it.

"You've got to *do* something!" That high voice was Eso, always ready for someone else to do something. "Get him to safety—wash his face—"

"Be still," growled a deeper voice. Amis's father. He knelt beside Gird, his face as gray as his beard. His hands shook as he reached out to his son. "Is he—?"

"He's dying—I saw the mace hit his face, and a horse trampled him—" Gird gestured at the pulped mess of Amis's back.

"And if they come back, they'll but hurt him more." Amis's father held his son's slack hand. "Gird—get a plank or bench."

Gird nodded, and backed away on his knees. He shivered, nauseated, and barely made it to the trampled verge before throwing up, the morning's food and a life's bile together. Then he went into the front room, where Mali stood with her fist against her mouth, white as milk, and ripped the legs off one of the benches without a word. The long plank banged against the doorpost as he went out, and he almost lost control again. Amis. Kindly, cheerful, steady Amis, who had taken him to the sheepfold gathering to meet Mali—who had farmed alongside his strip for ten years, who had never done one thing wrong but be where a mace could destroy him—

Amis's father and Gird wrestled Amis onto the plank; that long, lanky body felt *wrong*, as if it were a boneless sack of seedcorn. He was still breathing, a hoarse rattle, in and out, that bubbled the blood on his face. What had been a face. Gird thought of the cheerful brown eyes, the nose lopsided from a cow's kick, the wide mouth.

Amis's wife had fainted; Mali sat beside that crumpled heap, comforting the younger children, as Gird and Amis's father carried him through, all the way into the barton. There they sponged the blood off his back, rolled him over. Gird turned his head aside and retched again. They could do nothing. Amis's breathing filled the barton with pain. One of his brothers came, and stood beside them, watching. Amis's wife, finally, biting her kerchief, holding their youngest baby close. Mali came to stand behind Gird, and put a hand on his shoulder.

Amis never woke, and when he finally quit breathing Gird could not at first turn away. Only the noise of the returning Guard, angry voices and the clash of weapons in the lane, loosened the paralysis that had locked his joints in place. He stayed calm in the turmoil that followed, giving his evidence to the steward in a slow, deep voice that came to him for that occasion. Amis had never been known as a troublemaker; his lunge at the guard's horse was a grab for the child who had run unknowing into danger. The steward nodded, shrugged, remitted part of the death-fee, and evicted Amis's wife to live with Amis's father. Another family, strangers relocated from another vill, moved into it.

And Gird put a sack of grain at the far edge of the wood, with two stones on top of it. It was gone the next day.

PART II

Chapter Eight

The first scream brought him out of his musings; he looked across the ploughed strips to see nothing at first. Perhaps someone had spilled a kettle of hot water. He scratched the back of one leg with his other foot, and clucked to the oxen. They leaned into the yoke. Then another shriek, one he would have known anywhere. Raheli! He dropped the plowhandles, and started across the field at a run. Then the horses came, from between the cottages, and crashing through the back gate of his barton. Lords' horses, with the bright orange and green and yellow he had seen going in the manor gates the day before. Another scream, and another, shriller—one of the little girls? He had yelled himself before he realized it, a deep roar of rage and pain. Up the field, another plowman answered.

"Stop, you!" yelled one of the riders, waving something at him. Gird paid no mind, charging toward his own gate. Now he could hear a man's voice, yelling, and more screams down the lane. The same rider yelled "Guards! Ho!" The horsemen closed toward him, the horses plunging with excitement. Behind them now he could see footsoldiers in Kelaive's bright orange. The sun glittered on their helmets, on riders' buckles and saddlefittings, on the stubble of last year's grain. Gird took a breath, slowing to see how he might get by. Now one of the riders was above him, the tall dark horse snorting and prancing.

"Get back, fellow!" the rider said. Gird peered up at a narrow pale face. "It's nothing to do with you. Get back to work!" The voice had fear in it, as well as arrogance. Was he armed? Gird tried to circle the horse, but the horse spun, and blocked him. "Get back!" the man said, louder. Gird looked aside; the guards were almost on him, their cudgels ready. Another scream, this one a man's death-cry, ending in a gurgle. Gird flinched, and shivered—it had to be Parin, he was the only one inside. His belly churned; his vision blurred. Then pain stung him awake; the rider had slashed his back with a whip. He spun, fury once more driving out fear, but the guards had him, four of them. For all he could do, it was nothing—they had him face-down in the fresh-plowed furrows, choking on dirt, two of them on his back, as the screams went on—and then died away. When they let him up, the other plowmen were back at work, and the riders were gone, and the grim-faced guard sergeant gave him his warning.

He knew before he came inside what he would find. The shattered barton gate, the ewe he had brought in for nursing lying dead in the barton, her guts strewn wide, their one pig gone, the cottage doors smashed, the great loom broken: that was bad enough. But there lay Parin, his face one curdled mess of blood and shattered bone, and there lay Raheli, naked, the slight bulge of her belly that had promised so much to her and Parin. He knelt beside her, so full of grief he could not breathe. When he felt that first warm breath on his hand, he could hardly believe it. Alive? After the blow that had split her face all down one side, and drenched her in blood? After that blade or another had bared her ribs on one side, and sliced deep into her hip? After the beating, and the rape? He looked at the body he had not seen since she became a woman. Even at that moment, he noticed—and hated himself for noticing—the white beauty of her skin, the full young breasts, the long curve of back and thigh now streaked with blood. Her breath touched his hand again, and he drew a long shaky breath of his own. Alive. He had to do something—

He looked around the room again, seeing destruction everywhere, and out the front door, now splintered—something stirred, there. He could not leave Raheli, but he must; he had to get water, rags, something. He stood too quickly and his head spun. Staggering, he made it to the door and then crouched, heaving all he had eaten into the trampled torn dirt of the yard.

Then he looked up and saw the rest of it.

She must have been at the well, for the blood trail started there, and the water jug lay broken beside it. Girnis lay sprawled between the well and door, her slight body twisted as if she'd been thrown against the wall. And Pidi, where was Pidi? Gird found him on the far side of the well, fists jammed into his mouth, trying not to cry; a hard blue knot on the side of his head and a welt on his back.

He was shaking with rage and grief; he could hardly lower the bucket to the water. The weight of it full dragged on him, steadied him; he got it up, and scooped a handful for Pidi, who said nothing but drank it.

"Stay here," he said to the boy; Pidi nodded. Gird went to Girnis; she was alive, but unconscious. Her left arm was crooked, and swelling: broken. He glanced around for something to splint it with, and caught sight of someone, a kerchiefed head, over the sidewall.

It disappeared; he did not call. He found a piece of the splintered door, and tore a strip from his tunic. Girnis did not stir when he handled her broken arm. Should he carry her inside? No. Girnis would do well enough out here until she woke, he thought, and knew that he wasn't thinking as well as he should. But Raheli needed him. He took the bucket inside, breathing hard through his mouth. The cottage stank of blood and brains and slaughter. He had killed animals more cleanly—but he could not stop to think of that.

Raheli's face, if she lived, would have a scar from hairline to jaw. He was not sure she would live. The blade that had cut her had gone through into her mouth, come near her eye—might have broken her jaw or her cheekbone as well, he couldn't tell. Raheli had had the parrion of herbal wisdom from Mali; it was not his knowledge. Blood pooled under her head; her scant breaths gurgled. Blood in her mouth, what if she choked? He looked wildly around, and this time found the scattered bedding, the cooking cloths for straining, the cloths for women in their time. As quickly as he could, trying not to think beyond the immediate wound, he pressed the cleanest rags into her wounds. The long shallow gash along her ribs had nearly quit bleeding anyway; the deeper wound where the blade had met her hip oozed steadily, reddening the cloth. Her face—her face was hopeless, he thought at first, as blood soaked one cloth after another.

"Gird?" He jumped, swore, and turned to glare at the light that poured in the broken door. Then he saw it was a woman, though he could not make out her face against the light. "Is—is Raheli alive?"

"Just." His voice grated and broke; he wanted to burst into tears. Hard enough to be alone with this, but harder with someone else. "Let me see." She came up to him, and now he could see it was Tam's aunt, old Virdi. Her breath hissed out. "Aahhh—Lady's Peace, she's bad—"

"I know that." He had never liked Virdi, but she had the healing in her hands, so his mother had said. And no scorn to her for not saving Mali—healing in the hands was nothing in a plague of fever.

"The lord, he did this?" He thought he heard derision in her voice, and bristled. Next she would ask why he'd let it happen. But when he glared at her, her eyes were soft, not accusing at all.

"He did. I was—plowing. They—" He could not go on.

She nodded. "I saw across the fields—the guards knocked you down, there were too many. Lady's Curse on Mikrai Pidal Kevre Kelaive: may he never know peace."

He had never heard a woman lay a curse before, but there was no doubt Virdi had done just that. So simple? He shivered, suddenly cold. Her hand touched his head, dry and chill as a snake.

"Near broke your head, they did, too—" He had not realized that he'd been hit, but where she touched him was a heavy pain— and then it was gone, and she was rubbing her hands briskly on the hearthstone. She gave him a quick smile. "Rock to rock; the hearthstone's strong enough." She pointed, and he saw a little crack he didn't remember seeing.

Her hands on Raheli's head hardly seemed to have weight; they hovered, touched as light as a moth on a nightflower, retreated. She sighed, then lifted the cloths he'd laid on that torn face, and hissed again. "Get more water—and—" a quick look at the hearth, now fireless, "—go to Tam's, and bring a live coal."

"But will she die while I'm—?" Gird didn't finish the question, for she interrupted.

"Not if you're quick about it." She had poured the remaining water in the bucket into the one unbroken pot, and he took the bucket and went out. Pidi still crouched by the well, but now he was crying, shoulders heaving. Gird drew another bucket of water, and found the dipper somehow unbroken, caught in the hedge. He squatted beside Pidi.

"Come on, lad—let me see—" Pidi looked up, eyes streaming. "I—I couldn't—" He winced as Gird touched the lump on his head. "You couldn't stop them. Neither could I."

"But—but they—they hurt Raheli—and Parin tried to fight—"
"Pidi, listen. I have to get fire. Can you stay here?"

"Raheli? And—and Girnis! They—hurt her too!" The boy grabbed Gird's arm with both hands, threatening to overturn the bucket. Gird set the bucket carefully aside and gathered up his youngest child, letting him sob. He wanted to do that himself, would have given anything for a strong shoulder to cry on, but all the ones he'd known were gone. He patted the boy's back, carefully avoiding the welt on it, and carefully not thinking. Enough to comfort one who could be comforted. "I'm so sorry," the boy was saying between sobs. "I'm so sorry—"

"It's not your fault." Gird tried to keep his voice steady, soothing, as if Pidi were a sheep caught in a briar, a cow with her head through a gap. Finally sobs quieted to gulps. Gird unhooked the boy's hands and moved him away far enough to see his face. "Here—let me wipe that for you—" Pidi nodded, mouth set tight, and Gird cleaned his face. "Now—I still have to go get a firestart, from Tam's house. Will you stay here quietly?" Pidi nodded, solemnly, tears threatening again. "I'll be back," said Gird. Pidi said nothing.

He saw no one on the way to Tam's cottage, though he was aware of a stir in the village, of people watching him and ducking from his sight. All the doors were shut. He knocked on Tam's door, and Tam's wife, white-faced, opened at once. She paled even more when she saw the blood on his clothes.

"Virdi sent me for a firecoal," he said, as calmly as he could. Tam's children were huddled around the hearth, silent and staring. "Our fire's out." Tam's wife nodded. Without saying a word, she went to her hearth, and took a burning brand, far bigger than the custom was. She offered it with a stiff little bow, and he took it gingerly.

In the sunlight, the flame was pale, hardly visible; he could feel the heat of it as it blew back toward his face. He knew by that he was walking fast, too fast. Pidi waited in the yard, sitting now by Girnis. He nodded to the boy, and stopped to pick up some splinters of the door.

Inside, Virdi had Raheli's face clean of blood, but for the wound itself. She had her hand over Raheli's cheek, her expression withdrawn. Gird stepped carefully around her and laid the only fire pattern he knew, the shape the men used in the open. The brand from Tam's house lit it instantly, and warmth returned to his hearth. He went back out for the bucket, and picked up more wood. For an instant, he wondered if it was bad luck to burn doorwood, but then shrugged. How much worse could his luck be? He put the bucket down beside Raheli, and laid the wood carefully on the fire.

"Is there a boiler left?" asked Virdi suddenly. Gird looked around the chaos in the room, and then went to check in the back room. There he found a single metal pot, the one Mali had used for steeping her herbs, dented but still whole. He took it to Virdi, who nodded. "Good. Start heating water in it—put it near the fire, but not in it. And then clean your hands. I'll need your help."

They had Raheli's wounds bound, and her body covered with the cleanest cloth, when the steward came. All that time anger had grown in Gird's heart, anger he had controlled so long that he had half-forgotten some of it. Now it grew as swiftly as a summer stormcloud, filling him with black rage. He had tried so hard: he had suffered so much already. In spite of all he had brought up three of his own children, and two of Arin's—he would have had his first grandchild the next year—and the lords could not let even one hardworking farmer alone, in peace.

Yet when the steward came—an old man, now, slightly bent but still capable of rule—Gird said nothing of it. He heard what he expected to hear: he, as head of his household, would bear the penalty for his son-in-law's attack on the count's son and his friends, and for his own attempt to get to his cottage to defend them. The loss of the cottage he expected, immediate eviction, fines, loss of all "so-called personal" property, damages assessed for the breakage of the lords' property in the cottage.

"The count remembers you," the steward said slowly, his eyes drifting from the broken loom to the smashed door. "He will be content, he says, if you sign yourself and all your children into serfdom, become his property in name as in fact." He paused, and his voice lowered so that Gird could hardly hear it. "Were I you, Gird, I would flee: he'll name you outlaw, but you would escape for a time. Otherwise—you well understand what kind of man he is; he would take delight in all you fear, in far worse than you have seen, in this manor. I have done all I can."

"You serve him." That was all Gird dared say, and he clamped his mouth on the rest of it.

"I serve him—I gave my oath, long ago, to the count's father; had he not died young—but that's no matter. I break my oath by this much—to warn you, to say that for this night I can promise you no pursuit. Say you will clean and mend what you can by midday tomorrow, when you must be evicted: I will tell him that."

It was all the kindness left; years later Gird realized what the steward risked, and what he would suffer if anyone found out what he had done.

Chapter Nine

All the times he had thought about leaving, it had never been like this. He had imagined sending the children away somewhere (but where?), going himself to join the little band of rebels he had first met—but not this terrifying journey. He was sure they were leaving a trail a child could follow through the narrow wood. Anyone would expect him to go that way—but what other way was there? He could not have strolled past the manor itself with Raheli on his back.

It still worried him that he'd left the cottage such a wreck. It wasn't his fault, he knew that, but a lifetime's work and care nagged at him. He should have—

Ahead, two rocks clacked sharply together. Gird halted, breathing hard. Behind him, he could hear Fori's breathing as well, on the other end of the litter. Raheli was heavier than he'd guessed. Pidi, beside him, glanced up and Gird nodded. Pidi clicked two pebbles in his hand, mimicking the stones' sound. Another clack, this a triple. Pidi replied with the triple of triples Gird had taught him. Trouble, that was. Danger, trouble, need help—any of those.

Raheli moved on the litter, and moaned softly. Gird looked over his shoulder. Blood had seeped through the pack of moss on her face, staining it dark. He heard a twig crack, and looked ahead. There were three, coming down the slope. One was Diamod. He could have wished it was someone else.

"Gird—what is it?"

"You haven't heard?"

"Only the rock signals of trouble, that someone was needed. Yours?" Diamod looked past him at the children.

"Aye. My daughter's hurt bad; they killed her husband. Outlawed me, for what he did, and for trying to get to her—"

"I'm sorry." Diamod actually sounded sorry; Gird had been half-certain that he would dare amusement or scorn. "So—you're fugitives now?"

"Yes. I don't know if Rahi will live—"

"Later. Now we must get you away." Diamod waved the other two men forward, and they took the handles from Gird and Fori.

"These are smooth!" said one, clearly surprised.

Gird hawked and spat. "Scythe and shovel handles," he said. "I'm outlawed anyway; might's well bring something useful."

Diamod grinned at him, then sobered as he looked at the others. "Are all these coming?"

"Fori's my brother's son. His wife died last year, in childbirth. The other two are mine, and have no place in that village."

They set off again, faster for the unwearied strength of the two men carrying Raheli. Gird strained his ears backwards, expecting to hear any moment the cry of hounds, horses' hooves crashing in the leaves behind them. But he heard nothing, only their own hard breathing, their own footsteps.

They followed the water up out of the wood, past the cleft Arin had shown Gird all those years ago, where the Stone Circle visitors had waited for so many nights. Up a narrow, rocky defile, and carefully around the west slope of the hill, keeping as much as possible to the low scrub. Gird looked up once or twice, seeing folds of land ahead he did not know, but looked back oftener. When would the pursuit come, and how bad would it be?

By noon, when the sun baked pungent scent from the scrub,

they had found another watercourse, this one winding away to the south. Along its banks low trees formed dense cover. Diamod lagged far behind, watching for pursuit, as the others paused for a brief rest. Gird dipped water from the creek, and bathed Raheli's face.

She was awake again, lips pressed tightly together, eyes dull. He did not want to speak to her—what could he say?—but she questioned him. "Where—are we?"

"South of the village, beyond the hill. We had to leave, Rahi."

"Parin—they killed him—"

"Yes."

Her hand strayed to her belly, as if feeling for the child within. "I—don't want to lose the baby—"

"Virdis said you would not, unless you got fevered. She gave me herbs for you." He dug into the roll of clothing and bandages for the little packet of herbs. Rahi shook her head.

"I'm fevered now—I can tell. If I lose it—" Her voice trailed away, and her eyes fixed on some distance Gird could not fathom. Then she looked at him directly. "The little ones?"

"Pidi has a lump on his head, but he's all right. It would take more than a lump to damage him. Giri has a broken arm. Here— you need to drink—" Gird lifted her as gently as he could, but Rahi flinched and moaned. He could feel her fever burning through the wrappings Virdis had put around her. She sipped a little water, then shook her head. He laid her back down. She alone, of all his children, reminded him of Mali—she had that same hair, the same quick wit. He could not lose her. But her fever mocked him. Of course he could lose her, as he had lost his parents, his brother, his brother's wife, the babies that had died. He could lose her quickly or slowly, as the fever raged or died, or as pursuit caught them.

He looked around at the others. Giri, her arm bound tightly to her side, looked pale and sick; she had never been as strong as Rahi. Pidi, whose lump had matured into a spectacular black eye, sat watching Gird alertly. Fori, much like Arin but with Issa's slender build, sat hunched with his head down, breathing heavily.

"Fori?" Gird put a hand on his shoulder, and Fori jumped. When he looked up, his face was streaked with tears.

"I should have stopped them," Fori said, through sobs. "I—I should have been there."

"I, too—but we weren't. And if we had been, we'd have been dead as Parin is now."

"But she's—"

"Your cousin, and my daughter."

Diamod came back before he could say more, breathing hard as if he'd been running a long way. "I saw guards on the near side of that first hill, moving slowly. Not the way we'd come, exactly—I don't think they have a trail. But we can't stay here. We must move under cover, and keep moving."

This time Gird and Fori took the litter again, and the other two men took their bundles. One of them led the way southward, summering as Gird thought of it, keeping them along the creek bank as the water deepened and broadened, then leading them eastward, sunrising, up a tributary. Diamod lagged behind, overtaking them again near dark, when they'd stopped under a clump of pickoak where a spring came bubbling up from the rocks.

"They didn't follow," he said, before anyone asked. "They've put someone up on the hill—I saw a glitter up there—but no sign of real pursuit. We must stay out of sight of that hilltop, and no fire, but we can think now where to take the—your daughter."

Gird hoped his face did not show all he felt. "She's fevered now," he said, ducking his head. Raheli had said nothing, all the afternoon, but she seemed to be in a sick daze. He had gotten her to drink a little twice, but nothing more.

"She needs shelter, and a healer. Have you any family in another village?"

Gird shook his head. "Only my wife's—my dead wife's—family, over in Fireoak. But I don't know where that is from here, and even so they might not take her."

One of the other men turned to him. "Fireoak? My sister married into that village. They don't have much trade, those folk, but they're kindly."

"We can find Fireoak easily enough, but it will be days of careful travel. We're a day or more from the sheepfold where the dances are."

Gird nodded. "I know that."

"For healthy men it would be a day's journey, but carrying her, and with the others, it will be two, I think. Then from there to Fireoak is—"

"A day, like this. But it's the only shelter between, that fold."

Mali's parents, like his own, had been dead some years, but her brother was alive. He squatted beside the litter and laid a hand on Raheli's head.

"Mali's child?"

"Aye." Gird felt restless, in here where he could not see.

"We heard there'd been trouble your way. Your name was mentioned." Gird was sure it had been, if the guards had been by. "They said a man died—?"

"Rahi's husband, Parin. He was inside; he tried fight them off."

"Mmm. And you?"

He felt the rush of shame again. "I was out plowing—when I heard her scream, I tried—but the guards got me—"

Mali's brother shook his head. "None o' us can stand against them. It's no blame to you. Well. I reckon we can take her in, see if she heals—and the younger girl?"

"Has a broken arm."

"She's welcome here too. The lords come here rarely, and one woman—one girl—but the thing is—"

"You can't let us stay. I know that." Gird sighed, heavily. "I— I'm an outlaw now, we both know that. Trouble for you. But if you'll care for them—"

"We will."

"Then I'll leave now, before I bring trouble."

"Will you tell us where?"

"No. What you don't know, you won't be withholding. If Rahi lives, I may come through again sometime."

Mali's brother nodded. "I can give you a bit of food—"

"Save it for Rahi—I'm giving you two more mouths to feed, maybe three if she doesn't lose the child—"

"Never mind. We're glad to help Mali's daughters. May the Lady's grace go with you."

Gird almost answered with a curse—what grace had he had from the Lady this several years?—but choked it back. The man meant no harm, and maybe the Lady meant no harm either. He and Fori eased out of the barton, keeping close to the walls and low, until they came between the hedges that edged the fields of Fireoak. Back up the grassy lane—the plough-team's lane, he was sure—to the heavy clump of wood that reminded him of the way the wood had been when he was a child. Here no lord had thinned it, and the oak and nut trees made a vast shade.

Diamod was waiting, with Pidi; the others had disappeared. Gird and Fori scooped up the sticky paste of soaked grain, and ate it from dirty fingers. For the first time, Gird felt like a real outlaw. No fire, no shelter, no table or spoons—only the knife at his belt, and the farm tools he had carried away.

"And now?" Diamod asked. "What will you do now?"

Gird looked sideways at him. "What is there to do, but try to live and fight?"

"You had said you were thinking of teaching us what you knew of soldiering."

Gird wiped sticky fingers in the leafmold, and scowled at the result. "I had some ideas, yes. But your people—were they all farmers before?"

"Most of them. I was a woodworker, myself. There's a one-armed man who was a smith, but crippled for forging long blades."

"But most have used farming tools, sickles and scythes and shovels and the like?"

"Yes—but why?"

Gird had crouched by the trickle of water to scrub his hands clean; now he flipped the water from them, and leaned back against a tree. Something poked him in the back, and he squirmed away from it.

"You can't fight soldiers as an unarmed mob; we know that already. It takes too many—and too many die. Drill would help; having a plan and following it, not rushing around in a lump. But weapons—that's the thing. We'll never get swords enough, not with the watch they keep on smiths. I'd thought of making weapons from the blades of scythes or sickles, but that too would take a smith willing to work the metal, and then training to use them. I had just begun sword training myself; I'm not any good with a sword." He paused to clear his throat. Diamod was scowling, and now he shrugged.

"So? Are you still saying there's no way peasants can defend themselves?"

"No. What I'm saying is we have to use what we have. The tools the men are used to—the tools we can make, or that we have already—and then learn to use those tools for fighting."

Diamod looked unconvinced. "Are you saying that ex-farmers with shovels can stand up to soldiers with pikes and swords?"

"If we can't, then we're doomed. I don't know if they—we—can. But we have to try."

"And you'll teach us."

"I hope so. There's something else—"

"What?"

"Just an idea. Let me tell the others about it later."

Diamod led Gird, Fori, and Pidi through the woods that lay between Fireoak and the next holding to the east. Gird tried to keep in mind how they had come, but soon found all the trees, trails, and creeks blurring in his mind. That night they spent in the wood, eating another cold meal of soaked grain. The next day, they followed a creek most of the day, coming at last to a clearing where the creek roared down a rocky bluff. At the foot of the waterfall, a rude camp held a score of men.

In the center of the camp was a circle of stones around the firepit, symbolic of their name, but actually used for seating. The lean blackhaired man who appeared to be the leader did not rise from his stone when Diamod led Gird forward.

"So this is Gird of Kelaive's village, eh?" The man looked worn and hungry, as they all did. Diamod started to speak, and the man waved him to silence. "I'll hear Gird himself."

Gird stared at him, uncertain. So many strangers—not one familiar face beyond Fori and Pidi—upset him. He could not read their expressions; he did not know where they were from, or how they would act.

"Have you ever been out of your vill before?" asked the man, less brusquely.

"Only to trade fair, one time, and to Fireoak when I was courting," Gird said. The man's voice even sounded strange; some of his words had an odd twang to them.

"Then you feel like a lost sheep, in among wild ones. I know that feeling. Fireoak's in your hearthing, anyway—hardly leaving home and kin, like this. Diamod has told us about you—that you sent grain, the past few years, after your friend was killed—"

"Amis," said Gird. It seemed important to name him.

"And now you've run away to join us. Why?"

Gird got the tale out in short, choked phrases; no one interrupted. When he finished, he was breathing hard and fast, and the others were looking mostly at their feet. Only the blackhaired man met his eyes.

"Outlaw—this is what you chose. After telling Diamod you would not consider it—"

"While I could farm," Gird said. "Now—"

"You can't farm here," the man gestured at the surrounding forest. "So what skills do you bring us?"

Gird was sweating, wishing he could plunge away into the trees and lose himself. What did these men want? Were they going to grant him shelter or not? "I thought I would do what Diamod asked before: teach you what I know of soldiering."

Someone snickered, behind him. The blackhaired man smiled. "And what do you know of soldiering, after a lifetime spent farming? Did you bring swords, and will you teach us to use them? Or perhaps that scythe slung on your back will turn to a pike at your spellword? Diamod told me he had found someone, a renegade guardsman, he said, to teach us soldiers' drill, but what good is drill without weapons?"

The tone of the questions roused his anger, and banished fear. "Without drill you couldn't use weapons if you had them. With it— with it, you can use whatever comes to hand, and make a weapon of it."

"S'pose you'll lead us into battle wi' sticks, eh?" asked one man. Others chuckled. "Fat lot of good that will do, a stick against a sword."

"It can," said Gird, "if you've the sense to use it like a stick, and not try to fence with it." This time the chuckles were fewer; he could see curiosity as well as scorn in their faces.

" 'Course," said the black-haired man, "we've only got your word for it, that you can fight at all."

"That's true." Gird relaxed; he knew what would come of this. They wanted to see what Diamod had dragged in, but it would be a fair fight. "You want to see me fight?"

"I think so." The blackhaired man looked around at the others. "Aye—that's what we want. Show us something."

"Let'm eat first, Ivis," said one of the other men. "They been travelin' all day."

"No guest-right," the blackhaired man scowled. "Until this Gird proves what he is or isn't, I'm not granting guest-right."

"No guest-right," said Gird. He was surprised to find outlaws following that much of the social code. Food was more of the soaked grain, and a cold mush of boiled beans. Looking around, Gird saw only the one firepit, and no oven. The blackhaired man unbent enough to explain.

"Sometimes the lords hunt this wood, and their foresters use this clearing. So a fire here is safer than one elsewhere in the wood; folks is used to seeing smoke from about here. We tried to build an oven once, but they broke it up when they found it."

"Where do you go when the foresters come?" asked Gird.

"That you'll find out after you fight. *If* you convince us to let you stay."

When Gird had eaten a little, he stood and stretched. The others went on eating, all but a strongly built man a little shorter than he was. Gird glanced at the black-haired man, who grinned.

"You'll fight Cob; he's our best wrestler. Used to win spicebread at the trade fair that way, as a lad. Show us how a soldier fights, but no killing: if you're good, we can't afford to lose you or Cob."

"All right." Gird had seen Cob's sort of wrestler before; he would be strong and quick. But the sergeant had taught his recruits many ways to fight hand-to-hand, and which ones were best against which kind of opponent. Gird watched Cob crouch and come forward in a balanced glide, and grinned to himself.

Although he knew what to do, it had been a long time since he'd done it. He got the right grip on Cob's arm, and put out his own leg, but his timing was just off, and Cob twisted away before he was thrown. Gird avoided Cob's attempt at a hold, but the effort threw him off balance and he staggered. Cob launched himself at Gird, knocking him sideways, and threw a leg across him quickly. Gird remembered that—it took a roll, here, and a quick heave *there,* and suddenly he was on top of Cob. Under him, the man's muscles were bunched and hard. He was not quitting. Gird did not wait for Cob's explosion, but rolled backwards suddenly, releasing his grip. Cob bounced up and charged. This time Gird was ready; he took the wrist of the arm Cob punched at him, pivoted, and flung Cob hard over his shoulder onto the ground.

Cob lay blinking, half-stunned. Gird heard something behind him, and whirled in time to catch another charge, even as the blackhaired man said "Triga—no!" Triga's mad rush required no great skill; Gird used the man's own momentum to send him flying as well. He landed hard and skidded an armlength when he landed.

Cob whistled, from his place on the ground. "You could've made money with that throw, Gird. Teach me?"

Gird looked at the blackhaired man. "Well?"

"Well. You can fight—not many overthrow Cob. I'm sorry about Triga, but glad to see you have no trouble with him. We can use those skills."

"And the rest?"

The blackhaired man frowned slightly. "I am not the only leader, the Stone Circle is made of many circles, and each has its own. You must convince us all that this is something we need, and can use. I still do not see how sticks and shovels will let us stand against soldiers with sharp steel."

Gird started to say that he wasn't sure, but realized that these men didn't want to hear that. Those eyes fastened on his face wanted certainty, confidence, the right answer. The only answer he was sure of was drill. "You have to start with drill," he said. He knew they could hear the certainty in his voice about that. "You have to learn to work together, move together. Let me show you."

"Now?" someone asked, as if it were absurd to start something new so late in the day.

"You can't start sooner," said Gird, quoting the old proverb. Several of the men chuckled, but it was a friendly chuckle this time.

"Start with me," said the blackhaired man. "My name's Ivis." He stood and the rest stood also. Cob, cheerful despite his fall, had climbed to his feet, and reached a hand down to Triga.

Gird took a deep breath and tried to remember the expression on his sergeant's face. "The first thing is, you line up here." He scratched a line in the dirt with his toe. "You, too, Fori—come on. Pidi, just stay out of the way. Two hands of you here, and two behind, an armslength." That would make two ranks of ten.

When the front ten had their toes more or less arranged on the line he'd scratched, he looked at them again. They slouched in an uneven line, shoulders hunched or tipped sideways, heads poked forward, knees askew. Triga was rubbing his elbow. Those behind were even more uneven; they had taken his armslength literally, and the short ones stood closer to those in front than the tall ones. This was going to be harder than he'd thought. His boyhood friends had been eager to play soldier.

"Stand up straight," he said. "Like the soldiers you've seen. Heads up—" That sent one of them staggering, as he jerked his head up too far. Someone else chuckled. Ivis growled at them, and they settled again. Gird did not like their expressions: they weren't taking this seriously at all. Only Fori and Cob and Ivis looked as if they were even trying. "You three—" he said, pointing to them. "You get together here in the middle. And you others—look at them, how they're standing. Like that is what you need. Feet together, toes out a little. Hands at your sides. You in the back row, make a straight row—" Gradually they shifted and wiggled into something more like military posture. Gird wondered if he had looked like that at first. Maybe this was the best they could do, for now.

"Now you have to learn to march." He glared, daring anyone to laugh. No one did, but he saw smirks. His old sergeant would have had something to say about that, but he had never dealt with outlaws, either. "You all have to start with the same foot—"

"Like dancing?" asked Cob. Gird stopped, surprised. He'd never thought of it as like dancing, but all the dances required the men to step out with the same foot, or they'd have been tripping each other. He thought his way into the harvest dance he had led so many times. Wrong foot.

"Like dancing," he said finally, "but not the same foot. The other foot, from the harvest dance." Surely they all danced it the same way. "Think of the dance, and then pick up the other foot." Slowly, wavering, one foot after another came up, until they were all teetering on one foot. All but two had the correct foot. Those looked down, saw they were wrong, and changed feet. "Now one step forward." The double line lurched towards him, out of step and no two steps the same length. Gird felt a twinge of sympathy for his old sergeant. Had it been this difficult? "Straighten out the lines," he said.

He kept them at it until his voice was tired. By then they could break apart and reassemble in two fairly straight lines, and they could all pick up the same foot at the same time. But when they walked forward, their uneven strides quickly destroyed the lines. He was sure they could have danced it, arms over each others' shoulders, but they couldn't fight in that position. He'd told them that, and a few other things, and remembered some of the words his sergeant had used.

They were ready to lounge around, eating their meager supper, but Gird remembered more than his sergeant's curses.

"We must learn to keep things clean," he said.

"Clean!" Triga had scowled often; now he sneered. "We're not lords in a palace. How can we be clean—and why should we?"

"Soldiers keep themselves clean, and their weapons bright. I spent my first days in the guard scrubbing the floor, washing dishes, and scouring buckets. First, it keeps men healthy—you all know that—and protects against fevers. And second, it means that you know your equipment will work. A weapon's no good if the blade is dull. And third, I stink bad enough to tell any forester there's a poor man here: so do you all, after the drill. D'you want hounds seeking us? It's warm enough: we should all bathe."

Sighing, Ivis and Cob heaved themselves up, and the others followed. Gird led them to the waterfall. Once well wet, the men cheered up and began joking, splashing each other. Pidi had found a clump of soaproot, and sliced off sections with his knife. Soon the creek was splattered with heavy lather.

When Gird felt that the grime and sweat of the past days was finally gone, he washed his clothes as best he could, and saw the bloodstains from Parin and Rahi fade to brownish yellow. The other men watched him, curious, but some of them fetched their own ragged garments and tumbled them in the water. Gird smiled when he saw them laying out the wet clothes on bushes, as he was doing. Diamod brought him a clump of leaves.

"Here—rub this on, and the flies will stay away. Otherwise you'll be eaten up by the time your things are dry."

"I should've washed clothes first—now it's near nightfall. But I have a spare shirt."

"Most of them don't."

But even in dirty clothes, the men stank less, and carried them-selves less furtively. Gird, with a clean shirt tickling his bare knees, suggested another change in their customs.

"Why not bake a hearthcake on one of these stones? 'Twouldn't be bread, exactly, but it would be hot, and cooked—"

"If we had honey we could have honeycakes, an' we had grain," said Triga. Gird began to take a real dislike to Triga.

"There's always bees in a wood," he said crisply. "And stings to a bee, for all that."

"There's none knows how to make the batter, Gird," said Ivis. "We've no mill or flour. All we know is crush the grain and soak it—if you know better, teach us that."

Gird thought of the millstones left behind—but he could not have carried them and Rahi. He looked at the stones used as seats, and found one with a slightly hollowed surface. Then he went to the creekside, and looked for cobbles. He could feel the other men watching him, as if he were a strange animal, a marvel. But mill-stones, the cottage millstones, were no different. A hollowed stone, like a bowl, and the grinder. Some people had flatter ones, with a broader grinder. It had to be fine-grained stone, and hard. He picked up several cobbles he liked, and hefted them, felt along their smooth curves with a careful finger. Yes.

Ivis had the grainsack out for him when he returned. Gird won-dered if it was grain he'd grown, or someone else's contribution. It didn't matter. He dipped a small handful, and poured it onto the stone, then rubbed with the cobble. It wasn't the right shape—neither the bottom stone nor the grinder—and the half-ground grain wanted to spit out from under and fall off. He worked stead-ily, ignoring the others, pushing the meal back under the grinder with his finger. He was careful not to lick it, as he would have at home: thin as they all were, they must be keeping famine law, when all the food was shared equally.

When the first handful was ground to a medium meal, he brushed it into a wooden bowl that Ivis had brought. It was not enough to make any sort of bread for all of them, but he could test his memory. Cob brought him a small lump of tallow, and he took a pinch of salt from the saltbag he'd brought himself. Meal, water, fat, salt—not all he liked in his hearthcakes, but better than meal and water alone. He stirred it in the wooden bowl, while the fire crackled and Pidi brushed off the flattest of the stones facing the firepit. The tallow stayed in its lump, stubborn, and Gird remembered that he needed to heat it. He skewered it on a green stick, and held it over the fire, catching the drips in the bowl.

Finally it melted off, and he stirred it in quickly. He felt the stone, and remembered that he should have greased it. The stick he'd used for the tallow was greasy now; he rubbed his fingers down it, and then smeared the stone. The stone was hot, but was it hot enough? He poured the batter out. It stiffened almost at once, the edges puckering. Hot enough. With his arm, he waved heat toward it, to cook the upper surface. Mali had had the skill to scoop up the hearthcakes and flip them, but the only times he'd tried it, they'd fallen in the fire.

The smell made his mouth water and his belly clench. He looked up, and saw hungry looks on all the faces. Now the upper side was stiff and dull—dry, and browning. He hoped he'd put enough tallow on the rock, He slid a thin twig under it, and it lifted. He got his fingers on it—hot!—and flipped it to Ivis. Ivis broke it in pieces— each man had a small bite—and then it was gone. But if his fighting had gotten their respect, this had gotten their interest.

"I thought you were a farmer, not a cook," said Ivis.

"My wife was sick a lot, that last few years." Gird gestured at the bowl. "May I give my son that?"

Ivis nodded. "Of course. It's fair; he had none of the hearthcake itself." Pidi grinned and began cleaning the batter from the bowl with busy fingers and agile tongue. "But tell us—what do we need?"

Gird thought about it. "Millstones—we can use this, but we can't carry it along, not if the foresters come here. But we can put millstones in another place, if you have a particular place."

"Where I came from, we all had to use the lord's mill," said Ivis.

Gird shrugged. "That was the rule for us, too, but most of us had handmills at home. Always had. The lord's mill was a day's journey away—we had no time for that. And then if you did go, you'd have to wait while he ground someone else's, and might not get your own back. Anyway, we can have millstones for hand mill- ing—it'll take time, is the main thing. We can't have bread every day. Tallow, we need, and a bit of honey if it's available. Salt—I brought some with me, but we'll need more—"

"There's a salt lick downstream a bit," said Cob. "I can show you."

"And if we want lightbread, we'll need a starter. Do you ever get milk?"

"D'you think we live in a great town market, where we can buy whatever we like?" asked Triga.

From the tone of the response, others were as tired of Triga's complaints as Gird was. Gird waited until the others had spoken, then said "No, but I think you're not so stupid as you act." Cob grinned. Triga, predictably, scowled. Gird turned back to Ivis. "How long have you lived out here?"

"Me? A hand of years—five long winters. Artha's been here longer, but most don't stay that long. They move on, or they die."

"You've done well, on beans and grain."

"There's more in the summer. We find herbs, do a little hunting, rob a hive once a year—no one wants to do it more, with all the stings we get. We do get milk sometimes, when we venture in close to a farmstead. Not all of us, o' course. Milk, cheese, trade honey or herbs for a bit of cloth . . ."

Cloth, in fact, was one of the hardest things to come by. Gird, remembering his mother's hours at the loom, and the value of each furl, did not wonder at this. To share food was one thing; to share the product of personal skill was another. The outlaws had learned to tan the hides of beasts they hunted—"Stick 'em in an oak stump that's rotted and got water in it"—but good leather took more than that; many of the hides rotted, or came out too brittle to use for clothing.

As he listened to Ivis and Cob, and thought about all that this group needed, he thought back to his sergeant's comments about the importance of supply. Soldiers did not grow their own food, or raise their own flocks, or build their own shelters—this, so they could have the time to practice soldiering. But these men would have to do it themselves. Could they do that, and learn to be soldiers as well?

Chapter Ten

The next morning, Gird realized that the others were all looking to him for leadership, and not only in military training.

"Do we work on drill before breakfast, or after?" asked Ivis.

"After," said Gird, to give himself time. His clothes were still damp; he turned them over and hoped the morning sun would dry them. Then he eyed the trees, and realized it would be a long time before the sun came into the clearing. Breakfast was another cold mess of soaked grain. Gird was already tired of it. He was spoiled, he supposed, by having had a wife and daughter with a parrion for herbs and cooking. Pidi leaned against him as he ate, and Gird put an arm around him. He wished he could have left the boy with Mali's brother—he was really too young for this. Fori sat on Gird's other side, carefully not leaning, but clearly nervous among so many strangers.

"Do you have a plan beyond training us?" asked Cob. Gird glanced at Ivis, who seemed interested but not antagonistic.

"When Diamod first came to our village," Gird said, "he wanted to learn soldiering. Wanted me to teach all of you. I thought he meant *you* had a plan—whoever your leader was."

"We've tried things," Ivis said. "And the other groups—I know they have. Captured a guards' store house, one did, and burned it out, but that brought more guards, and they took prisoners—finally killed them. Robbed a few traders, but that's—we don't like to be brigands; that's not what we're here for."

"And that is?"

Diamod leaped into the discussion. "We've got to be the peasant's friend—free the peasants, somehow, from the lords—"

"That won't happen!" Triga stamped his foot in emphasis. "There's always been lords and peasants. But if we can make them understand they have to be fair—"

"Now *that* is what will never happen." Cob stamped both feet. "Lords be fair indeed! They wouldn't know how, and why should they? Nay, 'slong as we've got the lords over us, they'll do their best to keep us down, and take every bit they can. Does the farmer leave the sheep half a fleece, or feed a cow and not milk her?"

"A *good* farmer leaves the beasts alive and healthy," muttered another man. Gird could tell this was an old argument, comfortable in their mouths as their tongues were. He knew its byways as well, having heard them all in his own village. He cleared his throat, and to his surprise they all quieted and looked at him.

"You have no plan," he said, as if musing. "One wants to teach the lords how to rule, and another wants to end their rule, and I suppose some of you would like to go and live peacefully far away, if you could." -

"Aye—" More than one voice answered him.

"I used to think," Gird went on, "that it was best to work hard and live within the lords' laws. That if a man worked hard enough, honestly enough, everything would be right in the end. That's what my father taught me, and times I did other than he said, we all suffered for it. I determined to follow his advice, and trust he was right. But I was wrong." He paused, and looked around. Pidi was trembling a little in the arc of his arm; Fori's face was set. The others watched him closely, and did not move. "I told you a little—

about my daughter and her husband—but not all that led me here. It began long before, and over the years I built a wall of the stones I swallowed—stones of anger and stones of sorrow. A wall to keep myself at peace, and safety within—and it did not work." He ran a hand through his thinning hair, and scrubbed his beard. "I don't know if any law is fair, but the law the lords put on us is not fair, and no man can live safe under it. I don't know if all the lords are alike, but some of 'em—Kelaive, for one—are not only greedy, but cruel. They like to hurt people; they like to see people suffer. Such men cannot rule wisely, or fairly. And when such men rule, no one can live an honest life." He drew a long breath, gave Pidi a squeeze, and then pushed him gently away. He could not say what he was going to say, with his arm around his youngest child.

"I have taken that wall down," Gird said. "Those stones—those stones I will throw at our enemies. Those stones, which I bring to this circle—because the Lady herself cannot give us peace unless we drive off the alien lords who rule us."

"But we can't," said Triga. "We are too few—"

"Now, in this place, yes: we are too few. But there are more farmers than lords, more servants than lords. Few have joined you, as I did not join you, because they too think we are too few. They do not wish more trouble than they have. But if we can show success, they will come. I'm sure of it."

"Yes!" Cob stamped his feet again. "Yes, you're right. Gird's right," he said to the others. Most were nodding, smiling, clearly pleased with what Gird had said. And Gird, putting his arm around Pidi again, wondered if he could possibly perform what they were sure he had promised.

Serious planning began after a short review of yesterday's drill. He had realized that the clearing was really too small and too cluttered for serious drill; he could not march his two lines of ten five steps without someone having to step over or around a log or stone. And in the noise they made while drilling, a squad of mounted guards could have ridden up on them without anyone noticing.

"Do you have anyone out looking for foresters?" he asked Ivis.

"Usually someone goes downstream, and someone goes upstream," Ivis scratched his jaw and looked thoughtful. "We use stone clicks for signals. But today everyone wanted to hear what you said." In other words, Gird thought, just when it was most dangerous, they had no guard set. That would have to change.

"What about at night?"

"No, no one goes out at night. The foresters don't travel at night."

"But—" He wondered how far to go. Would Ivis be angry? It had to be said. "At night, you could see the glow of their fire— smell smoke or cooking food—and be warned."

"I suppose." Ivis didn't look eager to wander the forest at night; Gird could understand that. But Diamod had seemed to like sneaking about the village—maybe he could. He glanced at Diamod, who smiled brightly. He still did not understand Diamod, and he wondered if he ever would. The other men seemed to feel the way he felt—would have felt, if he'd left home under any other circumstances, he reminded himself. They were here because they had to be. But Diamod seemed to be enjoying himself.

"Someone should go out now, and be sure no foresters are coming," he said to Ivis. Ivis nodded, but did nothing. "Who will you send?" Gird asked.

"Me? But you're—"

"Do you *want* me to take over as leader? Is that what you're saying?"

Ivis sat silent a long moment, his face somber. Then he looked Gird in the face. "I haven't done much," he said. "Just—just tried to keep them together—talk to farmers about food—but I don't *feel* like a leader. I never did. They started listening to me after Rual died, but I never wanted it. They're used to me, but you'll do better."

"It's not something you and I should decide," Gird said, almost before he thought it. "If this is about fairness, and ruling fairly, then they should have a say."

"Triga will quarrel," said Ivis. Gird shrugged.

"Let him quarrel. He won't do more; he didn't like landing on the ground." He looked around at the others, now lounging around the clearing in the attitudes of men trying to hear a private conversation without seeming to listen. "Ivis and I were talking," he began, not raising his voice. They edged closer. "He asked me if I wanted to be leader."

"You! We don't even know you," Triga said. Predictable, Gird thought. He's so predictable.

"Quiet now—you can argue later." He put a bite into his voice, and Triga subsided. The others were attentive; he could not tell if they approved or not. "Ivis—do you want to tell them what you said to me?"

Ivis swallowed, gulped, and finally repeated most of what he'd said. "I think he'd be a good leader," he finished. "He's strong, and he has a plan. And he knows more than just soldiering. I'd rather follow him."

"And I," said Cob quickly, giving Gird a wide grin. "I want to learn how to fight like that."

"Yes," said some of the others, and "Gird—let's have Gird." Triga was obstinately silent until everyone else had spoken. They all looked at him, and he turned red.

"Come on, Trig," said Cob. "You know you want to—it's just your stubbornness."

"What if he's a spy?" Triga said. "How do we know he isn't a guard in disguise?"

"I'm not that stupid!" Diamod glared at him. "I was in his village: I met his friends. They told me a lot—" He gave Gird a long look, steady and measuring. "A lot about his past. They couldn't all have been lying. He's a farmer and a farmer's son, and if you think he's not, you can argue it with me. Knife to knife."

"Enough," Gird said. "We can't be spilling each other's blood over little quarrels, if we want to fight a war. Triga, d'you think Diamod's lying?"

"No." It was a sulky no.

"Do you think *I* am? I'll have no one in my army that thinks I'm a liar." He felt ridiculous, speaking of an army when what he had was twenty ragged, hungry, untrained men and one boy, but he saw the others straighten a little. If coward was a word to make men flinch and bend, maybe army was a word to straighten their backs and make them proud. He saw Triga's face change, as he realized that he might actually be thrown out of the group. Fear and anger contended; fear won.

"No—I don't think you're lying." Slightly less sulky, and somewhat worried.

"These others agreed to have me as their leader—do you?" He kept his eyes locked on Triga's; he could feel the struggle in the man.

"I suppose. For awhile. We can see." Cob and Diamod looked angry, but Gird shook his head.

"That's fair. You don't completely trust me, but you're willing to give me a chance." Triga's jaw dropped in surprise; he had been braced for an argument. Gird looked around at the others. "I told Ivis I would not take the leadership on his word alone. You have all chosen, as you have a right to do—and I thank Triga for trusting as far as he can. None of us can do more than that."

The others sat back, their expressions ranging from puzzled to satisfied. Triga said nothing, but looked as if he were chewing on a new idea.

"Now, We need to send out watchers, to let us know if anyone comes. Ivis says you usually had two; I'd like to send four—two of you, and my son Pidi and my nephew Fori. They need to learn the forest."

"It's my turn," said Ivis. "And Kelin—" Kelin was a slight brownhaired man with one shoulder higher than the other. He did not quite limp when he walked, but his stride was uneven. Gird nodded.

"Pidi knows many useful herbs," he said. "My daughter taught him."

Kelin grinned. "Then let him come with me: all I know is flybane and firetouch. And sometimes I miss firetouch until I'm already itching."

"Three pairs of clicks," said Ivis, as they left. "That's the danger signal. "You pass it on, whichever way it comes, and move away from it. Cob knows the trails."

When they had gone, Gird surveyed the clearing itself. If they had to leave it untouched, so that foresters who used it would not know they'd been there, he could not move the logs and stones used for seating to give more room for drill. They really needed a campsite the foresters did *not* use. This one could become a trap, particularly if his people became effective against the lords. So what did he need in a campsite? He thought about that as he roamed the clearing, pacing off distances, and trying to listen for clicks.

Water. Good drainage, and room for the jacks trenches he would have them dig; the disgusting stench just behind a trio of cedars was entirely too obvious. Level ground, uncumbered, for drill, but enough trees for cover. A cave would be nice, shelter from weather and a place to store food and equipment. While he was asking, why not a forge with a skilled smith? He remembered that Diamod had said one of the men had been a smith, a one-armed man— there he was. His name was odd, a smithish name: Ketik.

"Ketik—"

"Aye." He had a rough voice, and stood canted a little sideways, as if missing the weight of his arm. The stump was ugly, a twisted purple lump of scar. He wore no shirt, only a sleeveless leather jerkin.

"If we found another campsite, what would we need for a forge?"

Ketik stared at him out of light-blue eyes. "A forge? Don't you see this arm? I'm no smith now."

"If we had what is needed, couldn't you take an apprentice? Teach someone?"

Ketik snorted, a sound half-laughter, half-anger. "Could you teach someone to swing a scythe by telling them? Wouldn't you have to show them? Do you think smithery is so simple?"

"Not simple at all," said Gird quietly. "It is a great· mystery, and our village had no smith at all. We shared one with Hardshallows. But we will need a smith—"

"And not all are weapons smiths," Ketik said.

"I know. What I'm thinking of wouldn't take a swordsmith. But we would have to have our own forge."

"A good fireplace," Ketik said rapidly. "Fuel—fireoak is best. Someone to make charcoal, because you'd need to be able to refine ores sometimes. Leather for the bellows, and not the rotting, stiff mess these idiots make in old tree stumps. Real leather, properly tanned. Tools, which means iron: ore or lump iron from some smelter. Both are illegal. An anvil. Someplace with water, too, and a way to disguise the smoke. Satisfied?"

"We will need to move anyway," Gird said. "We might as well look for what we need."

"What we need is the gods' blessing and a fistful of miracles," said Ketik. He sounded slightly less irritated now, as if challenging Gird had eased his mind.

"You're right," Gird said. "But though we need Alyanya's blessing for a good harvest, we still have to plow and plant and weed and reap."

Ketik laughed aloud. "Well—you may be the leader we need after all. I never heard of a one-armed smith teaching smithery, but then I never heard of a farmer teaching soldiering, either."

Triga had come close while they were talking; now he said, "I said last autumn we should find a new campsite."

Gird nodded, ignoring the rancorous tone. "Did you find someplace you thought would be good?"

"Me?" Triga looked surprised. "They wouldn't listed to me."

"If you already know a place—"

"I know another place than this, but it might not be what you want."

"How far is it?"

"A half-day, maybe, or a little longer." He pointed across the stream. "Sunrising. It's swampy; the foresters never go there."

Gird opened his mouth to say that the last thing they needed was a swamp, and closed it again. If Triga was trying to be helpful, why stop him, "I think we'll need more than one place, but that sounds useful. If we're pursued—"

"It's like a moat, I thought," said Triga.

"As long as we have a bridge over it—one they can't see."

"Gird—about the grain—do you want us to grind more today?" That was Herf, who had been tending the fire when Gird awoke. Triga looked sulky and opened his mouth; Gird shook his head. "Triga, tomorrow or the next day I'd like to see your swamp. Right now, though, the grain comes first."

Triga said "I could go look for a path through the swamp."

"Good idea." Gird had never seen a swamp, and had no idea what one would look like. Were they flat? Sloped? Did they have high places that were dry? "If you find a dry place inside it," he said slowly, "like the castle inside the moat—?"

"I'll look." Triga actually seemed cheerful—for him—as he waded across the stream and turned to wave back at them. Gird shook his head and turned to Herf.

"Now. How much grain do we have?"

When Herf showed him their meager food stores, and the way they were kept, Gird could hardly believe the band had not starved long ago. Sacks of grain and dry beans were sitting on damp stone under a rainroof made of small cedars with their tops tied together. Gird prodded the bottom of the sacks and felt the telltale firmness of grain rotted into a solid mass. Beans had begun to sprout through the coarse sacking. Herf had tried to store onions and redroots in a trench, but most of them were sprouting.

"I know," he said in answer to Gird's look. "Once they sprout, the redroots are poisonous. But I couldn't dig them in any deeper here, without proper tools. The ground's stony."

"Well." Gird squatted beside the trench, and brushed the leaf-mold off a healthy redroot sprout. "My da used to tell about his granda's da—or somewhat back there—about the time before the lords came, when our folk grew things in the woods."

"In the *woods?*"

"In fields, too, the grain—of course. But redroots and onions and such—some we don't grow now—along the streams, and in the woods. We can't eat these—maybe we should plant them now, and harvest in the fall."

"We can still eat the onions—"

"Some of them, yes. But why not plant the others? Spread 'em around in the wood—no one'd recognize them as plantings, and they'd be where we knew—"

Herf frowned, thinking hard. "Then—we could grow the greenleaves, too, couldn't we? Cabbages, sorli—"

"Maybe even sugarroot." Gird poked at the leafmold. "This here's good growing soil for some crops. Herbs, greenleaves—grow 'em along the creekbank, we could. You know how hard it is to haul water to the greenstuff in summer—we could plant it where it needs no help."

"Aye, but breadgrain and beans—we can't live on greenstuff and redroots alone."

"Right enough for now—you get your grain from farmers, right?"

"Or steal it from traders—but that's rare."

"When we take it from farmers, they go hungry—so we can't afford to let any rot—"

"It's the best I could do!" Herf puffed up almost like a frog calling.

"I'm not saying it wasn't. But if we find a new campsite, maybe we can do better. Besides—did you ever see the big jars the lords use?"

"Jars?"

"Aye. Brown, shiny on inside and outside. Like our honeypots but bigger. They're almighty heavy and hard to move, but grain and even meal stay dry inside them."

"And where would we get such? We don't have a potter."

Another miracle to wish for, thought Gird. They needed some pots—at least small ones. In his mind's eye, his future campsite had sprouted another fireplace, although it wavered as he looked at it. He'd never seen a potter's workshop. He knew they had a special name for the hearth in which they cooked their pots, but not what it looked like. But he could see as clearly as if he stood there the kitchen of the guard barracks at Kelaive's manor, with the great jars of meal and beans, the huge cooking kettles, the shiny buckets, the longhandled forks and spoons, the rack of knives. If he was going to have an army, he would have to have a kitchen capable of feeding it—and storerooms—his head ached, and he shook it. What he had was a sack and a half of grain, some of it rotted, less than a sack of beans, a few sprouting onions, and redroots that might be edible in half a year. An open firepit, two or three wooden bowls, the men's belt knives. He sighed, heavily, and heaved himself up.

"All right. We'll grind some of that grain, and make hearthcakes tonight. But we're going to need more grain, and I know the villages are short right now. Some of the men hunt, don't they? How often do they bring anything back?"

"Not that often. There are only two bows, not very good ones, and the arrows—"

"Are as bad. I can guess that. Anyone who can use a sling, or set snares?"

Herf shook his head. Gird added those skills to the list in his head, and told himself not to sigh again. It would do no good. He wished he hadn't sent Fori off; the lad had a talent for setting snares, and had once taken a squirrel with his sling. Come to think of it, slings could be weapons too.

"All right." He raised his voice. "Come here a bit, all of you. There are some things need doing." The men came closer, curious. "If we're going to be an army," he said, "we have to organize like soldiers. Food, tools, clothing—all that. We're starting with what we have. The first thing is to get all the rotten grain and beans apart from what's good, and protect the good from the wet. Then we're going to plant the sprouted redroots, scattered along our trails, so that we'll have them next fall. They'll get bigger, you know, and double or triple for us. Who here has used a handmill?" That was usually women's work, although many men helped grind the grain. Two hands raised. Gird nodded at them. "Herf will give you the grain—you saw how I did it yesterday. We're making enough hearthcakes for everyone tonight. Unless the foresters show up, of course."

By midday, all the clothes washed the previous evening were dry. Gird pulled on his trousers happily; he did not feel himself with his bare legs hanging out. The two volunteer millers had produced almost a bowlful of meal, and Herf had used Gird's clean shirt to hold the little good grain in one sack while he scraped out the spoiled and turned the sack inside out. The bottom end was beginning to rot. Without Gird having to suggest it, Herf decided to rip out the stitching there and sew the top end shut, so the weakest material would be at the opening. Since he seemed to know how to use a long thorn and a bit of twine to do it, Gird left him alone. Two other men had gone out in both directions along the creek, with the sprouted redroots, and were planting them. Gird reminded them that there was no good reason to plant them close to that campsite, since they would be moving somewhere else.

Fori appeared unexpectedly in midafternoon with a pair of squirrels he'd knocked down, showing off to Ivis with his sling. He had skinned and gutted them already, and had the skins stretched on circles of green wood. Gird grinned at him, delighted. But two squirrels would hardly feed twenty hungry men—they had no soup kettle. Herf had the answer to that, showing Gird how hot rocks dropped in a wooden bowl could make the water hot enough to cook without burning holes in the bowl. By this time, he had all the good grain in one sack, and the dry beans separated from the damp, sprouting ones. Gird had wondered if they could also grow beans in the wood, but beans liked a lot of sun. Reluctantly, he had buried the smelly remnants of spoiled grain and beans. Now Gird sliced up onions, his eyes watering and burning, to go in with the squirrels and one dry, wrinkled, unsprouted redroot. Herf added the beans he'd put on to soak that morning.

The guards came back in the dusk to the smell of roasting hearthcakes and squirrel and bean stew. Gird had already found another, besides Diamod, who would be willing to stand night guard; these two had eaten, and when Ivis and Kelin returned with Pidi, the night guards went out. Gird had also drilled the others, in the afternoon, and insisted on their cleaning up. He was pleased to notice that Ivis and Kelin stopped to wash hands and face in the creek before approaching the fire.

They had only three bowls to eat from; these passed from one to another, along with the two spoons. But compared to the night before, it was a festive meal. Even Triga made no complaint. Ivis came to sit by Gird, and said, "I made the right choice."

"It won't always be like this," Gird said, thinking of all the things he had to do. "We were lucky that Fori got those squirrels."

"But it feels different." Ivis wiped his mouth with his tattered sleeve and grinned, teeth bright in the firelight. "You know what to do."

Across the fire, Fori was basking in the praise of older men; Pidi was showing Herf the herbs he had brought back in his shirt. They were feeling at home here; Gird wondered if the young adjusted more easily. He was not sure what he felt. The blinding pain when he thought of Rahi was still there; when it hit, he found himself turning in the direction of Fireoak, *willing* himself across the woods and fields between to be with her. She might be dead by now, or still struggling in fever. He could not know.

He was beginning to know the men around him, and already knew that several of them would have been friends if they'd grown up in the same village. Cob reminded him of Amis, with his matter-of-fact friendliness. Ivis was more like Teris—responsibility made him truculent, but once freed of it, he was amiable and mild-tempered. Gird told himself that these were mostly farmers—men like those he'd known all his life—and in time would be as familiar as the men of his village, but for the moment he could not quite relax into kinship with them.

That night before he dropped off to sleep, he made an effort to speak individually with each of them, to fix their faces and names in his mind. Then he burrowed into a drift of leaves, with Pidi snuggled close to his side. It was still hard to sleep, in the open, knowing he had no cottage to return to, but he was tired, and the strain of the past few days overcame him.

The next morning brought complications. Instead of cool spring sunshine, the sky was cloudy, and a fine misty drizzle began to penetrate their clothes. The foul stench of their ill-dug jacks oozed across the clearing. Gird was sure they could smell it in the next village, wherever that was. He wrapped his leather raincloak around the sacks of grain and beans. The night guards arrived back at camp hungry, while Herf was struggling with the fire. Smoke lay close to the ground, making them all cough. After the previous night's feast, plain soaked grain seemed even more dismal than usual. Gird's joints ached; he wished fervently for a mug of hot sib. He heard low grumbles and mutters, and Triga's voice raised in a self-pitying whine.

This would never do. Gird strode back into the center of the clearing as if the sun were shining and he knew exactly what to do. The men looked up at him, sour-faced.

"Triga, what did you find yesterday?" Triga, interrupted in mid-complaint, looked almost comical. Then he stood up.

"I found that swamp I told you about—" Someone groaned, and Triga whipped around to glare in that direction.

"Never mind," said Gird. "Go on—and you others listen."

"I walked all around it—that's why I came back so late. There's three little creeks goes into it, and two comes out. I don't know what the middle's like yet—there wasn't time—"

"Good. That's where we'll go today."

"All of us?" Herf asked. "It's raining."

"It's raining here, too," Gird pointed out. "You'll get just as wet sitting here complaining about the rain, as walking along learning something useful. Maybe we'll find a cave, and can sleep dry."

They didn't look as if they believed him, but one by one his fledgling army stood up. He grinned at them.

"But first," he said. "We're going to do something about *that.*" And he pointed toward the jacks. "It stinks enough to let anyone know a lot of men have been here, and it's making us sick as well."

"We don't have no tools," someone said. Kef, that was the name. Gird grinned again.

"I brought a shovel, remember? I'll start the digging, but we'll all be doing some—because there's more to it than just shoveling."

He had spotted a better site the day before. Now he took his shovel and tried it. Here a long-gone flood had spread across the clearing below the waterfall, and left a drift of lighter soil, almost sand. He started the trench he wanted, and gave the shovel to Kef. "That deep, and straight along there," he said. They really needed a bucket, too, but they didn't have one. He'd have to use the wooden bowls for the ashes. The men watched as he scooped ashes and bits of charred wood from the side of the firepit into one of their bowls. "You, too," Gird said, pointing at the other bowls. "We're going to need a lot of ashes."

"But I though ashes only worked in a pit," said Ivis.

"Best in a pit. But a trench is like a little pit. Ashes on top, then dirt, after you use it."

"Every time?"

"Every time—or it won't work. The guards kept a pot of ashes in the jacks; I started doing that at our cottage later, and ours smelled less than most." He looked at them, noticing the squeamish faces. "The worst part," he said carefully, "is going to be burying what's already there." He was pleased to note that no one asked if they had to.

It took longer than he'd hoped, with only the one shovel and small bowls to carry ashes, but at last they had the worst of the noisome mess buried, strewn with ashes, and a new bit of clean trench for that morning's use. Gird covered it up himself when they were all done, and marked the end with a roughly cut stake poked in the ground.

"Now we clean up," Gird said, "and then we go look for Triga's swamp. He's right—if we can find a safe way into it, that the foresters and guards don't know, it could be a very handy place."

Chapter Eleven

Triga led the way, with Gird behind him, and then the others. Gird had asked Ivis to be the rear guard, staying just in sight of the others. Within the first half-league, he was wondering how this group had survived undetected so long. They talked freely, tapped their sticks against trees and rocks as they passed, made no effort to walk quietly. Finally Gird halted them.

"We're making more noise than a tavern full of drunks. If there's a forester in the wood anywhere, he's bound to hear us."

Ivis turned a dull red. "Well—Gird—we don't like to come on 'em in surprise, like—"

"The foresters? You mean they know—"

"It's sort of—well—they'd have to know, wouldn't they? Being as they have to know the whole wood. But what they don't actually *see* they don't have to take notice of. My brother's one of them, you see, and—"

"And on the strength of one brother, you trust them all? What about the guard?"

"Oh, the duke's guard is a very different matter—very different indeed. But they don't venture into the wood except when the duke's hunting. And then they're guarding him, not poking about on their own."

"And—duke? Your lord isn't Kelaive?"

"Gods, no! I've heard about him, even before you came. Our duke's Kelaive's overlord, just as the king is his."

"So the foresters of this wood know that a band of outlaws lives here, and expects you to make enough noise coming so they can avoid you. What if they change their minds? Surely your duke's offered a reward"

"My brother wouldn't take a reward for me," Ivis said earnestly. "And if he captures the others, there I'd be, right in the middle."

"What if he's transferred, or killed, or one of the other foresters gets greedy?" Ivis said nothing in answer; from his expression, he had thought of this before and tried to forget it. Gird looked at all the others. "Listen to me: an army does not go about expecting its enemies to get out of the way. We can't fight like that. Cannot. Perhaps Ivis's brother has enough influence on the foresters of this wood, but we will not always be in this wood. We have to leave it someday, and you must know how to move *quietly*. And we must be alert—we must find the foresters before they find us, and never let them know we were near. Understand?" Heads nodded, some slowly. "Now—the first thing—no talking while we march. No banging on stones or tree limbs. Walk one behind the other, far enough that if one man stumbles, the others don't fall too. Triga, you should be far enough ahead that I can just see, and you shouldn't be able to hear us—you listen for anyone *else*. If you go too fast, I'll click pebbles twice; if I click three times, stop. You give two double clicks if you hear foresters. Ivis, if you hear anything behind us, give two double clicks. The rest of you—if you hear two double clicks, stop where you are and do not make a noise. Clear?"

Again, heads nodded. Gird hoped that there were no foresters out that day, so they could get in at least one practice before it was needed. He waved Triga ahead, waited until he was almost out of sight on the narrow trail, and started off himself. Behind him, the noise of the others was much less, although he could hear an occasional footfall. Triga led them fairly quickly, and Gird had a time keeping him in sight and avoiding obvious noisemakers. But his followers grew even quieter, as if they were listening for themselves, and learning from their own noise how to lessen it.

The double-click he had been half-waiting for startled him when it came. The others had frozen in place; Gird took a final step and a stick broke under his foot. He grimaced, and looked back along the line. Cob, behind him, grinned, wagged his head, and made the shame sign with his fingers. Gird shrugged and spread his hands. When he looked ahead, Triga had stopped just in sight. Gird could hear nothing now but the blood rushing in his own ears, and the faint trickle of water somewhere nearby.

The click had come from behind him, and now he saw a stirring in the line, silent movement as one man leaned to another and mouthed something. Gingerly, Gird took a step back toward Cob, placing his feet carefully on soggy leaves and moss. Cob leaned back to get the message, then forward to Gird.

"Ivis. Said we were a lot quieter, but should practice stopping. He may do it again."

Gird wished he'd thought of suggesting it, but at the same time wanted to clobber Ivis. His heart was still racing at the thought of being caught by foresters. He nodded, instead, and murmured "Tell him not too many—we have a long way to go." Cob nodded, and passed the message back. Gird waited what he thought was long enough for it to reach Ivis, then waved Triga on, and started again himself. He almost trod on the same stick, but managed to stretch his stride and avoid it.

Triga's swamp, when they came to it, appeared first as softer mud in the trail, and then a skim of sib-colored water gleaming between the leaves of some low-growing plant with tiny pink flowers. Ahead was an opening in the forest, with tussocks of grass growing out of the water.

"We have to turn here, if we're going around it," said Triga softly to Gird. The others had come up, but were squatting silently in the dripping undergrowth on the dryest patches they could find.

"Have you ever been out in it?"

"When I was a lad, once. There's someplace out there with plum trees; I could smell the flowers."

Gird sniffed. It was just past blooming time for the plums in his village, but wild plums came both earlier and later. He didn't smell any.

"Did you find the trees?"

"Finally—after I got wet to the thighs, and then when I got home my da beat me proper for running off from the goats—but there's a dry hummock somewhere, with plums."

"Right out in the middle, I'll bet," said Cob. "O' course, we're already wet."

"There used to be a path partway in," said Triga. "Follow me and step just where I do." And with that he was off again. The others fell into line.

Triga's way led alongside the bog, and finally came close enough so that Gird could see how big it was. Despite the drizzle and fog, he could just make out the forest on the other side, a dark massive shadow. In the bog itself were islands crowned with low trees tangled into thick mats. After a short time, Triga came out from under the trees, and stepped onto one of the tussocks. It trembled, but held him up as he took two steps and hopped to another. Gird looked at it distrustfully. How deep *was* that dark water? And what was under it?

"One at a time," he said, and reached a leg across to the black footprint Triga had left. He didn't like the way his foot sank in, and stepped quickly to the gap between tussocks. The mud sucked at his feet, and let go with a little plop. Across the gap, and onto another tussock. Now he was out in the open, where anyone could see him—anyone sitting snug under the forest edge, for instance. His neck prickled. One of Triga's footprints had a finger of murky water in it; when Gird stepped there, his foot sank to the ankle.

"I don't like this," said someone behind him, and someone else said "Shhh!" Their feet squelched on the wet ground, and Gird cursed silently as icy water oozed through his boot.

Only six of them had started into the bog, when the first foothold gave way and Herf found himself hip deep in cold, gluey muck. He yelped; three gray birds Gird had not noticed fled into the air with noisy flapping wings and wild screeches. Triga stopped and looked back, grinning. Gird said "Wait!" as softly as he thought Triga would hear.

They could not explain what happened without talking; Gird sweated, but endured the noise as best he could, while they established that yes, Herf had stepped carefully in the now-sinking footprint, and yes, all the footprints had been getting wetter, and no, it was clear that nobody else could make it. Herf, sprawled across the tussock with one leg stuck in the mud, was grimly silent.

"All right," Gird said finally. "First we get Herf out, and back on solid ground. Then all of you in the forest start circling the bog, and looking for other ways in. Don't get stuck."

"Don't walk on moss," Triga added. "It looks solid, but it won't hold you up."

"We can't come back the way we came in," Gird went on. "So Triga will have to find us a way across. And now we know that a group trying to follow us would bog down—"

"Although the tracks are easy to see," said Cob.

"Right. If we use this, we need a way in that we can all take, and that they can't see."

Getting Herf loose was no easy matter, and involved five men getting themselves wetter and muckier than they had intended. Two more got stuck, although not as badly.

In the meantime, Gird and the others perched on tussocks noticed that water was creeping up around their feet. "We have to keep moving," Triga said, unnecessarily, and went on, aiming for one of the brush-covered islands. By the time all of them had made it there, to crouch under the thick tangle of limbs and new leaves, they were mud to the knees and breathless.

"I didn't know it would be worse with more than one," said Triga. Gird accepted that as an apology, and nodded. At least some of the little trees were plums, tiny fruits just swelling on the ends of their stems. Water dripped on him, sending an icy trickle down the back of his neck and along his spine. He hoped his raincape was keeping the grain and beans dry. If he had to be wet and cold, it should be for a good purpose.

"We'd better go on," he said. "And if there's a way for each of us to pick his way safely—that might be better than stepping in your tracks."

"It's that kind of grass." Triga showed them again. "Not that other, with the thinner blades; it grows on half-sunk moss, and you can go right through. This stuff is usually half-solid, but you have to keep moving. Try to pick your way several tussocks ahead, so you don't have to stop except at places where trees grow. All those are safe. I think."

"Look at this," Cob said. He pointed to a delicate purple flower on a thin stalk. "I never saw anything like that."

"They grow in bogs," Triga said. "A little later, the whole bog will be pink with a different flower—the same kind, but larger. The purple ones grow only on the islands."

Gird looked at him. This sounded less and less like the knowledge gained on one clandestine visit as a child. Triga reddened.

"No one could find me here," he said. "I used to come here a lot, before I left home."

"And not after?"

"The others didn't want to see a swamp, they said."

"Well, we're seeing it now. What else do you know about it?"

Triga began to lead them across the little island to the bog on the far side. "There aren't many fish, for all this water. Lots of frogs, though, and little slick things like lizards, but wet. Birds—different kinds you don't see anywhere else. Some of them swim in the bits of open water, and dive. Most of them wade, and eat frogs and flies. Flowers. One island has a wild apple grove, and one has the best brambleberries I've ever eaten. Wild animals: something like a levet that swims, long and sleek, and levets, of course. Rabbits sometimes—I've surprised them grazing the grass on the islands. Deer come to the edge to drink and once I saw one where the apples grow. They jump very fast and carefully."

They began to cross to the next island, this time picking individual ways, with much lurching and staggering. But no one fell in the mud, and they all arrived safely and somewhat drier, but for the rain. This island had fewer trees, and starry blue flowers as well as the tall purple ones.

"In midwinter," Triga said, as if someone had asked, "the bog may freeze on top, but you still can't trust the moss. If the ice is thick enough to walk on, then it's safe, but not otherwise. Most years it freezes that hard after Midwinter. But the thaw comes early—I don't know why—and I've put a leg through the ice more than once."

This time they did not pause, but went on across the island and back onto the bog. Gird lurched and barely kept himself from falling into the muck.

"I'm thinking this might make a better farm than a castle," he said.

"Farm?" Triga glanced back at him, teetered, and regained his balance.

"Plums, apples, brambleberries, all guarded by this muck. I'd wager that in full summer the flies are fierce."

"So they are. The worst of them aren't out yet, the big deerflies."

"Onions would grow on the edges; redroots on the islands."

"Some of these grasses have edible seeds," Triga said. "My

mother's father, he showed me some of 'em. As much grain as wheat, almost. That's what the birds come for, the swimmers."

Gird was about to ask how the swimmers could find space to swim, when they came to a stretch of open water. Under the dark sky, with the drizzle falling, it was impossible to tell how deep it was. "Now what?"

"We've gone too far down. Turn up this way, upstream."

Gird could not see any movement in the water; it lay blank and still, dimpled like hammered pewter by the falling rain. Grunting, he followed Triga to the right, trying to pick his way. Eventually that space of water narrowed, and narrowed again, until he could leap across to a tussock that lurched under him. He grabbed the tallest stalks, and managed not to fall. Something hit the water with a loud plop behind him; he broke into a sweat again.

"Frog," said Triga. "Big one—he'd be a good dinner."

"You eat *frogs*?"

"What's wrong with that? They're good."

Gird shuddered, and tried to hide it. That was the explanation for Triga's attitude, he was sure. Anyone who would eat frogs would naturally be quarrelsome and difficult. "They're . . . cold. Slimy." He remembered very well the little well-frog he'd caught as a boy: the slickness, the smell, the great gold eyes that looked so impossible. His father had shown him frogspawn down in the creek, and he'd prodded it with a curious finger. It had felt disgusting.

Triga shrugged, looking sulky again. "It's better than going hungry. Food's food." He gave Gird a challenging look. "I ate snakes, too." Gird's belly turned. What could you say to someone who ate snakes and frogs?

"You eat fish, don't you?" asked Triga, pursuing this subject with vigor.

"I had a fish once." Gird remembered the bite or two of fish that he had eaten on his one trip to the trade fair as a youth. They had bought a fish, all of them together, and tried to cook it over their open fire. He could barely remember how it had tasted, though the smell was clear enough. It hadn't been as filling as mutton. He met Triga's expression with a grin. "The fish in our creek were about a finger long—the little boys caught them, but no one ate them."

From the looks on the others' faces, Triga's revelations about fish, frogs, and snakes were explaining his behavior to them as well. As if he'd realized that, he led them on faster, landing with juicy splashes on his chosen tussocks. Gird followed at his own pace, carefully. Snakes, too. There might be snakes out here, worse snakes than the striped snakes that wove through the stems of the grain, or the speckled snakes by the creek. He wanted to ask Triga how big the snakes in the bog could be, but he didn't want to admit he didn't know. Did they swim?

A sweet perfume broke through his concern about snakes, and he realized they were almost to an island whose scrubby gnarled trees were covered with palepink blossoms. Apples. Gird drank in the delicious scent, so different from the rank sourness of the bog itself, or the faintly bitter scent of the purple flowers. He climbed onto the rounded hump of solid ground with relief. Triga had thrown himself flat on dripping grass, and seemed back in a good humor; he smiled as Gird and the others crawled under low, snagging limbs to join him.

"This was always my favorite," he said. "Wild apples here, and crabs at the far end, two of them."

Gird crouched beside him. "What I don't understand is what made the islands. Why isn't the bog all bog?"

Triga shrugged. "I don't know. The way each island has its own trees and flowers, it's almost like a garden—as if someone planted them that way. But who or why I have no idea."

"Are any of the islands large enough for a camp?"

"No—probably not. I thought so, but now I see just six of us on one of them, I realize they're too small. The biggest has nut trees— not as tall as most nut trees—that would give good cover around the edge. But I think even twenty of us would crowd it. Certainly if you're going to be finicky about the jacks. Out here I always perched over open water."

The drizzle had stopped, but the apple limbs still dripped cold water on them. Gird looked out between the twisted trunks and caught a gleam of brighter light glinting from water and wet grass. It reminded him of something. He sat quiet, letting the memory come . . . he'd been crouched under another thicket, another time . . . dawn, it was . . . and the shadow had come, the thing that claimed kinship with the elder singers, but claimed also to be different. Kuaknom, it had been. Gird looked across the wet and dripping bog, now slicked with silver as the sun broke through for a moment. There across the uneven wet mat of moss and grass was an island, its trees like miniatures of the forest, bright flowers shining along its shore.

"I know who planted this," he said. It had come to him, with the beauty of the moment, the glittering, brilliant colors outlined in silver light.

"Who?" asked Triga.

"The singers. The old ones." He shivered as he said it. Was it bad luck to name them? Would it bring the illwishers here?

"You know *them*?" asked Triga, sitting bolt upright.

"No . . . no, but I know the tales. And I met one of their—the ones that went wrong, the kuaknomi."

"Gods take the bane!" Triga flicked his fingers twice, throwing the name away. "Don't speak of them!"

"But the others. I know they did. A garden, you said, each island like its own bed of flowers or fruit. I don't really like it, Triga, but it's very beautiful."

"Even the frogs?"

"Even the frogs."

The sun vanished again behind low clouds, and by the time they reached the far side of the bog, a light rain was falling. Cob scraped the muck from his worn boots with a handful of moss.

"I never thought I'd be so glad to find a muddy trail in a forest," he said. "And now we have to walk all the way back around to get home."

Gird gave him a warning look, and he was quiet. They all were, listening to the many sounds of the rain, the almost musical tinkling of the drops of water in the bog, the soft rush of it in the leaves overhead, the plips and plops of larger drops falling to the forest floor. Where, Gird wondered, was the rest of his troop?

Rock clicked on rock somewhere in the wet distance. One click. What was that? Gird peered around, seeing nothing but wet leaves and treetrunks. His heart began to pound heavily. He blinked rain off his eyelashes, and wished fervently that he'd let the damned grain rot, and taken his leather cape along. Then at least he wouldn't have rain crawling through his hair, trickling down his neck. He didn't mind arms and legs; he was used to being wet— but not his *head*. From the expressions the others had, none of them liked it. Hats, he thought to himself. We have to make hats, somehow. Every summer the women had plaited grass hats that lasted the season; they threw them away after harvest.

"Were we quiet enough?"

Gird leaped up and barely stopped the bellow that tried to fight its way from his throat. Ivis was grinning at him, along with the rest of the men who had gone around the bog. Rage clouded his vision for a moment as his heart raced. He felt he would explode. They were all watching, with the wary but smug look of villagers who have just outwitted a stranger. Another cluster of raindrops landed on his head, cold as ever, and it was suddenly funny. They *had* outwitted him, as fair as any trick he'd ever seen.

"You—" he began, growling over the laughter that was coming despite his rage. "Yes, damn you, you were quiet enough." A chuckle broke loose, then another. "Now let's see how quietly you can march home, eh?"

They were not as quiet, for the rainy spring evening began to close in fast, and they had to hurry. When they came to the clearing, Gird was glad he'd told Pidi to stay and mind the fire; they all needed to crowd near the glowing coals. Pidi had cooked beans, flavored slightly with the herbs he'd gathered.

Next morning was damp and foggy, but not actively raining. Gird woke stiff and aching, with a raw throat. Around him, the others were still sleeping, Pidi with the boneless grace of all small children. Gird pushed himself up, cursing silently, and crouched by the fire-pit. He held out a hand to the banked fire—still warmth within. But dry fuel? He peered around in the dimness. Someone—Pidi, he supposed—had made a crude shelter of stone, and laid sticks in it. They might be drier than the rest. He poked the fire cautiously with one of them, uncovering raw red coals. After a moment, the end of the stick flared. Dry enough. He yawned until his jaw cracked, then coughed as the raw air hit his sore throat. Sleeping wet in wet clothes—he hadn't done that for years. He'd never enjoyed it.

Alone in the early morning gloom, he let himself sag into sour resentment. Forget the hot sib. What he needed was a good stout mug of ale. Two mugs. Maybe they could build barrels and brew? No, first they had to have a dry place to sleep. A drop of cold water hit his bald spot. No, first they had to have hats. He added more sticks to the fire. Some of them steamed, hissing but enough were dry to waken crackling flames. Someone across the clearing groaned, then coughed.

"Lady's grace, I hurt all over," he heard someone say. He felt better. If he wasn't the only one, it didn't mean he was too old for this. Another groan, more coughs. "I'd give anything for a mug of ale," said another man. "Sib," said someone else. "Anything but beans or soaked wheat," said yet another. Gird felt much better. The soldiers had grumbled in the barracks, when he was a recruit. They'd grumbled when it rained and they had to work in it; they'd grumbled when it was hot and sweat rolled out from under their helmets. Grumbling was normal. He was normal. And he knew exactly what the sergeant had done about grumbling.

"Time to get up," he said briskly.

A startled silence. A low mutter: "Gods above, *he's* up. He's got the fire going." He heard more stirrings, and turned to see men sitting up, clambering to their feet, rolling over to come up on one elbow. He grinned at them.

"Can't fight a war in bed," he said. Utter disbelief in some faces, amused resignation in others. Pidi, who had not walked to the bog and back, came over to the fire, all bright eyes and eagerness.

"I found most of the roots and barks for sib." He showed Gird a small pile which Gird would not have recognized. "There's no kira in sight of camp, and you told me not to leave—"

"Good for you," said Gird. "Do you know how much of each?" *He* certainly didn't. Pidi nodded.

"But it takes a long time. Do you want me to start it?"

"Go ahead. We need it."

While Pidi started the sib, Gird went off to the new jacks trench, along with several others. Already the camp smelled better, he thought. Certainly the men looked better, even grumpy and stiff as they were. That hike in the rain had accomplished something.

"We need to set up work groups," Gird said without preamble, as they gathered near the fire. "A hand to each group—" They began shuffling themselves into clusters of five. Gird had thought of assigning them to groups, but decided to let them pick their partners—for now, at least. With his knife, he shaped chunks of bark peeling from a fallen limb into the familiar tallies of the farmer. "One notch for food, two for tools, three for camp chores. Two groups get a food tally, and one hand each for the others. We'll drill after breakfast, then the groups go to their assignments—"

"What's food for?" asked Triga. "We're the ones get to eat?" No one laughed. Gird shook his head.

"Those with a food tally go looking for food: hunt, gather herbs, tend the things we plant, later. Ivis, how did food donated by farmers come to you? Did someone tell you it was there, or did you go ask?"

"Every so often someone would come to the wood, and leave a feathered stick in a certain tree—that's for Whitetree, the nearest. Fireoak usually brought the food itself, put it just inside the wood. Diamod traveled about so much, he'd know, or he'd see it and bring it in, or come get us to carry it. And sometimes, when things were very bad, one of us'd sneak into the village and beg."

"Which is dangerous for them and for us both. And I suppose too much hunting would bring the foresters, wouldn't it?"

"Aye. They don't mind rabbits and hares and such, but the duke likes his deer hunts."

"Well, we'll have to do something. Fori's good with his sling, and he can set snares: that's something you can all learn. We need a better way to let the villagers know when we need something, and what it is. With a few more tools, we might be able to gather more food and lean on them less." Gird handed the first food tally to the group Ivis was with. "You know the local village; you've got kin there. Find out what they can send, and when. What is the most trouble to them. When they've had trouble, and what gave them away. If they can't send food, find out if they can send sacks, boxes, a bucket—anything we can use to store or prepare the food we have. Even little things: a small sack is better than none."

"The other food tally." Gird handed it to the group Fori was with. "Go some distance away from this camp, and then look for anything edible you can find. Birds' eggs, birds in the nest, rabbits, squirrels—most creatures are having young about now; look for their hiding places."

"Frogs?" Triga was not in that group, but he spoke up anyway.

"When you're carrying the food tally, you can catch us frogs, Triga," Gird said.

"And you'll eat them?"

Gird swallowed hard. "I'll do my best. Now—you *are* with the tool tally. You all know we need a lot of things we don't have. Another shovel, axes, chisels. A shepherd's crook would be handy for pulling down vines with edible berries; a drover's stick for beating nuts from the nut trees next fall. We need pots to cook in, bowls to eat from, baskets or sacks to carry what our gatherers find, spoons, buckets, rope: every one of these will help us make more of what we need. Whoever holds the tool tally will work for that day on one of the things we need."

"I can make baskets," Triga said. Everyone stared at him; usually women made baskets. He reddened. "I used to plait the grasses in the bog," he said. "First just for something to do, and then to see what I could make."

"Could you make a basket from anything around here?" asked Gird. He did not want to make another trek to the bog so soon.

Triga stared around, uncertain. "Maybe . . . I can try . . . but it may not work right the first time."

"That's all right. If you find a way, it's time well spent. Any of the rest of you like to whittle?" One man raised his hand. "Good—why don't you start whittling some spoons, and bowls if you find the right chunks of wood. You others try it—anything's better than nothing."

"What about the guard we send out to listen for foresters?" asked Ivis.

"From the last group, those with camp chores tally. Two go out, and three will have plenty to do here. Gathering wood for the fire, tending the fire, and some other things I've thought up. But first— we didn't do any drill yesterday, so let's line up."

This time they lined up quickly and almost evenly. They all started on the same foot, and they marched almost in step from the firepit to the stream, still in lines. Wavery lines, but lines. Gird showed them how to turn in place to the right and left, and then had them march around the camp as a column of twos. They had to weave in and out of trees, and they were soon out of step, but the pairs did manage to stay side by side. By this time Gird was warm and had worked the stiffness out, so he sent the two groups with food tallies off, and picked two guards from the camp chores group. One of the remaining three he sent in search of the driest wood he could find, one sat by the fire, and Gird beckoned to the last.

He had had the idea that they could weave lengths of wattle, as he'd used for the barton gate, and the fence between his smallgarden and his neighbor's. Wattle laid at an angle against a log might give some protection from wet. He explained what he had in mind to Artha, a very tall, loose-jointed man nearly bald on top. Artha had vague, hazy blue eyes, and the least initiative Gird had seen.

"But I don't—that wattle, now, we allus made it wi' the sticks i' the ground, like. Put the sticks down in the wet mud, my granda he said, and then put the vines through, back and forth, back and forth—"

"But the sticks don't *have* to be in the ground," Gird said. The times he'd mended his gate, without ever taking it down, he knew that. Artha stood slack-handed, his jaw hanging. Gird realized that this was going to take firmness, as if Artha had been a child. "Artha, bring me some sticks, about so long—" He spread his arms to show the length.

"All right, but I dunno how you'll do it lessen you put them sticks in the mud first—"

"Never mind, just bring me the sticks." Artha ambled off, and Gird searched up and down the streambank until he found a willow sprouting multiply from the muck. He cut the pliant sprouts and stacked them.

By midday, Gird looked around the busy campsite and smiled to himself. The voices he heard all sounded content; one man was even whistling "Nutting in the Woods." His sergeant and his father had both been right: idleness was a fool's delight, and work brought its own happiness. Triga had created one lopsided basket from the same willow sprouts Gird was using, and then torn it down to make it "right" as he said. Now he was halfway through again. It didn't look quite like any basket Gird had seen, but it was going to be a useful size, he could tell. The man who liked to whittle—Kerin, that was—had turned out three recognizable spoons. He'd pointed out that he needed something to rub them with, to finish them, and one of the others had experimented with Gird's collection of cobbles. Gird and Artha had made one length of wattle, not quite an armspan wide by twice that in length. Gird held it up to the light: it would no more keep water out than a basket, he thought. But it would support something *else*. Leaves? A deerhide?

Late afternoon brought the food gatherers back. First came the hunting and gathering group, with a miscellany of edibles. Birds' eggs from different kinds of nests: small, round and beige, pointy and blue with speckles, streaked with brown on beige. They'd found a rabbit's burrow, and while the blind, squirming kits had been very small, there were eight of them. Fori had knocked another squirrel out of a tree, and they'd found a squirrel nest—but that led to near disaster, when Fori, precariously wrapped around the slender bole, had met a furious mother squirrel face to face. Fori had come down faster than he went up, losing skin off his arms. "But I have a nose, still," he said. They had also, on the advice of one of the others, dug up the roots of the thick-leaved grasslike plants that grew along the stream lower down. One man had the bight of his shirt full of last fall's nuts: some were rotting or sprouting, but some were still whole and sweet.

Ivis's group had come back with little food, but other important treasures. "Gars says he never used his granda's old stone tools— even his granda didn't—but look—" and he emptied a well-worn, greasy leather sack. Gird looked at the odd-shaped bits of stone curiously. He could remember seeing clutter like that in someone's cottage . . . and old Hokka had used a sickle set with tiny stone blades. But he'd never used stone tools himself. "They're sharp," Ivis said, as if he'd asked. "Gars thinks some of them had handles— wooden handles—but I don't know how they'd fasten. But you can cut with them." Some were obviously blades, thin shards of stone like broken pottery. Others were rough lumps with a sharp edge, like handax heads, or chisels. Kerin poked at them.

"I could use these . . . it would be easier to make a bowl with this than a knife . . ." Gird nodded; that got him off the hook.

"Fine—try them, and if you can teach someone else—" He turned to thank Ivis, but Ivis was still grinning.

"That's not all. Look here—" Wrapped in a wet cloth, he had brought seedlings of the common greenleaves: cabbage, lettuce. . . .

The villagers had liked the idea of the outlaws growing some of their own food, and he'd been given as much as he could carry without crushing it. One of the men carried a small round cheese, and another had a large lump of tallow. He had also thought to ask for things Gird hadn't mentioned: beeswax, soap, thread. "Best of all—" Ivis nodded at the last member of his team, who pulled a bundle from under his shirt. It was cloth, something rolled into a lump—but the deepest, most intense blue Gird had ever seen.

"What is *that*?" he asked.

Ivis grinned. "You know the lords won't let us have blue clothes—"

"Yes. I never saw any."

"This is old, from my granda's time. He used to say that the blue was expensive—it came from some kind of blue stone, from far away north—but before the lords came it was a favorite color. Good luck color. Anyway, my brother says if you're serious about overturning the lords, best we'd have some blue shirts."

Gird unfolded the bundle carefully. Two blue shirts, each decorated with intricate embroidery around the neck, flowers and grain in brilliant colors. The old woolen cloth was as sound as ever. "Where had they kept this? Not even a moth hole . . ."

"I don't know. My brother's the eldest; he knew about it and I didn't. But I do remember my granda's stories. What do you think?"

"I think it's good luck," said Gird, refolding the shirts carefully.

Chapter Twelve

On a bright, blustery day in early summer, Gird led his troop eastward through the wood. There were twenty-four of them now, and every one of them carried his own spoon and bowl as well as his own belt knife. Each had a hat, plaited of grass and oiled against rain, and a staff about his own height. Each had three flat hard loaves of bread tucked into his shirt. And they marched quietly through the wood, with Diamod scouting ahead, and Triga bringing up the rear.

They were on their way to meet another of the Stone Circle groups two days away; Diamod (as usual) made contact. Behind them, the forester's campsite was clean and bare; they had moved all their gear some days back to another site Gird had found. Gird found himself about to whistle, and didn't. They were all doing well, including the new ones. He'd been surprised when three more came from his old village; a friend of Fori's, Teris's son Orta, and Siga, a single man about ten years Gird's junior.

They had told him all the latest news: how the steward had come to Gird's cottage only to find it stripped to the bare walls. He had taken that for Gird's impudence, but the villagers had done it, hiding every pot, tool, and bit of cloth. Gird had felt tears burning his eyes when the boys showed what they brought—his people, his neighbors, had cared that much, to risk themselves to save his things, and then to send their sons with it. Irreplaceable treasure indeed: two hammers, three chisels, his awl and his axe, a shovel blade, a spokeshave, a plane, a kettle, a longhandled metal spoon, firetongs, the cowhides that had been stretched across the bed-frames, a furl of cloth that still showed rusty bloodstains . . . "We couldn't carry it all," Orta had explained. "But if you go back, or send someone, there's more."

His eyes still burned, thinking of it. He blinked the tears away, and told himself to keep his mind on the journey.

Part of that involved watching out for forage along the way. They had all learned, since he came, to make use of whatever food came along. Gird had even eaten one of Triga's frogs; he was sure it wriggled in his throat, but he had to admit it tasted like food. More or less. Some of the others refused, but most followed his lead. He still didn't like frogs for dinner, but better that than hunger. Now he scanned the undergrowth on either side for edible berries and fruits, herbs and mushrooms. Fori, still the best slinger in the troop, would be watching the trees for squirrels or levets.

Gird wished it had been possible to leave Pidi with someone. The boy was too young for this, he told himself again—but then again, the boy was not as young as he might be. The black eye had faded, leaving only a faint dark stain beneath, but the little child he had been, thoughtless and carefree, had not come back. Pidi seemed happy enough—he laughed sometimes, and scampered through the woods like a young goat—but he would never be care-free. It would have happened in time, Gird knew, but—he shook that thought away. There was no safe place for Pidi. Home had not been safe. That led him to Rahi, and the black sorrow pierced him again. She had lost the child, in fever, and when he'd last heard, a few days ago, she was still too weak to get up.

A gust of wind roared by overhead, whipping the forest canopy and letting a flash of sunlight through. *The Windsteed in spring seeks the far-ranging Mare* . . . he thought, clicking his tongue in the rhythm of the chant. This was late for the Windsteed's forays, but what else could it be? He accepted the omen, and let the wind blow away his dark thoughts. It never paid to argue with the gods, any of them.

That night he insisted that their temporary campsite be set up as neatly as the old one. No one argued. Fori lopped a sapling to make a handle for the shovel blade, tied it snugly, and began digging the jacks trench. They would have no fire, but they ate their beans (cooked the night before) from bowls, with spoons. Even plain beans tasted better that way, not scooped up with fingers. Almost before he said anything, the correct tally group had gathered up bowls and spoons to wash them in the creek by the camp; when they were done, everyone stripped down and bathed.

The full measure of what he had accomplished became obvious when they met the other Stone Circle group the next afternoon. They had come out of the wood, and angled between some brush-covered hills, and down a crooked stream bed. The other group had a guard out to meet them—that much Gird could approve—but they could smell the camp long before it came in sight. He noticed that his men wrinkled their noses as well. He had not intended to bring them in as a formal drill, but they began to fall in step, rearranging themselves into a column.

They came into a space set off by a rocky bluff on one side, and house-high thickets of pickoak on the others, to find unkempt men lounging around a smoking fire. Someone had stretched a line between two trees, from which flapped something intended as laundry, but Gird could not recognize one whole garment. His own troop fairly strutted into the clearing, and came to a smart halt without the command he forgot to give. The others stared at them, wide-eyed as cattle staring over a gate. The one who seemed to be the leader, a redhaired man whose sunburnt nose was peeling, stared as hard as any. Then he got up from his log.

"I don't believe it. Diamod, you said these were farmers?"

Diamod smirked. "I said these were farmers who had learned soldiering. Was I right?"

"You—and *you* must be Gird." The man came forward, looking Gird over with interest.

"I'm Gird, yes."

"And you were a soldier?"

"Years ago I was a recruit. Then a farmer. Now—what you see."

The man looked along the column, and swallowed. "What I see is hard to believe. How long have you been training them?"

Gird squinted, thinking. "Since late-plowing time. I was finishing plowing the day it happened."

"I didn't tell him *everything*," Diamond interrupted.

"And you did that much that fast. Can you teach us?"

"I might, aye. But there's more than just marching in step."

"Swordfighting, of course. Or do you use spears?"

Gird laughed. "We don't use swords or spears—where would we get them?"

The man's face fell. "But—what do you fight with? Not just sticks, surely."

He had not intended this kind of entrance, or a display of the other things he'd been teaching his men, but this was a chance he could not overlook.

"Aruk!" he said. Behind him, twenty-four sticks came up, to be held stiffly in front of each man. Gird took a step forward, clearing the necessary space, and said, "Form—troop." This was tricky; they'd only been doing it right a few days, and it looked anything but soldierly if someone forgot. Properly, it took them from a column to the parade formation in smart steps and turns, each pair coming forward and spreading to the sides. It might have been wiser to simply face the column right or left and pretend that was the same maneuver—but if this worked, it was far more impressive. He did not look around; he wanted to see how these others reacted. From the even tramp behind him, and the heavy breathing, they were doing it right. From the faces in front of him, it looked professional.

Now he turned, as neatly as he could, and looked at his troop. They had all made it into place, still with sticks held vertically before them. Now came the interesting part. He gave the commands crisply, and the sticks rotated: left, right, horizontal, vertical, all moving together in an intricate dance of wood. No one was off-count today; he was proud of them.

"But—" the redhaired man said. Gird spun around to him.

"You fight with a sword?"

"Not very well yet, but—"

"These sticks are longer than swords. You can't fence against a sword, no, but you can poke with it—just as you'd poke cattle through a gap. D'you think soldiers are harder to move than cattle, if you hit them right?"

"Well—no. But I thought—"

"If you want to learn from me—what's your name, anyway?"

"Felis."

"Felis, if you want to learn from me, the first thing is to clean up this stinking camp!" He had not quite meant to be that rude, but a gust of wind brought the foulness thick into his lungs.

"But what's that got to do with—"

"Yes or no."

"Well, yes, but—"

Gird glared around at the men in the camp, most of whom were sitting up more alertly now, sensing a fight coming. Two were not; they lay against the rock face, with another crouched beside them.

"What's wrong with them?" Gird asked, pointing.

Felis glanced that way, then shrugged. "Sim has some kind of fever, and Pirin has the flux—"

"And you ask why the stink matters! Didn't you have jacks where you came from? Didn't the grannies teach you about any of that?"

Felis flushed dark red. "We don't have any tools, hardly, and it's not so easy out here away from the towns—"

Gird snorted. He felt good, the righteous anger running in his veins like stout ale at harvest. "You thought soldiering was easy? You thought fighting a war was going to be easy?" His sergeant had said something like that more than once—he had the rhythm right, anyway. Felis glared at him, but said nothing. Gird went on. "You ask any of these men—Ivis, or Diamod—if *we* had more than this when I started. You ask them if someone can smell our camp from as far away."

Some of the men were standing now, coming forward slowly. Gird could not tell if they came in support of their leader, or from curiosity. Felis looked around, seeking support.

"There's no way—we don't have good ground here, for digging jacks and such. It's hard enough to find enough to eat, and—"

A taller man intervened. "So what would you do, stranger, if you had command here? Or is it all talk?"

Gird raised his brows ostentatiously. "Do you want us to show you? Or had you rather live like this?"

"Show us!" Felis spat. "Go ahead—let's see what you can do."

"Your people must help," Gird said. Felis shrugged.

"I won't make them. You can try."

"You're giving me command?" There was a moment's absolute silence, on everyone's indrawn breath. Felis paled; his jaw clenched. Then he spread his hands.

"For one day, for what you can do. I'll be interested. Of course, we've nothing to share for supper." Gird was sure that was a lie, but he smiled.

"We brought our own, and enough for return," he said. Then he turned his back on Felis, taking that chance, and dismissed his own men "—to your tally groups."

Raising his voice to reach all the men in the camp, he said, "You have two bad problems. The first is your jacks, which is making you sick with its filth. No need to ask where it isn't—but you need a good deep trench far away from the creek."

"The ground's all rocky hereabout," said the tall man. "We can't dig it with our fingernails."

"Fori." Gird put out his hand, and Fori handed him the shovel blade. "Here's a shovel, if you can put a handle to it. Anyone here can cut a pole, or—"

"I'll cut a pole," said the tall man. He turned on his heel and stalked off. Gird watched him for a moment, then went on.

"What do you have to carry things in?" he asked the group at large. After a moment's silence, someone pointed to the kettle on the fire, and a large wooden bowl. Gird smiled at them. "That's more than we had," he said. "We had no kettle. But we don't dirty a kettle with filth. Triga, I'll want some baskets. Any of you men know how to make a basket?"

"A *man* make baskets?" asked one with a low whistle. Gird put out his hand to stop Triga (and Triga's arm was there—predictable as always) and said "Don't laugh; Triga's a good enough soldier to know that supplies help win wars. Learn from him; we need baskets to haul that stinking waste into the hole you—" He nodded at the tall man who had cut his pole and was bringing it back, "—are going to dig for it."

"I'm not moving any of that filth!" snarled someone across the firepit. Gird heard mutters of agreement, and the amused chuckles of his own men.

"Move the filth, or move yourselves," Gird said. "It's killing you—and you know it."

"That's not all," came Ivis's voice from behind him, "he'll have you bathing, and if you get a cut, he makes you scrub it out with soaproot. Besides, nobody wants to eat in this stench. Just get rid of it."

Gird grinned at his people, and walked over to the firepit. The kettle on it gave off a thin steam, but he could not tell what was in it. The overall stink was too strong. "What is it?" he asked the man tending the fire.

"Grain mush. It's been grain mush for months, 'cept when someone snares a rabbit, or finds a berry patch."

"No bread?"

The man squinted up at him. "You a housewife? I never learned to make bread. Besides, it takes things we don't have."

"You'll get them." Gird patted the man's shoulder, and left him peering backwards, stirring ashes instead of the fire.

Now for the sick men. He knew he'd been lucky that none of his own troop had sickened yet. Although he'd tried to nurse his mother and Mali, he knew very little of the healing arts. Cleanliness, of course—everyone knew that the fever spirits thrived on foul smells and dirt. They grew fat and multiplied on what made healthy men ill. It was nearly impossible to be clean enough to keep them all away (his mother had insisted that even a speck of old milk left in the bucket could feed enough spirits to ruin the next batch) but the cleaner the better.

The stench worsened as he neared the sick men. One of them had red fever patches on his cheeks; his breath was labored, almost wheezing. His eyes were shut, and he didn't pay any attention to Gird. The other, pale and sweating, had vomited; the man with him was wiping his face clean. Gird felt a tug at his sleeve, and turned. Pidi, almost as pale, had come up beside him.

"I picked some breakbone weed on the way—it might help for the fever. But I didn't bring any flannelweed."

"Boiling water," said Gird. "See if they have another pot, and be sure you get the water well upstream." Pidi went off, and Gird forced himself to squat down beside the sick men. The caretaker glared at him.

"Ya canna' do aught for 'em. This'n'll die by morning; feel his head." Gird reached out to the fevered man, whose forehead felt like a hot stone—dry. "And this'n, bar he stops heaving, he'll go in a day or two. He's lost all he can, below, and I can't get 'im to the jacks we got, let alone the jacks you say you'll dig."

"You know flannelweed?" Gird asked. The man shrugged.

"I'm no granny, with a parrion of herbs. What be you, man or woman?"

Gird took hold of his wrist and squeezed until the bones grated; the man paled. "Man enough, if strength makes men. But I'd be glad of a woman's parrion of healing, if 'twould save lives. Have you sought a healer?"

"Aye. Felis brought one from the vill, a hand or more of days ago, when it was just Jamis here. But she was like you, all twinchy about the smell. Said we'd have to clean it up afore she could do aught. So's Felis told her what he told you, and she huffed off, about holding her nose."

Gird let go of the man's wrist, and picked up the rag sodden with vomit. "This'll do him no good here, but to make him heave again." He tossed it away, and turned back to the sick man, who was staring at him with the frantic look of a trapped animal. "If we can find flannelweed, and get you to a clean place—I'll try, at least." He made himself touch the man's hands, filthy as they were, and managed not to flinch when the man clutched at him.

"Please, sir—please—"

"I'll try." Gird looked at the sulky caretaker. "You can go clean up; I'll get my people to carry them."

"You're welcome to it." The man stalked away, clearly furious, rubbing the wrist Gird had bruised.

Gird looked around. Herf, in the tally group for camp chores, had picked up the stinking rag on a stick, and was carrying it toward the stream. He could hear the solid chunks of the shovel at work somewhere among the pickoaks. Ivis came up.

"Are you going to want to move them? I can have someone cut poles—"

"Yes, and I'll need a bucket of clean water, if you can find one. Does anyone but Pidi know flannelweed?"

"I'll ask. Those rags on the line aren't really clean, but they're cleaner than that—" Ivis pointed to the sodden rags under the two men.

"We'll need them, but not here. No sense in dirtying them now." Gird unhooked the sick man's fingers from his hand, one by one, and stood up. Pidi was coming back down the slope with a bucket of water—had he had to go all the way up to find clean? Triga, Gird saw, had a cluster of men around him—presumably he was making a basket and showing them how. Artha—who, Gird wondered, had told him?—was carefully scooping ash from the cool side of the firepit into a sack of some kind. The cook looked furious, but wasn't interfering.

Gird went to look at the stream, and shuddered. It looked as if hogs had wallowed in it, and it smelled worse. All along the banks, except at a crossing, were the uncovered remnants of a long encampment. Flies swarmed over them, rising in a cloud when he came near. Some of the filth had fallen into the stream and was far too wet to shift easily. It had been foul so long that rocks in the stream were slimed with luxuriant green weed, its brilliant color clear evidence of the steady supply of filth. It would be best to move the camp entirely, but he could not do that by himself.

"Gahhh." Diamod had come up behind him. "This is worse than I recall. But perhaps you've changed my nose for me."

"It's a damned shame," said Gird. He was angry again, but this time with a slow, steady anger that would burn for days. "It's hard enough to think of fighting the lords, with their soldiers and their weapons. We can't be fighting ourselves, too. There's no village this bad; these men came from better. They should know."

"So did we, but we didn't do it until you made us. Be fair, Gird, when you were a boy, did you do more than your father demanded? Or your sergeant?"

"I grew to a man," Gird said, growling, and forcing away the memory of his boyhood sulks. Had his mother really had to threaten beatings to get him to clean the milk pails? Had his father clouted him more than once for leaving muck on the tools? He sighed gustily. "True, I was the same way. But now—they're men, they should know better."

"Teach them, like you taught us."

"I wish I could move the camp. Now. This moment."

Diamod grinned. "Tomorrow, maybe: the way you're going, you could do that."

Gird stared moodily at the mess near his feet. "We can't move all this tonight. Ashes, I suppose for the rest." He turned and called Artha. "There may not be enough—but try to spread ashes on all of this. Up-stream and down. Don't step in it."

"No, Gird."

On his way to see how the trench was coming, Gird passed Triga, who held up one of his "fast" baskets, a flat, scoop-shaped affair. "Gird, it might go faster if we had something like a hoe, to scrape the stuff right into the basket." A solution creating another problem, Gird thought, but one of the local men looked surprised and said "We have a hoe—course, it's just wood—"

"Fine," said Gird. "Triga, I don't think we can move it all tonight, but see what you can do with that." Triga nodded, not sulky at the moment. It had to be eating frogs, Gird thought, that made a man so touchy on some things so reasonable when given a problem to solve.

The steady thunk of the shovel led him to the trench diggers. The tall man who had cut the pole for the shovel handle was jabbing the dirt with another, pointed pole to loosen it for the man with the shovel. Four others—two of Gird's, and two locals—were picking out rocks ahead of the shovel. The trench was deep enough, and reasonably straight, but it would never hold the accumulation on the banks of the stream. This would do for current and future use.

"Fori—" Fori was on the shovel at that moment; he looked up. "We're going to need another hole for the old stuff. Not a trench;

just a pit. Let's put it farther back in the wood, away from this."
Fori nodded, and shouldered the shovel. The other men looked
from Gird to Fori, and back to Gird. "Artha's got the ashes; I
told him to go ahead and use them where they are, but he can
get more."

"Does Triga have carriers yet?" asked Fori.

"Yes, and a hoe for scraping up." Gird glanced up at the sky; it
wasn't long until sundown. "We can't finish tonight, but we can get
a start on it."

The tall man leaned on his pole and looked at Gird. "You remind
me of my da. He was always one for starting a job now."

Gird smiled. "I was just thinking of my own da." He turned
away, sure that Fori could handle that little group by himself. By
now, Pidi should have hot water—and he'd forgotten that he'd sent
Ivis to find someone to find flannelweed. And where were the food
tally groups?

Back in the clearing, he noticed a controlled activity. Pidi
crouched over a bucket of steaming water, chatting with the local
cook, who looked much less sulky. Felis, of all people, was gathering the dry rags off the line. Ivis, Cob, and Herf were crouched
near the sick men; a stack of sticks had appeared by the firepit;
and much of the clutter of the campsite was gone, replaced by
clumps of gear that he suspected were not really organized. But it
looked better, and he could walk across the open space without
tripping over bits of wood and someone's rotted boot. His own
men and the locals were moving about as if they had something to
do and were doing it. The cook waved to him, and Gird veered
toward the firepit.

"This boy says he's yours—right?"

"Right." Gird tousled Pidi's hair. "My youngest."

"You got nerve, dragging your boy along to a war."

Gird gave him a hard look. "I had no choice. They threw me
out of my holding, because my daughter's husband tried to defend
her—and I hit one of them—so did Pidi, for that matter, boy that
he is."

"Oh. Your daughter—she died?"

Gird could feel his head beginning to pound; Pidi laid a hand
on his arm, and he realized he'd made a fist. "No. She's alive, last
I heard, but she lost the baby. And she may die. I don't know."

The man gulped, and looked away. "I'm sorry." After a pause,
in which Gird tried to get his temper locked down again, he said,
"The lad brought me herbs, for flavoring. Wild onions, too. Most
lads don't know that."

"His mother and sister both had a parrion of herbcraft. Pidi learned quickly."

"This's not ready, Da, but it might help." Pidi pointed to the steaming bucket, in which Gird could now see leaves steeping. He sniffed the sharp-smelling steam.

"At least it smells good." He dipped some in his own bowl, and took it over to the sick men. Now he'd have to remember not to eat from his bowl until he could wash it. But Ivis had found a wooden cup the fevered man had used. Gird poured the hot liquid into it carefully. Ivis and Cob had stripped off his clothes, and washed him with the clean water they'd brought. Gird had no idea what the fever was; the man had the sour smell of sickness, but nothing he could recognize.

"Will he rouse at all?"

Ivis shrugged. "He opened his eyes when we first touched him with the wet cloth, but said nothing."

Gird held the steaming cup under the man's nostrils; they twitched. "Let's lift him, and see if he'll drink."

Cob looked worried. "The healer in our village said if they're not awake, don't make them drink."

"Just a sip." Gird was sure the man was really dying, but felt he had to try. Ivis lifted him, and Gird held the cup to his lips. When he tried to pour a little in, it dribbled back out. Gird sighed. "Well. If he wakes, we can try again."

"Do you think he'll wake?"

"No. But I'm no healer; I could be wrong."

They turned to the other man. Gird helped Herf bathe him with clean water, and wrap him in the cleanest clothes they could find. Gird hated touching the man's clammy skin; it reminded him of tending Issa, who had been sick so often. They gave him a drink of clean water; he did not heave it up at once, so Gird felt more hopeful. He looked across the campsite, and saw Triga and someone else dragging loaded baskets away toward the pickoaks. Artha was back at the firepit, gathering more ashes.

"Do you think they would share our food?" asked Cob. That was what Gird had been thinking; he simply did not know.

"If they would, we'd have them in our troop before midnight," said Ivis, grinning. "I still think it was that first hearthcake, Gird, that settled your place in our camp."

Gird grinned back. "You were tougher than that. I thought it was Fori's squirrels. But you know the customs: if they eat our food, and we don't eat theirs, that's their obligation and our protection. And they've already said they won't share."

"Felis said it. Felis may be wishing he hadn't been so clever."

"We can offer." Gird stood up and headed for the firepit again. At this auspicious moment, one of his food tally groups returned, gleefully carrying the carcass of a young pig.

"If they won't share now," breathed Herf, "they're so crazy we don't want them."

"How did they get that?" muttered Gird. "They haven't been down robbing some farmer's pigsty, have they?" When the commotion died down, he learned that they'd come across a sounder of wild swine, feasting on mushrooms and old acorns under the pick-oaks. One fell to a lucky shot by one of the slingers Fori had been trying to teach.

"I guess there were enough of us, so the most of them ran, and that one—it just knocked him flat, and then we landed on him, and slit his throat."

"And the others didn't come back. We were lucky." Gird looked at his smug foragers, spattered with blood and dirt, and then around at the locals, who looked as hungry as wolves.

"We caught him, but he lived in your wood," Gird said loud enough for all to hear. "We would share the feast."

The local men in the clearing looked at Felis, who spread his hands. "All right. But all we have is grain mush."

Gird breathed a sigh of relief. They *should* share food both ways; that made the obligations equal. "We would be glad to share freely, all we have with all you have." He would like to have insisted that all of them, locals and his men alike, clean up before eating, but with the stream so foul that was impossible. He called his troop together, while the cook and Diamod fashioned a spit for roasting the pig, and supervised the washing of hands in clean water. No one argued; they seemed almost proud to demonstrate their superior habits to the locals. That led to a flurry of handwashing by the locals as well, and Gird was content.

Soon the smell of roasting pig overcame the worst of the camp's stench. The cook caught the dripping juices off the pig, and stirred them into the mush, along with salt from Gird's pouch. By the time the pig was done, Gird's appetite had returned full force. With roast pig, mush, and the bread they'd brought, everyone had plenty to eat, and the conversations around the firepit were friendly. Then one of the locals got up and sauntered toward the creek.

"Use the new trench," said Gird. The man stopped.

"But it's dark. I couldn't find it."

"Cob, help him."

The man opened his mouth to complain and shut it again. Cob was up, with a brand from the fire. "This way," he said.

"But we always—" the man said, looking at Felis.

"Do it," Felis said. "They fed us our own pig; they can tell us where to put our own jacks."

Gird was up before dawn; the rank smell had gotten into his dreams, and he'd been pursued through dark tunnels by something with poison fangs and bad breath. His own men were curled up neatly enough under the edge of the pickoaks, where the smell was least. The locals were sprawled anyhow around the firepit. Gird went to the jacks, then picked his way to the firepit and poked up the fire. It was going to be a clear day, but dew had soaked the stones; he dared not sit down until they dried. He went to look at the sick men, and found that the fevered one had died in the night. The other was asleep, breathing easily. He put more wood on the fire, until it crackled, and then took a bucket and started upstream. On his way back, he met Fori with the other bucket.

"I thought this must be where you were," said Fori. "And I knew you'd want more good water."

"Another fifty paces up, there's a clean creek coming in from one side. I went up that to a pool—I think there's a spring under it."

"That's what Pidi said, when I asked him. Felis is asking for you."

"Is he?" Gird went back down, stepping carefully as the water tried to slosh out of the bucket. Felis would have waked with one of two plans, and Gird hoped the man had sense. He doubted it; anyone who couldn't stay out of his own mess could hardly be called sensible. Besides, it was never easy for a man to give up leadership.

Felis, however, had taken a third route Gird hadn't thought of. "I talked to everyone," he said, as soon as Gird came into the clearing. "They want to follow you. They think you know how to run an army." Gird set the bucket down by the firepit, and blinked. He hadn't expected Felis to ask the others himself, privately.

"What about you?" he asked.

Felis darkened with the easy blush of the redhead. "I wish I had done what you did," he said. "I wish I'd thought of all that. All I thought of was fighting itself—I kept trying to learn swordfighting—"

Gird met his gaze. "Do you want to learn my way, or go your own?"

"I'll stay, if you'll let me."

"You fooled me," Gird said. "I thought you'd be angry, and go away."

"I *am* angry," said Felis. "But you did it fairly, and not to make me angry. Did you?"

"No. At least—" remembering his own anger of the day before, "—at least, I didn't start that way. It seemed such a waste."

Felis's followers had been watching their conversation from a distance, furtively; when Gird and Felis smiled at each other and clasped hands, everyone relaxed.

That day was spent cleaning up the camp as best they could, while the new members learned how Gird's system worked. Supper was less a feast, for no lucky catch rewarded that day's hunters. But the camp stank less, and Pidi had given two draughts of flannelweed to the man with flux. He had not died, at least, and had not heaved all day.

"What now?" asked Felis, as they sat around the dying fire. "Are you going to drill us for a few hands of days, and then go take over another group?"

Gird yawned and stretched. He was very tired. "No," he said. "No, I have another plan. The Stone Circle must learn drill, and all the soldiering possible, but we'll never have enough outlaws to fight a war. We've got to have a way to train *everyone*. At home. While they farm, or make pots, or whatever it is they do."

"How?" asked Cob, beside him.

"Tomorrow," said Gird. "I'll explain it all tomorrow."

Chapter Thirteen

The newcomers, Gird discovered, had already grasped the idea of traveling quietly, with scouts ahead and behind. He led them back up the stream they had camped beside. The sick man looked as if he would definitely recover; they carried him in a pole-slung litter. All of them carried some piece of equipment, for Gird did not intend to return to that camp until it had had time to clean itself.

"I suppose you want us to dig a jacks trench every time we stop?" asked Felis.

"Yes." Gird was ready to glare, but Felis merely shook his head, and grinned. They were halted for a noon rest on the shady side of a hill, where the scrub grew barely more than head-high.

Summer heat shimmered on the slopes around them, and baked pungent scents from the scrub.

"So will you tell us your plan now?"

Gird looked around at the others. They were all listening; he wondered how they would react. Was there a better time? He thought not. But instead of answering Felis directly, he asked, "How many men did you have when you started?"

Felis frowned thoughtfully. "I didn't start it—but there were three hands when I came. Then Irin died, and then two more came, and then six, but one of them died soon; he'd been hurt. Three hands, four—it went up and down."

"And how many other groups are there, and how large do you think they are?"

Felis began tapping the ground, as if a map, to remind himself. "I heard of one away westward—beyond your village—Diamod went there once and said they had less than two hands of men. North and west, another, but I heard that one was captured and killed, all of them. Two hands, maybe three. South and east, someone told me of a large group: five or six hands of men, maybe more. But I heard they have fields, and can feed themselves."

Gird nodded. "That's what I thought. There may be more groups, but nowhere more than the farmers can support. We can't feed ourselves. So a day or two of travel between groups—each one drawing food from two or three villages—and the villages are so poor. Four hands is a large group; five is too large for most. And without proper care for the food they *do* get, some of it is wasted. Diamod told me several years ago there were enough in the Stone Circle to fight a war, but ten soldiers here and fifteen there and twenty over here don't make an army. They have to be together. Organized. Training together."

"But I don't see—"

"We need the Stone Circle: we need a place for men to go when they've been outlawed or have lost their holdings. But we need an army more. And we need an army that can feed itself during training, house itself during training, clothe itself—"

"It's impossible!"

"No, I don't think so." Gird let his eyes wander from face to face. "We were all farmers, craftsmen—we fed ourselves, housed ourselves—and in the evenings, off-season, we sat around our bartons or our homes and talked."

"Yes, and you yourself would have nothing to do with fighting when you still had your holding," said Diamod boldly.

"That's true, because you wanted me to sneak away and teach

you drill—go away from my home, and my work, and risk discovery both ways, to teach strangers. I say now I was wrong. But what I told you then still has force. Suppose you had said, 'Let *us* teach *you* how to fight and defend yourselves—here in your own village, you and the men you know best fighting shoulder to shoulder to protect your own against the lords.' Do you think I might have answered differently?"

A long silence. Diamod opened his mouth and shut it. Felis pulled a grass stem, chewed it, and spat it out. The others said nothing, but all the faces conveyed shifting thoughts and emotions. Finally Triga said, "You mean for us to go into villages and teach farmers what you've taught us—by ourselves?"

"It won't work," said Herf suddenly. "It can't—the lords would see it, their guards would. Right under their noses, peasants drilling? They'd be hung on the spikes by nightfall."

"There aren't guards stationed in every village," said Ivis. "If they would have their own scouts out, to see anyone coming—"

"Better than that," said Gird. "Think how our villages are built. Every cottage, nearly, has its own—"

"Barton!" said Fori, eyes suddenly alight. "Walled in—no one can see, but over the back gate—"

"That's right," said Gird. "Bartons. Big enough to teach a few men to march together, use sticks. No one notices when the men go into a barton of an evening, or the noise that comes out of it— men telling jokes, drinking ale—" He could suddenly feel it, the mellow flow of liquid down his throat that would ease his joints and make the old stories new again.

Felis pursed his lips. "Not everyone in the village will do it— what about those who don't? What if they report it?"

"Start small. One or two, let the locals decide who else to ask. Nobody in my village would've reported it to the steward, though some wouldn't come. Let 'em stay home. And if the guards do come, what's to see? A group of men talking and singing, same as any evening."

On face after face, Gird could see the idea take root and grow. He watched its progress through the group. It would work; he knew it would work. It had come to him in a flash of insight so intense that it waked him out of a sound sleep. He had been planning to try it, but the attack on Rahi had come first.

"So: you train us, and we train them. Just those of us here could reach five, six hands of villages, and if every village trained four hands of men—"

"But would we try to move in with them? Someone would surely notice that—"

Gird nodded. "I know. I'm not sure what the best way is, but I'm sure that training the farmers at home is part of it." He stretched, relieved that they seemed to understand his point and agree. "But right now, each one of you must know everything *I* know—and be able to teach it. And if you know something I don't, you must teach me."

"You don't know everything?" asked Felis slyly.

"No. I didn't know how to plait baskets or cook frogs; Triga taught me that." Triga grinned and raised a fist. "We all share some knowledge—the farmers among us, at least. But many of us have special skills, something extra, which we can share with others."

By Midsummer Eve, Gird had both groups drilling with sticks. They camped apart, for he still could not feed both at once. One campsite lay just within the east side of the wood, and the other was near (but carefully not in) Triga's bog. But the flow of information, skills, and supplies went back and forth almost daily. They drilled apart three days, and came together on the fourth, to practice larger group movement outside the forest, on a grassy hillside.

Both camps had the clean, tidy look of a good master's workshop—and it was a workshop, as Gird explained often. If they had an army someday, of farmers who had trained in their bartons, they would have to have camps in the field, and those camps would have to have jacks, kitchens, shelters for wounded, space to store supplies. Here, in small groups, they could learn what worked, and later they could show others.

As summer days lengthened, the food-gathering groups were able to bring back more and more supplies. Gird insisted that some of these be stored for emergencies. They dried fruit on lattices of plaited grass, cut the wild grain and threshed it, dug edible tubers, honed their skill at slinging and throwing. Archery was harder. Of the four bows between the two groups, one had broken early, and it seemed no one could make good arrows. Still, the best of them occasionally hit a bird or rabbit. Each camp had its own handmill, and when there was grain to grind, they had bread. Gird toyed with the idea of trying to brew some ale, but they really couldn't afford the grain. Maybe after harvesttime, he thought—next winter would be cold and dismal enough, without giving up ale entirely.

Gird rotated all the men through all the tally groups, but noticed which had special abilities. The whittlers, sure of an appreciative audience, worked even when not on actual tool duty, fashioning spoons and bowls, dippers and pothooks. Some of the men took to the old stone tools, and one liked to spend his spare time chipping new blades from flint cobbles. No one sneered, now, at those who could make useful baskets, or sew neat patches.

On Midsummer Eve, lacking ale, they drank the fresh juice of wild grapes and sat out under the stars, singing the old traditional songs. Like Midwinter, Midsummer was a fireless night, but this one was not dark and cold. In the freshness before Midsummer dawn, when every sweet scent of the earth redoubled its strength, Gird lay in the long grass and wished they could have women with them. The other men, too, were restless, remembering the traditional end to all those traditional songs, when the brief hours of darkness were spent first hunting the elusive flowers said to bloom only that night, and then celebrating them. Gird thought of his first night with Mali, of all the Midsummers he'd spent with her. A breath of air moved, wafting still more scent past him, and he rolled up on one elbow. She had been dead, and he had not gone back out, but now he was out, and he could not stop thinking about it.

Of course it would not do. He made himself get up and walk around the others, who pretended to be asleep. The two or three who were really asleep risked dangerous dreams, on Midsummer night. They snored, or muttered, and tossed uneasily. He did not wake them, walking farther away into the stillness. Dew lay heavy on the grass, gray-silver in the starlight, in the slow light of dawn that rose from the east in faintly colored waves.

Two days later, he had just come from the eastern camp, and was nearing the other, when Diamod met him on the trail.

"I have to tell you something," he said. Gird stopped. He had made a rule that they not talk on the trail, even when chance-met like this. But Diamod's expression declared this an emergency.

"What, then?"

"Your daughter Raheli—"

Gird's heart contracted; his vision hazed. "She's dead." Despite the two reports he had had, he had continued to worry, sure that she might yet die of her injuries or her sorrow. He had worked harder, to keep himself from thinking about it, but her face haunted him.

"No—she's come."

Relief and shock contended; he felt that the ground beneath him swayed "Come? You mean—come *here*? They wouldn't keep her?"

"They would have been glad to keep her; she would not stay. She has come here, and she insists she is joining us."

"No!" That was loud enough to send birds squawking away in the forest canopy overhead, and loud enough for any forester to hear. Gird bit back another bellow and lowered his voice. "It's impossible. She can't—"

"You come tell her that. She followed me here from Fireoak— I didn't even know she was following until I reached the wood, and then I couldn't—I didn't think I should—send her back. Or that she'd go."

Rahi alive, and well enough to walk so far—that was as much as he'd hoped. More. He wanted to see her, hold her, know she was whole and strong again. He remembered the blood on her face, on her body. When he looked at Diamod, the man seemed to have understood his very thought, because he nodded slowly.

"Yes, she has a terrible scar, and no, she seems not to mind. She wore no headscarf. Something else, she's dressed like a man."

Gird shook his head, shrugged, could not think of anything to say. Most headstrong of his children—how was he going to convince her to leave? If she had come this far, it would not be easy, and if she refused to obey him, it would cause him trouble with the men.

"What has she said to the men?" he asked Diamod.

"She said she was your daughter, and must see you. She had told me she meant to stay, but when I left she had said nothing else to the others."

"Thank Alyanya's grace for that," said Gird. He shivered, flicked his fingers to avert the trouble, whatever it had been (and he could guess well enough) and started on toward the camp.

The other men were all busy, carefully busy and carefully avoiding the tall, strongly built person in trousers and man's shirt who sat motionless on a log, back toward him. Gird paused to look at her. From that distance, in that garb, she looked like a boy, her short dark hair (she had cut her hair!) rumpled, her big hands busy with a knife on a stick of wood. What was she whittling? When had she learned to whittle—or had she known, and he not known it?

He came toward her; the other men's glances at him alerted her, and she turned, then stood. She stood very straight, as she had when expecting punishment in childhood—she had been the one of his children most likely to defy him. Now he could see the ruin that blow had made of her beauty, a scar worse than her mother's, puckering the corner of her mouth. Her jaw had been broken, by the unevenness of it now. Her eyes held nothing he had seen before, in her years as child and maid and young wife. They might have been stones, for all the softness in them.

He could not bear it. He could not bear it that his daughter, his (he could admit it to himself) favorite, could look at him so. "Rahi—" he began. Then he found himself reaching for her, sweeping her into his hug despite her tension when she felt his hands. She stiffened, pushed him back, then stood passively. That was worse. He held her off, searching her face for some part of the girl who had been. "I'm sorry," he said. "I didn't think—"

"I came to stay," she said, as if it were a ritual she had memorized. "I came to fight. I am strong. I have no—no family ties."

"Rahi—!" He was appalled. But she went on.

"No child, no husband, nothing—but the strength of my body, the skill of my hands. I can be useful, and I can fight."

The other men had vanished, into the trees. Gird did not blame them; he was grateful for their tact. He was also sure they were listening avidly from behind every clump of leaves.

"I can't marry again," Rahi went on. "I'm—too noticeable. Imagine going before a steward or bailiff. And the healers say that fever may have made me barren, as well as killing my—the—child. And I don't want to marry again. I want to do something—" She snapped the stick she'd been whittling, and flung the pieces away. "Something to end this, so no other young wife will see her husband die as I did, and then have it be his wrongdoing—" She looked up at Gird, eyes suddenly full of tears. "I have to do this, Gird, here or somewhere else."

She had not called him Da, or the more formal father: she had called him Gird, like any of his men. That was another pain, even closer to the deep center of his heart where father and child were bound in ancient ties. He blinked back his own tears, and brushed away those that had run down his cheeks. His beard was wetter than he expected.

He tried to stay calm. "Rahi, love, we can't have women here, in the camps. Not to fight—and it's not fair otherwise. It's not safe."

"Was I safe tending my own hearth at home?" she asked bitterly. "Is any woman safe? Are we safer when the strongest men are off in the woods playing soldier?" Gird grasped at the weak end of that.

"That's going to change; I thought of a way for men to learn soldiering in the villages." He explained quickly, before she could argue, and when he finished she was nodding. "So you see—" he said, easing into it.

"I see," she interrupted. "I see that the men will get some training, and then you'll take them away to a battle, leaving the women unprotected."

"That's not what I meant!"

"That's what it will be. You know that. Remember, years ago, when you told me I was as good as another son? After Calis died? I know many girls aren't that strong—but not all men are as strong as you, yet you've got Pidi here—little Pidi that I can sling over my shoulder—and you think I can't—"

"It's not just strength. You know that." Gird was sweating; he could feel it trickling down his ribs, and his hands were slick with it. "What about—you know—all those women things—"

Rahi stared at him a moment, and then snorted. A chuckle fought its way up, and she was suddenly convulsed with laughter. "Oh, Da—oh, Lady's grace, it still hurts when I laugh, but—You mean you never *knew*?"

"Knew what?" He could not imagine what she thought was funny about the problems having women in camp could bring.

Her hand waved, vaguely, as she tried to stop laughing, and hiccuped instead. "Mother never told you? All those years and you thought—" she shook her head, laughing again. Finally, eyes streaming tears, she regained control. Now, flushed from laughter, she looked like his daughter again, like her mother—all the warmth and laughter that Mali had brought into his life regained. Gird stared at her, halfway between anger and delight. She took a long breath, with her hand to her side, and explained "Da, women have ways—herbs, brews—we're not like cows, you know. We're people; we understand our bodies. If it's a bad time—and I agree, fighting a war would be a bad time—we take care of it and don't make a mess. I can't tell you; it's *our* knowledge."

"But Issa—"

"Oh, Issa!" Rahi shook her cropped hair. "It doesn't work for some women, or they won't bother—that kind wouldn't want to learn soldiering anyway." She chuckled softly, a gentler sound. "I thought I would never laugh again, and here the first time I see you, I disgrace myself—"

"It's no disgrace to laugh," Gird said. He wanted to reach for her again, hug her, stroke her hair as he had when she was a small child. But she was a woman, and a woman who had suffered too much to be treated as a child. "Even after sorrow—it comes, sometimes, when no one expects it."

Rahi nodded. "Mother used to say it was the Lady's way of making it bearable. Tears in joy, laughter in sorrow, she said, were a sign of the Lady's presence." She reached out to him, her hand almost as large as his own, and patted his shoulder. "There—now I've grieved, and laughed, and called you Da again, which I said would not do, were I your soldier. But I'm staying."

And from that decision he could not budge her, not then nor

that night nor the next day. Their argument was conducted in the spurious privacy of the camp, with everyone not listening. Between bouts, Rahi demonstrated her usual competence, fitting her contributions of work and skill in effortlessly. Gird began to notice covert grins, sidelong sly looks at her, at him. The skin on the back of his neck itched constantly from being looked at. His ears felt sunburnt. Rahi did not take part in the drill sessions, but she was clearly watching and learning the commands.

After the afternoon's stick drill, Ivis lingered when the others dispersed to their assigned groups. "Your daughter—" he said, his eyes down.

"Yes." Gird bit it off. He was going to have to talk about it, without having solved it, and it could do nothing but harm.

"You told us."

"Yes." He'd forgotten that, by this time. He looked at Ivis, who was staring past his shoulder. Gird resisted the temptation to look around—was Ivis looking at Rahi?

"She's a lot like you," Ivis said.

"She's—what?"

"Like you. Gets things done. Strong—more than one way."

Gird grunted. He could see where this was leading, and he didn't like it. Had Rahi been talking to them behind his back?

"She hasn't said anything, but we couldn't help hearing a little . . ."

Gird squinted up at the bright sky showing between the leaves, and asked himself why Mali hadn't had all boys. Life would have been a lot simpler. "She wants to stay; you all know that. She can't. She's stubborn, like her mother." *And me,* his mind insisted silently. "Stubborn on both sides," he admitted aloud. "But it's impossible."

Ivis dug a toe into the dirt and made a line. "She's not like most women."

Gird snorted. "She's like all women. Wants her way, and expects to get it. But with Rahi, it's even more so. Her next older brothers died, in a plague. That may have been it, though Mali—my wife— she was a strongminded woman too." As if she were alive again, he heard her voice in his ear, as she had warned him that first night at the gathering. *I will not guard my tongue for any man,* she'd said, and she'd kept that vow. Along with all the others. And had taught Rahi the same, if teaching had anything to do with what was born in the blood. He could feel his own blood contending. If only Rahi had been his son—but then it might have been Rahi dead, and his (her?) wife left. Gird shook his head. That was too complicated; what he had was complicated enough. How could the men respect a leader who couldn't make his daughter obey?

"We think she's earned it—if she can, if she's strong enough—"

"Strong enough! Of course she's strong enough; that's not the point."

Ivis cleared his throat noisily. "Gird—it *is* the point. To us, anyway. You've worried about some of the men here having the strength to lead, or the courage when it comes to a real fight. She's—she's your daughter, and we know what happened. She should be here."

Gird stared at him. "You think that? But if I let her—what about others?"

Ivis cleared his throat again. "The—the one thing I did hear her say, to Pidi, was that women could train at home too. In the bartons."

In the bartons I don't have yet, Gird thought furiously. In the bartons that are safe—if they are safe—only because the men always gather in the bartons. Again a memory of Mali forced itself into his consciousness, the day of their wedding when she had faced the ridiculous ceremonies with no embarrassment whatever. Were women really just humoring men with all that squealing and shyness? Could they—he had no doubts about Rahi, who could probably ride wild horses if the chance occurred—could *other women* really learn to fight, use weapons, *kill*—alongside men?

Ivis was watching his face with a wary expression. "She said I shouldn't say anything to you," he said.

Gird glared at him. "I thought you said you hadn't talked to her!"

"I haven't. I would have, but she wouldn't. Said it was up to you and her to work out, and I should stay out of it."

"Giving you orders, eh?" For some reason that amused him; he could feel Rahi's resentment of someone's interference, her fierce determination to convince Gird by herself.

Ivis grinned, catching the change in Gird's mood. "You notice I didn't obey."

"So how many of them agree with you?"

Ivis relaxed still more. "I didn't talk to all, but all I asked agreed that they would let her stay."

Gird muttered one of the old guards' curses he hadn't used in years; Ivis clearly had never heard it and didn't understand. "Go away, then. I want to talk to her." Ivis vanished, as if whisked away by magic. Gird looked around for Rahi. There she was, grinding grain as placidly as any housewife by her hearth. He had a sudden sinking feeling, as if a hole had opened in his chest, and let his heart fall out on the ground. Could he possibly be about to do what he was going to do? He swallowed against the feeling, and called her. She looked up, smiled, and came to him. He noticed that she had, even in that moment, scooped the ground meal into a bowl, and laid another atop it to keep out dirt.

This time he looked her over as if she were a real recruit. Within a finger of his height, broad shouldered, as Mali had been. Thin, from the fever, but with strength in her arms. The scar down her face made her too distinctive to send into a village or town—but she could still see out of both eyes, and had two good arms and legs. He had men with less. She stood there calmly, not arguing. Not intending to change her mind, either; he could feel the force of that determination as if it were heat from a fire.

"I don't think you understand," he said without preamble, "how hard it is for me. I've already seen you lying at my feet in a pool of blood. I don't think I can stand seeing that again."

Her face paled. "You don't understand how hard it is for me," she said. "I *lost* that blood, lost my husband, lost my child, and could not strike even one good blow to stop it. I *know* I cannot stand that—I will not be that helpless again. Not ever. Either you teach me, or—I don't know, but I'll learn somehow."

"And die somewhere I never know," Gird sighed, near tears again. "And that will be my fault, as it was my fault for not protecting you before. You give me a hard choice, Rahi." She opened her mouth, but he shook his head. "You would say, as your mother said often enough, that it is a world of hard choices. All right. I give in, on this one thing. But if this kills you, Rahi, make sure it is not because you failed to learn what I could teach."

If she felt triumph, she did not show it. Only in the corner of her eye, the little wrinkle twitched, whether from surprise or delight, he could not tell, and would not ask.

"And you were right," he went on, "to call me 'Gird' when you first came. If you would be a soldier, then it is for that you are here, and not as my daughter."

She nodded, gravely. "Yes, Gird."

"And if you—if you need—" Now her eyes crinkled in what could only be laughter. Gird glared at her. "Dammit—!"

"Gird, if I cannot stay as a soldier, for some reason, I will tell you at once, and go. But it is not likely, even without what I know of herbs: the healer said so."

His arms ached to hold her, comfort her, restore to her the promises of her childhood—the promises all children should have. But it was too late for that. She looked content with what life had left her; he had no choice now himself. Her future was no more doubtful than his—and, he thought sourly, the only doubt was *when* they'd be strung on the spikes, not if.

But when she returned to grinding, and he saw by the glances passed around the campsite that everyone understood, and accepted his decision (he could not believe many of them actually approved) he was able to return to planning with a lighter heart. If he could establish training in the villages, bartons full of trained men—his mind put other women in that picture, and he hastily blanked them out—in time they would outnumber the lords and their guards. Would any of the guards come over? They had come from peasant ranks. If they saw their friends and family actually fighting, would that make a difference? He let himself imagine a series of battles in which the peasants stood their ground, in drill array, using their sticks and shovels, pushing back the guard and then the lords themselves. Of course, he still didn't know whether the sticks would work as he saw them in his head.

He sighed. Time to start the next level of training. He had in mind straw-stuffed dummies tied onto logs, to simulate horsemen. It would help if he'd ever actually ridden a horse, and knew in his own body how firmly a horseman could sit. He'd seen men bucked off—he remembered trying to ride calves—but that was not like a soldier on horseback firmly in the saddle. Still, it ought to work. If they could unseat horsemen, they could ambush mounted patrols. Even more important, if they could unseat horsemen—even one horseman—even a straw dummy tied to a log—it might convince the farmers in their villages that it was worthwhile spending all those hours learning to drill and use a stick.

Making the straw dummy was quick work, in the hot days of tall grass and long afternoons. Cob suggested weighting the body with rocks; Triga had the even better suggestion of seating a real person on the log, and pulling him off slowly—to see how a person felt—and then making the dummy feel the same. That turned into several days of experiment, with one after another trying to keep his seat on the log with friends pushing and pulling from one or both sides. Gird took a turn, wondering if it felt anything like riding a real horse, or if it could be a way to learn. It was easy to wrap his long legs around the log and hang on, but hard to keep his balance when someone yanked his arm. After his second fall, he watched Ivis on the log.

"We don't need the straw dummy," he said, "As long as we pad the ends of our sticks, and remember that this one is a friend. Whoever's up can tell us which moves are hardest to counter."

The rider—Ivis, then others—was equipped with a reed "sword" and laid about vigorously to simulate resistance. Slowly at first, then with increasing confidence and speed, they all learned where to strike a rider to throw him off balance. The game became so popular that Gird had to remind them that there were other ways—and enemies—to fight, or they would have spent all their time knocking one another off logs.

Rahi, in the meantime, had merged almost invisibly into the troop. Gird was acutely aware of her presence for the first few days; then he went off to the other camp, and when he returned it was as if she had always been there—but as a soldier, not his daughter. She did not avoid him, exactly, but she did not spend her free time with Pidi, or with Gird, and even seemed to steer clear of Fori. She had her place in drill, and made no more than the usual beginner's mistakes. As he would have expected, she learned fast. Gird waited for something to go wrong, but nothing did.

It was now nearing harvest. After harvest the fieldfee collectors would be out; Gird wanted to introduce his barton idea to at least a few villages before then. For that he needed seasoned older men, men the farmers might trust as similar to themselves. They had to be proficient in the drill (although he didn't expect them to teach the farmers much in the short time until harvest—but they had to impress them.) And—perhaps most important—they had to be reliably close-mouthed. He himself would go, of course. Ivis had developed into a trusted lieutenant, as had Cob. Diamod was known in five or six villages as a Stone Circle organizer. Fells, who might have been another possibility, had broken his wrist on his last "ride" as a target, and would not be fit until after harvest.

After long discussions, Gird chose four villages to test his idea: Fireoak, Harrow (where Felis's group had supporters), Whitetree, where Ivis's brother lived, and Hardshallows. Cob and a man from Felis's group went to Harrow, Ivis to his brother, Gird to Fireoak, and Diamod to Hardshallows. They were to spend no more than two nights in the village, and talk to no more than five men.

Chapter Fourteen

Coming into Fireoak on a late summer day, as an active rebel organizer, was very different from leaving it as a fugitive who had only the ghost of an idea for rebellion. The two of them joined a stream of workers coming in from the fields: harvest markers, who went into the fields before harvest to make sure the boundary stones didn't roll an armspan one way or the other—herders prodding slow-moving cows toward home and milking time. Gird flared his nostrils, enjoying the scent of cow. He had never understood those who thought cows stank. Pigs stank; dogs stank; even people—but cows had a rich, joyful scent, as befitted animals who lived on fresh grass and herbs. Their droppings had never disgusted him. Someone—he could not right then remember who—had told him once that a man should keep only those animals whose smells were pleasant to him.

The Fireoak farmers and herdsmen knew perfectly well the two were outlanders, but they knew Diamod and had heard of Gird. They sauntered down the lane, dusty and brown as the farmers with them, and no one spoke to them. Slow, traditional talk rolled by: harvest chances, taxes, a remedy for stiff ankles followed by a joke about the cause, comments on cows and weather and the uncommon number of rabbits that summer—a joke directed at Gird, which he well understood and knew better than to answer.

"Pop up and down everywhere, they do," someone said a second time, to see if he would rise to the bait. "Got so common, we might think they's people."

Then the village, with its familiar cottages, the wattle fences between smallgardens, the walls of bartons rising behind. It was at once strange and the same: so like his own village, and yet not his village—and his village was not his village. Gird sniffed: bread, cheese, the vegetables they had not yet planted for the camps, ale somewhere—his mouth watered. Children wandered about, too thin but not yet starving, noticing the strangers but warned away from saying anything by quick gestures from their elders.

He would have passed Mali's brother's cottage, if Diamod had not jabbed him in the ribs. It looked different by daylight, from

161

the front. He remembered Rahi's harsh feverish breathing in the barton out back, the gray light of dawn when he'd eased out the gate into the field beyond. Now he saw a low fence enclosing a ragged smallgarden, the beaten path to the front door. And in the door, a thin girl, yellowhaired, who held one crooked arm as if it pained her. Her face whitened, and she ducked inside. Gird turned to see Diamod wink before he walked on.

Gird came to the door, stepped out of his boots, and said "Girnis?"

Mali's brother's wife, a face he barely remembered from that one night, said "You're Gird? Gods above, what do you mean— come in, don't stand there!" Gird picked up his boots and ducked beneath the low lintel. It was dark inside, and would have been cool if not for the fire on the hearth. By that flickering light, Gird could see Girnis standing flat against the wall between a loom and a wheel.

"Is—is Rahi—?"

"She's alive, and well, and stubborn as ever." Gird looked at the wife, whose lips were folded together. What had he walked into? He had not asked Rahi all that had happened here, but perhaps he should have.

"I thought—" the woman began, then closed her mouth, and twisted her hands, and finally said again "I thought you were leaving Girnis with us. To be ours."

"I did," said Gird, surprised. "I said so; I was grateful."

She looked at him hard, then her mouth relaxed a little. "You didn't come to take her?"

"Of course not! Why would you think—"

"Raheli left. When she didn't come back, we thought she was with you, or dead—we didn't hear of anyone being killed. And then we thought, if you wanted her, you might want Girnis, but she's—"

"She's not Rahi." She was the child of Mali's illness, the twin that lived, but never as vigorous as a singleton. "I wouldn't take her. Girnis, let me see you."

Girnis came to him, shyly but now unalarmed. Her arm had healed a little crooked—not so bad, when she held it out. But she stood with it up, as if it were still in its bindings, and it was thinner than the other.

"Does it still hurt you?" he asked. She nodded.

"Mother Fera—" she glanced toward the woman, "—says I should move it more, but the joint hurts, Da, when I try."

"Let me feel." Gird took her arm, conscious of its thinness, and the faint tremor—nervousness? pain?—that met his touch. He bent and straightened it slowly, stopping when he met resistance and heard her indrawn breath. He could feel nothing wrong but stiff-ness, but he was not a healer. "I'm sure your aunt has tried heat," he said, "and herb poultices. I think myself it would be good to move it more. Sometimes things hurt when they're healing. A few times a day, anyway—I think you could do that." She nodded, solemnly. She was quiet; she had always been quiet, the quietest of his children, but not slow. Just quiet, in a house full of noisy ones.

The woman had moved nearer; she looked less alarmed. "We've had an offer for her," she said. "She has a mixed parrion, she says?"

Gird nodded. "Yes. She has Mali's parrion of herbcraft, and Issa's—my brother's wife's—parrion of embroidery. Issa was a weaver, as well, but died before Girnis learned enough."

"I am a weaver," the woman said. "I can teach her, if her arm strengthens. But—will you let us arrange the marriage?"

"Of course. I told you—if you in your kindness will have her, she is your daughter, and yours is the right to speak for or against."

He heard boots in the barton, and stiffened, but the woman called through the house: "Gird's here. It's all right."

After that awkwardness, he was surprised to find that Mali's brother was enthusiastic about the possibility of training within the village.

"Of course, the bartons," he said. "You're right, Gird, and I don't know why we hadn't thought of it before. Had no one to teach us, I suppose. I know—let me think—I know two hands of men who would join here, at once. What about weapons?"

"Drill first, then weapons," said Gird. He and Barin were sitting on the cool stones of the barton, drinking ale to celebrate. He could feel a delicate haze leaching the tiredness from his bones.

"What about women?" asked Barin.

"Mmm?"

"You've got Rahi now. I'm Mali's brother, after all; I remember what she was like and how relieved the family was when you offered for her. Will you take women like that in?"

Gird shrugged. "*I* would myself, but I can't force another group to do it. What about you?"

"I don't like the thought of seeing my wife—but after all, she could be cut down for no reason, as Rahi was. Most of them won't want to anyway, but for a few—why not?"

The following night, five other men visited Barin's, presumably to finish an open barrel of ale before the beginning of harvest, when it was bad luck to have one. They talked village gossip until the stars were thick and white, then Gird spoke his piece. Less open than Barin, they still agreed it was a good idea. The longer they talked it over, the more they liked it—except that only two of them thought women should be allowed to join.

"They talk too much," said one of the men. "Let them find out, and it'd be all over the village by dawn."

Barin laughed. "And who was it let out the secret of Kinvit's lover, last winter?"

The others burst into laughs; the man who had complained of women talking too much said "But it wasn't my fault!" Gird chuckled. It was always the same; the loosest mouths complained that others gossiped. *Their* tales were always true, and if the wrong story got out, it was never their fault. Finally the man came around, laughing at himself. "All right," he said. "I got drunk; I opened my mouth, and out fell Kinvit and Lia, doing what Kinvit and Lia had been doing since harvest. No nosy old granny could have done worse." But he was still opposed to having women training in the village. Gird did not push him, letting Barin do most of the talking. They would all know, by now, about Raheli; they would all assume that Gird had a special reason for allowing women to fight. And that was perfectly true.

In the end, the men voted to organize a barton meeting, and gradually recruit new members. Gird promised to send someone— "It may not be me," he pointed out—to train them. "Consider him a sergeant," he said at first, but even in starlight he could see the dislike they had for that name, associated as it was with the lords' tyranny. "What would you call him, then?"

They talked back and forth, suggesting and arguing, until one of them said "We're like a bunch of cattle milling in a pen, waiting for the herdsmarshal to set us on our way."

"Marshal!" said Barin, smacking his leg with his fist. "That's good—and it's not a word we would fear to have overheard. Marshal. And the rest of us are—"

"Yeomen," said Gird. "That covers all of us, farmers and craftsmen alike. Any but lords. And no one will ever know, from talk of it, what it is."

"I do like that," Barin said. "The yeomen and the marshal meet in the barton tonight. As long as we need only those two ranks—"

"But we've got another!" It had come to Gird in another of those flashes of insight. "Marshal—that's one of us traveling, coming to train you. But even in the village, you'll need a leader—that's the yeoman-marshal. And then yeoman for everyone else."

"And someday—" Barin said. He didn't have to finish. They all drained the last of their ale, and stamped their feet in agreement. Gird could see it—the flow of men out to the Stone Circle, to learn. The flow back in, to train those in the bartons . . . and back out, to the fight they all knew must come, and then back, to take up their peaceful lives. As natural as breathing, or the cycle of seasons. He knew from experience that ale could make things seem simpler than they were in morning's light, but this was going to work.

Work began in earnest when he returned to the camp and conferred with the others who had gone out. All the villages had shown an interest—not surprising, since they had talked to men already known to be Stone Circle sympathizers. Two of the others had noticed that the villagers shied from the usual military rank terms of sergeant and captain, but they had not come up with alternatives. They nodded when Gird told them about marshal, yeoman-marshal, and yeoman.

"That'll do," said Ivis. "They won't mind that—it's nothing like the guards. Best of all, we can talk about it in front of anyone— even a guard sergeant—and he won't know what it is." Gird nodded.

"They thought of that, too."

"Will we all be marshals?" asked Cob. "I mean, when we're drilling here, that's going be to confusing."

"None of us are marshals yet," Gird said. "And some of us may be better than others at teaching. Besides, we still don't know enough." In his mind, the wheel of the year turned, grinding the moments away. How long before the first snowfall? Before full winter? Four bartons to train, this winter—maybe more. "After harvest," he said, "we need to bring one man from each village here, to drill with us, and see how the larger units work. When the taxes are paid, no one takes much notice if someone travels to visit relatives. In the meantime, our own harvest: I hear the fieldfees are up again, and we cannot starve our allies."

For the next few hands of days, they drilled only briefly, spending most of their time gathering food and preparing it for storage. No casual nutting and berrying, this time, but a planned harvest of the woods and fields, that must be done before the lords came to hunt, in the days after the fieldfees were paid. Gird had planned food storage sites both in and away from the camps, so that if one were found and destroyed, others would be safe. They could not hunt, and risk foresters preparing for the lords' visits seeing their smoke or smelling the blood, but they could gather fruit, tubers, berries, and stow them away. Into storage pits lined with rock went redroots and onions: their own harvest had been abundant. Other roots and tubers, bulbs and nuts, were stored with them, along with apples and plums and dried berries, bundles of herbs, strips of necessary barks. Their own baskets stored grain as well, harvested from the edges of common pastures, along streambanks, and in Triga's bog. Gird moved from place to place, checking the growing stores, and trying to foresee what hazards they must survive.

After harvest, the lords would come to hunt the large wood; Gird moved everyone to the tangle of hills where Felis's group had lived, and the only game worth hunting was wild boar. If they stayed out of the pickoak scrub, living uncomfortably in the lower brush, they should avoid the occasional hunting party with a taste for pig. The men grumbled, but only slightly. Gird found work for them even in the chest-high thickets of brush.

"We might need to come this way and hide, and it would be good to have paths they can't see from the opposite hill." So his troop crawled and twisted through the thick growth, hacking out paths wider than the rabbit-trails they found. Rahi sniffed the hacked ends of the scrub, and said she thought some of these were medicinal, stunted by soil or dryness. She began making a collection of twigs, bark, roots, and brewed a variety of pungent bitter concoctions which she insisted he taste. They all made his tongue rough up in furrows; they tasted as if they ought to do something good. One made him sweat profusely.

At last Ivis's forester friends sent word that their duke and his friends had returned to the city; the forest was theirs for the winter. By this time the autumn rains were beginning, turning their trails to cold gray mud. Gird wished he had a stone cottage, with a great roaring hearth; his knees ached constantly. Instead, he had the three main campsites he'd found for winter, two backed into the south face of a hill, and one deep in a grove of cedars and pines. His favorite had a clean-running creek, small but adequate to their needs, and the surrounding trees had all dropped their leaves, letting in the low winter sunlight. The other south-facing camp had a larger stream, but he was somewhat worried about floods, come spring. Even in the slower autumn rains, they had to cross the stream on fallen logs. The men called that one Big Creek, and the other Sunbright; the most secluded campsite they called Cedars.

No one grumbled when he insisted they go right on working, rather than huddle in the first shelter they could contrive. He did not know if they were learning to think ahead, or if they simply accepted his orders. But wet and cold as it was now, winter could only be worse. The shelters he had planned went up quickly: wattle frames for side and roof, thatched with whatever they could find, mostly wild grass. Gird realized, as they wrestled with the grass between rains, that he should have had them out scything it earlier. Next year, he thought. And by then he would need another scythe or two. And some sickles. They smeared mud on the insides of the walls. Triga suggested another plan: poles braced against a tree, lashed together, and then wattle woven to make a circular peaked shelter. After building a couple like this, he admitted that it took more work, and gave less interior room, but the two they had made a welcome change, like extra rooms, during that winter.

The newly designated yeomen marshals arrived for their training while this was still going on; Gird had to stop for a couple of days to give them intensive training. But they were almost as impressed with the troop's camp organization as with the drill. This, in turn, helped convince the last doubters among his soldiers that such organization was important. If it could impress strangers, then it was not just a matter of comfort.

The yeomen marshals stayed a hand of days; on the last day, Gird discussed with them the way they'd organize and train during the winter.

"By spring," he said, "I'd like to have your yeomen ready to drill with another barton. Someday we'll have to have bartons able to come together quickly."

"What about recruiting new bartons?" asked the yeoman-marshal from Hardshallows. "I know you wouldn't want to risk it in your old village—the steward, I hear, is still furious about you, and the men who left after you—but we're less than a day's walk from Hawkridge to the west, and not much more from Millburh, down our own stream."

Gird had hoped no one would suggest that yet; he had wanted to be sure the barton idea would work before starting more. But he could not actually stop them—these were not *his* men yet—all he could do was make them sneaky, if they'd already decided. In the pause, while he tried to think how to answer, Barin from Fire-oak spoke up.

"I think we should wait until we have at least two—maybe three—hands of yeomen, all drilling well. How else could we show them what we mean? And if—I don't mean to be illwishing, but if this doesn't work—if we find that our neighbors *do* tell the lords' men, then better only a few bartons die, than many."

Gird nodded, glad he hadn't had to say it himself. "Barin's right, I think. If your barton grows and prospers, and you're sure it's safe, then I will not tell you not to tell the next village. But we're like a man starting a journey with a heavy load: it's better to take a few slow steps, and be sure it's balanced and will hold, than to set off at a run and have the whole thing fall apart." His hands mimed the falling load, and they all laughed. "One village at a time. I think myself it would be better if only one in each barton knew the name of the yeoman marshal in other bartons."

"But if he dies?"

"Each of you tell one of your yeomen—not someone you usually work in the field with—how to contact *us*, here. And let us know the name of that person. Later, everyone will know everyone, but for now, as Barin said, *if* someone tells, it's better that only a few die."

When the yeoman marshals had left, Gird and his troop used the hand of days between the last of the autumn rains and the first of the snows to transport and stow the food and supplies the villages had given them, cut and haul wood for their fires, and add such refinements to their shelters as time and ingenuity allowed. When that first bank of blue cloud rolled across, cutting off the slanting autumn sun, and dropping the temperature, Gird felt that they were as well prepared for winter as possible.

This did not mean he had thought of everything. His own well, in the foreyard of his cottage, froze only in the bitterest winters, and only after midwinter. The clear-running creek that was one of the reasons for choosing Sunbright froze solid before Midwinter, and they must either melt snow and ice for water, or carry it (a cold, heavy load that sometimes froze before they got it home) from a spring some distance away. He had thought to dig the jacks trenches ahead, before the ground froze, but had not realized that the "loose" dirt from them would freeze, and have to be chopped into chunks to fill the trench.

Problems had the advantage of helping Gird keep everyone busy. In the villages, winter boredom led to quarrels and occasional fights. Here, such dissension could be fatal. So his four tally groups had assigned chores, and whenever the weather allowed, Gird chivvied everyone out for a march or drill practice. He divided the groups slightly differently. One brought food from storage, and another cooked it, while the camp chores group had to maintain the fire, the jacks, and the supply of water. The tool groups were set to repairing tools broken or chipped, and to making useful items for the camps. One of the things the villages had sent (at Gird's request) was yarn; Rahi taught several of the men to knit, using smooth-polished twigs as needles. Knitting was an unusual parrion;

she had had it from Mali's brother's wife, in the time she lived there, and liked it much better than weaving.

Midwinter was a different kind of problem. Gird had always known when Midwinter was coming because the village headman said so. Here, he realized, everyone thought of him as headman, and he should know when to celebrate Midwinter. He looked up, at a heavy gray sky. The days were still getting shorter, so it wasn't Midwinter yet. He felt that it would come in a hand or two of days, but he did not know when it would be, or how to find out. But missing the Midwinter celebration was unthinkable.

He asked the others. Most thought it would be "soon" but no one had an exact date. Would it matter? At that thought, a colder chill ran down his neck. Of course it mattered; Midwinter and Midsummer were the ends of the axle on which the year turned. He had to know. He had to find out. Now that the men knew he did not know, they were looking at him nervously.

"How did you find out last year?" he finally thought of asking Ivis.

Ivis flushed. "Last year—well—we all went into one village or another, near Midwinter, and celebrated there." And before Gird could decide to do the same, he said, "I don't think we can, this year—we're too many."

"True, but we can ask." Ivis' village was too far away, across the wood, but one of them could make it to Fireoak and back. To Gird's surprise, Fori asked to go.

"I can stay with Barin, and ask about Girnis. And the barton."

Gird nodded. "Good—but be sure you're back *before* Midwinter."

Fori set off the next morning with a sack of food and everyone's prayers. Gird watched all the faces staring afer him, and said, "Since you're all so glad to be outside, get your sticks." A general groan, but not so dismal as he'd expected.

Stick drill had progressed a little farther. Felis, once his arm healed, was able to demonstrate what he had learned of swordsmanship. Gird suspected it wasn't much, but he himself had never gotten that far. One thing he did know was the length of swords Kelaive's guards had used. He asked the others; the duke, Ivis said, carried a longer sword, but no longer than from waist to ground. He had seen him standing with its tip resting on the ground. So, Gird thought, a sword could have a blade that long, or shorter. He asked his one-armed smith, who mentioned curved blades and broad-bladed swords, but agreed on length. That meant that a longer stick could fend off a sword—not fence with it, to lose chips as the sword chopped—but if the stick could hold the swordsman back, the sword could not harm the person with the stick.

It seemed reasonable, but they had to test it. Slowly, Gird insisted. Carefully. No more broken bones, if possible. Felis took those of his original group who had learned the most about swords, and these faced Gird, Cob, and a few others Gird thought he could trust to stay calm.

The sticks were nowhere near spear length, but about the length a man would choose as a walking staff, or for guiding cattle. So far they were not all the same length, although a broad hand would cover the difference. Gird had watched them in use over the past season, noticing carefully what went wrong most often, when the sticks clashed in ranks, which grips did not hold. Now, with Felis well again, they would see. He felt a little silly, standing there with a real stick facing an imaginary sword, but what else could they do?

Felis waggled his wooden "sword" and swiped at Gird. Gird lowered his stick, and pointed it at Felis, who sliced at it. Before the "sword" struck, Gird jabbed the stick at Felis's face. Felis jerked back, and his sword stroke went wild.

"Wait," said Felis. "Try that again, slower." It would not be slow in battle, but they were only learning. Gird nodded, let Felis begin his sideways swipe with the sword, and then jabbed again. Again Felis jerked his head back, and this time, while he was still off balance, Gird jabbed again, and got him in the chest, gently. Felis grunted, then straightened. "I can't—I think I'm just not good enough—but if you keep poking that at my eyes—I have to back up."

"Let Cob and Arvan try it," said Gird, stepping back, Arvan advanced with his "sword" and very little enthusiasm, to meet Cob. Here Cob was the shorter by a head, yet with the length of his stick he could force Arvan off balance.

"It's too easy," said Felis, scratching his thick red beard. "These sticks we're using for swords don't have the weight of a real weapon. If someone got a blow in, it would jar your stick aside—"

"But could they?" Arvan was frowning. "Cob, just hold it still— let me try." He swung hard at the stick, and managed to bat it aside, but it swung back on rebound, and Cob needed little force to control it.

"But suppose there were more than one swordsman," Felis said. "If you have more than one coming in, you can't just poke one. The other one will poke you."

"That's what the formation is for," Gird said. "If it works." This time he and Cob lined up facing Felis and Arvan. When they lowered their sticks, and jabbed, the two "swordsmen" found themselves giving ground, flailing uselessly with their shorter weapons.

"Just remember," Felis said, "that even an accidental blow with a sword is going to take chips off that stick. It won't last forever. Can you do real damage with it?"

"I don't know." Gird tapped him in the chest again. "If I did that much harder, you might fall down; I might even break your breastbone, or a rib."

"You'll have to swing it to knock someone flat, most times." Triga, watching, entered the discussion. "And if you swing it, that gives time for a fast swordsman to slip in and kill you."

"*And* if you swing it," Felis pointed out, "it can foul on someone else's stick who's fighting another opponent."

"Mmmph. I thought we could try this—hold still, now, I won't really hit you hard." Gird jabbed at Felis's face, then tapped his chest, and then slid his bands down to swing the stick like a flail. But Arvan chose that moment to dart in and put his "sword" to Gird's neck.

"Like that," Felis said, grinning at Arvan and Gird both. Gird glowered at Cob.

"And where were you, partner?"

Cob looked rueful. "Standing watching you, when I should have been watching Arvan. We have more to learn, yeomen."

"We could whittle a point on these sticks, and fire-harden it," said Triga.

"It's still not going to go through any kind of armor. Even if it did, it would catch there, and I'd be standing there with a dead soldier on the end of my weapon, looking foolish." Gird scratched his beard vigorously, as if that could clear his head. "I thought if we hit them in the chest hard enough—or in the belly—that would knock them down, maybe even out."

"Hit them in the face—that makes 'em back up, and they'll worry about losing an eye—"

"True, but—" Gird thought about that. "We need a way to kill them, or we'd be standing all day poking poles at them. I did think of some farm tools—the shovel, the mattock, the scythe—but they all have to be swung. And you're saying, aren't you, that anything we swing will be clumsier than a sword?"

Felis half-closed his eyes, and began swiping the air. Gird stared, then realized he was imagining himself swinging various farm implements. Gird tried to guess which, from Felis's movements, but except for the sickle (a short swing, with a snap to the wrist) he could not be sure which was which. Felis opened his eyes, made a few passes with his "sword," and grinned. "I think there's a chance with a mattock—and even a scythe, though the grips would have to be moved around. But it wouldn't be easy."

Gird heaved a dramatic sigh. "None of this is easy. If it was easy, someone would've done it long ago."

Rahi spoke, for the first time in a drill session. "What if two or three worked together? One with the stick, to force the swordsman's attention, and one or two with weapons more likely to kill, but slower."

"That's fine, if we outnumber the enemy," said Felis. "But in battle—"

"Wait," said Gird. "That might work—and we had better outnumber them, Felis, facing steel with wood. Let's try it."

Felis shrugged, but stepped forward again. This time Rahi stood beside Gird with one of the sickles. She was on his left, but then looked at her sickle and quickly changed sides as Gird lunged at Felis. Felis backed, his attention necessarily on the stick in his face. When Rahi came forward, he tried to swing at her, but the pole caught him in the angle of neck and shoulder. Arvan swung at Rahi, but missed as Cob's pole got him in the chest, and then poked again at his face. Rahi could easily dodge Felis's wild strokes, and she swung, stopping just as the sickle tip hooked into his side. Then, slow for the exercise, but smoothly, she swung back, pivoting, to come forward again and take Arvan in the belly. They all stopped and stood up.

"It works in slow motion," said Felis doubtfully. "And I don't know how we'll practice it fast, not without killing each other."

"We still need someone with a stick for every swordsman." Gird scratched again, and stared at the stick. "And some behind with the other weapons, the killing weapons. Not that the sticks can't kill. But there's something I'm not seeing. Anyone else?"

"Well—you ever see that old-style stickfighting, on fair days?" asked Cob.

"No—the only fair-day I ever went to had one wrestler not as good as you, and a man who could throw knives."

"They started it like a dance," Cob said. "One man tapping a drum, and them tapping the sticks together. It was pretty, like watching horses in a field, tappity-tap. Then they started going faster, and faster, and about then I realized it was a kind of fighting. I'd have learned more, only I was there to make a few crabs wrestling, and my friends had bet on me. I asked one of them later, and he said it was old, something our great-great-grand-das would have known about."

"Do you remember any of it?"

"Only the first bits, the slow part. But it'd be good practice, anyway. Get us used to the feel of something hitting the sticks."

It took longer than Gird would have expected before he could match Cob's pattern; his knuckles felt as if he'd hit them with hammers. And that was with both of them being careful. Triga, who'd been to the same fair, and thought he remembered the stickfighting very well, tried to start fast and ended up sucking his split knuckles ruefully. At least he wasn't angry—but there had been no frogs to eat for days. Arvan picked up the movements quickly, as did Felis, but Padug, who had been Felis's other star pupil at swordsmanship, was slower than Gird. By the time Fori came back, to announce that Midwinter Feast should be celebrated in eight days, most of them were still fumbling their way through this new drill.

Midwinter itself was the coldest and darkest Gird had ever known. No one was sick—Alyanya's grace—but that meant no excuse for any fire whatever. And the rituals of Midwinter had always involved the whole family: each member had his or her assigned role. He had asked the men, and located an eldest son, youngest son, the oldest and youngest overall. Rahi had to take all the women's roles; Gird hoped the gods would understand and accept their intent, and not demand the precision only a whole family could provide.

At dusk on the first night, all their fires were quenched, and the hearths brushed clean. Water, fire, ritual earth (though they had no garden or ploughland), each handled with due reverence—the icy air breathed with respect and affection both. Rahi, not surprisingly, remembered all the women's verses: she had been, once, the youngest daughter, then the eldest, and with Mali's death and her marriage, Alyanya's representative in Gird's home. Together, finally, hands cupped around symbolic light, they sang the Darksong. That was in the middle of the night, when Torre's Necklace stood high overhead. From then until dawn, they huddled together, telling old tales of their childhoods, their fathers' tales as far back as any could remember. Their breath steamed silver in the starlight, each speaker like a tiny chimney. Then—best of omens—a clear dawn to Midwinter Day, and Rahi set the circle pattern of twigs for the new fire. In a great circle, hand to hand, they watched her light it, on the lucky third spark.

They had their feast, as well, for Gird had hidden a comb of honey, and dripped it liberally over hearthcakes and grain mush. Besides that, they had deer, hunted safely long after the lords had gone back to their city. They feasted in comfort, around the roaring fires, and spent the second long night singing more songs than Gird had ever heard. All it lacked was ale; he missed the warmth in his throat and belly, though not the aching head when he woke.

The rest of that winter was hard, but not as hard as he'd feared. When the snowmelt began, with the myriad tinkling music of dripping icicles, they were all still healthy. No one had lost fingers or toes to the cold; no one had had lung fever.

Twice he'd been able to send men to the four original bartons, to check on their training. All had a full three hands or more in training; Hardshallows had five. And they were still recruiting, though cautiously. Fireoak had discovered a man who thought Kelaive would pay him for rebel names. He had changed his mind, Barin reported, when they explained it to him personally. Fori's report of that explanation was fuller than Barin's; the barton had expressed their opinion of him with force—the man would limp for awhile. Gird winced, but accepted it. Better one man beaten than many killed—or even one. He felt slightly better when he found, still later, that the one who had hit the man in the head with a pot was his wife, now an accepted barton member.

Hardshallows reported that it had indeed started a daughter barton, down in Millburh. Growing slowly, but Millburh had a resident guard post, almost a fort. They had to be careful. As the weather lifted, the barton in Ashy, Felis's old village, sent word that it, too, had contacted another village: Three Springs, which had passed the word to two other vills in the same hearthing. As soon as the spring plowing was over, those bartons would be sending elected yeomen marshals to train with the main force.

It was all moving faster than Gird had expected. He still could not quite believe that he'd been away from his own home almost a year—and was alive, leading a growing number of disaffected peasants in what was clearly going to be an army. And yet they'd had no clashes with the lords, no trouble with any of the guard forces. It would be easy to be careless, moving through the green and fragrant woods of spring, with flowers starring the pastures beyond, with the birds carolling overhead.

We don't have an army *yet*, he reminded himself firmly.

Chapter Fifteen

All that spring and summer, the movement spread, like ripples from a dropped stone. The Stone Circle began to become what it had always claimed to be, the center of a wider movement of rebellion. The first bartons ventured out of their villages to drill with Gird in the fields. Their yeomen marshals contacted Stone Circle supporters in other villages. Distant Stone Circle outlaws, living wild in the woods and hills, sent messengers to find out what was happening. Gird would not let any more stay with him; he knew they could not support more where they were. But he sent those he thought would make good teachers and leaders, both to new bartons and to outlaw groups. Gradually—sometimes painfully—he discovered which of his people could do that work, and which of the outlaw groups were honest rebels, and which were brigands.

He insisted that the groups he led provide as much of their own food as they could. That summer was even busier than the one before, as strangers came and went, learning and taking back what they'd learned, while the work of supporting his own troops still had to be done. He saw no end to it, the things he had to do, remember, foresee. But he noticed that some of his people were learning to think ahead for themselves, learning to think how something used one way for a lifetime could be useful for doing something else.

He heard, late that summer, that a distant barton had ambushed a lord's taxman, and shook his head. "That'll start us trouble," he muttered.

Triga cocked an eyebrow at him. "You were hoping to have a war without trouble?"

"I was hoping to have a war when we were ready for it. Not in bits and pieces, here and there, where they have the advantage."

"What I heard was the barton got the money, all of it, and killed the taxman and his two guards. Sounds to me like the barton had the advantage."

"As long as they didn't take anything that can be traced. Where can they spend those coins? And on what? I hope they've sense enough not to go to a smith. They start trying to buy weapons, and we'll see trouble we haven't thought of yet." Gird doubled his own outposts and guards, expecting the worst. Sure enough, mounted patrols swept through the country, both in the wood and beyond in the hills. Gird's men were very glad of their low paths through the scrub. They came back to find that one of their winter camps, Sunbright—deserted now for several hands of days—had been found. The patrol had destroyed the little they'd left behind, and they would certainly know where it was the next winter.

But the patrols, after that double raid, stayed away. From their contacts in the villages, they heard of more trouble—searches of cottages and barns for illegal weapons, men taken on suspicion of rebel activity and beaten or—in two cases—killed outright. Only one of these was actually a Stone Circle supporter, and he had not been a member of the local barton (being, as the yeoman marshal put it, too hotheaded to wear a hat without its catching fire.) These searches and arrests actually increased support for the rebels: after all, if you could be arrested for nothing, why not join?

Gird split his group into threes, and sent each one to a different area for the rest of the summer. They drilled together only a few times, and cautiously, with watchers on all the nearby heights. During harvest, and the lords' favorite hunting time after it, more patrols came. But they'd been expected, and they found nothing but the same deserted camp they had found before. Once the winter storms began, Gird knew no more patrols would come. That winter was like the previous one, except that he began to try to keep accounts of his troop. He had begun with simple tallies, marked with wheatear, sickle, and flower, but he needed lists of all his people, and their villages, and the bartons and their yeoman marshals. Rahi brewed a brownish ink, but he had nothing like the smooth parchment the sergeant had had to write on. He struggled for awhile with the pale inner bark of a poplar, but finally gave up in disgust. He hated writing anyway.

That spring, the spirit of unrest made the whole countryside uneasy. Gird was not quite sure now how many bartons there were. The long winter months were ideal for conspiracy; each barton wanted to claim a daughter barton or two. That meant more than doubling, over the winter. Requests came in for Gird himself, or one of his senior instructors, to come inspect and drill not just one barton, but several. Gird and the others agreed on basic rules for drilling bartons together—how far the drillground must be from any village, what kinds of lookouts to set, what the signals would be, and what common commands all bartons should know. But he knew it was futile; in time, they would be discovered.

On those days of drill, Gird noticed first one blue shirt, then another. They had three at the camp now. Those who wore the blue held themselves proudly, aware of defiance. Gird insisted they have another shirt or cloak to throw over it, should an enemy show up. It would be hard enough to switch from drill to some innocuous activity, without having to explain away a forbidden blue shirt.

They could not, in these short sessions, teach all the new people all they themselves had learned. Gird felt the push and pull of time, the sense of things moving fast and slow at once: the lords could not long remain unaware of all that went on around them, but his people were not ready yet. They needed more time, more drill, and he needed to know more himself. When he thought of gathering all the bartons, in a full army, and meeting the lords with theirs, he was terrified.

Time ran out before he was satisfied with himself or the bartons, after Midsummer and well before harvest. He had gone to the gathering place for the sheep of five villages, so much like the pens where he had met Mali, but far to the north and east. Norwalk Sheepfold, they called it locally, the usual stone-walled shelter, back to the winter winds, with a fenced yard before it. It lay in the hollow of grassy hills, a half-morning's walk from the nearest village, where no troops were stationed anyway.

As usual, Gird came to the meeting site before anyone else, met the shepherds who would be their lookouts, and gave his instructions. Then he squatted in the lee of the sheepfold, eating a chunk of hard cheese, to wait for the first barton to arrive.

When it came straggling along, hardly any two yeomen in step, and weapons every which way, Gird winced. He knew it had formed recently, but that did not excuse the shambling, uncertain line, the complete lack of organization. He began, as always with a new barton, with an attempt at an inspection. As always, he found more than one thing wrong.

"You got to take care of yer own scythe, Tam!" Gird yanked the blade loose and just stopped himself from throwing it on the ground. They couldn't afford to lose a single scrap of edged steel. But every single time he had to check the bindings himself—it was enough to infuriate the Lady of Peace herself. Tam's jaw set stubbornly; the others stared, half-afraid and half-fascinated. Gird took a long breath and let it out. "This time get it tight," he said, handing Tam the blade. He could feel the tension drain away as he went down the line, looking at the other scythes. Most were in reasonable shape, though he wondered if they really would hold against horses or armor.

Fifteen men and three women. Eleven scythes, one pruning hook, two sickles, three shepherds' crooks, two simple staves. Everyone had a knife, and all but one of them were sharp. Before they began the actual drill, he looked around the skyline. Nothing but a flock of sheep to the north, whose shepherd waved from the rise. Safe.

"All right. Line up." They had done this before, taught by Per who had learned from Aris, who had learned from Gird the year before in Burry. They moved too slowly, but they did end up in straight lines, three rows of six. Tam was still trying to jam the end of his blade into the notch of the pole, tamping it against the ground. Maybe he'd learn, before he died.

"Carry." They stared at him, then half the group remembered that that was a command, and wobbled their weapons, clearly unsure where the "carry" position was. *Don't rush it,* Gird reminded himself, remembering the defections after his last temper tantrum. *They have to learn from where they are, not from where they should be.* "Carry," he reminded them. "On your left shoulder—this one—because you have to be able to carry your weapon a long way, and without hitting anyone behind or beside you, or catching on theirs." He reached out and took a scythe from someone—Battin, the name was—in the front rank, and showed them. "Like this."

By the time they were all able to follow the basic commands at a halt, the sun was nearly overhead. Gird looked around again. The northern flock was out of sight over the rise, but another moved now across the slope to the west, and its shepherd waved elaborately. Good. Two more bartons coming to drill. Even so, even with the shepherd's signals, he would take the usual precautions.

"Weapons into the sheepfold," he said. "Another barton's coming in." Much more quickly than before, they obeyed, laying the scythes out of sight behind the low walls of the pens. Two of the women began to cut thistles with their sickles, gathering them into their aprons. The men with shepherds' crooks leaned on the low-roofed lambing hut and began talking sheepbreeding. The others hid in the lambing hut itself. Gird sat on one of the walls, and caught his breath.

"Sir? Gird?" That was Per, the nominal yeoman marshal of this barton.

"Just Gird, Per. You've got a good group here." It would be a good group after a year of enough to eat and heavy training, but it would do no good to say that.

"I'm sorry about Tam's scythe. I—there's so much I don't know—"

"Don't worry. You can't do it all; that's why I tell them they have to maintain their own weapons. You've done a lot: eighteen, and fifteen scythes."

"Three women," muttered Per. Gird shot him a glance.

"You believe the lords' sayings about women, Per?"

"Well, no, but—"

"Our women have suffered with us all these years. We never kept them safe; they've borne the lords' children, and lost them if they had one touch of magic: you know that. Now they ask to learn fighting with us: if our pain has earned that right for us, theirs has earned it for them."

"But they're not as strong—"

Gird bit back another sharp remark, and said instead, "Per, we don't ask anyone to be strongest, or stronger. Just strong enough."

"Whatever you say."

"No. Whatever you finally see is right—dammit, Per, that's what this is about. Not just my way—not just Gird instead of your lord or the king, but a fair way for everyone. You, me, our women, our children. Fair for everyone."

"Fair for the lords?"

Gird snorted, caught off guard. "Well—maybe not for them. They had their chance." He pushed himself off the wall. The incoming bartons had joined somewhere along the way, and were marching some thirty strong, all in step and clearly proud of themselves. He could not tell, at this distance, exactly what weapons they carried, but at least some of them were scythes. Per's foot began to tap the beat as the formation came nearer. Gird let himself think what they could do with some decent armor, some real weapons. They were marching like soldiers, at least, and impressing the less experienced group he'd been working with. He called those in the lambing shed out to watch as the yeoman marshal of Hightop brought the formation to a halt.

They had a short rest, then all three bartons began drilling together. Almost fifty, Gird reckoned them up, a half-cohort as the lords would call it, most with staves. For the first time, Gird could *see* them facing real troops, the lords' militia, with a chance to win. He marched them westward, away from the sheepfolds, got them reversed, reversed again, and then tried to convince them that when the column turned, it turned in only one place. Those behind were not to cut the corner, but march to the corner, and turn. Again, and another tangle. He sorted it out, and got them moving again.

It was then that a shepherd's piercing whistle broke through the
noise of their marching. Gird looked around, already knowing what
it had to be. There, to the east, a mounted patrol out of Lord
Kerrisan's holding; already they'd been spotted. He saw the flash
of sunlight on a raised blade. His mind froze, refusing to work for
a moment. Someone else saw them, and moaned. He turned to
see his proud half-cohort collapsing, some already turning to run,
others with weapons loose in their hands. The sun seemed brighter;
he could see every detail, from the sweat on their faces to the dust
on their eyelashes.

"We have to get away," said Per in a shaky voice. He heard the
murmur of agreement, a grumble of dissent.

"We'll never make it," breathed someone else, and a heavy voice
demanded "Who *told* them we were out here?"

"It's a random patrol," Gird answered, without really thinking
about it. "A tensquad, no spears—if they'd known we were here
they'd have sent more, and more weapons. Archers, lancers." He
glanced at the horsemen, now forming a line abreast. One of them
had a horn, and blew a signal. Two of the horsemen peeled off,
rode at an easy canter to either side. "They're circling, to pen us—"

"But what can we do?" asked someone at the back of the clump
that had once been a fighting formation.

I ask for a sign, and I get this, Gird sent silently to the blazing
sun. *Lord of justice, where are you now?* A gust of wind sent a
swirl of dust up his nose, and he sneezed. "I'll tell you what we
can do," he said, turning on his ragged troops the ferocity that had
no other outlet. "We can quit standing here like firewood waiting
the axe, and *line up! Now!*" A few had never shifted; a few moved
back, others forward. Two at the back bolted. "*No!*" To his surprise,
his voice halted them; they looked back. "Run and you're dead.
We're all dead. By the gods, this is what we've been training *for*.
Now get in your places, and pick up your weapons, and *listen*
to me."

The others moved, after nervous glances at the slowly moving
horsemen, back into their places. Gird grinned at them. "And get
those weapons *ready!*" Far too slowly, the scythes and sickles and
crooks and sticks came forward. At once Gird could see what was
wrong, besides not having anything but a knife and short cudgel of
his own. They could face only one way, and he knew, knew without
even trying it, that they'd never reverse in formation, with weapons
ready. There had to be a way—what could work? In his mind, he
saw his mother's pincushion, pins sticking out all ways—but then
how could they move? There was no time; the horsemen were

closing, still at a walk, but he knew they would break to a trot or canter any moment. They must be a little puzzled by a mass of peasants who weren't trying to run, weren't screaming in fear.

"We have to kill them all," Gird said, as calmly as if he knew they could do it. "When they're close enough to fight, they can recognize you. The only way you can be safe back on your farms, is if you kill them all. That's what all this drill is for, and now you're going to use it." All those eyes stared right at his, blue and gray and brown. He felt as if someone were draining all the strength from his body; they were pulling it out of him, demanding it. "You can do it," he said, not pleading but firmly, reminding them. Never mind that this wasn't the best place for a small group of half-trained peasants to fight a mounted troop. Make do, make it work anyway. Miss this chance and you'll not have another. *I'll be safely dead,* he thought wryly.

Almost automatically, the formation had chosen the side facing the horsemen as the front. Gird walked quickly along it, nodding, and then, talking as he worked, shifted those on the flank and rear to face out. "If they come from two directions, we have to be ready. You turn like this—yes—facing out, and you behind him— yes, you—you put your crook here. You, with the stick—poke at their eyes."

"But do we hit the horse or the man?" asked someone behind him. This group had never drilled against even imaginary horses.

"The horse," said Gird. "If you hurt the horse, either it'll run or the man will fall off. Now think—you want to open a big hole—"

He heard the hoofbeats louder now, and faster. Sure enough, they were trotting towards him, eight horsemen with their swords out and shining in the sun. The horses looked huge, and their hooves pounded the dry ground. The two sent around the peasant formation had stopped: clearly they were intended to prevent run-aways. The horsemen yelled, a shrill wavering cry, and Gird yelled back, instinctively. His motley troop yelled, too, a sound half-bellow and half-scream of fear. Two of the horses shied, to be yanked back into line by their riders. The peasants yelled again, louder; the riders spurred to a full charge. Belatedly, the other two riders charged the back side of the formation.

He was still thinking *I hope this works* when the riders crashed into the block of peasants. The horses' weight and speed drove them into the formation, but five of them died before they cleared the other side. Gird himself slammed his cudgel into one horse's head, leaping aside to let it stagger past into the sickle of the woman behind him. The rider missed his swing at Gird, but got the woman's arm; someone buried a scythe in his back before he could swing again. Two riders were dragged from their mounts and stabbed; another took a scythe in the belly before sliding sideways off his horse, screaming. Gird saw one of the women with a simple pole poke one rider off-balance; someone else caught his sword-arm and stabbed him as he fell.

It was over in minutes. Ten horsemen lay dead or dying on the ground; seven horses were dead, two crippled, and one, spooked, galloped away to the west. Gird looked around, amazed. The woman who had lost an arm sat propped against a dead horse, holding the stump and trying not to cry. Eight were dead; two others badly hurt. But—but peasants on foot, with no weapons but the tools of their work, had defeated armed men on horseback. Not an equal fight, but a real one.

He knew he should say something to them, but he couldn't think of anything fitting. He looked around the horizon, and saw only the sentinel shepherd, waving that no danger neared. Per came up to him, bleeding from a gash on his scalp, bruised, amazed to be alive. They all were. Per nodded at the woman who'd lost an arm, and said "Gird—I see now."

"Do you?" He felt a thousand years older as his fury drained away. It had to be better to die this way, fighting in the open, than rotting in dungeons or worked to hunger and sickness, but those silent bodies had been people a few minutes before. That woman had had two hands. He nodded at Per, and walked over to crouch beside her. Someone else had already torn a strip of cloth from her skirt to tie around the stump. "You—?"

She had gone pale, now, the gray-green pallor before fainting or death, but she managed a shaky smile, and moved her other hand, still gripping the sickle. "I—killed the horse."

"You did."

"I—fought—they—died—"

"Yes."

"All?"

"All."

"Good." With that she crumpled, and before they had finished sorting out the dead and wounded, she had died.

"Noooo!" That scream came from one of the other women, who fell sobbing on the dead one's body. Then she whirled to face Gird, her face distorted. "You let her die! You—you killed her—and this is what happens—" She waved her arms to encompass the whole bloody scene. "You said fight to live, but she's dead, and Jori and Tam and Pilan—" Her voice broke into wild sobbing. Gird could think of nothing to say: she was right, after all. The woman had died, and seven others, and the two worst wounded would probably die, even if their lord didn't notice their wounds and kill them for that. The ten horsemen had probably had lovers or wives, maybe children—the weight of that guilt lay on his shoulders. But another voice, thick with pain, spoke out.

"Nay, Mirag! Rahi's dead, but she died happy, knowing she'd fought well. Not in a cage in the castle, like young Siela, when she tried to refuse that visiting duke, and not hanging from a hook on the wall, screaming for hours, like Varin. Gird promised us a chance, not safety."

"You say that, with that hole in you, with your heart's blood hot on your side? What will Eris say, tonight, when she has no one beside her: what will your children say?"

The man coughed, and wiped blood from his mouth. "Eris knows I'm here, and she knows why. If she weren't heavy for bearing, she'd be here herself, and the little ones too. This is best, Mirag. Rahi's satisfied, and I'm satisfied, and if you keep whining along like that, I'll say out what I think should happen to you!"

The woman paled, and her mouth shut with a snap. The man looked at Gird.

"She's not bad, Marig—Rahi's her sister."

"I'm sorry," It was all he could say. Marig shrugged, an abrupt jerk of her shoulder; the man beckoned with a finger and Gird went to him.

"D'you know much of healer's arts?" Gird shook his head "Might should learn, then. If I'd been able, I'd've put a tighter band on Rahi's arm. You'll need that craft, Gird."

"You'll get well, and be our healer," said Gird, but the man shook his head.

"Nay—this is a killing wound, but slower than some. Blood'll choke me, inside. But you'd best get all away, before more trouble comes."

A flick of memory, of his old sergeant's words long ago, came to Gird. "We won't leave wounded here, to be taken and questioned."

The man grinned tightly. "I hoped you'd think so. Make it quick, then."

"Is there anyone you'd—?"

"You'll do. You made it work." Gird grimaced; he had to have someone else agree, or it would feel like simple murder. He called Per over, and Aris, the yeoman marshal of Hightop. The wounded man was still conscious enough to give his assent again, and Aris, slightly more experienced than Per, saw at once why it must be done.

But neither would do it. So Gird took his well-worn dagger, and knelt by the man's side, and wondered how he'd feel if he were lying there, bleeding inside and choking, and how he could be quickest. Worst would be weakness, another pain that did not kill. So he put the whole strength of his arm into it, slicing almost through the man's neck.

The other badly injured man was unconscious, having been hit in the head, and then trampled under a horse. He quit breathing, with a last gasping snort, just as Gird reached him. Then it was only the hard, bloody work of dragging the corpses together onto a pile of brushwood and thistles, stacking what weapons they could use to one side. The group from Per's barton left first, to enter their village as best they might without attracting attention. They dared not carry any of the spare weapons, and Gird cautioned them not to take personal belongings from their friends' bodies.

"They'll know someone was here," he said, "to start the fire. But if you're carrying a tool or trinket someone recognizes, they'll know you, too, were part of it. This way it can seem that everyone from this village died, and it might spare you trouble." Not really, he knew: there was going to be trouble for everyone—but there had always been.

They seemed calm enough, even Marig. She had quit sobbing, at least, and she laid the locket she'd taken from her sister's neck back on her without being told twice. "Can't we even take Tam's scythe?" one man asked. "We don't have that many." His own crook had shattered. Gird shook his head again.

"With so few scythes, everyone will know that Tam's is with you. It'll be taken, but not to your village." He nodded to Per, who started them off, in trickles of two or three, moving indirectly.

Aris had the other two bartons ready to move out; each one carried his or her own weapon, and some them carried a second, taken from the fallen. Gird dithered over the swords. For one of them to be found carrying a soldier's sword meant instant death— but to lose all those blades—In the end he let them decide, and ten volunteers belted swords they could not use around their peasant jerkins.

"Are you sure you need to burn the bodies?" Aris asked. Gird said nothing; he'd never imagined doing anything else. It was in all the tales. "We'll need a good start of them," Aris went on, when Gird didn't answer. "They'll have horses near enough—we don't know but what the smoke could be seen a long way, and the horses

might come anyhow, and find us on the way. I don't know—I don't
know if I could lead another fight today."

"You could if you had to," said Gird, plunged once more into
how different it was in stories and reality. But Aris made sense, and
he looked at the stacked bodies. The smoke would draw attention;
someone would come, and that someone would likely be mounted,
and ready for trouble. No smoke, and another patrol would go
looking for the first—might not find them right away—but to let
the dead lie out unprotected? He squinted up, and saw the first
dark wings sailing far up. That alone would draw attention.

"All right," he said, finally. "No fire." *Lady, bless these dead—
these brave and helpless—* Aris nodded, clearly relieved, and set
off with his bartons. Gird angled away from them, his own new
sword heavy at his side. *Did I do the right thing?* he asked himself.
Am I doing the right thing now?

He looked back from a farther ridge, some hours later, and saw
a column of dark wings. The woman's face came to him, that face
so composed, even as she died, and the thought of dark beaks
tearing her face, gouging out her eyes—he stopped abruptly, and
threw up on the short grass, retching again and again, and scrubbing the dried blood on his hands. Nor could that be the end of
it: he had started something, back there, that no crow could pick
clean, and no fox bury the bones of—he had started something, like
a boy rolling a rock down a hillside, and the end would be terrible.

Word of the Norwalk battle spread as fast among the lords as
among the bartons. Gird, sifting reports from his runners and spies,
spared a moment for amazement at the varying interpretations. By
the end of the first day, that column of carrion crows had attracted
another patrol. By the end of the second, the little village of Berryhedge had been put to the torch, and the villagers—those who
had not fled the first night—were dead or penned in the nearest
fort's yard, to be dealt with at the next court. The other two bartons
had made it home safely, and so far their stolen blades had not
been discovered. Bruises and cuts alone were not suspicious; too
many of the farmfolk suffered injuries in their work year-round for
that to be a sign of collaboration. But all the lords' guards were
alert, watching for smoke from illicit fires, searching for weapons,
stopping travelers on the roads. It was, some said, a huge army—
an invasion from the neighboring kingdom of Tsaia—the private
war of one lord on another—the peasant uprising that had been
feared so long. On the strength of one escaped horse, and its tracks,
someone even decided that it had been an attack by cavalry, using

peasants as infantry. No, argued another: it was an alliance of horse nomads and peasants.

To Gird's surprise, some bartons now wanted to march out looking for patrols to fight. He reminded them of the dead and wounded, the village destroyed. But this was the first time that his people had fought, in military formation, against their old enemies, and they were elated.

"I can't see why you aren't happier about it," Felis said. "It worked, just as you said it would. Losses, yes: you had warned us, no war without deaths, without wounded. We understand that. But it worked. If we keep drilling, keep working, we can stand against them. And there are more of us; the numbers are on our side."

"I am happy." Even to himself, Gird did not sound happy, and he knew it. "I am—I just see the other side. Felis, we have only one real chance: we have to do it *all,* and do it right, because if we don't, then everyone who dies has died for nothing."

"It's not for nothing; it's for freedom." Felis scratched his sunburnt nose, and stalked around a moment before coming back to plant himself in front of Gird. "Look—you found a way for us to stand against their weapons and their training. It worked. Not even with the best of us, who've been training years now, but with one barton so new they hardly knew their left feet from their right. If you can do it with that, you can do it with anyone. Lady's grace, Gird, the day you walked into our camp I wouldn't believe you could get my men to pick up their own filth. But you did. What's wrong now?"

Gird could not answer. He knew, as he knew the ache in his bones, that it was not that easy. It could not be that easy. But they needed him to say it was, to cheer them on, to give the simple answer he knew was not enough. He felt himself resisting, as he had once or twice when the steward put pressure on him, as if he were a tree, rooting himself deep in the ground. The one thing he knew, the one thing he had to give, was his own certainty when he was right—and if he did not know he was right, he could not say it.

Felis, he could see, did not like his expression or that refusal to rejoice in their victory. Nor did others, who visibly damped their own glee when he was around. He should do it—but when he opened his mouth, stretched it in a smile, nothing came out. *We won,* he told himself, and the depths of his mind, cautious as any farmer to the last, said *We won that time.*

He was not even sure what it would take to win, in the way he meant win, in the way that would bring lasting peace. He threw himself into more planning, trying to calculate how many yeomen they had by now, and where, and trying to picture the larger country in which his war would now take place. A few soldiers had defected, men ordered to burn their own villages, or seize their own relatives, men who faced in adulthood what Gird had faced as a boy. They knew more of tactics than he did, and insisted that he had to have support in the towns, as well as the farms.

Meanwhile, the conflicts continued. Another ambush, and another. A guard encampment attacked at night; another village burned, and its fields torched. Like it or not, ready or not, it was on him; he must fly on that wind, or be left behind. Gird drove himself and those he knew best, traveling far to meet the yeoman-marshals of other bartons, to speak to those who were not sure, who were afraid. By autumn, he was moving far beyond the villages and fields he knew best, trusting those he had trained to keep his own group working, to find a safe wintering. This next year would see whole villages rise—even before planting time—and he had to be ready to lead his army in the field.

Chapter Sixteen

Something rasped, in the dry winter bushes, a sound too small for a cry, too great for a wild thing slipping away. Gird crouched, stock still, wondering whether to run now or investigate. It could be—it was probably—a trap. Someone had talked, and the town guard were out here to catch him. The sound came again, and with it another, like a sob choked down. Trickery, it would be. They were trying to lure him that way. But even as he thought this, he was moving, carefully as he might, threading his way through the prickly stiff brush.

In the gloom, he nearly stepped on the naked, bruised body that lay curled on its side. He stooped, after a hard look around that showed nothing but more brush. A man, an old man with thin gray hair and beard. One eye had been gouged out; the other showed only bloodshot white behind an enormous bruise. The man's pale skin bore many bruises, scratches where the bushes had torn at him, whip marks on his back, burns on his hands and feet. Yet he was alive, his breathing unsteady and loud, but strong enough, and he had a steady pulse at his neck.

Gird squatted on his heels, considering. It was already cold, and would be colder with full night. An old man, beaten and burned, missing an eye—he'd likely die by morning, left here with no covering and no care. But inside the town, the barton waited. Even now they'd be gathering, waiting for him, waiting for the hope that only he could bring. And the old man might die anyway. Gird touched the old man's shoulder, then wished he hadn't, for the bloodshot eye opened.

"No . . ." breathed a tremulous voice.

"You're safe," said Gird, knowing he lied, but not what else to say.

"Cold . . ." came a murmur.

"It's all right." His mind went back to his own home, the times he'd teased one of the women for that soothing "It's all right," when it wasn't. He could understand that now. It didn't make things all right. With a gusty sigh—too loud a sigh, he thought instantly: it would carry in the quiet twilight—Gird stripped to the waist and laid his shirt, sweaty as it was, on the old man's body. He had to have his dark jerkin for later . . . but he could spare the shirt.

"I'll help you," he said, and put his arm under the old man's shoulder. Groaning, and obviously trying to smother it, the old man managed to get his arms into Gird's shirt.

"You—should not—"

"I can't leave you here to die," said Gird. He couldn't help it that the words came out harsh, not comforting. He was late, and he was going to be later yet, and if he had to climb in over the wall, he was very likely to be seen.

"Who?" Now wrapped in the shirt, the old man had recovered scraps of his dignity; he asked with little volume but much authority. Gird chose to misunderstand the question.

"Who beat you? I don't know; I just found you. You don't remember?"

The old man held up his hands—longfingered, graceful hands, for all the ugly burns—and said softly, "Esea's light be with you, the High Lord's justice come to you, the Lady of Peace lay her hand on your brow—" He paused, as Gird scrambled back, careless of noise. "What's wrong?"

"Don't curse me!" It was hardly louder than the old man's murmur, but the anger in it carried.

"Curse you?" The old man chuckled, a breathy sound much like the whuffling of a horse. "Lad, it's a *blessing*—I'm giving you my blessing. Don't you know that much?"

Gird shifted uneasily. "What I know is, the longer we stay here, the likelier we'll be seen. Whoever beat you—"

"The senior priest at Esea's hall," said the old man. He was sitting up on his own, now, looking with apparently idle curiosity at the burns on his feet. "He called me a heretic, and held what he would call a trial by fire. I call that torture, but the law permits it. And as I lived still when he was done, they stripped and beat me and threw me off the wall."

"You should be dead!" said Gird, and then reddened, realizing how it sounded.

The old man chuckled again. "That's what the high priest said, in other words—that I should be dead, for the harm I'd done and might do, and he did his best. The gods, however, sent you—" He reached around, in the gathering darkness, as if groping for a staff, then stretched his hand to Gird. "Here, then. Help me up."

"But you can't—"

"I can't lie here in the cold in your shirt. Come now—give me your hand. It's not so bad as you think." Gird reached out, and felt the man's hand slide into his. It was bony, as old hands are, with loose skin over the knuckles, but stronger than he expected. And he could not feel, against his own horny palm, the crusted burns he expected. The old man staggered once, then stood, peering about. "Ah—" he said finally. "There they are." Gird looked, and saw nothing but the chest-high bushes disappearing into evening gloom. "If you will wait," the old man said, more command than request, and he plunged into the tangle without making a sound. Gird waited, although he was definitely going to have to climb the wall. The barton would be wondering if he'd been caught.

When the old man came back, he had a very dirty ragged garment slung around his shoulders, over Gird's shirt, and some kind of covering on his feet. It looked, in that light, much like the rags peasants wore wrapped around their feet in winter, when they had nothing better.

"Now, lad," he said, far more briskly than Gird would have thought possible. "Now we can go into town without fear."

Gird opened his mouth to argue, but instead found himself retracing his path through the bushes, the old man's hand clenched firmly on his elbow. The old man's other hand held Gird's staff. Without fear? Did the old man plan to ask the gate guards to let them in, when he'd been beaten and left for dead? What was he?

When they came to the gates, the postern was still open, and the last few townspeople were hurrying in. A row of torches burned brightly, lighting their faces for the guards to see. Gird tried to shy aside, into the shadows, but the old man's hand forced him to walk right up the middle of the trade road, into that golden light. He thought frantically how he could get out of this without alerting the guards, and glanced sideways at the old man.

In torchlight, the old man looked altogether different. Smaller, crook-backed, with a dry seamed scar where his eye had been, not the red dripping socket Gird had seen. Almost bald on top, and a wisp of pure white at his chin, a patched leather cape over a rough wool shirt (and it doesn't even look like my shirt, thought Gird), patched leather breeches on bowed legs, feet indeed wrapped in dirty rags. He leaned on Gird's arm, and the staff, as if his legs could hardly bear his weight.

"Ho, there!" One of the guards stepped forward, lifting a torch to peer at their faces. "And who be you, coming in so late—don't know your face!"

Gird opened his mouth, and found a name in it. "Amis of Barle's village, m'lord, and m'father's father Geris, come to pilgrimage at th'shrine."

"Should've come earlier; the gate's closed to outsiders."

At this the old man mewled, an infantile wail of misery and disappointment. The guard grinned, insolent but not unkind. "Never seen anyone needed a miracle more, and that's a fact. Got any honey to sweeten the sib, Amis of Barle's?"

"Honey, m'lord?" Gird let his jaw hang down stupidly, and patted his "grandfather's" hand. "We's no bees, m'lord, that's for them's got orchard trees. But we's barley-cake—" He fished in his jerkin for the stale end of barley cake he'd saved from breakfast, and offered it. Whatever was going on, he was supposed to pretend stupidity and meekness. The guardsman looked at him, long and steady, then pushed it back. "If that's all you've had, coming in from so far, keep it. Now, gransire, we've had an upset today, and I'll have to see your hands before you enter."

"Hands?" asked Gird before he thought. The one on his arm squeezed hard, hard as a strong young man, and released him. The guard nodded.

"In case a thief tries to sneak back in," he said. "He's hand-branded, that one, and we're to look at all strangers, especially those with one eye gone. I'm sure your gransire isn't the thief, but I must look." And he took each of the old man's knotted hands, and looked at the palm. So did Gird—and saw nothing but old pink skin, marked by heavy work. The guard jerked his chin up. "Get on in, fellow, you and your gransire, and be sure you're not

up to any mischief this night. Beggars' steps on the winter side of
Hall, and no laying up in someone's doorway."

"Thanks, m'lord." Gird found himself pulling his forelock before
he thought of it, and edged by the guard with care for his
companion.

Once through the town's wall, the old man used his grip of Gird's
elbow to guide him toward the main square. The streets were busy
yet, full of people who knew exactly where to go. Gird had his own
directions from the gate, but he went where the old man wanted
him to—he had no choice.

In the square, a few stalls still had shutters open. A bakery, its
main doors closed, sold the remnants of the day's baking out a
broad window. From one stall came the sour smell of bad ale, from
another the stomach-churning scent of hot oil and frying meat. Gird
swallowed his hunger, and found that his tongue now responded to
his own will.

"I've somewhere to go," he said gruffly. "Can you find a safe
place?"

"Better than you," said the old man. "Could you have come
through the gates alone?"

Gird grunted. Of course he couldn't, not that late, but if it hadn't
been for the old man, he wouldn't have been that late. "I don't
understand you," he said. "You were hurt, you could hardly
move—"

"We can't stand here in the open talking," said the old man. "I
want my supper." This last became a weak whine, suitable to the
aged cripple he seemed to be, and Gird was not surprised to see
a couple of guards walk by, scanning the faces as they went.

"I don't have anything but that barley cake," said Gird, and
added unwillingly, as the guards paused, "Granther, you know that.
It took all coppers we's got to make this trip for your eye. Here—"
He fished out the barley cake, and broke it, as the guards watched.
The old man took his share in a shaky hand, almost whimpering
in his eagerness. A drop of spittle ran down his chin into his beard,
glittering in the guards' torchlight.

"Beggars' steps over there," said one of the guards gruffly, gesturing across the square. Gird bobbed his head, hoping he looked
stupid and harmless. The guards moved on, stopping to joke with
the baker's lass, as she reached to close the shutters at the window.
The old man touched Gird's arm, pushing him gently towards the
beggars' steps.

When they sank down on the lowest of the five steps, Gird
stuffed his piece of barley cake back into his jerkin, and said again

"I have somewhere I must go. Can you stay here? Will they find you?"

In the dimness, the old man's face was suddenly more visible, as if a candle had been lit inside it. "Lad, I can stay here, or go, or stay with you, and they will not find me—have you seen nothing this evening?"

"Riddles," said Gird. "You give me tricks and riddles—"

"I give you light in darkness." The old man's face shone brighter, then dimmed. "But the blind cannot see light, and think darkness is reality."

Gird stirred on the cold step, not sure what he could say. The old man was mad, and no wonder, with what he'd been through. He must have been one of *them*—perhaps one of their elder mages—and he'd angered someone. They'd taken their revenge, and wrecked his mind as well as his body. Probably as bad as the rest of them, when he was whole, but now—"I need to go now," he said, as gently as he could. "I'll come back you."

"Yes," said the old man. "You will." He bit off a chunk of the barley cake, and started chewing it. Gird watched a moment, feeling a strange confusion in his mind, then shook his head and got up.

The meeting place, when he finally found it, was a merchant's storeroom crowded with nervous men, at least a dozen of them, and lit by two candles. He'd expected only the elders of the barton, but apparently others had insisted on coming. Was this a trap? He tried to see the corners of the storeroom as he gave the password again, but darkness lurked behind bales and boxes as if it were alive and twitching. His neck itched; he wanted to whirl and look behind himself, but he controlled that urge.

Calis, the only man he'd met before, limped forward to shake his arm and then grinned broadly at the rest. "I told you he'd come. Whatever happens, he'd come."

"He's late." That was a square-built, black-bearded man, with a look of authority and the weathered face of someone out in the open most of his life.

"He's here. That's what counts." Calis shook his arm again. "Lady bless you, Gird, for coming. You'll lead us, eh? Make us free?"

Calis had not sounded that simple back in Harrow, when he visited that barton's drill. Then he had seemed a possible leader, someone who could organize a barton, start its training. Gird looked around as calmly as he might, trying to figure out what had gone wrong here. Fifteen men, no women—that was still common enough, despite his urging. None very young: quite right, at such a secret meeting; young men talked too much. None very old. Four held themselves with a kind of furious rigidity: men used to command, perhaps, pretending a passivity they could not feel? Gird smiled at the black-bearded man. "Hurry makes the fleet fall, and the aim wide: I came as I might, to come safely."

"You would preach safety in war?" That was another of the four he'd noted, a tall brown bear of a man leaning against the stacked boxes across from him.

"I preach nothing, being no priest. As Calis will have told you, I expect—" He glanced at Calis, whose gaze slid past him. So. Trouble indeed. "I teach what seems obvious to me, that wild rebellion against the king but causes death and torment."

"And this is what we came for?" The brown man pushed away from the boxes to confront him. "We came to hear the same song the priests sing: obey, submit, seek peace from the Lady in your hour of death?"

"Gird, *tell* them. Tell them what you told us at Harrow."

The worst trouble: treachery. Their first rule was never to mention one barton in another, to say only "there" or "that other place" or "his barton." Gird shook Calis's hand from his arm, but without violence, and tried to decide where the worst danger lay. He could not fight fifteen, were they all of the same mind, but it was just as likely that Calis had tried to entrap honest rebels as well as one rebel leader. If he could but find them out, and lead them. A dense silence packed the room thicker than the men. Someone behind the black-bearded man coughed. Was it a signal?

Gird glanced around the group, meeting all eyes but Calis's. In the candlelight, all glittered; he could not tell false from true. He lifted his hand for silence, though all were quiet, and began.

"You know the times are bad. You know they're getting worse. Bad enough when peasants are murdered at their work, when wives and mothers are raped and beaten, left for dead with their babies crawling in their blood. Worse, when the craftsman's skill is bought with pain and threats, when a smith must make shackles and chains for prisoners, not plows and harrows for farming. Bad enough when merchants' goods are stolen for the rich, and they must cheat the poor to survive." He looked from face to face. There one closed, tight with anger—for old wrongs, or for his words? Another sat slack-jawed, as if he could drink Gird's words in, taste them on his tongue. There in the dim shadows at the back, two heads leaned together, mouth to ear.

"You know there's been fighting—everyone knows that. Men and women have died, for trying to save their own lives. You know that all the times farmers and craftsmen and merchants have tried to fight against trained soldiers, they've been killed, and their families with them. What I'm telling you is about another way."

"A way for peasants to fight soldiers?" asked the black-bearded man.

"A way for peasants to *be* soldiers." Gird paused. That was the nub of it, and enough to have him hanged. He sensed a stirring back in the shadows. Well, he need not mince words now, having already convicted himself, and maybe boldness would gather a few to his side. "The difference between soldiers and hopeless fools willing to die is training. Not fine swords, nor magic, but training— the training soldiers have."

"And you can give us that training?" *That* voice came from wealth and privilege, with its arrogant sonorities. Gird smiled straight at it.

"I? I'm a farmer: I *give* nothing. But I know how you can *earn* that training, and that's my reason here." Out of the gloom sea-green eyes stared into his. He could just make out a foxy brush of hair, a slender figure no longer lounging in the shadows but upright, alert. Odds it was some noble's son, come to spit rebels with his guards around him to keep him safe.

"Gods know, farmers give nothing." That voice again, this time clearly belonging to green eyes and an arrogant set of head and shoulders. "That sounds like kapristi talking, if a farmer knows what kapristi are." He didn't, but he caught the muttered "Gnomes!" of another.

"Farmers earn their bread," Gird said, working his toes in his boots to ready himself. It had to come soon. "As craftsmen do, and merchants too, most times. What's earned feeds; what's given rots the belly. What's taken—" He stopped as light dazzled his eyes, light that polished the blades drawn against him. He saw no source, but it centered on the brown man.

"What's taken belongs to the taker," said he, amusement ruffling the edge of his voice. "Traitors taken, in this town, belong to me." He stood easily, weaponless, but from behind the stacked boxes had come two guards, with pikes, and four of the other men had drawn swords. To Gird's surprise, the green-eyed man wasn't one of them: his face drew back, shocked into loss of its earlier dignity. Calis stood dithering, clearly wondering whether to seize Gird or retreat to the safety of shadows.

"What's taken," Gird said, meeting the brown man's eyes, "chokes the taker." His fingers clenched and loosened, and he realized then that he'd left his stout staff with the old man on the beggars' steps. *Idiot* he told himself. *You're asking the gods for a miracle.* The brown man gave a smile that might have been genuine admiration.

"You're brave, at least—no whining craven like most of your type. Too bad you didn't choose honest soldiery, fellow—"

"I tried," said Gird, keeping his voice level with an effort. He was not sure why he bothered to answer, save that he had no plan, and saw little help in the faces of others. "As a lad, I joined my count's guard right willingly. But then—"

"What?" asked the brown man, lifting a hand to halt the guards who had moved a step nearer. Gird looked at him, seeing nothing like the vindictive arrogance of his own count. Those eyes might have been honest; that mouth had laughed honestly, at things worth amusement, not at others' pain. Well, it would serve nothing, but he would tell this man the truth, and if one of them lived after his night, that one would know it had been told.

"The lord of our village came from the king's court with his friends, to celebrate his coming of age. One of the village lads chose that confusion to steal plums from the lord's orchard—" Gird paused, and the man nodded for him to go on. Despite himself, his voice trembled over the next phrases, and he forced more breath into it, almost growling at the end. "So our lord had him taken, which was just enough, and had him tormented and finally maimed, which was not just, not for a few plums. And he enjoyed the sight, gloating over the boy's pain, and I—" He stopped again, drew in a great breath. "I was hardly older; I'd known Meris all my life." His accent thickened, he could tell the brown man had trouble following it now. "I knew—I knew someday they'd tell me the same, to hurt or kill some poor lad as only wanted a handful of plums or a truss of grapes. Kill m'own folk, maybe, if in a bad year th'cows wandered. I couldna do that—could not—and so I ran, and it fell hard on my own folk even when I came back."

"You're from Kelaive's domain," the brown man said, softly. "That insolent pup, worst of a bad litter. I'd heard that tale differently."

"Certain so, if *he* told it," said Gird, caught up as always in that old pain, but also, suddenly curious to know how Kelaive told it.

"Not from him: his sergeant told one of my guards, and it passed to me on one long march—a good soldier ruined, he said, by a bad lord's whim, and the blame fell on him, too, for not knowing how to keep you." The man shook his head. "Well. You know the law, that's clear, and your place in it. You had a bad master; that's no excuse—"

"And what would be?" asked Gird, his voice tight with unshed tears and old anger still caged. "Would my mother's death, when that count refused the simples of the wood to us? Would our hunger, in a bad winter when Kelaive danced in the king's hall and laid double taxes on, to buy himself more gowns? Would my daughter's pain, her own babe by her lover dead, and her raped to bear a stranger's child? Cows stolen to make his feasts, sheep taken to give him wool—by all the gods, we farmers may not give, but we take better care of our least creatures than you lords do of us. Prod an ox and it kicks, and even a beaten cur will turn and bite your heel—"

"Peace, fellow!" The brown man stared at him. "Esea's dawn, but you've a long tongue in your head, and wit in that thick skull. A hard use dulls most tools, but those of high temper—" He stopped, gestured, and the four drawn swords rasped back into their sheaths, though the guards stayed as they were, poised just behind him. "See here: would you take service with me, you and your family safe from Kelaive, and quit this nonsense? You'll be killed, elsewise, and your family take the brunt of Kelaive's bad will: by law I must report those rebels I seize."

He might have done it, had not Calis seized his hand and rushed into speech. "Yes, Gird, yes! He's a good lord, he is, and fair and just—he'll keep his word to you—" But under the rush of words was fear, and in the other eyes he saw the same fear trembling. He shook off Calis's hand, and met the brown man's eyes.

"You will protect me, you say." The brown man nodded, gravely. "But what of these others? You may be trying to be a good lord, sir—" The sir came out slowly, but inexorably, "—but here are those who thought you bad enough to join a plot against you." He waved his hand around at those who clearly wished they could be invisible. "You may be better than Kelaive—I dare say you are, and it should be easy enough. But you can't protect all those that need it, and it looks like you haven't protected all your own, even."

The brown man looked around; Gird watched the men flinch as he looked at each one slowly. "Cobbler. Wheelwright. Cloth merchant. Baker's helper. You think to make a government out of such as these, farmer? Who'll make your laws? Who'll judge in your courts?"

"Honest men, sir." He didn't want to say "sir," to someone who would either kill him, or be killed, this night, but he found himself doing it anyway. And he could not hate this man, who was so much more reasonable than Kelaive.

"Honest *merchants*?" Scorn edged the brown main's voice. Gird noticed one of the men stiffen: that had gone home. "You think to find honest judges from a tangle of merchants who pour water in the milk, or chalk in flour they sell you. Or among farmers who put the bruised fruit in the basket first, or craftsmen who put as much base metal in gold or silver as they can?"

"As near there as among nobles, sir," Gird said, and braced himself for the blow that would surely come. The brown man glared at him, showing anger for the first time. "At least among common men, of different trades, there's a chance they'd stick to a measure, not make different weights and measures for each case."

"Damn!" The brown man clenched his fist then opened it. "You *are* a man, after all. I hate—it's too bad you cannot bring yourself to take service here." He glanced aside, at the black-bearded man who had been one of the swordsmen. "Remember what I said, Caer? Squeeze the mud, and it turns to stone; beat the ore and get gold: from the pressure we put on them, such comes out. I would be proud if son of mine had courage to speak so before a deadly peril, had wit to think in bondage." He turned back to Gird. "Death it must be, but a man like you does not fear death. I swear no torment; come quietly and I'll ensure the headsman's single blow. If you must fight, then I cannot interfere, and not all wounds kill cleanly."

For some reason he could not define, Gird felt a change in the room's atmosphere, as if a shutter had opened, letting in fresher air and truer light. He smiled at the brown man. "Sir, it's not my way to give in so easily. But I will admit that had my lord been like you, I might not be here."

"Were my subjects like you, Gird, I might not be here either." He looked around again. "Out of these weaklings, these trimmers, you'd make an army? Were you to have the chance to try, I'd wish you luck of it, but worry none."

Some bright image stung Gird's mind, and he said "Well—if you have no worry, you could let me train them, as a wager, and see if they can withstand trained arms."

The man laughed openly. "Well, indeed, fellow! Wit and tenacity combined! Let you train a score or so of malcontents to harrass my guards, and for a wager—that passes wit, Gird of Kelaive's domain, and near approaches madness. And I should be mad to take such wager."

"But why are you here, if you fear nothing from them?"

The brown man scowled, and a quick flicking glance to the green-eyed youth in the shadows conveyed some urgent menace. "You ask much, fellow. But if you think only subjects have troubled

families, and because you will soon be dead, I'll tell you. That—"
He flicked a hand at the green-eyed youth. "That's my son, one of
them. a true-son, of my lady's breeding. I came because he came,
and knew he came because that bold tailor, there, came to me and
warned me. My son's of an age to seek adventures, to throw off
fatherly wisdom, and stir up excitement—to seek, in a word, such
midnight meetings, secret societies, all that."

"I tried to tell you—" began the youth, but his father's gesture
stopped him.

"He would say that he's done this for me: the lad lies, and all
my beatings never stopped him. He feels deprived, that his brothers' share of my wealth is larger. They've increased it; he's squandered his. So he joins conspiracies against me, but with no real
conviction. He'd most likely have confessed this one in another
season."

"Your son. You love him?"

"Love! He's my son; he's my blood and bone—but he's as craven
as any of these fools about to spend their last breath in prison."

"You'll put him there too?"

"Him? No; he's my son. I may send him off to serve with the
king's army against the nomads, though. Let him freeze his rump
in an icy saddle for a winter, and see if he learns wisdom."

"And so a rich young man, who's had all the chances to do
better, gets off with a half-year's exile from home, while the poor
wretches with him must die—"

"It's necessary," said the brown man roughly.

"Oh, it's necessary," said Gird slowly, drawling it out in caricature
of his own peasant accent. "And it's that makes it necessary for us
to fight. When it comes down to it, your justice is to save your
own blood, and kill what stands in the way."

"So does anyone!" snapped the man, his patience clearly fraying.

"No, sir. I've seen it myself, villagers sharing their few bits of
food so the fewest died. We was all hungry, sir, each one of us,
but we didn't grab for self alone. You don't have to believe it, but
I've seen, and I know, and so does most of these others."

Suddenly, as if he were suspended in the air at the very top of
the room, Gird saw himself from outside, his own heavy-boned
weatherbeaten face, his shaggy thinning hair, his heavy arms gleaming with sweat, his old leather jerkin a little loose where the past
months of travel had thinned his belly. Baggy-kneed breeches,
patched and stained, worn boots badly in need of resoling, no weapons but fists like knotted lumps of hardwood.

And he saw the brown man, and even into the brown man's

mind—saw the slight awe the brown man felt, and the fainter tinge
of disgust that such a lout should speak sense, when his own son
had none. He saw the candlelight quiver on a guard's helmet as
the man shifted slightly; he saw the sides and backs of the other
heads watching him. And he saw the green-eyed man, that had
looked older but was only a youth, sliding a throwing knife from
his sleeve, as he looked at his father.

He was back in himself, yelling *"No!"* in a bellow that raised
dust from the boxes, and throwing himself at the brown man so
fast that the guards could not react. He hit the brown man square,
and knocked him sprawling, just as the blade came spinning out of
the dark, catching light and flickering. It missed them both, and
stuck in the floor, quivering. The guard on that side had seen the
blade whirl past; he turned to face the thrower. The other guard
moved forward to swing at Gird, but met instead the black-bearded
man, who had yanked his sword out to take Gird from behind.
Their weapons rang together, and Gird managed to roll off the
brown man and get out from under them.

Then a second blade flashed through the light and caught Calis
in the throat, even as he pointed a finger to the green-eyed man.
"Traitor," he said. "Call my father in, will you? Try to warn
him?" And as Calis choked in his blood and died, the green-eyed
man had his own sword out, and came into the fight on his own.
He caught the black-bearded man under the ribs from behind, then
parried the guard's pike stroke and danced away. "Brother in law,
are thy ribs sore enough?" The black-bearded man had fallen,
hardly an arm's length from Gird, and blood rolled out from
beneath his hand. The brown man scrambled back, grabbing the
fallen swordsman's weapon.

Gird saw this in a strange inside-out way which left him dazed
for the moment. He had wedged himself between two boxes, and
tore at one with his hands, hoping to loosen a slat he could use to
fight with. Now the other three swordsmen had their weapons
out—but not all on one side. Two struck at the brown man, one
defended; one of the pikemen, by this time had fallen to another
thrown knife, from whom Gird could not see.

Of all the outcomes to such a meeting, he'd never imagined this,
a fight between nobles—and not only nobles, but father and son.
Across the room, he saw one of those he thought true rebels slip
toward the door. Another caught his eye, lifted spread hands. What
could they do? Clearly nothing, but escape—this was no brawl for
unarmed men to meddle in. He could not help watching, though,
as the father stood ground over the black-bearded man, fencing

cautiously against his son's supporter. It was madness to stay—the son must have arranged his invitation, planning to blame the father's death on a stranger, a troublemaker from another land. Yet—as he saw from the edge of his vision another of the onlookers slip out the door—yet he had to know who would win, who would be pursuing him.

The fight went on, the clash of blades surely loud enough to draw notice. None of the combatants bothered with Gird; he might have been a spectator at a wagered match. He wondered if any of those who left were going to alert the city guard. He wondered more at what he saw. The green-eyed son, for all the faults his father claimed, a most skillful swordsman, pressed his father's ally back. The second guard, after a few cautious chopping strokes with the pike, tried to pin his opponent in a corner, but he was taken from the side, by the third man, who opened his belly. The guard groaned and sagged to the floor.

Now the brown man and one friend faced three: his son and his two allies. Gird eyed the fallen pike: he could use *that* if he got hold of it, but how? And to what use should he put it, besides escape—and he could escape now, if he would. Instead, he watched, fascinated, the struggle before him. The brown man, when his guard fell, gave no sign of fear or alarm, but fought the more hardily, his blows coming swift and strong against two, while his remaining friend fought his son. Yet he had to yield ground, backing away from his wounded son-in-law. The green-eyed man opened a gash in his opponent's arm, just as the father managed to slice deeply into one of the two he faced. That one dropped his sword tip to grab at the wound, and the father's sword slid into his neck. But not unscathed—his other opponent stabbed deeply into his thigh, and he staggered. In an instant, he recovered, so that his eager opponent, careless, found himself transfixed on a blade that pierced him to the backbone. His legs failed, and he sagged from the blade, dragging the brown man's arm downward.

Then the son turned, from a deathstroke to his father's friend, and raised his sword. And then Gird moved, scooped up the guard's fallen pike, and swung it like a quarterstaff to knock the son's sword aside. Leaping over the welter of blood and bodies, he tackled the son as he might have tackled a runaway calf, bearing him to the floor with his own great size.

Silence, curiously loud in his ears. Someone groaned; several someones breathed harshly. Under him, the green-eyed man heaved up without success; Gird put a knee in his back and dared look back at the carnage.

He met the level gaze of the brown man, the father, now tight-ening a belt around his bleeding thigh. When he had it knotted to his satisfaction, the brown man pushed himself to his feet, and moved unsteadily to Gird's side, looking down with an expression Gird could not read.

"Well, Jernoth, you've given me quite a problem this time. What can I do with you now?"

"I never meant this—" The voice was husky and strained, with what besides Gird's weight on his back Gird could not tell.

"Maybe not: but you meant mischief enough. What can I do?"

"Kill him," said Gird, without thinking. The brown man's intense gaze shifted to him.

"Kill my son? Who, if others die, might be my heir?"

Gird felt the tremor beneath him, the shiver of hope. "You'd have killed me, sir, as hasn't done you any harm, but saved your life twice this night. Why not him, that did the harm with intent? Do you think such a one should rule—do you think he'll be better than Kelaive?"

"Quiet, you stinking serf!" said the captive. "It doesn't matter what you want. I'm a noble; he won't kill me."

Gird ignored this, and looked straight at the brown man's drawn face. "Sir, a farmer has to cull as well as foster: it's part of good husbandry. Isn't a ruler like a farmer, seeking to improve the quality of his domain?"

"My son—blood of my blood—"

"Your son tried to kill you, and not even openly, in challenge. He's the cause of all these deaths. He was plotting you say, and not for the first time. Any farmer culls stock; foresters cull trees. You'd cull us peasants. Try the knife's edge on your own cheek, before you shave another. Sir."

The brown man picked up the pike Gird had used, and placed the point against his son's neck.

"Get off him."

"Are you—?"

"Get off him, fellow." Gird slid back, catching the son's elbows as he tried to get his arms under him.

"He's lost less blood than you, sir."

"Indeed. And I'm supposed to think you care which of us lives? Such as you hate all nobles; you'd be glad to see us all dead."

"No." Gird sat on the son's hips, one hand clamping the other's elbows behind his back, and fished in his jerkin for the roll of thongs he kept handy. He got it out, plucked one from the tangle, and quickly lashed the younger man's elbows together. "No, sir, I don't hate you, personally. I think you don't see clearly, but you may be trying the best you know how. At least you aren't like Kelaive. And I'm not going to let your son up to kill you, with you so weak."

"And you weren't thinking of taking this pike to me if I fell?"

"No. That's not what I'm here for." He pushed himself up, wondering if the brown man would now swing at him with the pike. He was unhurt; he ought to be able to dodge it easily enough.

"No. I suppose you weren't." The brown man regarded him thoughtfully. "You were here to teach my subjects how to fight my army, but you weren't here to play my son's game and kill me." His eyes closed briefly, and he sighed. "Damn. What a tangle this is—and I wonder why the city guard hasn't been beating the door in? We've made noise enough. Perhaps Jernoth bought them off, too."

"There's no one you can trust," said Jernoth savagely. His father let the pike rest heavier on his neck, and he was silent.

"He could be right," the brown man said. "And I'm not sure I could fight my way home, like this." He looked at Gird. "And what about you?"

"I've no wish to die, when your traitor son lives, and no wish to spend time in your dungeons, either."

"No—damn you, fellow, you keep making calm sense when any normal serf would be shivering in a heap. The others all ran away, and I doubt they're sleeping sound now. What are you, anyway? Have the gods laid a call on you?"

"No." Gird shook his head firmly. "My folk followed the Lady of Peace; she teaches submission. And your gods support you."

A clatter of boots on the street outside stopped him; something crashed into the shop beyond the door.

"You should have run when you could," said the brown man.

"You could acknowledge my help," said Gird. Then the guards were in the room, their torches sending wild flickers of bright orange across the calmer candlelight. They skidded to a halt, their pikes at Gird's back.

"M'lord Sier," said the one with a knot of bright yellow at his shoulder. "Someone reported noise—" His voice trailed away as he looked around him.

"Treachery, sergeant," said the brown man.

"This lout?" asked the sergeant.

"No." The brown man smiled at Gird. "That fellow came to my aid; the traitors lie dead, all but one." He looked down at his son, and the sergeant's breath hissed in.

"Lord—Jernoth, m'lord?"

"Lord Jernoth. And two of these others." He pointed, and the sergeant's breath hissed again. Clearly he recognized them all. The brown man's orders brought him to quick attention. "Sergeant, send word—I will need a cart; I've been wounded. This—fellow—" He waved a hand at Gird. "If he had not saved me, you would have a new sier this night; he is a stranger, but welcome in the city for three days, for his service. See he gets a tally from the guardhouse, meals and beer; I brought nothing with me, not so much as a copper crab."

"Yes, m'lord Sier." The sergeant eyed Gird with dubious respect.

"And then Lord Jernoth must be straitly confined until I pass judgment; it is ill done to hurry such a decision." This he said facing Gird directly; but somewhere in the tone of his voice, Gird sensed that he would come to follow Gird's advice.

From there, things went smoothly; the guards bound the young man more securely, then hauled him to his feet and away. Another tended the brown man's wounds, and yet another had already sped away with messages. The sergeant opened his belt-pouch with deliberate slowness, and pulled out a flat wooden tally, one end stamped with the Sier's mark.

"This here's a meal tally, good at any inn but the Goldmark or the White Wing—them's only for nobles." He took his dagger and made three scores across the tally. "That's for a day's food and beer; they'll break off the end each time, to the next line. Understand?"

"Yes, sir." Gird wondered if he was really going to get free this easily.

The sergeant lowered his voice and went on. "What I heard was there was a meeting of conspirators, to hear a stranger, an outsider who came in to start trouble. Have any idea who that was?"

"Me, sir?" Stupidity was always a safe mask for a peasant.

"And then here you are, without a mark on you, but the Sier says you saved his life. Me, I wonder if you meant to do that—but his orders is my life, as they say, and he says let you bide here three days on free meals and beer. All I say is, you'd best be gone by sundown that third day, or the sier might have remembered something he wants to ask you. I would."

"Yes, sir."

"And I don't suppose you'll be having any quiet little meetings with rebels while you're here, either."

"No, sir."

"All right. Go fill your belly, and stay out of my sight."

Gird went out into the dark street, only to be stopped by an arriving troop of guards, who let him go when he showed his tally. He tried to walk like someone with honest business, but the events of the past hour or so were beginning to touch his feelings, as well as his mind. When he got to the main square, he edged his way around it, touching the walls of one building after another, until he found the beggars' steps.

Chapter Seventeen

"You had an interesting evening?" The old man's voice was soft, but clearly audible. Gird jumped, then crouched quickly beside him. "Here's your staff," the old man said, brushing his knuckles with it, as if he could see in the dark. Gird clutched at it, consoling himself with its smooth oiled strength. If only he'd had it with him . . .

"You'd have gotten yourself killed," the old man said, even more softly.

"You—what do *you* know about it?"

"Shh." Gird felt a strong, bony hand on his forearm, and the faint warmth of the old man's body leaning against his. In the brief silence, he was aware of other movement on the beggars' steps, movement that might have been the restlessness of disturbed sleepers.

The old man's body was warmer than he'd thought at first; along his right side he began to feel as if he sat before a fire. He had not thought he could sleep, but now he felt himself sinking into that warmth, as the exhaustion of the day and the night's exertions landed on him. It was so comfortable—and he could not, at the moment, feel threatened.

He woke at dawn, when the great bells of Esea's Hall rang out to declare the sun's daily triumph. The sound crashed through him, shaking him out of peaceful dreams, and for an instant he thought he was being attacked. The old man's hand on his arm quieted him. Gird looked around wildly. The others who had spent the night on the beggars' steps were stirring, sitting up, stretching. The man beside him—was someone else. He jerked his arm back.

"Easy," the old man's voice said, out of a different face. "It's just a face." It wasn't a *very* different face, after all: still old, still with the same basic shape. He looked less feeble, this morning, and was certainly not blind—"A miracle, remember? We came for that."

"But—"

"We should find something to eat." The old man stood, and Gird unfolded himself, less stiff than he'd expected to be. "What is that?" the old man asked.

It was the tally the guard sergeant had given him. "It's—I can get food, at an inn. A tally from the sier."

The old man's wispy white brows raised. "So—the sier himself. I knew it was important, but—"

Gird had had enough of the old man, who was certainly not the helpless, tortured creature who had aroused his pity the evening before. "I will share my breakfast with you, but then—"

"You wish I would go away. I worry you, don't I?" That face was not guileless at all; Gird was more than worried. Whatever this was—and he was no longer sure it was a man and not some kind of demon—it kept forcing him into impossible situations.

"I have business," Gird said, through clenched teeth. "I only wanted to help you, and—"

The thin hand, so very strong, slid under his elbow and gripped his arm as if to steady a fragile, tottering oldster. "And you think I've brought more danger on you, more trouble. And you think *I* was blind, as I know you are. Come along, Gird Strongarm—I know you, and you will know me better before this day is done."

As before, he could not shake that grip, and found himself walking where the old man willed. To the public fountain, to wash his face and hands. To a cheap inn, where he bought hot, meat-stuffed rolls from the serving window, getting double the amount because he refused the ale that the servant offered. To a crooked alley, where they leaned against the bulging wall of a baker's oven, and ate the rolls, while cats wound around their ankles, begging. The food steadied him, and restored the town walls and streets to their normal colors, no longer bright and scintillating as if he had a fever, but ordinary, subdued, under a gray wintry sky.

"You are better now," the old man said, still clutching his elbow. Gird looked down at him.

"In body, yes. But you—what are you?"

"What I told you. A priest of Esea, presently in difficulty with his fellow priests. You have my gratitude for your service—"

"You didn't need me!" Fed, awake, alert, Gird had been remembering that whole sequence of events. "You only seemed hurt—you tricked me."

"No." The man's voice was low. "No—I could have died. I almost did. You do not understand—you could not—all that happened to me, or what my powers are. But I was near death, when you found me: that is true. You saved my life."

"But you healed—" Gird could not quite say it; his fingers wanted to make warding signs.

The man sighed. "Gird, we need to talk, you and I. You have done me a great service; so far I have done you only a small one, which you don't yet realize. You do not trust me—and no, that's not reading your mind; you smell of fear. But we should both leave this town, before we find more trouble than your strength or my powers can handle. Will you trust me for that?"

"I know I have to leave," Gird muttered. "He said so, and—and I don't know towns, that well. But I have tallies for two days more."

"Which no one will be surprised if you use to get food for travel, and then leave. That's what the sier would expect you to do. If you stay in Grahlin, they'll begin to wonder if you have more people to meet."

"Can I use the tallies again so soon?" asked Gird, staring at the ragged break on the end as if he thought it would speak to him. The old man chuckled, but it was a friendly chuckle.

"We don't have to go to the same inn. Besides, the sier gives these tallies to many men—to anyone on his service that day. Didn't you notice that the inn servant scarcely looked at you?" Gird had not noticed; he had been trying to see if anyone were following them. "You can use both tallies at one inn; tell them you want food to travel. They'll be used to that."

So it proved. His request brought no comment, and the servant handed over a cloth sack bulging with bread and cheese, and a jug of ale. On the old man's suggestion, Gird had retained the bit of wood with the sier's mark on it, left when the last of the tally was broken. That got him past the gate guards with hardly a glance. The old man had left ahead of him; Gird was tempted to go out the other gate, but felt it would not be fair.

The old man waited just out of sight of the gate, squatting in the windshadow of a tree beside the road. As Gird came alongside, he stood up and began walking with him, steadying himself with Gird's staff.

"Let me start with what is strangest to you," he said without preamble. "My powers and my knowledge."

Gird grunted. He was trying to think how he was going to explain to the others that his foray into the town had been not only useless, but disastrous. They had lost their one contact; the sier knew his face. Worse, the sier knew he had active enemies. Yet they needed someone in this town; it was sitting right there where the trade road met the river road, and soldiers based here could ruin any plan he might make for the whole area. That might be more than a year away—he knew that—but still the town could not be ignored.

He jumped as the old man's hand bit into his elbow. "Listen," the old man said. "You need to know this."

He did not need to know anything except how to get the old man to leave him alone, he thought sourly. They did not need a renegade priest of their enemy's god who might revert to orthodoxy at any moment and turn them in. But the twinge of pain got his attention, and he listened unwillingly.

"I am a priest of Esea," the old man repeated. Gird managed not to say that he knew *that* much. "You clearly think of Esea as a power of evil—from the way you reacted to my blessing. But Esea, in old Aare, where your lords came from, is the name we give the god of light. The sun is his visible form, but it is not the god."

"*Sunlord, Sealord, Lord of Sands and Chance . . .*" muttered Gird, unwillingly.

"You learned that verse in childhood, no doubt. So far as it goes, it's accurate enough. Our people worshipped Esea, the Sunlord— though only peasants called him Sunlord. Sealord, that's Barrando-wea. Ibbirun, the Sandlord—more feared than worshipped. And Simyits, god of chance and luck. We had other gods, many of them, including your Lady, Alyanya the fruitful." The old man looked at Gird calmly, as a man might look at an ox he was thinking of buying. "Tell me, what do you have against Esea?"

"Esea's the lords' god. He brings droughts, dries springs, over-looks wells. The *merin* hate him, and he withers the flowers we bring to please them."

"I see. Because you think of Esea as the Sunlord, and in dry weather you see more sun?"

Gird shrugged. "I'm no priest. But so the grannies said, in our village. If there's a drought, never let a priest of Esea near the wells: they'll call the sun's curse on them, and the water will fail."

The old man snorted. "Do they think priests need no water? That we need no food, so a failing harvest means nothing?" Then he shook his head. "No, I'm sorry. It's natural enough, that you'd blame outlander gods for your troubles, and even more natural, when your rulers are as bad as they are."

"Yes, but you—"

"I'm human. As human as you are: not a demon, not a god. I

am of the old blood, of Aare—kin to your lords, if you look at it like that." He walked on a few paces, glanced sideways at Gird, and said, "I see you do look at it like that. And no wonder. But there is much you do not know. The old Aareans had powers, all of them, which none of your people had. Now this cold land has thinned our blood, some say, or the gods of your people have sought vengeance. I think all that is ridiculous."

Gird fastened to the little he had understood. "You are the same blood as the lords—as that sier, or my old count?"

"Not close kin, but of the same origin—from Aare across the sea."

"But—I have seen no powers, in the lords." Even as he said it, he remembered the uncanny light that had come to a dusty, dark storeroom when the sier willed it. "Except—"

"Except last night. First with me, and then with the sier." He caught Gird's hand as he was about to make another warding sign, and said, "Stop doing that. It won't work, because I'm not what you think, but it is annoying. You'll convince anyone on the road I'm an illwisher." There was no one on the road, before or behind. Gird scowled. The old man sighed. "Gird, our people *had* power, and now most of them don't, or they have little. I have, and the sier has, and of course I know about the sier—I have known him for years. We have talked together, dined together—I've been his guest—"

Gird struggled to break the grip on his wrist; the old man was feeble—had to be weaker than he was—but he could not get free. He yanked back again and again, panting, without success. The old man merely smiled at him, a sunny, friendly smile of perfect calm and joy. "Let—me—*go!*" Gird said finally, when force had not worked.

"When I'm sure you have understood what I'm saying. Not until." The same quiet smile, but Gird felt the threat behind the words.

"Understood, or accepted?" he asked, still angry.

"Understood. Esea's Light, Gird, if I had wanted to charm the wits from you, I could have done it any time."

"Could you?" He glared at the old man, wondering if that had been the answer all along. Had he been charmed into thinking the man hurt, charmed into taking him into the city, charmed into going unarmed into that trap? That peaceful smile seemed to fill his eyes, as if the old man were suddenly larger; warmth and peace seeped into his mind, washing the anger away. But he clung to the core of it, stubborn as a stone in the earth: he might be shifted, but he would not be changed. The old man sighed, at last, and that imposed warmth and peace left him abruptly. He was shivering in a cold wind, aware of sleet beginning to sting the left side of his face.

"Well. Maybe I couldn't, at that. Not now, anyway. The gods must know what they're doing." The old man shivered now, too. But he was still smiling, if ruefully.

Gird looked around. They were on a rise, where the wind could get at them from any angle, and the sleet bit into him. The road ran on eastward, past an outcrop of rock that offered no shelter. Downslope to the right, downwind, scrubby grass thickened to knee-high scrub, and he thought he could see trees in the distance. "I'm cold," he said. "I'm going to find shelter, and if you won't let go of me, you'll have to come too." He was sure he could drag the old man, if he couldn't get rid of him.

"Good idea," the old man said, and nothing more until they had tramped through the scrub into the meager shelter of a leafless wood. Gird hunkered down behind a fallen log, and dug into the dry leaves. Deep enough. He pointed, and the old man crouched there, releasing Gird's wrist. Gird found fallen branches to stack on the windward side, then piled leaves to cut the wind under the log. He kept working, as the sleet came down harder, to cut poles and make a low roof over them. The first flakes of snow floated between the chips of falling sleet as he finished, and crawled under it.

The old man had dug out the leaves to form a nest, and huddled in it. Gird put the sack of food and the jug where he could reach them, and squeezed close to the old man. He was not as cold as Gird had expected—but then he had never been as feeble as Gird expected. Beyond the edge of the shelter roof, more flakes danced. The hiss and rattle of sleet lessened, and that magical silence that heralds falling snow spread around them. Snow clung to the edges of fallen leaves, forming a fantastic tracery until more snow covered the ground in unbroken white.

Gird stared at it. He had slept fireless in winter before, and he had food and ale, but how was he going to get back to his troop? He had expected to spend some days in the town—to leave with enough food to reach the next town—and then to return, with a guide, through three different bartons. He had come to the town from the south; now he was east of it, in a country he had never seen, which was rapidly disappearing under snow. Snow in which his tracks would be all too obvious, in which he could not hope to travel unnoticed. In which he could starve, or die of cold. Beside him, the old man snored, the easy sleep of the old. *He* was warm enough, and unafraid—and what did he have to be afraid of, if he could heal himself of such wounds as Gird had seen? If they had been real.

Gird reached out and pulled the sack of food to him. Don't look too far ahead, his Da had said. There are times to plan for planting and harvest, and times to eat the food at hand, and be grateful. Inside were bread, cheese, a slab of bacon, an onion. He looked at the sleeping man, and sighed, and put the sack aside again. They could share it when the old man woke.

As it happened, the old man woke before he did; Gird had not meant to fall asleep, but the silence and monotony had done it. Outside the shelter was dark, cold, and the silence. Within, the old man had made light, and radiated warmth like a hot stone. He was holding his finger—his *glowing* finger—to a ragged chunk of bacon, which sizzled and dripped onto bread beneath it. It had been the smell of cooking bacon which roused Gird, and it was the sight of it cooking at the old man's touch which sent him out into the dark and cold in one panic-stricken rush.

"Come back!" the old man cried. "I was cooking it for you!"

Gird crouched in the snow, uncertain, shivering . . . half with fear, and half with the cold. Snow caressed his head, his cheeks, his arms and hands, icy kisses like those of the snow maidens that lived in the far north. The old man's head poked out of the shelter. "It's all right. It won't hurt you. I promise." What good was the promise of someone who could cook bacon with his finger, and make light out of nothing? What good was the promise of someone who could change faces? But the smell of the bacon went right to the pit of his belly; his mouth watered. A lump of snow fell on his head, and he shuddered. Fear and warmth and food, or cold and hunger and—more fear. He was moving before he knew it, back to the shelter, praying fervently to whatever gods might be out this dark night to protect him from one old man.

Once face to face with him again, Gird could find nothing specific to fear. His hands were the gnarled and bony hands of any old man, holding out now a chunk of bread with a chunk of hot bacon on top. Gird looked at the food, but did not take it. "We must share," he said hoarsely.

"I don't like bacon," the old man said, almost wistfully. "A slice of a lamb roast now, or even beef—but I never could eat bacon without trouble. Go on, you take it."

Gird looked him in the eye. Could he not know the customs of Gird's people? Were their people so different? "We must share," he said again. "I cannot take food from you, if you do not take it from me." Or rather, he thought to himself, I *will not* take it and put myself in that kind of relationship.

The man shrugged. "It was yours to start with, I merely cooked it. You don't prefer it raw, do you?"

Gird sighed. Either he was ignorant, or he was being difficult. His head ached, and he didn't want to explain it, but he was going to have to. "It's important," he said. "You cooked it; that means you have the hearth-right, the fire-right. I cannot take—no, I *will* not take your food unless you take some from my hand, because that would mean you were my—you had the right to give or withhold food, and I needed your protection."

"Oh." The old man looked surprised, but drew his hand back. "Is *that* why your people first brought food to ours when they came?"

"Did they?" Gird had no idea what had happened when the lords first came. "What did your people do?"

"Made a very large mistake, I think," said the old man, as if to himself. "What should they have done?"

"Were they seeking aid in hunting, or against an enemy? Or were they starving?"

"No—at least not as the chronicles tell it."

"Then if they wanted an alliance of hearthings, they should have offered food of their own, and all shared."

The old man pursed his lips. "And what would it mean to you, if they ate the food offered, but offered none."

"That is the way of accepting the giving hearth as the leader—as the protector."

"Could they offer something else, in exchange? Arms, protection?"

Gird shook his head. "No—what protection could someone without food offer? The strong hearth has food to offer; the weak accepts it, and gives service for protection. If they wish friendship, it is as I said: food shared, both ways. Or more, if more than one are meeting. Famine rule, that can change things, but not always."

"Famine rule?"

"In famine, all share equally, without obligation, even if only one provides. But it must be declared, and accepted."

"This is worse than I thought," said the old man, grimacing. "We were so *stupid*!" He put the bread and bacon down, and said, "Will you take something from the sack and share it with me?"

"I can't cook it," Gird said, frowning. It didn't have to be cooked food, of course: bread was already cooked, and cheese was cured. But he had not actually provided this food—it belonged to the sier, who was an ally of the old man. Some people might argue about that. "Do you accept it as my food?"

"Yes."

"Then I offer this cheese and bread, my hearth to yours." Gird set the bread and cheese between them, then broke a piece from each and held out his hand. The old man took the pieces gravely, and offered Gird the bread and bacon again. This time Gird took it, hoping the bacon was still hot. But he waited until the old man had taken a bite before taking one of his own. The old man had not said the ritual words, but he was sure of the intent, and between only two, that was enough.

The bacon was still warm, and succulent; the grease-soaked bread made a comfortable fullness in his belly. Gird ate quickly, wasting no time, but his mind was full of questions. As soon as he had gulped down the last bite of bread, he turned to the old man.

"What did you mean, your people had made a mistake?"

The old man, eating more slowly, had not finished; he swallowed the cheese in his mouth before answering. "Gird, among my people the customs differ. Offering food is the sign of subservience: servants offer food to masters. I'm afraid when your people came bringing food, my people thought they were acknowledging their lower rank."

Gird sat quietly a moment, thinking this over. The food-bringers, food-givers, ranked *lower*? When everyone knew that those who can afford to give without taking in return are the wealthy and strong? It was backwards, upside down, inside out: no one could live with a people who believed that. They would kill each other. They would believe—that the strong and wealthy are those who can take without giving—He found he was saying this aloud, softly, and the old man was nodding. "But that's *wrong*," he said loudly. His vehemence was swallowed in the snow, lost in that white quiet. "It can't work. They would always be stealing from each other, from everyone, to gain their place in the family."

"Not quite," said the old man. He sighed heavily. "Then again, maybe that's part of the reason why things have gone so badly up here. Back in Aare, there were reasons for that, and safeguards. At least, I think so. It had to do with our magic, our powers."

"Like the light. And cooking with your finger?"

"Among other things, yes. Among our people, rank came with magic—the more magic, the higher rank. One proof of magic was the ability to take, either by direct magic, or by compelling—charming—someone to offer whatever it was as a gift."

Gird thought carefully around that before he let himself answer, but it was the same answer that sprang first to mind. "But how is that different from the bullying of a strong child, who steals a weaker's food, or threatens him into giving it up? It is stealing, to take like that." And it was precisely what the lords had been doing, he thought. What they had always done, if this man was telling the truth.

The old man also waited before answering, and when he spoke his voice was slower, almost hesitant. "Gird, our people see it as the natural way—as calves in a herd push and shove, seeking dominance, as kittens wrestle, claw and bite. Yet this doesn't mean constant warfare in a herd, only a mild pushing and shoving: the weaker ones know their place, and walk behind—"

"But men are not cows!" Gird could not contain his anger any longer; he felt as if it were something physical, bright as the light he still did not understand. "We are not kittens, or sheep, or birds squabbling in a nest—"

"I know." The old man's voice, still quiet, cut through his objection as a knife cuts a ripe fruit. "I know, and I know something has gone very wrong. But in our own home, in Aare, that sparring for dominance among our folk had its limits, and those limits were safe enough to let our people grow and prosper for many ages. We were taught—I was taught—that with such power comes great responsibility—that we were to care for those we governed as a herdsman cares for his herd—No, don't tell me, I understand. Men are not cattle. But even you might use that analogy—"

And he had, the night before, talking to the sier. Gird shivered, not from cold, when he thought of it. No wonder it had gone home, if the man thought of his common folk as cattle already.

"I still think it's wrong," Gird said.

"It may be. But right or wrong, it's the other way 'round from your people, and that means my people didn't understand them from the beginning. We assumed your people intended to submit, agreed to it without conflict: that's what our chronicles say. So whenever your people resisted, our people thought of that as a broken contract—as if you had gone back on your word."

Gird tried to remember what he had heard of the lords' coming. Very little, though he had heard new things from the men he had been training. Most of the stories began after that, with the settlements growing near the new forts and towns, with the "clearing" of old steadings, the forced resettlement of families, the change in steading custom to conform to the new village laws. Everyone had thought the lords knew they were unfair, knew they were stealing—

but had they not known? Had they thought that all they did was right, justified by some agreement that had never been made?

"Not all," the old man said. "Some things were forbidden in old Aare, which our people do here. The worship of the Master of Torments, for example: that they know is evil, and those who do it are doing it knowingly against the old laws. A contest of strength or magery is one thing, but once it is over, the winner has obligations to the loser, as well. But the basic misunderstanding, Gird, I believe I discovered tonight, from you. Your way seems as strange to me, I confess, as mine must seem to you—but strangeness is not evil. What we do with it may be evil."

"When you offered me that food," Gird said, "were you then declaring yourself lower in rank? Or were you trying to fool me into thinking that's what you were doing?"

The old man started to answer, then stopped, then finally said, "I thought—I think I only meant to calm you, to make you think well of me. In one sense, that is claiming a lower rank, because it means I care that you think well of me—in another—I don't know. I didn't think, I just did it."

"I felt," Gird said carefully—carefully, because he did not want to hurt this old man, even now, "I felt like a stubborn animal, being offered a bait of grain if it will only go through the gap."

A grin, across that close space. "You are stubborn; you would not deny that. I did not mean you to feel that, but given what your people think about offering food, wouldn't anyone feel so in such a circumstance? Have you ever—"

"Yes." Had the men he had fed felt that way? Demeaned, degraded? But it was not always so; he had taken food himself, gladly, acknowledging temporary weakness. Sick men had to be fed by healthy men, children by adults, infants by mothers. Was milk from the breast demeaning to a baby? Of course not. Yet—he worried the problem in his mind, coming at it from one side then another. The old man sat quietly and let him alone. "There are times," he said, "when it is right to be the one fed. Times no one minds. If someone's sick or hurt—or children—but grown folk, healthy grown folk—they feed themselves. In a way, living on another's bounty is like being a child again. Maybe that's why it means giving obedience."

"Probably." The old man nodded. "It's interesting that you have the importance of having food to give, but absolute prohibition against taking it by force from each other. The force is used against the land, I suppose, in hunting or farming."

"Not against," Gird corrected. "With. To help the land bear more. Alyanya is our Lady, not our subject."

"So you see even the gods as those who can give, not those who take?"

"Of course. If they have nothing to give, they are not gods, but demons." Gird nodded at the cold dark beyond their shelter. "As the cold demons steal warmth, and the spirits of night steal light from the sun."

The old man smiled. "This day is stealing my strength, Gird, and I cannot hold this light much longer. Not if I'm to have warmth enough until dawn. But before the light goes. I have an apology. I have withheld the courtesy of my name, although I knew yours. I am Arranha, and I am glad to have you as companion in this adventure."

Gird turned the name over in his mind; it was like nothing he had heard. "I thought the lords had many names—four or five."

"So they do, but priests have only one, and mine is Arranha." With a last smile, Arranha let the light fail—the light Gird had yet to understand, and the cold, snow-clean air gusted for a moment under the shelter. Gird felt Arranha curling up in his leafy nest, and thought of walking away. But he could not blunder through a wood in the dark and snow, not and hope to live until morning. With a silent but very definite curse, he lay down, wriggling his way into the leaves until he was curled around Arranha. His back was cold, but Arranha, protected on the inside, was warm as a hearth. Gird was sure he could not sleep—then began to worry that they might sleep their way into death in the cold—and then slid effortlessly into peace and darkness.

Chapter Eighteen

The next morning was cold and raw but Arranha was awake, and a milder warmth filled their shelter. Gird rubbed his eyes, and looked out to see snow covering all, under a gray sky: the light was silvery. The old man sat hunched, staring at his hands. Gird watched him warily. Was he about to do something? Was he doing something now, something Gird could not see? Then a cramp in his back jabbed him, and he had to stretch. Arranha turned to him, and Gird continued with a yawn that cracked his jaws.

"Sorry," he said afterwards, but even to himself he did not sound sorry. Arranha merely smiled. Silently, he divided the rest of the bread and cheese, and Arranha shared it. The jug, when he shook it, was full. He looked at the old man, who smiled again.

"I filled it with snow, and melted it. It's not ale, but it will do." Gird sipped, found it water with only the faintest taste of the ale that had been in the jug, and drank thirstily. Arranha went on. "It is not snowing now, and I think it will not for some hours. If you wanted to travel, now is a good time."

Gird scratched his jaw beneath his beard. "What about you? I would help you to someplace safe."

Arranha laughed aloud. "Safe? For me? Gird, I am safer with you than anywhere else I can think of, in the world of men."

"But surely you have friends—"

"None so rash as to harbor me now, when Esea's Hall of priests has declared me heretic and traitor. They intended to kill me, Gird—you saw that."

"But—sir—" Gird tried to think how to put it. The man was a priest, and had great powers, but he would hardly be accepted by Gird's troop of peasant rebels. He began as delicately as he could. "I have my work—you seem to know that, and what it is—and the people I work with, my people, they—they won't take to you."

Arranha showed neither anger nor surprise. "You do not want me with you?"

Gird found he was scratching his ear, this time. "Well—it's nothing against you yourself, but—you're one of *them,* sir. One of the lords, and that's who we're trying to fight. Sir."

"Do you know what you're fighting for, Gird, or is it all against?" Gird must have looked as puzzled as he felt, for Arranha explained. "Do you have a vision of something better, a way to live that you want, or are you fighting only against the lords' injustice and cruelty?"

"Of course we have ideas," Gird said. They were bright in his mind, those pictures of what the world should be like. He was sitting at the old scarred table in his own cottage, with Mali and the children around it, all of them with food in their bowls, laughing and talking. In the cowbyre were his three favorite cows, all healthy and sleek; his sheep were heavy-fleeced and strong. He could look around the room and see his mother's loom with a furl of cloth half-woven, tools on their hooks, Mali's herbs in bunches, the sweet smell of a spring evening blowing in the window. Outside would be the fields, with the grain springing green from the furrows, the smallgarden already showing the crisp rosettes of vegetables, the beans reaching for their poles with waving tendrils. From other cottages as well he could hear the happy voices, even someone singing. He felt safe; he knew the others felt safe. That was what he wanted, what they all wanted.

"Can you tell me?" asked Arranha gently.

Gird tried, but the memories were too strong, too mixed: sweet and bitter, joyful and sorrowful, all at once. His voice broke; his eyes filled with tears that were hot on his cheeks, and cold on his jaw. "It's just—just peace," he said.

Arranha sighed. "Coming to peace by starting a war is tricky, Gird. You've never known war; I have."

Gird set his jaw, and blinked back the tears. "It's war enough, when my family and my friends die for nothing."

"No. It's bad, but it's not the same. You're starting something bigger than you can see. Much bigger. You need a better idea of where you're going, what you will need. Do you know anything at all about law?"

Gird sniffed, rubbed his nose on his arm, and thought about it. Law. There were the customs of his village, and the customs all his people shared, from the days when they lived in steadings within a hearthing. Then there were rules the lords made, and that law he had had to memorize when he was a recruit. "A little," he said cautiously. Arranha looked at him, as if wondering what that meant, and sighed again.

"This is going to take longer, and it would go better in a warmer place. Where would *you* go from here?"

The abrupt change of topic jarred; Gird wondered what the old man was up to. Something, surely. But he was tired of arguing, of his own emotions. Let the old man come along, at least for now. "We left the city by the east gate," Gird said. "And then we walked east, and then south but only a little. So back south, and a little west—I don't know this country well, up here."

"The way you're speaking of, there's a village called Burry—is that what you meant?"

"Aye." In Burry, the barton was already five hands strong, and the yeoman marshal had relatives in three other villages.

"Can we reach Burry today?"

"No. But there's a place—" Gird did not want to talk about it, and Arranha did not press him. He ducked out of the shelter, into the distanceless light of a cloudy day over snow. They were going to leave tracks, clear ones, and the place they had slept would be obvious even if he tried to take down the shelter. But he could not see the road from here, or hear any travelers. Perhaps no one would happen by until another snowfall.

He led Arranha further into the wood, away from the road. The silence scared him; it felt unnatural. He reminded himself that he was not used to being away from a village in winter. Even near camp, he could hear the noises of other people. It might be nothing but this unfamiliarity that had his neck hair standing up, a tension in his shoulders. Arranha picked his way through the snow with little apparent effort, though he left tracks. Gird made sure to look, every so often.

When they came to the trail Gird had taken toward the city two days before, he almost walked across it without recognition. Its white surface lay smooth in both directions, trackless. He turned and led Arranha along it, as he looked for the place they could shelter overnight.

It was getting darker, and he was afraid he might not recognize it in snow, when he spotted the three tall cedars above a lower clump, and turned off the trail. Arranha had said nothing for hours. Now he said, "Is this a village?"

"No—it's an old steading. Cleared by your folk, to settle a village." He wasn't sure that was why it had been abandoned; it might have been much older than the lords' coming. "It's empty," Gird added. "No one lives here, or nearby." He pushed through the bushy cedar boughs, shivering as they dumped their load of snow on him, and entered the old steading. He bowed, courteously, to the old doorstep, still centered between the upright pillars that had held the door. On either side, broken walls straggled away, outlining the shape of the original buildings in brushstrokes of stone against the white snow.

When he looked back, Arranha had pushed through the cedars as well, and was bowing as Gird had, though he looked uncertain of his welcome. So he ought, Gird thought. This was old; this had belonged to no one but his own people, and Arranha was a stranger.

"Do you know how many lived here?" Arranha asked.

Gird shook his head. "It was a steading; my Da said a steading was three or so families. Less than a village—four hands, five? A large steading might have more, but I think this one was small." He led the way again, past the empty useless doorway, along what had been the outside of the main building, to an angle of low wall in what had been an animal shed or pen. Here two corners had survived the original assault and subsequent weather, to nearly enclose a space just over an armspan wide, and two armspans long. Gird thrust his hand into the cold snow in the larger space outside, feeling about, and grunted. "Here—help me lift this." *This* was a lattice, woven of green withes and vines, and lightly covered with leaves; it would have been unnoticeable lying flat among the ruins. Now, it fitted across the space between the walls, an instant roof.

"You knew this was here—you had it ready!" Arranha sounded excited for the first time.

Gird let himself grin. "Aye. Thought it up. Looks like nothing but old walls, but it's as good as a house. Almost." He had lifted his end carefully, so that the snow did not slide off; it was heavier that way, but it would look less obvious. He hoped. When they had it braced in place, he looked at it again. Those two side walls had been intended to support a slanted roof, he was sure—he hoped his roof would slant enough to drip on the wall, not inside. The end wall should be lying within the enclosed space; he reached into the snow again, and found the end. He pulled it out, careful to bring its load of snow with it. This piece was light enough for one to move; he shifted it until it almost closed the gap. Now they had a small house, its walls chest-high, topped with a slanted roof with its back to the north wind. Its floor was almost snow-free, because that snow had come out with the end wall.

"You thought this up?" asked Arranha.

"Not all of it. I thought of wattle for temporary roofs, in our camps, but others thought of leaving sections where we might need them. And a man in Burry thought of putting the piece down where you might want no snow when the shelter was built." As he talked, Gird braced the foot of the wattle enclosing the end with rocks. His hands began to go numb; he blew on them. Then he reached into his jerkin, and brought out one of his thongs. "We have to tie the roof on, or any little puff will blow it away." Arranha took the hint, and began lacing the roof to the end hurdle.

Inside the shelter, it was quite dark. Gird felt around in the protected corner, and found the dry sticks he'd bundled, and the little sack of meal. He thought of the time it was going to take to start a fire with a firebow, and sighed. It would be sensible to ask Arranha to start the fire with his finger—if that worked, and if it cooked bacon it should—but he hated to ask a favor of a lord.

"If you would let me, I will start the fire," Arranha said quietly. Gird backed out of the shelter and looked at him. No visible haughtiness, just an old man pinched with cold after a long day's walk in the snow.

"In that far corner, then. There's wood; I'll find more."

Arranha nodded and ducked inside the shelter. Gird did not stay to watch; he gathered an armload of wood, and came back to a shelter that let chips of light out between the chinks of the wattle.

Inside was warmth and firelight—none of Arranha's magicks. Was Arranha tired, or simply being tactful? Gird did not know, or care; he was glad enough to see a warm fire. The jug was nestled near the fire, and Arranha had found the niche in the wall with the cooking bowl. He had poured the meal into the bowl, but looked as if he did not know what to do next.

"Let me." Gird reached for the bowl, and felt the side of the pot. Warm, but not hot enough. He scrabbled around the floor of the shelter for small pebbles and pushed them into the fire. "For cooking," said Gird, to Arranha's surprised look. "I'll drop them in the jug, to make the water hot quicker. That way it won't crack the pot."

By the time the mush was done, Gird was ready to eat the bowl as well. He swallowed hard, handed the bowl to Arranha first, and forced himself to match spoonful for spoonful the pace Arranha set. They scraped the bowl clean; with a sigh, Gird took it outside to scrub it clean with snow. After a final visit to the outside—Gird insisted on showing Arranha the proper place to use as jacks—they came back to the fire, ready enough for a night's sleep.

Or so Gird expected. Instead, Arranha did whatever he did to brighten the light until Gird could see as clearly as in daylight. From the recesses of his clothes, he pulled a scroll. Gird blinked. The man had been naked; Gird had given him a shirt. Then he had had clothes of some kind—but Gird still didn't have his shirt back—and now he was taking things he had not had out of clothes he had not had. He did not like this. But the alternative was, again, a cold night alone in the woods—and here was warmth and light and someone alive. He gave Arranha the look he would have given one of his men who pulled a stupid trick, but Arranha did not react to it.

Arranha pointed to the scroll. "Can you read that?" Gird peered at it, his long-forgotten struggles with reading sending cold sweat to his brow. The list looked familiar, the lengths of line and numbers made it certain.

"No—but I know what it is. It's the Rule of Aare. I've seen it before; we had to learn it in the Kelaive's Guard."

"And what does it mean?" Gird stared at him, and Arranha nodded encouragingly. "The first one, for instance. What does it *mean*—how does it tell you to live?"

"Surrender none," said Gird. "That's obvious enough. Grab and hold what you've got. Don't quit. Don't give anything up."

"And what is 'anything'?"

"Anything—oh, lands, I suppose. Money. Power. Whatever they've got that they value—"

"Value," said the priest, in that tone that made Gird think he meant more than he said. "Things of value—think, Gird." He was thinking, and it made him restless. He wanted the ale he had had the night before, to ease the ache in his joints. He wanted to get out of this cold cramped shelter and take a walk across open, sunlit fields. He scowled, hoping that it would pass for thought, and ready to be angry if the priest laughed. The priest did not laugh. "Value," he said again. "Gird, what do you value most?"

"Me?" All the usual answers raced through his mind: money, food, ale, the pleasures of the body, possessions, a better bull for his cows. Then slower, deeper, the people he knew, the way of life he wanted to live. But for that he had no words, no way to say it. "Not just money," he said slowly. "Not things to buy or use, exactly. Friends—a good master, fair dealing in the market and at tax time—family—" Children, he would have said, but it was ill-luck to name them.

"Peace," said the priest, casting that name over ordinary life without turmoil or undue trouble, as Gird himself had said that morning. "Justice." And that stood for all the fair dealing, market or court or steward's assessment, for a lord who would not trample young grain on a hunt, or refuse the use of medicinal herbs in his wood. "Love," the priest said last, and it covered family and friends well enough, all the complicated relationships that made a life more than existence.

"But the law—" began Gird. The priest held up his hand, and Gird stopped short.

"The *old* law," said the priest, "said nothing of peace or justice or love, because everyone agreed on their importance. And the first Rule, 'Surrender none' meant precisely that none of these should be given up: not peace, not justice, not love."

"But—" began Gird again, and again the priest stopped him.

"Surrender none," the priest repeated, this time in a tone of command that would, Gird was sure, have held an army spellbound. "None—none of the Rules themselves, and none of the great goods the Rules were intended to preserve. Our people have forgotten that. Our priests have forgotten that. We have taught them the wrong meanings of those simple commands, and it is these, acted out, which brought them to such actions as trouble you. They think they are meant to grasp more and more, and hold it tightly, sharing it with none, when they were meant to surrender no opportunity of doing right, of spreading Esea's light, the High Lord's justice, Alyanya's peace."

Gird thought of the other Rules, so painfully learned when he was a recruit. If indeed the first meant *that,* then how could the second, the third, be interpreted? "One, for me, and one, for you" had looked, to a peasant boy, like a clear description of the present situation: one rule for the masters, and one for the serfs.

"No," said the priest, with a sigh. "It's easily read that way, and that is in fact the way they read it *now,* paying tribute to Simyits the Two-faced, the Trickster, the lightfingered lord of luck and gambling. But it reminds us to share, as children do, as we did tonight—one spoonful for you, and one for me. Your people do the same."

"But the others?"

"Define the vigilance necessary to protect the code: touch not, nor ask, nor interfere, where it is not necessary, where it is not your business; but if it is, then go far, swift, silently—never let justice lack because of distance or time or idle chatter. Face the door, yes: evil overwhelms the careless. Learn all the arts, to judge fairly, but staying alive is imperative, or the good judge cannot exist to judge."

"It's—it's like a grape-leaf," said Gird, his mind awhirl. "On one side dark green, shiny, and on the other silvery fuzz—can it be the same Rules? And even if it is, what matter to us? We were never *of* them."

"Gird, if a man use a stick to beat a cow, instead of guide it, does that make the stick evil? Would you burn the stick, for being a bad stick, or clout the man?"

"The man, of course, but—"

"The Rules of Aare were a tool of law, a stick, if you will—once men used them well, to guide themselves to better actions, and now they use them badly, to beat other men. You're going to need a stick like that; before you throw this one on the fire, take another look at it."

"It still sounds like trickery," said Gird. He looked closely at the priest, watching for anything he could interpret. Nothing but interest. "If the Rules can be read both ways, then there's something wrong with them. Why not write laws that can't be read wrong?"

"Try it," said the priest. A smile twitched his lips. Gird felt the back of his neck getting hot. Somehow the man had made a trap, and he'd walked in. Even though he didn't feel the teeth yet, it was still a trap.

"I could," he muttered sourly, thinking hard. What was the trap?

"It's not that hard to say a man shouldn't steal his neighbor's sheep, or put offal down his neighbor's well."

"And if the sheep got into his garden, or the neighbor had stolen something from him?"

"If we had fair courts, to settle the first problem—"

"Very good. And how will you make fair courts?"

The priest was taking him seriously. The trap must have very fine teeth, because he couldn't feel them yet, and the man was asking what he'd thought about before.

"Fair courts should have someone who knows something about the argument—the kind of argument—"

"Another serf?" asked the priest. This was extraordinary, and Gird paused to look again for any signs of ridicule. None.

"I've wondered about that," he said cautiously. "A farmer to judge disputes between farmers, a tanner to judge between tanners. But then if a farmer and a tanner have an argument, who? If it's someone who started as a peasant, say, then he'd need some training, same as if he wanted to be a soldier."

"Let's suppose you have your judge," said the priest. "A fair man, who knows enough of both sides to understand it, then what?"

"Plain laws that anyone can understand," said Gird. "Fair dealing between master and man, between crafter and crofter. If the law says 'no stealing' that's plain enough—"

"And what is stealing?" asked the priest.

"Taking what's not yours," said Gird. "That's obvious."

"But think, Gird. We all take some things that aren't ours: air, water, sunlight and starlight—"

"The water in my well was mine." Gird clung to that. Air? Sunlight? He'd never thought of himself as "taking" them. There was plenty left for everyone else.

"The water in your well came from somewhere else, and someone else put it there. Have you done one thing to make it grow, as you work to make your cabbages grow?"

"No." He'd never thought of it that way. It was his well, as it had been his father's well, and he had felt lucky to have a well of his own. His well, his water. But he *had* worked, himself, to get each year's crop of barley and oats and cabbages and onions, to take the cows to be bred, to birth the calves. He himself had fed and brushed his animals, pruned and manured his trees, plowed and harrowed and planted and harvested his fields. The water was just *there*, more in a wet year and less in a dry year, but always there, without his thought. Given, like the air and the light. And he had taken.

"Would you call that stealing from the gods?" asked Gird. Or, he wondered to himself, were the gifts of flowers and herbs to the *merin* spirits really a form of payment, and not praise?

"No, I think not. They gave us to this world, and gave to it also those things we need and cannot make for ourselves, by any labor. To take a gift is not stealing. But I wanted you to think about your law. If you want more than riots, if you want more than killing the magelords and then each other, you must have law."

Before he could stop himself, Gird blurted "But don't know anything about it."

Arranha smiled. "You were just saying you knew what kind of laws you wanted. And once you knew nothing about fighting, but you learned. You can learn this, if you care enough about it."

"From you?"

"From me you can learn some, but not all. You don't trust me, even now—" He looked closely at Gird, as if to see into his mind. Gird hoped the uneasy feeling inside wasn't the priest's inner sight. "So we must find you teachers better suited to your nature and experience. What do you know of the kapristi, the gnomes?"

"The gray rockfolk? Dire fighters, fair dealers, is what I've heard. Not much friends with humans—"

"Not with *our* folk," the priest agreed. "Before we came your people had no problem with them. Some of ours . . . well, you've heard me admit that our folk have gone widely astray from Esea's path, and not alone in their treatment of you. Some of the wildest thought the kapristi were easy prey, being small and seeming meek. Tried to hunt them, ahorse and afoot. Ignored their boundary markers, tried to move you peasants onto their land to farm or mine."

"And?"

"And were deservedly killed by the kapristi. That's not what my former colleagues would say, of course, but it's true. They never tried to invade human lands, or attacked humans where they had not been attacked. But once roused, those small gray folk are as dangerous fighters as any you could hope to train. As well, they live by a code of law that they boast is the fairest and most settled in all the worlds and peoples."

Gird could not keep back a grin. "There is such a law?"

"They claim so. I have met them myself, Gird, as a student of law. They like my people little, but they were fair and just with me. But it is a strict law, so strict that I doubt you'll find humans agree to follow it. They take no excuses, the kapristi, as they make none; they value fair exchange so highly that they believe free gifts are dangerous, fostering slackness. Would you go so far?"

"No, among our people, gifts are a sacred duty. Alyanya's blessings are gifts—"

"Yet the gnomes would say you return fair exchange, duties of worship, for such apparent gifts, or the gods take vengeance. That's their explanation for what's gone wrong with our people. Impiety, failure to return proper service, and the gods punish by withholding the gifts."

"And what do you say?"

Arranha sighed, "I say that my people have erred, by being ungenerous. We value free gifts, even if we misinterpreted your people's offer of food. Perhaps free gifts are dangerous for gnomes; for humans I think they are necessary. But with the loss of powers came fear, so our people grasp more, and give less, than they did. This hurts you, and you, in turn, will hurt them. That cycle has no end, unless you wish it—unless you declare an end, someday, and forgive the rest of the injury."

Gird felt his forehead knot. "What has that to do with justice?"

Arranha smiled at him, serene once more. "You will find out, Gird, when it is time."

Gird felt unaccountably grumpy at that, as if he were a child being told to ignore adult concerns for now. He was, after all, a grown man—widowed—the father of grown children. Arranha seemed to read this on his face. "I'm sorry," he said. "I didn't mean to confuse you. You are no child; I know that. But I do not know myself exactly why the god sent me to you, or you to me. I was as surprised as you, when you stumbled onto me in that ditch. The god wants something from both of us—"

"Not *your* god!" Gird said.

"Then yours. Believe me or not, as you will, but I have been a priest, a true priest, and I know: your god has shaped your life to some purpose, and I am now part of that purpose. I think—I believe—that some part of that is helping you learn how to shape the future beyond the coming war. Whoever leads your people needs to know more than soldiering."

Gird ducked his head. Of course he had thought about it, wondered if the gods had drawn him toward the leadership that now seemed certain. But it did not do to question them too closely, to bring yourself to their notice. The old man was strange, too strange; he wished he'd never found him. And yet—something about him attracted, as the warmth of a fire in cold attracted. Certainly he knew that they must plan for something beyond war; it was what had bothered him since Norwalk.

"I don't know," he said. "I just don't know."

"But you will," Arranha said softly. "You will know because you must know, and you will teach others."

Suddenly this solemnity in a tattered shelter in snowy woods, this serious discussion of legalities and philosophies, struck Gird as ridiculous. He snorted. "Aye—I can see now: the great gods who could choose you or anyone else will choose a peasant who can hardly read—a serf and son of a serf, who is better with cows than people—to teach a whole people about law. That's wisdom."

Arranha leaned forward. "Do not mock them, Gird. If they have chosen you—and I think they have, and you suspect it, beneath that banter—they will make you what they need. Better clay that can be shaped to their will, and then fired, than broken shards of earlier firings."

The laughter had gone, fleeing down the hollow corridors of his mind a nameless fear. "I am not mocking," Gird said. "I was wishing for miracles."

"Those, too, you may have. For now, you have me: no miracle, but an Aarean with some small magicks."

"Which once I would have called miracles," said Gird, sighing. "Well, Arranha, you may be right. But at the moment I cannot stay awake." The old man chuckled, released his light, and Gird fell asleep in the glow of the banked coals of their fire.

The next morning was colder, but brighter, as the clouds began to break and a thin sunlight poked through them. Gird and Arranha dismantled the shelter; Gird gathered more wood to replace what they'd used, and tucked it into the corners of the walls. Arranha watched as Gird tried to scatter snow over the wattle sections, now laid flat again. Gird wondered if the face he wore now was truly his own, healed of the injuries, or a face maintained by magic (how?) to fool him. And how was the barton at Burry going to react to this man? He could not lie to them, and pretend Arranha was other than he was.

"Do you ever wonder how our magicks work?" asked Arranha when they had started along the trail.

Gird, who was ahead, swinging his arms to warm up, shook his head. "I never saw any, until I met you. Not save the healer's hands that some have, to take away the pain and lay it aside."

"Your people have *that*?" Arranha's voice had sharpened.

"Some of them. Not many." The cold air speared into his lungs; he had to talk in short gasps, and wished Arranha would ask no more. But he could feel the pressure of Arranha's curiosity at his back, as if it were a stinging fly between his shoulders.

"You've seen it yourself?"

"Felt it m'self. Take the pain of a headache, or a blow. Lay it aside, on something doesn't feel pain, like a rock." He blew out a great cloud of steam, trying for rings. It was good luck to blow rings, the holy circle. "Most of 'em use herbs, for fevers. Singing charms, for demons, if they have the parrion—" He stopped, aware of the intensity of Arranha's interest. Had he said more than he should?

"Singing charms—" murmured Arranha. "Esea's light, what we've missed! What's a parrion, Gird?"

"Parrion's a girl's—" Well, how could he explain? "It's—what a mother gives—or an aunt—family things. My mother, she had a parrion of weaving. Certain patterns were hers, and the loom—but it's not like giving someone a cow. The steading—the family—knows a girl's ability. Her parrion is that, plus what the women give her. I don't know all of it; men don't have parrions, exactly."

"So that's it! Gird, in the old chronicles, my people record that yours used to have a group of elders in each—steading, is it?—and mentioned parrion. But it's not recorded what that was."

Gird nodded, on surer ground now. "Three elders, there were. One was of the hunters, one of the growers, and one of the crafters. The hunter was a man, the crafter a woman, and the grower might be either."

"And the crafters were weavers? Potters?"

"Toolmakers, builders, anything we made. Of course all know something of it—anyone can build a wall." Even as he said it, Gird wondered. Anyone could build a wall if someone good at building walls gave directions. Some walls were better than others.

"Hmm. Did women make weapons?"

"Of course. Why shouldn't they?"

Arranha crunched along several strides before answering. "Among our people, it's thought bad luck to let women make weapons. Their blood shed during the making could weaken the weapon's hunger for blood, make it weak."

Gird stopped short and turned; Arranha nearly crashed into him. "Blood *weaken?* You mean you don't blood your hearths, or your foundations?" From the shocked expression on Arranha's face, they did not. Gird's mind whirled. These lords were even stranger than he'd thought. To take food without giving meant strength, but blood shed meant weakness: another refusal to give, he thought that was. Yet they had magical power to heal themselves—why should they be afraid to give blood where it was needed? And what would this mean in a war? He was not about to explain the power of giving

blood to this alien priest. But Arranha was quick, he had seen it
for himself. His eyes widened even more, and his mouth fell open.

"It's—the giving again. Esea! I would *never* have thought of that.
The food giver is stronger—the blood giver is stronger—and *that's*
why our people found women ruling your steadings. And that's
why your people follow Alyanya: the Lady gives harvest—food—
and blood. I—am—amazed." He shook his head, like someone
recovering from a hard blow. Then, softly. "And I see that you can
never accept our laws. If you are to have your own, you will have
to forge them from your own beliefs."

Gird, although he heard this, felt a fierce exultation warming his
whole body. He had been afraid of the lords so long, afraid of their
cruelty, their wealth, their power. It had never occurred to him
that they might be *afraid*, that they might be weak where his own
people were strong.

But Arranha was still talking. "Gird, remember: if this is the
strength of your people, and you are their proper leader, then it
will be demanded from you—you will be their symbol—"

Gird shrugged. "Do you think I'm afraid to give?"

Arranha looked at him a long moment. "No—you've shown that
you can. But I think you do not understand how much you may
have to give—"

Gird shrugged again, this time irritably. "I may die; I know that.
It's likely. We all may. More than that, no man can give." Arranha
started to say something, closed his mouth, and shook his head.
Gird cocked an eyebrow at him, but the old man merely waved
for him to lead the way.

So what had *that* been about, Gird wondered, as he continued
toward Burry. He had already lost his wife, most of his children,
his home, his beloved cows (he wondered who was milking the dun
cow, and if she had settled again). The children he had left might
die, and that would hurt—that would worse than hurt; he knew he
could hardly live through it, if more happened to Rahi or Pidi or
Girnis. He himself could be captured, tortured, killed—but he
could not imagine anything else. And by being where he was, he
had consented to those losses, if they were demanded of him.

"I still think you should talk to the gnomes," Arranha said suddenly, after a long silence.

"I don't know any gnomes," Gird said. That should settle that.
Besides, he had a winter's work to do with the bartons, keeping
the training going. He would send someone else to recruit in
another town, someone who had been in a town before, maybe.

"I do," Arranha said. "They have much you need to know. For

example, leaving law aside, have you ever drilled two or three cohorts together? Do you know how to place them on a battlefield when cavalry threatens? Do you know what to do about archers? Or the kinds of magical weapons my people have?"

"We won at Norwalk against cavalry. We practice pushing men off horses," said Gird, feeling stubborn. Of course it wasn't really pushing men off horses; it was pushing men off logs, and he had to hope it was much the same thing. Arranha had said that the gnomes had fought the Aarean lords—and won. He would like to know how they'd done it. What he could remember of the sergeant's lectures on tactics had most to do with controlling unruly crowds, clearing the village square, hunting wolves. He had a sudden terrible vision of what his ignorance could mean if he led all his bartons out to battle and did something stupid—so stupid that the lords won easily, and his own people were dying, captured. He shook his head, banishing that ill-luck.

"Besides," he said, "you say the gnomes give nothing away. Why should they teach me soldiering for nothing? Or law?"

"You might have something valuable to trade," Arranha said. Gird waited for him to explain, but he didn't. So what did he have? Nothing but his own strength, the allegiance (for now) of some hands of half-trained peasants, his own burning desire for peace and justice. Arranha had said the lords violated the gnomish borders. But would they trade for that, when they could defend themselves as well as Arranha said? Would they trade bad neighbors for good?

"Would you talk to the gnomes if they would talk to you?" asked Arranha, breaking into this line of thought.

Soldiering beyond what his sergeant had taught, ways to make laws fair for everyone. Would it work? He had nearly got himself killed in that town, for knowing so little; he did not want to be the one to get all his men killed. And he did want peace, and justice, on the other side of battle. What would the others think, if he went to the gnomes? He thought about that. He had good marshals, now, who could keep the camps going, keep the bartons going, until he came back. It would be a season or more, he knew. But was he trusting Arranha because of some wicked magic?

"I will think about it," he said, looking back to see Arranha's expression. "I would need to tell my—my friends."

"Of course. If you would take my advice, go to them without me—so you can be sure there is no power of mine involved—and discuss it. If they agree, and you agree, then I will take you."

PART III

Chapter Nineteen

Winter wind had scoured the sky clean of clouds, autumn rains were past. The next clouds would bring serious snow, but that was likely days away. Gird followed Arranha across the frostbitten grass, his farmer's mind noticing every sheep dropping, every wisp of wool caught on a thornbush.

"I feel uneasy, out in the daylight like this," he said finally, when a fold of ground hid them from the wood in which they'd spent the night.

Arranha gave a brief smile back over his shoulder. For an old man, he was remarkably quick across country. "We are beyond Gadilon's domain, remember?"

"They wander beyond, often enough."

"Not this way. Kapristi taught Gadilon's sires caution, Gird. It was his great-great-grandfather who tried to start a war with them."

"I still can't believe—"

"—that those little folk could defeat the magelords? Nor could my people, at first. But you, you want to defeat them with peasants—is that so different?"

"Well—we're bigger—"

"And not so disciplined. Even with the bit of drill you learnt from your count's sergeant. You need more; your people need more: law and drill both, which to the kapristi are but branches of the same tree. Or, as they would say, two ends of one rod."

"Rod?"

"Measuring rod, or staff of justice. *One measure suits all lengths:* that's one of their sayings. *One law serves justice; many laws serve misrule.*"

"I think I will like that," said Gird slowly. "That's a problem I know, well enough—right there in the Rule of Aare, it is, though you say it wasn't meant to be like that."

Arranha smiled peacefully at him. "Truth is greater than either of us, Gird. I might mean to speak truly and be mistaken: I'm no god. And you might find it where you didn't expect it."

A little higher on the slope, something marked the rough grass . . . a straight line, he realized, that went on across the slope, and around the edge of the hill, to reappear on the next elbow west. He could not tell if it went beyond that. Neither fence nor wall nor plowed furrow—but a line in the grass, as if it had been closely mown perhaps two handspans wide. He nudged Arranha. "Is that the track of some demon?"

"You saw it! Good. That's the kapristi boundary line. Many humans don't notice—"

"Any farmer would," said Gird. "How do they mow it so evenly? How do they keep the line? I don't see any endstones."

"They don't need endstones: it's their domain, and they set the line where they will. Our people no longer dispute it, and yours never did, being wiser."

"And now?"

"Now we call, and then wait. Remember what I've told you: they're absolutely honest and fair, but they demand the same of others. They give nothing; fair exchange is their rule. They will not take simple courtesies amiss, but they will not return them. Expect no thanks, if a bargain is struck, and don't expect to get any more for asking please." Arranha led the way up to the boundary, and called upslope in words Gird did not know. "Kapristi speech, of course," he answered Gird's question.

"But no one's around," said Gird.

"No humans, no. But a dozen kapristi could be a stone's throw from here, and you'd not know it unless they wanted you to. This is *their* land, Gird; make no assumptions about what you do not know."

I'm not, Gird thought silently. He watched the slope above them, as it roughened into rocky outcrops of some gray stone streaked with black. Rockfolk. Elder folk, like the blackcloak, the kuaknom, he had seen. Like the treesinging elves he had not seen. Even more like the dwarves of legend, who sang gold out of the deep mountain rocks, and made jewels by squeezing rock in their hard fists. Folk created before humankind, who might see humans as he saw the Aarean magelords: intruders, dangerous, enemies.

Rocks moved, coming down the slope. He blinked warily, and they were not rocks, but small gray men. Kapristi, not men, he reminded himself. Gnomes out of fireside stories, all cautionary: what happened to the man who tried to cheat a gnome, the woman who hired a gnome to clean the chimney, the child whose goats strayed over the gnome's boundary. As a child, he'd thought that last story silly, but back then he'd assumed that the gnome lands had a tall wall around them, that the boy must have pretended his goats got in as an excuse to climb the walls and see for himself what treasures the gnomes had.

The gnomes (he felt slightly more comfortable with his peoples' name for them in his mind) moved with steady precision, nothing at all like men slipping and clomping down a slope. Six of them, all looking (to his eye) much alike. They loosed no shower of stones, no bits of turf, to roll before them. They had narrow clean-shaven faces (or did they not grow beards?) under close-cropped dark hair. Although they barely came up to his chest, he could not have confused them with boys—no boy moved with such economy, or had such hardness of face. They all wore gray: belted jerkins over long-sleeved shirts, narrow gray trews tucked neatly into gray boots. Jerkins and trews might have been leather; the shirts were wool.

Meanwhile, Arranha had bowed and spoken again in their angular tongue. Gird heard his own name mentioned, and glanced at Arranha, then looked back at the gnomes. The apparent leader was looking at him, a speculative look that made Gird feel like a carthorse up for sale. He could feel his ears and neck getting hot. Finally, Arranha turned to him again.

"Gird, this is Lawmaster Karik—that's not all of his name, but that's the polite way for a human to speak to him. I have told him about you, and he has agreed to speak with you. He has not, however, agreed to let you enter kapristi lands: he will speak with you here, across the line."

If it had not been for Arranha's gaze, Gird would have turned on his heel and stomped away. They didn't trust him, that's what it was, and he had done nothing to earn their distrust. *Yet*, said a voice in his mind. Arranha had told him of the Aarean nobles' attempt to take gnomish lands; they had reason to distrust humans.

Gird choked back all he wanted to say, and bowed awkwardly at the gnomish leader.

"Lawmaster Karik—"

"Gird? You have no clan-name?"

"Dorthan Selis's son was my father; but our clan name was lost. Our lord was Kelaive, whose subject-name I refuse."

"Ah." A gabble of gnomish between the leader and another of his group. Then the leader turned back to Gird. "It is that you have no master? No clan? No allegiance? You are without law?"

Gird stared. What were they driving at? He looked at Arranha, who said nothing, and wanted to smack that smug smile off the priest's face . . . except that it wouldn't work. He cleared his throat, and then realized that a wad of spit could be misunderstood. He swallowed it. The gnomes waited, motionless but not unattending.

"Lawmaster Karik, our lord destroyed our law." That got attention; he could almost feel the intensity of their interest. "I came seeking law—a way to make things fair."

"*Things* are fair, human farmer: it is living beings who may choose unfairness. Are you a god, to know justice and give judgment?"

Gird shook his head, hoping the gnomes had the same gesture. "No god at all, Lawmaster, but a man seeking knowledge. I know *un*fairness when I see it: short weight, shoddy work, carelessness that causes injury, stealing and lying—but Arranha has taught me that knowing wrong is not all I need to do right."

"And he brought you here? Or did you seek us on your own?"

"I—he would have taught me his rules, Lawmaster. He showed me that the magelords have broken the Rules of Aare, changed their meanings . . . but I want nothing of those old rules. I want new rules, better rules, that cannot be so misunderstood."

The Lawmaster turned to Arranha. "Here is a strange being. You told us once that the serfs had no wit for law."

"I was wrong." Arranha bowed, first at the Lawmaster, then at Gird. "When Gird and I first met, I thought he was a common outlaw—a rabble-rouser who wanted only vengeance for injuries done. And indeed, he had suffered injuries enough. But he has more—"

"Indeed." The Lawmaster's dark, enigmatic gaze returned to Gird. "And you, Gird son of Dorthan son of Selis, you must know we give nothing: that is fairness, good for good and evil for evil. What can you give, for the knowledge you seek?"

"My pledge. Arranha said you had no law between your people and ours except by steel. If our side wins, I pledge a rule of law that protects all boundaries, yours and ours, and my own strength to enforce it."

"You could be killed in a season, and your debt to us would not be paid. Or your cause could fail, easily enough . . . though I hear you are trying to teach discipline to idle human rabble . . ."

"Not idle, Lawmaster, but by the magelords' illwill."

"Hmph." The Lawmaster looked hard at Gird, then said, "Will you give the pledge of your hand and heart, to do all in your power to restore justice to these disputed lands?"

"Yes."

"Then come over the boundary, and I will teach."

For all that he had thought he was nervous under an open sky, Gird found that winter season mured in the gnome's halls almost intolerable. Rock beneath his feet, rock overhead, rock walls never far away on either hand. Nothing to see but rock, however finely dressed. He saw no beauty in the austere fluting of columns, the majestic proportion of the ceremonial halls. His hosts soon knew this, and his most constant guide once sniffed, "If you want splendor, Gird, if you want stone wrought into the likeness of beasts and birds and trees, studded with shining jewels and clad in gold and silver, if you want harp music and singing, you should have chosen our cousins. Dwarves chose splendor; they are all gold and blood, generous or deadly as the passion takes them. But you wanted law, you said, and that is what we live."

"You do trade jewels," Gird said. He had seen them once, laid in a precise pattern on black cloth for an apprentice to value.

"We do. We are rockfolk, after all; the rock speaks to us as trees speak to the sinyi." The gnome sighed heavily at Gird's blank look. "*Elves*, that is: the first born singers, those of silver blood. The rock is ours, and the rock returns to us in its treasures what we give of wisdom and loyalty."

"Like cows," Gird murmured; the gnome glared him.

"It is nothing like cows. You *eat* cows."

Gird did not argue—he could not win arguments with the gnomes—but he thought it was the same. He had loved his cows, cared for them, and out of that love and care had come the bounty of milk and meat and hide.

Most of his time, especially at first, he spent with Lawmaster Karik in a quiet, brightly-lit room lined with shelves full of books— the first he'd ever seen—and scrolls.

Lawmaster Karik insisted that Gird must learn to read and write—to gnomish standards—and calculate with their figures. "Law is too important to be left to your memory," he said. Gird could tell that this, like most that he said, was not negotiable. "You must write it down, and in courts of law it must be there for reference. Likewise contracts: you understand the importance of honest exchange, but how can that be adjudicated if the terms of the contract are in question? It must all be written down."

"But my people don't usually read and write," Gird said.

"They must learn." Lawmaster Karik tapped the heavy slates on which he had marked the gnomish runes. "If it happens that some cannot learn, then someone who reads and writes must stand for that person before the law. We have few so lacking in wit; we must hope that among your people it is also rare. Is it true you know nothing of written speech?"

Gird felt himself flushing again; in a moment he would start sweating. "They—I tried to learn, when my lord's guard recruited me."

"Well? Can you read, or not?"

He was sweating; he felt huge and clumsy and stupid next to the precise gray figure of the gnome, whose face never showed emotion. "Very little," he said unwillingly.

"You will learn. As it is a necessary precondition to your learning how to devise a workable system of law for your imperfect people, and as we did not ascertain before we contracted with you to teach you law, it is to our loss that this is assigned, and you will not incur any greater obligation because of it." The gnomish clerk who accompanied Lawmaster Karik to the lessons noted this down; Gird suddenly realized that what he had done originally had also been put down as a written contract. "You must learn rapidly, Gird, if you are to be in time to begin your war in the correct season."

To Gird's surprise, the gnomish script came easier than the Aarean had—or perhaps it was the absolute lack of distractions, and his fear that he might have to stay there forever if he did not learn. More quickly than he dared hope, he was able to sound his way through a passage of law that the gnomes had translated for him. They had turned aside his attempts to learn their language: "There is not time," all of them said.

"If it is when a contract made that one party agrees to hold the other not liable in case of death, then it is lawful for the death of that second party to clear the obligation from his own heirs, but if that second party has partners in work, then it is not lawful, even if it is so when the contract is made." Gird came to the end of that proud of his ability to read, but unsure of the implications for a farmer whose cow dies before it is delivered to the buyer.

Lawmaster Karik said, "A cow cannot be a party to contract: the death of the cow has nothing to do with it. It is the death of the farmer that might apply, if the buyer agreed that the farmer's death meant the farmer's heirs need not deliver the cow."

"But if he has not paid for the cow, why should he expect it if the farmer has died?"

"Suppose he has paid for it, expecting it to come."

"That's not how we sell cows," Gird said. He knew about that; no farmer in his right mind would pay for a cow that did not stand foursquare and in milk before his eyes. The Lawmaster looked at him, and he felt that he must have said something stupid.

"Let it not be cows," the Lawmaster said, "Even among men, it is common that one buys something for delivery later. One may provide cloth to a tailor, who will make clothes of it. One may send fruit or cheese or grain to a fair, and expect goods or coin to come back." Gird had to admit that some people did things that way; he thought it was unnecessarily risky. "You, yourself," the Lawmaster insisted. "You send men out to bring back supplies, do you not?" He did, but most of those were gifts, not paid for, and he knew very well what the gnomes thought of that. To prevent more argument, he nodded.

"So if someone buys something not present, and the person selling it should die before delivering it . . . then, if it was agreed beforehand, his death cancels the debt?"

"That is what that passage says."

"But does the seller's heir keep the price?"

A flicker of interest on the Lawmaster's face. "An excellent question! That is in the following passage, which you may now read."

Gird cursed himself silently, and put his thick finger on the first symbols of the next line. Another miserable passage of legalese. The matter turned, he learned as he read, on whether the goods exchanged for the undelivered goods were perishable, consumable, or durable. If someone traded soft fruits for grain, the grain to be delivered, the soft fruits might have spoiled, or been eaten, before the nondelivery occurred (counting, the gnomish law specified, the days between making the contract and expected delivery, before nondelivery could be charged.) Perishable goods fell under one section of law, and consumable goods under another.

"For example," the Lawmaster said, "if someone trades cloth to a tailor for clothing made . . . if the tailor cuts the cloth, but then dies before the garment is made . . . you see that cloth is consumable, and properly so. That is a different situation from a tailor who sold that cloth to someone else, and then died. In the first case, supposing the original contract to have had a death clause, the tailor's heirs would not have to return the cut cloth. But in the second, they would owe the price they received for it."

The more he studied, the more Gird saw that the gnomish law did make plain sense. Absolute honesty, absolute fairness in exchange: all the laws came down to this, and nothing intruded. They had a rigid rank structure, but rank had nothing to do with law . . . at least, the law of exchange, which made all equal . . . that "one measure for all" that Arranha had mentioned. He could see how it would work among humans—at least, among humans who wanted it to work. It was what he wanted for his people, fair laws; surely they all wanted the same.

Lawmaster Karik began to give him simple cases to examine. Gird found judging harder than he had expected, particularly when

Karik insisted that intent and circumstance made no difference to the law.

"If someone means well, but does ill, the ill is still done—and the consequences still exist. Besides, if intent forgives wrong, then any wrongdoer can claim good intent."

"But it's obvious," said Gird. "I could tell if someone meant to do wrong, or just erred."

"Could you? Suppose someone stole a measure of grain, claiming it was to save a family member from starving . . ."

"Find out if the person is starving," said Gird promptly.

Karik shook his head. "Suppose the thief had plenty of grain of his own, but chose to steal someone else's rather than fulfill his own family obligation. Suppose the thief had money, with which to buy grain, but again chose to steal it. Suppose—"

"All right." Gird held up his hand. "I understand. But surely there are times when circumstances make a difference."

Karik nodded slowly. "There are. No code of law can speak to all circumstances, even among gnomes, and among your undisciplined people I foresee great confusion. But for every exception you make to a rule, Gird, more will try to force their circumstances into that exception. As plants growing between set stones force them apart, the roots of the plants seek every weakness in the stone." Gird suddenly realized that Karik identified with the stone—that all the rockfolk would—where his sympathies had always been with the plants that broke stones apart. Even when it meant mending a wall, he had admired the delicate mosses and ferns that had persevered in their attack on it. He pushed this thought away, and came back to the subject. He had always assumed that the gnomes would feel as he did about Kelaive's treatment of Meris, that the punishment was far more than a boy's prank deserved Now he asked.

Karik listened to all the details before saying anything. Then he had questions Gird had never thought of, and only after offered his opinion.

"The right relation of punishment to wrongdoing is a subject in itself," he began. "In our law, the obligation is to restore, so far as possible, the right relation between the parties. Thus if you should steal a measure of grain, you would have to replace it—or its value—and also pay a fine to the court, to cover the cost of trying the case. We use punishment only for younglings, but some human systems extend punishment to adult humans, and in our view fail to distinguish properly between punishment and restoration. Some things, of course, admit of no restoration: injury that results in permanent loss of function, death, the breakage or loss of some singular, irreplaceable object. This is difficult to judge, although we have standards.

"In the case you speak of, you are not arguing that the wrongdoer was not guilty, but that the punishment was too great. On that basis alone, I would agree. But if the fine for a theft of so much fruit were a certain amount, the thief's age would make no difference. Circumstance should not change the judgment, assuming the law to be just in the first place. Kelaive seems to have had no law beyond his own pleasure: this does not make the boy's thieving less wrong, but adds another wrong—the lord's wrong—to it."

"I still think there are times—" Gird began. Karik waved him to silence.

"You have never lived under a just code of law; you cannot be expected to understand how it would be. We shall do our best to teach you, and hope you can teach others, and in time your people may approach justice." With that Gird had to be content.

In the course of learning law, Gird answered the gnomes' questions about the way he organized his troops. He had not forgotten what Arranha said about the gnomes' fighting ability. Perhaps he could find something to trade for their knowledge—but nothing occurred to him. The offer came, to his surprise, from the other side, many hands of days after he had made good progress with Karik.

He and Arranha met with a group of gnomes in one of the formal halls; Arranha had explained that he'd been asked to translate. After a few exchanges of formal greetings, one of the gnomes spoke steadily for several minutes. Finally Arranha turned to Gird.

"They would like to contract with you to provide military knowledge in return for your help in a specific battle. They think you need this knowledge, and may not win your war without it; they have been impressed by your diligence in your study of law, and your lawful nature. But, they point out, you seem to have no knowledge of strategy, and little of tactics. This they can provide. Are you interested?"

Of course he was interested, but for what kind of battle did they need his help, if they could defeat the magelords on their own? He framed that question as tactfully as he might, for Arranha to translate, but the gnomes could follow his speech well enough and began to answer at once. They could give him no details until they knew more of his abilities, but they wanted the Aareans lured into a trap . . . the Aareans were too wary, now, to come after gnomes if nothing else was involved.

Gird stared at the blank grayish faces, all too aware of his own limited experience. He wanted—no, *needed*—the expertise they had; he had been allowed to see a unit of gnomish guards drilling once, and he lusted after that knowledge. But what would it cost? By their own law, they had to deal fairly with him . . . though his notion of fairness went far astray from theirs. Was this a place in which they overlapped?

They did not rush him. He sat a long time, or so it seemed, in silence, and when he finally nodded, and then slowly read the contract and signed his name—shakily, but legibly—they bowed stiffly and left him alone with Arranha.

The next day, Lawmaster Karik introduced him to Warmaster Ketik, who turned him over to Armsmaster Setik. Not for the first time, he wondered if the gnomes chose their names to sound like beetle-clicks. It was not a question he could ask. Armsmaster Setik had the first scar he had seen on a gnomish face, two of them, in fact. Gird had expected a larger, brawnier gnome, but Setik was built like all the rest. He walked around Gird like a child around a trade-fair wrestler, looking him up and down, then snapped a question at the interpreter who had come along.

"Are all humans your size, he asks?"

Gird shook his head. "No—they come from this high—" he gestured, "to this high—a hand taller than I am. Some are built thin, and some heavy, at every height."

"And what are your weapons?"

Gird listed them—the ones they'd used so far, and the ones he'd thought possibilities. The Armsmaster listened in the usual expressionless silence, and then uttered a brief comment which the interpreter did not immediately explain. "What?" asked Gird finally. The interpreter's mouth twitched.

"He said 'Ridiculous!' "

Gird felt the back of his neck getting hot. It was *not* ridiculous; he had won a battle with just those weapons. The Armsmaster watched him out of black, shiny eyes like seeds. Gird struggled with his anger, all too visibly he was sure, and said, "It worked well enough." This time the Armsmaster's question was obvious enough that he began answering before the translator finished, squatting to draw on the floor with his finger the little battle of Norwalk Sheepfolds. The Armsmaster sat on his heels, watching, absorbed in the recital. But ultimately unconvinced; when Gird finished, he began a rapid commentary in gnomish, and Gird knew, before the translator began, that it was critical.

"He says you were lucky. He says you made fundamental errors in placement of scouts, signalling methods, and in choice of ground.

He says if you do that very often, you will kill all your people and lose your war."

Gird had long suspected that his apparent success at Norwalk Sheepfolds had been more luck than skill, but he did not like hearing that hasty analysis by someone who hadn't even been there. Someone who was used to drilling with experienced (and disciplined) gnomes, who would not have to stop a panicky rout just before a fight, who had time to pick the right ground, and dependable people to work with. He wanted to say all that, until the gnomes understood, but the Armsmaster's shiny dark eyes offered no sympathy. He wanted to say they'd won anyway, despite his mistakes (if the problem had really been his mistakes) but he met a closed, expressionless face that was not about to change its mind.

"So what should I have done?" he asked, not quite successful at keeping the sarcasm out of his voice.

"He says you will know when he has finished training you."

Gnomish military training was to the training his old guard sergeant had given as Mali's cooking had been to his mother's. He had been proud of his troop's drill—now, for the first time in his life, he saw absolute precision, and realized how sloppy even his old sergeant had been.

"It did not require much to impress peasants who had nothing," the Armsmaster said. The three units of gnomes who had just shown off would have impressed anyone, Gird was sure. They had moved forward, backward, sideways, opening and closing ranks, had marched one unit through another, and had come out the other end of a long string of commands in the same close, crisp formation they'd begun. "You will not get this, from your humans who are not all the same size and shape. But you can come closer than you have."

Gird felt like a clumsy, not-too-bright recruit again, trapped in the middle of a formation of gnomes not quite shoulder high on him. But he learned—learned not only how to move, but why. That notion of a pincushion that he had had, when he ran around turning his people in place at Norwalk: that had a name, and the right commands to achieve it whenever he wanted, from any other formation. He had always assumed that he needed a large uncumbered space for drill, the gnomes taught him to move a unit quickly and precisely in a room cluttered with supplies, to judge the space available and come up with the commands needed.

He discovered that the wrestling ability which had dumped both Cob and Triga was the very first level the gnomish younglings learned. Armsmaster Setik dumped him repeatedly, no matter what approach he took. "You're too short," he complained once, bruised and winded from several hard falls. "I can't get a grip on you—and besides, you rockfolk are stronger." Setik grabbed his wrist and pulled him up.

"We are not stronger. We know how to use our strength. Can you lift that?" *That* was a barrel of meal. Gird shrugged, and tried. It was heavy, but he had lifted heavier. Setik put his arms around it and heaved, but it did not lift. "You see? You are stronger, in plain strength. It can be very useful. But you do not know how to use that strength. You want to jump at me and do the work yourself. Make me do the work."

They drilled with sticks very similar to those Gird's people used. Setik insisted they must all be the same, no matter the size of the fighter. Gird thought that was another expression of the gnomish need for order, but Setik disagreed. "First: they must all be the same so that your fighting formation can have the same intervals without chancing an accidental blow. Second: they must all be the same so that when one breaks, or someone drops one, that fighter will be comfortable with any replacement. Each weapon has its own best blows; some are similar, but in battle a single mistake chances death. Chance is your enemy, Gird—do not depend on luck. Depend on skill, drill, strength, endurance, tactics: what you know, what you can do. If that is not enough, chance will not save you."

"But what about our tools? I thought we could use farm tools—we did use them."

Setik snapped a command at one of the others, who went jogging off to the gnomish armory, and returned festooned with agricultural implements. Setik picked up a scythe. "Show me how your people used this at Norwalk."

Gird hefted it, enjoying as always the very balance and swing of it, then shifted the handgrips for a better overhand stroke, and lifted it. It made an awkward chopping weapon, harder to control than a mattock, but it could reach over others and deliver a solid blow to a head or back. He had seen only two of the successful strokes, both oblique downward swings that ended in a soldier's back. He demonstrated on the straw-filled leather dummy set up in the middle of the chamber.

"I thought at first of swinging it as usual," he explained. "It could take off a leg. But the backswing's too dangerous—there's no way to control it in formation."

"That's what I thought." Setik scratched his head. "We had a weapon more like a mattock, used with a similar stroke but easier to handle because it balances better. That great long blade out there, and the curving handle, make this one very unbalanced. And even you, with your strength, could not swing it sideways at head level."

"Even if I could, the greatest danger is to the person on my left and behind. I've seen someone killed like that in harvest, a scythe-tip buried in his belly."

"Good *individual* defense," Setik muttered. "One man against several armed—that might work. Sharpen the outer edge of the blade as well. But not a good formation weapon. I suppose you use the shovel like the pole?"

"Yes, but it has that edge."

"Hmmm. What we call a broadpike. It would also work with a sharp downward stroke, but that would not fend off the enemy's. These little things you mentioned, sickles and firetongs and such— good for brawls, maybe, or defense when surprised by an enemy while working—but not for your army." Setik went down the list, explaining and demonstrating why each tool was not worth using as a weapon, "unless you have nothing else. But I would not waste my time drilling with them. If you are fighting with trained units against real soldiers, you need a formation weapon. We use polearms, to give us reach, a hauk in close fighting, and archers . . . do your people know archery at all?"

A hauk, when Gird asked, was a short stick, a club, which could be used for training, or for cracking heads—it reminded him of the guards' billets and maces. The gnomes in formation had hauks thrust into their belts behind their backs, ready to grab when needed. Gird learned how to handle all the gnomish polearms cor- rectly; Setik recommended that he settle on one, fairly easily made, for his own army. "A simple spike on the end of your pole will do," Setik said, "and any smith can make that from scrap metal— those scythe blades, for instance. A real pikehead is better, and you could use broadpikes, but that takes more metal, and more skill in smithing. Sharpening the pole itself is better than nothing, but wood alone is not likely to penetrate metal armor—if that's what they're wearing."

Setik knew exactly how footsoldiers with pikes should maneuver against cavalry; Gird's rude guesses, based on practice with men on logs, came close but would, Setik said, cost him too many sol- diers. Archers were the worst threat; the gnomes dealt with enemy bowmen by having better bowmen of their own. Gird was not sure his people could learn that fast. He himself had never been better than average with a bow. And the art of making good bows and good arrows—strong enough to be useful in war—had passed from his people to the Aarean lords. Peasants had not been allowed to have bows, or make bows; what they had now could take small birds and animals, but no more. Setik shook his head, and explained to Gird again just how much damage an unopposed group of archers could do. The implication was clear: learn this, somehow, or die for its lack. Gird began to consider who among his people might know a clandestine archery expert—someone far to the north, who might have friends or family among the horse nomads, whose bows the Finaareans respected, perhaps.

Days passed; Gird was no longer sure how many. The gnomes did not celebrate Midwinter, and refused to interrupt his lessons for it. He hoped the gods would forgive him, this once—perhaps, since he was underground, among gnomes, they would not know. That didn't seem likely; the gnomes certainly thought that the High Lord, the great Judge, knew everything above ground or below.

He felt stuffed with new knowledge, things that made perfect sense during the lessons but came apart in his mind afterward like windblown puffballs. The Warmaster had been appalled to discover that Gird had no idea how many of the lords there were, or how many soldiers they had. That Gird could not draw an accurate map of Finaarenis and the surrounding lands. That he did not know who the king was, or how the king was related to the various nobles, or how the land was governed. They poured all this into him, day after day, every minute of his waking hours filled and overfilled with new knowledge. He had never known there was that much knowledge in the whole world, and he wished he hadn't found it out. Even with the gnomes' organizing skills, he found himself remembering the name of a town when he wanted the number of stones of grain needed to feed a hundred men on march for two hands of days, or coming up with the right way to place scouts to watch a tradeway when he wanted the command that split a column marching forward into two columns, one of which was veering off to the right. He could imagine himself in the midst of battle calling out the exceptions to liability for delivery of spoiled perishables instead of the right commands, and he sweated all the worse for it.

This struggle was no easier that he did not know how long it would last: how long he had to learn what—he now agreed—he needed to learn. Years would not have been enough; he had started with a bare half-year, if he was going to lead the war in the next season. He would have fretted about that, if he had had time. Instead, the worry seeped into his other thoughts like a drop of dye into water, coloring every moment with fear he had not named.

He would have discussed it with Arranha, but the priest was often away when Gird returned to his assigned quarters and fell into bed.

At last, with no warning (at least nothing he had noticed) he and Arranha were summoned to the largest of the ceremonial halls, where a crowd of gnomes had assembled. Silently, Gird noticed; there was none of the whispering or chattering of a human crowd. Lawmaster Karik (one of the four or five he had finally learned to recognize at sight) led Gird to the front of the chamber, and spoke lengthily in gnomish. Then he turned to Gird.

"It is time to send you out, if you would be at your encampment before your people are sure we have killed you. Remember your contracts with us; we have delivered to you that which we promised. You have your obligation."

At least he knew the correct response. "I acknowledge receipt of your knowledge and training; I admit my obligation, and swear to fulfill it to the length of my life."

"Witnessed." That brought a stir, and the chorus from all. "Witnessed."

A chill went down his back. He fully intended to carry out all he had promised, but that "witnessed" meant uncounted gnome pikes at his back if he failed.

Chapter Twenty

He had known he missed the sun—even the thin, cold sunlight of winter—but not until he came out into that remembered beauty, and rested his gaze on a horizon impossibly distant, did he know how much. Tears stung his eyes. It had hurt, in ways he could not define, to have his vision trapped between walls so long. It had hurt to have sounds reverberating in those walls, quiet as the gnomes had been. It had hurt to smell no live wind, with its infinitely varying smells, its constantly changing pressures on his skin. They had led him out into a morning of softly falling rain, a cold spring rain that still held a threat of late snow. Between the showers that fell curtainlike here and there he could see long tawny slopes, dark patches of woodland, the soft lavender and muted burgandy of sap-swollen buds coloring what had been gray. He heard the soft whisper of the rain on sodden grass, the distant gurgle of water running away downhill, a vast silence between the sounds where nothing would echo. Cold and damp as it was, it soothed the inside of his nose, easing with smells of wet earth and rock the dry itch from a season underground with only rockdust and gnomes. His own human smell, that he had been aware of as unlike the others, disappeared into that freshness.

"We will see you at Blackbone Hill," said Armsmaster Setik, who had come out with Gird. Arranha was staying behind awhile, but had told Gird he would follow him later. Gird wondered if Arranha knew about Blackbone Hill; the gnomes mentioned the name only when Arranha was not around.

"Yes," said Gird, drinking in another breath of that air, wondering why the ragged, uneven landscape of duns and grays seemed so much more beautiful than the careful sculpting of the gnomes' halls.

"You have the maps."

"Yes." As he looked at the land, now, the maps he had been taught to use seemed to overlay it. He would go *that* way, and find a tiny watercourse to lead him north and west, then leave that one by a steep-browed hill, and find another beyond the hill, and then the wood he almost thought of as *his* wood . . .

"And—" Setik looked up at him with an expression Gird could not interpret. "I found it most satisfying; for a human, you are— are not unlike a kapristi in some ways."

Gird turned, surprised. The Armsmaster had been even less outgoing than his other instructors, if possible. Gird had assumed he would be glad to rid himself of a clumsy human oaf. Setik's brow was furrowed slightly, his scars pulled awry.

"You are by nature hasty, as all the lateborn are: hasty to laughter, to anger, to hunger—but you forced foresight on yourself, and withheld haste. You have a gift for order, for discipline, for what we mean by responsibility."

"You are a good teacher," Gird said.

The gnome nodded. "I am, that is true. But the best teacher cannot turn a living thing from its nature: I could not make stone grow and bear fruit like a tree. I could not teach a tree to fly. Even among us, who are much alike, some have less talent for war than others. You have it, and you have what is rare with us—what war requires that the rest of our life does not need, and that is a willingness to go beyond what is required, into the realm of gift."

Gird was both puzzled and fascinated. All he had heard, from Lawmaster Karik, showed the gnomes' distrust of gifts, and until now he had not suspected the gnomish soldiers thought differently.

Setik smiled suddenly, a change as startling as if rock split in a manic grin.

"War calls for more than fair exchange; we soldiers know what the lawgivers cannot understand. Even among us, I say, are some who freely give—and in war that giving wins battles. You have that; from what you say, it is a human trait." Abruptly, he stopped, and his face changed back to its former dourness. "Go with the High Lord's judgment," he said. Gird glanced back at the entrance to the gnomes' caves, so nearly invisible; there stood several others, watching and listening.

"You will not take thanks," he said to Setik, "but among my people it is rude to withhold them. I will thank the gods, then, for sending me to such a good teacher of war, and ask their grace to keep my mind from scrambling together what you so carefully set apart."

If he had believed the gnomes had any humor whatever, he would have said Setik's black eyes twinkled. "Soldiers of one training are as brothers of one father," the gnome murmured. "Go now, before someone asks awkward questions."

Gird nodded, saying nothing past the lump in his throat, and headed downslope. He stepped carefully across the boundary, and did not look back until he had traveled well out of sight of that unambiguous line.

The gnomes had shown him a small, exquisitely carved model of the lands they called *gnishina,* all drained by the great river Gird had never yet seen, from the western plains to the sea. All his life Gird had lived among low hills and creeks whose windings made no sense to him. He had thought the world was made lumpy, like redroots in a pan, until he saw the gnomes' country, with great mountains rising behind a line of hills.

The model made sense of what had seemed random hummocks. He had not understood the gnomes' explanation, but the great concentric arcs of rock were obvious enough, with the river dividing them like the cleft of a cow's hoof. Rows of hills, variously shaped by the different kinds of rock in them (he understood that much; everyone knew that red rock made rounded slopes, and white rock made stepwise ones) bowed sharply away from the river, to run almost parallel to the southern mountains as they neared them. Between the hills ran the creeks and rivers, all tributaries of the Honnorgat. These stream valleys had formed natural routes of travel. Moving a large force north or south was easiest near the Honnorgat; moving it east or west was easiest away from the great river.

Once more under the open sky, he could interpret the hills before him for what they were: the flanks of a great arch. Going north, he would cross white rock to yellow, and yellow to brown, then travel west to come back to yellow and white. Just so a man might run his finger from the side of a cow's hoof to the cleft, then forward to the point—and find hoof wall again. More importantly, with his understanding of the whole region, and the maps the gnomes had provided, he would know where he was—where his army was—and how to get where he wanted to go. He hoped.

Human lands were scarcely less perilous than the gnome prince-doms, though their perils were less uncanny. Gadilon might not trouble his gnomish neighbors, for fear of their retribution, but he had no intention of letting a peasant uprising unseat him. Gird was hardly into that domain when he saw the first patrols, seasoned soldiers whose alertness indicated respect for their new enemy. Whatever had happened while Gird was underground with the gnomes, it had ended all complacency in the outlying holdings. Gird spent an uncomfortable half-day lying flat among dripping bushes as the patrols crossed and recrossed the route he had planned to take. When dark fell, he extricated himself, muttering curses, and edged carefully around the hill and down a noisy water-course. Here the water noises would cover any he made.

Even with his caution, he was nearly caught. If the sentry had not coughed, and then spat into the water, Gird would never have known that the dark shadow of a boulder was actually a person. He stopped where he was, wondering if he'd been seen. Another cough, a muttered curse. Gird crept away from the stream's edge, feeling the ground under his feet carefully. He could not stay here, and he could not go back—not without knowing where the other soldiers were. He made his way into the tangle of rocks on that side of the stream, and eased his way up onto one of the huge boulders. From that height, he could just see a twinkle of firelight downstream and below. The sentry had probably been told to climb where Gird now was, but up here the night breeze was cold and raw; the man had slid down to get out of the wind. Gird flattened himself on the cold hard stone and thought about it.

With his gnomish training in mind, if he'd been the person responsible for that camp, he'd have had sentries upstream and down, and scattered through the woods. Scattered where? His un-gnomish experience told him that men, like the sentry whose cough had revealed him, cared for their own comfort. No matter how wisely a commander had sent them out, they would each choose a place that combined the maximum of personal safety and comfort with sufficient—to that individual—performance of the assignment. If he could figure out what that was, he could get around the camp in safety. If he made a mistake, they would all be after him.

One simple answer was to backtrack upstream and swing wide around the camp. That would work if he didn't then run into another patrol. He could think of no reason why Gadilon would have another patrol out to the south, but who could read the lords' intent? Or he could try to angle away from the stream, through the brush and woods, and hope to avoid any other sentries without losing so much ground. If the streamside sentry represented the distance from the camp that all of them were posted, that should be possible. He was still debating this with himself when he heard horses' hooves in the distance, a cry of alarm from the camp, and a trumpet call. The sentry below him gasped, and started back for the camp at a run, falling over rocks and bellowing as he went.

Gird stayed where he was, trying to understand what was going on. More lights appeared: flickering torches moving between the trees. Loud cries, shouted commands, responses from distant sentries. He felt a little smug that they were coming from the radius he'd guessed. He wished he could get closer, and had started down from the rock when he heard the unmistakeable clash of steel on steel. More yelling, more screams, more noise of hoofs, weapons, another trumpet blast cut off in mid-cry. He could hear noise coming his way, as several men thrashed through the undergrowth, stumbled over obstructions. They came near enough that he could hear their gasping breath, the jingle of their buckles and mail, the creak of leather. Behind them were more; someone shouted "There they go!"

With a crunch of boots on gravel, they were beneath him. He could just make out two or three dark forms against the starlit water, the gleam of starlight along a weapon's blade. One there was wounded, groaning a little with every gasping breath. Gird lay motionless, hoping no one would notice the large shadow flat on the top of the boulder.

"Don't let 'em get away!" he heard from downstream. "Follow that blood trail." One of the men below him cursed viciously.

"We got to move," he said. "They'll find us, and—"

"Per can't go farther," said another. "We'll have to fight 'em off."

"We can't." A pause, then, "We'll have to leave 'im. He's the blood trail, anyway. They find him, dead, they'll think that's it."

"No! They'll know he couldn't have got this far alone. 'Sides, he's my sister's husband; I'm not leaving him."

"Suit yourself." One of the shadows splashed into the stream, and started across. The other threw a low-voiced curse after him, and backed against the rock on which Gird lay.

Now the pursuers were in sight, the light of their torches swinging wildly through the trees. Gird saw rough, bearded faces, men wearing no livery, or even normal clothes, but the skins of wild animals roughly tanned and crudely fashioned. They carried swords and pikes, stained already with blood. Gird dared not lean out from his perch to see the men at the foot of his rock—but he suspected that they were Gadilon's soldiers, in his livery, and these others were—what? Not any he had trained, he was sure, but who? Gadilon's peasants?

He slid back carefully over the crest of the boulder, hoping that their attention was fixed on the men below. What happened then was clear enough by the sound of it: a low growl of anticipation from the pursuers, a challenge by the one man still able to fight, and bloody butchery thereafter. It did not last long. One of the attackers said, "There was another—look here, he took to the water."

"No matter. We'll find 'im by day, or let 'im carry word to his lord—he'll get no comfort of it. One back from each patrol will do us no harm." Then the speaker raised his voice to carry over the stream's chuckle. "Hey—you coward! You count's man! Go tell yer count what happened, and tell 'im 'twas Gird and his yeomen! Tell 'im to shake in 'is boots, while he has 'em to shake in."

Gird felt the blood rush to his skin at that; he nearly jumped up where he stood to deny it. How *dare* they use his name! His ears roared with the pressure of his anger; as his hearing cleared, he heard one of the men laugh.

"Diss, what're you playing at? D'you really think the count'll believe this night's work was Gird's?"

"What do I care? If he thinks it's peasants, he'll ride his peasants harder, and spend less time looking for brigands. If he blames every robbery and ambush in his domain on peasants, isn't that good for us? And if he doesn't believe it—if he thinks to himself it's a trick of brigands—he'll wonder why brigands would lay that crime on peasants. If maybe we're allies. And the peasants . . . if they'll skimp to send grain to Gird's yeomen, why not to us—if we convince them we're with them."

Gird dug his fingers into the rock to keep himself from plunging right into that—which was the same, he knew, as plunging a knife in his neck. The brigands all laughed; he heard them stripping the bodies of the count's soldiers, before they left them naked and unprotected in the night, to return to the fire and carousing with the guard-sergeant's ration of ale. Gird heard them ride away, in the hours before dawn. He waited until he could see clearly before slithering down from his perch, stiff and miserable, to see for himself what they'd done.

The dead soldiers looked no different from any other dead; he had not forgotten, in his half-year with the gnomes, how the dead looked and smelled. He squatted beside them and closed their eyes with pebbles. They were enemies, but not now his; he had not killed them, and he felt he owed them that basic courtesy. They had stiffened; he could not straighten their limbs. But he found mint already green beside the creek, and laid a sprig on each of them. Then he plucked a handful of it, and went toward the deserted camp. There he put mint on each of the dead, soldier and brigand alike, unsure why he was doing it except that it felt right. This was not his fight; he disliked both sides with equal intensity.

The brigands had stripped the soldiers of weapons, armor, clothes, and money (or so Gird judged, finding a couple of copper crabs trampled into the ground), but had left behind what food they had not eaten themselves. Gird saw no reason not to take it. He stuffed the flat loaves and half a cheese into his shirt. At the soldiers' picket lines, he found the cut ends of ropes where the brigands had stolen the horses; continuing downstream, he found another dead soldier, the downstream sentry.

He went as warily as he could, aware that he now had two sets of enemies: when Gadilon found out about his patrol, these hills would hum with soldiery, but at the same time the brigands would not be happy to find a real Gird in their midst. By midday, he had put a good distance between himself and the site of the brigand attack, but he felt no safer. The gnomish maps told him that he needed to cross all Gadilon's domain, south to north, then open sheep pastures shared between several lords and peasant villages, before he would be back in territory he knew by sight. The nearest barton—as of the previous fall, he reminded himself—was a group of shepherds who called their settlement Farmeet.

His most direct route took him across a trade road that connected Gadilon's towns with those in Tsaia to the east and Ierin, the most southwesterly town in Finaarenis. The gnomes had pointed out that he must, eventually, control traffic on this road in order to secure either southern quadrant of the realm. Like the River Road, along the southern bank of the Honnorgat in the north, the southern trade road allowed the lords to move soldiers and

supplies easily from one fortified town to another. Gird himself
found moving across country easier, but the gnomes had insisted
that no organized army could travel like a single man or a small
group.

Gird made it to the road with only one more close brush with
a patrol (he had hidden in a dense cedar as the men rode by
underneath, discussing the deaths of their friends in the ambush
Gird had seen. He was dismayed to find that they assumed peasants
had done it—and that the peasants and brigands were in league.)
Now he peered from a thick growth of plums, all white with bloom,
at a rutted track that seemed deserted. A horseman had ridden by
sometime before; he'd heard the hoofbeats, and he could see fresh
tracks overlying older ones. He leaned forward a little, shivering
the plums, and the bees in the blossoms lifted with a whine to
their buzz. Bees didn't bother him (he wondered where their hive
was), but he still could not tell if anyone was on the other side,
watching. The soldiers had said something about closing the trade
road, keeping the peasants from using it or crossing it. That would
take sentries all along the way—surely they weren't doing that—
but he would hate to take an arrow in the neck finding out.

Something chuffed, across the track. Gird held very still. A deer
burst through the plums there, paused in the track, ears wide and
tail high, and chuffed again. Even as Gird heard the snap of a
bowstring, an arrow thunked into the deer and it staggered, limped
a stride, and fell awkwardly. Three men dressed alike crashed
through the undergrowth, lashed the deer's carcass to a pole, and
disappeared back into the wood on the far side of the road, without
a glance toward Gird. Their silent cooperation convinced Gird that
they worked together constantly, but he had no idea whether they
were foresters, soldiers, or brigands. Or, for that matter, poaching
peasants. He could hear their progress through the wood; taking a
chance that anyone else watching would be attracted by that noise,
he darted across the road and into the trees, then swung wide of
their path.

He wished he dared speak to them. That archer had been powerful and accurate; that's what the gnomes said he needed. If those
were peasants, poaching deer, then he might find a useful follower.
More likely an arrow, he reminded himself. Too risky.

He made it safely to Farmeet, only to find the shepherds far less
outgoing than he remembered from the summer before.

"I heard you was taking on Gadilon's patrols," said one of the
shepherds, not quite looking at Gird. "Heard as you come on 'em

sleeping, and killed 'em lying there, and took their clothes and all . . ."

"No," said Gird. "That was brigands."

"How'd you know?" They were all very still, sitting hunched as shepherds do, their long crooks angling up over their shoulders.

"I was there, hiding from the soldiers, when the brigands came." They said nothing, but he could feel their disbelief. It was unlikely, he had to admit; to such as these, unlikely was nearly the same as impossible. Only a complete story would do; they would suspect anything less. Keeping his voice low and matter-of-fact, he told it all, from first sighting the sentry to laying mint on the bodies.

"Good you did that," said the oldest shepherd, nodding. "Shows respect to the Lady, that do. Proper to do it for both sides, too."

"They said they was you?" asked another.

Gird nodded. "They did, and they meant it to confuse both Gadilon's men and our people."

"We heard things this past winter." The oldest shepherd poked the fire. "You'd gone down to the underworld, we heard. Talked to that one—has the horned circle, you know what I mean?"

"Liart—" breathed Gird.

"Aye. No good, that one. Them's follows him likes hurting. Our lord's got some like that in his service. Heard you made bargain with 'im, anyhow. That's where you were, eh? Is it?"

"No." Gird wondered where that story had come from, the lords or the brigands or simple imagination. "No, I was with the kapristi—the gnomes, the little rockfolk."

"Ah. They're not *his* followers, what I hear."

"No. They follow the High Lord; I went to them to learn about law—what's wrong with the lords' law, and what might replace it."

A younger shepherd spat. "Anyone can see what's wrong with the lords' law—it don't take muckin' about underground to see that."

"Hush, Dikka. This'll be more, what Gird's talkin' about."

"When this war's over," Gird began, hoping they could think that far ahead, "we'll have to have fair laws, if we're to have peace. Most of our people don't remember how it was before the lords came. What we do now's a mix of our old customs and their laws— it makes no sense, as anyone can see—you're right there. But what to do about it—that's something else."

"And you saw beyond the war, to the peace? Ah, that's good." The oldest shepherd finally turned to look directly at Gird. "You want the peace, do you? And not just the fighting?"

"That's right."

"And you know a fair law for all of us then, when it's over?"

Gird shook his head. "I know a way to devise such a law—but it will mean many of us working on it. You, too, perhaps."

"Not me—but I'll be glad to think on it, that someone is. So you've naught to do with the horned chain?"

"No." He let it stand baldly, like that; they looked at him a long moment, then all nodded.

The oldest shepherd said, "You have an honest look, and nothing that fits one of the horned chain worshippers. So I say—" gathering the others with his eyes. "I say he *is* Gird, and not that fellow as stopped by a hand of days ago, claiming Gird's name and asking our help."

"What!" They had said nothing of this before. The old man grinned, showing the gaps in his teeth.

"Aye—another Gird was here, if we believed him, which we didn't. Big fellow, like you in that. Grinned a lot with plenty of teeth. Said that great powers was with him—and us if we joined him—and the lords would be cast down and trampled in the dust. Our sheep'd grow fat and have golden fleece, the way he told it— you'd think he'd been talking to the Master Shepherd and not the Master of Torments."

"So what did you do?" asked Gird, fascinated. The shepherds all chuckled.

"Do? We's no more'n stupid old shepherds, lad. Us can't think o' none but sheep and wool—can't make an onion from a barley-corn, nor sheep of mice, no more'n make soldiers of th' likes o' us, can you now?" The exaggeration of their accents was so pronounced that Gird found himself grinning; they grinned back, well pleased with his reaction. "He wanted a barton here; we said we's no bar-ton—we's shepherds, not farmfolk. He says what's Farmeet, then, as he's been told it's a barton—and we says it's a bitty sheepfold, no more'n that, just a lambing shed and pen. He was not happy wi' us when he left."

Gird sniffed elaborately, reference to the old saying about onions and barleycorn, and said, "I smell an onion in this seedsack, so I do—" They laughed uproariously.

"It works both ways," the old shepherd admitted. "No onions from barleycorns, but no hiding an onion from anyone with a nose. But them's certain as they smelled stupid, afore ever they got here; we's no reason to argue with 'em."

"How many?" asked Gird. The old shepherd held up his hands and spread them twice: four hands of men, about the size he'd expected.

The little Farmeet barton had only two hands of yeomen: six

men and four women. It would probably spend the entire war herding its sheep, shearing, spinning wool, but it had already served him well.

From Farmeet, he made it safely to Holn, where the rumors the brigands had spread had not yet come. Other rumors had. Already conflict had started, and the lords were raising all their troops, planning to crush the peasants before the summer came. They would move, Gird was told, on Kelaive's domain first, sweeping east across the lands where he had been known to dwell. Gird's own people had runners in all the southern villages, waiting word from him; Holn's runner had already gone to tell Ivis and Felis he was back, and another runner waited any message he wanted to send.

What he wanted, desperately, was a pause in time—a few days when nothing happened, so that he could get back with his own troop and make plans. But it could not be, and he understood it. He listened late to the yeomen of Holn, spreading the maps the gnomes had provided and running his finger along the lines. Then he slept, for a few hours, and had a last conference with the barton, warning them about the brigands who claimed his name. He had no time to stop and teach them the new drills the gnomes had taught him; they would have to learn later, when they rose. For now, he must get to his own troops as quickly as possible.

Although he knew the country near Holn, he was glad to have a local guide, who knew just where the patrols had been going. The first bits of green were showing in hedge and wood; wild plum frothed white, and tiny pink flowers starred the rumpled grass that had green at its roots. Cold wet air gusted past him, carrying occasional snowflakes, spurts of rain, and gleams of unsteady sunlight. He could smell the growth in it, the spring smell that made new lambs throw their tails over their backs and frisk as he and his guide went past. There was a pasture with cows, the herder in his leather cape standing hunched against a flurry of hard raindrops, and here was a ditch brimful of racing water, clear as deep winter ice in a bucket. Gird would have frisked if he could, and he chuckled to himself at the thought of a middle-aged farmer-turned-rebel, throwing his tail over his back to dance in a spring rain.

They saw no patrols that day, but between showers Gird thought he saw a smudge of dark smoke blowing away somewhere to the east. He asked his guide, who shrugged.

"There's been burnings, this winter past. A whole grange, we heard of: every bit of grain and hay lost, and the stones cracked, some of 'em. The lords were making everyone burn the stubble in the fields, last harvest, so's no one could hide in it. Hayricks, too, some places."

From Holn to Sawey, where Felis waited in the barton of a farmer called Ciri. It was dark, quiet but for dripping off the roofs—too quiet for a village on an early spring evening. His guide led him to the back gate, clicked the pebbles in his pocket together. Someone answered the clicks from within, then pushed the gate open for them. Inside was the good smell of food, cows, leather, oiled wood, and the sight of friends' faces. They hugged, smacking each others' shoulders. The gnomes' impassive dourness faded from Gird's mind—these were men, humans that he knew, faces alive with passion for one thing after another.

"At last," Felis said. Others echoed him. Gird took a deep breath. There was no going back now; there had been no going back from Norwalk, but now he could not hesitate. It was truly "at last" and he must do what he had come to do. They were watching him, relieved to see him but still a little uncertain. Hoping he was over whatever had bothered him after Norwalk Sheepfolds—*needing* him to be over it—but unsure that he was. They reminded him of boys watching a father whose uncertain temper determines the quality of their life. *I am sure,* he told himself. When he smiled at them, their faces relaxed.

"At last which?" he asked Felis, intentionally lightening the moment. "At last I am here to settle an argument, or so that you can tell me you don't want me, or—"

"You know," said Felis, rubbing his nose. How, Gird wondered, had it gotten sunburnt so early in the year?

"I do, but I'm not sure you do. Yes, this is the year, and yes, I have learned things we can use, and yes, we start now. Tonight."

He felt the change in the tiny enclosure: relief, eagerness, and—as always—fear.

"I told you," said one of the local men, in the corner. Gird smiled at him, raising an eyebrow; he flushed. "Some said you'd say wait, like you did last year, but I knew. I knew you had not lost your courage."

Felis jumped into that. "Only a few, Gird, and no one—"

"It's all right." He felt calm and light, certain now where he was going with this group, and for the next few days. After that—"I could not say what I thought was wrong; you know that saying things is not my skill. I'm a plain farmer, same as any of you. I was as glad as any, we'd won at Norwalk, but I knew something was wrong, and now I know what."

"And that is?" asked Felis, a challenge in his tone. Gird stretched, and let himself hunker down in a corner comfortably.

"You've heard of the gnomes' soldiering, haven't you?" Felis scowled, but nodded. "Well, they've taught me a lot. Norwalk *was* lucky. I had to learn better—and I have—and with what I know now and you can learn quick enough, even the gnomes think we can win."

"What did you trade them?" asked Ciris, whose barton it was.

"Our—*my*—pledge that we would respect their borders, deal fairly with them—" That got nods, and muttered agreement. "— And our help in one battle: they want to trap the magelords in a place called Blackbone Hill."

This caused less comment than he'd expected; if the gnomes wanted their help, they must think Gird's was good, and that meant good fortune. Gird had his doubts, but wasn't about to share them. Not yet.

"We're not in the same camps," Felis told Gird, when the other men had left and he and Gird were sharing a heap of straw. "The patrols began to come too close. Ivis thought we'd do better spread through several bartons. He said his forester friends told him the duke was planning a raid around Midwinter. So we left, and let out word to one of the brigand gangs that the camps had supplies in them. They moved in; the duke's men caught them—and recognized them, too; the leader's someone the duke's wanted for years. We hope that's convinced the duke that *his* peasant uprising was really a brigand gang in his wood. Ivis's brother agreed to say in the duke's court that the leader had been coming to him, threatening him."

Gird shook his head, half in admiration of their ingenuity, and half in concern. "Not all brigands are that gullible," he said, and told Felis about that other band he'd run into.

"So what will you do?"

"Fight my war, and let them fight theirs. People will recognize the difference soon enough." He told Felis about the shepherds of Farmeet. Felis chuckled.

"Everyone thinks farmers are stupid, and shepherds are the stupidest: lords and thieves alike. But tell me, what is 'your war'—how will we fight, and when, and where?"

"And have I seen the gods themselves, and is the overworld paved with gold and walled in crystal? You want all the answers at once? In the dark?" Beside him, Felis made a sound between a snort and a sniff; Gird relented. "All right. What I heard is that the lords have raised their army, and plan to start by clearing from

Kelaive's domain east. We will take all the bartons from Hardshallows eastward, and move north—away from them, for now—and
strike for the River Road."

"Why?"

"Even if we won here, we'd still be caught between the south
trade road, the River Road, and the trade road between Finyatha
and Ierin. Their supplies would flow freely; ours would not. If we
cut the River Road, we've cut Finyatha from Verella, in Tsaia—"

"Tsaia! You're not thinking of fighting there—"

"Tsaia's king is kinbound to this one. The gnomes say things are
as bad there. Our bartons on the east reported interest in neighboring vills inside Tsaia."

"But I don't know where Tsaia *is*, except eastward."

Gird grinned, in the darkness; Felis sounded as much affronted
as frightened. That was good. "You will know, when we get there.
Now: this is what we must do to win in Finaarenis alone. We must
be able to feed ourselves, control the food supply—and that means
the trade roads, as well as protection for the farmers, and certain
towns—"

"You sound—different—" Felis sounded uncertain again.

"I am, in a way. It's all very different than we thought. It's more
than raising three or four bartons at a time to attack a small force.
Right now the lords have trained soldiers with good weapons; they
have stores of supplies; they have control of towns and roads—and,
if we're honest, of much of the countryside. We should have more
yeomen overall, but you know how it is—if we seem to be losing,
some of those will go home and forget they ever heard of us. Our
people have almost no experience, our weapons— Oh. That
reminds me. Changes there, too."

Felis rolled over; the straw rustled. "All right. I'm convinced.
You've come back ready to lead us to glory, full of as many new
ideas as when you came into my camp that first day. But unless
the gods put their touch on you, you still need sleep, and so do I."

Chapter Twenty-one

In less than a hand of days, Gird stood facing his first army: the bartons from Hardshallows, his own village, Fireoak, Whitetree, Harrow, Holn, and the original two Stone Circle groups. After his experience with the gnomes, their "straight" lines looked crooked, and their marching seemed as ragged as goats dancing along a path, but he said nothing of that for the moment. They were there, bold, timid, nervous, confident, in every possible mood he might have expected. With them had come the food he had told them to put by for this purpose; each had brought his or her sack of grain and beans, onions and redroots, even strips of dried meat.

What he had not expected so soon was the ragtag clutter of refugees that had come with them. His own village had come all in a lump, convinced that anyone left behind would die. After all, everyone knew where Gird had come from, and Kelaive had never been slow to make reprisals. Most of Hardshallows followed its yeomen, for the same reason, and Fireoak, in the same hearthing, feared the same trouble.

So besides the yeomen, Gird had all the others to worry about: small children, pregnant women, old men and women who could scarcely totter. They knew nothing of camp discipline. He had to double, then triple, the size of the jacks; smoke from the cookfires marked the sky with unmistakeable evidence of their presence. When nothing happened for a few days, the oldest and youngest began to treat it as a holiday—spring, and no work to be done. Grandparents sat and chattered, children screeched, mothers festooned every bush with laundry.

Most of those who were young and strong wanted to join the bartons—better late than never—but Gird took only a third of them. The others he assigned to his traditional tally groups, with Pidi (now beginning to show his growth) to teach them the necessary foodgathering and camp skills. This group he knew could not keep up when the army began to move, but he had no safe place to send them; they would have to do as best they could.

As for the bartons, he had all of them change from varied farm tools to the long stick and the hauk for weapons. The farm tools went to the nonfighters, with a few hours of instruction. Once all his units had the long sticks, drilling them began to look more like drilling a real army. Gird imagined good, hard, steel points on the ends of those sticks, but what they had were sharpened wood: not good enough, but cheap and available. He imagined a lot more drill, but they had no more time than they did steel.

What he did have was willing spies. When the enemy army set out from Finyatha, runners passed the word from barton to barton. Gird knew within a few days, while the army was still days north of Hardshallows.

"Why don't we move *now?*" asked Ivis and Felis. Gird tapped the map the gnomes had made him.

"We can't be sure they aren't getting information the same way we are."

"But no one would tell the lords about us—not farmers—"

"Felis, think. They burned Berryhedge, didn't they? Took the survivors, beat them—do you think there's anything about the Berryhedge barton they don't know? They burned three other villages we know of last winter, taking prisoners each time. Some yeomen got away; some didn't. Some of those they caught will have told all they know—from pain, from fear, from hope of saving a child ... whatever. Most of our people want to be free, but many of them are scared—and so they should be. Some of those scared ones will help the lords, simply out of fear."

"But I still don't see why—"

"Look again. If they know we're moving north, they'll most likely turn and come after us. They could catch us on the move, before we get to the River Road. I don't know all that country; I need to see it, so that when we come to fight there, I can choose good ground."

"The gnomes taught you that, too?"

"Yes." He looked up, and saw a sulky expression in Felis's eyes. Ivis was merely puzzled. "Felis, I'll be glad to teach you all the gnomes taught me—to teach all of you—but right now I don't have time. Now. When the army has passed the lower ford, there, they'll be unlikely to turn back until Hardshallows. In spring, that stream runs deep and rough. That gives us time to get well north of them before they turn—and if we're lucky they'll go on to my old village, to get word from the steward there."

Cob said "What about the lords' magic—did you learn anything about that? Is it real, and what can they do?"

"It's real." Gird rumpled his hair with both hands. He could have done without that question. The next would be what could he do about the lords' magic, and the answer was, nothing. "Some of them have lost it—that may be why they've changed for the worst. They're afraid they'll lose all their power without their magic to fight for them. But some have enough left—they can make light, call storms, compel men to obedience, change their faces—"

"Are you sure?"

"Yes. Lucky for us that most of them don't have it any more; we'll be fighting soldiers who have no more magic than we do."

"Better weapons," said Cob gloomily.

"Better for fighting unarmed peasants. Remember that most of 'em have been sitting around guarding some noble's home; the ones that have experience got it with horse nomads—not with foot troops who use polearms. They belong to different lords; they'll have a divided command; they aren't used to drilling together. We are."

The lords' army did exactly what Gird had expected. They moved at a leisurely pace down the trade road from Finyatha toward Ierin, waited for a contingent of troops from Ierin, then swung southeast-ward, following the west bank of the Blue all the way to Hardshal-lows. His spies told him they burned that deserted village after fording the stream, then stopped to celebrate a victory. Supposedly, the enemy forces now numbered about 300 soldiers, and that many again of servants, guides, packers, and other noncombatants. This was by no means all the force the lords had at their disposal. Ivis's duke was rumored to be on his way with his personal guard—a hundred strong, some of them fresh from the northern frontier.

By this time, Gird and his army were on the move. His original Stone Circle troops now numbered just over fifty; these he consid-ered his best trained and hardiest. The bartons already risen con-tributed over a hundred, and the newest yeomen—the hardiest of the refugees—added another sixty or so. Then there were the refu-gees themselves, some of whom might be able to fight, at least a single blow: over two hundred of them.

Moving this motley group turned out to be harder than Gird had expected. Although he and his Stone Circle troops were used to traveling, many of the others had never been out of their villages until now. They did not understand maps, and the farther Gird led them from familiar country, the more unhappy and nervous they became. Some of the older people simply stopped, refusing to go on. For the first few days, it seemed that Gird was constantly being asked to persuade someone's father or mother to keep going. "Not another step!" burned itself into his memory, along with "How many times have I told you—!" addressed to a wailing child.

It was not what he'd planned. It was not anything like what the gnomes had advised. But what could he do? They were his people; he had to take care of them. He led them by the safest ways he could find, avoiding villages where soldiers were quartered. He could not hide the movement of so many from everyone, but most of the peasants would not report them. What worried him were the few who might.

Gird paced back and forth nervously. It was much harder to hide a camp for three hundred than a camp for fifty; the jacks stank almost as far as the road when the wind blew right, and he could not convince his yeoman marshals that any guard sergeant would know what that smell meant. They would not make the trenches deep enough, and insist that the users cover it all. As for the cookfires—he looked back over his shoulder at the wisps of smoke rising into the forest canopy. At least they had trees here, and something to cook. He had to remember that, and the times when they'd had nothing. Farmers around here had been generous, though it was hard to persuade them to stay on their farms and grow food when their barton training gave them confidence. They wanted to fight, now, not plow and plant and reap. He himself would have changed places gladly, in peace, but they wouldn't believe it. For a moment he felt a scythe in his hands, the lovely long swing back and forth, the bite of the blade into ripe wheat. But that was past, and now he had a camp to care for.

"Gird?" Raheli had come up to him, more quiet-footed than he would ever be. In the dimming evening light, the scar on her face stood out whiter than ever.

"What, lass?" His lass she would always be, the child he had held in the moments after birth, the laughing girl who had put flowers on the endstones and danced in the starlight with her lover . . . the girl he had not been able to protect. He could not get away from that.

"There's trouble nearby; a runner came in."

"How much trouble?"

"Farmer's place burning, soldiers all around."

"One of ours?"

"They say not. He came to a meeting awhile back, over to Whitford, and he'd been giving food to the local barton, but not drilling there. 'Tis said he's a lord's bastard, and got his cottage-right that way."

Gird grunted. Peasant jealousy again. "Not his fault, if it's true. Family?"

"Young wife, two children. Quiet man, they said. Hard worker, but kept to himself."

Gird interpreted that his own way. If his village had resented his getting the cottage, they'd have made life hard on him; such a man might keep to his own hearth with good reason. Had the soldiers interpreted his solitude as rebellion? "What of him and the family?"

Raheli shook her head. "Don't know yet. Soldiers took two off along the road, but it looked like a woman and girl." Her voice shook; Gird's would if he spoke, and he knew it.

"They killed him, then," Gird said huskily. "Otherwise, they'd take him along." To watch, to feel his own shame. The same shame and rage he felt still, when he thought of it. He turned away, blinking back the tears. "Well—we'll have to keep a good watch; there's naught more we can do."

It was near dawn when a sentry found someone crawling through the wood on elbows and knees, sobbing. Instead of killing the intruder at once, he dragged him along to the main campsite. Gird, coming from the jacks to the cookfire in hopes of a quiet mug of sib, heard the commotion as the sentry reported to the night marshal.

"What's this?" he asked, strolling over. The sentry's catch was a lean, dark-haired man who stank of smoke and burnt wood. He stood hunched and shivering, his hands cradled to his chest.

"Says he's a farmer, got burnt out," said the sentry. "Says they beat 'im, burned his hands."

"Come to the fire," Gird said. The sentry and the night marshal both helped the man, who staggered as if he was near collapse. They got him seated by one of the firepits, where the flickering light of the morning cookfire showed a strongboned face smudged with ash and soot. A welt stood out along one side of his face; one eye was swollen, and his hands, when he held them out, were blistered on the palms, as if someone had forced them onto a hot kettle. His shirt was scorched up one arm, with the red line of a burn beneath.

"You need to drink," Gird said. The morning cook had shifted to the other side of the firepit; he reached for the dipper in the sib kettle and paused. "Is your mouth burnt? Would cool water be better?"

"Water," the man said faintly. Before Gird could get up, the cook had turned away, and came back quickly with a bucket of cold springwater. Gird held a dipperful to the man's lips. He sucked it in noisily, swallowing so fast he nearly choked.

"Easy. There's plenty." Gird filled another dipper, and glanced at the cook. "Where's Rahi? We're going to need a good poultice for his burns." The cook nodded, gave another stir to the porridge, and went off. When the man had finished the second dipper of water, he shook his head at the offer of another.

"Thanks . . ." he said. Tears made a clean track through the dirt on his face, glittering in the firelight. "I—I thought—"

"You're safe," Gird said. It was not strictly true, but he was safer here than where he had been. "What's your name?"

"Selamis." An unusual name for a peasant, Gird thought, but Rahi had said he might be a lord's bastard. Some of them had unusual names. The man's mouth worked a moment, then he said, "It's—not a village name. I'm not from there."

"It's not a man's name that matters," said Gird. "Selamis is as good as any other. I'm Gird—that's Jenis, and that's Arvi." He craned around to look. "And the cook's Pirik. How did you get away?"

Selamis grimaced. "Tunnel—you—your men said, at Whitford that time, we should all have a way out, tunnel or hole in the wall, something like that. I had one in the woodshed, just under my barton wall. Not big. They threw me in there, after—after they were done—and said they'd take me off to the duke's court come morning. So—I managed to move th' wood, get the trap up—"

"With your hands burned like that? Brave man." Gird flexed his own hands, imagining how it must have hurt to move anything.

Rahi came then, with her bags of herbs and a chunk of tallow. "Get him clean," she said to Gird without preamble. He nodded, and dipped a bowl of water from the bucket the cook had left there. While Rahi worked the tallow and herbs together in a bowl to make a poultice, Gird washed Selamis's hands gently, then his arms and face. The man winced, but did not cry out. Rahi smeared the burns and the welt on his face with her poultice, and bound his hands in clean rags. "It will hurt," she warned. "Anything touching burns hurts, even air. But it will keep them clean, and under the blisters they should heal without much damage."

Once he was bandaged to Raheli's satisfaction, Gird and the night marshal, Arvi, helped Selamis to the jacks and then settled him on a blanket. By then it was dawn, light enough to see the paler line around his mouth from pain and shock. Gird told one of the others to keep an eye on him; he himself had more than a day's work to do. He half expected the soldiers who had burnt the man's farm to come looking for him, but his scouts reported that all the soldiers from that farm had headed back to the nearest town.

It was afternoon before he came back to see Selamis in daylight.

The man was drowsing uneasily, twitching and shifting in the blanket. He muttered indistinct words that sounded almost like an argument, then cried out and woke completely. Tears stood in his eyes. Gird squatted beside him, and laid a hand on his arm.

"Pain, or worry?"

"It—hurts a lot."

"Aye. I'm sorry we've nothing better. Are you hungry yet? Can I bring you water?" The man nodded for water, and Gird fetched it, then lifted him to drink. When he was through, Gird let him down gently.

"How many people do you have here?" the man asked, looking around. Gird blinked, thinking.

"Oh—two or three hundred, maybe more. It varies. Does that surprise you?"

"I thought—bartons—a few men each—"

"Some bartons are small, no more'n two or three hands of men. Others are larger. But you weren't in a barton."

"No. I—they didn't like me much." The expression on his face was curious; Gird would almost have said spoiled, but the man was too old, and had worked too hard, to be a spoiled child.

"Rumor says you're a lord's bastard." He watched for a reaction, and got it. Selamis's face closed, hardening; his eyes seemed to chill from warm brown to the color of icy mud. "You won't let me stay?"

"Why wouldn't I? I care more for honesty and courage than blood; that's what all this is about." That had surprised the man; Gird wondered again just what he'd been through.

"My—my sponsor assigned me that cottage," the man said quickly. "I didn't have anything to do with old Kerith being evicted; I'd have taken her in myself, but she wouldn't come—"

"I'm not blaming you," Gird said. Clearly someone had, and Selamis still felt he had to explain himself. He could believe that the local barton might have shunned the man, unfair as it was. But unfairness at the top made everyone unfair. "Here you will have the trust you deserve: if you are honest and brave, you will find loyal friends who care not at all who your father was—or your mother, for that matter. If you've suffered from both lord and peasant, you may find that hard to believe, but it's true."

"You're peasant-born?"

Gird laughed. "All the way back, near's I can find out. Farmer after farmer, born to plow and plant and harvest, to tend my stock."

"But they say you're a great general," Selamis said. Something

in the tone rang false; Gird looked at him a moment, but couldn't
place what bothered him. He laughed again.

"I'm no great general, lad; I know how to do a few things well,
and keep doing them. As long as they work, we'll survive. The gods
have been with us, so far."

"You believe they care who wins a war down here?"

"You don't?" Gird looked him up and down. "You don't think
the gods gave you a bit of extra strength, to open your trap door
with burned hands? You don't think they hid you from the soldiers
as you came through the night—that they led you to our camp?
I'd say you've had some bounty of the gods already—"

"But my family—"

Gird laid a hand on his shoulder. "I'm sorry. The last thing you
need now is a scolding, and you still weak from what happened.
I've cursed the gods myself, more than once, in such trouble." He
patted the man's shoulder, and levered himself up; his knees
seemed stiffer every day. "I'll talk to you again, but for now you
rest."

He had gone only a few steps, when Selamis called "Gird—"
Gird turned. The man's face had gone white again, and he was
shaking.

"What's wrong?" Gird asked, coming back to his side.

"I—I can't—" Selamis shook his head violently.

"Can't what?"

"I can't *lie* to you!" That came out loud enough to attract atten-
tion; Gird glared at the faces turned his way until they turned back.
He knew they would be listening anyway. He sat heavily beside
Selamis, facing him.

"What's this now?" he asked, in the tone that had always gotten
the truth from his children. Selamis had started crying, the rough,
painful sobs of someone who cried rarely. "Easy, now, and tell me
what it is you've lied about."

"They sent me," Selamis said, so softly that Gird could hardly
hear him between sobs. "They sent me."

"Who? The soldiers?" Selamis nodded; Gird chewed his lip,
fighting back the rage that spurted up in his mind. He looked away;
he was afraid of what Selamis would see in his face. "Sent you to
spy on the camp? To betray us?"

"Yes." That was as soft as the other; he heard fright as well as
misery in Selamis's voice. Gird waited it out, staring at his fingernails, until Selamis went on. "They—they killed my son. Said
they'd—they'd keep my wife and daughter—in prison—so if I
didn't come back they could—could—"

"I can imagine," Gird said. He could hear the iron in his own voice. When he closed his eyes it was as if he could see all of them together, all the men and women and children taken hostage in the past years—beaten and raped and tormented and killed—he opened his eyes, and stared hard at the leaves on the ground in front of his knees. "Why you?"

"Because I'm a lord's son," Selamis said bitterly. "He—he put me there, where everyone hated me; he knew I would have no friends, no one to turn to. They said I owed it to my father, that my only hope was with him. I would—if he had asked, as from a son, I would have done anything for him, but they *forced* me—"

"And your hands? Was that to make us believe?" Selamis shook his head. "No. That was the guard captain; he knew me before, as a boy. Just to remind me what he could do, he said. He's one of them—the horned circle—" His head rolled again. "I can't—I can't stand it—what they'll do to her—to my daughter—and I can't lie to you—what can I do?" Gird pulled him up and cradled him in his arms. There was nothing to do but endure, and Selamis surely knew that. Yet the pain the man was feeling would be like the pain he felt when he found Rahi—when Amis was killed—when Meris was tortured. He held Selamis with all the love he felt for all of them, all the ones who suffered in person or through those they loved.

"It's all right," he said, knowing as always that it was not all right, not yet. It was as much promise as reassurance. It would be all right someday; he would make it that way, make a world in which such things did not happen—or if they did, someone who cared would work to change them.

"But my *daughter*, my little girl! I have to go, I can't—"

"You can't go. You're hurt. And you can't betray us now; you don't really want to. You want to save your child, as any father would—as I did, and failed. I won't lie to you, Selamis. Your child may die, and die horribly. I can't promise anything better for her. But you can help me, help me make a better land than this." Selamis was still sobbing, but less wildly. When he was finally silent, Gird laid him down gently. "You are a brave man, Selamis. Brave to come here, brave to tell me—and brave enough for whatever comes of it." He left him then, and told one of the healers to watch Selamis closely. She peered at Gird, as if she could see his churning belly and the rage in his heart, but said nothing. He was grateful for that.

He was not grateful for the wariness of his marshals, who accosted him before he made it to the cookfires for his supper.

"Are you sure he can be trusted?" asked Felis, "I heard he was sent—"

"He told me that himself," said Gird. "If he tells me himself, that stands for something."

"He might have thought we'd heard something from the villagers."

"Have we?"

Felis scowled. "No. But we might. He wasn't liked."

"He wasn't liked because he was some lord's bastard, and the lord arranged a cottage for him. One of theirs was evicted. Not his fault. He wasn't in their barton because they didn't want him, but he gave food. They've got his wife and daughter, threatened him with what you'd expect if he didn't betray us—and *he* told me that. Himself. That's not like a spy."

"Not if he's told you everything," Felis said. Behind him, Ivis and Cob said nothing, but their eyes agreed.

Gird's own doubts vanished in a perverse determination to have Felis be wrong. "We'll watch him, but I say he's honest, and we can trust him. Are we to make the same mistakes they do? It's a man's own heart says what he is, not his father's bloodline. Men aren't cows."

"No, some of them are foxes." Felis stomped off, his own fox-red hair bristling wildly. Ivis and Cob laughed.

"He could be right, all the same," said Ivis, dipping out a measure of beans. "No better way to convince us he's honest than to confess something. I've done it m'self as a boy."

"And what if he *is* honest? How would you have an honest man act?" Ivis shrugged and did not pursue the subject. The next day, when Gird insisted they move on, Selamis was able to walk. Rahi said it would be many days before he could use his hands.

They had been threading their way between the domain of Ivis's duke and that of a count, to his east. North of that, they would come into the domain of the sier Gird had saved. Although the main lines of the hills ran across their way, gaps existed: ways known to herders, hunters, foresters. Gird had his scouts out all around; for several days they found nothing but their own people.

Then about midmorning on the fourth day, the forward scouts reported that soldiers were blocking the next gap to the north. Gird halted the ragged column and thought about it. They could swing west, here, between two lines of hills, and take the next gap . . . but that would mean stringing his whole line out, down on the streamside. Here that meant open land, arable. They would be trampling young grain they might want to eat, come winter . . . and they would be visible from hills on both sides. Downstream, west-ward, was a largish village with a permanent guard detachment. Could the blocked gap be intended to push him into a trap?

"How many in the gap?" he asked his scouts.

Fingers flashed. "Two hands. Four in sight, and the others in the trees on either side."

"Did they see you?"

"No—I don't think so." The scouts exchanged looks, agreed on that, and went on. "One of 'em said as how it was boring. They'd been told to guard the gaps—all of 'em—but they didn't think anyone'd come this way, not with the good bridge downstream."

Two hands of guards, but well placed in a narrow gap. The noise of battle would bring more—that had to be the intent, that or some similar trap. Overbridge, the village, had a barton but Gird had not called on it yet. His scouts reported that the Overbridge farmers seemed to be at normal work in their fields. Gird looked around. All his people were watching him, waiting for him to make a deci-sion. The longer he waited, the more nervous they would be—and the more likely that some child would get loose and go off noisily, to reveal where they were.

"Six hands," Gird said. He pointed to Felis and Cob. "Three each from yours. Ivis, have four hands ready for support, if we need it. The rest close up and be ready to get everyone across and through the gap *quickly*. If there's a real fight—if they have more hidden that the scouts missed—they'll have reinforcements coming, from both upstream and down. That won't hurt us as long as we know it's coming, and have reached higher ground before they do." He placed pebbles on the ground to show them what he meant. "If they do come after us, let 'em get right up in the gap, and then turn on 'em. Be sure you don't cross the water until all of us are across and out of sight. If they see us, I want them to think we're all the trouble they have."

Six hands of men—three from the original Stone Circle outlaws and three from Fireoak barton—followed Gird and the original forward scouts. They crossed the rushing little river upstream of the gap, at a narrows where the forest almost met across the water, going single-file as quietly as they could. Then they worked their way upslope, hoping to flank the ambush. Gird was not at all sure this would work; he would have expected his own maneuver. But if the guards were still expecting ignorant peasants, they might have no one on the hilltop to watch for it.

His idea almost worked. Gird spotted one of the guards at the moment the guard spotted him, and yelled. More yells, and the noise of movement. Gird held his group still. It was possible that the guard had not seen them all, and in a moment he would know where all the guards were.

"Come out here, you!" the guard said. "Who are you, skulking about in the woods?" He sounded as much nervous as angry.

Gird did his best to look frightened; he could hear the others clearly now, and then they came in sight. Seven . . . eight . . . nine . . . in yellow and green uniforms. They carried short swords; two had bows slung over their shoulders. That was a mistake; he hoped they would not realize it in time to cause him any trouble.

"Answer me, serf!" said the guard, bolder with his friends around him. "You know the rules: no one's allowed on the hills now."

Gird would like to have said something clever, but he couldn't think of anything. The man was three long strides away—farther than that for the men behind him—and Gird would have to be fast or the bowmen might get their bows into action. Someone behind him, trying to move closer, rustled the leaves; the guard's eyes widened. "Are there more . . . ?" His voice rose, as Gird charged straight ahead.

They had swords in hand, but swords could not reach him. Not if the others came in time. Gird thrust the point of his stick at a face that had blurred to a white blob; the man staggered back. Someone's sword hacked at his stick; he felt the jolt, swung the tip away, and jabbed forward again. The guards were yelling, surprise and fear mixed together. Gird paid no attention to them; he could see his own men on either side of him, jabbing again and again at the soldiers who flailed wildly with their swords, stumbling into trees. The two bowmen backed quickly, reaching for their bows.

"Bowmen first!" yelled Gird—the first thing he'd actually said, in words, and lunged at one of them. His stick caught the man hard in the chest; it didn't penetrate, but the man staggered and fell. He gave Gird a look of such utter surprise that it almost made Gird back a step—but instead he thrust again. This time the point caught the man in the neck, slid off to one side, and pinned his shoulder to the ground. Gird leaned on the pole. It was surprisingly hard to force the point in . . . but the man was clawing at his throat, his face purplish. Gird pulled the stick back and clouted him hard on the head. The soldier fell limp; when Gird checked, he was not breathing.

Around him, the fight was ending in a wild flurry of blows, counterblows, and bellows. The sharpened sticks worked, but clumsily: driving a sharp point of wood through clothing and flesh took strength and weight; once spitted, the enemy was even harder to free. Most of Gird's people had done what he did: use the point to fend off attack and throw the swordsmen off balance, then finish them with a blow to the head. It worked because they outnumbered their opponents, but Gird knew that would not always be true.

"Get their weapons," Gird reminded his people, as they finished off the last of the soldiers. "Knives as well: we can use everything. All their food, any tools." The dead soldiers had not worn armor. Gird shook his head over that; they must have assumed that the peasants had no weapons worth wearing armor for.

"Boots?" asked one of his still barefoot yeomen.

Gird nodded. "Clothes, if you want 'em. Felis, take two hands and go downslope; watch for their reinforcements. We made enough noise to rouse a drunk on the morning after. Cob, you take a hand back to hurry our people along." Gird helped drag the bodies into a pile out of the way. He did not bother to look for herbs of remembrance: these were his enemies; he had helped kill them, and it would be an insult to lay the herbs on them. Only one of his people had been hurt, a young yeoman who had a knife wound on the arm to remind him that fallen enemies were not necessarily dead.

Chapter Twenty-two

Soon he could hear the rest of his people coming. They were hardly past, moving much slower than he would have liked, when he heard hoofbeats from the stream valley. No one had said anything about a mounted contingent nearby, but it made no real difference. Felis sent a runner back up: twenty horsemen, five bowmen and the rest with swords. Dust back down the trail, as if more were coming, though he couldn't say if those were horsemen or afoot.

"Good," said Gird, surprising those around him. He hoped it was good; it would be good if they won. "Fori, take eight hands—go *that* way—" Downstream that was, "—through the woods two hundred paces, then go downslope and wait for my call. You'll be coming in on their flank or rear. The rest of you, come with me."

The entrance to the gap trail offered the horsemen a gently rising slope from the narrow fields near the river, a slope gradually steepening as the trees closed in. Gird placed his troops across the point of this triangle, inside the trees, with the center set back a horselength. He watched the horsemen as they rode back and forth near the river, clearly looking for signs of a crossing. One of them went upstream, and came back at a gallop, yelling. The group milled about, then formed into a double column and headed for the gap trail.

Gird was surprised at that. Could they really be so stupid? Sunlight glinted off their breastplates and helmets—these would be harder to kill, but they were trusting too much to their horses and weapons. At the last moment, as the leaders came under the edge of the forest, some caution came to the leader, for he held up his hand and the troop reined in. The bowmen had their bows strung; they reached for arrows. Gird gave the signal anyway. On either side, his men ran out, carefully keeping their formation, poles firm in their hands.

The rearmost horses squealed and tried to back away: their riders spurred ahead. Two bucked, and one unseated its rider, who fell heavily. The first two riders had also fallen, shoved from their saddles by skillfully applied poles. One lay stunned; the other had rolled up quickly, and was doing his best to defend himself with his sword. Behind him, the other riders had tried to charge forward, but their horses shied from the sharp points of the sticks, swerving and rearing. The riders cursed, spurring hard; they could not reach Gird's men with their swords, and any who were separated were quickly surrounded, and pushed out of the saddle. Three of the bowmen, however, had managed to set arrow to string. Two of the arrows flew wide, but one—by luck or skill—went home in the throat of the man about to unseat the bowman. He managed to fit another arrow to his string, and this one narrowly missed Gird. Now his companions realized what he was doing; the remaining horsemen clumped together, protecting the bowmen in their midst, so that they had time to shoot again and again.

Gird smacked the man nearest him with the flat of his hand. "We've got to get them *now!*" he bellowed. His people surrounded the horsemen several men deep, but were showing no more eagerness to face the frightened horses' hooves than the horses were to face their poles. "Stand there and they'll get you all!" he said, flinging himself past those in front to snatch at one horse's bridle. Its rider aimed a vicious slash at him; Gird ducked, and thrust his belt-knife into the underside of the horse's jaw. The horse reared, screaming and flailing; Gird caught a hard blow from one hoof, but lunged again. His men yelled; he saw another dart forward, and another. The bowmen could not hit them now without shooting through their own companions. Horses and men screamed; it smelled like a butchering. Gird grabbed for another bridle, and nearly fell; he had slipped in a gush of horse blood. Too bad, his mind said as if from a distance, that we have to kill the beasts for their riders' sake. And where, his mind went on, are those others that made the dust cloud?

As if in answer to that question, an even louder uproar erupted somewhere behind him. Gird whirled, slipped to one knee in the carnage, and staggered back up. There—downstream a little—it sounded as if Fori's group had engaged the enemy support without waiting for Gird's call. Or had he called? He couldn't remember. He was out of breath, and his leg hurt. When he looked down, he could see a rent in his trousers. The horse's hoof, probably. He took a deep breath, and bellowed. Those who looked around, he waved toward the new noise. "Fori's men," he yelled. "Get in *line*, idiots, before—" his breath and voice failed together. Someone put a shoulder under his arm; he would have shoved help away, but for the moment he could not. He let himself be helped to the edge of the trampled ground.

Someone handed him a waterskin; he drank, wincing as someone else prodded the gash on his leg. Now he could breathe, and see: all the horsemen down, and half the horses, in a welter of blood. Some of his own dead this time, more wounded. Tending them were women he distinctly remembered from the refugee group . . . what were they doing down here? He had to get back to the fighting, he reminded himself. When he tried to get up (when had he slid to the ground against this tree?) his leg refused to take his weight.

"Your arm—" said someone behind him.

"It's my leg," he growled, but glanced at his arm anyway. A bloody gash had opened it from near his shoulder to his elbow; he stared at it, surprised. He didn't remember that. A broad-faced woman with tangled reddish hair sluiced the blood off with water from a bucket, laid a compress of leaves on the gash, and wrapped it tightly with a strip of cloth. She touched his head; he winced and pulled back.

"Quite a lump," she said cheerfully. "We might's well call you Gird Hardhead as Gird Strongarm."

"But Fori—" he said.

"Quiet. It's all right."

He wanted to say it was not all right, not until the fighting was done and they were safely away. But something with teeth had hold of his leg, and was trying to pull it off. He blinked, grunted, and resolved the monster into two people, one of them holding his leg still while the other cleaned out the ragged wound. It seemed to hurt a lot more than it had; he didn't know if that was good or bad.

"Gird?" That was Fori's voice; Gird fought his way through the haze of pain and exhaustion to focus on Fori's face. Pale, but unmarked; he looked more worried than anything else.

"I'm fine," said Gird. He would be fine; it was not all a lie.

Fori grinned. "It worked," he said. "Just like you wanted: we took their reserves in the flank before they knew we were there. And then the others from here—from the first fight—came and got them between us. We lost a few—"

"How many, each side?" Thinking about the fight might clear his head.

Fori's hands flicked, counting it up. "Eight hands of reserves, afoot—our match. Then four hands of horsemen, and two hands in the gap itself: fourteen hands, seventy altogether. All dead. Of ours, eight dead, and four hands wounded, some bad."

Cob's head appeared beside Fori's. "Gird—we're going to move you now."

"Move me! I can move myself!" He lunged up, but firm hands pushed him down.

"No. We aren't going to lose you because you walked all your blood out." Gird would have fought harder, but his body did not cooperate. He let himself relax onto the rough litter, and endured a miserable bouncy trip to whatever ridiculous site Cob or Felis had picked for a camp.

He woke to firelight, and listened to the voices around him before opening his eyes. He knew at once he was indoors, in some large, mostly bare room. It did not smell like he imagined a prison would smell, and the voices around him sounded tired, but satisfied, happy, quietly confident. Then, in a lower tone, someone said, "What about Gird—do you think—?"

"He'll be fine," said the voice of the red-headed woman who had tied up his arm. "If he hadn't tried to fight the whole battle himself—"

"Did you ever see anything like it!" That was no question; the speaker's voice carried raw emotion. "Throwing that horse down like a shepherd throws a lamb—"

Did I? wondered Gird. He could remember nothing but the first horse rearing over him, and the hoof raking his leg. Now he came to think of it, that had been the other leg, not the one with the bad gash.

"—Like something out of a tale," the young voice was going on. Others chimed in, a confusion of details almost as chaotic as the battle itself. Gird felt himself flushing. They made it sound as if he'd waded single-handed into the entire Finaarean army.

"If *he* dies—" began someone else in a hushed voice.

Gird opened his eyes. "I am not going to die," he said firmly, glad that his voice carried his intent.

Several men laughed. "I told you," said Cob. "He's too stubborn to die." Under that confidence Gird could hear relief in his voice. He tried to hitch himself up and pain lanced through his head.

"Don't move," said the red-headed woman beside him.

"You could have said that before I did." Gird cleared his throat. With the headache, his other pains awoke again, and he wished he'd stayed asleep.

The woman grinned down at him. "Cranky patients get well faster," she said. "Soup?"

"Water." She and another supported his shoulders as he drank, then propped him up. The various pains settled down to a steady but bearable level, and he realized he was hungry after all. And curious: what exactly had happened, and where were they, and who had taken over when he fell on his face? Someone handed the woman a bowl of soup, and she lifted Gird's head so he could drink it.

He saw movement in the group around the fire. Then his most experienced fighters were around him. "You're wondering what happened," said Felis, almost smugly. Gird glared as best he could. Felis had become a good leader, but he could be unbearably smug.

"We were all standing around the riders, having poked and prodded them into a huddle, wondering what to do next, when you jumped out and—"

"I remember that," Gird said. "It's what comes after—"

Cob shrugged. "You grew about four hands taller, sprouted wings and horns, and started throwing horses around like sheep. No: you didn't really get bigger, but you *looked* bigger. Yelling your head off and covered with blood, and you did throw at least one horse right on its side—I saw that, and so did everyone else. The rider that sliced your arm—you threw him, too, across one horse and into another. The riders panicked, even the bowmen. I think we could have stood there watching you finish them all off, but that was boring after awhile, so we tried it for ourselves."

"What hit my head?"

"I didn't see that. We heard the others coming, and Fori's attack yell, and you told us to go help him. I ran off with my group; when I got back, you were sitting against a tree, not saying much of anything, while Elis here cleaned you up. It was hard to tell which blood was yours."

Felis broke in. "The new formations work perfectly, Gird. Even in the trees—I admit I'd wondered if that practice going between trees was good for anything, but now I know it is."

"Of course, we outnumbered them," said Ivis. "Two to one."

"More than that." Gird shifted, testing the limits of his pain. "They were stupid enough to come to us in pieces. We had three to one on the first group, more like five to one against the horsemen."

"But—oh." Gird could see by their faces that they were working this out for themselves.

"Remember what I told you. What counts is how many against how many at the point of contact. If they're not in the fight, they don't count."

Fori spoke up. "But we were even against their reinforcements, at first. And we were moving them—I think we could have won."

"Probably. I hope so. But you'd have had more losses, and a harder fight. We're good, lads, and better than before, but it never hurts to let them make it easy for us. If we can take them at good odds, why not? Now—where are we?"

They chuckled, slightly sheepish chuckles. Cob said. "You aren't going to like this."

"What?" He tried to roar, but it didn't come out as a roar, more as a peevish growl.

"We're in Overbridge. In the soldiers' barracks."

"You *idiots!*" That time it did come out as a roar, and faces turned to him. He struggled to sit all the way up, and nearly made it.

"Listen to me." Cob had a hand on his chest, with weight behind it if he didn't lie back. He lay back, simmering. "There are no more soldiers in Overbridge. The ones we killed were stationed here; the barton is sure none got away. The nearest beyond are past Burry, at a road crossing. We sent word to Burry—and you know the Burry yeomen." He did know the Burry yeomen, as determined as any; if they swore no one would get through from Overbridge, no one would. "This village is delighted with us—those guards camped here all winter drinking up the ale and rolling the local girls, even a few with babies coming. We killed them without trampling the fields, or involving the local yeomen. They *begged* us to come in, offered us food, even the little ale the guards hadn't found—"

"Ale—" said Gird meditatively. *That* should dull his headache. "But we can't stay here," he said, looking around to see if he could spot a likely jug.

"Of course not." Cob reached back, and someone handed him a jug. He dangled it in front of Gird's nose. "But for one night, while certain persons take their well-earned rest—"

"You do have sentries out?"

"Of course. Don't we always do what you tell us?"

Gird heaved himself up on his uninjured elbow; someone behind him helped him up until he was braced against the wall. He got his hands around the jug, and sniffed it. Yes, just what he needed. He took a long swallow that warmed his throat on its way down. He offered the jug to Cob, who shook his head.

"I've had some. Now, about our wounded: three of them won't be able to travel for days, maybe weeks—" Gird took another swallow, and felt the edge come off his aches and pains. Behind the throb in his head, his mind was beginning to work again. Wounded who could walk tomorrow—in two days—not for a long time. Members of the Overbridge barton who wanted to come along rather than stay home and farm. Villagers who wanted to meet the man who had thrown down a horse. Felis wanted to tell him about the weapons they'd taken from the dead soldiers and those found in the armory. Ivis had questions about food supplies for the next march, and Rahi—when had she appeared at his side?—Rahi had one of her herbal brews that puckered his mouth after the ale.

He woke next in the cool colorless light of dawn, his head pillowed on Rahi's lap; he looked up to see her slumped gracelessly against the wall, snoring. His head throbbed; he could not tell if it was the ale or the lump. He tried to reach up to scratch his itching hair, but chose the wrong arm; his wince woke her, and she smiled at him with a look that turned his heart. He could not stand for her to be here, for her to be leaning over him as he had so often leaned over her.

"You put me to sleep," he said quietly, holding her gaze. "You told them to give me ale, and then you had that brew—"

Rahi grinned. "You needed the rest, and you'd have stayed up all night, arguing and keeping everyone awake. Besides, we wanted to clean your wounds again. That hurts."

"Not so badly now," he said, moving arm and leg gingerly.

"You told us, clean makes fast healing. And we have two healers, now. From Overbridge."

"We still need to move, leave here before someone comes." Some large army they could not handle, a commander smarter than the one that had let Gird pit his entire force against three separate smaller ones.

But that day was spent reorganizing after the battles. Gird fretted less as he realized it was not entirely faked for his benefit, and less still when one of the healers had time to draw the pain from his head and lay it on the soldiers' hearth. Where, she insisted cheerfully, it really belonged. He thought to ask about Selamis, who had been traveling with the noncombatants, since he could not hold a weapon.

"He looks bad," said Ivis. "Sad, miserable—I suppose part of it's the pain. But his wife and daughter—he can't help thinking about them." Ivis's losses were far in his past, a young wife dead of fever, children never born alive. Gird thought he knew the anguish Selamis was feeling now (where was Girnis, his other daughter? She had married a lad from Fireoak, but neither of them had come to the wood when Fireoak village broke up. He had not asked Barin about her, not wanting to know.) He looked around but did not see him. Ivis interpreted the look correctly, and said "He's explaining the accounts to Triga."

Gird felt as if someone had poked him with a pin. "Accounts? He can read?"

"So he says." Ivis could not, and was glad of it. "Says he can calculate, too. And write."

"I'll keep him busy," Gird said. "We need someone who can keep track of what we have."

Meanwhile, his army had gathered all the clothing and equipment the soldiers had had—those with no shoes or boots tried on the soldiers' until they found some that fit or were comfortably large and could be stuffed with rags or tags of fleece. The soldiers' clothes, washed in the stream and dried on bushes, became shirts and tunics for those with no clothes, and patch material for those whose clothes needed patching. In the soldiers' kitchen were the huge cookpots he remembered, and longhandled utensils. The heavy storage jars would be impossible to carry along (and now, he thought, I know why their army needs wagons), but the food stored in the pantry would fit into sacks. They had fifty-nine swords now (some had broken during the fights), four bows gathered after the battle and another forty found in the armory. Gird spared a moment's thanks that the soldiers had chosen to go after them with swords instead of carrying those bows along. Best of all, the armory had racks of pikes, eighty of them.

Gird limped over to the racks and touched one gleaming tip. He lifted it from the rack and felt the balance. Not *that* different from the sticks—the gnomes were right about that, too. And if they carried them for a few days, the new weapons would feel normal.

"That should go through a little easier," Felis said behind him. Gird noted that Felis did not specify *what* it would go through easily. He knew that some of them were still shaken by their own violence, by the knowledge that they, too, were men who could kill.

"We have the gods to thank for this," Gird said. He turned and looked at those who had followed him into the armory. They all nodded; eyes down. "We earned the victory this time. But it will not come so easily again." They did not like hearing that, but it was the truth, and he could not lie to them. He had won at Norwalk Sheepfolds in spite of his own mistakes, because the enemy had not expected anything. He had won here, as easily as he had, because of the enemy's mistakes. Some day he would face a commander who made no mistakes, and then—He shook his head. Time enough for that later. Now they must thank the gods who had been with them, who had helped them.

His people had no rituals for celebrating victory in war, because they had not fought a war—at least not in living memory. Gird conferred with the oldest men and women he could find; none of them knew the right ritual. In the end, Gird combined the thanksgiving ceremonies for Alyanya's permission to open the ground— which should hallow their use of the steel they carried—with the harvest prayers for those who had died in the past year. Sweating with both nervousness and pain, he limped from the soldiers' barracks to the bridge over the stream, and threw in a ritual handful of grain, of flowers (gathered that day by village children), of mint leaves. The oldest granny laid a fire in the center of the village square; he led everyone in a slow dance around it. The fire burned bright, upright and clean: did that mean the gods were satisfied? He did not know. He felt both sadness and contentment, grief worn out with time, as the harvest lament always left him. The fire spurted up, suddenly, burning blue as the summer sky; Gird felt a wash of heat across him, as if he'd been dipped in it—but he was not burned, and the fire had fallen back to its wooden roots in an instant. All the hair stood up on his neck. *They said something*, he told himself. *And I'd better figure out what it was. . . .*

It had looked simpler on the model in the gnomes hall. Gird wiped sweat off his forehead and scowled at the stragglers moving along the trail past him. Go north like this, they'd said, and capture this stronghold, they'd said, and then send part of your force over here to capture this other stronghold which controls ... it had made perfect sense. There, with gnome soldiers. He could almost understand the gnomish disapproval of undisciplined humans.

He had not planned the capture of the Overbridge guardpost, and it had fallen into his lap, eighty good pikes and all. He had neither planned nor expected the other results of that victory: the bartons that had suddenly decided to leave home and join his army, the lords who decided to punish him by burning farmsteads where no one yet had even thought of joining him, the utter confusion and chaos which had erupted in a few hands of days all over the central part of the kingdom. He *had* planned a march north to the River Road, to isolate (if not capture) Grahlin, the city in which the Sier of Sorgrahl ruled, and he was instead spending days he could not afford in skirmishes with the sier's very capable mounted patrols. Remembering that brown man and his courage, he was not surprised to find that the sier made none of the mistakes other commanders had made.

He would have been glad to avoid Grahlin, but it was important for several reasons. It controlled access to the Honnorgat along one of its major tributaries, the Hoor. It sat athwart the River Road, which here bowed away from the Honnorgat to avoid seasonal flooding at the confluence with the Hoor. And the sier's large garrison would be as much trouble behind him as it was in front or on either flank.

It would have been easier—much easier—without all his unexpected allies, especially the noncombatant followers. They had no place to go; he understood that. But he wished fervently that they would find another no-place besides his army. They could not move quickly, and would not move silently. Even now, when his face should have warned them away, some of the children were calling out to him. The adults shushed them, only after the fact.

At the moment, he was trying to work his way to the west of Grahlin. They had tried it before, but this time Gird hoped that the sier would be busy with eight hands of men who had gone east, with forty of his precious pikes. They were supposed to convince the sier that they were leading the whole army that way, but if these stragglers didn't move faster (and more quietly) a stupider man than the sier would realize what was happening. Even as he thought that, the last of the noncombatants trudged by, and his rear guard grinned at him. He knew only about half of them. The rest were new, from the incoming bartons.

Gird fingered the tally sticks tucked into his shirt. Eight hands of pikes was less than a quarter of his army now; he found it hard to keep the rapidly changing numbers in mind. New people came in daily, supplies flowed in and out like water in a basket dipped in and out of a river. The gnomes had insisted that no one could manage a war without knowing his own and the enemy resources, but he could not do that if they kept changing. At least he would soon have someone who could *really* write and cast accounts. Selamis had been able to read everything Gird showed him, including the maps, and he said he could write. When his hands healed, they'd know.

The rear guard had passed; its marshal nodded at Gird, who fell in beside him. This was—Adgar, he remembered. Once of Felis's troop, then his own—the kind of man he liked as marshal, a solid farmer.

"I got the word by runner," Adgar said. "The sier's men took the bait, and are chasing our eight hands eastward."

"Lady's grace be with them," said Gird. His scouts had not reported any nearby enemy troops eastward, but things changed fast. "Our front's crossed the Hoor, and made it over that first ridge."

"Be nice if they could get right up to that guardpost without being spotted." Adgar hawked and spat. "We could use more pikes."

Gird said nothing. The sier's men, he was sure, had their weapons with them, not hanging on an armory wall. They would have to earn any pikes they got from Grahlin. Something stung his sunburnt ear, and he swatted it. In another hand of days they'd either stop to find flybane or be eaten alive.

By midday, the end of the rear guard was across the Hoor; the noncombatants were supposed to be sitting quietly in the woods, while the front waited for the rearguard to close up. Gird moved up to lead the rearguard, and noticed that his ragtag followers were following orders, for once. Heat and exertion had given them the will to stretch out in the shade and wait. Even the children were silent as he led the rearguard past them. He wished he could rest; he had gulped swallow after swallow of cold Hoor water and his belly gurgled. The ridge beyond was steep; he stumped up it, using his stick, until he saw the blue rag tied to a low limb. He halted, and clicked the pebbles in his left hand.

More clicks answered. Cob stepped out of the thick undergrowth, and waved him on. "It's working," he said. "They left the guardpost as soon as they saw our patrol go across the road." It had been a small group—purposely small, to draw out the guard detachment without giving them any reason to call for help.

"Horses?"asked Gird. Cob nodded.

"But they're fast, the fastest we have, and the land's broken down there. Good cover." He did not add, as he might have days earlier, that if all went well those guards would soon have better to do than chase fugitives. He knew from experience now that all did not always go well.

He led Gird up to the front now, where his other forty pikes would lead the rest across the open ground between the hill and the guardpost. If Gird was right, few if any were left inside. If Gird was wrong, they were going to be full of arrows, but he would not think of that. Instead, he took a last look at the sun, hoped the "fugitives" had had enough start to lead the guards a good distance away. Then he nodded at Cob, and set off at a quick walk across the short grass.

It felt very open, out here under the sky, away from hedges and trees. In the shadow of a distant clump, cows stopped chewing to watch them walk by. Gird forced his eyes away from the cows and their calves and back to the guardpost. It was designed like a fort in miniature, but its walls were no higher than barton walls. Most of the time it functioned as a toll station, collecting a fee from travelers using Grahlin's bridge over the Hoor. It did boast a tower, all of three men high, from which a sentry could survey the bridge and the road into Grahlin. Or, as Gird thought, the road *away*.

So far no alarm had come from the guardpost. Gird squinted at its tower; he could see no one up there. But a thin column of smoke climbed into the sky from somewhere in the guardpost. He muttered a curse. At the least they had left a cook behind—a cook who might chance to look out a window idly. He looked along the road as they neared it. Nothing westward—so he should hope, having sent a small group to block the road well out of sight of the guardpost. Eastward, this late in the day, no traffic moved between Grahlin and the bridge, as he'd expected.

Now they were on the road itself. Gird sent units around both sides of the guardpost, which continued to look as innocuous as a cottage, including the smoking chimney. The little tollbooth on the road was empty. The guardpost's main entrance, a heavy wood gate, was closed, but the postern stood open. Gird had planned to break down the gate, which a drunken guard in a tavern had reported to one of Gird's fascinated agents was "only there to impress serfs; it wouldn't keep out a hungry ox, let alone a determined soldier." But given an open postern—it was either a trap or great good fortune.

Great good fortune turned in an instant when the cook—a tall woman with two buckets of garbage in her meaty hands—backed out the door into the men Gird was sending in. She let out a scream that would have shaken slates from a roof, and flailed about with the buckets. In the narrow space of the postern, they couldn't get at her without killing her, and no one wanted to do that. Then her screams roused the hand of guards left at the station, and Gird heard them blundering around inside as they tried to figure out what was going on.

"*Quiet!*" Gird bellowed. To his surprise, the woman was instantly silent, her mouth hanging open. Her eyes bulged out in almost comical panic, and she dropped the buckets with a loud clatter. Gird took her by the shoulders, moved her aside, and said "Be still." She nodded, still with her mouth open. "Follow me," he said to Cob, and plunged through the door.

Already one of the guards had arrived at the narrow passage that led to the postern; Gird lunged with his stick, wishing he'd had sense enough to take a pike instead. His weight and speed forced the man back, but the wooden point would not go through the breastplate. He jabbed again and again; the man retreated, but slowly. Now he was out of the passage. Another guard came up beside him. Cob leaned on Gird, giving him more weight to use. That was fine, but he couldn't use the point on more than one at a time, and the passage was too narrow for two to stand abreast. He would have to push his way out, and take his chances until Cob and the others got through.

He took a deep breath, and bellowed a wordless cry as he lunged. The guard backed two steps; Gird hit his chest hard, and the man staggered and went to one knee. *Faster*, Gird told himself, shortening his grip and running out the end of the passage. Cob and the others were at his heels; he struck at the second man's face. Then Cob was beside him, then another. Cob had a pike, and the man who had fallen died on it. Gird saw a stairway up the outside of the tower, and a man halfway up. He had a horn, and was lifting it to his lips.

Gird threw his long stick, end over end. It spun in the air like a wheel; the man saw it coming, dropped his horn, and screamed. He ducked; the stick hit the stone above him and shattered. Gird had no time to watch this. One of the others had jumped at him as he threw. Gird threw himself to one side, and pulled his hauk from his belt. The sword knocked a chip from it, and the guard grinned triumphantly just as someone else's pike took him in the back. Gird grabbed the sword out of his hand, and looked around.

Four guards lay dead or dying; the small courtyard was full of Gird's men, and the guard on the tower stairs was slumped against the wall.

"Sling," said one of Gird's men smugly. Fori was not the only one, now, who could hit something with a slung stone.

"We're not through," Gird reminded them. "Get this place secure, and get four—no, six—hands to the bridge." He went for the tower, and panted his way up the steps. The guard there was unconscious; Gird dumped him off the steps for someone else to kill, and continued to the top of the squatty tower.

From there he could see dust rising from the distant horsemen who were chasing his fast patrol. A score of them, at least, by the dust. Below, he heard the noise settle into the busy murmur of purposeful activity. He looked the other way. There were six hands—most of his remaining pikes—almost to the bridge. Almost a third of them were wearing blue shirts. Gird grinned. His yeomen had begun wearing them when they expected a good fight. Gird himself still had the one Ivis had brought to their first camp, but he was saving that for the day they really needed luck.

Today they needed only the time the fugitives were buying. Gird had all his yeomen in place well before sundown, when the pursuers might be expected to return. A carefully selected group of followers straggled across the fields, although they did not straggle nearly so well when they tried. They kept closing up into neat lines, until Gird yelled at them again. The returning horsemen, trotting briskly in formation toward their own guardhouse, could not help but notice the milling mass of people in the field; they turned aside to investigate. As soon as their backs were to the road and the guardhouse, Gird's signal sprung the trap, and up from roadside ditch and out from the enclosure came the yeomen with their long sticks and their new-won expertise in unhorsing cavalry. One, indeed, wheeled instantly and rode for the bridge to alarm the city beyond, but found himself cut off by the pikemen.

Gird hurried his people into position for the reaction that was sure to come. He wanted both ends of the bridge secure, breastworks on the rocky west bank of the river, a defined perimeter that included the guardpost and the bridge. Late that night, he was sitting over a table in the guardpost with Selamis, interpreting the records that they'd found.

"This is tolls," Selamis said. "Last year by this time they'd had— let me see—almost twice as much road traffic. Numbers and weight are both down. So his income will be down—"

"But he's rich; he'll have treasure in a storehouse—"

"He has to pay his troops, feed his troops, pay his suppliers. Where do you think his money comes from?"

"Fieldfees," said Gird, almost bitterly. Selamis shook his head. "Fieldfee's the least of it. Road tax, bridge toll, market tax, building tax, death fees, marriage fees—not just on farmers, on everyone. Smiths won't make his weapons for nothing. He has to find them the raw metal, pay someone to bring it here." Selamis's hands were still tender, but he could turn the pages himself now. "Look at this. Cloth merchants' stonage last year—"

"Stonage?"

"Stones' weight—didn't your village use that?"

"But cloth is furls."

"Not in bulk. The rough measure of stonage is what team it takes to start the wagon on the level. If you've ever been in a big market town, in the square, you'll have seen the tracks, where they test it. The town's market judge has a hitch—can't use the traders' horses, they could be trained wrong. Double-double-hand-stone, a thousand stones, that is, if a pair starts it. If it takes another pair, it's counted as two, and so on. It's only rough; I was told once that a thousand-stone load will break down to more than that, unloaded, but it takes too long to do that. Most lords just raise the load-fee." Selamis liked to talk, and explained things clearly. Gird was fascinated at the variety of knowledge a lord's bastard had collected. When he asked, Selamis shrugged and seemed to answer frankly. "I was in his household until I was shoulder high to a grown man— they taught me reading, writing, figures, something of law and more of custom. Their custom."

"And then fostered you to farmers? Why?"

"I don't know." That was a door slammed in his face. "I suppose my father decided he had enough bastards around."

Gird thought of asking which lord had been his father, but thought better of it. The man was upset enough already. He yawned, honestly if tactfully, and suggested a few hours sleep before the inevitable attack from Grahlin. As it happened, the attack did not come at dawn, when Gird had expected it, and he got almost a full night's sleep before someone woke him up to ask his advice in an argument between two families whose children had started a fight.

Once he'd dealt with that (giving each child involved an unpleasant camp chore which took him far away from the others: the mothers might have thought of this, and let him sleep), he went out to look at the bridge by morning light.

Chapter Twenty-three

Full daylight, and nothing moved on the road between the city and the bridge. Gird stalked along the lines, glowering into the distance. He could not attack the city; he knew nothing about attacking cities. They had to come out here, where he could fight them. So far the sier had been willing to do that, and Gird had assumed he would come to get his guardpost and his bridge back.

"I don't like this," said Felis, when the sun was a hand higher. Gird didn't like it either. He wondered what the sier was doing instead of sending his troops out. That brown man would not give up his power easily. Even as he thought this, a shout from the bridge brought his head around. He could see nothing but one of his own yeomen waving an arm; he waved his in reply and jogged on.

Under the bridge in the early morning, the Hoor had flowed steadily northward, toward the Honnorgat. Now, even as Gird watched, that flow diminished, the water's color changing from clear green to murky brown. Then it was gone, and the wet rocks and mud gleamed in the sun before they dried. Fish flopped frantically in the puddles, splashing the water out. Sinuous gleams flashed up the bank and into weeds: watersnakes.

"Esea's curse," someone said softly. Gird felt trapped with everyone looking to him for answers he did not have. He had never seen a river disappear like that, and neither had anyone else he'd known.

"Fish," said someone else, and he saw several of his yeomen slithering down the bank to grab for fish in the puddles.

"Get back!" he yelled. Whatever it was had power to spare; where a river disappeared it could return. His people stared at him, and turned to climb back out. He wondered how much water they'd drawn, how many buckets and skins and jugs they had for their need. Expecting the worst, he sent someone to check on the kitchen well at the guardhouse; it was empty, which did not surprise him.

What surprised him was that nothing happened. Around midday, a runner came in from the eastern contingent reporting that they had fought two stiff engagements, come off intact, but had to retreat up the River Road eastward. That meant they could not help if he needed them, but he had expected that. The fish trapped in their puddles died, and stank by mid afternoon. The nearest creeks to the west were barely trickling; beyond them, the flow seemed normal. Gird sent a small party north to the Honnorgat; they reported that the big river seemed completely normal. Although it was not particularly hot for the time of year, everyone felt thirsty—which was partly the knowledge that they had no source of water, Gird knew.

He sent those who could not fight away westward, with a score of yeomen, to make camp by the nearest good water source. He hoped it would stay good. He had a feeling that the sier had decided to move to a new battlefield, one on which Gird had no strengths at all.

Afternoon wore on to evening, cloudless and still. As the sun set, the sky took on a strange bronze-green color; everything seemed to glow from within in that uncanny light. No one had actually suggested that they might abandon their position, but Gird noticed too many sidelong looks, too many whispers. He wished he had even the ghost of an explanation to give them. Instead, he had an itch between his shoulder blades and the feeling that something very bad was going to happen when he least expected it.

Early in the night, he decided to pull back his people on the far side of the bridge, except for the scouts dispersed in the fields. He felt a little better then, but not much. He was bone-tired; he'd walked the lines all day, trying to see something that would explain what was going on. But he could not settle to sleep. Most of the others had, worn out with tension, but Gird stalked back and forth, in and out the gate, grumbling to himself.

He had just been to the jacks when he heard a resonant *pooot* that sounded like a novice hornplayer, followed by a shattering crash that resolved into a splash-edged roar. The ground trembled beneath him. Gird spun to see water erupting from the kitchen well, glittering in the starlight, higher and higher, a trembling column far higher than the tower. Cold mist washed over him, then a splatter of drops, then a flick of solid water falling. The ground bucked and groaned; he fell heavily. He saw the well split, as a cracked waterskin splits if squeezed. Water roared out of a cleft in the ground, waves of it now rolling toward him.

No one could have heard him, but no one needed to. That noise, and the shaking ground, had everyone awake and moving. But the guardpost's enclosed space was already knee-deep in water, water that surged and heaved, seeking a way out. *At least the main gate's open,* Gird thought, struggling to keep his feet in the racing water. He was soaked already, and the water was rising. Other struggling shapes in the darkness clung together; screams rose over the deep-bodied roar.

"The gates!" Gird yelled. "Get out the gates!" He didn't know if anyone could hear him, but it felt better to yell. He fought his way through the water, now thigh-deep, and lost his footing just as he came to the gates. The water threw him, tumbled him, dragged him toward the dry riverbed, but before he reached it was shallow enough for him to get back to his feet. He angled away from the river, shouting for his marshals. In the starlit, windless night, he could see only the vague shapes of guardpost, toll station, and bridge, dark moving blurs that might be his men, and the glittering surface of racing water.

Then the ground heaved again, and the guardpost disintegrated into individual blocks of stone and pieces of wood, as a final gout of water spurted even higher, and fell with an indescribable noise on the mess below. Gird's ears ached with the silence that followed; his yeomen's cries seemed thin, more like buzzing flies than human sounds. He was cold, cold all the way through, wet and shaking. He looked toward the distant city, and saw a faint glow move through the air toward it, to vanish behind its walls.

Anger followed fear so closely that he was still feeling the chill when he found himself bellowing at his people to be *quiet* and pay attention.

"What *was* that?" came a plaintive wail.

"Magic," Gird said firmly. "Now—who's where? Felis? Cob?"

Answers came, shakily at first, and then more firmly. Not everyone. Cob had been inside, sleeping in the guards' barracks; he hadn't answered. Gird shivered, remembering the way the guardpost walls had wavered. Anyone who hadn't made it out before they fell could be crushed—or drowned. Gird splashed through the water, only ankle-deep now, to the near end of the bridge. He looked down, unsurprised to see water in the river, rising water. Too late for the fish, but the frogs croaked happily. If I were the sier, Gird thought, I would attack while the enemy was still disorganized. How long did the sier expect him to be disorganized?

He got most of his wet, shivering, miserable yeomen back into some kind of order, weapons in hand. One watchfire, on the west side, had survived; he sent a hand of men across the River Road to search for dry fuel. With a makeshift torch in hand, he clambered into the jumbled mess of fallen stones and mud that had been a tidy guardpost. Orange light glistened on wet rock, gleamed on stretches of rippled mud, and turned the slow but steady flow over the lip of the kitchen well to a fiery glaze. Some of the odd shapes were bodies: a naked foot stuck out from under a stone, a dead face, mouth clogged with mud, screamed silently from its pool of water. Gird shuddered. Someone in the darkness coughed, then retched. Someone else groaned.

All through the rest of the night, they searched the wreckage for anyone alive. Most of those in the ruins of the guardhouse were dead or dying, crushed by fallen stones or drowned—or both, it was hard to tell. Daylight made visible to all what those with torches had seen in the night: an uneven pile of rubble, mud, and the smashed remains of whatever had been inside it. One by one they dragged the bodies out. Too many bodies. Gird raged inwardly at the unfairness of it. Felis, red hair thick with mud, crushed when the tower fell: he had been a burr in Gird's boot, from the first day, but he had also done his best. Cob was alive, but lame; a falling stone had smashed his foot. Gird looked at all the bodies, all the injured. Twenty-three dead, eleven injured who could not walk. Worse than any battle he'd fought so far. They would have to dig a grave—and for that matter, new jacks. They would need litters for the injured. Food—all the food stored in the guardhouse was gone. He was not sure whether to trust the water that still came from the shattered well, trickling away through the mess. It came to him suddenly that no one had blessed this well for a long time. Its *merin* might have deserted it, or been angry with the men who took its water and gave no thanks. Perhaps that had made it vulnerable to the magelord's magic.

He sent someone to find herbs for the dead, and flowers for the well. If any good spirit still lived in that water, he wanted it to be happy, to know that the men there now respected it. He laid the proper herbs on each of the dead, muttered prayers for their traveling souls, and scattered the flowers on the water. They swirled in an unseen current. Gird took that as a sign that the *merin* accepted his offering, and dared to taste the water. It was sweet.

"Do you know what it was?" asked Cob, when Gird paused beside him.

"Magic," Gird said. "The sier's magic, I'd guess."

"What can we do against it?"

Gird shrugged. He had no weapons against magic, nothing but Arranha's word, and the gnomes' word, that the magelords were losing these powers, that he could defeat them with ordinary soldiers.

"If that's what they used to be like," Cob said, "I'll quit cursing my grandfather's grandfather for giving in. No one could stand against that."

Gird cracked his knuckles. "I don't know. Most of us are alive, and he's not come out to fight us yet. Maybe it takes something out of 'em."

Cob spat. "He hasn't come out to fight because he doesn't need to. He can do this again and again—"

"If he could do it so easily, he would have before." Gird spoke slowly, feeling his way into the truth. "He sent his soldiers, his patrols, because that was easier, until we blocked the road that he needs. Besides, he hasn't followed it up. If he could, I think he would; he's not a stupid man."

"You know him so well." Cob rarely indulged in sarcasm; Gird thought it was the pain of his foot.

"I met him, last year," Gird said. Cob stared at him. "When I came to visit the barton—what I thought was their barton. It was a trap, but not for me alone."

"And you met the sier?"

Gird nodded. "Met him and—" He did not want to tell Cob all the details of that meeting. "He's—an interesting man," he finished lamely. Cob gave him a long look.

"It should make a good story sometime. If we live to hear it." He tried to shift his legs, and bit back a groan. "Last thing I needed—damn that rock!"

What bothered Gird most was not knowing what else the sier could do. If he could dry up a river and then send water out a well, breaking the ground around it, what could he do with fire? Could any one of Gird's cookfires turn into a huge inferno? Could the sier move hillsides the way he had moved water? Or call a whirlwind? If he could move water at such a distance, could he influence men directly, even kill? Twenty-three dead now—in minutes—at no risk to the sier or his army. He shook his head as if flies were after him; this would not do. He needed to know more.

Selamis, called back from the nonfighters, stared at the sodden ring of destruction in apparent shock.

"You're a lord's son," Gird began, Selamis's eyes came back to him, wary now. "I met one of their priests, who said they'd had great powers before, but now these were waning. He said one reason the magelords bred with our people was in hopes of getting more mages. Do you know anything about that?"

Selamis didn't answer for a long moment, his eyes roving across the mud and rubble. "I never saw anything like this," he said finally.

Gird grunted. "Did you ever see the lords use any magic?"

"Yes. My fa—they could make light. Some of them did, anyway. I saw one *call* someone once, I suppose you'd say. A quarrel among servants, almost a brawl, and when he came they all quieted, even smiled. Not like they were hiding the anger, like they didn't feel it."

"What did he do?" Gird had not missed the change in Selamis's tone when he spoke of servants.

"He gave his judgment, scolded one—but they didn't mind. They couldn't, with that feeling."

"You felt it too?"

"Partly. It was—" Selamis seemed to struggle for the right words, his hands waving a little. "It felt good," said finally. "Peaceful, like a hot afternoon. Safe."

"Mmm." Gird thought what that could mean for a commander. To have his soldiers feel safe, confident—he remembered that the brown man, the sier, had given him a feeling of confidence. He had thought he didn't want to kill the sier because of his own attitudes; had the sier been influencing him? And if he could do that, could he make others feel fear and confusion? He asked Selamis.

"I never saw anything like that," he said. Gird eyed him thoughtfully. Something about the man seemed odd. He was only ten years younger than Gird, but seemed younger than the other men his age; Gird kept wanting to call him "lad." Was that his magelord blood? Arranha had said the lords discarded their halfbreeds who had no magical talent: was that why Selamis had been fostered away?

"Did you ever do any magic?" he asked bluntly. Selamis's eyes widened, then narrowed.

"No." It was a flat no, inviting no more questions. Gird ignored that.

"That priest I met, he said bastards with magic were adopted in, and those without fostered away as small children. You talk as if you stayed with the lords longer—did they think you might have it?"

Selamis reddened, and turned away. "I have no magic. I am only a bastard, and my father sent me away—he never said why. I hadn't done anything wrong—" *But to be a bastard,* Gird thought, *without the talent they hoped to breed in you.* He didn't like the whine under Selamis's words. A few years of luxury too many; perhaps he thought he should have had it forever.

"What about fire? Could they make something burn, something far away?"

"Like this?" Selamis looked around. "I don't know. Light a fire, yes, by touching the wood, but I never saw anyone do it from a distance. Except—" His brow furrowed. "—the priests of Esea, in Esea's Hall, once. They said it was the god lighting the fire on the high altar, but I always thought it was the priests; they had that look, that concentration."

So Selamis had been to Esea's Hall—with his father? Gird did not ask; he had more immediate worries.

"Is there any effort to it? Does it tire them?"

Again a curious expression crossed Selamis's face, caution mixed with something else Gird could not interpret. "I think so. I remember hearing that."

"So if one man, say, did that with the water, then he might be too tired to do more today?"

"He might." Selamis pursed his lips. "They said it was like any other strength—a weak man would be exhausted from lifting what a strong man could carry easily. The man who did this might have been able to do more, or this might have been the work of more than one using all their strength."

Gird scrubbed at his face; he felt he had been awake forever. "And you could not say which, could you?"

"No." Selamis looked around again. "Did you lose the maps, in that?"

Gird had forgotten his maps and the records he had found in the guardpost. "I—must have." They would be crushed under the rocks, soaked and blurred, even if he could find them. He glared at the rubble. "Now what will I do—I can't draw maps!"

"I can," Selamis said. "My hands are almost healed—and I remember the maps well enough. Let me look; I might find something." He stepped carefully onto one of the tumbled stones.

"Go ahead," Gird said. He didn't think Selamis would find anything useful, but there was always a chance. Others had picked through the rubble salvaging what they could; though most of what they found was smashed beyond repair, some weapons survived intact.

Around midmorning, two of his scouts returned to say that at least sixty foot soldiers were on their way, carrying pikes. With them were a score of bowmen. Gird could just see the dustcloud. He had only a few bowmen worth the name, although his yeomen had been practicing with the bows taken at Overbridge. He had plenty of time to withdraw, but he did not want to withdraw. He still had almost twice as many yeomen as the reported force, and thirty of the good pikes. Unless the sier could make the river itself flood, they should be able to hold the bridge, at the least. He sent all his wounded west, to stay with the other noncombatants.

"You're sure about this?" Cob asked. Gird could feel the attention of others; he wished Cob had not asked.

"Sure enough," he said. "He wants it, or he wouldn't have done all that. We thought it was important before; now we know it is."

"But if he has more magicks—"

"We'll pull back. Ordered retreat—" He had never actually done that, but the gnomes had told him how it should work. "They can't take us with sixty, even with good pikes—"

"Alyanya's grace," said Cob, wincing as someone bumped his foot. He had tried to insist that he could stay. Gird insisted that he go. He wished he could do the same with Rahi, who was perfectly healthy, but he knew better than to try. She had taken all his ideas about women, and her individual situation, and recast them into something that he did not yet understand. It was hard to think of her as his daughter, although the memory of her as a child and young woman still lived in his heart. He knew she had killed, now—he had been told, after Overbridge, about Rahi—but he still thought of her with her bag of herbs, her poultices.

He realized that he was standing there thinking about Rahi because he needed someone to replace Cob, and she was the logical choice—would have been, if it weren't that she was his daughter, and a woman. He had *said* it was the same rule for everyone—had he meant it? His mind flicked over the other possibilities. His senior people already had their responsibilities. There was Selamis, but he was new; he had never even drilled with them. He wondered if he could blame it on gnomes. They had been worse than surprised when he told them that women were in the bartons. But Arranha had said that the magelord women were trained to war— or had been.

He looked around. Cob had never said anything, but Gird knew Rahi had been his chosen second. She was busy now, supervising Cob's unit in raising the breastworks on the downstream side of the bridge. They had no shields that would hold against arrows; they would have to crouch behind their scanty walls and hope. Maybe he wouldn't need to say anything at all. But as if she felt his gaze on her, she looked around, and waved.

The enemy force came in sight now, marching along at a good pace. Gird felt his belly tighten. They looked ordinary enough, and if he'd had real pikes for all his yeomen, he'd have been confident.

It was going to be hard, bloody work with wood alone against their armor and steel, but it could be done. Had been done. Gird placed his few bowmen on either side of the bridge, where they would have the broadest target.

They came closer. Behind the soldiers with pikes he could just see the bowmen. He heard a shout, and they halted as neatly as even the gnomes could have wished. Their bowmen drew and released; the arrows flew up and burst into flames. Gird stared, as surprised as if a cow had suddenly grown fleece. Someone in his own lines screamed, then chopped it off.

The flaming arrows landed close behind his lines, but no one was hit. By that time, another flight was in the air; belatedly, Gird told his own bowmen to let fly. The second enemy flight fell closer. One missed Gird by a fingersbreadth; he felt the heat of the frames. His own bowmen saw their arrows angle away from the formation, as if they had struck something.

"What is *that*?" someone asked. Gird had no answer. He was beginning to wonder if his two-to-one advantage was an advantage at all. The enemy bowmen released another flight, the yeomen were looking anxiously up to watch the arrows fall. Two of them were struck full in the face. Another four were struck as well, and all six burst into flames, as if they'd been soaked in grease. The other yeomen backed away from them, and at that moment the enemy pikemen charged across the bridge.

Gird's bowmen tried again, and this time hit some of the enemy, but most of them made it to the breastwork. Even as he rallied his yeomen, Gird realized that he had made more than one serious mistake. They had never fought across a breastwork before, for one thing. Raising it for protection from arrows—which hadn't worked anyway—had meant raising it higher than his people usually thrust with their sticks. They were awkward now, handicapped by the breastwork, unable to coordinate their moves as usual. And although they had practiced against each other, they had never faced a trained polearm unit before. The sier's soldiers knew exactly how to handle their pikes over a wall—Gird's yeomen had no advantage of reach, and the disadvantage of poorer weapons and training.

Worse was to come. Rahi's yell brought his head around, and he saw her pointing downstream, to the north. He could just see the cloud of dust, and the dark dots within it that were men on horseback. One of the gnome warmaster's favorite sayings raced through his head: "War rewards the prudent and farseeing, and punishes the unwary. It is what you do not know about your enemy that destroys you." He had not known horses could ford the Hoor down-stream from the bridge; he had not known about that kind of fire arrow; he had not known that he did not know. He was not sure he knew what would get them out of this alive.

Already some of the sier's pikes were atop the breastwork, forc-ing a wedge into his line. If they divided his force, all was lost. Gird raised his voice over the din, calling them back to rally around him. Rahi looked over her shoulder, nodded, and got her unit rearranged into a tight mass, backing away from the breastwork one careful step at a time. Keris, on the upstream side, did the same, not quite as neatly. The sier's pikes overran the breastwork and pressed them hard, but the yeomen managed to come together and sort themselves into rows and columns again.

Gird could just see the approaching cavalry over the heads of the fighters. Would they surround his force, or attack one side? And how would the sier's commander order the pikes? He felt no fear, only disgust with himself for leading his people into this trap—a mistake from start to finish—and the stubborn determination to get them out if possible.

The sier's commander (Gird had finally picked out the dapper little man in a helmet decorated with streamers) had no doubts at all. He disengaged abruptly what had been the front, shifted his pikes sideways, and left Gird's flank open to his bowmen. Gird's own archers, gifted for once with both initiative and skill, let fly before Gird even realized what had happened, and skewered the front rank of enemy bowmen. But the second rank sent fiery arrows into Gird's closely-packed troop—and anyone hit was instantly engulfed in flame. Gird himself tripped one victim and tried to roll him, but the man was dead—consumed—after the second scream. Gird hardly felt the blisters rising on his arms for the cold chills that raced down his back. It had to be more magicks—no fire burned like that. His formation rolled; he could feel their terror. Frantic, his bowmen tried again, downed four more of the enemy.

And the enemy pikes slammed into what had been their right flank.

Gird struggled with his own fear and confusion, shouted orders he only hoped were right. Their poles were as long as the enemy pikes—just longer—they *could* hold them off if they made no mis-takes. He threw himself into that line, giving his yeomen his own energy, his own strength. His line stiffened, straightened ... and behind him, he heard the cavalry coming, a thundering roar.

War is full of mistakes; it forgives none. The gnomes had said that, too. Sometimes the winner was the commander who made the fewest mistakes, or managed to correct them. Gird spun, with a final slap on the shoulder to one of the line facing pikes, and bellowed encouragement to those facing horses.

This, so apparently dangerous, they had done before. The yeomen braced their sticks and pikes, ready to prod the riders off balance. The horses, as usual when faced with an obstacle too large to jump, slowed, shied, ducked away from the line. Their riders spurred them on, whacked them with the flats of their blades, but the horses refused. Gird would have called his line to attack, but he could not do that with the pikes opposite. He heard a yell from the remaining enemy archers, and several horsemen turned aside, to return with archers riding double.

"Look out!" someone yelled, as if there were anything they could do. The archers grinned—six of them, Gird counted. The riders backed off slightly; those with archers mounted turned their horses' heads away, so that the archers had the best possible angle. Gird sent up a wordless prayer to any god who might be paying attention—though he suspected he had been stupid enough to make them all turn their backs—and received no miracle. The archers made a slow and elaborate dance of taking arrows, nocking them—

"Front two, *now*—second two, reverse!" It was outrageous, hopeless, and impossible, but better than standing like sheep in a pen. The front two ranks on that side of Gird's formation followed him in a ragged charge at the horsemen; the second two—who had been supporting the two on the pike side—spun and faced outward to replace them. Gird did not stop to see if it worked, or how neatly they turned. He was running straight for the mounted archers, screaming as loud as he could; when he saw one archer draw, the arrow aimed at him, he threw his stick, end over end, and dove for the ground.

He felt the heat of the flames, but the arrow missed him. The horse, alarmed at an attack from the rear, crowhopped and whirled, fighting its rider; the archer grabbed too late for the rider's belt and slid off, landing hard on his back. He heard screams: one of his men had been hit by a fire arrow. But more had followed Gird's lead; horses squealed and bucked, spun and reared, and all but one archer fell off.

The other riders tried to cut Gird and his yeomen off from the fallen archers. Gird ducked under one horse's neck, got his arm under the rider's leg and heaved; the man fell off the opposite side, cursing, and cut his own horse trying to strike at Gird. The horse squealed, shied, and collided with another in time to spoil that rider's stroke. Gird had his hauk out, and popped the next rider hard on the knee. He heard it crunch. Then he saw one of the archers, standing, with his strung bow over his shoulder, reaching up for a lift onto horseback. The rider was leaning out and the archer took his wrist. Gird's hauk got the archer in the angle of neck and shoulder just as he left the ground. The man sagged, pulling the rider down and sideways; before the rider realized his danger, Gird had yanked back on the archer, and dragged both off the horse. He put a deliberate heel on the bow as he smashed the archer's head, and then the rider's.

"Gird! Here!" He followed that yell and found a tight cluster of his men, protected by their sticks, holding off a milling crowd of horsemen. Gird dived into that protection just as a sword opened a gash across his shoulders.

"We got the archers," said one of the men proudly.

Without archers, the horsemen could not quite reach and kill the yeomen; Gird was able to maneuver the survivors of his raid back into the main group. These had recovered enough control to withstand the pressure from the sier's pikemen, though Gird realized he no longer outnumbered the enemy by anything like two to one.

Time passed, with sweating, grunting, miserable fly-bitten flurries of effort and equally sweating, miserable, and fly-bitten stretches of exhaustion, when both forces had run out of breath and will. The sun moved on towards evening, and Gird had not been able to move his yeomen anywhere. But no reinforcements had come for the sier's troops, either. They were locked together like two stubborn bulls that have shoved head against head without yet establishing dominance.

What broke the stalemate was Gird's twenty other yeomen, coming back from the distant campsite to find out why they had had no orders. They came marching along, singing "The Thief's Revenge" as loudly and unmelodiously as twenty men could do, while behind them came such of the noncombatants as wanted to flourish a shovel or pick and learn to march in step. In actual numbers, they were too few to matter, but as fresh troops coming onto a field where all are exhausted, they had an effect beyond their numbers. The sier's men withdrew a step, and then another. Gird did not order a charge; he was near falling down himself, and knew his yeomen did not have strength left for a charge. The sier's pikes withdrew an armslength, a pike's length—the horsemen rode between, and the sier's pikes turned to march away. Gird let them. He was glad enough to see them go.

There was no question of holding his position. Too many had

died, demonstrating that he did not have what he needed to hold it. Gird watched the low evening sunlight gild the backs of the sier's men as they withdrew to the far side of the bridge, and formed again. His own yeomen gathered the bodies of their dead, ignoring the sier's fallen. It would be foolish to strip the bodies in sight of their companions. Too many, too many: Gird cursed his foolishness, his stupidity, and even the time he wasted cursing them.

"At least you got us out of it," Rahi murmured, as he gathered them again to march away.

"No thanks to me," Gird said. "I got us into it."

"You always said a lesson that leaves bruises is never forgotten."

He looked at her, but her steady eyes did not reproach him. "I said that?"

She grinned, a white flash out of her dusty face. "Often and often. When that witch of a dun cow kicked me. When Gori hacked his ankle with the scythe—" Gori, her older brother, his first son, who had died of a plague. Rahi went on. "One of your favorites, that was, along with 'Think first, and you won't bleed after.'"

Gird snorted. "I didn't remember that one, did I? Gods above: I thought about what I would do, not what they would do."

But if Rahi did not reproach him, others would. He would reproach himself for this day's stupidity. He would learn from it— he had to, to make the deaths worthwhile—but he would not forget that he could have chosen differently, and those men and women would still be alive.

Chapter Twenty-four

In this chastened mood, Gird spent the next hand of days ensuring that his camp was as safe as it could be. He examined those who wanted to train as yeomen, and assigned them to units to replace those who had died. He visited the wounded, steeling himself to endure criticisms which no one actually voiced. He was sure they said more behind his back.

To his surprise, his recent defeat brought in as many recruits as his earlier victories. Hardly a day passed without one or three or six men or women straggling into camp, asking a chance to train and fight for "the new day." Some had traveled hands of days from distant farmsteads; others came from villages and towns only a few hours away. Some were enthusiastic youths, children—as Gird saw them—hardly off their mothers breasts. They stared wide-eyed at his veteran yeomen; he could practically see "glory" written on their foreheads. When he tried to explain how hard a soldier's life could be, they hardly listened, their eyes wandering to the alluring strangeness of campfires, women in trousers carrying pikes, men practicing archery. Gird sighed, turned them over to one of the more dour yeoman-marshals, and tried to ignore their eager glances when next he passed them as they scrubbed pots or dug jacks trenches.

Older recruits posed other problems. Some had a grievance against a particular lord, and wanted Gird to ensure vengeance. These could turn sour when they found that everyone had a grievance, and Gird thought no one's private reasons more important than another's. Some were obviously the misfits of their villages, quarrelsome bullies who thought Gird would supply weapons and food and an excuse for their violent behavior. Some were spies, as Selamis had been originally, some were crochety old men who were sure they knew how Gird should run his army, and some were soldiers changing sides, born peasants and now returning to their people—who *also* knew how Gird should run his army. Few of them shared Gird's concern for the time *after* the war, for the kind of land they would have. And they all knew less than they thought they did.

Gird dealt with these as well as he could. What bluff honesty and forthright explanation could do, he did, but when that failed he resorted to his strong right arm and a voice that could, as one of his marshals said, take the bark off a tree at twenty paces. He had the least patience with whiners and those who could find, as the saying went, one grain of sand in a sack of meal.

The army grew, nonetheless, and Gird found that Selamis's ability to read, write, and keep accounts was invaluable. He no longer had to keep in his head the members of each unit, with its marshal and yeoman marshal. Selamis suggested—tactfully—changes in nomenclature, preserving the name "barton" for the original use, and calling tactical units "cohorts" no matter how many bartons went to make them up. Gird agreed, after scowling at Selamis's neat script for a long moment. The gnomes had had names for the units, based on size, from the five-gnome *pigan* to the hundred-gnome *gerist*, but the language of his own people had nothing but "horde" and "skirra." The former meant everyone in the steading or hearthing who could fight, and the latter meant a small raiding party sent to steal livestock. He did not like using one of the mage-lords' words, but cohort was better than the others.

With Selamis and his most experienced yeomen, Gird worked out a new, more uniform, organization. His cohorts were upwards of 120 hands—though the term "hand" began to fall out of use with the larger unit. Each cohort would have a marshal, and at least four yeoman-marshals. Where bartons had joined to form cohorts, their yeoman-marshals would serve, otherwise the most experienced yeomen could be chosen. Each cohort would divide into tally-groups for camp work, and each tally-group would be supervised by the yeoman-marshal for that section. When the army divided for some reason, Gird would appoint one of the marshals to command whatever group he himself was not with—which led to the title of "high marshal" for such a situation, and—over Gird's initial protests—"Marshal General" for himself.

"They don't have to call you that," Selamis pointed out.

"Thank the gods! Why should they? A general is one of those fancy officers in gold-washed armor with a plume to his helmet; I'm not—"

"But you are, in one way. Commander of the whole army. It's for the records, Gird, and if you send orders—"

"Flattery." Gird eyed Selamis dubiously. The man had good ideas, but he had too many of them, too fast, and was too tactful by half in presenting them. Gird could not doubt his bravery—he had asked to start training while his hands were still sore—but he could not overcome the feeling that Selamis was just a little too smooth.

Somewhat to Gird's surprise, the sier had caused no more trouble—no patrols had come in pursuit, and the guardpost near the bridge was left a pile of rubble. Gird's eastern troop—half-cohort, he reminded himself—returned after several hands of days, full of their own stories of battle. They had "almost" held the sier's cavalry; they had seen no sign of magicks.

Ivis made no comment on Gird's mishaps, but did get him aside to discuss Selamis. "Are you making a yeoman-marshal out of *him?*"

Gird raised his eyebrows. "I hadn't thought. Why?"

"He wasn't in the barton in his village."

Gird sighed. "We went over that. He was an outsider; he'd been given someone's cottage—"

"I don't entirely trust him." Perversely, Ivis's distrust made Gird feel obligated to defend Selamis.

"He's not like us, I'll admit, but he's good enough."

"He was telling Kef what you thought about the lords' powers," said Ivis. "As if you'd told him to. Did you?"

"Well—no. But I don't see that it matters, unless he lied about it. What did he say?"

"Just what you've told me, mostly, and you thought the others should tell you if they'd heard anything more."

"That makes sense. If I'd thought of it, I'd have done the same."

"Yes, but—" Ivis shook his head. "I can't explain it, but he's—he's not solid."

"His wife and daughter died. We heard three days ago, from someone who saw it. He knows—that would unsettle anyone." Gird did not say how Selamis had taken the news; he was not sure himself what that white-lipped silence meant, that was followed so soon by apparent calm. He looked off across the camp, where Selamis at that moment was chatting with someone while scrubbing a kettle. Harmless enough; what was it that unsettled Ivis? Gird remembered that Diamod had unsettled him, with the difference between farmer and craftsman, an indefinable shift in attitude.

By this time they had moved the main camp, shifting west away from Grahlin, and south along one of the arcuate band of hills. Only one of the gnomish maps had been recovered; Gird was trusting Selamis's memory for the rest. The maps looked much the same to him, barring the use of a brush instead of a pen.

The larger camps, and richer resources of summer, allowed refinements he had missed before. One of their number claimed to have made his own brews before, and combined the seeds of early-ripening wild grasses with gods only knew what to produce a potent brew. The taste varied widely from batch to batch, but no one was asking for flavor. Gird found it relaxing to sip a mug in the evening after dark, when the weight of the day's worries seemed to bow his shoulders and put an ache in every joint. It had been a long time—many years—since he could end most days in a pleasant if hazy mood. He had, he told himself, earned it.

It was on one such evening, after a day spent settling the petty disputes which so often infuriated him, that he found himself faced with six newcomers, all women, and all with a grievance. His head had ached since before dawn with the coming storm that drenched the camp in afternoon, and brought a foul stench from the jacks. No one else admitted to smelling it; he'd had to bellow at the marshals before they reassigned their tally groups to digging a new one. Even after the storm, it was hot and sticky, with hardly a breath of breeze and clouds of stinging flies; nothing would dry, and his boots were sodden. For supper they had only cold porridge left from the morning; the storm had caught them by surprise, and all the fires had gone out. So Gird had retired to his favorite stump with a pot of Selis's brew, and let the stuff work the day's irritations out of his consciousness.

He was not happy to be interrupted by the newcomers, and the woman who talked the most had a sharp, whining tone that set his teeth on edge. She had a complaint about the duke's steward in their village, and a complaint about the barton's yeoman-marshal, who did not welcome women. She wanted to tell him in detail about a legal dispute involving one woman's husband's mother and a promised parrion which had then been withheld, as proof of the unreasonable attitude of the steward. His eyes glazed after awhile. He was acutely aware of her disapproval, and that made him even less willing to be sympathetic. The other five women stood shifting from foot to foot as they listened, clumping behind Binis, the speaker, as if she were some sort of hero able to protect them. She didn't look much like a hero, a tall scrawny dark-haired woman with a big nose and very large teeth, hands too large for her wrists . . .

He never did remember when the vague annoyance sharpened into active dislike, and the dislike into anger. Along the edge of his memory was the sight of Binis's face, the expression changing from surprise to dismay to anger and contempt, the faces behind hers mirroring hers as if she were in fact the only real person there— his memory blurred, after that. The next thing he knew, Kef had waked him with the news that Binis was gone, and with her the five newest yeomen. That was the next morning, broad daylight, far later than he usually woke.

"She's gone to tell the sier where we are," warned Kef. "You really made her furious—"

"I said what I had to." Gird rubbed his face, hoping the headache would go away, and wondering what, in fact, he had said. He hadn't drunk that much, and the stupid woman shouldn't have kept nagging at him.

"I know, but—" Kef peered at him. "You should be careful, Gird; that stuff Selis makes would take the hair off a horsehide."

"I'm *fine*." He wasn't, but he would be with a can of cold water over his head and something to eat. If they had anything left. He clambered up, stifling a groan as stiffness caught him in every joint, and looked around.

Something was wrong. He couldn't tell exactly what, but instead of the busy, determined life of the camp he sensed uneasiness, an almost furtive bustle in the distance, and ominous stillness around him. None of his cohort marshals were nearby, and yet he saw no drill in progress, and heard no tramp of feet out of sight. He smiled at Kef, and started toward the hearth. It was bare; the fire burnt out and the stones barely warm. One cookpot sat to the side, and in it was one cold sodden lump of porridge.

"That's yours, then," said a woman walking by—Adar, he remembered after a moment. Widowed, mother of two surviving.

"You've eaten?" he said to Kef, who was still hovering near him.

"Oh yes. Hours ago. I mean—"

"You mean I overslept because I was drunk," said Gird, and prodded the porridge to see how firm it was. He broke off a smaller lump and ate it with difficulty, watching Kef's eyes. They wavered, not meeting his gaze.

"Well—you had a lot to do last night—"

"Is that what they all think?" He took another small lump, and gulped it down without trying to chew it. The stuff would hold slates on a roof in a gale, he thought.

"Oh no. I'm sure they don't—although some—I mean someone said, but I don't know who—"

Gird finished the porridge, cold and gluey as it was, and thought about it. Rahi'd told him to be careful about drinking too much, but she'd always said that. Tam and Amis, too—but that was years ago. And some people always complained that others drank too much. Far as he was concerned, it was those who had neither head nor heart, trying to deny others what they themselves couldn't enjoy. Yet he remembered old Sekki well enough, who always smelled of sour ale and staggered when he walked, day or night— who died in a stinking puddle of his own vomit, one night. The sergeant had pointed him out to Gird and the other recruits—and he knew the sergeant's warnings against drunkeness didn't come from lack of taste for it.

So—had he been drunk last night, and had he thrown away five good yeomen (he wouldn't count Binis) by losing his temper in a drunken rage? Evidently some of the others thought so. Could they all be wrong? They'd all been wrong before, but so had he.

His head throbbed, and the porridge sat uneasily in his belly. He hadn't been really drunk, but then again he had to consider how the others felt, what they thought. He picked up the cooking pot and started for the creek.

"Where are you going with that?" came a sharp voice from behind him. He turned, and grinned at Adar. She reddened.

"Going to clean it," he said. "Don't we have a rule, that laggards to table clean the pot?"

Her mouth fell open, then shut with a snap. "But you—but you're—"

"I can dip water and scour, Adar," he said mildly. "And one thing about rules, they're for all of us. I'm no different." He turned away before she could offer, and stumped down the bank. The first splash of cold water went on his face, then he dipped the pot, scooped up a handful of sand and small gravel, and swirled it around. When he felt with his fingers, the gluey coating of dried-on porridge was still there. Blast. He'd have to really work at it. He looked around for rushes or reeds. Adar was standing on the bank, watching him.

"Here," she said. "This makes it easier." She handed him a lump of porous gray rock, very light for its size. Scrapestone, or scourstone: he remembered seeing similar lumps for sale in city markets, priced far above a village peasant's ability to pay. Mali had always used rushes. But the scourstone took the porridge off the pot quickly, and his knuckles hardly hurt at all. He gave the stone and the rinsed pot back to her.

"Does it pass your inspection?" he asked.

A smile tugged at her mouth. "Better than my breadshovel did yours. I never would have expected *you* to know how to clean pots."

He thought of saying it was simple enough, like most women's work—which had been his father's comment when his mother was sick—but he thought better of it. Simple work could be hard, and since it had to be done, better those who did it should take pride in it.

"When my mother had fever," he said, "my father bade me do kitchen work—my brother's wife was sick, too."

"Ah. And can you cook?"

He grinned, remembering burnt porridge and bread that baked stone hard outside but soggy within. "No, not well. I've tried, and we didn't starve, but no one would choose my porridge or bread. The Lady gave me wit to plow and raise the grain, not prepare it." He did not mention his hearthcakes, which had helped him win over a campful of hungry men. They were poor fare compared to real food, and he knew it.

"You have a brewer's taste for ale," she said, then colored again. "I'm sorry—I didn't mean—"

"Yes, you did. And I gather you all agree. How much *did* I drink last night?"

"Too much," she said. "A pot or so, that I know of."

He wanted to explain about the pain in his knees and hips and shoulders, the steady ache that sapped his strength some days, the tension and fear, that ale relieved. But he remembered—and knew she remembered—the tonguelashing he'd given young Black Seli for getting drunk in a tavern and blabbing about the nearest barton. Black Seli's excuse had been a fever, and he hadn't put up with it. *Rules are for all of us. I'm no different.* Why had he said that, right out loud. It was true, but still. No one knew how hard it was, dragging a mob of ignorant peasants through one battle after another. He looked at Adar, and realized that she was not going to accept that argument. Neither would he, if someone else gave it.

Gird sighed, heavily, and said, "Well, you may be right. Times before, I drank too much, and I thought I had my reasons."

"Most men have," said Adar, "At least they say so."

"Yes. Well, I can't stop last night now—"

She cocked her head at him. "No—and you can't stop the results of it, either."

He had not thought Adar was so forthcoming. She'd been a quiet one, hardly speaking in drill, always busy at some task but never chattering with the other women. *You said women had brains too,* he reminded himself. *You said men should listen to them.* But it was different, Rahi or Pir and this stranger. He wasn't going to justify himself to her, and he wasn't going to make promises, either. He climbed the bank, regaining the advantage of height, and looked down at her.

"I'll have to try," he said. Then he went on, to hunt for at least one of his cohort marshals.

Kef caught him halfway across the camp, by which time Gird was sure that the problem was much bigger than he'd thought. All the firepits were cold, when someone should have been brewing sib and baking for the noon meal. Those few he could see all looked to be tying up bundles.

"Gird! Red Seli wants to see you." Kef was breathless; he must have run some way. "Back there," he said, waving an arm to answer Gird's unasked question. "In the woods near the spring."

"Where are the other marshals?" asked Gird. Already he knew they might have deserted.

"Ivis took his cohort up the river, to gather fuel; Sim's looking for a better campsite—"

"Better than this?" Gird looked at the clean-running creek, and the heavy woods around that hid them from almost all directions. And they had watchers on the high rocks, the only point that overlooked the camp.

Kef looked down. "They're afraid Binis will tell," he said. "Or those new ones."

"So they all decided to move while I slept."

"They tried to wake you, but—" Kef's voice trailed off. Gird's headache was no worse than the pain in his heart. *He* had told them the importance of a leader's ability to stay alert, to wake quickly and able to deal with emergencies. He had shown them— and would they distrust him now, because only once he drank too much ale? Could he not have *any* relaxation?

He remembered the gnomes suddenly, their stern faces and inflexible rules. Their warmaster would have had something to say about "relaxation," and not what he would like to hear.

"What did I say to Binis?" he asked Kef.

"You don't remember?"

"If I remembered, I wouldn't need to ask you, now would I? Tell me."

Kef looked down, scuffed his toes in the leafmold, and then stared past Gird's shoulder. "You said—you said you didn't care what the steward had done, that the yeoman-marshal had a right to run his barton any way he pleased, and if he didn't want a gaggle of whining women treating war like a village brawl over oven-rights that was fine with you, and if she didn't have a better reason than that for joining up, she'd never last a day of camp discipline— that you had enough half-witted, lovesick wenches hanging around already, bothering your soldiers with nonsensical notions—that for all you cared she could take her ugly face to the duke and see what good it did her—"

"I said *that?*"

Kef nodded. "More than that—and livelier than that, if you take my meaning. You brought up every god I heard of, and a few I haven't, and threatened to unbreech her in front of the whole camp and tan her backside."

"Oh gods." His heart sank. He had never suspected himself of that kind of thing. He thought Binis was ugly, and just the sort of woman he disliked, but that was no excuse for what he'd said.

"That's when Rahi tried to get you to be quiet—"

"Rahi—!"

"And you told her to shut her damnfool mouth or you'd show her you were still her father—?"

"Mmph." Humor pricked his misery. "I daresay she didn't take that well."

"No—she said ale was no one's father, and stormed off—that's when Binis left. And the others."

Gird scrubbed his head with both hands. Worse than he'd thought. Worse then he'd ever imagined—how could he have *done* such a thing? He could see, with the clear vision of the morning after, just how that would affect all the women. He had had no problems with them before; they had done all he asked of any soldier, and now—he shivered. "Where's Rahi?"

Kef was staring at the ground again. "Gone. She went off with Sim. I—I think she'll be back."

At least his son had been far away, off scouting with a small group in the west. Maybe he could get this straightened out before Pidi came back. He had the feeling it was going to take a long time, and a good bit of unpleasantness.

"Well. Thank you for telling me." That surprised Kef; he had expected anger, Gird could see. "I needed to know what had set everyone off. Now I do, and I'm not surprised."

"You're not?"

Gird shook his head. "No—why would I be? I didn't know what I was saying, Kef—you don't have to believe that, but I didn't. That's not an excuse; I've told you all that, and it has to apply to me, too. I was wrong to get drunk, wrong to say all that to Binis—"

Kef scuffed the ground again. "That yeoman-marshal, he did say as how she's hard to live with—always picking quarrels, complaining—that's why he didn't welcome her—"

"That's as may be." Gird took a deep breath, and it out in a long sigh. His head still hurt, but he could see, between the waves of pain, what he should have done, and would have to do now. "I was still wrong, and I can't afford to be wrong like that. Red Selis first, and then I'll find the other marshals: we need to have a conference."

Red Selis, who had taken over Felis's unit after the guardhouse defeat, was so relieved to find Gird sober, cooperative, and reasonable that he looked almost foolish. Gird did his best to project calm confidence. They discussed the transport of water to an alternate campsite, if one were found, and the possible storage of some equipment near the spring in case they came back to this site later. When all this was settled, Gird looked Red Seli straight in the face.

"I played the fool last night, and you have cause to mistrust me—what about it?"

Red Selis' face turned redder than his hair. "Well, I—I was going to say, sir—since you mentioned it first—it's not that we don't trust you—"

Gird resisted the temptation to shake him. "Of course you don't, right now: what I'm asking is, do you want to quit? Go home?"

"Quit!" Startled, Red Selis stared slack-jawed a moment, then shook his head. "No, 'course not. Just for one bit of temper? It's just that—I dunno, exactly, but—"

"If I'd done that in the midst of battle, it could've killed us all," Gird said harshly. "If someone else had, I'd be ready to break his neck for him—might even try. It's worse for me—I'm supposed to be showing you how. Tell you what, I never knew it to take me like that before—not that I recall. It won't do: you know it, and I know it. That's well and good: no more of it for me. But to mend last night's bad work—I have to know if you'll trust me on this, long enough to see that I mean it."

"Well—yes." Red Selis looked thoughtful. "I never—I mean I thought you'd be angry, like, that we'd seen you—"

"I am angry, but with myself. It's not your fault."

"'Twas *my* cousin made the brew—" muttered Red Selis. Gird had forgotten that.

"It's not his fault either. You've heard me say it to others: the rule's the same for all. I was flat stupid, that's what it is, and it won't happen again." As he said that, he wondered—how was he going to tell when he'd had too much? Surely it wouldn't mean giving up ale altogether? He could see sidelong looks from those of Red Selis's cohort who were close enough to hear. At least they were there, and not on their way home.

By nightfall, Gird had visited each of his marshals. Sim had not found a really good campsite; the army was dispersed among several temporary sites, and, to Gird's eye, had lost perhaps one in seven. He didn't do a formal count, and no one told him. Gird had not seen Rahi all day; he had not wanted to ask Sim about her. He had asked the marshals to gather everyone briefly, and in the dusky forest light of early evening he faced his army in a clearing not big enough for them all. He could feel hostility, fear, and even more dangerous, detachment—too many of them had decided they didn't care what he did.

"How many of you," he began, "saw what happened last night?" Arms waved, and a general growl of assent. "And how many of you saw it coming? How many noticed I was drunk before that?" Fewer arms, and a subdued mutter. Finally one clear voice from behind a screen of trees.

"I seen it days ago, the way you started goin' to the ale-pot every night. Said to my brother, you just watch, and he'll go the way of our uncle Berro, see if he don't, and you did." That brought a scatter of chuckles, but some nodding heads.

"Well," Gird said, "you were right. I just hope your uncle Berro never made such a fool of himself, and never said so much he wished he hadn't said."

"I always heard as how drunks say what they really mean," said someone else, challenging. A woman's voice. Gird had expected that.

"My Da said, the first time he found me drunk, that a drunk's mind was two years behind him, at least." He paused, looked around, and felt a flicker of interest from them. "If you'd asked me, back when I had a home and a wife and children, if I thought women could make soldiers, I'd have said no. I'd never seen one, and neither had any of the rest of you. When Rahi came, my own daughter, I doubted her at first. But she had nowhere to go, and I knew my own blood was in her."

"And you told her—"

"Aye. Drunk, which I shouldn't have been, I told her a bunch of nonsense. Maybe I do think that, down in the old part of me, in my past. But here and now, I mean what I've said afore about women. You know what that is, and how I've made the rules here. And kept them, until now. I let my own daughter—and you that have daughters know what that costs—choose to put her body in front of pikes and swords. I meant all I said, and my pledge is still that what laws we make afterwards will be fair to women as to men."

"Fine, then, when you're sober—but what if you're pickled in ale when you write the laws?"

"I won't be." He waited a moment, to see how they'd take that, and was surprised at the change in the atmosphere. Most of them were listening, were believing him. The others were uncertain now, no longer detached or hostile.

"I may be pigheaded, but I'm not that stupid: I made a mistake, a big one, and it's cost all of us, not just me. I'm not going to do it again."

"Going to let someone tell you to quit?" asked the same woman's voice. Gird had not thought farther than keeping away from ale altogether.

"Good idea," he said, surprising her. "Who would you trust?" A long pause was followed by several muttered suggestions, mostly marshals. The woman spoke up again.

"Rahi?"

"Tell you what," Gird said. "I'll talk to Rahi, Cob, those others you mentioned—and as far as the ale goes, they can tell me what they think. Is that fair?"

This time almost all of them agreed. "But what about Binis?"

asked another woman. Gird nodded, and waved quiet those who tried to hush her.

"She's right. What I do from now on is one thing, but what I did to Binis and those others is another—something I have to deal with. What I thought is I'd go after her, find her. Apologize—"

"No! She'll turn you in."

Gird shrugged. "If she does, it's better than her setting the sier on all of you."

But this provoked more discussion and argument. Gird waited it out. Finally, Red Selis seemed to speak for most when he said, "It's already happened; if she's gone to the sier, then she's gone— we don't want to lose you as well. If she comes back, you can apologize then."

"She won't be back," said someone else. "But the redhead has the right of it. You're no good to us dead or captured."

"I should tell her—" Gird began, when a voice behind him spoke out.

"Tell her what?" It was Rahi; he turned to see her standing there as if she'd never been anywhere else.

"I'll tell *you* I'm sorry," he said. "About last night—I didn't know how drunk I was."

"Very," she said. Her mouth quirked. "More than I ever remember. I hope you learned something from it."

"I did. And I was going to find Binis, and tell her—"

Rahi shook her head before he finished. "Best not. I've got her settled for now, best I could do."

"What?"

"Where did you think I'd gone off to? Someone had to be sure she didn't put the sier's men on us right away. I let her have her say—and she's got a tongue on her almost as bad as yours, when she's roused—and finally convinced her she wouldn't get any profit out of the steward, besides it not being everyone's fault. But she hates you still, and she'd be glad to do you an injury if she could. You can't mend it; best end it."

The meeting broke up into clumps of people talking, a few arguing, some coming to Gird to thank him for speaking, some edging around him. He spoke to all who approached him, feeling Rahi's attention at his back like a warm fire. Finally everyone wandered off into the gloom, and she came up beside him.

"You were stupid," she said quietly. He heard the steel underneath.

"I was. I don't know—"

"Mother said when you were young you drank like that sometimes. Came home ready to fight anyone."

"I don't remember—before I met her, yes, but after—"

"Only a few times, she said, but when she was dying she bade
me watch for it. Help you if I could."

"You helped me here. I'm sorry, Rahi." He would have hugged
her, but she stood just too far away, his daughter no longer, making
sure he knew it. That, too, pierced his heart with a pain as great
as all the rest.

She heaved a sigh much like his, and her hands turned, gesturing
futility. "I don't think you can understand what your ways have
meant to women—beyond what you saw in it." He raised his brows,
inviting her to speak, but she shook her head. "You can't understand; you've never been where we were. But don't take it back,
whatever you do. Not for me or for any of us. You'll lose—lose
more than soldiers from your army, if you do."

"I don't mean to, Rahi. You keep me straight, eh?"

She grinned, a little uneasily. "I'll tell you you're drinking too
much, and you'll curse at me."

"To no effect; the gods know what curses to take seriously. I tell
you now, when I'm sober—do it, and I'll listen, or you can lay a
hauk across my skull and let sense in. Did you hear me tell the
others? Well then—it goes for you, too."

Chapter Twenty-five

In the next few days, there was no sign that Binis had carried
out her threat to expose the army to her sier. Gradually, by ones
and twos, those who had fled returned. Gird, having apologized
publicly, would have liked to forget it had ever happened, but knew
that it had. In fact, the longer he thought about it, the worse it
seemed: first a defeat, and then a drunken temper tantrum. He
would have to do something to redeem himself.

His first choice of action was the disruption of a taxday at a
market town west of them. Most towns had a garrison of troops,
either belonging to the local lord or to the king. This made enforcement of special fees and taxes much easier. As well, the townsfolk
felt even more at risk than poor farmers, and were less willing to

lend their skills to Gird's supporters. Although most farming villages now supported a barton, few towns did, and those bartons were small and timid.

This time, Gird made sure, through his spies, that none of the lords were actually in Brightwater before he planned his attack. He would face fewer than a hundred soldiers—well trained and equipped, but unsupported by magicks—and he had the support of bartons in all the surrounding farm villages, as well as shaky support from a faction of artisans in Brightwater itself.

Brightwater lay in a valley between two ridges, just where a stream had cut the western ridge to join the one that ran northward toward the Honnorgat. Most of Gird's army had been east of it; he moved two cohorts onto the ridge west of the town, and waited. The town was too small to infiltrate beforehand; even with the summer fair approaching, the local troops were being cautious. He could not count on help from the two hands of yeomen in the barton there, either; they had formed only that winter, and had no regular place to drill. But as he'd expected, the approaching fair, and the incoming traders, distracted the local soldiers; they kept close to the town, scrutinizing traders, and did not bother to scout the woods. Once the fair began, the soldiers gave up even a pretense of patrol. They had enough to do in the town and the meadows around it. Traders who had not made it through to Grahlin on the River Road had turned aside and come here; the fields south of the town were thick with their camps.

On the day before the tax would be collected, a second contingent of soldiers arrived from Finyatha, wearing the king's colors and carrying pikes. Selamis, watching this with Gird, announced that the enemy now had 150 soldiers in the town. Gird scowled, and sent scouts to check back along all the roads to make sure there were no more surprises. Then he called Rahi over.

"We'll want every yeoman who can carry a weapon, and they need to be *there*—" He pointed across the valley to a wood below an outcrop of streaked yellow rock. "When we come down here, the fight'll slide that way, and they'll be placed right to land on 'em—"

"You're sure?"

"Naught's sure but death, but it should be so. They can't go the other way, without getting into the rapids where the streams come together. Handy of the Brightwater folk to build their town on *this* side of the river. If things go well for us, I'll want our reserves right down there by the bridge when they retreat that way."

In the event, it happened as Gird had planned. His two cohorts

made it to the edge of the fields just south of the town unobserved;
the traders who might have seen him were in the market square,
complaining bitterly about the tax being exacted. The soldiers stood
around the market square, menacing the traders. The few traders'
servants took one look at Gird's ragged but determined army and
dove under the wagons, too scared to give an alarm. By the time
they reached the town's inadequate wall, with its gates standing
wide for the fair, a few soldiers did see the peasants coming, and
tried to sound an alarm, but in the confusion of a fair that alarm
went unanswered until Gird and his men were well inside the town.

It was less a battle than a bloody slaughter, as his first cohort
took a section of guardsmen in the rear. They had been stationed
around the market, to keep merchants in until the tax had been
collected; they could not turn and combine fast enough to defend
themselves. Many of the people in the market had their own grievances, and joined in the fight with savage glee. Gird saw one woman
lobbing cheeses at a line of soldiers just before they fell; a shepherd
yanked back one man's head in time for a yeoman's knife to slice
his throat. Gird's battle plan dissolved as everyone entered into the
fray on one side or the other. When the tax officer fell, a swarm
of peasants and merchants tore at the sacks holding the fees, and
dove after the shower of coins that spilled out.

On the other side of the market, the soldiers had chance to
regroup and settle themselves to fight. Their trumpets blared signals; they locked shields and started forward. Gird managed to get
his cohorts back together, not without difficulty, and forced a way
through the surging crowd, even as the crowd fell away from the
soldiers' swords.

The two groups met in the market square; Gird's had the advantage of numbers, and forced the soldiers back into one of the narrow lanes opening onto the square. At this point, the citizenry
re-entered the fray by throwing things out of windows—mostly at
the soldiers, but some of the missiles landed on Gird's group. When
a ripe plum splattered on his head and dripped sweet sticky juice
down his face, Gird was instantly reminded of that first row in his
own village. He kept his cohorts moving, and the soldiers, increasingly unsure, retreated faster.

The town gates on the east opened onto a narrow strip of land
between the walls and the river; as with most towns, the bridge
was not in the town proper. Here the soldiers tried to rally, but
they had no real hope against Gird's larger number and longer
weapons. They backed raggedly south, along the town walls, toward
the fields where the traders had camped, and the bridge that would

let them across the river to a road leading safely north. But Gird's reserves were just where he had expected, and the soldiers were caught between.

Gird was just ordering the bodies stripped of weapons, when a stream of bellowing men ran out of Brightwater's east gates. His cohorts reformed instantly. The men slowed, and a small group approached cautiously.

"Who's in command?" asked a tall, heavyset man in a trader's gown. He was used to command himself, by his voice. Gird stepped forward.

"I am Gird."

The man's worried expression eased. "Gird—I've heard of you. You have to do something! They're rioting in there; they've killed the council, and they're looting in the market—"

Gird shrugged. "What did you expect? I daresay they're hungry."

"But you—but I heard you were different—that you had studied law or something of that sort, that you had some notion of order."

Gird gave him a long, level look. "Are you asking me to bring order to the city?" He heard a stirring in the ranks behind him, but ignored it.

The man's eyes shifted, and he turned to glance at the other equally worried men behind him. Gird noted that they all looked prosperous; their clothes had no patches and their faces had good flesh.

"Well, I—I can't. I don't know anyone else—they said you could control the peasants."

"Is that what you want?" asked Gird of the others. A few nodded; the rest looked confused. Gird felt a sudden surge of excitement. Was this the start of the new society he had dreamed of? A chance to set one town on the right path? It was a chance, whether or not it was the right one. He nodded, abruptly, and saw on their faces that they were more glad than frightened. He hoped his cohorts would agree. He turned to them, scanning their faces quickly. Some looked as confused as the traders; some looked eager, and a few angry or unwilling. Those he called out, and sent as scouts to patrol the roads.

"We've been asked to help Brightwater regain its order," he said. One of the merchants mumbled something; Gird ignored it. "I want no looting, no idle mischief: you know what I mean. These are our people, same as farmers; we need them and they need us. We'll let them see if they like our rule, if they think it's fair."

He took in only one cohort, replacing wounded with sound yeomen from the others, and marched them in as if for drill practice.

The crowd in the market dispersed, to stand flattened against the walls. He could hear some dispute at a distance, angry voices and clangs and clatters; that would have to be dealt with, whatever it was, but for the moment he had to control the center of town.

It looked far worse than the count's courtyard: dead bodies, some that stirred, broken pottery and foodstuffs scattered and trampled, market stalls torn down, broken, their awnings ripped and flapping in the breeze. Once he had his troops in the market square, it occurred to him that he had never explained how to organize a city. He wasn't sure himself.

The traders and merchants who had come after him now sidled up, looking even more alarmed. "You have to say something!" hissed the leader. Gird nodded, but let his silent gaze pass across the square, catching the eyes of those who watched, noting their expressions. Then he nodded, sharply, and raised his hand for silence.

They stared back at him, much like the first men he had met in the wood. Perhaps the same common-sense would work with them. "You've heard of me," he began, not sure they had. "I'm Gird; we're peasants seeking a better way to live. We fight the lords who tax and tax—" A ragged, halfhearted cheer interrupted him; he held up his hand again and it ended. "You've seen peasants fight before, out of desperation, but we are not desperate. We know a better way, a fairer way, and we want to see that for everyone. These men—" he pointed at the traders, "—came out and asked me to bring order to Brightwater. I would rather bring justice—is that what you want?"

A sulky-looking man slouched against a wall yelled out, "What matters what we want? You got the weapons; you'll do what you want."

Gird shook his head. "No: if Brightwater prefers chaos to order, you may have it. Do you?"

"Me? I want my rights, that's what I want."

"That's what we want for all." Other heads nodded. Gird noticed unfriendly looks aimed at the sulky man. He raised his voice to carry beyond the square and said, "Where is Jens, the harnessmaker's assistant?"

"Here!" Gird had never met Jens, yeoman-marshal of the Brightwater barton, but he liked the compact young man with bright blue eyes under a mop of chestnut hair. Jens had his entire barton together, and they were standing in what could pass for a double row.

Gird turned back to the others. "This is the yeoman-marshal of

Brightwater barton. He will help me restore order, and bring justice to your town. He knows you, and you know him; what he says is said in my name." He looked at Jens. "Do you know what fighting is still going on? Are there more lords' men here?"

Jens shook his head. "No, sir. I think that noise is at the council chambers, people taking things, but no more soldiers."

"All right then. We need this square cleaned up—" Gird looked around. "Wounded by the well, so the healers don't have far to go for water. Dead outside the walls—we'll need men to dig graves. Those whose stalls are broken, you can start repairing them." He pointed to the woman he remembered throwing the cheeses. "You—what about your stall?"

She pointed at a jumble of broken wood and ripped cloth. "That was it, sir, and how I'm to get another I don't know—"

Gird pointed to two of his yeomen. "Help her fix what she can. Selamis—" Selamis was at his shoulder, staring bright-eyed around. Gird glared at him. "*You* can take accounts—who had what space, who needs help to repair stalls or houses. Anything else you find out." He looked at Kef, one of the marshals he'd brought along. "You take a half-cohort and settle that riot, or whatever it is. Rahi, you take the rest and make sure everything else is quiet."

Gird stayed in the square with Selamis, trying to get a sense of the town's organization. It was far more complex than his village, or the army. The artisans were not simply "craftsmen" as he had supposed: each craft had its own standing in the town, and rivalry between crafts became apparent as he listened. Within each, too, were hierarchies and rivalries. So a tanner's apprentice might jostle a dyer's apprentice with no more than a curse in response, but a potter's apprentice ranked a tanner's. The finesmith had nothing to do with the blacksmith, and Brightwater boasted both a weaponsmith and a toolsmith. In Gird's village, anyone might peg a bench together or frame a cowbyre; here carpenters and joiners were separated by custom and caste. He wondered what Diamod would say about that, then remembered that Diamod was off scouting. Then there were merchants, some as specialized as the salt seller, and some as general as the importer who handled any and all goods transported across the mountains, from needles to silks to carved buttons in the shape of sea monsters. The houses towered two and three stories tall; those of the wealthiest were clustered in the southwest corner.

An uneasy stillness gripped the town soon after Gird's yeomen occupied the soldiers' guardhouse. Gird did his best to keep everyone busy, insisting that streets must be cleaned of dead bodies

("Yes, the rats too!" he had yelled at someone who asked) and
debris. When it was possible, he restored goods to the merchants
who had owned them—although he could not clean and mend what
the fight had soiled and broken.

He settled such minor disputes as were brought to him the first
day with what wit he could muster, although some of them seemed
frivolous. Why would someone in the aftermath of a battle want a
judgment against a neighbor for using the neighbor's balcony as
one end of a laundry line? Why pick this moment to complain
that someone's son was courting a daughter without the father's
permission? He realized that the Brightwater yeoman-marshal,
though well-known and considered to be honest, had the low status
of a "mere" harness-marker's assistant; whatever he said on an issue
was immediately appealed to Gird. Gird might have found this
funny (after all, they were preferring the judgment of a discottaged
serf), but he had no leisure to savor the joke.

That night, Gird found himself invited to dine with the principal
traders, who had, he was sure, their own ideas about his notions
of justice. They offered beef and ale, raising their eyebrows when
he refused the ale, and insisted that they each take a bite of the
bread he brought before he would eat of their meat.

"We had heard you liked ale," one of them said, too smoothly.
"If you prefer wine—"

"I prefer water," Gird said, smiling. "In war, I've discovered, the
drunkard has half the men of a sober man, and less than half
the wit."

They laughed politely, and came to the point rather sooner than
he expected. What did he mean by justice, and how would he
insure that traders would be respected and treated fairly? Gird
answered as the gnomes had taught him: one law, the same for all,
of fair weights and measures. A market judicar, backed by a court
to which all parties could appoint representatives. He sensed that
some of the traders were satisfied by this (he had never believed
that all traders were inherently dishonest), but that one or two
were appalled. One of these last walked with him back to the
guards' barracks, complimenting him on the discipline of his troops.
Gird felt as he had when the steward complimented him on the
sleekness of a calf.

"And you yourself," the man went on, his voice mellow as the
ale Gird had not drunk. "So different from what I'd expected—
truly a prince of peasants." Gird controlled his reaction with an
effort. Did the fellow think peasants had never heard lying flattery
before? The calf the steward had praised so highly had been taken

as a "free gift" to his count's marriage celebration. "I'm sure you will not misunderstand—" The voice had a slight edge in it now; Gird braced himself for the thorn all that rosy sweetness had been intended to conceal. "Some of my colleagues are—alas—less than frank with you. They have their own standards, not perhaps what you would understand, being so honest yourself."

Gird was tempted to say "Get on with it, man! Is it gold you want, or someone's life?" He merely grunted, and walked on a little faster. The man's hand touched his sleeve, slowing him. Gird glanced ahead, to the torchlight where his men were on guard at the corners of the market square.

"There's fair, and there's fair," the man was murmuring, his hand still on Gird's arm. "A man like you, peasant-born—good solid stock, I always say, Alyanya's good earth—" That came out of him as harshly as a cough; Gird would have wagered that the man had never given Alyanya a thought in his life. "I just want you to know I'm your friend; you can trust me. And as a token, I have a little gift—" The little gift came heavily into Gird's hand, round and smooth, with a slightly oily feel. He knew without looking that it was gold, the first gold he had ever touched. With anger and revulsion came curiosity: he wanted to peer at the coins, to see if it was one of the fabled gold seadragons, or the more common (by repute) crowns. He opened his hands and let the coins ring on the cobbles of Brightwater's main street.

"You dropped something, trader!" he said loudly. Heads had turned at the sound of gold hitting stone; he himself would not forget the almost musical chime, or the edges of the five coins against his fingers.

"You stupid fool!" The trader's voice was low and venomous. "You might have been rich, powerful—"

"I might have been your tool, or dead," said Gird softly. Then, louder, "Best pick them up, *sir;* there's been enough coin scattered today."

"If you dare tell anyone—" began the trader, crouching and scrabbling over the cobbles for his coins. "I'll—"

"You're threatening me?" Gird's voice rose, the day's frustrations and his anger getting the better of him. "You snivelling little liar!" The trader's hand slid into his gown, and the torchlight glinted on a thin blade; Gird batted it aside, hardly aware of the shallow gash it gave him. He could heard his men coming to see what was going on. His second swing felled the trader as if the man had been a shovel leaning on a wall. Gird stood over him, sucking his knuckles.

He wished the man would stand up, so he could knock him down again.

"What happened?" Jens, the Brightwater yeoman-marshal had come with the others. Gird didn't answer until they had all arrived, perhaps two hands of his own yeomen and those citizens of Brightwater who had been on the street and brave enough to hang around when trouble began. He looked around the circle of faces.

"This one came with me into the city, tried to bribe me, and pulled a knife when I refused his bribe. Tried to tell me the *others* were dishonest."

Jens snorted. "That doesn't surprise me. Short weight, scant measure, stone-dust in the meal, and it's been said for three years that it's his bribes to the council chair that preserved his license to trade here. They're not all bad."

"I didn't think so. But it's this sort of thing I'm going to get rid of." Gird looked around the faces again, seeing varied expressions from glee to worry. "An honest man doing honest work should be able to survive that way—one reason he can't is cheats like this. If you want my help, that's what the cost is to each of you—I won't tolerate bribes, cheats, lies. One rule, the same for all, and fair enough to let a man live if he's willing to work honestly."

"And women?" asked one of the two women there. He nodded. "And women. Same rule—no more being cheated because only a man can hold a cottage or craftcot. Earn the pay, get the pay."

"I'm for that," she said. Gird wondered who she was, she looked smaller than any of his women, but her face had the same resolute expression.

"What about him?" asked Jens. "Are you going to kill him?"

Gird was startled; it had never occurred to him, but from Jens' voice and the reactions of the townsfolk, no one would think it odd if he sliced the man's throat on the moment. "No," he said. "We've proclaimed no laws—he could claim he didn't know—"

"Not if he was dead," someone muttered. Gird ignored that.

"It's got to be fair," he insisted. "The lords kill for whim; we don't." That *we* included those around; he saw by their faces that they realized it, and were surprised. "No, this'n goes back to his own wagon, out there, *with* his money, all of it, and the other traders must know." As he said it, he realized that he would have to do part of it himself. They were still not accepting Jens or even one of his own marshals. He wished he could have a mug of ale; his belly needed it. He pushed that thought away, and pointed to two of his men. "Simi and Bakri—you carry him. I'll come along and explain. Jens, you come too: I can't stay here forever, and they're going to have to learn to respect you. The rest of you—back to your posts, and call out replacements if you need them."

Fires were still flickering in the traders' field; Gird could see a cluster of dark forms around the one where he had eaten. He hailed them, as his yeomen carried the trader toward the fire. By the time they laid him down, he was beginning to stir and groan.

"This man," Gird said, "told me some of you were dishonest, and then he tried to bribe me. I dropped his gold on the street—he got it back, threatened me, and then drew a knife." He pulled up his sleeve, and showed the fresh gash still dripping blood. "So I knocked him down, and here's his purse. Anyone here know much he had, so they can verify it?"

The other man who had seemed upset at Gird's original comments on fair trading scuttled forward. "I'm his partner—I know—" and then his voice trailed away. Gird could imagine what he was thinking. Supposing he did know how much his partner had had, should he give that amount, or something higher—and claim Gird had stolen it—or something lower, and let Gird keep the bribe he would be sure Gird had taken. Gird looked past him to the trader he had already picked as the most trustworthy. He had asked Jens about him, on the way out, and Jens said he had a reputation for fair dealing.

Gird carried the purse to the trader. "He gave me five coins, gold I think, but he picked them up when I dropped them. Would you hold his purse?"

Reluctantly, it seemed, the trader reached for it, and then upended it into one of the wooden bowls they'd eaten from. "Five gold crowns," he said. "Three silver crowns, and two copper crabs." He stirred the coins, picked up one of the golds, and bit it, then examined it closely. "And this one is false—poor Rini, he couldn't even bribe honestly." Several of the others chuckled. The trader looked hard at Gird. "I presume you have a reason for bringing him back here rather than slitting his throat for him?"

"I don't do that," Gird said. The gash on his arm was beginning to sting, and he felt suddenly foolish and countrified, standing there with his sleeve torn and blood dripping down his hand. He did not like the feeling, or those who made him feel so. It should have been obvious why he came; it had been obvious to him.

"Well." The trader cleared his throat. "He won't trouble you again, I daresay, and if you intended to be sure none of the rest of us offered you bribes, I may say that some of us would not, anyway."

He sounded almost angry; Gird realized that from the trader's point of view they might resent being lumped with the dishonest one. "I didn't think all of you would," he said. "But it seemed fair to return him here, where he was known, and make sure you knew his purse was with him."

"Oh." The trader's voice had changed. "You were not accusing us of being his accomplices? Of sharing the bribe?"

That had not even occurred to Gird; it opened new insights into the ways merchants thought—not reassuring. "No," he said firmly. "I thought before that most of you were honest, but one or two—" he carefully did not look at the unconscious man's partner, "—were less happy about what rules I might make. I spoke to you, sir, because you seemed honest before, and Jens said you were."

"Jens? Oh—that—uh—"

"The yeoman-marshal of Brightwater barton," Gird said.

"I thought he was a harness-maker's—"

"I was a farmer," Gird interrupted. "And now I'm the marshal-general." It was the first time he had used the title Selamis had come up with; it felt strange in his mouth, and sounded strange on his ear. He went on before the traders could comment on it. "We consider all yeomen equal, whatever their skill. Yeoman-marshals guide each barton; marshals train yeoman-marshals and command cohorts."

The traders looked a little dazed; the one who had been speaking before said, "Is it like a guild, then? More like that than an army, it seems—"

Gird knew nothing of guilds, and did not want to admit it right then. "It's enough of an army to fight a war with," he said. "But we think beyond war, to the way people should live in peace." Their faces were still blank, carefully hiding what they thought. Gird felt the day's work heavy on his shoulders, and wanted a quiet place to sleep before anything else. "You take charge of him," he said to the traders, waving at the one who had opened his eyes, but still lay flat. Then he turned and headed back for the town.

He would have fallen into bed without even cleaning the knife-gash if one of his men hadn't insisted on washing it out. They had saved him a bed—a real bed—in the barracks. He was asleep as soon as his head went down. He woke in full day, with sunlight spearing through the high, narrow windows and all the other beds empty. Someone had pulled his boots off, and laid a blanket over him. He felt stiff and dirty; somehow it was worse to sleep clothed in a bed, inside.

Outside he could hear what sounded like normal town noises. No screams, no clash of weapons. He stretched, shoved his feet into his boots, folded the blanket, and looked around. Weaponracks on the walls, but no weapons: the soldiers had used them the day before, and his men had them now. He could smell cooked food. He followed the smell and came to a wide-hearthed kitchen. Someone at the hearth looked up and saw him.

"There he is. Bread? Cheese?"

"Both." Gird looked around. "Where's the jacks? And a well?" He followed gestures and found the jacks, then a long stone trough fed by a pipe in the wall of the barracks court. A thin trickle leaked under the wooden plug; when he pulled it out, a stream of cold clean water raced along and out the open drain at the far end of the trough.

"Clean shirts inside," called someone from within. Gird pulled off his filthy one and used it to mop himself with water. Someone had left a chunk of soap—real soap—on the rim of the trough. He scrubbed, feeling more human by the moment. For that matter, he might as well be clean all over; he shucked his boots and trousers, and scrubbed himself all over. Yesterday's gash on his arm reopened, stinging, but it looked clean, a healthy pink. When he was done, he replugged the pipe, and looked for somewhere to lay his wet clothes. Rahi was standing in the kitchen doorway, chuckling and holding out a blue shirt.

"You!" He could not have said why it bothered him then, but somehow being found wet and naked, alone in a walled yard after his bath, was not the same as bathing with others in a creek or pond. He dropped the wet clothes, snatched the shirt, and then held it away. "Blue? But I don't have a blue shirt—"

"You do now. Go on, put it on; they're asking for you, a whole gaggle of them." She had brought trousers as well, somewhat too large but clean and whole. As he dressed, she picked up his wet clothes, sniffed them, shook her head and dumped them back in the trough. "These'll need more than rinsing."

That day Gird found himself having to explain in more detail than he had yet devised just how he thought the law should work. He discovered men of law, who explained at great length why his simple measures would not do, and why the law had nothing to do with justice, and a great deal to do with precedent, custom, and the maintenance of commercial stability. Gird listened until he could not stand it, and then roared at them; they turned pale and disappeared, and he thought no more of them. He let each craft, each kind of merchant, present an appeal: Selamis sat beside him and wrote them all down. Brightwater had plenty of clerks who could read and write, but Gird trusted Selamis more than the strangers. He was not surprised to notice that Selamis talked easily to the merchants, even the richest, or that they seemed to prefer him to Gird.

Then he gave them all his plan, which combined (he thought) absolute common sense with absolute fairness and honesty. When everyone complained, he was sure he'd gotten it right: it pleased no one completely, but everyone slightly. Somewhat to his surprise, the grumbling died off, and the townsfolk and traders went back to their work. He had expected more trouble, not shrugs and winks and return to business as usual.

Many of his yeomen had never been in a town as large as Brightwater. Gird spent the next several days straightening them out, and insisting (until his voice nearly failed) that his rules applied to them, too. It was always possible that a townsman's gift of a pear or meat pasty to the man patrolling the street was not intended—or taken— as a bribe, but Gird could see clearly where it might lead. If someone wanted to give supplies to the army as a whole, as the farm villages had done with their gifts of food and tools, then Gird insisted it had to be done openly. Selamis had to record the gift, and then Gird would distribute it among all the cohorts as needed. Only a few yeomen were obviously looking for bribes, or extorting gifts, whichever way it could be described. Gird shocked his followers and the townsfolk by discharging those few, publicly, and explaining why. After that, the problem seemed to disappear.

He himself had a chance to see inside a rich man's home for the first time, when the surviving master merchants and craftsmen invited him to dine. He had never really thought about what would go into all those rooms, had envisioned even a king's palace as a glorified peasant cottage, but with everything whole and in abundance. The guard barracks had reinforced that notion: it was larger than his cottage, but the furnishings were much the same. Now, when he stepped onto glazed tiles of blue and white, when he saw the tapestries hung from walls, the carved and inlaid chairs and tables, the shelves crowded with things whose purpose he could not even guess, he realized how wrong he had been. The dining hall lay at the back of the house, facing a walled garden—but a garden made more for viewing than using. No cabbages, no redroots, no onions or ramps—but bright ruffles of color he did not even know. Two fruit trees were trained against opposite walls; their fruit gleamed like jewels among the leaves.

The meal itself surprised him as much as the house. He had assumed rich men ate more of the same food that he ate—what else was there? He peered suspiciously at a translucent yellow-

green liquid in a glossy blue bowl, and waited until the others had
dipped their spoons (their *silver* spoons) into it before trying it. It
tasted like nothing he had ever imagined; he could have drunk a
kettleful of it. That was followed by a stew of vegetables and fish,
then a roast of lamb, rolled around a grain stuffing flavored with
herbs. He had not known lamb could taste like that. Then came a
dish of fruit with a honeyed sauce, then an array of cheeses, white,
yellow and orange.

By this time, he had had more food than his belly would hold
with comfort. The merchants nibbled on, watching him covertly.
He wondered if they knew he was calculating how many of his
yeomen just one such meal would feed. They might—and they
might be worrying about it, too. He looked around the room, noticing the soft-footed servants who had brought and removed all those
dishes. One of them met his gaze with an angry challenge; Gird
gave him a slight nod. He refused the last three courses, explaining
that he never ate so heavily in the midst of the day, and when he
left he felt as if he should take a bath and wash it all off.

"And that's an honest one, they say," Gird reported to Selamis
and several of the marshals that evening. "Not so rich as the one
the mob killed, not cruel or unfair to his laborers and servants. I
saw just that one part of the house, from the entrance to the dining
hall—but if the rest is anything like it—"

"It would be," said Selamis, the corners of his mouth twitching.
Gird glared at him.

"You know all about it, I suppose; you may even know what that
green stuff was that looked like ditch-water and tasted—oh, gods
know how it tasted, but it was good. But men like that, they have
a lot to lose. They've done well under the lords; they won't stick
with us if they don't do well under us. But if we bend the rules
for them, we're betraying our own people."

The marshals nodded seriously, but Selamis lounged in his seat,
almost smirking. Gird wanted to clout him. It was hard enough
making the marshals accept him when he was invisibly efficient;
when he put on airs, it rubbed everyone's hair backwards. Gird
glowered at him.

"I suppose you think *you* should have gone to that dinner? You,
who would know all the names for that kind of food, and which of
those pesky things on the table were for what use? I see the way
they talk to you first—maybe they should've asked you." Gird
paused for breath, puffed out his cheeks, and made a rude noise.
"But they didn't ask you, Selamis: they asked me. They know where
they stand with me, even if they don't like sharing table-space with

a big stupid peasant who doesn't know what to do with a silver spoon. You're in between: not one nor t'other, not true peasant nor true lord. *We* don't care if you're a bastard or not, but they do. Yet you push it in our face that you're more like them."

Selamis had gone first red, then white, then red again. "It's not my fault," he said, glaring at Gird. "I can't help it that I know figan soup when I hear of it, or what the things are. Or that the better—the merchants and such are comfortable with me."

"No, I suppose not." Gird was half-ashamed that he'd let his temper loose, but the silent support of the marshals, who had never liked Selamis that much anyway, stiffened him. "What is your fault is the way you use it. If you're one of us, *be* one of us; don't be smirking in your ale when you know something we don't."

From the traders he found out where the king's army had been all this time. It seemed that after reaching Gird's village, they had had word from Gadilon about an army harrassing his domain—an army headed by a terrible, cruel commander named Gird. Gird thought back to his near encounter with the brigands in Gadilon's forest, and managed not to laugh. The king's army was busy, the traders said, in the south and east, convinced that that was the main peasant force. And the traders had heard only vague rumors of trouble in the north until they were near Brightwater—and then the rumor had said the trouble was up on the River Road, near Grahlin.

"We were near Grahlin," said Gird, not specifying when, or why they'd left.

"I don't expect the king has heard that yet," the trader said. "Sier Sehgrahlin has much of the old magicks, but not the way of calling mind to mind. Even if he could, the king could not hear, nor any with him. There's no one much left with that, but the king's great-aunt, and she's too old to matter."

"Where is she?" asked Gird.

"In Finyatha, of course, in the palace. Amazing lady; she came to the market there once, when I was a boy, and my grandfather sold her a roll of silk from the south. She looked at me and said 'Yes, you may pet my horse,' and my grandfather clouted me for presuming. I never asked; she saw it in my mind. She told my grandfather so, and he said I shouldn't even have been thinking it, and clouted me again."

"What was the horse like?" asked Gird, suddenly curious.

"A color I'd never seen; I heard later it was favored in Old Aare: blue-gray like a stormy sky, with a white mane and black tail, and what they called the Stormlord's mark on the face, a jagged blaze that forked. But it was the fittings that fascinated me: that white mane was plaited in many strands, each bound with bright ribbons that looped together. The saddlecloth was embroidered silk—I was a silk merchant's child, I could not mistake that. Then when she mounted, she sprang into the saddle like a man—and rode astride, which the horse nomad women do, but no merchant woman I had known. My grandfather told me later all the magelords do, men and women alike, but they think it is presumptuous in lower ranks."

Gird returned to the topic that seemed to him more important. "But if she is the only one—and the sier Grahlin has no such powers—then his messengers must find the king's army before the king will know and come north?"

"Yes. If he even calls for him: did you not know that Sehgrahlin is the king's least favorite cousin? They have been rivals for years; Sehgrahlin refused to send his troops on this expedition, although he has some up north, guarding against the horsefolk. He will not like to ask the king for help, that one; he will do his best to drive you out of his domain with his own powers."

He had done that, Gird thought, but what more would he do? He asked the merchant, who shrugged. "He might help Duke Pharaon—they've hunted together a lot, and he once loved Pharaon's sister—but he married into the Borkai family. Those he would help, but they lie away north of you, north and west, right on the nomad borders." The trader knew what the gnomes had not—or what they had not bothered to teach Gird—which lords lived where, and how they were related. Gird had Selamis write it all down, although he suspected Selamis might know some of it already. Then he asked about the one magelord family the gnomes had mentioned, and the trader's expression changed. "Marrakai! Where would you have heard about them? They're not even in Finaarenis; Marrakai's a duke in Tsaia. No magicks, that I know of, but probably the best rulers in both kingdoms: honest, just, and put up with no nonsense. If that brigand you say is using your name wanders into Marrakai lands, he'll find himself strung high before he knows it."

The trouble with towns, Gird realized when he had been there a hand of days, was that they were harder to leave than villages. He would like to have had a town allied to him—but he could not hope to protect Brightwater against a full army. No army had come, but one might. Their barton had grown, swelled with sudden converts, but he didn't trust that. The newly elected council of merchants and craftsmen wanted him to stay (one told him frankly that it was cheaper to feed his army than pay the bribes and taxes of the earlier rulers) but he had not won his war. When the gnomes sent word that it was now time to redeem his pledge to help them at Blackbone Hill, he was glad of the excuse—but he left most of his army near Brightwater, under the command of Cob, whose broken foot was nearly healed.

Chapter Twenty-six

Under a milky sky, the crest of Blackbone Hill loomed dark and inhospitable. Gird had expected the darkness, but not the shape, which made him think uneasily of a vast carcass, half-eaten. Sunburnt grass, like ragged dead fur, seemed stretched between the gaunt ribs.

"There's them says it's a dragon," Wila, his guide, said nervously. Clearly he thought it was something. Gird forced a grin.

"If 'tis, 'tis dead, long since."

Wila shook his head. "There's bones, up there. All black, black inside and out. Seen 'em myself."

"Dragonbones?" Despite himself, Gird shivered. No one had seen a dragon, but the tales of Camwyn Dragonmaster proved that dragons had lived, and might still. Even the lords believed in dragons; one of the outposts up on the western rim was called Dragonwatch.

"Dunno." Wila paused, and hooked one foot behind his knee, leaning on his staff. "All the bones I seen was too little, unless a dragon has almighty more bones than other creatures. If they'd been normal bone, I'd have said fish or bird—something light, slender. But black like that—and no one could think that hill's just a hill, like any other."

Gird glanced upslope again: true. Something about the shape of it, malign and decrepit, made the hairs on his neck crawl. "Why's anyone live here, then?" he asked.

"Well, now." Wila switched feet, and leaned heavily into his staff. Clearly this was a question he'd hoped to answer. "In the old days," he said, "before the lords came out of the south on their tall horses, this was uncanny ground. The Threespring clans claimed the east side for spring sheep grazing—it's not so bad then, with new grass and spring flowers. The Lady tames all, you know," he added, and

dipped his head. Gird nodded, and swept his arm wide, acknowledging her bounty. "Then the Darkwater bog folk, they claimed
herb right to the western slope, and the land between rock and
bog."

"Herb-right to *that?*"

"Aye. In the old days, that is, when the Darkwater bog folk gave
half the herbalists in this region, they gathered the Five Fingers
from that very rock, the Lady's promise to redeem it, they said."
He peered closely at Gird. "You do know the Five Fingers—?"

Gird nodded. "But where I come from, only the wise may say
the names—I have heard, but cannot—"

"Ah—yes. I forgot. You're from the overheard, aren't you?"

"Overheard?" Gird hadn't heard *that* term.

"Where the kuaknomi overhear the blessings and overturn them.
That's what I was taught, at least. Where the kuaknomi overhear,
only the wise may say the name of any sacred thing, lest a prayer
be changed to curse."

"They don't come here?"

"Well—there's them as says Blackbone Hill has felt their touch,
but aside from that, no. We have the truesingers here, the
treelords."

"Elves?"

Wila snorted, then coughed. "That's coarse talk of them, lad.
What they call themselves is truesingers. Sinyi, in their tongue."

"You *speak* it?" Gird could almost forget the coming battles
for that.

"A bit." Wila put both feet on the ground, and picked the staff
up. "Best be going, if we're to be past the Tongue by dark." And
despite Gird's questions, he would say no more about elves, but
led the way at a brisker pace than Gird expected from someone
his age. What he did say, briefly and over his shoulder, had to do
with the human settlement now nestled at the hill's steeper end.
"Lords forced it," he said. "Broke apart the Threesprings clans,
and settled a half of 'em here, and put in two brothers from the
bog folk, and set them all to digging in the hill. Came out as you'd
think: fever and death, broken bones and quarrels, but the lords
want what comes out the mine shaft, and never mind the cost.
Send more in, when too many die. It's a hard place, Blackbone,
and no hope for better."

"But the barton—"

"Oh, well. The barton's together, and they'll fight—they're good
at that. Come the day—"

Come the day, Gird thought, and no one will have to live in a place like this, ever again. The black, disquieting hill loomed higher as they plunged into one of its gullies, angled downslope, then up and across to another. He had been days coming here, after the gnomes' message arrived, passed from one guide to another.

Blackbone was as bleak as its hill, a cramped village of dark stone huts locked in by steep slopes. It stank, not with the healthy smells of a farming village, but with rot that would never become fertility, human waste and garbage piled on barren stone. A thin dark stream writhed behind the row of dwellings, too quiet for its rate of flow. Wisps of sulphurous steam came off it. As a mining village, it had no farmsteads; the barton, Gird found, had adapted to circumstances, and met in the mine itself.

"They dunna come 'ere," said the yeoman-marshal, Felis. "They come to the outside, we got to haul it that far, and load their wagons. Inside they dunna come."

Gird found it hard to endure even the outer tunnel, as daylight faded in the distance. Now he was out of sight of the entrance, sweating with fear, and hoping the barton would think it was the heat. Around the gallery where they drilled, torches burned, smoking. In that dim and shaking light, the men and women looked like nightmare creatures, monsters hardly human. He had already noticed that they were all grimed with the black rock. Now their eyes glittered in the light, the whites unnatural against dark-smeared faces. He glanced up, seeing the dark rock overhead far too close.

One of the women grinned, teeth white against the darkness. "You're no miner, eh? The rockfear gripes you?"

No use to pretend. "It does. I'm a farmer, used to no more than a bit of roof between me and the sky."

She laughed, but not unkindly. "At least you don't lie. Lead us out to fight, then, and you'll be free of this rock." The emphasis on "you" caught his attention.

"And you? Do you want to stay here?"

"Nay—but what do I know of farming? I'd go to other mines, could I." Some of the faces nodded agreement, others were still, with a stillness Gird had never seen.

He had no time to wonder at that, for the detailed plan of battle had to be made that night. Now that he'd seen for himself the shape of the land, the way the dark rock loomed over the wagon road into Blackbone, he could mentally place his few archers where they could do the most good. The barton members nodded when he spoke, but he wondered if they understood at all. None of them were archers. Most of them had never been out of Blackbone in all their lives. They knew digging and hauling, enough carpentry to build ladders and simple boxes, and not much more. They'd been drilled with picks and shovels. Gird felt the edges filed onto the shovels and wished he could have such metal for better weapons.

One of the men nodded. "They 'ad to give us good steel, see, or it wouldn't be no use against this rock."

"But no smith," said the woman who had asked him about rock-fear. "They brings us the tools, but takes no chances we'll make swords."

Deep in the ground, away from natural light, Gird lost track of time and would have gone on all night, but they had candlemarks for measure, and brought him back out to sleep under the sky. He almost wished he'd stayed within, for the air stank worse than in the mine itself, and he felt smothered.

The next day, his troops arrived. None of them liked Blackbone Hill. He saw the looks sent his way, noticed how they angled away from the line of march, as if they didn't want to set foot on that dark stone. He hated it himself, felt a subtle antagonism through his bootsoles. What if he was wrong? What if the power of Black-bone turned against them, preferred the lords? The gnomes had said it would not, but they were, after all, rockfolk. Their goals were not his goals.

Threesprings barton, kinbound to Blackbone, had sent twenty-seven yeomen, the largest contingent. They were all darkhaired, dour, barely glancing at Gird when he spoke to their yeoman mar-shal. A third of them were women, all as tall and thickset as the men. Longhill, barely a day's march away, had sent fourteen: its best, the yeoman marshal assured Gird. Deepmeadow, Whiterock Ridge, Whiteoak, Hazelly, and Clearspring had been on the march two days each. Some of them had never been so far from home; they clutched their weapons and foodsacks as if they expected the rocks to sprout demons. Westhill, the most veteran of this lot, had marched four days across the rolling hills. Their sturdy cheerfulness heartened the novices more than Gird could; he did not explain that Westhill had no village to return to, for the lords had burnt and salted it over the winter.

Blackbone barton greeted these allies with restraint—or, as Gird saw it, with total lack of enthusiasm. A few words passed between the Threesprings yeoman marshal and a Blackbone man, a mutter of family news, as near as Gird could make out, but nothing more. Longhill clearly expected no better; the yeomen smirked and sat quietly without attempting conversation. The others, barring West-hill, clumped up nervously and stared roundeyed from the taciturn

Blackbone yeomen to the higher slopes of Blackbone Hill. Gird made his way from one barton to another, doing his best to reassure and cheer them.

Blackbone barton itself actually broke the ice with a contribution to the evening meal. Short of supplies as it was—as any remote mining village without farmstead support would be—the village nonetheless made a very potent brew and had saved it, as their spokesman said "For the day." Now the chunky little jugs passed from hand to hand, raising spirits or at least numbing fears. Gird, mindful of watchful eyes, took but one pull at a jug before passing it on. The story of his drunken rage had traveled farther than he had; he knew he dared not risk another, and certainly not before a battle.

By dawn, he had them all in position. They looked fewer in the morning light, when he knew an enemy was coming, and the land itself looked larger. Could they possibly hold the narrow throat, choke the lords' soldiers from the village?

Eight bartons. Near two cohorts, by his new reckoning, though he had none of his marshals along. And there, coming along the stone-paved trade road, were the mounted infantry, the archers he feared so much, the light cavalry, and—he squinted—and a small troop of the lords themselves, mounted. So—so the gnomes had been right. Whatever they got from the Blackbone mines was important enough to bring them out themselves. He could not read their devices, or recognize them by the colors they wore; the traders had told him all that, and Selamis had written it down, but Selamis was not here to remind him. Lords were lords, he thought to himself, and what difference did it make if he faced sier or duke or count—any and all would be glad of his blood, and he of theirs.

Because he was looking for it, he noticed that the lords' troops also disliked the touch of Blackbone Hill, and veered slightly until sharp commands brought them back. He told himself that the horsemen would have trouble on the slopes. Would horses, too, flinch from Blackbone? He hoped so; they were ruinously outnumbered otherwise. Perhaps he should have brought some of his regular troops—but there would have been no way to move that many that far without opposition, and he had had no time for additional battles. He looked over at Wila, who could see down into the cleft where his few archers waited, and held up his hands three times. Wila passed the signal on. If they could take the archers out, then his people could stand against a charge. Horsemen couldn't spread wide on that uneven slope. He hoped.

The clatter of hooves and boots rang loudly from the stones on either side of the track. Gird kept his head down, trusting his carefully placed archers to choose their targets wisely. He heard the twang of one bowstring, then another, then shouts from below. So it began, again, and he squeezed his own hands hard an instant, fighting down that last-moment fear that caught him every time. He stood, and waved his arm.

In that first scrambling rush downslope, Gird could see that his archers had done their work well; many of the lords' archers were down. Arrows flicked by, close overhead. A few of those below had found cover, and returned a ragged flight. Someone beside him staggered and went down, hands clutched to chest. Ahead of him, the front line of yeomen, with the best weapons, had engaged the mounted soldiers, unseating many of them and killing horses. The slope and sunrise gave them advantage, and Gird's archers continued to pick their targets wisely.

"Get the lords!" he bellowed, reminding them.

But the attack lost momentum, foundered. No arrows found the lords on their tall horses; Gird could have sworn he saw arrows slide aside, as if refusing to menace the magelords. The lords themselves drew no weapons he could see—not then—but their soldiers regrouped with amazing speed. They paid no attention to the wounded and fallen among them, striding over bodies as if they were merely more rocks. Gird had called for all his bartons to attack when he thought he saw the enemy crumbling, but now he had no unseen reserves, and the ground no longer favored him. Either his people were spread out along the road, outnumbered at each point, or he could call them to clump on the road itself, and try a frontal attack—exactly what he had not wanted to do with the weapons he had available.

Furious with himself, and with the gnomes who had advised this battle plan, Gird watched his ambush degenerate into a lengthy slaughter. Now that they were sure the rocky slopes held no more surprises, the lords and their soldiers pushed forward strongly on the road itself. Already they were beyond the range of Gird's archers, who would have to come out of cover to find targets. The yeoman marshals were looking over their shoulders now, expecting Gird to come up with something—some plan—and he could not think of anything. Could he hold them together? Would a rout be worse than this? Why had he ever thought the gnomes could design a battle plan for humans? He had to try something. He called them all in, trying to slow the enemy advance along the road. That might give someone a chance to escape.

It had been a mistake. It had been a disaster, and now the end

would come. Gird held the retreat together, as foot by foot they
were forced back through the village into the maw of the mine.
He had been so sure that taking out their archers would be enough.
It might have been, without the lords themselves there, with their
wicked magicks. Their troops, who might have broken and fled—
would have, Gird was sure—still moved forward, as if they had no
thought at all, as if they could suffer no wound or fall to no death.
Yet they fell, and died, and were trampled by their own. The faces
he could see did not change expression even in death. Too far
behind for any of Gird's weapons to reach, the lords sat veiled on
their tall horses, watching, performing whatever magicks they could.

Here was still more evidence that some of the lords still had
potent powers to call on. Rocks split, air hummed and thickened
in his throat, unnatural light rippled over the battle, making it hard
to see. And so he was going to die under a mountain of rock,
because he had believed the wrong story. There wasn't any way
out of this, but if he *did* live, he was going to have a few choice
words for Arranha, if ever he caught up with him again.

He shifted to one side as the mine closed around them.

"Go on!" bawled the Blackbone yeoman marshal in his ear. "Let
us take this."

"It was my bad idea." Gird smashed his club into a shoulder,
and ducked aside from a pike. "I should be last—"

They fought side by side for a few moments, as the soldiers
charged again. Then the momentum of that charge dissipated, and
they could retreat further into the dark shaft without immediate
risk. The soldiers were cursing the darkness, stumbling over loose
rocks and the fallen.

"Hurry *up*," the yeoman marshal said. "Afore the lords get in,
and make they magical lights—"

"But we should make a stand," Gird said. "I'll do it—a few
others—"

"Never mind!" The yeoman marshal yanked Gird's arm hard.
"Leave them to it; they'll find out—"

"What?" He couldn't see, in the dimness, anything but a flash
of teeth.

"It's in the charm," said the man, almost gleefully. "Come with
me." *What charm was that*, Gird wondered. It was that or be left
in darkness, and Gird came. Dying inside a cursed mountain wasn't
his idea of the way to die, but what choices did he have? None,
like the rest of them. All around, in the darkness, he heard the
rasp of feet on stone, the groans of the wounded, the heavy breathing. Deeper into the blackness, and deeper, twisting and turning

through passages that were sometimes tight for a single man, and other times so wide that three or four abreast must reach out with hands to feel the walls. Gird clamped his fear within him, and tried to think, without success.

When the dim bluish light of a gnomish lamp blossomed nearby, he could not believe it. All around were faces equally surprised, mouths open. A firm, cool hand gripped Gird's, and he looked down to see the warmaster who had set this battle's plan.

"It is for you to command," the warmaster said. "No human noise!"

"Silence!" Gird bellowed and no one spoke. He bent to the warmaster, full of his own questions and complaints, but the warmaster's expression stopped him.

"It is that they are within, the outland lords?"

"Yes."

"You marshal your humans, follow my orders."

"Yes." There was nothing more to say. Whatever the gnomes demanded, he would have to perform, both by his contract and by the logic of the situation.

"Then go. Follow that one—" the warmaster pointed. "Go far and swift."

"You don't need our help?"

The warmaster's face conveyed secret amusement. "Human help for rockwar? Go."

Gird waved, and the others formed up to follow him, as he followed his guide. It occurred to him, as they plunged once more into a narrow dark passage, that the gnomes might have planned all this just to lure a few lords underground—though he hated to think that.

All he could hear behind, though he strained his ears, was the noise of his own people shuffling along. His guide carried a lantern, so he himself could see where to put his feet, but the others stumbled in darkness. At last, a dim shape of light ahead, that widened and brightened to daylight. He squinted against the light, and then as he came out, stopped short. They faced a gloomy sunset, a few rays of somber light escaping beneath heavy clouds. And that meant—he shook his head, to clear it. They had walked *through* Blackbone Hill? He peered up and over his shoulder. There it was, that gaunt, misshapen spine arched slightly away from them.

Ahead the gnome set off downhill, in that measured but tireless tread, and Gird waved the foremost of his people on. He would stay to see the last of them out, and silence questions.

By dark they were far below the hill, coming into marshy ground.

The blackwater bogs, Gird thought. The gnome stopped suddenly, and Gird nearly ran into him.

"Here is good water." The lantern light glittered from a pool that looked as black as the rock of the hill. But when Gird dipped a handful, it was clear, trembling in the light, and tasted sweet. Others knelt, dipped for themselves, and drank thirstily. He could hear the splashes, and the moans of the wounded behind him in the darkness. The gnome touched his arm to get his attention. "This is water that runs clean, and the bog clans know safe ways from here. Do you acknowledge debt?"

There was no alternative. "You have brought us from danger to safe water: I acknowledge owing."

"That is fair. This is the exchange: no humans to go beneath that hill. To gather the herbs of the field, to pasture flocks, it is permitted. It is not permitted to delve in the rock, or build aught of the loose rock of the surface. Granted?"

"Granted." Gird sighed, nonetheless, thinking how he would have to argue the miners into it. He wanted to ask why, but knew he would get no answer. And he was tired, desperately tired. He wanted to know how many they'd lost, and if the wounded would recover, and he wanted to fall in his tracks and sleep.

"What of the magelords?" he asked, determined to get something out of this exchange.

The gnome smiled. Gird remembered that smile from his months in their princedom. "It is not a place for humankind, within that hill. The magelords took what was not theirs; knowing, they took it. We return justice."

The ground heaved, thudding against Gird's feet, and a shout went up from his people. Trees groaned; their limbs thrashed briefly as if in a gust of wind. In the lantern light, the water in the pool rocked and splashed like water in a kicked bucket. Gird looked at the gnome, whose smile broadened.

"Justice," it said again. "No pursuit."

When dawn brightened behind Blackbone Hill, the marshy forest looked much less threatening. Delicate flowers brightened the hummocks of moss; butterflies flicked wings of brilliant yellows and oranges in and out of the sunbeams. They had halted beside an upwelling spring of clear water, that flowed into an amber stream between thick-trunked dark trees. A clearly-marked trail led away downstream from their campsite, and the gnome—who had stayed with them until daylight—said that it led safely to an old settlement of the bog folk, now abandoned, but on another safe trail to Longhill.

Gird counted up his survivors. Only five of Blackbone itself had survived. Their kin from Threesprings had lost but three, and still remained the largest barton. Longhill had lost seven of fourteen; Deepmeadow had lost eight of twelve. Whiterock Ridge had lost all its archers, but no one else, and Hazelly lost only one. Clearspring and Westhill had lost two each. But of those living, a quarter were wounded, unfit for work or fighting for many days.

And the survivors were anything but satisfied with the way the battle had gone.

"You didn't tell us they rockfolk'd be involved," said the yeoman marshal of Hazelly. For someone who had never fought at all before, he was surprisingly pert, Gird thought.

"Us wouldn't've let 'un fight in th'mine unless they'd been there," said one of the Blackbone survivors, "They told us away last winter they'd no more patience with the magelord's thievery." He peered at Gird through the morning mist. "But they didn't say what t'would cost *us*. They said you was the best leader—"

Before Gird could answer that, someone from Threesprings broke in. "Ah, them rockfolk! Suppose it was their plan, too, warn't it? And you their hired human warleader?"

"They didn't hire me," Gird began, wondering how he was going to settle this lot. They had good reason to grumble, but so did he; it was not his fault the gnomes had kept the main part of their plan from him. So had the Blackbone Hill folk, for the matter of that.

Westhill, more experienced in living in the country, had done most of the work to make the camp liveable. The others learned quickly, if unwillingly: the Westhill yeoman-marshal had a tongue sharpened on both sides. Gird began thinking what to do with this ill-assorted lot. Some of them, from the villages that no longer existed, could come directly into the main army. Others might go home for a time, though the areas of peace shrank day by day.

In a few days, the mood had settled; those who had been most badly wounded were either mending or dead, and everyone else had decided to stay with Gird or go home in a huff. There were only a few of the latter. The rest had begun to recast the tale as they would tell it to friends at home. Gird noticed that the lords' troop grew, and the lords' magicks became ever more spectacular, as they retold it to each other. The survivors from Blackbone Hill itself—including some who had hidden in the houses until the fight passed by, and then escaped around the hill—seemed glad to go to Threesprings, where they had kin.

Gird himself climbed back up the trail to take a last look at the west side of Blackbone Hill in broad daylight. It had not changed, that he could see, and he felt no desire to walk on it again.

He made his way back across country toward Brightwater, with the Westhill yeomen. On their way, they found ample evidence that the war was spreading. Twice they fought off attacks by mounted patrols; once they blundered into the path of a large infantry force, and got away only because they were fitter than their pursuers. Gird wondered where that force had been going; as far as he knew, he had no one active in that direction. They passed more than one burned-out village, inhabited by peasants who fled into the woods when they approached, and slunk out behind them to work the fields.

Gird led them in a careful circle around Grahlin; they were near Burry when they met someone recently from Brightwater, a yeoman Gird remembered only vaguely. His news was mixed. The king's army claimed to have killed Gird, between Gadilon's domain and the gnome lands to the south; it had then marched north, celebrating that victory by burning any village whose lord reported it as rebellious. For some reason, it had gone east, rather than returning in its tracks, and was now at the eastern border of Finaarenis, preparing to march home on the River Road.

"So," Gird said, putting a blunt finger on the map. "That group we saw was probably going to join the king's army. Well. When they get to Grahlin, the sier will have much to tell them, and we can expect them in Brightwater sometime after harvest, no doubt."

According to later reports, the king's army had met with scattered but brisk resistance on its march north; bartons Gird had never heard of had fought individual and combined engagements. In the meantime, Gird's main force had control of the valley in which Brightwater lay, from just south of the River Road all the way to the southern trade road. They had taken two lords' residences, although only servants were there: the lords were off with the king's army, and their families were safe (for the moment) in Finyatha.

Putting all this information together with Selamis and the senior marshals, Gird thought he still had numerical superiority, but most of his troops were ill-armed and had no defensive armor at all. They were short of supplies, in part because Gird did not want to squeeze the remaining farmers. Some smiths had come over to the rebels, it was true, but they had little metal for them to work.

As the summer waned, Gird remembered the gnomes' warning that he must win in one season, or find an ally with money or troops—or both. They had suggested one, which he had been reluctant to approach.

Chapter Twenty-seven

Not for the first time, Gird felt well out of his depth. These wooded hills had taller trees than any he'd known; following a gurgling creek between two of them, he felt he was sinking deeper and deeper into unknown lands. Far overhead, the leaves just changing turned honest sunlight to a flickering green, as unsteady as the water beside him. Most of the undergrowth still showed the heavy green of summer, but one climbing vine had gone scarlet, as if the tree itself were bleeding. Gird shivered when he saw that.

If he had not spent that winter with the gnomes, he would never have come here, so far east, to meet a lord reputedly not so bad as the rest. But if he had not gone to the gnomes, he would never have survived his second season of war. If they had been right about other things, perhaps they were right about the Marrakai.

"Ho!" Gird jumped as if struck, and then stood still, peering about him into the confusion of leaves. Then a man in green stepped out on the trail he'd been following. His guide? Or was it a trap? The man had a staff like his own, and a bow slung over his shoulder. "Are you from the Aldonfulk hall?" the man asked.

"Yes," said Gird. The man moved like someone well-fed and well-rested, full of confidence. The lord himself? Then he remembered what he was supposed to say. "Aldonfulk Lawmaster Karik ak Padig Sekert sends greetings to the lord duke Marrakai."

"Ah. And Kevre Mikel Dobrin Marrakai returns those greetings, through his kirgan."

Gird struggled his way through the names he had heard only in the gnomish accent, and the references, to remember that the kirgan meant heir of law and blood. He stared as the young man came forward. Black hair, green eyes as the lords had sometimes, a face young but already showing character. That sier in Grahlin would have been glad to have such a son. The young man smiled.

"And you must be Gird, the scourge of the west, that we have heard so much about. I'm Meshavre, called Mesha."

"But you're a—" He didn't want to say it, but the young man said it for him.

"A lord's son? The enemy? I hope not that, at least. Yes, Kirgan

Marrakai, in formal usage, but this meeting you is hardly formal. Do not your people use one name only, at least in this war? Call me Mesha, then, and I will call you Gird."

He was used to command; his voice carried the certainty that Gird would do what he wanted because he asked it, and he (that voice conveyed) would ask nothing unreasonable. Gird could imagine him dealing with dogs and horses, with wounded men, with crying women, all of them calming under that voice and obeying it. Yet it was reasonable, what he said, and Gird could see no good reason to disobey, nothing that would not make him feel foolish.

"Well," he said, to gain time. "Mesha. Whatever you think of rebellious peasants, that's the first time I've called a nobleborn by a pet name in all my life." He met the young man's eyes squarely, to find surprised respect. Mesha nodded.

"My father was right, then, as were the kapristi. They said you were different, and told long tales of you; my father had heard some of those same tales from Finaarean lords."

"Who told them differently, I would guess," said Gird. He liked the young man; he couldn't help it. Was that the charming he'd been warned about? But the gnomes had said the Marrakai magic had gone long ago, that these lords were no longer magelords except by inheritance.

"I heard only one of them, from the sier whose life you saved. He was divided in his mind; if all the rebels were like you, he might be your ally. But come: let me bring you to a safe place to rest and eat. There's a forester's shelter, down this way." And without another word, Mesha turned and started down the trail. Gird followed, still half-afraid of a trap. But why then would the young lord meet him alone in the first place? Why not simply put an arrow through him from behind a tree?

The forester's shelter had three sides of stone, the front open to a firepit ringed with stones. Tethered beside it were two horses, a brown and a gray; a small fire crackled in the firepit, and something was cooking that sent a wave of hunger through Gird's belly.

Duke Marrakai was an older version of his son: heavy black hair and beard, green eyes, and a powerful body. Gird was aware that the two of them, father and son, could easily kill him if that was what they had in mind. But so far neither made a move against him. The duke was himself stirring a pot of some dark liquid, and Mesha moved quickly to unpack saddlebags: bread, cheese, onion, apples, slabs of meat. Gird unslung his own thin pack, and put his remaining loaf of bread with the other. Mesha looked startled, but his father nodded approval.

"We thank you, Gird, for sharing." His voice was deep, and Gird had no doubt its bellow would carry across a battle. "Mesha, show Gird the spring."

The spring came up beside a flat rock. Gird knelt and held his hand over it; the surface rippled a little with the flow. He muttered the greeting for its guardian spirit, and looked up to find the kirgan watching him curiously. "You don't speak to it?" he asked. Mesha shook his head. Gird looked back at the spring; surely it was glad to be recognized. He bent and scooped up a handful of icy, clean-tasting water. It made Gird's teeth ache. He filled his waterskin after Mesha drank.

"Do all your people talk to springs?" asked Mesha. Gird retied the thong that held the skin closed for travel.

"Whenever we take water from the earth, we thank the Lady, and the guardians. It's only courteous."

"Even from a well?"

"Of course." Gird looked at him. "If you give something to someone, don't you expect thanks? We cannot live without water, without the rain falling and the springs rising."

"Yes, but—is that why peasants—why your people—tie flowers and wool to the wellposts?"

"Yes, and if this were a spring on my land, I would bring gifts at Midwinter and Midsummer. Perhaps someone else does that here."

Mesha looked as if he would ask more, but didn't. Instead he waved at the clearing behind the shelter. "Over there, behind that cedar, is the jacks for this shelter. 'Tis far enough from the water, my father says." Gird had no need then, but wondered how long they thought he would stay.

They came back to find Duke Marrakai pouring the dark liquid into thick-walled mugs. "Do you have sib, in your country?" he asked Gird. Gird nodded. "Good. I like it with more tikaroot than most, though that makes it more bitter; this has honey in it."

It might be poison, but why? Gird took a mug and sipped cautiously. A strong flavor, thicker and darker than his people made it. After another sip or so, he decided he liked it well enough. The duke had his knife out, and cut the bread and cheese into slabs. Now it was Gird's turn to be surprised, for he held his hands over the food and used a form of blessing Gird had never heard: "Thank the Lady," had been enough for him.

Marrakai and his son took Gird's bread first, which forced him to share theirs. He wondered if they knew the significance of that among his people. Arranha had not, but these were supposed to be different. One bite stood for all; he might as well have cheese and apples. They ate in silence, as hungry men do; Gird, being hungriest, was most aware of his own eating. There was enough to fill his belly, and he took it. Mesha and his father ate slowly, so that they finished all together.

Then Duke Marrakai turned to Gird. "You are not oathbound to me, or to any with whom I share oaths: we are as strangers, among whom is no rank. Call me Kevre, if you will." Gird stared at him: a peasant call a great lord, a duke, by one name? He nodded, trying to cover his confusion. Marrakai went on. "We have shared food; among our people, that used to mean peace, and sometimes alliance. If it is not so among your people, I will not hold you to those obligations—but if you want first truce, and then perhaps alliance, let us speak of that."

Gird wondered if there had been ale in the sib; he could hardly believe what he was hearing. Alliance? With a duke of Tsaia? That the gnomes had had some reason for sending him here, he'd been sure, but this went beyond all hopes.

"Sir—Kevre—" That would take getting used to; the "sir" still came easily to him. "Among our people, shared food declares peace, at least for that meeting. And sometimes more—if something is being decided, then food shared means agreement." He did not mention obligation, intentionally: let the Marrakai duke show what he knew.

"Yet you were trailhungry when you came; it would be unfair of me to bind you by that—"

"Are you bound?" asked Gird boldly. Marrakai nodded. "I am. Both by custom and by my own honor. I knew what I did when I ate of your bread, and gave you mine; therefore am I bound. While you are here, in my domain, you are my guest; neither I nor mine will harm you, nor let harm come to you."

Gird nodded. "And I thought of what it meant, Kevre, when I put my food with yours, and when I saw you take it, leaving me only yours to eat. I said nothing and ate: that binds me, by the law the gnomes taught me, and by the custom of my people." He grinned at Marrakai. "Of honor I cannot speak, since I was taught that we peasants had none, but I can see right and do it."

"Which is honor enough for anyone," said Mesha quickly. His father gave him a sharp glance, but nodded.

"Mesha's right. So here we are, you my guest and I your host, both of us brought here by an interest in gnomish law. What law *have* the gnomes taught you? Is that your message?"

Gird tried to put his scattered thoughts in order. "Sir—Kevre—the gnomes taught me their law, and something of past times, and how the old customs of our people were like and unlike the High Lord's law."

Marrakai frowned. "Do they call Esea and the High Lord one thing and the same?"

"I'm—not sure. What they said was that the High Lord had been for the Aareans in the form of Esea. But they themselves consider the High Lord the source of justice. The judge."

"Yes. That I knew. The High Lord's Law, as they say. You know of the Rule of Aare?"

Gird nodded. "A priest of Esea taught me, but he was outcast, for claiming that the Rule of Aare meant differently than the king's law said."

"You met Arranha?" Marrakai shook his head. "Gird, I am well rebuked: I had not thought any peasant leader, no matter how worthy, would be familiar with Arranha's heresies *and* gnomish law. Are you sure you are not a scholar, rather than a fighter?"

Gird felt himself redden. "I did not choose fighting; I would farm if I could. But—"

"But you could not. My pardon, Gird; it is no time for jesting. But Arranha! I have not met him myself, although I have heard from his horrified colleagues all about his views. I think myself he's right. The oldest documents in my archives are from Old Aare, and from these it is clear that the interpretation of the Rule has changed, over the generations. I have tried to convince our king to return to the intent of the Rule."

"Would he?"

"Felis? No. None of them see it as I do, although some agree that great wrongs are being done in its name. Some would abandon the Rule entirely, seeing no hope of reform, and some are, unfortunately, profiting so well that they see no reason to change."

"Some like wrong itself," muttered Mesha. "The Verrakai—"

"I name no man's motives," said Marrakai firmly. "You know what I think, but that's not at issue here. There are bad men in any realm, and in every family."

"Not like that," said Mesha. Gird looked at him and wondered if he spoke as freely to his father in his own hall. "Taris is merely foolish."

"Judge all by the same rule," said Marrakai. "If you would name Verrakai wicked, for gambling with lives, then consider Taris's loss of those steadings—were there not men and women farming them,

who came under another's power? How is that different? We have
been fortunate to have so few, but we are not gods, to be perfect."

"You punished Taris; Duke Verrakai gave *his* son jewels when
he—"

"Enough!" Gird noticed that Mesha was instantly silent, but
clearly unconvinced. Marrakai turned to Gird. "My nephew, whose
father was killed years ago, gambled away some of his father's
lands—which to me is dishonor, for the care he owed those who
lived there. Lands are not like ring or sword. As for the Verrakai—
have you heard of them?"

Gird shook his head. "Only that Verrakai is one of the dukes of
Tsaia, a great lord of the east."

"A great lord, if wealth counts for all. I would not speak of him,
Gird, without need. Our families share no great love, and I cannot
be fair."

Gird looked from one face to the other, and said nothing. After
a moment, Marrakai sighed, and went on.

"That's beside our purpose. The kapristi may have told you that
long ago my father's father's father resisted our king's attempt to
invade their princedom across Marrakai lands. When they routed
that invasion, and made a pact of peace with the Tsaian throne—
as they did with the king of Finaarenis for the same reason—the
kapristi noted our action on their behalf. They counted themselves
in debt to Marrakai. My great-grandsire argued that what he had
done was right—that he had laid upon them no debt—but they
argued in return that by our law he had not been obligated, and
so it went, until they agreed on a settlement. From that day on,
we have dealt evenly with kapristi. As you know, they accept no
gifts and give none, but with those they consider upright, they deal
willingly and fairly."

"That is so," said Gird.

"Of course I knew of the unrest in Finaarenis; there is unrest in
Tsaia, for the same reasons. And I had heard of you: after Norwalk
Sheepfolds, everyone heard of you." Marrakai paused to drink more
sib, and offered Gird another mugful. Gird took it, nodded, and
Marrakai went on. "A peasant turned off his land turns outlaw:
that's nothing new. That peasant joins a rebellious mob, burns hayricks, ambushes traders: that's nothing new. But a peasant training
other peasants to march, to use their daily tools as weapons, to
fight trained soldiers—not only training them so, but leading them:
that was new. And not at all to most men's liking. Most lords, at
least. And then you disappeared entirely, after saving Sier Segrahlin's life. Dead, most thought, or frightened into flight.

He had to ask, though he was sure he knew the answer, and the question itself could anger Marrakai. "Is it because you fear this for yourself? You would give me help, and for what—to let your domain abide?"

Marrakai was not angry, but his son was. He shook his head, at both Gird and his son. "What I fear is long war, with all the lands laid waste and no justice gained. They have not begun to fight back, Gird, not with the worst magic. You will see far worse than you've seen: poisoned wells, fields ruined for long years, unless you find someone with magic to restore them. You did not win quickly; they know, now, what they face. Yet you must fight. I understand that—it had gone too far, and your lords have no intent to mend matters. Am I afraid? Of course. I have children too; I have lands I love, people that depend on me. Worse, I have an oath I swore to our king, when he took the crown. I cannot take my own soldiers into this, except to defend my own lands, without his permission, which he will not give."

"Why obey a wicked king?"

Marrakai sighed. "Felis is not wicked, merely weak. He has wicked advisors, some of them—if he had only had the sense to marry his rose, as he called her, instead of that sister of Verrakai's— but that's not wickedness. Gird, I pledged my loyalty to him, to the king of Tsaia both as king, and as the man Felis Hornath Mikel Dovre Mahieran Mahierai. If I go to war against his will, then I have broken my word, and if my word was ill-given, foolishly given, it is still binding on me. It would not be on everyone; some can free themselves with less trouble. I cannot. I cannot do it and be who and what I am, the self I respect. I have argued with him, pled with him, stormed at him, and finally left court—with his entire consent, because he was tired of hearing me. But that one thing I cannot do."

Gird felt the unshakeable substance of the man, as unyielding in his way as the gnomes. He had never found anyone to give such an oath to; the oaths he had had to give the steward he had never felt as binding. A peasant did what he must to survive; honor was something the lords sang of, in ballads.

"You disapprove?" asked Marrakai. Gird shrugged and shook his head.

"I have no right to approve or disapprove. It is right to keep a promise, that I'll agree, and if that is how you see your duty to your king, it may—must—be right for you."

"I wonder sometimes," said Marrakai. His lips quirked in a rueful smile. "What I propose to do is, in the eyes of many, just as bad as marching my own men out to face his. Fine wit, one of my tutors said, splits hairs, but split hairs make weak ropes to hang a life on." Gird said nothing; he could not follow that. Marrakai seemed to understand, for he shrugged in his turn. "Let me be clear, then: the gnomes sent word that you were the best of possible leaders to the revolt surely coming in Finaarenis. Last summer I thought you might come, and heard instead of your campaigns—"

"Not all of them mine," said Gird, rubbing his nose. "That fellow in the south—"

"I expected confusion of tales," Marrakai said. "But some were surely yours. The gnomes said you might—with the High Lord's judgment—win in one season, but they expected not. You would need gold for good weapons, they said, and possibly troops, and they were unwilling to provide either. They thought I might, for my own reasons." He looked at his son. "There is one of my reasons: Mesha will not succeed to my lands as long as Felis is king. He was too forthright at court, worse even than I am." A chuckle escaped him; Gird noticed that the young man's ears were bright red. Marrakai shook his head. "We are not good at hiding our opinions, we Marrakai; it has been so for generations. My grandfather said someone dropped yeast in the mix when the gods shaped the first of us; it bubbles out at inconvenient moments."

Gird looked from one to the other. He knew nothing of the lords' way of living, but he would expect no great tact from either of them. Curiosity pricked him. "What did you do?" he asked Mesha. The young man turned even more red than before, but his eyes twinkled. He started to answer, but his father waved him to silence.

"*What* does not matter, save that he spoke the truth as he saw it, and that was too stony a mouthful for the king's dignity to chew and swallow. I'll not have it a common jest, Mesha, I told you that: I'm proud of your honesty and courage, but it is wrong to make tavern gossip of your liege lord."

"He's not *my* liege lord," Mesha said, eyeing his father warily. "He will not take my oath—he said it—and thus—"

"I named you heir, and my oath binds you. Gods above, lad, this is no time for your antics! We are near enough the traitor's blade as it is." The younger man sat back, averting his face, and Marrakai turned to Gird. "I'm sorry, Gird: it is discourteous to withhold the tale, and yet I cannot let him tell it. Forgive me that discourtesy, if you will, and accept in its stead my support."

"Support?" Gird was still confused by the rapid exchange between father and son.

"Yes. You need weapons; I can supply some, and gold to buy others. You may need sanctuary; my woodlands are open to you, and my troops will not permit others to cross the boundary, if you should be pursued. If my peasants wish to organize—bartons, do you call them?—then I will make no objection. Your war will spread into Tsaia—it must, because our king is allied to yours—and you must win in both kingdoms if you are to win at all." He paused long enough that Gird wondered if he had finished speaking. "What I want is much like the gnomes asked of you: I want your assurance that you will do your best to organize a society *after* the war, in which order and law prevail—and that you do not urge your followers to massacres and destruction beyond the necessities of war."

"I'm doing that already," Gird said.

"So I had heard, but the stories were confused enough I was not sure which stories were of you, and which of your more fanciful selves. I can see for myself that you are not a man who hates easily, who would kill or rape for the pleasure of it; I know, from my own life, that war is a fire that cannot be caged in a hearth. This has already been bloody; it will be worse. I want to know I am supporting someone with a vision of peace beyond the war."

"Yes." Gird saw the futility of more words; how could he explain his vision? But his calm certainty seemed to convince Marrakai, who nodded shortly, and then stood.

"Gold I brought with me; you may take it as you go. Mesha will guide you to our borders, and introduce you to trusted men of my personal guard. Weapons—you will have to provide transport beyond my borders, but I can supply 250 pikes, whenever you can take them, and heads for the same number, if you have the poles."

Once again Gird found himself handling gold coins, this time in daylight, openly. Coins of both kingdoms were minted with the same values: Tsaian crowns were traded in Finaarenis often enough to cause no comment. He let his fingers rummage among them, enjoying the feel, and looked up to see a wary expression on Marrakai's face.

"They're so—heavy," Gird said. "And they feel—they feel so different against my skin. It's no wonder some men become misers, and want to touch gold all the time."

"Had you never felt gold before?" asked Mesha.

"Once. Someone tried to bribe me." Gird poured the coins from his hand back into the leather bag Marrakai had handed him.

"You cannot be bribed?" Mesha asked.

Gird met his eyes. "Between this gold and my heart is the memory of my daughter, raped and bleeding, her dead husband, my closest friend, struck down for nothing. I could be bribed, I daresay, but not with gold." The young man looked alarmed, but Marrakai smiled.

"I have trusted the right man, then. Fare well with that gold, and your memories."

Mesha, on the way to the Marrakai border, shared knowledge as precious as the gold he carried. "My father says I cannot tell you what I did to be banished from court and my inheritance, but he said nothing about what I *saw.*" He explained the kinds of magicks the lords might use, and the tools needed for each, and the cost. He knew nonmagical counters for some of them, because the Marrakai, having lost their magicks early, had had to defend themselves from rival mages.

"It's said the best defense is a pure heart, but none of us has one pure enough, if we even knew what the gods meant by it. Men were not made perfect, I say, and come nearest perfection as fools when they deny their mistakes."

Gird nodded. "I've made plenty. It's a rare young man sees that, but you have a rare father."

"He's—different." Mesha walked on some strides before explaining that. "I knew that before I knew why; I could see it in the way others treated him. They're afraid of him, although they have greater powers."

"I hope for your peoples' sake that you are different the same way," said Gird.

Mesha looked at him, started to speak, and then, after several minutes of silence, tried again, his face turning red even as he spoke. "What is it like, being a peasant?" When Gird did not answer at once, he turned away, ears flaming, and hurried on. "The harpers sing of simple country joys, of the delights of the farm. My father's people seem happy enough, but they would not tell me, would they? I asked my father, and he said go and try it—but my tutor brought me back."

Gird thought at least part of Mesha's curiosity was genuine interest, something he had had no chance to pursue in a place he was so well known. He looked, to see the young man staring at the ground as he strode along.

"I liked farming," Gird said. "It's hard work, but I grew up with it; I was good at it. Have you ever milked a cow? Swung a scythe? No? Well, it came natural to me. Digging's no fun, but it has to be—plowing, planting, harvesting, all that's the good part. Seeing Alyanya's grace fill the baskets and barrels. Weather's weather, the same for all. What's bad comes from other men—from the lord taking more and more in field-fee every year, from death-fee and marriage-fee, from losing the right to gather herbs and firewood in the forest, all that. Having to take grain to *his* mill, instead of using our handmills, and having to buy ale from his brewery, instead of brewing our own. Going hungry, when there's no need but to pay the taxes, seeing our children thin and sick, while his plump young-lings ride by on fat ponies, trampling our fields."

Gird looked over to see how Mesha was taking this; the young man's face was sober, neither angry nor disapproving.

"Never think the troubles of peasants are little ones, Mesha. Hunger gnaws at you; the hunger of your family, of your children, hurts worse than your own. To feel the winter wind strike through ragged clothes, to have no fire in the house, and then the steward comes, smelling of meat and new-baked bread, to demand a special tax because the lord's courting a lady, or his lady has had a child, that's the bad part of it. Our lord, Kelaive, said peasants were lazy cowards: said it with his plump belly full of food we raised, with his well-fed soldiers around him, and we listened, shivering in a cold wind, or baked by summer sun. The steward said we should understand his greater problems. Greater than hunger? Greater than cold, than sickness, with healing herbs denied? Can there be worse than choosing which child shall have a crust of bread?" He could say no more; he felt the blood beating in his ears, the breath storming through his lungs.

"I'm sorry," Mesha said.

"It's all right," said Gird, blindly walking on.

"It is not, and it is not right that I did not know." Mesha sounded angry now, and not with Gird. "My father is a better man than that. I know it." But Gird heard the uncertainty in his voice.

"I hope so," he said, carefully making his voice light and easy. "As you will be."

"I would tell you of things my father has done, but I see now that it is not enough, not for me. I must *know* how our people live. He has asked me before to take over a village, but I wouldn't—"

Gird was surprised to find himself relaxed again, "You are young, Mesha. When I was young, I did not look for pain. I trained as a guard under that very steward—not looking, not seeing. My fam-ily—I thought they were fools, and I would show them all. After all, as a guard I ate their food, wore their clothes, brought money home—real coppers—to my father. And boasted of it. That's what hurt worst, later—that I had boasted, while my sisters and brothers went hungry and I was full."

"You—you do not hate me?" That was a boy's voice, a boy's naked desire to have an older man's respect.

"No. I do not hate you, or even—by this time—Kelaive. I hate what made Kelaive greedy and cruel, what made my father cringe before even his steward, what has kept you—who would, I daresay, be just and generous if you could—from knowing what you need to know." Gird smiled at the young man's worried face. "Be at peace, Mesha, while you can; long life brings enough battles to every man's door."

Once he crossed the border into Finaarenis, Gird began arranging transportation for the promised pikes. It would have been easier to sneak them across country before the summer's war erupted; the gnomes had advised him to go to Marrakai first. But he wasted little energy on regret. Before the leaves fell, all his pikes were over the border.

Chapter Twenty-eight

Meanwhile, his people told him, the war had hardly slowed for harvest. The king's army had split, one column going to Blackbone Hill, where they found only ruin. The other had started west along the River Road, but when it reached the lands controlled by Sier Segrahlin, the sier had refused the king's army passage. Rumor had it that the king and the sier would not mend their quarrel, whatever it had been, until an enemy army lay at the gates of Finyatha.

"We could arrange *that*," said Gird, laughing.

"Could you?" Arranha, to Gird's surprise, had come to Brightwater. He wore the same face Gird remembered, and seemed content to live with Gird's army and to endure the nervous glances of the other yeomen who distrusted anyone who had been a lord.

"We must someday," Gird said. "But having fought the sier, I would prefer not to do it again, if we can avoid it."

Arranha smiled at him. "You are acquiring prudence, then? I thought he might give you trouble. If his powers last, if he is not killed by a rock falling on his head, or lung-fever—"

"Can he be killed so? When my bowmen aimed at lords, the arrows flew astray."

"As I understand that form of magic—and it is not my own—one must know of the attack to defend against it, like a man holding up a shield over his head. If someone surprises him, he has only the strength of his bone."

Arranha had brought additional reminders and suggestions from the gnomes. "Not free gifts of information, you understand. I was told that they consider this to fall under the original contract; they're pleased with what you accomplished at Blackbone Hill."

Gird snorted. "They damn nearly got us killed at Blackbone Hill; they didn't tell me what they were doing, or that they'd been talking to the miners—"

Arranha laughed gently. "But you survived."

Another surprise of that homecoming was Selamis. After Gird had scolded him for not letting go his aristocratic background, he had seemed to fit in better. Once more, he was almost unnoticeable. Gird had begun to make use of his special knowledge, taking it for granted that Selamis would know which lord was related to whom, and what the news the traders brought meant. But until he left for Marrakai's domain, the other marshals had still been wary of Selamis. Several had come to him privately, and asked him not to make Selamis a marshal, or give him command. Gird had had no intention of doing that anyway. Now, however, they all seemed at ease with him. The marshals had discovered how handy it was to have someone able and willing to write and keep accounts—and someone whose face everyone knew, but who had no actual command. Selamis, Gird heard with some surprise, had stopped a street brawl—and he had patched up a quarrel between two of the newer marshals—and he had convinced the ranking merchants that the Brightwater yeoman-marshal was worth hearing.

"I thought you were crazy," Ivis said, on Gird's first night back. "A lord's son, troublemaker in his village—I know, you said he wasn't, but we had one in our village and you never did. Now—he's not that bad. You know what Cob's been calling him?"

Cob leaned over and punched Ivis. "Hush. Gird won't approve."

"What, then?"

"Luap," said Ivis, snorting with glee. "You know—the lords' own term for a bastard who can't inherit. Rank but no power. Cob's been calling him our luap."

Gird looked hard at Cob, who had the grace to blush. "It's not as bad as it sounds," he said defensively. "He's the one taught me the word, and made a joke about it. Spends all his time with us high-ranking folk, marshals and you, and has no command of his own. So I took it up, and he just grinned."

"Joke or not, I don't like it."

"Why not?" That came from the subject of discussion himself, who flung a leg over the bench, clapped Gird hard on the shoulder, and faced him squarely. "No one's ever liked the name my father gave me: you said yourself Selamis was a strange name. I am a luap: my father's bastard, and your trusted assistant in all but command. They'll tell you I've practiced, and learned fighting, but I'm still best at keeping accounts."

"Yes, but—" Gird shook his head, uneasy about something in the guileless, open face in front of him. If it didn't bother the man, it should. But this was one argument he lost; he found that many of the yeomen had fallen into the habit of speaking of "the luap" or "that marshal's luap." With Gird's return, and Selamis's return to Gird's side, it quickly became "Gird's luap." Gird still called him Selamis, though he sometimes slipped.

Later that fall, the lords changed their strategy. They had not been able to trap Gird's army all summer, and he had inflicted sharp losses on them. So they turned their attention ever more strongly to the land which supplied him with soldiers and supplies, forcing the evacuation of farming villages, burning them out if they resisted, stripping the countryside of resources. They had armed soldiers supervise the harvest, after which the fields were burnt; for hands of days the sky was streaked with smoke, and ash dusted travelers. Livestock they drove to the lords' fortified towns or dwellings, and any they could not confine under guard were slaughtered to feed the soldiers.

This work proceeded at different rates in various parts of the kingdom. Some lords were loathe to lose the produce of villages they had established, and counted instead on quartering more of their own soldiers among them. Some did not have the resources to reduce or move more than one or two villages that autumn. Those that survived could choose to try escape, or wait and hope that the coming spring would change things. But Gird found more and more refugees wandering, some seeking him and some looking for any safe place to spend the winter.

His own force controlled the valley lying south and east of Brightwater. This provided a large grain harvest—large, that is, until he measured it against his increasing needs. The town of Brightwater, all the little villages, his army—the grain would feed so many only if it were carefully managed, and by his own laws (he felt the teeth of a joke in this) he could not seize it. Some, of course, would not trust him, and yield it willingly. His own followers had sometimes less patience than he did; he found himself scolding his own as often as the others about the need for fairness, the evils inherent in bullying.

"It's not the same thing," Ivis argued, one dank late-autumn day, when a cold rain had blackened the falling leaves to a silent dark carpet. "If we're fair in distribution—in famine law—and all share equally, then it's not bullying. Bullying benefits the taker—"

"So it does—and so it does here." Gird blew his nose noisily on a bit of dirty fleece and rubbed it on his sleeve. His head was pounding, his ears felt full of water, and he was sure this was more than a fall chill. He could not feel this sick with a mere chill. "It benefits us—the takers—because then we have more to distribute fairly, and our own share—as well as others—is larger."

"But it benefits *everyone*."

"No. Not the ones who lose—who have larger shares now. Our way is right, Ivis, and better than theirs—I know that. But part of our way is *how* we do what we do, not just what we do."

"If we all starve it won't do them any good—"

"We aren't starving yet. Besides, while I won't bully our people, I don't have anything against taking from our enemies."

"I thought you said we weren't ready to assault their fortified places."

"A grain caravan isn't fortified." Gird did not bother to explain, the way his throat was hurting, that he'd suggested to outlying bartons that they attack grain caravans. Some of them were successful—successful, too, at running off herds being moved from the deserted villages. More and more bartons began even bolder actions: ambushing any guard unit unwary enough to camp outside walls, or travel carelessly along the roads and trails. Clashes between small groups of rebels and small units of guards soon convinced the guards to move only in larger numbers.

Winter snows had always meant the end of military actions, but this winter brought no peace, only the slowing of movement. Gird, struggling to codify his laws with the help of Selamis and Arranha in Brightwater, sifted the reports from distant villages. Here a barton had ambushed a lord and two hands of guards, killing all of them and leaving that domain open; there two bartons had fought off a brigand attack, only to fall to the soldiers who came onto the scene when the battle was almost over. The merchants and craftsmen of Tarrho, a town about the size of Brightwater near the eastern border, had decided to overthrow their lord and declare their freedom—then the servants and laborers had rioted, overthrowing the merchants in their turn. Tarrho's small barton had tried to bring order, but had the trust of no faction; after bitter fighting that left many dead and the city without supplies of food, brigands rode in, looted everything, and set it afire. The king's messengers declared it was the fault of Gird and his rebels; the barton's survivors, who arrived in Brightwater before Midwinter, explained what had really happened.

"A good many of them brigand bands claims to be your yeoman, Gird," the yeoman-marshal said. "Nobody knows, for sure—I mean, if they aren't one of yours already, they don't. So they're afraid of your name, and the bartons."

"That's why we need to have our rules known," Gird said. "If they know we have rules, and what they are, and they see that we stick to them, then perhaps they'd trust us."

"Maybe." The yeoman-marshal did not look convinced. Gird peered at him.

"What do you think it would take?"

"Well—sir—I think they need something to see. We can say we have rules, but that's not enough, not for city folk used to looking up law in a book."

"Which is why I'm writing it down," said Gird, slapping the table and jostling Selamis's tools. He pointed at the younger man. "This is Selamis." He still would not say *my luap*. "He writes a better hand than I do, one anyone can read."

"That should help," the yeoman-marshal said, craning his head to see what was on the top sheet.

"It's very simple," Gird said. "I told him, we have to get it all into no more than four hands of rules—if people can count their fingers and toes, they'll be able to remember them."

And gradually, copy by copy, the first simple laws that later became the Code of Gird spread from barton to barton, even into the towns. Of necessity, these rules were suitable for a time of war; Gird could not possibly work out all the laws needed for trade and commerce in peacetime. But he was sure of his intent: cruelty was always wrong, and always harmed the community. Honesty and fair dealing were good, and helped it.

In the bitter cold and deep snows of winter, no army could march far. Stragglers came to Brightwater and the villages where Gird had some of his army encamped—starving, ragged, sometimes dying of cold even as they staggered to a fire. Gird himself traveled from one camp to another as best he could, trying to make sure that food and warmth were shared fairly among them. He knew, without needing the gnomes' advice, that he would have to win in this coming year—at least he would have to control most of the farmland, so that his people could grow food again. Otherwise his army would starve, and then the lords would win without a fight.

Food stores dropped lower and lower. His yeomen did not grumble much, seeing Gird's belt as tight as theirs. But the soft cries of hungry children pierced him as if they were all his own. He hardly saw Rahi or Pidi, these days; Girnis had disappeared into the dust of war and he knew nothing of her. But the children in the camps were always with him, a reminder of what he was fighting for, and what would be lost if he failed.

It was in the first days of coming spring, uncertain weather that could bring thaw or hard freeze from day to day, that he took one of his cohorts out to seek food from one of the villages that had promised it the year before. They marched four days, south and east down the valley, across a ridge, and down another valley. Gird had sent a runner ahead. But instead of a yeoman marshal, or the barton, come to meet them, he found the entire village standing grim and unwelcoming in a snow-swept meadow nearby. They would not, they said, give anything—not one stone's weight of grain or handbasket of dried fruit. Begone, they said, before you bring the lords' wrath down on us. Gird nodded, and looked them up and down individually.

"What it comes down to, you don't trust me."

The cluster of ragged men and women said nothing. He hadn't expected them to admit it. No one met his eyes. Behind him, his cohort, even more ragged than the peasants from the village. He could hear their breathing, the rasp of pebbles under their feet when they shifted in place. He could feel, as if it were a hot iron, their rapt attention on the back of his neck. His own belly knotted with hunger; he knew theirs were empty too.

Gird tried again. "You agreed with us last year, you remember that?" He stared right at the headwoman, who stared at her feet. But she nodded, slowly. "Yes—you said you'd share your harvest with us, feed us, to help us win against the lords—"

"You didn't win." That voice was bitter, but low, from the back of the group. Gird could not tell which dark-wrapped head it had been, or whether man or woman.

"We haven't won *yet*," said Gird. "But we're a lot closer—Lady's tears, did you think it would be all one battle? We told you—"

" 'Twas a bad winter," said the headwoman, still avoiding his eye. "And them folokai got after flocks, near took the whole lamb crop."

"Tell 'em all, Mara," said the same bitter voice, louder this time.

"The lords come," the woman said. Now she looked up, and Gird could see a fresh scar across her face, the mark of a barbed lash that had almost taken her eye. "They said we had to have more than we could show. They said we'd been giving it to rebels, and they said they'd have no more of it. They took a child from every hearth—they come here, and where was you? Away, is all we know. No help. Help for help, that's what we say, and you've given no help."

"I'm sorry," said Gird. Now all the faces looked at him, all scarred one way or another, all bitter. All betrayed. He wanted to say *It's not my fault*, but knew that wouldn't help. They had protected many of the villages, in the past year: he thought of all those skirmishes and battles, the cost of it to his army. This year, given supplies enough, they'd control more territory, and fewer villages would suffer. But here they had not protected the people, and the people had changed their minds.

"They come oftener," the woman went on. "Check the fields, check the stores. Leave us bare enough for life, they do, and destroy the rest. Threaten the fields, if we give aught to rebels."

Could he promise they would not come again? Did he have the strength yet? Gird tried to think, but he wasn't sure. And a false promise would be worse than no promise. And if he told them how close he was to moving his lines on another league or so to the hills, would these betray him to their lords? Were they lost to him entirely?

"Gird?" That was Selamis, as usual. He had, no doubt, come up with some clever idea for saving the situation. Gird wished he could be properly grateful. He waved the man forward. Selamis muttered "The Marrakai gold?" in his ear. Well, it was a clever idea. Probably not what the Marrakai agent had intended the gold to be used for, but it might work. Although—if they went buying food, to replace what he bought, their lords would surely notice *that*, too.

But he had to try. His mouth dried, thinking of all possible consequences. "We have a bit of gold we found—"

"Found!" That was not a promising tone. Someone spat juicily; it splatted on the rock a bare handspan from Gird's boots. "They told us you brigands'd have gold—and what they'd do if we come to market with it. You're no better than they are, that's a fact. Take our food for your army—they do the same. Both raids us, neither protects—not them from you, nor you from them, and there's not a hair of difference."

He could not, even hungry as he was, drive these folk farther. Like it or not, they were the reason for his fighting, and he could not harm them—yet. Could they use the gold at some market? One of them might pass for a trader, perhaps—someone robbed on the road? That was common enough. Would that pesky priest wreathe his magicks for them, make someone safe in the towns? He might, but he would want something for it, and Gird did not yet trust him.

"We're not the same, and I think you know it. But you've had more trouble than you could stand; I understand that. We won't take it by force, but you think of this—one child from each hearth *now*—do you think that will satisfy them? I lost more than that, before I broke free. You need not be as stupid as I was."

"You lost children?" Others shushed that voice, someone in a leather cloak, but Gird answered it, counting them on his fingers.

"My first two sons died of fever; the lord refused us herb-right in the wood. My wife lost two babes young, one from hunger and one from fever. My eldest daughter they raped; killed her husband. The babe died unborn. My youngest son they struck down; he lives. Another daughter they struck down, breaking her arm; I know not if she lives or dies. And my brother's children, that I'd taken in: two of them dead, by the lords' greed. And that's children. I lost friends, my parents, my brother. You ask yourselves: if they can take one child, will they stop there? Will all your submission, all your obedience, get you peace and enough food? Has it *ever* worked? You can sit here and let them take you one by one, or you can decide to fight back."

And he turned, glared at his own unhappy men, and marched them away. No one called him back, but he was not surprised to find three of the villagers following his cohort when they had gone some distance—and ready to join him.

Still, such incidents made him touchy. He was trying to stretch a small bowl of gruel one day, when two of his marshals reported that the villages to which they'd applied had refused to give or sell supplies, on the grounds that they'd been raided by brigands. His patience snapped.

"I am so *sick* of this!" It came out louder than he meant, and he'd meant it loud enough. Everyone fell silent, watching him, which only made him angrier. He lowered his voice to a growl, all too aware that his growl was audible farther than some men's shouts. "All this dickering, like a farmer trying to work down the price of a bull. All this haggling with thieves and bullies, craft guilds and village councils. Any idiot should be able to see what we're doing, and the worth of it. You'd think they *liked* being yoked and driven by the magelords, the way they kick and snap when we free them. The Lady of Peace herself would be driven to fury, the way they are. By the gods, we're trying to make them free, and make things fair, and they won't see it!"

"We might as well *be* brigands," said Herrak. It was not the first time he'd said something like that, and Gird disliked the whine in his voice. "The way they are, what difference does it make?"

"It makes a difference to *us*," said Gird. "There were brigands before; they never helped the farmers. If we're only robbers, all should be against us. What I can't see is why *they* don't see the difference."

"We need to win," said Selamis, smiling. He had the honeysweet lilt to his voice that Gird hated; it worked on the crowds, most times, but it was not plainspeaking.

"What do you think, I should go to the brigands and recruit *them*?" He meant it as a jest, but the quality of the silence told him the others had thought of that before. Seriously. Selamis was paring his nails with a knife; he gave Gird that sideways look that Gird disliked.

"Some of them might be more like us than you think. Leaderless farmers thrown out of their villages—isn't that what you started with?"

Cob sat up straight and glared at Selamis. "We were not brigands. We may have been disorganized, lazy, filthy, and incompetent, but we were not brigands."

Selamis smiled at him. "That's what I meant. But your lord called you brigands, I'd wager." Cob was not mollified; he glowered at Selamis. But Ivis nodded.

"He did. And maybe—you were good with us, Gird, and if you found even another cohort by full spring—"

Gird mastered his anger with an effort. Late winter had always been the worst time for quarrels, even in the villages: empty bowls and enforced idleness made everyone irritable. "I suppose you have a particularly saintly brigand in mind for me to recruit?"

"I can't promise saintliness, but these last two villages both claim that the brigands near them muster a cohort or two. And there's a man who can guide you to their camp."

"I'll think about it." He would have thought about it between other things for a long time, but the next day a stranger came bearing an offer—written, Gird was surprised to see—from that very brigand captain. He had been a soldier, he said, and turned his coat when the war began. He had much to offer Gird, and would meet with him—in his camp. Gird talked to Arranha. The old priest shook his head and spread his hands.

"You put your life in the hands of Sier Segrahlin, Gird, and came out of that alive; if you want to chance this brigand I have no reason to think you'll do worse. Will you take a cohort of your own?"

"No. We don't have the food now to move them that far, and have them look like anything but starvelings. That won't impress him or his men. I'll go alone, and wear my best boots."

"You might like to consider something." The big man's face was dark with more than weather; ancient dirt outlined every crease, and his heavy dark hair was greasy. But the dagger with which he was paring his filthy nails was spotless, its edge gleaming.

"I might," said Gird, accepting the dirty clay pot one of the other men offered without enthusiasm. Gods only knew what kind of brew would be in it. He sniffed as unobtrusively as possible. The big man's shrewd eyes missed nothing.

"If you want ale, we've got it. *That's* just water—spring water, from over there." His head jerked, and Gird's eyes followed, to a glisten of water among rank weeds across the clearing. Gird sipped, cautiously. It tasted like spring water, untainted by any herbs he knew.

"You're the peasant's new general, I hear," said the big man. He waved his hand, and a woman in a striped skirt, a pattern Gird had never seen, brought over a wooden tray. On it were a loaf and two wooden bowls half-full of stew. The stew had slopped onto the tray, making a gray puddle, but it smelled good. "Here," the man said, breaking the loaf and offering both chunks to Gird. Gird took the smaller; the man frowned, but passed him one of the bowls.

"I'm not a general," Gird said. He nibbled the bread: coarse and sour, but no worse than his own baking.

"General, captain, leader, whatever you want to call it. You're commanding them now—"

Gird nodded. No use hiding it, and by rumor this one would never tell the nobles.

"You need troops." The big man dipped his own chunk of bread in the stew, and stuffed his mouth full, then bit it off savagely. "I have troops."

Gird looked around at the men huddled at the cookfires, being served by the two women. "These?"

"Among others. More than you have, peasant general." The words were slurred with chewing.

"Then you want to join us?"

The man swallowed that mouthful, took another, and finished it before answering. "You need us. I think *you* want *us*."

Gird dipped his own bread into the stew and took a large bite.

Better meat than he'd tasted since spring. "Good stew," he said. The man frowned at him, but said nothing. Gird looked past his shoulder at the others, and found eyes staring back at him that quickly looked away. He put his bowl down, and leaned forward, fists on knees.

"I need people who want to make a better land."

The man's eyes widened, and then he laughed, an explosive gust that sprayed spittle an armspan. "Better land! What kind of talk is that? Is that what you peasants think you're doing?"

"If it's not, we're nothing but outlaws."

"And you think that's so terrible? Simyits' fingers, Gird, we've been outlaws so long most of us don't know where we come from, and do we look so starveling to you?" The man pushed up his sleeve, and squeezed a meaty forearm. "See this? Show me the peasant with as much meat on his bones—not you, not anyone you know. Besides, you're all outlaws: the lords have a bounty on you, same as us."

Gird was aware of ears stretched long to hear their words. "We're outlaws because we had no choice. Because the magelords' law gave us no way to live within it. Given a fair chance, I don't know many as 'ud live outside the law. All I ever heard of outlaws, they was mostly men driven off their lands by some greedy lord."

The man hawked and spat, not too near Gird's feet. "Aye, it's unfairness drives most men to the woods. Some of us was stolen away young, or born to free fathers. But we're all free now, that's the thing. Free, and with no wish to put our necks under the yoke again."

"The magelords' yoke?"

"Any yoke." The man spat again, this time a hairs-breadth nearer. Gird thought it was deliberate. "See here, Gird, I'll be straight with you. We're free, and we want to stay free. You talk of a better land: just what do you mean? A better king? A better tax gatherer?"

Some of the others had come nearer. Gird had noticed before that they were well-fed; now he could see the glint of weapons in their hands. "No king," he said. "The magelords brought kings to our land; we had none before."

"Who told you that?" It was a long, lanky redhead well behind his leader.

"The gnomes," he answered. He would have gone on, but the collective intake of breath stopped him. "What's wrong?" he asked.

"You deal with *gnomes?*" The big man sounded both angry and afraid.

He was not sure how to answer. Would they understand that

bargain he'd made, or would they fear gnomish incursions? "I learned of old times from the gnomes," he said finally. "And of law."

The big man's eyes slewed to left and right, meeting others and picking up control as visibly as a man picks up the reins of horses in harness. Gird felt a cold draft down his back. Something he'd said had changed their minds—and not for the better.

"I would not call it better for the rule of gnomes or gnomish men," said the leader.

"They seek no rule in human lands," said Gird. "They abide by their laws, which forbid that."

"But you learned law of them—and from them learned what you would do to make the land better?"

"It's obvious enough what would make it better. Honest dealing between one man and another, one craft and another. Fair judges. Taxes there must be, but fair, and no more than a man can pay and still live decently. From them I learned what is needed to make such things exist, what rules groups need."

The big man's teeth gleamed as he grinned. "Fair dealing, eh? And who's to say what's fair, with no king? The gnomes?"

Gird shook his head, pushing away his doubts. This was familiar ground, at least, and perhaps they would listen. "Not the gnomes; they have their law, for themselves. We need a law, a rule, for us—for all of us. We decide what's fair, all of us, in council—as our forefathers did, in the old days of steading and hearthing." Talking fast, he explained more of the plan he and his friends had worked out. But he knew soon enough that they listened with only idle interest. When he finished, the leader was shaking his head.

"That's fine enough for farmers, and village bakers. Do you think the finesmiths will sit elbow-to-elbow with stinking tanners and pig farmers mired to the knees? And what about us? We have none of the crafts you mentioned. What do you think such as we will do, in your 'better land'? Do you really think I'll take up plowing and reaping, or Pirig will return to herding sheep?"

"Why not?" asked Gird, though he was sure he knew. "It's honest work, and without the magelords' interferences—"

"Because I'm not what you call an honest man," said the big man, leaning toward him. "You want honest, you go to the gnomes, and much good it will do us! Should I push a plow or swing a scythe, when my skill is with sword and handaxe? Will your better land have a place for soldiers?"

Gird raised his eyebrows. "Soldiers? Is that what you are?"

"Close enough. Strong men with weapons: call us brigands or soldiers, it matters not. Soldiers are but brigands in uniform."

Gird bit back the angry reply he wanted to give; this was no time to lose his temper, or his head might go with it. "Some are," he said in as mild a tone as he could manage. The other man sank back onto his rock. "But if life's to be better for all, *our* soldiers must be more."

"Your soldiers! Your half-starved peasants who know less about swordplay than the worst fighter in my band."

Gird smiled at him, with clear intent. "If your swordplay's so skilled, then why haven't you freed yourself of the militia's scourge, these past years?"

"It's not all swordplay!" yelled someone from the back of the crowd that had now gathered.

"Exactly," said Gird to that unseen voice. "Fighting a war's more than swordplay; my peasants may be clumsy with blades, but they know that much. You've tried your way, and it didn't work—now you want my help—"

"No!" The big man had jumped up; something had pricked him there, something Gird might use if he could figure out what it was. "I don't need anyone's help! We could sit here, fattening on the spoils of your war, *peasant*, preying on both sides. I offered *you* help, help you need: men and weapons. I don't need your pious words, your gnomish law."

"And what did you want, in exchange for your help?"

"Only what you give others who bring in troops for you: that you name me marshal—even high marshal—along with those others."

"I think not," said Gird, and bent down to pick up his bowl. As he'd expected, the big man came at him, seeing a clear target. As he'd planned, the bowl of cooling stew went into the big man's face, and he tucked and rolled away from the knife. His feet jammed into the big man's belly, and then he was up, balanced, fist cocked, as the big man choked and gasped on the ground. He kicked the man's knife away. The other men had started forward, but now ringed about him, uncertain.

"Soldiers must trust each other," said Gird loudly. "I must trust my marshals, and my marshals must trust the yeoman marshals, and those trust their yeomen—or nothing works in battle."

"I'll *kill* you," growled the man on the ground, between gasps.

"Get up and try," said Gird. Someone snickered, in the crowd, and he felt that others felt the same way. But the ring surrounded him; he could not have escaped if he'd tried. He didn't try, and they came no closer, more curious than angry.

The big man finally clambered up, his dirty face grim. "You—you should have killed me when you had the chance, fool!"

"It's not my way to knife a helpless man who is not my enemy."

"I am now." said the big man. He glared around the ring. "You—why didn't you hold him?"

"Why?" asked the same redhead who'd spoken before. "You started it. Take him yourself; he might hurt me." More chuckles, this time more open. The big man flushed.

"So I will, then, and you'll miss your fun after—I'll let Fargi take his skin. As for you, Gird, I hear they call you Strongarm, not rocktoe: if you have strength in that arm, use it."

"Aye," said other voices. "No more wrestlers' tricks: fight Arbol manlike, fist to fist."

Stupid, Gird thought, remembering the gnomes' acid commentary on human brawling. But stupid or not, his one chance of surviving this ill-chanced venture lay in the strength of his arms and the hardness of his fists. The big man crouched, then rushed him. Gird sidestepped, jabbed hard into the man's ribs, and took a glancing blow on his own. So that worked—if he ever saw the gnomish warmaster again, he'd have to tell him. *If you must use fists,* Ketak had said, *learn to use them well.* The big man was throwing a flurry of blows at him now, blows Gird took on his own arms, keeping them away from his face. His own punches were landing on shoulders, arms, and body; the other man was quick enough to protect his own face, ducking behind his fists like a river-crab behind its claws. He heard the other men mutter, call encouragement to their chief; he tried not to hear any of that.

Then the other man kicked out, catching Gird on the shin. He dropped his guard for a moment, and took a hard blow to the side of his head. For some reason, that made him laugh: the memory of his father once telling him he'd be safe in a brawl, having a head made of solid stone. He saw on the other man's face surprise and a touch of fear at his laugh—well, so he should be afraid. For all the big man's extra weight, he was no stronger, his shoulders not quite as broad—and *he* had eaten all his supper, and taken a kick to the belly.

Gird let himself grin. The man himself had chosen fists, when he might have skewered Gird with a sword—did he not realize he had chosen Gird's best weapon? The other man gave back, footlength by footlength, as Gird hammered him. He hardly felt the return blows; he had not had such a wholly justified excuse for pounding someone in a long time. In battle he had to be thinking of the whole, had to be looking ahead—in training he had to be watchful that he did not cripple one of his own. But now, here, he could let out all the frustration and rage of the past year, and whether he lived or died, he would have the satisfaction of pulping that arrogant face that thought itself too good to be a peasant.

Now the other man had given up attack, and was trying to defend himself from Gird's blows. Gird drove him back with two, three, four short jabs to the body, and then loosed his favorite swing, all his weight and shoulder behind it, to crack the other's jaw and drop him like a loose stone. The big man went down, twitched, and lay still. Gird flexed his hands, and sucked a cut. Nothing broken, though they'd be stiff in the morning. As his temper cooled, he could feel the lumps on his ribs that would be bruises, and the throbbing of his kicked shin.

The mutters around him now were awed. He looked deliberately from face to face, wondering if they'd attack him, knife him. He would not have a chance against so many. But although two knelt beside their leader, and someone brought a bucket of water, the ring widened, giving him space. He heard a complaint, quickly squelched, about a wager, and realized that some of them had gambled on the fight—he should have expected it, but he hadn't.

"Is that how you won your army, then?" asked one of the men. Gird shook his head.

"No. But I find it useful sometimes. My—Da used to say the only way to get an idea into some heads was to break them open and let the light in." Open laughter now, a little uneasy but genuine amusement. He felt slightly guilty for the lie, his father having been Alyanya's servant to the end, but his instinct said that letting these men know he'd ever been in the militia would be a mistake.

"An' now?"

Gird looked at the speaker, licked his knuckles again, and said, "Now what? He tried to take me, and I flattened him—that's between us. There's nothing between you and me unless you make it so—are you challenging?"

"Nay, not I. What I meant—d'you claim command of us?"

"He can't!" said someone behind him. Gird did not turn.

"No," he said slowly. "That's not what we fought about. You'll choose your own leader—for all I know, you'll choose him again."

"But about joining your army—"

Gird shrugged. "You heard what I said. I'm looking for men as want a better land later, and those that'll be honest yeomen now. Those that do can come with me; those that don't had better not. We may be skinny and hungry, but we do know how to deal with those as try to stick a knife in our back or steal from us." He nudged the fallen leader with his toe.

"We could kill you now," muttered one of the men just at the edge of his sight. Gird laughed, and saw the surprise on their faces.

"Killing's easy—you could kill me, and the magelords likely will. So then what? Killing me won't get you into my army. Make up your own minds; I'm going home." He turned, and stared hard at the men who had crowded close behind him. Like dogs, they wilted under a direct stare, and shuffled, making a gap for him to walk through. His back itched; it would take only a single thrown knife, a single sword-thrust. But he could not have fought his way out anyway. Behind him he heard a sudden argument, curses, and more blows ending in yelps. Someone else was taking over, he guessed, wondering if they'd come after him. He walked on, into the trees, not looking back. Looking back would do no good.

He had gone some distance when he heard running behind him on the trail. Gird slipped aside, crouching in the undergrowth to crawl back down parallel to the trail, and saw four men and the woman in the striped skirt jogging along. All were armed; the first watched the trail keenly, and stopped them about where Gird had left the trail.

"He can't be that far ahead of us," said one.

"Wait—I don't see—"

Gird stood up; they heard the rustling leaves and turned, clearly startled and alarmed.

"Why did you follow me?"

"We—I—wanted to join you," said the first man.

"I heard you let women join," said the woman.

Gird stepped out onto the trail, warily enough. "I do, if they're willing to take orders like anyone else. But we have rules you might not like."

"There's better than *him*," said the first man, jerking his chin in the direction of the brigands' camp. "I'd rather fight than steal."

Chapter Twenty-nine

Spring rains that year delayed everyone's movements. Gird drew and redrew his battle maps, revising his plans over and over again. His cohorts were most effective as he'd used them before, striking swiftly against small concentrations of the enemy, where they could outnumber them and control the surrounding country. But if the supply situation stayed as bad as it was, he could not do that another year; he would have to confront the lords' armies directly, win and control larger areas, to ensure the safety of food-producing lands and those who farmed them. Should he do that early, or late, after wearing down the lords' armies with raids? What would it cost him, in unsown grain, in next year's harvest?

In some areas, the lords were not allowing their peasants to plow and plant; in others, the farmers were guarded by soldiers. Gird shook his head at that. Why would they think he'd raid during planting time? His own forces protected an area in the Brightwater valley; over the winter he had urged all the farmers to form bartons and learn drill. Most of them had. Now his army protected them during planting, and he hoped they could protect themselves during the fighting season.

He began moving his army eastward, one cohort at a time, cloaked in the rains and leaving less trail than if he moved everyone at once. Ivis had found a good shelter two days' journey away, overhanging ledges that opened into a sonorous cavern. Gird himself went back and forth with the first two, then spent several days in Brightwater, settling accounts with Marrakai gold and hoping the town would be there when he got back. If he got back. Then he headed out with the last cohort, noticing that despite all his care, the tracks left by the others were as clear as any map ever drawn, one brown scrawl of mud after another across the new spring grass.

Roads, he thought to himself. *We'll need good roads, when it's over.* What they needed now was good luck, the gods' gift of miracles; remembering the other times he'd wanted miracles, and what he'd actually received, he was not willing to ask. He felt unusually grumpy; he had banged his knee hard on the doorpost going out of the barracks, and it still throbbed. The damp raw air seemed to bite into the bruise, rather than soothe it. He hawked and spat, catching an early fly; that cheered him.

By nightfall, he felt he'd been marching for half a year. His feet were damp and cold; he pulled off his worn boots and pushed his feet near the fire, rubbing them. A fine drizzle hissed in the flames; smoke crawled along the ground, making them all choke and cough. Gird thought longingly of the barracks in Brightwater—even that merchant's house, with the brazier in the center of the table, where several men could sit around it and talk. He would never think like a merchant, but he had gotten over some of his first astounded contempt. He told himself to be glad he had a good leather cloak; time was when the drips off the trees would have wet his bare head. But it didn't work. He was cold, stiff, damp, and without reason homesick for his own small cottage, with his own fire on the hearth, and his own family around him. He said nothing; the others were quiet as well, on such a dismal evening.

The next day's march brought them to the rock shelter and cavern, where most of his army was gathered. He plunged again into the familiar problems: how large to make the jacks, how many sacks of grain and dried fruit did they have and how long it would last, where the nearest sources of supply were. He was more than ready to pull off his boots and stretch out near one of the fires for a rest when Selamis insisted that he had to speak to Gird privately.

Gird followed his assistant deeper into the cave, annoyed once more at Selamis's fidgits. They didn't have time for such nonsense.

"Here." The younger man's voice, hardly above a whisper, halted him.

"I'm here," growled Gird, trying for patience. "What is it now?"

Instead of answer, soundless light answered him. Between Selamis's clutched fingers shone a rosy glow, steady as daylight. His eyes glittered in it, squinted almost shut. Gird, through his own shock, saw the taut lines of his face, the tears that trickled down those quivering cheeks. He looked down, terrified, at his own hands, but they were outlined only from without, by Selamis's light.

"What—" His voice broke, and he swallowed, tried again. "What *is* that—what did you find? Where?"

"In me." The man's hands spread a little; the light glowed steadily between them, sourceless, rose-gold: the light of spring evenings hazed with pollen, of autumn dawns among the turning leaves. Or of friendly firelight, welcoming. Gird shuddered, and fought back a rising terror.

"You're a—a *mage?*" And almost simultaneously, rage shook him.

You lied to me, he thought. But Selamis's face showed more fear than even he felt, fear not of him, but of the light.

"I don't know." The man spread his hands farther apart, sighed, and the light vanished. Far back up the passage, Gird could hear Raheli arguing still about how many onions should go in tonight's kettle—so it was still the same world, the same time. "I told you," the voice went on in the darkness, "that I am a lord's bastard. But I didn't tell you—"

What this time, Gird wondered, remembering the many things his so-called luap had not told him until circumstances forced it. Would the man never find truth, and cease his lying?

"I was bred for magic." It came out in one gulping rush. Gird said nothing, listened to Selamis's breathing as it slowed again. "They do that now—"

"I asked you about that," said Gird softly. It made sense, now. "Go on," he said, more gently than he might have a moment before.

"I—I had none they could find," his luap said. "That's why they sent me away—the real reason."

"You know," Gird began as delicately as his nature allowed, "if you'd just tell me the whole damn truth to start with, we wouldn't have these little problems."

"I know. But if you'd known—"

"*Damn* it, I'm not a monster!" His voice echoed off the walls, most monster-like, and then he had to laugh, muffling it as best he could. "Oh lad, lad, you are too old for these tricks. I can believe your heritage of blood, true enough, the way you never trust outright—"

"Trust is dangerous," muttered Selamis.

"And you trusted me with this." As always, the rage and mirth had passed quickly; he felt a pressure to reassure this frightened man, a certainty that he must be saved for them.

"It has to be the magic," Selamis said, his voice now steady but very soft. "But I don't know—"

"When?" asked Gird, rather than let him entangle himself in his uncertainties.

"Two days ago, when we came. Raheli asked me to come back here and see if anything threatened. I fell over a ledge, just beyond here, and suddenly felt I'd fallen a long way. It was dark—darker than this—utterly dark inside and out, despair and grief. What I fear in death, only worse."

Gird grunted. Darker than this end of the cave, after that uncanny light had left it, he could not imagine. Fear? They all

feared, but Selamis was braver than he knew. He had a storyteller's
gift of tongue, that was all, that let him talk himself frightened.

"Then I called on Esea," the luap went on. Darkness pressed on
Gird's shoulders, so hard he nearly gasped. Esea! Was he so much
a lord's son he still reached for their god in his trouble? "And the
Lady—both of them. Light came to my mind—not as memory of
light, but light itself, within." Gird felt the hairs prickling on his
arms and neck as the luap talked. "Silver as starlight, cool. Then
under the silver light flowers grew in a wreath, but colored as in
sunlight, sweet-smelling: the midsummer's wreath, fresh-woven.
But the light was silver yet." Gird's eyes filled with tears, and he
felt them hot on his cheeks. Not magic, then, but the gods' gift?
It had to be. "Then the light came, in my clenched hands, just as
I showed you, and in the light I could see the symbols on the rock."

"The *what?*" Gird muted that roar even as it came out. Again
the light bloomed in front of him, the same serene rosy glow, but
this time the luap's face was calm.

"Come on. I'm supposed to show you. They said tell Gird."

"They?" He didn't expect an answer, and got none, following the
luap over that ledge of rock to a bell-shaped chamber in the cave.
In its center was a smooth polished floor, inlaid with brilliant patterns. Something glittered there, as if faceted, but the light was too
dim to make it clear. Selamis stepped around it, and Gird followed,
eyeing it doubtfully. Selamis stopped before a recess in one side
of the chamber.

"There," he said.

The light in his hands brightened. Gird looked uncertainly at the
wall, as the designs became slowly visible, then glowed of their
own light.

"It's something about elves," Selamis said, when Gird said nothing. "And something about the rockfolk, and something about the
gods—"

"And men," said Gird, tracing one line with a blunt thumb, for
he did not put the pointing finger, the shame finger, on anything
that might be sacred. Something rang in his head, a sound he later
thought of as the ringing of a great bone bell, his skull rapped by
the god's tongue—but at that moment he was conscious only of
the pressure, the vibration shaking wit and body alike.

When it ended, he was flat on his belly on the cold stone, eyes
pressed shut, and he heard Selamis's equally shaken breathing
nearby. He opened his eyes deliberately, rubbed his palms on the
stone, and then over his head.

"You might have told me you were the *king's* bastard," he said, mildly enough he thought. Selamis had already come to a stiff crouch, the light still glowing between his hands.

"I should have." It was the first time he hadn't made an excuse. Whatever had happened had affected him, too. "I—I should have."

"You could be the heir. Bastardy's no bar, not with magic."

"I—don't have that much—"

"They should never have let you live." Gird heaved himself up, shook his head, and glanced cautiously at the graven designs. Now he could barely tell what they were, interlacing curves and patterns that meant more than any ordinary man could understand. Or should. He looked over at that mysterious pattern on the floor. "What's that?"

"I don't know."

"Huh. Bring your light, can you?" The light came, and Selamis with it, almost affronted to have Gird interested in something else. He could make nothing of it, even with more light and finally shrugged. "Well. Whatever that is, now we know what you are— do we?"

"King's bastard. Outcast. Light-maker." Selamis's voice was bitter.

"Do you want that throne, king's bastard?" The growl in Gird's voice made the chamber resonate. "Is that what it is, you'd like a peasant army to put you on your father's throne, let you rule instead?"

"*No!*" That howl, too, resonated, a reverberating shriek that seemed to pierce the stone itself. "No. I want—I just want—"

"Safety." Now it was contempt that shook the air.

"There is none." A mere whisper, but Gird heard it. He looked across the comfortable, cozy light into a face that had grown into its years. Almost.

"Right you are, lad. No safety, no certainty, and hell to pay if the others find out who you are. Is that what you see? Or do you also have the foreseeing magic?"

"Some, yes. Since the light came."

He would not ask. Pray to the gods for favor, yes, and make the sacrifices his people had always made, but he would not ask the future. That was for the wild folk, the crazy horse-riders, and the cool arrogant lords who had no need to ask, because they knew.

"I will not be what he is," Selamis said. "I renounce my own name, and name myself luap—I swear I will not inherit that throne, that way, that habit of being—" It sounded like a vow to more than Gird, and Gird did not interrupt. "I am no true heir; I renounce it." But the light glowed on, even when he spread his hands wide.

Gird waited, then into the silence said, "Lad, you can no more renounce what the gods give—that magic—than I can the strength of my arm or the knowledge of drill that forced me into this in the first place. I've been that road; it turns back on you."

"I will not be the king!" shouted the luap, eyes wide.

"No. You will not be the king. But you cannot divide the king's blood from your blood, or the king's magic from your mind. You have only the choice of use, not the choice of substance."

"What can I do?"

Gird's belly rumbled, and he had a strong desire to hawk and spit. Clearly that would not do in this place; he didn't want to find out what would happen if he did. *Grow up,* he thought to himself, but to the luap said, "For one thing, you can guide us back out. I'm hungry." Then, at the indignant expression, he said "By the gods, you're half-peasant: use sense. You can be who you are, and do what is right. What's so hard about that?" Then he strode away, past the patterns on the floor that seemed to have tendrils reaching for his feet, and stumbled into the ledge. "*Damn* it," he roared. "Come on." His shin would hurt for days, he knew it, and there was too much to do and not enough time.

No one said anything when he came out of the shadows to the cookfire, the luap at his heels. The onions in the stew had everyone belching. *They can smell us in the king's hall, right across the land,* Gird thought, going out to the jacks, but he wasn't worried. He would have to think about the luap, but not now. Now he had to think about the army, and the king's army, and where would be best to meet them.

His one advantage was the willingness of the people to help him; he knew where the king's army moved, but the king's army must search for him. The king had left Finyatha again, and this time Segrahlin rode with him (so the word came), and every lord who could make magicks of any kind. And their well-fed soldiers, rank on rank of them, and their horsemen, who now had learned to armor the horses as well.

Thus he was in no mood to be cooperative when Selamis cornered him again the next night, and wondered, in too casual a tone, if Gird were going to name him a marshal in the coming campaign. Gird stared at him, momentarily speechless.

"I can't give you any command now," said Gird. "You can see that, I hope—"

Selamis glowered silently. When he was sulky, he *did* look almost aristocratic.

"And it's going to be damned hard to explain why I'm not. Blast you, you might have *thought*—"

"Would it have done any good to tell you sooner?" Gird did not like the self-righteous whine in that voice. Selamis had lied, and liars had no right to be self-righteous.

"Whether it would or not, you didn't. You didn't tell me, and didn't tell me, and if you hadn't had that—that experience—" He couldn't say it aloud, that Selamis had used magic, that he was a mage. It terrified him still, though he hoped he was concealing his reaction. The saying was that liars weren't much good at spotting others' lies. He hoped it was true.

"If I'd had no magic, it wouldn't have done any good to tell you."

"You think it's done *good?*"

"Well, I meant—if I didn't have magic, then my birth didn't matter—"

Gird rounded on him. "By the Lady's skirts, you're *still* thinking of the throne, aren't you? You still think your *blood* and your gods' cursed stinking *magic* give you some sort of right to power?"

"It wouldn't be the same—"

"You're right it wouldn't—because you're not getting within leagues of that throne, my lad. Forget that. You can make pretty lights, and your father is the Finaarenisian king. And that means *nothing*, not one damn thing, to me or any other peasant—"

"It means something to the nobles," said Selamis stubbornly. "You said that yourself. If they knew—"

"They'd slit your stupid throat. How can you be so *dense?* I've seen smarter stones, that had at least the sense to roll downhill. No. You're the king's bastard, and not alone in that, I'll wager. You've got a bit of magic, enough to scare girls with—"

Light blazed around them, and a cold fist seemed to squeeze Gird's heart in his chest.

"It scares *you*," said Selamis, furious, his handsome face distorted. "Quit pretending it doesn't. Admit it."

But there was rage and rage, and Gird's grew out of deeper roots than pique. He forced one breath after another out of stiff lips, and felt his heart settle once more into a steady rhythm. Without his thought, his powerful arm came up and smashed Selamis in the face. The light vanished, as Selamis measured his length on the ground.

"You stupid, stupid fool," said Gird, almost calmly. He squatted, made sure that Selamis was still breathing, then looked around. Could they be lucky enough that no one had seen the light Selamis made? No: there in the gathering dusk someone hurried toward them. Gird sighed, gustily. He ought to kill Selamis, quickly and painlessly, before he woke. He should have done it before, when he first realized the man had lied, and lied again. The fool had renounced his claim before the gods; that alone should have settled him. Now he, Gird, would have to explain everything, and it was the worst possible time to tell everyone that they had the king's bastard in their camp.

He was frowning over the supply rolls when he realized that Selamis was awake and staring at him. He glanced over and met a furious look.

"You hit me," said Selamis, in a hoarse whisper. His head probably hurt; the bruise on his face made it look lopsided.

"That I did. You showed me what you were."

"Why do you assume I'll be *bad*—?"

Gird put down the notched tally stick reporting the grain harvest in Plumhollow Barton and looked hard at Selamis until he wilted. "You know what you did: you lied, and lied, and lied again, and then lost your temper and used your magicks on me. Is that what any of us would want in a king, if we wanted a king at all? Should I believe that a crown will make you honest, teach you patience and mercy, give you wisdom? You seem to think you'll be a good king, better than your father. You might argue that it would be hard to be *worse*. But I'm not helping a liar, a lackwit, or a hotheaded fool onto a throne, where he can put his foot on my neck again. No."

Selamis's eyes closed, briefly, and the hand Gird could see stirred. Was he up to magicks again? But the eyes opened again, and the hand relaxed. "I'm sorry," he said. "I shouldn't have done that—"

"No more you should. Where'd you be if you'd killed me, eh?"

"I—I didn't think—"

"True enough. And does *not thinking* make a good king?"

"No." It sounded sulky, but then Selamis's face must have hurt a lot. A sigh, then, long and gusty. Gird didn't look up. "What are you going to do now?"

"I ask myself that," said Gird, picking up the single tally from the smithguild and running his thumbnail along the nicks. "I should have killed you, back when I first realized you were lying, and I definitely should have killed you last night. But I'll tell you what, lad, I'm a bad keeper of accounts, and you're good at it—and sometimes the best milker is the worst for kicking the pail."

"You'll let me live because I can read and cast accounts?"

"For now. But use those magicks just once more and you're dead."

"Did I hurt you?"

Gird's hand went to his chest before he thought; he glanced at Selamis and met his eyes. "Yes, and you might have killed anyone less stubborn. What did you think you were doing, eh?"

"I didn't really know—it just seemed as if I could press—"

"Don't. Don't even think about it. As soon hand a child of three Midwinters a pike to play with, and hope no crockery breaks."

"I'll be loyal," said Selamis, but it carried little conviction.

Gird put the tally down, and faced him squarely. "You will be loyal, lad, because I will break your neck myself if you're not. You have no more choices, no more room to maneuver. I've told the marshals what they must know; what you must know is that your life depends on my good word. And if they think you've charmed me, magicked my good word, they will kill you. And if you try charming one of them first, the same. If you find that too harsh, consider your father's way of dealing with traitors. We will kill you quickly as we may—but we will not let you loose again to misuse your talents."

Gird shifted east and south, taking two smaller holdings easily when the outnumbered garrisons fled, and winning another with a stiff fight: he needed the food enough to make the losses worthwhile. One of the fleeing lords had magic enough to poison the wells and blast a field to dry ash. Gird wondered if anything would ever grow in that gray grit. The others' fields might make a harvest, if nothing went wrong through the summer. The one that fought gave them, unwillingly, their first magelord prisoners.

The lord was dead; whether he had had magicks or not, he had fallen to pikes. His wife, several servant women, and the children— wholebred and bastard—had barricaded themselves into a wholly inadequate tower. Gird's yeomen battered the door down easily and dragged them out. Gird looked at the woman. But for her long robes, so unlike anything the peasant women wore, she looked like any other woman her age. She had borne children; she looked to be carrying another. The children were children: a stairstep gaggle, in all states from wild terror to infant placidity. The servant women were trying to gather them in their arms, soothe them.

Gird felt his head throbbing. He had never really thought about prisoners, and certainly not women and children. He had assumed that the lords would all be killed in battle, somehow, and he wouldn't have to worry about it. Now he did. The woman—the *lady,* he found himself thinking—looked as if *she* expected death. Or worse. The servants were unsure, glancing from the lady to his yeomen.

"She was about to stab the children," said one of the men holding her. Gird came closer. Brown hair, eyes with flecks of blue and green and gold. Her chin came up and she braced herself to face him.

"You didn't want to kill the children," said Gird.

"Better me than you," she said. Her voice was calm, almost toneless, the voice of someone who had given up.

"I'm not going to kill the children." What was he going to do with them? Where could he send them? But he was certainly not going to kill them; that was what lords did.

"What, then? Torture them for your amusement? I know what kind of games you peasants play." She had gone white, sure of what he would do; in the rage that followed, he almost did it, but one of the children broke loose from the servant women, and ran straight to him, pummeling his legs and screaming. Gird leaned over, wrapped the child in his arms and lifted him. Her? The mite had braids; did the lords braid boys' hair as well as girls'? The woman struggled frantically when Gird picked the child up, but quieted when she saw Gird hold the child carefully.

"Quiet, child," Gird said to the girl. He would assume it was a girl. She screamed all the harder, red-faced, tears bursting from under tight-shut lids. *"No!"* he yelled down at her. Silence followed; the child sniffed and opened her eyes. Remarkable eyes, blue flecked with gold, eyes he could drown in. He looked across at the lady. "You do not know the games peasants play, lady, if you think we torture children. It is the pain of our children that drove us to this war. Is this one yours?" White-lipped, she nodded. "A lovely child. I hope she has a long life." He set the child down and pushed her toward her mother. "Go, little one."

It was still no solution. He caught the sidelong looks, the low-voiced comments he was meant to overhear. As he toured the stronghold, learning more about fortifications than the gnomes had ever bothered to tell him, he wondered what he was going to do with them. The dungeon, when he found it, drove that thought out of his mind briefly, for there were the fates the lady had feared, knowing them too well. Gird swallowed nausea and rage, as his yeomen helped the pitiful prisoners up to daylight. He fingered the torturer's mask of red and black, wondering which of the dead men above had worn it. There on the wall was a larger version of the same mask, leather stretched over wood and painted in garish stripes. Beneath was a circle of chain, with barbs worked into the links. Behind him, his yeomen murmured, angry. Gird yanked the mask and circle off the wall, careful not to let the barbs prick his hands, and nodded to the other equipment.

"Take this all up and burn it. We'll leave nothing like this behind us." The words rang in his mind as he went back to his prisoners. *Nothing like this behind us* meant intent as well as material objects. He wanted to crush something, hurt someone, but that was what had started the whole mess.

The lady was crouched, with her children, in a corner of the outer wall, with a jeering crowd around her. They fell silent when they saw Gird, and he waved them away, but for a few guards.

"I think you know what I found below," said Gird. She would not meet his eyes, this time. She had known. Had she condoned, even encouraged? "I found the mask, the barbed chain—"

"I told him," she said, looking at her clenched hands. "I told him we were never meant to follow Liart. That our only hope was Esea's light, and if it failed, we should greet the long night peaceably. But he would not. He would not admit his powers failed, that his children might not have all he had been given. I told him nothing was forever, that men rose and fell like trees, like—like wheat, even, brief as that is. That we could not win safety this way."

Gird reached out and took her hands in his. "Look at me. Yes, like that. Did you, yourself, kill anyone? Did you send anyone to the torturers?"

Her head shook once, side to side; she said nothing, staring into his eyes with those multi-colored eyes of hers. Was she trying to charm him? Could she?

"Did you truly try to stop him, your husband?"

"Yes. But he would not listen."

Gird released her hands. "Well, then: you listen to me. If I find you've lied, that you helped with that filth, your life is forfeit. Otherwise, it depends on you. Will you redeem the evil your husband did?"

Her eyes widened; she had not expected that. "How could I do that?"

"Come with us, work to heal those who are hurt."

"I have not the healing gift—and besides, I am—" she gestured at her belly, just swelling her robes.

"Where do you think peasant women go, when they're thrown off their land and are pregnant? As for healing gift, if you can boil water and wash bandages, you will earn your keep—though I admit it's little enough, until this war's won."

"And I will be the slave of slaves, for your delight?"

His mouth soured. "No, lady, I would be delighted to have everyone safe at home, no one a slave to anyone."

"And if I don't agree?"

Gird shrugged, and stood up. "I suppose we can turn you out, chase you away from our camps, and let you find your own keep, if you can. Can you?"

"Not as I am," she said. "All right. I will take your offer." The unspoken *for now* seemed to hang in the air around them. Gird had the uneasy certainty that this would not be the last such problem, and he was not at all sure he had found the best solution.

The next day, he watched the lady—now garbed in the more practical peasant clothes—and her children set off with those of his wounded he was sending back to the rock shelter. He had had to argue harder than he liked with his own yeomen, to extract their promise to treat her fairly. The children they would have taken happily; he sensed that they wanted him to kill the lady, but feared to say it. Selamis—the *luap*, he reminded himself—had not offered his opinion, and Gird had not asked it. He had returned to being the efficient keeper of accounts and carrier of messages.

One of the new problems of this year, with the larger army was his inability to see what was going on across the field of battle. Now he knew exactly why the soldiers' officers rode horses: they were above much of the dust and all the bobbing heads and weapons. This count's stables had held many horses. Some of them were dead, but the others could be useful. He could barely remember how it had felt to ride that mule, back in his youth, but it would have to do.

The stables yielded five live, unhurt horses. Two were tall and leggy, one was a pony (*for the children?* Gird wondered) and the other two were nondescript animals of middle size. He was not even sure how to saddle and bridle them, but some of his ex-soldiers were, and quickly had all but the pony tacked up. These experienced riders mounted and tried the animals out. One of the tall ones began to fret and prance; it was lathered on the neck almost before it was ridden at all. The other tall horse seemed quieter, but on the second circuit of the courtyard went into a fit of bucking and dumped its rider in a corner. Gird knew he didn't want either of those. The other two horses were more obedient, but his experienced riders said neither was suitable for a novice. He could not afford a broken leg right now, Gird told himself, so he'd better keep using his legs for what they were meant for: walking. Maybe he could stand on a rock?

Two days later, as he was moving the army north again, he saw an old gray carthorse plodding through a narrow wood. One of the food scouts waved, hopefully. Meat? Gird waved back a negative. He really would like a horse; he had always wanted to ride a horse. Not someone's trained warhorse, but a plain old horse that would plod along, and let him learn without breaking his legs for him. He had no way to catch a horse, but he wasn't going to eat his desired ride, not yet. Besides, they still had meat from the horses back at the count's stronghold.

At the midday break, an old gray horse grazed only a few pike-lengths from them, ripping up the grass with delight. Was it the same horse? Gird could not tell. He could tell one cow from another across a field in the fog, but horses were horses to him, with color and size their only distinction. This one had the usual big dark eye, a pink-freckled nostril fluttering with each breath, burrs in the long hairs of its fetlocks—he realized that the horse had come a lot closer. He had to look up to see its back, its slightly swayed back. Ought to make it easy to stay on, he thought. The horse blew a long slobbery breath over his leg, mumbled the edge of his boot in its lips, and sighed.

He could probably grab its mane and hang on long enough for someone to get a belt or something around its neck. The horse's lips brushed his arm, gently as human fingers, and softer. Gird reached up to a tangle of yellow-gray mane that felt surprisingly silky. The horse yanked its head up, and Gird came to his feet. Everyone was watching him, silently. He looked at them, shrugged, and stroked the horse's neck. It stretched its head out, shook it sideways, and gave an elaborate yawn, showing a mouthful of heavy, slightly yellow teeth. Gird stroked its shoulder and barrel. He loved the feel of a healthy animal, and although this one had looked dirty from a distance, the coat felt sleek and clean under his hands. It must be someone's stray.

He found himself atop the horse bareback, holding the rope of an improvised halter, hardly aware of the sequence that put him there. The horse had sidled this way and backed that way until Gird had had to climb on a rock to keep stroking that sleek coat; he had wanted to keep stroking it. Then in some way the horse had indicated an itch, a flybite, on the opposite shoulder, and Gird had leaned across to scratch it, and there was a fly biting lower down, and he had leaned farther—and found himself lying belly-down across the horse's back. It had stood motionless until he made the obvious move of throwing a leg over.

It was much easier to see, from up here. He could see all the cohort beside him, and the ones ahead and behind. He could imagine how much easier this would make guiding a battle. But he had never imagined the effect of horseback riding on the unaccustomed rider. At first he was tense, then he relaxed and enjoyed it, and then—all too soon—his muscles and tendons began to complain. About midafternoon, he couldn't stand any more of it, and managed to slide off—which was harder than he'd supposed. His feet burned and tingled unpleasantly, until he walked the blood back out of them. The horse followed Gird as if he were tied, although Gird had forgotten to take hold of the rope.

He climbed on again the next morning. He was stiff in places he had never been stiff, but the horse had found another rock to stand beside. His legs loosened up quickly; he found the rocking motion pleasant. Something about the feel of the gray horse between his legs gave him confidence. He wondered if this was what the horse nomads felt, what made them raiders and not farmers. Of course, they rode real horses, war horses, and not gentle old carthorses. The back under him heaved a little, and Gird grabbed for the mane. Surely the horse had not heard his thought, and taken insult! He tried to think of something complimentary, just in case, and was rewarded with a relaxed back and springy walk.

His original intent, in coming north again, was to intercept the king's western movement at a site where the ground gave him advantage. The king, however, had recognized that same situation, and put his army to a forced march to intercept Gird's. Unluckily for Gird, the runners who would have brought him this information were captured. If he had not chosen to ride, for the first time, out beyond his scouts, he would have led them into a trap. As it was, the gray horse stopped with a snort, planting its feet firmly in the road, and refused to budge. When Gird tried to swing off, it whirled, nearly unseating him, and then started smartly back down the trail at his first experience of a trot. He clung to the mane desperately, afraid to fall at that speed; when it slowed, where his forward scouts were, they had taken that return as an alarm.

"I don't know," Gird said, glad to slide down now that the horse was standing still. It looked past him back up the trail, and snorted. "It saw something it didn't like; animals can smell and hear better than we can."

His scouts slid forward, to reappear not long after with word of a large enemy force lying right across the route Gird had planned to take. Gird looked at his maps again. Any other route to the same ground would take them several more days, and the enemy might easily trace them and reposition themselves. Straight ahead he might get a slight advantage from a slope, but he'd have to engage in woods where the pikes were far less handy than swords. He frowned. Back down their trace a half-day or so was a passable field, a large natural meadow, backed by a steep forested ridge behind several lower hills. They had come the long way through it, to avoid the hills, but he could hide several cohorts back there.

It was the best he could do, and it would do only if the enemy decided to come after them; they could not sit for long without starving. He gave his orders, and then had someone give him a leg back up onto the horse. Old worn-out horse it might be, but it had saved him, and maybe the war. He stroked its neck, as he waited for the last cohort to reverse. Strange that an old carthorse should be so willing to carry an untrained rider, and so gently, but he would be foolish to question such good fortune. The horse heaved a huge sigh, and butted his foot with its soft nose. Gird scratched its withers, and his own head, contented for the moment.

His army reversed and marched back down its trace without attracting immediate mounted pursuit—the only kind Gird feared. They were on his new-chosen field a little after midday. It was not as good as he remembered: there were bramble patches near a small creek, and muddy areas under the fresh green grass. But such as it was, he had no choice. He moved his army back, under the edge of the trees, to encamp, sent his scouts well out, and set to work to improve the site as best he could. By nightfall, he had word that the enemy was coming, on more than one trail. The largest group followed his own trace, but another was moving in from the northeast, on one of the alternate trails. So, he thought. He had been right—no escape that way, even if he'd tried it.

Chapter Thirty

In the predawn stillness, he could hear a single bird calling from far away, high on the hill's slope. His army slept. As quietly as he could, Gird made his way past the banked firepits, past the line of sentries, to whom he nodded without speaking, and started up the hill. Here, beyond the camp, he walked through layers of fresh summer scents, the night smells of open country. A patch of pale tiroc flowers poured out heavy sweetness; in the hot daytime sun, they hardly had an odor. Down from the heights came a waft of cedar, a sharp bite of wild thyme. A goat had brushed against the bushes here; its sharp pungency banished the other smells for a moment, until he'd climbed past it.

Ahead, the hill was dark against the early dawn glow. Something rustled in the bushes, a frantic frightened scurry as some small animal fled. The bird called again, closer now. It was no bird he knew, with that exquisite rippling flow of music. Gird looked back. Light had seeped into the upper sky, and far to the west the land began to show its shape, the hilltops their color. He climbed on, very aware of the smells and sounds, the feel of the cool air on his bare arms, the texture of the leaves that brushed against him, the feel of the stone or soil beneath his feet.

He came to the hilltop sooner than he expected. Behind, below, the ragged and smelly army lay hidden in shadow. He heard a distant clatter of pots, and wondered what the cooks would find to put in them. More roots and herbs, no doubt, and they still had two sacks of meal. Not much for a whole army. But morning hunger had been part of his life from childhood; farmers were always out working at dawn. He had this brief, private moment before the day's cares.

Far over the rim of the world, the sun rose up, the light by which truth could be seen, as Esea's priest had named it. Against the low slanting light, Gird saw the myriad furred tufts of grass, rose-gold, forming a dancing curtain of rose, veiling the sun's impossible brilliance, transmuting it to grace and delicacy. He stood bemused, as he had once long ago on his farm, on that silver starlit evening. All was gold now, gold and rose together, shifting veils softening piercing brilliance; the scent of it rose up around him, a column of rose-gold incense. He had just time to think *This is a vision,* when the hill slipped out from under him and he hung suspended in gold and rose draperies. Now he looked west again, over the land new-lit by the sun, where soft gold light filled the valleys like wine, and a harder radiance chiseled the hilltops into clean, unblurred beauty. Despite the haze of gold, he could see far, to the distant mountains on the edge of Finaarenis. He had dreamed of them as cold, gray, uncaring crags, but now they stood serene and gracious, great castles awaiting their lords. He seemed to see within them, to the arched and echoing halls where the rockfolk harped and sang and crafted jewels and gold into treasures worthy of such castles. Now he looked north, across the light, to the great river and beyond, seeing at a glance all its laughing little tributaries, and the great loom of the moors and the broad steppes.

There the horse nomads roamed, with bright embroidery on their boots, narrow streamers blowing from poles by their tents, herds of shining horses. Above them romped the Windsteed, flaunting a cloudy tail, and broad across the grassland the Mare of Plenty ranged on tireless hooves. Behind her, grass sprang tall and green, and her hoofprints filled with clear water.

He would have been frightened if it had been possible; he retained enough of his wit to know that. But it was not possible. He lay quiet in the gold and rosy veils, looking where he was bid, seeing the land as it was, as the gods saw it, as it could be: in the broad light of day, peaceful villages of farmers, orchards restored and fields once more fertile. Flocks of sheep on the hillsides, herds of cattle in river meadows. A market fair, in some town that might be built where a burnt village had been, with fair measures given, and fair weights enforced. Children splashing in a shallow ford, a woman riding a horse, a bright helm on her head, cottages with tight roofs and mended walls, rows of bright flowers. The vision pierced his heart, brought scalding tears to his eyes. This—he had almost forgotten—this was what he wanted, not an obedient army, helpful farmers, even victory in battle, but this peace, this plenty, this justice.

With the tears came his release from the dream. He felt himself falling, but slowly, like goosedown or a dandelion tuft; felt gentle arms around him; heard a murmuring voice he could not quite follow. Flower petals drummed feathersoft on his bare arms, against his face, drying his tears, and when he came to himself, he was standing in a drift as white as snow in the broad morning sun. He reached his arms into the cool petals, lifted them, buried his face in them. Alyanya's sign, it had to be—but beneath the fragrance was a faint bitter tang of cold wet earth in autumn. Promise and warning, then, and he but a peasant. Laughter rang about him, so joyous that he smiled before he realized the sound had been within him.

"Dammit!" he burst out, unthinking. "You won't ever make anything simple!"

And the voice that answered him then was cold, clean and precise as starlight.

—No. I did not make anything simple.—

Gird's knees gave way, and he fell into the flowers. *That* was not Alyanya, by any reckoning, and he could not pretend to himself not to know who it was. *Ask for a word from the gods*, he thought crazily, *and beware*—

But the knowledge he had asked for without really wanting it was pouring into his head, overfilling it as if someone stuffed a sack with wool.

Promise: it was possible to win that peace for his people.

Warning: it was not *his* peace.

His fault? he wondered.

No answer, only certainty. All the symbols the priest had taught him, all the gnomes had shared of their lore, flickered through his mind as quickly as the counters on a trader's account board, a rapid clicking that ended with the crashing finality of stone falling onto stone. As it was now, as reality lay, that peace was possible, but he was forfeit.

He had thought he did not care, until he knew it was certain. Now, in a silence he realized was more than normal, he lay face down in Alyanya's flowers and had leisure to consider if he meant in truth what he had said so often. I would give my life, he'd said. I will risk, he'd said. I could be killed as easy as you, he'd said to frightened yeomen.

But that had been *risk;* the spear might thrust in his gut, or not. The sword might slice another's neck. So far it always had been someone else, and he knew now he'd half-expected it always would be.

Now . . . *certainly* die? Never enjoy that peace? Never sit with his grandchildren around him, telling his tales of the old days?

He was suspended again, this time in the vast caverns of his own mind: cold, darkness, fear beneath him, and nothing at all above. If he fell *now* nothing would slow his fall; he would not land in Alyanya's flowers. His own mind—he knew it was that, and no gods' gift of vision—painted all too vividly a picture of the land after his fall. No peace, but the ravages of the magelords, the scavenging of brigands. More dead bodies bloated in the fields for crows to pick clean; babies and children and young and old: he saw all their faces. Innocent beasts, cows and horses and sheep, lame and wounded, wandering prey for folokai and wolves. And he saw his own death then, the death of an old man, bald and feeble, when he could no longer forage from his hideout in distant caves: he fell to folokai, and the crows followed.

Death either way, then. *It should be easy,* he told himself fiercely, *to buy that peace with an early death.* It was not easy. On his tongue he tasted the ale he would not drink, the roast he would not eat, and in his hands he felt the warm bodies of the children— o, most bitter!—he would never hold. *It is not easy!* he screamed silently into silence. His own mind replied tartly that nothing was easy, nor ever had been—and he opened his eyes and blinked against the snowy petals.

It was not easy, but he had done other things that were not easy. He had seen his mother die, and Mali that he loved, and his daughter near death at his feet. He had seen the best friend of his youth trampled under the lords' horses; he had seen wells poisoned and fields burnt barren. He took a deep breath, holding all these things in his mind, all the pain he could remember, all the love he'd had for family and beasts and trees and land—love that no one else ever knew, because he could not speak it. He tossed it high, with his hope for life. And felt it taken, a vast weight he had not known he carried.

The petals vanished, though he could feel their softness yet, and their perfume eased his breathing. He was all alone on the hilltop, though he heard someone crashing through the bushes on the upward trail.

"Gird! Marshal-general!" One of the newer yeomen, to whom that title came naturally. Gird took a breath, and hoped his face did not show all that had happened.

"What?" he called back, hearing in his voice a curious combination of irritation and joy.

"They're coming! They're already out of the wood!"

Gird swung to look north, and they certainly were. Horsemen first, the low sun winking on polished armor and bit chains, gleaming on the horses themselves, gilding the colors of banners and streamers and bright clothing. Some of those were surely magelords. Behind them, shadowy in the dust already beginning to rise at the edge of the wood, were the foot soldiers, rank after rank. His mouth dried. How many hundreds did they have? He had thought he had more—one thousand, two thousands, three. . . . The horsemen halted just far enough out on the meadow to let the infantry deploy behind them. Gird searched the wood on the far slope for the archers they would surely have sense enough to send out in a flanking movement. His own archers were supposed to be up on the end of the ridge, guarding against archers getting into his rear. He hoped they were alert. He had no fear of the horses or foot soldiers getting back there; the ridge behind him to the south was safe as a wall.

Below him, he heard his own army coming into order. He started down the hill, hoping the enemy had not spotted him atop the hill. He put his hand up to his hair, thankful that he hadn't put on his salvaged helmet yet.

At the foot of the hill, the gray carthorse stood as if it were waiting for him. Someone had found a saddle for it, and a bridle. Even so, the horse had positioned itself beside a rock. Gird climbed on, wondering even as he did why he found it so natural that the horse was making itself useful. Cob came running up with his helmet, and offered a sword. Gird shook his head. He hadn't learned to use a sword yet, and a battle was no time to try something new. The horse was new enough.

His cohorts had formed; he rode past them, checking with each marshal. The faces blurred in his eyes; his mouth found the right names by some instinct, but only Rahi's stood out distinctly. She gave him her broad smile, and the gray horse bobbed its head. Rahi's cohort laughed. He wanted to tell her, and no one else, what the god had told him, but he could not. That kind of knowledge had to be borne alone. He noticed, without really thinking about it, that over half of his yeomen had managed to find a blue shirt to wear; it was beginning to look like a uniform.

For a time it seemed that the enemy might simply stand on the far side of the field and stare at them, but after a time they moved forward. On the north, the broad-topped wooded ridge sloped directly into the meadow, but on the south, Gird's side, three distinct low hills lay between the sharp southern ridge and the more level grass, with the sluggish creek running east to west along it.

Gird had done what he could in the limited time he had to make this ground as favorable as possible. He had archers on the north face of all three hills, as well as the blunt end of the southern ridge. He had had pits dug, in the mucky ground near the creek, lightly covered with wattle and strewn with grass. This would, he hoped, make both cavalry and foot charges harder, and prevent easy flanking of his troop. His main force was arrayed before and between the two more eastern hills; the western hill seemed undefended, but in addition to archers had several natural hazards. Against the lords' reputed magicks, he had no defense but Arranha's comment that a mage could not counter what he did not expect. He hoped they would not expect the small, doomed, but very eager group that he had left well hidden on the south face of that north slope, directly in the enemy's rear, with orders to stay hidden until the lords were busy with their magic elsewhere.

Now the king's army moved; for the first time, Gird saw the royal standard that he had heard about, a great banner that barely moved in the morning breeze, then suddenly floated out, showing its device. Gird had been told it was a seadragon; by himself he would have thought it was a snake with a fish's tail. Each of the

lords with the king had his own banner, his or her own colors
repeated in the uniforms of the soldiers—and, if the gnomes were
right, his or her own separate battle plan. That was supposed to
be another advantage to his side. They looked pretty enough, like
the models the gnomes had shown him: one hundred all in yellow
and green, then two hundreds in blue and gold, then a block of
orange, and a block of green and blue. Gird assumed that the lords
were in the rear, those mounted figures in brilliant colors that
seemed to glow with their own light. Even as he watched, he saw
bright-striped tents go up, servants hanging on the lines. Smoke
rose from cookfires newly lit. For some reason, that show of confidence infuriated Gird. *Win it before you celebrate it,* he told
them silently.

The cavalry screen drew aside on either flank, and the foot soldiers advanced. Most of them still carried sword and shield; some
units had pikes; a few had long spears. Gird frowned; those could
cause him a lot of trouble. But watching them advance, he realized
that they were not accustomed to that extra length. Evidently someone had decided to make a weapon that would outreach his pikes,
but the men carrying them had not had enough drill. Behind the
swordsmen and pikemen came the archers. Over the winter, Gird
had tried many versions of a shield that would stop arrows but be
light enough to carry, and easily dropped when both arms were
needed for the pike. Nothing worked perfectly. His foremost
cohorts had small wooden shields that might protect their faces
from arrows near their utmost range, but most trusted to their
stolen—no, salvaged—helmets and bits of body armor.

The first enemy flights of arrows went up; Gird's marshals
shouted their warnings, and all but the stupidest looked down. The
enemy made a rush forward, discovering a moment too late the
pits Gird's army had dug. These were not deep enough or large
enough to keep the enemy back, but they slowed the rush just as
the archers, following it, came within range of Gird's archers.

More angry than hurt, the enemy foot soldiers floundered
through the mud, hauled themselves out of the pits and flung themselves on at Gird's unmoving cohorts. The enemy lines were no
longer lines, and behind them their own archers were falling to
Gird's. They did not care; they looked, to Gird on his old gray
horse, like any young men who have made fools of themselves in
public. Their officers, bellowing at them from the rear, didn't seem
to have much effect; a second and third line staggered into the
pits, tried to jump across and failed, and fought their way out, to
storm up the gentle slope toward Gird's cohorts.

The marshals watched Gird; he watched the straggling but furious advance. Those few seconds seemed to stretch endlessly, as if he had time to notice the expression on every face, whether the oncoming eyes were blue or grey or brown. Then the first ones reached the mark he had placed, and he dropped his hand, with the long blue streamer that served as their banner.

His cohorts moved. One step, two: cautious, controlled, their formations precise, he thought smugly, as any gnome's. Where the king's soldiers had expected last year's sharpened wood stakes, they met instead the steel pike heads that Marrakai gold had bought. The first died quickly, almost easily, a flick of the pike it seemed, from where Gird sat on the gray horse. He knew better, from having been there himself. Then the ragged lines caught up with each other, and the slaughter began.

Pikes outreach swords, but swordsmen and axemen can form a shield wall hard for pikes to breach, if all are brave. Whether it was courage, or the kind of magicks Gird had seen at work at Blackbone Hill, the soldiers of the king were brave. At first Gird's cohorts advanced, step by step, down that gentle slope, pushing the king's men back into the trampled mud and treacherous pits. Then the king's cavalry swept east, toward Gird's right flank, and back down the near side of the creek, avoiding the pits he'd dug at that end of the meadow.

This was not what he'd hoped they would do. He had hoped they'd be seduced by the apparent gap on his left flank, between that and the westmost hill. It should have looked like an easy way to get right round behind him. But apparently they'd been looking for something more quick than easy. And if he didn't do something—quickly—they'd be on attacking his flank with only the archers uphill to hinder them.

The gray horse seemed to understand this almost as quickly as Gird; he was picking his way neatly but rapidly across the gap between the center and the eastmost hill without jolting his rider at all. Gird looked around him. There—that cluster of bright colors up under the trees must be the lords and the king. So far they'd done nothing magical, but he had no doubt they would. And there, across the creek and coming his way, were the enemy cavalry.

Gird bellowed loud enough that the gray horse flattened his ears; the nearest cohort marshals turned, and caught his signal, then saw the rushing horses. He would have wheeled the gray horse around, but the gray horse leaped onward, straight at the oncoming cavalry. Gird hauled on the reins, to no avail.

"I know I said it would be nice to slow them down, but we

can't—one horse—one rider—" Was this to be his destined death, charging uselessly an entire wing of cavalry? But they were almost on them; Gird shrugged, and swung the pole his blue banner was tied to.

Pole and rag took one horse in the face; Gird nearly lost the pole, and his seat, but managed to keep both, and duck a swipe from a curved blade. The gray horse swerved under him; he grabbed for mane and hung on. All around were horses, most of them swerving aside and one frankly running backwards before it slipped and fell, rolling on its rider.

Then they were in the clear, Gird with his banner and the gray horse with a disgustingly smug cock to its ears.

"I want to go back," Gird said between his teeth, as if the horse were a recalcitrant child. It shook its head, blew a long rattling snort, and picked up an easy lope back toward the battle. He saw a dozen or more horses down, some with arrows in them. He saw the back of the enemy cavalry, trying to charge again and again into two of his cohorts of pikes. The armor on the horses, heavy padded canvas, would have protected them from sword-strokes of other mounted fighters—not from pikemen on foot. Gird wondered if they realized that, or simply never thought of it. He felt the gray horse tense under him, and braced himself for whatever it might do.

What it did was outflank the enemy cavalry, working its way up and over the knee of the eastmost hill without putting a hoof wrong, and return Gird to his observation post on the central hill. From here he could see that that particular cavalry sortie would be thrown back without much danger. His own center was not advancing now, holding place to support the right flank under pressure, but that did not concern him. More worrying, some of that bright-clad group of nobles who had been back under the trees were moving forward. Several of them, clustered together, raised their arms.

He had not expected the well to spout water, the year before, and he did not expect the storm that gathered like a boil atop the ridge behind him, and spat lightning into the trees. Wind rushed irrationally *down* the slope, bringing fire and smoke with it. Shrill screams rose from both sides, louder from Gird's camp followers, who found themselves caught between a forest fire and a battle. Then the wind stilled, as suddenly as it had started, and Gird saw that the little group of mages had fallen to the ground. Behind him, the fires still burned, but less fiercely, and the new wind direction took the smoke and flame upslope, away from him.

His eyes still stung and watered; he could barely see across the meadow to the king's party. Had it been his hidden archers who killed those nobles, or someone else? The momentary lull caused by the onrushing fire had given way to renewed din of battle. His cohorts were inching forward again, by the half-step now, the wounded shifting back as they had practiced, the fallen trodden underfoot. He could do nothing about that, not yet.

The enemy spearmen had finally made it to the front of their lines; they proved as clumsy as Gird had hoped.

Even so, they made rents in the cohort they faced, and it could not advance. For hours, it seemed almost for days, the two armies were knotted in battle. Their lines staggered back and forth, gaining and losing an armlength, a footpace. The noise was beyond anything Gird had imagined, so loud that individual screams and blows merged into a hideous roar.

He concentrated his attention on the details of it, sending his own voice above the rest when necessary. The enemy's reserve archers, mounted, tried a sweep past his left wing. This was the maneuver he'd been looking for: would they support it? At least half the remaining enemy cavalry, and—yes—behind the screen of battle, a cohort or two of infantry. They thought the west hill empty, available; Gird smiled to himself. He might be only a stupid peasant, but he had learned a few things. That trap would spring itself, but he had to set the main one now.

Once before, the arrival of his camp-followers bearing almost useless "weapons" had convinced an enemy that he had vast reserves. The lords had been telling themselves that the peasants were all rebels at heart; they had only to count to know how many peasants were on their own lands, and fear the worst. Gird had taken the chance that the king and his advisors would follow the trails they had followed through the ridges, trails where horses and pack animals could go, where armies could march without fighting their way through prickly undergrowth. Gird marched that way where he could, and he knew they had trailed him back to this meadow. So they would think that what they saw, and what might be behind the little hills, was the worst of what they faced. That was, in fact, the truth, but would they believe the truth when a pretense fit their deepest fears?

He rode the gray horse a little up the slope, above the dust of the battle, to where he had a clear view across the meadow to that forested ridge behind the king. The king would have scouts atop it, for a certainty —if his people had not found them yet. But that would do him no good. Gird waved the pole with its long blue streamer twice. An arrow whirred past his head as the horse neatly sidestepped. Evidently some archers had decided he was worth hitting—well, he'd told his own to take out archers first, and anyone on horseback next.

Shrill yips from the western hill told him that the first part of his plan was working. His archers were falling back, coming around the slope into the hollow between the two hills—not a deep hollow, but one with its own peculiarities. The enemy archers should be making for the hilltop; he thought the cavalry would swing around, trying to take him in the rear, and so came the signal he had been waiting for.

It was amazing how many pits five thousand yeomen could dig in less than a day. Gird thought they could have dug a trench all across the meadow, but trenches could be jumped, and pits cleverly placed where horses must go between rocks of a rockfall—pits just too wide to jump easily—are a most effective cavalry trap. Thanks to the land and the Lady, he thought piously, for that fortuitously placed rockfall between the hill and the ridge behind it, where many horsemen could get into trouble out of sight of the rest of their army. His archers, having slipped around the hill to the rockfall, were busy; the enemy archers above them, on the hilltop, found themselves unable to see what was going on. Those that tried to come down the south face of the hill to support the cavalry found the scour of the rockfall dangerous in more than one way. The others could—and did—let fly into the backs of the cohorts Gird had between the west and the central hill. He had anticipated this; those cohorts gave way, bending back around the hill; the archers found themselves having to shoot downhill into a confused mass of their own and Gird's troops.

One unwary captain in the king's forces saw that withdrawal as weakening, and urged his own cohorts on to flank those retreating. Gird smiled grimly. His left flank was now anchored by a wall of rock three men high—out of sight of that rash captain, up the little creek that looked so innocent. His troops stood on rock ledges, while their opponents were in the creek, or the mud on its other side. When they reached what they thought was his flank, they would find themselves standing on the far side of a pool of deep water, with no way out but the way they had come in. His archers would find them easy targets.

Meanwhile, the knot of bright-clad nobles across the field was moving again—perhaps it been only exhaustion that felled them. Gird squinted; he was sure he saw someone still on the ground. Out of the trees across from him came yet more cohorts of infantry, more squadrons of cavalry, and some—he squinted, shook his head, and looked again—some did not look human. Magicks, he told himself firmly. It's only magicks. Masks and costumes and fancy ways of frightening people into doing what you want. He wished he knew if the king's whole reserve was committed now.

Below him, the main forces contended as they had all morning, in a heaving, sweating, bloody, snarling mass. If it comes to plain fighting, he had told his marshals, if it comes to simple pounding each other, we win: we'll pound harder, and take more pounding. The king's army now outnumbered his in the center, but his center had not given back at all. They leaned into their pikes with every thrust, grunting with the effort.

Then the king's new reserves hit the back of his force, giving it that extra weight—man against man, those in front were forced forward by that pressure, onto the waiting pikes. They died, had to be shaken from the pikes, and others were already there, already being killed—and again, and again. Gird saw the shiver in his ranks, the realization that something new had entered. The marshals looked aside, trying to find Gird; he caught their eyes and waved with his free hand. Then he took the long pole and signalled his last reserve, across the meadow and up on the ridge behind the king's camp.

It seemed to take forever for that reserve to appear; he had told them to hide neither on the ridgetop nor near the bottom. In the meantime, his center sagged backward, and the enemy, heartened, drove forward with renewed energy. Gird had hardly time to see the first of his reserves clear the trees, yelling their heads off and sprinting downhill toward the enemy rear, before he was down in the thick of his own battle, supporting the center.

Fighting on horseback was completely different, he found. He had dropped the banner-pole, no longer needed—from here they would fight to the death, win or lose; he had no more decisions to make—and pulled his hauk from his belt. It was good for bashing heads, and bashing heads from above worked as well as when he was afoot. For one moment he thought of Amisi, and shoved the thought aside.

Later, when he heard it in songs, the battle of Greenfields (as the meadow became known) sounded much tidier than it had been in reality. The songs didn't mention the several times he was knocked off the horse, and remounted by some helpful soldier, or the blow to his knee that had him limping for a quarter year, or the near-rout when the enemy's last cohort of reserves turned out to be masked magelords with their power in hand. The songs certainly did not mention that long and miserable night after the battle, with the forest fire still burning its way south, or the cries of the wounded that never ceased. And somehow in the songs, that gray horse turned white. Gird was sure he had not aged that much in one day.

He remembered stumping through what had been the enemy's camp, swarming now with squads of his own yeomen gathering up supplies and weapons. The king's tent had gone up first, larger than many houses Gird had seen, with interior rooms walled in fluttering embroidered panels. He had had musicians with him (two had been killed, almost accidentally, when Gird's reserves tore through the camp; the others had been found crouched around their instruments), and a man who painted pictures on lengths of fabric. He had started a picture of the king, victorious, returning with Gird's head, but offered to change the faces for only ten gold pieces. Gird shook his head, and wondered what kind of king would take musicians and painters to battle.

The king was dead. He did not look much like Selamis, but fathers and sons did not have to look alike. He had been a tall man, dark haired as many magelords were, and in death his eyes had only the dull color of a fish found dead on the shore. Gird had found Sier Segrahlin's body, spiked with arrows from behind; he felt no guilt at that, but wished he could have talked to that brown man. They had almost understood each other, across a gulf no one else wanted to bridge. He still wondered, occasionally, if the sier had charmed him that night.

The songs listed the dead magelords, as if to remind the listener that these were all real. Gird did not even look at all of them; he had seen bodies enough. They had killed the wounded as quickly and painlessly as they could; they had killed all the magelords they captured; they dared not do less. At least there were no children with them.

He did not understand why he was still alive; his vision of the morning had been so clear, so certain. He felt curiously suspended, as he had after the Norwalk Sheepfolds, unable to rejoice in the same way as the others, though he felt a deep contentment. So many had died, and he had not, yet he had been sure he would— he had been almost *promised* he would. Nor had Rahi died, or Pidi; he found them both alive, marked but certainly not mortally wounded. But when he touched them he felt no more and no less than he felt for any of his yeomen: they were all his children, in some way he could not define.

He remembered coming back to his own encampment, holding

the wounded and dying, speaking what comfort he could, until he fell asleep and woke to find that someone had covered him with a stolen piece of the king's tent. All that day and the next, as the crows and flies fought with them, he tried to bring order and restore health to that trampled and discolored ground. "Bury them all," he said, "Or burn them—even the magelords, yes: we had the gods' gift of victory, we owe them respect."

The songs began that first night, with the talk around the fires of those who could talk, and by the next night a few were trying to fit words to familiar tunes. The dead king's surviving musicians were glad to help. Gird was more than a little amused that the first version he heard of what became "Gird at Greenfields" was set to "The Thief's Lament"—the very song with which he had been taunted for cowardice.

PART IV

Chapter Thirty-one

Greenfields broke the king's power, and gave Gird control of the main grain-growing regions of Finaarenis. But it was not the end of the war. Those lords who had not joined the king's army, for whatever reason, were now sure destruction loomed. Some walled themselves in Finyatha; others fled toward Tsaia. Heirs of lords killed at Greenfields squabbled over inheritances now in jeopardy; rich merchants, who assumed a peasant government would have no desire or need for fine goods, appealed to the remaining lords for help.

Gird knew all this, and much of it he had anticipated, but his first problem was securing the year's limited harvest. Where there were no lords, there might be brigands. He split his army into sections, put each under a high marshal, and sent them to settle the countryside. He himself rode for the north, crossing the Honnorgat for the first time in his life on the gray horse, which seemed less like a broken-down carthorse every day. He could stay on at a trot now, although he preferred the swinging canter. Most of his marshals had caught a horse and learned to stay on it, as well. It made supervising a march or a movement much easier, and messages could pass far more quickly. Feeding the beasts was another worry, but men could not eat grass, and horses could. In summer, at least, they could afford a few horses.

Rumors of the king's defeat spread even faster than Gird expected. In the north, he and his column found mostly deserted, looted manor houses, and celebrating peasants. Few of his recruits had come from the north—in fact he had trouble understanding their speech—but they seemed genuinely pleased with his success. He wondered if the quickly-established bartons in each village would ever amount to anything, and prayed that war would not test them.

Finyatha offered a different problem. Largest and richest city of the north, the seat of the Finaarenisian kings, it hung just out of his reach like a tempting plum. Most of its people were common folk, as everywhere, but at the moment it swarmed with magelord refugees. He had no knowledge of siegecraft; common sense told

him that assaulting those walls with pikemen would do no good—
a much smaller force on the walls could defend it. He thought of
trying to divert the river, but remembering Segrahlin's tricks with
water decided that some mage inside could simply call water into
any well he wanted. In the end, he left it alone, and like an overripe
plum, it fell on its own. One party of magelords tried to escape
along the River Road to Tsaia; most of those fell to raiding parties,
Gird's or brigands. The rest were too weak to keep control of the
city. When the disruption inside reached the gates, and the fighting
erupted into the fields outside, Gird's column—which had been
waiting at a distance—marched in with little difficulty, to the apparent delight of all.

The gray horse brought Gird into those stone streets as if carrying a king; cheers racketed off the walls, and the flowers of summer fell on his shoulders, Alyanya's blessing. Then the horse
pranced into the courtyard before a towering stone structure that
seemed to spring, like trees, from the roots of the world itself, and
reach skyward with every stretched finger. Between its arches, great
windows had stood; they were shattered now, glittering fragments
crunched beneath the horse's hoofs. A few pieces still clung to
their frames, reflecting brightness against the cool darkness inside.
The horse knelt; Gird stepped off and looked around. It was a hot
day, blue-skied, and the courtyard had blue shadows under every
ledge of gray stone. The very air shimmered; he blinked. Was it
the air, or his eyes?

Arranha stood on the steps, between splintered doors. Gird
would have been surprised, but could not quite feel it. "This was
Esea's High Hall," Arranha said, as if he were a guide. "It became
something else, something worse, and Esea's blessing was withdrawn." He shook his head. "I warned them, but they thought
they could extract more power by bringing darkness and light so
close together."

Gird could not follow this, but he did follow Arranha into the
partly ruined building. It soared overhead, high arches of stone,
one after another rising from fluted pillars, making a space reminiscent of a great forest. At the far end, where a circular window had
been, sunlight fired the lower arc to a silver crescent. Gird felt
hairs rise on the back of his neck. He swallowed.

"You must see this," Arranha was saying, "because you must
decide if the gods demand this building be torn down. I myself
would hate to see that; it's the most beautiful in the north, to
my eyes. But the people know what went on here; you must see
for yourself."

What he had to see was evidence enough that the magelords had lost all sense of right and wrong. Arranha tried to explain what they thought they were doing; to Gird, who had never sailed a ship, did not know a lodestone from any cobble in the river, who did not *care* about the theory behind it, it was simply disgusting and grotesque. An excuse, as he saw it, for some to bully others, to excuse their own cruelty on religious grounds. Here were the same symbols he had found in that count's dungeon: the barbed chain, the masks with horns and spikes, painted to terrify, the instruments whose only purpose was pain. The place Arranha had led him to stank of old blood, death, and fear. He heard a nauseated gulp beside him, and turned to see Selamis at his side; he had followed Gird, as he often did, without speaking or asking permission.

"Don't make it worse," Gird said. "Go spew outside if you must. But this is your *real* inheritance from your father." The younger man made it to the outside before he threw up. When he came back—to Gird's surprise—he looked grim but in some way satisfied.

Gird came back out to find a crowd of those who had suffered under the old, and wanted his justice. His, he thought. The blue summer sky pressed down on him. Another than Alyanya had given him that victory; what did *he* want here? Justice, and all that came with it. The Hall?

The evil, he told them, is not in the stones, but in those who did wrong. Justice will rule here, the High Lord who judges all things rightly. He himself went to the crypt under Esea's altar and scrubbed it until it stank no more of all that had happened in it. He brought in the holy herbs for the dead, and lay them reverently on the floor. He came up to find the crowd still standing, and scolded them as if they had been his yeomen for years. Cleaning before building, he said, waving his arms at the shattered glass in the courtyard.

With Finyatha fallen, the other lords in Finaarenis fled to Tsaia, where the Tsaian king gathered an army to retake that land and save his own. Gird ignored that for the present. They had not time before winter to mount a campaign; the Marrakai told him all he needed to know of preparations. He himself was back in Bright-water before snow fell, with Selamis and Arranha, to plan for the coming year.

Despite the destruction of farming villages and fields, they had more food than the year before. The lords' granges had held a surprising amount; some had burned, but more had been saved. Many other goods were found in more abundance, though the distribution was not as even as Gird would have liked. But he did not interfere with anything but gross injustice. If these people were to help make their own fair laws, they would have to start by making some mistakes.

In spring, the fighting spread eastward into Tsaia. Gird had not realized how far the barton organizations spread—not only in Marrakai lands, but beyond. Barton after barton rose, combined with its neighbors, and elected a marshal: most were competent. The Tsaian royal army which had at first treated the very idea of a peasant army with contempt, even after the defeat in Finaarenis, fell back again and again. Gird did not want his Finaarenisian troops to invade Tsaia: they had fought for their own freedom, in defense of their own homes and families. That much he had felt confident— that Alyanya, Lady of Peace though she be, could understand and condone. Invading someone else's land, even for the best reasons, did not seem the same.

But Ivis, his high marshal in the east, had no such worries. Bartons were bartons; yeomen were yeomen; in any fight between peasants and lords, he wanted to be one of the leaders. Several cohorts volunteered to go to Tsaia with him. Gird, working hard on the new and—he hoped—simple legal system that would enable men to live in peace and deal fairly with one another, let him go with only a warning.

The legal code was, in fact, turning out to be much harder than he had expected. If he made the laws simple, they were so general that someone would claim not to know how that general principle could be applied in a particular instance. If he made the laws precisely applicable to common situations, someone would come up with an uncommon situation and claim to have found no guiding general principle. Gird tried to ignore the twinkle in Arranha's eyes, but finally admitted that he had been as naive in law as in war.

"Not that you won't end up with better law than we've had," said Selamis, quite seriously. "I think it's coming quite well."

"Some of it," growled Gird. It had been so simple to say that no one should beat up someone else, but now he was faced with honest merchants who had pursued thieves, and husbands convinced that they must beat their wives. And how much beating was beating? If a thief, once caught, kept fighting and had to be clouted before he would come along to a magistrate, was that a lawful or unlawful beating? Gird had insisted that the right to beat, within marriage, was both limited and equal for both sexes, but enforcement proved beyond his means. He felt at times like the father of a roomful of quarrelsome children, each of whom insisted that the other one started it.

Mercantile law proved equally tricky. Gird himself had gone around to three markets, taken a sample weighing stone, and found that no two were the same. He had one of the Brightwater masons cut one that matched the middleweight stone, had several more made to balance it, and replaced all the Brightwater weightstones with the standard. As the mason turned out more standards, Gird sent them to nearby markets, and insisted on their use. Prices danced up and down with the new stones. Gird assumed they would settle to something equivalent to those before, but his mental analogy—a chip on a bucketful of water, after shaking—did not satisfy him.

At least this year most of the arable land was under cultivation, and his noncombatant camp followers had returned to their homes or settled in partially deserted villages nearer by. Some of the bartons had dispersed as well, those that had villages to return to. Food should not be a problem, if the war stayed in Tsaia.

As the war receded eastward, the land that had been Finaarenis settled back into farming and trade. Some lands were blighted, some wells ruined; peasants shrugged and moved on. Some fields grew rich green grass over bones the crows had picked; those they avoided for another year. Gird moved from Brightwater to Grahlin, amused now to see how small a town it really was, that had seemed a city to him. Esea's Hall there had been burned, by the local inhabitants; they showed him the charred foundations proudly. He moved on east, to camp near the Tsaian border for a time.

Tsaia fell, at last, with blue-shirted farmers calling themselves "Gird's Yeomen" holding the king captive in his own dungeon. By the time word came to Gird, the king had escaped—and been found dead, of a magelady's anger. The two messages came on the same day, in Ivis's difficult script. Gird had tried to insist that his marshals, at least, must learn to read and write, but some had struggled as hard as he himself. He looked up from puzzling his way through it, having read it aloud, to meet Selamis's steady gaze.

"So," he said. "You are the last surviving magelord of rank, if you look at it the way you once did."

Selamis shook his head. "No, you know I don't."

"You feel no slightest flicker of desire for that throne? They say it is lovely." The throne of Finaarenis had been hacked to bits before Gird saw it.

"None. That was not my throne anyway, even if they wanted a king."

Gird drew a long breath. "I suspect they do; there's a different feel over there. Marrakai said their king was foolish, not cruel, and Marrakai is anything but a fool. It's a land that might take lords, if they were not mages."

Selamis looked down, pensive. "And where is a land that will take mages, if they are neither lords nor evil?"

"You think of yourself? You are safe with me."

"I think of others like myself. I cannot be the only bastard with magic in his blood, that will someday bring him death at the hands of those for whom all magic is evil. Even some of the pure blood— that lady you sent away, and her children."

Gird cocked his head. "If I had magic in my hands—if I could bring light, as you and Arranha can, whenever I needed a light to find my way; if I could light a fire with it, and never be cold—I would find that tempting. I would want to use it, first for myself, and then for those I loved, and then—I don't know, friend luap, as you would be called—"

"I wish you would just call me Luap, as the others are doing now—"

"And forget who you are? I wish I could. But I see no way to use magic well, to have that much power others cannot share, with no force to bar misuse."

Selamis waved at the papers Gird had been working over, another revision of the first part of his Code. "Your law?"

"Law without force behind it is but courtesy: for love or greed, men do things they should not, and law must have a hard hand to knock those hot heads into sense. For ordinary men, the law can serve, but what force can bind a mage?"

Selamis laughed aloud. "You did it yourself, Gird—a good knock to the head, as you say, and there I lay."

Gird laughed too. "Yes, an untrained mage. By the gods, d'you suppose if I'd felled that sier in the first place he would never have fought against us?" A ridiculous idea, but he was in the mood for it.

"Mages are children first, Gird—good parents can teach them law."

That sounded reasonable but he still had his doubts.

Then the Tsaian king's killer sought sanctuary in his camp. He wondered what she would say about his death. *Magedead,* the report had been, from someone who claimed to know what that meant. *A royal ring on his chest, and briars grown over him, in bloom even in this season.* The season was autumn. Late autumn.

"Bring her in, then," he said to Selamis-now-Luap.

"She's a mage," said Selamis. He meant more by that; Gird looked at him sharply.

"So?"

"She's one of them, but not one of them."

"One trying to do good, like the Marrakai?"

Luap looked away. "Not precisely. She had lived for years as a sheepherder."

"A *mageborn* lady?"

"So those who knew her say. In exile from the Tsaian court, for some wrangle there—"

"And she comes to us. Why? Did she say?"

"She says you must know how the king died, and hopes you will let her take service with us."

Gird stared at Luap. "Is she a fool, this magelady? Take service with *us?* Why not join Marrakai, if she's what you call a good mage?"

Luap shrugged. "I don't know. Will you see her?"

Gird shifted in his seat. "Oh, I'll see her."

She was tall, and even in armor conveyed a lithe lightness, a supple strength. It set Gird's teeth on edge. This one had never, he was sure, borne a child or suckled, had never so much as cared for a sister's child. Dark hair, braided snugly to fit beneath the helm she carried under her arm. Skin pale as ivory, flushed with rose at the cheeks, eyes used to command, bright and piercing. Before he could speak, she had spoken.

"The king is dead, and by my hand," she said. "If you do not allow murderers in your army, you will not want me. Otherwise—"

Gird felt that his head was full of apricot syrup: sweet, cloying, thick. He dragged his thoughts through it, just able to think *So this is what that charming is about!* Whatever had happened to the magicks of the other magelords, this one had full measure and running over. He struggled with his tongue, which wanted to say "Yes, lady," and dug his fingernails into his palms. It helped a little.

"I wish you'd stop that," he said, somewhat surprised at the even tone in which it came out.

Her mouth opened, and her cheeks paled. "You—are not afraid."

Humor tickled the inside of his mind, thinning the rich syrup of her magicks. "No, but I am getting angry. I don't like tricks."

"It's not a trick," she said. The pressure of her sweetness increased; it was hard to breathe.

"Trick," insisted Gird, through the honeyed mist over his eyes. "Same as luring a fly to honey, and swatting it. You might try honesty."

All at once, the magicks were gone, his mind clear, and the woman's face had gone all white around the mouth. *That* had gone home hard, though most of the magelords didn't seem to regard honesty as much.

"I did," she said between clenched teeth. Without the magicks, her face was older, not unlovely, but no longer a vision of beauty and terror. The dark hair had silver threads in it; the face had fine lines, a touch of weather. "I tried honesty, back then, and that brought me exile. And when I tried again, my duty to the king— ah, you would never understand!" She turned away from him, a gesture Gird read as consciously dramatic.

"You killed him," Gird said, deliberately flat across that drama.

"I killed him." She faced him again, and now he saw tears glittering in her eyes. Did she really care, or was it all an act? Women he knew cried noisily, red-faced, shoulders heaving, not one silver tear after another sliding down ivory cheeks. "I trusted him; he was my liege. And then—"

He was tired of her dramatics, and wholly out of sympathy with her kind of beauty. "Spit it out, then, lass, or we'll be here all day—" It was the tone he used on his own folk, the young ones, the frightened ones. On her it acted like a hot needle: she jumped and glared at him.

"He sent me away because I would not give up my weaponcraft and magery to be his queen, or so he told me then. I loved him dearly, and thought he loved me; there was no Rule requiring me to give up the sword as queen. I thought it his whim, and tried to talk him out of it, but he would not. I went into exile heartsore, like any girl whose betrothed turns her away. When he was imprisoned I knew it; he called in the way of our folk, though he had no need to call *me*. I would have come. When I took him from the prison where *your* folk had him, when I'd fought our way past the walls to safety, he told me he'd sent me away because of foretelling. Because he'd been told he'd need me someday. So he set conditions he was sure I would not understand nor agree to, to force me to refuse him, and then to leave the court. I had been honest those years, true to him and his memory: he had lied to make use of me. No love, no children, no freedom for my own life—"

It was the sort of thing the women talked about, back home, stories and gossips about unfaithful lovers, men cheating women of a promised marriage, women's vengeance on them. The men, Gird had to admit, had their own gossip, muttered into their mugs of ale, or half-whispered from man to man during shearing time, with guffaws and backslappings. Still, it sounded just as petty from this magelady as from any village girl; he was surprised she hadn't come up with something better.

"And for that injury you killed him?"

"For that, and for the king he was not. By Esea's Light, he had enough of the old Seeing to know what went on. Marrakai would have helped him stop it if he'd wanted to, but he could not be bothered."

"And from that act of—honesty—" Gird let the word trail out, and watched the blood flood her face. "You came here, and used your magicks on me. Why?"

"I thought you would not give me hearing, but kill me first. It was only to buy that much time—"

"And you found that time worth the cost?"

"It did you no harm," she said.

"You." Gird leveled both index fingers at her. "It cost *you*, mageborn lady. It cost you my trust."

"But—"

"NO!" He hammered the table with both fists. "No. You listen, mageborn, and then see if you want to dare our mercy. This you did, this use of magicks to charm me into listening, this is exactly what we despise. To keep yourself safe and put others in peril, to use weapons we cannot bear: this is unfair, unjust, and we will not let you do it."

"What do you know about justice?" she snapped.

"More than you. I would not use my strength against a child to take what was not mine—no, not if I hungered. I know what fair exchange is—"

"You've been talking to kapristi—"

"Aye, and listening, too. Weight for weight, work for work, honest labor for honest wages, no chalk in the flour and no water in the milk: that's fair exchange."

"And what did you exchange for this wisdom?" She was still scornful, ready to be very angry indeed.

"What they asked for it: when we gain the rule, to bind ourselves to respect their boundaries evermore. To allow gnomish merchants in our markets, at the same fair exchange humans use."

"*That* is all they asked?"

" 'Tis more than they got from you, all these years, so they said. They want a peaceful, ordered land nearby, one content with its borders; they want fair dealing." Someone came in then, an excuse to dismiss her. But he could not quite dismiss her from his mind. Her image clung there, disturbing. He wished she would leave; it was going to take all his influence to keep the others from attacking her. They might even think she had charmed him.

Several nights later he heard music from the far side of camp. Strings, plucked by skillful hands, and sweet breathy notes of something not quite like a shepherd's reed pipe. A voice, singing. He stiffened. He knew that voice, knew that honeygold sweetness. *Damn the woman,* he thought. *Her with her arts, she'll get us all killed.*

He chose a roundabout way to her; he could not have said why. Perhaps the sentries would be less alert, listening to the singing? But no. They challenged him, every one, with a briskness he found irritating rather than reassuring.

She sat well back from the fire, cradling the roundbellied stringed instrument and listening to another woman play a wooden pipe three handspans long. Gird watched her from the shadows. That long bony face, the hollows of the eyes—she had grace, he had to admit. Her hands moved, her fingers began touching the strings again, bringing out mellow notes from her instrument. They wove around the pipe-player's melody and tangled Gird's attempt to follow either instrument alone. One of the men began to sing, a horse-nomad song. "Fleet foot the wind calls, run from the following storm—" The magelady joined in, again that golden tone he mistrusted. Her voice ran a little above the tune, patterning with it, but in no mode Gird knew. He scowled, ready to be angry. All at once her eyes met his. Her voice slipped, and found itself again.

No. He would not listen to her. He would not look at her. She was betrayal, treachery: she had killed her own king. Magelady, born to deceit and mastery. He was himself: peasant: Mali's husband. *Mali's dead,* whispered some dark corner of his mind. Raheli's father, then. Broad and blunt, and liking it that way—he would not let himself be seduced by mere grace and golden voice.

She was surpassing beautiful. He tried to think of her body as no more than the body of an animal, a sleek cow he had seen and coveted, a graceful horse. He focused on her hands, now racing over the strings to finger some intricate descant to the piper. It was not the same song. For how many had he stood here, fascinated, watching her? Those long-fingered hands, strong and supple, that long body. He met her eyes again, dark eyes older than her years, full of sorrow.

She knew. She knew he watched, and how he watched. Rage roiled up in him: she was charming him again, even now. He glared at her; she looked back, sorrowful and unafraid. Calm. *Kill me now,* her look said. *I did not do this.* Yet, if it was not charm, why wasn't she disgusted at his interest? A peasant, a coarse man old enough to be her father—

Not so, came her voice in his mind. *You are not so old, nor I so young.*

No disgust? *He* was disgusted, with himself. How could he think of such a woman, as a woman, after Mali's loyalty and Raheli's tragedy? What had he fought for, if not to remove such women from power?

Time had passed, the fire only warm ashes under a dark sky. The others had fallen asleep. Only she remained awake, watching him as he watched her. Magicks, he thought disgustedly.

"Not so, lord marshal," she said. Aloud, in her own voice, but quietly.

"Reading minds is magicks."

"That, yes. The other—if it be magic at all, it is older far than mine."

"I—would like to hate you."

"With reason." She turned away, and folded around the melon-bellied instrument a trimmed fleece. "But you cannot, lord marshal, any more than I hate myself. I did not come here to unsettle you."

"Wind unsettles water," he said, surprising himself. Where had *that* come from?

She laughed softly; it had an edge to it. "Yes—wind. But you are not water, lord marshal—Gird. You are what you said—good peasant clay. Do you know what the rockfolk say of clay?"

"No."

"Sertig squeezed clay to rock. And rock squeezed makes diamond, fairest of jewels that gives light in darkness."

He grunted, surprise and superstitious fear together. He had consented to be rock; the other, half dreamed of, still wholly terrified him. And diamonds were jewels, and jewels belonged to the wealthy, to such as this lady: he would not so belong. But his mouth opened, and he spoke again.

"I have dreamed of you." He had waked sweating and furious; he had not spoken to her since.

She looked away. "I thought you might. I'm sorry."

"You—you are like no one—"

"I am myself. Once—a name I will not use again. Now, what *he* called me, an autumn rose, a last scentless blossom doomed by frost—"

"You like that word. Doom."

"Gird, I know myself, and my future: it is the chanciest gift our people had, but in me it is, like the others, strong. I will have no

children; my time is past." She met his eyes squarely. "And you,
who have children—you think you could give me some?"

He felt suddenly hot. Now she was smiling, but it had no warmth
in it.

"I know your dreams, Gird; your eyes speak of them. A magelady's body—a magelady unwed—what is she like? You see the
foreign shape of my face, my hands, and you wonder about the
rest." From musing, her voice roughened to anger. "Ah, Esea! You
will believe it my magicks no matter what I do! And I have tried,
if you had the wit to see it, to be invisible to you, to draw no eyes,
least of all yours."

"It was your sorrow." That, too, came without his thought. Yet
it was true. She had tried no charms on him or anyone, after that
first meeting, but the stress of her sorrow drew eyes to her.

"Look, Gird: I will show you, and then if you are wise, if the
gods are truly with you, you will know that in this I am honest."

He opened his mouth, but her gesture silenced him, for she had
thrown off her cloak, and begun unlacing her shirt. If he said anything *now*, someone might wake, and the explanations would be,
at best, difficult. Her fingers moved quickly, deftly, stripping off
her clothes with no more apparent embarrassment than he would
have had in his own cottage. It should have been too dark to see
her, but she glowed slightly, a light he knew was magelight.

She had the body he had imagined. Long legs, long slender body
untouched by childbearing; her hips were like a young girl's and
her breasts—he ached to touch them. Even Mali as a girl had not
had such breasts, the very shape of his desire. But through the
beauty he had expected he perceived the barrenness she had
claimed. Like some graceful carving of stone, set up in a lord's hall
for amusement: he could engender nothing there. His hands
opened, closed; instead of the imagined softness and warmth, there
was hardness and cold.

She wrapped the cloak around herself again, dimming the glow
until he could just make out her face. "You see?" A thread of
sorrow darkened that golden voice. "It is not you, Gird; it is a
choice I made, long years ago: obedience to my king. Service, not
freedom. Death, not life."

"It's wrong."

Her brows rose. "You are my judge?"

"No, but—" There had to be a way to say it, that meant what
he meant. "Serving things rightly, that can't be serving death. Loyalty's good, I'll agree there, but it's not all—what you're loyal *to* must
be worthy."

"Wise clay, lord marshal." Her voice mocked him, but her face was uneasy. "Where did a peasant learn such wisdom?"

"It's only sense," Gird said stubbornly. "Peasant sense, maybe: we serve life in our work. Growing crops, tending beasts—that's serving life."

"I erred, as I've admitted. A mistake, believing the king was true, and worth my obedience. A mistake I remedied, you remember." Her voice had chilled again; he thought she did not truly believe it was a mistake.

"So you said." He was grumpy, annoyed with his body which had not admitted what his mind knew—no comfort there. A man his age, to be so put out—he was disgusted with himself, and with her for rousing that interest. On the way across camp, he stumbled into one thing after another, knowing perfectly well it was his own temper making his feet clumsy.

Arranha. The old priest was one of them; perhaps he could explain. Gird sought him out, not surprised to find that Arranha was awake, peaceably staring at the stars.

"And how is the lady?" asked Arranha. Gird felt himself swelling with rage, to be so easily read, and then it vanished in a wave of humor. He folded himself down gingerly, to sit beside the priest.

"She is herself," he said.

"Too much so," said Arranha. "A bud that never opened, eaten out within. She has the body of a girl, but no savor of womanhood."

Gird opened his mouth to let out surprise; his ears were burning. "She is lovely," he said, after a decent interval.

"Cold," insisted Arranha.

"Well—yes. And yes, I looked; she showed me—"

"She wants you?"

"No. I had never seen anyone like her—not to speak to—and I suppose—it was my own curiosity."

"Natural enough." Arranha shrugged that off, as he did other things Gird could not anticipate. "Which curiosity, I gather from your words, has now vanished. I would pity her, myself, were she not capable of better."

Gird chuckled. "I thought you said we all were capable of better."

"True. But great talents draw envy, even from tired old priests sitting up all night. Gird, she might have prevented much evil, had she listened to good counsel. It was not all heedlessness of love: she has the foreseeing mind. She chose not to listen; she chose in spite of her knowledge. She could not have saved the king, I daresay—from all I ever heard of him, as foolish a young man as ever sat on a throne. Not wicked, in any active sense, but silly and shallow. But she might have saved more than she did, and I can't forget that. Nor should you. If she ever quits making a singer's tale out of her lost love, she'd make you a fine marshal, but you'll have to change her course."

"I have enough to do, without teaching mageladies."

Arranha shrugged. "If a weapon falls into your hand, you either learn to use it, or your enemy uses it against you."

Luap looked up as a strong, slender hand slapped down on the account rolls. He started to complain, but the look on the magelady's face stopped the words in his month. She was white around the lips—with fury, he was sure—and he half-recalled hearing Gird's bellow only a few minutes before.

"You!" she said, in a voice that had some of Gird's bellow in it, though not so loud.

"Me?" He could not help noticing the hilt of her sword, her fine and reputedly magical sword. The jewel set in the pommel glinted, as if with internal fires. And every bit of metal she wore glittered, bright even beneath the cloth that shaded him from midday sun. Her eyes, when he met them again, seemed to glitter as well, fire-bright and angry. What could he have done? She had always seemed remote, but calm, when speaking to him.

"You," she said, very quietly now, "you have mageblood."

Luap shrugged, and looked away. "Common enough, lady; if you look closely, there's bastards aplenty in this army."

Her hand flipped this half-truth away. "Bastards in plenty, yes, but those in whom the mageblood *stirs* and wakes are few enough."

He stared at her, shocked almost into careless speech. But he caught the unspoken question back, and tried to school his face. He could see by her expression that she wasn't fooled, or maybe she could see his thoughts. She nodded at him, mouth tight.

"Yes. I do know. You have the magic, the light, and you know it. You could be what I am, were you not obedient to that—that *churl* out there!" Her arm waved. Luap felt a bubble of laughter tickle his throat. "That churl" must be Gird, whatever he'd done this time to anger the lady.

"It may be so," he said, trying to keep even the least of that laughter out of his voice. "There was a time I thought so, but truly, lady, I have no desire for it now."

She rested both fists on the little table and leaned close to him; he could smell her sweat, and the onion on her breath from dinner. It did nothing to diminish her beauty, or her power. "It has nothing

to do with your desires, whatever your name really is. It is given
to you, like the color of your eyes, the length of your arm: you
cannot deny it." He said nothing, facing her with what calm he
could muster. Her eyes looked away first, but she did not move.
Then she straightened up, with a last bang of one fist that crumpled
the supply roll. "No. You are more than just a bastard, and you
must learn it."

Suddenly she was alight, blinding him at first, and then the heat
came, scorching heat that blackened the edges of his scrolls. Without thought, he grabbed for power, and threw a shield before him,
swept the scrolls to safety behind him.

"Stop that!" he said, furious and frightened at once. She laughed,
a scornful laugh he remembered from his earliest childhood, the
laugh of one whose power has never been overcome. Above his
head, the fabric caught fire, the flames hardly visible against her
brightness and the noonday sun.

"You have the power; you stop me!"

It was challenge, challenge he had never expected to face, that
Gird would never have had him face. And he felt within a surge
of that uncanny power, whose ways he had never learnt, never
dared to explore. But as he had startled Gird, perhaps he could
startle her, and so he let it out, in whatever form it might choose
to come.

It came as a fiery globe, that raced at her; she slapped it away,
first with a laugh and then, when it surged again against her hand,
with a startled expression. She drew her sword, now glowing as
brightly as she, and swiped at the globe. Luap would have been
fascinated, if he had not also been involved. He could feel a vague
connection between himself and the globe, as if he had a ball of
pitch at the end of a long and supple reed.

With a final *pop* like a spark from sappy wood, her brilliance
vanished. Luap blinked. Her shadow stood behind her, lean and
black; the sun was overhead—he realized then that he was alight
as she had been. She was staring at him, her first expression changing to respect, and then awe.

"You," she said, in a very different tone from her first approach.

"Yes?" Whatever was in his voice, it worked on her. Her mouth
moved, but she said nothing. Finally she shook her head, and managed speech.

"Do you know *whose* bastard you are?" she asked. Luap kept
his mouth shut tight; if *this* was where she was going, he was not
going to help. But she nodded, slowly, as if this confirmed something she'd hardly dared imagine. "The king's," she said quietly.

Calmly. "You have the royal magery; it could not be anyone else—
and I think you knew, Luap. I think you chose your name of war
precisely."

"And if I did?" he asked, relaxing slightly. The shadow behind
her blurred, as if his light dimmed. He could not tell; his eyes still
refused to answer all his questions.

"If you are the old king's son, born with his magery—"

"They said not," said Luap. "Like all bastards with no magic, I
was fostered away—"

She laughed, this time ruefully. "Luap, they erred, as you must
have known long since. You are his heir—in blood, and in magic—
and the evidence is right here—in what just happened. Show this
to any of the old blood, and you would inherit—"

"Inherit!" For an instant his old dream sprang up, bright as ever,
but anger tore it away. "Inherit a kingdom torn by war? Inherit
the fame my father had, that made men glad to see him dead?
Inherit his ways?"

Her voice lowered, mellowed, soothed him as honey soothes a
raw throat. "You have thought of it, Luap; you must have. He was
a proud man, a foolish man . . . even, in some ways, a cruel man.
He should have had more sense than to foster *you* away. None of
our people have done all we should. But you—you know better.
You could be—"

"I could be dead," said Luap. He wanted to hit her; he could
feel her attempt to enchant him like a heavy weight of spring
sunlight. It had been bad enough to go through this once. He
shook his head at her. "If you had asked me two years ago, lady,
I might have been foolish enough—I *would* have been foolish
enough to agree. What my father did to me—the vengeance I
wanted, the power I had always envied—yes. I would have. Even
a year ago, maybe. But I've learned a bit, in this war. Even from
you."

"*Even* from me? You mean, because of me, you would not—?"

"Not you alone. But, lady, I can see what Gird sees now; I can
see the cost of your counsel, down to the last dead baby, the last
poisoned well—"

"We are not *all* evil!"

"No. But—you tell me, lady, what it is that made you angry this
time? What sent you here to work behind Gird's back?"

She whirled away from him; he let his own power flow out to her,
and she turned back, unwilling, but obedient—recognizing even as
she fought it the source of her compulsion. He released her, and

she staggered. "He—he's an *idiot!* He knows no more of governing than any village bully!"

Luap chuckled. "He is an idiot, that I'll grant. But he's far more than a village bully, and if you can't see that, you're not seeing him yet for what he is."

"He lets those fools of merchants blather on, bickering about the market rules—"

"What should he do, crack their heads for them?"· Luap could see she had thought of that, with relish. He shook his head at her. "Lady, Gird's as likely to lose his temper and bash heads as any man I've ever known. If he lets them bicker on, wasting time as you'd say, then he has his reasons."

"He claimed they would obey rules they made better than rules he gave—and yet he won't let them make the rules they *want* to make. Insists that they and the farmers must agree what is a ripe plum, nonsense like that."

"Nonsense like that matters, to those who grow the plums, or pay good coin for them."

"And that brings up coin. D'you know he's planning to call in and melt down all the old coinage? No more copper crabs and gold crowns, but stamped with wheat-ear and poppy. I tried to tell him what that would cost: the finesmiths don't work for nothing. He wouldn't listen. And he asks of me what he does not understand—"

"He wants you to give up your grievance, as he made me give up mine."

"Your heritage, he's made you give up."

"One and the same. My grievance: being born of royal blood, and thrown out to live in a peasant's world. Having the royal power, and being denied its use. The world, in short, not to my liking."

"It's more than that!"

"Not really." Luap grinned sideways at her. "Lady, I've known peasant lads enough, furious because their father favored another brother, because the steward was unfair, because the world was. Grumbling, sour, envious, resentful, quick to take offense and seek vengeance for every slight. So was I, though I hid it, thinking myself too good to admit such feelings, though they burned in my heart." He paused, to see how she would take this. She listened, though he suspected it was only because she knew he was a king's son. He took a deep breath, hoping no one would interrupt them, or come close enough to overhear what only Gird, so far, knew of his past.

"When I married, lady, I loved my wife as a prince might love a scullery-maid: just so much, for her beauty and her skill. Our children: I saw them in my mind, clothed in royal gowns, and hated the reality of their broad peasant faces, their rough hands. You are unwed: you cannot imagine what this means of love foregone, of wasted years, when I might have been rich in hearts-ease. Then as Gird's power grew, my master—who should, I knew, have been but a courtier at *my* court—commanded me to join the army, gain Gird's confidence, and betray him. I would have done so, for the reward he promised, but he did not trust. He took my wife, my children—killed my son, to make his point, and held them captive against my behavior. The wife I had never loved as I could have, the daughter I thought too plain: I saw in their eyes, as the soldiers took them away, a trust I had never earned. *Then* I began to love them, but it was too late." The old pain struck to his heart again, and tears blurred his vision. He blinked them away, and saw on the magelady's face a curious expression. He hoped it was not contempt: he could feel rage rising in him like a dangerous spring; contempt from her would set a fire under it. She said nothing.

"So I came to Gird, as one driven into rebellion by injustice, but I meant to betray him, only he was gentle, that night, with my injuries, and something—I could not do it. I told him, about my family, and he cried: great tears running down his face, his nose turned red—I could not believe it." He waited until she asked.

"And then?"

"And then they died, as my master had promised, and I could do nothing. In the market square at Darrow, before a frightened crowd—someone told me about it later, not knowing whose wife it had been. And I—I hated Gird, almost as much as my master, for having done nothing—though there was nothing he could have done. When I discovered my powers, I had thoughts of claiming my own place, somehow. Making things better, being the king that should have been, in a land where no one suffered. A boy's dream, after a beating. Crowns and palaces for all, meat and ale and honey on the loaf—"

"You could have—"

"I could *not*. Gird knocked me flat, when I tried my powers on him, and rightly so. I didn't see that at the time. But if you've wondered why I have no command, that's why. He could not trust me. The marshals still look at me sideways, but Gird knows I'm different now. So could you be, if you'd give up that old wound you cherish."

"I do not cherish it! The ruin of my life—!"

"Only if you choose so. Lady, listen to me. You have lost something: who has not? It is what we make of what's left that counts.

I lost my wife, my children, lost them even before they were taken, in the blindness of my pride in blood. I lost a crown, the way you see it. You stayed away from this war; you have not seen what I have seen, or learned the lessons it taught. My loss is as important as any other, and no more important than any other. King's son, bastard, widower, childless by war, a luap in every way: I have lost or renounced all command, being unfit for it."

"And this is what you and Gird want me to do?"

Luap stretched his arms high over his head, easing the knot in his back. By her tone, she was at least thinking about it, no longer quite so sure of herself. "Gird wants you to quit thinking you're a special case. I would have you consider the fruits of freedom: freedom from your past. What good is that old anger doing you now? What good is it doing any of us, when you would lure me into a conspiracy to undo what all these men and women have died to do? You, lady, best know whether you are as unfit for command as I was."

Her expression shifted, from half petulant to something approaching respect. "I—never doubted my ability to command, when it should be time. Not until now—"

"Yet you never took the field. And why come here, to your people's enemies? And why stay?"

"I'm not sure." She looked down, and away, and anywhere but his eyes. "I did not take the field . . . because the king did not call me, as he called other nobles. After I killed him, I thought . . . I knew that none of our people would accept me, the king's murderer. Why should they? I'd broken my oath to him, why not join his enemies? My own act placed me there, it seemed."

"And what did you think Gird would do, pat you on the head and tell you the king had treated you badly and deserved your vengeance?"

She flushed. "I didn't know. I don't suppose I was thinking clearly. As for why I stay . . . where would I go? Back to Tsaia to pick sides in that contention? Away from here, where some peasant terrified of magery is like to split my skull with an axe while I sleep?"

Now she met his eyes again, with an expression he had never seen on her face, honest bewilderment and the first glint of humor. "I set out to save the king, and killed him; after that, what could I dare intend, that would not go awry?"

Chapter Thirty-two

Gird had been right; Tsaia preferred lords to peasants, if peasants to mages. There the followers of cruel gods had all been magelords, or their close kin. When the bartons rose, some found their own lords with them, against those they most hated and feared. Duke Marrakai, though accused of treachery by Duke Verrakai, proved his loyalty in most men's eyes by supporting a Mahieran for the throne. The Rosemage, as Gird called her, assured him that the candidate had no more magical ability than a river cobble. He was not sure he believed her, but he did believe Arranha, who said the same thing.

He was, as he had never expected to be, alive and a hero. Everyone knew the big blocky man in blue (it seemed simpler to keep wearing that color; when he didn't, someone would give him a blue shirt "to remember by") on the stocky gray—almost white now—horse. Children ran out to meet him on the way, calling to him, running beside the horse. If his route was known, there would be bits of blue tied to branches, blue yarn braided into women's hair, blue flowers, in season, thrown before him. If he surprised a village, they would drop their tools and gather, beg for his blessing, bring all their problems for him to solve.

He found that they wanted him—his physical touch, his presence, his listening ear—far more than they wanted his ideas. They had each their local heroes—someone who had fought with him at Grahlin or Greenfields, Blackbone Hill or Brightwater. Every little ambush, each battle, had its heroes, and they had all gone home, if they lived, to tell the tale their own way. Gird heard with some astonishment that he had thrown a horse and rider "so far the crash was not heard when they landed" in one battle, and someone who had lost a leg and survived (Gird remembered the man clinging to his hand, begging for death) came hopping up without it to hug Gird and pound his back and show off his children.

But when he tried to speak to them of the future, only a few paid heed. The others were busy with their work, with lives deferred. They had won, and life was good; they feared nothing but the lords' return, and needed nothing but Gird's friendship.

Some were interested in the legal reforms he instituted. Merchants, craftsmen, and even a few former farmers—but their interest in abstract justice and perfect fairness gave way to factional argument far more often than Gird had hoped. Eventually, after hours and days and even seasons of wrangling, one group would agree on a particular rule, only to have those who had not attended the original conference refuse to follow it. Then everyone appealed to Gird, and he found himself making the very judgments he had called on others to make.

Most folk understood the need to have some armed force for protection, both locally, against brigands, and regionally, in case of invasion. But fewer wanted to support the barton and grange organization Gird envisioned, with adequate, uniform training for yeomen, yeoman-marshals, marshals, with regular drill for all yeomen even in times of peace.

He was troubled, as well, by the feeling that he had had since surviving the battle at Greenfields. He had been told that he could not see the peace he would bring, and here it was, all around him. Either the gods were wrong—and he could not believe that—or he had misunderstood. He didn't believe that, either. Which meant that the peace he saw was somehow not real. Something was wrong with it, as something had been wrong after Norwalk Sheepfolds. He had asked then if it was his fault that he would not see true peace, and had had no answer. He asked himself the same question now: was the wrong here his fault? Had he failed in something he should have done, that would have brought true and lasting peace—had he withheld something he should have given?

His own memories reminded him of his mistakes; the victories others boasted of in his name seemed to him full of his miscalculations, deaths he'd caused by his stupidity or carelessness. That one fit of drunkenness, which left a legacy still; even now, even when everyone called him Father Gird, someone would take the mug from his hand with a kindly smile, when he'd had what they thought was enough. He had done what he set out to do—free the land of its bad rulers—but every time his gray horse ticked a hoof on a skull, or he saw the white end of a bone turned up as someone plowed a field, he shuddered.

He traveled widely, urged on by that vague but persistent uneasiness. Everywhere he went he seemed to see prosperity returning, as farms returned to burnt-over fields, as once-deserted villages hummed with life. His people had more flesh on their bones; foreign traders complained of their scant profits, but kept returning. So did wealthy craftsmen who had thought a peasant kingdom

would have no need of their abilities. His new coinage, which the
magelady had so complained about, circulated more freely than the
old ever had. When Luap first mentioned what he saw as the problem, the continuing bitterness between former magelord landhold-
ers and tenants, Gird scoffed at him.

"They won't hurt children," he said. "The adults, maybe, but—"

"I've talked with Autumn Rose." Luap said the name without
embarrassment; Gird still thought it was silly. If she wanted to
conceal her real name, she could have taken any simple one. She
had changed, over the years, but she still had what he thought of
as lordly arrogance. He let himself remember the first time she
had laughed at herself, admitted that she could be as ridiculous as
anyone. Was it then that she began to change, to give up her old
grievance against the dead king. She had made, as Arranha had
predicted, a good marshal when she finally quit dramatizing her
lost love. He realized his mind had wandered, as it did more often
now, and came back to find that Luap was watching him, patiently.
Luap went on. "She thinks it will get worse. There are too many
of the halfbred children, and sometimes the power sleeps a generation or so, cropping out unexpectedly. Besides, you said not all the
adults were guilty, that if they wanted to live under your laws they
would be safe."

"So I did, and so they are." He hated it when Luap was patient
with him, as if he were a doddering old man; it made him grumpy.

Luap shook his head. "If they come so far as your courts, they
are. Many don't. There was a man killed in the south, near Kelaive's
old domain—" The regions had not been renamed; Gird decided
they needed to do that next. The very name Kelaive wakened old
angers. "—a younger son, he could make light with his finger,
enough to light a candle. Stoned, Gird, and no one will admit to
having anything to do with it. You can lose your temper and stab
someone in a rage, or bash his head with one rock, but stoning—
that takes time, and many people."

"What did they say he'd done?" He must have done something,
to arouse that kind of anger.

"They don't say, because no one admits to doing it. Cob's your
high marshal down there; you know he's sensible." He had always
liked Cob, whose blunt, matter-of-fact approach to life had not
changed through war or peace. He still limped, from the foot broken outside Grahlin, but never complained.

"What does Cob say?"

Luap pulled out the message and read it aloud. "Tell Gird he
must do something, perhaps send the mages away."

"Away *where?* Where would people trust me to send them? Those here don't want to live in Tsaia, won't go back to Aarenis—and they say there's nothing left in Old Aare. Besides, if I send them away, that kind of folk will worry that they're plotting together. I hear enough of that on the east side now, worrying that Tsaia will invade. It'll wear itself out, in time; what takes years to grow can't wither in a moment."

He went back to the maps, determined to eliminate Kelaive's name before the day was out. The old names, the folk names, belonged: Burry and Berryhedge (four families lived there now, in the ruins) and Three Springs. Get rid of the lords' newfangled names; he would agree that some of their family members were innocent, but no need to honor a bad name by putting it on a map. He was uneasily aware that some bartons had indulged in more looting and destruction than he would have approved if he'd been there, but he was sure—he hoped he was sure—that that had been a single overreaction to years of oppression.

Another year went by, and another. He put on weight; his old belt gave way one day in the middle of a court session, to everyone's delight. Someone ran to bring him a strip of blue leather; he insisted on paying for it (he was, after all, sitting as judge) and wore it thereafter. He still rode out from the city that had been Finyatha and was now Fin Panir, visiting villages and towns, following that old restlessness. He had to admit that Luap was right in one thing; it was taking much longer than he'd expected to reconcile the common folk to the continued presence of surviving mage-lords and their children. It would come, he was sure of it: at some point they would recognize what they lost in this continual picking at the past. Mali had told him that, all those long years ago, when he had held a grudge against Teris: all life soured if you held anger.

He was working by an open window one hot afternoon when he saw the furtive movement of those who know they're about to do wrong. One, then another, slipped past beneath him, heading around the corner toward whatever lured them on. He was not really curious; it was too hot, and his feet hurt even in slippers. Then he heard children's shrill voices, and someone yelled "I'll tell Gird!" in the very tone in which one wrongdoer informs on another. Sighing, he pushed himself away from his desk, put his feet into his largest pair of boots, and was downstairs when the threatened information arrived. "Something" was going on "down the market way" that he wouldn't like. The marshal, the barefoot child informed him "made no good of it." Then the child was gone, with a flick of a smile that could mean anything from "I started it" to "I know you'll fix it." Both could be true.

He followed the furtiveness he'd observed before, and saw more hurrying backs. Odd that someone's back could reveal intent, he thought. As much as a face, perhaps more. Then he saw a crowd, in the lower market, where the livestock pens were. At the moment, their backs had the look of guilty curiosity.

He felt the crowd's mood shift even before the growling mutter began. *Not again*, he thought. Couldn't the fools understand? Why did they start this nonsense again, now, when all was won, and only ruin could follow such anger?

Those at the back of the crowd moved instinctively away from his determined stride, even before they recognized him. Their voices followed, then raced ahead: "Gird—it's Gird—*he's* coming—" A lane opened for him, leading him toward the trouble.

There was Luap, as he had expected, and the Autumn Rose. She held the shoulders of a whip-thin, dark-haired lad whose face was a mass of bruises and scrapes, eyes barely visible in the mess. Blood dribbled from his broken nose and split lip. Gird could see the lad shaking, and no wonder. Across from them was a yeoman of the local grange, Parik, sucking raw knuckles. When he saw Gird, he glowered, no whit repentant.

Luap, uncharacteristically, said nothing. The Autumn Rose looked past Gird's ear, an insult he would have thought but for the warning that leapt into her eyes. So. He looked back at Parik, seeing in Parik's eyes the confidence that came from knowing he was not alone in this.

"Well?" Gird's voice cracked, as it had been doing since Midwinter Feast and that disastrous dance in the snow. He swallowed the lump and awaited an answer.

"That'n used magicks," said Parik, in a tone well-calculated to sting without justifying rebuke. He merely looked at the lad, and then gave a final lick to his own knuckles.

"You're accusing him of misusing magicks?" asked Gird mildly.

"Nah—they all seen it. He's a magelord's brat, should never have lived this long, and needs mannering, if he's to live any longer." Parik made a show of patting his tunic back into place.

"And you thought it your job—?"

"He put fire on me," said Parik, as if explaining something difficult to a dull child. "He put fire on me, so I put m'fist on him. Like you says, Gird, or *used* to say, simple means for simple minds." He laughed, a little too loudly, and Gird heard nervous sniggers elsewhere.

He closed his eyes, suddenly so tired he felt he must sink to the ground. He had told them, and told them, and explained, and argued, and shouted, and broken their stubborn heads from time to time, and even, when his breath ran out, spoken softly, and here they were, just as bad as ever. Just as bad as the magelords, barring they used fists instead of magic. *Gods*—! he thought, then stuffed the prayer back. Ask their help and get their interference, like as not. He opened his eyes to find everyone staring at him. Give them an answer, a judgment: he had to, and he could not.

"The Marshal?" he asked. His voice was unsteady; he could see their reaction to that, like a child's to a parent weeping.

"Don't need no Marshal to know right from wrong," said Parik, bolder now that Gird had not unleashed his usual bellow. "S'what you taught us, after all: don't need no priests, no crooked judges, no lords—and 'specially no magelords—"

Gird looked at Luap: Luap white-faced, gaze honed to a steel blade that sliced into Gird's mind. Luap, who had warned of this, whose warning he had ignored, thinking it special pleading. It was to Luap he spoke, in a conversational tone that confused the others.

"You were right, and I was wrong. Are you still of the same mind?"

Luap's face flooded with color: surprise. "I—yes, Gird."

"They are not *all* Parik." And that was special pleading, *his* special pleading. Luap nodded, taking it seriously. He had not hoped for so much compassion.

"Talk to *me!*" yelled Parik. Gird watched the Autumn Rose transfer her gaze to him, as deliberate as someone shifting a lance; Parik paled, but did not retreat. "Is that it, then? Are you hiding behind your pet magelords, using their power to charm us?"

"WHAT!" That time he had the old strength in it, and Parik backed up a step. Fury lifted Gird to his full height, pumped power into the fists clenched at his sides, as he stalked towards Parik, stiff-legged. "I never hide; I never did. There are no magelords, Parik, because *I* led you and the others to fight free of them. Mages, yes, and some mere children, like this lad here—but no magelords. No, Parik."

Parik backed up another step, blustering. "But—but that lady there—she looked at me—"

"I'm looking at you, Parik, and seeing a bully who'd be a lord as bad as ever we fought, had he the power."

"Me? But I just—"

"You just beat a lad half your size, for using magicks you said, but you brought no accusation to the Marshal—"

"Donag, he don't want to be bothered with little stuff like that—"

"Then Donag must not want to be Marshal; that's what Marshals do, is deal with 'little stuff like that' and keep big hulks like you from bruising their knuckles breaking lads' faces—"

Gird heard a growl from the crowd, concentrated over *there*—disapproval, backing for Parik. Maybe Donag as well? Could one of his Marshals be supporting this madness?

"He used *magicks!*" yelled Parik. "He put *fire* on me!"

"And what had you done, eh?" Gird glanced around at hostile faces, frightened faces, confused faces. "What started it all?"

"Parik's boy complained," said someone softly, just audible under the shifting crowd noise.

Gird swung toward that sound, and located a face that fit the voice. "Parik's boy?" he asked.

Silence fell, in the center. Parik scowled at the young woman who edged her way to the front. Neither beautiful nor ugly; a quiet face, clear-eyed and determined. She looked straight at Gird, as if afraid to look elsewhere—certainly not at Parik.

"It was Parik's boy, sir—Gird. He'n the others was playing, playing the stick game, y'know?"

He knew: a boy's gambling game, easily disguised as something else if disapproving adults came by.

"Julya—" began Parik angrily, but the girl went on, ignoring him. "That lad, he has quick fingers—he's a tailor's apprentice now, and I've watched him with a needle—and he won twice running. Then Parik's boy said he was a cheat, and a magelord's bastard, and the lad said he was no bastard, and Parik's boy jumped him, and Parik grabbed him, held him for his boy to hit. That's when the lad made fire on his fingers, to make Parik let go—" Her voice trailed away.

"You—you just want to lie with a magelord's son, you Julya—" Parik's voice had a nasty whine to it. The girl reddened but stood her ground.

"I don't want to lie with you or any of *your* hardhanded sons, that's the truth. And I won't see you lying about what happened and not tell."

"Here now! What's going on here!" That interruption was Donag. Gird merely looked at him when Donag got to the center of the crowd, and Donag wilted. "I heard something—" he started to say.

"Awhile back, I heard something," said Gird. He hardly knew what he was saying: a great space in his head rang off-key, like a cracked bell, and his vision was uncertain. "Awhile back I heard trouble—which you, Marshal Donag, should have heard. And then I heard that you did not care to hear such trouble. Or so Parik said."

In the quick glance that passed between Parik and Donag, Gird saw as much trouble as he feared. Anger gave him the energy he needed to round on them all, but before he had two words out, Donag interrupted.

"Gods blast it, we've tried for years! You keep telling us they weren't *all* bad. You keep telling us the children aren't their fathers. And yet we *still* have mages working their magicks on us and our children. Look at Tsaia—they have a king again, of the same mageborn line—"

"He has no magicks," said Gird heavily. "That was his great-uncle—"

"So he *says*," Donag growled. "So they all say. 'We have no magicks—we were born without—' And then some mageborn spawn of Liart burns an honest yeoman—"

"An honest yeoman who was doing coward's work, holding a lad for his lad to beat! And look at the damage: Parik has not even a blister, and just you look at the lad's face. By the wheatear and corn, Donag, if the lad had bitten Parik—as any lad would, to get away—you'd no doubt claim that was magicks."

"He could poison his bite," muttered someone.

"Donag, think! If the lad could charm someone, why didn't he charm Parik's boy—or Parik—into letting him alone?" Donag's face did not change; he was not thinking, or even listening. Nor were the others. Gird tried something new. "Suppose we exile them—send them all away. Will that satisfy you? Let the boy go, and any like him."

Parik and Donag both opened their mouths, looked at each other, and then Donag spoke. "If we let them go, they'll come back. Same as mice or rats or snakes—let 'em go, they'll breed and come back worse'n ever." Gird heard a murmur of agreement from the crowd. He wanted to tell them that what bred and multiplied here was their own fear, but he knew it would do no good. He struggled for words, and none came. He could feel the mood deepening, one frightened and angry person reinforcing another's fear and anger, as one bell vibrates when one near it is struck.

Black murder hung over the crowd, a veil of hatred and fear. Some had wrapped themselves in it, as if it were a literal cloak of supple velvet, welcoming the darkness. Others stood hunched, frightened, unsure which was worse, the growing darkness or the spear-bright danger of the mageborn.

Luap gazed at him, calm, almost luminous. For the second time,

Gird felt that crevice open in his mind, and Luap's voice flowing through, cool silver water from a spring.

—We will not fight—he said. —We will not break your peace—

My peace! Gird would have snorted if he could. Some peace, with the city in wild turmoil; even Alyanya's peace could not still this storm.

—*My peace*— echoed in his mind, in the great empty cavern still clangorous with the crowd's noise. —*Do you want my peace? Do you want justice?*— As once before, he could not confuse that voice with any other.

Out of his emptiness, out of his pain, he cried—silently, as the crowd listened in momentary silence—for help. To the gods he had tried to serve, and feared, and refused to ask before, he cried for help.

Again, as at Greenfields, he was snatched up from the ground, whirled in a storm of fire and flowers and wind high above the city. But only for an instant. Then he found himself standing where he had stood, but no longer empty. Overflowing, rather, with utter certainty. Full of light, of wisdom, of mellow peace thick as old honey in the comb.

It was still hard. His head would burst, he was sure; his mouth was too small for the breath he drew; he could barely form the words that he must speak. They had strange shapes, awkward in his mouth, as if thought were sculpted into individual shapes not meant for human speech.

With the first words, the crowd stilled. He could not hear himself; he was balancing himself on those internal forces. Incredibly the thought sped by that this might be what women felt at birth—stretched beyond capacity, control relinquished to forces they could not name. Then he was drenched in a torrent of bright speech he must somehow say, its meaning racing past his mind faster than he could catch it. He felt the hair standing upright on his arms and legs, the prickle of awe becoming a wave of sheer terror and joy so mingled he could not tell one from the other. It was so *beautiful*—!

And as he spoke, and tried to hold himself upright, he saw the crowd change, as if someone had thrown clean water on a mud-caked paving. The hatred and fear lifted in irregular waves, leaving some faces free of that ugliness, others still stained but clearing.

After the first wrenching outwash of it, he was more aware of the crowd, of his own voice, of *what* he was saying. The words were strange to mouth and ear, but he *knew* what they meant, and so, somehow, did his hearers. Peace, joy, justice, love, each without loss of the others, engaged in some intricate and ceremonial dance.

More and more the dark cloud lifted, as if his words were sunlight burning it away. Yet they were not *his* words, as he well knew. Out of his mouth, through his mind, had come Alyanya's peace, the High Lord's justice, Sertig's power of Making, and Adyan's naming: these powers loosed scoured the fear away.

That effect spread. Beyond the crowd gathered in the courtyard, beyond the city walls, across the countryside, the light ran clean as spring-water, lifting from fearful hearts their deepest fears, banishing hatred. Gird knew it happened, but dared not try to see, for the effort of speech took all his strength, even the strength he had been given. Sweat ran off his face, his arms, dripped down his ribs beneath his shirt, and still the great words came, and still he spoke them.

Now the darkness writhed, lifting free of his land, like morning fog lifting in sunlight. But it was not gone. He knew, without being told that when his words and the memory of them faded, it would settle again. And he could not stand here forever. Even as he thought this, the flood of power in his mind, faded, leaving him empty once more, but light, a rind dried by sunlight.

—It is not over—He had no doubt who *that* was. If he could have trembled, he would have. It had to be over: what else could he do? He could not live long as he was now. As he watched, seeing now with more than mortal eyes, the darkness contracted, flowed toward him. He closed his mind to it, as he had closed it to hatred so often before. It would not take *him*, even now, even weak as he was. But in his head the pressure grew again, forcing its way out, forcing an opening.

—Do not push that away: take it in. Take it *all* in, and transform it for them—

"I can't—" But he could, and he could do nothing else. With a despairing look at the crowd, at Luap, at the buildings that stood high around the market, even the top of the High Lord's Hall against the sky, he shrugged and relaxed his vigilance.

Now the great cloud of hatred and disgust pressed on him. He drew it in, doggedly, like a fisherman dragging a large net full of fish into a small, unsteady boat. It hurt. He had forgotten how painful it was to be that frightened, how hatred prickled the inside of the mind like a nestful of fiery ants, how disgust tensed every internal sinew. He had complained of his emptiness, to himself, but he had found those great clean rooms of his mind restful. There the spirit's wind had had space to blow; there he could go for quiet, for renewal. Now those spaces were filling, packed tighter and tighter, with stinking, slimy, oozing, crawling nastiness.

Envy, spite, malicious gossip like cockleburs, wads of gluttony like soft-bodied maggots, a sniggering delight in others' pain, thoughts and fears more misshapen, harder to hold, than the bright words he had found so painful. He felt himself grow heavier, as if he were filling with literal stones and muck, felt himself cramping into ever more painful positions as he tried to hold it all, and bring the rest of it in. Like a tidy housewife whose home is invaded by raucous vandals, he tried to protect some small favorite crannies of his mind, long-furnished with joyful memories—and failed. The stink and murk of it found every last crack, and filled them all. He felt himself creak, the foundations of his mind almost shattering from the weight. What would happen then?

He had it all. He dared not open his mouth, lest something vile leak out. The faces around him were stunned, horrified—he could not imagine what his face looked like, but it must be worth their horror. *Transform,* the gods had said. And just how? That ungainly, rebellious mass struggled to get out, and he *squeezed.* He did not feel the stones beneath his knees, then his hands—he felt only the terrible crushing weight of fear, the compression of hatred.

Through scalding tears Luap saw that homely, aging face transformed. *Like the High Lord's windows,* he thought. From outside, they looked dark—until at night a light woke them to brilliance. Now light illuminated Gird, almost too bright to watch, and from his mouth came rolling the words they all understood without quite hearing them. Beside him, the Autumn Rose murmured a counterpoint to Gird, her face radiant. Then she was silent. Luap felt his own heart lift, expand—and then his sight, as if Gird's speech awakened all his magegifts at once. He saw clinging darkness rolling away, lifting, knew in his bones precisely what Gird was doing, and what would come of it.

He could not bear it. It should not be Gird, who had earned a peaceful age, a time of rest. He should be the one. But when he opened his mouth, it was stopped, and the breath in it.

—You have other tasks—

He would have argued, but he had scarce breath to stay on his feet, and when he recovered, Gird was silent. Above them the cloud visible only to a few shifted, as if it were living spirit meditating attack. Gird was staring at it, mouth clamped shut just as so often before. Then—then his eyes widened, and his jaw dropped in almost comic surprise. Again Luap tried to move to his side, to help however he could. But again he could not move. Gird shrugged, then, and eyed the cloud doubtfully.

Even as he watched, Luap was thinking how he could record this in the archives. What would be believed, what would be too fantastic even for the superstitious, what would cause controversy, and what bring peace? He had no doubt that this was Gird's death. The man was too old, too battered by his life, to survive this.

—No one could—As he swayed under the pressure of that answer, he wondered if that was what Gird had heard.

And then the cloud settled on Gird, condensing, becoming, in the end, visible to everyone. That dark mass had no certain form, no definite edges. It weighed on him, pressed against him, until he sank first to one knee, and then the ground. They could not move to help, not until he lay flat, hands splayed on the stone, struggling to rise, to breathe—not until the darkness vanished, and Gird lay motionless.

Luap knew before he reached Gird's side that he was dead. His flesh was still warm, his broad blunt hands with their reddened, swollen knuckles still flexible, almost responsive, in Luap's. Luap blinked back his tears and looked at the crowd. Silent, awed, most of them had the blank and stupified look of someone waked from deep sleep. A few were already weeping.

But the air around them had the fresh, washed feel of a spring morning after rain. Inside, in the chambers of his heart where he had struggled to wall up ambition and envy, Luap knew that walls had fallen, and nothing was there but love.

Epigraph

"Gradually it was disclosed to me that the line separating good and evil passes not through states, nor between classes, nor between political parties—but right through every human heart—and through all human hearts."
—Alexander Solzhenitsyn, *The Gulag Archipelago*

LIAR'S OATH

Prologue

The king—Falkieri Amrothlin Artfielan Phelani, once Duke Phelan of Tsaia and now ruler of Lyonya—sat before the fire, brooding, his fingers tented together before his face. "I have heirs enough now; my lands are safe. It is time to undo the damage my folk did long years since. Time to redress old grievances, time to bring ancient enemies together in peace."

"Are you sure this is your task?" The woman stood by the fireplace, leaning one arm on the mantel; it shadowed her face, but the firelight brought out the gleam of silver in her belt, in the hilt of a dagger at her hip, and glinted from the crescent symbol of Gird that hung from a thong around her neck. And in shadow or sun or firelight, nothing dimmed the silver circle on her brow. Paksenarrion, paladin of Gird, the king's friend and former soldier.

"I'm sure. My grandmother, that Lady you met, said the present ruin was in part my fault—I cannot argue. And the original problem, too, comes from my ancestors." He gestured to the table behind him, with its litter of scrolls and books. "The Pargunese, in their rough way, have the right of it: they were free Seafolk, whom my ancestors sought to enslave—"

"As they had enslaved the Dzordanyans?"

"Perhaps. I don't know that, but I do know—I am sure—that the Old Aareans routed the Seafolk from their homes. They came here, to the Honnorgat valley, and settled the north shore of the river as far up as they could sail or row—and then found themselves faced with the Aareans again, moving north from Aarenis."

"A long time ago," said Paksenarrion, frowning.

"Very long, for humans." The king smiled briefly. He himself looked no older than she, though in truth he could have been her father; he had not seemed to age for a score of years. He would live as long again, or more: his elven mother's inheritance. "But when I asked my lady grandmother, she confirmed the Pargunese account. They sailed upriver; the Tsaians and human Lyonyans came over the mountains. And a few have memories of complaints made then, and wars begun then. The Pargunese and Kostandanyans have quarrelled with Tsaians and Lyonyans as long as any human remembers. And now with Sofi Ganarrion's heirs loose in Aarenis, with Fallo and Andressat at odds—"

"Not all that is your fault," Paksenarrion said. She moved to the chair across the firelight from him and sat down. "Surely you know that."

"As I know what *is* my fault," he said. "A king must never excuse himself. Gird would say that."

"Gird did," she said wryly, with a grin. "But how will you proceed?"

He stared at the fire, as if it had answers to give. "I must find some way to convince the southerners that I do represent Old Aare as well as the north. You remember Andressat: those old lords believe no northern title. If it were possible to find some buried talisman, some ancient relic . . ."

"Is a sword worth more than a swordsman?" Paksenarrion rested in her chair as if weightless; no hawk ever had more vigilant eyes.

"No, but I'm not likely to find a convenient army of Aareans ensorceled for an age, ready to my command—" He stopped abruptly; she had held up her hand. Her face seemed closed a moment, then she grinned as happily as the young girl he remembered.

"Are you not? Can you doubt the gods' influence, sir king, in asking *me* here?"

"I would never doubt the gods where you're concerned, but what—?"

"Kolobia," she said, Kolobia. His breath caught in his throat. Where she had been captured by iynisin, the elves' cruel cousins who hated all living things, who corrupted the very stone by dwelling in it. Where she had lost what made her what she was, a paladin of Gird . . . he thought of what she had gone through to regain it and winced away from the memory. She shook her head, impatient with his sentiment. "Kolobia," she said again, joyfully. "Luap's Stronghold—the sleeping knights there—"

"But you told me they waited some god's call to wake—"

"So Amberion said, when we found them. But as you know the Marshal-Generals have sent scholars there to read through their archives; they have not shared all they learned abroad. Those were not Gird's closest followers, as we first thought, but mageborn, descendents of those lords against which Gird fought. And in their own time, they believed themselves descended from the lords of Old Aare."

"Were they?" he asked.

She shrugged. "How can we know? We know what they said of

themselves in their records, but not if they spoke truth—or even knew it."

"And you think I should try to wake them?"

"I think you should ask the gods, and possibly your elven relatives. The scholars found as many mysteries as answers; they are not sure why the stronghold was founded, or why an end came—even what the end was. The records end abruptly, as if it came suddenly, or as if the writers expected no one to read their words again."

The king stood and paced the length of the room without speaking. Then he came back to the table, and leaned on it, as if reading the maps and books thereon. She watched him, silent.

"I know the way," he said finally. "I know, and cannot tell you, how to wake the sleepers . . . but without knowing why they sleep, and if some great power intended another awakening for them, dare I intrude?"

"The gods will tell you, if you listen," she said. He grunted; she always said that, and for her it was true: she listened, and the gods guided her. That was the essence of a paladin. For himself, it was more of a struggle. A king could not merely follow; a king had to understand. She had said more than once that paladins were not meant to govern.

"And what of the iynisin in Kolobia?" he asked. "If I waken the sleepers, what about them?"

A shadow crossed her face, as well it might. "Sir king, if you could persuade your elven relatives to explain more of the iynisin presence there it would help us all. In all the records from Luap's time, there is no mention of iynisin, and only one or two comments of some mysterious danger. The neighboring kingdom was said to believe that demons of some kind lived in the canyons before Luap came. Perhaps they thought iynisin were demons, but that doesn't explain why Luap and his folk never saw them."

"It would help," the king said, "if we knew more about Luap himself: who he was, and why he journeyed there, and what he thought he was doing."

Chapter One

Fin Panir in summer could be as hot as it was cold in winter; every window and door in the old palace complex stood wide open. Luap had started work early, before the heat slicked his hands with sweat to stain the parchment. Now, in midmorning, the heat carried ripe city smells through his broad office window. He paused to stretch and ease his cramped shoulders. For once Gird had not interrupted him a dozen times; he had finished a fair copy of the entire *Ten Fingers of the Code*. He reached for the jug of water and poured himself a mug, carefully away from his work. Could he write another page without smudges, or should he quit until evening's cool? He wondered, idly, why he had heard nothing from Gird that morning, and then remembered that a Marshal from a distant grange had come to visit. Doubtless they were still telling stories of the war.

He stretched again, smiling. It was nothing like the life he had imagined for himself when he was a boy, or a young farmer, but somewhat better than either of those vanished possibilities. As Gird's assistant and scribe, he had status he'd never had before; he was living in the very palace to which his father had never taken him. And he knew that without him, Gird could not have created, and revised, the legal code that offered some hope of lasting peace. His skill in writing, in keeping accounts, in drawing maps, had helped Gird win the war; his skill in writing and keeping records might help Gird win the peace.

"Luap . . ." One of the younger scribes, a serious-faced girl whose unconscious movements stirred him brought her work to his desk. "I finished that copy, but there's a blot—here—"

"They can still read it," he said, smiling at her. "That's the most important thing." She smiled back, shyly, took the scroll and went back downstairs. He wished he could find one woman who would chance a liaison with him. Peasant women, in the current climate, would not have him, as some had made painfully clear. They had suffered too much to take any man with known mageborn blood as lover. The few mageborn women who sought him for his father's name he could not trust to bear no children; he suspected they

434

wanted a king's grandson, and in his reaction to their pressure he could understand the peasant women's refusal. As for those women who sold their bodies freely, he could not see them without thinking of his daughter's terrible death. He needed to feel that a woman wanted him, the comfort of his body, before he could take comfort in hers.

But he knew that would not happen, any more than wishing would bring back Gird's wife or children, or restore any of the losses of war. All the Marshals had lost family; everyone around him had scars of body and mind both. His were no worse, he reminded himself, and decided to work on another page. Work eased his mind, and kept it from idle wishes—or so the peasants always said, in the endless tags and ends of folktales that now colored every conversation. He was lucky to have his work indoors, in this heat, or in winter's cold. He was lucky to have Gird's understanding, if he could not have his indulgence.

He had just pulled another clean sheet toward him when he heard the old lady's voice all the way up the staircase. He covered his inkwell; perhaps he would be needed. With that accent, she had to be mageborn, and with the quaver in it, she had to be old. The young guards, he suspected, would have no experience with her sort.

"I don't care what you say, young man." A pause, during which some male voice rumbled below his hearing. "I must see your Marshal-General, and I must see him now."

Luap rolled his eyes up and wondered how far the respect for age would get her. Her voice came nearer, punctuated by puffs and wheezes as she came up the stairs.

"Yes, it *is* important. It is always important to do things right. If your Marshal-General had had the advantages of good education, he would know that already, but since he has not—" A shocked interruption, from what Luap judged to be a very young yeoman, whose words fell all over each other in disarray. He grinned, anticipating the old lady's response. She did not disappoint him. "You see, young man, what I'm talking about. You're very earnest, I'm sure, and very dedicated to your Marshal-General, but you cannot express yourself in plain language with any grace. . . ."

Just as he realized that she would inevitably end up in his office, the yeoman's apologetic cough at the door brought his eyes to the spectacle. She was, undoubtedly, mageborn: a determinedly upright lady with snowy hair and slightly faded blue eyes, who dressed as if the former king were still ruling. A pouf of lace at the throat, a snug bodice with flaring skirt and puffed sleeves, all in brilliant reds and blues and greens: he had not seen such clothes since childhood. Luap wondered how that gorgeous robe had survived the looting. Then, with the appearance at her back of a stout, redfaced servant in blue and brown, he realized she must have impressed her staff with more than her money. The younger woman gave him look for look, challenging and defensive both.

"This is the Marshal-General's luap," the yeoman said. He was sweating, his eyes wide. "He'll be able to help you."

"I want the Marshal-General," the old lady said. Then, as Luap rose and came toward her, she raked him with a measuring glare, and her voice changed. "Ohh . . . *you'll* understand. Perhaps you can help me." Whatever she had seen convinced her he was one of *her* kind. Behind her, the peasant woman smirked, and Luap felt his ears redden. Of course everyone knew about him—at least that he had mageborn blood on his father's side, which was not that uncommon. But the way this woman said it, she might have known who his father was.

The old lady favored him with a surprisingly sweet smile, and laid a long fingered hand on her chest. "Could I perhaps sit down?"

Luap found himself bowing. "Of course . . . here . . ." His own chair, onto which he threw a pillow. She rested on it with the weightless grace of dandelion fluff, her rich brocaded robe falling into elegant folds. The peasant woman handed her a tapestry bag, then settled herself against the wall. The old lady rummaged in the bag, her lips pursed, and finally drew out a strip of blue gorgeously embroidered in gold and silver; it glittered even in the dim indoor light.

"You will understand," she began, peering up at Luap with a smile she might have bestowed on a favorite nephew. "They all tell me that the Marshal-General doesn't like fancy things, that he was a mere peasant, but of course that's nonsense." Luap opened his mouth, then shut it slowly at the expression on the peasant woman's face. Best hear the old woman out. "Being a peasant doesn't mean having no taste," she went on, looking up to be sure he agreed. "Peasants like fancy things as much as anyone else, and some of them do very good work. Out in the villages, you know." She seemed to expect some response; Luap nodded. "Men don't always notice such things, but I learned as a young wife—when my husband was alive, we used to spend summers at different vills on his estates—that every peasant vill had its own patterns. Weaving, embroidery, even pottery. And the women, once they found I was interested, would teach me, or at least let me watch." Another shrewd glance. Luap nodded again, then looked at the peasant woman leaning against the wall. Servant? Keeper? The woman's expression said *protector,* but it had to be an unusual situation. Few of the city servants had stayed with their mageborn masters when Fin Panir fell.

"So I know," the old woman went on, "that Gird will like this, if he only understands how important it is." She unfolded the cloth carefully, almost reverently, and Luap saw the stylized face of the Sunlord, Esea, a mass of whorls and spirals, centering a blue cloth bordered with broad band of silver interlacement. "For the altar in the Hall, of course, now that it has been properly cleansed." She gave Luap a long disapproving stare, and said "I always told the king, may he rest at ease, that he was making a terrible, terrible mistake by listening to that *person* from over the mountains, but he had had his sorrows, you understand." When he said nothing, finding nothing to say, she cocked her head and said "You *do* understand?"

"Not . . . completely." He folded his arms, and at her faint frown unfolded them. "This cloth is for the Hall, you say? For the High Lord's altar?"

She drew herself even more erect and almost sniffed. "Whatever you call it—we always called Esea the Sunlord, though I understand there has been some argument that the High Lord and the Sunlord are one and the same."

"Yes, lady." He wondered what Arranha would say about this. For a priest of the Sunlord he was amazingly tolerant of other peoples' beliefs, but he still held to his own.

"I could do nothing while the Hall was defiled. And of course the cloths used then could not be used again; I understood that. But now that the Hall is clean, these things must be done, and done properly. Few are left who understand that. You must not think it was easy."

"No, lady," Luap said automatically, his mind far astray. How was he going to explain her to Gird? How would Gird react?

"First," she said, as if he'd asked, as if he would be interested, "the wool must be shorn with silver shears, from a firstborn lamb having no spot of black or brown, neither lamb nor ewe. Washed in running water *only,* mind. And the shearer must wear white, as well. Then carded with a new pair of brushes, which must afterwards be burned on a fire of dry wood. Cedar is best. Then spun between dawn and dusk of one day, and woven between dawn and dusk of another, within one household. In my grandmother's day, she told me, the same hands must do both, and it was best done on the autumn Evener. But the priests said it was lawful for one to spin and another to weave, only it must be done in one household."

She gave Luap a sharp look, and he nodded to show he'd been paying attention. He wasn't sure he had fooled her, but she didn't challenge him. "It must be woven on a loom used for nothing else, the width exactly suited to the altar, for no cutting or folding of excess can be permitted. No woman in her time may come into the room while it is being woven, nor may touch it after; if she touches the loom while bleeding, the loom must be burned. Then while it is being embroidered, which must be the work of one only, it must be kept in a casing of purest white wool, and housed in cedarwood."

Luap nodded, tried to think of something to say, and asked about the one thing she hadn't mentioned. "And the color, lady? How must it be dyed?"

"Dyed!" She fairly bristled at him, and thrust the cloth toward his face, yanking it back when he reached out a hand. "It is not dyed, young man; that is fine stitchery." Now he could see that the blue background was not cloth, but embroidery. He had never seen anything like it.

"I'm sorry," he said, since she clearly expected an apology. "I don't think I've ever seen work that fine."

"Probably not." Then, after a final sniff, she gave him a melting smile. "Young man, you will not guess how long I've been working on this."

He had no idea of course, but a guess was clearly required. "A year? Two?"

She dimpled. How a woman her age had kept dimples he also had no idea, but they were surprisingly effective. "*Ten* years. You can't work on this all day, you know. No one could. I began when the king made that terrible mistake; I knew what would come of it. I tried to warn him, but . . ." She leaned forward, conspiratorial. "Would you believe, the king thought I was just a silly old woman! You may have been my mother's best friend, he said, but she only liked you because you were too stupid to play politics. Safely stupid, he said. You needn't think I'll listen to you, he said, you and your oldfashioned superstitions, *Well!*" Old anger flushed her cheeks, then faded as she pursed her lips and shook that silver hair. "When I got home, I told Eris here—" She waved a hand at the peasant woman. "I told her then, I said, 'You mark my words, dear, that hot-blooded fool is leading us straight into trouble.' Though of course it didn't start *then,* but a long time before; these things always do. Young people are so rash."

A movement in the passage outside caught Luap's eye—Gird, headed downstairs on some errand, had paused to see what was going on. For someone his size, he could be remarkably quiet when he wished. From his expression, the old woman's rich clothing and aristocratic accent were having a predictable effect on his temper. *Go away*, Luap thought earnestly at Gird, knowing that was useless. Then *Be quiet* to the old lady—equally useless.

She went on. "And that very day, I began the work. My grandmother had always said, you never know when you'll need the gods' cloth, so it's wise to prepare beforehand. This wool had been sheared two years before that, carded and spun and woven just as the rituals say: not by my hands, for there are better spinners and weavers in my household, and I'm not so proud I'll let the god wear roughspun just to have my name on it. Ten years, young man, I've put in stitch by stitch, and stopped for nothing. The king even wondered why I came no more to court, sent ladies to see, and they found me embroidering harmlessly—or so the king took it." She fixed Luap with another of those startling stares. "I am not a fool, young man, whatever the king thought. But it does no good to meddle where no one listens, and my grandmother had told me once my wits were in my fingers, not my tongue."

Gird moved into the room, and the old lady turned to him, regal and impervious to his dangerous bulk. He wore the same blue shirt and rough gray trousers he always wore, with old boots worn thin at the soles and sides. He stood a little stooped, looking exactly like the aging farmer he was.

"Yes?" she said, as if to an intrusive servant. Luap felt an instant's icy fear, but as usual Gird surprised him.

"Lady," he said, far more gently than her tone deserved from him. "You wanted to see the Marshal-General?"

"Yes, but this young man is helping me now." Almost dismissive, then she really focused on him. "Oh—*you* are the Marshal-General?"

Gird's eyes twinkled. "Yes, lady."

"I saw you, riding into the city that day." She beamed on him, to Luap's surprise. "I said to Eris then, that's no brigand chief, no matter what they say, even if he does sit that horse like a sack of meal." Gird looked at the peasant woman, who gave him the same look she'd given Luap. Gird nodded, and turned back to the lady. "Not that you could be expected to ride better," she went on, oblivious to the possibility that a man who had led a successful revolution might resent criticism of his horsemanship. "I daresay you had no opportunity to learn in childhood—"

"No, lady, I didn't." Gird's formidable rumble was tamed to a soft growl. "But you wished something of me?"

"This." She indicated the cloth on her lap. "Now that you've cleansed the Hall, the altar must be properly dressed. I've just this past day finished it. Your doorward would not allow me to dress the altar, and said it was your command—"

"So you came to me." Gird smiled at her; to Luap's surprise the old lady did not seem to mind his interruptions. Perhaps she was used to being interrupted, at least by men in command. "But we have a priest of Esea, lady, who said nothing to me about the need for such—" He gestured at the cloth.

"Who?" She seemed indignant at this, more than at Gird "What priest would fail in the proper courtesies?"

"Arranha," said Gird, obviously curious; surely she could not know the names of every priest in the old kingdom.

"*Arranha* . . . is *he* still alive?" A red patch came out on either cheek. "I thought he had been exiled or executed or some such years ago."

"Ah . . . no." Gird rubbed his nose; Luap realized his own mouth had fallen open, and shut it. "You said you were in the city when it fell—when we arrived. Surely you came to the cleansing of the Hall?"

"No." Now she looked decidedly grumpy. "No, I did not. At my age, and in my—well—with all due respect, Marshal-General, for those few days the city was crowded with—with noise, and pushing and shoving, and the kinds of people, Marshal-General, that I never—well, I mean—"

"It was no place for a lady of your age and condition," Gird offered, twinkling again, after a quick glance at Eris, the peasant woman. "You're right, of course. Noisy, rough, even dangerous. I would hope your people had the sense to keep you well away from windows and doors, most of that time."

"In t'cellar, at the worst," said Eris, unexpectedly. "But the worst was over, time you come in, sir. Worst was the other lords' servants smashin' and lootin' even as the lords fled. Runnin' round sayin' such things as milady here shouldn't have to hear. Though it was crowded and noisy enough for a few hands of days. And when th' yeoman marshals sorted through, takin' count o' folks and things. But they didn't seek bribes, I'll say that much for 'em."

"They'd better not," said Gird, suddenly all Marshal-General. Even the old lady gaped; Luap, who had seen it often enough not to be surprised, enjoyed the reactions of others. He had never figured out what Gird did to change from farmer to ruler so swiftly,

but no one ever mistook the change. "So," he went on, this time
with everyone's attention, "you did not come to the Hall that day,
and had not known Arranha was with us? You should know that
I've known him for some years—he'll tell you in what tangle we
met, if you wish. I knew he'd been exiled, and nearly killed, but for
all that he's a priest of Esea, one of the few left alive these days."

"He's a fool," said the old lady, having recovered her composure.
"He always was, with his questions into this and that and everything. Couldn't let a body alone, not any more than a bee will give
a flower a moment's peace to enjoy the sun. Always 'But don't you
think this' and 'Well then, don't you see that' until everyone was
ready to throw up their hands and run off."

Gird grinned. "He did that to me, too. You know he took me to
the gnomes?"

She sniffed. "That's exactly the sort of thing I'd expect. Gnomes!
Trust Arranha to complicate matters: mix a peasant revolt with
gnomes and both with religion." The flick of her hand down her
lap dismissed Arranha's notions.

"Well, it worked. Although there were times, that winter, when
I could happily have strangled your Arranha."

"He's not *ours*," the old lady said. "A law to himself, he is, and
always has been. Although you—" She gave Gird a look up and
down. "I expect you give him a few sleepless nights, and all the
better."

"But my point," Gird said, now very gently, "is that Arranha is
the only priest of Esea now in Fin Panir, serving his god within
the High Lord's Hall, and he has not said anything about needing
such cloths . . . although your years of labor should not be in vain,
you must know that we are not such worshippers of Esea as your
folk were."

"Even he—even he should realize—" Abruptly—Luap wondered
if it were all genuine feeling, or a habit known to be effective with
men in power—the old lady's eyes filled with tears that spilled
down her cheeks. "Oh, sir—and I don't mind calling a peasant *sir*
in such a case—I don't care what you call the god: Sun-lord, High
Lord, Maker of Worlds, it doesn't matter. But he must be
respected, whatever you call him, and I've made these . . ." A tear
fell, almost on the cloth; when she saw it, her face paled, and she
turned aside. "I must not—cry—on the cloth—"

Eris came forward, and offered her apron, on which the lady
wiped her damp face. "She really believes, sir, that if the altar's
not cared for, it'll come bad luck to everyone. It's no trick, sir, if
that's what you're thinking."

The old lady's hands, dry now, fumbled at the cloth, to fold it away safely. She didn't look up; her shoulders trembled. Luap felt a pang of emotion he could not identify: pity? sorrow? mean amusement? Gird sighed, gustily, like his horse. Luap knew what he wanted to say; he had said it before. *You should have worshipped better gods* he had told more than one mageborn survivor who wanted enforced tithes to rebuild the Sunlord's lesser temples. Only Arranha's arguments had kept him from forbidding Esea's worship altogether, although Luap couldn't see how the god could be responsible for his worshippers' mistakes. What he could see were any number of ways to placate the old lady without causing trouble among Gird's followers. Give the cloths to Arranha, and let him use them once or twice . . . the old lady would not make the journey from her house too often, he was sure. Agree to use them, then not—only she would care, and she would not know.

But he knew as well that Gird would not take any of these easy ways out. He would refuse her utterly, or agree, and use the damn cloths, and leave Luap to explain it all. Or Luap and Arranha together, an even less likely combination. Luap squeezed his eyes shut, wishing he could think of a deity who might be interested in this minor problem, and untangle it with no effort on his part.

"Luap," said Gird. Here it came, some impossible task. He opened his eyes, to find Gird's expression as uncompromising as ever in a crisis. One of those, then. "You will take this lady—may I have your name?"

"Dorhaniya, bi Kirlis-Sevith," said the old lady.

Eris spoke up again. "Lady Dorhaniya, as a widow, was entitled to revert to her mother's patronymic and her father's matronymic, sir. . . ." As if Gird really cared, but he smiled and went on.

"Luap will escort you, Lady Dorhaniya, to confer with Arranha. I presume there is some ritual . . . you do not merely lay the cloths on the altar yourself, at least not the first time."

"N-no." Her voice was shaky. "N-no. Properly—" Now it firmed; clearly the very thought of propriety and ritual gave her confidence. "Properly new cloths are dedicated by the priest . . . it's not . . . it's not a *long* ceremony," she said, as if fearing that might make a difference.   ·

"I understand. Then you will need to speak to Arranha, tell him what you've done, and have him arrange it."

"Then you will—you give your permission?" She looked up, flushed, starry-eyed as any young girl at her first courting. Gird nodded, and her smile widened, almost childishly, the dimples

showing again. "Oh, *thank* you, Marshal-General. Esea's light—
no—" and the smile vanished. "If you don't honor Esea—"

"Lady," said Gird, as to a frightened child, as gently as Luap
had ever heard him. "Lady, I honor all the gods but those who
delight in cruelty; in your eyes, Esea's light is kindly. May Esea be
what you see; you need give me no thanks, but your blessing I will
take, and gladly."

She had not followed all that, by the bewildered expression, but
she put out her hand, and Gird gave her his. She stood, then, and
said "Then Esea's light be with you, Marshal-General, and—and—
then I can rest, when I see the altar dressed again as it should be."

Chapter Two

Arranha had a favorite walled court, on the west side of the
palace complex, edged with stone benches and centered with a
little bed of fragrant herbs. Against one wall a peach tree had been
trained flat: something Luap remembered from the lord's house in
which he had grown up. Most mornings, Arranha read there, or
posed questions for a circle of students. Luap led Lady Dorhaniya
by the shorter, inside, way, ignoring her running commentary about
who had lived in which room, and what they had done and said.
When he reached Arranha, the priest responded with his usual
cheerfulness to the meeting.

"Lady Dorhaniya! Yes ... weren't you—?"

She had flushed again, whether with anger or pleasure Luap was
not sure. "Duke Dehlagrathin's daughter, and Ruhael's wife, yes.
And you—but I'm sorry, sir, to so forget myself with a priest of
Esea."

"Nonsense." Arranha smiled at Luap. "This lady knew me in my
wild youth, Luap, and like her friends gave me good warnings I
was too foolish to hear."

She softened a trifle. "I blame my sister as much as anyone, she
and your father both. If he had not tried to force a match, or she
had accepted it—"

"I would be a very dead magelord, having fallen honorably on
the turf at Greenfields with my king," said Arranha. "If, that is,
your sister had not knifed me long before, for driving her frenzied

with my questions. She threatened it often enough, even in courtship."

"Well . . . that's over." With a visible effort, the old lady dragged herself from memory to the present. "And my business with you, Arranha, is about the Sunlord, not about the past."

At once, he put on dignity. "Yes, lady?"

She sat on the stone ledge beside him, and recited the whole tale again. Arranha, Luap noted, actually seemed to listen with attention to each detail—but of course it was his god whose rituals mattered here. But when she started to pull the cloth from her bag and unfold it, Arranha put out his hand.

"Not here, lady."

"But I wanted to show you—"

"Lady, I trust your piety and your grandmother's instruction, but you have now told me—Esea's priest—about them. From here, the ritual is his, not yours or mine. Give me the bag."

She handed it over, eyes wide, and Arranha held it on outstretched hands. A pale glow, hardly visible in the sunlight, began to gather around it. Luap realized that the sun seemed brighter, the shadows of vineleaves on the wall darker . . . stiller. No air moved. The glow around the bag intensified, became too bright for eyes to watch. Luap felt a weight pressing down on him, yet it was no weight he knew, nothing like a stone. Light. But very heavy light.

Abruptly it was gone, not faded but simply gone; he blinked at the confusing afterimages of light and shadow. A cool breeze whirled in and out of the courtyard. And the bag on Arranha's outstretched hands lay white as fresh-washed wool, only less white than the light itself. The old lady sat silent, mouth open, eyes wide; her companion's face had paled, and even Arranha had a sheen of sweat on his forehead.

"Lady, your gifts are acceptable, and we can now, with your help, restore Esea's altar to its proper array."

"What *was* that?" Luap asked. Arranha merely smiled at him and shook his head; a fair answer. He offered his arm to the old lady, who roused suddenly from her daze and stood, more steadily than Luap would have expected.

"You should come too," Arranha said, as he guided the women toward the High Lord's Hall. Luap knew better than to ask why; he suspected the answer had to do with his ancestry, and only hoped Arranha wouldn't think it necessary to tell the old lady about *that*. He tried to think of a duty he must perform, right now, somewhere else, and couldn't—and in Arranha's presence, he could not make one up.

Fortunately for his composure, the walk through the maze of passages and little walled yards that had grown around the old king's palace kept the old lady breathless enough that she had no questions to ask. When they finally came to the great court before the High Lord's Hall, Arranha led the way straight across it to the main entrance. Whatever the doorwards may have thought, they offered no challenge to Arranha and Luap.

Inside, the coolness of stone and tile and shadowed air. Most of the windows shattered when the city fell had been boarded up. Luap supposed that someday artists would design new windows to fill the interior with manycolored light, but for now Gird had no intention of spending the land's wealth on such things. The great round hole in the end wall, above the altar, had been left open, for light, and through it the sun's white glare fell full on the pale stone of the floor, a bright oval, glittering from minute specks in the slabs of rock. Luap noticed how it was all the brighter for the shadows around it, focusing the eye on what lay within the light.

Arranha walked up the Hall, followed by the other three, their footsteps sounding hollowly in that high place. They walked through the sun, and back into shadow, halting when Arranha did, then moving at his gesture to stand at either side, where they could see. At the altar, he bowed before laying the bag atop it. His prayer seemed, to Luap, unreasonably elaborate for something so simple as the consecration of a handwoven cloth for its covering, but he omitted none of the details the old lady had mentioned, from the selection of the animal, to the washing and spinning and weaving. From time to time, he asked the old lady for the name of the person who had performed each rite. At last, he came to some sort of conclusion. By then Luap was bored, noticing idly how the sun's oval slipped up the floor, handspan by handspan, as the morning wore on. Arranha's shadow appeared, a dark motionless form; when he looked, the sun blazed from Arranha's robe. It shifted minutely to catch the edge of the altar, which would be in full sun any moment.

Abruptly, in silence, Arranha came alight. As if he had turned in that instant to the translucent stone of a lamp, his body glowed: Luap could see the very veins in his arms, the shadows of his bones. Once more he prayed, this time in a resonant chant. Without haste, yet swiftly as the sun moved, he opened the bag and drew out the cloths, unfolding them with cadenced gestures. In the full light of the sun, that rich embroidery glittered, shimmered, gold and silver on blue. Arranha's hands spread, and passed above the cloth. Its folds flattened as if he'd soothed a living thing. Blue as smooth and deep as the sky . . . light rose from the altar, as light fell from the empty window, to meet in a dance of ecstasy.

Luap did not know if Arranha kept on chanting, or if he fell silent. Until the sun moved from the altar, as it passed midday, he stood rapt in some mystery beyond any magicks he'd thought of. Then the spell passed, and he looked across to find the old lady's face streaked with tears; she trembled as she leaned on Eris's arm. Arranha folded the cloths, just as ceremoniously, and returned them to the snowy bag for storage. Then, stepping away from the altar, he turned to her.

"Lady, Esea accepts your service, and I, his priest, thank you for your years of diligence."

She ducked her head. "It is my honor." From the way she said it, Luap wondered if she had anything else in her life to look forward to. He smiled at her when she looked up, but none of them said anything as they left the Hall. Back outside, she seemed to have recovered her composure, and turned to Luap with a sweet smile.

"You will thank the Marshal-General for me? I will come again, but now—I am a little fatigued. Eris will see me home; please don't trouble yourselves."

"Of course, lady," he said. He might have offered to escort her anyway, but she'd already turned away, and something in Arranha's expression suggested that Arranha wanted to talk to him out of the old lady's hearing. For a few moments, Arranha was silent, then he shook his head abruptly and smiled at Luap, a smile twin to the old lady's, before leading the way back to his own chosen courtyard. There he waved Luap to a seat on the stone bench and sat beside him, hot as it was now in midday. Luap was about to suggest that they find a cool inside room in the palace when Arranha shook his head slowly. "I had forgotten her, you know. Until you brought her, I had not thought of Dorhaniya for years."

"You knew her," Luap said. "A . . . duke's daughter?"

Arranha sighed, and nodded. "Yes—longer ago than I care to think." He gave Luap a searching look, then went on. "You need to know some of this, and you probably don't remember it."

Luap felt himself tense, and tried to relax; he was sure Arranha saw through that, as he did through most pretense. "Don't remember what?"

Arranha peeled a late peach with care, and then handed it to him before starting to peel another for himself. Luap bit the peach fiercely, as if it were an enemy, and Arranha talked as he peeled.

"You need to know that we both saw you, as a child. Dorhaniya and I."

"What!" It came out an explosive grunt, as if he'd been punched in the gut, which is what it felt like.

Arranha gave him an apologetic look. "I didn't remember, until I saw her, and she started talking. Then, thinking of places we'd met before, I remembered. She will remember, too, once she thinks of it. She's the kind of old woman who thinks mostly of people, and where she's seen them. She will tease at her memories, Luap, until your boy's face comes clear, and then she will come to ask you. Be gentle, if you can; that's what I'm asking." He started eating.

Luap could not answer. He had locked all that away, that privileged childhood, a private hoard to gloat over when alone. Now he realized that no one had ever claimed to know both of his pasts ... the nobility had left him strictly alone, a pain he had thought he could not bear, and the peasantry, where he'd been sent, had not known him before. He did not even know, with any certainty, just where his childhood had been spent. It had never occurred to him, during the war, that he might come face to face with anyone but his father who had known him ... that the other adults of his childhood might still exist, and recognize him.

He felt that a locked door had been breached, that he had been invaded by some vast danger he could hardly imagine. His vision blurred. In his mind, he was himself again a child, to whom the whole adult world seemed alternately huge and hostile, or bright and indulgent. He could remember the very clothes, the narrow strip of lace along his cuff, the stamped pattern on the leather of his shoes. And someone else had seen that—someone who knew him now—someone who could estimate the distance between that boy and this man, could judge if the boy had grown as he should, even if the boy had potentials he had never met.

"I—didn't know—" It came out harsh, almost gasping. He could not look at Arranha, who would be disapproving, he was sure.

"I'm sorry." Arranha's voice soothed him, sweet as the peach he'd eaten and which now lay uneasily in his belly. "I was afraid she would tell you and cause you this grief in a worse place ... here, you are safe, you know."

He would never be safe again ... all the old fears rolled over him. He had been safe, secure, in that childhood, and then it was gone, torn away. The farmer to whom he'd been sent had not dared cruelty, but the life itself was cruelty, to one indulged in a king's hall, a child used to soft clothes and tidbits from a royal kitchen.

All around, the walls closed in, prisoning rather than protecting. He could hardly breathe, and then he was crying, shaking with the effort not to cry, and failing, and hating himself. Arranha's arm came around him, warmer and stronger than he expected. He gave up, then, and let the sobs come out. When he was done, and felt as always ridiculous and grumpy, Arranha left him on the bench and came back in a few minutes with a pitcher of water and a round of bread.

"I daresay you feel cheated," Arranha said, breaking the bread and handing Luap a chunk. "Those were your memories, to color as you chose, and here I've pointed out that others live in them."

Luap said nothing. He did feel cheated, but it was worse than Arranha said. Someone had invaded his private memories, his personal space, and torn down his defenses. The only thing that had been his, since he had had neither family nor heritance.

"I don't remember much," Arranha said, musing. "You were a child; I was a priest, busy with other duties. Not often there, in fact."

Luap noticed he said *there* instead of *here,* which must have meant he had not been brought up in Fin Panir—at least, not in the palace complex. That made sense; he remembered a forecourt opening on fields, not streets. He got a swallow of water past the lump in his throat, and took a bite of bread. If Arranha kept talking, he could regain control, re-wall his privacy.

"Someone pointed you out. I was in one of my rebellious stages, so I remember thinking what a shame it was—"

"What?" That came out calmly enough; Luap swallowed more water, and nearly choked.

Arranha chuckled. "Well—she's right, Dorhaniya, that I was troublesome. I questioned—as I do to this day—whatever came into my head to question. Her sister threatened more than once to cut the tongue from my head—and might have done it, too, that one. Anyway, I not only thought the lords' use of peasant women was wrong, I thought it was stupid—and said so. You were an example: a handsome lad, bright enough, eager as a puppy, and by no fault of your own the hinge of great decisions. All the talk was of your potential for magery: not your wit or your courage, not your character or your strength. I thought you had the magery, but that fool of a steward had frightened it out of you; others were hoping you had none."

"Why? Didn't the king have legitimate heirs?" He would be reasonable; he forced himself to ask reasonable questions.

"You didn't know—? No, of course, how could you? Luap, the

king's wife lost four children, either in pregnancy or birthing, and died with her last attempt, who was born alive but died within the year. By then he had taken the fever that left him no hope of children, even if he married again. He did, in fact, but to no purpose. He had sired you just before his wife's death; his older bastards had shown no sign of power, and most—for three were the children of a favorite mistress—died in the same fever that left him sterile."

Luap had never thought of his father as a king with problems. Whatever the king's problems, they could not have been as great as those he gave Luap. It gave him a strange feeling to hear him spoken of, as an archivist might write of a figure of history. In his mind he could see the very phrases that might be used of such a king.

"And his brother and brothers-in-law, and his cousins—all would have been glad to have him die without an heir. As in fact he did, before you were grown."

"But—but then the king Gird killed was not my father?"

"Oh no. Although when Gird told me you were the king's bastard, that's who I thought of, naturally. It was the simple answer, and like so many simple answers, it was wrong." Arranha shook his head, presumably at his own foolishness. "Seeing Dorhaniya again brought it back to me, and then I realized the child's face would grow into one very like yours. The king Gird killed was . . . let me think. First there was his brother, but he died in a hunting accident. So-called. Then his eldest sister's husband, who caught a convenient flux. The king Gird killed was the fourth, or fifth, since your father, a cousin."

"But she said she knew him—when she was talking about mistakes—"

"Well, she knew all of them. So did I. Her father was a duke, her husband one of the cousins—not one who became king; they killed him, I've forgotten how. She did know your father—"

"Does Gird know?"

"Know what?"

"That the king he killed at Greenfields—the king who defiled the Hall—was not my father?"

"I . . . I would have thought so, but . . . perhaps not." *Does it matter?* was clear on his face, then his expression changed. "I see. Of course he must be told, in case he doesn't know. You are not *that* man's son; you would have been the heir, but of a different man. A better man than that, though not much wiser. I'm sorry, Luap, but your father was, for all his troubles, a blind fool. I said it then, and spent a year in exile for it, and I'll say it now, to his son."

"He . . . didn't hate me?" It took all his courage to ask that; it was the deepest fear in his heart, that he had somehow earned his father's hate. Against it he had mounted a fierce defense—it wasn't his fault, it wasn't fair.

"Esea's light! No, he didn't hate you. He put all his hopes on you, but understood only one thing to hope for, and pushed too hard. He was desperate, by then, but that doesn't excuse him."

"No." Luap stared at the pavement under his feet. He had held that grudge too long; he was not ready for a father who had had problems of his own, who had been desperate, who had placed a kingdom's weight on the hope that his latest bastard would grow to have the tools of magery. He was not ready to consider how a king might be trapped by something more honorable than his own pleasure. "My . . . mother?" For the instant it took Arranha to answer, he held the hope that she had been mageborn too.

Arranha gave a minute shrug and spread his hands. "I'm truly sorry; I know nothing about her. When I saw you, she was nowhere in evidence. A tutor had you in hand, and bragged to the king of your wit."

"I don't remember her." He said that to his locked hands, staring at his thumbs as if they were the answer to something important. "I never knew—except that I couldn't ask. It made them angry."

"I daresay it frightened them as much as anything. You know the peasant customs: the mother's family determines lineage. We overrode that, whenever our law intruded into the vills, but quite often the peasants evaded our law one way and another. If you had found your mother, if she had claimed you, her people might have helped her get you away and hide you."

"But she didn't." Luap strained for any memory of his mother, forcing himself to imagine himself an infant, a child just able to stand. Surely he would remember who had suckled him, that first deep relationship; surely he could raise it from the deep wells of memory. A face hovered before him, dim and wavering like the reflection of his own in a bucket of water.

Arranha shrugged again. "It's likely she couldn't. She may have been sent far away; she may have died. That I don't know. Your problems were not her fault, Luap, any more than they were yours."

Too much too soon. His mind ached, overstretched with new and uncomfortable revelations. He had had it all organized, he thought, his past tidied into a coherent tale of childhood wrongs and struggles flowing logically into the conflicts of his adult life. He had constructed it of his own pain, his own understanding, and he had become comfortable with it. Now he must revise it, and found he was unwilling to do so. Tentatively, somewhere in his head, a new version began to take shape, safely remote from the other . . . something he could revise, to bring it into conformance. A tragic king, struggling against destiny—an equally tragic peasant victim, a child doomed from the start to be less than anyone's hopes, including his own.

He spent the rest of that day pretending to write, hoping no one would ask what he was doing. He wanted no supper, but knew that if he did not eat with the others, someone would ask questions. So he forced the food down, complained with the others of the heat, and spent a restless night by his window, staring at a sky whose stars held no messages for him.

The old lady returned days later, as Arranha had predicted. In those two days, Luap had struggled to regain the balance she had disrupted. Arranha had told Gird which king had really fathered him; Gird had grunted, scowling, and then given Luap one of his looks.

"What difference d'you think it makes?" Gird had asked. Luap felt abraded by the look and the question, as if the mere fact of stating his real parentage had been an evasion, or a request for something Gird could not approve. He realized he'd hoped for understanding, for Gird to move toward a more fatherly or brotherly relationship, but now he saw that could not happen. Anything that reminded Gird of his father's blood and rank—even this, which should have made it better—aroused the old antagonism.

This day she came early, before the late-morning heat. He heard, again, her voice below, and went down to meet her. *Be gentle,* Arranha had said; he wasn't sure he could be gentle, but he could be courteous. She wore a dress equally costly, but different, from the day before, more blue and less green in its pattern. Lady Dorhaniya's servant gave him another warning look, as he led them toward an inner room on the ground floor. He had no idea what it had been, but recently it had housed scribes copying the Code from his originals. These, at his nod, left their work gladly enough. The room had a high ceiling and tall narrow windows opening on a court shaded by trees and edged with narrow beds of pink flowers; it held night's coolness and the scent of the flowers as well as the tang of ink and parchment.

"No need to climb the stairs," Luap murmured, offering her a chair. Lady Dorhaniya smiled, but tremulously. Clearly she had something on her mind.

"Thank you, young man. Now let me just catch my breath—"

"A drink of water?" The scribes kept a jug in their room; he poured her a mug. She took it as if it were finest glass, and sipped.

"You should sit down, young man. What I have to say is . . . is very important to you."

Luap tried to look surprised. "I thought perhaps you'd come about something in the Lord's Hall."

"No. It wasn't that." She peered at him, then sat back, nodding. "I wasn't wrong, either. I may not be as young as I was, but I've not lost my memory, for faces. Tell me, these men call you Luap, but do you know your real name?"

"I've always been told it was Selamis," Luap said.

"Ah. You have reason to wonder?"

He shrugged. "Lady, by what I was told, my mageborn father chose my daily name, and gave me no other—common enough with such children."

"You know that much," she said, her eyes bright. "Do you know which lord fathered you?"

"I've been told it was the king," Luap said with more difficulty than he'd expected. "But many bastards dream of high birth."

She bent her head to him, in so graceful a movement that he did not at first recognize it as a bow. "Then I will confirm what you were told: you were the king's son—not this recent king, but Garamis. I saw you many times as a small boy, and you have the same look about the eyes you had then. Your mother was, it's true, a peasant lass—a maidservant in the summer palace—but some said she had mageborn blood a generation or so back."

Even knowing it was coming didn't help. He felt the same helpless rage and fear that had overwhelmed him while listening to Arranha. This old lady, so secure and decent, had *seen* him, remembered him. She had seen his mother, no doubt; she had known his father. He shivered, and looked up to find them both staring at him. The old lady's servant—Eris, he remembered—had a look he could interpret as contempt.

"Does it bother you?" Lady Dorhaniya asked. Her eyes were altogether too shrewd. "You were a charming boy, very well-mannered, and you've grown to a charming man. . . ." It was almost worse, though he could not explain it. If he'd been a bad child, cruel or wicked or dull, that could justify what had happened to him. If his father had been the last, most wicked king, that could justify what had happened to him. But he could see, against the inside of his eyelids, the child he had been, the child she was now describing so carefully . . . the child who wanted so much to please, the child alert to the wishes of those who cared for him. "—you brought me a little nosegay," she said. "So thoughtful, for such a young boy. . . ." He had learned that from a mageborn youth, a few years older, and found it impressed ladies visiting; he had made nosegays for all of them. "—and recitations. Your father had you stand up one night before dinner, and speak the entire text of *Torre's Ride*. You must have been nine or so, then—"

That he remembered; it had been just before he was sent away, and at first he'd thought it was because he'd made an error. His tutor had scolded him for it. He had known, then, that the king commanded that performance, but not that the king was his father. And then the steward had come, with a false smile on his face, to take him to an outlying vill and deliver him to the senior cottager.

"—Just before your dear father died," Lady Dorhaniya said. "I don't expect you remember it. They closed the summer palace, and I suppose you went somewhere else."

She could not know where "somewhere else" had been—to someone like her, the closing of one palace meant the opening of another. His mind, running ahead on its own track, tripped on the memory of "—your dear father died," and came back to the present. "He died after that—not long after that?"

"Yes, that's what I was saying. Before Sunturning, it was, and then Lorthin took the throne, and sent my dear husband into exile for a time. So of course I wouldn't have been to the summer palace even had it been open."

"What—" His mouth had dried; he swallowed and tried again. "Did you know my mother—I mean, her name?"

"You don't remember—? Oh—yes; they sent her away when you were just walking. Her name . . . no, I don't . . . but she was a comely lass, never fear. Darker haired than your father, but with red in it; that's where you got the red highlights in your hair, and your eyes are more like hers. Your face is his, brow, cheek and chin."

That didn't help; she seemed to realize it, for she made one of the meaningless comforting sounds old ladies make, and reached to pat his knee. "There, young man—young prince, I should say, for you alone survive of the royal blood, though it won't do you much good. You've nothing to fear in my memories of you. . . ."

But I do, he thought, feeling himself squeezed between intolerable and conflicting realities. Already I have much to fear from you, and I can't even tell what it is . . . but I feel it. "I . . . don't remember much," he said with difficulty. Even as he said it, details he had forgotten for years poured into his mind as pebbles from a sack, each distinct. Yet it was not a lie, for he could not remember what he most wanted to at the moment, what this old woman had looked like, which of the many noblewomen she had been. He could not remember what she remembered; he had nothing to share, no memories that would make sense to her.

"I expect you remember more than you want, sometimes," she said, surprising him again. He had scant experience of old women, and none of his own background; when he met her eyes, they seemed filled with secret laughter, not unkind. "Most men remember the bad things; my husband, to the day he died, remembered being thrashed for riding his father's horse through a wheatfield near harvest. Yet in his family he had the reputation of being a rollicking lad no punishment could touch. You look now as you did then—sensitive enough to feel a word as much as a blow. That's why I thought, perhaps, my memories could help you. Show you the way you seemed to others—"

"No!" It got past his guard, in a choked whisper; then he clamped his lips tight. Tears stung his eyes. He swallowed, unlocked his jaw, and managed to speak in a voice nearly his own. "I'm sorry, Lady Dorhaniya, but—that's over. It's gone. I don't—don't think about it—"

She sat upright, her lips pursed, her expression unreadable. Then, as if making a decision, she nodded gravely and went on. "Prince, you cannot put it aside that way. It's true, the world has changed; you have no throne, and no royal family to sponsor you. But you must know your past, and make it your own, or you cannot become whatever Esea means for you."

The god's name startled him; he started to say that he was no worshipper of the Sunlord, but stopped himself. Instead, he said, "I swore that I would give up all thought of kingship."

She nodded briskly. "Quite right, too. Pursuing such a claim could only bring trouble to the land and people. And you have had no training for kingship. But this does not mean that Esea has no path lighted for you."

Luap shrugged, easing tight shoulders. "As Gird's chronicler, scribe, assistant . . . it seems clear to me that this is my task." Listening to himself, even he could hear the lack of completion; he was not surprised when she shook her head.

"For now, prince. For now, that is your task, and see that you do it in the Sun's light! But you have more to do—and don't laugh at an old woman, thinking me silly with age." For an instant, she looked almost fierce, white hair and all, though he had not laughed, even inside. "You have a position no one else can share: you are the royal heir, though you have no throne. But you—and only you—can lead your own people—"

"Which of my people?" Luap asked irritably. She was beginning to sound like the Autumn Rose, and he had a sudden vision of that dire lady in old age, still pursuing his irresolution with her own certainty.

That got him a long straight stare; he could feel his face reddening. "That," she said severely, "was unworthy of you. You know quite well I meant your father's folk, the mageborn. I would have thought Arranha would have spoken to you. . . ."

"He has," said Luap, suddenly as disgusted with himself as she seemed to be. "He and the Autumn Rose both. I am supposed to do *something*—but no one can tell me what, or how, or even more how to do it without breaking my oath to Gird—" *And the gods.* Sweat came out on him. What kind of leadership could he give, without using magery he had sworn not to use? What kind of leadership without usurping Gird's authority?

"Of course no one can tell you," Lady Dorhaniya said tartly. "You are the *prince;* you inherited the royal magery—oh yes, I have heard that, too. As the prince, the Sunlord's light is yours, do you choose to ask such guidance. Have you?"

To such a question only a direct answer was possible. "No, lady," said Luap, sweating. He had had a child's knowledge of the gods when he was sent away; after that, among peasants, he could not have worshipped the Sunlord even if he'd wanted to. He had not wanted to; he had been abandoned by his father and his father's god, and he would not pay homage to either of them.

"Well, you should. Esea knows you had a poor enough childhood, with that prune-stuffed steward and whatever happened after your father died, but the fact remains that you are what you are, and unless you learn to *be* that, you're as dangerous as a warsteed in the kitchen." She looked around for her servant, and then hitched herself forward. Luap rose and offered his arm. "Yes—I must be going. I've said too much too soon, it may be. But your father, prince, had more sense than his brothers; somewhere in your head you have it. I suggest you ask the Sunlord's aid, and soon." Then she stopped again. "And who is this Autumn Rose you mentioned?"

That he could answer. "A mageborn lady, a warrior from Tsaia, who joined Gird's army after—"

"Oh, *her*. The king-killer. Some nonsense about her having been involved with the king before his marriage." Lady Dorhaniya sniffed. "She was a wild girl, willful, always storming off about this and that. It's one thing to learn weaponlore, if you've the strength and stomach for it, and another to be starting quarrels just to have the chance of settling them. Not that the prince—later the king— wasn't as bad, for he loved to watch her flare out at things. So she's calling herself Autumn Rose, is she?" From her tone, that was just more foolishness.

"Do you know her name from before?"

The old lady's eyes twinkled in mischief. "Of course I do, but if she hasn't told even Gird, why should I tell you? I doubt she has much family left to be embarrassed, but it's her business, silly as she is." Luap could not imagine anyone thinking Autumn Rose silly. Dangerous and difficult, but not silly. "You might just tell her it sounds more like a title than a name."

Luap grinned. It had not occurred to him that the old lady would have known the Autumn Rose, or, knowing her, might disapprove. She sounded as she might about an errant granddaughter. "I think of her as Rosemage," he said. "Some call her that."

Another sniff. "It would not hurt either of you to ask Esea's guidance," she said. "You've no time for foolishness, either of you, at your ages." Then, with a last nod, she left, leaning only slightly on Eris's arm. Luap followed silently to the outer door, then climbed the stairs to his office. He felt even more unsettled than usual. Everyone wanted something from him, but none of them agreed on what it was. All the decisions he'd made so firmly, in good faith, seemed to be coming apart, unravelling in his hands like rotting rope.

Chapter Three

Through the hottest days of summer, Luap kept to his work. Gird wanted copies of the newest version of the Code spread widely by late harvest; he asked no more about Luap's real father, only about how the copying proceeded. Aside from the heat, the work suited Luap well. He could concentrate his mind on accuracy, on the precise flavor of a phrase, on Gird's intention and its best expression. He had little time for memory, though he found forgotten courtesies creeping into his speech. "It's that old lady, eh?"

asked Gird. Luap agreed it probably was, or perhaps Arranha. He tried not to think about it, and claimed his work prevented visiting Dorhaniya until he'd finished the Code. It was safer not to think of it, to submerge himself in Gird's plans, to become, if he could, the eldest son or younger brother that Gird so desperately needed.

But at last the copying had been done, and in the cooler fall weather, he had more than an excuse to leave Fin Panir—he could best be spared to carry the copies to the larger granges, where more copies could be made to send elsewhere. So it was that on a dank autumn day he found himself peering along the bank of a stream for the overhanging rock and dark entrance to a certain cave.

He did not let himself wonder why he chose not to stay overnight at Soldin, knowing he could not reach Graymere by sundown. When the chill autumn drizzle thickened to gusts of rain, he made for the cave directly. It was the only thing to do. It was logical, reasonable, and he did not have to manufacture an excuse.

It bothered him slightly that he could think of making an excuse. He had legitimate business, Gird's business, in Soldin and Graymere both. No one would have questioned his spending a night in the cave, even if anyone had seen him. The yeoman-marshal in Soldin had suggested that he stay the night there, but obviously saw nothing amiss in Gird's luap choosing to press on, even in bad weather. Young and earnest, he expected such dedication in Gird's personal staff.

Luap had wondered if other travelers used the cave . . . surely they did. But on this dank, dripping evening no smoke oozed from the entrance, and no tethered mounts or draft teams snorted or stamped as he legged his own mount along the creek bank. A pile of blackened rocks marked a firepit, obviously in recent use—but not today. He would have it to himself, unless someone showed up later. He hoped no one would, but he was grateful to the previous users, who had stacked dry wood inside the entrance, out of the rain.

He got his fire going, and went out to gather more wood to dry beside it. Someone had improved the path down to the creek, cutting steps and anchoring them with stone; the single plum he vaguely remembered had suckered into a thicket, now dropping their narrow leaves to the sodden ground. By the time he had found wood to replace what he expected to use, it was nearly dark.

His wet cloak steamed as he set his traveling kettle to boil. So did his horse's coat, and the smell of horse expanded, he thought, to fill the cave as well as his head. Wet wool, wet horse . . . almost as bad as the stench of their army, the last time. And then someone else had done the cooking. His head felt heavy, stuffed with thick smells and memories . . . including that final memory, of Gird's fist against his skull. He ran his hands over his wet hair as if feeling for that old lump. There—it had been there, and another bruise on the other side, where he'd fallen against stone.

He had eaten his soaked wheat and beans, and a lump of soggy bread that wrapping had not kept dry, had gone out into the fine rain to use the jacks he'd dug, and was back in the cave's relative warmth and dryness, when he admitted to himself just why he had chosen that trail, that day, in that weather. Of course he didn't expect anything to happen. He had had his revelation, first from the gods, and then from Gird: you are a king's son, and (or but) you can't be a king. One revelation to a lifetime, Gird had said after Greenfields, and would explain no more than that.

But for Luap it had happened here, and he still did not understand it. As with the rest of his life, he had been shown something, a small glimpse of some mystery, and then it vanished. He had learned to hoard such glimpses, to keep them hidden deep in his mind, until he found another—and another—and could try to make them fit some pattern. He had learned, he realized, in all the ways Gird despised . . . that he himself despised, when he thought how he admired Gird . . . but ways he could not change. Not now. Gird had all the pieces of his pattern—had always had them. He had always known who he was, and what his place was, growing out of his own ground like a young tree. Luap had had sidelong looks, sly taunts, occasional brief phrases, whispers, suggestions, riddles. "Don't you know, boy?" he remembered an older youth had asked once. "Only bastards don't know who their fathers are." The boy had been yanked away by someone in guards' uniform, and disappeared; Luap never saw him again.

He sat staring at the flames, ignoring the dancing shadows on the walls that shifted, bowed, straightened in answer to the flames' movement. He had come back because . . . because he was going back in there, to the place where he got one straight answer, for once in his life, and might—no matter what Gird said—get another.

But that means, one of his inner voices said, *that you are not content to be Gird's luap.* Was that true? Alone in the cave, in the orange firelight, he let himself think about that. *Feel* about that. He did not resent Gird. Gird had won his heart, that first night, when he had had to confess his duplicity, when Gird had let him sob out the agony of loss. Gird had defended him against the other peasant leaders. And even the blow that felled him had been, he realized, justified. In the years since, he had come to believe that Gird, with all his peasant coarseness, all his human failings, had the intrinsic greatness of an ancient tree, or a mountain.

Yet he did not want to be *only* a luap forever. He let himself remember, cautiously, his life before the war. His wife and children were long dead, their suffering ended. He would regret his treatment of them for the rest of his life . . . but that was in the past. Tonight . . . tonight, he would like to have had a woman beside him. A child leaning against his knee. A place where he, not Gird, was paramount. A kingdom, however small, in which to be king.

Here, inside a whole mountain, on a black night of dripping rain, no one would see him use his power; no one could see his light. It could not be betrayal if no one knew. He felt his way to it cautiously, even here—a little light, just enough to see by—and his hands enclosed it, glowing. He felt the hairs rise on his arms. He could still do it; it had not vanished. Despite Arranha's assurance that it would not, he had doubted. Around him, in the throat of the cave, the walls showed their stripes of gray and pink and brown. There was the ledge over which Gird had stumbled . . . there, the opening beyond.

Gingerly, he edged toward it. The little chamber opened, then enclosed him, as if he completed it. Its walls held the same graved patterns he remembered, that Gird had traced with his thumb, that Luap had devoured with his eyes, trying to remember them. Spiral on spiral, coil in coil, lacing and interlacing. He turned, slowly, following the pattern . . . it felt *strong,* and meaningful, but he could not read it. A bad taste came into his mouth: another failure.

On the chamber's floor, curiously clean of dust, multicolored tesselations glowed in his light, inviting. A different pattern, in which color as well as line interacted, in which his eye was teased, frustrated, satisfied, and finally released with a *snap* that echoed in his head. He looked up.

And up.

He stood, not in the small bell-shaped chamber of the cave, but in a lofty hall, larger than the Lord's Hall in Fin Panir, lit by unshadowed silvery light. He could see no windows, no source for the light. He stood on a pattern like that on which he began, but set on a raised dais large enough for a score to stand uncrowded. All his hair rose; cold chills shook him; his own pulse thundered in his ears.

At last he could hear and see clearly again, only to find great silence and unmoving space about him. He did not want to speak, and risk waking whatever power held sway here, but courtesy demanded some greeting. In his mind, he recited the opening phrases to the first ritual he remembered, something out of his childhood, the morning greeting to the Sunlord. Around him, unbroken silence changed its flavor from austerity to welcome. Was he imagining it? He took a slow, shuffling step forward, away from the pattern. Nothing. He was not sure what he half-expected, but he felt like a child exploring forbidden adult territory. For an instant, such a moment flashed before his eyes, a tower bedroom crowded with furniture, rich hangings, a bed piled with pillows, and the furious eyes, four of them, that glared at him before an angry voice rose and whirled him away on its own power.

No. He was grown, and whoever that had been must have died in the war, if not before. He fought down the fear that trembled in his knees and walked forward, off the dais, across a pattern of black and white stones, to the high double arch that closed the end of the hall. Not truly closed, for he could see less brightly lit space beyond, but he didn't want to walk under those arches. At the top of one, a harp and tree intertwined; on the other, a hammer and anvil. He shivered: he could not imagine a place where elves and dwarves would both choose to carve their holy symbols. He turned back.

The dais, at that distance, seemed apt for a throne; he closed his eyes, and let himself imagine seeing one there, and himself— no, not on the throne, but walking up the hall toward it. His imagination peopled the hall with vivid colors, the richly dressed lords and ladies of his childhood. Music would fill the hall, harp and drum and pipe, and from that celebration no one would be sent away, solitary, to cry in the dark. His power prodded him from within, responding to some influence he could not directly sense.

He opened his eyes. He could still see what it would be like, but—he shook his head to force the vision away—that was daydream, and this was—if not reality—at least something less tuned to his wish. It lay empty, gracefully proportioned, but blank stone, not filled with the friends he had never had.

Soon he realized that it must be all under stone somewhere, for in his cautious exploration he found no window, no door, no hint of outside weather or time. Fresh air, in currents so gentle he could not detect a source, lighted corridors and chambers, all carved of seamless red stone, all empty, all silent but for his footfalls echoing from the walls. No sign of living things, not the Elder Races he assumed had built it, or the animals that should be inhabiting any such underground warren. He dared not explore too far; he went cold again at the thought of being trapped here forever, in some vast nameless tomb, if he lost his way back to the main hall.

Then it struck him that he might be trapped anyway. Would the pattern work again, and if it did would it bring him back to the cave he knew? Trembling, he placed himself on the dais, on the pattern, as precisely as he could. With a last look around, he concentrated on the pattern, and his own power. A cold shiver, as if touched by ice, and he was back in a bell-shaped chamber. The same such chamber? He intensified his own light, and went back toward the cave mouth . . . to find there the embers of his fire, his blanket, his damp socks now dry on the hot stones. He felt almost faint with relief.

All that night he sat crosslegged with his back against the rock, hardly aware of the rain outside or the smell of horse. In his head, the puzzle pieces would not merge, made no sense. What kind of place was this? What kind of place was *that*? Twice he found himself on his feet, headed back to the chamber to see if it would work again, and twice he forced himself back to the fire. He shouldn't try it again until he'd thought it out, and thinking *at* it wasn't the same as thinking it out.

Should he tell Arranha? He could imagine the priest's eager questions, his childlike curiosity. Arranha would tell everyone else, hoping to stumble on someone with more lore, if it were but fireside tales. He didn't want others to know yet, not until he knew more himself. The Rosemage would want to come try it for herself; she might keep it a secret from everyone but Gird, but she would not let the knowledge rest idle—she would insist that he *do* something with it. And telling either of them meant that Gird would find out, and Gird would not overlook the use of magery if he found out through someone else. So—should he tell Gird first? That would mean admitting the use of magery, unless he could claim that the pattern acted without his power—and lying to Gird was always, no matter how good the reason, tricky. At best. At worst, Gird would hit him again (he rubbed his scalp, remembering).

The next day, in the rain-wet woods between Soldin and Graymere, he argued with himself and his internal images of Gird, Arranha, the Autumn Rose. Surely the gods would not have given him the power, shown him the inner cave, if they had not meant him to use them. In his head, Arranha agreed, pointing out that using magery where no one could see it, where it could affect no one but himself, was very like using no magery at all. It had not been oathbreaking, because he had not sought power, or influenced anyone, or taken command unbidden. The Autumn Rose also approved; he imagined her striding along that vast hall as if she owned it: she fit that sort of space. She would want to know where it was; she would want to know who had been there before, who built it, who used it now. He had a moment's vision of her confronting a troop of very surprised dwarves somewhere in those warrens, and almost laughed.

Gird, though. Gird stood in his head foursquare and awkward. *You used magery*, that image said, scowling. Only a little, and it didn't hurt anyone, he answered. And look what I found. *Excuses*, said Gird's image in his mind. *Truth's truth, lad: you swore to give up the mage powers, and you used them.* Even in his own mind, Gird had the stubbornness of a great boulder in a field, or a massive oak; he felt that his own arguments scratched around and around, going nowhere and moving that obstruction not even the width of a fingernail.

By Graymere, he'd convinced himself to tell the Autumn Rose and no one else until she'd had a chance to try the pattern herself. She might agree to keep it secret from Gird until she had used it, or tried to; perhaps Gird would accept that if Luap explained he had wanted confirmation from someone else before "bothering" Gird. Between Graymere and Anvil, by way of Whitberry, he changed his mind, and planned to tell only Arranha. Arranha, for all his skewed approach to things, would be more likely to know what those symbols carved in the arches meant, if there had been a time when elves and dwarves worked stone together. Approached carefully, he might be willing to keep this secret, at least for awhile. But on the long, muddy track back to Fin Panir from Anvil, he realized that he would have to tell Gird, and risk the consequences. If Gird found later that others had known, he would not forgive— he would not even listen. His one chance was to tell Gird first, and hope that curiosity had not completely abandoned the Marshal-General.

He wanted to keep it secret. He wanted one place, one small corner of his life, in which Gird had no standing. He rode hunched against the wind, eyes slitted, remembering that vast silence, that sense of absolute privacy. He did not have to decide *now*—for certainly he was the only one to have this knowledge. As long as he did not choose to share it, he could have his secret kingdom. His mind flinched from the words—he was not to seek a kingdom. It was more like the memories he had once held privately: a secret, but nothing so dangerous as a kingdom.

But he would have to tell Gird, he argued to himself. It would not be honest to do otherwise. Although it *would* be important to pick exactly the right time to tell Gird—when the Marshal-General was in the right mood, when he had no pressing worries, when they had ample time to discuss it. From experience, he knew the first few days back in Fin Panir would be a chaotic jumble of work. It might easily be a hand of days, or two, before he could find time to tell Gird about something which, after all, was of no practical importance to the Fellowship.

"Luap . . . sir?" Luap glanced up to see a strange yeoman in the doorway, twisting his conical straw hat in his hand. "It's about Gird. . . ."

Luap realized he had not heard anything from the other end of the corridor for a long time. He had been working steadily through the mass of accounts and correspondence that had, as he expected, kept him at his desk every day since his return. Gird had been out much of the time, busy with court work. Now his heart faltered—had Gird died? But the man was already speaking, concern overcoming nervousness.

"He come in for a meal like he does so often," the man said. "And then he sees this old friend from back at Burry or some-such place. And they gets to talking and taking a bit of ale, you know. . . ." His voice trailed away. He didn't want to say it. Luap sighed.

"You'd like someone to help him home?" he asked.

The man nodded. "This friend, see, he's eggin' him on, like, and Gird won't listen to the innkeeper or even the cook. . . ."

Luap realized that he'd seen the man before after all. He worked in the stables at the largest inn down by the lower market. He groaned inwardly. It was going to be a hard job getting Gird back up the hill. "Do you have a spare room, perhaps?" he asked.

"Well . . . I suppose maybe, but after what he called the innkeeper . . ."

"I'll come now," said Luap, standing. Whom could he call? He'd need more arms than two, if Gird had drunk his fill. He flung his blue cloak around him, and took the stout stick that had become a Marshal's insignia, though all knew he was no Marshal. A glance out the window of the room across the corridor located Marshal Sterin, and a yell brought him in, sweaty and cross from drilling novices.

"Gird?" he said. "What's the Marshal-General want now?"

"A friend's help to come home," said Luap. "He's down at the Rock and Spring."

"Ahh . . ." Sterin cut off whatever he'd almost said, with a glance at the man from the inn. "Met an old friend, did he?"

"From Burry, this man thinks. Got to talking about the war—"

"I see. We'll need another, and it can't be a novice. Too bad Cob's not here. Tamis Redbeard?"

"Good," said Luap. Tamis Redbeard stood a hand taller than he did, and could probably lift Gird in one hand. If he wasn't fighting back.

They could hear Gird and someone else before they came in sight of the inn. Singing, none too melodiously, one of the songs written after Greenfields. A small crowd loitered outside the inn, a few lucky ones close enough to peer in the windows. It parted like butter before a hot knife, then flowed back as seamlessly, as Luap led the others through the door.

"There was a man rode out one day
Upon a horse, a horse of gray
And all along the people saaaay
He must be such a king, oh . . ."

The man from Burry, or wherever, had one arm around a post, and one around Gird's shoulders. He had reached the green stage; Luap thought he would vomit in a moment or two. Gird had still the flush of early drunkenness, a red rim to each eye and a glitter in them.

"Marshal-General, we've need of you up the hill," Luap began. It wouldn't work, but he could start with respect and good sense.

"No court today," said Gird, head thrust forward. He belched, grinned at his companion. "So we're just taking a bit of ale, like, and singing the old songs. No harm in that. Everybody's got to have some time—"

"No, it's not court," Luap said. "It's something else."

"I know," said the other man, slurring the words. "You think we're drunk and ye've come to nursemaid th' old man." Luap glared at him; that would end any chance of Gird cooperating. Gird glowered, first at his companion and then at Luap.

"Is that what it is, you think I need a keeper?"

"No, sir. We've need of you, that's what I said."

"And you need me so much you brought two Marshals along? Can't you ever tell the truth, Luap? Did you think I wouldn't know Sterin and Tamis, big as they are, with their staves?"

Luap gritted his teeth. It was not *fair*, in front of all these people, and in such a cause. Confront drunks directly and start a brawl— even Gird said that, when he was sober. It wasn't as if he himself hadn't used subterfuge on other drunks, from time to time. Rage scoured his mind, eroding the controls he placed so carefully. He opened his mouth, but Sterin was before him.

"Aye, Father Gird, if you'll have the truth of it, we was told you'd drunk more'n was good for you, and would be the better of friends to bring you home. Yer friend there's had more'n his fill; he's green as springtime berries, and the both of ye smell like ye've emptied a barrel—"

"Lemme alone," began the other man, when Sterin reached to unhook his arm from Gird's shoulder. Then he turned even greener around the mouth, his eyes widened, and he spewed across the floor, then fell headlong in the mess. Sterin had stepped back, not quite in time, and now gave Luap a disgusted glance. He shrugged.

"I'll get this mess clean," he said, meaning man and floor both. "You and Tam get the Marshal-General back before he doubles it." Luap fought down another surge of anger. Sterin was in his rights, as the senior Marshal present, but did he have to make it so obvious that Luap had no right of command?

"Yes, Marshal Sterin," he heard himself saying, the effort at courtesy clearly audible and destroying the effect he had meant to produce. He and Tam moved around the man from Burry, now struggling to sit up, and moved into position beside Gird. He put his arm under Gird's elbow, ready to lift or push or whatever would be necessary.

"Let's go now," he suggested, in the calm quiet tone that worked best with most drunks. Gird glanced from one to the other.

"I am not drunk." As always in this state, his words came slow, the peasant accent distinct. "My father wouldn't put up with it."

"Your father's dead these many years." Luap heaved, as effectively as he might have heaved at a live, deep-rooted oak. "Come on, now, man . . . you've got to get back home."

"No home." His forehead knotted. "Gone. Went away."

The other drunk, still pale from throwing up the first wash, tittered weakly. "I'm not that drunk," he lied. "*My* home didn't go away."

"Shut *up*," Luap muttered at the man from Burry. "Sterin—get him away." He had seen the expression on Gird's face before, the swift change from hilarity to grim sadness. It had something to do with whatever happened the morning of Greenfields, which Gird would not speak of—but he was more dangerous in this mood than any other. The man from Burry vanished, and in a few moments Sterin reappeared. Luap could feel the tension in Gird's shoulders, some mingling of rage and sorrow.

"No home," Gird said again. "Never . . . it will never be. . . ." All around the eyes stared, the ears listened; Luap could almost see the legend growing. In a moment someone would decide it was prophecy, that Gird had the foreseeing gift beside all his others. He caught Tamis's eye, and Sterin's, and gave a minute nod. "It is not finished!" Gird's voice sharpened, and Sterin, who had reached for his other arm, stopped to give Luap a worried glance. Somewhere outside, Luap could just hear pattering hooves of sheep or goats, and a voice calling to them. Everyone in sight was silent, motionless, waiting Gird's next word. And this, too, he would have to explain, somehow, when Gird sobered up the next day, for all that some thought the gods spoke truly to men drowned in wine.

"It is not finished!" Gird said again, louder. "Not until mageborn and nonmage live in peace, not until the same law rules farmer and brewer, crafter and crofter, townsman and countryman. Not until they agree—" He paused, breathing hard, as if from battle, then he shook his head. "And they won't," he said quietly, sadly. For all Luap's recent annoyance, he found himself moved, almost to tears, by that tone. "They want what cannot be—" He turned to face Luap. "You do, whether you know it or not—and they—and maybe I myself wish for what cannot be." He spoke still quietly, but with such intensity that everyone around stood breathless, straining to hear. "It should not be so hard, by the gods! To agree to live in peace: what's so hard about that? Or is it because I didn't die at Greenfields?"

Luap stared at him, feeling the hairs rise on his scalp and along his arms. Die at Greenfields? What did he mean? He peered around Gird to meet on Tamis's face the expression of what he felt: fear and confusion.

"They told me," Gird said, now almost conversationally, "that I would not live to see the peace. I came down from the hill to die— and then lived. Is it that?"

"Thank Alyanya's grace you *did* live, sir," said Tamis quickly, and Sterin murmured something similar. Luap couldn't say anything; his mouth was dry, his tongue stuck to the roof of it. He had never believed in the drunkard's truth, but this was truth if ever he heard it.

But Gird was shaking his head. "My head hurts," he said. "It's hot. I think—I think I'll go back—if you'll settle with the innkeeper, Luap?"

He walked off, not quite steadily, Tamis and Sterin at either elbow, leaving Luap to pay and—since Sterin had gone—to help the innkeeper in mopping the stinking floor. *That's what I'm good for,* Luap thought. *Pay the bills, keep the accounts straight, clean up after him.* That wasn't a fair assessment, and he knew it, but he indulged himself a little anyway. It wasn't fair that Gird had called him a liar in public, when he was only trying to be tactful.

When he had finished mopping, much of the crowd had melted away, as crowds do. Not as interesting to watch a sober man mop a floor as watch a drunk foul it . . . and Gird hoped to make a strong and peaceful society out of these sheep? The innkeeper accepted his coins with a sour look, although he'd added a sweetener to the total. "Great men!" the innkeeper said, leaving no doubt that he was still angry. "I'm not saying a thing against what he did, y'understand, but that doesn't give him th' right to call honest men thieves or cowards."

Luap couldn't decide if an apology would do any good, and his momentary silence seemed to irritate the innkeeper even more.

"I know what you're like," the man went on, feeling each coin ostentatiously before putting it in his belt-pouch. "You won't tell me what you think, but anything I say goes straight to *him.*"

"He's not like that," Luap said.

"Huh. He's not, or you don't tell him everything?" Shrewd hazel eyes peered at him. Luap shrugged.

"Tomorrow he'll be sorry he insulted you; surely you know that. Bring it up at the next market court, and he'll fine himself and apologize before as large a crowd as heard the insult."

"Oh, aye. Apologies don't mend broken pottery or put wool back on a shorn sheep. My da said them's don't make mistakes don't have to waste time on apologies." Luap wondered where the innkeeper had been during the war. The innkeeper answered that, too, in his final sally. "We've had royalty in here, you know, before the rabble—before the revolution. Dukes, even a prince of the blood. Knew how to hold their wine, they did, and it wasn't any of this cheap ale, neither."

Luap's temper flared. "Well, you've had another prince of the blood, for what that's worth."

The innkeeper's eyebrows went up. "Who, then?"

"Me," said Luap, turning to go, sure of the last word. But the innkeeper cheated him of that, as well.

"But raised with peasants, weren't you then? Makes a difference, don't it? It's not like you're a real prince, just some summer folly, eh?"

And if that's not enough to sour a day, thought Luap as he

climbed back to the upper city, there's maudlin Gird, who will no doubt spout more difficult prophecy I'll have to explain.

Down below conscious thought, he was not aware of the relief he felt: another day in which he had a good reason not to tell Gird about the cave.

Chapter Four

Raheli leaned against the barton wall, arms folded, watching the dancers through the open grange door. Out of courtesy for her, to spare her the long walk to the traditional sheepfold, they had brought the musicians here . . . they were dancing *here* . . . and she could do nothing but watch. She knew the music, the same as she'd heard all her life, and every step the dancers danced. She could remember, as if it had been yesterday, the night when Parin's hand on her arm changed her from girl to woman. When the dance had changed from entertainment to courtship, and they had begun the dance of life that ended with his death.

She tried not to think of it; she had pushed it aside, so many times, from the moment the mageborn lords had broken his head. She would not let herself brood on it; it did no good. But the old songs ran into her heart like knives; for an instant she almost thought she felt the flutter of that life she had never actually borne. Her child, and his. The face that had come to her in dreams, as her mother had said her children's faces had come. She could smell the very scent of him, feel the warm skin of his chest against her cheek.

The dancers shouted, ending one dance, and a short silence fell. In the torchlight, the dancers' faces wavered, bright light and black shadow, as strange for a moment as ghosts. Raheli had the feeling for a moment that Parin and the child both were in there, some-where, waiting for her. She had pushed herself off the wall before she realized what she was thinking. Her movement had caught someone's eye; before she could return to her place, she saw people watching her. She would have to go in, and greet them. She tried to smile, and walked forward.

"Rahi! The Marshal's back!" yelled some of the younger yeomen. A way opened for her. They had been dancing a long time; the grange smelled of sweat and onions and the torches and candles, more like a cottage during a feast than a grange. "Now we can dance the Ring Rising."

They meant it as an honor. They could not know she had danced the Ring Rising with Parin, that first time. Rahi blinked away scalding tears, put off her old grief, and accepted the role they demanded of her. The musicians finished their mugs of ale, and picked up the instruments again.

Ring Rising had been, Gird told her once, older than any other dance. Something about it had to do with the old Stone Circle brotherhood, that Gird had turned into the Fellowship, in his own way. But long before, so the oldest tales went, the dance had raised stones, rings of stones, on hill after hill, until the mageborn came and struck them down with their new magic.

Hand in hand with her senior yeoman-marshal, Belthis, Rahi began the dance to the beat of the finger-drums. Couple after couple fell in behind them. It felt strange to dance this indoors; the walls seemed to lean inward, pressing on them. What if it did move stones? Rahi concentrated on the intricate steps, feeling her way back into the rhythms. Heel, toe, side, back, skip forward, stamp. A step, a double-stamp. Now a double line of couples, two concentric rings, then a swirl that twisted them to interlocking rings, dancing in and out of each other's patterns. Soon all there had joined in, children and elderly as well as the young adults. Rahi found herself moving through four interlocked rings, touching hands with one partner after another for a quarter-turn, then swinging to find another.

It was in the midst of the dance, with the grange full to bursting of music and dancers, that she came face to face with her dream, the child she would have borne. Dark hair, dark eyes, Parin's smile, soft fingers, light-footed and blithe. Her breath caught in her throat, but they had danced the pattern and separated again before she could get a word out. Tears burned in her eyes; she felt them on her cheeks, on the scar ... and someone she could not see for tears put an arm around her shoulders, making sure she did not falter in the dance, until her breath came easily again.

It was not fair. It had never been fair. She rejected bitterness as instantly as she would have fear. Fairness had nothing to do with it, and everything, and was all Gird had wanted, and more than she would ever have. From bootheel to the top of her head, she felt the beat of that ancient dance, and from hand to hand the warmth and love of her people, and in the middle where the cadence and warmth met, she could feel her heart beating, expanding and contracting, as if it had grown larger than her chest.

Around her the faces glowed, all the children her children, all the men and women her brothers and sisters, her aunts and uncles, fathers and mothers. Her own scars bound her to them, to all those maimed or sickened by life's disasters. *Her* people, with their ancient link to land and deeper magic than the mageborn would ever know . . . and it had not been fair, but she would make it fair. Light and dark, true and false, as simple as the realities they had all endured: hungry and not hungry, cold and not cold, pregnant and not pregnant. She felt herself rising above them, lifted on their affection and trust like a leaf on a summer wind, like the stones of the great rings in which peace and plenty dwelt. Here was the child she had lost, and the love she had lost, and here she would serve.

When the music stopped, she did not know it; she came to herself slowly, realizing silence and space around her. The torches had burned low, but gave a light unusually steady. Then, as she drew a long breath, the murmurs began. The senior yeoman-marshal of the grange bowed to her. "Marshal—it was our honor."

"My pleasure," she replied, hardly thinking. She felt different, but could not yet define the difference; she would have to think about it later. She glanced around. They were all watching her, most smiling, as if she were the favorite grandchild at a family gathering. *Once, I was,* she thought, and felt the scar on her face stretching to her grin. Now they moved closer, touching her arm, her shoulder; her heart lifted, suddenly exultant. She could have hugged them all, but had no need—she could tell by their expressions that they felt what she meant, just as she felt what they meant. Once, and again, she had a place, the place she had thought lost forever.

The next morning, she set out for Littlemarsh barton with a lighter heart than she'd had for years. She felt in place, comfortable; she thought of Gird suddenly with a warmth that surprised her. Could he have felt estranged, in these past years? She thought of him once more as a father, as the father he had been to her. Not perfect, not with his temper and his occasional bouts of drunken depression, but a man who loved his children even more than his beloved cows. For the first time in years, she let herself think of her mother: her face came to memory only dimly, but her words, her movements, the very smell of the bread she made and feel of her strong arms were as clear as if she'd died the day before. That was what she'd hoped to be—another woman like her mother—but time and chance had stolen that from her, as the lords' cruelty had stolen her mother's life, robbing her of peaceful old age.

Yet this morning, bitterness could not swamp the better memories. Mali had laughed a lot; even her scoldings had held warmth and good humor in their core. They had been, within the limitations of hunger and cold and fear, a family drenched in love. From that love, Gird had found the strength to hold and lead an army; from that love she herself had found the strength to come back from an easy death, lead others in battle, and care for them after. For all that had gone wrong, all the wickedness loosed on innocents that she had seen, love and caring had not abandoned the world— or her.

"Alyanya's blessing," she murmured, feeling the tears run over her face, knowing they were healing something. She was not cut off, alone, alienated from her people, a useless barren woman who could only hope for death. She had a family: all of them. She had given her blood, though not in childbirth, and this day she knew that gift had been accepted, by the gods and by her people.

I will go to Gird, she thought, half in prayer and half in promise. *I will tell him he has a daughter again, and not just another Marshal.* In her mind's eye, she saw him grin at her; she saw his arms open; she felt the welcoming hug she had told herself she would never seek again.

Raheli dismounted stiffly. After six days in the saddle, she felt every one of her old wounds, and twice her age. She led her brown gelding into the stable, shaking her head at the junior yeoman who would have helped her. Taking care of her own mount came naturally to a farm girl. She stripped off the saddle and rubbed the sweat marks with a twist of straw. The junior yeoman had brought a bucket of water and scoop of grain; when her horse was dry, she put feed and water in the stall and heaved the saddle to her hip, closing the stall door behind her. Gird's gray horse, in the next stall, put its head out and looked at her.

"You," she said, with emphasis. The gray flipped its head up and down. Cart horse, she thought. Da should know better than that. She would never forget how it had shone silver-white in the sun at Greenfields. Here, in the dim stable, it looked gray enough, but she knew its coat would shine in the sun. It took her sleeve in its lips, carefully, its eyes almost luminous. She rubbed its forehead, scratched behind its ears, and it opened its mouth in a foolish yawn. "You don't fool me," she told it, and it shook its head. "Right." Gird had loved cows, from her earliest memory, as much or more than people; she wondered that the gods had sent him a horse and not a magical cow. A snort from the gray horse. "I know—I'm not supposed to know the gods sent you." She herself had discovered an affinity with horses, and the gray had responded much as others did, with its differences in addition.

Out of the stable, across the inner courtyard. In her Marshal's blue, with the saddlebags that proclaimed her a visitor from some outlying grange, she found a way opened for her in the crowds (they seemed like crowds) that thronged the court and the passages of the old palace. The two guards at the outer door had nodded to her, not questioning her right to enter. Up the stairs, along the corridor, to the office where Luap—she had come to calling him that after Gird did—kept accounts and made the master copies of Gird's legal decrees. She looked in—empty, but for the sick lad she'd heard about, asleep again. Gird's office, near the end of the corridor, was empty too. She frowned. Usually this time of day one or both of them were at work here. She left her saddlebags on his desk, and went down to the kitchen.

"Rahi!" One of the cooks on duty recognized her at once. "When did you get in? How long can you stay?"

"Just now," she said, pouring herself a mug of water. "I'm not sure how long I'll be here yet—where's Gird?"

A sudden silence; eyes shifted away from her. She felt her heart quicken even before the first woman said anything. "Oh—he's not feeling too well today. Nothing serious—"

He'd gotten drunk again. She was sure of it. She had come here to make peace with him, to restore their family, and he had gone off and gotten drunk. Rage blurred her vision, and she fought it down. She would not ask these people; it would embarrass them. She made herself smile. "Well—if he's not up to work, perhaps I could find something to eat?"

"Of course." In moments, a bowl of soup and a loaf were before her. "I don't know if you remember me . . . ?" The woman looked to be her own age, or a little older, not so tall and plumper. Rahi tried to think, but nothing came back to her. "Arya, in the third cohort of Sim's . . ." the woman prompted.

Yes. Arya had been thinner—they all had—but strong and eager, one who never argued about camp chores, either. "I do now," Rahi said, pulling off a hunk of the warm bread. "You taught us all a song about the frog in the spring, I remember." She hummed a line, and Arya grinned.

"You look like your da when you smile," she said. "But dark hair . . ."

"My mother," said Rahi, around the bread, relaxing. Arya had come from a vill much like her own; the talk about which parent a child resembled was as comforting as old tools. Next the talk would turn to their mothers' parrions.

"Since you're here . . ." Arya said, then paused, floury hands planted firmly on the table. Rahi swallowed the bread in her mouth and waited. Arya looked away, but didn't move, and finally came out with it. "There's some of the Marshals saying that now the war's over, there's no need for women to be taken into the bartons. There's some of them saying the Code's too partial to wives. Have you heard of that?"

Rahi nodded. "Mostly in the bigger towns, is where I've heard it. Mostly from men who weren't in the fighting at all, crafters and traders and such."

Arya sat down across from her. "It's the same here, but some of the Marshals—I'd have thought they'd have more sense—some of the Marshals have taken it up. Taken it to Gird, even. I heard it myself, one evening: pecking at him like crows at a sack of grain, all about how there's no need for it now, and the women won't make good wives or mothers if they're always drilling in the bartons. That in the old days our women had parrions of cooking or healing or clothmaking, not parrions of weaponwork."

"He won't listen," said Rahi. "He lost that argument a long time ago." She didn't realize she was grinning until she felt her scar stretch; she was seeing in her mind's eye the blank astonishment on Gird's face that day in the forest camp.

"For you, maybe," Arya persisted. "He would never try to stop you—but what about the rest of us?"

"But you're a veteran," Rahi said. "No one could put you out of the barton now—"

"Not exactly. Not yet." Arya spread her hands. "I shouldn't be bothering you, maybe, but you were the first—and we all look to you. Some of us don't intend to be wives, or go back to farms; we like what we're doing now. And if anyone can keep Gird from taking it away—"

"Don't give it up." She knew now what was coming, and hoped to head it off with a short answer.

"That's what I say," said the other woman, coming now to sit beside Arya. She was younger, darker, with the intensity of youth. Rahi wondered if she had ever been really tired. "It's not up to Gird; our lives aren't something for him to give or take. Arya's a veteran, same as anyone else who fought; why shouldn't she live however she wants? It's not like she was a mageborn lady who needed watching."

"But you know yourself, Lia, it's not that easy—"

"Gird always said nothing's easy that's any good—isn't that right?" The other woman faced Rahi with a challenging stare.

"But are you really afraid he'll change the Code?" asked Rahi. "I'm not the only woman who's a Marshal, you know." But some gave it up, she reminded herself. Some went home, back to a family if they had one, or to start a second family if they'd lost husband and children. When she ran through the list in her mind, perhaps half the women who had won Marshal's rank still held it. In her own grange, fewer women came to the drills as the memory of war faded, as fear of invasion lessened. She had not pushed them, she suddenly realized, as she pushed the men—she had accepted all the usual reasons: pregnancy, a new baby, a sick child, an ailing husband or parent.

"It's not just the training," the other woman—Lia—went on. "Who wants to fight in a war, after all? I was too young for fighting then; I train now because Arya tells me I should. Without her, I'd wait until trouble came before I picked up a sword. But the rest— you know how it was. Under the lords' rule, women could hold no land, even as tenants; in the city, women couldn't rent buildings or speak before a court for themselves. *Father's daughter; husband's wife; son's mother*—that's how it was for all but the mageborn ladies. My mother was a widow; she had no son. She had to ask her brother for houseroom for us, and I had to take him for my da. If the war hadn't come, he'd have married me to the tanner's son, and taken his share of the bride-price. The mageborn didn't have that problem—that woman everyone calls the Autumn Rose, or the Rosemage—"

Rahi snorted; she couldn't help herself. Arya grinned. "I remember what you called her, Rahi."

"Don't say it!" Rahi held up a hand, chuckling. "I've been told often enough how rude I was. Am. And if my mother were alive, she'd say throwing a name at someone is like throwing mud at the sky. It always comes back on you."

"But what I meant was it was different for them," said the younger woman, earnestly. "Their ladies had the right to choose; they had the right to learn weaponscraft—"

"Easy, Lia," said Arya. "Rahi knows all that, none better." She took the younger woman's hand in hers, squeezed it. "Rahi's not going to let her da, even the Marshal-General that he is, change

the laws back and put free women under men's thumbs again."
The look she gave Rahi said *Are you?* as clearly as words.

Rahi shook her head, and bit into the bread as if she hadn't
eaten in days. It made her uncomfortable, the way so many women
acted around her, as if she were a sort of Marshal-General for
women, and Gird was the one for men. Whenever she traveled,
women would come to her with their problems, things their own
marshals should have handled, things she had no idea how to handle. She supposed she deserved it: she had been the first, and the
arguments she'd used on Gird still seemed reasonable. But when
she heard them coming back at her from someone else's mouth—
and when some women went far beyond anything she'd ever
meant—she never knew what to say.

They didn't want to hear what she really thought. If she had had
a family to go back to . . . if she had been able to bear children
. . . she would not be a Marshal. She would have been happy to
center a family as her mother had; she would have enjoyed (as, in
her short time as a young wife she had enjoyed) the close friendship
of other women in a farming village; she would have liked growing
into the authority the old grannies had, when younger women came
to her for help, one of the endless dance of women who passed
on the knowledge and power that came with the gift of life. The
peasant folk had always had a place for those who loved for pleasure, not bearing, but most of those married for children, and loved
where they would. She had no way to understand those who were
content outside the family structure, women who not only loved
women but wanted no home as she knew it, wanted no children.

And even with those whose needs she understood, she felt she
was the wrong person to help. She wasn't the right age, the right
status. To be one of the old grannies, you had to be a wife and
mother first; you had to give the blood of birthing, the milk of
suckling, proving your power to give life to the family, before you
could share it abroad. She was no granny; she was barren, a widow,
a scarred freak who would not fit in. The comfort she had felt at
the dance vanished, and she blinked back the tears that stung her
eyes, hoping the others did not notice, and finished her meal. Her
past was gone, no use crying over it. That cottage would not rise
from the rubble; those poisoned fields would not bear grain in her
lifetime, and Parin would not rise from the dead to hold her in his
arms, however she dreamed of it. And hers was not the only such
loss; the only thing to do was go on. She struggled to regain the
vision that had brought her to Fin Panir. She had said she would

do what her people needed; if these women needed her, she must be what they asked.

"I don't think Gird would change the Code that way," she said slowly. "Not just for me, but because he really does believe in a fair rule for everyone. But I'll keep my eye on it, how about that?"

"And on that luap of his," said Arya, scowling. Rahi looked up, startled. He had seemed loyal to Gird, these last years—was he changing?

"What about him?"

Lia sniffed, and Arya's scowl deepened. "He's too thick wi' that Autumn Rose, is what. And that old woman that brought fancy cloths for the altar in the Hall, she's been telling him he's a prince—"

Rahi shrugged. "Gird knew that, and told others. So?"

"But she *treats* him as one. What if he starts thinking he'd rather rule than be Gird's luap? What if he has another child? What if the other mageborn are turning to him . . . eh?"

Rahi considered this. She had never liked Luap as well as some, or disliked him as much as others; in later years she'd come to think of him as important, even necessary, to the success of Gird's purposes. A bit too confident in situations where an honest man wouldn't be confident, but as Gird had said, if the gods could make a commander in war from a plain farmer, anyone could change. Yet—she doubted the gods had anything to do with Luap's change, if it was a change. "I don't know," she said. "You know I don't like the Rosemage, but Luap—he's not the same as he was when I first saw him, and he's not to blame for his father's acts."

"If you say so." Both women had a sullen look Rahi could not interpret; she wondered what Luap had done or said.

"Rahi!" A man's voice, from door to the courtyard. Marshal Sterin, she remembered after a moment. "When did you reach the city?"

She looked at the angle of sun through the tree in the courtyard. "Perhaps a hand ago." Then it occurred to her that he had phrased his question curiously. Why? Why "reach the city" instead of "arrive?"

"Th' old man's had a bad morning," Sterin said, coming in. The two women got up, silently, and went back to their work. Sterin sat where they had been. "He'd gone down to the lower market, on some errand, and met an old veteran from Burry."

She had figured it out for herself; she didn't want to hear it from Sterin. "He went drinking with him, did he?"

"Yes. We got him home all right, but—" Sterin leaned closer;

Rahi noticed that he looked worried. "Did he ever talk to you about Greenfields? About *before* Greenfields?"

"No." She had not seen him before Greenfields, except that one glance across the field; she had heard from others that he came down from the hill just before the battle started, and looked, they said, "strange." By the time she saw him again, they had other things to talk of than the morning—and by the time she thought to ask, a season later, he would not speak of it. Everyone knew he would not speak of it.

"He said something," Sterin said now. "He was drunk, yes, but his voice changed, and he said things. . . . I wonder if the gods gave him the words."

Rahi doubted that. She waited; Sterin was silent a moment then told her the rest.

"He said he should have died, at Greenfields, and that all the troubles we have now come because he didn't."

"What!"

"Aye, that's what he said. Plain as if he was in court, giving judgment. 'I should have died,' he said, 'and that's what's wrong.' The gods gave him a vision that day, he said, of a land at peace with him dead, and shattered with war if he wasn't willing. Well, we were there, you and me, Rahi—we know how he fought. He didn't save his skin by shirking danger; he and that horse were right in the middle of the battle. When he charged the magelords' cavalry, I thought sure he'd be spitted."

"Yes," said Rahi, trying to remember anything but a confusion of noise and fear and stench. She could remember faces in her cohort, the thrust of pike and spear, the moment she slipped and fell, and someone yanked her up, but she could not remember anything of the shape of the battle. She had heard about Gird's charge at the cavalry, but hadn't seen it. All she knew was that it ended, at last, with the old king dead and victory for the peasants.

"So if the prophecy was that he'd have to be willing, I'd say he was—he proved that. Yet does that mean the prophecy was wrong, or he's remembered it wrong, or is this something new?"

"I don't know." Rahi shook her head fiercely when Sterin kept looking at her. "I don't, I tell you. He gets drunk sometimes, you know that, and drunken men spout nonsense. Why believe it's prophecy? He may not remember anything of that morning but the end of it."

"You could ask him," Sterin suggested. "Maybe he's willing to talk about it now, the morning after . . . maybe to you, especially. You are his daughter—"

She started to blurt "Not anymore!" as she had so often, insisting on her separation from all that *daughter* meant, insisting on her status as a yeoman and then a Marshal. But after all she had come here to regain that family name, and angry as she was at him for being drunk at such a time, she could not now deny that he was her father. "I'm a Marshal," she said, after too long a pause. "Just like you: a Marshal."

"If something's gone wrong, something more, we need to know it," Sterin said. "People heard, Rahi: people heard him say that, in the inn and on the street. They will talk; they will make stories about it. Luap is worried, too," he finished, as if that would change her mind.

Rahi snorted. "Luap worries: that's his duty. He thinks he'll have to change the records, that's what it is." But Sterin still looked worried, his blunt honest face creased with it. "All right, I will ask. When he wakes, when I can see him." Another task set her because she was Gird's daughter, another burden she'd never asked for and did not want. The entire time she'd been insisting she was only a yeoman like any other, a Marshal like any other, people had expected her to have Gird's ear: find out this, please make sure he does that, don't let him do this other. Make him change the Code, don't let him change the Code, tell him the Code will never work, explain that granges need more grange-set and that the farmer shouldn't have to pay grange-set in a bad year. She wondered if anyone bothered Luap asking for Gird's favor—it was his job, after all, to deal with such things.

Sterin left the kitchen, clearly relieved to have handed her the difficulty. The two cooks did not come back to chat, for which Rahi was glad. She wanted a few minutes of peace to think about all this, and decide which end of the tangled knot to grasp. Perhaps she should start with Luap, assuming he hadn't been drunk, too. She wished she could stay in the kitchen, with its good smells of baking bread and stew and bean soup. She wished she could discuss it, parrion to parrion, with Arya, going back to the comfortable time when the way to chop onions, or season a soup, or preserve fruit, had been the most important topic of the day. She had not cooked, really cooked, for years; she eyed the great lump of dough Arya pummelled and wished she could sink her own hands into it.

But she would have to talk to Luap and Gird, bearing the grievances of some women and the fears of some men, worrying about prophecies and law instead of bread and meat. She sighed, finally, and pushed herself away from the table. Her bowl went into the washpot; she doused it and rinsed it and set it aside before Lia could intervene, and grinned at the surprised younger woman.

"My parrion was cooking and herblore," she said. "In the old days." Arya looked up at that.

"D'you still?"

"No—not much. I've five bartons and the grange to oversee, and the market courts as well."

"Someday we won't have parrions," Lia said. "Someday we'll be able to choose what we like."

Rahi just managed not to stare rudely at her. "Parrions *are* what you like; I had my mother's gift for it, and nothing made me happier than using it."

"Not me," Lia said. "I'd have learned leatherwork, if I could, but my uncle said girls must choose needlework, weaving, or cooking. And at that, he wouldn't let me choose, but left it to my aunt."

It must be the city way, Rahi thought. "A parrion is a talent," she said firmly, "talent and learning both. If you're not happy as a cook, why not learn leatherwork now?"

"It's too late, and none of the leatherworkers would have me as prentice," Lia said. She seemed to grow angrier as she talked about it, as if Rahi's interest were fat dripping on hot embers.

"There's a woman in my grange does that work," Rahi said slowly. "She's got a girl prentice." She was realizing that even now she understood very little of the structure of city crafts; had city women been restricted in their parrions? Had the village girls? None of them, after all, were ever swineherd or tanner or—except in emergencies—drove the ploughteams. She had assumed those differences resulted from the magelords' rules, but they didn't really know all that much about their own ancestors. How much of what she saw now, in the villages and towns, was new, a still fragile structure?

Lia shrugged, the shrug of someone more ready to complain than change, if change requires effort. "It's all right; I'm here and doing useful work. And with Arya."

Another tangle. She wondered who would know how the crafts had been organized, which were traditionally men's and which women's. And how Gird could possibly come up with a law that would satisfy those who remembered the past and those who wanted a wholly new future.

Chapter Five

Patiently, Luap trimmed another goosequill for the boy who might, if he lived long enough, make a scribe. The broken quill had not been the boy's fault; he could not control the spasms of coughing when they came. Garin was asleep now, and when he woke would find a new quill ready-trimmed. Luap wished he had better skills, some magic to heal whatever raged in the boy's lungs. So few had his gift of language, almost elven in its grace. He concentrated on that task, to avoid thinking about Gird's "prophecy," and the rumors already coming back to him in colorful variety.

"You spoil them," came a voice from the doorway. Luap set his lips in a smile and turned. Not the woman he'd wanted to see, this gray morning, but Gird's unmanageable daughter, back from the eastern wars to quarrel with her father . . . or so he saw it. In all fairness, Raheli often had the right on her side, but she had even less tact than Gird, if that were possible. And with Gird sleeping off a drunken binge, her tongue would be all edges; he wondered when she'd arrived, and if anyone had told her yet. In answer to her complaint, he tried a shrug with one shoulder. She scowled.

"The boy's sick," he said. "It's not his fault. I don't trim quills for all of them."

"I should hope not. D'you have the latest version of the Code?" Just the slightest emphasis on "latest"; whatever she thought of Gird's incessant revisions, she would not criticize her father to him. In the same way, copying her father's courtesy, she had continued to call him Selamis long after everyone else used Luap. Now she and Gird both used his nickname more often than not, but he remembered their care to preserve his own identity.

"Three copies." He stood, foraged in the pigeonholes above the work table, and handed her one, hoping that hint would keep her from taking it.

"Good," she said cheerfully; he anticipated what she would say and managed not to wince visibly. "Then I can have this, and you'll still have some . . . I'll have copies made for the eastern granges. You won't need to worry about it."

The end of his tongue would never heal, he was sure, from biting it. Rahi's eyes challenged him, daring him to argue. Tall as Gird, not quite as broad, though the padded tunic she wore gave her more heft than she owned, she stood foursquare in his doorway and dared him. Despised him. *Lord of justice,* he let himself pray, and then dropped it. She was Gird's daughter; he was Gird's luap; he had no right to do whatever he thought of.

Not that she'd ever know what he thought of. *That* he hid far inside, from both Rahi and Gird . . . that Rahi reminded him of his dead wife, that he had waked from dreams of stroking her scarred face back into beauty with his magery, erasing the ruin of war, pretending (how long would such pretense last? he had demanded of himself) that she was Erris come back . . . and making her love him, as Erris had.

Which would never happen, no matter what magery he used; he could not do it.

"It would be a help," he said mildly, handing over the thick roll, enjoying her surprise at his cooperation. She even relaxed, a rare sight, and came forward to take it, bending then to look at the sleeping boy.

"One of yours?" The implication was clear: one of *his* meant one of the mageborn. Luap shrugged again.

"I don't know, to be honest. No parents he can remember . . . he came out of the taverns here in Finyatha. Voice like crystal, and had taught himself to read. He has a talent for words, that one, and takes in knowledge as damp clay takes footprints. The singer's gift is no commoner in my father's people than in my mother's—" At that not-subtle reminder of his dual heritage, he saw the long scar on her face darken. He went on smoothly. "—so he could belong to either, or both."

"That priest says the mageborn need no training to wake their powers." *That priest* was Arranha, but Raheli would not say his name. She liked nothing mageborn, and Arranha's mildness irked her, giving no excuse for her dislike.

"Not to wake, but to use . . . or at least, to control." Luap wondered what she was getting at now.

"So how can Gird say the children are safe?" She sounded puzzled more than angry, but underneath that puzzlement Luap sensed a decision already reached. She did not understand her father's reasoning, and would go her own way.

"I'm not sure—"

Her hand flashed outward, demanding silence; Luap bit off the rest of his words and waited. "I'm trying, you see, to follow him. I know it is not the child's fault, to be mageborn, to have the magicks inborn, any more than it is a strong child's fault to have strength. But the magicks are weapons; it's like handing a strong child a sword or a pike—pots will break, if not heads. If the powers can wake without training, and it takes training to control them—but we cannot let them be trained, lest they turn against us—"

"Why would they?"

Her eyes were dark, her mother's eyes Gird had often said, but they seemed full of light as a hawk's eyes, staring through him to distant lands he could not see. "Why would they not, knowing we killed their parents . . . or most of them? Knowing their magicks gave them power of vengeance, power of rule . . . why would they not turn against us?"

"You don't trust fairness? Gird does."

She did not quite snort at that, but she glared, this time directly at him. "Fairness! Gods know we need fairness, and demand it, but for all the fairness lodged in human hearts you might whistle down a hedgerow forever, hoping to call out a skreekie with a bag of gold. I've seen little enough fairness, nor you either. Fairness would have had you on a throne—"

"Fairness forbade me," said Luap. "Your father—Gird—trusts fairness. In the end, he says—"

"In the end, when all men are wise and honest . . . and do you, too, believe that will happen?"

He had changed this much: he could not lie to her, even though he wanted Gird to be right, and her to be wrong, as much as he'd ever wanted anything. "No," he said. "I don't. But I think it's worth working toward."

"Men and women aren't gnomes," said Raheli, as if he'd argued that point.

"No," he said. "They aren't." He wished she would go. He wished she would go now, quickly, before the Autumn Rose arrived . . . or he wished the Rosemage had his sensitivity and would delay her arrival until Rahi left. But she would not deviate a hairsbreadth from her way, that one, and if her way now aimed at more than her own pride's joy, it was still a straight uncompromising trail. *Go away,* he thought at Rahi, knowing it would do no good. Even if she could feel a pressure from him, she would resist it.

"Will you marry again?" she asked, in a tone consciously idle. He knew it was not. Several of the men had offered for her, before she made it clear to everyone that she would not remarry. She probably thought women had offered for him.

"I doubt it," said Luap. "You know my story . . . and besides, a man marries to have children. What could I offer mine, but suspicion?

You—everyone—would think it meant I was still thinking of the throne."

"I thought you might marry . . . her." Only one *her* lay between them. Luap said nothing, but Rahi persisted. "You know. Calls herself a rose . . . I say thorny. . . ."

Luap closed his eyes against the explosion: the Autumn Rose was in hearing distance, only a pace or so away. Silence. He opened his eyes, to find Rahi lodged in his doorway like a stone in a pipe, and the Rosemage's light streaming around her like water.

"You don't have to like me," the Rosemage said. "You don't have to understand one tenth of what I have done—"

"I understand quite well." Rahi's accent thickened; her back held the very shape of scorn.

"You do *not*." The Rosemage angry regained her youth; color flushed her cheeks and her light blurred lines of age and weather. Luap's mouth dried. He was bred to find her beautiful; her voice and the magic she embodied sang along his veins. Despite himself, he could not believe that the peasants knew what real love was. They could not feel this wholeness, this blend of body, mind, spirit, magery. "You hate me for things I never did; you despise me for not doing what in fact I accomplished."

"You never bore a child." Rahi, like her father, seemed to condense in anger: immovable, implacable.

"That's not *fair!*" That shaft had gone home; the Rosemage's light flickered, and true anguish edged her voice. "You know it's not—its—"

"It's women's warring," Rahi said, her own voice calm now that she felt her victory. "And for all that, lady, neither have I. You could have thrown that back at me." She glanced over her shoulder at Luap. "Don't marry this one, or they'll never believe you a luap." Before either of them could answer, she'd shouldered past the Rosemage and disappeared down the corridor.

"That miserable . . ."

"Peasant she-wolf is the term you're looking for," Luap said softly, nodding to the still-sleeping boy. "Prickly, a trait you both share. Is it, in fact, an effect of barrenness?" He hated himself for that, but he dared not show his very real sympathy, not now. Her face whitened, as her light died, and then her intellect took over.

"I don't know. Possibly. Her people, with their emphasis on giving as the sign of power, would obviously value childbearing . . . but all peoples must, or they die away. So she and I, childless, though each with good reason, know we cannot meet our own standards. I never thought of it that way, but it could be." She sounded interested now, not angry. She hitched a hip onto his work table, and swung the free foot idly. Even relaxed like that, she had more grace than Rahi.

"I try to think what the difference is, between her and Gird," Luap said. "Surely it's not that women bear grudges more—at least, Gird says his wife never did. But Rahi is not going to trust us, not ever."

"Not *me*, not ever." The Rosemage's hands clenched, then relaxed. "I suppose you've heard the full name she gave me?"

Luap had, but he was not about to admit it. She waited a moment, then went on. "I suppose it doesn't matter. I might even think it funny, if crude, if she'd pinned it on someone else. Thorny bottom . . . and she's as thorny as I am. . . ."

"True enough." Luap let himself smile in a way that had, in his youth, worked its way among girls. "And here I am, poor lone widower, caught between you two briars, like a shorn wether in a thicket."

She laughed. "You? Don't try that with me, king's son; you are no gelding. Far from it."

"By choice. . . ."

"By choice and good sense, you've chosen to father no more children. You know what would come of it; you would not risk the land or the child. But you need not forswear the love of women, especially women who can't bear children. And the two of us—you may feel caught between us, but not in impotence."

"I do wish," Luap said, turning away as he felt his face grow hot, "that you were not my elder in years and experience. It's difficult." He hoped she had not caught his surprise: he had not thought that he might lie safely with barren women. Already his mind ran through the possibilities.

"So it is. So I might intend it to be. D'you think I like having that name tacked to me? Do you not realize that she has seen to it that no man will even ask?"

"Are you suggesting—?"

"Maybe." She eyed him; he wasn't sure she understood what he'd meant. When the boy stirred, choked, and began coughing, he was glad.

"Easy, lad." Luap lifted the boy's shoulders, offered a spoonful of honeyed fruit juice. He felt a constant tremor, as the boy tried not to cough.

"And how are you today, Garin?" the Rasemage asked.

"Better, lady." The boy's lips twitched, attempting a smile, then another cough took him. He curled into Luap's arm; Luap stroked his hair. This boy would say "better" on his deathbed, which, if he didn't really improve, this would soon be.

"You *could* heal that," came the Rosemage's murmur, just within hearing. Luap could feel his teeth grating; he could *not* heal it, not without claiming the king's magic as his own, using it . . . and he had sworn he would not. Sworn to himself as well as to Gird, to the gods he believed in a little more each year. His father had used magery for darker aims, yet Luap believed he had intended better . . . surely as a boy he had not been wholly cruel. He had never asked any who might know, including the Rosemage.

"You know better," he said to her, wishing he dared a slap of power at her and knowing she would laugh at him even if it worked.

"Even the peasants know we had healing powers once," she said conversationally. Garin's coughs slowed; he gasped, his heart racing beneath Luap's hand.

"Little enough lately," Luap said. "Gird says he heard rumors, tales from old granddads, nothing recent. You say *you* lack them."

"Mmm." She didn't pursue it, for which he was less grateful than he felt he should be. By her tone she would pursue it later. Garin lay back, spent and silent, barely able to sip a few spoonsful of broth. He was going to die, and not sing those songs, and although there was no way Luap could blame Gird, he did anyway. Gird cared for this boy no less than any other, but no more. It had seemed to Luap that if he could interest Gird, if he could only get Gird to understand *why* the boy was important, he would then do something and the boy would live. What that something might be, he could not of course define. But Gird's response had been, as always, impersonally compassionate. He hated seeing anyone suffer; he had sat beside the boy while Luap slept, on the worst nights, comforting him as tenderly as a mother; but he had shaken his head at Luap's vehemence, insisting that this boy's death was no more tragic than another's.

Was it because so many of his own children had died or disappeared? Because Raheli would bear him no grandchildren? Or was it the gnomish influence?

"I can't believe Gird would really mind that," the Rosemage said softly. Luap started, and glanced at the boy, who lay dozing now, unaware. "Healing, I mean."

"I can't do it." His hands had fisted; he flattened them with an effort. "Arranha says I'd have to claim all the magery—that it would be like trying to see only green, or only red, to use only the healing. And he's not even sure I've got it. Besides, as you very well know,

I promised Gird and the gods that I would not become a magelord. No more magicks: that's what I said, and what he holds me to."

"You've asked him about this?"

"Not specifically, no. He knows, though. He knows what it would take, and my oath binds me." Never mind he had broken it more than once, by intention and later by accident. Never mind that time in the cave; no one would know that until—unless—he told. Where he could, he was loyal to it.

"You should ask him. He's a farmer; they care about living things. For healing, he might let you try—"

"No." His power bled into that; the word ached with power. She looked at him, opened her mouth, and shut it again. He wondered if she knew he was lying. He wondered so many things she might know, and he dared not ask—better that she think he knew already, or didn't care to know, than that he hungered for that knowledge he lacked.

"I hope he's better soon," the Rosemage said, putting out a hand to Garin's hair. Then she left, without saying more, and Luap sat struggling with his unruly desires.

Soon enough he heard, from down the corridor, Rahi's voice raised to Gird, and Gird's gusty bellow in reply. He did not want to know what she said, or what Gird said to her; he could imagine it well enough. Gird's taste for ale had been nearly disastrous once in the war; he'd conquered it then. Now, in peace, why shouldn't an old man have some pleasure? But Rahi would have none of that; he had overheard much the same quarrel before. She would drag up times past, from her childhood; Gird would glower for days.

The silence, abrupt and startling, drew him from his musings. Had the woman murdered him? Had he clouted her? He heard what might have been sobs. Should he investigate, or leave them to settle things?

"You blundering old fool!" Rahi said. She had waited in the corridor, trying not to hear Luap and the Autumn Rose, trying to calm herself, but when she looked in Gird's door, her anger flared again. Gird slouched against his work table, eyes red-rimmed and bleary. He and his clothes were clean enough, but the room still smelled like a hangover. "I come all the way to Fin Panir to—to tell you something important, and you've gone off drinking with some lout who probably wasn't even a veteran—"

"He was!" His voice rasped, as if he had a cold as well as a hangover. "He was from Burry, and I remembered him—"

"Better than you remembered your vow not to drink so much."

She bit back the other words she wanted to say; disappointment soured her rage. She had hoped for so much from this meeting. She needed so much from it.

"We're not at war!" Whatever energy he'd summoned to achieve that bellow brought life to his eyes, "It's not the same thing!"

"It's still wrong." Rahi realized she was going to cry an instant before the tears came, but too late to turn away and hide them. Sobs choked her as she fought them down; she could say nothing. Gird's face changed, concern replacing anger.

"Rahi! What is it, lass?" He was still bigger than she, more massive; the hug she had imagined enclosed her before she knew it. He pulled her head to his shoulder and stroked her hair, murmuring soothingly. She gave in to it, and let her tears fall. When they ceased, she felt odd, empty. Gird released her before she actually moved, and waited silently for what she might say. She wished that blowing her nose could take longer; she wasn't sure what that would be.

"I . . . wanted to change my mind," she said at last.

"About marrying again?" he asked. His voice held a note of hope. He had insisted all along that she could remarry, even if she could not bear children. With all the orphans war had made, he'd said, she could have a dozen children.

"No." She took a long breath, swiped at her face with her sleeve, and looked him in the face. "I said once that I was your daughter no longer, only your soldier. But you're right, the war's over."

"Lass—" A tentative smile, that widened when she managed to smile back. He reached out again, and she moved into another embrace. "Rahi, lass, you don't know how I've needed that. . . ." She felt him sigh. "And there I was drunk, as you said. You're right, it was stupid."

"It's all right," said Rahi softly, "but not if you keep doing it." She felt his chest shake with an almost-silent chuckle.

"Eh, that's the daughter I remember. Tell me now, what changed your mind?"

Rahi told him about the dance in her grange, and the way she had felt restored to family connections. "And so I thought you might be feeling the same—not fitted in, with no vill or family—"

"I have, sometimes. I've tried to tell myself they're all my kin, but I know they're not. After Pidi disappeared that winter—" Gird shook his head. Raheli remembered her younger brother, her only surviving sib, riding off into the snow and never arriving at the next grange. She had not known until spring that he had disappeared;

she would never know what had happened. That was the spring she had almost hated the grain that sprang green in the furrows.

"Da," she said, feeling that old comfortable word in her mouth again. "Da, I still can't marry—I still can't have children—"

"I know. It's all right, Raheli Mali's child, it's all right." His eyes squeezed shut a moment; she saw the shine of tears when he opened them.

It was not all right, but it would be later. She still felt angry that he had been on another drunken binge; she could see by the color of his face and the change in the texture of his skin that he was not well. But her impulse had been right, to restore the family link she herself had broken—not broken, she told herself now, but set aside.

They sat awhile in silence, one on either side of the work table, then Rahi remembered the other good reasons she had found for coming the long way to Fin Panir. He had set her saddlebags on the floor; she retrieved them, and spread out her grange records and the comments from the past year's courts.

"The soil's different, where I am now, from home—where we lived before. The Code allows for easing the grange-set in a dry year, but where I am the farmers lose grain more often to mold in a wet year. If you allow the local Marshals to adjust the grange-set based on the yield of sound grain—that wouldn't take a complete revision of the Code—"

"Ummph. You're right. It already says at the Marshal's discretion, so if we struck out 'because of drought' that would do. What else?"

"We had an odd case last spring come into the grange-court: a man, not mageborn, claimed to do magicks a new way."

"A new way?"

"As scribes study writing, he said, so he studied magicks and performed them—for a fee. The judicar brought him to me because some of the people wanted him killed as a mageborn using forbidden power, or as a demon. When I investigated, it seemed to me that he performed what he agreed to, although I found the fee unduly high. And he had none of the appearance of a mageborn, and explained his magicks sufficiently that I feel sure he was not."

"So what did you do?" asked Gird.

"Treated it as a matter of commerce. As someone in an unknown profession, of no registered guild, he had to demonstrate that he was honest and gave good weight, so to speak. The Code allows Marshals to impose a good-faith tax on newcomers who have no guild to speak for them, until their honesty is proven. He had not earned that much with his little shows of colored fire and magic crystals. I told him plainly that too many people disliked all magic for me to keep him safe, and if someone broke his head for him, he'd have only himself to blame. He got out of town safely enough, for I told the judicar and those listening that I would not take lightly an injury done him when he had done none yet himself. Since then I've heard nothing; he never came to the next grange west."

"A new kind of magic . . ." said Gird. "I wonder what could be."

"He thought of it as a craft, not some inborn talent, and I believe he was honest in that, at least." Rahi frowned. "But without a guild, without knowledge of what his work is worth—assuming it's honestly done—we have no way of knowing if his price is fair."

Gird leaned back and tucked his fingers in his belt. "I suspect we can't protect the sort of fool who will pay a man to work magicks. You were right, Rahi, to treat it as commerce, as a matter of contracts. Make sure he fulfills what he said; the buyer must decide if the price is fair." He shook his head. "Though where we can fit *that* into the Code, I don't know. I'll talk to other Marshals about it."

"I . . . quarreled with Luap, on the way here," Rahi said. "It's not his fault; I was angry about you." She felt a childish pleasure in confessing that; he had always been more understanding with the child who confessed wrongdoing.

"He's easy to quarrel with, this harvest time," Gird said. "I don't know what's bothering him, unless it's the old lady with her notions about royalty."

"Someone mentioned an old lady. . . ." Rahi said. He looked as if he wanted to tell the tale; she wanted, at this moment, to listen to him talk.

"A good woman," Gird said, lips pursed. "Her servant Eris says so, and so does Arranha. Widowed years ago. Very pious: but for worshipping the Sunlord, she's much like old Tam's mother, back home. She came in asking permission to put altarcloths she'd embroidered in the great Hall; it was clear she meant no mischief, so I said she might talk to Arranha about it."

"But she's mageborn? She knows Luap's the king's son?"

"Aye. She knows more than that—seems he's not the last king's son, but one before that. Garamis, his name was. She saw Luap himself as a child, when he lived in some lord's house. It's that, Arranha says, which upset him, though I can't see why it would. Until we're the oldest, if we live that long, there's always someone who knew us as children. What harm in that?"

Rahi thought about it. It had been years since she had seen

anyone from her vill. Would she feel anything strange if she met someone on the street who remembered her as a child? No—she had enjoyed being that child, that young woman. She would like to meet someone who remembered that. Had Luap not enjoyed being that boy? Surely it must have been easier than growing up a peasant child.

"It's the change, I expect," Gird went on. "Having to leave the lord's house for a farmer's cottage; he's said before that was hard. He's tried to forget that first bit, in recent years. And now she brings it back. One of the yeomen even told me she calls him 'prince.' "

"But she shouldn't!" Rahi was more shocked than she'd expected. Gird shook his head.

"She's an old lady, lass. As stubborn as any village granny, for all she wears a fine dress and wears jewels. You know yourself that arguing with old ladies is like plowing water. If she wants to call Luap prince, she will; all I can do is hope it won't go to his head." He tried to stretch again and grimaced. "As yesterday's ale has gone to mine. I'm too old for that, you're right."

Rahi grinned at him. "Remember the time that old dun cow got after me, for trying to ride her calf?" Gird's slow smile widened, and he began to chuckle. "You told me that fools earned their lumps."

"So I did. But that's enough of that, lass, or I'll decide you're only my Marshal again. Marshals don't lecture me—"

"I would," said Rahi boldly. Gird groaned.

"You would, and your mother would have made a fine Marshal. Will you give over, now?"

"Aye. Shall I make up with Luap?"

"You might soothe his prickles a bit, and you might keep the edge of your tongue off the Autumn Rose, too. Don't think I missed that bit of the quarrel."

He had surprised her again. He could always do that, manage to know what no one suspected he knew, manage to do what no one suspected he could. Yet once he had done it, it always seemed right, inevitable.

"She irritates me," Rahi said, "like a bed of nettles."

"And why did we gather nettles?" He did not wait for her answer. "Because the plant is not evil, but harsh, and needs the right cook. Nourishing inside; irritating outside. There's virtue in the Autumn Rose you've never found, lass: take it inside next time."

Rebuke for rebuke, and although it stung, she could feel that he was right. She had never looked for anything in the Autumn Rose but what she knew she disliked. Finding that, she had been satisfied to despise her. She tried a last defense. "I have heard gossip that they might marry, Luap and the Rosemage."

"Neither of them are such fools," Gird said. "Nor are you, to believe it."

"Well, if that's your wish, I will study to adopt her as a sister," Rahi said, half-joking. "No more quarrels, by my will."

"You could have a worse sister," Gird said. "She is as true as Luap once was false. Strange to us, but true." He sounded very tired, now, and Rahi realized that it was nearly noon.

"I could make you a brew," she said, half-shyly. "If Arya will let me use her hearth—"

His eyes brightened a moment. "That black stuff? No one else can do it right, lass, and if you'd fix that I'd be grateful."

"Take your rest, then, and I'll be up with it when it's done." This felt right, felt normal, even if it was the result of a drinking bout. She had Mali's parrion, and her own skill; she knew she could mix healing brews better than most. She settled Gird with a cloth over his eyes and his feet propped up, then went back to the kitchen to ask permission to use the hearth.

She found Luap there, with a cook she had not met; Arya and Lia, the woman explained, had finished their day's work. "Bakes the best bread, Arya," the woman said. "But she trusts me to finish it now. I'm Meshi."

Rahi explained what she needed, eyeing Luap, who looked completely comfortable as if he had been there awhile.

"Of course. No need to ask. The herbery's through there—I expect you know—and I'll just fetch the pot—" Meshi was a bustler, whose brisk busy movements around the room could make it seem crowded with only a few people in it. Rahi went out to the herbery, wondering why Luap seemed so relaxed with someone like that, and so tense with people she found more soothing. She found the herbs she needed, hardy aromatics that could be picked green until the first hard freeze. The rest of the ingredients were in the pantry, in neatly labelled pots and sacks: the same roots and barks used in cookery, most of them.

She set to work acutely aware of Luap watching her. Had he ever seen her at her own parrion? She couldn't remember. She chopped, grated, and squeezed, as each ingredient demanded, then put all to simmer on the hearth. Meshi bustled past her one way and then the other, chopping vegetables into bowls, stirring them into a huge kettle of stew, taking Arya's last batch of bread from the oven and putting the loaves on racks to cool, washing up behind herself as if she had an extra pair of hands. Rahi did not miss the looks Meshi gave Luap, or the occasional sharp glance she herself received. When she had the pot simmering to her satisfaction, Rahi offered to help with whatever Meshi had planned.

"Oh, dear, no—no need." Meshi hardly paused in her path between pantry and kitchen. "I'm not rushed. Just you sit there and keep an eye on your own pot, so I won't worry about it." She came back from the pantry with an apronful of apples, and sat down to peel them. Rahi, rebuffed, ventured a smile at Luap. He nodded and gave her a smile that seemed more forced than natural . . . although after their earlier encounter she had to admit that only a forced smile would be natural.

"Meshi likes to feed people almost as much as I like to eat," he said, with a nod to the cook. She smiled warmly at him, a curl of apple peel dangling from the knife.

"I like to feed those as know good cooking from bad," she said. "Luap's one to know if I change a single spice in my preserves."

"My parrion was cooking and herblore," Rahi said, feeling unaccountably shy.

"Was it now?" Meshi looked up, interested. "I thought you looked more deft than most who cook for need and not love. And you gave that up to be a Marshal, eh?" Rahi wondered where Meshi had been during the war. She looked to be Luap's age, and perhaps, like many city people, she had simply stayed home and hoped the war would not disrupt her life.

"I had no choice," Rahi said, feeling her face flush. She had assumed that everyone knew her story. "And now—"

"Raheli has no village to return to," Luap said smoothly. "Surely you knew, Meshi. . . ."

"Oh." Now it was Meshi's turn to flush. "I'm sorry. I should have known . . . it's just these dratted apples . . . all full of core and I wasn't thinking—" Her hands twitched among the peels.

"It's all right," Rahi said. "I must get used to those who don't know the whole story."

Meshi turned to her. "As you had a parrion for it, would you want to help with these apples?"

"Of course." Rahi moved to the table, and picked up an apple. "Sliced or just cored?"

"Sliced, not too thin." Meshi put an earthenware bowl between them. "If old Gird's feeling better by suppertime, he'll have some of it."

They worked companionably until all the apples were sliced. Rahi got up to sniff her brew, and Mesbi continued with her apple dish.

Luap had snatched a slice on his way out, and Meshi laughed at him. "That man! There's not another in this place like him. Those two, Arya and Lia, they don't like him for being half mageborn, say he puts on airs, but I don't see that. He likes to eat, but what man doesn't?"

"He's been with my—with Gird a long time," Rahi said, stirring the brew. It smelled about right; she found a cloth to wrap the hot pan, and a mug for Gird to drink from.

Meshi stopped short and looked at her. "It's hard for me to believe, Gird being your father. Him so fair and balding, and you so dark—"

"My mother," Rahi said. "She was dark."

"Ah. And a parrion of cooking, like you? Surely it came from her family, for old Gird, bless him, can hardly boil water."

Rahi laughed, surprising both of them. "I know. When my mother died, he had to cook—and I learned very quickly."

"It's none o' my affair," said Meshi in the tone always used by those who say it anyway, "but your Da needs a family. Why not come here to live? You'd be happier in your parrion than off somewhere being a Marshal."

Rahi smiled at her, but shook her head. "I have to be a Marshal," she said. "I don't quite know why, but I know it's right." Then she took the brew upstairs, and woke Gird from a restless doze. When he asked her the same question, she was ready with the same answer . . . and he smiled at her and agreed.

Chapter Six

"I want to see the Marshal-General," Aris said. Seri pressed close behind him.

"Run off, lad, and tell your Marshal your troubles," said the big guard. The skinny one said nothing, but his eyes laughed. Aris felt his anger glowing, and fought it back. He knew what the Marshal-General thought of boys who lost their tempers. They had not come this far to make fools of themselves.

"The Marshal-General," he said again. "It's t-too imp-portant for just our Marshal."

Brows went up on both guards. "Oh?" said the skinny one. "Would your Marshal agree?"

Aris just stared at them, one after the other. Finally the skinny one flushed, shrugged, and said, "Gran'ther Gird won't mind young'uns. He never does." The big guard glowered, but finally shrugged as well.

"All right, but you stop first at Luap's and ask if the Marshal-General's got other business right now. Upstairs, second door on the right." He stepped aside, waving a vast meaty hand. Aris and Seri scampered past. The guard yelled after them, "No running! This isn't some alley, brats!" Seri giggled. Aris was at the landing before he figured it out: alley brats, just what everyone called them, but the guard hadn't meant it that way. Exactly.

"We made it," she whispered. "I didn't think—"

Aris shushed her. Another flight to a passage . . . panelled walls, a floor of patterned wood, dark and yellow. Once it would have been polished; now it was clean, but scuffed. The first door on the right was closed. The next, open, gave on a sun-barred room lined with shelves. A tall man in Girdish blue sat at a table, facing away from them, looking at someone on a low pallet under the windows. Aris peeked around the door . . . the youth on the bed lay pale as milk, bones tight under the skin of his face, eyes deep-shadowed. Seri, bolder now that they were upstairs, rapped on the doorpost. The tall man swung around, finger to lips, then stared at them, clearly surprised. With a glance at the sleeping youth, he rose and came to the door.

Aris had heard the tales. Gird's luap, the Marshal-General's scribe and friend, was supposed to be mageborn on his father's side. *Royal,* whispered some. King's bastard. Uncanny, born with great powers but promised not to use them. Can't trust that kind, most muttered, making one or another warding sign. Their Marshal said the same, glowering when another leaf of Gird's Code came down, scribed in the luap's elegant hand. To Aris, he looked like just another tall, dark-haired adult. An uncle or father, not a grand-father, and no more magical than a post. Seri pinched him. His mouth came unglued, and he said, quietly enough, "Sir, they said downstairs to tell you we've come to see the Marshal-General."

The tall man had graceful brows, but they still rose. "Children, now, they're letting in to pester the Marshal-General? Or do you bear a message from your Marshal or some judicar who could not come himself?"

"It's *our* message, sir!" Seri pushed past Aris; she knew his temper and its limits. Her single braid hung crooked over her shoulder, already fuzzy with escaping hairs, for all that she had rebraided it neatly just before they came into the Upper City. "The Code says, sir, that all come equal before the Code—"

His wide mouth quirked. "True, young judicar, but it also sets up the courts in which to try cases; not all come before the Marshal-General."

"This does." Seri gave him a flat stare for his amusement, and his face sobered. "It is a matter the Marshal-General must decide, and we must see him. If he cannot see us now—"

"If you'll allow, I'll let him know you're here; so far as I know he has no one with him." The man slid past them, and strode down the hall. Aris looked at Seri, not knowing whether to follow or not. She leaned against the doorpost, peeking in.

"I wonder if he's dying."

Aris looked too. Unbidden, his magery stirred; he squashed it down. "I think he must be," he said.

"You should," Seri said, flicking him a glance. "Even if we haven't seen the Marshal-General yet."

"It's against the Code; it's not right."

"You should." He wondered if the Marshal-General himself were that certain; Seri had the rooted integrity of a tree, that cannot be but what it is. Were all the old peasant breed like that, so sure of themselves, so all-of-a-piece? What would it feel like? He himself, his magery flickering inside him, often felt he was made of shadows and flame, shapeless except in opposition to each other. He could just remember, in his early childhood, someone explaining that light existed by itself, but shadows only when something stood before the light. Now Seri nudged him into the room. "Go on, Aris. I'll tell the Marshal-General—"

The boy—man?—on the bed was older than either of them; Aris could tell that, but not how old he was. He would be tall, if he stood, and would grow taller yet, if he lived. *Can I?* he asked himself. He had never actually healed someone so close to death, not a human person, not someone so large. Did that make a difference? He wasn't sure. Seri nudged him again. She would not give up, but she had no parrion of healing, the way her people thought of it. *Our* people, he reminded himself. He and Seri were one people, whatever anyone else said. She had stood by him in the grange, and he would stand by her . . . meanwhile, he felt his mage powers lean toward the sick youth, as if they could reach out of himself.

He came closer. From the shallow, uneven movement of the chest, he deduced lung trouble: he knew that much from animals. Was the thinness from that, or from not being able to eat for coughing, for lack of breath? With a sudden lift, he felt the power take him over, an exhilaration like none other unless birds of the air felt this way, swooping and gliding. He let himself flow with it, barely aware that he murmured words he'd overheard in childhood. His hands glowed; he laid them carefully on either side of the youth's sleeping head, ran them down to his shoulders, then over his chest. Something prickled in his palms, harsh as nettles or dry burs. He wanted to pull back, but knew he must not. Behind him, he heard Seri's indrawn breath, but he paid no attention to it. She had seen him do this before; she always gasped, but he had learned it meant nothing. She would watch and wait, and be there when he had done.

Darkness retreated slowly, grudgingly, from his light; he could feel, in his hands, the slow withdrawal of something dire from the youth's body. He had no name for it, and it didn't matter. The light either worked, or it didn't; when it worked, it healed old wounds as well as new ones, fevers as well as wounds. If he could hold his focus until all the damage had been repaired, the youth would wake whole and free from pain, healthy as if he had never been sick.

But that was the limit: his own strength, his own concentration. He could feel the sweat trickling down his face; he knew his sight narrowed to a single core of light, and he dared no attention to interpret what his eyes could see. Only with the vision of power, which perceived each strand of disease or injury, which knew when the light had worn or driven it away, dared he perceive. Hearing had gone, and most of eyes' sight, and even the sense of where he was, when the last dark shadow fled. At once, his power snapped back into him, and with it, all his strength. He fell, knowing he was falling, trusting Seri to be there, to catch him, as she had been from the first time he'd used this power.

Hearing returned while he was still crumpled untidily on the floor. Seri's voice, sharp, and a deeper rumble somewhere overhead.

"—because *I* told him to, sir! He would not break your law, but—"

"Will you just stand back, child, and let me see the lad. I'm not going to hurt him. He's fallen."

"He always does," said Seri, somewhat more calmly.

Another voice—the man they had first met. "You mean he's done this *before?* Healing?"

"Yes, of course. He's always done it, until the new Code came out, and the Marshal said he couldn't. That's why we came."

Aris managed to open his eyes. His vision had not cleared: would not, for some little time. But he could see Seri, standing stiffly, ready to fight if she had to, and the man whose office this was, and a great lump of a man who must be the Marshal-General. Aris swallowed, with difficulty, and smiled. "Please don't worry," he said to the Marshal-General. "I'm all right."

The man grunted, and came nearer; Seri moved out of his way, scowling. "You're the color of cheese-whey, lad, and your eyes no more focus on me than a newborn's. If this is 'all right,' I would hate to see you sick or wounded."

"Is *he* all right?" Aris asked. The Marshal-General, so close, looked even bigger, heavier, almost as if a great oak had chosen to move and lean over him. He glanced down, half-expecting roots instead of worn boots.

The other man answered, in a lighter, clipped voice that carried some emotion Aris could not read. "He's got the color you had before; he's sleeping peacefully and breathing normally, and I could swear he's gained a half-stone. . . . I suppose we'll know when he wakes."

The Marshal-General's hand, hard and warm, cupped Aris's chin. He felt no fear; here was nothing uncanny, but strength and gentleness allied. Less frightening than his father's steward had been, less frightening than his father, for that matter.

"Lad—from what your friend says, you knew you broke the Code, to use such magic."

"Yes, sir." He didn't try to explain.

"Your friend says you did it because she told you to—was it then her fault you broke the Code?"

He could feel himself turning red, hot to the ears. "No, sir, of course not!" He quoted carefully: " 'Let each yeoman take heed for his own deed, for if one counsels wrongly, yet the ears which listen and the hands which act belong to the doer.' "

"Mmm. You have learned to recite, but yet you do not obey. What then should the judicar say, in such a case?"

Behind the Marshal-General, Seri opened her mouth; Aris shook his head at her. "It is my deed, and my fault, sir. I know that. But . . . but the boy was so sick, and if I waited he might not live. That's why we came, to ask you to amend the Code to allow healing. The judicar should say I was wrong, and punish me—but you, sir, can amend the Code."

"To save you punishment?" The Marshal-General's face gave nothing away to his still blurred vision. Aris shook his head. "No, sir. Even if you amend the Code, I broke your rule before you changed it. But others who heal won't have to be punished later."

"Alyanya's flowers!" Strong arms gathered him into a rough embrace. "D'you really think I'd punish a boy who healed another, who gave his power until he looked near death? If you need punishment, the way your power wounds you is punishment enough. I had thought the healing magery all destroyed, and all rumors of it lies, with the sick charmed perhaps into thinking themselves well. But I saw this myself, saw you heal—"

"It's not really me, sir; it's the power," said Aris. He was too old to let himself be comforted like this, but he wished he weren't. He had never had that much of it. "It's the light—"

"I don't doubt it's some god's power," said the Marshal-General. "But you're the one they gave it to, and you're the one must decide how to use it. Now: the two of you will come with me, and have more to eat than you've had lately, by the look of you."

Aris found himself standing, but with the Marshal-General's arm half-supporting him. His vision reddened, then cleared; he looked at the youth on the bed, who had slept through all this undisturbed. *He's tired,* Aris thought. Seri gave him one of her looks; he was not sure what it meant, but he would find out. She always told him. The other man, the Marshal-General's luap, had another look, or series of them, that flickered across his face like cloudshadow over a meadow. In the aftermath of using his power, when he felt unusually sensitive, he felt the man's own magery as something cold and hard, and wondered that he could have missed it before.

"Food," said the Marshal-General, and urged him forward. Then, to his luap, "I'll take care of these two for now, but find them a place to sleep. Wherever they've come from, they aren't going back today."

Out in the passage, with its scuffed patterned wood, and along it to the right. The Marshal-General said, as they passed a door, "That's my room, if you need me later, but I think you should eat and rest now. The kitchen's down this stair." Aris stumbled in the change from lighter passage to darker stair, and the Marshal-General's arm steadied him. Seri padded behind, silent for once.

The kitchen, warm, smelling of rising bread dough, some kind of stew, lit by both fire and windows open to an enclosed courtyard, promised safety and comfort. Aris sank down on a bench beneath a window and let himself relax. Seri sat beside him; the Marshal-General murmured to someone working at a long table, and fetched a cut loaf of bread. The other person vanished into a dark door, then reappeared with a jug and brought over jug and several mugs. A tall woman, that was, wearing an apron over trousers and tunic.

"Milk," said the Marshal-General, pouring it into the mugs. He handed one to each of them, and then lifted his own. Aris sipped, cautiously. Sometimes his belly objected to milk or meat after a healing; this time it lay quiescent. The milk slid down, cool and sweet. The Marshal-General sliced the loaf, and offered it. Seri fished a dirty lump of salt from her pocket and offered that on an open palm. The Marshal-General pinched off a bit without speaking, sprinkled it on the bread, and waited until she took a slice to bite into his own. Aris swallowed the last of his milk, and filled his mouth with bread and salt.

They had eaten bread and stew, and drunk more milk than Aris had had in several years, before Gird let them talk more about it. Aris felt sleepy with all the food; Seri looked ready to leap at some task, her braid already more than half loosened, the tendrils curling around her face, her eyes sparkling. In the kitchenyard, in the shade of an old apple tree, the Marshal-General looked like an old farmer, not a judicar—and certainly not like what he was. But food had not dulled his wits, Aris found.

"—and your father was a mageborn noble?" he asked. "Did he have the power of healing?"

"No, sir." Aris numbered his father's magery, what he knew of it, on his fingers: light, fire, sending arrows where he would. "He died when I was very young—" In the Marshal-General's war against the magelords, though it would be rude to say so. "—but no one ever said he could heal. Nor my mother either." Seri made a small noise; Aris hoped that would be enough for her. She had never liked his mother.

"And both are dead now?"

"No, sir." He said no more, even when Gird's eyebrows rose in a clear demand for more information. Seri took over.

"She went off with another 'un, sir, after the old lord was killed. He didn't want Aris, her new man didn't."

Gird looked at Aris; Aris said nothing. Whatever Seri thought, his mother was his mother, and he would not speak ill of her. Gird turned to Seri. "So, then—how long ago was this, and how long have you known him?"

Seri grinned, glad to take over "I've known him always; we grew up in the household together. Aris was youngest, and they were always busy—"

"And I was small for my age," Aris added. "Easy to misplace in a crowd."

"*And* you had none of your father's magery," said Seri. "He didn't know what you did have." She turned back to Gird. "My mother's sister was Aris's nurse; 'twas not her fault he grew no larger. But she was blamed for it, and then his mother wouldn't have him by because he fretted so about sickness. They thought he was afraid of it."

"I am," Aris said. "I didn't know what to do, then."

"And now you do?" asked Gird.

"Not . . . completely. There's too much—Seri's people have ways of healing with herbs I don't know, and she's told me of hearth-witches who can draw pain and lay it on stone or iron. But I know some of what I can do with magery." He yawned, fighting the sleep that tried to overwhelm him. He felt he'd been running for hours, or heaving stones. Why was healing, that required only concentration, such hard work?

"He needs to sleep," he heard Seri say. A chuckle shook the shoulder he leaned against.

"I can see that for myself, child. Let the lad rest, then, and you tell me your tale. You're not mageborn-bred, are you?"

A snort from Seri. "No, sir. Not a drop of magic in me, just peasant common sense." *You have magery, Seri, but it's not my kind,* Aris thought, then drifted into sleep.

He woke on a pallet on the floor, a clean soft pallet. The room was almost dark; the window above him glowed deep blue: late evening. He heard no one near, and stretched at leisure, his spine crackling. He loved to think of the little spine-bones clicking against each other in some language he didn't know. Cats stretched, but he never heard their spines crack. He blinked at the window; one star had pricked dusk's curtain. As he watched, another, and two more. He felt safe, and happy, and thought of going back to sleep. He would wake early, if he did, but no matter. Then he heard voices in the distance, coming nearer. Seri and the Marshal-General, still talking. He grinned in the dark. Seri could talk all night and half the day; now that she'd decided she liked the Marshal-General, he'd have a time getting rid of her. She had missed her grandfather after he died.

"He should be awake," Seri was saying. "And if he goes back to sleep now, he'll wake with a headache before dawn. He always does."

The Marshal-General's voice carried a hint of humor. "So what should we do, lass, to keep the lad healthy?"

"Feed him. He won't think he's hungry, but he needs it."

The light they carried warmed the passage outside, began to gleam on the edges of the furniture. Aris grabbed his wandering mind by its scruff. This was not the time to fall into a trance and let the light play in his mind. So far the Marshal-General had been understanding, but he mustn't push his luck too far. He sat up, rubbing his eyes, as they came in. With the candlelight, the window looked darker, more true night.

"Aris—" An edge to Seri's voice, a warning. Did she think he'd let himself be caught by light-trance in front of the Marshal-General?

"I'm awake," he said, yawning hugely. "Just woke." He looked for the Marshal-General; in candlelight, his broad lined face looked entirely different. "I'm sorry, sir, I fell asleep and keep yawning."

"Seri explained." A long pause during which Aris wondered if Seri had explained too much, then, "Come, lad—there's soup and bread left for you."

He stood without assistance, and didn't argue about the meal; Seri was right, as usual. By the time he'd eaten two bowls of soup, and three slices of bread, he felt solid to himself, firm on his feet. The Marshal-General, he saw, recognized the difference.

"So, lad—are you able to tell me your side of it, or would a night's rest improve your tale?"

"I'm fine now, sir." He felt Seri stir, beside him, but she said nothing.

"Good. You'll need the jacks, I expect, and then come up to my office; Seri can guide you." The Marshal-General pushed himself up and left the kitchen. Seri gathered the bowls and the end of bread.

"I'll help," said Aris, but she shook her head.

"You go clear your mind, Ari. The jacks are across the court, through the gate: there's torches. And the washstand's by the well. I'll do this." When he came back in, all traces of his late supper had vanished; the kitchen looked vast and bare in the candlelight, warmth radiating from the banked fire on the hearth. The cooks had put beans to soak; the faint earthy smell made him think of cellars and small-gardens. Seri took his hand, one quick clasp, then led him back upstairs. He thought he could find Gird's office on his own, but he was glad of her company.

She left him in the passage outside the lighted room, with a single hug. Inside the room, the Marshal-General sat with another man, the luap, and when Aris tapped at the doorpost, they both looked up to stare at him. "Come on in, lad," said the Marshal-

General. "Come and tell me your story, and Luap here will write it down."

Aris felt a mild reluctance to talk in front of the luap—Luap, he must be called—but with the Marshal-General's eye on him, he could not argue. He took the stool the Marshal-General pointed out, and wondered where to start. What had Seri already said? He didn't want to bore them. Luap, he noticed, had what looked like an old, rewritten scroll on the board in his lap. Luap smiled at him.

"Start by telling me your name, if you will, and what you know of your history."

Perhaps Luap had not taken down what Seri said. Aris began with his name, his father's name, the place of his birth. That was enough of family, he thought, and said, "When I found I could heal—"

"Wait." Luap held up his hand. "Were you the only child?"

"No, sir. But the youngest, by several years; my next older brother had already begun arms training when I was born. That's why I was so often alone with Seri and her family and the other servants; my parents were away at court, or visiting other domains, or—by the times I remember at all—at the war."

"Do you read, then?"

Aris nodded. "Until near the war's end, I had a tutor my father provided. He taught me to read and write and keep accounts, and I taught Seri—"

"A servant's child?" Disbelief edged the Marshal-General's voice at that.

"She's my friend," Aris said. "It was more fun, to have someone to read with, to write to, and as for accounts, she is faster than I. It was a game to us."

"So," Luap said, with a glance at the Marshal-General, "Seri was your companion in childhood, and much of that was during the war. Did your tutor instruct you in magery?"

"No, sir. He had none himself; he said my father would have me taught later, if I showed any ability. But then my father was killed, and my mother—" He stopped, feeling the heat on his face. His mother could not have known what he overheard; surely no child was supposed to hear things like that. He had tried to forget them.

"Seri said your mother married another lord after your father died in battle," the Marshal-General said. "Seri said the other lord didn't want to bother with you. Is that what you think?"

The last time his father had been home, his mother had said those things he wished he'd never heard. *I didn't want the last brat*, she'd screamed. *It's not my fault he's too young to help.* There was more, that he carefully did not remember. Then his father had come for that last moment, scooping him into a tight hug, telling him to remember. Not what he'd just heard, he was sure: his father could not have known, any more than his mother, that he'd been awake with a headache. *If only you had the magery,* his father had whispered. *But it's too late, now.* He had been frightened; he had started to cry, partly with pain of his headache and partly with fear, and his father had put him down gently and gone out the door.

Aris realized too much time had passed, and his hands had knotted in his lap as they did when he thought about his mother. "She— she grieved at my father's death," he said finally, in a low voice. "The lord Katlinha swore to protect her."

His throat closed on another memory he had not quite buried. The lord Katlinha's long black moustaches, which had fascinated him with their stiff curl. The lord's hand stroking Seri's cheek and neck, and the drawling voice in which he'd said, "Of course you can bring your sweetling, lad, though you're really too young to appreciate her. . . ." Something wrong: he had realized suddenly that Seri was frightened, Seri who was never frightened—her eyes dilated, her breathing shallow. "But you'll both have to mind me," the lord had said, laughing at something Aris couldn't understand, because Seri afraid was nothing to laugh about.

Then his favorite pup, the lame one, had chosen that moment to nip the lord's other hand, and the lord's hard bootheel had stamped. The pup squealed, Seri jerked free, Aris had flung himself at the injured pup, ignoring the lord's command to let the beast die. In the end the lord had shrugged. "I'll have you, lady, if it's your will, but I won't bother with that worthless scrap. There's no mageblood in him; you said you weren't willing, and no doubt you withheld yourself."

They had gone, and left him. He and Seri had run off to join the blueshirts, with the surviving servants, and spent the last of the war fetching water and digging trenches for the peasant army. That he could say; he could not say the other.

"The lord didn't want another son," he said, half-gasping with the pain of remembering it.

"And your mother?" The Marshal-General's voice held no anger, but also no space for refusal.

"Didn't . . . didn't want me," said Aris, eyes down. It was his greatest shame, that he had been the kind of boy a mother would not want.

"Did she know you had magery?" asked Luap.

"No, sir. She was sure I had none; my brothers, she said, had shown it younger than I did."

A silence followed. Aris looked up to see that the Marshal-General's face had contracted in a black scowl. Luap stared at nothing, across the room. Finally the Marshal-General shook out his shoulders and looked at Aris. "Well—she was wrong, quite clearly. When did you find out what powers you had?"

"It was the puppy." He hadn't told them about the puppy; he tried to make it brief, and avoid that difficult moment with Seri. A favored pet, accidentally injured, and the pressure of his grief. "The cowman had already told me I was good with animals," he said. "I liked the stables and byres; the beasts were quiet with me, and the men showed me how to work with them. But all I'd done was what they told me, until the puppy." The huntsman had said it was hopeless; the cowman had said the same. Broken spine, soon death, and the sooner the better; the huntsman wanted to put the pup out of its misery. He had burst into tears again, and again an adult had been disgusted with him, though this time not cruel. *Yer not cryin' 'bout the pup*, the huntsman had said. *Yer cryin' 'bout yer ma and da and that sun-lost count, may he die in the dark.*

He had held the whimpering, shivering pup, that had made such a mess in his arms, and felt Seri behind him, also shivering. Then the familiar prickle he had felt so often before without doing anything—without guessing what it was. His hands itched, stung, moved almost without his knowing. He ran a finger down the pup's back to the soft pulpiness where the count's bootheel landed. He tried to imagine what should be there, what it should feel like. The pup rolled in his hands suddenly, squirming, and slapped his face with its wet pink tongue . . . and he'd fallen asleep where he sat, with Seri holding his head.

By the time he'd wakened, the pup had run off somewhere; Seri, the cautious, had said it was best. Before he could argue with her, the remaining servants had rushed in with word of an advancing peasant army. He never saw the pup again, to be sure he'd healed it. But in the next few seasons and years, he had plenty of opportunities to try out his powers. Seri argued for caution, for secrecy, but later helped him use—and hide—what he could do.

"I thought at first it was for animals only," he explained, now once more calm, with the story far enough from his mother. "After what the cowman said—well—I asked to work with the beasts, wherever I was, and found I could help them. Seri said to start with little things, so if I couldn't do it, it wouldn't matter so much. Scratch on a cow's udder, a sore teat, lameness from stepping on something sharp, that kind of thing. I couldn't always heal it, but I could usually make it better. Then one place at lambing time, the shepherd wanted my help because my hands were so small—"

And lamb after lamb he delivered, in the cold rain of that week, had lived . . . they had all lived. The shepherd, who had taught him the old hard truth that sheep are born looking for a place to die, had taken his hands and spread them, looking for the gods' mark, he'd said. He'd found nothing, but Aris had slept for a week when the lambing was over, so deep asleep that Seri had had to clean him where he lay, like a baby. It was natural, then, when the shepherd's wife's next baby came out blue and still, for the shepherd to thrust the limp bundle into his hands and growl, "It's a lamb, lad—save it!"

"The baby lived?" asked the Marshal-General.

"Oh, yes. She's a healthy child; it was just something about the birthing." He paused, trying to think what to tell next. Not how frightened he had been; Gird wouldn't want to hear that. The shepherd had assumed his talent came from Alyanya; he himself wasn't sure. The only magery he'd seen was a dance of light by his father and brothers when he was very small, one Midwinter Feast. He'd been told Esea gave them magery, and that made sense, for the light dance. But healing? No one had even mentioned the possibility. In that remote village, once the war passed, all anyone cared about was sowing and tending and harvest, the daily routine, into which he fit happily. No one really cared how he healed, or where the power came from, so long as it worked.

"But you had no family—who'd you live with?" asked Luap, leaning forward. Aris grinned and spread his hands.

"After the war, sir, there's many not in the right place . . . we worked in well enough, here and there, until things settled a bit. Then that shepherd, he took us into his family."

"It must have been—" Luap coughed, spat, and went on. "It must have been very different from what you knew before." Aris did not miss the keen glance the Marshal-General shot at his luap.

"It was, sir, but—but for missing the people I knew, it was better."

"Better!" That from both of them, clearly surprise and disbelief.

Aris felt his face reddening. "Before, sir . . . my tutor and some others, they didn't think I should spend so much time with Seri, or in the stables with the animals. We've been lucky; I know that. Except for that one bad winter, we've always had enough, and we've always been together. Once I found out what I could do, what the feeling was for, I felt happier than I'd ever been."

"Hmmph." That was the Marshal-General, giving his luap another look Aris couldn't read. "Well, then: if things have gone so well, why come to me?"

This part he could tell without a hitch. From the shepherd's child, to another in the vill born apparently dead, from those to a child with fever, a man injured by falling rock, a woman poisoned by bad grain . . . he had begun testing his powers on people as well as livestock. When the village saw how each attempt at healing wore on him, they were careful in their requests, and Seri protected him as best she could. Then came the first request from a neighboring vill in the same hearthing, a child kicked by a plowhorse. Another, from another vill, then another and another. He had come to be known all through that hearthing, as the boy who could heal what herblore could not. Most of the time, he worked with animals, learning all he could of each kind, but when the calls came, he would go and heal the sick and injured. Seri stood between him and the world, the warm hand at his back, the one who remembered that he needed food after, the one who would sometimes scold those who hadn't tried herblore first.

"Then the Code came," Aris said, meeting the Marshal-General's gaze directly. "Of course we'd all heard of you, sir, and I'd seen a Marshal in the market towns. Our vill has a yeoman-marshal; Seri and I drilled with the other younglings as we grew tall enough. No one thought anything wrong about my healing and being in the barton as a junior. I don't know how many knew I was mageborn, but no one questioned me. Until last harvest-time."

Last harvest-time, the new Marshal of Whitehill grange had come to inspect each barton on his rolls, and with him, he'd brought the new version of Gird's Code. All the village stood in the barton to hear him read it, nodding their heads at familiar phrases—it wasn't that different—until the clause about magery.

Aris felt the now-familiar tremor in his hands, and locked them together. "It said, sir, that no form of magery could be tolerated, that what seemed good was really evil in intent and act, and forbade the mageborn to use, or anyone to profit by, magery. Of course everyone looked at me, and the Marshal stopped reading. 'Do you have a mageborn survivor in this vill?' he asked. Some nodded, and some didn't—I think they wanted to hide me, protect me. I raised my hand, and he called me forth. 'Do you practice evil magicks, boy?' he asked. Sir, I could hardly answer. I had healed, yes: that hand of days, I'd healed a serpent bite. But evil? I said so, that I had healed, and he drew back as if I'd thrown fire at him. Our yeoman-marshal stood up for me, then, and said I'd caused no trouble, nor had a bad heart, but the Marshal was firm that my magery was evil. If I had no bad heart, he said, I'd be willing to forswear it, never use it again. The people sighed at that, but he overrode them. I could not be in the barton, he said, if I used magery, nor could they harbor me. It was in the Code, he said."

"What did you do?"

"I said I was sorry, and would do so no more, though I couldn't see how healing was evil. He bade the yeoman-marshal watch me closely, and warned me that he would tolerate no magery in his grange." Aris looked at the Marshal-General again. "He said you knew best, sir, and if you said it was evil, then it was. I did my best, after that. The village folk were troubled in their minds; a few said I must have charmed them, to make my power seem good, but most wished naught had happened. They still came to me, many of them, when someone was sick, or a beast hurt. The yeoman-marshal tried to make them quit, but he couldn't. He asked couldn't I do something, short of using magery, but I don't have what Seri's folk call a parrion of herblore: I don't know any way but the power. And it came to hurt, sir . . . it rises up in me like water in a spring, when I see someone in need . . . I fell sick myself, late in winter, and Seri said that caused it. She said we had to come to you, because the Code is yours, and perhaps you didn't know that magery could be healing power."

"I had heard it could be; I never knew it so." The Marshal-General leaned forward; Aris could see doubt in his expression. "You say you had seen little use of magicks by your own folk before—did you never see someone charmed?"

Aris shook his head. "Not that I know of. Others have told me . . . it makes them think they want to do something, or like someone."

"And people do like you." The Marshal-General said that flatly. "Seri says everyone in your household liked you."

"You think I *charmed* them?"

"Perhaps you didn't mean to; a child may not know what it does. But I worry about it, lad. From what Seri says, even my own reaction to you. . . ."

Aris could not think of anything to say. He had been ready for anger, even punishment . . . but he had not expected this. The Marshal-General, looking steadily at him, apparently saw an expression that meant something, and relaxed, sighing.

"No, I don't think you are using magicks, not even without your knowledge. You're too relaxed; you weren't like that while healing. I've seen Luap here make light; he gets a faraway look. But I'm still worried. You seem a nice enough lad, no harm to you; Seri's talked my ears half off explaining about you and your family. Yet . . . there was a reason for the Code to forbid all magicks."

Aris let out the breath he had held. Gird waited, as if for Aris to say something, then went on.

"The magelords misused it, misused it so badly that what everyone remembers is the misuse, not the right use." He said "right use" as if it hurt his mouth. "None of us know what the right use would be like, not having seen it, so judging the difference—knowing when the use is right and when it's wrong—would be difficult, if any of us could do it at all. Tell me, lad, have you ever misused your healing magick?"

Aris had followed the argument Gird was making; it made more sense than what his own Marshal had said, that magery was inherently evil. He spoke his thoughts aloud. "I had thought, Marshal-General, that healing was good in itself—and because it was good, then that use of magery was good. I never used it for anything but healing; but . . ." He stopped, trying to remember all the details of each healing, even in that abstraction he noticed that Gird's luap watched him closely. "I suppose, sir . . . if the gods meant someone to die, for some reason, then healing that person would be bad, and not good. Or not being able to heal completely . . ." He remembered the child kicked in the head by a horse, whose life he had saved, but the child remained mute and subject to fits, dying a few years later of a fever . . . the parents had not sought his help then. He told Gird about it. "Perhaps that was a misuse of magery, although at the time, I thought only of the child's life."

Gird nodded. "It may have been, though I agree you did not mean harm. But I've seen a man who meant no harm bury the tip of his scythe in a child's belly during harvest: the harm is done, with or without malice. I am glad to see that you recognize that, that you are willing to consider what harm you may have done." He glanced at his luap before going on. "Have you ever used your healing magicks to gain something unfairly? To force others to do what you wished? To cause a pain that you might gain approval for relieving it?"

"No!" Aris heard his voice rise, childishly, and took a long breath before continuing. "Sir, I would not know how to cause a pain; the pains people come with hurt enough. I have—I have told people what they must do to help me, sometimes, as in pulling a broken limb straight, or cleaning a wound. As for gain—some have given me food, afterwards, and if that is wrong, then I have been wrong, but I never asked, sir. Seri will tell you."

"Seri," Gird said gruffly, "is a young lass growing into a woman,

and you are a young lad; in Seri's eyes you are a hero who will
never do wrong."

Aris felt his face burning; it took all his will to meet Gird's eyes.
"Seri doesn't lie, sir," he said through locked teeth. "She wouldn't,
even if she were—"

"A lass in love?" finished Gird when he hesitated. "You may be
right—but even if you are, I had to hear it from you. You are about
to cause me a lot of trouble, lad, and I want to be sure it's worth it."

"Cause you trouble?" The last thing he wanted to do was cause
trouble, and he could not imagine what trouble he would cause.

Gird's deep laugh surprised him. "Yes—how do you think your
Marshal will like it when I change the Code to allow healing? Or
the others who think as he does that all magicks are evil, that there
are no good uses of a bad tool? And Luap here will have a lot of
work to do, writing out new versions of the Code to be sent all
over. I will have arguments from the Marshals and others who are
afraid of any magicks; I will have complaints about changes—you
don't think that's trouble?"

He could hardly believe what he was hearing. "Then—"

"Aris, I believe your healing is good, and your intentions good.
I will insist on some restrictions, both for your own good and to
calm peoples' fears: you are still young, you would have guidance
if you were a farm lad learning to scythe, let alone someone who
can save lives. But of course you must heal, and more than that I
give you leave to train other mageborn in the use of that gift, if
you can. If anything will reconcile our peoples, it will be the right
use of magicks, using them to help and not harm."

Chapter Seven

Gird's ideas of proper guidance surprised Aris and Seri both. For
a hand of days, they lived in the old palace, free to run about and
meet the others who lived there. The lad Aris had healed woke to
comfort and health; he was shy at first, but soon treated Aris like
a favorite brother. Gird's luap tested their knowledge of reading,
writing, and accounting, and argued that they should be kept among
the clerks where those skills would be most useful. Aris decided
he liked the man, though he didn't want to spend all his time

hunched over a desk. He found Luap's mixture of grave courtesy and sadness fascinating, and hoped that he would be able to learn the healing magery. Seri, for once, did not agree with him: she didn't exactly dislike Luap, but she could not, she said, see any reason for Aris's fascination.

On the fifth day, Aris widened his explorations to the stables and cowbyres, where he met Gird's old gray horse.

"You're—you're not old at all," Aris said, staring wide-eyed at the gray. It looked nothing like a carthorse now, in the sunlight that speared through the doorway. Hammered silver, an arched neck, great dark eyes that looked Aris full in the face. Then it turned to Seri, whose breath caught in her throat.

"It's not just a *horse*," she said softly. The horse fluttered its nostrils and made a sound like a growl. Aris, entranced, put out his hand. Warm breath flowed over it.

"I don't think anyone's supposed to know," he said. The horse bumped his hand with its muzzle. He wanted to touch it, stroke that head and that glossy mane. With a twitch of its ear, it gave permission. His hands moved without his thought, gentling and caressing, as he would have touched any horse. He always liked handling animals; he felt better when he touched them. This was more; he felt strong, safe, and alert "Does Gird know?" he asked softly, into an iron-gray ear. The horse drew back its head and favored him with a look combining mischief and warning.

"No," said Seri, coming up beside him to fondle the horse's other ear. "Father Gird doesn't know, and he—" she meant the horse, "—thinks it's funny. And in the legends, no one quite believes it. They don't want to think about it. But how can anyone think you're an old broken-down carthorse?"

In the way of horses, each of them received the full power of one dark eye, then the horse seemed to collapse in on itself. Suddenly it was thicker, stubbier, paler—no longer hammered silver, but the dirty gray of white cloth left out to mildew and weather. The hollow in its back deepened; it stood hipshot, head sagging over the stall door. It yawned, disclosing long yellow teeth; its lids sagged shut over those remarkable eyes.

"But why did you show *us*?" Aris asked. He was sure it had, that the horse had its own reasons for revealing to them what it concealed from others. Without a change in shape or color, this time, the eyes opened, and the horse looked deliberately from one to the other. Aris felt the hair rise all over his body, as if he'd been dipped in cold water. He felt even more alert, as if some great danger had passed near. Every sense came to him sharply. He could hear a horse five stalls down licking the last oats from its manger, and another slurping water. The voices of men in the yard outside, bantering about their work, were almost painfully loud. He could smell everything, from the pungency of the horses to the smoke to the last apples frost-pierced on the trees in the meadow. He could feel the clothes on his body, the slick hair of the horse's neck, the pressure of the air in his nose that promised an autumn storm.

He glanced at Seri. She looked as if she felt the same. Her hair stood out from her braid as it did on cold clear winter days, more alive than some people's faces. Now she looked the old horse full in the face. "We're supposed to do something? *We* are? But we're newcomers; we don't know anyone. What—"

As if a large, warm hand had touched his shoulder, Aris felt calm rest on him. Not his calm: the horse's. The horse shook its head sharply. "Not yours, then," he said. "A god?" No answer, but it must be. A god wanted something from them, which meant they must give it, whatever it was. And they were to be ready—that much was clear—but whatever it was would come later, not now.

The gray horse yawned again, and when it was through stood looking even more aged and decrepit, if possible. "So," said Gird from behind them. "You've found my old horse." Aris managed not to look from the horse to Gird and back again. "He's a good campaigner," Gird said, rubbing the horse's poll, "but getting long in the tooth." The eye nearest Aris opened an instant; he felt the horse's secret laughter. "You said you liked cows, boy," Gird went on. "Come see ours. We've got two of the dun milkers and four of the spotted ones." Aris glanced back as they left the horse stables and saw the gray horse watching them.

Gird lavished the attention on the cows that Aris and Seri had given the old horse. He and the cowman discussed them in detail, from their broad black nostrils to their carefully curried tails. Gird ran his hands over them, looking inside their ears, stroking their broad sides and velvety flanks, feeling the udders for any inflammation. Aris liked the smell of cows, and their complacent belief that grass counted for more than anything else, but he could see that Gird's affection went beyond that. Finally Gird was done, and led them out into the meadow west of the palace complex. A few fruit trees, the remnants of a larger orchard, clung to their last leaves and some wizened apples.

"If you could live as you liked," Gird said, "what would you do between healings?"

Aris thought. "Well—I could work in the stables—or I suppose with your—with Luap in the copying rooms."

Gird looked at Seri. "I'd like to work with the horses," she said. "If Aris is, that is."

Gird nodded, as if that confirmed something he'd been thinking about. "That's about it. You two have lived and worked together for years, but—but if one of you died, what would the other do? You, Aris, are willing to do whatever's needful; you have the mageborn courtesy; you won't say what you want most, and I'm not sure you know. Seri knows, and will say it, but then thinks she must stay with you. I would not split brother from sister or friend from friend, but the two of you need to learn that you can live out of each other's pockets."

Aris felt cold. Would Gird send Seri *away?*

"I've been talking to Luap and the Marshals," Gird went on. "I don't like to see younglings cramped inside with scribe's work. Unless that's what you wanted most, I wouldn't have it so. You both need grange discipline, and you both need a chance to find your own balance. So here's my thought." He looked from one to the other, as if to be sure they were paying attention. Aris could hardly hear over the blood pounding in his ears.

"You, Aris, need to know herblore as well as your own magicks, and you need to be around others who heal in different ways. There's a grange in the lower city that has three women with parrions of herblore in it; they have agreed to teach you what they know, and the Marshal can supervise your use of your own healing. You will be a junior yeoman, as you were in your own barton; you will spend your days in grange work and healing and study. And you, Seri, seem like to grow into a Marshal someday. For you I've found a grange with a healthy group of junior yeomen; if you have the abilities I suspect, you will be a yeoman-marshal soon enough. And yes, before you ask, these are separate granges. But both are in Fin Panir, and you will live here, near me, for the first year. You will still be together part of every day; but you will learn to trust others, and work with others, not just yourselves."

This was so much better than what Aris had feared that he felt himself flushing with relief. "Thank you, sir," he said. Gird smiled at him, obviously well-pleased.

"All right, then," he said, "let's go down to the city, and I'll introduce you."

Marshal Kevis of Northgate Grange welcomed Aris as warmly as any mageborn could expect. "A healer, the Marshal-General tells me. Gods, lad, if we'd known about you during the war! But you would have been too young, then, I suppose?"

"I didn't know what I could do until later—at least, I thought it was only animals."

"Gird said that, yes. Well. Suriya is our oldest herblore-healer; she wants to meet you at drill tonight. Her daughter Pir and her niece Arianya are the others. We have the same drill-nights as the other granges here, and I'll expect you to attend unless you're sick—or do you get sick?"

"Yes, Marshal," Aris said. "I don't think I can heal myself—if I could, I wouldn't have gotten sick in the first place."

"That's sense. Well, then, be at drill, study healing with Suriya, and when someone needs your skill, come and tell me. If Suriya has nothing for you to do, there's always work at the grange. Gird says you'll be staying up the hill, with them—even so, you're to come to me before you go healing someone."

Aris nodded. He felt half-dressed, with Seri off somewhere else, but he understood what Gird was trying to do. Not split them apart, but teach them to grow on their own. When he asked, the Marshal had several chores he could do that day, until time for drill. The yeoman-marshal, a young man a few years older than Aris, put him to work chopping wood and carrying water.

Suriya was a gray-haired woman who looked old enough to be his grandmother. She laid a gnarled hand on either side of his head, and hummed, then nodded sharply and spoke to the Marshal. "He'll do. The Marshal-General was right, Alyanya bless him: Here, lad, see what you think of this—" She handed him a small cloth bag of aromatic herbs. Aris sniffed.

"I don't know much, but it smells like what my folk called allheal and itchleaf."

"So it is, lad, with a pinch of dryhand, for them as gets the sweats without need. Scribes use that sometimes, that shouldn't, for a natural sweat keeps the body pure, but they don't like smudges on their scrolls." She waved at two other women, who came nearer. "This is my daughter, Pir, and my niece who's just come into her full parrion. You'll learn from her first, if it doesn't bother you to learn women's things."

Aris shook his head. "No, why should it? The law's the same for all, and the gods gift whom they will."

The women looked at each other, the family resemblance clear in the angle of eye, the set of the mouth. "Well, then," said Suriya briskly, "we'll get along. Aris, your name is, so I've heard—has that a meaning, in mageborn speech?"

"I don't know," Aris said. "I think it may have been a child's name, and I never learned the other."

"Ah. Well. It's the wrong time of year to gather most herbs, but we've still some collecting to do: barks, roots, that sort of thing. We'll meet you here at sunrising tomorrow, shall we?"

Aris ran back up to the palace, excited and worried both. He found Seri in the same mood, but in her it came out in chatter. "I like our Marshal," she said. "I only wish you could be there—but I know what Father Gird means, and he's right. He's made me his yeoman-marshal's helper, already, and I had no idea how much work there is in a city grange. I missed you, but I like it."

That set the pattern for the next two seasons. Before dawn, both were off to their granges, to learn from the best their Marshals could find. They drilled with the junior yeomen, and both assisted the yeoman-marshals and Marshals in any grange work to be done. Aris spent hours with Suriya and Pir, sorting herbs into packets and sacks, learning to identify by smell dozens of different dried leaves, roots, barks. They taught him to brew some into thick dark teas to drink, and mash others to a paste with lard, to be spread on the skin. He went with Suriya to the people who asked her help. Many times his own gift did not wake; he simply watched as she applied her herbs, and saw how her very presence soothed the worried families. At night, back in the old palace with Seri, they compared notes. Her days, spent almost entirely in grange work, were very different from his. Beyond the usual drill, her Marshal had begun giving her extra classes in weapon skills. The first time she was allowed to use a sword, she came back almost glowing with glee.

"But Seri—" Aris didn't know how to disagree with her; in all their life he never had. But swords were for hurting people; he knew she could not really want that. Not Seri, whose warmth was almost a healing magic in itself. Besides, swordfighters—soldiers—died younger than most.

"I am not becoming a bloodthirsty warrior," she said, almost angrily. "You're as bad as my Marshal. Stopped in midswing, he did, to ask what I was grinning about and scold me for it."

"I know you're not bloodthirsty," Aris said, rubbing her shoulder where a knot of pain resisted his fingers. "That's why I worry. If you wear a sword, someday you'll have to use it, and you'll feel bad about it."

"I'll feel worse if I don't know how, and get killed. Or if others get killed because I didn't learn enough. The Marshal-General didn't like killing people, but he did it. He did it as quick and clean as he could." Seri, unlike Aris, had actually watched some of the final battles, despite being warned off more than once by the rear ranks. She had come back white-faced and shaky, but ready to help tend the wounded. Aris had stayed near the fires, tending the wounded as they came from the field as best he then knew, unaware that the pounding headache and itching of his palms came from something more than tending smoky fires and boiling whatever herbs someone gave him.

"I don't want you to die," Aris said softly.

"I won't," she said. "I will work hard, and be *very* good." It should have sounded arrogant, but it didn't.

By the time Suriya was ready to send Aris and Pir out to collect the early summer herbs in the fields far from the city, Gird had decided that the two should live away from the palace, in or near their granges. Aris moved his small pack down to Suriya's house, and slept on a pallet in the kitchen. He had been called out at least once every hand of days for a healing; it would be simpler to live here. But he knew he would miss Seri. The first time he had healed in Suriya's presence, she had gasped and turned pale. Now she knew what to do, what he needed of rest, quiet and food afterwards. But her hands, warm and strong as they were, were not Seri's hands; he never felt the same afterwards until, in his rare free time, he could get up to the grange where she lived and worked, and tell her what had happened. She seemed cheerful enough, but her face always lighted up when he came, as if she, too, needed the familiar audience for her own tales.

The young man strode into the courtyard like someone who had never been thwarted. *Marrakai.* Luap struggled against a lance of envy that pierced him. He had known, as a boy, what the Marrakai were; he had been taught, in those early years, the high nobility of both realms. He fought the envy down, refused that easy resentment. Marrakai, according to Gird, had lost their magery early, and adapted. Gird no doubt thought he had much to learn from the Marrakai. Perhaps he did, though he was sure that learning to live with the loss of a talent was not the same as learning not to use one.

The young man went to one knee before Gird, surprising everyone, including Gird; Luap saw the flush of red that darkened his neck.

"Get up, young Marrakai: we don't do that."

"You have my respect, Marshal-General." He stood straight now, almost quivering in eagerness for something . . . Luap could not imagine what. What could a man like that need from Gird?

"Aye, well . . ." Gird rubbed the back of his neck with one broad hand. "You have mine as well, and your father. How is he?"

The young man grinned. "He's still in some trouble with the king, Marshal-General. For all the king needs his support, he wishes it need not be so."

"That bad, eh?" Gird waved the others aside, called Luap with a look, and sat heavily on the bench beneath the plane tree. "Here—sit and talk." He reached beneath the bench and pulled out a water jug. "Thirsty?"

"No, sir—Marshal-General." The young man leaned back, and stripped off his dusty gloves. "My father thinks the king will settle. He's not like the old one; he's got sense and no wish to evil. But he finds it hard to forgive my father's support of the peasants."

"I thought your father was going to stay at home and pull his woods up around his ears."

The young man shook his head. "That was not his nature, Marshal-General, as I think you know. He could no more ignore a war than a fine horse can ignore a race . . . it began with sanctuary given to fugitives from other domains."

Luap watched the Kirgan closely. The boy had Gird's confidence and no wonder: he hung on Gird's every word, eyes wide with admiration. Luap eyed the thick, lustrous cloth of his tunic, the oiled leather, finely tooled, of his belt, the carved bone hilt of the dagger in his obviously new boot. He remembered cloth like that, boots like that; the boy was rich, and had enjoyed a lifetime of such riches . . . which was fine; Luap could understand that. What he could not understand, or accept, was the way Gird accepted this youth, and his equally rich and powerful father, as friends.

I have served you honestly, he said silently toward the back of Gird's head, and pushing aside the memory of that time when he hadn't. *And I would have been this boy's master . . . but you never trust me this way.*

"But in spite of that your father is satisfied?" Gird asked. Luap had already told him that, as had the first messengers back from troubled Tsaia. "He is sure the new king has no such powers?"

"He swears it," the Kirgan said. "He considers the Mahierian branch the best choice, for all it angers the Verrakaien." Luap wished he knew more about the Verrakaien, who seemed, by the rumors, to be as powerful as the Marrakai but utterly inimical to them. Rumor also gave them the largest remaining store of magery, along with whispered tales of its source. He watched the young man's face, wondering how Gird was so sure the Marrakaien were telling the truth.

"And he has not taken the field at all?"

"No, although some of the local bartons sent volunteers. You did know that father allowed the bartons to organize openly?"

"Oh, yes." Gird's deep voice broke into a chuckle. "That news reached us quickly, I suspect." It was not quite the .reaction the Kirgan had expected; Luap recognized the flicker of eyelid, the tension of shoulder quickly controlled. "Luap—"

Luap recalled himself and said, "Yes, Gird?"

"The Kirgan Marrakai confirms our reports that Tsaia's new king has no powers of magery, and that the merchants and craft guilds support his rule, while our supporters have mostly returned to their homes. I see no purpose in pursuing the war, with the most dangerous magelords dead—"

"Except the Duke Verrakai, Marshal-General," murmured the Kirgan.

Gird's shoulders lifted. "Far to your eastern border, Kirgan, and well beyond my reach. Those of you who know him best must do as you think wise, but you are not asking my aid, are you?"

"Well—no." He had the look of one who would have taken help if it had been offered, and had been hoping for that offer.

"Then I see no cause for quarrel between your land and this. Is that not what your father meant by sending you?"

"Well . . . yes. To ask, rather, if it satisfied you."

Gird heaved the kind of sigh that Luap had learned was intentionally dramatic. "Lad, I would be happiest if all the kingdoms lived in peace and plenty, but that's not like to come in *my* lifetime. Men delight in quarrels, as cows in summer grass. But your father's gold bought our freedom, in those steel points we used to let the mageborn blood run out—" Luap could not see the slightest flush, any sign that the youth considered mageborn blood his kin. Gird had told him the Marrakaien magery had been lost long before. How long? Long enough to consider themselves peasants? Not likely, with that air of mastery, that rich embroidery on sleeve and hem, those supple boots, that elaborately tooled belt. Was their friendship then pretense? What other motive could the Kirgan Marrakai have, coming to Gird, than that which he spoke openly?

He felt uneasy, all along his side, as he walked the Kirgan to the common dining hall. Gird had said, with a look that might have been meaningful (but which meaning?) to take care of him.

"He's not changed." The Kirgan sounded happy about that. Luap eyed him.

"Did you expect him to?"

"No. I suppose not. But my father told me that men in power

often do." A pause, in which they entered the dining hall, and Luap's look quelled those who would have challenged the Kirgan. He showed the young man where to wash, and led him to the serving table. Would he expect fancier food? No—he dipped into the mutton stew as if he liked it, tore off a hunk of bread just as Luap did, and sat on the bench as if his rump were used to no better. "I saw that myself, in the new king we have."

"Ah." The new Tsaian king, which Duke Marrakai had backed against other contenders. "You are at court much?"

"Only to carry my father's messages. He says court life is not healthy for young men—or for him, at present." The Kirgan chuckled as he said that, and Luap smiled responsively. He could not decide if the young man's frankness were what it seemed or not. He wished the Rosemage were there; she had known Duke Marrakai when he was young, though she would not talk much about him.

"So—has your new king changed?"

The Kirgan looked thoughtful and clasped his fingers as if that would help him decide what to say. "He was . . . they had always made fun of him. I heard that in the years I was in Valchai's household. The king—the old one, I mean—had the mage powers our family had long lost, and some said that his cousin's lack proved his bastard blood."

A white rage shook Luap as a dog shakes a rag, then dropped him, leaving him hot and cold at once. He could feel his power struggling to escape, prove itself, but held it in check. He would not let this—this *boy* push him into anything rash. "Are the gifts then proof of pure blood?" he asked, as calmly as if discussing the color of a new calf.

"No. At least my father says not. Once perhaps they were, but when our folk came into the north, they began to fail, unaccountably and unpredictably. Some families accepted this as the gods' price for the gift of a great new land, and others fought it . . . but that you know."

"Yes." It was all he could say, through clenched teeth; luckily, the Kirgan seemed not to notice.

"At any rate, the new king had been considered of no moment so many years that some thought he would be unable to rule. He was known to spend his days in the stables, training his own horses and even grooming them."

"And what's wrong with that?" Gird asked, setting his own bowl down on the table and grunting as he swung his leg over the bench. Luap bit his lip. Even now, he'd find Gird down in the cowbyres of a morning, humming over some cow as he brushed her. For himself, if he never saw a cow except on the table, ready to eat, it would be well enough. The Kirgan flushed, and Gird relented. "I know: your great lords aren't supposed to do their own work. But if the man likes horses, how can he keep away? Still, he'll be busy enough now to have no time for that, as I have no time for farming. . . ."

"Would you go back to it?" No one else had asked, that Luap knew; trust a rash youth to open his mouth and say it.

Gird sighed. "Now? I—I like to think I would, if the chance came. I miss it, the smell of the grass and the cows, the feel of a scythe handle as the blade bites into the stems. But my farm's gone, my family's gone—and that's all part of it, you see. Not just any field, but the field I knew from boyhood, and the same cottage, and my family around the table. Friends beside me in the field, all that. If I went back to farming, took a vacant place, I'd have to do it all alone. That I don't want: their faces would hover over the table, and I—I'd be alone."

For a moment, Luap saw Gird in some cottage, surrounded by children and grandchildren—but it would not happen, and they all knew it. He suspected that Gird would make a less than perfect grandfather anyway.

The Kirgan said, "I have thought long on what you told me before, sir. I have been learning the skills of farming myself." He opened his hand to show Gird the calluses on his palm as if they were battle scars. Perhaps they were, Luap thought. Gird clearly approved, and his nod seemed to mean as much to the boy as any praise. What kind of duke would he make, with the attitudes he learned from Gird? As difficult as the blend of mageborn and peasant in Fintha, Luap could not imagine how it would work in Tsaia, with the mageborn retaining their right to rule. His envy ebbed, thinking on the difficult task the Kirgan would face as time went on.

When Arranha invited him to one of the courtyard discussions, Luap went hoping to hear something which would help him deal with his own confusion. Instead, Arranha spent the whole afternoon propounding the idea that common daylight and inspiration were analogous: that the gods gave light to see with eye and mind both, that the mere exposure of evil by such light somehow ensured its defeat, that all good men would naturally choose to be flooded with that light, so that any errors could be seen and corrected.

Luap could not explain what bothered him about that doctrine. Gird, somewhat impatient after a day spent settling quarrels between granges, had no sympathy with his imprecision.

"He's a priest, and a Sunlord priest at that. Why should you understand what he says?"

"He thinks we all should." Luap rolled the quill in his hand. "He thinks we should all understand the gods . . . that the Sunlord's light enlightens everyone. . . ."

Gird snorted. "There's some as stumble into holes in broad daylight. Granted, we all stumble more in the dark, but—"

"That's what I mean. If . . . if you're thinking about something *else*, if you're not using the light, you can run square into something . . . and if you're trying to see, you can see better in dim light sometimes than midday glare. I think the mind's light is the same, but Arranha doesn't."

"Mind's light, or god's light?"

"They're the same, aren't they?" At Gird's expression, Luap tried again. "I mean, once inside your head—how can you tell? Light is light."

Gird's expression might have been pity, or contempt, or some combination. "I think if you ever have a god in your head, Luap, you will discover the difference. Now—about those grange rolls—" And he refused, with a glower and another question about the grange records, to enter into that discussion again.

Luap puzzled over it himself, day after day. Somewhere in that concept of Arranha's something didn't fit his own experience, his own knowledge of himself. Was refusing knowledge the same thing as choosing evil? Was his desire for the privacy of his childhood memories, his instinctive distaste for Dorhaniya's reminiscences, the same as turning away from the light? He could not tell, and he could not tell if that failure meant something.

Chapter Eight

Luap did not, after all, have to decide when and how to tell Gird about that distant land. Gird himself suggested they travel together, when it became obvious that the Marshal-General's presence would settle some festering disputes in outlying granges. The cave lay on the obvious shortcut from one problem to another, and Luap took that as a favorable omen.

"I don't know that I like this any better than I did the first time." Gird's voice rang off the stone walls.

"You don't have a cold." Luap grinned over his shoulder. Gird had one hand on the wall, feeling his way. He wouldn't fall over the ledge this time.

"And you don't have that tone of voice you had." Gird's look was friendly enough, but unsmiling.

"Yes." Luap remembered the previous occasion entirely too well; he had been almost hysterical with fear and elation. Now his mouth went dry. He had sworn and been forsworn, all in less time than heating a kettle of water. This place was the very focus of Gird's distrust of him, however he'd proven himself since. How could he expect Gird to believe him now?

"Yes," he said again, flattening his tone to avoid the least taint of charm. "But I will tell you what I can. You remember that you, too, felt an influence here?"

"I felt the god's presence, not an *influence* like your magery." Gird had decided to be difficult; Luap smothered a sigh. Gird's expression, in the gloom, looked one with the rock walls. Luap felt as bruised by that as by his memories.

"I felt both." Luap paused, and thanked the gods' mercy that Gird did not comment. He drew another long breath and plunged on. "That inner chamber, floored and ringed with strange designs . . . ?"

"Umph" More grunt than word, it meant *Go on, I'm listening.*

"It can take you to a place."

That should have been clear enough, but Gird stared, eyes suddenly brighter in dimness. "Take you? How?"

"I don't know how. And—" forestalling another question, "I don't know where the place is, or why, or anything else. I don't know if it will take you, or only me. But I thought you should know."

Gird had that crafty look Luap most disliked. He would complain. He did. "Gods' teeth, lad, you keep thinking I should know things that don't help at all."

Damned mulish peasant, thought Luap, an indulgence he allowed himself only in the dark. Gird read his face too well.

"You told me to assess all magical dangers. This may be one. If I can go somewhere and return, so may others."

"*Your* kind."

"Or others. I think the Elder Races have used this."

"Gnomes?" Gird sounded almost cheerful about that; unlike Luap, he still got on well with his former advisors.

"I don't know. You might know the symbols I found in that other place."

"So—have you asked them?"

"Not without talking to you. I wondered if you'd try it with me."

"Try—you mean go *somewhere?*"

Luap nodded. Gird heaved one of those sighs Luap had learned were as dramatic as necessary. "Has the place gone to your head, then, as it did last time? Will you try another of your tricks?"

"No." Surely he knew that already.

"Well, then. Yes. I will. But—" a blunt finger hard against Luap's chest. "—But I still own a hard fist and strength to use it."

"I know." He let his own light come, in this hidden place, until it shone as bright as was needful, looking away from Gird's face in conscious courtesy. . . . Gird still hated to see magelight, even Arranha's. Then he led the way to the chamber for which he had no proper name, the bell-shaped space with its carved decorations, its inlaid design on the floor. "We'll stand here," he said, stepping boldly out onto it.

"You're sure?" Gird edged his boot forward as if he thought the smooth stone might be glass, and break. In here his voice echoed, waking a resonance more metallic than stony. He spoke more softly then. "I don't like this—the gods—"

"Will sense no impiety." Luap waited until Gird moved close to him, the broad shoulders slightly hunched, apprehensive. He stretched his own chest, wondering, in the last possible moment, if this was wise. But he had to try; the need for that squeezed his mind painfully. He felt inside for the power he had inherited, that the Rosemage was so determined he would learn to use. As if his feet were moving in a dance, he could feel the interlacing patterns below him in the stone, and his mind sang a response. . . .

And they stood in the great hall with its arches at the far end. He felt Gird's sudden shift of weight, heard the indrawn ragged breath, that came back out as a shaky whisper.

"*Somewhere* . . . you said . . ."

"This is . . . it. Wherever it is. Whatever it is." However it works and we got here, he went on silently, hoping Gird wouldn't ask about that. At least not yet. "We can walk around," he went on, taking a step off the pattern's center. He could damp his own magelight; the place lay under the cool silvery glow of deeper magic. Would Gird notice the difference? Gird did.

"More magicks than yours," he said. "And how big is this place?"

"I'm not entirely sure. I didn't go far." He watched Gird move around, and finally leave the pattern that here centered a raised area of the floor. The man could still surprise him . . . an old man, a peasant born, distrustful of any magicks . . . and here after being snatched from a cave to a hall, he was looking around with alert interest and no apparent fear. He could still taste the fear that had

choked his own throat the first time he'd come—but of course he'd
had no warning. No ... Gird was simply the braver man. He followed him down the hall, noticing without analyzing the odd ring
of their boots on the stone floor, the way the walls threw the sound
back less harshly than he'd expected.

"Harp and tree ..." Gird muttered, looking up at the carving.
"The treelords, the oldsingers, that would be. I wonder if the blackhearts ever had a place here."

"Blackhearts?"

"I may not have told you." A long pause, in which Luap tried
to remember if he'd ever heard of blackhearts. "And I'm not sure
this is the place for it. There's a feel ... a good feeling here." Gird
looked around. "Anvil and hammer ... Sertig's folk, then."

"Gnomes?"

"Nay. Dwarven; the gnomes follow the High Lord as judge. But
I heard the lore of Sertig there, and from the first smith I knew,
back in the woods. 'Tis said all smiths learned metalcraft of
dwarves, and the dwarves say Sertig hammered out the world on
his anvil. Gnomes themselves think the High Lord ordered chaos
as we might sort seed or stones for building—at least I think that's
what they meant."

"And elvenkind?"

Gird's face wrinkled. He had never said much about the elves,
receiving the first elven ambassador with evident embarrassment
and awe. "Think that their god made the world like a harper makes
a song, if I understood what I was told—and I doubt I do. A song's
not a thing, like a stone you can count, or a lump of iron you can
shape ... it's ... it's just a thought in the mind, until someone
sings it again. It's not really there, between singings. So how can
the world be a song?"

"Maybe it's not finished." But even as he said it, Luap felt a
shiver go down his spine ... the world *was*, as Gird said: you could
touch it, smell it, taste it. He could not imagine it as something
becoming, not in its essence. Humans might move across the world,
even change it, as the Aarean lords had laid waste some tracts of
forest, but its basic reality didn't change. He hoped.

Gird had grunted; now he prowled near the arches. "Dwarfkind,
elvenkind, and this ... I suppose ... is for the gnomes?"

"What—lords of light and shadow!" That was a magelord's oath,
and earned him a sharp glance from Gird, but he could not help
it. Luap swallowed an angular lump of confusion, and wondered if
he should tell Gird that the arch he stood under had not been

there before. Not there the previous trips, and not there a few—minutes?—ago when they'd first arrived.

"I don't remember seeing this at first," Gird said. His voice was husky; was he finally afraid of something? Luap swallowed again and forced the truth past his teeth, which wanted to grip it.

"It wasn't here." Gird gave him a long level stare. "I swear, Marshal-General—" in this context the title came easily, more easily than his name. "It was not here when I came before, and it was not here when we arrived."

Over his head the arch bore the single unflawed circle of the High Lord, glowing with its own light, as the harp and tree, and the anvil and hammer. Up either column ran the same intricate interlacing patterns as on all other columns in that place, patterns he had seen in weaving or pottery all his life, now graved deep in polished stone. Gird's hand reached out, drew back, went out again, thumbfirst, to follow one of the lines a short way.

"It must . . . must mean something. . . ." All the resonance had left his voice; his brow wrinkled. Of course it meant something; what else? But Gird stared up, mouth gaping as he leaned back. Luap wanted to say something, do something, but couldn't think of anything effective. He wanted to think Gird was disrespectful, but couldn't manage that, either. Gird reserved disrespect for humans. Now he gave Luap another one of his looks. "Did you go through, before?"

"Through one of these?" At Gird's nod, he shook his head. "I would not chance it, marked as they were. And it felt wrong."

"Humph." Gird shook his head, to what question Luap could not guess, and turned away from the middle arch to Luap's great relief. Back up the long, silent, echoing, empty hall, around the dais. "Back there?" Gird's broad thumb indicated the openings hewn in the wall. Luap felt himself flushing, though why he couldn't imagine.

"Yes . . . I did. Not far; I wasn't sure of the light, of the directions—"

"Show me." That was plain enough; Luap shrugged and led the way through the left-hand door. Heartwise, the peasant lore had it. Sunwise, to Arranha and the magelords. The passage ran as he remembered, with no surprising additions, level and dry, wide enough for three men to walk comfortably together. Gird crowded him, nonetheless. "Find any stairs to the outside?"

"No." That had worried him; he knew there must be ways out, for the air to be so fresh. But in his limited explorations, all he'd found were empty chambers and these passages. Around a corner, then another. Ahead the passage forked. "I stopped here, and went back."

"Wise, I would think." Gird licked his finger and held it up. "Ah . . . we'll try the left again."

"Doesn't it bother you?"

"What?" Then he grinned, mischievous; Luap could have smacked him. "You mean being understone like this? That's right— you came later. You knew I was with the gnomes, but not how long. All the winter that was, and never a day's clean light, or living air. An hour or so of this won't bother me."

He wanted to believe that negated the courage, but he knew better. Gird had earned the right to be casual here, in those months with the gnomes. He followed Gird left away from the junction of passages, hoping his trailsense would hold here. Empty corridor followed empty corridor. Rooms opened here and there, blank and empty, floors gritty under his boots. Gird seemed to know where he was going, and Luap followed, stubbornly forcing his fear under control. Finally Gird stopped, and leaned on the wall.

"I'm tired. This could go on forever."

"Mmm." Luap leaned on the opposite wall, and looked down at his scuffed boots. He felt as if the stone were leaning back against him.

"We'll go back." Gird sighed. "I'd like to know where this is— which mountains. Dwarves would know."

"Would they?" asked Luap. "If it doesn't come out somewhere, maybe they never saw the outside. . . ."

Gird snorted. "They had to, to take out the stone they cut. And I've heard they know stone by its smell and taste . . . that a dwarf will know a rock brought from leagues away. The gnomes could do that, and they said dwarves could too." He pushed himself off the wall. "Well. Back we go." He led the way again, and Luap came behind, trying not to look back over his shoulder at what might follow the clangor of their voices. "You found a good surprise, Luap, I'll give you that. Not like before, indeed." He led on at a good pace, and soon they came back to the great hall; they could hear their footsteps ring in it before they arrived, as if it were a bell.

Luap let out breath he had not realized he held. "How did you know your way?" He could ask, now that they were safe.

Gird's brows rose. "You didn't? You count the turns, the door-ways you pass, keep track of lefts and rights—"

And this was the man who formed half his signs wrong in writing, whose brow furrowed over a page of clear script, who could not reckon except by placing objects in a row and counting them. Luap managed not to shudder or glance back through the doorway. "And now?"

"Mmmm." Gird looked around, up, around again. "I would still like to see the *outside* of this rock."

And I, thought Luap fervently. He opened his mouth to say "Then we'll go back," and shut it, for Gird was strolling with perfect assurance—or what looked like it—down the hall toward the arches. He had never heard Gird pray, and he did not hear him pray now—but he was sure that pause before Gird walked under the arch with the High Lord's sigil had in some manner been a request for permission. He himself did not run to follow, because (he told himself) it was disrespectful—he walked, quickly and quietly, and was in time to see Gird standing straddle-legged at the foot of a narrow curving stair that rose into the first darkness he had seen in this place. Gird turned and gestured.

"Come *on*, Luap; if it didn't scorch me, it's not going to hurt you." Luap would have liked to be sure of that, but stepped gingerly through the arch, his heart pounding. It had *not* been there before, and now he had walked through it, and—he glanced back, to find the hall just as visible, just as empty, just as silent as before. From this side, too, the arches stood clear, each with its holy symbol.

Gird had already started up the staircase, grunting a little. Luap sighed and followed. He might as well. If something happened to Gird, he could not go back without him. The stair rose in a spiral around a central well; Luap tried to keep a hand on the wall, but felt that the stairs tipped slightly inward. The staircase had no railing; his stomach swooped within him like a flight of small birds. His legs began to ache. From silver light, they passed to dusk, and then to dark. Gird stopped abruptly, and Luap almost ran into him.

"Why is there no light here?" His voice sounded flat, almost as if they were in a tiny closet, then it rang back from far below.

"I don't know." Luap felt grumpy, and his voice sounded it.

So did Gird; he heard a grumbling mutter, then: "Well, *make* some, then." That was a concession. Luap called his light, dim enough after the gloriously clear light below, and close above Gird's head the stone sprang into vision, arced into a shallow dome, scribed with patterns as intricate as any below. Within Gird's reach was a doubled spiral; Gird reached a cautious hand toward it.

"You know that?" asked Luap.

"Gnomes used it." Gird's broad peasant thumb traced the spiral in, then out, missing none of the grooves. He looked up, and said, "At your will." Not to Luap; Luap's hair rose. Suddenly a gust of cold air swirled in, and he felt the sweat on his neck freezing. Above the red stone vanished, and out of a dark gray sky snowflakes danced down upon them. "Blessing," said Gird, and climbed on. Luap followed, pushing against the gusting wind and shivering in the cold.

He came out over the lip of the opening onto a flat windswept table of red stone. Gird crouched an armslength away, back to the wind, eyes squinted, hair already spangled with snow. Luap looked around. He had never seen anything like their surroundings. They seemed to be on the flat top of some mass of stone, like a vast building. To one side—in that storm he could not guess the direction—rock rose again, a sheer wall as if hewn by a great axe. On the other sides, their table ended as abruptly. Snow streaked the rock, packed into every crevice, but swept clean of exposed surfaces. Its irregular curtains cloaked more distant views, but gave tantalizing hints of other vast rock masses.

"Not a place I'd expect to find elves," said Gird. "Not a tree in sight. Gnomes and dwarves, though . . . I'm surprised we haven't seen them."

Luap shivered. "If we stay here, they'll find us frozen as hard as these rocks."

"Not yet. I've never seen any place like this—or heard of it, even in songs."

Luap sighed, and climbed the rest of the way out, shivering, to crouch beside Gird. "Probably no one ever saw it before." At Gird's look, he said, "Human, I mean. Gnomes, dwarves, elves, yes." He squinted, blinked, and realized that the snow came down less thickly . . . he could see downwind, now, to the dropoff and beyond. . . . "Gods above," he murmured. A wet snowflake found the back of his neck and he shivered again.

"Uncanny," said Gird. It was the same voice with which he'd come down from the hill before Greenfields, quiet and a little remote. As the last of the snow flurry wisped past, scoured off the stone by the incessant wind, Gird stood and looked at the wilderness around them.

It seemed larger every moment as the veils of falling snow withdrew, and a little more light came through the clouds. Vast vertical walls of red stone, cleft into narrow passages . . . Luap realized that Gird was moving toward the edge of their platform, and followed quickly.

"Don't get too near—"

"—the edge. I'm not a child, Luap." A gust of wind made them both stagger and clutch each other. Gird pulled back and glanced upward. "Nor a god, to stand in place against such wind. I will be careful." He looked back and up. "There are trees—up on that next level—" Luap squinted against the wind and saw an irregular blur of dark and white, that might have been snow-covered trees. He looked into the wind, and saw the edge of cloud, with light sky beyond it, moving toward them, visibly moving even as he watched. He nudged Gird, who turned and stared, mouth open, before turning his back to the wind again. "A very strange place indeed, you found. Not in the world we know, I daresay."

As the cloud's edge came nearer, the wind sharpened, probing daggerlike beneath Luap's clothes. He found it hard to catch his breath, but he no longer wanted to retreat to the safety of the magical place . . . he was too interested in the widening view. Light rolled over them from behind, as the cloud fled away southward and let sunlight glare on the snowy expanse. Luap squinted harder, suddenly blinded. Then, as his eyes adjusted, he stared until his body shuddered, reminding him of the cold.

Wall beyond wall, cleft beyond cleft, stacked together so tightly he knew he could not tell, from here, where those clefts led. Stone in colors he had not imagined, vivid reds and oranges, and far away a wall of stone as white as the snow—unless it was a snowfield on some higher mountain. And a distant plain, apparently almost level, glaring in the sunlight until his eyes watered.

"Not good farmland," said Gird. Now even he shivered; he swung his arms and added, before Luap could replay, "Now let's get back in; I'm famished with cold."

They struggled back against the wind, eyes slitted, and found the entrance by almost falling in. Luap led, this time, and nearly fell into the stair's central well when his boots slipped on inblown snow. He did not care. He felt that something had opened, inside his head, a vast room he had not known he owned, furnished with shapes he had not know he wanted to see until he saw them. *Beauty,* he thought, setting one foot carefully after another. *It's beautiful.*

Behind him, he heard Gird's comments about the impossibility of farming in land like that with inward amusement. He had nothing against farmland; he liked to eat as well as anyone. But these red rocks, streaked with snow were not meant for farmland. Trumpets rang in his head. Banners waved. *Castles,* he thought. And then again: *Beauty.* And then, slowly, inexorably, *Mine. My own land. My . . . kingdom.* As in a vision, he saw the arrival of his people, the mageborn, saw them come out into the sun atop that great slab of stone, saw the awe in their faces. He went down slowly, step after careful step, listening to Gird behind him. He did not notice how far they had gone before the cold wind no longer whistled down the central well; he simply assumed, he realized later, that the entrance would close itself.

He waited for Gird to reach the bottom of the stairs, and let Gird lead the way back into the hall. "I wonder if it's the same every time you go up," Gird said, in the tone of one who would find it reasonable if either way. Luap almost turned and went back to find out, but restrained himself. He could come again, alone: he could find out by himself if his land (he thought of it already as his, without noticing) was there. He didn't notice that he had not responded until he realized that Gird had stopped and was peering at him. At once he felt the heat in his face, as if he had been caught out in an obvious lie. But Gird said nothing about that.

"You must have been cold," he commented. "And now your blood's coming back: your face is as red as raw meat. Mine feels like it too." And indeed he was flushed, almost a feverish red. Luap felt an unexpected pang of guilt.

"I'm sorry—" he began, but Gird cut him off.

"Not your fault. I'm the one insisted we stay out up there so long. Brrr. It may be spring in Fintha, but it's winter here—let's go back, unless you have a magical feast hidden here somewhere."

"Alas, no," said Luap. He led Gird back to the center of the pattern on the dais, and reached for his power, this time with confidence. It seemed but a moment, a flicker of the eyelid, and they were once more in the cave's inner chamber. Gird coughed, and the cough echoed harshly, jangling almost. Luap led him out, with a concern more than half real, to their campsite just inside the cave's entrance. Their horses, cropping spring grass outside, paused to look, and Gird's old white horse whuffled at him.

Outside, the day had waned to a moist, cool evening. Luap built up the fire quickly, noticing that Gird still shivered from time to time.

"Are you all right?"

"Just cold." He sounded tired as well as cold. Luap wondered if that way of travel, which he found exhilarating, felt different for the one who was taken, like a sack of meal in a wagon. "I don't *like* caves," Gird said, peevishly. "They all have *something* . . . this one that chamber, the gnomehalls their secret passages and centers, and gods only know what in that place you found, whatever it is." He hitched himself around on the rock, and spread his hands to the fire Luap had built. "And I'm still not sure why you showed me that. Do you know yourself?"

"Not really." Luap put the kettle on its hook, and added more wood to the fire. He should have brought a keg of ale. That would have kept Gird from asking awkward questions . . . but Gird being Gird might have thought that a suspicious thing to do. "I thought you should know about it; I thought it should not be a secret."

"Umph. It was meant to be a secret, I'd wager. Meant to be, and kept a secret, all those years, until you stumbled into it. And that's something I've always wondered about—" He coughed, a long racking cough, and Luap offered him water. Gird gulped a mouthful, and coughed again. "Blast it! You'd think I was an old man, hacking and spitting by the fire." Luap said nothing, in the face of Gird's shrewd gaze. "So . . . is that what you think?" Luap managed a shrug he hoped looked casual.

"You're older than I am, but Arranha is older. To us you're just Gird." Not quite true; others had commented, this past winter, on that same enduring cough.

"That horse has slowed down," Gird said, jerking a thumb at the white blur standing hipshot just outside the cave. "He hardly moves out of an amble, these days." Luap looked at the horse, and met dark eyes that looked no more aged than a colt's. Gird never admitted anything unusual in his horse, but everyone else realized that it had never been a stray carthorse. Where it had come from, no one knew, but Luap had heard more than one refer to it as "Torre's mount's foal."

"Horses age faster than men," Luap said, ignoring the snort from the cave entrance. "And you were willing to sit out in that snowstorm longer than I was."

"That's true." Gird prodded the fire with a stick; sparks shot up, and shadows danced on the cave walls. He looked around. "It was homelier with an army in it."

Noisier and smellier, Luap thought, remembering quarrels and hunger. Now they had plenty of food, warm dry clothes without holes, warm blankets to sleep in. "Sib's ready," he said, lifting the lid on that aromatic brew. "We'll be back to a town tomorrow." If he was lucky, Gird would not get back to his previous topic. He dipped a mugful for Gird, another for himself, and set the loaf by the fire to warm. They had an end of ham, the mushrooms they'd gathered on the way, a handful of berries, a few spring ramps. Gird drank his sib in three gulps, then held his mug for more. Luap served him, silent and hoping to remain so. He offered a slice of warm bread, with a slab of cold ham. Gird took it as silently, and bit off a chunk.

Silence lasted the meal, then Gird belched and sighed. "Strange place. A long way from here or anyplace I ever saw. They don't look like the mountains near the gnome princedom. Elves . . . dwarves . . . they will not thank you for sharing their secret, when they find out."

"I thought perhaps they'd lost it." That sounded strange, even as he said it. "Forgotten it," Luap amended. "There's no sign anyone's used it."

Gird blinked. "But you haven't been watching. How would you know?"

"I—don't." He had been sure, from the utter blankness of the chamber in this cave, the empty hall *there*. No smells of occupation, no stir of air, no sounds. He was sure the place had been waiting for him, would be empty any time he returned to it, until he took others there. *If* he took others there. His heart quickened, and he took a long breath. He would not think about that now.

"How much sign did we leave?" Gird went on. "In a day or so, whatever snow we tracked in will have dried. That's large country, out there. You could take an army through this cave, a tensquad a time, and send them out into that, and a day later no one could tell."

Luap hoped his face showed nothing; he felt the sweat spring out under his arms and on the back of his neck. He cleared his throat and forced a shrug. "But until we know where *there* is, what good is that?"

Gird nodded. "That's sense. We're not wandering folk, any more; we have no need of more lands. There's plenty amiss here to clean up. You're right, lad; my mind just wandered a bit. And I should thank you for showing me, not keeping it to yourself. You're right; someone else should know it exists, someone human, I mean. But it's lucky we didn't know during the fighting. Some would've wanted to hide from trouble that way."

He almost told Gird then. His mouth opened; he said the first words that came into his head . . . and they were not those words. "It would have complicated things," he said, and ducked his head and pretended to yawn. Towers, walls, *castles* slid through his mind, peopled with mageborn men and women and children, living together in peace, far from the quarrels Gird never wanted to hear about, where he could learn the ways of his powers, and use them to prove they were not dangerous.

"Tires you, does it? Traveling that way?" Gird prodded the fire; Luap managed another yawn as the flames danced high for a moment, and nodded. He was tired but not from that. From being caught in the old trap of Gird's mistrust, from being penned in too small a pen.

Chapter Nine

Gird came from court as grumpy as Luap had seen him. "Your folk I expected to be difficult; mine I thought had more sense."

"What now?"

"A petition from over northeast somewhere, to have all the mageborn children tested for magical powers and then destroy them. The magery, not the children. I think. I don't know how many times I have to *tell* them—!" He broke off, scrubbing his forehead with a fist as if to wipe out the memory. "It will work in the end; it has to work."

"Maybe it won't," said the Rosemage quietly. "What then?"

"Not another war," said Gird. "We've had enough of that." That *no war* didn't mean *no killing* they all recognized. "Look at Aris and Seri; they're fast friends. They get along with both peoples." The Rosemage opened her mouth, but closed it again. Gird knew, as well as she and Luap, that few mageborn had Aris's talents, and few peasant-born had Seri's experience of friendship. You can't, Luap thought, make an alliance work because two children get along. More likely, Aris would trust too much in his own goodwill, and some superstitious peasant with no goodwill at all would bash his head in for him. That Seri would then gleefully avenge him wouldn't help at all. He wondered what Gird would do if someone killed Aris as a mageborn—would that finally convince him that the two peoples would never mix? Or would he ignore that as stubbornly as he'd ignored all the other evidence?

"We could leave," Luap said, as if continuing the conversation interrupted long before. No need to say how or where: Gird had not forgotten that.

"All of you?" Not quite disbelief, but a tone that made clear Gird's opinion. Root and branch, child and lady and old and young?

"All of us." Luap shut his eyes a moment, *seeing* them all in the echoing arches of that great hall, hearing in his mind's ear the voices racketing off stone. How could he feed them? "We could farm that other valley," he said. "Small-gardens . . ."

"Most of us aren't farmers," said the Rosemage. Damn the

woman—she should realize it was their best hope. "Small-gardens don't yield grain. . . ."

"There's a plain beyond," he said. "Maybe that would produce grain. Or something Arranha said, about the terraces used in Old Aare; we could build terraces. And if we aren't farmers now, more of us are than were. We can learn. Better that, than—"

"You want to run away!" Gird's anger blazed from his eyes. "You won't give it a chance!"

"I've given it a chance!" The moment he said it, he knew he'd lost; if only he had said *we* instead of *I*. He got his voice under control and tried to mend the unmendable. "Gird—sir—however much *you* want the mageborn to blend in, most of the others don't. They've told you themselves. Even some of the Marshals; you know why you didn't send Aris to Donag's grange. And Kanis, in the meeting two days ago—"

"Kanis is a fool," Gird said through clenched teeth. "And you're another. You ought to see it, you of all of us, if blood-right stands for anything. Does your mother's pain mean nothing to you? You are *ours* as much as theirs—" He flicked a glance at the Rosemage, not hostile, but acknowledging, and went on. "You could be the bridge between us, Luap, if you'd work at it, instead of haring off after some scheme to make yourself a comfortable niche with your father's folk. You don't have the right to say: the peoples must say. The mageborn, if they want to leave *on their own,* can go without you. They don't need you, except to cause them trouble: you've sworn to take no crown, and what can you be, without one, but temptation?"

"That's not fair!" He wanted to say more, but he had ruined his chance, and knew it. Gird would not budge now, not for a season or so. Yet he could not keep quiet. "You know I have traveled the land, more than you yourself, carrying copies of your Code, and trying to show your—the people—how harmless, how loyal, a king's son can be. And they don't trust me yet. What more can I do?"

"Quit saying 'my people' and 'your people,' for one thing. Quit thinking it, for another. The distance between a merchant trading across the mountains and a shepherd lass who's never been away from home is no less than the distance between the mageborn and the . . ." Even Gird wanted a name for the others, and though he refused to say "my people" the words hung between them in the impervious flame of reality. He cleared his throat, avoiding the term, and kept going. "If I can expect the merchant and the shepherd, the cheesemaker and the goldsmith, to live under one law, what is so hard about the other?"

The Rosemage warned him with her eyes, but he could not desist. Gird must someday see the truth, he was convinced, and if he kept at it, perhaps it would be sooner. He did take time to choose his words carefully. "Gird, you set no limits on craftsmen or merchants or farmfolk, so long as they stay within the law, but what would happen if you told farmers they could not farm, or weavers they could not weave?"

"Why would I do that?" Gird asked. "And what has that to do with—"

"The mageborn powers, Gird. You want them given up, as if they were wicked in themselves, rather than talents like a dyer's eye for color or a horse-trainer's skill with horses."

Gird cocked his head. "Talents like other talents? I think not, lad, and if you believe that you're fooling yourself."

"You let Aris heal: that's a mageborn talent." He hoped his envy did not bleed into his voice. Every time he saw Aris, his own talent ached within him . . . perhaps he too could heal, if only Gird would let him try.

"Healing is a gift of the gods. Yes, I know, it was said to be a mageborn talent, but what mageborn in my lifetime had it? had We saw no healing; we saw wounding and killing. I let Aris heal, yes, because some god's light shines through that boy like a flame through glass, but you notice I haven't let him do it without supervision. The gods I trust; his mageborn talent I trust no more than this—" He flicked his fingernails in derision. "Healing is a service; it's not a way of getting power over others. Will you—you of all people—tell me the mageborn don't use their talents to get power?"

"That's not *fair!*" It was already too late; Luap felt the last strand of control fraying. "You trust that Marrakai whelp—born and reared in the privilege you claim to despise. You trust a stripling boy of whom you know nothing but another child's report—and I've worked with you for years, gone everywhere at your command, and you don't trust *me*—"

"And why should I?" Luap had not seen Gird that angry at him for years. "You tell me that—and remember what you did, Selamis-turned-luap. The first time I saw Aris use magery, it was to heal, and he gave his own strength to it. The first time I saw *you* use magery, you tried to kill me, to force me to accept your rule. Right after swearing you sought no crown, you tried that—should I then trust you?"

"Then why did you make me your luap? Why expect me, whom

you don't trust, to join our peoples? Why not pick someone you do trust—that Marrakai Kirgan, or Aris?"

"To give you the chance to change, rare as it is." Now Gird looked more tired than angry. "D'you think I don't know men can change? The High Lord knows I have, from the boy I was, from the farmer I became, from my first year as a rebel. Some say no one changes, that cows can't turn to horses, or wolves into sheep—but I know change is possible. That's what I hoped for you, that you'd grow out of envy and lying, and into some understanding of responsibility. You've worked hard—yes, and I've praised you for it—but you've never given up wanting what you think you should have had."

"I . . . tried." His throat closed on the rest. He had given Gird everything he could, every talent he knew he owned, except the one Gird would not accept, the magery. And what he had really wanted, Gird had never given him—not easy praise, but the trust he saw given to others for nothing.

"I know you did. In your own way. But—how many more like you, who still want power, would reach for it if I let active magery return? Yes, it's hard on the mageborn to lift mud with a shovel when magic might do it, or rely on candles when they could have magelight—but it was hard on everyone else, when the mageborn chose to use their magicks as they did. We can't have that again; we can't have you, *trying* to control your wishes, and not doing it."

If he had not felt Gird's fist before, he would have thought the words hurt as much. Remorse lay a bitter blade at the heart of his pride: he wanted to throw himself down and plead; he wanted time to unroll its scroll and let him unsay what he had said. But it would take more than a change in the day's writing; he had years of error to undo, and time flowed like the great river, always one way, always down to death. He swallowed the knotted anguish, in all its confusion of meanings and feelings, as he had swallowed so much, and felt an insidious relaxation. He had tried; he had failed; he should have expected that. It wasn't his fault; he had done his best.

He wanted to shrug, but he knew that would anger Gird even more. Instead, he sat very still, avoiding everyone's eye. From the corner of his own, he could see the Rosemage's expression, composure over disappointment over frustration. She had as many layers as he did, was as different from Gird's singleness of heart as he was, yet Gird, though he did not fully trust her, never subjected her to the criticism he aimed at Luap. He glanced at Gird, ready to be dismissed again, only to meet a steady look of regret that almost broke his determination.

As if no one else were in the room, Gird spoke. "You know, Selamis, you reminded me of my brother from the day I first saw you. My favorite brother; he died in a wolf-hunt, years before the war started, but I never forgot him. I thought 'Here's Aris back again, and this time I'll protect him as he protected me.' There were some who didn't like your ways from the first; I argued that they were unfair. When you told me you had lied, and what had been done to you, I wept—do you remember that?" Luap nodded; he could not speak. "I knew that any man could be driven to lie by enough pain; I never blamed you for it. But you lied afterward."

I told the truth afterward too, Luap thought. *More often than I lied. You might give me credit for that.* Aloud, he said, "I'm sorry. I am not the man you would have me be. But since I am not, give your task to someone more fit to handle it, and let me go."

"I wish I could." Gird looked at him. "But you know why I cannot, if you will only face it. You are who you are, your father's son—and you came to me. That old woman knows, and Arranha: I know they've told you."

"And they've told *me* that my magery is part of it. That I must tap that power to do what you ask—yet you ask me to do it without. How? I have tried, and failed." For the time, his bitterness had vanished, leaving him at peace, a still pool in the calm before a winter dawn. "Since it is my lies that made you distrust my people—" There. He had said *my people* blatantly, just as he saw it in Gird's expression. "—rid yourself of me, and you and the others may be able to trust them."

"I don't want to trust them, you purblind fool! I want to trust *you.* I want you to deserve my trust." He had never heard such anguish in Gird's voice; it shook his certainty. "I want you to be the Selamis we all see you could be."

"And not the luap you all see?" The moment it was out of his mouth, he could have bitten his tongue in two. It was like slapping the old man's face; nothing would heal now. But Gird looked more sad than angry.

"No, not the luap. If you could think past your balls, Selamis, and past your own losses, you could see that not all fatherhood involves a woman, and not all kingship requires battle."

"I'm sorry." It seemed he was always saying that; it tasted of long chewing, its meaning leached away, its savor lost. Yet he meant it; he would say it until he died, if he must. He shivered, and made a warding sign; he hoped he would not need to be sorry so long.

"Well." Gird shook his head, refusing further debate on that subject. "You're not going; I need you. And your people are not going out to your mysterious land, wherever it is. We will work through this; if I can lead peasants to war, surely I can lead them into peace. Although I remember Arranha saying that would be harder."

Luap found the look on Arranha's face worse than anything he might have said. He wanted to scream back at it, he wanted to run from it, he wanted to be what all these people wanted him to be . . . that they expected him to be without explaining beforehand. He was supposed to guess, to figure it out from the hints that were enough for others but had never been enough for him. He could always see more than one direction behind each hint, always see more and more complicated patterns radiating from a simple one. Arranha would say more light would help, but more light simply revealed more complexity, more ways to go wrong.

"What is the one thing you truly want?" Arranha asked, after a silence that seemed very long to Luap.

Cascades of images flowed through his mind, each begetting a dozen more. Each made of dark and light, color and its absence, lines and spaces, textures. . . . "To be whole," Luap whispered, into the hollow space of his dream, the secret chamber of his mind, to which no god's voice had come. To have this space filled, this chamber habited, the voiceless voiced, the blind—but he was not blind; he had all Esea's light he could tolerate, and what it revealed was emptiness. "To be whole," he said a little louder, putting voice to something without a voice.

"To *be* something," Arranha said. Nothing colored his voice, neither approval nor disapproval. "Or to *do* something? Or to *have* something?"

Luap sat silent, trying to keep his hands still. Arranha's questions always had traps in them; that parallel series must mean more than it seemed, must be more than the reflection of his own words from Arranha's mind. He had been, he thought, plain enough. He wanted to be whole, more than anything. But to *be*? Not do? What did he want to be whole for? Had he a purpose? Had he some other desire which this phrasing veiled?

He wanted . . . he wanted to hear that voice, the one he had not found in the chamber that lay in no visible mountain, the one no one could find but himself. He wanted to hear that voice say . . . but that was nonsense. Children hoped to hear adults praise them; children hoped for approval. He was grown, a man old enough to have his first grandchildren on his knee, if his children had lived. It came to him in a sudden storm that his son had been killed, not as a whim of the soldiers sent to command his mission to Gird, but because he was a son—a potential heir in time of rebellion. Why had he not seen this before? Because his grief for the boy had eased before the much harder grief of knowing how his wife and daughter suffered when he did not betray Gird?

In the memory of his children, his longing for something only children wanted ebbed, leaving him aware of nothing but exhaustion and the hollow he so desperately wanted filled. "To be whole," he said finally to Arranha. In his own ears, his voice held conviction. "That's all. And—and I don't know what that would be. With magery, without . . . just whole."

Arranha's expression softened. "I wonder sometimes if any of us have understood what your boyhood was like. Did you have any feeling of being in a family?"

"No." Luap swallowed. "Or I supposed I may have, very young, but not later. I never knew where I fit; I never knew exactly what they wanted, except that I wasn't right." He did not try to express the memories that flooded him now: other children had brothers and sisters, parents, a pattern into which they fit. All those patterns excluded him; he had been defined, he realized, by negatives. *You're not my brother,* one boy had said, shoving him away when he would have made friends. He had learned not to ask the adult men if they were his father; he had learned not to ask women if they were his mother. When he had asked those questions, in his innocence, he had been thrust away: you are not my son, you are not my child. He had learned not to ask the most important questions that crowded his head, for that would risk the little he did have, the little he did know. And in the unknown spaces, he could make up his own answers, safe as long as he did not ask, did not seek the truth, which always told him what he was not. His dreams were not lies if he did not ask.

Arranha stared at his own hands as if they were new to him. "I have been an outcast most of my life—causing trouble, as Dorhaniya told you, even as a young man—but at least I always knew what I was an outcast *from.* I knew my father's face, my mother's hands; I scuffled with my brothers, teased my sister . . . and I cannot imagine what it would have been like without them. Would I have gone my own way, if I had not been sure what that was? What I was? Have I taken pride in being true to my own vision without realizing how lucky I was in having such a vision?"

"For some," Luap said, looking down, "the truth is a blessing. For others, the truth can only be pain."

"Surely not!" Arranha's voice shook. "Even if it seems painful, the truth is better than lies; light is better than darkness."

Luap did not argue. He had lost that argument a long time ago, as a small child. Safer to guard his dreams, his private corners of the mind, his small comforts: what truth could improve them? In his mind, Gird could be the loving father he had never had; in truth Gird loved him no more than anyone else, perhaps less. How could the truth be better? What could anyone build from truths that only took away, that never gave?

But he felt Arranha's gaze on him as he would have felt the sun's heat. For all his apparent gentleness, for all his mild good humor, the old man had his passions, truth and light among them. "You cannot be whole without truth," Arranha was saying. "You cannot be whole without the light."

But he was wrong. What would make me whole, Luap thought, is something to fill the dark places, the inside places that have never seen light.

For some days, he and Gird trod gingerly around each other, much like lovers who have quarrelled and want to make up. Luap said little, but remembered to say that little pleasantly, allowing no hint of his misery to color his voice. He drove himself in his work, beginning at the first hint of daylight, writing until his hand cramped and his arm ached, until he could scarcely stand. Gird gave his orders quietly, commended Luap on the neatness of the finished scrolls, asked necessary questions about accounts. And as time passed, Luap felt they were easier with each other. Gird would accept the help of a flawed luap as he would have used a flawed tool if a good one were not available. He himself basked in a gentle melancholy—resigned to his failure, to a future in which he satisfied no one, achieved nothing he wanted, never found trust or acceptance. He could at least be better than Gird's fears, if not as good as his hopes.

In this mood, he found strange pleasure in visiting Dorhaniya and enduring her mild scoldings, in seeing the Rosemage's doubts flickering in her eyes, in noticing how Arranha worried. He might not be what they wanted, but he had their attention. Perhaps it was not possible to be what they wanted—those several contradictory things they wanted. Perhaps the best he could hope for was their continuing interest and attention. It wasn't the trust he craved, but it was better than being ignored.

He had fallen into a reverie one day, staring blindly out his window as he stretched his fingers to ease a cramp, when he felt someone watching him. He turned. Aris stood beside the door, one foot hooked on the other ankle.

"You seem tired, sir," the boy said. He had grown at least a head in the past year, and was as skinny as ever.

"A cramp in my hand," Luap said, smiling. "A problem all scribes share."

"Would you like me to heal it?"

Luap stared. Would he expend his power on so small a thing? "No, Aris," he said. "It doesn't matter; it's just a nuisance."

"Father Gird asked me to see if I thought you had the healing magery," Aris said. "I told him I thought you would know best yourself, but he said he had forbidden you to try."

"Yes," Luap said with difficulty. "He did." Something about Aris's posture communicated unease, though he seemed relaxed. "And what do you think?"

"I . . . don't know, sir. Do you want that magery?"

I want all magery, Luap thought, and hoped it did not show in his face. "Yes," he said. "I would like to heal the sick and injured, as you do—it would be a great good. But I know so little of my powers I cannot say if this is one of them."

"Do you want me to attempt to find out?" The obvious answer was *Yes, of course,* but for some reason the obvious answer did not come. Why had Aris asked, instead of simply obeying Gird's request? Was he trying to convey another message?

"Can you?" Luap asked. "What would it take?"

Aris untangled his ankles and came into the office. "I'm not sure, sir. Perhaps if I held your hands—but I don't know if that would work. I've never done this before."

Reassuring. Luap wondered if he'd told Gird that, and how Gird expected to get useful information from so young and inexperienced an examiner. The proof that one could heal was a healing: what did it matter what a boy thought of the possibility? But it did matter; he could feel his heart pounding in his chest at the very thought of it. If Aris, whom Gird trusted, said he had the healing magery, surely Gird would let him learn to use it. He held out his hands for Aris to touch. The boy took them, his own hands warm and dry, their bony length promising size and strength later.

"Did you ever feel your hands itch when you were near someone hurt?" he asked. Luap shook his head. Aris peered at his palms. "You have scars here—what happened?"

"Burns," said Luap. He felt sweat start in his hair, under his arms. He did not want to remember that, not now. "When I first came to Gird's army," he said quickly, as if speed would protect him from the memory, "I had burned hands. They—the men who came to my farm—they burned them." He blinked away the tears and looked up to find Aris's bright eyes watching him steadily.

"I'm sorry," Aris said, almost whispering. "I can't do anything now. But perhaps that's why you don't feel it."

Luap sat back, shaken. What did the boy mean? That he had the healing magery, but didn't feel it because of the burns? That he had once had it, but the burns had destroyed it? Aris still held his hands, and now Luap felt a slow, langorous warmth moving through his own fingers and wrists, up his arms to relieve tension in the elbows he had not even known he felt. Then it receded, and he felt a coolness replacing the warmth. His own magery rumbled inside him like a simmering pot just coming to boil, and he shunted it aside. His head throbbed a moment, then eased.

"It hurts you not to use it," Aris said. "Does Gird know?"

"Do I have the healing magery?" Luap countered. Gird was this boy's hero; he would not complain of Gird.

"I don't know," Aris said, releasing Luap's hands. Luap flexed his fingers: no cramp now, nor any residue of tension. "I feel great power, but it's not like mine. That doesn't mean it's not the healing magery," he said quickly. "I can't tell."

And since he could not tell, Gird would not release him from his oath, and the power would continue to fret in its cage. Luap hoped the boy would not feel his frustration. He did not want to come between Gird and Aris, though he would have liked to convince Gird that his own magery had some good purpose.

Aris left, to report to Gird, and Luap stared blindly out the window. So long as Gird refused to see how many of his people— our people, Luap reminded himself—did not want his vision of peace, he could do nothing. He had to abide by his oath, even when Gird thought him foresworn, and hope that things would change. Either the peasants cease hating the mageborn—which he felt would never happen—or Gird recognize the problem and let him take the mageborn to safety somewhere else. Not *somewhere*, but there—to his own land that he had found.

In the meantime—he picked up his pen and went back to work— in the meantime he must be Gird's most loyal assistant and scribe. The work would ease his mind; it always did. And if nothing changed, if he spent his life this way, it could have been worse spent. He knew that; he accepted it, struggling to crush the doubts and desires that rose from his magery.

Chapter Ten

Luap and the Rosemage met on the road below Fin Panir; he had been to a barton with a message from Gird to its yeoman-marshal, and saw her coming along the road. He drew rein and waited for her. She looked best, he always thought, on horseback, her slenderness all grace, her innate arrogance appropriate to the task of mastering her mount. She wore her old armor; she often did, riding out, though it made her more conspicuous than he would have thought comfortable. Perhaps she did not think of it. But on this day, hot and sticky, he wondered how she bore the heat. As she came nearer, he saw the flush of sunburn on her cheek, on her nose.

Before he could say anything, she said, "I was a fool to wear armor on such a day, with no reason." Her gloves were dark with sweat. "Although I suppose I could consider it proper training. That's what I was taught: you don't know the day you will need to fight, so you must be trained for cold and heat both."

Luap smiled "I must say I'm glad I'm not wearing that."

"So you should be." She reined up beside him. "Gird's right: all these pretensions of our ancestors were more trouble than they were worth. There you are, in soft pants and shirt, with a hat that shades your head instead of cooking it—and I wanted to feel grand, so I'm basted in my own juice."

"Well, you'll be back in the city soon, and into a cool bath—"

"No such luck. I've agreed to teach a class in longsword—that's why I'm back so early—and while I can get out of this cooking kettle, I'll be in a hot banda soon enough."

They rode on to the city gate, and almost at once heard the unmistakeable grumble of an unhappy crowd. Luap might have turned up an alley to avoid it, but the Rosemage pressed ahead, straight toward the noise. Luap shrugged and legged his horse up beside hers. Traffic thickened around them, slowed, became the back of a crowd. Luap stood in his stirrups, peering over the nearest to see the usual small opening in the middle. A man had hold of a boy; and several people were yelling. He could not make out the faces at that distance. Just another brawl, he thought, and would

542

have backed his horse away. He looked at the Rosemage; she turned to him and nodded.

"We need to do something about this."

"Us? Why not a Marshal?"

"Didn't you recognize that boy? He's one of ours." She urged her horse on; around it, people backed away, scowling and muttering Luap followed, getting the same scowls and mutters, and handsigns that he knew all too well. These were the peasants who never forgot or forgave anything the mageborn had done; his skin prickled all over: Slowly, pace by pace, the horses forced their way into the crowd. One man, enormous of girth and shoulder, refused to give way.

"We don't want *you* here," the big man said. Luap thought he remembered the man as a troublemaker in the last assembly. At least he had the same build and resolute scowl as the one who had stood up in the back and told Gird he was an old fool to trust the surviving mageborn.

"Perhaps not, but I am here, and I'm staying. What is this?"

"None o' yer business, magelover! Think we don't know how ye put it in Gird's ear, and you with that fancy magelady at yer side?" That was someone much shorter, who ducked quickly into the crowd; even from horseback, Luap could not see the man's face.

"That's right, Luap," the big man said. "You always claimed to be no threat, a true luap, even a steer, but day after day we see you with that sorceress and that old mageborn priest. Think we don't know you lust for magery like a boar for a sow? Think we don't know you hoard every scrap of power Gird gives you, may his eyes clear? Seems every time he sits in a court, he's come more to favor your people: we know who to blame for that. And every year he ages; he's not half the man he was the day of Greenfields, but you haven't a handful of gray hairs yet. What're ye doin', stealing his life from him bit by bit?"

An ugly sound, not quite a roar, from the crowd, showed their agreement. Luap's horse flattened its ears and tail, and shifted nervously under him. He could not have spoken, for the rage and contempt that filled him—these *dolts*, these *fools*. to think this of him, to blame Gird for partiality to the mageborn, when anyone with sense could see that Gird trod a knife-edge between the resentments of his people.

Anger roared through him, a cleansing wind that swept away the memory of his own half-loyalties, his own errors.

"I would give him my years, if it would help," he said, in such a tone that the crowd stilled. He meant it at that moment. "I am but a child, and he my wise elder. What is this, that you will not let Gird's luap know?"

"A mageborn brat causing trouble, then," said the man, in the tone of one who means *And what will you do about it?*

The crowd opened just a little, showing a scrawny lad, much-bruised, in the grip of a husky man with his other fist cocked. Parik, that was, a member of one of the three granges in the lower city. His scribe's mind read the details off the last grange report: Marshal Donag, veteran of the war in its last year, and known for his dislike of the mageborn. Gird had commented on that when choosing another grange for Aris's training; Donag had later complained that he spoiled the boy. Parik he did not know, though he remembered the man's name on the grange rolls; he could not remember his craft or trade. He could not recognize the boy with all those bruises.

"Let him go." The Rosemage, in her gleaming armor, shone in the sun almost as if she had called her light. The crowd shifted slightly away from her, enlarging the central space. Even the man barring her way moved aside. "Is it Gird's way to batter children?"

"He's no child. He's a mageborn demon; he put fire on me." The man shook the boy, who wobbled and nearly fell.

"Let him go," Luap said, this time releasing enough of his own magery so that the man obeyed, as if his hands were not his own. The boy staggered across the open space to the Rosemage, bleeding from a broken nose and split lip, one eye rapidly swelling shut. She steadied him; Luap could feel her anger's warmth, like a banked fire, and hoped the boy would realize she was not angry at him. He was wondering how to get the boy to safety, how to send word to Gird, when he saw a disturbance in the crowd across the way. He saw sidelong glances, heard the murmurs that ran faster than an old man could walk, *Gird*. He hoped fervently that it was.

The crowd parted for him, reluctantly it seemed, and Luap watched that heavy-shouldered figure stalk into the sunlit opening. He could think of nothing to say; he watched Gird eyeing Parik and his bruised knuckles, the Rosemage and bruised boy. It had gone far beyond I-told-you-so, and Luap felt no satisfaction in that. Gird's glance had lost none of its edge; raked the crowd, and Luap saw many of them flinch from it.

"Well?" His voice cracked; Luap suddenly felt his own throat close in pity. Gird had not been well—really well—since Midwinter Feast, when he'd insisted on showing everyone how to do the Weaving dance in the snow, in and out of all the doors of the palace. It was monstrous that they would not let him rest and heal, that they kept pecking at him with one little problem after another.

Parik, insolent to the bone, tried to pass it off as the boy's fault, a misuse of magery, and then insulted Gird into the bargain, mocking the old man's sayings. Luap saw Gird turn pale, and hoped it was anger—it would have been anger, in the old days, but now it might be illness. Gird's next words did not reassure him; Gird's voice shook. The crowd stiffened; they did not quite growl. Parik pushed his luck, as such men always did, Luap thought, with a viciousness intended to break Gird's authority completely. He felt so angry he could hardly keep from attacking Parik—but Gird would not want that. He must fulfill Gird's trust, at least until Gird died. He was promising himself that he would kill Parik without pity the moment Gird died when Gird surprised him again.

Across that space, in the face of those who despised both of them, Gird met his eyes, nodded, and said, as casually as if they were relaxing after dinner; "You were right, and I was wrong. Are you still of the same mind?"

It could only be the plan he had forbidden so angrily. Luap felt the heat mount to his face; he stammered his answer. Of course he was of the same mind—but to say it *now*—!

"They are not all Parik." Luap winced; Gird, of all men, should not have to plead that way to him. He nodded. He saw that Gird understood that, trusted him now as he had never trusted him before. What Gird might have said next, he never found out, for Parik interrupted, furious that Gird would dare speak to a mageborn. Rude, loud, insolent—and this at last roused the old Gird, the Gird who had settled more than one dispute with his fist. He rounded on Parik with the same intensity, the same deep roar, stalked up to him as if he would as soon clout the lout on the ear as take another breath. Parik backed away, as so many bullies had backed away, making excuses. . . . Luap smiled inwardly. That would do him no good with Gird: excuses never did. Gird went on, inexorably as always, digging at the root of the matter: what really happened? Who did what first?

Luap had not noticed the girl before she spoke; he doubted anyone had. But the boy the Rosemage held shivered as she came forward. *He* knew her. The girl's evidence made it clear that Parik's sons had started the trouble, and then their father had intervened, to help his sons beat the boy bloody, for no more reason than being mageborn and deft-handed. Parik claimed the boy had "put fire" on him then; the girl claimed that if he did, it was to save his life.

Again an interruption, this time Marshal Donag, who tried

blustering and sarcasm. To hear him talk, Luap thought, you'd think he'd fought the whole war at Gird's side—or by himself, with Gird coming in at the end. He didn't really hear what they said, concentrating instead on being ready for the trouble he knew was coming. This crowd was as ripe for riot as the summer air for a thunderstorm. Thus it was only the Rosemage's gasp of surprise that brought his attention back to the actual words, and he was as astonished as any in the crowd when Gird suggested exiling the mageborn. ". . . Send them all away," he heard. "Will that satisfy you? Let the boy go, and any like him."

His own plans in Gird's voice; his own dream exposed, taken over.

But the crowd wanted none of it. Like the brooding menace of a dark cloud on a sultry day, the crowd's mood darkened, threatened; he could almost see the murderous anger. Luap struggled to meet it with calmness, to convey that he was not part of this—that he would not meet that anger with his own, that he would honor the oath he had sworn. As if he could reach Gird's mind with his own, he held his thought before him in clarity: *We will not fight. We will not break your peace.* He was sure they would die here, he and the Rosemage and the boy, and probably Gird as well, when the crowd finally stirred, but at least he would have kept his oath.

The change in Gird's expression, the shift from grief through resignation to wild astonishment, brought him back to full attention. All those who could see Gird were locked in the same pose: rigid, staring. All at once, the old man seemed to come alight, not the magelight he knew, but something else, something that made magelight look homely and comfortable.

Then Gird spoke. The words . . . the words had meaning, but no form; sound but no meaning. He could not follow them; he could not do anything else. They battered at him, shattering walls of reticence, caution, prudence, opening up spaces in his heart which he had hardly known existed. As a house unroofed by storm seems suddenly small and full of light, its furnishings dim and shabby in the open air, his mind looked strange to him. Yet as Gird continued to speak those words he could not quite hear, he felt cleansed. He had not wanted to furnish his mind's walls with such shoddy ideas, or its rooms with such ill-made decisions. He could let go, now, of his fears, his spite, his wish that things might have been different . . . he could trust others, as Gird was trusting him. He was scarcely aware of the tears that streaked his face, and only slightly more aware of the Rosemage's voice, murmuring a counterpoint to Gird's.

But this would kill him. Surely this would kill him. Luap blinked away his tears; it was not fair that Gird, who had earned a peaceful old age, should be the one to die of this. He wanted to help, wanted to do something to save Gird, but he could not speak. A voice spoke; he knew what it was, as Gird had always suggested he would if it happened. He had his command. This was not his task. Something else was.

Gird fell silent. Luap could tell that others had been affected as he was; faces had softened from angry hostility to the surprised bewilderment of children who do not understand. He looked up, and saw what might be the cloud such summer days breed, but one that boiled with malice ... he knew what it was, the dark malice of them all, in a form visible to some ... and now cleansed, but for how long?

Gird's face changed again, this time through disbelief to calm acceptance. The cloud contracted, condensing around Gird to a black fog that seemed to weigh on him, pressing in on him until he collapsed slowly. Even as he watched, even as he stood paralyzed by awe that such a thing could happen, Luap was aware of part of his mind trying to fit what he saw into words. He would have to write it; he knew that as surely as he knew this would kill Gird. He would have to write it, and how could he possibly convey, in mortal language, what he was seeing? No one could possibly believe it. The cloud thickened as it grew smaller, as Gird struggled to stay upright, and sank to one knee, then to both, then fell on his face. The cloud vanished, and Gird lay motionless. Luap knew he was dead, even as he found he could move again, and came to Gird's side to touch him.

In his own mind, in the faces of others, Luap saw changes he could not yet analyze. Fears vanished; all the nagging barbs of envy and irritation ceased ... sorrow pierced him, but he knew, even then, that sorrow would heal.

Free, a corner of his mind whispered to him. *You're free, now.* But in the silent space where he knelt, holding Gird's cooling hand in his, he felt not free but rebound to Gird's service. All the rancor, the quarrels of the past days ... none of that mattered. He had never realized how he loved Gird, how he respected him; he had fooled himself with his ambitions. *I'm sorry,* he said silently. *I will do better.*

In that peace of mind which perfect sorrow brings, he and the others carried Gird's body back up the hill, to lie in the High Lord's Hall a brief space before burial. Silence followed them, spread through the streets, and despite crowds packed breathless-close, no noise intruded. In one brief, almost cordial meeting, the Marshals then in residence in Fin Panir, Arranha, and Luap agreed that Gird should be buried in what had been the palace meadows, and his name carved in a stone of the Hall's nave. No argument, not even a hint of discord, marred that meeting, or the solemn ceremonies that followed. Messengers rode out at once to distant granges; Luap felt only sorrow that Raheli, at the eastern border of the land, could not possibly arrive in time for the funeral.

Despite the crowds that poured into Fin Panir from every town and vill and farmstead within two days' travel, the crowded streets never erupted into argument or brawl. People hugged each other, crying, then walked arm in arm, smiling through their tears. Peasant-born greeted mageborn, and mageborn greeted peasant-born, all at peace and willing to meet as equals. With hardly any formal organization—for the peasant folk had no tradition of elaborate funerals, and no one consulted the remaining mageborn—the city orchestrated a spontaneous ceremony unlike anything its citizens had ever seen. "It seems right," someone would say, and others would agree, as if they had had the same idea but had been slower to speak. They would have a procession from the city wall to the High Hall, and then follow as Gird's body was taken out to the meadow for burial. The family-centered verses of a village funeral would be spoken by volunteers, who had come forward to tell Luap "I want to say the younger sister's part" or "We want to sing the brothers' song."

Two elves brought a length of white cloth bordered in intricate blue embroidery, finer than any Luap had seen, to wind the body in, and herbs to preserve it until the burial. The Gnarrinfulk gnomes sent a squad of gnomish pikes to stand guard over the body. A squat, red-haired, bandy-legged horse nomad appeared the second day with a sack of horsehair he claimed was the forelock and tail of his clan's lead mare and stallion. The horse hair was to be plaited, it seemed, into rings for Gird's great toes and thumbs, the remainder to stuff a pillow for his head. When the nomad found no one skilled at such work, he muttered but sat down in the main court to do it himself. Then, before the funeral, he rode away. Luap hoped he was satisfied; the horsefolk made difficult enemies, and might easily consider that Gird's death dissolved any agreements with his successors.

The funeral procession began at the city gates, by the river. Veterans of the war marched, all in blue shirts or with blue rags around their arms; Marshals and yeoman-marshals marched with their staves; craftsmen and merchants and farmers walked in more ragged, but no less fervent, processions. Some groups sang, others marched in silence. Luap, along with the more senior Marshals, carried the poles on which the body rested. Out the palace gates to the west, into the meadows where someone (Luap had forgotten to think of it) had scythed the long grass and the city's gravediggers had dug the grave. Now the little group came forward, and said the ancient words familiar in every peasant village: the father's lament for a son, the mother's lament for her child, the older and younger brother and sister. No one had spoken for the role of wife, and since Raheli lived, no one could take her place as a child, but the crowd together sang the short farewell.

When Gird's body sank into the grave, and the first clods fell, the crowd wept as one, but they rose from that weeping refreshed again, sad but not despairing. Luap, standing by the heap of dirt, felt someone's arm around his shoulders, and looked up to see Cob at his side.

"I'd hoped not to see it," Cob said, shaking his head. "But then, when it came, I was glad—and that makes no sense at all. They say you were there?"

Luap's scattered wits came back to him. Cob, he realized, must have ridden fast to make it here; he'd been at his grange, a hand of days normal travel from Fin Panir. "I was there," he said. He felt tears rolling down his face again, as if a wound had opened.

"I was at the market," Cob said, as if Luap had asked. "There was some dispute the judicar couldn't settle, and they'd called me in. One of those days when you think everyone wants to quarrel and is looking for an excuse. I was ready to break a few heads myself, just to let some sense in, although I told myself it was the weather. Then like a weather change it came over us—I could see it in the faces of the others, as well as feel it. I even looked to see if the wind had lifted the pennants, or a storm had neared, for the change was that sudden, and that strong. One moment scowls and whines and angry voices; the next moment smiles and apologies and . . . I've never known anything like it. The two men who'd started the fuss turned to each other and shrugged, and the quarrel unknotted like greased string. I felt suddenly stronger and young again, convinced that Gird's latest revision wasn't silly after all, but would work."

Luap had not had leisure to wonder what had happened beyond the immediate environs of the city; he was both fascinated and surprised. Had no one else seen the dark cloud, or recognized it? "How did you find out what really—?"

"Gnomes," said Cob. "Don't ask me how they knew, because I

couldn't tell you. The rest of that day went by with everyone in a holiday mood, and no reason for it. I would have worried, but couldn't. Then that night, someone knocked on the grange door, and when I went to see, there was a gnome. 'Your Marshal-General is dead,' he said. 'He has taken away the darkness from your human sight; he has freed your hearts from unreasoning fears and anger.' I'd only met gnomes once before, at that Blackbone Hill mess you were lucky enough to miss; *they* didn't talk like that. Afore I could ask any questions, he was gone, and I heard the beat of their boots, running all in step in the darkness." Cob paused for breath, and cleared his throat. " 'Course, the darkness wouldn't bother them, living understone as they do. But then I roused my yeoman-marshal, and called out the grange, and before dawn I was on my way. Rode day and night, I did, as if I'd lost thirty years, changing horses wherever I could. Met your messengers at Hareth—"

"Come on back," said Luap. "There's plenty of beds here—"

"He threw me, you know," Cob said. "I was with him from the first, from the forest camp Ivis had, back in the Stone Circle days. I remember him coming in with his lad and his nephew, all hollow with hunger, and Ivis bade me wrestle 'im, and he threw me. Flat on my back, I was, before I knew what happened." He shook his head. "Not many of us left, that started with him there, and I don't suppose anyone from his vill at all, barring Raheli."

"I wish she had been able to get here in time," said Luap, meaning it.

Cob shrugged. "You sent word; that's all you could do. Rahi's got sense; she'll understand."

"And now what?" Cob scratched thinning hair. Every Marshal in Fin Panir and all those visiting had gathered in the old palace. "Th' old man's dead, gods grace his rest, and we've to decide what to do. Did he ever say, Luap, aught about what came next?"

"No . . . not really." Luap looked around the table. "He wouldn't be king, remember—I know he didn't want to see a return of kingship. He wanted just what he always said: one fair law for everyone, and peace among all peoples."

"So we've got a Code he revised every half-year, meaning he wasn't convinced it was one fair law yet, and quarrels enough to break his heart—" That was a Marshal from the east, someone Luap barely remembered from the war.

"Not now," Cob said. "No one's quarreling now—it's as if Gird himself cast a charm at us." Even that word, so potent for strife, brought no frown to any face. "It's in my heart that's about what

he did, him and the High Lord. Gave us some peace to sort ourselves out and have no more stupid quarrels, no more need to
knock heads. But we'd best decide how to do that before everyone
wakes up."

"We could have a council of Marshals," said Sekkin.

"We *are* a council of Marshals." Cob scratched his head again.
"Thing is, will that be enough? Gird himself knew we couldn't go
back to steading and hearthing organization, and the bartons aren't
large enough either, no more the granges. We've got to have sum-
mat up top, if not a king someone who'll do what Gird did, at least
in a way. . . ." His voice trailed off. No one could do what Gird
did, and they all knew it. Gird, for all his talk of every yeoman's
abilities, had known it.

Eyes came back to Luap. Now, if ever, he could take what Gird
had never offered, become Gird's successor. He knew the Code
better than any of them, having written more copies than he cared
to remember of each revision, and he had traveled more than most
of them, carrying Gird's letters to each corner of the land. It would
be logical—would have been logical, if he had been other than he
was. Might still be logical, except that he had promised Gird, albeit
in silence, in that last moment.

"I think," he said slowly, picking his way through possibilities as
if along a steep mountain path, "I think Gird thought of Marshals
selecting another Marshal-General. Perhaps a council of Marshals,
perhaps all of them—I don't know exactly what he thought. Whoever was chosen ought to have been a Marshal, I would think . . ."

"In other words, you don't want the job." Cob had Gird's directness, if not all his other qualities. Luap spread his hands.

"I was never a Marshal. As well, you know my heritage, my vow
to seek no command."

"Aye, but you're the one man might stand to both folk as the
right person to lead now. It's not like you're taking anything from
Gird; he's dead." Others nodded, around the long table. "You know
the Code and the land; you were his choice for many things. And
it's not like you'd be a king—you'd have plenty of Marshals making
sure you didn't revert to that nonsense."

It made sense, but he felt repelled. What he once might have
thought his due, for all the work he'd done, what he had wanted
when he thought no one would give it to him, he now did not want.
The thought of having to perform Gird's daily duties shepherded by
Marshals who would no doubt look for any deviation from Gird's
custom made his skin itch. If he took command—any sort of

command—it must be *command.* And besides, he'd promised Gird he wouldn't.

"It would break my vow," he said. Cob nodded.

"All right. Whatever anyone's said, you've always been true to Gird; I've seen that. It's not your fault who your father was, nor any of the rest of it. But that leaves us still with no decision."

He might have changed his mind if they'd pressured him more, but he felt that even with Cob the offer had been as much courtesy as anything else.

"I do think," Cob said, "that we ought to start calling you Marshal—you may not have sought command, but you've been doing Gird's work all this time. If you're not to be Marshal-General, you'll still be needed in any councils, as you were with Gird."

The word popped into his mind from some forgotten conversation. "Why not Archivist?" he asked. "Someone who keeps the records—that's what I really am. You all earned the title of Marshal, leading yeomen—I haven't done that."

"Makes sense," said Donag, down the table. "Like a scribe, only more so, eh? Judicar and scribe together, maybe. You'll write Gird's life, won't you?"

He had not actually thought of that, in spite of having written accounts of the war, battle by battle. He had been hampered by Gird's insistence that he include only the barest facts; the time he'd tried to explore the meaning of a battle to the morale of both sides, following a model in the old royal archives, Gird had insisted he rewrite it. "You don't know what they thought, or even what most of our people thought: you only know who was there, and who won." But it came to him in a rush how much good he could do, writing about Gird, making Gird come alive for later generations, so that those who had never met him would understand how great a man Gird had been.

"Yes," he said to Donag, to all of them, to his own memory of Gird. "Yes. I will write Gird's life."

Aris, dressing carefully to take his part in Gird's funeral procession, felt guilty that he felt no more pain than he did. He had loved the old man as the grandfather he had never known; he had admired him as the hero who had singlehandedly routed the wicked king. How could he be taking this so calmly? Only last Midwinter Feast, when his healer's eye had recognized that Gird's health was failing, he had spent several miserable days trying to hide his grief until Seri talked it out of him. He was not ready to lose Gird's wisdom, he told himself. He was not ready to lose that straight look, the one that made him feel as if Gird were seeing into his head, finding all the messier corners of his mind. Yet—he had cried only briefly. His appetite was good. He had carried out his duties as yeoman-marshal of his grange, to his Marshal's evident surprise and possible distrust. Could he really have loved and respected Gird, if he was acting so normally? Even Seri, usually level-headed and calm, had flung herself on Aris, sobbing wildly, in the first hours after.

You know better, said an almost familiar voice in his head. Better than what? he wondered, and answered himself: better than to think tears define sorrow. Of course he'd loved Gird, and Gird had loved him. But now they had to honor Gird's memory, and go on with the work.

He rubbed at a possible smudge on his belt-buckle and went out to face his Marshal's inspection. He had advanced from junior yeoman to senior yeoman with the others his age, as had Seri. To his surprise, he had been offered a trial period as yeoman-marshal in this, his second grange assignment. His first Marshal, Kevis, had recommended that he change granges for the next stage of training, and Gird had concurred. Seri's promotion had surprised no one, except perhaps the pompous Marshal she had once played tricks on. And now he would walk at Marshal Geddrin's side, at the head of the third grange formed in Fin Panir.

Geddrin, a massive man whose freckled face usually looked surprised, was frowning at his own image in a polished shield. By its shape, it had been captured from a magelord in the war. "Cut myself," he said out of the side of his mouth. Shaving was a new fashion in the past few years, taken from the merchants and much commoner in cities than in rural granges.

Aris wondered whether to offer to heal it. Geddrin had accepted Gird's word that Aris must be allowed to heal, but it clearly made him nervous to watch. And he might take the offer as an accusation of softness. He moved closer until he could see the cut, then whistled softly, "It'll drip, Marshal, sure's you start singing, where it is. Let me close it for you, and it won't stain the cloak. . . ."

"*Heal* it, you mean," said Geddrin, but without heat. "Say what you mean, Aris. But yes, go on—Gird's seen my blood before; I've no need to look like I was showing off for him."

"Yes, Marshal," said Aris. So small a wound, clean and new, took only his touch and enough breath to make his knees sag. It vanished, leaving Geddrin's face just as rough-scraped and freckled as before.

"If all the mageborn were like you . . ." Geddrin said, wiping the blade with which he'd shaved on a cloth, and slipping it into its sheath. He didn't finish that, though Aris knew the thought in his mind. If all the mageborn were like him, there would have been no war.

One step to Geddrin's rear, Aris led the grange's cohort of yeomen around to the city gates where the parade would start. There the most senior Marshals decided the order of march. Aris listened to the mix of accents, the muttered comments on various Marshals, the rumors already abroad over who would be the next Marshal-General.

"—An' I said to him, your Marshal may be a veteran but he's all hard stone from his eyebrows back. Old Father Gird was tough, but he wasn't stupid."

"What I always say is, the ones you've got to watch is them quiet ones. The nicer they are, the more they're looking for a way into your beltpouch, eh? Isn't that so?"

"—So there we was, Geris and me, not an arm's-length away from old Gird on that horse. An' he was bashing heads, lads, like you wouldn't believe, till one o' them poles got him under the armpit and I was sure he was killed—"

"*And* you and Geris got him back up on his horse. Alyanya's tits, Peli, we've heard that story every drill night since the war. . . ."

"I dunno why they don't get his horse, the way we always heard in the songs. . . ."

"*I* heard nobody's seen that horse these two days."

"Eh? T' old man's horse?"

A silence spread; Aris could pick out the speaker now. A tall, stout woman with graying hair, whose old blue shirt hardly stretched across her front. She nodded, decisively. "I heard it from my daughter, who heard it from a lad who cleans the stables. That very evening, he said, going to tell the old horse, he found the stall empty. And the latch fastened, he said, and that's what she told me."

An excited murmur ran through the crowd, though no one broke ranks; Aris shivered as if a cold wind had touched his neck. He had not had leave, in the days since Gird's death, to go up to the high city; he had assumed the old gray horse still dreamed in its stall. He looked beyond the dust-clouds rising from the crowd assembled to march, as if he half-expected to see a gray horse in a nearby field. But he saw no animals at all, and in a moment Marshal Geddrin called the grange to order.

Through the old massive gateway they marched, one grange after another, singing the old songs from the war, that Aris had learned as a child. Far ahead, the first marchers were soon out of time with those behind, but no one noticed or cared; those who had come to watch shouldered their way in among the marchers, so the entire route soon resembled a vast segmented monster in tortuous motion upward.

Aris gave himself up to the movement and emotion of the crowd, willing himself to melt into it, be part of it. Not until the silence around the grave did he think to look and see if Gird's gray horse was visible anywhere. He saw no horse in the crowd, or near the grave, or—when he narrowed his eyes to see beyond, to the far edge of the meadows—anywhere on the grassy expanse. Then a flick of cold air, sharp as a tail's lash across his cheek, drew his eyes upward. A fair wind, fresh and fragrant, blew tumbled clouds across the sky, and by some trick of eye and mind, one of them seemed to run, its mottled gray suddenly gleaming white in a streak of sunlight. Then he could not find it among the others, and when he dropped his eyes they were full of tears.

Geddrin's arm came around his shoulders. "S'all right, lad," he said. "It takes some longer to find their tears, that's all. I knew you cared—go on now, give him that gift." The tears ran down his face, and he felt the knot of grief inside loosen enough to let more fall. What he really wanted was time alone with Seri, time for both of them to cry together, and comfort each other. But Geddrin, unlike Kevis, did not know him well enough to know why he needed that. When he followed his Marshal and grange back through the city, he felt bruised and lonely.

Chapter Eleven

Even in the changing climate that followed Gird's death, Luap could not forget the cave and that strange place to which it had taken him. It had not been his imagination, a sort of dream or enchantment: it had taken Gird, too, the last man who could be fooled into believing what wasn't there. And Gird had seemed to say, in that crowded few minutes before his death, that Luap was right . . . that he should take his mageborn relatives and go.

Had that been a gift of knowledge from the gods, a private message to Luap before the general message he had given them all? Or had it been Gird's despair, the last of his human—and thus fallible—utterances? Should he act on it? Was the place even there, now?

As the new council of Marshals dithered about appointing a successor, Luap's mind wandered often, always in the same direction. As it was now, the mageborn didn't have to leave. Things were better, not worse. Gird's dream of compromise and cooperation might well come to pass. But did that mean that none of them could leave, or should leave? The Marshals were, if not as hostile, still clearly frightened by the idea of the mageborn using their powers. Using the powers safely required training . . . and that distant, empty land would be a safe place to acquire that training. No one there to be frightened by a sudden light, a clap of thunder, a gust of wind. No one there to argue that a child who could lift buckets of water from well to water trough could also lift coins from one purse to another. And if the mageborn learned to use their powers safely, with guidance in the ethics involved, then perhaps they could demonstrate to the others how such powers should be used, and that would erase the old fears, and even improve on Gird's vision.

"Luap!" Sterin touched his shoulder. They were all staring at him.

"Sorry," he said, feeling his ears redden. "I was trying to remember something and just . . . ."

"It's all right," said Cob, "but even if we bore you, you shouldn't go to sleep: you've got to keep the notes." He was grinning to take away the sting, but Luap felt it anyway.

"I wasn't bored." Of course he was bored; they'd been hashing over the same argument for a hand of days, with the same three or four people saying the same things, only louder. He was hot, his back in the sun from the windows in the council's meeting room, and he could smell the stables all too clearly. "There's something in the gnome laws Gird told me about one time, that I thought might help, but I just can't remember." Apparently that convinced them, or most of them; everyone shrugged and went back to the same things they'd said before. Luap took careful notes, even though he already knew what Foss and Sirk would say.

His own arguments continued in the same trails as well, but more smoothly, more logically, as time passed. It did make sense. The mageborn needed to learn to use their powers safely and properly; the safe and proper use of their powers would reassure those without them, as people recognized the safe use of any tool. They could not learn to use their powers here without frightening people, and threatening the fragile peace that Gird had bought so dearly. Therefore, they needed to find a place—far enough away that accidents or mistakes, common in learning, could hurt no one—to get that practice. Then the community Gird envisioned could be made of mageborn and former peasants, all using all their talents to the fullest, for the benefit of all. As for a place ... well ... it was logical to use a place which no one without the mage powers could stumble on by accident, and get hurt. The only such place he could think of was wherever the cave took him. Only a mageborn, he was sure, could do whatever he had done to make the pattern work.

It all made sense; it all fitted like the interlocking gears of a mill. If you start here, and the parts all fit, you come out over here, inexorably. Arranha had said that about logic: arguments are not made, he said, but found, by following all the rules of logic from any starting place. If the rules are not broken, the conclusion cannot be wrong, and has existed from the beginning of the world. He had not made it true that the only way to get to Gird's dream from present reality was by taking the mageborn to the distant land of red stone towers, but he had found out, by logic, that this was true.

Of course he still might be wrong, and he would have to test it. Arranha taught that all human vision lacked completeness. Conclusions must be tested. At the least, he would have to return to the cave and see if he still arrived at the great hall, and if the stair still came to the same outside. He would have to take someone else, as witness and test both.

He found it easy to arrange some days away, on a pretext of gathering material for his *Life of Gird*. Not entirely pretext, for he intended to do just that; he foresaw that his work would be the foundation text, the way that Gird would be remembered generations after those who knew him had died. He intended to make Gird's greatness come alive, breathe from the scroll, and to do that he wanted as much detail as possible. Still, he intended to visit the cave, and he was not going to tell the others about it until he knew if it still worked.

He arrived, on a mild sunny afternoon, in a very different mood than before. Sunlight glittered on tiny crystals in the gray rock; lush green grass and scarred bark showed where years of travelers had tethered their mounts. The creek purled over its stony bed, hardly disturbing the summer growth of mint and frogweed. Luap dipped a pot of water, and sniffed the mint's crisp aroma. He was aware that weather influenced his moods, but this was more than sun-induced relaxation; it was also the inner calm that had followed

Gird's death. He was not afraid, this time, of consequences; he was not stirred by useless ambitions or wracked by guilty memories. Signs of recent campfires in the cave did not disturb him; he knew that others sometimes used it for shelter while traveling.

When he had watered and fed his horse, he sat in the sun outside the cave, thinking about the stories of Gird he had heard so far, and how best to arrange them. In the old archives, the stories of great kings and mages began with a childhood full of portents. He wondered if all those tales were true. One young prince had been born, so the tale went, with heatless flames around him; another had brought frost-killed flowers to life in a snowstorm.

Gird's life, as others remembered it, was depressingly free of portents. He had found no one from Gird's original village, for one thing. Perhaps, he thought, squinting into the late slanting light, Raheli would know some childhood stories about her father. The few things Gird had told Luap weren't much use. He'd been chosen for the count's guard because of his size, and left it because of some misunderstanding. He'd never actually said what it was, but Luap assumed it was because he'd gotten drunk. That wouldn't be impressive in a legendary figure. A mother dead of fever; a brother killed by a wolf. Half a life spent farming, apparently with enjoyment—he certainly retained a fondness for cows and even scythed the meadows a few times at haying time.

Luap shifted on the rock he'd chosen as a seat. None of that made a good story. Who, in a hundred years or so, would believe that a simple peasant lad with no more training than that could lead an army to victory? It had happened, yes: It was true, yes: But it was not *reasonable.* He had to make it believable to people who had never seen Gird, who had no idea what force of character lay in that lumpish peasant head. At least, he thought, the man was bigger than average, stronger than most. That would help. He might have been handsome when he was younger; that would help, too.

As the sun sank, he rose and stretched, watered his horse again, and made his own tidy campsite well inside the cave. He needed no fire, but he needed an explanation for the tethered horse outside, so he rolled his blanket and set his pack at one end before calling his own light and going back to the inner chamber.

On this, his fourth visit, the bell-shaped chamber with its walls covered in intricate patterned relief seemed almost homey. He did not hesitate to step out onto the central design of the floor; he felt no real apprehension before calling on his power. As smoothly as ever, as swiftly and silently, he was elsewhere, in the grand high hall he remembered. It, too, looked familiar, and the third arch, which had appeared when Gird visited, still opened off the far end. He thought about going out, up the stairs, to the outer world, but decided against it. This much worked as it had; surely the same world would be outside. And now he wanted a witness to share the wonder. He returned as quickly as he had come.

The next morning, he went on as he'd planned. He interviewed a veteran farming newly cleared land, who remembered Gird telling about the first winter in the forest, and two more in the next vill, who wanted to complain about the current edition of the Code rather than talk about Gird himself. Most of them had only second-hand knowledge; he had known Gird as long as they had, but he wanted to be thorough. The details that would make Gird's life come alive later might come from anyone. By the time he returned to Fin Panir, he had two scrolls full of such tales. He had also decided that he must tell Arranha and the Rosemage, even though he foresaw awkward questions. With that decision made, he wasted no time, and the next day sent word to both asking them to meet him in his office.

The Rosemage, who had been teaching the more advanced yeoman to use a longsword, arrived with a bandage around her left hand. "Clumsiness," she said, before anyone could ask. "Mine, as well as the yeoman's. And no, it's not dangerous, and yes, I would let Aris heal it if necessary."

Arranha, Luap noticed, gave her the same smile he gave Luap. "Lady, no one doubts your ability."

She chuckled, pulling one of Luap's chairs to her, and sat down. "The class I was teaching no longer thinks I'm beyond injury, using magery to protect myself while thumping them. I think the fellow actually expected that his blade would turn aside rather than hit me. Luckily, he's still using wood. Unluckily for me, it still hurts." She had placed herself so that the injured hand could rest on a table, Luap noticed. He wondered if she were certain no bones had broken.

"We need to train more healers," Arranha said. "Surely there are others among us who have, or can learn, that magery. Luap, would the Council of Marshals approve the use of healing magery in someone other than Aris?"

"I'm not sure," said Luap, well-pleased that Arranha had given him an opening without needing any hints. "Aris had trained himself, in a time before the uses of magery were against the Code; whatever mistakes he made then, when he appeared here he functioned as a successful healer. That certainly influenced Gird's decision, and the reaction of the other Marshals. The Marshals know, in their minds, that a child with Aris's talent must learn to use it, just as a child must learn any adult skill, with many mistakes in the process—but in practice, they so distrust all magery that, without Gird, I suspect they would forbid it."

"Mmm. So the child would have to be trained to be approved, and would have to be approved to be allowed to train—is that what you're saying?"

"Yes. I may be wrong, but this is the impression I get." Then, before the others could speak, Luap went on. "In fact, I asked to see you because of just this problem and a possible solution."

The Rosemage looked up sharply. "A solution!"

"Yes. You weren't with us when I first discovered that I had some magery; Arranha may remember the incident—"

The old priest hid his expression behind folded hands, peering at Luap with bright eyes over his fingertips. "Are you certain you want me to tell all that tale?"

Luap smiled. "Enough know it already, or think they do. But I'll be brief: we were camped in a cave, lady, and deep within I found a small chamber and had a . . . what I suppose you could call a revelation. A voice spoke, naming the king my father. And my magery woke, so that I had light in my hands. Unfortunately, the shock of that so unhinged my wits that I tried to argue Gird into a command—and sought to use my magery on him to convince him. You tried that yourself; you know its effect."

"Gird knocked him flat," Arranha said when Luap paused for breath. "Told everyone—perhaps especially me—that he'd kill him the next time he used his magery. Luckily, by the time you forced that, lady, Gird had changed his mind."

"Not my most impressive moment," said Luap wryly. "But some years later, after the war, and after Dorhaniya told me my real parentage, I went back there. I was hoping for another revelation, something to rattle my mind."

"The study of logic . . ." muttered Arranha. Luap shook his head.

"Such studies settle *your* mind, Arranha, but don't help me. At any rate, I returned, while on a journey for Gird, and found something quite different. I found a place—a far place—to which magery can travel."

"A place." It was almost the same tone as Gird had used. "What sort of place? Where?"

The same questions, and he had hardly more answers. "It's a great hall and many chambers, all carved from living rock, and outside is a strange land of red stone, great towers and mountains and narrow steep valleys. Where it is from *here* I cannot say, but it's apparently in a colder land than this."

"And you can get there by magery . . ." Arranha mused. "So—"

"I took Gird once." Luap said. "That is the place I meant, the time we quarreled so about moving the mageborn. As far as we could tell, it was a great land empty of all people; I thought it would suit us well. He said no—but you remember the day of his death—"

"And you think that's what he meant, when he said you had been right, and he had been wrong? You think that was permission to take the mageborn there?" The Rosemage sounded doubtful, and in her voice he could doubt Gird's meaning himself.

"I think you should come see it. No one knew, but Gird and I; he's dead, and someone else should know. What I'm thinking now is that it's a place no one without magery could stumble upon, a place where the mageborn could learn to use their powers safely, without risking harm to others, and without a chance to use them wrongly: there are no peasants to rule. With such training and discipline, our people might be more acceptable to those without magery—at least, there would be no beginners' errors to be explained away."

"Ah, that makes sense." Arranha nodded, his eyes bright. "As weapons-practice is done in the bartons and granges, not in the marketplace or inside a home—this is a place for our young ones to learn properly." Luap kept quiet, waiting for the Rosemage's response.

"I'm surprised you didn't tell us before this," she said. Luap shrugged.

"Gird preferred that no one else know," he said. "He thought it was a secret best kept close, lest disaffected mageborn try to use the cave. Now, I think you two should know, but no one else, until you've seen the place and considered how it might be used."

"Tell us about it," said Arranha. "What sort of great hall? How large? How many could stay there at once?"

"I'd rather you saw it for yourself," said Luap. He could not possibly describe it all, and besides that, he wanted their reaction; he wanted to see someone like himself arriving.

"How far from here is the cave?" asked the Rosemage.

"A few days' travel by horse; it's between Soldin and Graymere. At this season, the ford at Gravelly should be passable, which cuts a day off."

"It will do my hand no harm to rest from teaching sword-work," the Rosemage said. "Why not leave tomorrow?"

Luap opened his mouth to protest, and then shrugged. If they were that eager, why not? He had planned to suggest a more elaborate, less obvious journey, with each arriving separately, by a different route, to meet by "coincidence" if anyone found out. "Very well," he said. "I'll tell Marshal Sterin or Cob that I won't be at the Council."

Traveling with Arranha and the Rosemage was nothing like traveling alone. Arranha wondered, aloud, about half the things he saw: what was that rock, and why did it break into squarish lumps when another rock the same color didn't? Why would any bird build a nest that hung swinging from a limb? If the weaving patterns of peasant women had the names of plants and animals, why didn't they look like that plant or animal? He noticed everything that Luap normally rode by without seeing it: tiny wildflowers, the speckles on river frogs, the relative numbers of red and spotted cattle in fields they passed. He greeted everyone they met on the road, and if Luap had not reminded him that they had a goal, would have stopped to talk of anything that caught his mind.

He's like a bur, Luap thought. Everything clings to him; he could stop and be stuck anyplace until some stronger attraction yanked him free. By the end of the first day, Luap was exhausted by the relentless intelligence with which Arranha attended to his surroundings.

The Rosemage, on the other hand, seemed to view the country as a military map: this position defensible, that one not. She said little, in contrast to Arranha, but the little she did say had to do with the possibility of brigands up a narrow valley, or the way someone with any knowledge at all could control the trade roads. Luap had not, since the war's end, felt nervous about trouble on the road, but he found himself eyeing places where travelers were vulnerable. Then Arranha would exclaim over some novelty, and he had to make some comment in response.

The cave, when they reached it on the fourth day, felt welcoming. Luap thought longingly of the silence in that distant hall, and was tempted to vanish there, leaving his companions behind. Instead, he took the horses to the creek, while Arranha and the Rosemage set up their camp inside. It was hot, even standing above cool water; he felt itchy and obscurely distressed. Here, with the water chuckling softly around the horses' fetlocks, with their gentle sucking, he began to relax. No one pointed out the swirl in midstream where something had come to the surface from below—he noticed it, which he would not have four days before, but in silence.

Arranha's horse lifted its head, water dripping from its muzzle, and yawned. It shivered its withers, and Luap saw its knees begin to buckle.

"No, you don't," he said firmly; the other two lifted their heads to watch as he yanked Arranha's horse back to dry land. It blew, spraying him in the face. Muttering, he got them all back from the bank and safely into the trees. The Rosemage was coming from the cave when he came in sight of it. She waved and came down to help feed them.

"I've never seen a cave like this," she said, almost eagerly. Sunburn had given her a rich color. "Where I was in Tsaia, the caves were dank little holes under graystone bluffs—big enough for one shepherd and a few sheep in a blizzard, no more. This thing's big enough for an army."

"That's what we had," said Luap.

"—And that chamber," she went on. "Arranha says those designs aren't anything from Old Aarc. If Gird didn't recognize them as his peoples', what could they be?"

"You've been in the *chamber?*" Anger raged through him; he had expected them to *wait*. It was his secret, after all.

"We didn't try to use it," the Rosemage said. Luap managed not to say anything sarcastic, and she went on. "Although it's thick with magery in there—I suspect anyone sensitive at all could trigger it." She put two handfuls of grain in the nosebag of her bay horse and tied it over the halter. "How long do you think we'll stay?"

"Not above a glass or so, I think. Time enough to see what Gird saw." Luap finished with the other two horses and led the way back to the cave. Deep inside, where dimness should have faded to blackness, a faint glow showed that Arranha had no qualms about using his magery here. Luap called his own light—if the old priest could be that bold, he wasn't going to chance falling over any stones.

As he came past the ledge where Gird had stumbled, Arranha said, "It's very interesting, this pattern."

"It's more than *interesting*," Luap said.

"Oh yes—I know—but my point is, I doubt if it's a pattern wrought by humans. It's not Old Aarean, nor any pattern of the northern branches, and you say Gird did not recognize it . . ."

"By the gods?" Luap felt a cold chill down his back and arms.

"Perhaps. But the Elder Races, particularly the sinyi, use patterns of power. Have you asked any elves about this, Luap?"

"No. Remember, Gird wanted it kept secret."

"Hmmm." Arranha's bright eyes glittered before he blinked and turned away. "Strange—he had scant love for secrets, in most things. 'Bury a truth, and it rots,' he told me more than once."

"Well—I never asked him if I could ask the elves; it never occurred to me. His reasons concerning the mageborn seemed so strong, to him—"

Arranha said, "I daresay it doesn't matter. You've used this pattern three times now; if it were a matter for elves, you would surely have heard from them."

Another shiver, as if icy water had funneled beneath his shirt; Luap twitched, but said, "Then let us go, and you judge what you see."

This time his mind clung to the pattern and the remembered place; almost before he could think, they had arrived. He did not know which face to watch. The Rosemage, to his quick glance, seemed almost turned to stone. Her face paled, then flushed; her eyes widened. Arranha, too, seemed stunned to silence.

Luap repeated the same prayer he had uttered the first time he came, and heard Arranha and then the Rosemage repeat it. Then he led the way off the dais.

"We can talk now," he said quietly, looking back. They had said nothing but the prayer. They were looking up, around, faces as full of awe as Luap had wished. The Rosemage brought her gaze back to him.

"It's—impossible," she said, shaking her head.

"That's what I thought the first time. That I had dreamed it, perhaps. But Gird saw it too."

"If the gods did not make this, they blessed it," said Arranha softly. "I have never felt such presence, not even in the Hall in Fin Panir when Esea blessed Lady Dorhaniya's belief."

Is that what happened? thought Luap. He felt uncomfortable thinking of Dorhaniya in this place.

Arranha had moved down the hall, slowly; now he approached the arches at the far end. The Rosemage stayed near the dais. "Do you know what this is?" called Arranha, his voice louder than any Luap had heard in this place. He was pointing at the arch with the harp and tree entwined.

"Gird said it might be an elven symbol," Luap said.

"As you should well know," Arranha replied. "And the other— that is surely dwarfish. And you did not think to ask them?"

Luap felt his face burning. For a moment he was not sure what to say, but the great place eased him, as it had before. "Gird saw what I saw; it was his decision. Perhaps he was upset enough with me that I had used magery to bring him."

Arranha did not reply, but walked, as Gird had, through the arch with the High Lord's circle above it. Luap followed, and behind him he could hear the Rosemage coming.

"Up those stairs," Luap said, "is a land unlike any I've seen. Bare red stone, deep canyons with trees and rivers—" He had not actually seen the rivers, but where there were trees, rivers must be also. "Not good land for farming, Gird said, but I think it would support a small number."

"Mmm." Arranha looked at the stairs. "Shall we go up, then?"

"Certainly." Luap led the way, wondering again why the light that filled the hall and passages below did not extend to this. Because it was an entrance? As before, the sound of their boots on the steps echoed off the floor below, and as before they came to a darkness close above their heads. But this time Luap called his light before it was too dim to see, and pointed out to Arranha the whorls and interlacements Gird had noted. He himself, this time, put his thumb in the groove and traced the interlocked spirals in and out, and Arranha prayed.

When the ceiling close above them vanished, Luap half-expected the snowy blast of his first visit. But even here—wherever here was—spring had come, and warm sunlight spilled down the stair. Only a light breeze stirred his hair as he climbed the last few steps and came out to the view he remembered so clearly.

It was still there. He had been afraid, in some corner of his mind, that it was less majestic than he remembered, but in the clear cool sunlight that land lost none of its grandeur. The vast blocks of red stone, the endless vista of stone and sky. He could see farther than before, but still had no idea where the place lay, or how deep the canyons were.

Arranha and the Rosemage reacted as he had hoped. "It's . . . like nothing I've seen anywhere," Arranha said. "Certainly it's not anywhere near Fintha, nor down the Honnorgat valley as far as I've traveled, nor like anything I heard of Aarenis or Old Aare."

"It's so—big," the Rosemage said. Luap glanced at her. Few things ever seemed to daunt her, but this did. "Even the sky seems bigger. And how do you get down from this, or up into those trees?"

Where Gird and Luap, in the cold and snow, had seen what might be the bristling thatch of a forest above another level of stone, now the forest showed clearly. It seemed to stand on the topmost level of the stone, far above their heads or across great crevices on other blocks, as if Luap's imagined city of castles were roofed with trees and not slate.

"We didn't stay long enough to find out," Luap told the Rose-mage. "It was snowing when we got into the open, and though the snow ceased, it had been blown away by a bitter wind. We were glad to get out of it."

"And you never came again, to explore?" Arranha asked. He had put back the hood of his cloak, and turned his face up to the brilliant sunlight. With his eyes closed, and his arms held out, he looked to Luap a little like a bird drying itself after rain.

"I had no time," Luap said, "and no reason. I suggested to Gird that he allow me to bring the mageborn here, when all that trouble started. But you know what he thought of that."

"Mmm. Yes." Arranha opened his eyes, as bright and penetrating as hawks' eyes. They seemed to have absorbed the brilliant light and now it poured from them. Luap blinked. It must be something to do with being the Sunlord's priest. Arranha stared in all directions, as if looking for something in particular. "I don't feel anything dire," he said finally. "I see no sign that anyone inhabits this land. Do you?"

Luap shook his head. "It felt empty to me from the first. That's why I thought it would bother no one if we came here."

"Lady?" asked Arranha of the Rosemage. "What can you sense about this land?"

"Its size," she said, her voice still muted by the land's effect on her. "It is so large, so empty . . . it does not care about us at all, did you realize? Everywhere in Fintha or Tsaia, there's a sense— I think the elves call it taig—that the land is almost aware, that it cares what we do. I've heard the farmers say a field is generous, faithful, or that another field is bitter and hard-hearted. When I had sheep, I felt that way myself at times, held in the land's palm. Nothing so grand as Alyanya's notice, but perhaps some of her power running over into the land itself. But here—" she shook her head. "If this is even in Alyanya's realm, it would be hard to think so. This land has no interest in us, in our welfare; it is neither generous nor mean. It has its own affairs, and what they are I cannot imagine."

"Does it frighten you?" asked Luap.

"No. Not as a threat would. But that indifference feels strange; I did not know how I had depended on our land's sensitivity until I felt nothing like it here."

"I felt it as cleanliness," Arranha said. "As if this were newmade land, its stone washed clean by light and water on the first day, untouched by history. And yet it feels old, at the same time. I wonder if it is just untouched by *our* history— we have no little stories about this rock or that, about who chased a stray cow into which canyon—and so we feel it has no history. Surely it must." His face sobered. "And surely we should know that history, however strange it is, before we lay our own upon it. As there are metals that must not touch, for they cause corrosion in each other, so there may be histories that must not be laid one upon another." He looked from one to the other; Luap wanted to argue that expression, but could not. Then Arranha sighed and shook his head. "No—I feel no menace here; the Rosemage is right. But it is in the nature of Esea's priests to seek knowledge and more knowledge, the god's light upon ignorance. We expect trouble to come from ignorance more than malice—our weakness, as Gird showed, but nonetheless trouble can come from ignorance. Here is a land— a great land, as the Rosemage has said—about which we know nothing, not even how to find our way to water. So I have qualms, which will probably be foolish in the end."

"I hope so," said Luap soberly. "I feel nothing but promise here, a promise of peace and—with enough hard work—security. If you have definite warnings—"

"No," said Arranha. "Nothing definite, and not really a warning. Just the awareness that what you don't know can kill you."

"We'll learn," said Luap, feeling confidence rebound in him. "And the first thing, I suppose, is to map the inside of this place, and find another outlet. Surely there is one." He gestured. "Shall we go back inside?"

Down the stair, under the arch, into the great hall. With their footsteps behind him, he could feel it a procession, almost a homecoming. He led them past the dais, into the corridors behind. To his surprise, he remembered clearly which turnings he had made, both on his own and with Gird. Both Arranha and the Rosemage were more uneasy than he felt; his courage rose as he perceived himself the boldest of the party. He chose a downward-trending ramp at one turning, and found himself in an unfamiliar passage.

"Listen!" The Rosemage held up one hand. They all held their breath. A distinct musical plink repeated at irregular intervals. "Water," she said finally. They followed the sound along the passage to an opening in one wall; it gaped a few handspans wide and high, dark within, unlike the regular doorways they had seen so far. Luap put his hand through, made his magelight, then looked. A chamber as large as the common dining hall in Fin Panir held clear water . . . he could not tell how deep, but he could see the stone below it clearly. Its surface lay within reach of his hand. Above, the chamber rose higher than the passage ceiling, marked here and there with the dark stain of dripping water. From a line around the chamber, Luap saw that the water rarely if ever rose as high as the opening in the wall. He stretched his hand down and touched the surface: ice-cold. He sniffed it: pure, with no hint of salt or sulphur.

"We need not fear thirst," Luap said. He stepped back; Arranha and the Rosemage both leaned in to look, kindling their own light. "Now if we can find a lower entrance—" He was sure a lower entrance existed. It must be there. Farther down, they found a great room that could only be a kitchen, with hearths and ovens cut into the stone. Here was a draft of cool air, sweet and fresh, from the chimney shaft. Another passage, that seemed darker, less full of that sourceless light. Luap headed for it. The spiralling stair had been darker . . . did all the outside ways begin where the light failed?

The passage ended in a blank wall; Luap was not surprised. Nor was he surprised when his own light revealed the same incised patterns on the passage wall to one side. He traced them carefully as before, and as before the wall melted away, letting in a fresh breeze, pine-smelling. The opening let in abundant light; Luap thought two horsemen could ride through it abreast. They looked out onto a narrow terrace supporting great pine trees, and heard the cheerful gurgling of water among rocks below. One tree, larger in girth than Luap could span, stood square athwart the opening . . . clearly it had grown there since someone last used the passage. Luap edged past it, and came out into the sunlight. Some small animal let out a squeak and fled upslope, a flurry of gray fur, hardly seen. High above a hawk squealed; Luap could not see through the pines where it flew.

"With running water so near, why store water inside?" asked the Rosemage, coming out into the sun. "There's enough in there for three rivulets this size." She had moved to the lip of the terrace, and was looking down into the minute creek, which made far more noise than its size suggested. Then, before Luap could answer, she had moved lightly downslope and skipped across, a matter of hopping on two rocks and grabbing the drooping branch of a bush on the far side. She climbed out of Luap's sight; he followed her, out from under the pines, and then realized how narrow the place was. The Rosemage stood atop a cottage-size boulder at the foot of a rock wall that matched the one they'd come out of. He looked up . . . and up. Those soaring red walls, so near and high that he could not see the flat shoulder of the mountain, or its higher forested crown, delighted him even from below. Nothing had ever looked so impregnable, so defensible. Once inside, no imaginable army could possibly harm him or his people.

Chapter Twelve

Once they came out of the passage, Luap began to wonder if he would ever get his companions back inside. Arranha clambered up and down the narrow cleft in which they had come out, observing the angle of the sun and attempting (as near as Luap could understand it) to determine from that where they were. The Rosemage followed the water up to its source, a crack beneath a wall of stone, and then down to its joining with the larger stream Luap had been able to see from above a stream that ran almost sunrising and sunsetting. She came panting back with her hands full of red berries, having seen, she said, two deer, fish in the stream, frogs and strange shapes of rock she wanted Luap to look at.

Luap followed her down the streambed. It felt like returning to childhood, when one could explore a new corner of the garden, or a stretch of meadow or woods. Surely he should be more careful, he thought, nearly turning his ankle on a loose stone, but he could not imagine how, in this unknown land, he should know what hazards to watch for. The walls on either side ended as suddenly as the walls of a building; he found himself looking across a wider space, with a noisy stream racing down to his right, to the facing wall. Low bushes, some laden with berries, tufts of a coarse tall grass, and—on this side of the narrow valley—no trees. The trees—more pines and others he did not know—filled the space between the stream and the foot of the opposite cliff.

The Rosemage touched his shoulder. "The deer . . . there." He followed her pointing finger and saw four of them, tails twitching nervously, ears wide. Then three of them returned to browsing. They seemed larger and grayer than the deer of Fintha, but he was not sure . . . everything seemed larger here. He gazed down the valley. On either side, high walls of red rock shut out any distant view. The valley seemed to widen somewhat at its lower end. He saw more trees there, many that were not pines. Up the valley, it narrowed, the walls closing in; it seemed to be cut off by another wall of rock. He tried to remember what he could see from above, but he could not make sense of it.

What he did understand was the sheer size of it. From above,

569

the larger valley had seemed a narrow slot, hardly wide enough to walk in, but he thought an archer would just be able to shoot across it. Hard to tell, with the steep slopes of broken rock below the cliffs, but if it were level . . . it would be large enough to farm. He tried to convert its irregular slope and shape to something approximating the teams and selions by which traditional fields were measured. At least they would have plenty of stone for building, if the day came they wanted to live outside the—he wondered what to call it, that vast hall understone. Castle? No . . . more a fortress, a stronghold. Stronghold: he liked that.

He imagined stone-walled cottages nestled against the walls, fields terraced and leveled, green with young grain, fruit trees trained against the foot of the cliffs. In his mind, laughing children played in the noisy stream, scampered along the narrow paths between plots of grain and garden vegetables, climbed the great rocks. He saw the harvest festival, with everyone gathered in the great hall, and a feast prepared in that huge kitchen; he could smell the food even now. He imagined caravans coming and going from Fin Panir, bringing news of the Girdish lands, bringing those who wanted to study Gird's life, taking back the freshly copied scrolls, the memory of great beauty.

"Luap!" That was Arranha, who had now made his own way down into the larger valley. "I think I know something of where we are."

"Oh?" At the moment Luap didn't care.

"But we'll have to go back, and then come back here, and do it again at night. On a clear night in both places."

"What?" The Rosemage looked as confused as Luap felt.

"I think we may be very far west of Fin Panir," Arranha said. He looked about, then headed for a sandy area near the stream. "Come here; I'll show you." Luap followed him; Arranha squatted and began drawing in the sand with a stick. "Here—this is the world." It looked like a circle to Luap, but he knew better than to argue. "If the sun rises here—sunrising—in Prealith on the eastern coast, it's overhead there before it's overhead *here,* in Fin Panir." He pointed to a spot near the center of the circle. "Now—if it's overhead in Fin Panir, where is it on the sunsetting edge of the world—here?" He pointed to the circle's rim.

Luap said, "Well . . . if it comes first to Prealith, and then to Fin Panir, then the other side of the circle will be . . . later. But are you sure about that?"

Arranha nodded. "You can see the sun move across the sky. It must be going from one place to another. Just as you walking past the High Lord's Hall, let's say, are first opposite one corner and then the next. Morning must be earlier as you travel sunrising, and later as you travel sunsetting. That's clear, isn't it?"

It wasn't clear at all to Luap. "And you got this from what you were doing up there?" He jerked his chin at the narrow cleft from which they'd come. Arranha nodded again.

"I was noticing how quickly the sun moved across that narrow space. When we came out, the sunlight came in the opening and lay full on the rocks above. Even as you and the Rosemage were coming down here, it moved far enough to put that in shadow. It occurred to me that if you had both large and small sandglasses, you could measure how long it took for the sun to cross that space, and thus how fast it moved . . . and from that discover how far apart any two places were. Far apart in the sunwise direction, that is." From his expression, he expected that to make sense to Luap. Luap glanced at the Rosemage; she was scowling in an effort to understand. Arranha sighed and tried again. "If you are walking, you know how far apart places are by how long it takes you to get there, isn't that right?"

"Yes, but—" But some roads were harder than others. Uphill took longer, hilly roads took longer. "—does the sun move more slowly in the morning?"

"No." Arranha frowned. "At least—I don't think so. I don't know if anyone's ever measured it with a sandglass. Perhaps the sun, as Esea's sigil, moves uphill as fast as down. That would be something to do, measure its progress before and after noon. I was assuming its speed stayed the same. If it does stay the same, then it travels across a certain space of the earth in each measure of time."

Clearly Arranha was going to keep explaining until Luap said he understood. He saw no chance of understanding, but he could, perhaps, save himself further confusion. "I see," he said.

Arranha smiled at him. "I knew you could follow that." The Rosemage stirred, as if she had a question, and Arranha turned to her. Luap shot her a glance over Arranha's head, and she made some quiet comment about the tameness of the wildlife.

"I think," Luap said, "that they see few people, if any." He was thinking to himself that there must, however, be something which fed upon the deer. Wolves? Bears? Would these attack humans in daylight, or should they return to the stronghold? He wanted to explore, but not foolishly.

"I'm going across," the Rosemage said. "I've never seen trees like those." Luap started to tell her to be careful, but didn't. She was older than he; she didn't need a keeper. She went slightly upstream, to a narrow place where she could jump from boulder to boulder and make her way across the stream and up a bluff of earth to the trees. Definitely pines, Luap thought, but so much larger than any pines in Fintha . . . and yet they looked small against the cliffs.

"I've seen similar trees in the Westmounts," Arranha said. "But there they grew in solid forests along the mountain slopes." As they watched, a bright blue bird flew from one of the trees, screeching, and into another. A smaller bright red and yellow bird flitted from bush to bush on the near side of the stream. A loud thud caught Luap's attention; he looked and saw that one of the browsing deer was stamping a forehoof. On the third stamp, the group bounded away upstream, leaping over the rocks as if they were floating. He looked around for the source of the danger, and saw nothing—but the Rosemage, working her way upstream through the trees. Arranha said, "There's plenty of wood in those trees . . . enough for fuel and building both, if we're careful. Some of them would have to come down anyway, to make fields. And that one in the entrance . . ."

"And there's more forest on top, if we can find a way to that upper level." He had no idea if the internal passages went that far. "We should be careful; these trees may take a long time to grow. But perhaps some are nut trees or have wild fruit, as these bushes do." He had lost sight of the Rosemage, and felt an urge to follow her upstream on his own side of the stream.

"I'll stay here," Arranha said, still peering at his designs in the sand. "I would like to find this out for myself."

Luap moved along the near bank of the creek, noticing how clear the water ran. He dipped his hand in. Cold, too, and sweet to the taste. The red rocks of the creekbed seemed to sparkle; when he looked closely he saw tiny flecks of gold. His heart pounded. It couldn't be *real* gold . . . but perhaps it was an omen. Certainly that might explain the almost magical shimmer of the cliffs in the sunlight, those myriad flecks of glittering gold. A frog popped up from the water to perch on a rock . . . the frog's skin, too, seemed dusted with gold. And the fish, hardly a hand long, that held its place in the current with its tail just waving, had speckles on its side of rose and gold.

It had not seemed hot, when they first came into this valley, but now Luap could feel the sun's heat reflecting from the cliff to his left. He noticed when it eased, and looked left to see another narrow cleft leading away in the direction of the one outside the stronghold. Should he explore it? No—it would take too long. He kept on his way, watching from time to time to see if he could see the Rosemage among the trees. He caught one glimpse of her, but she was still ahead of him, upstream. The sun baked him; he thought he knew now why the trees stayed on the other side. He was glad when the stream twisted, and he moved into the shade of its opposite bank for a few minutes. Here he found delicate flowering plants hanging half in the water, their starry blossoms stirred by the current. Ferns, too, clung here, and a low herb holding juicy berries just above the earth. A great rock hung out over the water on the other side, with a pine angling up from it.

"There's a very big fish in that pool," the Rosemage said. Luap looked up, and saw her lying stomach-down on the rock, peering at the water. "It's deeper than it looks." Luap squinted and found an angle where the reflections didn't obscure his gaze. What had seemed a pool perhaps knee-deep showed itself much deeper.

"How big a fish?" he asked, thinking of dinner. She held her hands apart to show him. Big enough for all of them, if he could catch it.

But he could not stop for that, and they could not stay past sunset—that much he was sure of. He scrambled past a fall of rocks and found that he was now on the same level as the Rosemage, some distance away. He could just see Arranha's white hair glowing in the sunlight downstream. The sun had moved too fast, he thought; he dared not go much farther. Echoing his thought came the Rosemage's call. "We should go back. . . ." From the tone she was no more eager than he. With a last look around, he spotted yet another cleft leading to the north, winterwards. From above, he remembered, he had seen narrow ridges of rock standing on end, finlike. Did each have its cleft, and could each cleft conceal another stronghold, or part of the same one? He tried to estimate how thick the fins were . . . thicker than the city walls of Fin Panir, thicker than half the city, he suspected. His skin prickled, imagining those walls hollowed out for dwellings, imagining the rock full of his people, his mageborn survivors, all secure in their stone castles. But the sun's angle warned him. He jumped down from that boulder and made his way as quickly as he could back down the stream.

Even so the sun had disappeared behind the cliffs sunsetting when he reached Arranha. The sky, still bright, gave light enough in the larger valley, but up in the small one, under the great pines, it seemed already dusk. Far overhead, he could just see the top of sunlit cliffs, still blazing red, but he stumbled over rocks in the gloom. At first, he could not remember exactly where the entrance lay; the tree in front of it obscured it more than he had expected.

But they found it at last, and after a last drink from the rivulet outside, came in to the silence and shadeless light of the stronghold.

None of them said anything on the way back to the great hall. Luap, counting turns and hoping that he remembered them all, had neither breath nor attention to spare for his companions. He had not realized how far down the sloping passages had taken them; going back uphill he could feel the pull on his legs. At last they came to the level ways he remembered clearly, and then to the hall itself. There they paused.

Arranha sank down on the dais, breathless.

"Are you all right?" the Rosemage asked. Luap felt guilty; he had not remembered that the old man might have even more trouble with the climb than he had.

Arranha nodded, but waited a moment to speak. "I'm . . . fine. Just tired. I haven't climbed so much in years. . . ."

"I'm sorry," Luap said. "I was trying to remember the turns—"

Arranha chuckled. "And I'd rather you remembered the turns, lad, than worried about me and forgot them. But we must mark the route, next time, eh?" In a few minutes he was able to stand. "I would like to see more—I would like to explore every passage and room—but I think we should return to your cave, Luap. My bones crave a night's sleep, with a blanket around me."

"We could come back and bring food," the Rosemage said. "And blankets. Spend a day or two here—"

"We can't leave the horses there, untended," Luap said. Then he and the Rosemage looked at each other, bright-eyed. "Bring them!" they both said. Luap went on. "We could explore more easily—see more—perhaps reach both ends of the valley in one day." He wondered if a horse would fit into that inner chamber. Its head, yes, but all of it? What would happen if all the horse didn't stand on the pattern? Surely it would all come, or all fail to come . . . not sever the beast. He shuddered. "Arranha's right," he said. "For now, we go back and have a night's rest."

Although he had not thought it took so long to go from the lower entrance to the great hall, when they emerged from the cave in Fintha, the last glow of sunlight was just fading from the sky. "I thought so," said Arranha, with some satisfaction. Luap presumed that meant his idea about distance and time, whatever it was, made sense to him.

"I'll feed the horses," he said, forestalling further explanation. Once more he led the tethered horses to drink, then fed them. Even after sunset, it was much hotter and stickier here than there; he missed the clean bite of that distant air. When he climbed back to the cave entrance, the Rosemage had a fire going, and had started cooking. He gathered more fallen branches for fuel, broke a few switches of flybane and stripped the leaves from them, and went back to rub the horses with the sticky sap. Arranha peeled redroots and sliced them for the pot, quietly for once. He offered no theories about the origins of redroots, the different ways they might be peeled or sliced. . . . Luap decided the old man was really tired.

He himself was tired, he realized, after sitting to eat the stew the Rosemage had prepared. He was stiff from the climbing, and mentally tired from the excitement. He wanted to talk about everything he'd seen, check his memories against theirs, and at the same time he wanted to fall asleep right where he sat. He took the pot to the river to clean it, and came back to find Arranha already asleep and the Rosemage yawning as she piled turf on the fire. So he lay down and dreamed all night of the red castles of his future home.

The next day dawned fair and hot. Luap woke early, and went down to water the horses. He wanted to escape to that cool, crisp air of the stronghold. He imagined what dawn might look like, rising above sheer red rock walls, the first sunlight spilling over the cliffs like golden wine. Here, the air lay heavy, a moist blanket on his shoulders; he was sweating already.

"It'll storm by nightfall," the Rosemage said. Her shirt clung to her, already sweat-darkened. She dipped a bucket in the river upstream of the drinking horses, and put her hand in. "It's hardly cool at all. Your country must be fierce in winter, but it's certainly cooler in summer."

"I know. I was wishing we could go back there today." He backed Arranha's mount out of the water, and fetched hers. "But we're short of fodder for the horses; we need to move on to the meadows and let them graze."

"They could graze there if we could get them there," she said. "If they'd fit into that chamber . . . but then they'd come out in the great hall. That's no place for horses." By the wrinkle of her nose, he knew she was thinking of the mess they could make, the damage they could do. True—that hall was no stable, and they would not have the means to clean it. And if a shod hoof damaged the pattern on the dais, could they get back? Best not to risk it. But he wanted to go back, wanted to taste that cold water again, breathe that air.

Arranha woke as they came back up. He, too, commented on the moist heat of the morning, and the difference from the crisp air in "Luap's country" as he called it. But he did not want to go back—not then. "At dawn, precisely, or sunset—yes. With a sand-glass to measure the time."

So after a cold breakfast, they saddled the horses and rode back toward Fin Panir. Just after midday, when they were too far from a village to find shelter, a violent summer storm broke over them, drenching them with rain so they rode the rest of the day with the odor of wet wool. Luap tried to fill his mind with the scent of those pines.

Raheli ran her hand along the shaft of the pike the yeoman had brought to replace one he'd broken in drill. Good seasoned wood, shaped well and rubbed smooth. She nodded her approval, and he grinned at her. He had the agility and grace of an ox, she thought, but made up for it with strength and goodwill. Now may I do as well, she thought, to amend my own faults. She had had so short a time with Gird to renew their family relationship, to feel how she might be truly an elder even without bearing . . . she still found herself mired in bitterness some days. She and Gird had not been meant to do new things, but to do old things well, she was sure. They had done new things because they must, not like those for whom this was their parrion.

Yet she did new things constantly. She had been listening to the women, since her visit to Gird, and even more since his death, noticing much she'd ignored before. She had, after all, lived in the one vill all her life until the day she still thought of as the day the war started. She had never been as far as a big market town, let alone a city; she had known nothing of how city folk lived, or peasant folk across the Honnorgat. Or even peasant folk before the magelords came. She listened to old grannies tell of their grannies' times; she listened to women who had the life she had lost, and women who wanted the life she had as a Marshal. Even mageborn women . . . they had not all been wealthy, arrogant mageladies who delighted in beating peasants. In fact, most of them were more human than she had imagined from meeting the Autumn Rose. She had met Dorhaniya now, and listened to stories that sounded much like those she'd grown up hearing at her own hearth.

So the burden that women wanted to place on her—the way they wanted to see her as the women's Marshal-General—bothered her less and less. She would not be *the* Marshal-General, but she could make sure that the code that bore his name remained fair to women. And that, she was convinced, began with women drilling in the bartons alongside men. Even to Gird, that had been what mattered: if the women risked the same in war, then they deserved the same from the law. Men could not argue against that, as they could if women did not willingly risk the same in times of danger. That women—as she knew from her own past—were always at risk did not help; being a victim won no respect.

Convincing the women of all that, in peacetime, was another matter. Once she thought of it, she quit accepting so easily the excuses that came to her, and applied the hard logic of the war she'd survived. If there were war, she said firmly to the woman (or more often man) who came to explain why Maia or Pir or Mali wasn't coming, she would learn to fight, or be killed. Have you all forgotten? Do you want to see the slaughter of untrained peasants again?

Gradually, she had increased the number of women in her own grange and bartons who actually appeared reasonably often of drill-nights. Ailing fathers and tired husbands found they could survive a cold supper; when they complained to Raheli, she suggested tartly that they come to drill with their wives and daughters. Some couples began to do so, and that heartened others. The young girls she caught early, insisting to their mothers that such drill would not make them unfit to bear. "I am barren because my husband and I did not know how to fight," she had said more than once. "Not because I fought in the war."

But it wasn't the reluctant ones who bothered her most. She had been reluctant herself; she knew what was in their hearts. And while she didn't share the feeling, she could understand those like Seri, who enjoyed drill for its own sake, and dreamed of using their weapons to protect others. No, the ones who bothered her were the few—usually town girls, she liked to think—who were eager to learn the drill, eager to learn weaponlore, and even more than that eager to shed someone else's blood. Those made her shiver. How could a girl, whose life should be risked in giving life, be eager to end it? She did her best to make explanations. This one had a brutal father; that one had been estranged from her natural family from birth.

If she had thought about it beforehand—and she hadn't—she might have thought that girls who had no interest in boys would be like that, but the difference between those who loved women and those who loved men ran across the difference between those who liked to hurt and those who did not. She herself had been angry, after Parin's death, after the loss of her child; she had been so angry she dreamed night after night of striking at others the blows that had struck her. She had expected to exult in mageborn blood, when her chance came . . . but in fact the first time she had hit an enemy she had almost dropped her weapon and apologized. The memory of that first battle in the forest, the feel of striking another human being, still came back to her on bad nights. She did not tell the young ones that—she had, after all, become good at soldiering, or she would not have survived—but she did not understand those who wanted to hurt others.

"Marshal?" A girl's voice brought her out of her musing. Raheli looked at her, noticing how the face had lengthened in the past year, how she had grown so much taller. This was not one of her problems, but a delight: a girl she would have been glad to have as a little sister.

"Yes, Piri?"

"The lads say you'll be looking among the junior yeoman for a yeoman-marshal—"

"Yes, from the eldest group. Whoever it is will be sent to another grange to work with that Marshal for a few years. Why?"

"Sent away—?"

"Yes. It would be hard on a lad to have his friends beneath him, wouldn't it?"

"Yes, Marshal." Piri had the dark hair and gray eyes common to this cluster of villages; now she flushed and looked down. "I just wondered, Marshal, if you ever thought of a girl."

"A girl? You?" Raheli was startled. Piri came to drill faithfully, but seemed perfectly suited to follow her two sisters into marriage. Had she quarreled with the boy she seemed most likely to marry?

"No—but there's Erial." As if anticipating her Marshal's reaction, Piri rushed on. "She's better at drill than most of the boys, she never gets tired, and she doesn't flirt."

"With boys," said Raheli drily. "She flirted with you last year, until you made it clear you preferred young Sim."

"Well . . . yes . . . but that won't cause any trouble because most junior yeomen are boys."

"And she asked you to ask me?" Raheli said.

"No . . . she didn't. I just thought . . ." Piti looked down. Raheli sighed. The two had been best friends as small children, then that simple relationship had been complicated for them by whatever god governed the loves of adults. Piri had a soft heart; she would not want to hurt her friend, but she felt uncomfortable with her.

"Piri, you're right that Erial is good in drill; she might make a good yeoman-marshal. But one thing any yeoman-marshal needs is a desire to take on that job. Yes, it would be easier on you if she moved away, or was busy with something like this . . . but none of

us can live Erial's life for her. She understands that you love Sim;
you must understand that she may not want to go away."

"If she asked would you consider her?"

"Piri, is she bothering you?"

"Not really—I mean she's not *doing* anything, but I know what
she's thinking about."

Raheli snorted. "I doubt it, child. Most of us think we can read
thoughts like scrolls, and yet we have no idea what's behind someone's eyes." She looked at Piri's red face thoughtfully. "Is it Sim?
Is he upset about Erial?"

Piti turned even redder. "He did say—that when I wasn't looking
he saw her watching me."

"Watching you. And Sim thinks no one has a right to look at
you but him, is that it? Boys! At that age, Piri, they're like young
bulls, jealous of everything. If he knew a sheep looked at you he'd
probably drive it away. No, lass: from what I've seen, Erial understands very well that you prefer Sim; she may not like it, but she's
no worse than you are and unless you have something more than
'Sim says she looks at me' you have no real complaint. What did
your mother say?"

"That Sim's a young cockerel crowing over his first pullet."
Raheli grinned; Piri's mother had come closer than she had. Sim
was much more gamecock than bull. "She said Erial'd been my
friend all my life and it was silly to fuss now. But I thought
maybe—"

"You thought maybe there was an easy way out that would please
Erial and Sim both, didn't you?" Piri nodded. "Piri, the easy ways
we see out of things are usually full of traps: think how we tempt
an animal into a pen. We make the gate look like the easy way out
of trouble. Learn to look on both sides of the gate before you walk
through it. Now. About Erial. If *she* wants to be a yeoman-marshal,
and she asks me, I'll consider it. Not for you, but for her and the
yeomen she will serve later. But she has to ask, and I don't want
you hinting to her in the meantime. Does Sim know you came
about this?"

"No, Marshal. It was my idea."

"Good. Then you don't tell Sim, because the way he is, he would
go straight to Erial and tell her."

Piti nodded, somewhat shamefaced, and turned to leave. Raheli
called her back.

"It wasn't a bad idea, lass, and I'm not angry. You're one that
doesn't like angry words or bickering: that's good. But sometimes
there are things worth angry words; you must have the courage to

endure the anger when it's needed. I know you have that courage, but you may not have recognized it yet."

Raheli was not surprised when Erial showed up later that day. Piri and Erial had been friends too long for communication to fail, no matter that certain words could not be said. Erial's approach, like Piti's, began obliquely.

"Marshal, do you think married women can become Marshals?"

"Become, or stay? A few wives commanded cohorts in the war, but those whose families lived preferred to return to them afterwards. I think it would be hard to do a Marshal's work and a wife's work as well. Even more, a mother's work. It would be like trying to be the wife of two families. Marshals are, in a way, the grange's wife and mother."

Erial grinned at her. "*You* are, Marshal, the way you visit everyone and help those in trouble."

"Good commanders were the same way: a cohort's not that different from a family. It needs food, healing, comforting, and someone to resolve disputes." Raheli wondered why Erial had started from that direction, but never missed a chance to teach. "Why did you ask—are you planning to combine the two?"

"No. You know better." Erial scowled and looked away.

"Some like you do, to have children. Half the time I see you, you've got all your cousins trailing behind; for all I knew you wanted some of your own."

"It's because my aunt's been sick; you know that. And they like to play marching games, but none of them remember the commands." Nonetheless, Erial had a sheepish look; Raheli suspected she enjoyed watching her cousins more than she would admit. She had lived with her aunt since her own mother died. "No—" Erial went on, sobering, "—it's about a friend, that I think would make a good Marshal, only she'd have to be a yeoman-marshal first, and she thinks she can't do that and be married."

"Piri," Raheli said, seeing no purpose in dragging this out.

"Yes, Pir. She used to talk about it a lot, learning to do what you do, protecting the vill—all until she got silly over Sim."

Raheli had no trouble with this one. "She's not 'silly over Sim'— she wants to marry him, and he wants to marry her. And I can't agree with you: Piri would not make a good Marshal except in wartime, if then—she had a youngster's taste for adventure, that's all, and now she's grown out of it." Erial opened her mouth, shut it, and scowled fiercely as a young wildcat.

"But I know someone else who would make a fine Marshal," Raheli went on. She hadn't meant to, but in thinking over the prospects earlier she'd realized just how outstanding Erial was. "If someone else wanted it, that is. Even though it would mean moving to another grange for part of her training, and who-knows-where after that." Erial turned red, then pale, and her eyes shone.

"Me?" she squeaked. It was a safe guess; there were only seven girls in the older group of junior yeomen, and Erial had to know she and Piri were by far the best.

"You." Raheli ticked off the reasons on her fingers. "You know the drill; you learn fast; you can teach—your cousins prove that. You have no betrothed to go into a decline when you leave. You don't stir up trouble with lads or lasses—"

"Sim's mad at me," Erial muttered.

"Sim's a young lad crazy about Piri, and jealous as . . . as a cockerel. That's not your fault. I'm not blind and deaf; I know how you've acted, and you haven't put pressure on Piri. Sim has. And you're the one who had that notion of being Marshal in the first place; Piri was following you, the way she always did until she veered off to follow Sim."

"You're saying I haven't grown out of it?" Erial asked in a shaky voice.

Raheli chuckled. "*And* you've got the resilience, the toughness, to survive some hard years with another Marshal, among strangers. And even more important to me, while you like the work and the weaponlore, you don't like to hurt people. Alyanya forbid, but if you ever had to fight in battle, you might like it more than I did— but you wouldn't turn cruel. I can trust you for that. So—do you want to be a yeoman-marshal?"

"Yes!" Erial said. Then her face fell. "No . . . no, I can't. There's my cousins; if my aunt dies—"

"We'll let Piri lead your cousins around for awhile: you'd trust her, wouldn't you? And if your aunt dies, the grange will help; you know you can trust me. Take your chance, Erial, when it comes. Unless you don't want it."

"I do." She glowed with delight; Raheli grinned at her.

"Now mind, you'll have some problems with the lads when they hear about it, and I don't want any nonsense. You're not a yeoman-marshal yet; I'll send you to—" And who would she send Erial to, who could be trusted? "—someone I trust," she said finally. She would have to look up the rolls; they really needed a better way of training youngsters who might become Marshals. Cob would be best, but did he have an opening? "Go on," she said. "I'll be along after awhile to talk to your aunt and uncle about you."

She sat at her desk, for once well content with her role as

Marshal and a woman other women could come to. It wouldn't always work out so neatly, any more than every loaf came from the oven with a perfect crust and crumb, but when it happened she could take pleasure in it. The next time she went to Fin Panir, she thought, she would bring up this matter of Marshals' training with the Council.

Chapter Thirteen

Luap and the others had been back in Fin Panir only a few days when Raheli arrived. She wanted, she said, to see what progress Luap was making on the *Life of Gird*. He showed her the racked scrolls of notes, explained about the interviews.

"Did you get the ones I sent?" she asked.

"Oh, yes. You are the only source I have for his early life, you know. Can you tell me anything more about his childhood? Anything that would fit well?"

"Fit well?"

"You know—something that would show the reader that he was going to be what he became. That story about his brother dying of an attack by wolves—where was Gird then? What did he do?"

Rahi stared at him. "Arin went out with the hunters; he was the elder. Gird stayed—you know my grandparents were still alive then, don't you?"

"I'm not sure." Luap pulled out the scroll she had sent and looked. "No—all you said here was that Arin died, and Gird succeeded to the tenancy."

Rahi frowned. "It's more complicated than that. It was before I was born; Arin and his wife Issa and their children, and Gird and my mother Mali, lived with their parents. Gird's and Arin's. The eldest son in each cottage could be called out for a hunt; I don't know if Arin had to go, or if he chose to, but he went with other men out to a distant sheepfold. When wolves came, he ran out after them; they tore him but were beaten off by others. Gird said when they brought him home, the steward came, and granted a sheep's carcass to the family. Even remitted the death-duty. But within a year, his father died, and the cottage and all the family

came to him. Issa and her children, his mother, his own children—
for I was born later that year."

"But Gird didn't go out to hunt the wolf that killed his brother?"

"No—the other men had killed most of them. And he had to do
the work Arin had done, as well as his own."

"It would have made a better story," Luap said. Rahi gave him
a strange look

"It's not a singer's tale," she said. "It's what really happened."

"Another thing I don't understand," Luap said, avoiding that
implied criticism, "is when he actually began working against the
magelords. From what you've written, and from what I heard others
say, his own liege was harsher than most, deliberately cruel."

"Indeed he was!" Rahi's face stiffened; her scar stood out white
as bone.

"Then Gird must have resented it all along; he was no man to put
up with cruelty lightly. Why didn't he join the Stone Circle earlier?"

"Do you think he never asked himself that?" She sounded angry;
Luap could not understand why. "Do you think no one else ever
asked? Why did he have to wait until the count's meanness killed
his mother and his wife, until starvation and disease picked off
children and friends, until his best friend died beneath the very
hooves of the lords' guard, until I—" She drew a long, shuddering
breath, and flushed and paled again. "Until they killed my husband
and nearly killed me, and I lost his first grandchild. Why did he
wait and wait? I don't know." She shook her head slowly; her accent
thickened. "I would not call it cowardice, nor stupidity. He knew
it was wrong; he knew it was worse; he thought—as much as I can
know what he thought—that the Stone Circle way would be no
better. It was throwing lives away, not saving them. He did give
grain, and pull his own belt tighter, that I know, once his friend
was killed. But he had sworn to follow Alyanya's peace, and seek
no mastery of steel."

"But *why?*" asked Luap. He had never heard Rahi speak even
this much of her father; he was fascinated.

She sat for some time in silence, her face grave. She, like Gird,
had gained weight with peace and prosperity; she had grown almost
massive, like a matron with many children. "You know he was once
in the count's guard," she said finally.

"I had heard that, back during the war; someone said it was
where he learned the craft of war. But others said he had been a
farmer all his life. Which was it?"

"I don't know this of myself," Rahi said. "I don't know if I should tell you; he never told me about it and I heard it only in bits and pieces, from my mother and the village women her age."

"If it made him the leader he was, it should go in his life," Luap said.

She nodded, slowly. "Very well—but understand that this is a tangled story, and I was a child when I heard it." He waved a hand to urge her on; she continued. "Gird was big and strong, even as a boy; the count's steward saw that and suggested he join the local guard. He trained part time, and his father had payment for his service. When he came to manhood, and would have been made a guard, the count chose to torture a boy who had stolen fruit, and Gird ran away. Arin—the same Arin the wolf killed—brought him back, and the count did not kill him, but the fine and the count's enmity destroyed my grandther's standing in the vill. So Gird gave up all thought of soldiering, and became a farmer in his father's cottage; he had learned, the women said, what came of following foreign gods of war."

"But he had been in long enough to have knowledge—" Luap prompted.

"No—it's before you joined, but remember that he spent that winter understone, with the gnomes. He said himself that what he learned from his old sergeant in the guards was to real soldiering as his own breadmaking was to my mother's. He knew a few things, more than the men who had just run away to live like animals in the woods—but he could not have led an army in war without the gnomish training." She stretched, then pushed herself out of the chair to prowl around his office and peer out the windows. "I think myself, Luap, that his very slowness, his very reluctance to oppose the magelords openly is what made it work. He had no hothead enthusiasm, no boyish illusions, such as I see in the lads and lasses in my grange, who dream of glory. He had a grown man's thought, slow but sure, and when he finally moved it was like a mountain shifting its place."

She looked back over her shoulder at him. "Of course, it would be nice to think he had been working against them secretly his whole life. If he had organized the Stone Circle, if he had planned it all. But if he had, that would mean he had planned to let his mother and mine die of fever, rather than risk the count's ban against harvesting herbs in the wood. It would mean he had planned to use the anger generated by one outrage after another to rouse the peasants . . . that his own anger was false, assumed for one occasion and put off for another. And a false man, Luap, could not have done what he did."

Luap felt hot. She had made no direct accusation, but he felt as he had often felt when Gird insisted on strict, literal truth where a little pruning of a tale would make it more effective. He had been thinking that she would like his story of Gird's life, the way he had emphasized what was really important, and treated the more noisome moments lightly, as necessary contrasts to the main theme. Now he felt uneasy about that.

"Now it's your turn," she said, smiling. "You have said you have part of it written, the part you know from your own experience. Read it to me."

He spread his hands. "Rahi, you've just told me things I didn't know, that will make some changes necessary. Not changes in what happened, but in what the events mean. I'm not writing for the people alive now, who knew him personally, but for those in the future to whom all our time will be as dim as eight generations back is to us. So I must make it clear not only what happened, but why—not only what Gird said, but what he thought."

She frowned at him. "I don't see why that would change anything from the war years."

"It would," Luap said firmly, now determined not to let her see the *Life* until he had added and adjusted and rearranged the new material. "Consider his interaction with the first Stone Circle group he met, for example. Cob has told me that they all thought he had been a soldier, not just a boy in training. It would have been different if he had been—"

"But the facts don't change," Rahi said. "What happened is what happened. At least for what you yourself witnessed, you should have no changes to make."

"I can't agree." He laid his hand flat on the work table. "When I have had time to consider what's already written, in light of what you've told me today, *then* I will show you—but not now."

She looked more puzzled than angry, though he had expected anger at any confrontation. "I don't understand, Luap. You wrote to tell me your *Life* was coming along well; you wanted me to see it; you clearly expected me to approve—and now you look like a man who knows someone else's gold has found its way into his pack."

"It's not that!" he said, feeling his ears redden.

"I didn't say it was—but I don't understand why you've changed your mind. Da said you had notions sometimes—"

Notions. Gird had said that about old women who accused each other of being witches. He had also said it about Luap, in one of their arguments. Luap struggled to find his dignity. "I do not have *notions,*" he said. "I am doing my best to make Gird's life memorable and accessible to people who never knew him. I want to do a good job. What you've told me today makes me realize that I haven't done as well so far as I thought. And I'd rather show it to you when I'm more satisfied with it myself."

"As you will." Rahi shrugged, as if to show she didn't care, but the tightness of her expression said otherwise. She was probably thinking *notions* even if she didn't say it again.

For the rest of that visit, she remained more pleasant than he expected, if somewhat cool. She did not quarrel with the Rosemage—in fact, Luap realized, she had not quarrelled with the Rosemage in a long time. She did not upset anyone at the Council meetings, except in quietly insisting that Marshals should accept and promote girls as well as boys in barton training.

"It's not necessary any more," Marshal Sidis said. "You know yourself Gird only allowed it because you started it, and you were his daughter. There's no reason for women to waste their time in training to use weapons, when there's no war."

"That's not so," Rahi said firmly. "You weren't there, but Cob can tell you—he was. Gird came to believe it was both necessary and right—the only fair way. Some say there's no reason for anyone to train, when there's no war—but without training, we'd have the same mess Gird started with. If we're to be safe from another invasion, we must know how to fight—and for the same reasons as last time, women need to know as much as men." She surprised herself by having little anger to control. Sidis, from the northwest, had hardly made it to the war before it was over; he had the title Marshal only because he had led his small contingent and Gird confirmed most such leaders as Marshals if they fought at all.

"The horsefolk women learn weaponskills," she added, "and they were never conquered by the magelords."

Sidis snorted. "No one can conquer them—they simply ride away."

The Rosemage shook her head. "The mageborn tried, Marshal Sidis, in the early years; they wanted to settle the rich pasturelands along the upper Honneluur but the horsefolk drove them back. And it's in our archives that the horsefolk women fought as fiercely as the men, making our defeat sure."

"That may be," said Sidis, "but if every glory-struck girl spends her days in the barton, who'll be weaving and baking, eh?"

"Do the glory-struck boys spend all their days in the barton, in your grange?" Rahi wasn't sure if it was his tone, or the dismissive gesture in which he had indicated that the girls were not serious, but now her anger stirred.

"Well, no, but—"

"And do you find they cannot learn to scythe a field or dig a ditch, because they swing a hauk at drill?"

"That's not what I meant, Marshal Raheli!" His use of her long name was the final flick of the lash.

"Wasn't it?" She had both hands flat on the table, the broad hands she had inherited from Gird; her mother's had been longer. "Have you forgotten, in the years of conquest, that *our* people know Alyanya's blessing comes with the gift of blood, and that women in birthing face the same death that comes in battle? Do you not think it might be well for girls to learn discipline and courage, that our people never fall to ungenerous hearts again? You sound as if you thought it was a bad habit our women picked up from the magelords."

"But then they want to be yeoman–marshals, and the boys complain if the girls are better. They don't think it's fair." Sidis said this as if it answered all objections, then reddened as he realized, from the expressions around the table, that it didn't. Cob almost choked on a laugh. Some laughed aloud. Even Luap smiled. Sidis shifted in his chair, and finally shrugged. "All right. You're Gird's daughter, and no one can argue with you about what Gird said. I still think—but what does that matter?"

"It matters," Rahi said. "It always matters, because what you really think will change the meaning of the words you say. If you think the girls are silly and glory-struck, while boys with the same visions in their heads are sensible and brave, every child in your grange will know it ... and the sensible, brave girls will find a reason to stay home. And they will be as I was, good young wives to be trampled underfoot of the first tyrant who comes to the door." He started to speak, but she shook her head at him. "No, Marshal Sidis, you must think again. I do not want some child like me, some young girl whose mind is all on baking and weaving, as you would have it, left with no way to defend herself. Even my father, even the man who led the army to victory, could not defend me when an enemy came: *that* is the hard truth of it. There's nothing glorious about a soldier's death, but a victim's death is worse. My father saw it that way, finally: he had seen me near death, when I had no chance to fight, and if I had died on the battlefield, it could not have been worse."

Cob raised his hand, and Rahi sat down. "She's right, Sidis," he said. "It's the old way, after all. Some even believed that women taking up weapons caused less disruption than men, because Alyanya's Curse could not apply."

"I never heard that." It was not quite a snort, but close.

Rahi leaned forward. "You're not a woman. The Lady of Plenty, Alyanya of the Harvests, requires that blood be given for any use of iron or steel in planting or harvesting, isn't that so?"

"Yes, but—"

"And for a man, that means his own blood on the blade: shovel, spade, plow, sickle, scythe, pruning hook, even the knife used to cut grapes. Some folk said—in our village it was said, but I know in others it was different—that Alyanya required the same for using a blade on an animal. Others said that sacrifice was to the Windsteed, or even Guthlac. A man who withheld his blood would be cursed, in his loins and his fields. But for a woman, Sidis, the Lady had already had her sacrifice of blood; a girl cut her thumb once only, to promise the blood of childbearing later, and could use an edged tool with no more concern for Alyanya's Curse. Even in Torre's Song, it is the wicked king who is cursed for bringing steel to flesh, while Torre herself . . ."

"All right." Sidis turned up his hand. "I submit. We shall have granges full of girls, and lads who cannot keep their minds on the drill—"

"If you make clear to them that death follows stray thoughts as an owl hunts mice, Sidis, they should be able to follow the drill. If a girl can distract them, I would hate to have them in battle." Cob, again, with a look at Rahi. "For that matter, look at young Seri, in training here. If it weren't for her, I suspect Aris would wander from healing to healing, help Luap with scribes' work, and never take drill at all. That girl would make a yeoman worthy of any grange, and she's been nothing but good for a dreamy-minded mageborn lad with more talent than sense."

Rahi thought better of Aris than that, but she agreed about Seri. She knew that Seri had cheerfully dealt with a couple of lads who were at the age to see her as a girl, not a fellow-yeoman. Her Marshal had told the tale for a season afterwards. "She wasn't angry, and she didn't make any fuss," he'd said. "Just bashed them once each, told them not to be silly, and got on with it. Now they're her friends, and they've quit smirking at the other girls, as well. Do their courting at the dances, like they should."

Sidis still looked angry and stubborn; despite herself Rahi felt a twinge of pity for him. She hated being argued down, herself, and she knew he would have to come to this on his own before he would really believe it. She tried to think of some way to make it easier for him. Nothing came to her; she wished she had her father's power. Then she remembered how often he had stopped an argument with his fist, and a snort escaped her. Sidis glared.

"I'm sorry," Rahi said. "It's just—I remember Da—Gird— settling matters with his fist. I didn't like it, but here I am doing the same thing with words. I think you're wrong, Sidis, but you have a right to be wrong as long as it takes to change your mind. I don't want you agreeing with me just because I'm Gird's daughter, or Cob is one of the most senior Marshals. Gird himself thought we should talk things out, even if he stopped the talk sometimes; he was right in that."

"I don't understand you," Sidis said. "You change your mind—"

"No. I don't. But I won't try to change yours by force."

He still looked confused, but he nodded. When the time came to vote on the matter, he waited until he saw how the others voted. Then he shrugged. "It worked for Gird," he said. "So why not? We can always change it back if we're wrong." And he tossed his billet on the pile for retaining women's rights in the grange organization.

After the meeting, Rahi was packing her things for the journey back to her grange when Sidis sought her out. "I wanted you to know it wasn't you I objected to, or any of the women who were actually veterans," he said "But most women up where I'm from didn't fight—in fact, most of the men didn't fight. They see the grange drill as something imposed from outside; it's the women who've pestered me to send their daughters home."

"So they don't see the worth of it, eh?" Rahi sat down, and waved at him to do the same.

"Aye. It was on the edge of the magelords' holdings, and even I remember that things weren't too bad until after the war started. That's when our Duke—the Duke that was—raised the fieldfees and imposed stiffer fines. We had less bad to fight about, and more to lose, and there's feeling now that the grange system's as bad as the magelords' stewards ever were."

Rahi whistled. "Perhaps they don't think they need anyone at all, is that it?"

Sidis twisted a thong and untwisted it. "That's what it seems, most times. They're good folk, but they don't look ahead much, and they think they can deal with their own lives better than anyone else." He looked troubled, someone telling an unpleasant truth about people he cared for. "I've wondered myself, now the mage- lords are gone, what we need all this drill for. I come here, and you all seem to know things—it comes clearer, like. But how I'll explain it to them—"

"Maybe they should do without a grange for awhile." Rahi leaned back against the wall, watching his face. He didn't say anything at first. "If they don't want it, if they aren't supporting it—maybe they have to feel the need first. Da always said you can't convince an ox it will need water in the middle of the work when you show it a bucket at dawn. You could find another place . . . even here."

"But—" His hands worked the thong back and forth, back and forth. "It's losing, that is. Giving up. If there's a grange somewhere, it should stay—"

"Not if it's not wanted." Rahi felt her way into this argument, hoping she was right. "We're not here to make things worse, after all. The granges started because people wanted them. It's true there has to be some kind of law—if those folk come to market in a town with a grange, they'll have to abide by the Code. But if it sticks in their throats, why not let be?"

"The other Marshals," Sidis muttered. "They talk of their granges growing, of founding new bartons. They'll think I did something wrong."

Rahi opened her mouth to deny that, and then stopped. To be honest, *she* thought he'd done something wrong. He'd come into the war, and then his position as Marshal, without any real conviction. And if she thought so, others might as well. She could not reassure him with her dishonesty. "If you made a mistake," she said, picking her words as carefully as she would have picked through a bundle of mixed herbs, sorting them, "—if you did something wrong, it sounds to me that your folk have made mistakes as well. You couldn't have done all the wrong. Our whole system began with the people, the peasants. If they aren't with us, we have nothing. Pretending we do leads right back into what the mageborn did, all that pretense about the lords protecting the people, and the people serving the lords. If the folk in your grange don't want a grange, it won't be a real grange no matter what you do."

His brows had drawn together, but his hands were still. "Some do—at least—"

"If they want it, they will make it work. Think about it."

"What would you think, Raheli, Gird's daughter, if I let the grange go—closed it, or however it's done?"

Rahi looked past him, seeing against the far wall of the room a stream of images from the war, and the years after. What might it have been like, to live in a village with a better lord than Kelaive? Or with no lord at all? Could there be farmers, village folk, who did not understand in their bones what the grange was for, and how it worked? Apparently so. "I would think you had tried," she said. "I hear the truth in your voice. But it's not my decision." She could not tell what Sidis thought of what she said; he merely nodded and went away, leaving her to ride out of Fin Panir later that day still wondering.

She took that uncertainty with her back to her own grange, and looked more carefully at the people who did not choose to come. She had heard no grumbling for some time, but did that mean satisfaction? Or that people grumbled where she could not hear them? She was not surprised when a letter from Fin Panir reported that Sidis's grange had dissolved, and he himself had given up his Marshalship. She hoped they would fare well, and hoped that her words had not formed his decision.

It was half a year before she came to Fin Panir again. Luap had finished his *Life of Gird,* and the Council wanted her approval. From the tone of the letter, she wondered what the other Marshals thought of it. They might have sent a copy, instead of a letter, surely it would have been easier to send the scrolls here, instead of dragging her to Fin Panir in the busiest time of the year.

A copy of the original awaited her in Fin Panir; the young yeoman who led her to a small room opening on an interior court pointed to it. "Luap said that was for you, as soon as you arrived."

Rahi stretched out on the room's narrow bed, and unwrapped the scroll. Luap's fine, graceful handwriting moved in even lines; she found it easier to read than her own crabbed script. "In the days of the magelords, in the holdings of one Count Kelaive, was born a child who would grow into Gird Strongarm, the savior of his people." Rahi wrinkled her nose at that. A bit flowery, not much like Gird himself.

She read on, her thumb moving down the scroll and holding it open. It couldn't be exactly like Gird, she reminded herself, because Luap hadn't known the young Gird. Even she had only village tales to rely on. But she felt uneasy, as if a hollow bubble were opening in her chest. She could not say, at first, just what it was, but something . . . something was definitely wrong. She put the scroll down and lay back for a moment. Would anyone else notice it? Did it matter, when so far as she knew, no one else had survived from their village?

She picked up another scroll, and began reading. This was set during the war; Gird was enjoying a mug of ale in a tavern—she stopped again, trying to remember. Tavern? When had they been in a tavern? The drinking she remembered had been in various camps in the woods; by the time the army was taking towns, he had not been drinking that much. She looked at the scroll more closely. It was, she decided after a bit, intended to be funny: the great war-leader relaxing with ale, becoming excited, almost starting a fight. Her shoulders felt tight; she remembered how dangerous Gird could seem, in those rare drunken rages from her childhood. It had not been funny at all. And worse than that . . . this was not real; she could think of no time when it really happened. She scanned along the scroll, looking for some reference, and found it. This was supposed to have happened after the capture of Bright-water, and before Shetley, but she remembered that time as clearly as the past half-year . . . Gird had not been in any tavern; he had been off trying to persuade brigands to join the army.

Luap had made it up. He had made up a good story, as men often did, but then he had put it in this work, which was supposed to tell Gird's story for all time. Rahi felt cold, then hot. How much had he made up? Was that what bothered her about the first scroll? She snatched it up, and read it carefully, with growing anger.

"You're not telling the truth!" Rahi's voice went up. Luap managed not to wince visibly. He had been afraid she would not appreciate what he had done, how he had turned the story of an ordinary farmer-turned-soldier into the shape of legend.

"I am telling the truth—I'm telling what it meant. That's what they need to know, not every little detail."

"It's a lie." She glared at him, Gird with brown hair and breasts, the glare he remembered all too well. "You're making it into a story . . . a song, like the harpers sing, that everyone knows is just a tale."

"Raheli, listen! If the harpers change the kind of tree a prince hid behind, because it rhymes—oak, say, instead of cedar—that helps the listener remember. It doesn't change anything important. The prince still hid behind a tree: that's what matters. If they say half Gird's army wore blue, when it was one person less than half, or almost two-thirds, why does that matter? The point is that we won at Greenfields. That's all I'm doing. I'm making sure people remember what it meant—what his kind of life meant—and they won't make sense out of the real details. You didn't yourself."

Would it work? For a moment he thought it had; her gaze flick-ered, as she thought about her own reaction. But then the angry glare came back.

"You're turning him into a lovable old gran'ther, using even his lust for ale—"

Luap shrugged that off. "Most men like ale; it makes him more human—"

"He *was* human! And his liking for ale cost us lives, you know it did."

"That's not the point—"

"It *is*, and it would have been *his* point. Was his point, at the last, remember? There's nothing good about it. . . . I remember after—" A long pause; he wondered which *after* she was seeing. "After my mother died, a bad stretch then; he came home drunk and sour with it, angry with everyone—"

"He had cause," Luap offered, sympathy he did not really feel.

"Everyone has cause," Rahi said. "But some do better. He did, later. And if you make it endearing, you diminish him—what it cost him to stop it, to change." In her eyes, *I never did that*, defiance but not quite pride. He knew she didn't, had sought, without admitting it, evidence that she was as fallible as Gird. As far as he could find out, she made none of Gird's mistakes; no drinking, no carousing, no wild flares of temper. Frustrating. He had never been able to maneuver Gird while Gird lived, and he could not maneuver Raheli, either.

He shrugged, as close to discourtesy as he allowed himself with her. "I'll change it back, then. You're his daughter; it has to please you—" He expected an explosion; instead he got a flat stare, and her nostrils widened as if she'd smelled something dead.

"I'm not . . . you're trying to make me feel bad about that, and I won't have it. He said you were slippery, and he was right about that." If nothing else. She didn't have to say that; it hung between them, something on which they agreed. She took a deep breath, and tried again. "I'm not asking you to improve the tale to please me; quite the contrary. I want you to tell the truth. Just the plain truth." If you can. He heard that, as if she'd shouted it.

"Even you don't believe the plain truth," he said, accenting "plain" just a little. "You weren't here; you're convinced it was something else than what we said."

She shook her head, the dark hair tossing back in a movement he remembered from his wife. His mouth dried. "*You* said things I found hard to believe—"

"Then ask the others! I know you did—"

She prowled his study, a thundercloud ready to burst. "What they said made even less sense."

His temper flared. "Then believe what you like! If I lie, and the others talk nonsense, what will you have in the chronicles, eh? Shall we just forget him, and all he tried to do?"

"You know I don't mean that." Again that level gaze. "We can't just forget him. But—"

He would try sweet reason, though it had never yet swayed her. "You hate having to hear it from me. You don't trust me; you never have, not even as much as Gird himself did, and you wish you'd been here yourself. Well, so do I. Then you could tell me what to write, and—" He stopped himself from saying *and if you lie, it's your oath forsworn, not mine.*

"I would not have said to turn a dark cloud into a dark beast," she said firmly. "Even if I'd seen such a cloud."

"I'll change it," Luap said. He could always change it back. "I simply have no idea how to write of *that* cloud so anyone years hence will know what I mean."

"Do you know what you mean?" That with a shrewd sidelong look that took his breath away, the very look Gird had given him so often.

"I—no. No, I don't. It seemed—I told you—as if all the wicked thoughts and shameful fears in every heart had taken visible form, a black blight thicker than a dust storm. But *what* it was ... I daresay only Gird himself knew. The words he spoke, that scoured it, lifted it, condensed it—those were no human words. I know that, and I've asked the elves—"

"And they said ?"

"They found I could not recall the shape of the words, could not repeat them—and indeed, it was as if they slipped past my ears—and would say only that Adyan might be pleased with Gird."

"And then he died, while you stood there doing nothing." That was unfair; he seized that unfairness and cloaked himself in honest resentment.

"It was the gods' will; none of us could move. I cried—dammit, Rahi, I told you that, and others must have—"

"Yes." She had turned away. He waited. Finally she turned back; her eyes were dry. "You cried; I cannot cry yet. Tears are cheap."

He hated her. He felt he had always hated her; he willed himself to forget the times he had been sure he loved her, when (surely) he had only loved her father, and of her father only that part she herself could not share. "Your tears," he said formally, in as steady a voice as he could manage, "your tears you can name the worth of. It is your right. The tears of others you have no right to shame." He felt dark, dire, brooding as a storm-cloud low over the western hills. Great, and in some sense noble, to chide her about that, standing up for the tears (he could almost feel his gathering to fall) of plain, simple men who rarely cried, whose tears tore apart the rock walls of their souls, great floods that ripped mountains asunder. He looked up to find her watching him, that flat peasant stare (how had he ever thought it attractive?), that hard mouth with no sweetness, a dried haw withered on a dead stem.

"You're too poetic," she said. "You will make it all pretty, make all the patterns match at the edges, as they do in the rugs we took from the mageborn houses . . . better you should learn from village weavers, who leave one corner open for the pattern's power to stay free, and able to work."

"You don't understand." She didn't. She couldn't. She could but she wouldn't. He did not know which, but only that she did not understand.

"Nor you." Her back to him now, a back broader than a woman's ought to be, shoulders bulking more than his own. He had an excuse, a scholar's hours, but she had no excuse for looking (to his now critical eye) like a stubborn ox. "I'll see you in Council," she said, and left the room without looking back. Luap's mouth held a dry bitterness; he made himself sit back down at the desk, but could not find words to pen. Council meetings had been going so well, until now; Raheli would ruin all that, he was sure.

Chapter Fourteen

And so she did. He did not know to whom she'd spoken when she left his office, or what she said, but from the way some Marshals looked at her she had spoken her mind. Whether about Gird or about him, Luap did not know. Others, who had heard she was in the city, but had not seen her yet, greeted her almost with reverence.

"Lady," said one, then actually blushed. "Rahi, I mean. Marshal. We're sorry we—"

"I know," she said, taking his hands in hers. It was, Luap thought, a very dramatic gesture. "Were you there yourself?"

"Not then, no—but I'd been out in the drillfields, and it didn't take long—"

"It's all right," she said. "I understand." Did she indeed, Luap wondered. Did she begin to understand what she was doing, with her fierce determination to leave Gird's life as blocky and unshaped as it had been in actuality? Why could she not realize that no story lived without shaping, without trimming here and filling out there? The point was to have Gird remembered.

Later that day, he hugged this certainty around him as he came into the Council meeting, expecting trouble from her, and those other Marshals who had not liked his *Life of Gird* as much as others. He had been able to hold them off by reminding them that Raheli, as Gird's daughter, must have some say. He had expected her to understand his purposes a little better than she had, to defend him to the others. Now—now it was going to be difficult.

Cob met him just outside the meeting room, and shook his head, though he smiled. "Luap, I could have told you not to try polishing clay. I know—you were trying to make the story fit the old songs, but you should have realized it would never pass Rahi."

Luap managed to smile back, shrugging. "I thought I'd done a good job, until she raked me over about it. I really think that of Gird, you know. I think he's that special."

"Special, yes. But Gird's old gray horse—can you imagine it tricked out in flowers and braids and a golden bridle? It was a horse for such a man: strong and brave, not a fancy magelady's pony. So with Gird—he never wore a fine shirt to the end of his life, and knew better than to try it. You've put lace on a plough, Luap, and neither the lace nor the plough looks the better for it." Then Cob's arm came around his neck. "But I will say, Luap, that it's the most *gorgeous* story I ever read, even though not much like Gird. Life would've been easier with your Gird running things."

The others, once the Council convened, took the copies of the *Life* which Luap had made for them, and Cob suggested that Luap explain his work.

"You probably know already that Marshal Raheli, Gird's daughter, doesn't like what I've done." Better get that out of the way first; they would realize he was being honest. "What I thought— what I wanted to do, was write a *Life of Gird* that would live through the generations, and show why we reverence him. He did more than just raise the peasants in a revolt and win the war . . . we know that. He tried to make a way for mageborn and peasant to live in peace with one another. He tried to devise a fair law which all could use." He paused and drew a deep breath, looking beyond the table out the window into a darkening courtyard. "It seemed to me that Gird was too large to fit on my page; I could not find the right words for him as he really was. So I read in the archives, all the lives of the old kings and warriors, and what we know of the songs the elves make, and tried to shape what I wrote

into something men and women could remember and chant by the
fireside a hundred sons' sons' lives from now. Gird is a greater hero
than any I found in the tales; it seemed to me I must show that
in the way I wrote of him." He sat down, with a nod to Raheli,
now calm and composed.

Marshal Sterin raised his hand, then stood. "I read Luap's *Life
of Gird* two hands of days ago. It seemed to me very fitting for
what Gird accomplished: perhaps more splendid than strictly necessary, but as Luap says, making clear to the future why Gird was
great. It's true I found some of the phrases flowery, but if that is
the mode in which men have always written of heroes, why not?"
He sat down abruptly, as if he'd finished any argument. Raheli
raised her hand, and at their nods stood in her place.

"He's a hero to you, to everyone: he *saved* everyone." She swallowed; her lips firmed. "He didn't save me." Before anyone could
answer that, she went on. "Oh, I know, that isn't fair. He didn't
want it to happen; he tried to fight and was outnumbered; he saved
my life after. But the plain fact is that he did not save me, and
what I remember includes that. My suffering was the price of his
action; he waited until afterwards to start fighting."

Luap closed his eyes a moment. Against the inside of his lids,
he saw his wife's face, the wife who had died—he had heard how
terribly—in a village market square because he had not protected
her. Gird had seen Raheli, but he had been able to heal her—or
at least get her away—while his own wife ... *You would not be*
her *hero, if she had lived,* his conscience told him. I am no one's
hero, he thought sourly, and opened his eyes again to find Rahi
watching him with all Gird's intensity. Her face changed; he wondered what had come into his.

"I'm sorry," she said. "Your wife—"

"Never mind." He waved that away; he could not tell Rahi what
he'd told Gird, that he had not really loved his wife until he saw
her dragged away, weeping in fear and shame. He hoped Gird
hadn't told anyone else, but he would not ask if she knew. "I can
see what you're saying, Rahi, but do you think it is valid for everyone? He did not save you, as I did not save my daughter, but does
that make what he did less important? Or less important that the
future should know about him?"

Cob stood, and looked around the table. "Most of you know that
I was with Gird from the first forest camp. Except for Raheli,
there's none else can say that now. I was there the day he came,
with his son Pidi and his nephew, a man near dead with grief but
determined to make something come of it. And that's when Raheli

still lay near death with woundfever and childfever, so though she is his daughter, I knew him longer as a leader in war." He grinned. "That's to stop anyone saying he knows what Gird would have wanted. I admit I don't. He was a plain man, and plainspoken, rough as the bark on an oak, but he knew as well as anyone the value of the old ways of saying things. And I've known our Luap from the day he first came, as well. To my mind, he's served Gird honestly all these years, and endured the taunts of them that didn't serve half as well. That's to stop anyone saying that what I say next comes from jealousy or dislike of Luap. It's not. I like him more now, and trust him more now, than I did that first year."

"Well then? What's your complaint?" asked Sterin, a bit flushed. Luap knew, as they all did, that Sterin had hardly met Gird before the war ended. He had organized and fought with a grange far from Gird's army; he had earned his Marshal's rank honestly, but resented the easy familiarity of those who had been Gird's friends.

"It's what I told Luap, before coming in here." Cob grinned at Luap, who could not help smiling back. Cob and Gird were wood from the same tree; whatever elevated Gird to greatness had been added to, not changed from, the essential peasant identity. "He's put lace on a plough; he's made Gird all smooth and easy, even his mistakes made decorative. Gird was a hero, right enough, but he was a plain man first: good bread and water—yes, and ale—not fine pastries and sweet wine. If the future knows him as a hero just like others, what good will it do them? He can help only those that remember him as he was."

"If he's remembered at all." Luap murmured that, not having permission to speak, but Cob turned to him sharply.

"Luap, he will be remembered. If not by your writing, then by fireside tales—and I grant—" He held up his hand. "I grant those tales and songs are likely to be even more astray. We've all heard some of them. But for this, for the story we most want told, I for one would like you to make it more like the man, plainer."

Luap nodded, expecting the vote that came. He would rewrite the *Life of Gird,* both now and again . . . and again, when some peoples' narrow ideas had died with them. He would not falsify— he *had* not falsified—what had happened, but he would choose his own way of saying it.

By the time they had settled other business, and finished the meeting, Rahi had cooled down. She came to him quietly, when the others had left.

"I know you don't agree," she said. "I know you thought you were doing the best for Gird's memory. You may think you'll outlive all of us, and maybe you will. But think about what Cob said, not my words alone. I am not that important; what happened to me happened to many, and I believe Gird would have come to his decision even without that. It might have made a neater pattern if Gird had been different. But he wasn't different; he was what he was, and it's that—the man he really was—that you must celebrate. The same man who did nothing all those years is the one who led us to victory, and at his death accomplished what his life could not. It makes no pretty pattern, but it's what really happened. He never asked anyone to believe something of him they had not seen; his *Life* must show what he really was, for that is what will help later."

Luap managed to smile. "I will do my best, Rahi." She asked no more, but went on out. He would do his best, his very best, to make Gird's life live in memory. She might not like it, but she might not be there to complain.

It occurred to him then that this might be another reason to move his people to the distant stronghold. There he could produce Gird's life as he knew was best, without interference. If—as seemed likely, given their age and health—he outlived the older survivors of the war, he might find less resistance to his version of events.

The only problem was that he could not tell his people where he was leading them because he still had no idea where that land lay from Fin Panir. Arranha's curious method of determining sun-wise distance had not been proven right in theory, let alone accurate. Besides, it would not work for distance summerwards or winterwards. It would not help at all to start riding west in the hope of finding the place; as narrow as those clefts and valleys were, they could ride right past it and never find a thing. Perhaps he should ask one of the elves or dwarves who would be in Fin Panir for the spring Evener: surely they would know where it was.

A few days later, he found time to ask Arranha's advice. The priest's study, with its broad work table and two chairs, looked out on the little sunlit courtyard where he often sat. But the spring sun had not melted all the snow in the corners. The old man sat by the window, wrapped in a parti-colored knit shawl, in a chair softened with pillows, looking far more frail than Luap expected.

"Ask the Elder Races? Of course—that's what I said in the first place." Arranha did not look up from the scroll he was reading; Luap recognized his own handwriting. "This bit here, in your *Life of Gird*—are you sure this is how it happened?"

Luap felt himself reddening. "I'm changing some things," he said. "Surely you heard that the Council asked me to."

Arranha waved a dismissive hand. "That's to be expected.

Nothing would please everyone the first time around. But I don't recall this conversation." He pointed, and Luap craned his neck to read the passage. He sighed.

"I was trying to make clear Gird's reasoning," he said. "At the time it seemed muddled, but later we could all see how it made sense."

Arranha looked up at him. "Luap, if you are telling the tale of people stumbling around on a dark night, you can't bring sunrise earlier so that you can see them stumble around. I remember this; Gird's reasoning *was* muddled, and it became clear later only because he himself straightened it out. If you make it too neat, it's not real."

Luap threw himself into the other chair in Arranha's study. "So I have been told," he said, trying not to let the resentment he felt color his tone. "Evidently I misunderstood the whole purpose of writing Gird's story. I thought the important thing was to have him remembered for what he did: freeing the peasants from oppression, establishing a new and fairer law, and his final sacrifice. I thought the details didn't matter, so long as people understood the structure of his life. That's why you can't write a life in progress: it has no shape yet. The shape you think you see cannot be the real shape."

"That's true enough, but—"

"But the Council—and now you—seem to think the details of the embroidery are as important as the design. I'm sorry. I thought making the whole design clear and easy to see was more important." He ran his hand up and down the chair's arm, enjoying even now the smooth curves and fine texture of the carving.

Arranha looked at him, that clear gaze which even Gird had found disconcerting. Luap remembered Gird telling the story of their first meeting, how the gaze of the old man's eyes unsettled him. "If you had been telling the story of a more conventional hero, I might agree: leave out the little inconsistencies. But Gird was in no way conventional, as we all know. He transcended all the easy definitions; he was a tangled mat of contradictions, heroic knotted firmly to unheroic. He fits no pattern, Luap, and it is that which you must make clear. Not trim and tuck and pad the old man to fit an existing model." He tilted his head slightly. "Why does this bother you? Why are you so determined to make Gird like any other hero of legend?"

Luap tried to subdue his anger, knowing that would move Arranha no more than it would have moved Gird himself, though for different reasons. His hands had clenched; he opened his fingers consciously, forcing himself to calmness. "Because I think that's what people remember. That's why the heroes of legend *are* alike, because that's what it takes for people to believe in them. If I told Gird's story exactly as it was, some would say he was no hero at all. They would disbelieve in his greatness precisely because it fit no pattern. Such a man, they would argue, could not have done those things; the gods would not work with someone who failed so often, and remained so muddled for so long. Even his death: think, Arranha—will any description in words of that cloud of malice and fear convince someone generations hence that Gird's death was more than a sick old man's vision? I can almost hear someone complaining that it was not enough, that he had done nothing to deserve the gods' favor, that cleansing all of us from all the dark desires of our hearts was less than killing a monster of flesh and blood."

"But it was more, of course," said Arranha.

"Of course it was." Luap heard his voice go up, and took a deep breath. "It was far more than that; we all knew it who lived through it. But later—I think of those in the future, Arranha, who will not have even the shadow of a real memory handed down from grandparents. To say that Gird was, for most of his life, as confused, frightened, and ignorant as they are will not make them believe in his greatness later. To say that he died uttering strange words, with no mark or wound upon him . . . well, so do many old people die, and if their families feel a sudden wave of relief and joy that the elder's struggle is over, that's no proof of the gods' intervention."

"So you do not trust Gird's own people to understand his real life?"

Luap shook his head. "No, I don't. I read all the old legends I could find, Arranha, and had the elders tell me the legends they recalled—of their own folk, not just mageborn tales. There's a difference, of course. The mageborn legends all name their heroes prince or king, princess or queen; the peasant legends are full of younger sons and daughters, talking animals, and the wise elder. But they still follow a pattern. The young hero looks like one—it's clear to friends and family that this is the hero. The hero never works with the evil he overcomes—he never submits to it. And he always knows what he's doing. I'll grant you, after knowing Gird I doubt this has always been true. But it's what people believed to be true, believed enough to remember. If I show Gird too different from that pattern, I don't think his legend will survive."

Arranha nodded. "Your reasoning is clear. But for that reason I suspect it's faulty in dealing with the life of someone who could no more reason than a cow can fly. Gird *felt* his way along, knowing the right as a tree knows good soil, by how it flourishes. In all my life, I never knew another like him, someone so infallible in his perception of good and evil, whose taproot sought good invisibly, in the dark. I learned from watching him that those with none of Esea's light—inspiration, intelligence, what you will—may have another way to seek and find goodness. Because Gird, as we know and can say with utmost respect, was not a man given to intelligent reasoning. Shrewd, yes, and practical as a hammer, but incapable of guile, which comes as naturally to intelligent men as frisking does to lambs." He laughed, shaking his head. "And I have only to think of Gird to find myself mired in agricultural images: listen to me! Cows that can't fly, tree roots feeling their way through the soil, frisking lambs—that's Gird talking through me, or my memory of him."

Luap could barely manage a smile in response to that. He felt colder than the raw early-spring day. He had not felt Gird's memory come alive while he was working on the *Life;* he had not felt Gird's presence at all, since the first days after his death. And if Arranha felt it, if others felt it, was that why they did not agree on his way of telling the story? Because they felt so close to Gird, they could not understand that distant ages would not have that feeling? He could not think what to say, how to ask the questions in his mind that troubled him without taking definite form. He waited a moment, one finger tracing the floral carving of the chair-arm, then reverted to his first topic.

"So you think I should ask the elves or dwarves where that pattern took us?"

Arranha's brows rose. "Yes, I said that. I admit I'm surprised you haven't already done so, though I suppose you've been too busy . . ."

"I felt—I wanted to finish Gird's *Life* first. But now—it will take me as long to rework it, and even then they may not like it. I just thought—"

Arranha's smile was sweet, understanding, without a hint of scorn; it pierced him just as painfully as Arranha's disapproval. "You just thought of your secret realm, a place of refuge. Quite natural. Yes, by all means ask them. But think of this, Luap: what will you do if they claim it as their own realm, in which we are not welcome?"

That had occurred to him before; he knew that was the root of his reluctance to ask. What is never asked cannot be refused: an old saying all agreed on. "The day I took Gird," he said, having thought long about it, "we saw at first only two arches, which I had seen before. But another appeared—"

"Gird saw this?"

"He saw three arches; I had seen but two, and saw two when we first arrived. You saw the third that is there now, with the High Lord's sigil upon it. When I told him there had been but two, he felt—I think he felt, for I admit he did not say it thus—that our presence, or at least his human presence, had been accepted." Luap had no idea himself what the appearance of that third arch meant, but trusted Gird's interpretation.

"I wonder if they'll see it that way. But better to find out now, before you take a troop out there and find you're intruding and not welcome. Will you ask the elven ambassador first, or the dwarves?"

"I had thought the elven. The legends say they're the Eldest of Elders."

"They will ask," Arranha said, "why you did not ask them before. Gird's will could not have withheld you past his death, not in their eyes."

Luap knew they would ask exactly that: another reason he had not asked.

The elven ambassador arrived a few days before the Evener. Luap had never been sure why the elves chose to recognize Gird or his successors; they had not, Lady Dorhaniya told him, ever come to the court in her lifetime. But from the first year of Gird's rule, an elf or two had come at Midwinter, Midsummer, and the two Eveners, at first asking audience with Gird, and then with the Council of Marshals Then the dwarves had begun to appear, on the same festivals, glaring across the Hall at the elves, who ignored them except to proffer an icily correct greeting. Some of Gird's followers preferred elves, and some preferred dwarves—the dwarves, Luap had heard, made good gambling and drinking companions. He himself found elven songs too beautiful to ignore.

This elf he recognized: Varhiel, he had said, was the closest human tongues could come to his real name. He stood taller than Luap as most elves did, a being of indeterminate age whose silver-gray eyes showed no surprise at anything. He greeted Luap in his own tongue and Luap made shift to answer in the same. He had discovered a talent for languages, both human and other; he particularly enjoyed the graceful courtesies of the elves. When the preliminaries were over, Luap felt his heart begin to pound. He should ask now, before he changed his mind. . . .

"When Gird was alive," he said, "I found a place which might have been elven once."

Varhiel raised his brows. "Once? What made you think it is not still elven ?"

"I found no elves there, or sign of recent habitation," Luap said. His palms felt sweaty. Why was this so hard?

Varhiel shrugged. "Perhaps it is a place we do not frequent; perhaps you came between habitations. . . but I doubt a place once ours would be abandoned." He picked a hazelnut from the bowl on Luap's desk and cracked it neatly between his fingers. "Where did you say this was?"

"I'm not entirely sure." Luap took a hazelnut himself, cracking it on his desk. He pushed across a basket for the shell fragments. "It's a long story . . ."

"Time has no end," the elf said He leaned back in his seat with the patience of one who will live forever, barring accidents.

Luap wondered what it would be like to feel no hurry, no pressure from mortality. He pushed that thought aside, and began his tale. Necessarily, since the elf could not be expected to take an interest in minor human affairs, he left out much of it. He told of his first visit to the cave, of his discovery of his mage powers, and of the later discovery that the cave and those powers transported him somewhere.

"Say that again!" The elf's gray eyes shone. "You travelled—?"

"Somewhere," Luap said, nodding. For a moment he felt he had been saying that word forever, telling one after another that he went *somewhere,* to meet the same incredulous response each time. "I don't know where. That's why I'm talking to you."

"Say on." The elf's wave of hand was anything but casual.

Luap tried to read the elf's expression as he described the great hall in which he had arrived, the arches out of it . . . and then Gird's journey.

"You took *another* there before asking our permission?" Luap had never seen an elf angry, but he had no trouble interpreting that.

"Gird was my. . . lord," he said. "He held my oath; all I learned went to him first." Then he realized that "there" had been said with complete certainty. "You know where it is?"

"Of course I know. And it is not a place for you latecoming mortals. You must not go again." The elf looked hard at him. "Or have you been more than those two times?"

"When Gird came," Luap said, side-stepping the question, "another arch appeared. One with the High Lord's sigil on it—"

"No!"

"—And thus Gird said our presence was accepted."

The elf stared at him. "Another arch . . . appeared?"

"Yes."

"When Gird came?" At Luap's nod, the elf sat back. "A mage-born human blunders into *that*, which we have kept inviolate for ages longer than your people, Selamis the luap, have existed . . . it is a clangorous thought."

"Gird walked through that arch," Luap said warily. He felt he must say it, but he did not know why he felt so. "He walked through, and then up the stair—"

"I hardly dared hope you had seen only the hall," Varhiel said. "And Gird would, yes—would have no doubt that he could walk through any arch he wished, or climb any stair, and I suppose he opened the entrance for you, did he? What was it like, your first view of that land?"

"It was blowing snow," Luap said. The memory could still make him shiver. Varhiel laughed.

"I'm glad. It is unseemly, but I take pleasure in the thought that at least one protection held against invasion. Now, I suppose, we must go to the trouble of destroying the patterns."

"No," said Luap. The elf's look reminded him he had no rights to argue. "Please," he said more softly. "Please listen—let me tell you the rest." As smoothly as he could, he told of his later visits, of the need for a place where the mageborn could train their powers to good, of Arranha's approval, and the Autumn Rose's. "They felt—we all felt—the holiness of that place, the great power of good that lies in it. This I'm sure would prevent any misuse of our powers, as our people learn to use them well."

"It is impossible," the elf said. "It is not your place; you did not make it; you do not understand those who did."

"But it is so beautiful," Luap said. He could feel tears gathering in his eyes, and blinked them back. Never to taste that pine-scented air, that cold sweet water? He could not bear that. Varhiel stared at him.

"You find that beautiful, all that bare rock?"

Luap nodded. "It eases something—I know not what—in my heart. And it's not barren—if you have not been there for years of human time, you may not know the trees that grace those narrow valleys."

"Canyons," Varhiel said. "That is what the Khartazh calls them, at least." He sighed. "If you find it beautiful, I am sorry to forbid it to you—but it is not yours. Even if I had the right to permit you, I would not, for I know why it was built, and under what enchantments it lies: it is not meant for mortals, and certainly not for humans. But I have not the right; you would have to have leave of the King—our king, of the Lordsforest, in the mountains far west and north of here—and I can tell you now you would not receive it."

"You could ask him," Luap said, in desperation.

"Ask him! You want me to ask the King to let a gaggle of late-comer humans inhabit a hall built by immortals for immortals? So you can practice your paltry powers in safety?"

Luap felt himself flushing. What he might have said he never knew, for the Autumn Rose came in at that moment. She had clearly overheard the last part of that.

"*I* will ask, of your courtesy, and as you are the ambassador, whose duty it is to carry requests from Fin Panir to your lord." Luap had not imagined that any human could approach elven arrogance, but the Autumn Rose angry came gloriously close. "Pray ask him, if you will, if he minds the corners of a deserted palace being home to those who have no other home, if they agree to be responsible for damages."

Varhiel stood. "Damages! Little you know, lady, what you say . . . little you know what damages such a place might sustain, or how to mitigate them. But as you command, and courtesy requires, I will take your message, and bring back his, which I am sure I could do without the effort moving from my seat. Yet you will have what you ask: the King's command, and speedily." He did not quite push past the Autumn Rose, yet she felt his movement, as a tree feels the gale that shreds its leaves.

She raised her brows to Luap. "If your meekness would not work, could it hurt to try my boldness? We shall see: I suspect Varhiel is not in his king's pocket any more than I am in yours, or the reverse. And you are a king's son; he owes you a king's answer."

"But if they're angry," Luap said. "If they never let us return—"

"Then we will find other mountains," she said. He wished he could believe her. He felt a cold wind sweeping through him; he could not bear to be barred from those red stone walls forever.

"Let's go there," he said suddenly. "Let's go now, before he returns."

She stared at him, eyes wide. "Luap—what is it? We can't go haring off to the cave now, and you can't get there by magery without those patterns . . . can you?"

"No. But—perhaps I could reproduce the patterns. It may not

be the place, but the patterns laid there—" He wet his finger and began to trace a design on his desk. "See . . . like this, and this . . ."

She frowned. "Luap—I've seen that somewhere else."

"The design? You can't have."

"No, I have." She stood motionless a moment, brows furrowed. Then she looked at him. "Luap, come with me."

"Where?"

"Just come." She grasped his hand, and when he asked if she wanted to find Arranha first, shook her head. Down the stairs, outside, across the courtyard, and into the High Lord's Hall. He was halfway up the Hall toward the altar when he remembered what she was talking about. Incised in the floor just behind the altar was a pattern he had never really noticed. "That's the same, isn't it?"

Luap bent over it. Here he dared not bring his own light, and the shallow grooves hardly showed in the dimness. "It . . . seems . . . the same," he said, tracing part of it with his finger. He dared not trace all of it, and vanish.

"In the old law," the Rosemage said, "*our* law, the man in a house has a better chance of keeping it. But you may be right that we need Arranha." Before he could say anything, she strode away, leaving him with his hand splayed out across the pattern as if to protect it.

Arranha, when he came, was inclined to shake his head. "It is not Luap's place, though he found it untenanted; we knew all along someone else had made it. If they forbid, we dare not object."

"But look at this." The Rosemage pointed to the pattern. "It's *here*, in the most important place of worship our people had in the north. You told us this was the first of Esea's Halls over the mountains. If it is their pattern, then why is it here? If it is here with their consent, then Luap has an heir's right to it . . . to its use, at least."

"I don't know," Arranha said. "If it is the same pattern, then what it might mean is that they made some agreement with our ancestors. That doesn't explain why there were only two arches until Gird came, though."

"We could see if it works," she said.

"And if it didn't?" Arranha said. "I've never known you to be rash, lady, before this?"

"*I'll* try it," Luap said suddenly. "If it doesn't work, then you will have the most excellent excuse to do nothing."

"You can't—" the Rosemage began. Arranha looked thoughtful.

"Perhaps you should. If it works . . . are you prepared to meet the elves in that place, by yourself? We could come along."

"No," Luap said "If all three of us vanished, who would help the mageborn? We all know that I am one of the points of stress. Without me, some of our people would be quicker to forget their heritage and merge with the peasantry. If one of us must risk, I should be that one. You both have the respect of the Council of Marshals; you can do anything I could do for our people here."

"Well said." Arranha nodded. "Go, then, and Esea's light guide you." As he spoke, the pattern glowed in the shadowy hall, just bright enough for Luap to see that it was clearly the same. He stood on it, motioned them away, and thought of that distant hall.

And was there, on the dais.

But not alone. Under the arch crowned with harp and tree stood an elflord, crowned with silver and emeralds and sapphires: Luap could not doubt that this was the King, the Lord of that fabled Forest in the western mountains. Under the arch crowned with anvil and hammer stood a dwarf, his beard and hair braided with gold and silver. His crown was gold, studded with rubies. Luap could not doubt he was the king of some dwarf tribe, though he knew not which one. On one side of the hall stood a company of elves, facing a company of dwarves. All wore mail styled as their folk wore it, and carried weapons. In the center of the hall, a gnome in gray carried a great book bound in leather and slate. Varhiel faced the dais, only a few paces away.

"I told them you would come," he said. "Without invitation, without courtesy . . . see now, mortal, what you dare by intruding here. This is not your place: you did not make it, you do not understand it."

Luap surprised himself with his composure. "Is that your king's word, Varhiel?"

"You may ask him yourself," said Varhiel; his bow mocked Luap, but Luap did not respond. He looked down that long hall at the elvenking, inwardly rejoicing to see the hall filled and alive as he had always imagined it.

But before he could speak, the elvenking spoke; his voice held a richness of music Luap had never imagined. "Mortal, king's son you named yourself: what king claimed you?"

No human words could be courteous enough for speech with this king; Luap felt himself drowning in that power. His magery responded, seemingly of itself, and he did not suppress it, allowing his light to strengthen. "My lord, my father died while I was young;

I have been told by those who knew both him and me that he was Garamis, the fourth before the last king."

"You claim the royal magery?"

Luap smiled before he could stop himself. "My lord, the magery claimed *me*, when I had long thought I had none." He felt his mind as full of light as his body; he might have been burning in some magical flame. Was this Esea's light?

"Varhiel said you claimed that when you brought Gird here, a third arch appeared, and on that basis you claimed a right to use this place. Where is that third arch?"

Luap started down the hall. Sure enough, he saw but the two arches he had seen when he first came. He felt the sweat start on his forehead. It had been there; it had appeared with Gird and had been there when he brought the Rosemage and and Arranha. Now he could not see it. Surely it had to be there, between the others, where a blank red wall stood.

"Show us this arch," the dwarf said suddenly. "If you are not *nedross*." He did not know much of the dwarf speech, but no one could talk long to dwarves without learning something of *drossin* and *nedrossin*. He looked again, saw only the bare stone. But, his memory reminded him, the elves are illusionists. At once a rush of exultation flooded him. He walked forward, past the ranks of elves and dwarves, through the very current of their disapproval, their determination to exclude him. He walked past the gnome, who stepped aside without speaking. He thought of Gird, of how Gird had strolled down this hall as if he had the right to walk anywhere. Could he be that certain? Yes. For his people, he could.

He walked to the red stone as if he expected it to part like a curtain. Two paces away, one pace: he could see the fine streaks of paler and darker red, the glitter of polished grains. "Here," he said, laying his hands flat on the cold, smooth stone. "It bears the High Lord's sigil; in Gird's name—" His hands flailed in air; he nearly fell. On either side of him, the columns rose, incised with intricate patterns: over his head the arch curved serenely, with that perfect circle at its height.

He struggled to control his expression; blank astonishment filled him. He heard, inwardly, a rough chuckle that reminded him of Gird. *Did you think I'd let you make a fool of yourself?* Luap shivered; he knew that voice. He wanted to ask it questions, but it was gone, leaving his head empty and echoing. And no time. From their arches, the elvenking and dwarvenking had come to confront him.

"Mortal, I see the arch. I do not see why you should be allowed to use this hall." This near, the elvenking's beauty took his breath away; it was all he had ever imagined a royal visage to be.

"My lord, it was my thought—and Gird's, for that matter—that such a thing meant either the god's direct command to come here, or their approval."

"For what purpose?" The arching eyebrows rose, expressing without words the conviction that no purpose would be justified.

"A haven for the mageborn—"

"You would use magery here?" That was the dwarf, a voice like stone splitting.

"This is magery," Luap said, with a wave that included the entire place. "How could one be here and not be using magery?" That came close to insolence; he felt his stomach clench, as if he'd leaned far out over a precipice.

The elvenking's eyes narrowed dangerously; Luap felt cold down his spine. "Mortal man, this is not human magery, but the work of the Elder Races, far beyond your magery—"

"Yet I came, and this arch appeared—I do not claim by my magery alone but with the gods' aid."

"And what gods do you serve?" Luap blinked; that was one question he had not anticipated. *The gods of my father, or of my mother? The gods of my childhood or my manhood?*

"I was reared both mageborn and peasant; I have prayed to both Esea and Alyanya . . ." he began. The elf interrupted.

"I did not ask from whom you sought favors, but whom you *served.*"

How could any man say which god he served—truly served? He might think he had rendered service, but the god might have refused it, or not recognized it. Possibilities flitted through his mind, an airy spatter of butterflies. He could think of only one he had served, and that one not a god. "I served Gird, mostly," he said. The elf's brows rose as the dwarf's lowered; he had a moment to wonder if those were two ways of expressing the same reaction, or two different reactions to the same words.

"And it was Gird's visit that brought this arch," the elvenking said.

"Yes."

The elf looked at him so long in silence that Luap felt his knees would collapse. Finally he spoke. "You convince me that you are convinced of what you say. But you do not know what you ask. This stronghold was made for another, not you. It was built to ward against dangers you do not understand and could not face. If you live here, you may rouse ancient evils, and if you do, it would be better for you that you had not been born. Yet . . . if you ask me, knowing that you do not know, and knowing that I say your people would find better sanctuary elsewhere, I will grant you my permission. But whatever harms come of it will rest on your shoulders, Selamis-called-Luap, Garamis's son."

"What dangers?" Luap asked. "What evils? I saw a land of great beauty, breathed air that sang health along my bones—"

The king held up his hand, and Luap could not continue. "I tell you, mortal man, that you would be wise to choose some other boon from me. Yet wisdom comes late or never to mortals; I see in your eyes you will have your desire, despite anything I say. Be it so: but remember my warning."

"And you will not say what that danger is?"

"It is none of your concern." A look passed from the elven to the dwarven king, and returned, which Luap could not read but knew held significance. His anger stirred.

"And why is it not? If the gods led me to this place, as I believe they did; if Gird's coming hallowed it for mortal use, as I believe it did and this arch proves; if then you know of some danger which threatens, why should you not tell me, and let us meet it bravely?"

Another look passed between the kings; this time the dwarf spoke. "You believe the gods intended this: do you think the gods do not know of the danger? Are we to interfere with their plans? No: you have our permission; that is all you need from us, and all we give."

Luap realized suddenly that he was hearing the two kings each in his own language, and understanding perfectly, yet he knew he could not speak or understand more than a few courtesies of his own knowledge. Such power, he thought, longingly; his own magery was but the shadow of theirs. But pride stiffened him; he looked each in the eye, and bowed with courtesy but no shame. "Then I thank you, my lords, for your words. As the gods surpass even the Elder Races, I must obey their commands as I understand them."

The elf looked grim. "May they give you the wisdom to accompany your obedience," he said. Then he turned to the gnome. "Lawmaster, record all that you heard, and let it be as it is written." He strode up the hall, and when he reached the dais, the elves vanished. The dwarf king came nearer and looked up into Luap's face.

"You may be a king's son, mortal, but it will take more than that to rule in this citadel. You are not of the rockblood; you do not know how to smell the drossin and nedrossin stone. The sinyi care for growing things and pure water; we dasksinyi care for the virtues of stone; the isksinyi care for the structure of the law. Now ask yourself, mortal, what the iynisin care for, and what that corruption means. We will not forgive an injury to the daskgeft." He turned, and his dwarves cheered, then burst into a marching song. Luap could no longer understand their speech: he watched as they followed their king to the dais and vanished.

That left the gnome, a dour person who gave Luap a long humorless stare. "Gird should have had more sense," it said. "I am a Lawmaster: this is a book of law. Do you understand?"

"Yes, Lawmaster." Luap struggled with a desire to laugh or shiver. How had Gird endured an entire winter understone with such as this?

"In this book will be recorded the contract between you and the Elder Races. Do you understand that?"

He did not, but he hated to admit it. "If we wake this danger, whatever it is, they will take it ill."

"They will withdraw their permission," the gnome corrected. "You are, for the duration of your stay here, considered as guardian-guests, not as heirs. You have the duty to protect this as if it were your own, but it is not your own, nor may you exchange any part of it for any value whatsoever. Is that clear?"

"I—think so. Yes."

"You have the use-right of the land, the water, the air, the animals that live on the land and the birds that fly over it, but no claim upon dragons—"

"Dragons!" Luap could not suppress that exclamation.

"Dragons . . . yes. There may be dragons from time to time; you have no claim upon them. You are forbidden to interfere with them. You may not, through magery or other means, remove this citadel to another place—" Luap had not even thought of that possibility. "—And you must keep all in good repair and decent cleanliness. You must not represent yourself as the builder or true owner, and you must avoid contamination of this hall with any evil. Now—if these are the terms you understand, and you accept them, you will say so now—"

"I do," said Luap.

"And then the sealing. You were Gird's scribe as well as luap; you know how to sign your name. As you have no royal seal, press your thumb in the wax." Luap signed, pressed, and the gnome laid over the blotch of wax a thin cloth. The gnome bowed, stiffly, and without another word walked to the dais, where he vanished.

Luap could not have told how long he stood bemused before he, too, went back to the dais, as much worried as triumphant. He arrived in darkness—not in the High Lord's Hall, as he'd expected, but in his cave . . . and realized he'd been thinking of it. Could he transfer directly? No. Back to the distant land, then to Fin Panir. The High Lord's Hall was empty; it was near dusk. Where had they gone, and why? Or had the elves wrapped him in such sorcery that years had passed, and they thought him lost forever?

"Almost," said the Rosemage when he found her in his office. "Four days is too long to stand waiting."

Quickly, Luap told her what he remembered of his meeting with elves and dwarves and the gnomish Lawmaster. He found it hard to believe it had been four days . . . but he could not remember everything. Something about danger, about *drossin* and *nedrossin,* about which of the Elders cared most about which aspect of creation . . . but none of that mattered, compared to the final agreement. The Rosemage grinned; she looked almost as excited as he felt.

"Well, then—and where is this fabulous place, now that we have permission to use it?"

At that moment, Luap realized he had not asked—that he had not been given a chance to ask. And he doubted very much that the Elders would answer any such question now.

Arranha was the least concerned about that; he was sure, he said, that he could figure it out by means of celestial markers. Luap, annoyed with himself for being so easily enchanted by the elves, grunted and left him to it.

Chapter Fifteen

"What happened?" asked Aris, as Seri came out of the Council meeting room. She grinned, stuck up her thumb, and then put a finger before her mouth. They scurried down the stairs like two errant children, across a court, through another passage, and then found an empty stall in the stable.

"It went just as we hoped," Seri said, when she'd thrown herself down on the straw. "I'm glad you suggested starting with the history, though."

"Makes you seem older," Aris said. He sat curled, with his arms

around his knees. It had been Seri's idea, all of it, but she had let
him help her shape it.

"They had to agree with that, of course, since they knew it: that
all the Marshals now were Marshals or yeoman-marshals under
Gird himself, they'd all led soldiers in the war. And they had to
agree that weaponsdrill in the barton, and marching in the grange
drillfields, isn't much like battle. Even Gird had to get them out
of the bartons and into mock battles before real ones. So they could
see where I was going, and some of 'em—Cob, for instance—were
already nodding when I said the granges needed something more.
He started in to propose just what I'd planned, so I didn't have
to bother."

Aris chuckled. "They'll like it better from Cob; he's one of them."

"And it doesn't matter to me," Seri said, with a wave of her
hand, "as long as we have that kind of training. After all, he was
in the war, not just scrubbing pots and carrying water like we were.
He'll know better how to set it up, now he's thought of it."

"But about the other—." Aris prompted.

"You won't believe it." Her grin lit up the stall. "He had just
gotten well started on laying out a training plan when the Rosemage
raised her hand and said she thought perhaps I'd had more to say.
Cob stopped short, shrugged, and asked if I did. So I told them
about our plan—"

"Your plan," Aris said firmly. "I didn't think of that."

"My plan, then. I told them how future Marshals would need
more training than just leading a gaggle of farmers around a hayfield, or even fighting in a mock battle once a year or so—that they
needed to be real Marshals, well-tested before being given command of a grange—and Aris, they *listened* to me. I said it all, all
we talked about: working up from yeoman-marshal, spending time
in two different granges, and then talked about having a place for
concentrated training." She paused so long that Aris had to speak.

"Well? What did they say?"

"Five or six of the older ones all started talking at once, about
how they didn't have to worry as long as they had veterans, and
how much it would cost, and that Gird never meant to have armies
roaming around stealing from honest farmers—then Raheli stood
up and they were all silent." Seri lay back in the straw and stared
at the high roof far overhead. "You know, I never realized how
much she's like him."

Aris sat up straight. "Like Gird?" He thought about it. They saw
her only when she came to Fin Panir, and often enough only from

a distance. They had heard stories, of course, but none of them made her seem much like her father.

"I know, it surprised me, too. All we'd seen, after all, was her from a distance, walking around. That great scar on her face, and her dark hair—she doesn't *look* anything like him. But when she looked at me, it gave me the same sort of feeling as the first time we met Gird. I don't know how to say it better than that she's an opposite of Luap."

"Warm, not cold," Aris mused, and looked up to see if Seri agreed. She was nodding vigorously.

"She has Gird's directness. I liked her at once, but if *she* was my Marshal I wouldn't dare try anything." She didn't have to elaborate on that; he knew about the tricks she'd played on her Marshal. It had been, she'd explained from time to time, the result of being separated from Aris. He had always kept her out of mischief. Not long after, they'd been reassigned to the same grange.

Now Aris came back to the main subject. "So Rahi stood up, and they were quiet, and then what?"

"She said it was a good plan. She said it should be in Fin Panir, and each grange should have the right to nominate two candidates a year, but not all would become Marshals."

"But you thought three—"

"Two, three, it doesn't matter. The point is, she approved. And— what you won't believe—the Rosemage stood after her, and approved as well. *She* argued for including the study of law and the archives as well. Said that knowledge of war was only part of a Marshal's training; that Marshals had to be able to act as judicars and recognize all kinds of things going wrong. The two of them started in, then, and it was almost as if they'd pulled the details of the plan straight out of my head." She threw her arms out, raising a cloud of dust from the straw, and sneezed. "Of course, I know they didn't, but it means we were planning in the right way."

"Huh. If you said something that got the Rosemage and Gird's daughter working together, it was definitely right."

"They should be friends," said Seri soberly. "They would fit together."

"Luap doesn't think so."

Seri wrinkled her nose. "Luap couldn't do what he does if they did, is what he means. But it's what Gird would have wanted. Think of it—the Rosemage could lead her people—"

"Not while Luap is the king's son, and she's an outlander."

"He could *let* her; he could tell them to follow her, and not him.

But he won't." Seri rolled over on her stomach and propped her chin on her fists, as if she were a child again. "He's ruining things."

"He's not!" Aris scrambled nearer and thumped her shoulder, then bent down to look her in the eye. "He's Gird's chosen luap, Seri: he is not ruining things."

She didn't budge. "You don't see everything; you're thick as bone some ways. I think the healing makes you see people differently. You don't see what they are; you see their needs." She rubbed the bridge of her nose for a moment before going on. "I don't think he knows it, I'll say that for him. I think he believes he's doing the right thing, what Gird would have wanted. But he got it into his head a long time ago that the Rosemage and Rahi were natural enemies, like a levet and a wren—"

Aris snorted. "And which of those two is a wren?" Seri smacked him.

"You know what I mean. He thinks that, and he can't see that they're made to be allies. Not friends, maybe, but allies. And so he treats them as enemies, and they see each other through his vision, except sometimes like this."

"Mmm." It was something to think about. Did the healing magery give him such a different view of people? Or was it the magery itself? Could that be why Luap saw the Rosemage and Rahi as natural enemies? But he had no chance to discuss that with Seri, for someone was calling her. She rolled to her feet; he sighed and scrambled up after her. They had little time together these days, and he treasured the brief encounters.

"Seri!" Now the voice was closer: Rahi, Gird's daughter. Aris followed Seri out of the stall. The older woman laughed, the first relaxed laugh he had ever heard from her. "I might have known you'd be off somewhere with Aris."

"Yes, Marshal," said Seri. Her braid had come half undone again, and she had straw in her springy curls.

"Did you come up with all that by yourself, or did Aris help?" Now that she was close, Aris realized what Seri had meant about her being like Gird. A bluntness, but without any brutality, a sense of great strength in reserve, a warmth . . . he found himself grinning back at her, more at ease than he usually was with the older Marshals.

"He did—"

"No, Marshal, it was all hers—" Aris broke off as his voice clashed with Seri's and they laughed. "She will give me credit I don't deserve: we talked about it, but that's all."

"Gird said you two were great friends—but he sent you to separate granges for training, didn't he?"

"Yes, Marshal, but that doesn't matter." Seri might have said more, but another voice hailed them; the Rosemage moved across the stable yard, Aris thought, like one of the graceful horses.

"There you are, Rahi—and with the younglings. They're a pair, aren't they?" Aris felt like a colt up for sale at the market when the Rosemage shook her head at them. "Hard to believe the two of you could be our children, when you come to Council with solutions for problems the other Marshals haven't thought of yet."

Rahi had flushed, but now seemed relaxed and cheerful; Aris wondered what had upset her momentarily. He wanted to look at her scar; he wondered if he could heal it, but he dared not ask. "Fair enough." Rahi said slowly. "One for each of us, that way."

The Rosemage shook her head. "They come as a pair . . . we've learned that in Fin Panir, if nothing else. Gird himself separated them for a few years, in training, but even he admitted they were the closest he had seen outside a few twins."

Rahi grinned; Aris noticed how the scar pulled at her mouth, making the grin uneven. "They don't look much like twins," she said.

"We're not," Seri said boldly. "We're not alike, but we fit together. Father Gird said that was stronger than two alike."

The two older women looked at each other, a measuring look, brows raised. "That's true enough," murmured the Rosemage. "But again uncanny wisdom for one so young."

Seri shrugged, with a side glance at Aris. "It's not my wisdom, but Gird's."

"Well, yours or Gird's, it's true enough. Now I—we—need to talk to you." The Rosemage looked at Rahi. "Don't we? It's a nice afternoon for a walk in the meadow out near Gird's grave."

"And no one will overhear or interrupt," said Rahi, smiling. "Of course we need to talk to these two. I hardly know them except by what I hear from Luap."

With the older women flanking them, Aris and Seri walked out the west of the stable complex into the meadows beyond. Once well out of earshot of the stables, Rahi said, "You didn't say all you had planned, Seri; I could tell that. What else?"

"Cob said it well enough," Seri said. "The details don't matter—I mean, they do, but it doesn't matter who does it right, only that it's done. I know I'm too young to be telling Marshals anything, let alone the Council."

"But you were *right*," said the Rosemage. "That's what matters, not age."

"Well . . . it's like food. If I have it, I share it; if they eat it, it's nourishing. It doesn't matter who gave the bread and who gave the salt, so long as the bowl's full."

Rahi chuckled. "Peasant wisdom, lady."

The Rosemage pretended to stumble. "You're calling me lady?"

Rahi shrugged; Aris thought she was embarrassed. "I can't remember your real name."

"I quit using it, it meant something noble in our language I never lived up to." From the tone, she had never said *that* to anyone before. Rahi nodded slowly.

"And my name meant 'fruitful vine'—so I perhaps have no right to it."

"Rosemage," said Aris, trying to head off emotions he did not understand, "is a difficult sort of name to use—I mean in talking *to* you."

"You're right, it is. It's actually Luap's nickname for me, a nickname of a nickname." Aris noticed that the others looked as confused as he felt; she sighed and explained. "Your father knew this, Rahi, but I don't know if you did. The old king of Tsaia, the one I killed, had called me 'Autumn Rose' in a sort of jest. A bitter jest to me, for I loved him. When I killed him, I felt I had killed my old self, with its unsuitable name, as well, and I told Gird I would henceforth be the Autumn Rose in truth. Luap turned that to Rose Magelady, and then Rosemage. As you say, it's more a name of reference than one of address. Arranha told me I was being silly, and now I agree—but it's too late to change back."

"Never mind," said Rahi. "I can call you lady as the others do, without it hurting my mouth. I still have some questions for young Seri."

"Yes?" Seri, like Rahi herself, had seemed less interested in the Rosemage's explanation than Aris.

"You may be right to have the senior Marshals set out the plan themselves, but I'd like to know how you would have done it. Perhaps some of your details need to be included—and I'm a senior Marshal; I could see that they are."

"Oh." Seri paused a moment; Aris could almost see the thoughts in her head, busy and humming like a hive of bees at work. "Well, it seemed to me that we needed Marshals capable of leading out a grange against small problems, like wolfpacks or robbers. And then we needed Marshals, or perhaps High Marshals, who could lead groups of granges against invaders. I know it's peaceful now, but it was peaceful before the mageborn came—excuse me, lady—"

"No need," the Rosemage said.

"—And even though Gird won the war with ill-trained troops, and no cavalry," Seri went on, "it would be easier—it would cost less blood—to have better training and maybe some horse soldiers."

"Knights," said the Rosemage.

"Not too many," Seri said. "Mostly it should be yeomen, as it is now, but there should be a few whose parrion—guild?—it is to learn how to engage in wars, so that we have that knowledge when we need it."

"You would have the training place here, in Fin Panir?" Seri nodded. Rahi went on. "And you would have the Marshals—let's stay with that for now—learn what?"

Seri ticked the items off on her fingers. Aris was proud of her, the way she was staying calm when he knew she was bubbling inside. "First, the Marshals must be reliable, honest, hardworking that's why I said they should have grown up in one grange, and then worked in another. They have to be old enough to become yeoman-marshals first, because you don't know if they're going to misuse power until they have some. Marshals shouldn't be bullies. Then they have to know the Code, and they need to know the Commentaries, too, because the Code's always changing and it probably always will. Marshals have to get along with everyone in the city—or town—all the merchants, crafters, and farmers. They may not be the strongest, but they have to be skilled in all the weapons our people might use, and they have to be good at teaching them. They have to know something about the mageborn, and about the horsefolk, and anyone else we find, because they have to judge whether there's been fair dealing."

When she paused for breath, Aris put in, "And she wouldn't mind if they were skilled in each craft, and born with every parrion in the world." Seri flushed red.

"It wouldn't hurt," she muttered.

The Rosemage chuckled; Aris thought she looked much younger than usual. "No, it wouldn't hurt, but how long do you think they could be in such training?"

"If they're made yeoman-marshal after their first year as senior yeoman," Seri said, "and then serve four years as yeoman-marshal, they'd be the same age as someone finishing journeyman training in most crafts. Surely a Marshal must have earned the same respect as a master in a craft, and most journeymen spend four to six years before they pass the guild. . . ."

"And in that four years they would have time for law and history and languages as well as military things," Aris said. "I think—we think—that Marshals should all have knowledge of healing crafts, as well. If they lead yeomen into battle, they should know how to treat wounds and camp sicknesses."

"So new Marshals would be over twenty-six," Rahi said. "Even thirty—"

"Weren't most of Gird's Marshals, appointed in the war, over thirty?"

"Yes, but that was a special case." Rahi looked thoughtful; Aris gave Seri a warning glance. Best let Rahi think it out for herself. "I wasn't close to thirty . . . but then . . ." Aris smiled to himself. He had expected her to see their logic. "You're saying that all Marshals should have that maturity, as Gird and his first recruits did?"

"Yes, because Marshals aren't just battle commanders; courage isn't all they need." Seri looked back and forth between the two older women. Aris watched them smile at each other, as if at the antics of favorite children.

"I think, Rahi, that these two have more maturity than some gran'thers I've seen." The Rosemage shook her head. "But don't you two get above yourselves, eh? I heard about the tricks you played when you first came, Seri."

"I wouldn't do that *now*," Seri said. Aris wondered. She hadn't meant any harm, and none had followed, but she could no more forswear mischief than he could healing. Tease, prick the pompous, and then hug the hurt away—that was Seri. "And besides, I don't know enough yet—I want to learn all the things I'm talking about—"

"And be the first truly educated Marshal?" The Rosemage whistled. Seri blushed, and Rahi reached over to tousle her already tousled hair.

"I keep telling myself it's a new world these younglings live in," she said. "It's not like where I grew up, nor you either. But sometimes it does startle me. I presume you know it's going to be hard, Seri?"

"Of course." Now she looked affronted "It's supposed to be hard, or it's not any good. I'll be tired, and grumpy, and even scared—"

"And dirty and hungry and hurting, if we do it right," Rahi said, no humor at all in her voice now. "And you will be scared, I promise you that."

"And you, Aris—" The Rosemage broke that tense silence. "Do you, too, look toward being a Marshal?"

"I—I don't know. I want to learn all that Seri does, but—I'd like to spend more time healing, if I could. Teaching it, too."

"Mmm. It will be interesting. . . ." The Rosemage and Rahi shared a look Aris could not interpret, but turned the talk to other things until day's end.

Aris licked the grease from roast chicken off his fingers and reached for the bread. Seri pushed the loaf within his reach with her elbow; she was too busy eating her own chicken to free a hand. He tore off a hunk of bread, wiped his fingers, and ate that before saying anything. He had not been this hungry since coming to Fin Panir. Across the little fire, two of the yeomen with them grinned.

"I wonder what gave th' Marshal th' notion t'play this game," said one of them around a mouthful of bread.

"If I find out," said the other, "I'll knock his nob for 'im, that I will. My da told me it was more work than it sounded in songs, and he was right. We've climbed five hills a day, I'd wager, and haven't walked down but one."

"And that one muddy," said the first yeoman. "Wi' rocks at the bottom." He crunched the bone of his chicken leg and sucked the marrow noisily, then belched with satisfaction.

"Rocks!" said the second. "I'll tell you about rocks—" Then, as Aris raised an eyebrow, he fell silent. Their Marshal's blue cloak swirled past, then the yeoman resumed, in a lower voice. "Like to broke my legs, I did, and the old man says 'That's what eyes is for, lad, to look where you put your feet.' "

Aris gave Seri a long took; she blushed and wiped her mouth and fingers with bread. *He* knew where the Marshals had found that idea, and who to blame. He knew she would have confessed, challenging the man to thump her if he could, had the Marshals not told them to keep quiet about whose idea it was. Once they'd decided the idea had merit, it hadn't taken them long to put it into practice. Aris had been thinking of maneuvers in the spring, marching over soft green grass under warming skies. He had imagined himself setting up a clean tent to which the injured would come for treatment. Instead, the granges in Fin Panir, all four of them, were sent out in the cold after-harvest autumn storms, to practice moving engagements in the hills southwest of the city. Three days' march to the hills had taught them all how little they knew of supply and camp organization (the veterans enjoyed pointing it out) and the hand of days in the hills proper had been a revelation even to them.

Aris took another hunk of bread. So far he hadn't been scared, except of not keeping up, but he had been cold, wet, muddy, tired, stiff, and hungry. He hadn't been needed to heal anything worse than blisters and bruises, for which most of the yeomen had their own pet remedies. Instead of a healer's tent, he found himself carrying a staff just like everyone else, and doing the same camp chores he had done as a boy. Even though he and Seri had been with the peasant army, even though he had once lived a much harder life, the years he'd lived in Fin Panir had taken the edge off. And tomorrow they faced the three days' march back, into the teeth of the winter wind. He wondered if they'd get to sleep tonight, or if the Marshals had some surprise planned for them, as they had on other nights. He hoped not. His eyes felt gluey.

Luap hardly believed what he saw, the Rosemage and Raheli eating elbow-to-elbow at the campfire, and both enjoying it. He was not sure what he felt. On the one hand, the two of them quarreling could knot his stomach. But on the other . . . he had always been able to move one by invoking the other's opinion. What if they really agreed? What if they became (he shuddered) *friends?* The Rosemage had always gotten along with Gird better than he did himself; if she made friends with Rahi, his whole rationale for withdrawing the mageborn could fall through.

Everyone knew how those two had loathed each other; if they could become friends, so could any other mageborn/peasant pair.

Beside them were Aris and Seri, a pair he already found inconvenient. He wanted Aris to come with him; he did not want Seri. But he knew Aris wouldn't leave her behind. He needed the Rosemage; he needed Aris's healing talents. He did not need Gird's troublesome daughter or that curly-headed young warleader who should have been born early enough to fight in the war.

He had come on this uncomfortable jaunt, he told himself, simply to chronicle the training exercise. Burdened with his sack of scrolls, his inksticks and pens, his folding table and a tent to keep them dry, he had not been tempted to take part in the training itself. Instead he instructed two of his more promising clerks in the art of field mapping, wrote up each day's notes as reported by the Marshals, and tried without success to devise a better way to render rough country visible on a flat surface. It had been tiring, difficult work, carried out under difficult conditions, but it had not been the same as clambering up hill and down to hold mock battles with another group of tired, rain-soaked yeomen. He knew that, he had been there in the real war. So he had stayed away from the evening fires, to avoid making his comfortable job any more insulting than it was already.

Tonight, though, the maneuvers were over—supposedly—and they would all march toward home in the morning. So he had brought out a jug of the peach brandy his favorite cook made, in hopes of sweetening the Autumn Rose's attitude. And there she sat, dirt and grease to the ears, joking with Raheli.

He walked toward them; young Aris saw him coming, and leaped up. "Sir—Luap—"

"Sit down, lad. You've worked a lot harder than I have." Other yeomen moved aside to give him room beside Aris.

"I wanted to ask you," Seri said, direct as always. "About those maps. Did you ever talk to the gnomes about mapping?"

How could the girl be that wide awake, that full of energy? Aris looked tired to the bone, but Seri—it must be the peasant endurance, Luap thought He remembered Raheli brimming with energy when others had been too tired to move. And Gird, despite his age, had nearly always been the first up in the mornings. "Once, after the fall of Fin Panir," he answered. "They'd come to talk to Gird, and he showed them my copy of the map they gave him." He chuckled. "They weren't impressed. I told them I had had to do it without the original; it was lost in the flood outside Grahlin that time—"

"Was that when the well exploded?"

He looked past Aris into that bright, wide-awake face, and past it to the two older women. Was that tone just a bit put on? Did Seri have some purpose besides what he heard in words? Rahi spoke up, as if he'd asked her to.

"Not exploded—but apparently the local magelord had magicked all the water in the river into it, underground, and sent it all out at once. It made an awful noise, and scared us silly."

"The water shot up in the air," Luap added. "Higher than any fountain, a column of water perhaps a man's height across. It was, only a little mud-brick fort and when the water hit, it came apart around us. On top of us."

"And the next day we had a pitched battle we never should have fought," Rahi went on. "Gird was too shaken by the flood, I think—he felt we had to hold the bridge. Cob's foot was hurt that night; he's limped ever since. And we lost others who'd been with us from the start—" She stared at the fire, her face, grim. That fiasco and Gird's sullen, drunken response in the next hands of days had almost ended the rebellion. Seri looked from Rahi to Luap.

"What I meant, sir, was that I wondered if the gnomes had

solved the problems you were having with the new maps. Do they have some way of showing the land, even when it's wrinkled up, so you can tell what part of a hill sticks out?"

"Not that I know of. By the time I had them to copy, of course, they'd been soaked and torn. We had to dig them out of the wet rabble, try to uncurl them without tearing them any worse, and then redraw them. Maybe there were marks that didn't show after that." Seri looked interested, alert, and—in another place and time—Luap would have been flattered by that alert interest. He had had few chances to teach her, but those few times he had enjoyed it. She came to everything with such enthusiasm, such eagerness to learn and do well, and those Marshals who had supervised her considered themselves lucky. But now he felt her intensity as a veiled threat—she and young Aris between them were up to something, and he could not decide what. Had they anything to do with the new friendship between Raheli and the Autumn Rose?

For those two were as amiable with each other as either with anyone else, now, and from the looks they cast at the youngsters, might have been their aunts if not their mothers.

"I brought something to warm cold hearts," Luap said, holding up his jug of peach brandy. "Who'd like a sip?" The Autumn Rose held out her hand, and he gave it to her.

After a sip, she handed it on to Seri. "Be careful, girl; it's stronger than it tastes. Did Meshi make that for you, Luap?"

"Yes; she spoils me." Safer to say it himself.

"True, she does," the Autumn Rose agreed. "Do you know I found her making spiced preserves one time, and she told me she didn't have enough for everyone—but when Luap came down the stair . . ." They all laughed; Luap managed a grin.

"It comes out even—the other cooks don't like me because she's so partial, and won't give them her secret recipe for the spiced preserves. I've thought of getting it from her, and telling them, just for peace in the kitchen, but—" He shrugged, and threw his hands out; everyone laughed, but with no sting in it.

"You know what would happen then," Rahi put in. "They wouldn't like you more, and Meshi would bang you on the fingers with a spoon every time you came in the kitchen. It is good; reminds me of my mother's preserves, but there's something else in it."

"Whatever it is costs enough to put cooks at each others throats," Luap said. "I think one of the spices must come from over the mountains." He took a sip himself, that warmed him all the way down. Perhaps it wasn't a bad thing to have Rahi and the Autumn

Rose friends. It seemed less threatening than it had, just as Seri's—or was it Rahi's?—ideas about the training of Marshals to replace those retiring seemed less threatening. He looked over at the girl—not really a girl, now. She would make a formidable Marshal in her day. He glanced at Aris. Would he take Marshals' training as well, or stick with his role as healer? He tried to imagine them both in middle age, and failed.

As sharply as a pinprick, his own vision of his stronghold intruded. He wanted to see Aris there, using his healing magery, teaching others how to heal. Seri did not fit. He had no use for a Girdish Marshal, a peasant with no more magical ability than any other peasant. What could she do? He wasn't going to raise and train an army; they would have no enemies to guard against, out there. Aris belonged, was one of his people by birth and talent, and she did not belong. She would hold Aris back, prevent him from learning what other mage powers he had. If they did not marry—and he was sure would not, though he could not have said why—it would be best for Aris to learn to get along without her, so that he could be with his own people. She would be happy enough in Fin Panir or elsewhere, busy with a grange.

How was he going to manage that? He watched Rahi and the Autumn Rose; clearly they, like Gird, thought the two belonged together. He would have to find some way of shifting them apart, bit by bit. He looked at Aris; the boy had deep circles under his eyes. This had taken more out of him than Seri; he was not, Luap told himself, as robust. He should be protected, his healing magery nurtured. That was too precious a talent to be squandered in mock warfare.

Chapter Sixteen

"You're going," said Seri. Aris looked up from the scroll he'd been studying Seri looked as she always did when she'd pulled off some mischief.

"And who's to be my guardian?"

"I am." She sounded as smug as she looked.

"You? But you're—"

She pointed to the badge on her tunic. "A Marshal-candidate in good standing, of known good character, approved by the Council. So we can leave whenever you like, and stay as long, and—"

To be free again—to ride out the gates, with Seri at his side, and no one to argue with him whether this one or that needed his healing more, no one to suggest he must conserve his power for greater needs—he felt a childish glee of his own, to match the sparkle in her eyes. "Tomorrow?" he asked, not really believing it.

"Good choice." said Seri. "I'll tell the cooks, and get our things ready. You finish that miserable compilation for Luap, and—I suppose you do have to tell him?"

"I should." Aris sighed. "But surely he knows—he was at the meeting, wasn't he?"

Seri rolled her eyes. "Meeting? What meeting? Can't a few Marshals get together and discuss minor matters without holding a formal meeting?"

"But then are you sure it's—"

"Raheli, the Autumn Rose, Cob, and Garig: is anyone going to argue them down? And they had discussed it with others—not *all* the others, admittedly, but enough to justify it. My directors agreed—in fact they had brought it up before I had And Rahi did suggest we go on and leave now—quickly—before the decision caused comment."

Her look said even more: it usually did. "I could leave within a glass or so," he said softly. "I could leave Luap a note. We don't need that much—"

She clasped his shoulder, and leaned close. "Even better. We'll take an afternoon ride." She waved her hand, "I'll go get the horses ready."

Aris turned back to the scroll. He couldn't concentrate on it; he had read it before, and knew that nothing on it would help him. He rolled it carefully, slid it back into its case, and the case back into the rack. He rummaged on the desk until he found a scrap of old parchment, scraped many times and fraying, to write his note to Luap.

He felt slightly guilty for not taking the trouble to find Luap, rather than leaving the note in his office, but he did not want to discuss his plans with the Archivist. More and more, in the past year or two, he had felt uneasy around Luap, and he could not explain why. Seri, he knew, felt the same way. He put the note where Luap could not miss it, then went to see if Seri had left anything behind. His pack, rolled neatly, lay on his pallet, and his box held only what he himself would have left behind. When he ran his hand into the center of the pack-roll, he felt the hard edges of coins—so she had thought of that, too.

With his pack under one arm, he didn't look like someone out for an afternnoon's ride—but then if anyone asked, he had permission to leave for longer than that. He remembered a Marshal saying once that an innocent heart was the best disguise, and on his way to the stables, no one seemed to look at him. Seri had both horses saddled, and her own pack strapped tight. Mischief lighted her eyes; her horse, catching the excitement, jigged sideways.

"I am hurrying," said Aris, to both horses as much as to Seri. His own snorted, as he snugged the pack straps, and mounted. He didn't have to ask which way—they would start as they often did, riding west and north into the meadowland beyond the city.

By sunset, they were out of sight of the city, beyond the range of their earlier rides in this direction. They had passed one village to the east, but now saw nothing, not even sheep, to indicate that another was near. Still, they felt safe; they could walk back to the city in one day if the horses pulled loose in the night. But the horses did not escape, and they rode off the next morning in high spirits. All that day they moved into country new to them, rolling land covered mostly in grass, with scattered groves in hollows and along streambanks. In the last span before sunset, they chose a grove near water to camp in.

"It's almost like being children again," said Seri. "When we used to go and make houses in the bushes, remember?"

"Yes, but now we know how to do it right." They had blown fluff from a seedhead for camp chores: tonight Seri had to dig the jacks, and Aris had to take care of the fire. Not that it mattered to either of them, Aris thought, but Gird's training held to the tally-group system, and it had come to feel natural. With the horses watered and fed, their own waterskins full, and their camp laid out properly, they settled in by the fire to talk.

"I wonder if we should take turns as guard," Seri said. "I know there's no war, and this is settled territory, but it's good practice—"

"Mmm." Aris leaned back. He had not ridden so many hours in a long time, and he knew he would wake stiff. "I don't sense any dangers."

"Nor I. But it's the right way to do things. I'll take first watch."

"All right." He looked at the fire for awhile, listening to Seri's footsteps on grass and stone. She went down to the spring, up the slope to the edge of the trees, and came back to the fire.

"Nothing now." He could feel her tension as if it was his own. In a way, it was his own tension, reflected like firelight. They both knew why they had needed to get out of Fin Panir, why they had needed to travel alone, but the years in the city made it hard to return to the easy communication of their childhood, when idea and response had flowed between them without barriers.

Seri sat back down with a sigh. In the flickering light, her face looked much older, and as heavily stubborn as Gird's had been. "Remember after Father Gird died?" she asked. Aris nodded. Because they were then training in separate granges, they had been able to talk for only a few minutes now and then—but they had had the same dream in the days after the funeral. "I always felt close to him," Seri went on. "From the first day we came. It was like having a grandfather of my own. Not that I didn't respect him, but—"

"It was much the same for me," Aris said. They had talked of this before; it was as good a way as any to ease into the real problem. "If I had been able to choose a father, I'd have chosen Gird."

"And then he died," Seri said. "Like any other father or grandfather, except it wasn't."

Aris looked at her. They had each tried to talk to the Marshals about it, and had had the blank looks given to those who have said something outrageous. They had learned not to talk about it, not to mention what was, to them, the most salient point of Gird's death. "I think," he said softly, "that they don't quite remember it. They know they felt better afterwards; they know they couldn't quite remember why they had been so angry—but I think they don't actually remember what happened."

"Luap does," said Seri. "Or he did, but that's not what he's put in his *Life of Gird.* He's made it a monster."

"How did you find out?" Aris had been wanting to see the *Life* for several years, but Luap gave him no chance.

"I heard from someone who heard Rahi complaining about it. She said he was trying to make it more like one of the old tales from the archives, one of the kings' lives tales."

Aris snorted. "That wouldn't fit Gird, no more than a crown would have."

"Rahi said he couldn't make clear what really happened, so he made up the monster so that people would understand. Only they won't, because that's not what it was."

"I wish he'd let me help," said Aris. "It could be written the right way, the way it happened. It wouldn't be easy, but that would be better than making up a false tale."

"Rahi said Luap can't see that—he thinks a false tale that makes sense is better than the true one no one will understand." Seri poked a stick at the fire, until sparks flew up. "Aris—do you ever feel Father Gird is still around?"

"Really? In person? Or just—feeling that he's there when he's not?"

"I'm not sure." She faced him directly. "Aris, those dreams we had after he died—those aren't the last ones I've had."

He wasn't surprised. Those hadn't been his last dreams of Gird, either. He nodded, and said, "Tell me about them."

"I can't, exactly. It's—it's as if he wanted me to do something, and I'm not sure what. If he *were* alive, he wouldn't be happy with Luap, that's certain . . . Luap's ruining it all."

That was the core of it, what they had needed to talk over far away from Fin Panir's many curious ears. Aris felt a cold chill down his back, as if someone had run a chunk of snow down it "I know. And I don't think he knows what he's doing . . ."

"How can he not!" Seri had finally let go her anger, and now it blazed in his mind as brightly as the fire she poked into brilliance. "He's a scholar; he surely knows if he writes truth or falsehood. He was Gird's helper so long, he surely knows what Gird would have wanted. Gird wanted mageborn and peasant living in peace, one people. Luap swore *oaths* that he would obey Gird and follow Gird's will, yet he's doing everything he can to push mageborn and peasant apart."

"Not quite everything," Aris pointed out. "If he really knew he was doing it, he could do worse—"

"Not without the Council noticing. He's just being sneaky." She glared at him. "Or have you gone over to them as well?"

He stared at her, shocked and horrified. "Seri! I couldn't!" Tears filled his eyes; if Seri thought he would turn into another like Luap, he wasn't sure he could bear it.

"You spend so much time with them," she said, her voice hard. "You do what Luap tells you; you hardly have time for anyone else—"

"I'm here," he said. "I left Fin Panir in the turning of a glass, on your word—how can you think I *like* all that, you of all people!"

"Then don't defend him," said Seri, "when you don't believe what you say. D'you think I can't tell what you really think? But if you won't say it, even to me, even alone in the dark wild, how is that different from him?"

Aris struggled to control his voice. "I have tried to be fair," he said. "Tried not to . . . to make hasty judgments. I saw—I see—Luap and the other Marshals, all quick to say what someone meant, and sometimes I know that's not what the other meant. So I look for the chance that someone like Luap, doing something I would not do, has at least a good reason, in his own mind, for doing it." He swallowed the lump in his throat. "But—you're right—I don't like what he's doing, and I haven't liked it, and I haven't been able to do one thing about it. I'm too young, and I'm mageborn, as he is—"

"And half the distrust you meet is for him," Seri said, now less fiercely. "They're afraid you're another Luap. When you were younger, and you were out and around more . . ."

"Which is another thing," Aris said. "I want to do more healing myself; I want to go more places, and it's the Council—yes, and Luap—who insisted I stay close and try to train other mageborn to heal. It isn't working, and I don't think it will, but they won't listen to me."

"Why not?"

"Why won't it work? I'm not sure. The Autumn Rose says the healing magery was rare anyway; it failed first, when the mageborn were losing their powers. I've found only one who responded to the training—"

"Garin—"

"Yes. And he exhausts himself when he closes a cut; the one time he tried to heal a broken bone, he fainted partway through and slept for a week."

"You did that, when you were a child—"

"Yes, when I'd worked with all those sheep. But he's a man grown, older than I am. The Autumn Rose found a girl said to have healed her family members of headaches and the like, but what she was really doing was charming them—they didn't feel the pain as long as she was there. That's not a bad use of charming— I've taught her to use it on more serious things—but it's not healing. You remember that Gird wanted me to work with peasant healers to learn herblore, and with the granny-witches to learn hand-magicks. I've learned a lot more about herbs, and most of the women with a parrion of herblore say if I were a girl they'd trade my parrion, though they don't think much of a man learning it. The grannies have watched me heal, and I've watched them lay pains on a stone, and neither of us learned how the other did it. Whatever they do is not in their power to explain, or mine to learn—and the same for what I do. They don't sense the light of health and the dark of fever or injury the way I do, but they do feel the prickling in their hands."

"I suppose that's something," said Seri. She frowned. "So you don't think you'll be able to teach anyone?"

"I don't know. Some child, perhaps, will be born with the talent, and I can help train it. But it's not like reading or writing—it's not something everyone can learn more or less well—and since I didn't have someone to train me, I really don't know what the training should be like." Aris leaned away from the fire as a gust sent smoke into his eyes. "Nobody wants to hear that, though: Luap is still convinced I could teach other mageborn to heal, and the other Marshals still hope I can work with the granny-witches. They don't want me to be the only one—and I wish I weren't." He struggled with the sorrow that always came when he thought of that, of being the only one who knew what he knew. He could share his skills by using them, but he had no one who could understand what his life was like, what it felt like to hold that power in his hands and pour it out.

"We can't let him ruin it," Seri said. For a moment he didn't know what she meant. She nudged him with her elbow. "Luap, that is. We can't let him ruin what Gird wanted."

"How can we stop him, if the Council of Marshals can't? And it's not *all* his fault. Remember what Rahi and the Autumn Rose were like before you worked on them?"

Seri ducked her head. "They should be friends; they should have been friends all along. You know that."

"Yes, and I know they weren't. That started before we came, a long time back, from all the tales. What I meant is that it's not only Luap who has strayed from Gird's dream. It's a lot of them, even Rahi. They never saw it clearly, maybe." Aris wondered again why not, when it seemed so obvious to him. They were older; they had known Gird in the war. Why couldn't they all have seen that what he wanted was good? A swirl of night wind brought flames snapping higher from their fire, and a gout of sparks lifted into the dark. Aris tried to keep his mind from following them, from the trance of light, but remembered that only Seri was here. He need not worry. He lifted his hand, in one of their childhood signals, copied badly from the huntsman, and let himself go.

Sparks flying on a dark wind . . . he felt the glittering heat, the potential fire, in each spark, and its frightening vulnerability. So small against the cold, the dark, and yet so bright, so hot. Were there sparks of darkness as potent? Could darkness spread, as fire spread, from its sparks? He let that thought go, and rose instead with another gout of sparks, high above the starlit land. Most sparks lit no fires; most died to ash in the cold wind, and most that fell found no fuel.

He came back to himself slowly, slipping from trance to the ordinary musing of any mortal around a fire. The ideas that had seemed so definite against the dark slipped out of his mind. The fire crackled, hissed, murmured. Behind him, one of the horses stamped and blew. He felt his skin tighten all over, fitting itself to him again. Where had he been? Only a thin blue flame danced above the coals; he could not at first remember why he saw the fire from below, why he was curled on the ground instead of a bed. Then he felt Seri's hand on his shoulder, solid and warm, as if she were the hearth in which a great fire burned. He took a long breath in, smelling the leather of her boots, the wool of his own shirt, the firesmoke, the horses nearby, even the wet herbs near the tiny creek. When he looked up, the stars seemed like a scattering of sparks . . . but sparks that would not die, that would never go out.

"And what did you bring back this time, Ari?" Seri's voice was almost wistful. He had never told her a story she liked better than one from his earliest childhood, and he had never been able to tell that story again. Like all the visions that came with light, it existed only in the moments of the trance itself, and his memory faded more quickly than a meadow flower.

"The sparks," he began, letting his tongue wander free. "If Gird's wisdom brought light, then the sparks flew out . . . but not all minds held the fuel to kindle them. Some would burn bright, but quickly die. Some would catch no spark at all. Many would come to the fire for warmth, but fear the sparks flying, lighting in themselves. . . ."

"But I feel it," Seri said. He turned over to look at her. He could see it in her, as he could feel it in her touch.

Aris pushed himself up. "You're right. You do."

"And so do you!" She sounded almost angry.

"I hope so. I used to think so, but—"

"But you've been listening to them. To *him.*"

Aris shook his head. "No—it's not that. I think—I think Father Gird saw things from his own side—as a peasant—and so for peasant-born it's a little easier to catch his vision. It all fits. When I try to think like you, I see it clearly, but when I try to see it like Lady Dorhaniya, or Luap, I see other possibilities. Gird didn't have any reason to trust magery; even with me, he wished my healing would work some other way. He had no place for magery in his mind, no place it would serve the dream and not harm it. He agreed my healing was good, but he would not have agreed that being able to lift stones by magery was good. He would think how they could be used to hurt people. What I know is how much the magery hurts if you don't use it. Again, he understood that about my healing power, but I don't think he realized that it's true of *any* magery. It's like—suppose someone said to you, 'Don't lead. Don't learn. Don't question anything.' "

Seri had been scowling, but at the last her face changed expression. "No one could tell me that! I have to, it's the way the gods made me—"

"Yes, and the mageborn who have magery *are* that way, just as you are eager to learn, curious about everything, quick to lead. Remember our childhood? You got whacked with a spoon often enough for being—what did the old cook say?—nosy, bossy, always asking questions. You couldn't help it, but what do you think it would've felt like if you'd tried to change?"

"I suppose . . . I'd have felt trapped, like a wild animal tied in a barn. Ugh!" She shivered. "Why did you have to say that? I don't like to think about it."

"But when I tried not to heal, you said you understood. . . ."

"I knew you were unhappy, and I knew you would never do anything wicked, Aris, but I didn't imagine—gods forgive me, but I didn't really think what it might be like. I was thinking of the people who needed you, that you could heal." She leaned against him, as she had in childhood. "I'm sorry, Ari. It just never occurred to me."

"It's all right." He leaned back, comforted by her presence, by the familiar warmth and smell of her. "But can you try to understand, now, why it's so hard for the mageborn who have those talents to leave them unused?"

"I suppose." The doubt in her voice had no real solidity; he knew he had won his argument. He waited. In a few moments, she spoke again, slowly, thinking it out aloud. "And I suppose it's as bad—or worse—for Luap. Is that what you're saying? He's a king's son by birth, but he never got to *be* a king's son. They didn't know he had the magery; he never had training in its use. Yet he has it, and it's as restless in him as your healing is in you, or my curiosity is in me. I wonder if the royal magery would be stronger?"

"Arranha says it is, that when it comes it either comes in full or not at all—and that Luap has it. I don't think Gird ever knew how hard it was for Luap, or recognized how determined Luap was to be loyal to Gird." He felt Seri shift against his side, and then relax again.

"I suppose," she said again. "I would think that for Gird—but then, Gird never asked me to do anything but be what I am."

Aris snorted. "Except the time you were playing those tricks on your Marshal." He could feel her suppressed chuckle; it finally erupted into a gurgle of laughter.

"Yes . . . well . . . even then he didn't ask me to be different, just reminded me that I was too young to know all the background, and too old to get away with it."

"I've always wondered—what *did* Father Gird do to you?"

Seri laughed again. "What do you think? Gave me a couple of smacks and told me to be glad he hadn't used his full strength. Told me to behave myself. If I wanted to be a leader, I'd have to set a better example to the junior yeomen—and that was true. It took me longer than I like to remember to straighten them out. They were a *lot* wilder than I was. 'Think you're clever now, lass,' he said to me, 'but what's to come of them if there's a real danger, and you're not there, and they won't trust the Marshal, eh?' Made me think, it did. He left me there another half-year, then put me in that grange down near yours."

"Good for both of us," Aris said.

"He thought so. You'd be a steadying influence on me, he said, and I'd be sure you didn't walk off a roof in a trance." Aris felt the twitch of her shoulder. "Come to think of it, he never did believe you could take care of yourself, any more than I do." As if on cue, Aris yawned, a great gaping yawn he could not smother before she turned and saw it. "And you can't," she said. "You were off there wherever you were, and you're half asleep now. Go on. I'll wake you to watch later."

Aris wrapped himself in his blanket, and slid into sleep as comforting as a hot bath, just wondering if Seri would wake him, or sit up all night thinking. The grip of her hand on his shoulder woke him to dark stillness; her other hand came across his mouth, warning. Before he moved, he felt some dire magery nearby. He slid a hand free of the blanket, and touched hers, tapping a message. Her hands left him, and he reached down and slid his own knife free. Where had he left the sword? Where was the danger? And from whom?

It felt like nothing he knew, no mageborn he had ever been near, not even his mother's last lover. Cold, ancient malice, a bitterness no love of life could touch . . . *iynisin*. Of the timbre of the elves who had so delighted him in Fin Panir, but of opposite flavor, this magery mocked all he had admired.

"Here's your sword . . ." Seri breathed, barely audible above the pounding of his heart. Aris flung the blanket aside and stood, staring into the darkness. He could just feel the warmth of the banked fire on one leg, but no gleam of coals lit the dark, and the stars' light seemed feebler than it had. The wind had died; he could hear nothing but felt one cheek colder than the other, proving the air moved. He felt Seri's movement at his back, a shifting from leg to leg more menacing than nervous. Then her quiet mutter of explanation: "I felt it first, then something dimmed the starlight. The horses aren't moving. Nothing is. I woke you—"

"I feel it," Aris said. "Iynisin." Saying the name aloud took great effort, but when it was out he felt less frozen. He bent and folded his blanket, felt around until he located the rest of his pack, and put it all well aside, in case they had to fight.

"The elves said that was a legend." Seri's voice wavered; he realized that she was really afraid. Seri? it was absurd; Seri had never been afraid.

"Doesn't mean it's not true." Aris moved to her voice, and leaned against her. His hands prickled; he laid one on her arm, and felt the demand of his healing lessen. She could not be sick—was he supposed to heal her *fear?* He let the power free, and felt it move from his palm to her arm, driving away whatever hindered her light.

Her *light.* Even as he withdrew his magery, knowing it had been enough, Seri burst into a glow as different from magelight as sun from starlight. Shadows fled away from them; Aris saw his own, black and dire, stretch to the edge of their hollow before he too caught light. His, though he had never seen it before, he knew to be magelight, the same as Arranha's. It had the quality of lamplight or firelight; he knew without trying that he could kindle wet wood with it at need. But Seri's ... Seri's was light only, the essence of vision, of knowledge, of inward seeing and outward seeing. Aris pulled his mind back from its favorite pastime, and had a moment to think how they must look, two glowing figures on a dark wilderness.

Then he saw the iynisin. All around the hollow, everywhere he looked, the blackcloaks, the beautiful faces eroded by hatred to shapes of horror. He could not tell how many, but he felt the weight of their malice as if each glance were a stone piled on his flesh. As if they knew the very moment of being seen, they spoke— two of them, voices clashing slightly as if they read from a script.

"Foolish mortals ... you have chosen an unlucky place and time to indulge your lust." Aris said nothing; Seri muttered, but not aloud. The iynisin went on. "You stink of Girdish lands, mortals; you trespass on ours. As we cursed your dead leader, so we may curse you, if we do not kill you and feed on your flesh."

This time Seri answered them. "If you think you cursed Gird, you haters of trees, you erred; he died beloved of the gods."

"And his line died with him." One of the iynisin came closer; Aris could not see that the others moved. "Only sunlight spared him the full power of the curse, but that much held. And he ventured out only near dawn . . . it is long until dawn, mortals, and no sunlight will save you."

Aris felt a burst of gaiety, unexpected and irrational. "Then we shall have to save ourselves," he said. "With the gods' help, if they find us worthy of aid."

"You cannot stand against *us*," the iynisin said. "See—" He pointed to the cluster of trees around the spring, where the horses were tied. Beyond, on the brow of the hollow, all the iynisin pointed downward. Aris stared: in the light he and Seri made, the trees shriveled, twisting in on themselves; their wood groaned and split. The new green leaves blackened, as if scorched. Under the trees, all the little green things that sheltered there shriveled as well. In the trees, one of the horses made a noise Aris had never heard. He felt Seri's back shiver against his; his sword felt loose in his grip as sweat ran cold down his sides.

"You call yourself a healer," another iynisin called. "Heal *that*, boy." They all laughed, a sound so close to beautiful that it hurt the ears worse than simple noise. Aris's hands itched, then burned; his healing magery demanded that he do something. But he could not go to the trees or the horses without leaving Seri, and he would not leave her. Could he do anything at a distance? He flung his power outward, toward the trees, but if it worked at all, it was the flurry of wind that whirled dead leaves from dead stems.

Not that way. The voice in his mind sounded impatient, like a master whose prentice had just done something wrong for the fifth time. I've never done this before, he thought back at it. *Think!* it bellowed. "Father Gird!" Aris said, almost squeaking in surprise.

"He can't help you," the iynisin said. The others laughed and sang. "He's dead . . . dead . . . dead . . ." And on that refrain they came forward, their black shadows streaming away behind them. Aris had just time to think what a ridiculous way this was to die, when he felt Seri lunge away from his back, and he nearly fell backwards into her. That stagger saved him; the blade aimed at his throat missed, and he had his own back up by then. He had not had as much training in weapon skills as Seri, but she had insisted that he go beyond the basics required of all yeomen.

His sword clashed on three; he was too busy to be scared, but a corner of his mind insisted he had no chance against so many.

He had no time to remember exactly what he'd been taught. He had to thrust, swing, and thrust again; an iynisin blade slid past too fast for his response and he felt it burn along his side. He sagged to one knee; another blade caught his swordarm, slicing deep; his fingers opened, and the sword fell. He heard Seri gasp, and a dark form leaped above him. He grabbed a boot, and yanked; the iynisin fell, cursing, kicked back then scrambled out of reach. His hands itched, intolerably; he had no strength to withhold the healing magery. It leapt from hand to hand, almost brighter than his mage-light, scalding first his wounded arm, then burning along his bones to reach his wounded side. With an intolerable wrench, his rib reknit itself, and the organs within returned to health. *So that's what Father Gird meant,* he thought, reaching for the sword.

Battle had now passed beyond him, for they had Seri backed to the rockface, her sword dancing in her own light, ringing a wild music off her attackers' blades. Her face had a withdrawn expression, showing neither fear nor anger. Aris ran forward, noticing how his light threw the iynism shadows back into themselves, caught between the two lights. He thrust clumsily at the first black-cloaked back he saw, wasting no time in challenge. Seri had told him often enough he should spend more time in grange and barton: he would admit she was right, if they lived. This close he could see the blood on her clothes, sense the heaviness in her legs. He did not wait for Gird's admonition. To send his healing to Seri was the same as healing himself; he hardly slowed his attack on a second iynisin while closing her wounds.

They turned upon him again, but he fought through the ring to her side, taking another slashing blade across his shoulders. This, as he set his back to the rock, repaid his healing of it with a pain the double of its cause. One corner of his mind wanted to think about that: to wonder at the discovery that he could heal himself, to consider why it hurt, when none of those he healed had ever complained of pain. Between him and this curiosity stood the memory of Gird, who would not put up with nonsense in the middle of a fight. First things first, the old man would have said.

"I thought they'd killed you," Seri said. Then, before he could answer, she said, "Shift sides." She lunged forward, and he slithered sideways behind her. He had come up on her right, her strong side; she needed him at her left.

"I, too," Aris said, trying to look sideways and to the front at the same time. He wished he'd practiced whatever it was she'd just done to make an iynisin lose its blade. Something slashed the back of his hand, and he dropped the sword again. His tendons and bones screeched their fury at his clumsiness as the magery pulled them back into place and knit them into strength; in the meantime, the dagger in his left hand had shattered. He snatched frantically at the fallen sword, and got it up just in time to save Seri from a killing thrust to the side.

The analytical corner of his mind decided that the pain was healthy after all; it was the compaction of all the pain normally felt during normal healing. As healer, he had used his magery to lift such pain from those he healed; part of his exhaustion came from absorbing that pain. But he could not do this for himself. Better, the analytical function went on, like a prosy lecturer who does not realize that outside the classroom a riot has started, better to mend the real damage than soothe the pain, if that is the choice.

"ARIS!" Seri's shout brought him out of that, to see the black-cloaked iynisin fleeing through the twisted trees and over the rim of the hollow. From behind them, above the rock-face, a light stronger than their own held all starlight at its core. It was that, and not their fighting, that the iynisin had fled.

Chapter Seventeen

Although Luap had been startled to find Aris's note, he realized that it might be wiser to bring up the idea of moving the mageborn when Seri and Aris were not in the city. They could only confuse the issue, and he had not yet formed a plan for convincing Aris to leave Seri behind. First convince the Council, and then talk to Aris. He rolled and unrolled a scroll as he thought about it. The details of the plan he had rehearsed so long flicked through his mind. How long, he wondered, would Aris be gone? Should he press for a meeting today? He thought not. Any appearance of hurry would plant some of those peasant hooves firmly in their muddled minds, ox-like. He remembered how it had been with his first version of Gird's Life.

He waited until the next regular meeting, two days later. The younglings, as he thought of them, had not returned. Some had noticed a column of smoke from far away, but that could have been anything. It was the season for storm-lighted grass fires, he reminded the worriers. And he had the feeling that they were unhurt, no matter what the smoke meant ... they would reappear when they were ready, cheerful and sturdy as always. And inconvenient, no doubt.

The meeting began on a sour note, because a complaint of witchcraft had been referred from a grange-court. A group of sheepfarmers insisted that a mageborn boy had cursed their flock, causing all the lambs to be born dead. They had beaten the boy, who had responded with an obvious burst of magery, setting a hayrick afire. The local Marshal had saved the boy, but wasn't sure the first accusation was correct—and the boy, he said, would never completely recover from the beating. He had come, with the boy and two of the sheepfarmers, to Fin Panir to "settle this once and for all," as he put it. Luap winced; this would make the Marshals edgy about anything to do with mageborn.

He watched the sheepfarmers, tall husky men in patched tunics, sit on the edge of the bench in the meeting room, as far from the mageborn boy as they could. He didn't entirely blame them. It was hard to judge the boy's age—Luap guessed about twelve—because of his strangeness. He had mismatched eyes, one that slewed wide, and a constant tremor that erupted in a nervous jerk to his head at intervals. The eye that looked ahead had an expression Luap had never seen before, cool and calculating it seemed, though his mouth dripped spittle when his head jerked. The Marshal, balding and scrawny (had he really been the one who saved Gird from being trampled that time?), explained that the boy had had a bad name in their vill from the beginning. And it was his limp—not the slewed eye or the tremor—that resulted from the beating.

The farmer's testimony came in slow, difficult bursts of thick dialect; Luap knew they resented the questions he asked, but he had to know what they said to keep accurate notes. They knew their sheep, they kept repeating, and while it's true that sheep come into the world looking for a way back to the high pastures, they'd had a fair crop of lambs every year until this lad took a dislike to 'em, and for nothing worse than being told to keep away from Sim's daughter who was carrying her first and feared the evil eye. They knew he'd cursed the sheep because he said so—or at least he gabbled a string of nasty-sounding stuff that must have been a curse, and right then old Fersin's best ewe bloated up and died. Within a day, anyway, and it wasn't the season for death-lily, neither. Then the ewes started dropping lambs too soon, dead lambs, all of 'em, as if someone had fed them bad hay with birthbane in it, but no one had. Wasn't any birthbane nearer than a day's ride.

The Council looked at the Marshal—one of many named Seli, called for convenience Bald Seli—and he shrugged. "They called me in when the first ewe died, and accused this boy. I said don't be calling down evil you don't need—that ewe could've eaten something. None of 'em knew what the words meant, that he used. And they had no proof he was mageborn, only that he showed up years back with no family, and a scrap of good cloth for a cloak. Then the lambs started coming, all dead. They didn't call me; I heard from you—well—one of 'em's son, a junior yeoman. Thought I should know, he said. I went up there and found they'd pounded this boy so hard they'd broken bones, and then he'd set the hay on fire. The way I understand Gird's law is if the boy did magery first, he's wrong, but if he was hurt first, he could use magery to defend himself."

"Burning hay's not defense," muttered one of the farmers, as if he'd said it before.

"It made you let go of him," the Marshal said, as if he'd said that before, too.

"Is he truly mageborn?" asked Luap. The boy flicked him a malevolent glance that sent shivers down his back. Mageborn or not, the boy was wicked.

"I don't know," Bald Seli said. "He won't say. Isn't there some way to tell?"

Everyone looked at Luap. Would they realize that it was a use of magery to detect magery, and thus required a breaking of the law to detect a possible breaker of the law? No, irony was beyond them. He thought of sending for Arranha, but decided against it. He let a little of his power come forth, a mere trickle, and spread it as a net, imagining a silvery web before him. If the boy had mageborn blood, and such power, it should color that web. He leaned toward the boy.

"Are you mageborn?" he asked quietly. The boy stared past him, his skew eye to one side and his focused gaze to the other. Luap turned to Bald Seli. "Can he answer questions? Has he ever talked with people in your vill?"

"Oh, aye," the Marshal said. "He never said much, but he made shift to ask for food, and answer yes or no. He didn't have our accent, but we could understand him."

"No, ye didn't!" The boy's voice was a peculiar skirl, rising and falling with no relation to the sense of the words. "Ye never understood me. Me. Never. Ye ask am I mageborn—I'm more'n mageborn. . . ." His words fell into a gabble Luap could not understand. The two farmers cringed against the wall.

"Careful, sir, he's doin' it again. He'll be cursin' the whole Fellowship next—"

To Luap it seemed that the boy's gabble was that of one who could not control his voice, like the very old who sometimes lost words and strength all at once. It did not sound as he had imagined cursing to sound, but the boy's cold gaze made him uneasy. He felt nothing in his net of magery to make him think the boy was mageborn—but he was not sure he wasn't, either The babble died away; the boy licked the spittle off his lips with an eagerness that frightened Luap again. He wondered what Gird could have made of this; it was beyond him.

Cob came up with their solution. "Take him into the High Lord's Hall," he said. "And get Arranha. If it's a curse, that'll be the place to take it off. We'll know what we're dealing with."

Luap did not want to go, but he knew he must. He watched two Marshals carry the boy, whose tremors and twitches seemed less a struggle to escape than the way his body worked. Arranha met them at the Hall doors, and seemed no more upset by this than any of the problems people had brought him. He looked at Luap.

"He's mageborn, in part, but he was also born flawed. Both in his magery and in himself."

"Did he curse the sheep?" one of the farmers asked.

"I don't know," Arranha said. He asked the boy the same question, but got no reply. "Bring him up to the altar," he said then, "and we'll see if the god can shed light on our dilemma."

But as they approached the altar, the boy exploded in wild squeals and convulsive movements so strong the Marshals could hardly hold him. "He's frightened," one of them said. "Maybe he thinks we sacrifice people."

The farmers muttered, and Luap thought he heard one of them say "Only a mageborn would think of that."

"Put him down, then," Arranha said. They laid the boy down as gently as they could, for all his thrashing about, but he began beating his head on the stone floor. "We need Aris," Arranha said. He laid his hands to either side of the boy's head, but instead of quieting the boy screamed, a piercing noise that echoed in the high vaults of the Hall. Then he twisted around and caught Arranha's thumb in his teeth. Luap leapt forward, as did others, and somewhere in the struggle to unlock the boy's teeth from Arranha's thumb, the boy quit breathing. No one quite knew when, or why.

After that, and its daylong aftermath of confusion, grief, and anger, Luap expected nothing but trouble when he introduced his idea the next day. He led up to it as carefully as he could,

explaining how a distant land could let his people learn to use their
skills to benefit others, but he was sure their minds were full of
the boy's malicious grin as he bit down on Arranha's thumb. When
he paused, he heard exactly the disapproving murmur he had
expected.

To his surprise, Raheli stood. The murmur stilled. Everyone
peered to see Gird's daughter.

"I believe him," she said. Then she looked at Luap, eye to eye,
gaze to gaze. "I believe him," she said more softly, and silence lay
heavily on them. "My father—Gird—" As if they did not know, he
thought. "Gird saw good in him; he was spared to serve Gird's
Fellowship." In a long pause, no sound broke the stillness; he saw
her take a long breath and wondered what would follow. "What is
the reward of a faithful luap?" she asked. None answered. She
looked around. "I will tell you, then," she said. "A faithful luap,
one who serves without enjoying power, one who stands beside, in
the place of, the inheritor, shall be recognized at last by the one
he serves. He shall stand before him, and be given his reward, the
respect of the people. This is Gird's luap: Gird will determine
his reward."

Luap blinked; that could be taken two ways, and one of them
he felt as a blade at his throat. "In the meantime," Raheli went
on, "we can give our respect. I believe him, that he will take his
folk to a far place and not breed up an army of invasion. You know
I have not trusted him in the past. If his stronghold were nearer,
I might be less willing to trust him now. But I believe he means
what he says, and I believe the distance will enforce a truce
between our peoples. My father wanted all to live in peace, but he
himself could not find a way to let the mageborn learn to use their
powers aright. That boy yesterday—if he had been brought up in
a distant land, he would never have caused the trouble he did here.
Arranha and Luap would have recognized something wrong in him.
I believe Luap in this—that Gird agreed to let them go, and to
this end." She sat down, and in a moment the murmur began again,
this time in a wholly different mood.

For that, and for some other reason he did not fully understand,
when the Marshal-General called on him again, he found himself
speaking with less forethought and grace than usual.

"Marshal Raheli has said more than I would claim—that boy
frightened me. It's true that I think our young people are best
trained elsewhere—some place where we can be sure their power
does no harm, that they have control of it, and know how to use

it for good. But that boy—Marshals, I cannot claim to understand that."

"But if you had such a child, in your distant place, you would not let him come back here to cause trouble, would you?"

"No." He shuddered at the thought. "I don't know what we'd do—but we would not let him loose on the world."

"What about Arranha's thumb?" asked another Marshal. Many of them. Luap knew, liked the old man even though they would not follow his god. Luap shook his head.

"We don't know. If Aris were here, I'm sure he could heal it. But Garin is not as skilled, or as powerful. Arranha says if the Sunlord wants him healed, he will be healed, but he's feverish this morning."

Bald Seli had attended the Council, though his sheep-farmers had already headed home. Now he spoke up. "Maybe I should have let them kill him, 'stead of bringing such trouble on us."

Glances flicked at Luap, each a minute but definite blow. "Maybe—but I think you did right," Cob said. "You were trying to be fair; that's what mattered. And I'll agree with Raheli, Gird's daughter, that if the mageborn had some safe place to teach their children, we might not have problems like this. At least not with the mageborn. It's not Luap's fault that the boy went wrong; for all we know he was cursed from birth."

To Luap's surprise, the other Marshals slowly came around to the same decision, and for much the same reasons. No one wanted to say good riddance to the mageborn—he was not even sure they thought that inwardly. Instead, the boy and his uncontrolled powers became the reason to agree that the mageborn needed a place to be trained properly. And they trusted Luap and Arranha to oversee that training and determine who might come back to the eastern lands.

"Will you take everyone? All the mageborn?" asked Bald Seli finally.

Luap shook his head. "I will take all who want to come, and try to persuade the younger ones that it's best. But some are too old, at least until we have established a settlement. Most of you know Lady Dorhaniya, for instance: she will certainly not come at first. Others are happy here, and get along well with those who are not mageborn—either they have no magery, or they are content not to use it. Unless you demand it, I expect they will choose to stay. Those who have little mageborn heritage, and whose families have no other mageborn blood, will almost certainly stay."

"I like that." Bald Seli said. "I remember old Gird saying we needed most to get along with each other; I'd hate to see that dream abandoned."

"So we'll give you all the troublemakers," Cob said to Luap with a grin, "and keep all the good ones—except you and Arranha, of course. And I suppose young Aris will come with you?"

Luap didn't want to start on that. "I thought to invite all mageborn who wanted to come—"

"But no others?" asked Raheli.

There was the crux of it. "I hardly thought any but mageborn would *want* to come," Luap said carefully. "Surely it would be as strange for them as a society wholly without magery is for the talented among us."

"But who'll do the work you mageborn don't know how to do?" asked Bald Seli. "Your folk don't know cooking and building and such, do they? They couldn't yoke a span of oxen and use a plough. . . ."

Luap nodded. "Some of those I think will want to leave are half-bloods, as I am . . . remember that I was fostered among farmers; I farmed, before the war." From the look on Bald Seli's face, he didn't quite believe it. Luap let a little humor seep into his voice, as he broadened his accent. "Aye, Var, coom up there; steady, Sor. . . ." His hands clutched imaginary plough handles, and his use of the traditional names for oxen brought smiles to more than one face. He grinned at Bald Seli. "My foster-father had me make my own yoke, same as anyone else. I've no doubt there are better farmers among you, but I made my crops and paid my field-fee and fed my family from my own work."

"I thought you'd been brought up in a big house." That was Kevis, who knew Dorhaniya.

"Only as a small boy. Then it was off to the farm, and no more big house for me until I came here." Luap glanced around the room. "I won't say all of us are farmers, or have such skills, but even for those who don't, it won't hurt them to learn." A shuffle of feet at that, agreement too strong for silent nodding. "We won't have to take the farmers and crafters you need here." Phrasing it that way, it could seem he was concerned for the welfare of those left behind. Which he was, in a way.

"But if someone wanted to come—I'm thinking, Luap, that if Aris goes with you, Seri will want to go too. You can hardly expect to separate those two."

"I wouldn't forbid it, certainly." Certainly not now, not when it could cause the failure of the whole plan. "But we don't want youngsters who wish they had magic powers wasting their time out

there, when they could be learning good crafts here." Others nodded, seeing the point of that. "As well, since it is for our people
to learn to use magery, it could be more dangerous for those without it. What I'm thinking of is more—more an outpost, say, where
our people go for special training. When they have it, some of
them—if you permit—will no doubt want to come back, and use
their powers for good purposes." More dubious looks at that, eyes
shifting back and forth under lowered brows. All the better: if they
forbade mageborn to return, then it was not *his* fault that the
peoples sundered.

"What about the archives?" asked another Marshal. "How can
you keep the archives and lead your settlement?"

Luap relaxed. This was something he had planned carefully. "We
have many good scribes now, those who can not only copy a text
accurately, but understand how to organize the archives. I can't do
both jobs—certainly not in the first few years out there—but I will
always be available for questions. Frankly, I think my successors—
those I will recommend—are as skilled as I am, if not more skilled.
I will continue to write, of course, but I doubt you'll miss my
contributions."

"But are these scribes Marshals?" asked the same man.

"No," Luap said. "Although there are at least three who have
been yeoman-marshals and might qualify for the new training, if
you felt it important. Certainly there are advantages in having an
Archivist who is also a Marshal . . . even though I'm not."

"As good as," Raheli said. "We've granted you Marshal's blue,
and the authority within the archives. I, for one, would prefer an
Archivist to have Marshal's training."

The Marshals discussed that for a time, and Luap realized that
they had made their decision, made it far more easily than he had
ever expected. They would argue about when he should go, and
who should be in charge of the archives after him, and how often
he should report . . . but they were letting him go.

So he told Arranha that evening, trying to cheer him up. Arranha's thumb had swollen to twice its size, and a red streak ran up
his arm. Suriya, the woman Aris had worked with in herblore, had
come to poultice it, but so far without effect.

"She didn't have to tell me it was a bad bite," Arranha said. He
sat with his eyes almost closed and the tense expression of real
pain on his face. "I knew that, from the malice on his face, the
way he ground his teeth on it, the way I felt."

"I wish Aris were here." Luap tried to sit still; he knew that Arranha needed quiet, restful companions.

"I, too. Young Garin has a lovely voice, but not a tithe of Aris's healing power. He eased the pain awhile ... suggested I have Bithya in, that girl Aris worked with ... but I'll wait. Perhaps I won't need her."

"Do you want us to send after Aris? Although I don't even know for certain which way he went."

"No ... no, don't trouble the lad. He needs this chance to show what he can do somewhere else, and if the gods don't choose to send him back ...." Arranha's voice faded. Luap felt a stab of worry. The old man could die of this, and then what? He needed him; they all needed him. Mageborn and peasant alike, they needed his wisdom, his determination to find the light in any tangled darkness.

"Rest now," he said to Arranha. "Is there anyone or anything ... ?"

"No ... don't bother."

Luap wondered if anyone else might help. Raheli, he remembered, had had a parrion of herblore. When he found her, she shook her head. "The woman Aris studied with knows more than I did, she and her daughter both. We talked about it."

"There's nothing more—?"

"Not without taking his hand off, and that's chancy, as you know. Sometimes it saves lives, but some die anyway."

"I thought of sending for Aris, but we don't know where he went, and Arranha says not to."

"Arranha's getting feverish. But you're right, we don't know where Aris is, and we have no way to find him." Rahi sighed. "It seemed like such a good idea, giving Aris his chance to travel and test his healing—and he and Seri might make a good partnership, if they had time together—but now I wish we'd waited." She stalked restlessly about the room for a moment, then said, "Well—and when do you think you'll start resettling your people?"

"I don't know I'd—you know Arranha and I had talked about it?" She nodded. "I depended on his advice, but now—"

"Now you may have to make all the decisions yourself. I hope not, for your sake as well. What will you do first?"

"Take others to see it. Start thinking how to make it workable— we should grow our own food, for one thing, and not have to transport it from here. There'll be plenty of work, hard work, to make it feasible."

She nodded. "There's something else: you need to think which mageborn to move first, and whether you want to gather them somewhere before you take them. Supplies for the first year or two, until your crops take hold. . . ."

"Supplies, yes." Luap grimaced. "Well—I did it for Gird; I ought to be able to do it now. But I don't even know how many mageborn there are, or how many will come."

But the familiar rhythm of planning comforted him in the days following, as Arranha grew sicker, the swelling worse. He began making lists: seed grain, vegetable seeds, tools for farming and tools for making tools. He knew of no mageborn smiths . . . could he hire a smith to set up there? And if he could, with what could he pay a smith's high fees? He found a master smith, and began asking the necessary questions; smiths were notoriously slow in giving answers. He went back to his lists. They would need a few looms— with skilled craftsmen and enough wood, they could easily copy the pattern looms. He paused, thinking. He had never worked wood himself . . . and that forest was very different . . . did that matter? Another question to ask a craftsmaster. He needed to know more about the skills of the people he would take—how many mageborn could weave, cook, plough, reap? So far as he knew, the work that needed doing—the work that would keep them alive—had never been done by magery.

Several times a day he checked on Arranha, who was unfailingly cheerful but visibly weaker each visit. To his surprise, others with no mageborn blood at all also visited. Rahi delayed her return to her grange and scoured the archives for anything on herbal treatments. Dorhaniya worked her way up the hill and arrived breathless and faint; Luap was afraid she would have a fatal attack as well. He insisted that she stay overnight in the palace; Elis agreed, and the next day Luap hired a cart to take her home. The men who had listened to Arranha's many lectures on light and wisdom came to stand by his door, peering in shyly but unwilling to intrude on a sick man.

Luap felt a deep guilt he could not explain. He knew it had not been his fault: the boy would have bitten anyone; he had been mindlost if not possessed by some evil. He knew it was not his fault Aris was gone—Rahi had confessed that she and the Rosemage and Arranha himself had connived at that. He knew it was not his fault that he lacked the healing magery. But he felt guilty nonetheless . . . somehow it *was* his fault—his fault that Gird's dream had not come true, and his fault that Arranha suffered for it. In reaction, he felt that his irritation was pardonable when one of the scribes made a mistake or spilled the ink. He got a morbid satisfaction out of scolding someone he would not ordinarily have scolded, and then lashing himself for being short-tempered.

He clung to his lists, and shared them with the Rosemage and Rahi. The Rosemage pointed out that he should require the mage-born to pay their own way, if they could: he was not a king, so he could not be expected to fund the expedition. Some of them were still wealthy; nearly all of them had something to contribute.

"They'd better," Rahi said lazily, leaning back on the cushions of a bench in the scribe's room. It was late night, and the scribes had long since ceased work. "If they don't have something to con-tribute, they'll starve."

"More than skills: money," the Rosemage said. "Clothes, tools, dishes, all that."

Luap had a sudden panic. "How are we going to transport all that? Either we have to take it to the cave, and try to stuff it in the chamber; or we have to take it into the High Lord's Hall— that doesn't seem right." He had a vision of the chamber choked with boxes, bags, sacks, bales of household gear ... of the mess creeping across the floor of the great hall. Yet it had to be done: they couldn't make everything out there.

"It will work," the Rosemage said. "You don't have to do it all yourself."

"No, but—" But it had been his idea, his plan, and his place ... his dream, in place of Gird's. If it came true, it would be his responsibility; he could not deny that. Gird had known, Gird had not started a war and then gone home to twiddle his thumbs and watch how it went.

"Scary, isn't it?" asked Rahi with surprising understanding. He looked at her, and she smiled. "Back before you joined, that very first battle, Norwalk Sheepfolds ... remember it from the archives?"

"Of course," Luap said. "Were you there? I thought—"

"No, I wasn't there. But it scared Gird—what he'd started. He wanted it; he thought it was the only way. But when it came, when he saw what it meant, that he could never go back and things would never be as they were, that scared him. And I thought that was what you were feeling."

"Yes," said Luap. "I suppose I am. I believe we have to do it, that it's the only way." The undefined warning the elves had given rose from his memory; should he tell them about it? No, for he could not tell them what he did not know himself. "If I'm wrong— if I forget something—"

"You can always come back for it. You will be coming back

quarterly at first anyway, to report to the Council and check on the new Archivist."

"That reminds me." Luap rummaged among the scrolls on his desk, glad to be distracted with something more pleasant. "I think we should keep a copy of the records out there, as well, and a copy of my records there should be transferred to Fin Panir each year. You know we found that mice and damp had damaged many of the old scrolls. This way, we would have complete records in two different places."

Rahi snorted. "You would have all the world scribes, if you could. Think of the hours of work—"

"Yes, but good records are important. Without them, we wouldn't have been able to clear up the land disputes of the past few years, for instance. And if we had better records of the early mageborn invasion, we might know more about what happened to the magery, and why the transfer pattern is graved in the floor of the High Lord's hall."

"Very well, but you'd best take more farmers than scribes or you'll be hungry"

"What are you going to do about Aris?" asked Rahi suddenly.

"Do? We can't find him; we have no idea where he's gone. We can only hope he comes back before Arranha dies."

"I didn't mean that: I meant about taking the mageborn away. Do you think Aris will go with you?"

"Of course he will," Luap said. "He's mageborn—more mageborn than I am. He has the most useful of mageries."

"And Seri?" asked Rahi.

Luap shrugged. "She's welcome, of course; I said that before. I don't think it's the best place for her; I doubt any without magery will find it comfortable. But we all know how attached she is to Aris."

The Rosemage stretched and grinned at him. "Yes—though you did your best to separate them, didn't you?"

Luap felt his ears getting hot. "I thought it would be easier later, yes. Evidently you two don't agree, and I'm willing to admit I was wrong about them. So I suppose I'll have a peasant-born Marshal as well as a mageborn healer—"

"—And Marshal," Rahi said. "Aris will probably pass the Council when Seri does."

"Is he keeping up his drill that well? I wasn't aware. Two Marshals, then, one of each. That should convince the more stiff-necked on the Council that we're being well watched and not up to mischief."

The Rosemage scowled. "Nothing will convince some thickheads. And they may not want to let Aris go; he's become very popular. If he does much healing on this journey, he will be under pressure to stay here. If Seri supports that—"

Luap shivered. "I hope not. Though to tell you the truth, if only he and Seri come back in time to save Arranha, I would trade that for having him in the new land."

Chapter Eighteen

The light strengthened, spread around them. "Well met, kinsmen!" came a ringing cry, so like the iynisin that Aris flinched. Then he realized that this held the true music.

"Elves," whispered Seri. "But we aren't their kinsmen—"

"Those are," Aris said, fighting for breath. The aftereffects of healing clogged his mind; he wanted to fall in a heap and sleep. "The iynisin—" But the elves were dropping lightly down from above now, bringing their own light, in which their expressions showed clearly: astonishment and consternation.

"But you're not—" said the first, then his mouth shut in a straight line.

"Who are you?" asked the next, after a similar look and recoil. "How have you made that light? Is this some new human magery? Are you in league now with the dark cousins?"

Aris had not known he could make such light, and now he did not know why it vanished, with a sudden shifting of shadows. "I am mageborn," he said. "But—"

"I am not mageborn," Seri interrupted. "I am a Marshal-candidate, from Fin Panir, and I have no idea why the light came." She still burned with it, brighter than their elflight but as steady. "But we are not in league with those creatures; they attacked us as we camped."

"In truth . . ." What must be the leader of this group appeared now, striding down the slope and around to confront them. Elflight, Aris realized, cast none of the harsh shadows his magelight had thrown; its radiance softened the shadows of Seri's light, though it did not dim its brilliance "You say you were attacked, by many?"

"Yes." Seri said. Aris glanced about but saw no bodies. He

thought he had killed at least one of those he struck from behind
. . . had they carried them away?

"If you were attacked," the elf leader said with such perfect
clarity that it seemed an attack of language, "then why do we see
blood only on your blades and clothes, while you stand unwounded?
Or are you such mighty warriors that you can without danger
engage a party of iynisin which might daunt even our band? For
that matter, where learned you that name, which is not commonly
used by mortal men?"

Around them now were the elves, all armed for battle as he had
never seen elves: terrible and grim they looked, in the light of their
magery He saw some of them look at the trees the iynisin had
cursed, and knew they would not forgive such an injury. He heard
the cries of one who found their horses, and sang the news to the
leader in that elvish tongue he had not learned. They will not
believe us, he thought to himself. Here we are unhurt—they will
believe we were with allies. His heart contracted. The elves had
never loved or trusted the mageborn, and with good reason.

"Aris healed us," Seri said. She wiped her blade on a hanging
shred of her tonic. "If you look, you will see he could not heal our
clothes." Then she looked more closely at the smear on the cloth.
"By—it has silver in it, this blood! Or is it your light?"

"Let me see," said the leader, stepping closer to her. He held
out his hand for her sword; she handed it over as if to a Marshal,
hilt first, across her fist. His brows rose, but he took it courteously,
then looked closely, then sniffed it. "Well," he said. "It is indeed
iynisin blood, lady, so whether it came from a quarrel among
friends or a meeting of enemies, we give you thanks for it." He
passed the sword to the others, each of whom examined it. The
leader looked at Aris. "You *healed,* she said. You have the healing
magery of your forefathers?"

"Yes, sir," Aris said. He held out his own blade. "And though I
fought with less skill, I did spill some of their blood." His blade,
too, the leader took and examined, then returned it, as another elf
handed Seri back her blade. Aris wiped his own, and sheathed it,
under those watchful eyes. When he looked up, the elf spoke.

"So you would say that you and this lady were beset by iynisin,
and fought them off, and you with your power healed your
wounds?"

"That is what happened, yes."

"A mageborn and a peasant together? A peasant with the power
to call light? And it *happens* that iynisin come upon you in this
place?"

Aris had no chance to answer; Seri broke in. "Yes, that is *true*. We came from Fin Panir, to—" She stopped, and glanced at Aris. What they had been discussing was no business of elves. The elf waited, brows raised.

"Seri and I were friends before we came to Fin Panir," Aris said. "Before Gird died. I came to ask him to allow me to use my magery to heal, and he granted that, but put us both in training there. We have little time together—"

"So you rode a day's journey away to find privacy?" The elf's question implied only one use of such privacy.

"No, we're on a longer journey." Aris gestured to his pack, which one elf was examining with care. "I have been granted permission to travel, and test my healing in other places; Seri is my—well— supervisor. The Council wishes a peasant-born to make sure I don't misuse my powers."

"They let a friend have this right?"

"I'm a Marshal-candidate," Seri said. In her voice was the certainty that a Marshal-candidate would tolerate no misdoings from anyone, least of all a friend.

"And his lover."

"No." Seri shook her head. "We have never been lovers; we don't need to be lovers."

"Ah. Rare in humans, though I have heard of it. Well, then, young mortals who are not lovers, can you explain how you called upon yourselves the malice of iynisin, or why you called on us with your light? We thought it was elflight, and you beleaguered elves: we came to your aid. We had seen magelight before—" Here the elf looked at Aris. "We would not have come for that, but this light—"he gestured at Seri."—is something we do not know and mixed with yours might be elflight." This time more gently, he asked her. "Are you sure you do not know how you called it?"

In that lessening of tension, with the elf's change of tone, Aris felt exhaustion sapping his strength again. Only immediate danger could keep him alert now, after such a day and night, after the healing power he had poured out. He heard Seri's explanation through a thick fog, and only realized he had fallen when someone caught him. Not Seri; he knew her hands. These were as alien as tree limbs: cold, strong, but not ungentle.

"—He's like this after healing sometimes," he heard her say. "Keep him warm—" He could not argue, but he could hear what they said, as they wrapped him in a blanket and laid him aside, while the leader still talked to Seri, and one of them stirred the fire and set the kettle back on it.

He listened to the voices, their sweet chiming voices and Seri's warm, practical peasant burr, comfortable as an animal's shaggy hide. She said nothing about Luap, but talked freely about her own training, Aris's training, the changes of policy that everyone discussed. Gird's legacy had been a government with few secrets, its issues argued openly in every market in Fintha. When the kettle boiled, he was able to drink a mug of the hot herbal brew, which opened his eyes and let him see that Seri's light had, at some point, gone out. Or back. She was telling the elf leader exactly what the iynisin had said, word for word as far as Aris could tell, and then describing the fight.

"I thought Ari had been killed; I'd been forced far enough away that I saw one sword go in—so I ran for the rockface. That way I had something at my back."

The elf leader nodded. "Wise—and this is your first real battle?"

"Yes . . . in the war, we were too young to do more than camp chores."

More raised brows. "You were too young to do camp chores, unless I read your age wrongly. But didn't you know your—Aris?—could heal his wounds?"

Seri shook her head. Her braid had come completely undone, and her hair looked like a wavering dark cloud. "No—he'd never healed himself before. We thought it worked only on others. When I saw him get up, I was as surprised as the iynisin. More, because they hadn't seen him; he came up behind them."

"I know why we didn't know I could," Aris said. His mind had caught hold of its familiar net of thought. They all turned to look at him. "It hurts—and the one time I tried it, that time I cut my hand on the sickle—"

"I remember," Seri said. "He was cutting wild grass for Gird's army," she said to the elves.

"—I thought to try it and it hurt a lot. So I quit."

"But it didn't hurt me," Seri said. "Or any of the others."

"No, and I think I understand that, too. You see—"

"Not now, Ari." Seri smiled to take the sting out of that. "You're not all the way awake yet." He was, but he wouldn't argue with her. If she wanted him to think it out somewhere else than with elves, he would. He sipped the bitter brew again, and wondered where her light had gone, and even more where it had come from. She shouldn't have been able to do that.

"What do you, young mortal, think of your friend's light?" That was the elf leader, pointing to him. Aris, in the midst of another sip, almost choked, and put the mug down.

"I don't know. I didn't know she could do it—I never heard of anyone coming alight but mageborn, and not all of them. And as you saw, her light was not the same color as mine."

"And you, she says, did not call light before: why this night, and not others? Did you never before need to see your way in the dark?" The sarcasm of the second question almost confused his answer to the first; perhaps Seri was right, and his wits lay more scattered than he thought. He hesitated, trying to gather them, before he answered, but the elves did not seem impatient. Only interested.

"We needed to see," he said finally. "Other times—it might have been useful, but I didn't really *need* it. Here—we felt the evil coming—"

"Did you call on the gods for aid?"

Had they? He could not quite remember. There had been a voice in his head—"Father Gird," he said. His voice chimed with Seri's, saying the same thing.

The elf leader frowned. "You're Gird's children? I thought only one of his children lived, a grown woman."

"Not really his children," Seri said, trying without success to smooth her hair. "But we called him Father Gird. Not to his face, it wouldn't have been respectful, but with each other."

"How old *were* you, when you left your homes?"

Aris tried to think. He wasn't entirely sure; the mageborn and the peasants reckoned age differently. "I had lost my front teeth," he said slowly. "I suppose we were—" He held up his hand. "—about this tall."

"Children!" the elf said. The elves spoke softly in their own language, a murmuring ripple, then the leader said, "So you called Gird your father?"

"Lots of people called him Father Gird," Seri said. "Or Gran'ther Gird."

"And you believe he spoke to you in your peril? How do you explain that?" Aris could not explain that, or the recurrent dreams he and Seri had had since Gird died. He shook his head. The elves spoke again to one another, and he tried to make sense of the beautiful sounds. He wished they would sing; he had heard elves sing at Gird's funeral.

He woke just at dawn, to find the elves standing in a circle around the two of them. Their elflight had drawn in around them, leaving Aris and Seri to the dawnlight. Seri looked as sleepy as he felt; in the cold predawn light, the dried blood on her clothes looked like smears of black mud. Aris scrambled up, uncertain of many things. The elven leader neither smiled nor frowned.

"We have no memory of any such as you," he said. "The blending of your lights last night . . . this is new. In all our memory, none of this lady's race has ever called such light, and we know no other living person with the magery among the mageborn." He looked at the cluster of trees, motionless now in their posture of anguish, blackened as if burnt, leafless, the ground beneath them ash-gray. "And there is the work of the iynisin, the un-singers, those who hate the living trees for the One Tree's choice. We found their blood on your blades . . . and I say we do not understand. We knew Gird, but we do not know you." The elves came together; their light brightened so that Aris could hardly see their faces. "We do not condemn you, for the iynisin blood you shed. But we do not commend you, for those trees which the iynisin blasted, and the creatures dead with them, and the spring now tainted. Heal that, if you can—if not, you have a long journey afoot, and the gods will deal with you."

The elves vanished, withdrawing their light with them; where they went, Aris could not see in the glare of the risen sun. He blinked; Seri came to him and put an arm around his shoulders. She was shivering; they both were. Around them, the new grass sprang, somewhat trampled but green and healthy; it stretched to the edge of the hollow. But the trees, and under the trees—all that was dead, not only dead but a death that held no promise of rebirth. Aris felt his mouth dry with fear as much as thirst. How could he heal that?

Gingerly, they moved into the twisted shadows of those twisted trees. The earth beneath felt dead, as if they walked on salt or iron filings. When they came to the horses—what had been the horses—Seri gave a choked cry and ran forward. Whatever magery the iynisin used had killed them as well, drawing them into strange unhorselike shapes as it worked, leaving the dead bodies hardly recognizable, the very hairs of mane and tail stiff as thorns. Aris moved past the horses to the spring, which the evening before they could have heard bubbling from here.

In its hollow, a plug of dirty wet earth like mucus, and a thin black stain along the line of the beck. It stank of death and decay, as disgusting a smell as the shambles in the lower market. Aris prodded the sodden earth with a stick that shattered in his hand. He was going to have to dig it out with his fingers. He shuddered; he did not want to touch the oozing slime. Behind him, he could hear Seri's boots scuffing the dead earth, the shriveled leaves. She was probably trying to do something about the horses, but he knew he had to clear the spring first. That was the earth's lifeblood.

He laid his hand just above the lowest part of the spring's hollow, trying not to smell it, and tried to feel his way into it. Nothing. Grimacing, Aris plunged his fingers into the cold, slimy mess and tugged. It felt worse than anything he'd ever touched. Gobs of cold stinking goo came off; he wiped the stuff from his hands on the ground beside the spring and reached in again. It's cursed, he thought to himself. There's nothing healthy in there at all; it's all gone wrong. Something warmer than the rest wriggled against his fingers and he almost cried out; when he yanked his hand free this time, he saw a dank tendril pull itself back into the muck.

Seri's hand on his shoulder felt as hot as a firebrand. "I hope Father Gird knows what he's doing," she said.

"He didn't do this," Aris said, wiping his hand on the dry earth again, and wishing he didn't have to put it back in there with whatever that was. "The iynisin did this." And us, he thought, because we came out here not knowing what we were doing.

"Can you heal it?" Seri asked, as calmly as if she were asking if someone could weave a fircone pattern.

"I'm trying," Aris said, putting his hand back on the damp hole. Was it any less slimy? Could he feel even a trickle of something that might be clean water?

"It doesn't look like it." Seri's face, when he glanced at her, gave no hint to any other meaning than the words themselves. "It looks as if you're digging muck out of a smelly hole—not healing a spring."

Aris felt a blinding rage, a white hot boiling fire that nearly escaped through his teeth. He clenched them, and looked at her through the flickering blaze. Her calm face . . . her eyes that were not looking at him, or the spring, or anything else. He saw the tears rise, glittering, in the early sun, and overflow; she did not even try to blink them away. His rage fled as suddenly as it had come. When he could get his breath back, he said "I can't reach my magery. You're right—I'm just digging and hoping."

"Aris!" She threw her arms around him so suddenly and so tightly that he lost his balance and they both nearly fell into the spring's hollow. "I'm *frightened*. I don't know what this means, what the iynisin were doing, what the elves meant—and the horses are dead and all the trees and there's no water and—"

She had never been frightened but once that he knew of; he had always relied on her. She had been awake last night when the iynisin came; she had fought with far more skill than he . . . and now she lay against him, shuddering all over like a frightened child. As they both were, he realized.

"I am too," he said. He could not even stroke her hair, not with his hands soiled by whatever curse the iynisin had laid on the spring. "I am, and I don't know what to do about it." For a long moment they huddled together. Oddly, saying aloud that he was frightened made the fright more manageable. It wasn't some nameless horror, some impossible alien presence: it was fright, the same ordinary fright that he had felt before in his life, worse perhaps because they were in real and not imagined danger.

As he thought this, warmth seemed to flow over him. He glanced up. The sun had risen well above the lip of the hollow by now, and its power seemed no less than it should be. He was frightened, hungry, tired . . . but alive, and warmer every moment. He shifted, and Seri too sat up.

"How silly," she said. "So that's what that kind of fright feels like. Ugh!" She shivered, but more as someone who steps unaware on spilled water than fear. "And it seemed to go on forever, but it couldn't have. . . ."

"No." Aris's hands had nearly dried. He looked at the moist hole, the gobs of wet muck he had torn out. "I wonder why I thought that would work. You were right; it needs real healing. And I can't."

"What if they come again?" Seri said. "It's daylight now; supposedly they can't come in daylight, but—"

Aris spread his dirty hands. "I don't know. We'll fight, I suppose, and if that's not enough, we'll die." Until he heard the words come out of his mouth, he did not know how serious he was. They might die; they might have died last night and if the iynisin came back they probably would. He didn't think the elves would come back to help them.

Suddenly it seemed ludicrous. Yesterday they had been eager to leave Fin Panir, eager to ride out into the unknown and find adventure, and all in one night they'd had more adventure than he had ever imagined. And he was tired, hungry, filthy, and quite ready to spend the rest of his days playing scribe to Luap, if only he could get back there.

Or was he? He met Seri's eyes, to find the same speculative look coming back at him. She, too, had gotten more than she bargained for, but now she was coming to grips with it. He didn't want to go back and be Luap's scribe, the tame healer of the safe city, doling out dollops of power to close cuts and ease bruises and mend the odd broken bone. It wasn't contempt for those sick or hurt . . . it was simply that others could do that. Herblore and time would heal most of it, and the healers he'd been training could do the rest. No—he wanted to find out if there was something only he could do. He had wanted a challenge, and here it was, and he wanted to meet it. He felt a smile stretch his grimy face. Seri grinned back.

"We were idiots," she said. "We came out here expecting nothing worse than a stray thief, when we knew—we *should* have known— that these empty lands are empty for a reason. We were playing at being careful, and it nearly killed us. It's not maneuvers: it's real."

"Right." Aris stood up. The spring still stank; the trees still arched in anguish over them. "So how much water was left in the kettle when the elves left?" Very little, it turned out. Aris sloshed it thoughtfully back and forth, and did not pour it into the mug Seri held. "Wait," he said. "I'm thinking of something. Let's go up and see if there's dew on the grass."

Out of the hollow, the wide plain lay lush and green; the dew they could lick from the grass refreshed without satisfying. Aris looked back. In full daylight, the hollow looked even worse. They could not leave it like that, even though it meant spending another night far from any settlement. He hoped the dead trees would burn.

The column of smoke rose, oily and rank, from the dead horses and twisted trees. They had lighted it from their campfire, after carrying their remaining gear, including the kettle with its swallow or two of water, up out of the hollow. Seri, who had served with her grange's fire patrol, had told Aris which way it would burn, sunsetting, away from the city.

"And this season, with the new green, it should not go far, and be no worse than a storm-lighted fire."

It looked worse; the trees writhed in the fire as if they were still alive, popping and cracking and showering sparks. The smoke twisted, billowed, clear evidence to anyone as far as the horizon that something dire had happened. A back gust whirled it up Aris's nose; he coughed and shook his head. They waited; the fire burned away from them at last, the trees shattering into fallen coals. Without their shape, the hollow looked naked, vulnerable. Aris whispered an apology without realizing he'd done it until Seri looked at him.

"I was thinking of the Lady, of Alyanya," he said. "You remember what you told me, long ago—that the springs are sacred because that's where she gives her blood to the world?"

"Yes." Seri's ash-streaked face looked years older than the day before. He thought his probably did too. "And defiling a spring is like raping the earth itself. And all we can do is burn—" Her voice broke.

Aris looked away, blinking back his own tears. His gaze followed the smoke column into the sky; he grieved at its stain on what had been clean blue from one rim of the world to the other. It rose more gracefully now that it had consumed most of its tainted fuel, its black ugliness paling to gray as it burned slowly along the grass. "Come with me," he said finally, taking the kettle and starting back down the slope toward what had been trees.

"Wait, Ari—it's too hot." Seri caught at his arm. Then as if she had touched his mind instead, she moved with him. They said nothing more, even when the heat of fire beat on their faces, even when the coals they could not avoid scorched their boots. Aris found the spring's deep hollow surrounded by smouldering logs; he kicked one aside and knelt on the hot soil. The spring's outlet, first plugged by the iynisin's foulness, had burnt to a solid cake of muck in the fire. Aris tipped the kettle, as carefully as if pouring into a tiny cup. He knew no words to say, but he heard Seri chanting.

The first drop of water seemed to hang long in midair, sparkling in the light of the sun like a great jewel. Aris watched it hit the center of the original spring. It sat on the surface a moment, then made a tiny round spot of darkness. The next fell, and the next. Aris strained to hold the kettle steady, to have each drop fall exactly on the one before. He knew that was important, though not why. The sound of each drop falling echoed in his ears, as if they were hoofbeats, drumbeats, the tramp of armies . . . he had to keep the pattern, make the intervals regular. Drop by drop, he emptied the kettle and the dry, baked earth clogging the spring absorbed it.

When the last drop had fallen, and nothing happened, he started to shrug and stand. Then he felt his power return, as unaccountably as it had vanished. His hands itched and stung, he held them out over the single drop of moisture. Seri's hands gripped his shoulders; he felt her as a great reservoir of power, and drew upon it, trying to force a way past the obstruction. But it was like trying to heal a block of stone; he could tell he was doing something wrong. He sat back on his heels, enduring the torment of his unused power.

Then he realized . . . he had been trying *his* peoples' way, using force where violation had been the original wound. How could he use his power without repeating that violation? He tried to imagine it trickling out, as the water had, drop by drop, to be absorbed or not, as the spring—as the Lady chose. He cupped his hand gently

over the damp spot, protecting it from the sun, the hot acrid air.
A gust of cooler air brushed along his face. He looked up.

The smoke had shifted shape with the change in wind. Now it
arched over him—over the spring—in almost the shape of a great
gray horse. *Gird?* he thought. It could not be Gird's old horse . . .
it was just smoke on the wind.

Thunder muttered; Seri's grip on his shoulders tightened.
Another gust of cold wind made his skin roughen; he felt a sudden
weakness as his power surged out of him as uncontrollably as a
lightning bolt. He squeezed his eyes shut; when he opened them,
rain stung his face. The sky had darkened, one of the spring storms,
he thought, coming up unseen in the shadow of the smoke. Lightning flashed, so near that light and sound came together: he felt
his teeth jar together. Rain fell harder, hissing on the hot coals that
had been trees. Steam rose in swirls, blown by the wind. Perhaps
the rain would waken the spring, when he had not. He huddled
with Seri under the storm's lash, until it cleared as suddenly as it
had begun. The last of the raindrops sank into that sterile soil; the
surface seemed to dry almost instantly.

He felt a great tearing sadness. They had cleansed with fire, and
the rain with water; he knew nothing else to do. He blinked the
rain out of his lashes and looked up.

The horse standing across the hole that had once been a spring
did not look like Gird's horse. It seemed made of air and cloud,
storm and smoke, all the colors of the sky, and all the power of
thunder. Its dark muzzle snuffed at the dry hole; its eyes accused.
Aris found himself talking to it as if it were mortal.

"The iynisin cursed it; we tried to cleanse and heal . . . but I
don't know how."

A sound between snort and grunt: a challenge. The delicate nostrils widened, sniffed at him, and over his shoulder to Seri. Then,
with deliberation, one forefoot went into the hole. Aris could not
see how deep; he could not look away from those eyes. He saw
the quick withdrawal of the hoof, a flurry of mane and tail, then
nothing as a final clap of thunder shook him to his face.

No rain followed: the sky arched unclouded overhead, with the
sun halfway down the afternoon sky. In the arch of the hoofprint,
as they watched, the damp earth darkened, sifted downward, and
a line of silver appeared: the sky reflected in living water. Slowly,
steadily, it widened to a circle, and the circle lifted to fill the hole.
Aris felt something in himself that echoed that movement, something filling a hole he had not known was empty.

"Aris, look!" Seri tugged at his shoulder. He turned. Where there had been blasted, sterile soil, covered with ashes and the burnt remnants of trees, a few green leaves showed. It could not be; it was too soon. But there they were, looking exactly like young sprouts anywhere. Aris touched one lightly; he felt only the surging growth of a healthy young seedling just emerging from its sleep.

Seri reached back to touch the water in the spring; he wanted to stop her but was too late. She put her wet finger to her forehead, then the nearest seedling. "Alyanya's grace," she said. Aris echoed her. Whatever else had happened, Alyanya had chosen to restore her spring. The spring gurgled suddenly, almost a chuckle of amusement and content; its water overflowed the central hole and swept down the little channel, sweeping away ash and sticks. Aris wondered if they dared drink from it, or if that would be sacrilege; Seri had no such doubts, and with another brief prayer sank the kettle in the deepest part of the spring. "She doesn't want us dying of thirst and making another mess," Seri said. "Drink your fill."

The water tasted of water, clean and pure as any springwater. Aris drank, and let it wash away the night's fear, the day's frustrations. When they had had enough, they went back to the gear they had left above the hollow. Not all had been destroyed in the fight, or in the fire; they had food enough for a day or so, and a change of clothes. Aris went to fetch another kettle of water, and found that the spring had swept the old channel clear as far as the deeper pool where they'd watered their horses the day before. He called Seri; they took turns bathing, with the other keeping watch above the hollow, and changed into clean clothes. Seri had washed her hair; it lay slicked to her head, braided tightly. Aris looked at the blood-stained rents in the clothes he'd been wearing. It was hard to believe that blood was his, that he had been wounded there, and there, and there, and yet was walking around in the sun with no wounds upon him.

"We should wash those before we mend them," Seri said, "but I don't know if it's right—"

"She's brought the water back, and its—she might see it as another gift, our blood."

"It's smelly dirt, is what it is," Seri said. Aris looked at her, surprised. He had said something like that, long ago, when she'd tried to explain her peoples' rituals in building or reaping. Now she wrinkled her nose at him. "All right. I know better. But washing dirty clothes is not the same as ritually blooding a foundation."

"It might be, if we thought of it that way," Aris said.

"It's not the same. Else anyone could treat a spring as a common washpot, and claim to have a ritual in mind." She shook her head, and the first tendrils of her braid came loose. "But—we need to do it, and we'd best get on with it."

In the cold water of the larger pool, the dried blood melted into faint pink streaks and left rusty stains on the cloth. A smell of blood rose more strongly as the water soaked into the stains. Aris scrubbed at the gray shirt, the gray trousers, the blue tunic . . . he had bled more than he'd realized, and felt almost faint thinking of it. He did not look too closely at Seri's washing; he didn't want to know how much she had bled. Finally they had all the blood out that would come out, and wrung the clothes as dry as they could. Aris watched the clean springwater cut through the hazy pink, watched it clear gradually, in ripples and swirls, the last taint of blood from the pool. Alyanya must not be angry with them, if she kept the spring open.

They spread their clothes on the grass, up above the hollow, in the evening sunlight, and considered whether to start walking back to Fin Panir or spend the night near the spring. Aris yawned so, that Seri finally suggested napping awhile.

"You had no sleep last night," Aris said. "I had some—I'll watch first."

"You're half asleep already," Seri said. "You wouldn't be able to stay awake—" And in the end Aris curled up where he sat and fell asleep.

Sunlight woke them both. Aris stretched, blinked, and sat up. Why hadn't Seri wakened him? She was awake now, looking around with a puzzled expression. "I slept," she said. "I wasn't supposed to, but—"

"It's all right. We're here, we're alive." He felt completely rested, alert, better than he had felt in a long time, as if sleeping on the living earth had restored him. He stood, and looked down into the hollow. A thin haze of green covered the black scars of the fire; along the line of the brook, it thickened to a brilliant streak of emerald and jade. It had come back so quickly—how could that be? Was the damage done by the iynisin so superficial? He could not believe that; he had touched that earth, the agonized limbs of tortured trees—those had not been minor wounds. The elves had not thought them minor. So this recovery meant some power had intervened, restoring what it could not heal.

He felt an urge to go back to the spring one last time before they set out for Fin Panir. After they had eaten, he and Seri went down the slope, sniffing the fresh green smell of growing things that replaced the stench of death and burning from the day before.

Even the horses' skeletons had crumbled, erasing the memory of their contorted, unnatural transformation and death. The spring rose, pulse after pulse of pure water trembling the surface, shaking the reflections of their faces as they leaned over it. Aris felt at one with it, with the power of Alyanya to bring life and growth, with the water and the growth of plants, with sunlight and the wind that blew through it, with Seri—as always with Seri.

When he looked up, two horses stood across from him, a bright and a dark bay.

Chapter Nineteen

Two horses, where no horses had been. Aris shivered. Surely they should have heard horses walking up on them. One of the horses reached across the tiny trickle of water and nosed his hair. The other reached toward Seri. He and Seri looked at each other, he suspected her thoughts were the same as his. But neither spoke. As in a dream, he put out his hand, and the horse—his horse, the dark bay—nuzzled it. He turned away from the spring, and the horse followed. He put his saddle on it, as if he had the right, and the horse stood quietly, switching its long, untangled tail at flies. Seri, when he looked, was saddling the bright bay as if she'd done it for years. And the bridles—he had thought the bridles burned with the dead horses, but discovered the bridle—or *a* bridle—in his pack. It fit the dark bay as if made for it. Still without a word, he and Seri lashed their packs to the saddles, then mounted.

Aris turned the horse's head toward Fin Panir. It did not move. He thought about it. Was it a demon horse, sent by the iynisin? He could not believe that. But it had been sent by *someone*, he was sure. Perhaps he ought to be thinking what that someone wanted. He didn't really want to go back to Fin Panir now, he realized. He had something else to do, though he could not think what.

"I don't want to go back," Seri said. Her eyes sparkled; her cheeks had color again. "Let's go on, and see where these horses take us." She reined hers around, and it pricked its ears to the north, winterwards.

"Good idea." Aris rode up beside her. His horse strode off with a springy stride that made riding a pleasure. He knew he should be stiff and sore, but he wasn't. He felt he could ride forever. Seri's braid swayed to the movement of her horse. For a time they rode in silence. Aris puzzled over all the things that had happened, most of which made no sense to him, but he did not feel ready to talk about them out loud. He felt as if he'd fallen into someone's story, as if powers he could not imagine were working on their own plans, using him as a stone on the playing board.

Seri spoke first. "If we were together like this all the time, it would help if you could fight better, and I could also heal."

Aris laughed. "It would be better if both of us could do everything anyone can do."

"I'm serious." Seri made a face at him. "If you were a better fighter, you wouldn't almost get killed right away—if you had, who'd have healed me? And if I could heal, then I could heal you—or someone else that needed it."

"I don't think good healers make good fighters," Aris said slowly. "I think it's—it's how, when I'm practicing, I can almost *see* the wound that I could cause. And I know what it costs me to heal it."

"Ah. Then that's why fighters—at least Marshals—should be healers as well. If we're to lead yeomen into battle, we should know what will follow. Not just what it looks like, but what it takes to heal it."

Aris shook his head. "But that makes it too easy, like the old stories of the Undoer's Curse: if you can make something right too easily, there's no reason to worry about doing wrong beforehand. Marshal Geddrin told me that, when I'd have healed every cut he got trying to shave himself: if I depend on you, he said. I'll never learn to keep a sharp edge and a steady hand."

Seri leaned forward and stroked her horse's mane where the wind had ruffled it. "But it's not easy for you; I've seen what it takes out of you. That's not the same as the Undoer's Curse. I still think there should be a balance. Those who must fight should also be healers, and those who heal should also be fighters. Otherwise I'm too proud of my fighting, and you're too proud of your healing. Or not you, maybe—"

"But the old healers are, some of the ones I worked with. You're right. Alyanya's the Lady of Peace, they say, and those who heal must never take service of iron . . . remember Gird, that time, when he told us about his boyhood? How his parents were angry that he wanted to be a soldier?"

"Yes, but it's Gird who healed the peoples at his death," Seri said, "and he couldn't have done that if he hadn't been a fighter first. Not because he wanted to kill people, but because—" She looked far over the rolling grass, then shook her head. "I'm not sure how to say it. I just know it's true. He had to be a farmer *and* a fighter to do what he did."

"The service of blood," Aris said softly. "Both ways—I hadn't thought of it before, but they're related. To give blood to the fields, to bring the harvest—that's like giving blood to the people—"

"But it doesn't always work."

"Nor does farming. Things go wrong, in peace and in war both. But what Gird did, he showed that it's the giving that matters. You can't hold yourself back." Aris smacked his thigh with his fist as the thoughts boiling in his head finally came clear. "That's it, Seri! That's the link between healing and fighting: the good healer withholds nothing that could help. If I don't go because I'm tired or sick, or if I am unwilling to risk the loss to myself because I don't like the person who needs me, then I'm a bad healer. If the fighter tries to protect himself—herself—then that makes a bad fighter. Even the training, working on the skills—both are long-term crafts, practiced because they may be needed, not today, but someday."

"Yes," Seri said. "And the other link is that the fighter who heals will never forget the cost of it—and the healer who fights will never condemn others for fighting at need."

They looked at each other as if seeing anew. "I still don't know what this is all about," Aris said finally, "but somehow I don't think Arranha will be able to help us with it. It's too much of Gird for that."

They rode the rest of that day without meeting anyone. Aris had no idea, now, where they were in relation to Fin Panir, and he did not feel it mattered. He was going this way because he was supposed to go this way, and his horse agreed.

The next day, they saw sheep spread across a slope far ahead of them, and angled that way without talking about it. By afternoon, they were close enough to see the hollow below, with a tight cluster of stone buildings; they could hear dogs barking as the sheep moved down slowly toward the hollow.

"They must think we're brigands," Seri said, frowning. "They wouldn't be penning them that early, else."

"We'd better change their minds," Aris said, "or we'll be spending another night on the hard ground." He turned his horse downslope. Seri followed. From their height, they could see the scurrying figures, the dogs working the sheep far too fast . . . and one broke away at a gate, bounding up the hill toward the riders, followed by a dark streak of sheepdog. A shrill whistle from below brought the dog to a halt, growling, then it raced back down the hill. The sheep, moving with the single-minded intensity of the truly stupid, made for the gap between Aris's horse and Seri's. Seri flung herself off her horse and made a grab for it.

"Idiot!" Aris said. Grabbing a determined sheep is harder than it looks, and jumping on one from above is chancy at best. Seri had a double-handful of wool and a faceful of stony hillside as the sheep, bleating loudly, did its best to jerk free. Aris swung off his horse and grabbed for a hind leg, then the other. With the sheep in a wheelbarrow hold, Seri could get a foreleg and then they could flatten the sheep out and decide how to get her back down to the fold.

A bellow from below caught his attention—and there, making surprising speed up the steep slope, was a tall man and a boy, with two sheepdogs. "Let loose o' my sheep!" the man yelled, when he saw Aris watching.

"She was gettin' away!" Seri yelled back. "We just caught 'er for you."

"An' sheep are born wi' golden fleece," the man yelled. "I know your kind. You catch sheep all right, and then ye make sure they don't escape—yer own stomachs." He waved the dogs on, and they came, bellies low, swinging in from either side. Aris started to rise, but then saw what the horses were doing. Each horse had put itself between a dog and the pair with the sheep—and the sheepdogs found themselves herded back as neatly as ever they'd worked a flock. The man and his boy stopped a short distance below. "That can't be," the man said, half in anger and half in wonder. "Horses don't do that."

"Ours do," said Seri, almost smugly. The sheep picked that moment to thrash again and kick her with the loose foreleg. "D'you want us to bring your sheep down, or will your dogs pen her for you?"

The boy came nearer, out of reach of his father's arm. "Aren't you robbers, then?"

"Not us," Seri said cheerfully. "Here—you take her." She beckoned, and the boy came up and got a foreleg hold on the sheep himself. At his soft voice, the sheep quit struggling; Seri stepped back and looked at the man. "I'm sorry we frightened you," she said. "We're not robbers, even if Ari does have your sheep by the hind legs. We thought we'd help you."

"You could help me," the man said slowly, "by letting go of my sheep." Aris shrugged, let go, and stood. The sheep scrambled up awkwardly; the boy still had a grip on one foreleg. "Let's go,

Varya—let's see what these folk do." The boy let go, and the sheep stood, ears waggling. He said something to her, and she followed a few steps. Then the man whistled, and waved an arm, and the two dogs closed in on the sheep. She edged her way downhill.

"You don't act like robbers," the man said then. "But I never heard of honest travellers . . . where are you from?"

"Fin Panir," Aris said. His horse walked up and laid its head along his arm. He rubbed the base of its ear absently, and then the line between jowl and neck.

"Girdish folk? Is that why you're wearing blue?"

"Yes," said Seri. "We're in training to be Marshals."

"Whatever that is," the man said. He stood silent some moments, and Aris had almost decided to mount when he said, "You might as well come down wi' us for the night; I don't want your deaths on my conscience."

"Deaths?" Seri asked.

"Aye. There's things in the dark—surely you know that. We don't take chances any more, between human robbers and those other things, the blackrobes, and sometimes wolves and that, things running in packs. We'd have brought the sheep down early even without seeing you. Come on, now. No time to waste. There's chores."

The farmer showed no surprise when Aris and Seri both proved handy at the evening chores. Perhaps, Aris thought, he didn't know there were people in the world who couldn't milk, who couldn't tell hay from straw, for whom wheat and oats and barley were all just "grain." The farm buildings were larger than those Aris had seen before, well built and weathertight. They met the farmer's wife, his other children, all younger than the boy on the hill. And they ate with the family, sharing some berries they had gathered that day.

"So what brings you this way, Girdsmen?" the farmer asked. "Is it part of Marshals' training to wander around frightening honest farmers?"

"No . . . the wandering, perhaps, but not the rest." Seri rested her chin on her fists. Aris watched the faces watching her, the children all intent and eager just because she was a stranger. The farmer's wife sat knitting busily, looking up only now and then as she counted stitches. "To tell you the truth, there's new ideas about how Marshals should be trained. Do you have a grange here?"

"Nay." The farmer sounded glad of it. "We had better things to do than get involved in your war and go around killing folk. We stayed here wi' our sheep, as farmers should. So all that about grange and barton and Marshals, all that means naught to us." He gave Seri a challenging glance, as much as to say *And take that as you please.*

Seri just grinned at him. "You were lucky, then. Aris and I had the war come upon us as children; we had to grow up hedgewise. Then Father Gird took us in—"

"Was that a real man, Gird, or just a name for whoever was leading?"

"A real man," Seri said. Aris could hardly believe that anyone doubted it; did these farmers never leave their little hollow? "He took us in, Ari and me, when we'd been living with farmers, because Ari has the healing magery."

"Mageborn!" The farmer glared at Aris; no one else in the room moved or spoke. "I let a mageborn in my house?"

Seri shrugged. "Father Gird let him in his house. And told everyone to let him use his magery. Healing's good, he said."

"Is it true, lad? You can heal?" The farmer's voice rumbled with suppressed anger.

"Yes," Aris said. "But not all things, though I'll try."

"Come on, then." The farmer heaved himself up from the bench, clearly expecting Aris to follow. He caught Seri's eye, and she rose as well. "What's that?" the farmer asked. "I thought you said *he* had the healing—why are you coming?"

"Gird said Aris must have someone to watch him," Seri said. "I travel with him for that reason."

"Huh. Don't trust him, eh?" By his tone, he approved: no one should trust mageborn.

"I do," Seri said, "and so do those who've worked with him before. But Gird set the rule, and the Council holds by it."

With a last grunt, the farmer led them upstairs. Aris had not seen stairs in a farmer's house before. He wondered if the farmer had taken over a small manor house. But he had no time to ask, the farmer flung wide a door on the left of the passage. There on a low bed lay a man near death from woundfever. "It's my brother," the farmer said. "He and his family lived here with us, and this is all that's left. They killed his wife and oldest child one night when we were out late, in lambing time. She'd gone out to bring us food. The younger children, two of them, died of a fever—they'd been grieving so, I think they had no strength. The others are with mine, of course. But a hand of days ago, maybe, he thought he heard voices outside, near the pens. He didn't wake me afore going out to see, and by the time I woke, and got outside, this is what I found. Heal him, if you can." His gaze challenged Aris.

"Do you know who did it?" Seri asked. The farmer nodded.

"Aye. They blackcloaks, that the magelord used to keep away with his mageries. Cost us plenty in field-fee, it did, and we were glad to see him go, but we didn't know what our fieldfee paid for until he was gone. It must have been his mageries that protected us, for now we see them, season after season, and if they keep coming, we'll soon be gone."

Aris knelt by the wounded man. He had been stabbed and slashed many times, but without a killing wound, almost as if the swordsman had wished him to live for awhile. The wounds drained a foul liquid that filled the room with its stench. "Did you try poultices?" he asked.

"Of course we did. D'you think we're all fools up here?" The farmer glowered. "M'wife's parrion is needlework, not herblore, but she knows a bit. She used allheal and feverbane, and you can see how well they worked. We took 'em off today, as it seemed to ease him. Please—" And now his voice was no longer angry. "Please, lad, try to heal him."

Aris was afraid it was too late, but his power burned in his hands. The women he had worked with had insisted on cleaning wounds first, before trying to heal them, but would he have time? He thought not: even as he watched, the man's flushed, dry skin turned pale and clammy, though he still breathed strongly. He looked at Seri, who stood poised as if for battle. "Seri—you wanted to know more of healing. Come here." Her eyes widened, but she came. "Think on this man as Gird would . . . a farmer, a father, beset by the evil that came upon us. Put your hands here—and I'll be here— and we'll see how your prayer works with my magery."

This time, the flow of power through his hands seemed like fire along a line of oil: both he and Seri came alight, as they had on the hillside when menaced by the iynisin. He heard the farmer stumble against the door and mutter, but he could not attend to it. Seri's hands glowed from within; he felt the flow of power from her, indescribably different from his—but he could direct both. He sent the power down the man's body, driving away the heavy dark- ness of the woundfever, then returning to mend the ripped flesh, the cracked bone, the torn skin. Seri's power, wherever it came from, seemed lighter somehow than his own, almost joyous. It seemed most apt against the sickness while his soothed the wounded tissues together. At last he could find nothing more to do, and leaned back, releasing his hands. Seri kept hers on the man's shoulders a moment longer, then lifted them. Instantly their lights failed, leaving the room in candlelight that now seemed darkness. But instead of the stench of rotting wounds, the room smelled of fragrant herbs and clean wind.

"What did you—" The farmer lurched forward, hand raised. Then the man on the bed drew a long breath, and opened his eyes. "Geris—" he said. "I—did I dream all that?"

"Dream what?" the farmer asked hoarsely.

"I thought—they came again. The blackcloaks. And you came, and I was hurt . . . I thought I was dying. . . ."

"You were," the farmer said. His voice was shaky; tears glistened on his cheeks.

"But I have no pain." The man looked down at himself. "I have no wound—and who are these people? Why have I no clothes?" He dragged the blanket across himself.

"Girdish travellers," the farmer said. "I—I'll get you clothes, Jeris." He turned and plunged from the room. The man they had healed struggled up, wrapping the blanket around him.

"You—will you tell me what happened?"

"Your brother asked us to heal you," Seri said. "We asked the gods, and it was granted us." Aris glanced at her. Was that what she'd done? He had done what he always did, using his own power. Like any talent, it came from the gods originally, but not specifically for each use.

"But—" The man shook his head. "Then it really happened, those blackcloaks? It seems now like a dream, an evil sending. They—they toyed with me; they would not quite kill me. And they laughed until I felt cold to my bones."

"Iynisin." Aris said. "That's the name we know for them. Evil indeed: we too have faced their blades—"

"And lived? But of course . . . you have healed me, so I, too, have lived despite the blackcloaks." The man still seemed a little dazed, which Aris could well understand. They heard the farmer stumbling back along the passage; he came in with shirt and trousers for his brother, and Aris and Seri edged past him out the door and went back downstairs. The woman and children all stared at them.

"He's alive," Aris said. "I've no doubt he'll be down soon." Two of the children burst into noisy tears and ran to hug the farmer's wife; the others looked scared. Then they all heard feet on the stairs, and the injured man came down first. His lean face still looked surprised, but he moved like a healthy man, without pain or weakness. Aris let out the breath he had not known he was holding. The farmer, heavier of build, stumped down the stairs after him.

"Thanks and praise to the Lady," the farmer said; his brother echoed him, then his wife and all the children. "Alyanya must have sent you," he said to Aris and Seri. "Did this Gird of yours follow Alyanya?"

"Alyanya and the High Lord," Seri said. Aris wondered at her certainty. He had always thought of Gird as following good itself, whatever god that might mean from day to day.

"And you are mageborn too, are you? I saw that light, which only the mageborn have. . . ."

"No," Seri said, shaking her head. "My parents were peasants, servants in a magelord's home. That light—I do not understand it myself, but it came upon me first when Aris and I were beset by those blackcloaks, as you call them."

"The gods' gift," the brother said. Aris wondered if he himself had looked like that when the elves came. "Are all Marshals, then, like you?" He looked at his brother. "Because if they are, Geris, perhaps we should turn Girdish; perhaps this is a sign."

"It may be a sign to us," Seri said, "or to you, but Marshals are not like us. They're older; nearly all are still Gird's veterans, those who led his troops in the war. I'm not yet a full Marshal. I'm in training. But Marshals are supposed to help and protect those in their granges; they study healing—at least the young ones do—but not all have more than herblore." *Yet.* Aris thought. Perhaps they would someday. Perhaps this has been a test given by the gods, instead of the Council of Marshals. He imagined future Marshals able to call light at need, able to heal. Perhaps the Marshals, and not the mageborn, would carry on his gift. It didn't matter, so long as someone did. He yawned, suddenly feeling the loss of strength that usually followed a healing. It had taken less from him this time. Because Seri helped? Because the gods were involved? He did not know, but he knew he would fall asleep here at the table in another breath or two.

Seri woke him at daybreak. He had been moved to a warm corner near the hearth, and covered with a blanket; he knew she must have told them to do that. Overhead, he heard muffled scrapes and thuds: the farmer moving around. Seri seemed indecently cheerful for such an hour. Aris scrubbed his itching eyes with cold hands.

"The horses are calling us," Seri said.

"They would be." Aris yawned again, and scrambled up, brushing at his clothes. They would be rumpled and smudged after a night on the floor. Seri opened a shutter, letting in the cold gray light of dawn. The farmer's boots thudded on the stairs. He paused when he saw them up, then shook his head.

"Now I can believe you're farmers' brats," he said. "Ready for chores, eh?"

Aris and Seri followed him outside. Heavy dew lay on the grass and bushes near the house, and furred the moss on the stone walls of the outbuildings. Seri drew buckets of water and Aris carried them to the different pens. When he came to the enclosure where their horses had sheltered, he stopped and stared. The horses snorted, nosing for the bucket. Aris poured it into a stone trough, still staring. The horses gleamed as if they had just been rubbed with oil. Of course he and Seri had rubbed them the previous day, but the girthmarks had showed slightly. Now nothing marred their glistening coats. Something tickled his mind, something he should understand, but it slipped away when he tried to follow it. A stronger flicker in his mind continued, strengthening, all through breakfast. Seri, he saw, felt it too.

"No," she said to the fourth or fifth invitation to stay. "No, we must go, today." And today meant as soon after breakfast as possible. Aris, moved by the same inexplicable urgency, took their gear out to the horses and found them already saddled. Seri, he thought, must really be in a hurry; he wondered when she had found time to slip out and saddle them.

They were well away before the sun entered the hollow, this time riding sunrising, into the light, as their need suggested. They followed a beaten track that ran along the high ground most of the time.

About halfway through the morning Aris said, "Do you think it's the gods, or Gird, or something else?"

Seri's frown meant concentration, not annoyance. "I've been trying to think. Up until the iynisin attacked us, everything seemed normal, didn't it?"

"I thought so. I was surprised that you'd gotten permission for us to leave, but nothing more."

"There was nothing strange about that; the Autumn Rose and Raheli and Cob all thought you should have the chance to travel and try your healing elsewhere, 'stead of becoming one of Luap's scribes. And they thought we'd do well together. Rahi said I'd been watching you heal even before Gird knew about it, so they might as well trust me."

"So it started with the iynisin attack," Aris said. "Or was it before?"

"Before?"

"When you were talking to me about Luap, about mageborn and peasant, and which I'd chosen."

"No." Seri shook her head. "It couldn't have been that."

"It didn't sound quite like you—the Seri I knew."

"How not?"

"Mmm. Angrier. And I couldn't believe you would stop trusting me, just because I tried to be fair about Luap."

"I'm sorry. I remember feeling suddenly furious, hot all over. You're right, that wasn't like me, most of the time." They rode in silence a few moments, then Seri turned to him with a strange expression. "You don't suppose . . ."

"What?"

"*Torre's Ride,*" she said softly. "It's a test, like *Torre's Ride*—could it be?"

Aris snorted. "That's ridiculous. It—" He grabbed wildly at the saddle as his horse bolted, bucking and weaving. Seri's exploded too, pitching wildly and then bolting in a flat run to the north. Aris managed to stay on until his horse, too, gave up bucking to run after Seri's. His breath came short; he felt sore under the ribs, and the horse ran on and on. By the time it slowed, they were far from the track they had been following; a wind rose, whipping the grass flat in long waves, obliterating the pattern of trampled grass that might have led them back to it.

"And now we're lost," he said to Seri, who was hunched over, fighting for breath.

"I'm right," she said a moment later. "And don't argue again. It's a test."

"Fine." Aris waited until he could breathe more easily, and said, "And perhaps we should start figuring out what kind of test involves iynisin, elves, thunderstorms, and horses that come out of nowhere and run forever without sweating." For the two horses were not breathing hard, and no sweat marred their sleek hides.

"And a dying man who needs our healing." Seri straightened up and stretched her back. "And getting lost." Then she reached over and grabbed Aris's arm. "Look at them."

He looked. Their two horses had their muzzles together, and each had one eye rolled back to watch its rider. "*They* know," he said. "You mischief," he said to his horse. He felt its back hump under him, a clear warning. "No, I'm sorry. Don't do that again; I'll fall off. But you do know, don't you?"

"Gird's horse," Seri said. Her eyes danced. "These are the same kind." Her horse stamped, hard, and shook its head. "Or—similar?"

Both horses put their ears forward and touched muzzles again, then blew long rolling snorts.

"Gods above," Aris said. "We are right in the middle of something—I wonder if Torre ever felt confused." He felt suddenly better, as if he'd solved the puzzle. But he knew he hadn't.

Seri grinned. "Remember when we were very young, and used to hide in the garden and tell stories?"

"Yes, and you always said you wished we could have a real adventure." Aris chuckled. "And I thought you'd grown out of that."

"Never," Seri said. "Nor have you; I remember who got stuck up in the pear tree." Her face sobered. "Father Gird wants us to do something," she said. "And even if we hadn't stumbled into the iynisin; he'd have found some way to test us. He wasn't one to send untrained farmers into battle."

"We're supposed to be trained already," Aris said. "All those years in the granges, as yeoman-marshals, as Marshal-candidates—"

"So we've survived the tests. We've learned to share our talents. We're more ready now than we were." Seri looked cheerful; Aris hoped she was right.

"When we find out what it is he wants," Aris said. "If we've finished the tests." Seri grimaced and put out her tongue.

The two horses stiffened, then threw up their heads and neighed. Out of a fold of the ground rode a troop of nomads on shaggy ponies. All carried lances; the nomads called out in their high-pitched voices.

They came back to Fin Panir leaner, browner, and far more cautious than they'd left. The gate guards didn't recognize them or the horses, but when they gave their names said they were wanted at the palace. "Why?" asked Seri. Aris thought he knew; his hands prickled. He led the way, his bay picking his way neatly through the crowded lower market.

"Aris!" Luap, crossing from the palace to the Hall, stopped in midstride. "Is it really you? We need you."

"Who is it?" He was already off the horse; Seri slid off hers. A stableboy came running out; the horses let themselves be led away.

"Arranha. A few days after you left—" Luap told the story as he led them quickly into the palace. "We've tried everything—herblore, young Garin—and it's not enough. He hasn't died—I suspect that's Garin's doing—but his arm's swollen to the shoulder and he weakens daily."

Aris said nothing. He loved the old priest; he wondered why the gods had let him leave Fin Panir if Arranha was going to be in danger. When he came into Arranha's room, he stopped short, shocked. Arranha had always been "the old priest" to him; he had known Arranha was older than Gird. But he had been so vigorous an old man, so full of life . . . and now he lay spent and silent, his body fragile and his spirit nearly flown. Awe flooded him. Was this Arranha's time, and had the god he had served finally called him? He could not interfere with that.

He put his hands on Arranha's shoulders; at once the magery revealed the dangerous fever in the wounded arm. It had seeped even past his shoulder, into his heart. Aris let his power flow out. He felt the resistance of a deepseated sickness, and worse than that Arranha's lack of response. He had given up; although he breathed, he would not struggle against death any longer.

Seri put her hands on his; Aris looked up, surprised into losing his concentration. "We work together," she said. He nodded. He could feel her power pulsing through his hands and into Arranha. "Gird loved and trusted him," Seri went on. "Gird wants him to live; he must help Luap with the mageborn in the west." Slowly, Aris felt the sickness yielding, first from Arranha's heart, and then fingerwidth by fingerwidth down his arm. The swollen tissue shrank; the angry reds and purples faded. He could feel that Arranha breathed more easily; his pulse slowed and steadied. Finally, even the purple bite marks which had oozed a foul pus faded, and Arranha's hand lay cool and slender on the blanket once more.

Arranha opened his eyes. "You called me back. Why?" Then he seemed to see them clearly and his expression changed. "*Both* of you! Seri, when did you learn healing?"

She grinned at him. "It's not like Aris's; I have to ask Gird what he wants."

"Gird. But he's not—"

"He's not a god; I know that. But he lets us know what he wants done."

Arranha pushed himself up in the bed. "I might have known. He saved my life outside the walls of Grahlin, and now he's done it again; I wonder what he expects of me this time." His gaze fell on Luap. "Don't look at me like that, Selamis: I'm well now. I'll be with you in the west; isn't that what you wanted?"

Raheli watched the Council carefully the morning Aris and Seri were to come in to make their report. Already rumors had spread, as fast as light from a flame: Arranha healed, a mageborn and peasant working healing magery together. She and the Rosemage had already conferred; they sat on opposite sides of the room where they could hear most of the murmuring and see each other. Luap sat in his usual seat, with fresh scrolls around him and his pen full of ink. The scribe he had nominated to take over his position sat behind him at a small desk, he would practice taking the notes.

But the Council concerned her most. In the years since Seri had maneuvered Cob into presenting her own plan for the training of new Marshals, the Council had changed character. Fewer of the rural Marshals bothered to come in to Fin Panir; some sent their concerns, and some ignored the Council until a crisis arose. Most of the Marshals who attended regularly had granges in Fin Panir or Grahlin, or vills within a day's ride of Fin Panir; they had plenty of yeoman-marshals to do their work while they attended Council. By the accidents of war, most of them had also been latecomers to Gird's army, gaining command because the earlier Marshals died in battle. Since they had not known Gird as well, they relied on the written Code, the growing volume of Commentaries, and Luap's version of Gird's life when considering some new policy. Raheli could still influence them, as Gird's daughter, as could a few others, but it grew harder every year. She had begun to regret her decision to refuse the Marshal-Generalship.

Aris and Seri appeared in the doorway. Both wore the gray shirts and pants of the training order, and the blue tunic of a Marshal-candidate. Raheli felt herself relaxing. No one could help liking those two; they had the cheerful steadiness that attracted goodwill. Aris looked tougher, his face tanned where it had been pale, his shoulders broader. Seri looked less concerned about him; she seemed full of confidence.

When they were called to account for their journey, they spoke in turns, but without formality; it did not seem rehearsed. Rahi had already heard part of the story the night before, but Aris's description of the iynisin curse on the grove and spring, and its healing the next day still awed her. When Seri told of the horses appearing, one of the older Marshals said, "Like Gird's old gray horse!" at once.

"We thought of that," Aris said. "But we are not Gird—we could never claim that importance."

"Nor did he," Luap said. Everyone stared; Luap rarely spoke in Council meetings, maintaining the distinction between the Marshals and himself.

"But go on," another Marshal said. "We can discuss this later. I want to know what happened next." So did they all, and questioned Aris and Seri about each last detail of their journey, including much that the two had not had time to tell Raheli. They had healed someone at a farm, they had found a tribe of horse nomads, and spent a few hands of days with them, learning their language and healing their sick. . . .

"Horse nomads? How could you learn so fast? And why heal them? We didn't train you and send you out to benefit them. Aris was supposed to heal yeomen who needed it."

Seri answered this time. "We cannot say how we learned so fast—it surprised us, and them, as much as it surprises you. But since the gods directed us there, they must have had some purpose. As for healing, that is the purpose of such power—to withhold its use is as evil as to misuse any magery."

"I don't like it," the Marshal-General said, scowling. "An honest peasant lass fiddling about with magery; that can't be right. I know you'll say Gird approved young Aris using his healing magery, under supervision. But that's not the same as Seri doing such things, calling light and all that."

Raheli spoke up. "Marshal-General, in the old days there are legends of our people having some great powers—consider the Stone Circles they raised. And Gird would have trusted peasants— especially someone like Seri who has served well in barton and grange—to use magery for the benefit of all."

"It's magicks, and magicks are evil," the Marshal-General said.

Raheli would have said more, but Seri leaned forward, smiling at the Marshal-General. "Sir, that magic by which Gird freed us all from fear and grief at his death; was that evil?"

"No, but—but that was not magicks; that came from the gods. Luap said so."

"And the gods granted this to me, sir—I did not ask for it; I didn't even imagine it was possible. It is not my talent. It is their gift. I would be ungracious to refuse it. Now if the Council requires that I not use it here, I will leave—but I will not renounce what the gods have given me."

That set off a stormy argument. Some said Seri was rebellious, haughty, ruined by spending too much time with a mageborn; others argued that she was right: if she had new powers, they must be the gods' gift, and she should use them. Through this, Aris and Seri sat patient and quiet, though Rahi felt angry enough to bash some heads. She wished Cob had been there.

Finally, when the argument died of its own weight, the cheerful steadiness of the two young people had its effect, and the vote the Marshal-General demanded, to force Seri to give up healing, failed. in the days that followed, both returned to their former training duties so quietly that it seemed the storm had never occurred. Aris spent more time in the drillfields and barton, and Seri spent more time with him, learning herblore, but otherwise they seemed unchanged.

As the year rolled on, Luap and Arranha together planned for the great move. By word of mouth, the plans travelled the land, and mageborn survivors began to trickle into Fin Panir. The strong and young, those known to have magery, would go first and prepare the land for planting. One by one, Luap showed them what became known as the mageroad. He still worried that they did not know where in real space the stronghold lay, but he felt he could not wait.

Chapter Twenty

Getting the first working groups funneled through the cave was almost as difficult as moving Gird's army, Luap thought. Aris had agreed to come to the stronghold with Seri "for awhile;" he would not say whether he would settle there permanently. In the wake of Seri's defiance of the Council, Luap chose not to press the issue. Surely they would find the new land fascinating enough once they had lived there for a time.

"*Here* we need not hide our abilities." The Rosemage eyed the canyon walls with a craftsman's look.

"The stronghold itself is large enough. . . ."

"For now. But it won't be. And we'll need tradeways: roads, passes, bridges. Look—" From her fixed stare, a line of light sprang to the nearest rockface a few spans away. A high screech ending in a *ping*, and burst of rockdust. A cylinder of stone wobbled, and fell out, leaving behind a clean, smooth, perfectly round hole. Luap stared at her, surprised once more. She reddened. "Of course, *you* could do more; I know that. And this tires me. But it will save our few numbers from spending all their time chipping stone."

It would that. Luap shivered, wondering if she were right in thinking he could do "more" when he had never imagined even so much. He shivered again, as the thought crossed his mind of what such use of power might say, to those with the ability to sense its use. As the smoke of a city could rise above it, reveal it, before its towers came in sight, could their magery make obvious their location?

"I wouldn't suggest it," the Rosemage went on, "if this were not
empty land, unpeopled. The rockfolk never accepted human magic
applied to stone; that was one of the quarrels the gnomes had with
us." Luap had not known that; he wondered if she knew it as fact
or legend. He wondered if the dwarven king he had seen would
object; he wondered why he had been given no specific warning
prohibition about that. The Rosemage continued. "If the rockfolk
lived in these mountains, we would have to have their permission."

"What about elves?"

The Rosemage shrugged. "They would not care, why should
they? They work their magery with living things, not lifeless stone."

"Gird told me once of the blackcloaks, who seem elves but are
not."

"Legends." The Rosemage stared not quite through him, and
he shrugged.

"Some are true."

"Yes, and some horses fly. No one will argue that Torre's magic
horse did not fly, or that the gods could not turn mountains on
their heads if they wished, but we never *see* a mountain balanced
on its peak. Elves are strange enough without making them into
two kinds of folk—" "She shook her head as he would have
answered. "No—I have heard the tales, too. Bright elves that come
by day, and dark elves that come by night, good elves living in
trees and wicked ones living in holes of the ground and poisoning
the roots of trees: children's tales. These people see duality everywhere, in everything, balancing a water hero against a sky hero,
stone against tree: night and day, storm and calm. That alone shows
it can't be true . . . it's too neat, a dance instead of war."

Luap drew a long breath, which tasted of nothing more dire than
pine. The way Arranha had explained the original Aarean beliefs,
the Rosemage's ancestors and his own had also believed in a duality,
but one soon fragmented into a great arch of deities and powers,
from the vicious to the benign. He had never really believed in
any of them, until Gird. He was sure Gird had not lied about the
dangerous being that had cursed him one dawn—Gird would not
bother to make up something like that, assuming he had the imagination. But he had not seen it himself; Gird could have been mistaken. He had been, after all, only a peasant . . . he would not have
known what it was, only what it told him. It might have lied, if
it had been as evil as Gird thought. And he did not want the
Rosemage's scorn.

"You have more knowledge, lady." Even as he said that, he wondered why his tongue chose *knowledge* over *wisdom*, which would

have made the compliment stronger. He drew another long breath of air as clean and cold and empty of human scent as any he had ever taken. "An empty land . . . a fine refuge."

"Good morning!" That was Arranha, moving far more briskly than a man his age should, Luap always thought. Since Aris and Seri had healed him, Arranha might have been ten years younger. "A fine day. So, lady, you have the skill of stonework?"

The Rosemage smiled at him. "In a small way, Arranha." From her tone, she did not think it that small. He peered at the hole. Luap pointed out.

"Ahh. Fine work, indeed; you have a straight eye. But you've done it the hard way; we don't need that precision in moving large blocks. We're going to need to move a lot of stone; best use the quicker ways."

"Quicker ways?" She was rarely flustered, but she looked flustered now. Luap took a guilty pleasure in that.

"With your permission." Not that anyone would refuse Arranha permission *here*, whatever Gird's folk might have said. Luap smiled and nodded; the Rosemage waved her hand. "There, then," said Arranha, pointing out the opposing rockface, a little distance down canyon. "Block the flow there, and we'll have a sizeable terrace to work with, once we have soil for it."

Arranha's mild expression did not change; the rock buzzed, then screamed like some dire creature mortally wounded. A dark line scored it, visibly darker and deeper with every heartbeat. Finally light flashed out from it, as if someone had poured boiling oil into its wound, and a chunk of red stone the size of a cottage leaned out from the cliff and fell gracelessly into the gorge. When it struck, Luap felt the shock in his boots and knees; a cloud of dust rose above the noise and every bird in the canyon took to the air. He had no time to watch that cloud vanish in the morning wind; the old priest had begun carving another chunk, and as it fell another. By the time Arranha quit, the low end of the gorge had a pile of broken rock chockablock in its neck, and the little stream had already backed up into a muddy pond. The Rosemage stood silent, arms folded, her brows drawn together.

"There now," Arranha said, a little breathlessly. "Yes, you can learn, lady. So can he." With his thumb he indicated Luap.

Not all could. Luap found it easy, and the Rosemage difficult, but not more so than her finer carving. But some could not sense the stone's inner grain, and wore out their power on cuts that led nowhere, mere slits in the stone, while others could not score even a nail's path in the stone by magery. Aris, whose skill in healing no one matched, could do nothing with stone but carry the smaller chunks to be stacked somewhere.

Luap admitted to himself that he liked that. He, the king's bastard, had that power in full measure; he could carve his own castle, depending on his own abilities. Day after day he labored, never letting his growing excitement affect his concentration on the task. As Arranha had taught, he felt for the rock's own internal structure, the grain and interleaving of its substance, and concentrated his power so that it fell away as he wanted, and left sound walls behind. He learned to anticipate even the shattering that followed those falls, so that the very blocks fell readily to hand, for the builders to raise into terraces.

Others of his people had other magery; man-long blocks rose at their will, and eased into place. Sooner than he had expected, the framework in the small canyon had been done, and the lowest dam laid in the large one. The Rosemage had found a passable route to the lower lands southward, a matter of one low pass and a twisted canyon outlet where the little river ran knee deep from wall to wall. Next year they would smooth that route for horse travel. No one knew what lay beyond, but the Rosemage and Arranha both insisted some humans lived there.

As nights chilled, and frost starred the pools of still water at dawn, Luap felt well content. He had made a good beginning, it was going to work. They could not plant the next spring, but the one after that he was sure they'd have enough level land for some grain. Gird's successor had promised food for four growing seasons, he should make it with one to spare. His careful planning seemed to lock into place like the blocks of stone forming the terraces; he took comfort in the evidence that his leadership was working.

Deep under stone the blackrobed exiles had long exhausted their own powers. Nothing they could do from within would free them, and through the ages the land around their prison lay vacant—a tangle of narrow canyons surrounded by deserts. Above, the battle scars of their defeat weathered away in winter snow and spring rain; grass and sedge, bush and tree, grew once more free of blight, until the few wanderers who came that way had no reason to suspect what lay imprisoned in one red mass of stone more than another.

Then into their prison of ancient magery the younger, less-skilled power came, fraying the barriers as if a caress from without were stronger than the many curses flung from within. Slowly at first, then more rapidly, the barriers withered. And silently, cloaked in that magery which even defeat could not wrest from them, the blackrobed spies went by night to search out their deliverers.

"Surely they have been warned," *said their leader, when the first spy returned with his tale of mortal settlement.* "Surely our noble cousins have told them—"

"No." *The spy smiled, a smile that should have been beautiful on such a face, but was not.* "For pride the sinyi will not speak our name; they have tried to erase all memory of us in the old lands. And they resented this one's ability to use the ancient patterns. He angered them."

"Blessings on him." *The tone conveyed a curse instead.* "And what did they say, those guardians of our . . . virtue?"

"Only that a great danger lay mured in this wilderness, which he would regret awakening."

The flash of bared teeth among them passed for human; one of the others chuckled. "Oh, he will. He surely will."

"Not yet," *said their leader.* "Here we have leisure to purpose more than a hasty vengeance on our wardens. We can do much better, by Arranha's aid. Think on it . . . these mortals will settle and multiply, will they? Let them prosper. Let them plant their filthy trees, and reap many crops of fine grain, all the while fattening like oxen, like swine, for our feasting. Leave them without fear—for now. Let their prince, who is too wise to heed warnings he does not understand, take pride in his wisdom. May he rule long, I say, for his fall will be sweeter. We are free now; we can wait and watch this feast in preparation."

A murmur of delight, chilling in its intensity, followed his words.

"But there are hazards," *the spy warned.* "An old priest of Esea—of the Light, alas—has keen wits. And two of the younger mortals—one of them a true healer—have met our kind before. Or suppose their prince dies before the feast is spread. They might all leave."

Their leader laughed aloud. "You name hazards what I name treasures! The priest is old, you say: he will surely die before long. We are in no hurry. And they have a true healer, and a prince without the healing magery, a prince we would have live long in complacent prosperity . . . how fortunate for us. Here's a web to tangle those lightfoot cousins of ours, a jest to sour their hearts and silence even the forest-lord at the end. One shall snare the other, and never suspect it. Indeed the Tangler will be pleased."

"But we cannot approach the Winterhall: that magery they did not touch, and it still holds strong against us."

Their leader smiled, then looked at each face in turn, the companions of his long exile. "No matter. We have won, before ever battle be joined. Can you doubt that an unwary mortal, whatever human magery he may have, will fall to our enchantments? We need not enter the Winter-hall, when we hold its prince's heart."

Sunrise on Midwinter: Luap no longer shivered, having learned the bodily magery from Arranha. He stood, on the eastern end of the rock platform, looking southeast as rose light flushed the snow, as a high wing of cloud grew feathers of rose and gold, then bleached to whiteness as the sun flared, blinding. Behind him, the song rose up, the song he had vaguely remembered from earliest childhood, sung now by all his people. Not quite all, he corrected himself; all the ones *here*, the best of the workers of old magery. Deep voices, high voices, all in towering harmony that rang off the nearby cliffs, the echoes seeming answers from yet other choruses . . . his skin prickled. The words were nothing like the peasants' short rhymed Midwinter chants; he could feel the longer flowing lines twining around each other, statement and response, question and answer, full of power as the singers themselves. "Sunlord, earthlord, father of many harvests . . ." echoed back from the facing cliffs, and behind him the choir sang of "springing waters shining in the sun. . . ."

He alone did not sing; he had sung the invocation in the Hall below, at Arranha's direction, and now (also at Arranha's direction) he stood silent, looking at the land, listening to his people, being— according to Arranha—the tip of the spear the first light touched, the one through whom the Sunlord would enlighten his people.

"If you are clear," Arranha had also said, last night. "You must be clear, the crystal to gather the light and spread it abroad."

He would be that crystal, he thought, banishing from his mind the faint doubt he had heard in Arranha's voice. If Gird could become what he had become, if from peasant clay had come first that stone hammer to break the old lords' rule, and then that . . . whatever it was . . . that he had become at the end, surely he, Luap, could be that clear crystal point Arranha spoke of.

Light speared from the sun's rim, just clearing the distant mountain. He squinted only slightly. *Take it in,* Arranha had said. *Fear nothing light; the god cannot darken your sight; only you can darken the god's light.* Fine, but a lifetime's experience made squinting easy. Gird's voice, it seemed, came into his head with the thud of worn boots on hard-packed earth. *Easy? And who said leadership's easy, lad?*

He forced his eyes wide, and felt that his head filled with brilliant light, radiance, glory. Slowly, the sun crawled upward; he watched, not thinking now, returning only praise for glory. At last its lower edge flicked free of the world's grip. Behind him, the singers fell silent. He stood motionless another long moment, then remembered his next duty. Arms wide, welcoming, he let his gaze fall to the little altar before him. *Light to light, fire to fire, sight to sight* . . . the peasant chant intruded, and he had to strain to remember what now he should say. "Lightbringer, firebringer . . ." His own power's fire given to the eight carefully laid sticks, no conceit of actual help to the Sunlord, Arranha had said, but willingness shown. And he must make that fire the hardest of the several ways he knew. A flame burst from the sticks, unsustained by them, unconsuming: his own power given freely. They would be saved to kindle the first fires after Midwinter Feast.

He quenched the fire, and turned. Arranha nodded at him; the others smiled. Beyond them, their shadows stretched blue across the plateau almost to the cliff beyond. In his mind, their numbers matched those shadows; he could imagine the beauty of so many voices, singing the Sunlord's praises. This year they would fill the terraces they had built; this year they would plant for the first time, and then . . . then others could come. Others of his people, and in a few years children born here, would raise their voices in song to speed the turning year.

Back inside, he called the Rosemage and Arranha into his own room. "I will be going, in a few days. If it goes well—"

"It should," said Arranha. "They were friendly enough last fall."

"I hope it will." Luap paused to sip from the mug of sib the Rosemage had poured him. He had not expected her to become his servant, but she had been doing him such services since autumn. At first it had felt very strange, but now he enjoyed it. "But some may object even if we take the dirt from fallow lands."

"You can't take it from the cursed lands," the Rosemage said. "Remember—"

"I know." He waved at her. Most of the old lords who poisoned their lands had done so with temporary magicks, having hoped to restore themselves to power. But a few, in the final days of the war, had chosen to use long-lasting curses which even now could not be broken. Generations, Arranha had said, would pass before that soil bore healthy growth. Luap had seen the blighted fields, black as charred wood and far less fertile . . . luckily they were few. He would not bring that curse back here to work its evil. "It's still going to be difficult."

"I had a thought," said Arranha. Luap looked at him. From the tone it was one of those thoughts that caused them all to feel that their minds had been twisted into bread coils. He nodded, and Arranha, smiling as usual, went on. "At one time, our people had the power to make much of a small supply. As the Sunlord's light brings increase to the fields, or one seed makes many after the growth of a crop—"

"Argavel's Lore," said the Rosemage.

"Yes. And it came with the usual warning: the gods' gifts must not be used lightly. Some of our ancestors used this too greedily, and lost it. But I asked Gird one time—"

"You asked Gird?" Luap could not keep the surprise from his voice.

Arranha nodded. "Of course: he was a farmer, and a good one. The priesthood or Esea had preserved a verse at the end of Arga-vel's Lore which implied, I always thought, that the *elements* had been unaffected by the decree that mortals might not usurp the gods' power of increase."

"So?" For once, the Rosemage sounded abrupt with Arranha; Luap was glad his tediousness bothered someone else as well.

"So we could no longer make a pile of gold rings from the pattern of one, or a platter of bread from one slice . . . but we might, I thought, have the power to make two lumps of clay from one, or two gusts of wind from one . . . you see?"

"And what had Gird to do with that?" asked Luap.

"He let me try, with a lump of soil. And it worked." Arranha looked pleased with himself. Luap felt he was supposed to get something more from this than he had yet figured out.

"So you—took a lump of soil, and you got two lumps of soil?"

"Five, altogether. It's harder than it looks. One needs a matrix of some sort. I was using sawdust. Rockdust would be better." Arranha smiled again, and then shook his head. "Gird was not impressed. He said you could get good soil by putting sawdust and cow droppings together, every farmer knew that much."

At last it came together in Luap's mind. "But you're saying you could use some good dirt and the rockdust we have to make more? I would have to bring only one fifth what we need?"

"Better even than that. It didn't occur to me while talking to Gird, but I should be able to use whatever you bring doubled, and then redoubled, and so forth." Luap wondered if his face was as blank as the Rosemage's; Arranha sighed at them. "It's the same principle as my way of cutting stone." *How,* Luap wanted to ask, but Arranha anticipated this and went on "Remember what I showed you about reflecting lines? Symmetry? This should work the same."

"How many of us can do it, do you think?"

Arranha shrugged. "As with the stone, we don't know. It may not be the same ones; young Aris may find multiplying earth more like healing than stonework, for instance. And it will not take many: doubling increases faster than you think."

Luap had chosen to return to Fin Panir after Midwinter Feast, and in the Lord's Hall before dawn. That should satisfy the new Marshal-General's finicky notions about magery, he thought. Everyone knew by now he traveled by magery; it was ridiculous to insist that he hide the fact. Particularly since he could time his arrival to alarm no one.

That had been his intent, at least, and he depended on his lookouts' report of the star positions to time his exit—but there was light enough in the Lord's Hall for a very frightened junior yeoman to see his arrival, and for Luap to see the youth's rapid flight, as well as hear it. Amused, Luap stepped from the incised platform below the altar and strode after him into the snow-streaked courtyard.

The yeomen on duty at the Council stairs were not amused. Roused from late-watch endurance by the boy's startled cry and plunge from the Lord's Hall door, they'd been prepared for something more dangerous than Luap: a demon, perhaps, or at least a ghost. Luap himself, familiar to them but not the boy, merely irritated them.

"You didn't have to scare the lad," said one, wiping his nose. "Comin' in th' dark like that—you could ha' been anyone."

Luap tried a smile, which made no difference in their expressions "I'd thought coming before dawn would be the least trouble," he said. "I didn't expect anyone to be there—"

"It's after dawn," the guard pointed out.

"Here it is. Where I was, it will be dark another span. This is nearer the sun's rising, and I forgot how much." Actually he was not sure how much sooner dawn came to Fin Panir, but they need not know that.

"Huh. Don't think of everything, do you? Well, if it's the Marshals you want, they'll not all be up yet?"

Luap thought of the years in which Gird was always up by dawn, at work by daylight. Some of the Marshals were like that still, but some, in Fin Panir, clearly relished the chance to lie abed warm on cold winter mornings. That had begun even while Gird lived, though the old man had not been above routing younger Marshals out himself.

"Something wrong, out there?" asked the other guard. He sounded hopeful. Luap laughed.

"No—all's going well, but I am supposed to report at intervals." The guards moved back into the windless angle of the building, and Luap moved through dim passages to the kitchen.

"You look fresh for someone who rode all night," said Marshal Sterin, hunched over a mug of sib. Another Marshal sat silent beside him. "Or did you come in late, and find a room?"

Luap chose a mug from the stack, and dipped himself a hot drink. "I came the mageroad," he said, not looking at them.

"But that still leaves you a long ride—unless you can come *here*—" By the change in tone, Sterin didn't like that possibility. His voice sharpened even more. "Or can you just flit from place to place at your will, regardless? I thought it was some special place you'd found, that made it possible."

"The Lord's Hall," said Luap, between sips. "The same pattern, or part of it, is incised in the floor near the altar. I thought you knew that." He could not remember which Marshals had been in Fin Panir the last time he'd come.

"Ah. So when you take the old lady, she won't have to ride a week to your hidden cave, eh?"

"No. That's why I came this way—" That was a reason they could accept, and even admire.

"How did you learn it worked here as well?"

Luap shrugged, and reached past them to a cold loaf; he could smell the morning's baking in the ovens. "Tried it once. I don't know what might have happened; my thought was that if it didn't work, I'd have come out in the cave anyway."

"Huh. Like jumping a horse over a fence in the dark," Sterin said, in a tone that suggested it took courage and stupidity in equal measure. Luap remembered now that he had been a stableboy before the war; he loved horses. "So—how do you like it out there? Is it good land?"

"It's rough," Luap said. "Mountains, narrow rocky valleys: it's going to be hard to farm, but it's ours."

"There's some won't mind thinking of the mageborn breaking their fingernails on hard work," said the other marshal in a carefully neutral voice.

"Work won't hurt us," said Luap. Let them think that, and gloat, while his people moved house-sized rocks with a finger's touch and magery.

Both men chuckled. "You learned something, your years wi' Gird," said the quieter one.

"And my years as a farmer," Luap pointed out. They looked as if they'd forgotten or never believed, but finally smiled at him. "When's the Marshal-General available?" he asked.

"Oh—time the sun hits the side court, he'll be done eating," said Sterin. "You don't want to bother him afore then—but you'd remember." Luap nodded; anyone who'd tangled with Marshal-General Koris before he had two mugs of sib and hot breakfast inside him remembered it. That he'd been just as unpleasant to the magelords during the war, especially that morning at Green-fields, had won him a Marshal's shirt and later advancement. No one doubted his courage, or his willingness to work (once he was up and fed) but Gird himself had learned not to disturb Koris at dawn without urgent reason.

"You want *what?*" The Marshal-General stared as if his froggy eyes would burst. Luap still found it difficult to believe they had chosen Koris, even though he'd been at the election. If only Cob had not been so adamant about staying with his rural grange.

"Dirt," said Luap again, being patient. "Soil. You know: what you grow crops in."

"You're going to take *dirt* back to your mountain fortress by *magery?*"

Luap bit back a sarcastic remark about the practicality of taking it any other way, and nodded instead. Still, through the ensuing argument, he had a vivid mental image of a caravan loaded with dirt headed for an unknown destination. "With your permission," he said. The Marshal-General scowled at the courtesy, and Luap cursed himself. He had forgotten how rude—honest, they called it—the Girdsmen were, in their own land. Among his people, he found himself thinking, courtesy implied no weakness; he had acquired the habit of smooth speaking. Here it could only get him in trouble.

"Well . . . let me ask the others." The Marshal-General had run out of reasons, but he was not about to give in.

Luap bit his tongue to keep from explaining again that they would not take *much* dirt; it could inconvenience no one to take a little dirt from some disused farmstead. He could have simply taken it, without asking, except that he had promised Gird, a promise he had so far kept. But Gird would not have had to ask anyone, he would have given his answer at once, and that would have been the end of it. In his mind, Luap asked Gird, and Gird—his

imagined Gird—growled assent, irritable at being disturbed for
such a trivial matter. Luap felt better. Gird would have let him
take the dirt, and this paltry successor to Gird's position would
accomplish nothing with his indecision.

"You will excuse me," he said smoothly to the Marshal-General,
not minding now that it ruffled the man so. "I have friends waiting,
whom I have not seen in more than a season. When the Council
has considered, perhaps you would let me know?"

Astonishment. Resentment. Envy. Anger. This was someone who
would always end in anger, for whom anger served every need.
"And where will you be," the Marshal-General asked querulously.
"Here in Fin Panir, or off in that haunt of magery?"

Already such a reputation! Luap wondered what the man would
have said if he'd seen them carving the very mountains to build
their terraces, and smiled to himself. That smile came into his
voice; he did not trouble himself to hide it. "I will be here, in
Fin Panir, some length of days, Marshal-General. Working on the
chronicles, and checking the copyists' work, as the Council
requested. Should your decision take longer, I may be there
awhile."

The Marshal-General sniffed. "We shall take what time we need,
to consider carefully all that might result from such a choice."

Luap struggled not to think *It's only dirt* too loud. The man's
eyes dropped again to his desk, then flicked up as if hoping to
catch Luap by surprise. Luap met that glance with blandness. "I
would not try to hurry you, Marshal-General."

Now the man flushed, and he rushed into explanation. "It's not
just my decision, you know. I'm not like a king—"

"It's quite all right, Marshal-General," said Luap. They had no
real hierarchy, having fought a revolution to end hierarchies, and
had discovered the function behind tradition with dismay. Gird,
taking a king's power, had never believed he held it, and in that
belief had used it casually, as if born with the rod in hand. His
successors, so far, had used it nervously, uncertain how much use
was needful. Even Cob, who had seemed to understand the need
for a single final leader, had not pursued his original plan. Luap
smiled again at the Marshal-General, and left.

For all that he felt alienated from the peasants who crowded the
streets, he enjoyed the city bustle. From the palace area, he went
down to the main market, noting how healthy, if rude, the population seemed these days. Red-cheeked men and women, bundled
warmly against the cold, hurried to and fro, meantime trampling
the snow to a dirty mess. When he came to the wider streets near

the market, he found more signs of improved trade and order. An oxcart of sand almost blocked the street, and two men shoveled sand over a thick lens of ice. The inn where Gird had gotten so disastrously drunk looked busy enough; he heard singing from behind its windows. Loud voices in the streets, cheerful but coarse; half the words were those *his* people never used.

He had remembered where Dorhaniya's narrow house stood, past the market, and up one of the crooked streets on the lower hill. When he knocked, Eris answered the door, as stolid as ever, but she smiled briefly.

"She's doing better," she said. "I'll tell her."

"I didn't know she'd been sick," Luap said.

"Oh. I thought maybe that was why you came—"

"No, I've been out in the new place—surely she told you?"

Eris shrugged. "I don't pay that much mind, to be sure. She's getting on, you know. She did say something—about a new place, and we might go—but she'll never shift out of her own room, again, let alone move the household."

"But—" He said no more. He had counted on Dorhaniya, old as she was; something about her eased his mind in a way no one else did. To her, he was the prince, the legitimate heir to the throne, and while she agreed he must never take the throne, she still gave him the deference, the respect, she thought due his birth.

"I'll tell her," said Eris again. "Please—wait here—she'll want to see you, but she'll want to dress."

He waited in a stuffy little room hardly warmer than outside. Perched on a carved chair that seemed designed to poke him in the spine if he relaxed, he looked around at a room lit by sunlight reflected from a snowy back yard, perhaps a garden in summer. Gradually, he recognized the contents, the tools and supplies of a lifetime's occupation for a woman of Dorhaniya's class. Baskets of fine-spun yarn in neat balls, two standing tapestry frames, another hand-frame with a half-finished design placed neatly on a table under the window. He stood, after another vicious poke from the chair, and went to the table. Outlined in a circle of blue, a white G and gold L intertwined, the stitches so tiny that, as with the altarcloth, he almost believed the design painted and not embroidered. He glanced at the frames. On one, another version of the G and L design, this one set in a blue rectangle bordered with red and white interlacing. To his eyes, it looked finished. The other, hardly begun, he could not interpret—something geometrical, he thought, in green and blue and red.

"She begs your pardon," said Eris, behind him; Luap turned

quickly. "She wants to see you, but wishes to have me put up her hair. Would you like something to drink?" She had brought a tray with a tall, narrow silver pot; the scent of the vapor rising took him straight back to childhood. What had it been called? Something he'd never tasted, but served to the adults in the afternoon. "Selon, perhaps?" said Eris, touching the pot. Luap nodded, more curious than thirsty. It looked as he remembered, darker than sib, with a hint of red, but clear. Eris poured into a cup thin as an apple petal, and shaped almost flowerlike, of five lobes. He took it, inhaled, and smiled at her. The impulse came to confide.

"I haven't smelled this since I was a boy," he said. Her answering smile was clearly ironic.

"I don't doubt," she said, in a voice that halted any further confidence. "No more trade to Aarenis or Old Aare; my lady's had the sacks hidden in her grain-jars more than half her life. It was her husband's, the Duke's—part of the marriage settlement, it was, for my lady's father craved selon, especially in cold weather. Hasn't been any in the markets since I was a girl, not even for the richest mageborn. Yet my lady'd rather starve than sell it." From her tone and expression, it was clear that Eris had never tasted it, and that it would never occur to Dorhaniya to share, and that Eris would resent any questions far more than her lady's thoughtlessness.

Luap sipped. A strange flavor, that fit well with its aroma: rich, exciting, an edge of bitterness (though less bitter than sib, and needing no spoonful of honey to ease it down.) By the end of the cup, he felt rested, as if waking from a night's sleep. Eris had left the tray on the table; he considered pouring himself another cup, but resisted the temptation. Lady Dorhaniya might want to share one with him, and it would not look well if he had guzzled the whole pot. But the tray also held a small plate, of the same delicate ware, with tiny pastries; he tried one and found it delicious. He had not suspected Eris of being that good a cook. He ate another, then another.

"She's ready," said Eris from the doorway. She turned and led the way up a short flight of stairs, and showed Luap into a room in the front of the house, overlooking the street. He stopped just inside the door, appalled. It had not been that long—surely it had not been that long! Exquisitely clean and groomed as always, she lay against piled pillows, silver hair elaborately dressed—but no longer the spry elderly lady he had known. Only her eyes still looked alive, and even there, he thought, he could see the faint veils of approaching death wrapping her gently away from the world. It could not be; he would not have it. He was making the safe place for her to live; she must live until he made it. He would heal her—he remembered then that Aris was in the new stronghold. Well, then, he would get Aris. He realized he was standing there, like any rude clod, saying nothing, and that she was smiling at him, the rueful smile of any grandparent observing a child in distress.

"You can't do it," she said, her voice as fragile as a frost-fern on the window. "It is not something you can cure."

"Aris—" he said.

She shook her head, once, very carefully, as if she feared it might come off. "No, my prince. Not even that sweet boy—man though he is—can defeat age. I'm glad you came back in time; I wanted to see you again."

He knelt by her bed, holding her hand in his and blinking back tears. It was hard to remember how he had resented her at first, when he felt she intruded on his childhood memories. Now it was as if he had always known her, as if she were part of his own family. "I wanted you to see it," he said softly. "I thought of you, as we carved the valley walls. . . ."

"I know," she said. "You told me. . . . I can almost see them in my mind, the way you said. A land made of castles, towers and walls, rose-red and pink and sunset-orange. I think of you standing there in the sun, atop a red stone wall, the wind blowing your cloak. Your place, your own land. Prince, if you never wear a crown, you will still have more than your father had, when you have your own land, at peace, with your own people around you."

In her soft old voice, the dream came alive; he forgot the surly guards, Sterin's doubts, the Marshal-General's obstructions. Already, the terraces lay green with springing grain, edged with vegetables, and fruit trees bore blossom and fruit on the same branch in a warm spring sun.

He blinked. Whoever did or did not have the power of charming men, Dorhaniya had it full measure, though he doubted she knew it. That vision had been hers, not his—for his included watchtowers on the height. "I came directly here," he said. "To the—to Esea's Hall; the same pattern is there, behind the altar. I could take you back, if only for—"

Her head turned slowly. "Prince, if you command, I will do even this—but I would not live to see it. Esea's light almost blinds me even now. Do not trouble yourself about me—think of the others you are working to save. Think of your friend Gird—"

"Gird?" The last person he wanted to think of right then, and the last he'd expected her to mention.

A sigh escaped her. "Prince, never forget him. He was—more

than a man, I think. A great man, at the least. Peasant though he was, the gods gave him light to see beyond the rest of us. And he was your friend, though he and you might both deny it."

"I . . . would not deny it."

"Wise of you." She drew a breath, and let it out slowly. "If I cough, prince, do not fret. Just wait." He waited; she did not cough, but did not speak for some time. Then: "Gird loved you, but as a man loves a son he does not understand. And so his advice to you could not be precisely fitted—but it was not bad, for all that. You were his luap; I would not have you disloyal."

"Disloyal?" His heart sank. Could she possibly imagine all he had thought? Hoped? And would even she consider it disloyal?

"Downstairs," she said. "In the room where Eris left you. You saw the embroidery?"

"Yes, lady." Was her mind wandering?

"Prince, I charge you to take as your crest that symbol." It was as if a tiny child had spouted legal theory, or a wren had given voice to an eagle's scream. Luap felt his jaw drop, and hastened to shut it again. It was not a voice to bear argument. "Gird and Luap—your initials intertwined. I think of you as a prince, as indeed you are, but Esea's light shows me you will prosper as Gird's luap only. Stray from that at your peril."

"But, lady—why do you think—?"

"Because—" Her old face crumpled, and her grip tightened on his hand. "Prince, I will not insult you—but remember an old lady's years. I had children; I had nieces and nephews enough, watched them grow through all the awkwardnesses of youth to adulthood, saw the same patterns in the adult as in the child, the same grain in the wood. It is not your fault; I could never blame you. But you know what I mean—don't make me say it!"

"I don't hate Gird," he said, almost whispering.

"That is not enough," she said. "You must love him. You must be his luap, truly his luap, before you can be the prince you are—or rather, the prince you were meant to be."

"To all but you, I have always been his luap."

"Then . . . to me also, be his luap."

"But, lady . . . you were the one who said I must be a prince; you encouraged me."

"Yes. I did." Her other hand plucked at the lace on the coverlet. "I did not always understand, until Gird died. I thought it was foolishness longer than I should have, all that about Gird's rule being one for both peoples. But it came to me when he died, that he was right: that was the only way. And if I encouraged you to think of your heritage, and that made you unwilling to enter into Gird's vision, then I was wrong and Esea may send me to the dark forever."

"You could not be so wrong," Luap said. He squeezed her hand. "You, who love the gods so much—how could they be angry with you?"

"Don't be silly!" Again that tone of authority that stung like a lash. "Selamis—no, *I* will call you Luap! If that will get through your thick head—how can you think of the gods as indulgent grand-parents? If I cause great harm, then of course Esea will be angry with me. I only hope I have not, or that I can cure it."

"You have not caused any harm," said Luap firmly. If he could do nothing else, he would soothe the fears of this dying old woman. "You are quite right; I am Gird's luap. I loved Gird from the day I met him, served him as well as I could, and will continue to honor his memory to the day I die. Don't fear I could forget him."

She had fallen back against her pillows again. "You will use the crest I made?" she asked, her voice unsteady. "You will be loyal?"

He kissed her hand. "I will use it," he said. "I will carve it into the very rock, if that will please you. And I will serve Gird's mem-ory as I served him in life." He meant that, and his voice carried all that conviction.

"Esea's light guide you," she said. She lay for awhile, eyes shut, breathing shallowly. Eris came in to sit beside Luap.

"It won't be long," she murmured. "Today, perhaps tomorrow."

Luap forgot time, and sat silently, holding that old hand with its soft loose skin, until the light failed outside. Eris went to fetch candles; when she came back, Dorhaniya's breathing had changed. She seemed to struggle, panting, then all at once lay motionless, each breath slower than the last. Luap waited long for the last, before he realized it had already come and gone. Beside him, Eris sobbed.

Chapter Twenty-one

"You can take a wagonload of soil, but no more," said the Marshal-General when he summoned Luap. By his expression, he expected Luap to argue.

"Thank you. Marshal-General," said Luap, "for your generosity."

"And you can't take it from any working farm," the Marshal-General went on, "or from any grangeland. You must find unclaimed land, and take it there."

"Of course, Marshal-General."

"And take it out the *other* way—we don't want a wagonload of dirt in the Lord's Hall."

Luap started to say that a wagon wouldn't fit into the little cave chamber, and realized that was what the Marshal-General hoped he'd do. He bowed instead. "Of course, Marshal-General; that would not be fitting."

"*And*," the Marshal-General went on, as if reaching for something at which Luap would balk, "and you will have a yeoman-marshal with you, to ensure that you take your soil as I said, from unclaimed land only."

Luap shrugged, as much in anger as resignation, but managed not to say what he was thinking. The Marshal-General stalked to his door, opened it, and beckoned to a short muscular woman wearing the blue shirt that most yeoman-marshals wore these days. Apparently he had already explained her task, for now he simply pointed to Luap and said, "Make sure, Binis, that he does what I said."

"Right, Marshal-General." She looked at Luap as if he were a thief on trial; he could feel his ears growing hot. He would, he decided, change her mind before he left, if he could not change the Marshal-General's. "When do we leave?" she asked Luap.

"After a friend's funeral," he said. "An old lady I've known a long time, a friend of Gird's—she died yesterday."

"Who?" asked the Marshal-General.

"Dorhaniya, who made the altar cloths for the Lord's Hall."

"A magelady," growled the Marshal-General.

"Gird thought of her as a pious old woman who cared more

about the gods than any quarrel of men," said Luap, putting a bite in it. "He enjoyed talking to her—but you weren't in the city then, were you?" He regretted that even as it popped out, for it would do no good to remind the Marshal-General that he had never been close to Gird. The man scowled even more darkly.

"Even Gird made mistakes," he said.

"I must go," said Luap, "but we can leave at dawn, day after tomorrow. Meet you in the kitchen?" He looked only at Binis, who glanced uncertainly from him to the Marshal-General. The Marshal-General nodded, then she did.

"But don't try to sneak out without me," she said. "I'm a tracker; I would find you."

"That's as well," said Luap, "since we'll be traveling in the midst of winter storms. I will depend on your tracking ability when the snow flies."

The Marshal-General grinned at him. "That's right . . . how are you going to dig your soil while it's frozen? You can't use your magery here; it's against the Code and your own oath forbids you."

"I may find a place and come back after the thaw," Luap said. "I have no intention of breaking my oath." Before the Marshal-General could say more, he added, "And I will of course find yeoman-marshal Binis if that is necessary, so that she can supervise."

He turned with a conscious flourish and left the Marshal-General's office—Gird's office, as he himself still thought of it. He spent the rest of that day with Eris, and greeted those who came to speak of Dorhaniya as if he were a family member.

At dawn on the second day, he came into the kitchen with his gear packed and ready to go. Binis was gossiping with a cook kneading dough, an older woman who gave Luap an open grin.

"We miss you, Luap! Do you still like fried snow?" He saw Binis stare at the woman as if she'd turned into a lizard. So . . . not everyone remembered, or knew, that he had had his own friends here? That not all of them had left?

"Ah . . . Meshi, no one makes fried snow like yours. This Midwinter Feast I wanted to come back for it. I don't suppose you saved any?"

"Saved! Fried snow keeps about as well as real snow in high summer, as well you know. If you want my fried snow, Luap, you'll just have to come when it's ready." She flipped the mass of dough into a smooth ball and laid a cloth over it. "I suppose you want breakfast before you leave, eh?"

"Anything that's at hand." Anything at Meshi's hand would be delicious; she had a double parrion of cooking.

"First bread's out." In a moment, she had sliced a hot loaf and handed it to him with a bowl of butter and a squat stone jar. "Spiced peaches," she said. "From our tree."

"You shouldn't," he said, as he always had, and added, "but I'm glad you did. Spiced peaches again!" He let a lump of butter melt into the hot bread, then spooned the spiced peach preserves onto it. The aroma went straight to his head.

"You don't have spices in that godslost wilderness?" Meshi looked shocked.

"Not yet; I'll buy some in the market to take back." The first bite, he thought, was beyond price; his nose and his tongue contended over ecstasy. Then he noticed Binis standing stiffly to one side, and gestured. "Come, don't you like spiced peaches?"

"Never had any," she muttered, but sat across from him and took a slice of the hot bread. When she'd put a small spoonful on it, she tasted it; her face changed. "It's—I never had anything like that."

"Can't make much," Meshi said shortly, setting down two bowls of porridge with emphasis. "Takes time, makes only a little. Can't serve it all the time." *Or to everyone* came across clearly in the little silence that followed. Luap wanted to eat the whole jar of preserves, but took the hint and started on the porridge. Meshi's gift held even with that. She waited a moment longer, for courtesy, then took the stone jar back and capped it. "It dries out," she said. Then she turned to Binis. "He tried to talk me into going with them, you know. Flattered my cookery, said how they wouldn't have proper foods for the holidays—"

"We don't," said Luap.

"—And I almost went," Meshi said, as if she had not heard the interruption. "But I had too many friends here who weren't going, and even for old Luap I wouldn't give them all up." Then she winked at Luap. "And, to tell the whole truth, I was scared of that magery—being taken by magic to some place I'd never seen gave me the shivers. So I couldn't. But I miss Luap, that I do, for he's one to notice who does the work, no matter what it is."

"He's mageborn," said Binis, around a mouthful of porridge.

"He's *half,*" said Meshi firmly, giving Luap another wink. "Half mageborn, which he can't help any more than any of us can choose our fathers, and half peasant-born, which isn't to his credit any more than his father is to his blame. And I'll tell you this, Binis, to your face and in front of his, if you have the sense you should have, you'll forget whatever our Koris said about him, and look at the man himself. I was here when Gird was still alive, and Luap's worth a gaggle of your Marshal-Generals."

Binis looked at Luap, then at Meshi. "Was he your lover?"

Meshi glared. "He was not. Is that all you girls can think of, these days, but who crawls in whose bed?"

Binis shrugged. "You seem fond of him, is all I meant."

"I like him; I trust him; and it's not his fault he's in bad with the Marshal-General."

"Mmm." Binis was not convinced; Luap didn't know if Meshi's words had made things better or worse.

They left the kitchen, bellies full and foodsacks stuffed, and walked down to the lower city. Binis walked a step behind, Luap noticed, and would not come up beside him even though the streets were not yet crowded. He had not been surprised to find that the Marshal-General would not lend horses from the grange stables; he had arranged to hire mounts and a pack animal from a caravan supplier. He had no intention of walking those trails in winter if he could help it.

As much to annoy her as because he had planned to, he stopped to buy spices—perhaps someone out west would take the trouble to make spiced preserves—and tucked the expensive packets deep in his clothing. The horses he had arranged for were saddled when he arrived, two stocky beasts and a smaller pony. He lashed the foodsacks and their other gear to the packsaddle, and handed the caravaner the sack of coins. He mounted; Binis still stood, holding the rein of the other horse, with a dubious expression. Finally, flushing, she scrambled up so awkwardly he realizes she might not have ridden before.

"I'm sorry," he said. "Do you not like riding?" it was the most diplomatic way he could think to ask.

"Never did." She sat lumpishly, her stirrups far too long and her grip on the saddle too tight.

Luap caught the eye of the caravaner, who bit his lip and said, "Just wait, yeoman-marshal, and let me get at them stirrups. You looked longer-legged than that standing on the ground." The man adjusted the stirrups, then said, "Bein' as it's winter, you might want stirrup-covers, eh?" He ducked back into the stable entrance, and came out with fur-lined leather hoods that tied to the stirrups and protected their feet from the worst winds. They would also, Luap knew, keep Binis's feet from sliding too far into the stirrup.

By the end of the first day's riding, he wondered why he had ever thought midwinter a good time for this. They had had no more than ordinary winter weather, snow no deeper than usual, but they arrived at the village's small grange stiff and sore. Binis could hardly get off her horse, but flinched away when Luap tried to help her. Luap would have had more sympathy for her if she had not made it clear that she blamed him for her discomfort, as if he had chosen to travel horseback because she could not ride. The Marshal, new here since Luap had left, made it clear he thought they were both crazy to be riding around the countryside in the wintertime. He was inclined to blame it all on Luap's magery.

"You may be able to keep yerself warm wi' your magicks, but ye might have had some concern f'the yeoman-marshal here." The Marshal had wrapped a blanket around her; she gave Luap a venomous look out from under the Marshal's elbow. Luap wondered if it would help to tell them he had not kept himself warm—his feet felt frozen, despite the stirrup-covers. From the look on both their faces, they wouldn't believe him.

"I'll see to the horses," he said, and went out. He was tempted to spend the night in the grange's lean-to barn; the horses were friendlier than his companions. But they would probably think he was performing wicked magicks out here by himself; he had better not.

When he came back inside, he heard the murmur of voices; it ceased when they saw him. The Marshal's own yeoman-marshal had joined them. He looked at Luap with the same accusing gaze, and Luap knew they had been discussing the wicked mageborn while he was outside. He found it hard to swallow his supper of ill-cooked porridge and heavy bread amid barbed comments about the luxuries he must be used to. He bit back one retort after another; his jaw felt sore. He tried to remind himself that all peasants weren't like this—Dorhaniya's Eris, for instance, or Cob or Raheli. But these three, and the present Marshal-General, exemplified everything he disliked about his mother's people. By the time he rolled himself in a blanket on the floor (Binis, of course, had the spare pallet), he was thoroughly disgusted with them.

That day and night set the tone for the whole miserable journey. Binis felt the cold more than Luap, but remained convinced that he was using magery unfairly to keep himself comfortable. He had no way to prove he was not. As his anger grew, he would have used his magery that way if he had known how. He tried, surreptitiously, but succeeded only in giving himself a throbbing headache made worse by the glare off the snow. And he was just as cold as Binis, he told himself, but she wouldn't believe it. He remembered, with a burst of satisfaction that he knew was unwise, that the woman whose complaints had driven Gird to a fit of rage had also been named Binis. It wasn't the same Binis, of course, but this one might have been that one's daughter. He didn't ask. He preferred to imagine it, in the privacy of his own head.

They arrived, two days later than he had expected, in Cob's grange. Here, at least, the welcome was as warm for Luap as for Binis. Cob, always lamer in winter, stumped awkwardly into the snowy lane to greet them.

"Luap, you look like a frozen sausage. Get off that horse, and come in to the fire. Vre—" That was his yeoman-marshal, a brisk young man. "Take their horses around back. Bring the packs inside. Ah, Luap, I've missed you. That scribe you left in charge is slower than a pregnant ox at a gate. And who's this?" Luap explained that the new Marshal-General had insisted he have a yeoman-marshal escort. "You? What does he think he's about? No insult to you, Binis, but no one needs to watch Luap. Alyanya's grace, *Gird* trusted him. That ought to be enough for anyone."

Luap took a step and staggered; he knew his feet were at the end of his legs, but he hadn't felt his toes since the village before. Binis, looking from him to Cob with a scowl, had made it to the grange door. Cob shook his head.

"You're going to look like me, if you keep that up. Need an arm?"

"No. I'm fine." He could walk, if he kept a surreptitious eye on his feet to be sure where they were. He made it to the door, across the grange, and into Cob's office. There a fire crackled busily on the hearth. Binis had already crouched beside it. Cob pulled a chair near, and waved Luap into it.

"Let him get his feet to the fire, yeoman-marshal—he's twice your age." Binis looked startled.

"But Marshal, he's a mageborn—he can use magicks to warm himself. . . ."

Cob snorted. "Does it look like it? Use your wits, Binis—he's famished with cold, as bad as you are." She looked at him, as if seeing him anew. Luap found it embarrassing.

"I'm warm enough," Luap said. Cob's welcome was as good as any fire, and his feet were already beginning to throb. Cob's yeoman-marshal, Vrelan, came in with the packs.

"Shall I fetch something to eat, Marshal?" Vrelan sounded eager to prove himself; Luap realized he was very young, probably born after the war. Cob sent him to the local inn—Luap had not realized there was an inn—and turned back to Luap.

"So how is the settlement coming? Will you get a crop in this next year?" With that opening, Luap could explain that he had come for fertile soil, and needed only a little. Cob grinned. "Take what you like—we've plenty in the grange fields."

"I can't do that. The Marshal-General specified I was not to take so much as a clod from farmland or grangelands, only from waste ground."

"Even if the Marshal offered?" Cob looked angry.

"That's right, Marshal," Binis said. Luap thought she would have been wise to hold her tongue. "That's what I'm to do, watch to be sure he doesn't take the wrong soil."

Cob looked at her; Luap recognized the look Gird had given that other Binis and held his breath. But Cob was not drunk, as Gird had been; he merely shook his head. "I didn't ask you," he said. "And I don't think that frog-eyed fool has the right to tell me what I can and can't do with a bit of earth from my own drillfields. He wasn't with Gird as long as I was." It was exactly what Luap had hoped he would say, all the long, cold, miserable trip from Fin Panir, but now he felt a hollow open inside him. Cob meant what he said, and he could take his soil and go home—but that would leave Cob in a mess.

"No," Luap said. "I didn't come here to start a quarrel between you and the Marshal-General."

"You didn't start it," Cob said, reddening. "That—" Luap was aware of Binis's interest, her ears almost flapping wide on either side of her head. And Cob had been Gird's friend, with Gird longer than almost anyone else still alive.

"No," he said again, and let a little of his power bleed into it. On Gird it had not worked; on Cob and Binis it worked well. Both sat quiet and stared at him. "I will not disobey the Marshal-General's orders on this, though I thank the friend who cared more to help me than advance himself." Neither of them said anything, and he was afraid he had put too much power on them . . . but then Cob shook himself, like a wet dog.

"All right," he said gruffly, not looking at Binis. "But I want you to know that I trust you. Now—where's that boy with the food?" He got up and left the office to Luap and Binis. Luap stretched luxuriously. The fire's warmth crept over him in exquisite waves; he could feel not only his throbbing feet, but a blanket-like warmth on his knees and thighs. He had not been this warm for days; the other Marshals had pushed Binis close to the fire. He glanced at her. One side of her face seemed flushed—from the fire or embarrassment, he could not guess.

"Are you warm enough?" he asked her.

"Did you really not have magicks for the cold?" she asked, without answering him.

"No," Luap said. He was not really surprised at her question; from the little they'd talked he had discovered her to have a literal mind and a tenacious grasp of the trivial. "I'm glad of a fire," he added, hoping this would divert her from the question he saw hovering on her lips. "If you are still cold, why not get a blanket?"

"I'm all right," she said. "Are you really twice my age?"

She was so predictable. She would ask next if Meshi were really his friend, and if he had slept with her, and then why the mageborn had gone to his stronghold . . . and so on, no doubt for hours.

"I don't know how old you are," he said. She scowled at that, looking for trickery in it. "And I don't really know my own years." Which was not quite true, but saved discussing it. She scowled again, not because she detected a lie, but because she had not been answered.

"Is Meshi, that cook, really your friend?"

He uttered a silent prayer to any god who might be listening to bring Cob back into the room. She would go down the predictable list, and it would drive him to saying something he would regret. For the first time, he felt he really understood Gird's rage that night in the forest. He answered all in a rush. "Yes, she's my friend; we met during the war. And she's not my lover and never has been, just as she said when you asked her."

Binis looked shocked; Luap stared her down. Cob came in, followed by Vrelan with a kettle wrapped in cloths, which he unwrapped and put on the hearth. "Better stew than I make; the inn's cook has the true parrion. And new bread, and a pot of custard."

"Marshal-General says Marshals should make their own meals," Binis said primly. Luap closed his eyes a moment. Didn't she realize—? Cob merely grunted, though his yeoman-marshal stared at Binis as if she'd sprouted green horns.

"I've cooked enough meals in Gird's army to last me, yeoman-marshal. When there's a good cook, who knows what she's doing, and needs the trade, I'm not going to eat lumpy porridge and soggy bread to please someone as won't get out of bed before midday. Gird could've milked a herd and ploughed two fields before Koris finishes breakfast." He dished out stew for everyone, breathing a little hard, and handed Binis her bowl with a stare. "And you go ahead and tell him, Binis, all I've said—he knows how I feel about him, and I know how he feels about me. But when all's said and done, he knows who fought beside Gird from the first day. I didn't *want* to be Gird's successor, but it was offered me. *He* had to argue his way into it."

Binis turned redder than the fire could explain, and ate her stew without looking up. Luap burned his mouth on the first bite, and slowed down. Cob was right—the cook had a parrion. Mutton stew could be almost as bad as lumpy porridge, but this had a savor he liked. Cob pushed over a half-loaf of bread and a dish of butter.

"You spoil me," Luap said, carefully not looking at Binis.

"No—we eat this well almost every day." Cob buttered a hunk of bread for himself and stuffed it in his mouth. Luap winced inwardly. He liked Cob, but the man had never acquired even as much polish as Gird. When he had refused the Marshal-General's position, he had apparently returned to his rural grange determined to be as much a peasant as possible.

Vrelan, meanwhile, sat in the corner opposite Binis, eating as rapidly as any hungry young man just past boyhood. He smiled shyly at Luap when their eyes met. He will want tales, Luap thought to himself. He will want stories of Gird, and stories of my distant land—he's got those dreamer's eyes.

Cob swallowed, then belched. "So—tell me, Luap, is that land what you hoped it would be?"

Luap nodded, and swallowed the stew in his mouth. "Yes—although it's even colder than this. I've never seen snow so deep. Luckily we need not travel in it, and the stronghold itself doesn't freeze. Though it's not really warm, either."

"Magic, is it?" This with a quick sidelong glance at Binis.

"No, the elves said it was the depth of stone. It stays about the same all year." Luap scooped up more stew before it cooled. His feet had quit throbbing and he felt almost sleepy. "We spent the time before snow building terraces," he went on. "Piled the rock up, had Arranha telling us how to level them."

"I thought you'd just level the valley floor," Cob said. "Isn't it a small valley?"

"Small and steep. Not just the sides, the floor as well. Level the whole thing and the new floor would be halfway up the mountains at the low end." Not quite, but it made a vivid image; Cob nodded, mouth pursed. "So we're doing smaller terraces, none more than three men high at the low end. Most less than that—it'd take too much soil to fill them otherwise."

"A lot of work," Cob said. "And so few of you—I suppose you found a way to use your magicks?"

Luap grinned at him. Cob would not demand, from a friend, but he was as curious as anyone else. "Yes, we did, though it still takes a lot of sweat and blisters. I must admit, it's good to see magery used the right way, for breaking stones and not people. And it keeps the few with magery too busy for mischief."

Cob shot another glance at Binis, who had finished her stew and was munching the end of a loaf of bread. "When you've finished, yeoman-marshal, you and Vrelan take back this pot and then check the horses. You can trust me not to let Luap out of my sight." His tone was pleasant but firm; she could neither resent that order, nor disobey it. Cob turned to Vrelan, "Since we have guests, get us a pot of their good ale, and see if they'll send a loaf of bread fresh from the morning baking." He gave the yeoman-marshal a few coins. Binis and Vrelan went out with the kettle, one cheerful and one scowling. When the outer door had shut behind them, Cob turned to Luap.

"There'll be things you don't want her repeating to the Marshal-General, I daresay, but you might share with an old friend. Tell me: did you find you had all the royal magery?"

For answer, Luap freed his light, and grinned at the expression on Cob's face. "I know—I shouldn't do that here, even though we are alone and you are a friend. You're a Marshal first, and I'm not supposed to use my magery. But I thought you'd like to see it."

"I'm glad for you, since you wanted it, but—glad to see it?—not really. Although it must be handy to have your own light, if you live underground. There are times I could use that. But—you built the terraces that way?"

Luap damped the light; the room seemed dark without it, despite the fire burning cheerily on the hearth. "We did," he said. "Some of us—it's strange, Cob, who has which magery. Our people have not tried to use it for work for a long time; I think that was a mistake. Some can move stones the size of this room—" Cob looked around, the whites of his eyes glinting in the firelight, as if worried that the room might take flight. "—And others can hardly shift a pebble. Most that have any magery at all can call some amount of light, enough to start a fire with. Aris, as you know, can heal. Were you in Council when he described his attempts to train others?"

"No. I missed that one." Cob prodded the fire and laid another split log on it.

"To make it short, he's found no one else who can do what he does. Some can heal lesser things, but at greater cost to themselves. He's hoping that some of the children will have that talent, that he can find it early and train it."

"I thought there was a girl—"

"Yes, so did the others—so did she, for that matter. It wasn't really healing; she could convince people they were not feeling pain, but what caused the pain got no better . . . unless it would have anyway. A useful skill, certainly, and a better use of it than charming someone into handing over their purse, but not true healing. Aris has worked with her, so she now recognizes when she needs to call him in and when it's safe to relieve the pain and wait for a natural healing." Luap sighed. "It's sad—the one magery we all wanted to have, that most people trusted, is the rarest. I had hoped to learn it; I can't. And Aris, so gifted, has little else but his light."

"I miss that lad," Cob said, shaking his head. "He loved Gird so, and Gird loved him like a grandson."

Luap felt a pang of envy and wrestled it down. Everyone liked Aris; he did himself. "We're lucky to have him," he said.

"And how's Seri doing, out there with all you mageborn?"

"Well enough. She has Aris, after all; they're still like two burs, though they don't seem likely to marry."

"Why not? Would you object?"

"Of course not," Luap said. "But since they came back from that long journey, back when she was still a Marshal-candidate, they've been different. I can't explain it, nor can the Rosemage, but we both recognized it."

"It's too bad," Cob said. "I was hoping their child might combine the two of them. Squeeze Aris and Seri into one person, and you'd have quite a Marshal-General." He stretched his legs to the fire. "You're looking better, now you've eaten—that sour-faced yeoman-marshal you're traveling with must have sucked the blood out of you."

Luap laughed. "It's not that. I didn't know she didn't ride, and she took it as an insult . . . and then she has trouble in the cold."

"She'd have died in the bad winter camps of the war," Cob said. "Or she'd have gotten over her foolishness. I hate to think of women like her becoming the next Marshals."

"How's Raheli?" That was the natural transition.

"Haven't seen her since the Council when she spoke for you. She'd mellowed a lot then, I thought. We talked a bit about Gird. I thought she should have been the next Marshal-General. She thought it shouldn't go from parent to child—but she has no children, so I didn't think that was a problem. She wouldn't do it, though."

"I thought the objection would come because—"

"Because she's a woman? So did I, though I don't agree. But

she wouldn't take it. She nominated me, in fact, but—I don't know, maybe I should've done it. It just didn't seem right. I *knew* Gird; he threw me flat on my back the first day he came into our camp, and I'm no more fit to take his place than . . . than a cow is. Nobody is, when you come to it, but I couldn't."

The door opened, and the two yeoman-marshals came in, shivering. "A wind's got up," Vrelan said "Old Dorthan says he reckons another storm's coming." Cob looked at Luap, his brows raised. Luap shrugged.

"I didn't like the look of the sky behind us today, but that's all I can say."

"You're welcome to stay all winter, if that's what it takes," Cob said. "But if a storm's coming, we've some work to do, with two extra beasts in the barn. No—" Luap had started to stand, but Cob waved him back down. "If this is a big storm, your help will be welcome come morning, but stay warm now."

"I'll bring more wood, at least," Luap said.

"If you're determined on it . . . there's a stack in the barton corner."

Outside, in the blowing dark, the cold wind took his breath away. Binis had gone with Cob and Vrelan; he found the woodstack on his own, and thought about moving some in by magery. But Binis might see, and that would do Cob no good. He lugged in several armloads before Cob returned. By then it had begun to snow, small dry flakes that stung his face.

Morning's light barely penetrated the blowing snow; Luap and Cob fought their way around the end of the grange and into the barn built against it, carrying buckets of hot water from the hearth. "We should have built peasant cottages, wi' inside ways to the cowbyres," Cob said, struggling to shut the door against the wind. The horses whickered, their breath pluming into the cold air. When they drank, their whiskers whitened almost at once. Cob nodded to the ladder. "If you can make the climb, it'll be easier for me." So Luap climbed into the narrow hayloft, and threw down enough for all the beasts at once, then climbed back down to help Cob feed them.

Later, the snowfall lessened, though the wind still scoured flurries off the drifts. All four of them went out to check on the poorer folk in the village. Luap had never had a clear idea of what a rural Marshal did when not holding court or drill. Cob apparently thought that a Marshal's job included everything no one else remembered to do . . . he was remarkably like Gird, Luap thought, in the way that he had made himself a caretaker for the whole village. He had Vrelan chop firewood for a family in which the man had a broken arm, and the mother was pregnant. He and Luap climbed up to mend a gap in the roof of one cottage, where slates had blown off overnight. Cob himself dragged one drunk out into the street and made him fetch clean water from the public well to clean up the mess he'd made on the floor, while the man's wife tried to make excuses for him. Binis, clearly astonished that Cob considered her available for such work, was kept as busy as the rest of them.

"It's like this," Cob explained after darkness had fallen and they were eating in the inn. "Some Marshals think we're just judges and drillmasters, but someone's got to do all the rest. Back afore the war, each village had its headman or headwoman, and in some places, even the magelords took care of their people. Everyone knew what needed doing and how to do it. They knew who really needed help, and who was a wastrel. But the war changed that. People may not live in the village they were born in; we've got crafters and merchants and gods know what all, living all amongst each other. And whatever you say about one fair law for everyone, some things just plain aren't fair. You don't make it fair by treating everyone alike, either. That's all I do—what the village head would have done, or a good lord: either one. Know the people, know who needs help, and who needs a good knock on the head to straighten 'em up."

"But you can't do it all yourself." Binis looked tired, but less sulky than the days before. Perhaps work agreed with her; Gird had always said it was good for the sulks.

"No," Cob agreed, wiping his bowl with a slice of bread. "No, I can't do it all, not even with young Vre, here. But that's what I tell them on drill nights—just as in an army, we're all parts of each other. If you let your neighbor go hungry, he's not likely to help you when the robbers come. Same way, if you're always asking for help, but don't give any, soon no one cares. I went after Hrelis today, you saw—the drunk. His wife's always coming for grange-gift, says he's sick. We know what kind of sick; Vre told me last night he was in here drinking and begging. So for him I have a bucket of cold water, but poor Jos, who got his arm broken helping someone reset a wheel, we'll do what we can for him. When his arm's mended, he'll be around here doing chores without anyone saying a word." He belched contentedly, and smiled at Binis. "But you're right—I don't do it alone. I don't have to check Morlan's widow any more, and I didn't have to find homes for the children whose parents were killed by lightning in the pasture last spring.

This grange is beginning to function as a village should—with care and common sense."

"And that's the other reason you wouldn't be Marshal-General, isn't it?" Luap asked. "You had in mind what a grange should be, but you wanted to show it, not tell people."

Cob flushed and looked away. "I'm no more skilled with words than Gird was," he said. "It's what he did, after all. He showed us—"

"And yelled at us," Luap said, grinning. Cob's dream was not his dream. but he knew it came close to Gird's dream . . . and he could see it was a worthy dream. "But it's going to take unusual Marshals to do what you're doing."

Now Cob grinned back. "Oh—well, that young Seri, you know, she used to talk of things like this. Her and me and Raheli and some of the others: we were thinking what a grange is for, when there's no war. It can't be just to collect money to send to Fin Panir." Binis started to say something, then stopped. Luap wondered if Cob had convinced her; he doubted it. But Cob had convinced him.

That day and the next, with the drifts too high for travel, they stayed in Cob's grange and helped with his definition of grange work. Luap found himself able to admit he had picked a bad time to come looking for soil, but that he'd wanted something to work with for spring planting. "And I was with Dorhaniya when she died," he said. "I'm glad I was there, though I'd hoped she'd like the new place. . . ."

"Tell you what," Cob said. "Come thaw, I'll find you a place to take your soil—there's unclaimed land between me and the next grange south. If I understand it, we'll thaw here before you will, so you won't lose much time. How would that be?"

"I don't think the Marshal-General would approve," said Binis. Cob gave her a look Luap would not like to have turned on him.

"I didn't ask you, Binis, and I'm not asking the Marshal-General. If it's unclaimed land, he can't deny it: he's already given his approval. Whatever his quarrels with Luap, the law says he's made a contract, and he can't back out now."

"But we're not supposed to help—"

"We're not supposed to act like bratty children quarreling over sweets, either." Cob glared at her, red-faced. "D'you think this is what Gird wanted? We won the war; the mageborn aren't our lords any more. Now it's time for peace, and peace means helping each other. And you might remember that Luap here was Gird's closest assistant: he did more for Gird than any of the rest of us, including your precious Marshal-General."

Luap had not expected that strong a defense, even from Cob. It embarrassed him, shook his certainty in the peasants' opposition— a certainty that Binis increased whenever she opened her mouth. Now Cob turned to him.

"How about it—will you trust me to find you some good soil, within the Marshal-General's limitations?"

"Of course, I will," Luap said. "I will come back to Fin Panir in early spring—your early spring."

"Good. That's settled. It'll save Binis here from riding all over the countryside in winter—I don't suppose you can whisk her back to Fin Panir by magery, eh?"

"Alas, no. We'll have to go as we came."

It was as cold a trip as the one out, but Binis seemed slightly less hostile; at least she seemed convinced that Luap, too, suffered from the cold. Luap hoped that Cob would not get in too much trouble with the Marshal-General while he was gone . . . but when he considered the two men, he thought Cob would come off well in any contest between them. So he returned to the stronghold with the embroidery Dorhaniya had given him, determined to prove himself to Cob as well as his own people.

"Now we can begin to move," the black-cloaked leader said. "For mortals time runs swiftly; they become accustomed to safety, and cease to watch for danger. They hope all will be well, and hoping so, believe it to be. A year, two years, of peace, and they think peace eternal." He paused for the scornful laughter, like a rustle of dry leaves, before going on. "We must learn more about them," he said. "Especially the prince. We must know them better than they know themselves—not a difficult task. For each weakness, we will provide the appropriate temptation . . . and remember, if we can use what they call their virtures to entrap them, so much the better."

Chapter Twenty-two

Luap returned to Fin Panir while the canyons of his own land were still choked with snow. This time, the guards at the High Lord's Hall merely shrugged when he appeared. The Marshal-General, he was told, was "in conference," too busy to see him; Luap found someone who claimed to know where Binis was. He went down to the lower city to visit Eris. Dorhaniya had left her enough to live on, she had said after the funeral, and her own skill at needlecraft would help.

"Sir," she said, when she answered his knock on the door. From her expression, she had not expected to see him again. Then she relaxed. "You've come for the banner?"

He had forgotten it, in the sorrow of Dorhaniya's death and the difficult trip with Binis. "No—or rather yes, I will be glad to have it, of course, but that's not why I came. How are you?"

"I miss her," Eris said. Then she stood aside and beckoned him in. "There's lots of them don't understand, you know. Why I ever stayed with her after the war, why I stay here now. She was just another rich mageborn, they say, just another foolish old rich woman." She led Luap back to the small sitting room he had seen before. "Of course that's true: she was old, and rich, and foolish, and mageborn, but that wasn't the half of it. You know: you met her."

"I know." Luap looked around. He had thought he could forget nothing he had seen, and yet he could not be sure nothing had changed. The embroidery frame was missing . . . but what else?

"I didn't stay just because she was rich, and I never wanted for anything while she was alive. It wasn't that."

"I know," Luap said again. He had never completely understood the bond between Eris and Dorhaniya, but it had nothing to do with gold or comfort: he knew that much.

"She was so—so dithery, sometimes. Her family—her own and her husband's—they both thought she was short of wits. That's why her father sent me to her when I was just a child, and she had only married the year before. Keep her going, they said, as long as you can; she's got no sense of her own. But they were wrong."

Eris sat down, and smoothed her skirt. Luap didn't know what to say. He felt that he should comfort her, but she needed nothing he could give. Except perhaps his listening ear, at the moment. "She knew people," Eris said. "She couldn't always say what she meant about them, but she knew what they were like inside. She knew her husband was a silly fool whose pride would get him in trouble with the king, but she never complained about it. She knew that sister of hers, the one who didn't marry Arranha, was mean to the bone, but she never complained about that, even when her sister cheated her out of her mother's jewels. I won't say she was never wrong, for she had a soft heart, but she wasn't wrong often."

Luap wanted to ask what Dorhaniya had thought of him, but he wasn't sure he wanted to know. She had seen through him several times that he knew of, commenting on fear or anger that no one else had ever seemed to see. She had scolded him, too; he would like to have known that he'd satisfied her afterwards.

Eris looked at him. "She liked you," she said. "She didn't think you were perfect, mind, but she liked you."

"I wish she'd lived to see our place in the mountains," Luap said. "I wish you would come." That popped out before he thought, and he wasn't at all sure he meant it. But Eris shook her head.

"I don't want to leave Fin Panir; I lived here in this house with her and it's got my memories. But I thank you for the offer; 'twas generous. She always said you were generous."

"Are you getting along all right?"

"Well enough. There's some as think I shouldn't be living in this house alone, that it's too much space for one person, but my lady left it to me, and the courts upheld that—" Luap had had to use all his influence there, for some considered mageborn wills to be invalid, and this was not an area Gird had thought much about. "—so I'll be all right. I may take lodgers, later, when I've decided what to do with the rest of her things."

She took him around the house, then, showing off the treasures of a vanished aristocracy, things that had survived because Eris and Dorhaniya's other servants had defended the house and her. Much of it did not interest Luap at all: the cedarwood needleboxes carefully notched for knitting needles and embroidery needles of all sizes, the little bags of fine grit for cleaning and polishing the needles, the many boxes of colored yarn and thread, narrow bands of lace and embroidery for decorating garments, and small rooms full of Dorhaniya's best gowns.

"I could cut these up for the cloth," Eris said, rubbing the skirt of one blue and green brocade between her fingers, "but I can't bear the thought. No one wears such clothes now; they'd be used for patches, or rags, and it's a waste." They were beautiful; he remembered how Dorhaniya had looked, and how the mageladies of his childhood had looked . . . how their gowns had rustled, how he had reached out to finger the cloth, the lace, and been slapped away.

More interesting to Luap were the bowls and vases and trays, the sets of fine tableware, the silver spoons. "She had to sell some of it, the last few years," Eris said. "But most of it's here. You don't have to worry that I'd go hungry, sir, not with all this."

"I'm glad," Luap said. He would have felt obliged to help her some way, and yet he had no wealth to be generous with. He touched one of the bowls almost guiltily . . . as a child he had been delighted with the beautiful things he saw, fascinated by the fine detail of tiny carvings, the play of color and gleaming light in rich fabrics and embroidery. Other things were more important, of course, but he wished that Gird had not been so convinced that plainness was a sort of virtue in itself. The peasants had made beautiful things as well, as beautiful as they could within the limits of the materials they had. They had never had silver and gold enough to make it into spoons or dishes, but he had no doubt they would have . . . how could anyone not prefer the feel and glow of silver, which never changed the flavor of the food being eaten.

Eris watched him, musing. "She would have liked you to have some of her things," she said finally. "But she did not know what you would like; you never said much."

Luap shook his head. "How could I? As a child, I had one life, and in manhood another: there was no bridge between them until I met her. I found it hard to talk about, as you know."

"But your eyes speak, and your fingers when you touched that bowl. I have more than I need . . . would you take a few things, in her memory?"

"She made the banner," Luap said softly; tears stung his eyes. "I have no right to anything . . ."

"Nonsense." Eris brushed her hands down her apron. "You have not asked; I have offered. That makes the difference. And since you have no right, as you say, you have no right to choose: I will choose, and you will take what I give you." Luap wanted to laugh, she must have spoken in just that tone to Dorhaniya when that lady "dithered" as she put it. He could easily imagine her settling her lady's mind to a decision. If Dorhaniya had felt half the relief he did now, it was no wonder she had been as loyal to her servant as her servant was to her.

"Thank you," he said, feeling less guilt and more anticipation. "I do—I would be happy to accept whatever you choose."

"Very well," Eris said. "You'll take her needlework for you back this trip; I'll make my selections and have them ready for you next time. Not more than a quarter-year, either—is that clear?"

"Yes, ma'am," Luap said. She shook her head, smiling.

"And don't be saucy with me: you were her prince, but to me you're just another half-mage." The joy fell from him like a dropped cloak; she saw it in his face and came at once to put her hands to his cheeks. "No—I didn't mean it like that. I cannot feel for you what she did; I have no magery. But you are more than just another half-mage to me: you are a man she trusted and admired, a man who was kind to her beyond the requirements of his place. I would not give you anything of hers if I did not also respect and admire you, in my own way." She gave his head a little shake. "Though if you could laugh a bit at yourself, it would be better for you."

"I'm sorry," Luap said, tasting the bitter salt of unshed tears.

"No—don't waste your time being sorry. Go and do what you need not be sorry for." Gird's advice, from another peasant, but this one had given him respect and admiration; Luap lifted his head and smiled at her.

"I will," he said.

Binis in the spring was slightly less sour than Binis in deep winter; she actually smiled at Luap briefly. He had debated walking the whole way to Cob's grange to accommodate her, but decided it would simply take too long. She had ridden it in bad weather; now she could ride in good. She did not argue or complain; perhaps she had anticipated this and practiced in the meantime. Despite the usual spring mud, they made good time, rising early to ride all day. They stayed in different granges than they had in winter, since they covered more ground each day, so Luap did not have to deal with the same Marshals. And this time, when they rode up to Cob's grange, Binis took both horses' reins without asking, and led them around back while Luap went in the open grange door. They had ridden late; Cob had started drill with three hands of yeomen who were bending and stretching together.

"Luap! I've been expecting you." He turned the group over to his yeoman-marshal, and came forward to clasp arms. "Where's your watchdog?"

"Putting the horses away," Luap said. Cob grinned at him.

"Getting her trained, eh? Using your charm on her?"

Luap winced and shrugged. "Don't say that; it sounds bad. And you know better. She rides better."

"She needed to." Cob looked him up and down. "And you could use some exercise, after days spent in the saddle, I daresay. Work out the stiffness, remind your legs what they're for?"

Luap groaned. "You—you're as bad as Gird himself. All right." He put off his cloak, loosened his belt, and joined the others. He had not really drilled in a long time; he had lost, he discovered, the suppleness he had had in youth and he could feel the tightness in his legs every time he leaned over.

But he recognized Cob's purposes. His yeomen might remember the man who had helped Cob in the blizzard . . . they would certainly remember the man who drilled with them, claiming no special place. He caught the sidelong looks; some of them knew his name. When Binis came in from putting up the horses, Cob asked her to lead the stick drill as if she were his own yeoman-marshal. Luap saw resignation and grudging respect on her face. She proved to be a reasonably good drill leader. Luap had not drilled with sticks in years; his palms soon felt hot. But he was determined not to quit, not with Binis leading. Cob limped around, giving advice to all, until he came to Luap.

"Take a breather; you're as old as I am, and this is young man's work."

Luap glared at him, half-amused and half-angry. "You got me into this."

"So I did, but I don't want you going back bloody-handed. I'd forgotten about the burn scars. You never did develop good calluses after that, did you?"

"Not on the one hand, no." Luap stopped, loosened his grip, and flexed his fingers. That would hurt in the morning; it hurt now. Cob took his hands and looked at them, lips pursed.

"Lucky we've a cold stream. Just wait for me." He stumped up to the front of the grange. "Binis, I want you and Vrelan to have them pair off for fighting drills. No broken bones, but a few raps in the ribs won't hurt my yeomen." Binis looked at Luap, and Cob turned to her. "You may not know it, yeoman-marshal, but in the war he had both hands burned. And you don't build callus on burn scars—I saw him try, in the war. Gird himself finally told him to drill only as much as his scars would bear. If you want to argue that—" He looked as dangerous as he ever had, Luap thought, a man sure of himself and his place in the world.

"No, Marshal," Binis said.

"Just keep in mind . . . Gird didn't say pain was good, only that getting good usually involved pain. Those aren't the same thing."

"Yes, Marshal." A dark flush mounted up her face; Cob put his hand on her shoulder.

"Sorry. We veterans can be rough-tongued; if I didn't think you knew what you were doing, I wouldn't let you supervise section drills." He gave her a little shake and came back to Luap. "Come on, now; we're getting those hands in cold water."

"You should have been a healer," Luap said. Cob had insisted that he keep his hands in cold springwater until his bones ached; then he'd put a salve on the worst places, and given Luap soft rags to wrap around his hands.

"I wish I were," Cob said. "You know, young Seri insisted that all Marshal-candidates learn something of herblore and healing. . . . I wish the gods would grant us just a bit of Aris's talent."

"I wish the gods would give everyone Aris's talent," Luap said. "He's always busy—too busy—and even working all day every day he can't possibly heal all he'd like."

"Is there no way to misuse it?" Cob asked. "Of course I don't accuse Aris—I know Aris—but if everyone had the power, could it be misused?"

Luap shook his head. "I don't see how. It can't be hoarded for self-healing; Aris can heal his own injuries, but it's painful, as is withholding healing from others. Aside from healing someone the gods want to call—Aris told me about a child kicked in the head, whom he healed but who never completely recovered—I don't see how anyone could misuse it. That doesn't happen often."

"Perhaps you're right. I know we need more healers, more who can do what Aris does. Herblore has its place, but it can't cure many things." Cob turned away a moment, rummaged in a basket, and came up with a lump of soil. "Here now—smell this, and see what you think."

Luap sniffed. It smelled earthy, alive, the way soil should smell. It was a dark, heavy clod, more clay than loam, but it would mix with the sand in the canyons, he was sure. "Good," he said. "In fact, better than good. Where's it from?"

"Southeast. Unclaimed land between granges, just as the Marshal-General required. I've found a cart and stout horse you can hire, although how you're going to get them into your cave . . ."

"I gave up on that," Luap said. "I'll take a sackful, or maybe two, on a pack animal. I can drag the sacks into position by myself." Or he could travel the mageroad alone, and bring back someone from the other end to help, but he did not tell Cob that. "We'll see what Arranha's *mathematics* does. According to him, we could start with this single clod."

"Good. We'll start in the morning, if that's all right with you." Cob leaned back in his chair. "Binis seems a bit less touchy this time."

Luap shrugged. "She's fine. The winter trip was my fault; it would have made anyone difficult."

"No—there you wrong yourself. You've never been one to complain about that kind of thing. But we'll see in the morning."

They arrived at Cob's chosen site, a meadow already greening, with new grass and pink flowers peeking through the dead grass of winter, by nightfall. Binis looked around. "Are you sure no one claims this, Marshal?"

"Very sure. I checked with the next Marshal over. There's a village blasted by magery between us, fields poisoned and dead, so there are fewer people than some years back, and neither of our granges spread this direction. This is just outside the dead zone, but you can see the land is well alive. Luap?"

Luap dismounted and dug his dagger into the turf, bringing up a small lump of thick dark soil. It smelled rich and fertile. "It's perfect," he said. He pulled out the two sacks he'd bought, and unlashed the shovels from the pack pony's saddle.

"You're not going to dig it *now*," Cob said.

"We're camping here, aren't we?" Luap asked. He grinned wickedly at Cob. "What was the first thing Gird taught all of us?"

"You give Vrelan that shovel and help me cook," Cob said. "I trust your cooking."

The next morning, Vrelan and Binis—she surprised Luap by offering—dug another narrow trench to fill the sacks with earth. "I know it's harder this way," Luap had said, "but a narrow trench will quickly heal; we don't want to leave the land open to harm." Soon they were done; Luap nicked his finger to produce a drop of blood which he squeezed into the trench. Binis stared at him, and he explained. "Alyanya's blessed me; when I was a farmer, I blooded my blade like everyone else."

They returned to Cob's grange that night, and the next day Luap and Binis set off for the cave, more than a hand of days away. He felt almost smug about surprising her with his willingness to drill, to dig a jacks trench, to offer his own blood in return for the earth. "I thought you would destroy all the old ways," she said as they rode. "*Our* old ways, I mean."

"Did you ever meet Arranha?" Luap countered. She looked blank. "The priest of Esea in the High Lord's Hall?"

"That old man in the white robe? No. They said he was a mage-lord who followed the Sunlord. That's what the war was against, magelords and bad gods."

Luap closed his eyes, fighting off a wave of anger. How could she be that ignorant, that stupid? "Arranha," he said between clenched teeth, "*helped* Gird fight that war. Arranha is the one who took Gird to the gnomes. You do know about that?"

Binis nodded. "They hated the magelords too, so they gave him pikes."

"No. They gave him training, and maps, and advice. Duke Marra-kai of Tsaia gave him gold to buy pikes."

"*Duke* Marrakai? Gird took gold from a magelord? I don't believe it!"

"He did," Luap said. "And his son visited Gird after the war, in Fin Panir; Gird liked him." He glanced at Binis; her lower lip stuck out, and she looked like someone determined not to believe that night follows day. She was certainly not going to believe that Gird, hero of the peasants' war, considered a Tsaian magelord and his son friends. "But about Arranha: Gird rescued Arranha from the mageborn who hated him—the priests who really did follow bad gods, as you call them—and they became friends." He thought a long moment. "Binis—did you ever meet *Gird?*"

She reddened. "No, not to speak to. I saw him a few times, in the city, but he was ... you know, he was the Marshal-General, and I was a child."

Hard to believe the years had gone that fast. Hard to believe that someone could be a yeoman-marshal, yet never have drilled with Gird, never have struck a blow in real battle. He'd known she was younger, much younger, but ... *We're getting old,* he thought suddenly. *All of us who knew Gird; all of us who really know what that war was about, and who was on which side.*

"Were you in the city the day Gird died?" Luap asked. Binis nodded. "And did you feel it?"

"I felt ... something," she said. "I remember how hot it had been, sticky. There'd been quarrels all day, up and down the street. My aunt got on me about something—I don't really remember— and I threw a pot at her. I knew it was wrong; I knew she'd tell my da, and my uncle, and the Marshal and they'd all be down on me again. I ran out the back way, up the alley toward the old palace, and I thought I'd run out in the meadows. They wouldn't know where to look. Everything was unfair; everybody was angry with me and it wasn't any of it my fault." Her voice had risen, remembering old grievances. Then her face smoothed out again, and her voice softened. "I remember . . . I'd run too fast, I couldn't seem to breathe, and I felt squeezed somehow, like stones were on me. And then all at once it was over. Like a storm passing, but there wasn't any storm. Stillness, but not sticky, not so hot. Calm, I guess you'd say. I had stopped running, and now I thought I'd go back."

Luap was afraid to break her mood, so they rode in silence some distance until the pack pony stumbled, and he reined up and dismounted to check it. Binis stayed on her horse, and as he lifted each of the pony's hooves in turn, she went on.

"I didn't know what'd happened right then. Not till after I was back at our house. My aunt—she came to me as I came in, said she was sorry, and I was sorry too, for breaking a good pot. I felt— I don't know how I felt, except that nothing hurt inside, the way it had since my mother died. All the quarrels seemed silly, but not anything to grieve over. Just put them aside and go on. Later the Marshal said something about Gird having taken a kind of curse off us, but in your *Life of Gird* it's not a curse."

"No one really knows," Luap said. "If it was a curse, or an evil spirit, or just ourselves . . . but we know whom to thank for lifting it."

"Yes, but—but I still get angry. I still see things go wrong, things happen that aren't fair."

"Gird didn't heal us, the way Aris heals," Luap said, thinking it out as he spoke. He swung back up onto his horse and nudged it into motion. "Maybe he couldn't; maybe even the gods can't. But he gave us a respite, and a taste of what real healing is. I think we're supposed to do the rest."

"Hmph." Binis scowled again. "But we're not Gird."

"True enough. But Gird wasn't Gird all along." Which was, he realized, just the point Raheli had made about his *Life of Gird*. Could she be right about that? No. She had been right about many other things, but on that he would not change his mind. No amount of talking or writing would convince people who had not known him that Gird had begun as a perfectly ordinary man . . . they would simply decide that he had not been a hero. Just as Binis could not accept a Gird who befriended mageborn and Sunlord priests, later generations would deny either Gird's early life, or his later accomplishments. And he could not take the chance that they might deny what Gird had done. He must make sure that Gird lived through the ages as the hero he had really been, even though that meant shaping his early life. He wasn't pretending Gird had been perfect—he understood how people could love someone more for his faults—but Gird's life had been entirely too unformed to last as a story.

"Cob says the magelords mistreated you," Binis said. "So why didn't you turn against them?"

Luap turned in the saddle to see if she was serious. She was. "Binis—what else would you call joining Gird's army, than turning against them?" He had been so careful to keep himself out of the telling of Gird's life—he had been trying to make Gird the center, as he should be—but if people like Binis didn't even know what Gird's luap had done, perhaps he should make another revision. She looked unconvinced; Luap tried again. "Binis, Cob is my friend from those days—from Gird's army. We fought on the same side. The magelords killed my wife, my children—" As always, tears came when he thought of that; he blinked them away. Binis was the sort to think he had pretended grief. "—And I did turn against them, the ones who had done it. I have the scars to prove it."

"But then why did you take up with them again afterwards?" The depth of ignorance in that question took his breath away. How could he possibly explain? "I mean," she said, putting the final peg in her assembly of faulty logic, "everyone knows you're the mage-king's son, and if you'd really turned against the magelords, you wouldn't have anything to do with them."

Among the rush of emotions came the cold thought that he'd never known one who needed Arranha's classes more: even he, not the brightest of Arranha's pupils, had learned not to use one word with two meanings in the same argument. Would she ever understand that the "them" he knew now were not the same "them" who had abandoned him in childhood and destroyed his family? Gird had known that. Raheli understood that; he realized how different she was from this sort of peasant, and how unfair he had been to blame her for the minds of those like Binis.

He even felt a trickle of pity for Binis herself, cramped into a narrow mind and unlikely to find a way out. In her, Gird's insistence that right was right and wrong was wrong, that compromises always cost more than could be easily reckoned, had turned to a rigid system unlike anything Gird himself would approve. What could he say to open a window in her head? Gird would have used his fist, likely enough, claiming that it took hard knocks to crack thick-shelled nuts ... but that was not his way, nor would Binis learn that way from him.

"The people who hurt me, who killed my family," Luap said,

"were killed in the war. I saw their bodies, many of them. The mageborn who survived were children and the very old, some women who had not even known me, let alone caused me harm. Should I hate them? Gird did not hate them."

"But they were the same sort. Magelords!" She made it a curseword. His magery growled within him, as if it could respond of itself to an insult. He fought it down, telling himself she was only saying what she had been taught.

"Are all peasants fair, kind people?" he asked instead. "Surely you've known some who cheated, who stole, who were unfair—?"

"Ye-esss . . ." She dragged that out, as if it came unwillingly. "But they've been cheated by the mageborn; it's not their fault." She eyed him, looking for a reaction. "The Marshal-General says most real thieves and brigands are part-mageborn anyway; that's why they're too lazy to work and be honest." *That's why he doesn't trust you, half-mage,* was as clear in her gaze as if written on parchment.

"You insufferable fool!" Luap's anger roared past his knowledge that losing his temper would only cause trouble. This time it was not Gird; this time it was not someone he respected; this time— this one time, maybe—he was wholly justified, completely right, and he was not going to pretend a subservience and shame he did not feel. He would wipe that smugness off Binis's face, that sly satisfaction in catching him off guard, that intolerable superiority. "The Marshal-General himself has mageborn blood—is *that* why he can't get up until midmorning? Does that make him dishonest enough to steal from the grange-sets honest peasants have sent in to buy himself fancy foods rather than eat porridge and stew with the rest? Or didn't you know any of that?" By her expression she had not known, and didn't believe. "Look it up in the archives," he said bitterly. "*If* you can read. His grandmother was raped by a magelord, just as my mother was. It's in the records, the great accounting Gird held after the war. His own mother reported it."

"You made that up," Binis said. "It can't be true. Besides, the Marshal-General's special: he has a right to sleep later and eat better food."

"Really! Gird didn't . . . but then you didn't know Gird, more's the pity." That rush of anger over, Luap felt the first twinge of fear. Lazy, selfish, and misguided the present Marshal-General might be, but he still had to work with him. So far the Council had sided with Luap on the larger issues, but he must not strain their patience by angering the Marshal-General on minor matters. He looked at Binis with more loathing than she perhaps deserved. She was the

Marshal-General's tool, less culpable because she was both younger and subordinate. He hated her. If not for his oath to Gird, he would use his magery now, and compel her to agree. He toyed with that idea for another furlong or so, imagining sending her back to the Marshal-General as a spy, as a mageborn tool. If she had said anything more, he might have, but she had the prudence of the naturally sly, and said nothing.

So the rest of the day passed, in uncomfortable silence. She asked once, in late afternoon, what grange they would stay at that night, and he replied that they would camp. He managed not to add, with the sarcasm he felt, that she should have realized that from the supplies he'd bought in Cob's village. He attacked the jacks trench as if it were a buried enemy, raising another blister on his hand, and she watched sullenly. They ate their supper in silence, and in silence passed the night and the morning's rising. Binis filled in the trench without commenting.

Luap rode in morose silence all that morning, inquiring of all the gods he could think of—and Gird—what else he could have done. The explanations and excuses looked shabby, spread out in his mind; he knew that Gird would have swept them away. Yes, the woman was stupid, smug, and difficult: that was *her* problem. He had not made things better with his flare of temper. He found himself arguing that Gird, too, had lost his temper with a difficult woman named Binis, but it would not work, and he knew it. All at once he was plunged into internal darkness, a wave of despair. How could he think of leading his people to any good purpose? Everything he'd ever done wrong came back to him in vivid pictures; he hunched over the horse's neck, wishing he could spew it all out and die, have it all over. The Rosemage would lead his people better. Or Aris and Seri, in partnership.

He had no thought of food, and Binis finally said, plaintively, "Aren't we going to stop and eat?" Another stab of guilt—had he compounded anger and rudeness with cruelty?

"I'm sorry," he said. "I—lost track of time." He reined in and looked around. At least he wasn't lost; he still recognized the shapes of hill and field. Beneath him, his horse sighed and tugged the reins, wanting to graze the fresh spring grass. "Yes. We can stop here, or go on a bit to that creek." He pointed.

"You look sick," Binis said with her usual tact.

Luap shrugged. "I'm sorry," he said again. He thought of apologizing for yesterday's anger, but Binis was not one to inspire selflessness; she absorbed it as her due. He dismounted, and let his horse graze. Binis found a convenient rock and settled to her food; he had no appetite for his, but realized he should eat anyway. He choked down some mouthfuls of bread and cheese. This would not do; they had several more days of travel together, and he had to find some way to get along with this woman.

He tried asking questions about life in Fin Panir; Binis gave short answers, and made it clear that he should know the answers already. He tried telling her about the war, how it had been to march these very hills and river valleys with Gird's army. She listened to that, but her questions revealed no grasp of tactics—he became very tired of her "Why didn't Gird just—?" She seemed to think all battles were great set pieces, with armies lined up on either side; she was sure that any villagers who didn't support Gird's army must have been part mageborn.

"They were hungry and frightened," Luap tried to explain. "Someone had to stay and plant the fields, but if the magelords caught them sharing food with us, they'd be killed—worse than killed." He remembered the thin faces, the desperation, the bodies displayed on hillsides. "Look there," he said, pointing to an ox-team busy with spring ploughing. The farmer had made a grisly decoration of skulls turned up by the plough. Binis shuddered; Luap thought he might have pierced her determination to simplify the past. He hoped so.

By the time they reached the cave, in a misting rain, Luap felt her presence as a great weight on his neck. He made a last try. "We had several cohorts in here," he said. "Worse weather than this, but also early spring. Gird had a bad cold. Lots of us did."

"Which spring?" she asked. This time she took the shovel to dig the trench; he thought that was a good sign.

"The spring before Greenfields," he said. While she built a small fire in the familiar ring of stones, he dragged first one sack of soil, then another, back to the chamber. She did not offer to help. The feeling grew on him that this was the most significant of his visits to the cave: the season, the weather, and the sullen peasant were all the same. Binis could easily stand for some hundreds of her fellows.

He felt this even more when he discovered that she expected him to take the soil to his stronghold by the mageroad, then return and go back with her to Fin Panir to report to the Marshal-General. "That way I can be sure you don't return and steal more," she said. Luap wondered briefly if she had anything between her ears but malice and stubbornness.

"Binis, if I had wanted to disobey the Marshal-General and steal more earth, I could have come here in the first place and never travelled with you at all."

"You wouldn't have dared," she said. "You can't disobey the Marshal-General." She said it in the way she would have said that stones fall or water is wet, someone stating a natural law.

"*I* could," Luap said flippantly, and instantly wished he hadn't. He already knew Binis had no sense of humor. She was scowling now, as if he had insulted her. "Listen to me: I did what your Marshal-General asked because I swore an oath to Gird. Not an oath to obey his successor, an oath to support him, and do no harm with my magery to his people. I saw no reason to quarrel with the Marshal-General; I have fulfilled his requirements, and I am going back to my land." *To stay,* he almost said. But he would return, to continue his work with the archives, and he did not mean to cause more trouble than he had.

"I won't let you," Binis said. "You have to take the sacks there and return."

The sheer stupidity of it, her inability to see that she had no way to compel him, almost made him laugh. He thought of agreeing, and then not coming back, which might at least teach her something about the limits of her power, but in this place he could not lie to one of Gird's people, not even one he was sure Gird himself would have knocked in the head. Gently, as if speaking to a dull child, he said "Binis, I am going and I am not coming back. You have food, two horses and a pony, and a clear trail. You're a yeoman-marshal and it's peacetime. You will be perfectly safe travelling alone, and there's a grange not a day's ride away. Now sit down and eat your supper."

"You're not going to do it," she said. She moved over to block his way to the chamber. Luap felt again the anger he had felt at Gird—and she was no Gird; he lifted his fist, and she blinked but stood her ground. He could not hit her. He had sworn not to use magery in this land . . . but it was gentler. His power flowed out and around her like honey around an ant; she struggled, but could not move.

"Farewell, Binis," he said, stepping past her. He moved quickly past her, into the chamber, and laid a hand on either sack as he called on his power.

Chapter Twenty-three

"What does the prince fear?" the black-cloaked lord asked his spy. "What does he love? These are the knots in which to bind him." He had sent many spies, over the years, and learned many things he expected to use in the future. But he had not yet decided on the exact way to approach the prince and use him to destroy the others.

"He is a king's bastard—not ever acknowledged," the spy said. "And like all such he doubts both his father's goodwill and the reality of his parentage. He fears ridicule—he fears disrespect—and he fears that he is not deserving of respect. He is beginning to fear age, as he sees those he respects dying or approaching death. He has a vision for his people, for this place, and he fears that as he ages he will lose control of them. That his vision will not survive."

"And he loves?" The tone was contemptuous; they did not believe that "love" existed, but they knew others claimed to be moved so.

The spy shrugged. "Insofar as he can, he thinks he loves his people. He believes they need his protection and wisdom; he takes pride in serving them. He is sure he knows best, and wants them to agree that he does. He loves his own will, but no more than many. He has a vision of himself as a great leader."

"Anything else?"

The spy smiled; he had been saving the best for last. "He was warned never to seek command, or take it; he was told he was unfit for it. Although he did not understand why he was considered unfit, he submitted to others. Now, having accepted the leadership here, he has broken an old oath. That is no consequence to us, but it bothers him: he will not let himself think of it, or admit that is what he has done." Others laughed; such self-blindness offered easy access for their enchantments.

The leader's brows rose. "Unfit for command? Not to our purpose. . . . I can scarcely imagine one I would rather see in his place. A bastard prince, a prince afraid of his own weakness, a prince afraid that age will erode his power, an oathbreaker . . . apt for our purposes, indeed! He should welcome our aid as eagerly as an overworked shepherd welcomes a well-trained sheepdog. So long as *he does not see the wolf beneath the dog's fur, we shall prosper as he does. Let him think on his losses, and fear more: let him grasp—and we shall have something for him to hold."*

Climbing up to the forested top of the mountain took longer than Luap would have expected. He was winded and sweaty when he finally made it over the rim and into the cool shade of the trees. It had been too long, he told himself, since he had climbed even as high as the terrace now below. The Rosemage looked almost as tired, but Seri and Aris were bubbling with energy.

"It's easy walking from here," Seri said. "And we marked our trail, the first time."

Luap nodded, still out of breath, and turned to look behind him, out over the rim. Now he could see much that had been hidden from the level below, while whole clefts and canyons had disappeared—they might have been only surface cracks in the rock. Others showed more clearly; he thought he could see a narrow green valley up the main canyon and then southward. Gird should have seen this, he thought. Northward a great gray angular mountain loomed, very unlike the red rock around them. Eastward, the higher mountains were white; he could not tell if it was rock or snow.

"We haven't explored all of this yet," Aris said. "Only toward the west, and only part of that. But we've found so many things . . . trees like this in places, and in others low round trees hardly larger than bushes. Grassy meadows, even a little creek right up here on top of the mountain."

"And game," Seri said. "Tame enough to touch, some of these animals."

"All right," he said, smiling at the Rosemage. "Let's see your marvels."

The two led them along the southern edge of the trees, where Luap could see between the trunks a plateau with similar trees across the canyon. It was, as they'd promised, much easier walking than the canyon itself; they reached the low end before the sun had moved three handspans on its way.

On this end of the mountain, no intermediate terrace broke its sheer cliffs. Luap crept cautiously to the dropoff and found himself staring down into a well of blue air, still shadowed by the cliff. Perhaps a bowshot away, a stone tower rose to a lesser height, partly eroded from the cliff behind. Below the steepest slopes, the hollow was filled with trees.

When he looked west, he saw across a lower cliff a vast low

plain, with mountains rising from it in the distance. "Is that where you thought you saw a caravan?" he asked.

"Not from here," Aris said. "Come along this edge, now." He led the way around a cove or bay of stone, toward another outlying point; it occurred to Luap that this end of the mountain had a shape rather like an outflung hand, fingers of stone defining angled coves between them.

"That's what we thought." Aris pointed back to the tower. "We called that one the Thumb." The next prominence was farther away than it looked—everything in this country, Luap thought, was farther away than it looked—but from it he could look through a break in the western cliffs. "There's a stream in there," Aris said. "But it's not the same one that's in our canyon. It comes from the north, and cuts through to the west."

Through the break, he could see a pale line, like a scratch, in the even tan of the distant plain. "That could be a trail, I suppose," he said. "You saw something moving along it?"

"Yes. And if you look south—there—you can see what might be a town."

Luap could see nothing but a jumble of shadows that might come from a pile of rocks or low buildings the color of the plain. Certainly it looked like no town he had ever seen—but nothing out here looked like anything he'd ever seen.

"There's nothing green until the next mountains," the Rosemage said. "What could they live on? Is it just bare rock?"

"I don't know." Seri flung out her hands. "But I think we could find a way out of here . . . look." She leaned out and pointed. "If you come down the canyon to that lower fall, and then angle around the Thumb—that tower—and then up the slope that sticks out from this . . . then you're close to the stream that goes out through that cliff. It's rugged, but we could build a trail—"

"After we've made sure our cropland bears," Luap said firmly. "We aren't here to explore; we're here to settle."

Seri looked a little disgruntled; Aris spoke up. "But, sir—if we can get out, then others—those we saw—could get in. It's only good planning to know if there's a back door in your house, and how to secure it."

"Why would anyone come into such rugged country?" the Rosemage asked. "As level as that plain is—"

"What you said before: here it's green, and there's water. Or perhaps they hunt up here; surely we have more game than the plain."

"Hmm. Well, I don't see that we'll have people to spare for that this growing season. Perhaps next year. Although if trade is possible, there are many things we could use." Luap looked around. "Just as I see things up here that we can use. More timber, for one, and game."

"And we found pine-nuts very different from those on the taller pines," Seri said, her enthusiasm rekindled. "And other plants to eat."

Luap glanced at the sun, now well past midday. "Show us what you can on the way back; I don't want to be benighted up here." Seri nodded; she and Aris led away from the western cliffs back over the mountaintop. In some places, the ground was broken; scrubby bushes and small trees struggled among the tumbled stones. In others, the groves of tall pines rose straight from level rock; little undergrowth impeded movement or sight between them. They came upon small meadows in little hollows; in one of these a gray stag in velvet looked at them a long moment before stalking away. And by the time they had reached the eastern rim and the trail down, the mountain threw its shadow over all below, so that dusky rose rock melted into dusky blue shades, layer after layer. Far to the east the white cliffs of the higher mountains still caught the light.

The Rosemage climbed down the trail first, then Luap; he thought his legs would give out before he stood at last on the level stone of the terrace. And he still had to climb down the stairs to the main level of the stronghold. Behind him, he was aware of Seri and Aris, both still full of energy. He rarely felt his age—he had been younger than many of Gird's companions in the war—but now he felt the years that lay between him and the two younglings. Even between him and his own youth. That war, he reflected, had been years ago: they had been children, and he had had children. No wonder they were excited with each new hill and valley they found. He wished he had as many years left to enjoy this land.

He pushed that worry away. He was younger than Arranha, younger than the Rosemage. He would live to see his dream fulfilled. And these two would be part of it. In this mood, he was willing to grant Seri and Aris leave to explore father, so long as they took their turn at the necessary fieldwork. Perhaps it would make them decide to stay; surely they would come to love this country as he did.

Arranha, at dinner that night, had his doubts about exploring the lands beyond the canyon. "Would it anger the elves or dwarves?" he asked. "Did they place any limits on your dealings with those folk?"

"They didn't mention them," Luap said. "They said I was not to claim ownership of this hall—or that I had built it. Of course I would do neither."

"That gray mountain we saw," the Rosemage said, changing the subject with less than her usual grace. "It looked to me as if it might have ores: did the dwarves say aught about that?"

"Not a word." Luap shook his head. "Why?"

"If there's silver, or gold," she said. "Even iron, for us to make our own tools and pots; you'll have no trouble getting a smith if we have metal. Or if we have gold to pay."

"That's much more sense than frolicking off to follow desert caravans around," said Arranha. "You brought the mageborn here to learn the use of magery in privacy, in safety. Involve us in someone else's business, and you're asking for trouble. But using the land's own wealth to trade back to Fin Panir, that's another matter."

"It's not far," the Rosemage said. "Even allowing for the way things seem close . . . I'm sure we could find a way to it.

Luap felt a vague discomfort; he had a vision of his folk flitting away in all directions like a flight of small birds when a cat pounces. "You're eager to leave, then?" he found himself saying.

"No—I don't think it's leaving," the Rosemage said, and gave him a steady look. "I think Arranha's right: our safety here depends in part on being unknown. We are few; surely whatever land lies there has more people in it. But if we can find materials we need, be they trees or metals, something to trade back to Fin Panir or hire artisans here, that makes more sense to me."

Luap raised his brows and looked at Aris and Seri, whose expressions wavered between wistfulness and chagrin. "And you two? You wanted to find out who lives out there, did you not?"

Seri gave the Rosemage a look. "It's—it's *practical*. In the military sense. Surely you see that we need to know who's at the back door, and how easily they could find us. Suppose someone's living in those western canyons—suppose they get a taste for the fish in our stream?"

"How far away do you think the gray mountain is?" Luap asked Aris. "Do you think it's as near as the western cliffs?"

"No—but I'm not sure how far." Aris looked worried, as he did sometimes when asked about things outside his competence.

"If it's just a matter of distance," the Rosemage said, "then the western cliffs—even that town Aris thinks he saw—are closer. I won't argue that. But there's nothing to the caravans and towns but danger—and the mountain might offer something better."

Seri looked stubborn. "It's dangerous not to find out what's out in the plain."

The Rosemage started to speak, then stopped, shook her head, and began again. "Seri—I know your Marshal's training covered defense; I know you are competent. But is this something you really think is important that way, or just an itch to explore?"

"We need to know," Seri said. She seemed to grow more compact, more peasantlike, even as they watched her. Aris leaned into the conversation.

"She's right—we do."

The Rosemage flushed; Luap felt a momentary tremor of excitement—was she going to lose her temper? She had not since they came, though he had seen her lips pinched more than once. Arranha spoke up.

"If the gods are telling you that, Seri, then there's no argument. You must find out, or someone must. We can look at the mountain later; it will still be there. Or one party could go each way."

"We can't have everyone going off at once," Luap reminded them. He felt again that vague disturbance inside, but had no time to attend to it. Later—later he would consider whether it had most to do with age or something else. Perhaps it was the thought of danger; danger either way, whether they left their neighbors unknown, or went to meet them. "Why not have Aris and Seri take a look at the western cliffs, see if there's any trail or road there? They need not explore so far as the town, not at first—not even leave the cliffs. That should take only a couple of days, I would think—?" He looked at Seri, who nodded happily. "In the meantime, you—" He looked at the Rosemage. "—you could be planning your route to the gray mountain, perhaps from up on the high level. When they get back, you could leave, and not be too long delayed." He smiled at her. "Would that do?"

"Yes . . . of course. Arranha?"

"I don't even know how far my bones will take me," Arranha said, smiling. "Perhaps you should choose another, younger companion for the journey. Find me an easy trail, will you?"

"That I will. I have no more love than you for clambering over rough ground."

The mood around the table now seemed lighter, warmer. Luap basked in it; he had headed off a quarrel. "I'll check the schedules," he said. "Perhaps Aris and Seri could start tomorrow or the next day."

The lowest terrace in the main canyon had been placed just above a turn, where the canyon angled south away from a tributary stream. That far, the trail had been made smooth, and Aris and

Seri had jogged down it easily. Now they turned north to follow the smaller stream around the Thumb. The tower looked taller from below. They came through the shade of the big trees that formed a grove where the streams met—not pines, this time, but broad-leaved trees whose deeply furrowed trunks and softly clattering foliage reminded them of riverside groves in Fintha. Small, bright-colored birds flitted through the leaves like butterflies; a bird they did not see gave a sweet rippling call. Up the smaller stream, the trees quickly disappeared and they walked among head-high bushes of juniper and thorn. Soon the stream disappeared, and though its steep bed rose steadily, it was incised even more deeply in the slope around it. They had started walking in the streambed when the water disappeared, because the thick growth close beside it made it impossible to walk on the bank. Seri, leading Aris up the narrowing bed, stopped suddenly with a little yelp.

"What?" asked Aris. He was not exactly grumpy, but the streambed seemed to hold every bit of the sun's heat, and he itched with sweat.

"That snake." Seri pointed; Aris looked past her. The snakes in Fintha were shy creatures, small brown or green serpents that looked like an old thong left on the ground until they moved. Here they had found similar snakes, though more brightly colored, curled on rock ledges. Aris had had to heal several snakebites. But they had not seen anything like the big yellow and brown patterned snake, longer than a man's leg and thicker than his arm, that moved with deliberation across the sand in front of them, worked its way up the bank, and vanished among the junipers.

"If that bit someone—" Aris said. He didn't know how to finish that. Was the snake venomous? In Fintha, snakebites were rare, and although some children suffered woundfever, no one died. Here they'd found that the bright-colored snakes could kill—the first person bitten had not bothered to have the wound treated, thinking it like the snakebites back home. But Aris could heal those bites, with no more drain on his power than a sprained wrist would cause.

"If they come that big, they might come bigger," Seri said. "I almost stepped on that one—for all its color, it looked remarkably like a stick until it moved."

The dry streambed led them back sunrising, into the sheltered cove between the Thumb and the next promontory. Sandy banks gave way to soil, then soil and rock. Seri climbed out, using the root of a pine to help.

"Plenty of trees here," Aris said. "Though it would be hard to

get the wood back upstream." The search for timber had been one
reason for this expedition.

"Until we build a road." Seri looked around. "Though it would
really make more sense for someone to live here, at this end. I
wonder how far back into the mountain the stronghold extends."

"Not this far." Aris looked across the slope to the mountain that
blocked their view to the west. "If we could terrace this, it would
give enough space for a pasture."

"Too far from the main settlement," Seri said. "Unless someone
lives here to watch—they could be stolen by those folk below, or
even escape." She drew a deep breath. "Well. We'd best go looking
for that pass, if we're going to find it today."

That meant coming back out of the shady cove, into the glare
of the sun, to scramble uphill between clumps of juniper. The
ground here was shattered rock, obviously the outfall of the cliffs;
in places it had worn to sand, but the nearer they came to the base
of the cliffs, the steeper and more rugged their way. They seemed
to struggle on forever, but the sun had not quite passed noon when
Aris realized they were going the same direction without climbing.
He was in the lead, then; he turned back to see Seri's head still
below his, and a view that took his breath away. He stopped, panting, and waited for her to catch up.

"Look at that," he said, when she came up beside him. They
were now, if he judged aright, at the level of the Thumb's base.
Beyond it, he could see to the south, a better view of the canyon's
new direction than he had had from the mountain-top. Looking
north, the ends of the first two promontories showed clearly; he
could not see the stream that had made its way among them to
an outlet west, but he assumed that going downhill would lead
him there.

They moved downslope and toward the next cove to find shade;
both of them were unusually careful about the ground on which
they sat. Aris thought that the people of the caravans might avoid
these mountains simply because of the many things that stung and
bit—that huge snake, the little crawlers with their poisoned tails.
He said that to Seri, who shrugged it off. "Each land has its own
hazards; I think it's the rough terrain. Horses would find it difficult
unless someone built trails. And if they have no magery, building
trails could take years."

Aris glanced back at the way they'd come. They could no longer
see the Thumb, having come around the next outflung wall of
rock—the pointing finger, he thought to himself. After a brief rest,
they started off again, this time downslope and angling as much

sunsetting as winterwards. They could see the notch in the western wall where the stream went through, but little of the land beyond.

"Should we head straight for it, or just go downhill to the stream?" he asked as they came out of the angle of the cove.

"It's easier walking up here," Seri said. "If we go to the stream, there'll be a lot of twisting about. And it looks as if deer use this— there's a trail here."

"Fine with me," Aris said. They worked their way down a rib of rocky soil that gradually narrowed on both sides, falling off more steeply to the north. Soon they were on exposed rock again, this time a ledge overlooking a sharp drop to another perhaps a man's height down on the north, though it sloped more gently to the south. "It didn't look like this from above," he said. Ahead, they'd almost reached the western wall, which came down in great steps to close off their ledge. "Maybe we should start heading for the stream."

Seri peered downward. The ledge below their ledge dropped to another, and then another. "If we get down, can we get back up? Remember that place up the main canyon . . . if someone came the other way, and dropped over, there'd be no way back."

"Not without wings," Aris said. "You're right; we'll go on to that wall. Maybe there's a way around." When they reached the wall, a narrow, well-scuffed trail seemed to lead along the very edge of the wall into the notch.

"My turn to lead," said Seri. Aris chuckled.

"You want to be the first to see out . . . go ahead then." Aris looked back at the rampart behind them, the steep rocky slopes changing abruptly to vertical walls . . . he could not guess how high. He glanced back once more as the angle of trail was about to cut off his view. Then he heard a confused noise in front of him, a muffled cry from Seri, and he ran forward.

The trail turned sharply back into a crevice of stone; Aris nearly went headlong over the edge. He dropped his stick and grabbed at the rockface. The rock he grabbed came loose in his hand but slowed him just enough that he could keep his footing. Then he could see them: Seri, struggling with two men, one of whom had a good grip on her braid, holding her head back while the other choked her. Aris charged, slamming the rock he still held against the first man's unprotected head with a satisfying thunk. The man dropped; Aris stepped on him with intent, and swung at the second, who had to let go of Seri's throat to block the swing. He didn't dare look at Seri; the man had a curved blade longer than a knife.

Aris shifted the rock to his left hand and drew his own dagger.

The man grinned, and swung the curved blade in a complicated pattern. Aris ignored that, and threw the rock at the man's face, using magery to improve his left-handed aim. The man flinched aside, which gave Aris time to grab another rock. The man swung, not at him but at Seri. Aris lunged, trying to protect her, but he stumbled over the man he'd knocked out. Seri managed to jerk her legs aside: the blade rang on the stone but did not shatter. Aris pushed his stumble into a roll, hoping to get under the man's guard with his dagger. It might have worked, but the man stepped back too far and fell backwards off the trail with a yell. A series of thuds and clatters, and a very final-sounding shriek suggested that he would be awhile climbing back.

Seri was on her feet now, still gasping; Aris could see the purple bruises at her throat. She smiled at him, and waved him away. He wanted to heal her, but he understood—first make sure no more attackers appeared. He checked the man he had hit with the rock, who lay unmoving, but alive. Farther down the trail—Aris lunged and yanked Seri to the ground just as an arrow clattered against the wall where she'd been. Now that he was touching her, he could heal her; he struggled to keep the anger he felt from contaminating the healing magery.

"I'm fine," she said a moment later. "Stupid, careless, and clumsy, but alive and well." Another arrow rang on the rock just below them. "How many?"

"I don't know," Aris said. "I saw one with the bow, and another behind, but the trail twists. It's an awkward aim for the archer. Notice they aren't yelling at us."

"I did. No help to yell for, or other enemies?"

"I don't know that, either," He looked back up the trail. Had they really been so stupid, walking along an obvious trail without any precautions at all? Game trails, he reminded himself bitterly, go up and down to water, or connect food sources, not along ridges where people would prefer to walk. "But we can't get back up there without making a very good target, and even if we did there's that long open stretch of ledge." And all the way back to the stronghold, they would be leading trouble home. And hadn't both of them decided it was too hot to wear helmets, and that swords were awkward weapons not likely to be needed? Two sticks and Seri's dagger, he thought, might not be enough.

"So we have to settle it here," Seri said. In that tone of voice it almost sounded reasonable. Aris heard a faint noise and glanced up in time to see that the unknown archer knew about lofting his arrows into difficult places. No—*two* unknown archers: there were two arrows rapidly falling. Luckily, a wind-current near the cliff deflected them, and both fell harmlessly beyond the trail. Others, Aris knew, might not. He did not know if his slight magery would work on arrows shot by someone else. Seri touched his shoulder. "That man—the first one—had a bow over his shoulder."

Of course. Aris had not really looked at him, beyond making sure he stayed quiet. Together, they got hold of a foot and pulled the man closer to the cliff. An arrow struck the man only a hands-pan from Aris; the man did not stir. Seri reached for the arrow that had struck the cliff first. "Now we have two arrows," she said. "Unless he's got more." It was harder than Aris would have thought to wrestle the bow and string from the man's shoulder, and when he had it in his hands he wondered how a little twisted bit of a bow could be much use. But when he had it strung, he realized it was more powerful than most. He yanked the arrow free of the man's body, and set it to the string. It felt strange, but he hoped what he knew of the longer, straighter bows of Fintha would serve. He peeked around the rock and saw the other archer also leaning far out to look. Release . . . and a touch of magery as the archer, seeing the arrow on its way, tried to dodge. The man yelled then, in terror at seeing an arrow follow his movements. Aris saw two others get up and start running back down the trail; the man he had shot lay still.

"Odd sort of quiver," Seri said, behind him. He looked back; she had found six more arrows stored in a length of hollow bone.

"They ran," Aris said. "And wherever they're going, they'll report strangers up here. I think we should follow them." He was ready to say why they should do something so foolish, without proper weapons or anyone knowing, but as usual Seri understood.

Seri nodded. "Not good neighbors. And you're right; we don't have time to go back and get tangled in arguments. We need to know more before we tell the Rosemage anything about this." Aris was sure she felt the same pull he did, the same urgent call to follow the fleeing men.

Nonetheless, they would not be so incautious again. Aris retrieved his stick. They stripped the first man of his leather tunic, a small round shield, and a curved blade. He had dark hair and an unkempt dark beard; under the leather tunic he wore a long sand-colored tunic or shirt that left his muscular legs bare below the knees, and peculiar openwork shoes of leather thongs. Aris looked over the edge of the trail, and saw a crumpled figure far below; it didn't move. The dead archer, when they came to him, yielded another bow, another blade, and more arrows, as well as a helmet that didn't fit either of them until Seri tucked up her braid. She decided that the first man's tunic didn't offer enough protection for its weight and smell; they discarded it. The trail beyond that was both steep and exposed; Aris caught a glimpse of those they followed more than once. Now he thought he saw four of them. He thought about shooting across the angle of trail, but they were moving fast, and he was not sure how far this bow would send an arrow, even with magery behind it. He didn't trust his judgment of distance in the clear air.

Chapter Twenty-four

The notch in the western wall had widened around them—though Aris took only hurried glances at the land below—when he heard horn signals echoing from the rocks around them. He stopped, flattening himself against the wall. Here the trail looped northward again, around the knees of the mountain that formed the western wall; he could not see directly west, but had a good view across the notch itself. He saw nothing moving, though the horns seemed to come from that direction. Sound could bounce off walls, he knew—could it bounce around corners? He and Seri moved cautiously forward. He wondered if they could climb above the trail, where the upper slope was now more broken rock than cliff.

"Yes," Seri said when he suggested it. "It's about time we tried something sneaky." Aris tested the rocks; they seemed firm enough. He pulled himself up into them, and worked his way over the top of the knee, keeping low, until he looked down on the next section of trail they had left.

He had been wrong about the number, or they had had a trailing guard. Five husky, bearded men huddled on the trail, speaking in a tongue Aris had never heard before. He didn't have to understand the words to know they were worried and afraid. The two with bows carried them strung, arrows in their free hands; the other three had their blades out. From somewhere down the trail, Aris heard the noise of many men. He flattened himself between the rocks, wishing that he'd found gray rocks to match his clothes. He caught a glimpse of movement, sunlight glinting off metal. The general noise came nearer, resolved into the scrape and tramp of boots on stone. Below him, the huddle of five stirred. Their voices came up to him, harsh and incomprehensible.

"Suppose they're rebels, like Gird," said Seri softly. She looked almost as worried as the men on the trail. That had not occurred to Aris.

"They attacked you," he pointed out. "Would Gird have tried to throttle you first, without asking questions?" Some of Gird's followers might, he thought. But if Gird had known, he would have clouted them; Aris felt no guilt at all about the man he'd bashed. Besides, the tension that had drawn him after these men had not been that of need, but of danger. He felt the danger now, far more from them than from whatever force was coming up the trail. "And you'd better take off that helmet—if I can see theirs—"

"You're right," said Seri. "Now—do we stay out of this, or assume the enemy of our enemy is a friend?" She had no time to say more. Around the corner of rock came a solid mass of men in rust-colored uniforms. As they caught sight of the five men on the trail, they let out a yell. One of the men below yelled back, the same word over and over. The men in uniform had bows, and drew them; the men below dropped theirs, and sank to their knees, arms wide.

"Fugitives giving themselves up," Aris murmured. That much he could understand, though not what kind of fugitives or why they had not left the trail to hide in the rocks, as he and Seri had done. More yells back and forth, all meaningless; two of the kneeling fugitives pointed back up the trail and said the same word repeatedly. He wondered what *biknini* meant.

"Telling about us," Seri said. "D'you suppose we were that frightening?"

"Perhaps—but I doubt we'd frighten that troop. They look well-trained." The bowmen were advancing in order, one step at a time, to someone's command. The fugitives knelt, their outstretched arms trembling. When the bowmen were perhaps twenty paces distant, and Aris had picked out the commander by his more elaborate uniform, they halted. The commander said something; the fugitives crept forward on their knees, arms still high, away from their weapons. One suddenly cried out, and tried to dash back up the trail. The two foremost archers loosed their arrows at once and the man staggered and fell, two black arrows in his back. The other fugitives stayed where they were.

Aris felt sick; watching someone else in danger was much harder than being in it himself. He watched the commander come forward, sunlight glittering on metal at his shoulder, on his ornate helmet, on the chain with a hanging pendant around his neck. Because the trail, even here, was scarcely wide enough for three men to walk abreast, he had to edge past his troop carefully. Unlike his soldiers, he had no beard, only long moustaches hanging below his chin. His heavy sword-belt of dark leather had a design worked into it in gold; from it hung a scabbarded curved blade on one side, and a short stick with a knobbed head on the other. He wore gloves and boots that matched his belt; the boots were knee-high, with tops turned down over them. Aris could see nothing of his face from above but the clean chin and drooping moustaches.

The captain and one of his soldiers walked nearer to the fugitives, and he gave an order, authority implicit in the tone. The fugitives shambled to their feet, one of them looking back to see their fallen comrade. The captain asked a question; the fugitives answered in ragged chorus, "Biknini!" Was that a plea for mercy, or a word for what they'd seen? Or something else entirely, an insult or curse? The captain gave another order, and the fugitives lowered their hands and put them at their backs; one turned, slowly, to face away from the soldiers. The captain yelled at them, and two more turned, grudgingly, partway. The fourth remaining stood as if frozen in place, trembling violently. The captain spoke to the soldier with him; the man pulled what looked like cord or thongs from his belt, and went forward to bind the captives' wrists.

He had just grabbed the wrists of the first man when Aris realized that the fourth was not paralyzed with terror but pretending it; he had drawn a long, narrow dagger from his sleeve. For the moment, the captain and the soldier with him were screening the fugitives from the archers; he no doubt thought the fugitives were far enough from their weapons, and sufficiently cowed, to make it safe.

That error nearly cost his life, as the first three fugitives whirled as one and grabbed the captain and his assistant; sheltered behind them, with knives laid against their throats, the fugitives began dragging them back up the trail toward their own weapons. The archers yelled, but wavered, clearly unwilling to shoot their own commander. Aris found himself standing before he knew it, and he and Seri yelled what later seemed silly, since the fugitives could not possibly understand, any more than they had understood the fugitives. "No, by Gird! Let them go!"

One of the archers let fly an arrow that wobbled up, then fell far behind them; it was clearly simple panic. The others, having glanced up once, kept their eyes and aim steady on the fugitives. The fugitives were not so steady. After one long terrified look, the one holding the captain let him fall and turned to run screeching back up the trail. Seri bounded up and across the hump, to cut him off on the far side. Two others cried out and fell to their knees, wrapping their arms around their heads. But one paused to stab the soldier he was holding before he, too, fled up the trail. The archers got him before he made the turn, then ran forward to swarm over the kneeling fugitives and protect their captain. The captain scrambled up and looked up at Aris, calling out. Aris stood, expecting any moment to find himself full of arrows. Then his hands tingled; he felt the need of the wounded soldier. He met the captain's eyes and smiled. The man stared, spoke a word, and the archers lowered their bows. Aris pointed to the wounded man, then held out his hand, palm up. The soldiers muttered and drew back as much as the narrow trail allowed. The captain gestured: *Come down*, that had to mean. He held his hand up, palm toward his men, decisively. *No attack.* But did he mean it? Was he honest? Aris had to take that chance; he knew the soldier would die without his aid.

He came down the steep slope carefully, using his stick. The soldiers pulled back, leaving him room on the trail. They had bound the two fugitives tightly, with a loop from the wrists around the neck, and a guard stood over each one with naked blade. Aris went to the fallen soldier. He had been stabbed in the chest—Aris wondered why the enemy had not simply cut his throat—and he had already begun to turn blue; his breath gurgled. His eyes were open, but unfocused as he fought for breath, but he saw Aris well enough to flinch.

"Don't be afraid," Aris said, hoping the tone would carry. "I will help you." He laid his hands on the man and felt the healing power flow out of him, a sensation that had become more powerful during his training. He could not explain it to others, but it could be as sharp a pleasure as withholding it was pain; although a difficult healing drained him, nothing else in his life gave him the same strong pleasure when it worked. He imagined the power surging along the man's torn blood-vessels, forcing out the blood choking his lungs and windpipe, mending every wounded tissue, restoring his strength . . . he noticed, in the vague way such things came to him, that the man also had a long-standing illness that recurred at intervals: this, too, the healing magery burned away. When he took his hands from the soldier's chest, the man blinked at him in astonishment: wide awake, obviously in no pain, and no sign of his injury but a short pink scar.

Aris looked around for the captain, and discovered that all the soldiers had also knelt, each with one hand on his head; the captain alone looked at him, astonishment clear on his sweaty face. Whatever he might have said was interrupted by Seri's shout from around the corner. "Ari! Come help me with this lout!"

"He will be fine," Aris said, to the captain, smiling. "I must go." He stepped over the soldier, who had not moved yet, and picked his way through the kneeling archers. Would they shoot him in the back? No. He made it to the corner and found Seri trying to drag the last fugitive by one foot.

"I whacked him in the head with my stick," she said, before he could ask. Together, they dragged the man back around the corner, where they found the soldiers just beginning to stand up; all promptly knelt again. "What is this?" asked Seri.

Aris explained. "And I suspect they think we're not human," he finished. "Perhaps they don't have magery." They dumped the fourth fugitive by the man the soldiers had shot, and Aris said, "I think we'd better make friends of these: it looks like they've been here awhile."

"Let's give them part of *Torre's Ride*," Seri said. "That's impressive."

They both held up their sticks, in the traditional gesture of minstrels who wanted everyone's attention, then began together the familiar old chant. "Hear now the tale of Torre, king's daughter, befriended of the gods, whose deeds divide the watches of the night. . . ." Together, they stopped and grounded their sticks. The captain stared, silent. Aris and Seri put out their right hands, palms up, and made a lifting gesture. The captain scrambled to his feet. Aris waved, indicating the other men, and made the lifting gesture again. The captain gave an order, and his men also stood, including the man who had been stabbed. The captain put his hand on that man's shoulder, then put his clenched fist on his chest, and extended his arm with hand open. That had to be thanks . . . heartfelt thanks? Aris thought so. He bowed, smiling at them, then turned to indicate the fallen fugitives: come get them. The captain smiled, and gave an order that sent two of his soldiers forward. Aris noticed that they left their bows behind; none now had arrows set to the string.

When the soldiers had dragged the fugitives back to the troop, the captain put out his hands, palm up. Then he pointed dramatically to himself, and said "Veksh." Aris wondered if this were his name, his title, or something else. The captain then pointed to one of his soldiers. "Veksh." So it could mean soldier, or man. Aris pointed to himself, and attempted the word with a questioning intonation.

"Veksh?"

The captain tossed his head, a gesture that could have meant anything to him but conveyed nothing to Aris. Then he pointed to one of the bound prisoners. "Veksh." So it probably meant man, not soldier . . . unless the fugitives were in a general class of warrior. And very likely the tossing head meant *no*. Aris pointed to himself again.

"Human. Mageborn."

Seri, following his lead, said "Human. Peasant." Aris hoped the strangers would not think that "mageborn" meant man, and "peasant" meant woman . . . he hadn't thought of that possibility until the words were out of his mouth.

The captain pointed back up the trail, then waved his arm . . . could he mean all that country? "Biknini." The fugitives had said that. The captain wasn't pointing at them, so it must not refer to individuals . . . a description of the land? Mountain, canyon, cliff? Aris decided that this was not going to work; he would try a more direct way. Moving slowly, he stepped nearer the captain, and with gestures indicated that he and Seri had been attacked by the fugitives and had killed three. Seri mimed her part well; the captain and his soldiers nodded as if they understood. He hoped that meant that a nod signified *yes*.

The captain pointed to Aris, then Seri—this time using a bent finger—and then made a circle with his arms, and threw the circle toward the distant canyons. Aris thought it was a very efficient way of asking if the two of them were all of their kind who lived over there. He shook his head, remembered that the captain had used a different gesture, and tried to copy the toss. Someone in the troop laughed; the captain turned on the unfortunate and said something scathing. Aris wished he knew what it meant.

Quickly, he used the same bent-finger point to indicate the captain, the man he had healed, and Seri and himself, then drew a circle with the same finger, and touched his chest. Slowly he made a fist of that hand, placed over his heart. He hoped they would understand that meant *friends*. Again the captain nodded, smiling, and repeated the gesture. He said something to the soldiers; one of them came forward with a bulging woven bag, and another with a leather bottle. Aris nodded to Seri; they pulled out the pouches they'd slung under their shirts. There on the trail, the captain offered a heavy loaf of dark bread, strips of dried meat, and water.

Seri and Aris laid out salt, dried fruit, and their much lighter travel bread. The captain looked worried; Aris smiled at him.

"It is our custom to share," he said, as if the man could understand. "we will accept food from you, if you will accept food from us." He let his fingers rest on their food, and the others' food, then waved toward the captain. Again, the captain repeated his gesture, then very slowly reached toward the salt. Aris nodded; and himself touched the bread. The captain nodded. Seri reached forward and touched the water flask. The captain nodded again. Slowly, with great care, they exchanged bites of food. Seri almost choked on the water and told Aris, "It's not water; it's wine." The captain looked worried until Seri smiled at him. They each took a mouthful of each food: Seri, Aris, the captain, and the man who had been wounded. Behind the captain, his soldiers muttered softly.

And now what? Aris thought, as that ritual ended, and the four stood again. Do we just walk back up the trail and forget them? Or should we go with them and try to learn their language?

The captain clearly wanted them to come along. His gestures were unmistakable. Aris felt reluctance rise in him, a chill resistance. Seri shook her head decisively. "No, we are guardians, we must go back." Conveying that in gestures took longer, a pantomime that involved, in the end, the captain, his soldiers, and even the captives. Seri and Aris indicated that they, like the captain and his soldiers, were guardians who must not leave their post, who had pursued dangerous invaders, but must now return. Once the captain got the main idea, he nodded vigorously, then began a mime of his own. They would come back? They would meet with him? Such friends should stay friends. They could hunt danger together. He pointed to the sun, and held up one hand, fingers splayed: a hand of days, Aris thought. He wants to meet us here in five days. He offered gifts: a medallion from his boots, the flask of wine. Seri took off the little medallion she'd carved of cedarwood, with the interlocking G and L that Dorhaniya had devised. The captain accepted it with a deep bow, touched it to his forehead, and turned to his soldiers.

"We'd better hurry if we want to be back over the notch by nightfall," Aris said, with a look at the sun's position. Much of the upward trail would be shadowed already. Seri nodded, and they started back uphill, around the angle of rock that would hide them from the soldiers. It was cooler walking in the shade of the rock behind them; Aris noticed that even on the sunlit slope across from them, the trail they'd come down hardly showed. When they were well into the shade, he asked, "Do you trust them?"

Seri looked at him. "Trust them? Not like you, but I felt nothing evil, did you?"

"No, except from the ones who attacked you. Brigands, probably, who prey on those caravans." They both looked back, and Aris caught a glimpse of something moving in the broken rock below, toward the streambed. "Seri—what's that?" They crouched low, trying to see into the shadowed angles of the lower slopes. More movement, stealthy . . . someone darting from cover to cover, two hurrying a laden pack animal. . . .

Seri and Aris exchanged looks; the same thought joined them. "The *other* brigands."

"Those were decoys," Seri breathed. "They were supposed to draw off pursuit, while the main party went up the streambed."

"I suppose we're lucky," Aris said. "We could've run into that lot down there. There's probably more of them."

"We have to tell the captain," Seri said. Aris agreed, though he wished it had been earlier in the day. Now they could not possibly make it back to their own canyon by nightfall.

"If we can see them down there, they might see us," Aris pointed out. "And they'd expect their people to be a lot farther along."

"They might think we're soldiers, giving up the pursuit."

"We can hope." Together they marched in soldierly fashion to the now-familiar angle of rock, then back into the sunlight. Looking downward from here, they could see nothing below that looked suspicious; the stream's outlet, far to the west, looked like a dry, gravelly bed. And the soldiers were also out of sight already on the twisting trail. They hurried on, almost running, until they caught sight of the moving troop ahead and below. "Now do we call, or—"

"We call; I don't want to be shot by their very efficient archers." She grinned at him. "Let's give them *Torre's Ride* again; maybe they'll remember some of the words." They started in on that again, and at once two soldiers in the rear rank turned and gaped. They heard the captain's voice; the troop stopped. Aris waved, then pointed downward. The captain spread his hands and gave another order; his soldiers stood in their ranks as he toiled back up the trail. He looked disgruntled. Aris went to meet him, and tried to convey with gestures that they had seen many people, with pack animals, far below them as they climbed back. It took longer than it should have; the captain seemed determined to misunderstand. But finally it was clear he did understand. With his own gestures, he showed that it would take far too long to reach the foot of the mountain, find the trail, and follow that band of fugitives through the notch; he wanted Seri and Aris to lead him on the upper trail.

Seri and Aris exchanged glances. It would be dark before they got to the notch; on the far side that exposed ledge would be difficult to traverse without light, and the fugitives would see a light that high. Yet the captain's request made sense, from his point of view. And they were reluctant to have strangers moving into the canyons while they were here, giving no warning to their own people.

"Yes," Aris said, nodding. "Come now." He and Seri turned and again led the way upslope. Behind them, the captain and his troop seemed to make an incredible amount of noise. Not until they had marched some distance did it occur to Aris to wonder about the prisoners. He looked back but could not see them. They reached the place where he had seen the movement below, but deeper shadow now cloaked the lower slopes; he could see nothing. And in the time it had taken to find the captain and retrace their path, all the other party might well have passed. He pointed it out, none-theless, and showed the captain with his hands how the fugitives moved.

From there to the notch was an uphill grind that tired even Aris and Seri. The soldiers had to stop repeatedly, and the sun had set well before they reached the place where Seri had been attacked, although enough skyglow remained to show the edge of the trail clearly. Scavengers had already found the bodies; Aris heard grunts and hisses as they neared it, and saw several dark blurry forms slither off the trail. He explained to the captain as if the man spoke their language; it was too dark to see most gestures or expressions.

The cold night wind had begun, and moaned softly through the notch, smelling of pine and wet rock. Aris and Seri led the way again, and in the last dayglow pointed out the ledge which they must follow to the base of the cliffs beyond. Aris moved out onto the ledge first. He could just see the ledges below in the starlight, one vague grayish slab after another, but he had to feel his way along. Seri, behind him, suddenly touched his back.

"What?"

"That glow." Aris turned, and saw the unmistakeable orange glit-ter of a fire in the distance, somewhere north and below.

"We still have to get off this ledge," he said. "Make sure the captain sees it, though." He made his way along gingerly, hoping that the large snake they had seen did not wander at night. The soldiers slipped, muttering what must be curses; their boots clat-tered on the rock until he was sure that they could be heard all the way back in the stronghold. Where the ledge slipped back under rocky soil, and scrubby trees began, he startled an owl. It flew away, hooting shrilly. "Now they must know," he said. Seri touched his shoulder again.

"It's farther than you think," she said. "Don't worry about it. Just let us get these men safely into some kind of camp."

Aris looked up at the looming cliffs ahead, their sheer flanks visible even in starlight. "The way we came," he said. "It'll be out of sight of that fire, and safe enough. One of us can go down the streambed to water." Soon the fire was hidden by a fold of ground, and then the massive projection of the cliff itself. The closer they got to the cliff, the colder seemed the air that poured off it, an invisible river. Aris led them to the edge of the forest; it was too dark to travel within it. There he waited for the captain; Seri put his hand over the captain's cold glove, and Aris pressed down: sit. The captain spoke softly to his men, and all sank to the ground. Aris felt legweary himself; he was glad to take out the food in his pack.

Somehow, even in the dark, they were able to share food among all of them. The captain assigned two men to guard, placing them where Aris suggested, upslope toward the north. Aris wondered whether to trust them, but he felt no warnings. He and Seri slept a little apart from the others, side by side, and woke stiff but rested in the first light of dawn. The cliffs across from them had begun to glow a dull orange, though the sun was not yet on them; behind, the taller cliffs of the main mountain were still deep rose, shadowed blue. In that dawn silence, he heard falling water, a merry irregular chiming like tiny bells. Following it, he found a spring dripping into a moss-cupped pool crowded with flowers, some the same as in the upper canyon, and one a curious lavender bloom he had never seen before. He filled his flask, and showed Seri the spring.

The morning found the captain more suspicious and less amiable, if his expression meant anything. Aris had never before imagined how difficult it was to convey the simplest meanings with gesture alone. He knew the captain wanted to know if their people lived in the same direction as the fire of the night before. He wanted the captain to know that they did not. He wanted the captain to understand that either he or Seri should go and warn the stronghold, perhaps returning with help; he could see that the captain didn't want to let either of them out of his sight. Or perhaps he was not used to sleeping on the ground in his uniform. Aris knew that made some people grumpy.

He tried drawing a map on the ground with a stick: here we are, there they are, and over here are my people. The captain's expression did not change. Seri said, "Let's go with them now—they won't be worrying yet." She pointed north, where they had seen the fire the night before, and gave the captain a wide grin. His face relaxed; he shrugged, smiled, and gave an order to his soldiers. Soon they were on their way, around the first "finger" and into the next cove, angling toward low ground and the streambed.

By the time they found a reasonable slope down to it, the sun had cleared the cliffs to the east, and glinted off the stream itself. They saw no smoke; Aris thought that the brigands probably put their fires out in daylight, so that smoke could not betray them. Aris had spotted a trail that he thought the others used coming down from the high pass; he stayed upslope of it until they reached the stream, which here ran swift and clear, alternating rocky stretches, gravelled pools, and sandbars. Seri touched his shoulder, but he had already seen.

There on the damp sand were the hoofprints of several horses, headed upstream; the captain grinned and clapped Aris on the shoulder. "Kreksh," he said. The hoofprints went across the sandbar, and up into rocks on the far side. The captain walked his fingers along the near side of the stream; clearly he wanted to get behind the fugitives. Aris nodded; that made good sense. He still worried about sentries. He did not know this country, and the fugitives clearly did. They must have someone watching down their back trail. He tried to indicate this; the captain smiled, nodded, and mimed cautious sneaking through the bushes. Aris pointed to the cove that now opened behind them—why not go into the trees? The captain looked up at the cliffs, as if he expected trouble from them, and shook his head.

Soon enough, the streambed itself led them into the trees. Aris felt safer; someone perched overhead on a rock could not see through the canopy.

They heard the brigands, and smelled the smoke of their fire, before they saw them. Voices echoed off the cliffs; Aris was glad he had insisted that the captain speak to his men about moving more quietly. The captain could understand what they were saying; Aris could not, but he could tell that they were relaxed, not on their guard at all. Aromatic smoke and the delicious scent of cooking meat made him hungry; he tightened his belt and crept on, cautiously.

When he came to the edge of the clearing, it was obvious that these brigands had lived there a long time. Three log huts, low but sturdy, backed against the cliff, and a rail fence kept the animals from straying . . . a motley group of horses and mules. They had butchered a mule—its head was displayed on a stick; its hide had been stretched from a tree-limb, weighted with stones. Aris guessed that they stole the animals from the caravans, used them to transport their goods, then ate them.

The brigands themselves were swarming over the loot they had stolen, spreading it out in the sun to gloat over. Aris saw lengths of striped cloth, some in brilliant colors, rugs, copper pots, and small sacks that the robbers opened, sniffed, then tied shut again. He had trouble counting them, but thought the number must lie between fifteen and twenty. He thought all were men until a woman came out of one of the huts with a baby at her breast, and another woman followed her.

The captain grinned again, and sent his men around the clearing. He showed Aris, with gestures, what he planned: his men would attack from behind, forcing the brigands to withdraw the way they had come even if they escaped. His men would have the higher ground, and beyond the notch he would have reinforcements. Seri touched the captain's shoulder, and pointed to a trail that seemed to lead away from the clearing on the far side, then to herself, brows raised. The captain nodded, and Seri began to work herself into position. It might be only a trail to a jacks, Aris knew, or it might be an escape route.

The captain's signal to attack was that same horn call that Aris and Seri had heard the day before. It came from the cliff behind the clearing, magnified by the walls until it sounded like a fanfare. The brigands dropped their loot, looked around wildly, and bellowed. The hut doors opened; more women poured out, and a few men either sleepy or drunk by their staggering gait. Some of the men outside ran for the huts—to get their weapons, Aris guessed—but the soldiers cut them down with arrows, staying in cover themselves. Those not hit with the first flight threw themselves on the ground, behind any cover they could find, and tried to crawl to the huts. The soldiers ran out, yelling as if they had an army behind them. Some of the brigands broke and ran; two—who had swords in reach—tried to fight and were cut down. One of the fugitives charged straight at Aris and the captain, sword swinging. Aris leaped forward, evaded a swing, and thrust hard with his staff; the man fell, gasping, and dropped his sword. Aris kicked it away behind him, and looked for Seri.

Several brigands had tried to get past her; Aris saw only the final head-splitting blow which she dealt the last of them. Then the fight—it could hardly be called a battle—ended, with most of the brigands dead, a few bound hand and foot, and the women huddled together under the soldiers' guard. The captain strode up to them;

the soldiers crowded around, laughing. One of the women screamed as a soldier grabbed her; Aris heard cloth ripping.

Seri and Aris pushed between them, and stood back to back on either side of the women; Seri said "No!" and Aris brought up his stick. The captain glared and said something, pointing to the women and then to himself. "No," Aris said. Behind him, the baby started crying, a thin pulsing wail; by the sound, at least two women were sobbing too. "No," Aris said again. "You can't hurt them; it's not right." He had no way to mime that; he hoped his tone would convey his determination. One of the soldiers muttered "Biknini daksht!" and grabbed at Aris's stick; Aris swung it out of his reach, and knocked him on the knee. The man fell back with a cry, and the others muttered louder, looking at their captain. He chewed his long moustaches, shrugged, threw his hands out and gave a command. The archers put arrows to their bows, and half-drew them. The captain pointed to Aris, then the women, then himself, and waved around at the archers.

One of the women said something more than a cry. The captain stiffened; his eyes opened wide, and he replied. The woman spoke again, in a low, hurried voice. Aris wished he had some idea what was being said. Whatever it was affected the captain; he bowed, stiffly, and gave an order that made his archers lower their bows. Then he bowed even lower and held out his hand. From behind Aris a woman stepped forth, wrapped in a blanket that now covered most of her head; her legs were bare and he thought she had on little under the blanket. She touched the captain's hand with the tips of her fingers and turned away. Aris saw wide-set amber eyes and a tangled mane of red hair. The captain shouted orders; his soldiers ran to the tumbled piles of loot and snatched up lengths of cloth. With great courtesy, the captain offered them; the woman took one and wrapped it around her, over the blanket, before walking into one of the huts.

"I think that's over," Aris said, lowering his stick. Seri moved around beside him; the women they had guarded eyed the cloth avidly, and when the captain nodded, snatched it up and ran for the same hut as the first woman.

"If only we knew what had happened," Seri said. She ran her hands along her stick, eyeing the soldiers. "Although I suppose we must now go with them, to make sure they don't mistreat these women on the way back—wherever that is. But if we're not back by tomorrow, our people will be worried."

Shortly the first woman reappeared, now without the blanket and wrapped in two layers of cloth that covered her to her ankles. She came first to Seri, knelt, and kissed her hand; then kissed Aris's. Aris was so astonished he could not react before she stood again and began talking to the captain.

He watched that interchange. Something in the captain's stance indicated that the woman was of equal or higher rank. A captive? He could not tell. The captain answered her, first briefly, then with a long spate of words that was, Aris finally figured out from the gestures, the full story of yesterday's chase and this morning's stalk.

Meanwhile the soldiers briskly packed up the rest of the loot, and searched the huts for more. The other women had straggled out with bundles and sacks; two more children appeared, both just able to walk. The soldiers loaded the loot on the pack animals, and looked from their captain to Aris and Seri. The captain looked at them, too, and spoke to the first woman. She pointed to the other women and nodded. The captain threw up his hands; the soldiers muttered, but unpacked one animal to saddle it for riding. The first woman and the two children rode; the other women walked, one carrying her baby.

Aris wondered what they would have done if he and Seri had not been there. He didn't like the thoughts that came to him. He had noticed that yesterday's prisoners had disappeared, and he was sure they were dead. He glanced at Seri, who grinned and nodded to the captain.

It was close to noon when the captain led them off toward the stream. They followed its windings deeper and deeper into the gorge that cut through the western cliffs. If he had had the leisure, Aris would have studied the odd colors and patterns of the rocky walls, but the captain, homeward bound, kept up a good pace. They stopped once to water the pack animals and eat the last of their food, but pressed on in the growing heat of afternoon.

The stream's narrow bed widened gradually; its water disappeared into a fan of gravel and sand. Aris looked back at the rampart of the cliffs far above; the mountains behind were invisible from here. They stood on a great hump of broken rock and gravel, the outwash of the stream, with a good view now of a cluster of buildings some distance away to the left. The captain looked back, and waved to them. Aris looked at the sun, about to dip behind distant mountains, and then at Seri. She still grinned, as usual, and it lifted his spirits. "Might as well," she said. "Maybe he'll feed us."

The captain had waved his shiny helmet, and blown his horn; soon Aris could see a mounted troop riding out to them. Well before dark, they were all mounted—on horses that seemed to Aris hardly larger than nomad ponies, though very differently shaped—

and riding toward the town. The captain seemed unsurprised that Aris and Seri could ride; Aris thought perhaps he had worn out his surprise earlier.

The town, when they reached it, was a cluster of low, mud-brick and stone buildings crammed behind a stout wall perhaps two men high. Aris had not seen any green fields, though in the gathering dark he could not see clearly; perhaps its fields were on the other side. Its narrow gate had a tall, heavy wooden door. Men in the long, loose shirts like those the brigands had worn came out carrying torches to light their way. Inside the gate, the buildings jammed wall-to-wall. Women crowded the narrow streets, crying out when they saw the woman on horseback, and then shrieking even louder when they saw Aris and Seri.

Chapter Twenty-five

Their first meal in the strangers' town combined new tastes with elaborate ritual. Aris could only hope that their hosts would not be offended by mistakes; he was soon completely confused about what was expected of them. They seemed to be part exhibition and part honored guest. He and Seri had been offered deep copper basins of warm water for bathing (the captain had mimed a bath for them); they had taken turns, glad to wash off the sweat and dirt of two days' journeying. Clothes, too, had been offered: long white robes with gray panels down the front— as close to the color they had been wearing, they thought, as the captain could find—went over wide-legged gray pants of the same smooth fabric. Aris found the robe deliciously smooth against his skin. He looked more closely at the gray panel, and realized it was brocade, glittering almost silver. Seri touched hers. "This is silk," she said. "Like the clothes Dorhaniya had, that Eris used to make those tunics for Luap." Their own clothes were taken away for washing—again, clearly mimed—but no one tried to touch their sticks or their daggers.

But the meal drove all concern for clothes out of mind. The captain had also bathed and changed; he appeared in a long robe similar to theirs, but in red and brown brocade. When he sat, on the pile of cushions placed for him on a colorful carpet, Aris noticed

that he had dark silk pants under his robe. Aris and Seri sat on
either side of him.

The room was lit by oil lamps and candles both, with polished
metal reflectors used to make it brighter where the diners sat. On
the other side of the room, a crowd of people stood, murmuring
among themselves. Aris wondered who they were; the captain
seemed to ignore them. Servants brought in low tables, then trays
laden with food. The captain dipped into a mound of steamed grain
and vegetables with a long handled utensil that had a flat, leaf-
shaped blade, and offered Seri the resulting lump. She looked
around for a plate or something resembling it; a servant held out
a flat cake that looked like travel-bread. She took it, and scooped
the food off the utensil; the captain repeated this ritual with Aris,
who did the same. Then the captain ate a single mouthful, and
waited until they had finished their serving. Every dish he offered
first to one of them, alternating the honor.

Aris liked the steamed grain, but not the sour little leaf-wrapped
rolls stuffed with meat and swimming in a sweet sauce, although
he was hungry enough to eat it anyway. A bowl of crispy fries he
realized with horror were fried insects; apparently the look on his
face was enough, for the captain shrugged and turned away. When
Seri also refused it, he shrugged again, dipped one in its accompa-
nying sauce (red flecked with yellow and green) and crunched it,
grinning. Another pile of steamed grain, this one colored a rich
gold, and fragrant with even more spices. . . . Aris liked that, and
the meat stew that came after it. Between each offering, servants
handed him a cup of water and a cup of wine.

By the time Aris felt stuffed, after tasting several dozen different
foods, all new to him, the table still held enough for a feast. The
captain waved his hand, offering more of anything; Aris shook his
head and patted his stomach, hoping the captain would understand.
Apparently so; he clapped his hands and servants came to remove
the tables. Other servants brought a small one, and on it put a loaf
of bread, a bowl of water, a large book and a scroll. The captain
smiled at Aris, then at Seri, and put his hand on the bread.

"Grish," the captain said. Aris blinked. He must be naming the
bread, unless bread stood for something else.

"Grish," he repeated. Then he laid his own hand on the bread
and said, "Bread." The captain repeated his word twice, and went
through the whole thing again with Seri. Then he touched the
water in the bowl.

"Sur."

Aris repeated that, and said, "Water." Again, the captain repeated the procedure with Seri. Then he pointed to the bread, and the water, and said "Bret. Waffer." Aris and Seri exchanged glances, pointed in their turn, and said "Grish. Sur." It was something, but didn't seem likely to lead very far.

Then the captain opened the book. Aris had heard of books: Gird had reported that the gnomes used books, flat pages that could be turned. But he had seen only scrolls, although it was easy to see how one could cut a scroll into short lengths and bind them together. This book had not only writing—the script looked very strange, as if it were made of random brushstrokes, yet those vertical columns could be nothing else—but also pictures. Clearly drawn in black ink, brilliantly colored, they were both beautiful and informative. The captain stopped at a page depicting a group of riders on horseback prancing past a grove of pines. He pointed to one of the horses.

"Pirush." When Aris and Seri had both repeated it, he said, "Pirush. Nyai pirush." He held up one finger. "Nyai." Pointed again to the horse. "Nyai . . . pirush."

"One horse," said Aris. He held up his finger. "One—" and pointed to the tree, "—horse."

Two horses, it turned out, were "teg pirushyin." Two men on the horses were "teki vekshyin." One man on a horse was "nyaiyi veksh." One pine tree was "nya skur," and two were "tag skuryin."

With the aid of the pictures and a natural quickness, Aris and Seri made some progress even that first night. Their experience with the horse nomads helped, because although the languages seemed nothing alike, they had learned how differently thoughts could be put into words. The captain, also quick to learn, picked up their "please" although he offered no equivalent; perhaps he simply used it in situations where he'd observed them using it, without understanding. By the time the captain rose to escort them to their guestroom, they could understand his words, "Sleep— tomorrow more" as well as his gestures.

They slept well, wakening to find that someone had put their clothes—clean and dry—in a neat stack beside the door. No sooner had they begun to talk softly than servants appeared with more basins of warm water. Aris and Seri washed and changed into their own garments; Aris noticed a faint but pleasant smell of spice.

The next day, Aris felt that one of them must return and explain to Luap what had happened. His combination of words and ges- tures, with reference to the pictures in the book, seemed to con- vince the captain, who offered a mount and an escort. Seri spoke up suddenly.

"Aris—why not try duplicating the pattern—perhaps in the ground out there—and going the mageroad?"

"Because I thought you should go, and you can't use the mageroad alone."

"They won't know that; if they see you use it, they'll be convinced I have the same power."

"And we don't know if they'll consider it proof that we're the biknini." The biknini, in the book, were dangerous-looking monsters, capable of changing from a cloud to a collection of spikes, horns, and hooves, to apparent human form. "And we don't know if it would work."

"It's the quickest way," Seri said. "If it doesn't work, you can still ride the horse. As ceremonial as these folk are, they may take drawing it as a prayer of some kind."

"It will be," Aris said. It was too good an idea to waste, though. The captain led the way outside the walls. Aris looked around, noticing a green patch some distance away with trees around it. Grainfield? His newly acquired language deserted him; he had to point. The captain nodded, said something Aris thought he remembered meant "grain" and offered with gestures to lead him that way. Aris shook his head, and looked for a smooth, level space which he could use for the pattern. He found what seemed a good spot, and gestured with his stick: please get back from this. With captain and a crowd watching, he drew the design, and when Seri nodded, stepped onto it. Would it work? He thought of the stronghold's great hall, and with a familiar internal wrench found himself there. Luap, passing through on some errand, stumbled, then smiled.

"What—have you found another pattern somewhere? And where's Seri? I thought you two were off exploring together."

"We were," Aris said. "Where's Arranha? I need to talk to both of you—we've met the people out there to the west." He wished he had thought to ask Seri to protect the pattern—since it worked at all, it might work the other way too, and give him a quicker way to travel back and forth. Would she have thought of that? Probably. "Just a moment," he said. "I have to try something."

Luap stared at him in some confusion. "People? Where? And how did you get back here without Seri?"

"Please," Aris said. "Go find Arranha, and the Rosemage, and I'll be back shortly." *I hope.* He concentrated on the pattern he had drawn, on Seri's presence, and found himself back outside the town, where the crowd was arguing and waving their arms about, while Seri stood calmly by, arms folded. When he appeared, silence fell instantly; half the crowd threw themselves on the ground, another group turned and ran for the gate, and the captain blanched. "It works," Aris said to Seri. "I've asked Luap to find Arranha and the Rosemage. If you can protect this pattern, I can come and go using it. Is it safe for you to stay?"

Seri grinned. "Now it will be. I think the crowd was giving our captain trouble."

Aris didn't want to leave her there, in danger, but she insisted. He took the mageroad back to the stronghold and found Luap, Arranha, and the Rosemage all waiting for him. As quickly as he could, he told them what he and Seri had found, and done; despite his sense of urgency, it was a long tale to tell quickly.

"Luap, if you take my advice, we will let Seri and Aris learn the language before we take action, but in the meantime I will post guards at the western end of our canyon." The Rosemage had not bothered to repeat her earlier concern and point out that a possible enemy now knew exactly where they were. She turned to Aris. "Aris, can you describe the way to that upper trail well enough that someone can find it, or will you have to lead them?"

Aris shook his head. "I'd best lead them; it's easy country to get lost in."

"Then Arranha or I will use your pattern to visit that town, and bring Seri back. She should be able to explain that she will return later. What do you think?"

It felt right to him; he nodded. Not until later did it occur to him that Luap had said little, and made no decisions himself. Arranha, they decided, would be less threatening a visitor. He could bring Seri back, or stay a day or so: not more than two. The Rosemage went to gather the few trained fighters to follow Aris down-canyon, and Aris went off to fetch his own weapons from the armory, tell his prentices where he was going, and fill his pack. His mind buzzed with questions. How many people lived in the western plains, and where were those caravans travelling from and to? How long would it take to learn the language? Could they trade with that town? Were they peaceful folk?

He led the group down the canyon at a brisk pace. The Rose-mage worried that the captain had already sent a troop of his own; Aris didn't think he would, but knew it was a possibility. He felt strange without Seri at his side, and wondered if Arranha were strong enough to protect her if things went badly in the town.

When they came to the notch, they had seen no sign of soldiers; Aris pointed out the route he and Seri had taken through the notch and then north toward the brigand encampment. The Rosemage, breathless, looked at him and shook her head. "You younglings! You covered all that ground and still had breath to fight and talk? At least I have some hard-won experience." She pointed out where she wanted the guardposts. "We need one of the stonecutters to come up here and carve them out; for now, we can build rock barriers of loose stone." She looked down toward the streambed. "You were right; we can't go straight down here without building another trail—but we'll put a lookout where he can see any approaches from the stream, as well."

By that night, Aris felt that no invasion could come from the town without being discovered. And the next day, Seri and Arranha returned; she slipped downcanyon to find him and tell him what had happened.

"Although the important thing is, the captain wants us to be allies against brigands. Makes sense to me; if brigands are living in that western end, they could be a threat as our people move down this way."

"What happened to the women we found?" Aris asked.

Seri made a face. "Hard to ask that; I don't have enough words yet. I tried, of course. If I understood what the captain said, one woman had been held captive, and her family is rich—they had a reward for her return. The others had been traveling with her, servants or friends or whatever. But I never saw them again, and the captain didn't seem to understand most of what I asked." She grinned. "Then again, I didn't understand most of what he asked, either. That book is impressive, but you can't draw pictures of the things we most wanted to say."

"What did they think when Arranha appeared?"

"They all threw themselves on the ground, even the captain. Perhaps they have more respect for old people, or perhaps they could sense he is a priest. Maybe it was his way of dressing, his long robes. But whatever it was, they treated him as if he were a direct messenger of the gods."

Aris punched her lightly. "In some ways, he is."

In the next day or so, after much discussion, Luap decided to let Aris and Seri contact the town as much as they wished, and encouraged them to learn the language. Since the strangers now knew about them, the original objections no longer mattered, and prudence alone suggested that they must learn more about these neighbors. He sent one of those skilled in cutting stone by magery down to carve guardposts where the Rosemage wanted them. Now that they had neighbors, he would need to think more like a ruler—

a member of Council, he corrected himself—and less like the head of a family. His people's very existence would depend on decisions he made, how he managed relations with these strangers. Within a few hands of days, a trickle of information began to flow between the town and the stronghold, as Seri and Aris learned more of the language.

"They call themselves the Khartazh," Aris reported, the next time he came back. "They have large cities to the north, and a king rules in one of them. They trade with the Xhim, far to the south, and over still more mountains in the northwest to folk who live along a seacoast." He frowned, staring at the map of the stronghold which Luap had been working on. "It's hard to believe they mean north*west*; the great sea is in the east: we all know that. The Honnorgat flows into it, the Immerhoft Sea is part of it—"

"Perhaps it goes all the way around the land," Luap said. He did not really care where the great sea was; he had never seen one, except on a map. Aris, he thought, was like Arranha in one thing—his curiosity could take him away from the point at hand to investigate all sorts of unimportant trifles. If it weren't for his own ability to remember what really mattered, if it weren't for his prudent leadership, his people could find themselves hungry and naked because no one bothered with the boring necessities. He shook his head, banishing that thought: it was unfair. He had many able helpers, and Aris could be practical when necessary. Perhaps he had an illness coming on; he would ask Aris later. But Aris's next word drove that thought from his mind.

"The captain has reported to his king, of course," Aris said. "The king sent word that his ambassador will meet with you at your convenience." Another practical problem, Luap thought, yet to listen to Aris one would think he had produced a solution instead.

"How long will that take?" asked the Rosemage.

"The captain thought it would be sometime in autumn; he says the great lords move as slowly as mountains."

"Then we could still go to our mountain," the Rosemage said with a glance at Arranha. "The younglings have had their fun—"

Luap smiled at her. "I'm not sure it was fun—or was it?"

Aris shrugged, smiling. "Enough that I'll admit we've had our turn. At least it worked out well. But can you spare one of us to be in Dirgizh, learning the language, if the Rosemage and Arranha leave?"

They might as well get all their adventuring done at once, and have it over with before winter. Luap wondered that he had not noticed, back in Fin Panir, the erratic behavior of these four. Now that he thought of it, he had seen, without recognizing, an inability to stick to a task. Arranha had been a rebel among the priests—rightly so, considering that priesthood, but it proved he was undependable in some ways. The Rosemage, after all, had turned against her first lord; even Gird had found her hard to manage. And the young ones had followed no one's pattern; they were likeable, goodhearted, but of the same difficult, questioning temperament as Arranha. A shame, since they all had remarkable talents, but the gods made no one perfect. He would have to learn how best to use their talents without letting their limitations damage the whole settlement.

Gird, he thought, would have imposed his will with a hard fist, but he, Luap, preferred to use more humane methods. It was not for him to command as Gird had; he was not a king, though he was a king's son. He would not make the mistakes his father had made. He would temper firmness with gentleness, where it did no harm. Let them have a loose rein; let them discover for themselves that his reasoning made more sense than their wild intuitions.

So he was careful to keep an even tone as he answered Aris. "As long as they're back when the ambassador arrives. The fieldwork is well in hand; you'd be spending much of your time on other things anyway. Seri, I think you should go; Aris, as our only healer, needs to stay closer until his prentices have more skill. We had another snakebite while you were gone."

"But I can use the mageroad," Aris said. "I could go back and forth each day. Spend part of the day in Dirgizh, and part of it here—"

"I'm not sure that's wise," Arranha said, relieving Luap of the necessity. "What's often seen becomes common; the mageroad is presently a mystery to them, and should remain one."

"I wish we had a horse trail out," Seri said. "Then I'd have a reason to bring our horses from Fin Panir." She and Aris had left their horses behind at first, when the Marshal-General had baulked at letting so many animals into the High Lord's Hall to use the mageroad. Farm stock had been needed first, and after all they had little pasture and no place to ride but the main canyon. Luap had been surprised that they agreed without argument, but he knew they missed their horses. He, too, missed riding a good horse; the few plow ponies they had were rough-gaited and clumsy on trails. Still, bringing that up now was another proof that she could be as erratic, as faulty in judgment, as Aris or the Rosemage. What could *her* horse matter?

"The Marshal-General is not likely to let us bring more beasts through the High Lord's Hall," the Rosemage said. "Even those. And you know we've never fitted a horse into that inner chamber of Luap's cave."

"I know—but if we had them we could ride out there—and it would be quicker going back and forth—"

"Seri." Aris laid his hand on hers. "I know you don't want to be in Dirgizh alone—but is there more?"

"No—just a feeling. They keep talking about demons in here, demons haunting the canyons. What if something happens while I'm away? While the Rosemage is away?"

"I won't command you to go, if it so distresses you," said Luap; at his tone, Seri flushed.

"I'm a Marshal; I have nothing to fear." The look she gave Luap had in it more challenge than respect. Then she grinned and relaxed. "In fact, it should be fun—they'll let me ride their horses, I can see how they drill their troops—"

"And you come back often and let me know," Aris said, almost fiercely.

"And Arranha and I will come back laden with gold and silver and jewels," the Rosemage said, laughing. "And we will all be rich, able to buy all those things in the market you've told us about. We won't have to dig the horse trail by magery; we can hire men to do it."

Luap thought they should have known better. If he had been asked, Arranha and the Rosemage would not have been his choice for the task of exploring the wilderness looking for gold. What did either of them know about it? Arranha, at his age, should spend his time in quiet study and prayer; the Rosemage, too, was no longer young, for all that she could wrap herself in magery so that none could see the silver threads in her dark hair, or the lines at her throat. But he could not argue with Arranha, who had been, in many ways, his mentor. He would never, he told himself proudly, use his power to overwhelm the old priest; if hints would not suffice, he would let Arranha do what he would.

The others talked on, their plans growing ever more grandiose and ridiculous. Luap listened, realizing his responsibility to protect them from themselves. They had talents he did not share, he thought with conscious generosity, but without guidance they would lead themselves—and everyone else—into a tangle of problems.

Aris busied himself, while Seri was in Dirgizh, by reorganizing his stores of herbs and bandages, teaching formal classes to his assistants and prentices, and exploring the main canyon for useful plants. When the Rosemage and Arranha came back from their mountain, when the ambassador had come and gone, and others could speak to the Khartazh as well as he and Seri, he hoped they could leave for awhile. The memory of the long rides with Seri, of the healings he had performed among the farmers, among the horsefolk, rose vividly in his mind. They could not stay forever in Luap's canyons; they had work to do in what he privately considered the "real" world. He missed Raheli and Cob; he even missed the Marshal-General.

Perhaps that explained why the Rosemage and Arranha wanted to explore the gray mountain—perhaps they, too, felt trapped in the canyon. He could not imagine Arranha lying about his motives, but—could anyone really take one look at a mountain and assume it contained gold or silver? The thought came into his mind that all four of them had been unusually distractible lately . . . he and Seri had felt a compulsion to explore the mountaintop, and then the western canyons, while the others took one look at that gray mountain and wanted to go there. None of them seemed to have time to talk things over, as they had when they first came, and when they did confer, their ideas went everywhere; they could come to few conclusions.

Had anyone else had similar desires? Aris intended to ask his assistants, but found himself instead confronted with an emergency that drove everything else out of his mind. Several children had eaten poisonous wild berries, and it took all Aris's skill and power to save them. By the time they were out of danger, he'd forgotten about his earlier concerns. He needed to find out which plants were poisonous, and make sure all the parents knew them; he needed to find remedies for snakebite and sting that could serve when he was not at hand. Luap was right, he thought: he had more than enough work to keep him busy right here.

Chapter Twenty-six

Luap had no idea what to expect from the Khartazh ambassador. Seri and Aris had described the soldiers and their captain in terms of weapons, and tactics. To his questions about what they wore, and what they looked like, they'd returned doubtful answers. "They're all sunburnt, of course," Seri had said. "Very brown."

"I think it's their natural skin," Aris had said. "Not just the sunburn. Perhaps a natural protection." Both had had much to say about the soldiers' gear, the use of headcloths to keep the sun from their helmets, the small, light horses they rode, the very different shape of their bows . . . but he had gained no insight at all into the men themselves. Nor had Seri been able to describe their language. She and Aris both were quick-tongued; they had learned the horse nomads' difficult speech with ease, and would no doubt learn this before anyone else, but she had spent the past hands of days in the west, with the Khartazh soldiers: she had not been back to teach him what she had learned. He would have to rely on her and on Aris for translation.

Although the captain Seri and Aris had met had told them it might be easily six hands of days before an ambassador would come ("at your convenience" Luap recognized as a term of courtesy, not a reality), in fact he had appeared in less than four. The earlier decision to allow Arranha and the Rosemage to go wandering off to explore the gray mountain now seemed less wise; Luap did not expect them back for days yet. In the meantime he was having to meet a royal ambassador alone, without their help, and it bothered him. He knew it had been his decision to let them go, but he had to fight off the temptation to blame them anyway.

He wished he knew more about protocol in royal courts. His was not, of course, a royal court, but the ambassador represented a king. He ought to show some magnificence, he thought. He had decided to offer the man a chance to rest and eat, if he wished, before their meeting; it was what he himself would want, after a journey up the canyon. He had a chamber prepared, with what luxuries they had brought, and hoped it would do. He had a sinking feeling that it would not.

Seri and Aris, in Marshal's blue, escorted the ambassador from the lower entrance to that chamber by a route that did not take him past the kitchens. One of Aris's prentices ran by the shorter way to let Luap know the man was inside.

"And he has moustaches down to *here,*" the boy said, excitedly. "And four servants with boxes and bags and things, and—"

"Did you hear whether he would eat and rest, or whether he wished to meet at once?"

"He was glad of a chance to rest, I think. I can't understand his talk, but Seri and Aris seem to. Aris said he'd come talk to you in a little while."

Luap waited in his office, forcing himself to do necessary copy-work to stay calm, until Aris appeared.

"Seri's staying beside the door," he said. "He's happy enough to rest first; he's used to riding wherever he goes, and that climb up into the mountains tired him. We should build a horse trail there, he said. I'd agree; if we ever want to trade, that would make it easier. He didn't think much of our horses when we got to them, but he rides well."

"What's he like?"

Aris shrugged. "It's hard to say. We barely understand each oth-ers' words; I think the captain we learned from has a different accent. He's very polite, but then that's what ambassadors are: it's his duty. He talked about some kind of demon that used to live in these mountains, but also about those who built the stronghold. They knew it was here, I think, but were afraid of something if they tried to come. Brigands, possibly; the captain said robbers had been in these mountains forever."

"I wish I could speak their language. It's awkward—"

"Perhaps not. He can't understand us, either. And misunder-standings can be laid on the language problems, not on any illwill."

"Do you have any idea what he wants? Why they sent an ambas-sador now, rather than letting that captain you met come talk to me?"

"If I understood them, they would consider that disrespectful. Once the captain had agreed that we weren't demons of some kind, he seemed to think we were something more than human. He would not dare, he said, to—I think the word means 'insult'—you by coming himself, when at the very least you should be welcomed by a royal ambassador, if not the king."

"What did you tell them about our settlement?"

"Not much—we're still learning the language. We tried to tell them that we had come from far away sunrising, and we had to travel by magery, not overland. That we lived in a great hall carved in the stone, and were friends of those who built it, not invaders." Aris looked doubtful. "I know that's not all the story, or exactly what you would have said, but it's the best we could do."

"That's fine—it may make us sound grander than we are, but that has its advantages. We don't want to be anyone's conquest."

"That's what Seri said, sir. Today, riding up the canyon, we could tell he was impressed, as much by the children playing in the stream and the fields as by the fields themselves. 'Is it safe?' he kept asking. 'You have not been attacked?' We said no, not by any worse than brigands, and his captain could tell him how we dealt with brigands."

"Good. We want peace with our neighbors, whoever they be. But trade could not hurt us, either." Luap stretched, easing tight shoulders. "Do you know anything of the way they spend the days? Would it be better to meet in the morning or evening?"

"I would think morning, not too early. Perhaps after an early breakfast?"

"Very well. I'd like you and Seri both to be there."

Luap chose to receive the ambassador in the great hall, where he had had two chairs and a table placed near the dais. The banner Dorhaniya had embroidered hung behind it. He awaited the ambassador in his Marshal's blue, which the Council had agreed he should wear even though his title was Archivist, not Marshal. He had shaved his face, since Seri reported that the captain had not had a beard, but the soldiers did.

Aris's messenger had brought word that the ambassador was on his way, and had withdrawn hastily. Luap's heart pounded; he felt a great weight on his shoulders. If he failed, if this man became an enemy, all his people would suffer. He turned to the doorway, struggling to appear calm. A moment more . . . then Aris paused in the door, standing very straight. It had not occurred to Luap before just how impressive a man he had become.

"My lord . . . the Khartazh ambassador." Or how formal; in Aris's deep voice, that sounded as courtly as anything he'd ever heard, and his bow was as smooth as if he did it every day. He said something in a foreign tongue; Luap assumed he was repeating his announcement.

The ambassador came through the door, and seemed to freeze in place an instant, his eyes roving up and around. Then he bowed very low, spoke, and waited in that position for Aris's translation. "Great prince, it is an honor . . ."

"We, too, are honored," Luap said smoothly. "Will you come forward and take a seat?" Seri, not Aris, translated for him. He was surprised; had they worked this out between them? The ambassador looked paler than he had expected, and almost frightened. What had he thought he would see? He himself noticed the long moustaches, the face otherwise cleanshaven except for a tuft at the chin, the hair hidden in an embroidered cap. He was not quite Luap's height, and his build was impossible to determine, robed as he was in richness that reminded Luap of the wealthiest mageborn women. Layer upon layer of cloth, slashed and puffed, embroidered and decorated with chips of shell and polished wood . . . he rustled as he walked forward, then bowed again. But for all that, his eyes were shrewd, the eyes of a man used to judging others. They were a strange golden-brown Luap had not seen before.

Luap waited another moment for the man to seat himself, then realized why he would not: he, Luap, was assumed to have the higher rank here. Slowly, as if that were part of his own protocol, Luap stepped back and seated himself. Slowly, eyes watchful, the ambassador sat in the other chair. Aris moved to stand at the ambassador's right hand; Seri came to Luap's. In the doorway, the ambassador's servants knelt, laden with their boxes and bags. The ambassador spoke again, looking at Luap. Aris translated: "I have brought gifts from our king, not worthy for one of your rank, but we beg you will accept them." The ambassador gestured, as if for permission, and Luap nodded. The servants came forward on their knees, and once in the hall began laying out an array of gifts.

A length of glowing scarlet cloth, edged in gold, tossed out to lie fanlike on the stone floor . . . a wide collar of black fur . . . a set of small pots of brasswork, with brilliantly enameled lids . . . a wide silver tray, on which a servant heaped mounds of preserved fruit, and smaller mounds of spices so pungent Luap could smell them from his seat. A belt of scarlet leather, stamped with gold sunbursts . . . matching scarlet gloves, deeply fringed with a gold sunburst on the back of each hand . . . and tall scarlet boots, stitched in sunburst patterns; the tops turned down to dangle tiny gold disks from them. Luap could not imagine how one could ride or work in such boots—they must be intended for ceremonial occasions. Finally, with a musical ringing, the eldest servant drew from its padded bag a necklace of many gold links and pendants, and laid it carefully on the black fur where it showed to best advantage. Luap tried not to stare like any farm child, but found it difficult. And what could he give in return? He had expected an exchange of gifts, but nothing like this. He had a few things from Dorhaniya's house that she had left him, but nothing so grand.

He nodded, smiled, and said "Our thanks for your graciousness; your people's workmanship is remarkable." That was too flat; he hoped Seri's command of their language was equal to improving it. He waited while she translated, then heard the ambassador answer, then finally heard Aris's translation of that.

"Prince, we are relieved to find you accepting these few gifts, all we had time to collect. It is the king's hope that you will grant us your blessing—" Aris looked uncertain; he turned and asked the ambassador something in his own language. Finally he resumed. "—the favor of those we think may be more than human, if not the gods themselves."

Luap had the uneasy feeling that he and Aris had both misunderstood something. But he went on as best he could. "We, too, would offer your king what trifles we have . . . nothing to equal this magnificence, but tokens of our friendship." The ambassador listened to Seri's translation of that with close attention; he seemed to relax a bit, and offered a tentative smile. Luap sat back in his chair, and sent Seri to fetch the gifts he'd made ready.

These she lay on the table between the two men. Luap himself unwrapped and displayed them—he hoped this would be taken for honor, not weakness. A sea-green bowl, in which Dorhaniya had once kept dried rose petals, filled now with the precious selon beans Eris had given him, a blackwood bow, and a richly decorated sword, part of the spoils of Fin Panir, which no Marshal would carry because of its origin and decoration. Luap had always enjoyed looking at it, but had to agree that it was better to look at than use.

The ambassador's eyes widened; he stared at the sword. "And the horse you rode yesterday," Luap added, "if it pleased you." Seri translated; the ambassador gave Luap a desperate look, then stood, his rich clothes rustling, and grasped the sword. Aris and Seri stared at him, both alert but unmoving. Luap wondered what he had said wrong. The ambassador said something that sounded formal, drew the sword quickly, and held it poised for an instant. Luap had that moment to think he was being attacked before the ambassador plunged the tip towards his own body.

"No!" Luap yelled, grabbing for the sword. Decorative it might have been, but it was sharp; it cut his hand to the bone. Aris and Seri tackled the ambassador and wrestled the sword away; Luap squeezed his wrist with his good hand and wondered what had gone wrong. Blood soaked his best gray trousers and splattered the floor; he could not wipe it up without letting go his wrist. He had bloodied the ambassador, too. . . .

"Sir!" The young men Seri had been training crowded the door. "What happened?"

"I don't know," Luap said through clenched teeth. His hand hurt more than he would have thought. "Help Aris with the ambassador—and don't hurt him. He wasn't after me; he was going to kill himself." In a few moments, two solemn young men were holding the ambassador, an easy task since he did not struggle. Seri had the sword; Aris came at once to Luap and took his hand.

"I can heal this," he said, with a sideways look at the ambassador. "Should we have him taken away?"

"No. Let him see." Whatever had gone wrong, Luap sensed, would not be made worse by a show of power. With Aris holding his arm, he dared to look at his hand. Two fingers dangled by a shred of skin; he saw bone and tendon laid bare.

"It's all right," Aris said. "Just relax." Easy for him to say. Luap thought—but he knew better. He leaned back in his chair, trying to relax, and let Aris work. The pain eased; he felt something tickle his hand, a feather-touch on the palm. When he looked again, his hand looked almost normal, if pale: the long gash was closing smoothly. It made him dizzy to watch; he looked past Aris to Seri.

"Do you know what happened?" She shook her head, and said something to the ambassador, whose reply was long and broken as she asked questions repeatedly. By the time she turned to him, Aris had released his hand; he felt no pain, and it looked normal except for the blood on his skin. The ambassador, he saw, was staring at it, wide-eyed; the man's servants had all put their foreheads on the floor.

"I think he thought you wanted him to kill himself," Seri said.

"What?"

"He keeps saying, 'He gave me the sword and told me to ride away.' "

"But that's not what we—what I—said."

"I know. But it's what it means to them. I think." Seri sighed, smoothing her tumbled hair. "He says if a king gives a servant such a sword—not a soldier's sword, but one with gold and jewels—it means the servant has displeased his lord and should kill himself. He was not sure that's what you meant, since you are not of his people, but the gift of the horse made it clear, because where could he ride that horse from here but to the afterworld? There is no trail back to his land."

"But I said the gifts pleased me," Luap said. "Isn't that what you told him?"

"I thought so." She asked the ambassador a question, and listened to his reply. "Yes, he heard that, but thought it was a joke—sarcasm. You liked the gifts so well you told him to die." Luap thought about that. What kind of people would think that way? Did he want to befriend people who thought that way?

"Tell him," he said carefully, "that among our people we do not make such jokes—we do not lie about things like that. The gifts pleased me. And among our people the gift of a sword is a gift of trust. Do you think he will understand that?"

"I hope so," Seri said. She talked, and the ambassador spoke to her, and she talked again. Luap watched the servants, who knelt motionless all this while. What kind of people had such servants? Abruptly, the ambassador yanked his arms free of the two young men, as if they had not been holding him at all, and threw himself at Luap's feet. All down his back, Luap saw, his outer robe buttoned with tiny black buttons ... he realized the man could not reach those buttons himself; he could not get dressed without servants. Luap looked down; the ambassador had taken his boots in his hands and was kissing them. He felt sick.

"Tell him to rise, and sit in his chair," he said to Seri. He could feel the hot flush on his cheeks. "Does he still think I'm angry?"

"He thinks he's disgraced his king, and will bring war on his people," she said, before speaking again to the ambassador. This time he rose, shook himself to resettle his clothes, and sat once more in his chair, his hands linked in apparent composure. Those strange amber-yellow eyes stared at Luap as if trying to penetrate his mind.

"I'm sorry," he said, directly to the ambassador. "I am not angry with you. Please do not injure yourself. As you can see, I am not hurt." Bloody, yes, and confused, but not hurt. "Please ask your servants to rise; I will have someone show them where to take the gifts."

Seri translated that, and the ambassador spoke a few phrases to his servants. They set to work repacking the gifts, without looking up. The ambassador continued, speaking slowly, and waiting for Aris to translate each phrase. "It is my shame. It is my mistake. Do not be angry with my king. Great lord, let your vengeance fall on me, and not on my king. Great prince, your wisdom excels all; be merciful."

Luap put out his hand; the man flinched but did not pull away when Luap touched him. "Do not fear. I am not angry." He smiled, and thought of a joke of Gird's. "Don't worry: when I am angry, you will know it." Seri gave him a look, but translated that. The ambassador blinked, and stared, and then essayed a tentative smile. "That's right," Luap said, as he would have encouraged a frightened child crossing the rapids.

The ambassador spoke again, this time more fluently. "He asks about the healing," Seri said. "And perhaps I should have told you before, but Aris healed a soldier: the captain may have mentioned that."

"Tell him we have various powers, but this we consider the gods' gift," Luap said. The man listened to Seri, and made a curious but graceful movement with his hands as he spoke again.

"He says his king would be honored by our friendship," Aris said. "But, sir—there's a problem with that word. The captain told us there were different words for friends—if I understood him— according to rank and intention both. I'm not sure what this one really means."

Luap smiled at the ambassador again. "I'm not sure we need to know at the moment, and any kind of friendship is better than war. Tell him I wish to bathe and change, and have the blood cleaned up; perhaps he would like to rest, or walk outside, for awhile, and we can meet later." This suggestion, translated, seemed to calm the man more than anything else. He rose, bowed deeply again, and seemed rooted to his place. Luap finally realized he was waiting for the "great lord" to leave first. He was afraid to insist on anything else, for fear of causing another dangerous misunderstanding.

Even a bath and a change of clothes did not completely dispel his shakiness. Seri had evidently assigned her entire group of trainees to help him; one of them took his blood-stained clothes away to wash, and two more hovered outside his door, eager to help with anything he could imagine. He asked for something to eat, and got a tray of bread, sliced meat, and fruit. While he was eating, Aris came in.

"Seri or I will stay with the ambassador until we're sure he's not going to hurt himself," Aris said. "He seems better, but—"

"He scared me," Luap said. "I never saw anything like that."

"You saved his life," Aris said. "We were impressed."

Luap found himself smiling. "You never saw me in the war, did you? I spent most of it as Gird's scribe, but he trained me, and his training stays." He looked at his hand. "And I'm glad you were here, Aris; I'd have lost those fingers. I hope I'm doing the right thing."

"Saving him?"

"No. Talking to him at all. Making agreements, or thinking about it." Luap shook his head. "What kind of people can they be, to take a gift as a command to kill themselves?"

"It's the language problem," Aris said. "He seemed nice enough, on the way in. We just didn't understand him, and he didn't understand us. What did you think of his gifts?"

Luap looked at the bundles piled in the corner of his office. "Gorgeous, but the Marshals back home wouldn't approve. Those boots—!" He had a sudden urge to look at them again, and bent to unroll the bundles. "And this fabric—it must be the same stuff as Dorhaniya's dresses . . . silk, I think she said." He felt the scarlet material; it slithered through his fingertips like water, smooth and cool and slippery. "Look at it."

"Mmm." Aris touched it, then stroked it. "Lovely feel. They gave us clothes like this the first night we spent with them, only in gray and white. This would make a fine tunic for Midwinter Feast."

"Only with a fur undershirt." Luap found the boots, gloves, and belt curled together. He tried a glove, and found it short in the fingers, made for a stubbier hand than his. "Can you imagine what the Marshal-General would say if I wore these in Fin Panir?" The boots, he could see, were also too short. He shook them; the gold disks chimed softly together. But the belt almost fit; he could punch another hole in it. It looked garish with his gray and blue, he thought, but against the red silk it looked perfect. He laid the leather things aside, and found the little sacks of spices. "I'll have to take some of these to Meshi, the next time I go back to Fin Panir. I had no idea they had such spices out here."

"I wonder if that's where ours came from," Aris said, frowning. "The spice merchants rarely say."

"Still hoping for a land route? I suppose it's possible. But until we can talk to these people and be sure we understand what they say, we can't know." Luap sniffed the sacks, one after another. "I'm sure this is one of the spices she uses with peaches and pears both. I wonder if she'd come out here, even for a short while, and teach our cooks." He rummaged again, and came up with the little brass pots. Set in a row on his desk, they looked like a set intended for some purpose. Each had a slightly bulbous bottom, eight delicate ribs, and a flat lid. The brightly enamelled lids, in blue and white and red, fit snugly, but Luap pried them up. Inside, the pots had been enamelled in a dark but brilliant blue. The largest would hold perhaps two handfuls of grain; the smallest perhaps five pinches.

"They would store spices," Aris pointed out. "I've always seen spices stored in boxes, but boxes let in damp."

"I wonder if the designs on the lids mean anything." Those swirls might be letters or symbols, he thought, but in no script he knew. "I suppose we could ask the ambassador, first making sure he had no weapon at hand." Almost before he knew it, he had found the leather sacks of preserved fruits, and dipped into one. It almost melted on his tongue, a confection of honeyed fruit and spice. "Try this," he said to Aris, offering the sack. "Whatever it is, the merchants in Fin Panir would pay dearly for it."

Aris tasted the sticky brown lump and his face changed. "Anyone would. I can't imagine what it is." He began picking up the many little sacks and sniffing them. "Here's another—no—it's not the same. This is plums, I'm sure." Together they explored the contents of each sack with the slightly guilty pleasure of children rummaging in a pantry.

"I suppose these should go down to the kitchens," Luap said finally. He and Aris looked at each, then both burst into laughter.

"Not until Seri's had a taste," Aris said. "And then I think I might classify these fruits as medicinal. At least until we can figure out how to make them."

"You'd better go relieve Seri, then, before I lose all self-control and gobble the lot of them. What I should do is take a sample to Meshi—if anyone can figure out how to copy them, she can."

Aris left, grinning, and said he'd send Seri down; Luap decided he might as well unpack the rest of the presents and figure out where to put them. He had laid out the fur collar on the back of one scribe's chair, the silver tray on his desk, and had the gold necklace in his hands when Seri appeared in his doorway. He grinned at her.

"Did Aris tell you about the honeyed fruit?"

Seri gave him a look he could not quite interpret. "Yes . . . he said I should come taste it. That's—what are you going to do with that?" Luap looked down at the necklace.

"I don't know. I can't wear something like this. Perhaps the Rosemage can. Or perhaps we can use it for trade in your town."

"No, we can't do that. They'll be upset; it's the king's gift. Although you could sell it in Fin Panir." She looked thoughtful. "Although I don't think anyone in Fin Panir could afford it."

"Tsaia, then," Luap said. He let the necklace slide through his hands onto the silver tray, and picked up one of the sacks of fruit. "Here—smell this, then taste it." Seri sniffed, then poked in a cautious finger.

"It's sticky."

"Yes, and it's delicious." He watched as she tasted it, but to his surprise she didn't react as he and Aris had.

"It's too sweet; it'd be better spread on bread." She didn't taste the others, but did approve the spices, and looked at the set of pots with interest. "Those could be signs from their script," she said. "I haven't seen much but the captain's watch list and the book we mentioned, but the shapes are similar. Fat and thin squiggles, it looks like to me, but I daresay that's what our script would look like to them."

"While you're here," Luap said, "Can you start telling me about their language? Even a few words would help."

"We started on that back in the town," Seri said. She fished out a grimy scrap of parchment covered with tiny script. "Aris and I used this for notes—it's fairly hard to read, but I can copy it for you." Luap cleared the scribe's desk and chair for her, and decided to have the gifts carried up to his own quarters to get them out of the way. The youngsters were glad to do that, eager to handle things that had come from outsiders.

Luap made sure the ambassador was given the choice of eating in his guest chamber, or with the others; he chose to eat alone. Manners, thought Luap. We've already discovered that we don't have the same manners, and he doesn't want to offend. Luap himself took the note Seri had made and started trying to learn a few words of the Khartazh tongue. He went out in the early afternoon, walking up and down the path reciting to himself. Words were easy; he'd always had a quick ear, so calling a horse a pirush didn't bother him. Seri had marked multiples: one pirush, two pirushyin. He practiced counting: not one or two pirushyin, but nyai pirush, teg pirushyin. The sounds felt strange in his mouth, as they had felt strange in his ears when the ambassador talked. But the structure of the language defeated him. He knew the language of the mageborn, which they thought of as Old Aarean, and the language of the peasants, which they called Speech. In between was the bastard tongue each race spoke to the other, now called Common. Each had its own ways of saying things, some easier than others. But this—this language seemed to make everything difficult. Seri had given him eight ways to say "Please come in"—not just a ranking from simple to ornate, but completely different words. Even the simplest greetings varied widely with the relative ranks of the speakers.

Thinking about the formality of the language, and what Arranha had told him about the Old Aareans, Luap decided that the Khartazh must be an old and very complex society. They would not be the same as the Old Aareans, but surely any old, complex civilization would have some attitudes in common. They were rank-conscious: that much was clear from Seri's first reports, and the language confirmed it. Wealth he could judge from the gifts he'd been sent, and attention to detail by the fine craftsmanship. They might or might not have magery—the ambassador's response to the morning's excitement could be taken either way—but they feared demons and had gods they respected. Arranha should have been here, he thought. Arranha would know how to interpret what they've already said and done.

He knew he could not wait for Arranha or the Rosemage. However the ambassador interpreted the morning's events, those amber eyes had been shrewd. The man would observe closely everything he saw, and report all of it. The longer he thought about the implications of that gold necklace, the silk, the heaps of spices, the set of pots, the more Luap worried that the Khartazh was more than it had seemed to Seri and Aris. What did they know of empires? He himself had read everything in the royal archives; he had listened to Arranha and Dorhaniya; he knew what Seri and Aris could not, how empires dealt with small princedoms on their flanks.

And it had been going so well. Why, he asked himself, couldn't the Khartazh have been some petty dukedom, no worse than a—a Marrakai? Why did it have to be what it so clearly was: a mighty and ancient empire, wealthy and sophisticated? And why did the ambassador have to come while the Rosemage and Arranha were off somewhere in the wilderness? He knew the why of that: he had agreed, in the certainty that nothing was going to happen until fall. So he would have to deal with this ambassador himself, and somehow convince the man that the mageborn were worth befriending and far too powerful to attack.

By late afternoon, he was ready to try again; he inquired and found that the ambassador had rested, eaten, and was willing to see him once more. His people had managed to get the bloodstains out of his good shirt and trousers, and get them dry again. His Marshal's blue tunic, so much thicker, had not dried; he put on one of the tunics Eris had made him. Remembering the ambassador's elaborate clothes, a length of brocade from Dorhaniya's dress could not be too formal. He wondered if he ought to wear the red leather belt, but decided against it; he had chosen his tunic for its color— the nearest to Girdish blue possible—and thought the belt looked garish with it.

This time, without the awkwardness of the gift exchange, things went better. The ambassador too had changed clothes; Luap realized that his blood must have splattered the ambassador's robe as well. Now he wore an over-robe of glistening black. Luap hoped it didn't portend anything dire. The ambassador bowed repeatedly on entering the room, but once he sat down seemed more relaxed. Luap knew he might be misreading the man's face, but hoped a smile meant the same thing for both of them.

To put his visitor at ease, Luap suggested, through the translators, that the ambassador might want to ask questions—some of which, he admitted, he might not be able to answer. The ambassador stroked his long moustaches and blinked. Then he said something which Aris translated as "Is this formal or informal?"

Luap thought about that. Either answer might be wrong, and give offense, but he had to answer. He turned to Seri. "Tell him it is informal, that I would not require formality from one to whom all our ways are strange."

The ambassador responded with a bow from his seat, and more apparent relaxation. "We are honored to be accepted without formality in your hall," was Aris's next translation of the ambassador's words. Before Luap could consider what that might mean in light of what he'd said, the ambassador went on, speaking in short phrases and waiting for Aris's translation. "It is clear that your people have many powers. Our king asks if you come in peace."

"Yes," Luap said, nodding. "We do not love war, though we are not without warriors." He hoped that would deter any aggressive tendencies; he watched the ambassador's face closely during the translation and his response to it.

"So our captain said." The ambassador let his eyes rest on Seri and Aris, one after the other, as Aris translated. "In our land, powerful lords rarely take the sword . . . it is common with you?"

Powerful lords—did that mean him, or Seri and Aris, or all the mageborn? "All our folk study weaponlore," he said, remembering Gird's sayings about peace and war; he paused there to allow Seri's translation to catch up. "We find it the best way to keep peace."

That earned a blink; the amber eyes narrowed, then relaxed. What he had said had gone home; he could only hope it was in the right target.

"Your folk did not build this hall?" was the next question.

"No," Luap said. "We are—" He had no word for it, really: they had not been given the hall, nor were they renting or borrowing it. "The builders," he said, "were our friends." That ought to make it clear: they had not built it, but they had permission to be there.

The ambassador sat straighter, if possible. After a long pause, during which Luap tried to think what he could have said wrong, the ambassador slid a thick gold ring off his finger and placed it on the table between them. Luap looked at the ring, and then at the ambassador. Was it a bribe? Another gift? A threat? A promise? The ambassador simply stared back at him. Finally Luap spoke.

"Your customs are different." He listened to Seri's words, which seemed a lot longer than that, and fretted at the need for translation. The ambassador looked anxious as he heard his version, then spoke again.

"He says that this ring is only a sign—a token—and that one more suitable will be brought later." A sign of *what?* Luap wanted to say. Aris went on. "He hopes you will permit the king to continue as your trusted steward. If you take the ring, he expects that you will not invade or use magic against them; if you refuse, he thinks you will conquer the Khartazh by force."

Astonishment swamped all other feelings, followed closely by triumphant glee. He had done it; he had bluffed an old, rich, empire into thinking itself menaced. But none of that must show, he felt the years of work with the scribes taking over. Blandly, almost casually, he said, "Tell the ambassador that I have no need for kingship of the Khartazh; his king may rule in peace. But I wear no man's ring—" Some memory of the horse nomad's ceremonial rings for Gird at his death came to him, and he held up his hands, thumbs upward. "—my thumbs are free."

Seri gave him a startled look before she began translating; the ambassador received those words with outward rigidity. Luap could tell he had made an effect. He felt another burst of satisfaction. Perhaps he was only a king's bastard, whose years in a palace had been far in the past—but it came back to those for whom it was natural. He was the prince, a true prince, with all the royal magery and the gift of command. He belonged here, dealing with a royal ambassador; he did not need the Rosemage or Arranha after all.

Chapter Twenty-seven

After that, the real work began. The ambassador had maps, and could procure others. Luap tried not to show how fascinated he was by the maps, which used a marking system he had not seen before, dividing the land into squares. He saw at once how useful that could be, and noted the accuracy with which their mapmakers had drawn the cliffs he had seen, the delicate shading that made clear which slopes were steep and which gentle. Here was the technique he had needed so badly back in Fin Panir . . . the Council of Marshals would be glad to see this.

But the ambassador's use of the maps impressed him in other ways as well. The Khartazh traded overland to great distances; they had heard of lands far east, across a vast desert, but regular caravans had ceased some dozen years before. *The war*, Luap thought. Gird's war. They had been declining before that for several decades. *The Fall of Aare*, Luap thought, the hairs standing up on his arms. Could it be? The ambassador recognized the selon beans Luap had given him—yes, they had been part of that trade, and spice and amber had gone the other way. Now—the ambassador shrugged—now the caravans moved mostly north and south. The names he gave meant nothing to Luap—Xhim and Pitzhla and Teth—nor could Seri offer any hint of a translation. He asked again about the eastern trade: water was too scarce on the western end of the former route, the ambassador said, and profits too chancy. His shrewd amber eyes seemed to ask. *What are you planning?*

In one moment of vision, Luap saw exactly what he would do. Here he had water, and safe shelter. That upper valley the Rosemage had thought of as horse pasture, with its opening to the high plateau above the plain: that would be the place for caravans to come. They would have to build a trail up from the desert below, and another into the western canyons and out to the town, but with magery they could do it easily in a few hands of days. Someone—Seri, he thought, or the Rosemage—would have to find a good trail from the base of their cliffs to the old caravan route south of them.

And then the caravans would come, bringing horses, cattle,

craftsmen, harpers, goods to trade and a market for the Khartazh's spices and silks. Luap could imagine the whole stronghold full of busy, talented workers all enriched by the flow of commerce. He drew a long, happy breath. If only the Rosemage and Arranha would come back with good news of ores . . .

Instead, they returned too soon, for Arranha had collapsed on the journey, and the Rosemage had struggled to bring him to the stronghold alive.

"We had just reached the gray mountain's foot when he clutched his chest and fell," she said to Luap. Aris was busy with Arranha, whose shallow breaths hardly moved the covering upon him. "I knew the climb out of the canyon had been hard on him; he said he found it hard to breathe that night, and didn't sleep well. But I thought he was better, or I'd have turned back."

She seemed to want reassurance; Luap nodded. "Of course you would; you couldn't know."

"He's so old. I didn't realize; he's always been so active, so lively of mind. And now—"

And now he was dying. From Aris's expression, no healing would serve. Luap felt his own throat closing. "I should have let him go with you, and made Aris and Seri wait," he said; he knew that had had nothing to do with it, but it was all he could think of. Now the Rosemage put her arm around him.

"You know that made no difference. Neither of us . . ." She stopped, blew her nose and wiped her eyes, then went on. "Neither of us can stop age when it comes; not even royal magery is proof against time."

Luap felt something shift inside him—not quite protest, but uncertainty. Curiosity. Was that really true? Had anyone ever tried to hold back age with magery? With the *royal* magery? It might not work with the very old, like Arranha (though how had Arranha stayed so vigorous so long?) but perhaps it would work with someone much younger, still strong.

But the immediate problem swept that from his mind. The Rosemage needed care as well as Arranha; she had the hollow-eyed look he remembered seeing in survivors of daylong battles. Luap called for Garin, and someone to help the Rosemage to her chamber; when she protested, he overrode her. "We all love Arranha; Aris is with him, and I will be with him. But I don't want to lose both of you. Bathe, rest, eat—let Garin ease what he can. You'll be needed later."

"But—someone said the ambassador had come early, had been

here—" She was trying to keep herself awake, upright, and focused; she would not let herself escape duty for comfort, even now. Luap put his hand on her arm, and let a little of his power seep into it, and into his voice.

"It went well; everything's going to be fine. Go and rest. I will tell you all about it when you wake." In the influence of his power, she staggered a little, and Seri moved quickly to support her and lead her away. "Take care of her," Luap said to Seri; unnecessary, since Seri would never do less, but it let others know he considered Seri in change.

Arranha sank quietly, without a word or change in his expression, all through that night. Before dawn, the Rosemage was back at his side; Luap was glad she had come while he was there. "What did Aris say?" she asked softly.

"That he was dying, that it was from old age, and that he could do nothing. I'm not sure that's true, because Arranha seems so calm—perhaps Aris eased him some way when you arrived. . . ."

"He had been calm since the first day. Then, he seemed anxious. He said things—but I wasn't sure he was aware of them."

"Said what?"

She shrugged, and hugged her robe around her more tightly. "I—I don't know if he meant it. Something about danger, about a darkness in the stone. But since he was dying, it could be that alone."

"Mmm." Luap thought about it. "When I climbed to the top of this mountain, I remember feeling that the light failed—but I thought it was being breathless from the climb."

"Yes, I thought of that. Especially coming back with him, places I had to carry him—my sight went dark more than once. That's why I didn't tell everyone at once and give warning. Even Arranha, who so served the light, might lose it at death for a time. Yet if it was a true warning, what was it about?"

"That mountain, perhaps? The gray one? Perhaps it has the gold you hoped for, but it's claimed by some rockfolk tribe; that would be danger, if we meddled with it."

"I suppose." She did not sound convinced, but neither was he. Most likely, Arranha's approaching death had shadowed his mind, and his words meant nothing to those who were not dying. She stirred beside him. "So—tell me about the ambassador."

He felt strange, sitting beside a dying man and talking of his own triumph—as he could not but see it—but it would pass the time. He kept his voice low, and began with the ambassador's arrival, putting in all the details he could think of. The Rosemage listened attentively, clearly glad to have something to fix her mind besides Arranha. When he described the ambassador's attempt to use the sword on himself, she gasped.

"And *you* caught the sword! What happened?"

Luap held out his hand. "I nearly lost fingers—you can't see a scar at all, for Aris healed it at once, but from here to here—" He pointed, then allowed himself a wry grin. "It hurt a lot more than I would have thought." Before she could ask more, he went on, explaining what the ambassador had thought, and what he himself had inferred from both the man's actions and his gifts. "A powerful ancient kingdom," he said. "More than a kingdom—more like the tales we had of Old Aare. They trade widely; I think they used to trade with Fintha in years past, perhaps before I was born. Powerful allies, if we are their friends, and dangerous enemies."

She looked worried. "I expect they will see us as easy prey."

"No." His power bled into that, and she looked at him with dawning respect. "They fear us now; they will do us no harm. Wait until his next visit; you will see."

She recovered her composure with an effort. "You are confident, suddenly." The warning not to be overconfident came across clearly.

He shook his head. "I saw the man; I dealt with him. Aris's healing power alone might have convinced them, or his use of the pattern to open the mageroad—surely you and Arranha realized that."

"I suppose . . ." Her voice weakened; Luap felt a rush of sympathy.

"You're still tired; let me fetch something to eat."

"No—I'm all right. I suppose—Arranha and I both felt they were hiding something—the ones we met in that town. Perhaps they were trying not to show their fear of the magery."

"That sounds reasonable. The ambassador seemed frightened even before we began, and if they have no magery of their own— if they cannot believe mortals have it—"

"You can't pretend we're elven!" She stared him in the face, shocked.

"Of course not!" Luap put a bite in his voice and she reddened. "We're mortals, not elves, and I could not pretend otherwise. What I was going to say—" He looked at her, and she looked away, still flushed. "Was that if they have no experience of mortals using magery, they may give us more respect for that reason. I went out of my way to say we were *not* those who had built the stronghold.

Still, if they are in awe of magery, our few numbers will not be a temptation to them."

"Yes. I can see that." A long breath. "Now that they know we're here, whatever we can in honor do to convince them we're too strong to attack—"

"Exactly," said Luap. "If we must balance magery against numbers to avoid confrontation—"

"But we could not fight them," the Rosemage said.

"Of course not." Luap nodded. "The point is to avoid that— avoid it ever becoming an issue. They seem to think that because we are here, where their legends place demons or monsters, that we must have greater powers than we showed. Of course we must not masquerade as elves, or claim their allegiance. Not only would that be dishonest, it would place us at greater risk. But they found Aris's healing power, and the mageroad, impressive enough. If they think of us as a small but powerful folk, who want only peace and trade, they will have no reason to test our strength."

"I see," the Rosemage said. She looked again at Arranha. Luap thought his death very near; he remembered that slow cessation, breath by breath, from Dorhaniya. "Do you think we should call Aris?"

"Both of them," Luap said. "They will want to be here." He rose and went to the door, where a boy dozed against the corridor wall, and sent the lad for Aris and Seri. Soon they came, sleepy-eyed and solemn. Aris nodded after he looked at Arranha.

"Yes—very soon. I could not heal him—" His shoulders sagged. Luap patted him as he would have a child.

"It's not your fault, Aris; no one heals age." The words felt familiar in his mouth, and he remembered that the Rosemage had said that first, many hours ago.

"I know, but we have no other priest. Who will perform the rites for him, and for the Sunlord?"

"I suppose I will," Luap said slowly. "What he taught me, at least; I am not trained as a priest of Esea."

"He was the last—" the Rosemage said, and then she was crying, her shoulders shaking. It echoed in Luap's mind: the last. The last priest of Esea, the last of his father's generation, the last link to the old world where his kind had ruled. With Arranha would die the knowledge that had comforted Dorhaniya—no one else was likely to know the rituals for making altar linens, or care. With Arranha would die memories of Gird shared by no one else—for neither Gird nor Arranha had told him all of the time they journeyed together to the gnomish lands. With Arranha would die quarrels among priests, theological disputes, conflicts of power, even such unimportant things as the questions he had asked Dor-haniya's sister, that drove her to anger. Arranha had connected him to his own past, had known the boy he had been, had known his father, had known men whose grandfathers came over the southern mountains from Aarenis, had been one of an unbroken priesthood stretching back to Old Aare.

Luap felt acutely aware of that loss. Gird's death had ended what he might learn from Gird, but there were still many peasants living in vills much like his, plowing fields, making tools, tending sheep and cattle. Arranha—what had been Arranha's vision, that died here with him? What had he thought, as a young man, would shape his life? What had really shaped it?

He stared at Arranha's quiet face, already as remote as a stone carving, and wished he could shake it to life and speech again. Now he knew the questions he should have asked—now, when it was too late. Now he knew what he did not know—would never know. Elders died, he thought. Elders died, and with them their personal visions died. If Gird had died at Greenfields, as he had said he should have, Gird's vision would have died there too. It had lived on because Gird lived on, and when he died it began to fray. . . .

Luap shied away from that thought, forced his mind from the thought that different people—himself included—had striven to engrave their own visions on what was left of Gird's. Instead, he thought of himself as an old man for the first time. He would be old soon, the elder on whom the others depended, as he had depended on Arranha. Here, in this stronghold and the land around it, lay his vision. When he died, what would happen to the strong-hold? To his people?

I did not seek command, he cried in his heart. *It is not my fault that it was thrust on me.* In that familiar echoing space, a comfort-able warmth rose. He might have come to it by accident, against advice, but he had nonetheless done well. His people prospered, and praised him. Perhaps he had not been fit for command in Gird's day—he would admit that—but now? Who else could have done what he had done? He hugged that to him, comfort for his genuine grief, as they carried Arranha's slight body to its resting place on the mountaintop, where the first sun each day could find it.

He must not die until it was safe, he thought on the way back down. He must shape it now, while he could, with all his strength, and be sure he did not die too soon. He felt the weight

of responsibility settle onto him ... his people had no one else
to depend on, now.

He spoke of this concern to no one. He might have discussed it
with Arranha, in the old days, but Arranha was dead; in the days
after the funeral rites, Luap found himself worrying the problem
of his own mortality whenever the pace of work allowed. He was
not afraid of death itself—he had proven that, he thought, in the
old days, on the battlefields of Gird's war—but he wanted to
accomplish something before he died. Gird would have approved,
he thought. Gird, too, had dreamed of establishing a people in
peace and prosperity—and that was all Luap wanted.

Always and ever, in the depths of his mind, the question tickled
him: was it really not possible to hold back aging with magery?
Could he not at least *try*? It couldn't hurt, surely ... not if he took
care. Even the appearance of youth or agelessness might help
impress the Khartazh, and the Rosemage had agreed that anything
harmless which had that effect was good.

*"And how is the prince, after the death of his priest?" the black-
cloaked leader asked his spy.*

*"He has recently thought of trying his magery—his 'royal'
magery, as he calls it—against aging," the spy said. "They have
told him it will not work, but he is not convinced. And now, of
course, he worries more than ever about the fate of his people if
he should age too soon."*

*"I believe he will find his magery strong enough for that," the
leader said "He deserves a long and healthy life." The black-cloaked
assembly laughed, their voices harsh as jangling iron.*

A few days after Arranha's funeral, Luap called Seri and Aris
into his office to look at the maps the ambassador had left him.
Seri's eyes lit up.

"Imagine the effect of these in Marshals' training," Luap said.

"Do they have any of the old caravan route?" she asked.

"You remember I asked the ambassador that, and he said he
would find out. But I have another idea. If we could find a practica-
ble route from the upper valley down to the plain, it might be
shorter and safer for caravans to come through there—and then
through our canyon to Dirgizh. Then we would have someone to
trade with, and a way for those who won't use the mageroad to
visit."

Seri frowned. "Do we need that? It's a long way for anyone to
come, and I doubt Girdsmen would ..."

"I think they will," Luap said. "That trade used to prosper; as Fintha recovers from the war, Finthans will have more to trade. You know yourself the spice merchants do well. We could be trading now, if the Marshal-General weren't so opposed to frequent use of the mageroad . . . imagine how easily we could sell the gifts the ambassador brought. An overland route should be acceptable to the Marshal-General."

"He's right, Seri," Aris said. "He's not opposed to trade; he's encouraged the trade south into Aarenis—" Luap had not known that; he wondered how Aris knew.

"And you want us to find a way through these canyons to the old eastern route?" Seri said.

"Yes . . . and I don't know whether you should begin by finding it from outside—from Dirgizh—or from the upper valley. But you're our most experienced explorers so far."

"We'll have to start now if we're to be done by winter," Aris pointed out.

"I hadn't thought you'd start this season," Luap said. "Until we have others who can speak the Khartazh language as well, I can't spare you more than a few days at a time."

"Then we'll start there," Seri said. "Aris can teach his prentices, and I'll teach the militia—"

"And me," Luap said, smiling. "I should learn Khartazh."

"And you," she said. "But you learn faster than most."

Even so, Aris and Seri managed a short trip into the upper valley. Deciding just where to start the climb out of the main canyon was hard enough. Two approaches ended in sheer cliffs they could not climb. Finally Seri climbed partway up one of the north-running canyons across from what they thought should be the best way.

"We didn't use our heads," she said when she came back down.

"Again?" Aris grinned at the expression on her face.

"It's not funny," she said. "We don't have much time and we've wasted too much. What we need to do is follow that game trail—" She pointed. "It disappears over that knob—"

"Which is too far to the right; the valley has to be right up over that fallen block."

"And we can't climb it. Think, Aris: the animals go everywhere. We follow the game trail and keep choosing the ones that go higher."

The game trail angled sharply up the steep slope; Aris found himself grabbing for rocks and bushes to help himself climb. By the time they were above the trees, he could see far down the canyon, and back up the one Seri had come out of. Above him, Seri's boots went steadily on, occasionally giving him a faceful of dirt.

"This is a lot worse than the trail to the mountain top," he said, gasping, when they stopped for a rest.

"We have more to climb." Seri tipped her head back to look. "Gird's toes: look at that. We should be goats to get up there— and how could anyone bring a caravan down?"

Aris looked down and wished he hadn't . . . the broken rock and loose soil below looked unclimbable. "We have to find another way out: I don't want to break both legs going down this!"

On the next stretch, they came out on rock that looked, Seri said, like cake batter or custard that had stiffened in pouring. It did not look like honest rock, Aris thought, and wondered what had formed those loops and layers. At least it didn't shift underfoot, and the angle of the corrugated surface made climbing easier. The slope eased; they could walk upright again, between odd little columns of the strange stone. Here Aris agreed—they looked exactly like the last bit of batter from a pan, dripping crookedly to one side or the other.

The game trails disappeared into a grassy meadow thick with late wildflowers—tall blue spikes and low red stars. Bees hummed past them busily. On their right, still higher cliffs rose; they seemed to be crossing a terrace that might, Seri thought, come out above the valley they sought. They could see a similar cliff face to their left; between, they assumed, lay the tumble of broken rock they'd been unable to climb.

From the meadow they passed into a pine-woods of trees smaller than those on the canyon floor, and came at last to a clear view of the upper valley. On either side, sheer cliffs rose from a level floor of green. A ribbon of silver wavered down the valley: a creek. They hurried down the slope before them, so much gentler than the one they'd climbed.

"It's odd that the rocks don't look the same on either side," Aris said. On the west, the same rose-red solid stone, streaked dark with ages of weather, looked exactly like the stone found so far in the main canyon. But the eastern cliffs were subtly different—an oranger red, more mottled than streaked, conveying, he thought, some weakness in structure.

"I wouldn't make my home in that," Seri agreed, as usual, with the thought behind his words. "But that grass, and that stream— think of this for horses. It's perfect." She bounded down the last of the slope and ran out on the grass, only to fall on her face.

"Seri!" Aris ran after her, and tripped on the deep sand just as she had. She was up already, her expression rueful.

"Sand," she said. "It's not a terrace like ours at all." Aris, face down on the sand, eyed the patch of green before him.

"And that's not real grass, either. Sedge."

"Oh, well, it's got water." Seri strode off toward the creek, and he followed her. When he caught up, she was laughing. "Water, I said! Look at this—it's hardly a knuckle deep."

"Soaking the sand," Aris said. He looked all around, at the sheer walls, the almost-level floor of sand, the glisten of water that had looked like a real stream. "A very strange valley indeed."

It was, he thought later, as they examined it in more detail, like a flattened miniature of the main canyon. Its sand floor was not as level as it had looked from above; it had miniature grassy terraces, small dunes of open sand, little sedgy bogs near quicksand, even a small cluster of trees whose triangular leaves sounded like gentle rain in the breeze. They spent the afternoon working their way up the valley; the stream deepened upstream, against their experience, and acquired a gravelly bed. To the east, a tributary valley opened, but they could see it was blocked at the upper end by a sheer cliff. The way out to the south lay, if anywhere, up a ravine garish with orange stone and odd black boulders. They pushed themselves into that climb, unwilling to spend the night in the valley, though neither could say why.

They looked back once, from a terrace about halfway up the ravine, to see the valley looking once more like a level swathe of grass. Just above the ravine, they found a sloping pine wood ... and more sand.

"It's softer than rocks to sleep on," Aris offered, when Seri's lip curled.

"And harder than rocks to walk on, and we do more walking than sleeping. It will take us longer to go where we need to go," she said. But they made a pleasant camp that night anyway, enjoying the knowledge that no one—no one at all—knew exactly where they were. Their small fire crackled and spat with the fat pine-cones and resinous boughs; the water they'd brought up from the valley tasted sweet with their supper of hard bread and cheese.

"Two of the most dangerous, alone, in our valley: we should take them."

"No. One is the healer. We need him, for the prince's downfall."

"Then the woman—"

"We cannot take one without the other, not without giving

warning. Patience, trust the prince's weakness, and wait. Vengeance long-delayed is all the sweeter."

"The woman is dangerous, I tell you," the complainer said. "There's an uncanny stink about her, something like the old priest had. She doesn't like the valley; she senses something—and that against our strongest protections."

"Then we will have the prince distract her," the leader said. "She will do us no harm if she's busy somewhere else—or worried about something apart from our kind of danger. She is Girdish; such mortals concentrate their minds on practical matters, and dislike magery. If she senses something, let her think it is only that of other mortals, no more."

The next day Aris led the way out of the pine grove onto an open upland; to their left, a curious conical hill of rough black rock looked like nothing either of them had ever seen. Far to the west, they could see the mountains beyond Dirgizh. Ahead, they knew, was the drop from their block of mountains—but which was the best way?

Seri pointed to the black peak. "If we climbed that we could see more."

Aris shrugged. "It's higher ground that way We might find rock instead of this sand." For the lower ground had small dunes of windblown sand, difficult to walk on.

They found the gentle slope toward the black hill much easier than the day before. Soon they were walking on rock again, rippled and curved like mudbanks in a stream. More and more of the land around them came into view. Looking back toward the upper valley and the main canyon, they could see only a jumble of red rock, cut with sharp blue shadows. The mountaintop above the stronghold stood out clearly, but not the canyons between. Southward, they began to see a lower plain beyond the mountains . . . and the high white cliffs of another mountain range to the east. Finally, as they walked among the jumbled black boulders of the black hill's base, they could see an edge.

Seri cocked her head at the black hill now close above them. It looked as if it were made of a pile of loose black rocks, some room-sized and most smaller. "Do you think we can climb that, or will it be like climbing gravel?"

Aris looked south, at a distant blue shadow he thought might be more mountains very, far away. "Do we need to, now? I think we can find our way to the edge of this without it. I wonder how far that cloud or mountain is. . . ."

Seri looked. "More than a day's travel. In this air, more than two." She scrambled up the steepening slope of the black hill, dislodging a shower of rough black rocks, and slid down again. "Not worth it, you're right. I wonder what the dwarves would call this kind of rock." She picked one up, and hit another, experimentally. The one in her hand broke, and she yelped. "It makes sharp edges," she said, holding out her gashed hand.

"And you want me to heal it for you," Aris said, shaking his head. "Will you ever learn to wear gloves?" He laid his hand over the gash and let his power heal it.

"Peasants don't wear gloves," Seri said scowling, but her eyes twinkled. She shook her hand, looked at the rock, and shrugged. "Come on—we'd better get this done today. I've got to work on those junior yeomen—or whatever we decide to call them—when we get back."

They came to the edge before midday, an edge even more impressive than the drop from the mountaintop into the western canyons. Swallows rode the updraft, the wind whistling faintly in their wings, and veered away as the two came to the edge and looked out. Aris thought he had never seen anything so beautiful; a vast gulf opened before them, with nothing to bind the sight until the line where earth met sky. He knelt to peer over the edge, cautiously. A sheer drop he could not estimate, then spiked towers, then steep slopes and finally rubble flattening gradually to the glitter of a fast-moving river. He looked along the river's path, and saw that it disappeared into sand some distance downstream. Upstream—the breath caught in his throat. Upstream he could see what this cliff must look like—its match on the far side of the river rose from the sand, all shades of red, rose, and purple, and looking eastward he saw those walls converge. But above the red rock— where only blue sky arched in their canyons—were higher cliffs of gleaming white.

He looked at Seri, whose face he thought mirrored his own astonishment. "It's—beyond words," she said. "I can't imagine why the dwarves don't live here—why it's not full of the rockfolk."

He started to say perhaps they didn't know, then remembered the dwarven symbol in the stronghold's great hall. Of course they knew. And had they abandoned this—this vast beauty of stone so strong that it sang even to mortals? "Perhaps they loved it too well to tunnel into it," he said. "As the horsefolk leave some herds free-running."

"Perhaps." Seri stared awhile longer, then shook her head sharply. "Well. We're not going to build a trail straight down *this*.

We'd better look for a place where we can. Maybe where the water comes down. . . ."

They worked their way east, staying close to the edge and looking over at intervals. This canyon narrowed rapidly at the bottom, while the upper levels were still far apart, and soon Aris spotted a sheer cliff with a waterfall. "That won't work," he said. "Even if it's passable from above, imagine that in a storm—it would wash out any trail we built."

They headed south and west again, crossing their own tracks, and found a place where a dry wash wrinkled the surface, deepening rapidly toward the edge. "It will be another cliff," Seri predicted. But when they looked, some flaw in the rock had formed a great fissure. Broken chunks the size of buildings stepped down toward the desert below. Aris looked at it doubtfully.

"I supposed we could try—go down as far as we could—"

Seri snorted. "We shouldn't be stupid twice in one year. We've already gotten into trouble—or what could have been trouble—when we used that robbers' trail without thinking about it. We're supposed to be Marshals—now think. If we go down, and can't get back up—"

"I could use the mageroad," Aris said, for the sake of argument. He enjoyed feeling more daring than Seri, rare as the chance was.

"If you slipped and cracked your head," she said, "I couldn't use it, and couldn't heal you. No—let's find some way to recognize this from below, and then figure out how to go around."

"From Dirgizh?"

"Right. From the old caravan route they spoke of. Now let's see. . . ." She lay flat, her head over the edge of the cliff, and looked toward the fissure, then the stream below. "It would be nice to have a grove of trees—"

"No trees." Aris said. He sat, his legs dangling over enough space to stack five cities cellar to tower, and looked over at the facing cliffs. Their fissure seemed to line up with a skinny spire of rock, much thinner than the Thumb, on that side. He pointed it out to Seri; her eyes narrowed.

"Yes . . . but from down there the line will be different. Let's see . . . we can see the stream, so if you stood on this side of it—"

"We should be mapping this," Aris said suddenly, wondering why they hadn't thought of that. Before she could remind him that they had brought nothing to map with, he said, "I know—we can't. But if we draw it on the stone several times, we should be able to remember it." He rolled back from the edge, and broke some brittle sticks from one of the stiff, spiny bushes that dotted the upper plateau. They drew what they saw, until both agreed on the proportions and shapes, and could reproduce it anew.

By then it was late afternoon; they would have trouble making it back to the pine wood by dark, let alone back to the stronghold. "No one can see us use the mageroad here," Aris said. "Let's do it." Seri nodded, and he found a sand-covered stretch, back from the edge, and graved the pattern carefully with his stick. The late-afternoon wind howled up the cliff, blowing sand into the pattern even as he drew it; he had to rework the pattern with deeper grooves, and then decided to mark it out with pebbles instead. Seri wandered about at a little distance, looking alternately at the great space below and beyond, and at the curious black hill behind them.

Suddenly she stiffened, and said, "Aris!" He looked over, to see her staring back at the confusing jumble of rock near the upper end of the little valley.

"What?"

"Something moved." She backed toward him.

"Look out!" he said sharply; she had nearly stepped on the end of the pattern he had completed with pebbles. She looked down, moved aside.

"Sorry," she said. Her dagger was out, he noticed with some astonishment. "Aris, something's over there—"

"Too far to bother us, if you let me finish the pattern and get us on the mageroad."

"I don't like it," Seri said. Aris placed the last three pebbles, stood, and took her hand.

"Then we'll leave. Come on, Seri, it would be stupid to wait here for whatever it is; it's getting late, the sun will be in our eyes—"

"Oh, well." She relaxed suddenly, and stepped carefully where he pointed. "It's probably only one of those wildcats—"

And they were back in the great hall, where their arrival brought bustle and excitement, and a summons from Luap to tell him what they had found.

"So this is what we think, sir," Aris said, summarizing their long report. "We need to approach from the lower end, both to locate the old caravan route east, and to find out if that water we saw is good. Then we'll need to consult with the best stone-carvers—you know I can't do that—and it will take at least a season of work to cut a passable trail for pack animals, and make sure it doesn't fall. If we can go now to the Khartazh, and find out about the caravan, perhaps next summer—after the fieldwork's done—work could start on the trail down. And the trail from here to the upper valley, and the trail out to Dirgizh, which really should come first."

"But what about the distance overland to Fintha?" Luap asked. "Won't you need to go all the way to Fintha to be sure that's where it comes out?"

"We'll go to Fintha, surely," Aris said. "But we think the horse nomads will tell us about the eastern end of the trail—and the merchants in Dirgizh and the next town south may well know about this end. Convincing someone to try it may be difficult . . . but I've noticed the merchants show an interest in renewing that old trade."

"With your permission," Seri put in, "we'd like to start by going to Dirgizh, as soon as possible, and follow the old caravan route east—then turn north and see if we can find our notch."

"How long do you think that will take?" asked the Rosemage.

"Hands of days," Seri said. "We don't know until we've gone. But it must be done sometime—"

"And then we'd go to Fintha," Aris said. "Take our horses, and go visit the horse nomads . . . they liked us well enough before."

"What you're telling me," Luap said, "is that it will be more than a year before we have a way for a caravan to come here—let alone before one actually comes. Two years, more like, or even three. . . ."

The Rosemage shrugged. "When we started, remember, we didn't know if anyone would ever discover an overland route; I think even three years sounds remarkably quick."

"The question," Aris said, "is whether this is worth all the effort. People will have to work on the trails instead of other things—"

"It's worth it," Luap and the Rosemage said together. Then she fell silent and Luap went on. "No land survives long without trade," he said. "Especially one so limited in resources as this. If our people are to have a permanent place—for those who can't, or don't want to, return—then we must have trade."

"And overland trade," the Rosemage said, "will disturb the Finthans less than continued heavy use of the mageroad."

"I wonder if Raheli would come?" Seri said suddenly. "I would like to see her again." Aris noticed that Luap had stiffened, but before he could ask why, Luap relaxed.

"I doubt she'll leave her grange for us," he said. "But of course she would be welcome."

Chapter Twenty-eight

Luap had made the decision to meet that first caravan at the upper end of the trail from the desert. All along the way, his people had planted bannerstaves; today the narrow pennants snapped loudly in a freshening wind. Blue and white, Gird's color and Esea's, alternated. He himself wore the long white gown they had found so practical in the dry heat of summer, and over it a tabard of Girdish blue. He had an uneasy feeling about that, but surely they need not ape the fashion of Girdish peasants, not out here. No one wore those clothes any more; he had put on that worn pair of gray homespun trousers and rediscovered how itchy his legs felt. So he had insisted on some garment of blue, for all of them, and most had chosen the simple tabard.

His scouts had reported the approaching caravan two days before. Last night's campfires had been at the base of the cliffs; soon they would be here. He was sweating, he realized, with more than heat. He wished he could see. Instead, he heard them first . . . the ring of shod hooves on stone, the echoing clamor of human voices, swearing at some unlucky mule. Then one of the youngsters waved to him, and he went to look over the edge. They were closer than he'd thought, toiling upward only a few switchbacks below, horses and men and mules all reduced to squirming odd shapes by the distance and brilliant sunlight.

One looked up at him, a face sunburnt to red leather, eyes squinted almost shut, unrecognizable. He had hoped for Cob, who had been, as much as any of them, a friend, but he had known how much Cob loved his own grange, how little he would look forward to a long journey into strangeness. The man's free arm waved, then he looked down again. Luap watched the slow advance. Seasons of waiting had passed faster than this; his throat felt dry, and he accepted the wineskin someone offered without really noticing it. The wine, cool and sweet, eased his throat, but the hot stone must, he thought, be crisping his toes. They would be even hotter, having climbed those sunbaked cliffs in the day's heat.

At last, the first of the caravan reached the top, two glasses or more after he'd expected them. Too late now to reach the

788

stronghold by dark; they would camp in the pine-wood just below. Luap walked forward to meet the first rider, and proffered the wineskin. The man's horse stood head down, sides heaving. He was still convinced he had never seen the man before when Cob's voice came out of that swollen, sunburnt face.

"By the Lady, Luap, you've chosen one impossible lair . . . no wonder you travel by magery!"

"Cob! I'm glad to see you!" And he was, even now, even when he half-wished the caravan had not come, that he could sever the ties with Fin Panir. Of all Gird's quarrelsome and difficult lieutenants, Cob had been the first to shrug and accept him, and the only one whose loyalty to Gird's luap had never wavered except at Gird's command.

"And I, you: you could have come out to the grange, your last visit." That loyalty had not blunted Cob's tongue, reminiscent of Gird's own. Now he looked Luap up and down, as Gird might have done. "Gone back to magelords' dress, out here? That'll do you no good with the Marshal-General, Luap."

Luap felt himself flush, and hoped Cob would take it for the heat. "Try it yourself, out here—it's better in this heat."

"Not me. I'll sweat more happily in my own clothes." Cob took a long pull at the wineskin and grinned. "Ahhh. No need to ask how your vines are doing. That's good, sweet as I like it. How much farther do we go today?"

Again, like Gird, that ability to switch quickly back to the practical. "The Hall's a half day or more from here, for such a large group. I thought we'd camp partway: there's a good spring, and pine-woods. We brought food, in case you were running low. We can be there well before sundown."

"Good." Cob's gaze ran ahead. "Follow the banners?"

"Yes. Shall we wait to start until all are up?"

"No need. As long as someone's here to point the way and give encouragement."

Cob led his horse slowly over the rippled stone; Luap walked beside him. At first they did not talk; Cob seemed glad enough to look around. Then he began to ask questions. Luap explained, as best he could, the interlocked system of canyons.

"We don't go into this one much; the upper end, that we call Whiterock Gorge, has good hunting now that we've hunted out most of our own, but as you know all too well, climbing back up from the big one with game would be difficult."

"That makes sense. How deep is your canyon, then?"

"Not as deep as this, but steep enough going in. We'll go through a tributary first, a curious place. A rockfall let sand drift in behind it; we're hoping to improve the soil and use it for farming later. It would make good pasture: the walls go straight up from level sand, like a great wall. If we closed off the upper ends, our horses would be safe there."

"No wolves? No wildcats?"

"Oh, we have both, but our hunters have thinned them. The wildcat here reminds me of the old tales of snowcats in the southern mountains—remember them? These are gray; you'd think they'd show up against the red rock, but they don't." The bannerstaves here led off into deep sand; Luap paused. "I'm sorry, but we've a stretch of sand here; the rock takes you to a dropoff no horse can manage."

Cob sighed. "When I get back to Fin Panir, I will never complain about hard ground or cold again. We had three days of sand at a time on the way, and I learned about it."

"It's not long—just to that grove of pines." Best not tell him now that half the next day's journey would be on deep sand.

Behind them, the line of sweaty, tired men and animals stretched out; Luap could hear the creaking of saddle leather, the grunts and wheezes of tired animals; men complaining; the pennants snapping in the wind. It seemed to take twice as long to reach the grove as he'd expected, but they were all under its shelter by sunfall.

Those he had left to prepare a meal had created a haven in the wood: a central fire, cushions and carpets laid out for tired men to lounge on, stew, roast meats, and even fresh bread scenting the air. Picket lines for horses and mules stretched back into the trees. By full dark, everyone had gathered around the fire to eat and talk. Overhead, stars glittered brightly in the clear air; Luap almost decided to set no sentries, to emphasize the safety in which his people lived, but changed his mind. Gird's followers had learned prudence the hard way; it would do him no good with them to seem careless.

He woke in the turn of night, to find Cob beside him, holding his arm.

"Luap—are you *sure* there's no one out here but your folk?" Cob's voice was so low Luap could hardly hear it.

Luap pushed himself up, and yawned. "Not out this way Why? Did the sentries call an alarm?"

Cob grunted. "Your sentries have become too used to safety: they're asleep. I woke up, went to the jacks, and went to speak to them—but found them curled up as comfortable as boys in a haymow.

Then I felt something—nothing I could define, a cold menace—like the look a thief gives in a dark alley."

At that moment a cold current of air coiled around Luap's shoulders and down his neck. He shivered, then recovered. "Cob— you've not been in mountains before. The night air's colder than you think, and at the turn of night it feels colder than steel. More than once when we first came, one of us thought something dire had passed, but we came to realize it was only the cold. The night may be still when the sun falls, but later on, these movements of air come, as if they were alive. But nothing more."

"Huh." Cob's head, in the starlight, looked frosted; Luap could not see his expression. "Well. If you're sure. But you might have a word with your sentries, just in case."

Luap groaned inwardly. Get out of his warm blankets to rouse sentries to watch for nothing? But nothing less would satisfy Cob, and after all, the sentries were supposed to be awake. He nodded, pushed the blankets aside, shivering again at the cold. "I'll stir them up. If nothing else, all these horses might draw a wildcat." Cob rolled himself back in his blankets, and Luap headed for the sentry posts.

Cold, clear air chilled his face, his hands; when he breathed, his chest felt bathed in ice. Even under the pines, starlight trickled through; beyond the trees, he could see a silvery glow over the silent land. A horse stamped, in the picket lines, and another was grinding its teeth steadily. Luap heard nothing he should not hear, and nearly fell over one sleeping sentry in the speckled shade.

He shook the man awake. "Wha—what's wrong?" It was Jeris, one of the youngest he had brought with him.

"You're supposed to be standing guard," Luap said. "Marshal Cob got up to use the jacks and found you all asleep."

"I—I'm sorry." In the dark, he couldn't see Jeris's face, but the voice sounded worried and contrite enough. "There was nothing— and it was so quiet—and . . . and cold, and . . ."

"I understand, Jeris, but with all these horses we must worry about wildcats or wolves. We haven't cleared this plateau, you know."

"Yes, my lord." The words came smoothly; in the dark, off guard, Luap suddenly realized how that would sound to Cob and the others.

"Don't say that," he said sharply. "They don't use that anymore. Just call me Luap, or sir, if you must."

"But my—but, sir, it's not respectful—"

"Respect includes doing what I ask, doesn't it? Don't use 'my lord' while our guests are here. It will upset them." And would Jeris remember? And remembering, would he obey? Or would he, in the spirit of youthful investigation, ask Cob why it would upset them? Luap shook his head and moved to the next post. Sure enough, all the sentries were asleep, and as he went from post to post, Luap himself began to feel a vague unease. Wouldn't *one* have stayed awake? Wouldn't one of them have wakened at the turn of night to use the jacks, as Cob had? For that matter, why were all the travelers sleeping so soundly?

But he could not hold that anxiety when he got back to the clearing; he wrapped himself again in his blankets, finding to his dismay that none of his body warmth remained, and was asleep before he realized it. He woke at the sound of the cooks working about the fire; half the travelers were out of their blankets already. For a moment or two, he lay quietly, trying to remember what had bothered him in the night, but he couldn't. It was a morning as clear as the day before, too beautiful for dark thoughts.

They started early, before the sun could strike heat from the rock. Down from the pines, into a narrow rocky defile. When they came around a knob to see the little tributary canyon below them, Cob drew rein. "So that's your future pastureland. You're right: it's perfect. There's even water."

"And quicksand," Luap said. "But we'll work that out. Be sure you follow the stakes."

Down the length of that little valley, so oddly shaped with its nearly level floor and its vertical walls. Then up again, into the morning sun, to climb around the rockfall, back into the shadow of the main canyon.

Luap led the way down that steep slope, uneasily aware that the signs of magic in use were all about them, plain to be seen if any of the visitors wanted to notice. Would they? Would they know what those smoothly carven walls meant? Would they realize that the natural canyon had not been blocked by natural falls of stone, filled with natural fertile terraces ready for planting? Cob knew, of course; he had explained it all to Cob. And the Council of Marshals knew, in theory—he had come out here to train the mageborn in the right use of their powers. But he knew they had no idea what that really meant, and the common yeomen in this group would never have seen magery used in all their lives. How would they react? In his mind's eye lay the image of this land as he and Gird had first seen it ... he could still hear Gird's dismissive "not farm land." Now each crop gave its own shade of green, its own texture, to the terraces; smooth green fans of grain, bordered by rougher, darker bushes yielding berries and nuts, a ruffle of greens and redroot vines. The fruit trees, just coming into bearing. . . .

"I thought Gird said this was no good for farming," said Cob, just behind him.

"We worked hard on it," said Luap.

"Mmm. You must have. You couldn't have taken this much soil, not through that little cave. Two sacks, is what I know you took."

"No, we didn't." He left that lying, and hoped Cob would do the same.

"Magery, I suppose," Cob said, and spat. "Well. It's what you came for, after all, isn't it? A place for the magefolk to do their magery without upsetting anyone?"

Even from Cob he had not expected that quick analysis and calm acceptance. Luap nodded. "Yes—although we had peace in mind more than magery to start with. And here it can't be used against anyone."

Cob peered up at the canyon walls. "No—unless enemies come upon you, which doesn't seem likely. The horsefolk don't come within hands of days of here, and who else could there be? Have you found any folk at all?"

"West of these mountains is flat land, with a caravan trail and a town—Dirgizh—that's a waystation for a folk called the Khartazh. They have a king somewhere north. They don't come into these mountains; they claim they're haunted by evil spirits."

Cob snorted. "Whatever you are, you're not evil spirits—unless they mean whoever was here before you and carved your original hall."

"I doubt it's either," Luap said. "Until we smoothed the trail, it was difficult for people, and impossible for horses. Robbers laired in the mountains just east of the trade trail and preyed on travellers; I think the king's men just didn't want to worry with 'em. It's easier to say mountains are haunted than to admit they're too rough for your taste."

"That's so. Like a junior yeoman I had in my grange back east, who was sure some mageborn had magicked his hauk. He could not believe he was really that clumsy and weak. It took me three years to convince him that he was his own curse. Speaking of that, how's young Aris?"

"Curse? Aris?"

"No, I'm sorry. He's his own blessing, I was thinking, unlike Tam back home. Are he and Seri still like vine and pole?"

Luap grinned. "Yes, but not married. You'd think they were still children."

"It may be best. Seri's not one to mother only her own children. What does she do?"

"She's our Marshal: insists on drill, cleaned those robbers out of the mountains between us and the trade route, set up guardposts—"

"Good for her." Cob's horse slid a little and he grunted. "You couldn't get out of here in a hurry, could you? Going up must be slower."

"That's one reason we'd like to keep some horses in that upper valley," Luap said. "Every time we take a party up and down this trail, we have to rebuild it. Foot traffic's not so hard on it; if we could climb up then ride out, that would help."

"The merchanters we travelled with kept going west and south; they say there's another trade route that way . . . and they've always wanted a shortcut. Do you think your—Khartazh, was it?—are on the other end of their road?"

"Oh yes. They talk about a time—probably before we were born—when caravans went east to Fintha every year. As near as I can tell, that trade declined after the fall of Old Aare, and stopped almost completely after the war started. If that trade resumes— and I hope it will—I would like to see caravans here; it would be a shortcut for them, and good for us. That's why we built the trail you climbed up, from the lower plain; I hoped to bring in caravans. But the trails are so rugged, maintaining them would be difficult."

Now they were off the last switchback of the trail, into the pines. He watched as Cob drew a deep breath. "Ah—this is better. Some shade for my face, a cool breeze." Here, two horses could go abreast; Luap reined in to let Cob come up beside him. "This is the last time I make this trip, mind. You can travel the mageroad with no more trouble than walking out of a room; I'm not blistering my old skin again just to see you."

"I'll take you back the mageroad, if you wish," Luap said.

"We'll see," said Cob, eyeing the green terraces, the flowering bushes, the berries, "Maybe I'll just stay here and live off your mercy."

Luap pointed. "Up there—that's one of the lookout posts Seri had us build." Cob squinted upward, blinking against brilliant light.

"Good to see out of, but cold in winter, I'd think. And if a wind blows—"

"No one's fallen off yet." Luap enjoyed Cob's awestruck look.

He liked knowing he'd surprised the man; he heard the murmurs from those behind with the same pleasure.

It was just on midday when Luap turned across the stream to the sunny side of the canyon; the walls seemed to shimmer in the light as if painted on silk. The little arched bridge, so delicate against the massive rock walls, rang to the horses' hooves. Cob stared at the narrow cleft of the side-canyon as if he could not believe it. "We're going in there?"

"Yes. It's not all a tumble of rocks; there's a trail." Again in single file, they rode up, into the cleft with its hidden pockets of old trees. The lower entrance stood open, as always in good weather. One of Seri's junior yeomen stood guard beside it, proudly aware of his good fortune.

"Go in and tell them the caravan's come safely," Luap said. "We'll need help with the horses."

"Yes, Luap," said the boy; Luap was glad for once that Seri's young trainees tended to scamp the courtesies. He slid off his horse, and took Cob's reins.

"Here—go on in and let Aris put a salve on your face if he can't heal it. I'll water your beast."

"I'm all right, here in the shade." Cob leaned against the rock, watching the others come up, and Luap handed the reins of both horses to one of his people who had come running out. That one did murmur "my lord" as he took the horses away; Luap hoped Cob hadn't heard it. Another appeared with a tray and tall cups of water slightly flavored with an aromatic fruit from Khartazh. Luap handed one to Cob, who was looking up at the great pines, around at the rock walls. "I wouldn't have believed it without seeing it, that's certain. And how you've managed to raise food in it—that's another wonder. Gird would have been proud of you, Luap." He sipped the drink, then smiled and emptied the cup. The servant took it and refilled it.

"I'm glad you think so." He wondered if Cob would still think that way when he'd seen how comfortable a life he and his people had achieved in so few years.

"Luap . . . I'm not here to check up on you." Cob's shrewd glance widened to a grin as Luap felt his face burning. "There— you see? You *did* think I would act as the Marshal-General's spy."

"Sorry," Luap muttered. So he had heard the servant's words.

"You should be! When have I ever agreed with him? No, if you and your folk are happy out here, and living comfortably and at peace, this is what I hoped to see. And if you transgress some one of the Marshal-General's many little rules, he won't find out from my report—not that he could do anything if he did. You're growing your own food; you're not taking anything from the granges any more."

"I see him when I report," Luap said. "I suppose I've come to think of you—of the others—as mostly like him."

"We're not. At least, not all of us. So settle down, will you, and quit looking so nervous. If you're playing prince out here, and all your people kiss your feet, it's your business. I won't, but if they want to, they can."

Luap forced a chuckle. If only he could believe that—but Cob, he knew, would not lie. Perhaps he did have a friend in this sun-burnt old peasant. "I confess, then, to allowing more deference than I would have in Fin Panir."

"Deference! Is that what you call it?"

Luap shrugged. "If you mean showing respect—"

"For rank and not for deeds. Yes. Although I suppose you have shown them deeds enough, out here, even if those deeds were magery." Cob nodded to the growing cluster of Girdish riders now dismounting and milling about the stronghold entrance. "We're making a tangle here—where would you have us go?"

"Which is greater, fatigue or curiosity?" Luap countered. "We have guest chambers, of course, and bathing chambers to wash off the trail grime. Or you can begin with food. Or you can let us drag you all over, showing off."

"I must admit food sounds good," Cob said. "I want to see that grand hall you told us about, but then food . . . and that lot had better start with something to eat." He beckoned to a younger man. "You may remember Vrelan, my yeoman-marshal."

"I do indeed," Luap said, smiling. Vrelan looked old for a yeoman-marshal now, and he wore the blue tunic of a Marshal.

Cob nodded. "Yes, he's Marshal Vrelan—just finished his training this last winter. We're finally training Marshals faster than establish-ing new granges, so we old ones can have replacements and the younger ones can get experience before taking on a whole grange. Considering my age and failing health—" by the tone of this voice, he was quoting someone he did not like, "—the Council decided that a younger Marshal should come along to report on your settle-ment. The Marshal-General would have sent Binis—"

Luap almost choked. Cob was grinning broadly.

"I thought that would get your attention. But I insisted on Vrelan, for his expertise in horsemanship and wilderness travel; Binis still rides like a sack of redroots." He cleared his throat and spat.

"Marshal Cob!" That was the Rosemage; Luap was surprised that it had taken her this long to appear. He had half expected her to meet them in the upper valley. She hugged Cob, then turned to Luap. "Seri says there's another gang of robbers holed up in those canyons somewhere; the Khartazh had a caravan attacked north of Dirgizh. We got the message yesterday. She's taken half the regular guards the long way around, and I'm about to leave to take the high trail and try to spot them from above. She wanted me to wait until you were back in the stronghold with your guards."

"Is Aris with her?"

"Yes, but Garin's here if anyone in Cob's group needs help."

"Then I suppose we'd better set the usual doubled guard, and let you go. Who's your second this time?"

"Liun, and he's up on top checking all the guardposts. He'll be down to report to you."

"Well, then." Luap shrugged at Cob. "I'd better get to work; come along if you like, and we'll get something to eat as we go past the kitchens." He felt almost pleased by the otherwise bad news. Cob would see how well Seri and the Rosemage had organized the militia; he would see busy, hardworking people, not idlers. The Rosemage turned away and strode rapidly up the passage. "Just let me tell Jens—" Quickly he gave his orders to one of the boys to provide food and a guide for Vrelan and the others. Then he headed for his own office, with Cob trailing.

It had become so natural to him that he hardly remembered his first feelings of awe and nervousness at being underground. Cob's wide eyes and quick breathing reminded him. "It doesn't bother you at all?" Cob asked, when Luap looked back, having just remembered Cob's lameness. He slowed, waiting for Cob to catch up, then forced himself to stroll as if he were not in a hurry.

"Not any more. It did at first, but we've been here now for several years and the walls don't cave in and the light never fails." He pointed out store-rooms, kitchens, the great water reservoir, as they passed them, and explained where the cross-corridors went. They came at last to the corridor behind the great hall, and the chamber where Luap had chosen to do his work. His scribe had heard him coming, and was looking out the door.

"Ah, Luap: did the Rosemage find you?"

"Yes—she's on her way. Where's the Khartazhi message?"

"Here, my lord." He handed over the woven pouch, like a miniature rug, in which such messages were carried. Luap opened it, and looked it over. The king begged his assistance in the capture or destruction of lawless robbers who had attacked two caravans in the past *thirg*—a thirg, Luap knew, was about six hands of days. The king's captain thought the robbers might number fifty—an unusually large band. The message finished with the flowery compliments he had come to expect in any communication from the Khartazh. "We could not send a formal answer, my lord, until your return . . . the messenger is waiting."

But Seri had already gone, as if she had the right to anticipate his commands. Luap wondered why some were born with the will to act, and others always awaited permission. "Then I'll dictate it now," he said. "Or—better—write it in my own hand. This is Marshal Cob, by the way, an old friend from Fintha. Why don't you fetch Garin, while I'm writing, and see if he has some salve for sunburn?"

"I can go," Cob said. "No need to bring anyone to me." Luap saw his gaze flick around the room, noticing the thick patterned carpets, the wall hangings, the stone ink-dishes, the racks of scrolls. He smiled at Luap. "I'm glad Vrelan will see this." Just enough emphasis on Vrelan to make his meaning clear to Luap . . . a visit from Binis would have been a disaster.

"I won't be long," Luap said. He pulled a clean scroll from the rack kept ready for him, and stirred the ink his scribe had been using. Cob nodded and withdrew; Luap hoped Garin could ease that sunburn—it almost made his own face hurt to look at it.

By the time Cob came back, he had finished that message to the king's captain, and seen his messenger on his way. He had also approved the revised watch-lists Liun submitted, and suggested to his personal staff that they minimize the formal courtesy for the duration of Cob's visit. The scribes flowed in and out of his office with reports, messages, requests; he dealt with them easily, as always, sensing around him the whole settlement in busy, organized activity. When Cob came in, Luap smiled at him and said "Now— you must come see what I found when I first came by the mageroad."

Cob's reaction to the great hall was as strong as Luap could have wished. He looked up and around. "This is . . . this is . . . it's all magery?"

"No—not now; it's real enough. It was done by magery, though, and not by ours. The Elder Races built it; they have never told us why, or why they abandoned it." No sense in repeating the vague warnings he had been given; if he didn't understand them, Cob certainly wouldn't.

"And those are the arches." Cob walked toward them, as Gird had, with perfect assurance that he could do so. Of course, he had not come by accidental magic. Cob looked up. "Harp, tree, anvil, hammer ... and the High Lord's circle. This is the one that appeared when Gird came?" Luap nodded. "I'd have been scared," Cob said.

"I was," Luap said. "Do you want to go up and see it from above?" He nodded at the spiral stair.

Cob shook his head. "Not today; my foot's climbed as far as it wants. Let's go find one of those kitchens full of food, eh?"

Luap smiled, and led him slowly back the way they had come. Cob seemed to notice everything. "Big as this place is, I'm surprised your people are moving out into the canyons: why do the work to dig out a separate dwelling?"

"Convenience, mostly. It may not look it, but the lower terraces are a half-day's walk down the canyon: it's easier to live beside the fields. And it's like the old palace at Fin Panir ... living in a small house is easier. To have privacy here, you have to spread out into all the levels, but when you've done that, you're a long way from the kitchens or the bathing rooms, or even a way out. Some things we have to do here, but families, in particular, seem to want their own dwelling."

"Ah. And do they make these dwellings the old way, or by magery?"

"By magery, for the most part. Most are small, one room deep and several wide, just in from the rockface. You saw the way this stone breaks, leaving wide arches? They build within that, using magery to help shape the broken stone into blocks and then lift them to form walls." He grinned at Cob. "They're very odd-looking houses, by eastern standards, but they're comfortable. Tomorrow or the next day I'll take you visiting."

By the next morning, all the travellers had rested and were eager to satisfy their curiosity. Some went out to the terraces in the main canyon to see how the mageborn farmed; some explored the passages of the stronghold itself, getting lost repeatedly. All climbed the spiral stairs at least once, to look out over the tangle of canyons and have the locals point out where they had been riding the day before.

"When will Seri and Aris be back?" Cob asked Luap at the midday meal. Luap shrugged.

"I don't know. It depends on which canyon the robbers are in. Look—" He put his hand down on the table. "This—my hand—is the mountain we're in—as if we were in the wrist. On the west end, six fingers stick out, with canyons between them—they could be in any one of those. That's why the Rosemage went up here—"

He pointed to his knuckles, "—to see if she could spot them from above and let Seri know."

"Why not have a permanent settlement there, and then you'd know?"

"It's the size: you don't realize how far away that is. And those canyons face west, picking up all the summer winds, very hot and dry: you can't farm in them." Luap reached for another slice of bread. "We're very few, you know, in a very large land."

"So you do this king's work for him, catching his robbers . . . ?"

"They'd prey on us if they could; some tried." Luap remembered those early encounters with an echo of the same fear he'd felt then: his people were so few, so vulnerable. "Once the Khartazh realized we were settlers, not brigands, it made sense for us to help keep those canyons clean of trouble."

"Ummm." Cob blew on his stew, as if it were still hot. "And what do you get from this agreement?"

That was, of course, the problem. "Not a great deal yet," Luap admitted. "But we can grow more food here than they can in the desert below the mountains. We take in fresh food to Dirgizh— the nearest town—for trade; they have superb weavers and smiths."

"Do they know you're mageborn?"

Luap pursed his lips. "They know we do some magery; I'm not at all sure they understand what 'mageborn' means to you and me. The king's ambassador, when he first came, saw Aris healing. They have legends, they say, of the builders of this stronghold, and at first thought we might be those beings, or their descendants. We haven't tried to conceal our powers, but neither have we tried to exaggerate them." Much. He thought Cob would probably not approve his strategy of subtly encouraging the Khartazh to think the powers they saw were the least of those actually held.

"They're a very formal society," he went on. "A very ancient, complex empire by their own account, and their craftsmanship and language support that. In our encounters with them, we have had to adopt a more formal, ornate style than is common in Fin Panir." He let himself chuckle. "I confess I rather like it—it's like a dance, making intricate patterns."

Cob looked at him. "I can see you would like that, but do the patterns mean anything?"

"All patterns hold power," Luap said. Cob's eyes widened; he realized he'd quoted a proverb learned from the king's ambassador. "The elves say that," he said, which was also true. "That's what they said when I asked how the mageroad works, why the magery alone wouldn't do, or why those without magery could not use the patterns. Patterns hold power, and those with power can both find, and use, the power in patterns."

"The patterns of language and manners as well?" Cob asked. "Are you saying that those with the most elaborate manners have the most power?"

"I—never quite thought of that," Luap said. He liked the idea; certainly it had been true in Fintha before the war. Would the peasants, who now had the power, develop more elaborate manners because they had it? Or did it work only the other direction? "I did think that the patterns show where the power is, in a way. The Khartazh, for instance: they have different ways to say something depending on the ranks of the people involved. That reveals the way their society is organized; if you know there are eight ways to say something, you know there are at least eight different ranks."

"Or eight different crafts," Cob said. "Each has its own special terms."

Luap wondered if he were missing the point on purpose, and decided not to pursue it. He wanted Cob to see how much they had accomplished, how well they were doing, not quibble over the interpretation of Khartazh social structure and language. "Would you like to see the farm terraces this afternoon, or would you rather visit one of the outlying homesteads?" Either one of those should provide plenty of innocuous conversation, he thought.

Cob frowned thoughtfully. "I'd like to see the farmland, I suppose. See what you've made of those two sacks of earth. But—is it all in the sun?"

"Not all of it. We'll take care of your sunburn." Luap asked the cooks for a loaf to take along, and led Cob down the side-canyon, back across the bridge, and into the shade of the pines.

"We can stay in the shade, here, while I explain what we did. In another glass, the sun will be off this terrace, and you can dig in it if you wish." He leaned against a tree-trunk and Cob leaned beside him. "Gird was right, in what he said: there was not a flat bit of earth in this canyon larger than my hand. But there was water—the stream—and Arranha knew how terraces worked. Now the little terraces you know—the ditches and dykes every farmer uses to keep wet fields drained and slow runoff on slopes—are the same idea, but we had to build bigger ones. The rocks came from the walls, by magery as I told you before. Then we had to shape and place them, some by magery and most by hand. That left us with a series of rock walls across the canyon—and notice all the terraces are fan-shaped, with curving walls."

"Because straight ends wouldn't stand flood?"

"Right. The canyon widens downstream—it doesn't look much like it, but it does—so the terraces reflect that shape. But what we had when I came to you for soil was a lot of broken rock heaped into the walls that now form the lower edge of each terrace. Look upstream there—" Luap pointed; Cob leaned out to see a curving, breast-high wall. "Downstream, the terraces are lower; the stream falls less rapidly. That wall is thicker than it looks—Arranha told us how far back to slope it so that it would hold. But that left us with spoon-shaped hollows to fill with soil. We had broken rock for the base, and plenty of sand—good drainage—but nothing with which to make good soil for grain and vegetables."

"So you brought two sacks of earth, about enough for two healthy redroot plants. . . ."

"And doubled it by magery. And doubled that. And doubled that. I know—" Luap held up his hands at the look on Cob's face. "I know, it seems impossible. It did to me. The only reason I rode off with two sacks was that Binis was with me, and I wanted to be free of her more than I distrusted Arranha's numbers. The short of it is that the mageborn used to have the power of doubling many things, but lost it—for misuse, of course. Some fool couldn't resist doubling gold and jewels, and another tried to increase crops. But earth was not under the ban: we could double a clod of dirt to two clods, and that two to four clods, and so on. Arranha said it would be enough, so we tried it. And it worked."

"But doesn't it take—I mean, I thought the larger the magery, the more power it took—the more it cost you."

"That's true. Supposedly the doubling should have been the same no matter what amount we doubled. But we couldn't think of it like that, so as the amounts grew larger, it was harder. What we had to do was double small amounts many times." Luap grinned as he remembered just how difficult and time-consuming that had been. He explained to Cob, who after awhile began to see the humor in magicians having to haul one sack of soil a few feet, double it, and haul it another few feet and do it again. "And when I think that I almost dumped it out loose—that would have been a real mess. If we'd had to move it shovelful by shovelful from one terrace to another—"

"How long did it take?"

"Longer than I planned for. We didn't make a full crop that year." He pointed. "We didn't finish upstream from that one, or go farther downstream than—the third, there, with the tall tree beside it."

"What about wood? I notice you haven't cut this area recently."

"We get most of our wood up on top—the very top of the mountain is heavily forested. Down here, we use the trees for shade—as you see—and as shelter for the herbs we need. Aris has found that some of the natives are also medicinal, but we have gardens of the same ones you'd find in Fintha."

"But as your population grows, will you have enough cropland?"

Luap shrugged. "If not we'll spread into neighboring canyons, as I said. This year we should have a good surplus. In another few years, the fruit trees should be bearing, too."

Cob nodded; if he was the friendliest of the Marshals, he was also the one Luap respected most, and most wished to have respect him. The rest of that visit went as Luap had hoped, although he and Cob were both disappointed that the Rosemage, Aris, and Seri did not return until the last day before the caravan must return.

"It was all very complicated," the Rosemage said. "They asked if we could give testimony at the trial, and then there was a message from the caravaners, sent north from Vikh, the next town south. Had you arrived safely, they wanted to know. The captain had to hear all about Cob and the new trail—he thought we would fly them in by magery, I think. Anyway, it all took much longer than we expected, or we'd have come back by the mageroad, if only for a day. We have messages from their king, by the way."

"And I have a letter for you, from Raheli," Cob said. He handed it to the Rosemage, who opened it and began reading.

"I wish I'd known," she said ruefully. "This needs an answer—I wish I could take time off and visit her—"

Luap, who had opened the king's message pouch, shook his head. "Not now, I'm afraid—he wants to send his heir to visit. We'll have a lot of work to do beforehand."

"One thing after another," the Rosemage said, shrugging. "Tell her I will come as soon as I can, Cob—and I *wish* we'd had more time."

But if they would return safely by the overland route, they must leave now. Cob would not take the mageroad and leave others to travel the hard way, and they all knew how the Marshal-General would react to the sudden eruption of horses, mules, and people into the High Lord's Hall. The Rosemage went with them to the edge of the mountains, and watched until they were safely down into the desert below.

"We'll be back," Cob bellowed cheerfully from halfway down. "Or someone will."

*   *   *

"They grow rich and fat," one of the blackcloaks grumbled. "Year after year, and for how long? Their horses foul our valley; their caravans clatter and gabble, loud as a village fair. Let us have a good feast now, and forget the rest."

"Are you truly one of us, or a half-mortal fool?" hissed the black-cloaked leader. "We have no reason to hurry: the fatter they grow, the greater the feast to come. The more folk who come, the more kingdoms or empires involved, the more chaos will follow their downfall. We shall topple not one princeling in a canyon, but all with whom he trades, if we bide our time and prepare. Will the eastern lands blame Khartazh? Will Khartazh believe it a plot of Xhim? Some mortals, at least, will think it a plot of the sinyi. Dasksinyi may turn against irsinyi . . . all is possible. In the meantime, we observe. We listen. We gather from their idle talk much we can pass to others."

"As long as the sinyi don't find us first," the grumbler said, undaunted. All hissed, a long malicious sibilance as chilling as wind over frozen grass.

"If the sinyi do find us," the leader said, "if the dasksinyi or irsinyi find us, it will be because some one of you was clumsy . . . some one of you was hasty . . . some one of you could not obey my commands and thought to outwit me. Then it would be better for that one to be brought before the forest lord, than before me." Silence followed; after a time he said, "Is that understood?"

"Yes, lord," came the response.

Chapter Twenty-nine

Years passed, peacefully enough. Each summer a caravan came, bringing news from the eastern lands that seemed increasingly irrelevant. Late each summer they left, taking with them the copies of the Code, of commentary and history, and taking also the memory of a high red land peopled with grave, courteous folk. As time went on, a few stayed, some of mageborn parentage and some not, but all intrigued by a way of life so different from their own. Craftsmen, finding a market for superlative skill; scholars; judicars intent on pursuing fine points of law; even a few Marshals, unhappy with changes in the Fellowship.

Some disliked the stronghold and its inhabitants intensely. They claimed to sense evil; they blamed the mageborn for using their powers. Their companions laughed—in the face of that peace, that prosperity, that hive of diligent workers who quarrelled so seldom and shared so readily, such suspicions reflected on those who voiced them. Perhaps the old magelords had been evil, but not that child charming a bird to sing on his finger. Not that woman whose magery lifted the bundles from the pack animals and set them gently in a row. The suspicious never returned—and some did not survive the trip home, having angered their companions with too many arguments.

For the first ten years or so, Aris and Seri travelled often, sometimes to Fin Panir, where their adventures furnished the substance of many a fireside tale and song. Their other adventures, in distant Xhim, on the vast steppes, no one knew but themselves and the gods. Luap worried, every time, that they might not return. Later, they spent most of their time—in the end all of it— in the stronghold, for despite Seri's warnings, the mageborn did not maintain active watchposts or keep up militia training unless she was there. They depended on the Khartazh to guard them on the west, and on the desert and mountains to protect them on the other sides.

By the time Cob died, Luap's position as a distant, powerful, but valued ally had become secure. His version of Gird's life, of the history of the war, spread copyist by copyist throughout the land. Power kept him young, something he concealed from each year's visitors as well as his own folk. He lived on, and the other witnesses to Gird's *Life* died, one by one, until he was the last who had fought in that army, who had known anything but the end of Gird's life.

The Council of Marshals even invited him back to be Marshal; his refusal won him support as a moderate, modest man, although the more violent said it proved his weakness. He noticed, in reports of the gossips, that Raheli's influence lasted beyond her own death. She was blamed for a militant and violent strain of Girdish rule that Luap was sure Gird would not have approved. He ignored the counter-arguments that she had compromised with Koris and his successor only to ensure that women retained their rights in the grange organization, that she herself, and her followers, had been moderate. Rahi's death left him free to write Gird's *Life* as it should have been—he would prove he was right, and she had been wrong. Aris and Seri still held Gird's original dream, and something in Aris's clear gaze kept Luap from openly admitting that he had no intention of reuniting the two peoples, not now or in the future.

The others were content to leave the eastern lands to their own affairs.

Luap's calendars of the western lands, meticulously kept though they were, interested Aris little. . . .

Aris climbed the last few steps to the eastern watchtower, aware that he no longer wanted to run up them. He didn't feel older, but he was, when he thought of it, acting older. He put down the sack of food and the waterskin without speaking to Seri; she was watching something in the eastern sky, and she would speak when she knew what it was.

In the changeable light of blowing clouds, the stone walls and towers seemed alive, shifting shape like demons of a dream. Clefts and hollows in the rocks gave them faces that leered and mocked the watchers, faces that smoothed into bland obscurity when the light steadied. Far below, he could hear the moaning of the great pines; up here, the wind whistled through the watchtower openings.

He felt on edge, his teeth ready to grip something and shake it, his hands curling into fists whenever he wasn't thinking about them. It was ridiculous. He was a grown man, the senior healer with students (none too promising) under him, too old for such feelings. He glanced at Seri, then stared. He rarely looked at her; he felt her presence always, so familiar that he did not need to see her. But now: when had gray touched that wild hair, and when had those lines appeared beside her eyes, her mouth? From vague unease, he fell into panic. Seri *aging*? Getting old?

As always, she reacted to his change of mood before he could move or speak. "Aris. What's wrong?" Her eyes were still the clear, mischievous eyes he had always known; her expression held the same affection. He shook his head.

"I—don't know. Something just—"

"I'm on edge too, and I don't think just from you." She turned to look out again, the same direction. "Maybe it's this weather; it's hard to see, hard to judge distance, even for landmarks I know. I keep thinking I see shadowy things flying in the upper canyons, something moving along the walls—but of course those are the cloudshadows, blowing all over." She sighed, rubbed her eyes, and sat down abruptly. "Whatever it is, if it's not nonsense, can't get here before we eat our dinner."

Aris unwrapped the kettle. "Kesil and Barha brought back a wild-cat and two stags; we have plenty of meat in this stew. And the bread is today's baking; Zil wanted you to have this fresh. He tried something new, he said. I'm to slice it from this end." Seri spooned

out two bowlfuls of stew, while Aris sliced the narrow loaf. "Ah . . .
I see . . . he filled it with jam."

"Before baking? Let me try." Seri took a slice and bit into it.
"Good—better than spreading it on after. And perfect with this
stew."

Aris leaned back against the stone wall, noticing how its chill
came through his shirt. Soon time to change to winter garb, he
thought. He munched thoughtfully, carefully not thinking about
how Seri looked, which was harder than it should have been. He
found he was thinking of how everyone looked; how old or young
everyone looked. Babies born the first few years had grown to
adulthood . . . men and women who had been much older now
looked it, white haired and wrinkled. Men and women his own
age—he did not pay that much attention to, outside of sickness,
and they were rarely sick. He frowned, trying to count the years
and *see* the progress of time on some familiar face. Luap? But
Luap had not aged at all. Had he?

Seri's warm shoulder butted against his. "You're worrying again.
Tell me."

He put down his bowl of stew, still nearly full, and saw that Seri
had finished hers. Her hands, wiping the bowl with a crust of bread,
were brown, weathered, the skin on the backs of them rougher
than he remembered. When he looked at her face, the threads of
gray in her hair were still there, *really* there. "You're older," he
blurted. Seri grinned, the same old mocking grin.

"Older? Of course I am, and so are you. Did you think this
magical place would hold us young forever?"

"But you—you never had children!" He had not thought of it
before, but now it seemed so obvious, with all the others having
children, with all the children growing up around them.

"Did you want children?" Seri asked, eyes wide.

"I never thought about it," Aris admitted. "Not until now. I just
wanted to heal people. . . ."

"That's what I thought," said Seri. She nudged him again. "You
had other things to do, and so did I."

"But—" He could not say more. He knew what "other things"
she had had to do; she had had him to look after, to care for when
he pushed his healing trance too far. And she had shared in the
same tasks as all the adults not busy with children: planting, harvesting, taking her turn at guard duty, drilling the younglings, working on whatever needed doing. She had many skills; she used all
of them.

"Aris." Her strong hands took his face and turned it toward hers.

"Aris, you are not like other men, and I am not like other women. We were never meant to be lovers and have a family like everyone else. We are *partners;* we are working on the same thing, and it's not a family."

"I suppose." A cold sorrow pierced him, from whence he could not say. Was he an adult? Could an adult have gone on, heedless of time, year after year, pursuing his own interests and ignoring the changes around him? Was that not a child's way?

"Think of Arranha," Seri went on. "He gave his life to his service of Esea. He could never have been a father. Think of the Marshal-General." He knew she meant Gird by that. "Did he marry and have another family? No. Or his daughter Raheli?"

Aris stirred uneasily. He had always wished Rahi would let him try to heal her, and had always been afraid to ask. Now it was too late; she had died without children, and he knew she had wanted them.

"Besides," Seri said, chuckling. "If everyone had children, as many as they could, with your healing powers, the world would be overrun with people. Would the elves like that, or the dwarves? And where would the horsefolk wander, if farmers moved out onto the grasslands? No, Ari: it's better as it is. You didn't think of fatherhood; I didn't care that much. If it makes you feel better, think that I took you as my child."

Aris felt his ears go hot; it did not make him feel better. He cleared his throat and said the first thing that came into his head. "But Luap hasn't aged."

The quality of Seri's silence made him look at her again. Eyes slitted almost shut, mouth tight, she stared past him into the wall. Then her eyes opened wide. "You're right. I hadn't thought. He's older than we are; we thought he looked old when we first saw him. And he *hasn't* changed. The Rosemage—"

"Some, not much." A few strands of white in her hair, a few more lines on her face . . . but that wasn't something he looked at, or thought about, much of the time.

"*He's* using magery." Seri's tone left no doubt which "he" she meant, or that she disapproved. "I didn't know he could do that. Will he be immortal, like the elves?"

"I . . . don't know." Aris had never considered that use of magery; he could not imagine its limitations or methods. "He must get the power somewhere—for something like that—"

"But you know I'm right," Seri said, her eyes snapping. "You know he's doing it—it's the only explanation."

"I suppose." Other possibilities flickered through his mind, to vanish as he realized they could not be true. Long lives bred long lives, yes: but not this long with no trace of aging. The royal magery itself? No, for the tales told of kings aging normally, concerned that their heirs were too young as they grew feeble. Could he be doing it without realizing it? Hardly. Aris knew Luap to be sensitive to subtleties in those around him; he must have noticed the changes, the graying hair and wrinkling skin, and known his own did not change. "I must talk to him," he said. "He must tell me what he's doing, and why."

"The *why* is clear enough," Seri said. "He doesn't want to die, that's all."

"I don't think so. I think it's more than that. You know he always has two plans nested in a third; for something like this he must have more than one reason."

"He won't thank you for noticing," Seri said, taking the last bite of her bread. "Not now."

Aris knew she was right, but felt less awe of Luap than he had for some years, now that he knew whence that unchanging calm had come. "I'll be back," he said, "to tell you what his reasons are."

"If he'll give them." She handed him the empty pot and cloth; Aris took them and fought the wind back to the entrance shaft.

Usually he met Luap several times in an afternoon, without looking for him, as they both moved about their tasks. Now he could not find him. Aris looked in his office—empty—and in the archives—also empty. He carried the pot back to the kitchen, where Luap sometimes stopped to chat with the cooks. They took the pot without interest; Luap was not there. They didn't know where he was . . . and why should they? they said, busily scraping redroots to boil. Aris looked in his own domain, where he found the others busily labelling pots of the salve they'd made that morning: the task he had given them. No Luap, and he had not stopped by while Aris was gone. Back down to the lower level, where the doorward at the lower entrance said yes, Luap had gone out some time before. He often took short, casual walks; he would be back soon, the doorward was sure.

Aris took the downward slope toward the main canyon without really thinking about it. Luap might have gone across to visit any of those who had hollowed out private homes in the fin of rock across from the entrance. He might have gone for a dip in the stream, though it was a cool day for that. But he walked most often out to the main canyon and across the arched bridge, so Aris took that route.

The main canyon, under the blowing clouds, looked as strange as it had from above. Aris paused on the arch of the bridge, and looked upstream and down. The wheat and oats had been harvested; the stubble in some terraces had already been dug under, while others looked like carding combs, all the teeth upright. Around the edges of the terraces, the redroots and onions made a green fringe against the yellow stubble. Down the canyon, he could see the tops of the cottonwoods turning yellow. Upcanyon, a few of the berry-bushes had turned dull crimson. For a moment he thought he saw a wolf slinking among them, but it was only a cloudshadow, that slid on up the canyon wall like a vast hand.

But no Luap. Aris walked on to the pine grove on the south side of the canyon, and found a child bringing goats back . . . the child had not seen Luap. He came back across the bridge, telling himself that he was being silly, that not seeing Luap for a few hours meant nothing. But his heart hammered; he could hear his own pulse in his ears.

"Aris—you're needed!" Garin waved at him as he went past the storeroom where the herbal remedies were kept.

"What?" His voice sounded cross to him; he saw by Garin's surprise that it sounded cross to others. "I'm sorry," he said. "What is it?"

"A child of Porchai's has fallen down the rocks—you know they've made that new place, the next canyon over—"

"I know it." And he'd told them to be careful, with three young children, all active climbers.

"A badly broken leg, the word is. The runner came in just after you were here before."

"I'll go," he said. "No, you stay—I'll take one of the prentices." He chose the one who had the sense to have a bag packed ready— Kevye, that was—and strode out. He would certainly find Luap when he got back.

The shortest route to the Porchai place lay through a tunnel cut through the fin that separated the two narrow canyons. Aris disliked the tunnel; he had argued against making it, despite the distance it saved those who lived on the far side. But convenience and speed mattered more to most people than his concerns about safety. The tunnel was cleared and lighted by magery; most of those who had need to go from one side-canyon to another used it. Aris rarely did, but could not justify leaving a patient in danger just to satisfy himself. He strode through quickly, hardly noticing the stripes of red and orange in the rocks on either side.

Irieste Porchai met him as he came out, crying so he could

hardly understand her. "You said be careful of the dropoff, and we were, I swear it. He was climbing up from the creek, and slipped—turned to look at something, I think."

"It's all right. He's awake? He can see?" But he could hear the child now, fretful whimpers interrupted with screams when anyone came near or tried to move him. He moved quickly to the sound, and found a small child lying twisted on the ground, the bones of his legs sticking out through bloody wounds. He knelt beside the boy, and put his hands on the dark hair. First he must be sure nothing worse had happened.

"Lie *still*," Iri Porchai said to the child. "It's the healer, Lord Aris." Even at the moment, he wished she had not used that title; he'd never 'iked it. But he'd never convinced the mageborn not to use it.

The child's head rested on his palms now . . . he let his fingers feel about through sweat-matted hair. A lump there, and a wince; a small bruise. He felt nothing worse, and his hands already burned with the power he would spend. He let the child's head down on a folded cloth someone had brought, and ran his hands lightly over the small body. The child looked pale, and was breathing rapidly: pain and fright, Aris thought. All the ribs intact, and no damage to the belly or flank. He looked more closely at the legs. Both were broken, and both breaks split the skin; on the left, one bone stuck out a thumbwidth; on the right, the child's flailing had drawn the bone ends back inside. With all that dirt on them, Aris thought. This would not be easy, even for magery. Aligning such badly broken bones, healing the ragged tissues . . . he would be here until after sunfall. He looked up at his prentice. "Kev—you'll have to steady his legs for me; we must be sure the bones are straight."

"Don't hurt me!" cried the boy, trying to thrash again.

"It won't hurt," Aris said, "if we get them straight in the first place." He wished he had Gurith's power of charming the pain away; this would hurt until the healing was well begun. "Come now—we'll be quick." He nodded to Kevre and to the adults who would help hold the boy still.

As Kevre moved the boy's legs to a more normal position, the broken ends of bone disappeared back into the wounds; he yelped but quieted quickly as slight tension kept the ends from wiggling. Aris laid his hands on the boy's thighs, and let the power take over.

His years of training and experience melded with that power so that now he knew what he had not known in his boyhood: he knew how the broken bones lay, how the thin strands of tendon and ligament had twisted, which of the little blood vessels had torn. He could direct his power more precisely, even into both legs at the same time, working down from the knee-joints, first aligning all the damaged bits of tissue, then forcing them to grow together, to heal as if they had not been broken. The bones were the easiest; they were easy to visualize, and being rigid were more easily controlled. Harder were the blood vessels and tendons, the torn muscles and ripped skin. Hardest of all were the innumerable bits of dirt, any speck of which could cause woundfever. Slowly, methodically, Aris directed the flow of power, concentrating on each minute adjustment. He knew by the boy's relaxation when the healing had progressed enough to ease the pain, but he was far from finished.

When the power left him, the child lay silent, watching him with bright brown eyes. Dark had come; magelight glowed around him from a dozen watching adults. Aris drew a long breath. He had not quite completed the healing before his power ran out; the bones and other tissues were aligned and firmly knit together, but he had not been able to replace all the lost blood. "Wiggle your toes," he said to the boy. A frightened look, that said *will it hurt?* as clearly as words, then both feet moved, and all ten toes wiggled. He looked at Irieste. "He'll need a lot of your good soup," he said. "As much liquid as he'll drink, and good meat to help replace his blood. I'm sorry; my power ended before I could replace that." He felt dizzy and sick, as usual, but he knew he would be all right. Kev helped him stand; his knees felt as if someone had hammered on them.

"Lord Aris, you need to eat something. . . ."

I need to sleep, he thought. But he could not fall asleep here; he must not worry the family. "We'll go back, Kevre." He leaned on Kev's arm more than he liked, and yet he could walk . . . how was it that he had used all his power, but had not fainted from it? his mind worried at the question, as if it had importance just out of reach. The family followed him into the tunnel, which he suddenly saw as an orifice in the body of some vast animal. Like walking into a blood vessel, or a heart . . . the prick of fear woke him enough to make walking easier. In that light, the red rock streaked with darker red and orange looked entirely too much like something's insides. He staggered, climbing down to the creek, and Kevre steadied him. In the stronghold, he wanted only a bed. Seri appeared, and started to ask a question, but her face changed.

"Ari! What happened?"

Kevre answered for him. "A healing, Marshal Seri; two broken legs. He's just tired. . . ."

"He's more than tired." Seri's arms around him renewed his strength; he could lift his head, now, and focus on the faces around him. She helped him to his own room, and pushed him onto his bed.

"I'm better," he said, smiling at her. She did not smile back; she was chewing her lip.

"You look half-dead," she said. "Kev says your power ran out before you finished the healing?"

Shame washed over him. "Yes. The boy will be all right; I finished the main part of it, but I couldn't do it all . . . it was just gone." Exhaustion clouded his vision; now that he was down, he could not imagine how he had stood and walked so far. "Sorry . . ." he murmured, and let himself slide into blackness.

When he woke, Seri sat curled in the corner of his room, wrapped in blankets. He tried to throw back his own covers, and she woke up and blinked at him. "So—you're alive after all."

"Of course I'm alive. You know I sleep after a difficult healing."

"I know that ten years ago you would not have called a child's broken legs a difficult healing."

Aris frowned, trying to remember. "I suppose . . . it's part of getting older. I don't have the strength I had."

Seri unwrapped herself and stood up. "I think it's something more. Remember what we were talking about yesterday?" He didn't; he felt that his head was full of wet cloth, heavy and impenetrable. "Luap," she said, leaning close to him. "Luap staying the same as the rest of us aged."

The conversation came back to him dimly, like something heard years before. "That can't be right," he said. He wanted to yawn; he wanted to go back to sleep.

"It is," she said "Come on—get up and eat." She pulled the blanket off him, and yanked on his arm. Aris stood, stiff and sore, and let himself be prodded down the passage, in and out of a bath, and into the kitchen.

"Breakfast's long past," said the cook on duty. "Where've you been?"

"He was healing last night," Seri said firmly. "He exhausted himself, and we let him sleep it out."

"Oh. Sorry." She spoke to Seri and not to Aris. "What does he need? Something hearty, or something bland?"

"He's hungry, not sick. Meat, if you have it."

"I've the backstrap off that stag; I was saving it for the prince." The cook looked at Seri again, and said, "But Lord Aris can have it; it'll give him strength." She pulled a slice from the deep bowl where it had been soaking in wine and spices. "There's soup, as well, in that kettle there—" She nodded at it. Seri filled two bowls, and brought them back to the table as the cook worked on the venison steak. She grabbed a half-loaf of bread from the stack on another table and tore it in two pieces.

"Here. Ari—get this into you." Aris sipped the hot soup, and felt its warmth begin to restore him. The fog before his eyes thinned; by the time the cook laid a sizzling steak in front of him, he was alert and hungry. He began to feel connected again. Seri said nothing, just watched him eat, and when he had finished the steak she handed him another hunk of bread. "Come on, now, we're going out."

"Out?"

"Yes." With a cheery thank-you to the cook, she led Aris out into the passage that led to the lower entrance.

"I should tell Garin where I am," Aris said. He had no idea how late it was, or if Seri had told his assistants and prentices where he would be.

"Not now," Seri said. Her grip on his arm might have been steel. He strode along beside her, more confused than worried. She slowed a little as they neared the entrance, and nodded casually to the guard she had insisted on posting there. She led Aris downstream toward the main canyon, but turned off the trail to a hollow between two trees. They had often sat there to talk in privacy; the stream's noisy burling in the rocks just below ensured that. Aris curled up in his usual place, with the tree-trunk behind him and a twisted root as an armrest; Seri stretched out, her head near his knees, her booted feet on a rock. "You went looking for Luap after we talked," she said. "Did you find him?"

"Not before they called me for the healing," he said. Suddenly tears filled his eyes. "I failed, Seri: I didn't have enough power. And who will follow when my power fails completely?"

"You did not fail," she said. "Something stole your power."

"What?"

"Listen. Yesterday, I felt something dire, remember? I've felt it before; I've never found anything I could point to. But when I started thinking about it, I realized that you've been having more trouble with your healings in the past few years—since we quit travelling, in fact. I looked up your records last night. Garin helped."

"You?" Seri's dislike of poring over archives had long been a joke between them.

"Yes. And since you insisted that I keep accurate notes of guard reports, I could put those together. I hadn't really noticed, but my comments about feeling an evil influence have been more and more frequent—and correlate with your most difficult healings. No—" She held up her hand as he opened his mouth to speak. "Wait and hear the rest. Think about it. Why haven't we noticed that Luap was not growing older? And how can he do that? You told me once that for the body, aging meant injuries unrepaired, illnesses not completely healed. You said that of course healing couldn't keep someone young—but what if it *could?* Suppose Luap gets his power from you—and that's why he's not aging, and you cannot heal as you did five years ago?"

"It can't be," breathed Aris. He closed his eyes; he felt as if he'd been kicked; his breath came short. It could not be; it was impossible. But inwardly he was not sure . . . or rather, he sure that in some way Seri was right. "Not on purpose," he murmured. "He couldn't—he wouldn't—"

"Aris, you cannot stay young forever without knowing it. He must know what he's doing. I'll grant this might not be the only way. It could be his own magery, or something the elves granted him. Something else could be sapping your strength. But taking these things together . . . why couldn't you find him yesterday, and why did someone need your healing just then?"

Aris stared at her, even more shocked. "You don't think he made that child fall!"

Seri reddened. "No—I suppose I don't, really. But it happened just when you were about to confront him, and I have not seen you so drained since you were a child. And I must tell you, I have had a prickling all along my bones since yesterday. There's danger coming."

Aris stirred restlessly. He knew something was wrong; when he thought about it, he had to admit he had been losing strength for several years. He had thought of that as age, when he thought of it at all. He had shrugged it off; his powers mattered only as they served the community, not in themselves. But he could not imagine Luap deliberately risking him—the most powerful healer—the way Seri suggested. Luap might be willful, even devious, but he had never been stupid.

"How could it be?" he asked. "I don't think it's true, but if it were true, how would it work?"

"I don't know. If we knew when it started—"

"We do." Aris realized that he had known that without knowing what the sign meant. "Remember the first time the king's ambassador came?" Seri nodded. "He commented then on how young Luap looked for his age; he said something about those who do not grow older being the wisest. I thought he meant the elves."

"I think he did. He meant the ones who built the stronghold."

"Well, I heard Luap talking to the Rosemage after Arranha died, and saying how lucky he was to look younger than he was—that it gave him an advantage in dealing with the Khartazh. He asked what I thought, and I said that age seemed to be loss of resilience—the skin stretches out, the joints stiffen. It might, I said, be like a failure to heal. We know that those badly wounded often seem older, even if they live. If it were possible to heal all injuries, even those so small we don't notice them, wouldn't that hold off age?"

"I doubt it," Seri said, scuffing the pineduff with her boot. "If it worked that way, everyone you healed would get younger."

"And you're right; they don't. I said so then, and the Rosemage said the gods meant time to flow one way, not slosh back and forth like water in a pan. But it might have given Luap an idea. If you're right about him, I think that's where it started."

Seri frowned. "But he doesn't have the healing magery. At least, you never thought so."

"No. The royal magery, yes: you saw him carve the canyon with it, and he can do many other things. But I've never seen him heal."

"Because healing is giving," Seri said, as if she'd just thought of it. "You pour out your own strength; Gird recognized that. Luap doesn't. He conserves; he withholds. He tries to do right; we've both seen him do the right thing where someone else might not. But it's calculation—he must figure out the right thing and then try to do it—he can't just feel it and do it, as Gird did."

"He's not selfish," Aris said quickly. Then, as Seri watched him without saying anything, he said, "Not in the usual ways, I mean. In times of shortage, he takes no more than his share. He lives simply, compared to any of the Khartazh officers."

"Would you give a wolf credit that he eats less grass than a sheep?" Seri asked. "And I am convinced he took your power, made you less able than you were, risked not only you but all who depend on you for healing. For that matter—" She rolled over and stabbed at the soft duff with a twig. "For that matter, how do we know that no children have the healing magery? Suppose he's stealing it from *them*? Before you could detect it, perhaps without knowing it—"

Aris shivered. He had a sudden vision of a hole in the bottom of the great water chamber . . . all the water swirling out that hole, eventually, if it were not refilled by rain. Had that happened to his power? Had Luap known, had he thought he was taking only a little, the overflow, and unwittingly taken from the very source? Or had he known—no. He could not believe that. He studied his hands, aware now of the signs of middle-age as clear in him as in Seri. "I think," he said slowly, "that something never existed in Luap that Gird had . . . as if a young tree grew with a hollow core, as those giant canes do, but then thickened around it. No one could see, from outside, but if that inside were what Gird gave *from*, then Luap might have nothing to give. He might try—as he has— but no one can bring water from a dry well."

"Whatever the cause, it was wrong," Seri said. Then she sighed, and scraped her hair back, looking at him with worry in her eyes. "And there's you. What are we going to do to restore your power? And the others; how are we going to find out how much else is wrong?"

Aris squirmed against the tree's bark. It felt comforting, that great vegetable existence at his back. "*If* you're right, the first thing to try would be the freeing of my own power. You say you noticed a change after we quit travelling?"

"Yes—within a year or so, at least."

"Then we should travel."

"But we can't—we can't leave the stronghold now!" He had never seen her so anxious. "I told you, I sense some evil. We can't leave them here, without help—"

Aris tried to feel around inside himself, the self he had thought so familiar, and find the hole out of which his power fled. He could not; he felt opaque to himself, and wondered how long that had been going on. Years? He could not tell. "I don't think I can free it here, so near him—and I don't know how far we'd have to go." When had they last been as far as the western canyons, the town beyond? He could not remember. Seri reached out and took his hand.

"You will do it, Aris. Look—let's try the mountaintop."

Exhaustion washed over him. "Today? Now?"

"Yes." She held both his hands; he felt as if warmth and strength poured out of her and into him. Very strange; he was used to that process going the other way. "Now," she said, pulling him up.

They reached the foot of the stairs without anyone commenting. Aris looked up the spiral. "All those steps," he said. Then he grinned at Seri. "I know. Gird wouldn't put up with whiners. If you're beside me, and old Father Gird will help—" He felt better, ready to face the long climb to the first plateau.

They came out into the midday light, another day of blowing cloud. Aris felt the wind pushing him sideways, but fought with it until he reached the trail to the high forest. He looked up, wonder- ing if the rocks meant to look unclimbable, or if it was his fault.

He made it up, grunting and puffing. The backs of his legs ached. Seri came up as lightly as a deer, he thought. She spent more time out of doors than he did . . . and why? he wondered. When had that started? It wasn't as if the mageborn were sickly, always needing him. But the accidents seemed to come just as Seri was starting somewhere, or when they'd planned a day away.

He headed off into the trees, taking the short way to the western watchpost. Seri caught up with him. "Let's go north, to Arranha's cairn."

"It's a long way," Aris said; he didn't feel like walking that far. Hard to remember that at first they'd come up every Evener to lay a stone on the pile.

"So? We're trying to find out if either of us can come out of the fog up here."

They had walked some distance when Aris realized he was moving more easily. He had warmed up, he thought . . . but it was more than that. He was breathing deeper, without strain; his head felt clearer. The racing patterns of light and cloud no longer seemed ominous, but playful. He noticed flowers in bloom up here that had gone to seed in the canyon below; he remembered years when they had always climbed the mountain to see the last wildflowers bloom.

Seri swung her arms and did a skip-step. "It may have nothing to do with Luap, but I still feel happier up here."

"And I." With renewed strength, he probed at himself, feeling again for anything wrong with his power. Vaguely, fuzzily, he sensed something wrong *there*. He prodded it as he would have a sore spot: how deep, how big, how inflamed? The familiar sense of something resisting the flow of healing magery . . . but this time resisting the flow *in* . . . he wondered if patients felt this.

He did not realize he had stopped, until Seri took his hand to tug him on. "Don't stop—it's getting better."

"Yes, but I—"

"A little farther. I'm feeling it too." She went on, and he followed, until his head cleared with an almost audible *snap*. He blinked; everything seemed brighter, the colors of leaf and bark and stone more sharply defined. Seri slowed. They had been walking in mature pine forest, the trees spaced well apart, with the sun slanting in between them. When they stopped, Aris could hear nothing but the wind in the pine boughs overhead. There before them was the pile of stones; some had fallen in the years when no one came. Aris stooped to replace them.

Seri rubbed her head hard with both fists. "It feels *strange*, but good. And you?" She picked up another stone and placed it.

"The same. Rather like a long fever breaking." Aris stretched out between two trees; he felt both exhausted and full of life. He wanted to eat a huge dinner, sleep, and get up well again. "And you were right," he said to Seri. "I won't accuse Luap, not yet, but *something* was interfering with my magery. It must have happened gradually—"

"And now," Seri said, sticking to the practical, "what are we going to do about it? About him?"

"Do? I—don't know. Did you find out what had been done to you?"

"Oh, yes." Her expression was grim. "Good, loyal Marshal Seri had to be kept from taking Aris out on misguided quests: she had to be convinced we were needed here, even though I should have seen that everything I tried to do, Luap managed to undo."

Aris thought about that. "I still don't think it can be Luap by himself. Something else must be involved."

Seri nodded. "And I think I may know what. Remember how the Khartazh worried at first that we might be demons in human form? All their legends said these mountains were full of demons. What if they were right?"

Certainty pierced Aris like a spear of ice. "And Luap didn't know—"

"No—although I do remember Arranha saying once that the elves had given him some kind of warning no one could understand."

"So your feeling of evil somewhere . . . could be that. It could have been spying on us all these years, making some plan—"

"And perhaps invading Luap's mind, making him prey on your power—" Seri shivered, and shook her head. "Which still leaves us with the practical problem of what do we do? They won't listen to us; we can't get them away, even if that is the right answer. I can try to cajole Luap into letting me double the guardposts, make some patrols, but it won't be enough if what I suspect is coming."

Aris looked at her. "We can either leave now—as soon as we can—and hope to strengthen ourselves enough at a distance to come back in force—or we can stay, and try to resist the influence here. It depends on how long we think we have; I suspect we have very little time."

"Yes." Seri gnawed on the side of her thumb like the child she had been, raked at her unruly hair, and sighed. "I should have realized earlier—"

"No." Aris was as surprised as Seri when his light came and flooded the space between the trees. "We don't have time for that; we must put aside regrets and guilt and do what we can now."

For the first time in many years, her light matched his; he watched the old confidence and courage flow back into her, the old enthusiasm kindle.

"They know," the black-cloaked spy said. "That Girdish woman Marshal—"

"I told you we should have killed her before now—" hissed one of the watchers.

"And I forbade. She kept the healer happy, unaware. What does she know?"

"That their prince has not aged, and that the power for that came from the healer, and not from the prince. That some magery prevented anyone noticing."

"And the healer?"

A soft unpleasant chuckle. "The prince had a sudden urge to go here, and then there—where the healer and woman did not think to seek. And we arranged a diversion—"

"Without asking me?" the edged voice of their leader brought absolute silence to the chamber.

"Lord, we had to do something. . . ."

"So. And you did what?"

"Loosened a stone beneath a child's foot; he fell, and required the healer. Such things are easy now, the way the mortals have burrowed into the stone. They have prepared their own doom, even as you, lord, said they would. We sapped more energy from the healer as he worked, and no one knew. He will sleep long, and waken tired and confused. It will give us a day, perhaps two."

"So . . . now, now at last we may act. True, the game has lasted just over a score of years—but for some of them it has been a lifetime."

A shiver of delight, hardly audible, disturbed the silence with the faint rustle of black robes. Eyes and teeth gleamed. They knew already which would go where, and do what. Immortal hatred burned in their eyes, immortal pride. Vengeance at last on the proud sinyi who had imprisoned them; vengeance at last on the mortals who had dared to meddle in immortal quarrels; vengeance on the foolish prince, and his more foolish followers. Through the stone itself, rotted from their malice, they moved in darkness and silence.

Chapter Thirty

The guard on the eastern post saw the smoke dark against the first glow of dawn, and sent for Seri, who sent for the Rosemage. By then the light had strengthed; they had to squint against the glow of the rising sun. The Rosemage eyed the smoke columns and said nothing. Seri said, "That's all the way to the head of the canyon, lady. Duriya and Forli are up that far. . . ."

"And the others?"

"The caravan route, the upper valley. Probably the other part of it, where we've been pasturing the horse herd."

"And your assessment?"

Seri scowled. "If we had enemies, if someone wanted to cut us off from the east, that would do it."

"And if they wanted to move on us, they'd be coming down, from higher ground. Like a spring flood."

"But we don't know yet it *is* an enemy. Or who?"

"You smell trouble as clearly as I do, Seri." The Rosemage, in morning sunlight, looked like an image made of silver and ivory, her hair concealed in a shining helm. "And I, since our lord Luap is not qualified in this, at least, will take a troop up the canyon to see what it is."

"Not alone," Seri said.

"No—but if it is magery of some sort, I will know it. I will send word."

"If you can," Seri muttered. "*They* haven't, unless that smoke is their warning." She meant those who had chosen to live at the head of the canyon, carving their home where the seasonal waterfall could make a glittering curtain for its porch. And those who lived in that first valley along the caravan way.

"Perhaps that danger surprised them," the Rosemage said. "It won't surprise me." She strode away, to the entrance of the stair down to the great hall. Aris, ignored in this exchange, sucked his cheeks.

"She *is* a warrior," he said to Seri. It was half-plea, half excuse.

"She is," Seri said, "but she's a long stretch of her life from a war. As are we all."

"She's the best we have," Aris said. Then, with a look at the expression on her face, he added, "Barring you, of course."

Seri turned on him. "Me! Don't be ridiculous. Aside from grange maneuvers, I have never been in battle, or commanded; I have the training, yes, but that's all. What I know—what I feel—" She stopped, brooding away eastward toward the distant columns of smoke. "I could have, Ari—and I can't tell you how I know, but I'm right in this. It was my parrion, but no one wanted it, and I had to find my own way to it . . . and now, when I'm older than Gird was when he commanded, now our lives may depend on it. Because you're right, even though it is ridiculous: I am the best we have. Better than the Rosemage, because like Gird I know what I don't know."

Aris touched her arm. "Seri—it's all right. It will be all right. It could be a fire, some child careless in learning magery—"

"No. Three fires, the same day, almost the same time? Have you forgotten our talk yesterday? No, it's an attack, from whom or what we can't know. But we had best find out."

Far below, the clatter of horses' hooves echoed off rock walls, coming to them as a confused stutter. A thin shout and the sweet resonance of a horn call reached them: the Rosemage must have flown through the halls, he thought, and put a flame on someone, to be out and moving so quickly.

"Find me a replacement," Seri said. "She's our commander, but if she doesn't come back—" Aris made a warding sign without thinking; she scowled at him. "This is not a child's game, Aris. Hurry."

Whatever the Rosemage had said, as she passed through, had affected the mageborn as a stick would an anthill. Aris heard the noise before he was well down the stairs, and met half a dozen on the way up. One only had the armband of a trained lookout; that one he grabbed and held until the boy actually met his eyes. "Go up, and do whatever Seri tells you," he said. "You're on duty now." Then he himself went on down. He knew what she would want; he could start seeing to it. And he could prepare himself for the healing that would be necessary.

In the great hall, no one ran: it never occurred to anyone that running was possible. But Aris hurried, stretching his long legs, and then jogged steadily along the corridors, dodging those who tried to grab his sleeve and ask questions. He caught a glimpse of Luap, who was surrounded by a sea of bobbing heads and waving arms. He saw a sturdy yeoman, half-mage, whom Seri respected, and waved him over. "Seri'll be coming down," he said. "She'll explain; wait for her, but tell anyone she would want."

In the kitchens, the cooks were heading toward the lower entrance; Aris called them back. "We're going to need food," he said firmly. "We'll have people coming in; we'll have marching rations to prepare—"

"The Rosemage took all we had—" grumbled one.

"Then start making more. In case of wounded, I'll want broth and soup, and I'll need space at one hearth for a row of small kettles of herbs."

"Stinking stuff," said another cook. "We won't have that in here—"

"You will," said Aris firmly. "I can't heal everyone; we'll need poultices and draughts. I'll send in one of my prentices with the kettles." He smiled at them until they withdrew, grumbling, to their hearths and ovens. A moment later, a messenger bearing Luap's armband came in with the same orders, but found the cooks at work. "C-commendations, then," he said, looking around with obvious surprise. "The prince thought you might have been upset."

The head cook glanced at Aris and away. "What, then—does he think we've no common sense, to know what's needed?"

Aris walked swiftly to his own quarters. Jirith, his steadier apprentice, was laying out an assortment of healing herbs. "Good lass," Aris said. "I might have known you'd be at work."

"I wasn't sure where to do the steeping," she said. He could tell by the tension in her jaw that she was alarmed, but her voice stayed steady. "The lower kitchen is closer to the main entrance, but the upper one to the infirmary."

"The lower," Aris said. "We'll clear a storeroom for use down there, if we have many wounded. Gods grant we don't." His mind tossed up the things he remembered from Gird's war, when he had not yet known he could heal. As if it were yesterday, he saw those wounds, heard the groans and screams, smelled the rotting bodies before they could be decently buried. This time, he thought, I know what to do. This time it won't be the same.

The Rosemage swung into the saddle of her gray horse, hardly aware of the turmoil her passage through the stronghold had generated. She felt at once vindicated and elated; she had *warned* Luap that all was not well; she had felt something, and he had insisted it meant nothing, and now—now she would prove she was right. Behind her, other hooves clattered on the stone, other riders mounted . . . she did not look back; she gave them the trust that they would be ready when she gave the command.

Outside, sunlight had just reached the bottom of the cleft into which the lower entrance opened. She could smell the resinous pines, the damp earth, the living air that always seemed fresher than the air inside. She sniffed, but caught no hint of any smoke but that of the lower kitchen ovens, fragrant with baking bread.

Two hands of men . . . that was all she had. It would have taken much longer to muster a larger number, so had the settlement spread from its early years. Had they counted on that, whoever they were? Were the smoke columns warnings, lit by their own people, or triumphal, defiant acts of a victorious enemy? Two hands of men—enough for casual brigands, but—she nudged her horse, and rode forward, out into the sunlight—not for anything serious. And her instincts told her this was very serious indeed.

Outside, turning downstream to the main canyon, she did glance back. Two hands, mostly full mageborn, with the lances they used against mountain cats and brigands, with swords and bows as well. She unhooked her signal horn from her saddle, and put it to her lips. The sound rang off the stone, echoed crazily from the main canyon wall across from the mouth of their smaller one.

She wondered if that had been wise, though they had used horn signals for years. Whoever caused the smoke would know someone had noticed, that someone was coming. But they might have known anyway—it might hearten defenders, help drive off attackers. She didn't believe that, but she hoped it.

At the main canyon, she held up her hand and the others gathered around her. "We cannot surprise them," she said. "Speed is our chance to do some good. But if things go badly, someone must get back to warn the others." She looked around, gauging their reactions. None of these were old enough to have fought in Gird's war. Some had helped drive the brigands out of their holes above the Khartazh caravan route; others had traveled with the caravans east, and fought horse nomads. She hoped that would be enough. She settled on the youngest. "You, Tamin: you stay well behind, and if I fall, ride back as fast as you can to the stronghold."

His young face looked even younger with the effort to be solemn, to live up to this. The others too looked serious enough.

"We will ride first to the head of the canyon; that's the shorter way, but we'll leave Tamin at the caravan trailhead. That way he can't be cut off. We have no idea who this might be, or what, so stay alert." They nodded; she turned her horse, crossed the stream on the terrace dam, and made her way up the shadowed south side of the canyon. Coming down they might have to trample crops; going up she was careful to use the trailway.

If it had not been for the smoke columns—the one at the canyon head visible even from here—she would have enjoyed that ride. The trail, two horses wide and well-packed after years of use, required no great skill; her big gray muscled its way up the steeper sections with ease. A light wind sang in the pines, and swayed the grain as they rode past it. They passed the narrow openings of the other two side canyons running north, all three separated by ribs or fins of rock that seemed slender in comparison with the great block which lay over the stronghold. Yet each was broader than the length of Esea's Hall in Fin Panir. She peered up at the canyon entrances, a little higher than the trail in the main canyon. All looked normal there. Should she stop to look? No, they must find out what the smoke meant, first.

The trail lifted over a hump of rock, and the caravan trail snaked back, up the first switchback. Ahead, the trail to the head of the canyon wound around house-sized blocks of stone at the outfall of the upper valley before angling left to clear the base of the mountain that formed the valley's eastern wall. She could not see from here what caused the smoke; it had changed color as they rode, and now the thick column thinned to a faint stream of ash-gray. And from here, close under the steep slope, she could not see the smoke that must have come from the upper valley itself.

"Tam, you'll stay here. No—wait—go across the stream, where you can see anyone coming down the caravan trail. Give us a warning, if you do, then go back to the stronghold and warn the others."

He nodded, and reined his horse away from the others. The Rosemage watched as the horse picked its way carefully across the stream, here fast-running over a rocky bed. She remembered when all the canyon had been that way, only small deep pools interrupting the stream's noisy rush. Tam turned, on the other side, turned, looked far above them, where she could not see, and waved. She was proud of him; he remembered to make that wave a signal, to indicate that he'd looked and found nothing amiss. She waved back, and legged her horse on.

She felt the skin of her back prickle; more than sunlight made her neck itch, her skin feel tight all over. When she had first come into this empty land, so vast and strange, she had felt this way often. They were so few; the land could swallow them and not even notice. But years had dulled that feeling; she had become used to the solitude, the wide sky, the great canyons empty of everyone but themselves. Now she felt again as she had that first year, when every rock seemed to shelter an unknown menace.

As they moved from the shadow of the cliffs to the broken rock beyond, sweat began to trickle down her sides, under the mail. She could never see very far ahead, and worried more and more that they might be ambushed. But nothing stirred, and no strange sounds alarmed her. The trail was narrower; although it had been built wide enough for two horses abreast, it had not been maintained as well. The horses plodded on, steadily and quietly.

Beyond the broken rock, the foot of the valley wall narrowed the canyon again. The stream here gurgled pleasantly, narrow enough to step across in most places, edged with mint and a plant with starry golden flowers. The trail wound back and forth across the stream, hardly more than a footpath. The Rosemage stopped and turned in the saddle.

"We must leave the horses," she said. "We can't fight horseback up this way, and we dare not be trapped where we can't even turn—"

"They cleared a forecourt, like, below the fall," one of her troop said. "There's room to turn there."

"Yes, but not in between." She didn't like this, any of it. Leave the horses and they might be stolen, or spooked. Take them, and they could be attacked easily from above, with bows or even rolled stones. And why hadn't she thought to leave the horses with Tamin, back at the trail division? Now she would either have to leave someone else to guard them, which meant having only eight with her, or tie them and hope nothing happened. She had lost her wits, she thought angrily. It was hard to think, hard to make any decisions; she half wanted to turn around and ride back to the stronghold. She dismounted, ending both the internal and external discussion, and the others dismounted as well. "We'll tie the horses," she said. If something spooked them, sent them back down the canyon, it would at least warn Tamin.

Despite everything, that walk up the steep trail to the clearing below the falls reminded her again why she loved this country. All along the creek, more of the starry yellow flowers, more tiny ferns, more beds of fragrant mint. Tiny golden frogs splashed into the water, arrowing across pools not much larger than a kettle to flip themselves onto a sunny stone. The canyon walls closed around them, making each stretch of trail a private room, almost a secret.

She could well understand why someone might want to live here, even though in flood or in winter snow it would be impossible to get out, to join the others in the stronghold. If she had had no responsibilities, she might have wanted to live here herself.

They came around a last twist to the clearing, a grassy circle edged along one rock wall by the merest trickle of water. The Rosemage stared. The last time she had seen it, fruit trees and vines had been trained all around the margin in rock-walled terraces above the seasonal floods. Those trees had been hacked to the ground; their green wood, slow-burning, had fueled the smoke that rose as if in a chimney, straight up the cliffs past the dwelling. They had not smelled it before, but now acrid smoke stung her nostrils. Behind her, a mutter rose; a wave of her hand silenced it. She let her eyes rove up the cliff, ledge by ledge, looking for any movement, ignoring for the time a trickle of darker smoke from the dwelling entrance. Nothing . . . no movement, no sound, until her gaze flowed into the sky and found dark wings already circling.

She moved cautiously around the clearing, keeping close to the wall. The trees had been cut with axes, the marks clear on their short stumps. A few branches had escaped the fire, their blossoms and tender leaves already wilted from the day's heat. Some of the carefully laid terraces had been broken apart, the stones flung several arm's-lengths. It could not have been done by stealth; it would have made considerable racket, to echo off the cliffs on every hand. The mageborn must have heard it—why had they done nothing? Because they had been killed first? She did not look forward to what they might find in the dwelling itself.

The lower, obvious entrance led to a small stable, carved of the rock. Here the families had kept goats and a couple of sturdy ponies to pack their fruit down-canyon and other supplies back up. Normally it was closed by a heavy door of thick planks; these were shattered almost to splinters. The Rosemage knew before she entered that the animals were dead; she did not expect the savagry with which they'd been flayed and butchered. Most of the meat had been taken, and the innards strewn to smear every bit of wall and floor with stinking slime. Here, for the first time, she found a footprint in the bloody mess: it could have been human, by its size and shape, a foot cased in soft leather, not boots with heels.

From the stable, an inner stair led up into blackness. The Rosemage considered, decided to use the outside approach to the family's own chambers. This, outside, meant climbing a series of ledges, zig-zagging up the curving cliff. When she had visited before, a notched log had served to cross one gap which now required a careful leap.

The main entrance had served as a front porch, a low stone wall protecting small children from the drop to the clearing below. No water trickled past it now, but she remembered how beautiful it had been when the falls ran. She glanced out, down-canyon, surprised as always at the way the land hid its real shape. From here, the side-canyons were invisible; she could not tell where the stronghold lay.

But she could not stand gazing at lost safety, not now. She waited until half her band had made it that far, then called her light. It flickered for a moment as shock blurred her mind. There they were, the two families, the bones unmistakable through charred flesh, square in the entrance to the rest of the dwelling. A few ends of wood indicated that the household furniture had fed that fire. Stinking smoke trailed along the cave floor and made her cough. She moved forward.

"We have to know," she said. "Maybe someone escaped, maybe a child found a hiding place—" In her light, she could see walls smeared with blood and filth and smoke. As she edged past the smoldering pyre, she realized that the passage had been systematically dirtied with the corpses before they were burned—she hoped they had been corpses then, not still living. Nausea cramped her belly, her throat, and she fought it down. She had to remember how the cave dwelling had been laid out. She heard someone retching behind her, but the stench of death and burning was so bad nothing could make it worse.

Two families, both fairly young; they had shared this passage, a dining hall, a large kitchen with two hearths, and the wide space behind the waterfall. On either side of the passage had been each family's sleeping rooms and private space. She could not remember all of it; she wasn't sure she'd been shown all of it. She went into the first opening she found, on the left, and found the remains of a loom, smashed, and the cloth ripped away, hacked and smeared with blood. In the next, only the splinters of whatever furniture had been there, probably taken to fuel the fire. Someone had walked through the pool of blood on the floor before it dried, leaving footprints like those in the stable. Chamber after chamber, on one side the central passage or another, had only destruction, blood, the smell of horror.

Her mind could not take in the whole thing. It seemed to fragment, to split into five or six minds, each attending to only one part of what she saw and heard and felt. Had they been surprised? Had anyone fought? Where had the attackers come from, and who were they? Could she find more clues?

In the kitchen with its double hearth, its concession to the

kitchen rights of two women of equal rank, she found the first sign
of resistance. A pothook, marked as if by a sword-slash. A broken
knife, stained with blood. The Rosemage sniffed it, trying out what
her magery might tell her. A strange odor seared her nose, woke
terrible fears. Not human, not this blood. But what? She called the
most experienced of the huntsmen, who sniffed and then shook
his head.

"Nasty, lady, you're right about that. But it's nothing I've smelled
before, not here or anywhere. It has a . . . a tingle in it, a ringing,
almost a sound."

"It's wicked," the Rosemage said. She felt something in the atmosphere as a smothering wave of evil. "And it knows we're here."

But nothing more happened, as they searched each chamber
carefully. They found no survivors, only the bloodstains where each
had been killed and gutted. They found no clues but the odd-
smelling blood on that one blade, and the evidence of the pothook,
that the attackers had used swords. And the sense that some great
evil, some cold and incalculable menace, lurked about them.

The Rosemage was almost surprised to find that it was still daylight outside when she came back to the ledge behind the dry
waterfall. Her head ached; her mouth tasted of smoke and death.
The others were all white-faced and grim.

"We must find out if those in the narrow canyons are safe, and
warn everyone," she said. "Belthis, you go—tell Tam what we've
found, and rouse the stronghold. Then check the first of the side
canyons. Those two oldest lads of Seriath's were planning to live there
this summer; they'd started a rock shelter last year. Get them out of
there, if they're alive, then make sure the next side-canyon's safe."

"Should those people leave?" asked Belthis.

"No. Remember—the west wall of that's the east wall of the
canyon outside the stronghold, and there's the tunnel." The next
side-canyon east had seemed a good place to expand the settlement's living quarters, but it had proven inconvenient to have to
go around the spine of rock between them. The Rosemage wondered just how far along that tunnel had come . . . she had not
kept up with such things lately. But if they lost the upper canyon,
if an enemy attacked, that tunnel could be dangerous.

They must not lose the upper canyon—they could not, if they
only knew what they faced. And she must find that out, before
worse came upon them. "Go on," she said to Belthis. "Have Tam
talk to Seri, as well as Luap, about defenses. Messengers must go
today to the lower canyon, to the western valleys."

He gulped. "And what shall I say about you, lady?"

"That I am trying to find out what manner of enemy we face."
She followed him out from under the ledge, into the cleaner air
that still smelled of smoke, and wished she need not stay.

Aris had chosen his room, and had his healers at work making
it orderly and handy, when Seri came to find him. She was wearing
the mail she had ordered from the Khartazh, and it jingled slightly
as she moved. The expression on her face combined decent concern
with pure glee.

"I had the word out before *he* said anything." Her eyes sparkled;
though she was trying to stay solemn, she looked very much the
mischievous child she had been.

"How many?"

"Not as many as I'd like." She scowled a moment, thinking, then
went on. "We've lots more who could fight—who may have to
fight—but of the ones trained solidly, either Girdish or magery,
we've fewer than twenty hands—a bare cohort." She didn't say
why; she didn't have to. Luap had decided, when the Khartazh
proved true to its treaties, that they did not need a large armed
force. Training took time from more important things. "Of course
I don't suppose there's ever been a commander who didn't want
more soldiers," she added. Then, looking at him closely, "And how
are you?"

Aris shrugged. What bothered him most was Seri going out to
fight; they both knew that, and there wasn't any use saying it. "I'm
following our plan." The one he and Seri had worked out together,
in case Luap's assumptions about the safety of the region were
wrong. The Rosemage might be Luap's ranking military commander, on the strength of her background, but Seri had trained
the young men and women, mapped each canyon, and planned the
details of defense. She had also, in the early years, led more than
one expedition against the brigands.

"Good. If nothing interferes with her, she should have a messenger back here by midafternoon, at least. Then we'll know something—" She paced the small room, her hair springing free with
every stride. "I've got the old guardposts all manned, messengers
on the way west—"

"To the Khartazh?" Aris asked. That had been a decision point
in their plan, one they had argued over, taking opposite sides in
alternation. Seri shook her head.

"Not just yet. I want to hear the Rosemage's report." Then she
flushed, aware what that sounded like. "I mean—"

"I know what you meant." Aris grinned. "You *are*, you know. You might as well admit it."

"Luap hasn't said anything," she muttered, still red.

He could think of several reasons for that, none of them good. He felt once more the emptiness, the coldness, he had felt when he realized that Luap was using magery to extend his own life. Images raced through his mind, all ugly: an empty skull, rolled along the stone by a high wind; a headless man staggering, falling, dying. If Luap had lost—whatever made him a leader, whatever made him care—then they were all lost. And what kind of leader would choose to live long, and watch his people age and die?

Not Seri. He had another clear vision of her, from one of the early raids against brigands, leading the way up a narrow ledge. She might have stayed back, knowing her value to them as a trainer, or even commander, but she always led—she never pushed. She would have been, he knew, a better leader than Luap; in her own land, in distant Fintha, she would have made a good Marshal, and probably come close to Marshal-General, for everyone liked and trusted her. But here, Luap's refusals constrained her, like a plant grown in too small a pot.

Luap, when he came down, looked both calm and elegant. "The Rosemage can easily handle any little raiding party of brigands," he said. Aris looked at him, thinking what one of the cooks said aloud.

"And if it's not just a little raiding party?"

Luap smiled, "Then we can gather everyone in here, and defend it; once those doors are closed, no brigands can open them."

"But the crops—" someone said.

"We can replant; we can trade to Khartazh if we need to. We have reserves of both food and money. And if it's some invading force, horse nomads gone crazy or something, we can call on the Khartazh for aid." That smile again, confident and calm. "As you know, we have close trading ties there; the king has promised to be our brother."

Seri poked Aris in the back. When he didn't move, she poked him harder, then hissed in his ear. "Ask him to—" But Luap was already talking again.

"I know there are some of you who would like to see me call out our guard. Seri, I know you've been training them for years—" Aris dropped his hand and grabbed Seri's wrist even before she moved. He knew how that tone would affect her. "—But we don't yet know what we face," Luap said, reasonably. "Better to give an early warning and let families pack up their goods on the chance they might have to come here."

As if a heavy iron trapdoor fell on stone with a great clang, Aris felt something *shift* in his head: something final. From the expression on Luap's face, he had felt something too, and all the mageborn crowding around had the same startled, wide-eyed look.

"What was that—?" began someone. Aris felt an icy certainty, and again saw it mirrored in the other faces. He knew what it was; he knew . . . and by the time they had reached the great hall, others knew it too.

There, each beneath the appropriate arch, stood two figures that Aris knew at once were rulers of their folk. More than their rich clothing, or their crowns, their bearing proclaimed their sovereignty. The elven king carried a naked sword in his hands; the blade glowed blue as flame. The dwarf king bore an axe with the same light. Both looked grim and angry. Between them, but not *in* Gird's arch, stood a gnome all in gray, holding what seemed to be a book bound in slate and leather.

Luap went forward to meet them, as an aisle opened through his own people. Aris followed close behind him.

"Selamis Garamis's son, you have broken your word with us; you have loosed that which we bound long ago, in spite of our warnings."

Chapter Thirty-one

Aris felt a cold wave wash him from head to foot. He had not known Luap had made a contract with elves and dwarves—what contract? The elven king continued.

"We revoke our permission; we lay a ban upon you. The patterns of power you enjoyed will not longer suffer your use. You must scour the evil from this land, or be forever mured in this hall."

"But what *is* it?" Luap asked, all in a rush. Then he took a long breath and said, more slowly, "My lords, I do not know what you mean. We do not yet know what the smoke portends; my people have gone to find out. We have waked no evil that I know of—"

"Then you are blind and deaf, mortal, and your pretensions of power all are lies! You were warned; you were told to beware your neighbors, to walk softly and keep watch: you have not. The very air stinks of evil; the rock tastes of it; the water; the trees wither in its blast—and you claim you do not see?"

"But then—if you revoke your permission—you want us to *leave*?"

The dwarf spoke. "Mortal, we could wish you had never been, save that that would be to walk with cursed Girtres Undoer. What you have done cannot be undone; it must be mended, if that be possible, by the one who broke the covenant. Thus we command, who have that right."

"But—how? What do you mean?" Aris could hear the tremor in Luap's voice, and smell the sweat that sudden fear brought out on him. He himself stood watchful, wondering.

The elf spoke again. "You are barred from the use of the patterns to make your way elsewhere, lest the evil you waked travel with you, and bring dishonor on the patterners. You are forbidden permission to live here, where you have polluted a holy place with evil; the living water and all green things will no longer do your bidding. You must fight free on the land's skin, cleansing it from the evil you waked, or die here—your deaths payment for what evil you have done."

Aris could not see Luap's face. His voice, when he spoke, was low and halting. "You—cannot condemn all these for my failure, if indeed I failed. Not all are guilty; we have children, young people. . . . Let them escape by the mageroad; I will stay and fight. . . ."

"A people abide the judgment of their prince," the gnome said in a colorless voice. "If the prince errs, the people suffer: that is justice."

"But it's not *fair*!" Luap cried. "You have never told me the nature of this evil—I don't even know what I did, or did not do, or what it is you speak of!"

In the silence that followed that outburst, Aris heard running footsteps coming toward the hall. One of the youngest of the militia ran in, gasping, bearing a broken knife in his hand. Without ceremony, he said, "This is it! This is what the Rosemage found!" Luap turned his back on the kings, and reached out a hand.

"Let me see that." The young man held it out; Aris intercepted it as a strange, almost-forgotten smell tickled his nose. Luap scowled, but Aris brought the broken blade to his nose and sniffed.

"Iynisin," he said. Luap recoiled, snatching back his hand. Aris turned to the kings. "This is iynisin blood—is that the evil you meant? Are iynisin the evil, or the servants of it?

The elvenking spoke. "You are right, mortal, in your surmise: that is iynisin blood, and they are now awake and powerful in this place, where once they had been banished and trapped in stone. Your prince paid no heed to our warnings; one by one he broke the terms of that agreement by which we gave permission, and used his magery in ways no mortal should. Now the evil has come upon you; now the pattern comes to its necessary end." For a moment, compassion moved across his face like a gleam of light between clouds. "We take no joy in the suffering of those innocents among you, but we cannot risk evil escaping from hence to ravage wide lands. Escape may be possible for some of you—but not by magery. Those roads are closed until another of your people comes by land."

"We have caravans every year," someone said.

The elf smiled without mirth. "They could not come up the trail from the great canyon against iynisin arrows; you have lost the upper valley. It will be long, even in our perception, before a Finthan walks into this hall."

The gnome spoke again. "I, the Lawmaster, witnessed this contract the day it began; I witness now that it was broken by Selamis Garamis-son, and that the lords of elves and dwarves declare it void and state the penalities openly. So it is, and so it shall be recorded." He took from among the pages an irregular cake of wax. "This was your seal, Selamis: it, like your word, is broken." He dropped it, stepped upon it, and ground it with his heel. Aris noticed that Luap had turned white as milk.

And with no more words, they vanished. Luap stared around him; his eyes seemed sunken in his head. Those who had rushed to the great hall stared back, but no one dared speak. Aris moved forward. "Let the prince have his peace," he said. "Go to your homes and prepare for whatever comes; gather what food you have, what you can carry—"

Murmuring more and more loudly, casting looks back, they went, at first slowly and then all in a rush. Luap stood alone in the midst of the great hall, silent and motionless. Aris looked at him, then shook himself. They didn't have time now—he had to find Seri and await the Rosemage's return.

"What will it take to recapture the upper valley?" asked Luap. It was after the turn of the night; the air tasted bitter and stale. Aris wasn't sure if that was the lurking evil, or simple exhaustion. They had been in conference for a long time, Luap and all the older inhabitants, with explanations and non-explanations flying back and forth.

"Were you listening?" the Rosemage said, her voice edged like steel. "We cannot take the upper valley with the forces we have, not if we bring everyone in from the western valleys, not if we ask aid from the Khartazh. Which, by the way, I would never recommend."

"Why not?" Luap had laid his hands palm to palm, a gesture that meant he was withholding blame for the moment only.

"Luap, the king could not hold these canyons before we came; he could not do it now. We are his friends so long as we are useful, and we have been useful because we drove out the brigands that preyed on the caravans. Even if he would help, and could help, his price would be more than I want to pay."

"We have gold," Luap said.

"It is not gold he will want, but lives. Which of our people will you send into slavery?"

"Nonsense." Luap slapped the table. "We have gold; we have other wealth. We are not poor wanderers—"

"Strength is your heritage," Seri said suddenly. All heads turned toward her; Aris stared. "Arranha told Father Gird that, remember? Your people believe that the strong take, and prove their strength by taking. If you lack the strength to protect your own, what does that make you?"

The mageborn went white to the lips; silence held the room. Seri looked around, meeting each gaze with her own challenge.

"What the lady has said, and what the Khartazh king will see, is that you—we—are no longer a strong ally, to be respected. If we cannot hold these canyons, we come out of them suppliants, beggars, no matter what wealth we bring with us. Can we stand against the Khartazh on open ground? No: and so that wealth can be taken as easily as you once took the land from the people of Fintha and Tsaia. The Autumn Rose does not trust the king of the Khartazh, nor do I."

"But some are already living there; some have married into families—"

Seri shrugged. "It may be they will fare no worse than other foreigners who settle in his realm—but they will no longer be favored foreigners, when this citadel falls. We must hope for mercy; we cannot demand justice."

"Then what do you suggest?"

"We must try to send word to Fin Panir and stop the caravans: perhaps one can get through, by following the main stream out its gorge. That route is passable, though difficult. We must use what magery we have to seal off the upper valley—and the upper end of the main canyon—and hope that gives us time for the children and those who cannot fight to make their way elsewhere."

"But where? If we cannot go back to Fintha—and you will not seek aid of the Khartazh—where else can they go?"

"They cannot go back to Fintha by the mageroad, but some, if we are careful, might make it overland with a returning caravan. Some might go to Xhim."

A growing murmur of dismay. The older mageborn knew they would not be welcome in Fintha, not as long as the present Marshal-General ruled. None of them wanted to face the long journey to strange and unknown lands.

"There must be another way!" Instantly several other voices echoed the first man. "Have you even *tried* the mageroad?" asked another. "Why should we believe elves?"

"It won't," Aris said. "Can't you feel the difference?"

"I'm going to try," said the man. Luap started to stand, but said nothing as the man walked quickly to the dais, stepped onto it, and closed his eyes. Then the man fell, as if someone had hit him hard; he made no sound but lay crumpled on the dais. Aris went to him quickly, felt for his pulse, and looked back at the others.

"He's dead." Someone screamed.

"Silence!" Luap rarely raised his voice; now it rose above the scream and commanded them all. Aris wondered how much of his royal magery went into it; he felt his own throat close, refusing speech. "I will confer with the Rosemage, with Aris, and with Seri," Luap said. "You will await my decision. Go now."

Luap dressed for the conference with care. If he looked slovenly, they might panic; his people—any people, he reminded himself—relied more on appearances than they might think. White and silver gray, to remind them of his power, touches of rich blue to comfort any who still worried about Gird's view of things. He combed his dark hair—still unfrosted—and congratulated himself on his decision to preserve his youthful vigor. They would need a strong man, not an aged one, to bring them safely through this crisis. Most of them seemed not to notice, but if anyone did—if anyone, in a panic, mentioned it, he could point out that it was proof of his great power. It could not be as hopeless as the elves had said; nothing was hopeless. He had survived too many things in his life to believe that, and his experience mocked the despair he had felt earlier. What a fool he had been, to let those things upset him.

It bothered him that he could not quite think what to do, what solution might come, but he was sure he would in time. He might even find a solution the elves had not thought of. They so hated their once-relatives that they had refused to admit the problem . . . if they had only *told* him, from the beginning, like any honest person would, all this could have been avoided.

He found the beginning of the meeting tedious. The Rosemage gave her report not once but a dozen times, answering the same questions over and over. Each head of a family had to express shock, dismay, worry. Somehow they managed to entangle old grievances in the present emergency, dragging in all sorts of irrelevancies. Why could they not see that there was no time for this? He quit listening, and began trying to plan some effective action. The next caravan would arrive in the spring; they must get control of the upper valley by the time it was due. They could not fight successfully in winter . . . his eyes narrowed, as he tried to think where in the upper valley a small force could shelter for the winter, to be sure the iynisin stayed away once evicted.

"What will it take to recapture the upper valley?" he asked in the next pause. He hoped that would get their attention and force them to think about the real problem, not who made what minor decision a decade before.

Everyone stared; the Rosemage looked as angry as he'd seen her in years.

"Were you listening?" she asked. He let his brows rise; he stifled the urge to say no one had said anything worth listening to, and let her rattle on. They were too unsettled yet, he decided, as the Rosemage and Seri refused to consider going to the Khartazh; they were still full of complaint, unreasonable, unready to think their way through to answers. When Keris Porchai insisted on testing the mageroad himself (Porchai, who had been slower to learn its use in the first place than most of the mageborn) Luap let him go; when he died, that was the perfect excuse to end the meeting. He would take his few chosen assistants and see if he could knock sense into them in privacy. He would need all of them, and they must quit acting as if he were a halfwit.

He used his power on them, as he rarely did, for the sheer pleasure of seeing it work: one word, and he could silence them all, even Aris. They obeyed, as they had to, leaving in a rush. He wondered if they knew how lucky they were, to have had a gentle, unambitious prince. Until now. Now only his ambition could save them; he would have no more time to be gentle. He led those he had named to his office, and turned with what he intended as a calming smile.

Instead, he faced rebellion. Hardly had he begun to explain what he thought of doing, when the Rosemage flashed out at him.

"You have not aged: surely you know this."

"Of course," he said smoothly. "It served its purpose. . . ."

"You used the royal magery for yourself!" The Rosemage glowed, as full of light as a fire, as the sun. "What might have held that evil away from the entire settlement, you used to spare your own years—"

"I held the evil I knew or suspected away from here *by* using it so, by seeming ageless: have you forgotten how that convinced the king's ambassador? You are the one who reminded everyone how dangerous the Khartazh empire is. *This* evil I knew nothing about."

"And you stole that power from Aris—"

"No." Luap shook his head. "My own magery served well enough. I would not have taken aught from him."

"But you did," Seri said. "Did you not realize that he has less healing power now than a hand of years ago?" Her voice conveyed utter certainty.

"It cannot be." Luap's face sagged; he felt as if all his years had come upon him at once. "I would not have done such a thing. It's impossible."

Seri shook her head. "It is not impossible, and it is the only explanation we have. Aris's power has waned, year by year, as you did not age. Let the Rosemage test your power, and she will find the flavor of his. Perhaps you did not know. . . ."

"You had no healing magery of your own," the Rosemage reminded him. "How, then, have you remained hale and strong so long? You must realize that the healing magery and control of age are closely allied." Her voice shook; she was, Luap realized, very near tears. "It may be too late, but you must release your magery to its proper purpose."

"It is too late," Luap said, looking at his fingers. "The elves say that, and I believe them: they make unsteady allies, but they do not lie, and they know more than we of the iynisin." He attempted a smile. "I have not even seen one."

"I have," Seri said. He had not known that. Her blunt face, weathered from years in the brilliant sun and dry wind, had lost the bright promise of its youth, but nothing could dim her eyes. Now, as she looked past him into the memory where that iynisin had been, he felt a pang that was almost guilt. She should have stayed in Fintha with Raheli; he should even have allowed Aris to stay, if necessary. She was Gird's child as much as any of his blood; she belonged there, and she might die here, because of his selfishness.

If, indeed, he had been drawing on Aris's power. He still could not believe that.

"Let me see," the Rosemage pled, her long hands reaching for his. He seemed to see her doubled, the beautiful woman she had been when he first met her, overlaid by the woman she had become. When had her hair gone silver? When had those lines marred the clarity of her cheek and jaw? An insidious hum along his bones urged him to ignore all that: what did it matter, after all, if one woman aged? He could lay an illusion over anything unpleasant. The important thing, surely, was his reign, his kingdom, his power.

Then her hands grasped his with a touch like fire. He could feel her power in his wrists, her magery only just weaker than his, her skill in using it as great or greater, for she had had the early training. Swift as light moving across the face of a cliff, picking out each hollow and ledge, her magery swept along his nerves, into the chambers of his mind. He could not sense what she found, but she recoiled in horror, eyes wide.

"You—you do not even know, do you?" Her voice was a whisper hardly loud enough to hear. Seri, after a quick glance at the Rosemage, stood alert, as if ready for battle.

"What is it?" Seri asked, not looking away from him.

"He . . . was invaded." The Rosemage scrubbed her hands on her robe, as if to remove the touch of his skin. "I cannot tell when—or I might, but it would take longer. You were right; he has been drawing on Aris's power, though I do not think he knew it. I am not sure how much Luap is left, to be honest."

Luap felt something stirring uneasily deep in his mind, like a hibernating animal prodded in its den. What was it? He tried to explore, to do for himself what the Rosemage had done, and met a vague reluctance—no opposition to meet head on, but the sensation that things would go better if he didn't bother. "I don't know what you mean," he said to the Rosemage, in a voice he hoped was reasonable. "I am the same Luap as always."

"No," she said, with a decisive shake of her head. "That you are not, whatever you are."

He wanted to scream at her, insist on it, but Seri stood there, poised for anything he might do. She looked less angry than he would have expected to find that he had been stealing power from her beloved Aris, but he knew she was dangerous. He tried to gather his magery around him, the comfortable cloak he had had all these years, and the Rosemage stirred.

"No,"she said, as if she knew what he was thinking. "No, you cannot do that, not again. I won't let you."

The sleeping monster stirred again, then arose, flooding his mind with its anger. "You!" he said, not knowing or caring if he spoke his own thoughts or those of the thing within him. "*You* not let me? You old woman, I mastered your magery years ago, when first we met: you should remember that. And I can master it now." It was in his hand, as reins in the hand of a master teamster; he could feel the power straining to be free, to strike. His light filled the chamber; his will—

And Seri came alight. He nearly gaped in astonishment. A *peasant*? Had she been mageborn all along? But her light met his and did not mingle; his eyes burned. Where had he seen such light before? He squinted against it, his eyes streaming tears.

"You will not harm her," Seri said. "The gods will not permit it."

"It is too late," the Rosemage said. Luap looked at her; she struggled against tears. "I served one bad king: I killed *him*. Now I have served a bad prince through another exile. I will not kill you, Selamis, but I will serve you no longer. I will serve what remains of our people, and kill only those creatures of the dark. Fare well, Seri and Aris: if you ever come again to Fintha, I hope you bring peace between our peoples. As for you, Selamis, I can neither curse nor praise you; I pray instead that Esea's light will show you what you have become, and the High Lord will judge fairly how far you consented." She pushed past Aris, out into the corridor. Luap could not doubt it was for the last time, that she meant what she said. She had never said anything she did not mean. He wanted to scream after her, beg her to stay, but the shadowy presence inside him forbade it.

"What did I do?" he asked himself as much as those around him. "What went wrong?"

Seri, still alight, came near on one hand, and Aris on the other. "Perhaps," Seri said, "it is what you did not do. Give me your hand." He would have refused, but she had it already; Aris took his other hand, and they joined theirs. In that instant, he saw the thing within him, which like a soft maggot had found his hollow core, soothing and comforting him as it nestled there, growing to fill what emptiness it enlarged. Now a mailed and glittering malice, the self's armor against self-knowledge, raised its claws in mock salute and leered. He knew it chuckled in delight, its long purpose fulfilled.

"*NO!*" Not so much scream as moan, with all the intensity of the feelings he had not felt for years. He squeezed his eyes against the sight, but for the eyes of the mind there are no lids. Shame scalded him. Seri's light, and Aris's, flooded his mind, left no shadowy corners, revealed everything Gird had revealed those long years before, but worse. Tears ran down his face; he remembered all too clearly trying to tell Gird he would have been a better king. Better? The presence in his mind mocked him: Could any have been worse? Had any kin of his, any of those royalties whose prerogatives he envied, ever been as feckless, as vicious, as to let such an enemy into such a sanctum? "I'm sorry," he said; the echo of the many times he had said that reverberated through his mind.

He would have been glad to die, but death was not offered. "Is this what you wanted?" asked Seri. He shook his head; that was not enough. He had to answer aloud.

"No," he said hoarsely. "It is not."

"Did you know what you were doing?"

"No." He remembered all the warnings, and how sure he had been that he knew better, that he had outgrown those warnings.

"Then throw that filth out," she said. Luap stared at her; surprised he could see her through his tears. Throw it out? How could he? "You must," she said, more gently, as if she could see every thought in his mind. "You must; no one else can."

He had no more strength; he felt it running out of him like blood from a mortal wound. "I can't," he whispered.

"You were Gird's friend ," Aris said, unexpectedly. "You can." All those times he and the others had faltered to a halt in mud or hot sun, certain they could not march another step, and Gird had bellowed at them, rain or sweat running down his weathered face ... and they had taken the next step, and the next. If Gird were here, would he dare say "I can't"? No. He could almost hear the old man's gruff voice, feel that hard fist once more. He had to try again. "Get out," he whispered to the presence within him. "Get *out!*"

You'll die came the response. Its sweet poison soothed; he felt himself responding as he had, unwittingly, all these years. *You have no chance but me.* Disgust at himself, and the memory of Gird, gave him strength to resist.

"Get OUT!" He felt Aris and Seri joining their power to his, yielding this one last time to his command as his magery proved too weak ... and then the presence, whatever it was, fled away down the wind of his anger.

And left him once more empty, hollow, guilty, hardly able to stand. Seri and Aris supported him; as his strength returned, he could see them more clearly. No longer "the younglings" he had both admired and envied, but weathered and graying, well into middle age.

"I can't—I don't know what to do?" His voice came out rasping and feeble as an old man's.

"You've made the right start," Seri said. "Now you might try asking the gods."

Luap winced. He had not, he realized, really asked the gods anything for a long time. He had never really wanted to know what the gods wanted of him. He had spent those times in the yearly festivals when prayers were normally offered giving complacent reports on his own genius, looking for praise in return. Now he had no choice; unpracticed as he was, he must ask. He let them lead him back to the great hall, and tried to fix his mind on the gods he hardly knew.

Chapter Thirty-two

He knew at once it was no dream, not as he had dreamed before, and his first thought was that Gird had not warned him what meeting a god was like. Where had the space come from, he wondered, in which he hung suspended, like a thought in some vast intelligence? At once his mind clung to that notion, and began elaborating it, an activity he recognized even as it continued: protective flight into logic, the mage's trance.

A face appeared before him, a man's face of near his own age, he thought. Unlike dreams, it carried no emotion with it—a stranger's face, weathered by life into interesting lines. It stared aside, not directly at him, and he watched with his usual attention, looking for clues to character and motivation. A face used to command, to the obedience of others, to hard decisions . . . it was turning now, toward him. Eyes a clear cool gray met his, *caught* his, across whatever gulf of time and space lay between them. Commanded him, as they had (he could tell) commanded so many others. Now he could see the head above the face, bearing a crown—a *crown*?

A king. A king's face, and not the one he had seen last, dead, on the trampled earth of Greenfields. And not Tsaia's king, past or present, nor the black-bearded king of the Khartazh: those faces too he knew, and this was something else. A god? He thought not, though awe choked his breath. He tried to look aside, and could not. Slowly, inexorably, the rest of the man's figure became visible. A king in green and gold, the gold crown in his hair shaped of leaves and vines. Something about the clothes seemed foreign, strange: he could not say what. Slowly, as the drifting of morning fog, he began to see the room around the man ... its panelled walls, its broad table littered with scrolls and books, its carpet like a garden of flowers, manycolored. Someone else ... across the room, a woman whose weathered face wore a curious ornament on the brow, a silver circle ... but in a trick of light she seemed to fade and he could not see her. The king said nothing ... did he see Luap as well as Luap saw him?

Then, "You." The king's voice, deep, resonant, carrying power as a river carries a straw. "You are part of it; you will help."

He did not want to answer a wraith, a dream, whatever this was, but from his mouth came the honest bleat of fear he felt. "I can't." Even if he'd wanted to, he had no more help to give, not even to his own people. Could he explain *that* to a wraith, a messenger, whoever this was? The iynisin could not get in, through no power of his but the original power of those who had sculpted the fortress ... but he and his could not get out.

"You will wake them?" That voice came from the glare he could not see, where the woman had seemed to stand. The king's face turned aside, and Luap almost sagged in relief. It was like facing Gird again, on his worst days—and worse, that he had now failed at what he'd promised.

"I must," the king was saying. "They close the pattern. I cannot explain—"

"No matter." For an instant, Luap could see her again, this time as if through a white flickering of flame. She had a smile that rang aloud, louder than laughter would have been; when she chuckled, softly, he realized again that his senses were rapt in some strange magic. "I think you've missed your mark, sir king. What you seek to wake has not slept."

"What?" The king looked again, deep into Luap's eyes, a look he felt as a sword probing his vitals. "How can that be? I sought along your memories, to find the place—"

"While thinking of the reason you sought them, a reason many lives old, did you not?" The king's eyes never wavered from Luap's, but he nodded. The woman went on. "You found what you sought, then, but—Gird's teeth, my lord, I can't understand how you will get them out, and still leave what we found."

"Nor I." The king took a breath, and let it out slowly, now

watching Luap with obvious wariness. "You—" and there was no doubt which of them he addressed. "You are of Gird's time, are you not? And someone who knew him?"

Luap was not aware of speaking, but he knew he spoke in some manner the king understood. "I am Luap."

"Yes." One word, in that tone, and Luap wondered what the king saw in his face. What Gird had seen? He hoped not, but the king's next words were not reassuring. "You are not . . . what legends made you."

No time to ask that, not of such a king. "I was Gird's friend, until his death; his chronicler, after."

"You have Aarean blood."

He could not help it; his chin lifted. "I am a king's son." He did not trouble to explain which king.

"And your mother—?"

Damn the man. Luap struggled once more with the envy that never died, and said, "A peasant woman. I never knew her, past infancy."

To his surprise, that stern face softened a little. "I am sorry. My mother, too, died when I was young, and I had a . . . difficult time."

Difficult, Luap thought bitterly, could not have included being tossed out to fend for himself in a peasant village. "I have the royal magery," he said, uncertain why he said it.

"I suspected you might. Some of you, at least." The king turned away again, and spoke to the woman. Luap wondered again why she was so hard to see, for a white fog lay across her image. "If you're right, and we have opened a gap between times as well as places, how should I proceed?"

"I have no idea." The fog intensified, then she appeared, much nearer, peering past the king's shoulder. "You truly are Luap?"

He found it hard to answer, even in this nebulous state. "Yes. . . ."

Her eyes widened; humor quirked her mouth. He was reminded, for no reason he could imagine, of Raheli in one of her rare good moods. "Gird—understood you, did he?"

Tears flooded his eyes and ran down his cheeks before he could blink them away. What he might have said vanished in the storm. Her brow puckered; the ornament centered it, serene and unchanging.

"It's all right," she said. "Don't worry . . . he understands."

"Who?" asked the king.

"Gird. He shelters you as well, Luap." He had thought the king's voice commanding; he had never imagined a woman with such power. Light and tears blurred his vision to a white glow. "It will be well," she said; her voice came to him as a warm arm around his shoulders. "King's son, listen to the king." Then he could see again, the king's face expressing rue and tenderness. For her, he was sure.

"Lady—dammit, Paks, you will unnerve me, as well as him."

"Sorry, my lord." She had moved from his sight, though he knew, as if he could see, that she had stretched out in a chair at one end of the table.

"You aren't really sorry." It sounded like an old quarrel between them, worn comfortable with time.

"No—but he needs your help, as you need his. Tell him, sir king." She did not need to say "then listen" aloud; it was implicit in her tone.

The king raised his brows; Luap's knees would have shaken if he had been aware of them. Not a man to anger, he thought wildly. As bad as Gird. As good? Not another one, he thought; gods save me from heroes! As if she had heard his thought, the woman chuckled again, out of sight, but with no scorn in it.

"I am Falkieri, Lyonya's king," the king began. "You won't know of me—and was Lyonya even a kingdom in your day?"

"Ah—I had heard tales—" Such tales as no one believed, he'd always thought, but so had the iynisin been, until they attacked. And what did the man mean, "in your day—"? Was this foreseeing, this trance? He had thought that gift lost utterly; even the Rosemage, even Arranha, never suggested he might have that power.

"Good. I am half-elven, and if the old tales be true, and your father was a king, then you are half-Aarean. Is that so?"

Half-elven. He had never heard of mortals and elves together; his skin shivered at the thought of the iynisin who waited outside the hall's protection. "My father was a magelord, sir king—" Odd way of speaking, that seemed, after the Rosemage's description of court life, after the florid formality of the Khartazh. Plain, even. "They came from Aare, but old Aare is no more. So they say, who have traveled the south; I have not."

"Magelord . . . and that means?"

"Some of the mageborn retain the powers all once had. I myself have some—but much diminished, if the tales be true, from those with which the magelords came."

The king sighed. "As I suspect it was my magic that called you, it is but courteous that I explain why. Your ancestors, king's son, had long abused the powers they held before they came to this land. No blame to you, but when the pot's broken, it matters not who spilled it—all must clean. Long and bitter wars have followed every trail your ancestors took; the Seafolk they raided and scourged from the eastern coasts fled seaward, and found this land, only to find your people moving into it from the mountains. Generations of war—which I, as a young man, helped to fight. Injustice on injustice, which I now feel called to redress."

"You?" That got out; Luap clamped his lips on the "alone?" that would have followed.

"I have an heir. Several, in fact. I have a trustworthy Regent—" The king's glance went aside, to where the woman sat out of Luap's gaze.

"And Council," she put in. "You know my limitations."

"If Gird sends you elsewhere on quest now—" the king began.

Another warm chuckle. "I'm not *that* old; you were still commanding the Company—"

"But—"

"And I'll make no promises I can't keep." Luap flinched, and hoped the king didn't see. From something in her voice, he knew it as truth: she had never made promises she couldn't keep, and had kept promises he didn't want to contemplate.

"I know. And you know my meaning. King's son, I am going back to a place where I made grave errors; I will try to put them right. I need your help, and that of your people—Gird's people— to bring justice to Aarenis and even to Old Aare. Now—"

As if that pause released his voice, Luap heard himself asking "Who is she?"

"A paladin of Gird," she said, a bright shape once more wavering at the king's shoulder. "Does that grieve you?"

She had chosen the very word. Whatever she was, he could not be. "Paladin?" he asked, clinging to the unfamiliar word.

"Gird's warrior," the king said. "Sworn to his service, under his command."

Awe choked him again. "You've—*seen*—him?" Faster than speech could be, the hope ran through his mind that Gird had not mentioned him; shame made his ears burn.

"In my heart," she said, bringing a fist to her chest. Now he could see clearly; a big fist, scarred with work or war, and a face that had seen a life's trouble without hardening to bitterness. A yellow braid hung over one shoulder. "Don't worry," she said again. "Gird will help you."

Even the Sunlord wouldn't help him, he thought miserably. If this was foresight, no wonder the gift disappeared; it would drive him mad, one more instant of it. He squeezed, trying to close his eyes, but could not. "Not me," he said, with difficulty. "I—erred. Stupidly. Again. He warned me, but I thought—I could read, you see. I was smarter."

"Smart enough to cut yourself with your own sword?" asked the king. His smile was rueful again. "I did that, too." He flicked a glance at the woman. "We kings' sons have much to learn from peasants, Luap."

The rush of laughter came as suddenly as the tears, as despair; he gulped it down. "So . . . so Gird said. And Rahi." At the king's look of incomprehension, he added "Gird's daughter."

"I never knew he had a daughter," said the woman; Luap winced, suddenly quite aware of the reason. He had left Rahi out of the chronicles where he could, helped by her own belief that being Gird's daughter meant nothing special. If these folk were indeed from far in the future, when some at least of the records must have been lost, Rahi's part might have vanished.

He could think of nothing to say about Rahi. He could think of nothing but his guilt, and the iynisin outside, waiting.

"You're afraid," the woman said. "What is it?"

Her voice soothed, warmed. "Iynisin," he said. Best get the tale over with quickly; this vision had lasted a long time already. Without sparing himself, he told of the decision to move all the mage-born to the canyons, and how he and the others had used their powers to smooth the way, to make the canyons liveable. Then of his dealing with the Khartazh, and his decision to use his power— he thought only his—to keep him young. And then the iynisin, whose influence at first escaped notice, until that morning's attack, and then of the judgment of elves and dwarves that sealed the mageroads against them.

They stared at him, the two faces unlike but the same expression. "We will die," he said, facing it for the first time. "All of us. If we can't go out to plant and harvest, or trade . . . we will starve."

"What would you?"

"Escape, of course. Can you—"

"No." The king's face was grim. "I have no magicks to bring so many so far, from such a length of years. What I had thought to do was wake those found sleeping in your Hall—" Luap opened his mouth, and the king raised a hand to silence him. "Paks saw that, years ago. I presume that was you and your remaining warriors. She traveled by the pattern—the mageroad, you call it?— back to Fin Panir, where the Girdsmen rule; I had thought to ask you to go that way, or to another end—for some went elsewhere,

the time Paks used it. But you are not now sleeping in that hall—
at least, the man I talk to is not—"

"Sir king." The woman's voice carried power again; again she
reminded him of Raheli. If Gird's daughter had been fair instead
of dark . . . he shivered, suspecting that she was Gird's daughter in
a way he had never been his father's son. "If he is not sleeping,
yet we found him sleeping—if peril threatens which he cannot
escape, and fighting will not serve any good—Gird knows I understand the iynisin—" She turned to Luap. "They captured me, for
a time." Luap shuddered; her eyes were steady below the circle on
her brow. "Perhaps you can suggest a way for him to save his
people in that enchantment."

The king's eyes came alight. "And then—"

"And then perhaps a call to wake will actually awaken them."

"But—" Luap cut that off. To sleep but awaken only to another
danger, to whatever distant war the king had in mind, to waken
only to more guilt, more peril . . . what purpose was that? Even if
it could be done, why not simply die, and be done with life?
Despair seized him again, and all he could remember were the
numberless lies, the many times he had dodged trouble, to let it
fall elsewhere. The face of his dead wife swam before him, for the
first time in years; he heard his daughter's pitiful cries as they
dragged her away. He could hear his own voice, the perpetual
whine that Gird had accused but he had never heard. And he had
robbed even Gird's daughter of her due, in shaping the chronicles
as he had. He would be better dead; he would only ruin another
man's dream.

"All the others with you?" asked the woman. She had read his
thought again, or it showed on his face for all to see. Now she
shook her head slowly. "No—they can have a better death than
that, to fall once more because you fell. And for you, too, death is
not the answer."

"How?" All his rage, all his sorrow, all his weakness; they knew
everything now, or should have. "I was their king; I failed them!"
He squeezed his eyes shut, trying to hold back the tears, then
stared at her through that wavering pattern. "How many? Tell me—
how many were left?"

"I . . . don't remember. Fifty, perhaps. A few more or less. I was
not counting them, and the High Marshals left them in peace."

"We have more than that—some hundreds—" He could not
reckon them up; their faces flickered through his mind too fast to
count. Somewhere they had records, he was sure of that. "Children,
parents, old people . . . not just warriors. . . ." He shook his head.

"Few warriors; we were a peaceful people." That too was his fault; guilt squeezed him harder.

"Yet there are warriors with you," the woman said. "Two of them: who are they?"

He had forgotten: the dream or vision had taken him so far away that he had lost any memory of Seri and Aris standing near, holding him. He tried to see, tried to remember, but the woman went on as if he had spoken, her voice suddenly lighter. She spoke to them, not to him, some greeting that they answered, though he could not really hear it.

"I should never have been a prince," he said, not knowing to whom he said it. Perhaps to himself, perhaps to Gird's memory.

The woman spoke to him again: "What do you mean?"

"Do you know what my name means?" he asked. Irony flavored the thought, even now.

"Luap? It's your name: that's all I know."

Luap looked for mockery on her face, and found only compassion and mild interest. "It means 'one who holds no command,'" he said, "Or 'one who does not inherit.' Some called bastards that, when they meant to be kind. I was Gird's luap—his scribe, his helper, his friend—but he forbade me command, and in the end I took the name of my position. Then he died."

"Killing the evil monster," the woman said, nodding.

"No. That's what I wrote, thinking it more understandable than what he did do . . . and what that was I cannot say: you would have to have been there and experienced it. But he died, and released me from my oath—or so I thought. As you see I sought command. And this is what came of it."

"You—oathbreaker?" That was the king, for whom command had no doubt come early and with no qualifications. "You seized your command against your oath to Gird?" No doubt, from the tone, what the king thought of that.

"At Gird's death, he said he was wrong—about our peoples." There was too much to explain, no way to make it clear. Luap found he could say nothing more, though his memories clamored for expression. "I thought," he said finally, "that he meant I was free to bring my people here, and take command here—only here—if they agreed. And they did." A long silence; he saw both faces clearly. "I was wrong," he said then. "I thought I would be better than my ancestors; I was worse. And I don't know what to do. Aris and Seri—" He could only hope that the woman now knew who Aris and Seri were. "—told me to pray, and when I prayed, I saw you."

The king grimaced; the woman laughed—not cruelly, but in genuine amusement. "I doubt it will be so easy, Luap, but are you willing to try?"

"Try *what*?"

"If you got into this by taking command you should not have had, relinquish it."

"How?" How could anything lift that weight from his shoulders? Who would take it? Yet he longed to hand it over, all his pride with it—anything, if only the wrongs he had done could be undone.

She grinned at him, and he could not help but feel better. "*There* is a king," she said. A real king, she did not say, but meant. "Would you follow such a king?"

That was the king he would like to have been; a last stab of envy took his breath, a last certainty that *that* king had had an easier life, and then he felt the tears running down his face. "I would," he said.

"Then be the luap you were: give Falkieri, Lyonya's king, command, and obey him."

Could he trust this stranger seen in a dream? Luap shrugged; he could not trust *himself*—this man, he was sure, could be no worse, not if he had a—what had she said, "paladin of Gird"?—to help him. "I will," he said, and looked the king in the eyes. The king looked back; Luap would have flinched if he could, but then the king's eyes warmed.

"Tell me about your people," he said. "Tell me about your land, and what you know that might help us save them."

"This is what you must do," the king said finally. Luap nodded. He felt eased, though it was not over. "Your people must go—now—tonight—with your paladins to guard them."

"My paladins?" He had no paladins he knew of, nothing like that woman with her strange ornament and her laughing eyes.

"Paks says your Marshals are paladins: Seri and Aris, is it? Yes. They must go with them, or your people have no chance at all. Then you will need some for a rear guard, who cannot expect to escape."

"The militia, I suppose," said Luap. His lips felt stiff. Seri's militia, he might as well have said, for he had had nothing to do with it for years.

"You will stand guard," the woman said. "Where we found you, on the stone arch there above the entrance of your Hall."

"There isn't an arch," he said. "The mountain falls sheer. The arches are in other canyons."

She shrugged. "By the time we come, it will be there; I saw you as a vast guardian shape, protecting that approach and the upper entrance from all harm, in Gird's name."

Luap would have protested: he wanted death, not an eternity of waiting, of the memory of all his errors. He wanted to ask how long he would stand there, how many hands of years. But he had given his oath; this last short time he could be true to it. As if she understood, the woman smiled at him.

"You loved this land," she said. "You will be able to see its beauty all those years." She did not say how many; perhaps she did not know. Despite himself, through all his guilt, that brought him joy. It was a mercy too great, and bought at too dear a price; tears scalded his face again.

"And I will need the use of your royal magery," the king said, as if asking for the use of a spoon or knife. "I must command your people, through you, and this is the only way."

"I—very well," Luap said, hardly able to speak. "Go ahead." He was aware of his voice, speaking the king's words, but it seemed to come from some distance, as if he hung suspended between the vision and the place his body stood. He heard himself explaining, asking for volunteers for the rear guard, directing everyone to go now, to snatch up only what they could carry. Aris and Seri looked stubborn, and would not have gone with the others if something— he could not know what—had not intervened; he saw their faces change. Sorrow fought with hope, reluctance with eagerness. Seri embraced each of her militia in turn, then turned to Aris; hand in hand they led the others out of the great hall.

Then the king's magery and his own twined in the last acts of power, preparing the enchantments that would let his survivors rest, that would place him once more where he had first seen his kingdom and imagined himself a king.

He stood poised on a great stone arch on the eastern end of the mountain; he could feel neither heat nor cold, neither wind nor rain nor snow, neither hunger nor thirst. Above him, above the clouds that blew past in the seasons, the stars wheeled in their steady patterns; he knew them all. Beneath him, in the hollow heart of stone, his warriors rested at peace, until they should be called to rise again.

Beyond his mortal vision, but within his dream, on the dark night his watch began, he had seen the fragile human chain make its way down the canyon. He had seen the glowing figures of those he had not recognized as more than Marshals; he had heard the cries of those who fell; he had known that some lived, that some survived to reach far Xhim and the sea beyond, and a few—a very few— returned to the eastern lands to tell of a disastrous end to his adventure. But they had all been children when the stronghold fell, and their tales, though he could not know it, were dismissed as children's make-believe and soon forgotten.

He knew when the Khartazh soldiers came to visit, and found demons abroad once more, and saw the western canyons fill up once more with brigands who preyed on the caravans of the west. He knew what they said, how they mocked the folk who had once lived there, who had disappeared so suddenly.

He stood guard on the stone, year after year and age after age, bound to that place by his own magery and the magery of those who built it. In time the iynisin retreated to their lairs of stone; in time the trees grew again, in time the snows and floods of years tore down the terraces and left the canyon once more "no good for farming," as Gird had said, with all the soil so carefully placed scoured from the canyons to dry and bleach on the desert far below. In time the stone beneath him crumbled, leaving him suspended on a vast arch of stone. He could not tire, but he could hope for an ending, a completion of the pattern once begun, a better completion than he had himself designed.

He knew it would come, because he had begun it. The paladin would come, and restore the mageroads; the king would wake his warriors. Then his long watch would be over; he would be freed to go before the gods. He knew that would come, because the king had promised, and the paladin had given her word, and they were not liars: he could trust their oaths. It did not depend on his.

It is said in Fin Panir that the first paladins came out of the west, in a storm of light, riding horses so beautiful they hurt the eyes to see. A man and a woman, it is said, but no one remembers their names.